The Collector's Book of
WESTERNS

The Collector's Book of
WESTERNS

Selection by
ROSEMARY GRAY

Wordsworth Editions

In loving memory of
MICHAEL TRAYLER
the founder of Wordsworth Editions

I

Readers who are interested in other titles from
Wordsworth Editions are invited to visit our website at
www.wordsworth-editions.com

For our latest list and a full mail-order service, contact
Bibliophile Books, 5 Datapoint, South Crescent, London E16 4TL
TEL: +44 (0)20 7474 2474 FAX: +44 (0)20 7474 8589
ORDERS: orders@bibliophilebooks.com
WEBSITE: www.bibliophilebooks.com

First published in 2010 by Wordsworth Editions Limited
8B East Street, Ware, Hertfordshire SG12 9HJ

ISBN 978 1 84022 649 2

Text © Wordsworth Editions Limited 2010

Typeset in Great Britain by Antony Gray
Printed and bound by Clays Ltd, St Ives plc

CONTENTS

The Long Stories

THE SHORT STORIES

THE VENGEANCE OF PADRE ARROYO

GERTRUDE ATHERTON

1

PILAR, from her little window just above the high wall surrounding the big adobe house set apart for the women neophytes of the Mission of Santa Ines, watched, morning and evening, for Andreo, as he came and went from the *rancheria*. The old women kept the girls busy, spinning, weaving, sewing; but age nods and youth is crafty. The tall young Indian who was renowned as the best huntsman of all the neophytes, and who supplied Padre Arroyo's table with deer and quail, never failed to keep his ardent eyes fixed upon the grating so long as it lay within the line of his vision. One day he went to Padre Arroyo and told him that Pilar was the prettiest girl behind the wall – the prettiest girl in all the Californias – and that she should be his wife. But the kind stern old padre shook his head.

'You are both too young. Wait another year, my son, and if thou art still in the same mind, thou shalt have her.'

Andreo dared to make no protest, but he asked permission to prepare a home for his bride. The padre gave it willingly, and the young Indian began to make the big adobes, the bright red tiles. At the end of a month he had built him a cabin among the willows of the *rancheria*, a little apart from the others: he was in love, and association with his fellows was distasteful. When the cabin was builded his impatience slipped from its curb, and once more he besought the priest to allow him to marry.

Padre Arroyo was sunning himself on the corridor of the mission, shivering in his heavy brown robes, for the day was cold.

'Orion,' he said sternly – he called all his neophytes after the celebrities of earlier days, regardless of the names given them at the font – 'have I not told thee thou must wait a year? Do not be impatient, my son. She will keep. Women are like apples: when they are too young, they set the teeth on edge; when ripe and mellow, they please every sense; when they wither and turn brown, it is time for them to fall from the tree into a hole. Now go and shoot a deer for Sunday: the good padres from San Luis Obispo and Santa Barbara are coming to dine with me.'

Andreo, dejected, left the padre. As he passed Pilar's window and saw a pair of wistful black eyes behind the grating, his heart took fire. No one was within sight. By a series of signs he made his lady understand that he would place a note beneath a certain adobe in the wall.

Pilar, as she went to and fro under the fruit trees in the garden, or sat on the long corridor weaving baskets, watched that adobe with fascinated eyes. She knew that Andreo was tunnelling it, and one day a tiny hole proclaimed that his work was accomplished. But how to get the note? The old women's eyes were very sharp when the girls were in front of the gratings. Then the civilising development of Christianity upon the heathen intellect triumphantly asserted itself. Pilar, too, conceived a brilliant scheme. That night the padre, who encouraged any evidence of industry, no matter how eccentric, gave her a little garden of her own – a patch where she could raise sweet peas and Castilian roses.

'That is well, that is well, my Nausicaa,' he said, stroking her smoky braids. 'Go cut the slips and plant them where thou wilt. I will send thee a package of sweet-pea seeds.'

Pilar spent every spare hour bending over her 'patch'; and the hole, at first no bigger than a pin's point, was larger at each setting of the sun behind the mountain. The old women, scolding on the corridor, called to her not to forget vespers.

On the third evening, kneeling on the damp ground, she drew from the little tunnel in the adobe a thin slip of wood covered with the labour of sleepless nights. She hid it in her smock – that first of California's love-letters – then ran with shaking knees and prostrated herself before the altar. That night the moon streamed through her grating, and she deciphered the fact that Andreo had loosened eight adobes above her garden, and would await her every midnight.

Pilar sat up in bed and glanced about the room with terrified delight. It took her but a moment to decide the question; love had kept her awake too many nights. The neophytes were asleep; as they turned now and again, their narrow beds of hide, suspended from the ceiling, swung too gently to awaken them. The old women snored loudly. Pilar slipped from her bed and looked through the grating. Andreo was there, the dignity and repose of primeval man in his bearing. She waved her hand and pointed downward to the wall; then, throwing on the long coarse grey smock that was her only garment, crept from the room and down the stair. The door was protected against hostile tribes by a heavy iron bar, but Pilar's small hands were hard and strong, and in a moment she stood over the adobes which had crushed her roses and sweet peas.

As she crawled through the opening, Andreo took her hand bashfully, for they never had spoken. 'Come,' he said; 'we must be far away before dawn.'

They stole past the long mission, crossing themselves as they glanced askance at the ghostly row of pillars; past the guardhouse, where the sentries slept at their post; past the *rancheria*; then, springing upon a waiting mustang, dashed down the valley. Pilar had never been on a horse before, and she clung in terror to Andreo, who bestrode the unsaddled beast as easily as a cloud rides the wind. His arm held her closely, fear vanished, and she enjoyed the novel sensation. Glancing over Andreo's shoulder she watched the mass of brown and white buildings, the winding river, fade into the mountain. Then they began to ascend an almost perpendicular steep. The horse followed a narrow trail; the crowding trees and shrubs clutched the blankets and smocks of the riders; after a time trail and scene grew white: the snow lay on the heights.

'Where do we go?' she asked.

'To Zaca Lake, on the very top of the mountain, miles above us. No one has ever been there but myself. Often I have shot deer and birds beside it. They never will find us there.'

The red sun rose over the mountains of the east. The crystal moon sank in the west. Andreo sprang from the weary mustang and carried Pilar to the lake.

A sheet of water, round as a whirlpool but calm and silver, lay amidst the sweeping willows and pine-forested peaks. The snow glittered beneath the trees, but a canoe was on the lake, a hut on the marge.

2

Padre Arroyo tramped up and down the corridor, smiting his hands together. The Indians bowed lower than usual as they passed, and hastened their steps. The soldiers scoured the country for the bold violators of mission law. No one asked Padre Arroyo what he would do with the sinners, but all knew that punishment would be sharp and summary: the men hoped that Andreo's mustang had carried him beyond its reach; the girls, horrified as they were, wept and prayed in secret for Pilar.

A week later, in the early morning, Padre Arroyo sat on the corridor. The mission stood on a plateau overlooking a long valley forked and sparkled by the broad river. The valley was planted thick with olive trees, and their silver leaves glittered in the rising sun. The mountain peaks about and beyond were white with snow, but the great red poppies blossomed at their feet. The padre, exiled from the luxury and society of his dear Spain, never tired of the prospect: he loved his mission children, but he loved Nature more.

Suddenly he leaned forward on his staff and lifted the heavy brown hood of his habit from his ear. Down the road winding from the eastern mountains came the echo of galloping footfalls. He rose expectantly and waddled out upon the plaza, shading his eyes with his hand. A half-dozen soldiers, riding closely about a horse bestridden by a stalwart young Indian supporting a woman, were rapidly approaching the mission. The padre returned to his seat and awaited their coming.

The soldiers escorted the culprits to the corridor; two held the horse while they descended, then led it away, and Andreo and Pilar were alone with the priest. The bridegroom placed his arm about the bride and looked defiantly at Padre Arroyo, but Pilar drew her long hair about her face and locked her hands together.

Padre Arroyo folded his arms and regarded them with lowered brows, a sneer on his mouth.

'I have new names for you both,' he said, in his thickest voice. 'Antony, I hope thou hast enjoyed thy honeymoon. Cleopatra, I hope thy little toes did not get frostbitten. You both look as if food had been scarce. And your garments have gone in good part to clothe the brambles, I infer. It is too bad you could not wait a year and love in your cabin at the *rancheria*, by a good fire, and with plenty of frijoles and tortillas in your stomachs.' He dropped his sarcastic tone, and rising to his feet, extended his right arm with a gesture of malediction. 'Do you comprehend the enormity of your sin?' he shouted. 'Have you not learned on your knees that the fires of hell are the rewards of unlawful love? Do you not know that even the year of sackcloth and ashes I shall impose here on earth will not save you from those flames a million times hotter than the mountain fire, than the roaring pits in which evil Indians torture one another? A hundred years of their scorching breath, of roasting flesh, for a week of love! Oh, God of my soul!'

Andreo looked somewhat staggered, but unrepentant. Pilar burst into loud sobs of terror.

The padre stared long and gloomily at the flags of the corridor. Then he raised his head and looked sadly at his lost sheep.

'My children,' he said solemnly, 'my heart is wrung for you. You have broken the laws of God and of the Holy Catholic Church and the punishments thereof are awful. Can I do anything for you, excepting to pray? You shall have my prayers, my children. But that is not enough; I cannot – ay! I cannot endure the thought that you shall be damned. Perhaps' – again he stared meditatively at the stones, then, after an impressive silence, raised his eyes. 'Heaven vouchsafes me an idea, my children. I will make your punishment here so bitter that Almighty God in His mercy will give you but a few years of purgatory after death. Come with me.'

He turned and led the way slowly to the rear of the mission buildings. Andreo shuddered for the first time, and tightened his arm about Pilar's shaking body. He knew that they were to be locked in the dungeons. Pilar, almost fainting, shrank back as they reached the narrow spiral stair which led downward to the cells. 'Ay! I shall die, my Andreo!' she cried. 'Ay! my father, have mercy!'

'I cannot, my children,' said the padre, sadly. 'It is for the salvation of your souls.'

'Mother of God! When shall I see thee again, my Pilar?' whispered Andreo. 'But, ay! the memory of that week on the mountain will keep us both alive.'

Padre Arroyo descended the stair and awaited them at its foot. Separating them, and taking each by the hand, he pushed Andreo ahead and dragged Pilar down the narrow passage. At its end he took a great bunch of keys from his pocket, and raising both hands, commanded them to kneel. He said a long prayer in a loud monotonous voice which echoed and re-echoed down the dark hall and made Pilar shriek with terror. Then he fairly hurled the marriage ceremony at them, and made the couple repeat after him the responses. When it was over, 'Arise,' he said.

The poor things stumbled to their feet, and Andreo caught Pilar in a last embrace.

'Now bear your incarceration with fortitude, my children; and if you do not beat the air with your groans, I will let you out in a week. Do not hate your old father, for love alone makes him severe, but pray, pray, pray.'

And then he locked them both in the same cell.

THE BRIDE COMES TO YELLOW SKY

STEPHEN CRANE

1

THE GREAT PULLMAN was whirling onward with such dignity of motion that a glance from the window seemed simply to prove that the plains of Texas were pouring eastward. Vast flats of green grass, dull-hued spaces of mesquite and cactus, little groups of frame houses, woods of light and tender trees, all were sweeping into the east, sweeping over the horizon, a precipice.

A newly married pair had boarded this coach at San Antonio. The man's face was reddened from many days in the wind and sun, and a direct result of his new black clothes was that his brick-coloured hands were constantly performing in a most conscious fashion. From time to time he looked down respectfully at his attire. He sat with a hand on each knee, like a man waiting in a barber's shop. The glances he devoted to other passengers were furtive and shy.

The bride was not pretty, nor was she very young. She wore a dress of blue cashmere, with small reservations of velvet here and there and with steel buttons abounding. She continually twisted her head to regard her puff sleeves, very stiff, straight and high. They embarrassed her. It was quite apparent that she had cooked, and that she expected to cook, dutifully. The blushes caused by the careless scrutiny of some passengers as she had entered the car were strange to see upon this plain, under-class countenance, which was drawn in placid, almost emotionless lines.

They were evidently very happy. 'Ever been in a parlour-car before?' he asked, smiling with delight.

'No,' she answered, 'I never was. It's fine, ain't it?'

'Great! And then after a while we'll go forward to the diner and get a big layout. Finest meal in the world. Charge a dollar.'

'Oh, do they?' cried the bride. 'Charge a dollar? Why, that's too much – for us – ain't it, Jack?'

'Not this trip, anyhow,' he answered bravely. 'We're going to go the whole thing.'

Later, he explained to her about the trains. 'You see, it's a thousand miles from one end of Texas to the other, and this train runs right across it and never stops but four times.' He had the pride of an owner. He pointed out to her the dazzling fittings of the coach, and in truth her eyes opened wider as she contemplated the sea-green figured velvet, the

23

shining brass, silver and glass, the wood that gleamed as darkly brilliant as the surface of a pool of oil. At one end a bronze figure sturdily held a support for a separated chamber, and at convenient places on the ceiling were frescoes in olive and silver.

2

To the minds of the pair, their surroundings reflected the glory of their marriage that morning in San Antonio. This was the environment of their new estate, and the man's face in particular beamed with an elation that made him appear ridiculous to the Negro porter. This individual at times surveyed them from afar with an amused and superior grin. On other occasions he bullied them with skill in ways that did not make it exactly plain to them that they were being bullied. He subtly used all the manners of the most unconquerable kind of snobbery. He oppressed them, but of this oppression they had small knowledge, and they speedily forgot that infrequently a number of travellers covered them with stares of derisive enjoyment. Historically there was supposed to be something infinitely humorous in their situation.

'We are due in Yellow Sky at 3:42,' he said, looking tenderly into her eyes.

'Oh, are we?' she said, as if she had not been aware of it. To evince surprise at her husband's statement was part of her wifely amiability. She took from a pocket a little silver watch, and as she held it before her and stared at it with a frown of attention, the new husband's face shone.

'I bought it in San Anton' from a friend of mine,' he told her gleefully.

'It's seventeen minutes past twelve,' she said, looking up at him with a kind of shy and clumsy coquetry. A passenger, noting this play, grew excessively sardonic, and winked at himself in one of the numerous mirrors.

At last they went to the dining-car. Two rows of Negro waiters, in glowing white suits, surveyed their entrance with the interest and also the equanimity of men who had been forewarned. The pair fell to the lot of a waiter who happened to feel pleasure in steering them through their meal. He viewed them with the manner of a fatherly pilot, his countenance radiant with benevolence. The patronage, entwined with the ordinary deference, was not plain to them. And yet, as they returned to their coach, they showed in their faces a sense of escape.

To the left, miles down a long purple slope, was a little ribbon of mist where moved the keening Rio Grande. The train was approaching it at an angle, and the apex was Yellow Sky. Presently it was apparent that, as the distance from Yellow Sky grew shorter, the husband became commensurately restless. His brick-red hands were more insistent in their prominence. Occasionally he was even rather absent-minded and far-away when the bride leaned forward and addressed him.

3

As a matter of truth, Jack Potter was beginning to find the shadow of a deed weigh upon him like a leaden slab. He, the town marshal of Yellow Sky, a man known, liked and feared in his corner, a prominent person, had gone to San Antonio to meet a girl he believed he loved, and there, after the usual prayers, had actually induced her to marry him, without consulting Yellow Sky for any part of the transaction. He was now bringing his bride before an innocent and unsuspecting community.

Of course, people in Yellow Sky married as it pleased them, in accordance with a general custom; but such was Potter's thought of his duty to his friends, or of their idea of his duty, or of an unspoken form which does not control men in these matters, that he felt he was heinous. He had committed an extraordinary crime. Face to face with this girl in San Antonio, and spurred by his sharp impulse, he had gone headlong over all the social hedges. At San Antonio he was like a man hidden in the dark. A knife to sever any friendly duty, any form, was easy to his hand in that remote city. But the hour of Yellow Sky, the hour of daylight, was approaching.

He knew full well that his marriage was an important thing to his town. It could only be exceeded by the burning of the new hotel. His friends could not forgive him. Frequently he had reflected on the advisability of telling them by telegraph, but a new cowardice had been upon him. He feared to do it. And now the train was hurrying him toward a scene of amazement, glee and reproach. He glanced out of the window at the line of haze swinging slowly in towards the train.

Yellow Sky had a kind of brass band, which played painfully, to the delight of the populace. He laughed without heart as he thought of it. If the citizens could dream of his prospective arrival with his bride, they would parade the band at the station and escort them, amid cheers and laughing congratulations, to his adobe home.

He resolved that he would use all the devices of speed and plainscraft in making the journey from the station to his house. Once within that safe citadel he could issue some sort of a vocal bulletin, and then not go among the citizens until they had time to wear off a little of their enthusiasm.

4

The bride looked anxiously at him. 'What's worrying you, Jack?'

He laughed again. 'I'm not worrying, girl. I'm only thinking of Yellow Sky.'

She flushed in comprehension.

A sense of mutual guilt invaded their minds and developed a finer tenderness. They looked at each other with eyes softly aglow. But Potter often laughed the same nervous laugh. The flush upon the bride's face seemed quite permanent.

The traitor to the feelings of Yellow Sky narrowly watched the speeding landscape. 'We're nearly there,' he said.

Presently the porter came and announced the proximity of Potter's home. He held a brush in his hand and, with all his airy superiority gone, he brushed Potter's new clothes as the latter slowly turned this way and that way. Potter fumbled out a coin and gave it to the porter, as he had seen others do. It was a heavy and muscle-bound business, as that of a man shoeing his first horse.

The porter took their bag, and as the train began to slow they moved forward to the hooded platform of the car. Presently the two engines and their long string of coaches rushed into the station of Yellow Sky.

'They have to take water here,' said Potter, from a constricted throat and in mournful cadence, as one announcing death. Before the train stopped, his eye had swept the length of the platform, and he was glad and astonished to see there was none upon it but the station-agent, who, with a slightly hurried and anxious air, was walking toward the water-tanks. When the train had halted, the porter alighted first and placed in position a little temporary step.

'Come on, girl,' said Potter hoarsely. As he helped her down they each laughed on a false note. He took the bag from the Negro, and bade his wife cling to his arm. As they slunk rapidly away, his hangdog glance perceived that they were unloading the two trunks, and also that the station-agent far ahead near the baggage-car had turned and was running toward him, making gestures. He laughed, and groaned as he laughed, when he noted the first effect of his marital bliss upon Yellow Sky. He gripped his wife's arm firmly to his side, and they fled. Behind them the porter stood chuckling fatuously.

5

The California Express on the Southern Railway was due at Yellow Sky in twenty-one minutes. There were six men at the bar of the Weary Gentleman saloon. One was a drummer who talked a great deal and rapidly; three were Texans who did not care to talk at that time; and two were Mexican sheep-herders who did not talk as a general practice in the Weary Gentleman saloon. The barkeeper's dog lay on the boardwalk that crossed in front of the door. His head was on his paws, and he glanced drowsily here and there with the constant vigilance of a dog that is kicked on occasion. Across the sandy street were some vivid green grass plots, so wonderful in appearance amid the sands that burned near them in a blazing sun that they caused a doubt in the mind. They exactly resembled the grass mats used to represent lawns on the stage. At the cooler end of the railway station a man without a coat sat in a tilted chair and smoked his pipe. The fresh-cut bank of the Rio Grande circled near the town, and there could be seen beyond it a great, plum-coloured plain of mesquite.

Save for the busy drummer and his companions in the saloon, Yellow Sky was dozing. The newcomer leaned gracefully upon the bar, and recited many tales with the confidence of a bard who has come upon a new field.

' – and at the moment that the old man fell downstairs with the bureau in his arms, the old woman was coming up with two scuttles of coal, and, of course – '

The drummer's tale was interrupted by a young man who suddenly appeared in the open door. He cried: 'Scratchy Wilson's drunk, and has turned loose with both hands.' The two Mexicans at once set down their glasses and faded out of the rear entrance of the saloon.

The drummer, innocent and jocular, answered: 'All right, old man. S'pose he has. Come in and have a drink, anyhow.'

But the information had made such an obvious cleft in every skull in the room that the drummer was obliged to see its importance. All had become instantly solemn. 'Say,' said he, mystified, 'what is this?' His three companions made the introductory gesture of eloquent speech, but the young man at the door forestalled them.

'It means, my friend,' he answered, as he came into the saloon, 'that for the next two hours this town won't be a health resort.'

The barkeeper went to the door and locked and barred it. Reaching out of the window, he pulled in heavy wooden shutters and barred them. Immediately a solemn, chapel-like gloom was upon the place. The drummer was looking from one to another.

'But, say,' he cried, 'what is this, anyhow? You don't mean there is going to be a gun-fight?'

'Don't know whether there'll be a fight or not,' answered one man grimly. 'But there'll be some shootin' – some good shootin'.'

The young man who had warned them waved his hand. 'Oh, there'll be a fight fast enough if anyone wants it. Anybody can get a fight out there in the street. There's a fight just waiting.'

The drummer seemed to be swayed between the interest of a foreigner and a perception of personal danger.

'What did you say his name was?' he asked.

'Scratchy Wilson,' they answered in chorus.

'And will he kill anybody? What are you going to do? Does this happen often? Does he rampage around like this once a week or so? Can he break in that door?'

6

'No, he can't break down that door,' replied the barkeeper. 'He's tried it three times. But when he comes you'd better lay down on the floor, stranger. He's dead sure to shoot at it, and a bullet may come through.'

Thereafter the drummer kept a strict eye upon the door. The time had not yet been called for him to hug the floor, but, as a minor precaution, he sidled near to the wall. 'Will he kill anybody?' he said again.

The men laughed low and scornfully at the question.

'He's out to shoot, and he's out for trouble. Don't see any good in experimentin' with him.'

'But what do you do in a case like this? What do you do?'

A man responded: 'Why, he and Jack Potter –'

'But,' in chorus, the other men interrupted, 'Jack Potter's in San Anton'.'

'Well, who is he? What's he got to do with it?'

'Oh, he's the town marshal. He goes out and fights Scratchy when he gets on one of these tears.'

'Wow,' said the drummer, mopping his brow. 'Nice job he's got.'

The voices had toned away to mere whisperings. The drummer wished to ask further questions which were born of an increasing anxiety and bewilderment; but when he attempted them, the men merely looked at him in irritation and motioned him to remain silent. A tense waiting hush was upon them. In the deep shadows of the room their eyes shone as they listened for sounds from the street. One man made three gestures at the barkeeper, and the latter, moving like a ghost, handed him a glass and a bottle. The man poured a full glass of whiskey, and set down the bottle noiselessly. He gulped the whiskey in a swallow, and turned again toward the door in immovable silence. The drummer saw that the barkeeper, without a sound, had taken a Winchester from beneath the bar. Later he saw this individual beckoning to him, so he tiptoed across the room.

'You better come with me back of the bar.'

'No, thanks,' said the drummer, perspiring. 'I'd rather be where I can make a break for the back door.'

Whereupon the man of bottles made a kindly but peremptory gesture. The drummer obeyed it, and finding himself seated on a box with his head below the level of the bar, balm was laid upon his soul at sight of various zinc and copper fittings that bore a resemblance to armour-plate. The barkeeper took a seat comfortably upon an adjacent box.

7

'You see,' he whispered, 'this here Scratchy Wilson is a wonder with a gun – a perfect wonder – and when he goes on the war trail, we hunt our holes – naturally. He's about the last one of the old gang that used to hang out along the river here. He's a terror when he's drunk. When he's sober he's all right – kind of simple – wouldn't hurt a fly – nicest fellow in town. But when he's drunk – whoo!'

There were periods of stillness. 'I wish Jack Potter was back from San Anton',' said the barkeeper. 'He shot Wilson up once – in the leg – and he would sail in and pull out the kinks in this thing.'

Presently they heard from a distance the sound of a shot, followed by three wild yowls. It instantly removed a bond from the men in the darkened saloon. There was a shuffling of feet. They looked at each other. 'Here he comes,' they said.

8

A man in a maroon-coloured flannel shirt, which had been purchased for purposes of decoration and made, principally, by some Jewish women on the east side of New York, rounded a corner and walked into the middle of the main street of Yellow Sky. In either hand the man held a long, heavy, blue-black revolver. Often he yelled, and these cries rang through a semblance of a deserted village, shrilly flying over the roofs in a volume that seemed to have no relation to the ordinary vocal strength of a man. It was as if the surrounding stillness formed the arch of a tomb over him. These cries of ferocious challenge rang against walls of silence. And his boots had red tops with gilded imprints, of the kind beloved in winter by little sledding boys on the hillsides of New England.

The man's face flamed in a rage begot of whiskey. His eyes, rolling and yet keen for ambush, hunted the still doorways and windows. He walked with the creeping movement of the midnight cat. As it occurred to him, he roared menacing information. The long revolvers in his hands were as easy as straws; they were moved with an electric swiftness. The little fingers of each hand played sometimes in a musician's way. Plain from the low collar of the shirt, the cords of his neck straightened and sank, straightened and sank, as passion moved him. The only sounds were his terrible invitations. The calm adobes preserved their demeanour at the passing of this small thing in the middle of the street.

There was no offer of fight; no offer of fight. The man called to the sky. There were no attractions. He bellowed and fumed and swayed his revolvers here and everywhere.

The dog of the barkeeper of the Weary Gentleman saloon had not appreciated the advance of events. He yet lay dozing in front of his master's door. At sight of the dog, the man paused and raised his revolver humorously. At sight of the man, the dog sprang up and walked diagonally away, with a sullen head and growling. The man yelled and the dog broke into a gallop. As it was about to enter an alley, there was a loud noise, a whistling, and something spat the ground directly before it. The dog screamed, and, wheeling in terror, galloped headlong in a new direction. Again there was a noise, a whistling, and sand was kicked viciously before it. Fear-stricken, the dog turned and flurried like an animal in a pen. The man stood laughing, his weapons at his hips.

Ultimately the man was attracted by the closed door of the Weary

Gentleman saloon. He went to it, and hammering with a revolver, demanded drink.

The door remaining imperturbable, he picked a bit of paper from the walk and nailed it to the framework with a knife. He then turned his back contemptuously upon this popular resort, and walking to the opposite side of the street, and spinning there on his heel quickly and lithely, fired at the bit of paper. He missed it by a half-inch. He swore at himself, and went away. Later, he comfortably fusilladed the windows of his most intimate friend. The man was playing with this town. It was a toy for him.

But still there was no offer of fight. The name of Jack Potter, his ancient antagonist, entered his mind, and he concluded that it would be a glad thing if he should go to Potter's house and by bombardment induce him to come out and fight. He moved in the direction of his desire, chanting Apache scalp-music.

When he arrived at it, Potter's house presented the same still front as had the other adobes. Taking up a strategic position, the man howled a challenge. But this house regarded him as might a great stone god. It gave no sign. After a decent wait, the man howled further challenges, mingling with them wonderful epithets.

Presently there came the spectacle of a man churning himself into deepest rage over the immobility of a house. He fumed at it as the winter wind attacks a prairie cabin in the North. To the distance there should have gone the sound of a tumult like the fighting of two hundred Mexicans. As necessity bade him, he paused for breath or to reload his revolvers.

9

Potter and his bride walked sheepishly and with speed. Sometimes they laughed together shamefacedly and low.

'Next corner, dear,' he said finally.

They put forth the efforts of a pair walking bowed against a strong wind. Potter was about to raise a finger to point the first appearance of the new home when, as they circled the corner, they came face to face with a man in a maroon-coloured shirt who was feverishly pushing cartridges into a large revolver. Upon the instant the man dropped his revolver to the ground and, like lightning, whipped another from its holster. The second weapon was aimed at the bridegroom's chest.

There was silence. Potter's mouth seemed to be merely a grave for his tongue. He exhibited an instinct to loosen his arm at once from the woman's grip, and he dropped the bag to the sand. As for the bride, her face had gone as yellow as old cloth. She was a slave to hideous rites, gazing at the apparitional snake.

The two men faced each other at a distance of three paces. He of the revolver smiled with a new and quiet ferocity.

'Tried to sneak up on me,' he said. 'Tried to sneak up on me!' His eyes grew more baleful. As Potter made a slight movement, the man thrust his revolver venomously forward. 'No, don't you do it, Jack Potter. Don't you move a finger toward a gun just yet. Don't you move an eyelash. The time has come for me to settle with you, and I'm goin' to do it my own way and loaf along with no interferin'. So if you don't want a gun bent on you, just mind what I tell you.'

Potter looked at his enemy. 'I ain't got a gun on me, Scratchy,' he said. 'Honest, I ain't.' He was stiffening and steadying, but yet somewhere at the back of his mind a vision of the Pullman floated, the sea-green figured velvet, the shining brass, silver and glass, the wood that gleamed as darkly brilliant as the surface of a pool of oil – all the glory of the marriage, the environment of the new estate. 'You know I fight when it comes to fighting, Scratchy Wilson, but I ain't got a gun on me. You'll have to do all the shootin' yourself.'

10

His enemy's face went livid. He stepped forward and lashed his weapon to and fro before Potter's chest. 'Don't you tell me you ain't got no gun on you, you whelp. Don't tell me no lie like that. There ain't a man in Texas ever seen you without no gun. Don't take me for no kid.' His eyes blazed with light, and his throat worked like a pump.

'I ain't takin' you for no kid,' answered Potter. His heels had not moved an inch backward. 'I'm takin' you for a damn fool. I tell you I ain't got a gun, and I ain't. If you're goin' to shoot me up, you better begin now. You'll never get a chance like this again.'

So much enforced reasoning had told on Wilson's rage. He was calmer. 'If you ain't got a gun, why ain't you got a gun?' he sneered. 'Been to Sunday-school?'

'I ain't got a gun because I've just come from San Anton' with my wife. I'm married,' said Potter. 'And if I'd thought there was going to be any galoots like you prowling around when I brought my wife home, I'd had a gun, and don't you forget it.'

'Married!' said Scratchy, not at all comprehending.

'Yes, married. I'm married,' said Potter distinctly.

'Married?' said Scratchy. Seemingly for the first time he saw the drooping, drowning woman at the other man's side. 'No!' he said. He was like a creature allowed a glimpse of another world. He moved a pace backward, and his arm with the revolver dropped to his side. 'Is this the lady?' he asked.

'Yes, this is the lady,' answered Potter.

There was another period of silence.

'Well,' said Wilson at last, slowly, 'I s'pose it's all off now.'

'It's all off if you say so, Scratchy. You know I didn't make the trouble.' Potter lifted his valise.

'Well, I 'low it's off, Jack,' said Wilson. He was looking at the ground. 'Married!' He was not a student of chivalry; it was merely that in the presence of this foreign condition he was a simple child of the earlier plains. He picked up his starboard revolver, and placing both weapons in their holsters, he went away. His feet made funnel-shaped tracks in the heavy sand.

THE BLUE HOTEL

STEPHEN CRANE

1

THE PALACE HOTEL at Fort Romper was painted a light blue, a shade that is on the legs of a kind of heron, causing the bird to declare its position against any background. The Palace Hotel, then, was always screaming and howling in a way that made the dazzling winter landscape of Nebraska seem only a grey swampish hush. It stood alone on the prairie, and when the snow was falling the town two hundred yards away was not visible. But when the traveller alighted at the railway station he was obliged to pass the Palace Hotel before he could come upon the company of low clapboard houses which composed Fort Romper, and it was not to be thought that any traveller could pass the Palace Hotel without looking at it. Pat Scully, the proprietor, had proved himself a master of strategy when he chose his paints. It is true that on clear days, when the great transcontinental expresses, long lines of swaying Pullmans, swept through Fort Romper, passengers were overcome at the sight, and the cult that knows the brown-reds and the subdivisions of the dark greens of the East expressed shame, pity, horror, in a laugh. But to the citizens of this prairie town and to the people who would naturally stop there, Pat Scully had performed a feat. With this opulence and splendour, these creeds, classes, egotisms, that streamed through Romper on the rails day after day, they had no colour in common.

As if the displayed delights of such a blue hotel were not sufficiently enticing, it was Scully's habit to go every morning and evening to meet the leisurely trains that stopped at Romper and work his seductions upon any man that he might see wavering, gripsack in hand.

One morning, when a snow-crusted engine dragged its long string of freight cars and its one passenger coach to the station, Scully performed the marvel of catching three men. One was a shaky and quick-eyed Swede, with a great shining cheap valise; one was a tall bronzed cowboy, who was on his way to a ranch near the Dakota line; one was a little silent man from the East, who didn't look it and didn't announce it. Scully practically made them prisoners. He was so nimble and merry and kindly that each probably felt it would be the height of brutality to try to escape. They trudged off over the creaking board sidewalks in the wake of the eager little Irishman. He wore a heavy fur cap squeezed tightly down on his head. It caused his two red ears to stick out stiffly, as if they were made of tin.

At last, Scully, elaborately, with boisterous hospitality, conducted them through the portals of the blue hotel. The room which they entered was small. It seemed to be merely a proper temple for an enormous stove, which, in the centre, was humming with godlike violence. At various points on its surface the iron had become luminous and glowed yellow from the heat. Beside the stove Scully's son Johnnie was playing high-five with an old farmer who had whiskers both grey and sandy. They were quarrelling. Frequently the old farmer turned his face towards a box of sawdust – coloured brown from tobacco juice – that was behind the stove, and spat with an air of great impatience and irritation. With a loud flourish of words Scully destroyed the game of cards, and bustled his son upstairs with part of the baggage of the new guests. He himself conducted them to three basins of the coldest water in the world. The cowboy and the Easterner burnished themselves fiery red with this water, until it seemed to be some kind of a metal polish. The Swede, however, merely dipped his fingers gingerly and with trepidation. It was notable that throughout this series of small ceremonies the three travellers were made to feel that Scully was very benevolent. He was conferring great favours upon them. He handed the towel from one to the other with an air of philanthropic impulse.

Afterwards they went to the first room, and, sitting about the stove, listened to Scully's officious clamour at his daughters, who were preparing the midday meal. They reflected in the silence of experienced men who tread carefully amid new people. Nevertheless, the old farmer, stationary, invincible in his chair near the warmest part of the stove, turned his face from the sawdust box frequently and addressed a glowing commonplace to the strangers. Usually he was answered in short but adequate sentences by either the cowboy or the Easterner. The Swede said nothing. He seemed to be occupied in making furtive estimates of each man in the room. One might have thought that he had the sense of silly suspicion which comes to guilt. He resembled a badly frightened man.

Later, at dinner, he spoke a little, addressing his conversation entirely to Scully. He volunteered that he had come from New York, where for ten years he had worked as a tailor. These facts seemed to strike Scully as fascinating, and afterwards he volunteered that he had lived at Romper for fourteen years. The Swede asked about the crops and the price of labour. He seemed barely to listen to Scully's extended replies. His eyes continued to rove from man to man.

Finally, with a laugh and a wink, he said that some of these Western communities were very dangerous; and after his statement he straightened his legs under the table, tilted his head, and laughed again, loudly. It was plain that the demonstration had no meaning to the others. They looked at him wondering and in silence.

2

As the men trooped heavily back into the front room, the two little windows presented views of a turmoiling sea of snow. The huge arms of the wind were making attempts – mighty, circular, futile – to embrace the flakes as they sped. A gatepost like a still man with a blanched face stood aghast amid this profligate fury. In a hearty voice Scully announced the presence of a blizzard. The guests of the blue hotel, lighting their pipes, assented with grunts of lazy masculine contentment. No island of the sea could be exempt in the degree of this little room with its humming stove. Johnnie, son of Scully, in a tone which defined his opinion of his ability as a card-player, challenged the old farmer of both grey and sandy whiskers to a game of high-five. The farmer agreed with a contemptuous and bitter scoff. They sat close to the stove, and squared their knees under a wide board. The cowboy and the Easterner watched the game with interest. The Swede remained near the window, aloof, but with a countenance that showed signs of an inexplicable excitement.

The play of Johnnie and the grey-beard was suddenly ended by another quarrel. The old man arose while casting a look of heated scorn at his adversary. He slowly buttoned his coat, and then stalked with fabulous dignity from the room. In the discreet silence of all the other men the Swede laughed. His laughter rang somehow childish. Men by this time had begun to look at him askance, as if they wished to enquire what ailed him.

A new game was formed jocosely. The cowboy volunteered to become the partner of Johnnie, and they all then turned to ask the Swede to throw in his lot with the little Easterner. He asked some questions about the game, and, learning that it wore many names, and that he had played it when it was under an alias, he accepted the invitation. He strode towards the men nervously, as if he expected to be assaulted. Finally, seated, he gazed from face to face and laughed shrilly. This laugh was so strange that the Easterner looked up quickly, the cowboy sat intent and with his mouth open, and Johnnie paused, holding the cards with still fingers.

Afterwards there was a short silence. Then Johnnie said, 'Well, let's get at it. Come on now!' They pulled their chairs forward until their knees were bunched under the board. They began to play, and their interest in the game caused the others to forget the manner of the Swede.

The cowboy was a board-whacker. Each time that he held superior cards he whanged them, one by one, with exceeding force, down upon the improvised table, and took the tricks with a glowing air of prowess and pride that sent thrills of indignation into the hearts of his opponents. A game with a board-whacker in it is sure to become intense. The countenances of the Easterner and the Swede were miserable whenever the cowboy thundered down his aces and kings, while Johnnie, his eyes gleaming with joy, chuckled and chuckled.

Because of the absorbing play none considered the strange ways of the Swede. They paid strict heed to the game. Finally, during a lull caused by a new deal, the Swede suddenly addressed Johnnie: 'I suppose there have been a good many men killed in this room.' The jaws of the others dropped and they looked at him.

'What in hell are you talking about?' said Johnnie.

The Swede laughed again his blatant laugh, full of a kind of false courage and defiance. 'Oh, you know what I mean all right,' he answered.

'I'm a liar if I do!' Johnnie protested. The card was halted, and the men stared at the Swede. Johnnie evidently felt that as the son of the proprietor he should make a direct inquiry. 'Now, what might you be drivin' at, mister?' he asked. The Swede winked at him. It was a wink full of cunning. His fingers shook on the edge of the board. 'Oh, maybe you think I have been to nowheres. Maybe you think I'm a tenderfoot?'

'I don't know nothin' about you,' answered Johnnie, 'and I don't give a damn where you've been. All I got to say is that I don't know what you're driving at. There hain't never been nobody killed in this room.'

The cowboy, who had been steadily gazing at the Swede, then spoke: 'What's wrong with you, mister?'

Apparently it seemed to the Swede that he was formidably menaced. He shivered and turned white near the corners of his mouth. He sent an appealing glance in the direction of the little Easterner. During these moments he did not forget to wear his air of advanced pot-valour. 'They say they don't know what I mean,' he remarked mockingly to the Easterner.

The latter answered after prolonged and cautious reflection. 'I don't understand you,' he said, impassively.

The Swede made a movement then which announced that he thought he had encountered treachery from the only quarter where he had expected sympathy, if not help. 'Oh, I see you are all against me. I see – '

The cowboy was in a state of deep stupefaction. 'Say,' he cried, as he tumbled the deck violently down upon the board – 'say, what are you gittin' at, hey?'

The Swede sprang up with the celerity of a man escaping from a snake on the floor. 'I don't want to fight!' he shouted. 'I don't want to fight!'

The cowboy stretched his long legs indolently and deliberately. His hands were in his pockets. He spat into the sawdust box. 'Well, who the hell thought you did?' he enquired.

The Swede backed rapidly towards a corner of the room. His hands were out protectingly in front of his chest, but he was making an obvious struggle to control his fright. 'Gentlemen,' he quavered, 'I suppose I am going to be killed before I can leave this house! I suppose I am going to be killed before I can leave this house!' In his eyes was the dying-swan look. Through the windows could be seen the snow turning blue in the shadow of dusk. The wind tore at the house and some loose thing beat regularly against the clapboards like a spirit tapping.

A door opened and Scully himself entered. He paused in surprise as he noted the tragic attitude of the Swede. Then he said, 'What's the matter here?'

The Swede answered him swiftly and eagerly: 'These men are going to kill me.'

'Kill you!' ejaculated Scully. 'Kill you! What are you talkin'?'

The Swede made the gesture of a martyr.

Scully wheeled sternly upon his son. 'What is this, Johnnie?'

The lad had grown sullen. 'Damned if I know,' he answered. 'I can't make no sense to it.' He began to shuffle the cards, fluttering them together with an angry snap. 'He says a good many men have been killed in this room, or something like that. And he says he's goin' to be killed here too. I don't know what ails him. He's crazy, I shouldn't wonder.'

Scully then looked for explanation to the cowboy, but the cowboy simply shrugged his shoulders.

'Kill you?' said Scully again to the Swede. 'Kill you? Man, you're off your nut.'

'Oh, I know,' burst out the Swede, 'I know what will happen. Yes, I'm crazy – yes. Yes, of course, I'm crazy – yes. But I know one thing – ' There was a sort of sweat of misery and terror upon his face. 'I know I won't get out of here alive.'

The cowboy drew a deep breath, as if his mind was passing into the last stages of dissolution. 'Well, I'm doggoned,' he whispered to himself.

Scully wheeled suddenly and faced his son. 'You've been troublin' this man!'

Johnnie's voice was loud with its burden of grievance. 'Why, good Gawd, I ain't done nothin' to 'im.'

The Swede broke in. 'Gentlemen, do not disturb yourselves. I will leave this house. I will go away because' – he accused them dramatically with his glance – 'because I do not want to be killed.'

Scully was furious with his son. 'Will you tell me what is the matter, you young divil? What's the matter, anyhow? Speak out!'

'Blame it!' cried Johnnie in despair, 'don't I tell you I don't know. He – he says we want to kill him, and that's all I know. I can't tell what ails him.'

The Swede continued to repeat: 'Never mind, Mr Scully; never mind. I will leave this house. I will go away, because I do not wish to be killed. Yes, of course, I am crazy – yes. But I know one thing! I will go away. I will leave this house. Never mind, Mr Scully; never mind. I will go away.'

'You will not go 'way,' said Scully. 'You will not go 'way until I hear the reason of this business. If anybody has troubled you I will take care of him. This is my house. You are under my roof, and I will not allow any peaceable man to be troubled here.' He cast a terrible eye upon Johnnie, the cowboy, and the Easterner.

'Never mind, Mr Scully; never mind. I will go away. I do not wish to be killed.' The Swede moved towards the door which opened upon the stairs. It was evidently his intention to go at once for his baggage.

'No, no,' shouted Scully peremptorily; but the white-faced man slid by him and disappeared. 'Now,' said Scully severely, 'what does this mane?'

Johnnie and the cowboy cried together: 'Why, we didn't do nothin' to 'im!'

Scully's eyes were cold. 'No,' he said, 'you didn't?'

Johnnie swore a deep oath. 'Why, this is the wildest loon I ever see. We didn't do nothin' at all. We were jest sittin' here playin' cards, and he –'

The father suddenly spoke to the Easterner. 'Mr Blanc,' he asked, 'what has these boys been doin'?'

The Easterner reflected again. 'I didn't see anything wrong at all,' he said at last, slowly.

Scully began to howl. 'But what does it mane?' He stared ferociously at his son. 'I have a mind to lather you for this, me boy.'

Johnnie was frantic. 'Well, what have I done?' he bawled at his father.

3

'I think you are tongue-tied,' said Scully finally to his son, the cowboy, and the Easterner; and at the end of this scornful sentence he left the room.

Upstairs the Swede was swiftly fastening the straps of his great valise. Once his back happened to be half turned towards the door, and, hearing a noise there, he wheeled and sprang up, uttering a loud cry. Scully's wrinkled visage showed grimly in the light of the small lamp he carried. This yellow effulgence, streaming upward, coloured only his prominent features, and left his eyes, for instance, in mysterious shadow. He resembled a murderer.

'Man! man!' he exclaimed, 'have you gone daffy?'

'Oh, no! Oh, no!' rejoined the other. 'There are people in this world who know pretty nearly as much as you do – understand?'

For a moment they stood gazing at each other. Upon the Swede's deathly pale cheeks were two spots brightly crimson and sharply edged, as if they had been carefully painted. Scully placed the light on the table and sat himself on the edge of the bed. He spoke ruminatively. 'By cracky, I never heard of such a thing in my life. It's a complete muddle. I can't, for the soul of me, think how you ever got this idea into your head.' Presently he lifted his eyes and asked: 'And did you sure think they were going to kill you?'

The Swede scanned the old man as if he wished to see into his mind. 'I did,' he said at last. He obviously suspected that this answer might precipitate an outbreak. As he pulled on a strap his whole arm shook, the elbow wavering like a bit of paper.

Scully banged his hand impressively on the footboard of the bed. 'Why, man, we're goin' to have a line of ilictric streetcars in this town next spring.'

' "A line of electric street-cars",' repeated the Swede, stupidly.

'And,' said Scully, 'there's a new railroad goin' to be built down from Broken Arm to here. Not to mintion the four churches and the smashin' big brick schoolhouse. Then there's the big factory, too. Why, in two years Romper 'll be a met–tro–*pol*–is.'

Having finished the preparation of his baggage, the Swede straightened himself. 'Mr Scully,' he said, with sudden hardihood, 'how much do I owe you?'

'You don't owe me anythin',' said the old man, angrily.

'Yes, I do,' retorted the Swede. He took seventy-five cents from his pocket and tendered it to Scully; but the latter snapped his fingers in disdainful refusal. However, it happened that they both stood gazing in a strange fashion at the three silver pieces on the Swede's open palm.

'I'll not take your money,' said Scully at last. 'Not after what's been goin' on here.' Then a plan seemed to strike him. 'Here,' he cried, picking up his lamp and moving towards the door. 'Here! Come with me a minute.'

'No,' said the Swede, in overwhelming alarm.

'Yes,' urged the old man. 'Come on! I want you to come and see a picter – just across the hall – in my room.'

The Swede must have concluded that his hour was come. His jaw dropped and his teeth showed like a dead man's. He ultimately followed Scully across the corridor, but he had the step of one hung in chains.

Scully flashed the light high on the wall of his own chamber. There was revealed a ridiculous photograph of a little girl. She was leaning against a balustrade of gorgeous decoration, and the formidable bang to her hair was prominent. The figure was as graceful as an upright sled-stake, and, withal, it was of the hue of lead. 'There,' said Scully, tenderly, 'that's the picter of my little girl that died. Her name was Carrie. She had the purtiest hair you ever saw! I was that fond of her, she – '

Turning then, he saw that the Swede was not contemplating the picture at all, but, instead, was keeping keen watch on the gloom in the rear.

'Look, man!' cried Scully, heartily. 'That's the picter of my little gal that died. Her name was Carrie. And then here's the picter of my oldest boy, Michael. He's a lawyer in Lincoln, an' doin' well. I gave that boy a grand eddycation, and I'm glad for it now. He's a fine boy. Look at 'im now. Ain't he bold as blazes, him there in Lincoln, an honoured an' respicted gintleman. An honoured an' respicted gintleman,' concluded Scully with a flourish. And, so saying, he smote the Swede jovially on the back.

The Swede faintly smiled.

'Now,' said the old man, 'there's only one more thing.' He dropped suddenly to the floor and thrust his head beneath the bed. The Swede could hear his muffled voice. 'I'd keep it under me piller if it wasn't for that boy Johnnie. Then there's the old woman – Where is it now? I never put it twice in the same place. Ah, now come out with you!'

Presently he backed clumsily from under the bed, dragging with him an old coat rolled into a bundle. 'I've fetched him,' he muttered. Kneeling on the floor, he unrolled the coat and extracted from its heart a large yellow-brown whiskey bottle.

His first manoeuvre was to hold the bottle up to the light. Reassured, apparently, that nobody had been tampering with it, he thrust it with a generous movement towards the Swede.

The weak-kneed Swede was about to eagerly clutch this element of strength, but he suddenly jerked his hand away and cast a look of horror upon Scully.

'Drink,' said the old man affectionately. He had risen to his feet, and now stood facing the Swede.

There was a silence. Then again Scully said: 'Drink!'

The Swede laughed wildly. He grabbed the bottle, put it to his mouth, and as his lips curled absurdly around the opening and his throat worked, he kept his glance, burning with hatred, upon the old man's face.

4

After the departure of Scully the three men, with the cardboard still upon their knees, preserved for a long time an astounded silence. Then Johnnie said: 'That's the dog-dangedest Swede I ever see.'

'He ain't no Swede,' said the cowboy, scornfully.

'Well, what is he then?' cried Johnnie. 'What is he then?'

'It's my opinion,' replied the cowboy deliberately, 'he's some kind of a Dutchman.' It was a venerable custom of the country to entitle as Swedes all light-haired men who spoke with a heavy tongue. In consequence the idea of the cowboy was not without its daring. 'Yes, sir,' he repeated. 'It's my opinion this feller is some kind of a Dutchman.'

'Well, he says he's a Swede, anyhow,' muttered Johnnie, sulkily. He turned to the Easterner: 'What do you think, Mr Blanc?'

'Oh, I don't know,' replied the Easterner.

'Well, what do you think makes him act that way?' asked the cowboy.

'Why, he's frightened.' The Easterner knocked his pipe against a rim of the stove. 'He's clear frightened out of his boots.'

'What at?' cried Johnnie and cowboy together.

The Easterner reflected over his answer.

'What at?' cried the others again.

'Oh, I don't know, but it seems to me this man has been reading dime-novels, and he thinks he's right out in the middle of it – the shootin' and stabbin' and all.'

'But,' said the cowboy, deeply scandalised, 'this ain't Wyoming, ner none of them places. This is Nebrasker.'

'Yes,' added Johnnie, 'an' why don't he wait till he gits *out West*?'

The travelled Easterner laughed. 'It isn't different there even – not in these days. But he thinks he's right in the middle of hell.'

Johnnie and the cowboy mused long.

'It's awful funny,' remarked Johnnie at last.

'Yes,' said the cowboy. 'This is a queer game. I hope we don't git snowed in, because then we'd have to stand this here man bein' around with us all the time. That wouldn't be no good.'

'I wish pop would throw him out,' said Johnnie.

Presently they heard a loud stamping on the stairs, accompanied by ringing jokes in the voice of old Scully, and laughter, evidently from the Swede. The men around the stove stared vacantly at each other. 'Gosh!' said the cowboy. The door flew open, and old Scully, flushed and anecdotal, came into the room. He was jabbering at the Swede, who followed him, laughing bravely. It was the entry of two roisterers from a banquet-hall.

'Come now,' said Scully sharply to the three seated men, 'move up and give us a chance at the stove.' The cowboy and the Easterner obediently sidled their chairs to make room for the newcomers. Johnnie, however, simply arranged himself in a more indolent attitude, and then remained motionless.

'Come! Git over there,' said Scully.

'Plenty of room on the other side of the stove,' said Johnnie.

'Do you think we want to sit in the draught?' roared the father.

But the Swede here interposed with a grandeur of confidence. 'No, no. Let the boy sit where he likes,' he cried in a bullying voice to the father.

'All right! All right!' said Scully, deferentially. The cowboy and the Easterner exchanged glances of wonder.

The five chairs were formed in a crescent about one side of the stove. The Swede began to talk; he talked arrogantly, profanely, angrily. Johnnie, the cowboy and the Easterner maintained a morose silence, while old Scully appeared to be receptive and eager, breaking in constantly with sympathetic ejaculations.

Finally the Swede announced that he was thirsty. He moved in his chair, and said that he would go for a drink of water.

'I'll git it for you,' cried Scully at once.

'No,' said the Swede, contemptuously. 'I'll get it for myself.' He arose and stalked with the air of an owner off into the executive parts of the hotel.

As soon as the Swede was out of hearing Scully sprang to his feet and whispered intensely to the others: 'Upstairs he thought I was tryin' to poison 'im.'

'Say,' said Johnnie, 'this makes me sick. Why don't you throw 'im out in the snow?'

'Why, he's all right now,' declared Scully. 'It was only that he was from the East, and he thought this was a tough place. That's all. He's all right now.'

The cowboy looked with admiration upon the Easterner. 'You were straight,' he said. 'You were on to that there Dutchman.'

'Well,' said Johnnie to his father, 'he may be all right now, but I don't see it. Other time he was scared, but now he's too fresh.'

Scully's speech was always a combination of Irish brogue and idiom, Western twang and idiom, and scraps of curiously formal diction taken from the storybooks and newspapers. He now hurled a strange mass of language at the head of his son. 'What do I keep? What do I keep? What do I keep?' he demanded, in a voice of thunder. He slapped his knee impressively, to indicate that he himself was going to make reply, and that all should heed. 'I keep a hotel,' he shouted. 'A hotel, do you mind? A guest under my roof has sacred privileges. He is to be intimidated by none. Not one word shall he hear that would prijudice him in favour of goin' away. I'll not have it. There's no place in this here town where they can say they iver took in a guest of mine because he was afraid to stay here.' He wheeled suddenly upon the cowboy and the Easterner. 'Am I right?'

'Yes, Mr Scully,' said the cowboy, 'I think you're right.'

'Yes, Mr Scully,' said the Easterner, 'I think you're right.'

5

At six-o'clock supper, the Swede fizzed like a fire-wheel. He sometimes seemed on the point of bursting into riotous song, and in all his madness he was encouraged by old Scully. The Easterner was encased in reserve; the cowboy sat in wide-mouthed amazement, forgetting to eat, while

Johnnie wrathily demolished great plates of food. The daughters of the house, when they were obliged to replenish the biscuits, approached as warily as Indians, and, having succeeded in their purpose, fled with ill-concealed trepidation. The Swede domineered the whole feast, and he gave it the appearance of a cruel bacchanal. He seemed to have grown suddenly taller; he gazed, brutally disdainful, into every face. His voice rang through the room. Once when he jabbed out harpoon-fashion with his fork to pinion a biscuit, the weapon nearly impaled the hand of the Easterner which had been stretched quietly out for the same biscuit.

After supper, as the men filed towards the other room, the Swede smote Scully ruthlessly on the shoulder. 'Well, old boy, that was a good, square meal.' Johnnie looked hopefully at his father; he knew that shoulder was tender from an old fall; and, indeed, it appeared for a moment as if Scully was going to flame out over the matter, but in the end he smiled a sickly smile and remained silent. The others understood from his manner that he was admitting his responsibility for the Swede's new viewpoint.

Johnnie, however, addressed his parent in an aside. 'Why don't you license somebody to kick you downstairs?' Scully scowled darkly by way of reply.

When they were gathered about the stove, the Swede insisted on another game of high-five. Scully gently deprecated the plan at first, but the Swede turned a wolfish glare upon him. The old man subsided, and the Swede canvassed the others. In his tone there was always a great threat. The cowboy and the Easterner both remarked indifferently that they would play. Scully said that he would presently have to go to meet the 6.58 train, and so the Swede turned menacingly upon Johnnie. For a moment their glances crossed like blades, and then Johnnie smiled and said, 'Yes, I'll play.'

They formed a square, with the little board on their knees. The Easterner and the Swede were again partners. As the play went on, it was noticeable that the cowboy was not board-whacking as usual. Meanwhile, Scully, near the lamp, had put on his spectacles and, with an appearance curiously like an old priest, was reading a newspaper. In time he went out to meet the 6.58 train, and, despite his precautions, a gust of polar wind whirled into the room as he opened the door. Besides scattering the cards, it chilled the players to the marrow. The Swede cursed frightfully. When Scully returned, his entrance disturbed a cosy and friendly scene. The Swede again cursed. But presently they were once more intent, their heads bent forward and their hands moving swiftly. The Swede had adopted the fashion of board-whacking.

Scully took up his paper and for a long time remained immersed in matters which were extraordinarily remote from him. The lamp burned badly, and once he stopped to adjust the wick. The newspaper, as he turned from page to page, rustled with a slow and comfortable sound. Then suddenly he heard three terrible words: 'You are cheatin'!'

Such scenes often prove that there can be little of dramatic import in environment. Any room can present a tragic front; any room can be comic. This little den was now hideous as a torture-chamber. The new faces of the men themselves had changed it upon the instant. The Swede held a huge fist in front of Johnnie's face, while the latter looked steadily over it into the blazing orbs of his accuser. The Easterner had grown pallid; the cowboy's jaw had dropped in that expression of bovine amazement which was one of his important mannerisms. After the three words, the first sound in the room was made by Scully's paper as it floated forgotten to his feet. His spectacles had also fallen from his nose, but by a clutch he had saved them in air. His hand, grasping the spectacles, now remained poised awkwardly and near his shoulder. He stared at the card-players.

Probably the silence was while a second elapsed. Then, if the floor had been suddenly twitched out from under the men they could not have moved quicker. The five had projected themselves headlong towards a common point. It happened that Johnnie, in rising to hurl himself upon the Swede, had stumbled slightly because of his curiously instinctive care for the cards and the board. The loss of the moment allowed time for the arrival of Scully, and also allowed the cowboy time to give the Swede a great push which sent him staggering back. The men found tongue together, and hoarse shouts of rage, appeal, or fear burst from every throat. The cowboy pushed and jostled feverishly at the Swede, and the Easterner and Scully clung wildly to Johnnie; but, through the smoky air, above the swaying bodies of the peace-compellers, the eyes of the two warriors ever sought each other in glances of challenge that were at once hot and steely.

Of course the board had been overturned, and now the whole company of cards was scattered over the floor, where the boots of the men trampled the fat and painted kings and queens as they gazed with their silly eyes at the war that was waging above them.

Scully's voice was dominating the yells. 'Stop now! Stop, I say! Stop, now –'

Johnnie, as he struggled to burst through the rank formed by Scully and the Easterner, was crying, 'Well, he says I cheated! He says I cheated! I won't allow no man to say I cheated! If he says I cheated, he's a – !'

The cowboy was telling the Swede, 'Quit, now! Quit, d'ye hear – '

The screams of the Swede never ceased: 'He did cheat! I saw him! I saw him – '

As for the Easterner, he was importuning in a voice that was not heeded: 'Wait a moment, can't you? Oh, wait a moment. What's the good of a fight over a game of cards? Wait a moment – '

In this tumult no complete sentences were clear. 'Cheat' – 'Quit' – 'He says' – these fragments pierced the uproar and rang out sharply. It was remarkable that whereas Scully undoubtedly made the most noise, he was the least heard of any of the riotous band.

Then suddenly there was a great cessation. It was as if each man had paused for breath; and although the room was still lighted with the anger of men, it could be seen that there was no danger of immediate conflict, and at once Johnnie, shouldering his way forward, almost succeeded in confronting the Swede. 'What did you say I cheated for? What did you say I cheated for? I don't cheat, and I won't let no man say I do!'

The Swede said, 'I saw you! I saw you!'

'Well,' cried Johnnie, 'I'll fight any man what says I cheat!'

'No, you won't,' said the cowboy. 'Not here.'

'Ah, be still, can't you?' said Scully, coming between them.

The quiet was sufficient to allow the Easterner's voice to be heard. He was repeating, 'Oh, wait a moment, can't you? What's the good of a fight over a game of cards? Wait a moment!'

Johnnie, his red face appearing above his father's shoulder, hailed the Swede again. 'Did you say I cheated?'

The Swede showed his teeth. 'Yes.'

'Then,' said Johnnie, 'we must fight.'

'Yes, fight,' roared the Swede. He was like a demoniac. 'Yes, fight! I'll show you what kind of a man I am! I'll show you who you want to fight! Maybe you think I can't fight! Maybe you think I can't! I'll show you, you skin, you card-sharp! Yes, you cheated! You cheated! You cheated!'

'Well, let's go at it then, mister,' said Johnnie, coolly.

The cowboy's brow was beaded with sweat from his efforts in intercepting all sorts of raids. He turned in despair to Scully. 'What are you goin' to do now?'

A change had come over the Celtic visage of the old man. He now seemed all eagerness; his eyes glowed.

'We'll let them fight,' he answered, stalwartly. 'I can't put up with it any longer. I've stood this damned Swede till I'm sick. We'll let them fight.'

6

The men prepared to go out of doors. The Easterner was so nervous that he had great difficulty in getting his arms into the sleeves of his new leather coat. As the cowboy drew his fur cap down over his ears his hands trembled. In fact, Johnnie and old Scully were the only ones who displayed no agitation. These preliminaries were conducted without words.

Scully threw open the door. 'Well, come on,' he said. Instantly a terrific wind caused the flame of the lamp to struggle at its wick, while a puff of black smoke sprang from the chimney-top. The stove was in mid-current of the blast, and its voice swelled to equal the roar of the storm. Some of the scarred and bedabbled cards were caught up from the floor and dashed helplessly against the farther wall. The men lowered their heads and plunged into the tempest as into a sea.

No snow was falling, but great whirls and clouds of flakes, swept up from the ground by the frantic winds, were streaming southward with the speed of bullets. The covered land was blue with the sheen of an unearthly satin, and there was no other hue save where, at the low, black railway station – which seemed incredibly distant – one light gleamed like a tiny jewel. As the men floundered into a thigh-deep drift, it was known that the Swede was bawling out something. Scully went to him, put a hand on his shoulder and projected an ear. 'What's that you say?' he shouted.

'I say,' bawled the Swede again, 'I won't stand much show against this gang. I know you'll all pitch on me.'

Scully smote him reproachfully on the arm. 'Tut, man!' he yelled. The wind tore the words from Scully's lips and scattered them far alee.

'You are all a gang of – ' boomed the Swede, but the storm also seized the remainder of this sentence.

Immediately turning their backs upon the wind, the men had swung around a corner to the sheltered side of the hotel. It was the function of the little house to preserve here, amid this great devastation of snow, an irregular V-shape of heavily encrusted grass, which crackled beneath the feet. One could imagine the great drifts piled against the windward side. When the party reached the comparative peace of this spot it was found that the Swede was still bellowing.

'Oh, I know what kind of a thing this is! I know you'll all pitch on me. I can't lick you all!'

Scully turned upon him panther fashion. 'You'll not have to whip all of us. You'll have to whip my son Johnnie. An' the man what troubles you durin' that time will have me to dale with.'

The arrangements were swiftly made. The two men faced each other, obedient to the harsh commands of Scully, whose face, in the subtly luminous gloom, could be seen set in the austere impersonal lines that are pictured on the countenances of the Roman veterans. The Easterner's teeth were chattering, and he was hopping up and down like a mechanical toy. The cowboy stood rock-like.

The contestants had not stripped off any clothing. Each was in his ordinary attire. Their fists were up, and they eyed each other in a calm that had the elements of leonine cruelty in it.

During this pause, the Easterner's mind, like a film, took lasting impressions of three men – the iron-nerved master of the ceremony; the Swede, pale, motionless, terrible; and Johnnie, serene yet ferocious, brutish yet heroic. The entire prelude had in it a tragedy greater than the tragedy of action, and this aspect was accentuated by the long, mellow cry of the blizzard, as it sped the tumbling and wailing flakes into the black abyss of the south.

'Now!' said Scully.

The two combatants leaped forward and crashed together like bullocks. There was heard the cushioned sound of blows, and of a curse squeezing out from between the tight teeth of one.

As for the spectators, the Easterner's pent-up breath exploded from him with a pop of relief, absolute relief from the tension of the preliminaries. The cowboy bounded into the air with a yowl. Scully was immovable, as from supreme amazement and fear at the fury of the fight which he himself had permitted and arranged.

For a time the encounter in the darkness was such a perplexity of flying arms that it presented no more detail than would a swiftly revolving wheel. Occasionally a face, as if illumined by a flash of light, would shine out, ghastly and marked with pink spots. A moment later, the men might have been known as shadows, if it were not for the involuntary utterance of oaths that came from them in whispers.

Suddenly a holocaust of warlike desire caught the cowboy, and he bolted forward with the speed of a bronco. 'Go it, Johnnie! Go it! Kill him! Kill him!'

Scully confronted him. 'Kape back,' he said; and by his glance the cowboy could tell that this man was Johnnie's father.

To the Easterner there was a monotony of unchangeable fighting that was an abomination. This confused mingling was eternal to his sense, which was concentrated in a longing for the end, the priceless end. Once the fighters lurched near him, and as he scrambled hastily backward he heard them breathe like men on the rack.

'Kill him, Johnnie! Kill him! Kill him! Kill him!' The cowboy's face was contorted like one of those agony masks in museums.

'Keep still,' said Scully, icily.

Then there was a sudden loud grunt, incomplete, cut short, and Johnnie's body swung away from the Swede and fell with sickening heaviness to the grass. The cowboy was barely in time to prevent the mad Swede from flinging himself upon his prone adversary. 'No, you don't,' said the cowboy, interposing an arm. 'Wait a second.'

Scully was at his son's side. 'Johnnie! Johnnie, me boy!' His voice had a quality of melancholy tenderness. 'Johnnie! Can you go on with it?' He looked anxiously down into the bloody, pulpy face of his son.

There was a moment of silence, and then Johnnie answered in his ordinary voice, 'Yes, I – it – yes.'

Assisted by his father he struggled to his feet. 'Wait a bit now till you git your wind,' said the old man.

A few paces away the cowboy was lecturing the Swede. 'No, you don't! Wait a second!'

The Easterner was plucking at Scully's sleeve. 'Oh, this is enough,' he pleaded. 'This is enough! Let it go as it stands. This is enough!'

'Bill,' said Scully, 'git out of the road.' The cowboy stepped aside. 'Now.' The combatants were actuated by a new caution as they advanced towards collision. They glared at each other, and then the Swede aimed a lightning blow that carried with it his entire weight. Johnnie was evidently half stupid from weakness, but he miraculously dodged, and his fist sent the over-balanced Swede sprawling.

The cowboy, Scully and the Easterner burst into a cheer that was like a chorus of triumphant soldiery, but before its conclusion the Swede had scuffled agilely to his feet and come in berserk abandon at his foe. There was another perplexity of flying arms, and Johnnie's body again swung away and fell, even as a bundle might fall from a roof. The Swede instantly staggered to a little wind-waved tree and leaned upon it, breathing like an engine, while his savage and flame-lit eyes roamed from face to face as the men bent over Johnnie. There was a splendour of isolation in his situation at this time which the Easterner felt once when, lifting his eyes from the man on the ground, he beheld that mysterious and lonely figure, waiting.

'Are you any good yet, Johnnie?' asked Scully in a broken voice.

The son gasped and opened his eyes languidly. After a moment he answered, 'No – I ain't – any good – any – more.' Then, from shame and bodily ill, he began to weep, the tears furrowing down through the bloodstains on his face. 'He was too – too – too heavy for me.'

Scully straightened and addressed the waiting figure. 'Stranger,' he said, evenly, 'it's all up with our side.' Then his voice changed into that vibrant huskiness which is commonly the tone of the most simple and deadly announcements. 'Johnnie is whipped.'

Without replying, the victor moved off on the route to the front door of the hotel.

The cowboy was formulating new and unspellable blasphemies. The Easterner was startled to find that they were out in a wind that seemed to come direct from the shadowed arctic floes. He heard again the wail of the snow as it was flung to its grave in the south. He knew now that all this time the cold had been sinking into him deeper and deeper, and he wondered that he had not perished. He felt indifferent to the condition of the vanquished man.

'Johnnie, can you walk?' asked Scully.

'Did I hurt – hurt him any?' asked the son.

'Can you walk, boy? Can you walk?'

Johnnie's voice was suddenly strong. There was a robust impatience in it. 'I asked you whether I hurt him any!'

'Yes, yes, Johnnie,' answered the cowboy, consolingly; 'he's hurt a good deal.'

They raised him from the ground, and as soon as he was on his feet he went tottering off, rebuffing all attempts at assistance. When the party rounded the corner they were fairly blinded by the pelting of the snow. It burned their faces like fire. The cowboy carried Johnnie through the drift to the door. As they entered some cards again rose from the floor and beat against the wall.

The Easterner rushed to the stove. He was so profoundly chilled that he almost dared to embrace the glowing iron. The Swede was not in the room. Johnnie sank into a chair, and folding his arms on his knees, buried his face in them. Scully, warming one foot and then the other at a rim of the stove, muttered to himself with Celtic mournfulness. The cowboy had removed his fur cap, and with a dazed and rueful air he was running one hand through his tousled locks. From overhead they could hear the creaking of boards, as the Swede tramped here and there in his room.

The sad quiet was broken by the sudden flinging open of a door that led towards the kitchen. It was instantly followed by an inrush of women. They precipitated themselves upon Johnnie amid a chorus of lamentation. Before they carried their prey off to the kitchen, there to be bathed and harangued with that mixture of sympathy and abuse which is a feat of their sex, the mother straightened herself and fixed old Scully with an eye of stern reproach. 'Shame be upon you, Patrick Scully!' she cried. 'Your own son, too. Shame be upon you!'

'There, now! Be quiet, now!' said the old man, weakly.

'Shame be upon you, Patrick Scully!' The girls, rallying to this slogan, sniffed disdainfully in the direction of those trembling accomplices, the cowboy and the Easterner. Presently they bore Johnnie away, and left the three men to dismal reflection.

7

'I'd like to fight this here Dutchman myself,' said the cowboy, breaking a long silence.

Scully wagged his head sadly. 'No, that wouldn't do. It wouldn't be right. It wouldn't be right.'

'Well, why wouldn't it?' argued the cowboy. 'I don't see no harm in it.'

'No,' answered Scully, with mournful heroism. 'It wouldn't be right. It was Johnnie's fight, and now we mustn't whip the man just because he whipped Johnnie.'

'Yes, that's true enough,' said the cowboy; 'but – he better not get fresh with me, because I couldn't stand no more of it.'

'You'll not say a word to him,' commanded Scully, and even then they heard the tread of the Swede on the stairs. His entrance was made theatric. He swept the door back with a bang and swaggered to the middle of the room. No one looked at him. 'Well,' he cried, insolently, at Scully, 'I s'pose you'll tell me now how much I owe you?'

The old man remained stolid. 'You don't owe me nothin'.'

'Huh!' said the Swede, 'huh! Don't owe 'im nothin'.'

The cowboy addressed the Swede. 'Stranger, I don't see how you come to be so gay around here.'

Old Scully was instantly alert. 'Stop!' he shouted, holding his hand forth, fingers upward. 'Bill, you shut up!'

The cowboy spat carelessly into the sawdust-box. 'I didn't say a word, did I?' he asked.

'Mr Scully,' called the Swede, 'how much do I owe you?' It was seen that he was attired for departure, and that he had his valise in his hand.

'You don't owe me nothin',' repeated Scully in his same imperturbable way.

'Huh!' said the Swede. 'I guess you're right. I guess if it was any way at all, you'd owe me somethin'. That's what I guess.' He turned to the cowboy. ' "Kill him! Kill him! Kill him!" ' he mimicked, and then guffawed victoriously. ' "Kill him!" ' He was convulsed with ironical humour.

But he might have been jeering the dead. The three men were immovable and silent, staring with glassy eyes at the stove.

The Swede opened the door and passed into the storm, giving one derisive glance backward at the still group.

As soon as the door was closed, Scully and the cowboy leaped to their feet and began to curse. They trampled to and fro, waving their arms and smashing into the air with their fists. 'Oh, but that was a hard minute!' wailed Scully. 'That was a hard minute! Him there leerin' and scoffin'! One bang at his nose was worth forty dollars to me that minute! How did you stand it, Bill?'

'How did I stand it?' cried the cowboy in a quivering voice. 'How did I stand it? Oh!'

The old man burst into sudden brogue. 'I'd loike to take that Swade,' he wailed, 'and hould 'im down on a shtone flure and bate 'im to a jelly wid a shtick!'

The cowboy groaned in sympathy. 'I'd like to git him by the neck and ha–ammer him' – he brought his hand down on a chair with a noise like a pistol-shot – 'hammer that there Dutchman until he couldn't tell himself from a dead coyote!'

'I'd bate 'im until he – '

'I'd show *him* some things – '

And then together they raised a yearning, fanatic cry – 'Oh–o–oh! if we only could – '

'Yes!'

'Yes!'

'And then I'd – '

'O–o–oh!'

8

The Swede, tightly gripping his valise, tacked across the face of the storm as if he carried sails. He was following a line of little naked, gasping trees, which he knew must mark the way of the road. His face, fresh from the pounding of Johnnie's fists, felt more pleasure than pain in the wind and the driving snow. A number of square shapes loomed upon him finally, and he knew them as the houses of the main body of the town. He found a street and made travel along it, leaning heavily upon the wind whenever, at a corner, a terrific blast caught him.

He might have been in a deserted village. We picture the world as thick with conquering and elate humanity, but here, with the bugles of the tempest pealing, it was hard to imagine a peopled earth. One viewed the existence of man then as a marvel, and conceded a glamour of wonder to these lice which were caused to cling to a whirling, fire-smote, ice-locked, disease-stricken, space-lost bulb. The conceit of man was explained by this storm to be the very engine of life. One was a coxcomb not to die in it. However, the Swede found a saloon.

In front of it an indomitable red light was burning, and the snowflakes were made blood-colour as they flew through the circumscribed territory of the lamp's shining. The Swede pushed open the door of the saloon and entered. A sanded expanse was before him, and at the end of it four men sat about a table drinking. Down one side of the room extended a radiant bar, and its guardian was leaning upon his elbows listening to the talk of the men at the table. The Swede dropped his valise upon the floor, and, smiling fraternally upon the barkeeper, said, 'Gimme some whiskey, will you?' The man placed a bottle, a whiskey glass and a glass of ice-thick water upon the bar. The Swede poured himself an abnormal portion of whiskey and drank it in three gulps. 'Pretty bad night,' remarked the bartender, indifferently. He was making the pretension of blindness which is usually a distinction of his class; but it could have been seen that he was furtively studying the half-erased bloodstains on the face of the Swede. 'Bad night,' he said again.

'Oh, it's good enough for me,' replied the Swede, hardily, as he poured himself some more whiskey. The barkeeper took his coin and manoeuvred it through its reception by the highly nickelled cash-machine. A bell rang; a card labelled '20 cts' had appeared.

'No,' continued the Swede, 'this isn't too bad weather. It's good enough for me.'

'So?' murmured the barkeeper, languidly.

The copious drams made the Swede's eyes swim, and he breathed a trifle heavier. 'Yes, I like this weather. I like it. It suits me.' It was apparently his design to impart a deep significance to these words.

'So?' murmured the bartender again. He turned to gaze dreamily at the scroll-like birds and birdlike scrolls which had been drawn with soap upon the mirrors back of the bar.

'Well, I guess I'll take another drink,' said the Swede, presently. 'Have something?'

'No, thanks; I'm not drinkin',' answered the bartender. Afterwards he asked, 'How did you hurt your face?'

The Swede immediately began to boast loudly. 'Why, in a fight. I thumped the soul out of a man down here at Scully's hotel.'

The interest of the four men at the table was at last aroused.

'Who was it?' said one.

'Johnnie Scully,' blustered the Swede. 'Son of the man what runs it. He will be pretty near dead for some weeks, I can tell you. I made a nice thing of him, I did. He couldn't get up. They carried him in the house. Have a drink?'

Instantly the men in some subtle way encased themselves in reserve. 'No, thanks,' said one. The group was of curious formation. Two were prominent local businessmen; one was the district-attorney; and one was a professional gambler of the kind known as 'square'. But a scrutiny of the group would not have enabled an observer to pick the gambler from the men of more reputable pursuits. He was, in fact, a man so delicate in manner when among people of fair class, and so judicious in his choice of victims, that in the strictly masculine part of the town's life he had come to be explicitly trusted and admired. People called him a thoroughbred. The fear and contempt with which his craft was regarded was undoubtedly the reason that his quiet dignity shone conspicuous above the quiet dignity of men who might be merely hatters, billiard-markers or grocery-clerks. Beyond an occasional unwary traveller, who came by rail, this gambler was supposed to prey solely upon reckless and senile farmers, who, when flush with good crops, drove into town in all the pride and confidence of an absolutely invulnerable stupidity. Hearing at times in circuitous fashion of the despoilment of such a farmer, the important men of Romper invariably laughed in contempt of the victim, and, if they thought of the wolf at all, it was with a kind of pride at the knowledge that he would never dare think of attacking their wisdom and courage. Besides, it was popular that this gambler had a real wife and two real children in a neat cottage in a suburb, where he led an exemplary home life; and when anyone even suggested a discrepancy in his character, the crowd immediately vociferated descriptions of this virtuous family circle. Then men who led exemplary home lives, and men who did not lead exemplary home lives, all subsided in a bunch, remarking that there was nothing more to be said.

However, when a restriction was placed upon him – as, for instance, when a strong clique of members of the new Pollywog Club refused to permit him, even as a spectator, to appear in the rooms of the organisation – the candour and gentleness with which he accepted the judgement disarmed many of his foes and made his friends more desperately partisan. He invariably distinguished between himself and a respectable Romper man so quickly and frankly that his manner actually appeared to be a continual broadcast compliment.

And one must not forget to declare the fundamental fact of his entire position in Romper. It is irrefutable that in all affairs outside of his business, in all matters that occur eternally and commonly between man and man, this thieving card-player was so generous, so just, so moral that, in a contest, he could have put to flight the consciences of nine-tenths of the citizens of Romper.

And so it happened that he was seated in this saloon with the two prominent local merchants and the district-attorney.

The Swede continued to drink raw whiskey, meanwhile babbling at the barkeeper and trying to induce him to indulge in potations. 'Come on. Have a drink. Come on. What – no? Well, have a little one, then. By gawd, I've whipped a man tonight, and I want to celebrate. I whipped him good, too. Gentlemen,' the Swede cried to the men at the table, 'have a drink?'

'Ssh!' said the barkeeper.

The group at the table, although furtively attentive, had been pretending to be deep in talk, but now a man lifted his eyes towards the Swede and said, shortly, 'Thanks. We don't want any more.'

At this reply the Swede ruffled out his chest like a rooster. 'Well,' he exploded, 'it seems I can't get anybody to drink with me in this town. Seems so, don't it? Well!'

'Ssh!' said the barkeeper.

'Say,' snarled the Swede, 'don't you try to shut me up. I won't have it. I'm a gentleman, and I want people to drink with me. And I want 'em to drink with me now. *Now* – do you understand?' He rapped the bar with his knuckles.

Years of experience had calloused the bartender. He merely grew sulky. 'I hear you,' he answered.

'Well,' cried the Swede, 'listen hard then. See those men over there? Well, they're going to drink with me, and don't you forget it. Now you watch.'

'Hi!' yelled the barkeeper, 'this won't do!'

'Why won't it?' demanded the Swede. He stalked over to the table, and by chance laid his hand upon the shoulder of the gambler. 'How about this?' he asked, wrathfully. 'I asked you to drink with me.'

The gambler simply twisted his head and spoke over his shoulder. 'My friend, I don't know you.'

'Oh, hell!' answered the Swede, 'come and have a drink.'

'Now, my boy,' advised the gambler, kindly, 'take your hand off my shoulder and go 'way and mind your own business.' He was a little, slim man, and it seemed strange to hear him use this tone of heroic patronage to the burly Swede. The other men at the table said nothing.

'What! You won't drink with me, you little dude? I'll make you then! I'll make you!' The Swede had grasped the gambler frenziedly at the throat, and was dragging him from his chair. The other men sprang up. The barkeeper dashed around the corner of his bar. There was a great tumult, and then was seen a long blade in the hand of the gambler. It shot forward, and a human body, this citadel of virtue, wisdom, power, was pierced as easily as if it had been a melon. The Swede fell with a cry of supreme astonishment.

The prominent merchants and the district-attorney must have at once tumbled out of the place backwards. The bartender found himself hanging limply to the arm of a chair and gazing into the eyes of a murderer.

'Henry,' said the latter, as he wiped his knife on one of the towels that hung beneath the bar-rail, 'you tell 'em where to find me. I'll be home, waiting for 'em.' Then he vanished. A moment afterwards the barkeeper was in the street dinning through the storm for help and, moreover, companionship.

The corpse of the Swede, alone in the saloon, had its eyes fixed upon a dreadful legend that dwelt atop of the cash-machine: 'This registers the amount of your purchase.'

9

Months later, the cowboy was frying pork over the stove of a little ranch near the Dakota line when there was a quick thud of hoofs outside, and presently the Easterner entered with the letters and the papers.

'Well,' said the Easterner at once, 'the chap that killed the Swede has got three years. Wasn't much, was it?'

'He has? Three years?' The cowboy poised his pan of pork, while he ruminated upon the news. 'Three years. That ain't much.'

'No. It was a light sentence,' replied the Easterner as he unbuckled his spurs. 'Seems there was a good deal of sympathy for him in Romper.'

'If the bartender had been any good,' observed the cowboy, thoughtfully, 'he would have gone in and cracked that there Dutchman on the head with a bottle in the beginnin' of it and stopped all this here murderin'.'

'Yes, a thousand things might have happened,' said the Easterner, tartly.

The cowboy returned his pan of pork to the fire, but his philosophy continued. 'It's funny, ain't it? If he hadn't said Johnnie was cheatin' he'd be alive this minute. He was an awful fool. Game played for fun, too. Not for money. I believe he was crazy.'

'I feel sorry for that gambler,' said the Easterner.

'Oh, so do I,' said the cowboy. 'He don't deserve none of it for killin' who he did.'

'The Swede might not have been killed if everything had been square.'

'Might not have been killed?' exclaimed the cowboy. 'Everythin' square? Why, when he said that Johnnie was cheatin' and acted like such a jackass? And then in the saloon he fairly walked up to git hurt?' With these arguments the cowboy browbeat the Easterner and reduced him to rage.

'You're a fool!' cried the Easterner, viciously. 'You're a bigger jackass than the Swede by a million majority. Now let me tell you one thing. Let me tell you something. Listen! Johnnie *was* cheating!'

'Johnnie?' said the cowboy, blankly. There was a minute of silence, and then he said, robustly, 'Why, no. The game was only for fun.'

'Fun or not,' said the Easterner, 'Johnnie was cheating. I saw him. I know it. I saw him. And I refused to stand up and be a man. I let the Swede fight it out alone. And you – you were simply puffing around the place and wanting to fight. And then old Scully himself! We are all in it!

This poor gambler isn't even a noun. He is kind of an adverb. Every sin is the result of a collaboration. We, five of us, have collaborated in the murder of this Swede. Usually there are from a dozen to forty women really involved in every murder, but in this case it seems to be only five men – you, I, Johnnie, old Scully, and that fool of an unfortunate gambler came merely as a culmination, the apex of a human movement, and gets all the punishment.'

The cowboy, injured and rebellious, cried out blindly into this fog of mysterious theory: 'Well, I didn't do anythin', did I?'

HOW SANTA CLAUS CAME TO SIMPSON'S BAR

BRET HARTE

IT had been raining in the valley of the Sacramento. The North Fork had overflowed its banks and Rattlesnake Creek was impassable. The few boulders that had marked the summer ford at Simpson's Crossing were obliterated by a vast sheet of water stretching to the foothills. The upstage was stopped at Grangers; the last mail had been abandoned in the tules, the rider swimming for his life. 'An area,' remarked the *Sierra Avalanche*, with pensive local pride, 'as large as the State of Massachusetts is now under water.'

Nor was the weather any better in the foothills. The mud lay deep on the mountain road; wagons that neither physical force nor moral objurgation could move from the evil ways into which they had fallen, encumbered the track, and the way to Simpson's Bar was indicated by broken-down teams and hard swearing. And farther on, cut off and inaccessible, rained upon and bedraggled, smitten by high winds and threatened by high water, Simpson's Bar, on the eve of Christmas Day 1862, clung like a swallow's nest to the rocky entablature and splintered capitals of Table Mountain, and shook in the blast.

As night shut down on the settlement, a few lights gleamed through the mist from the windows of cabins on either side of the highway now crossed and gullied by lawless streams and swept by marauding winds. Happily most of the population were gathered at Thompson's store, clustered around a red-hot stove, at which they silently spat in some accepted sense of social communion that perhaps rendered conversation unnecessary. Indeed, most methods of diversion had long since been exhausted on Simpson's Bar; high water had suspended the regular occupations on gulch and on river, and a consequent lack of money and whiskey had taken the zest from most illegitimate recreation. Even Mr Hamlin was fain to leave the Bar with fifty dollars in his pocket – the only amount actually realised of the large sums won by him in the successful exercise of his arduous profession. 'Ef I was asked,' he remarked somewhat later – 'ef I was asked to pint out a purty little village where a retired sport as didn't care for money could exercise hisself, frequent and lively, I'd say Simpson's Bar; but for a young man with a large family depending on his exertions, it don't pay.' As Mr Hamlin's family consisted mainly of female adults, this remark is quoted rather to show the breadth of his humour than the exact extent of his responsibilities.

Howbeit, the unconscious objects of this satire sat that evening in the listless apathy begotten of idleness and lack of excitement. Even the sudden splashing of hoofs before the door did not arouse them. Dick Bullen alone paused in the act of scraping out his pipe, and lifted his head, but no other one of the group indicated any interest in, or recognition of, the man who entered.

It was a figure familiar enough to the company, and known in Simpson's Bar as 'The Old Man'. A man of perhaps fifty years; grizzled and scant of hair, but still fresh and youthful of complexion. A face full of ready, but not very powerful sympathy, with a chameleon-like aptitude for taking on the shade and colour of contiguous moods and feelings. He had evidently just left some hilarious companions, and did not at first notice the gravity of the group, but clapped the shoulder of the nearest man jocularly, and threw himself into a vacant chair.

'Jest heard the best thing out, boys! Ye know Smiley, over yar – Jim Smiley – funniest man in the Bar? Well, Jim was jest telling the richest yarn about – '

'Smiley's a danged fool,' interrupted a gloomy voice.

'A particular low-down skunk,' added another in sepulchral accents.

A silence followed these positive statements. The Old Man glanced quickly around the group. Then his face slowly changed. 'That's so,' he said reflectively, after a pause, 'certingly a sort of a skunk and suthin of a fool. In course.' He was silent for a moment as in painful contemplation of the unsavouriness and folly of the unpopular Smiley. 'Dismal weather, ain't it?' he added, now fully embarked on the current of prevailing sentiment. 'Mighty rough papers on the boys, and no show for money this season. And tomorrow's Christmas.'

There was a movement among the men at this announcement, but whether of satisfaction or disgust was not plain. 'Yes,' continued the Old Man in the lugubrious tone he had, within the last few moments, unconsciously adopted, 'yes, Christmas, and tonight's Christmas Eve. Ye see, boys, I kinder thought – that is, I sorter had an idee, jest passin' like, you know – that maybe ye'd all like to come over to my house tonight and have a sort of tear round. But I suppose, now, you wouldn't? Don't feel like it, maybe?' he added with anxious sympathy, peering into the faces of his companions.

'Well, I don't know,' responded Tom Flynn with some cheerfulness.

'P'r'aps we may. But how about your wife, Old Man? What does *she* say to it?'

The Old Man hesitated. His conjugal experience had not been a happy one, and the fact was known to Simpson's Bar. His first wife, a delicate, pretty little woman, had suffered keenly and secretly from the jealous suspicions of her husband, until one day he invited the whole Bar to his house to expose her infidelity. On arriving, the party found the shy, petite creature quietly engaged in her household duties, and retired abashed and discomfited. But the sensitive woman did not easily recover from the shock of this extraordinary outrage. It was with difficulty she regained her equanimity sufficiently to release her lover from the closet in which he was concealed and escape with him. She left a boy of three years to comfort her bereaved husband. The Old Man's present wife had been his cook. She was large, loyal and aggressive.

Before he could reply, Joe Dimmick suggested with great directness that it was the 'Old Man's house', and that, invoking the Divine Power, if the case were his own, he would invite whom he pleased, even if in so doing he imperilled his salvation. The Powers of Evil, he further remarked, should contend against him vainly. All this delivered with a terseness and vigour lost in this necessary translation.

'In course. Certainly. Thet's it,' said the Old Man with a sympathetic frown. 'Thar's no trouble about *thet*. It's my own house, built every stick on it myself. Don't you be afeard o' her, boys. She *may* cut up a trifle rough – ez wimmin do – but she'll come round.' Secretly the Old Man trusted to the exaltation of liquor and the power of courageous example to sustain him in such an emergency.

As yet, Dick Bullen, the oracle and leader of Simpson's Bar, had not spoken. He now took his pipe from his lips. 'Old Man, how's that yer Johnny gettin' on? Seems to me he didn't look so peart last time I seed him on the bluff heavin' rocks at Chinamen. Didn't seem to take much interest in it. Thar was a gang of 'em by yar yesterday – drownded out up the river – and I kinder thought o' Johnny, and how he'd miss 'em! Maybe now, we'd be in the way ef he wus sick?'

The father, evidently touched not only by this pathetic picture of Johnny's deprivation, but by the considerate delicacy of the speaker, hastened to assure him that Johnny was better and that a 'little fun might 'liven him up'. Whereupon Dick arose, shook himself, and saying, 'I'm ready. Lead the way, Old Man: here goes,' himself led the way with a leap, a characteristic howl, and darted out into the night. As he passed through the outer room he caught up a blazing brand from the hearth. The action was repeated by the rest of the party, closely following and elbowing each other, and before the astonished proprietor of Thompson's grocery was aware of the intention of his guests, the room was deserted.

The night was pitchy dark. In the first gust of wind their temporary torches were extinguished, and only the red brands dancing and flitting in the gloom like drunken will-o'-the-wisps indicated their whereabouts. Their way led up Pine Tree Canyon, at the head of which a broad, low, bark-thatched cabin burrowed in the mountainside. It was the home of the Old Man, and the entrance to the tunnel in which he worked when he worked at all. Here the crowd paused for a moment, out of delicate deference to their host, who came up panting in the rear.

'P'r'aps ye'd better hold on a second out yer, whilst I go in and see thet things is all right,' said the Old Man, with an indifference he was far from feeling. The suggestion was graciously accepted, the door opened and closed on the host, and the crowd, leaning their backs against the wall and cowering under the eaves, waited and listened.

For a few moments there was no sound but the dripping of water from the eaves and the stir and rustle of wrestling boughs above them. Then the men became uneasy, and whispered suggestion and suspicion passed from the one to the other. 'Reckon she's caved in his head the first lick!' 'Decoyed him inter the tunnel and barred him up, likely.' 'Got him down and sittin' on him.' 'Prob'ly bilin suthin to heave on us: stand clear the door, boys!' For just then the latch clicked, the door slowly opened, and a voice said, 'Come in out o' the wet.'

The voice was neither that of the Old Man nor of his wife. It was the voice of a small boy, its weak treble broken by that preternatural hoarseness which only vagabondage and the habit of premature self-assertion can give. It was the face of a small boy that looked up at theirs – a face that might have been pretty and even refined but that it was darkened by evil knowledge from within, and dirt and hard experience from without. He had a blanket around his shoulders and had evidently just risen from his bed. 'Come in,' he repeated,' and don't make no noise. The Old Man's in there talking to mar,' he continued, pointing to an adjacent room which seemed to be a kitchen, from which the Old Man's voice came in deprecating accents. 'Let me be,' he added, querulously, to Dick Bullen, who had caught him up, blanket and all, and was affecting to toss him into the fire, 'let go o' me, you darned old fool, d'ye hear?'

Thus adjured, Dick Bullen lowered Johnny to the ground with a smothered laugh, while the men, entering quietly, ranged themselves around a long table of rough boards which occupied the centre of the room. Johnny then gravely proceeded to a cupboard and brought out several articles which he deposited on the table. 'Thar's whiskey. And crackers. And red herons. And cheese.' He took a bite of the latter on his way to the table. 'And sugar.' He scooped up a mouthful *en route* with a small and very dirty hand. 'And terbacker. Thar's dried appils too on the shelf, but I don't admire 'em. Appils is swellin'. Thar,' he concluded, 'now wade in, and don't be afeard. *I* don't mind the old woman. She don't b'long to *me*. S'long.'

He had stepped to the threshold of a small room, scarcely larger than a closet, partitioned off from the main apartment, and holding in its dim recess a small bed. He stood there a moment looking at the company, his bare feet peeping from the blanket, and nodded.

'Hello, Johnny! You ain't goin' to turn in agin, are ye?' said Dick.

'Yes, I are,' responded Johnny, decidedly.

'Why, wot's up, old fellow?'

'I'm sick.'

'How sick!'

'I've got a fevier. And childblains. And roomatiz,' returned Johnny, and vanished within. After a moment's pause, he added in the dark, apparently from under the bedclothes – 'And biles!'

There was an embarrassing silence. The men looked at each other, and at the fire. Even with the appetising banquet before them, it seemed as if they might again fall into the despondency of Thompson's grocery, when the voice of the Old Man, incautiously lifted, came deprecatingly from the kitchen.

'Certainly! Thet's so. In course they is. A gang o' lazy drunken loafers, and that ar Dick Bullen's the ornariest of all. Didn't hev no more *sabe* than to come round yar with sickness in the house and no provision. Thet's what I said: "Bullen," sez I, "it's crazy drunk you are, or a fool," sez I, "to think o' such a thing." "Staples," I sez, "be you a man, Staples, and 'spect to raise hell under my roof and invalids lyin' round?" But they would come – they would. Thet's wot you must 'spect o' such trash as lays round the Bar.'

A burst of laughter from the men followed this unfortunate exposure. Whether it was overheard in the kitchen, or whether the Old Man's irate companion had just then exhausted all other modes of expressing her contemptuous indignation, I cannot say, but a back door was suddenly slammed with great violence. A moment later and the Old Man reappeared, haply unconscious of the cause of the late hilarious outburst, and smiled blandly.

'The old woman thought she'd jest run over to Mrs McFadden's for a sociable call,' he explained, with jaunty indifference, as he took a seat at the board.

Oddly enough it needed this untoward incident to relieve the embarrassment that was beginning to be felt by the party, and their natural audacity returned with their host. I do not propose to record the convivialities of that evening. The inquisitive reader will accept the statement that the conversation was characterised by the same intellectual exaltation, the same cautious reverence, the same fastidious delicacy, the same rhetorical precision, and the same logical and coherent discourse somewhat later in the evening which distinguish similar gatherings of the masculine sex in more civilised localities and under more favourable auspices. No glasses were broken in the absence of any; no liquor was uselessly spilt on floor or table in the scarcity of that article.

It was nearly midnight when the festivities were interrupted. 'Hush,' said Dick Bullen, holding up his hand. It was the querulous voice of Johnny from his adjacent closet: 'Oh dad!'

The Old Man arose hurriedly and disappeared into the closet. Presently he reappeared. 'His rheumatiz is coming on agin bad,' he explained, 'and he wants rubbin'.' He lifted the demijohn of whiskey from the table and shook it. It was empty. Dick Bullen put down his tin cup with an embarrassed laugh. So did the others. The Old Man examined their contents and said hopefully, 'I reckon that's enough; he don't need much. You hold on all o' you for a spell, and I'll be back'; and vanished into the closet with an old flannel shirt and the whiskey. The door closed but imperfectly, and the following dialogue was distinctly audible: 'Now, sonny, whar does she ache worst?'

'Sometimes over yar and sometimes under yer; but it's most powerful from yer to yer. Rub yer, dad.'

A silence seemed to indicate a brisk rubbing. Then Johnny: 'Hevin' a good time out yer, dad?'

'Yes, sonny.'

'Tomorrer's Chrismiss, ain't it?'

'Yes, sonny. How does she feel now?'

'Better rub a little furder down. Wot's Chrismiss, anyway? Wot's it all about?'

'Oh, it's a day.'

This exhaustive definition was apparently satisfactory, for there was a silent interval of rubbing. Presently Johnny again: 'Mar sez that everywhere else but yer everybody gives things to everybody Chrismiss, and then she jist waded inter you. She sez thar's a man they call Sandy Claws, not a white man, you know, but a kind o' Chinemin, comes down the chimbley night afore Chrismiss and gives things to chillern – boys like me. Puts 'em in their butes! Thet's what she tried to play upon me. Easy now, pop, whar are you rubbin' to – thet's a mile from the place. She jest made that up, didn't she, jest to aggrewate me and you? Don't rub thar . . . Why, dad!'

In the great quiet that seemed to have fallen upon the house the sigh of the near pines and the drip of leaves without was very distinct. Johnny's voice, too, was lowered as he went on, 'Don't you take on now, fur I'm gettin' all right fast. Wot's the boys doin' out thar?'

The Old Man partly opened the door and peered through. His guests were sitting there sociably enough, and there were a few silver coins and a lean buckskin purse on the table. 'Bettin' on suthin – some little game or 'nother. They're all right,' he replied to Johnny, and recommenced his rubbing.

'I'd like to take a hand and win some money,' said Johnny, reflectively, after a pause.

The Old Man glibly repeated what was evidently a familiar formula, that if Johnny would wait until he struck it rich in the tunnel he'd have lots of money, etc., etc.

'Yes,' said Johnny, 'but you don't. And whether you strike it or I win it, it's about the same. It's all luck. But it's mighty cur'o's about Chrismiss – ain't it? Why do they call it Chrismiss?'

Perhaps from some instinctive deference to the overhearing of his guests, or from some vague sense of incongruity, the Old Man's reply was so low as to be inaudible beyond the room.

'Yes,' said Johnny, with some slight abatement of interest, 'I've heerd o' *him* before. Thar, that'll do, dad. I don't ache near so bad as I did. Now wrap me tight in this yer blanket. So. Now,' he added in a muffled whisper, 'sit down yer by me till I go asleep.' To assure himself of obedience, he disengaged one hand from the blanket and, grasping his father's sleeve, again composed himself to rest.

For some moments the Old Man waited patiently. Then the unwonted stillness of the house excited his curiosity, and without moving from the bed, he cautiously opened the door with his disengaged hand, and looked into the main room. To his infinite surprise it was dark and deserted. But even then a smouldering log on the hearth broke, and by the upspringing blaze he saw the figure of Dick Bullen sitting by the dying embers.

'Hello!'

Dick started, rose, and came somewhat unsteadily towards him.

'Whar's the boys?' said the Old Man.

'Gone up the canyon on a little *pasear*. They're coming back for me in a minit. I'm waitin' round for 'em. What are you starin' at, Old Man?' he added with a forced laugh; 'do you think I'm drunk?'

The Old Man might have been pardoned the supposition, for Dick's eyes were humid and his face flushed. He loitered and lounged back to the chimney, yawned, shook himself, buttoned up his coat and laughed. 'Liquor ain't so plenty as that, Old Man. Now don't you git up,' he continued, as the Old Man made a movement to release his sleeve from Johnny's hand. 'Don't you mind manners. Sit jest whar you be; I'm goin' in a jiffy. Thar, that's them now.'

There was a low tap at the door. Dick Bullen opened it quickly, nodded 'Good night' to his host, and disappeared. The Old Man would have followed him but for the hand that still unconsciously grasped his sleeve. He could have easily disengaged it: it was small, weak, and emaciated. But perhaps because it *was* small, weak, and emaciated, he changed his mind, and, drawing his chair closer to the bed, rested his head upon it. In this defenceless attitude the potency of his earlier potations surprised him. The room flickered and faded before his eyes, reappeared, faded again, went out, and left him – asleep.

Meantime Dick Bullen, closing the door, confronted his companions. 'Are you ready?' said Staples. 'Ready,' said Dick; 'what's the time?' 'Past twelve,' was the reply; 'can you make it? – it's nigh on fifty miles, the round trip hither and yon.' 'I reckon,' returned Dick, shortly. 'Whar's the mare?' 'Bill and Jack's holdin' her at the crossin'.' 'Let 'em hold on a minit longer,' said Dick.

He turned and re-entered the house softly. By the light of the guttering candle and dying fire he saw that the door of the little room was open. He stepped towards it on tiptoe and looked in. The Old Man had fallen back in his chair, snoring, his helpless feet thrust out in a line with his collapsed shoulders, and his hat pulled over his eyes. Beside him, on a narrow wooden bedstead, lay Johnny, muffled tightly in a blanket that hid all save a strip of forehead and a few curls damp with perspiration. Dick Bullen made a step forward, hesitated, and glanced over his shoulder into the deserted room. Everything was quiet. With a sudden resolution he parted his huge mustaches with both hands and stooped over the sleeping boy. But even as he did so a mischievous blast, lying in wait, swooped down the chimney, rekindled the hearth and lit up the room with a shameless glow from which Dick fled in bashful terror.

His companions were already waiting for him at the crossing. Two of them were struggling in the darkness with some strange misshapen bulk, which as Dick came nearer took the semblance of a great yellow horse.

It was the mare. She was not a pretty picture. From her Roman nose to her rising haunches, from her arched spine hidden by the stiff *machillas* of a Mexican saddle, to her thick, straight, bony legs, there was not a line of equine grace. In her half-blind but wholly vicious white eyes, in her protruding under lip, in her monstrous colour, there was nothing but ugliness and vice.

'Now then,' said Staples, 'stand cl'ar of her heels, boys, and up with you. Don't miss your first holt of her mane, and mind ye get your off stirrup *quick*. Ready!'

There was a leap, a scrambling struggle, a bound, a wild retreat of the crowd, a circle of flying hoofs, two springless leaps that jarred the earth, a rapid play and jingle of spurs, a plunge, and then the voice of Dick somewhere in the darkness, 'All right!'

'Don't take the lower road back unless you're hard pushed for time! Don't hold her in downhill! We'll be at the ford at five. G'lang! Hoopa! Mula! *Go!*'

A splash, a spark struck from the ledge in the road, a clatter in the rocky cut beyond, and Dick was gone.

Sing, O Muse, the ride of Richard Bullen! Sing, O Muse, of chivalrous men! The sacred quest, the doughty deeds, the battery of low churls, the fearsome ride and gruesome perils of the Flower of Simpson's Bar! Alack! she is dainty, this Muse! She will have none of this bucking brute and swaggering, ragged rider, and I must fain follow him in prose, afoot!

It was one o'clock, and yet he had only gained Rattlesnake Hill. For in that time Jovita had rehearsed to him all her imperfections and practised all her vices. Thrice had she stumbled. Twice had she thrown up her Roman nose in a straight line with the reins, and, resisting bit and spur, struck out madly across country. Twice had she reared, and, rearing, fallen backward; and twice had the agile Dick, unharmed, regained his seat before she found her vicious legs again. And a mile beyond them, at the foot of a long hill, was Rattlesnake Creek. Dick knew that here was the crucial test of his ability to perform his enterprise, set his teeth grimly, put his knees well into her flanks, and changed his defensive tactics to brisk aggression. Bullied and maddened, Jovita began the descent of the hill. Here the artful Richard pretended to hold her in with ostentatious objurgation and well-feigned cries of alarm. It is unnecessary to add that Jovita instantly ran away. Nor need I state the time made in the descent; it is written in the chronicles of Simpson's Bar. Enough that in another moment, as it seemed to Dick, she was splashing on the overflowed banks of Rattlesnake Creek. As Dick expected, the momentum she had acquired carried her beyond the point of balking, and, holding her well together for a mighty leap, they dashed into the middle of the swiftly flowing current. A few moments of kicking, wading and swimming, and Dick drew a long breath on the opposite bank.

The road from Rattlesnake Creek to Red Mountain was tolerably level. Either the plunge in Rattlesnake Creek had dampened her baleful fire, or the art which led to it had shown her the superior wickedness of her rider, for Jovita no longer wasted her surplus energy in wanton conceits. Once she bucked, but it was from force of habit; once she shied, but it was from a new freshly painted meeting-house at the crossing of the county road. Hollows, ditches, gravelly deposits, patches of freshly springing grasses, flew from beneath her rattling hoofs. She began to smell unpleasantly, once or twice she coughed slightly, but there was no abatement of her strength or speed. By two o'clock he had passed Red Mountain and begun the descent to the plain. Ten minutes later the driver of the fast Pioneer coach was overtaken and passed by a 'man on a Pinto hoss' – an event sufficiently notable for remark. At half-past two Dick rose in his stirrups with a great shout. Stars were glittering through the rifted clouds, and beyond him, out of the plain, rose two spires, a flagstaff and a straggling line of black objects. Dick jingled his spurs and swung his *riata*, Jovita bounded forward, and in another moment they swept into Tuttleville and drew up before the wooden piazza of The Hotel of All Nations.

What transpired that night at Tuttleville is not strictly a part of this record. Briefly I may state, however, that after Jovita had been handed over to a sleepy ostler, whom she at once kicked into unpleasant consciousness, Dick sallied out with the bar-keeper for a tour of the sleeping town. Lights still gleamed from a few saloons and gambling-houses; but, avoiding these, they stopped before several closed shops, and by persistent tapping and judicious outcry roused the proprietors from their beds, and made them unbar the doors of their magazines and expose their wares. Sometimes they were met by curses, but oftener by interest and some concern in their needs, and the interview was invariably concluded by a drink. It was three o'clock before this pleasantry was given over, and with a small waterproof bag of india-rubber strapped on his shoulders Dick returned to the hotel. But here he was waylaid by Beauty – Beauty opulent in charms, affluent in dress, persuasive in speech, and Spanish in accent! In vain she repeated the invitation in Excelsior, happily scorned by all Alpine-climbing youth, and rejected by this child of the Sierras – a rejection softened in this instance by a laugh and his last gold coin. And then he sprang to the saddle and dashed down the lonely street and out into the lonelier plain, where presently the lights, the black line of houses, the spires, and the flagstaff sank into the earth behind him again and were lost in the distance.

The storm had cleared away, the air was brisk and cold, the outlines of adjacent landmarks were distinct, but it was half-past four before Dick reached the meeting-house and the crossing of the county road. To avoid the rising grade he had taken a longer and more circuitous road, in whose viscid mud Jovita sank fetlock deep at every bound. It was a poor preparation for a steady ascent of five miles more; but Jovita, gathering her legs under her, took it with her usual blind, unreasoning fury, and a half-hour later reached the long level that led to Rattlesnake Creek. Another half-hour would bring him to the creek. He threw the reins lightly upon the neck of the mare, chirruped to her, and began to sing.

Suddenly Jovita shied with a bound that would have unseated a less practised rider. Hanging to her rein was a figure that had leaped from the bank, and at the same time from the road before her arose a shadowy horse and rider. 'Throw up your hands,' commanded this second apparition, with an oath.

Dick felt the mare tremble, quiver and apparently sink under him. He knew what it meant and was prepared.

'Stand aside, Jack Simpson, I know you, you damned thief. Let me pass or – '

He did not finish the sentence. Jovita rose straight in the air with a terrific bound, throwing the figure from her bit with a single shake of her vicious head, and charged with deadly malevolence down on the impediment before her. An oath, a pistol shot, horse and highwayman rolled over in the road, and the next moment Jovita was a hundred yards away. But the good right arm of her rider, shattered by a bullet, dropped helplessly at his side.

Without slacking his speed he shifted the reins to his left hand. But a few moments later he was obliged to halt and tighten the saddle-girths that had slipped in the onset. This in his crippled condition took some time. He had no fear of pursuit, but looking up he saw that the eastern stars were already paling and that the distant peaks had lost their ghostly whiteness and now stood out blackly against a lighter sky. Day was upon him. Then completely absorbed in a single idea, he forgot the pain of his wound, and mounting again dashed on toward Rattlesnake Creek. But now Jovita's breath came broken by gasps, Dick reeled in his saddle, and brighter and brighter grew the sky.

Ride, Richard; run, Jovita; linger, O day!

For the last few rods there was a roaring in his ears. Was it exhaustion from loss of blood, or what? He was dazed and giddy as he swept down the hill, and did not recognise his surroundings. Had he taken the wrong road, or was this Rattlesnake Creek?

It was. But the brawling creek he had swam a few hours before had risen, more than doubled its volume, and now rolled a swift and resistless river between him and Rattlesnake Hill. For the first time that night Richard's heart sank within him. The river, the mountain, the quickening east, swam before his eyes. He shut them to recover his self-control. In that brief interval, by some fantastic mental process, the little room at Simpson's Bar and the figures of the sleeping father and son rose upon him. He opened his eyes wildly, cast off his coat, pistol, boots and saddle, bound his precious pack tightly to his shoulders, grasped the bare flanks of Jovita with his bared knees, and with a shout dashed into the yellow water. A cry rose from the opposite bank as the head of a man and horse struggled for a few moments against the battling current, and then were swept away amidst uprooted trees and whirling driftwood.

* * *

The Old Man started and woke. The fire on the hearth was dead, the candle in the outer room flickering in its socket, and somebody was rapping at the door. He opened it, but fell back with a cry before the dripping half-naked figure that reeled against the doorpost.

'Dick?'

'Hush! Is he awake yet?'

76

'No – but, Dick? – '

'Dry up, you old fool! Get me some whiskey *quick!*' The Old Man flew and returned with – an empty bottle! Dick would have sworn, but his strength was not equal to the occasion. He staggered, caught at the handle of the door and motioned to the Old Man.

'Thar's suthin' in my pack yer for Johnny. Take it off. I can't.'

The Old Man unstrapped the pack and laid it before the exhausted man.

'Open it, quick!'

He did so with trembling fingers. It contained only a few poor toys – cheap and barbaric enough, goodness knows, but bright with paint and tinsel. One of them was broken; another, I fear, was irretrievably ruined by water; and on the third – ah me! there was a cruel spot.

'It don't look like much, that's a fact,' said Dick, ruefully . . . 'But it's the best we could do . . . Take 'em, Old Man, and put 'em in his stocking, and tell him – tell him, you know – hold me, Old Man – ' The Old Man caught at his sinking figure. 'Tell him,' said Dick, with a weak little laugh – 'tell him Sandy Claus has come.'

And even so, bedraggled, ragged, unshaven and unshorn, with one arm hanging helplessly at his side, Santa Claus came to Simpson's Bar and fell fainting on the first threshold. The Christmas dawn came slowly after, touching the remoter peaks with the rosy warmth of ineffable love. And it looked so tenderly on Simpson's Bar that the whole mountain, as if caught in a generous action, blushed to the skies.

LEFT OUT ON LONE STAR MOUNTAIN

BRET HARTE

THERE WAS LITTLE DOUBT that the Lone Star claim was 'played out'. Not dug out, worked out, washed out, but *played* out. For two years its five sanguine proprietors had gone through the the various stages of mining enthusiasm; had prospected and planned, dug and doubted. They had borrowed money with hearty but unredeeming frankness, established a credit with unselfish abnegation of all responsibility, and had borne the disappointment of their creditors with a cheerful resignation which only the consciousness of some deep Compensating Future could give. Giving little else, however, a singular dissatisfaction obtained with the traders, and, being accompanied with a reluctance to make further advances, at last touched the gentle stoicism of the proprietors themselves. The youthful enthusiasm which had at first lifted the most ineffectual trial, the most useless essay, to the plane of actual achievement, died out, leaving them only the dull, prosaic record of half-finished ditches, purposeless shafts, untenable pits, abandoned engines, and meaningless disruptions of the soil upon the Lone Star claim, and empty flour sacks and pork barrels in the Lone Star cabin.

They had borne their poverty, if that term could be applied to a light renunciation of all superfluities in food, dress or ornament, ameliorated by the gentle depredations already alluded to, with unassuming levity. More than that: having segregated themselves from their fellow-miners of Red Gulch, and entered upon the possession of the little manzanita-thicketed valley five miles away, the failure of their enterprise had assumed in their eyes only the vague significance of the decline and fall of a general community, and to that extent relieved them of individual responsibility. It was easier for them to admit that the Lone Star claim was 'played out' than confess to a personal bankruptcy. Moreover, they still retained the sacred right of criticism of government, and rose superior in their private opinions to their own collective wisdom. Each one experienced a grateful sense of the entire responsibility of the other four in the fate of their enterprise.

On December 24, 1863, a gentle rain was still falling over the length and breadth of the Lone Star claim. It had been falling for several days, had already called a faint spring colour to the wan landscape, repairing with tender touches the ravages wrought by the proprietors, or charitably covering their faults. The ragged seams in gulch and canon lost their harsh outlines, a thin green mantle faintly clothed the torn and abraded hillside. A few weeks more, and a veil of forgetfulness would be drawn over the feeble failures of the Lone Star claim. The charming derelicts themselves, listening to the raindrops on the roof of their little cabin, gazed philosophically from the open door, and accepted the prospect as a moral discharge from their obligations. Four of the five partners were present. The Right and Left Bowers, Union Mills and the Judge.

It is scarcely necessary to say that not one of these titles was the genuine name of its possessor. The Right and Left Bowers were two brothers; their sobriquets, a cheerful adaptation from the favourite game of euchre, expressing their relative value in the camp. The mere fact that Union Mills had at one time patched his trousers with an old flour-sack legibly bearing that brand of its fabrication was a tempting baptismal suggestion that the other partners could not forgo. The Judge, a singularly inequitable Missourian, with no knowledge whatever of the law, was an inspiration of gratuitous irony.

Union Mills, who had been for some time sitting placidly on the threshold with one leg exposed to the rain, from a sheer indolent inability to change his position, finally withdrew that weather-beaten member, and stood up. The movement more or less deranged the attitudes of the other partners, and was received with cynical disfavour. It was somewhat remarkable that, although generally giving the appearance of healthy youth and perfect physical condition, they one and all simulated the decrepitude of age and invalidism, and after limping about for a few moments, settled back again upon their bunks and stools in their former positions. The Left Bower lazily replaced a bandage that he had worn around his ankle for weeks without any apparent necessity, and the Judge scrutinised with tender solicitude the faded cicatrix of a scratch upon his arm. A passive hypochondria, born of their isolation, was the last ludicrously pathetic touch of their situation.

The immediate cause of this commotion felt the necessity of an explanation.

'It would have been just as easy for you to have stayed outside with your business leg, instead of dragging it into private life in that obtrusive way,' retorted the Right Bower; 'but that exhaustive effort isn't going to fill the pork barrel. The grocery man at Dalton says – what's that he said?' he appealed lazily to the Judge.

'Said he reckoned the Lone Star was about played out, and he didn't want any more in his – thank you!' repeated the Judge with a mechanical effort of memory utterly devoid of personal or present interest.

'I always suspected that man, after Grimshaw begun to deal with him,' said the Left Bower. 'They're just mean enough to join hands against us.' It was a fixed belief of the Lone Star partners that they were pursued by personal enmities.

'More than likely those new strangers over in the Fork have been paying cash and filled him up with conceit,' said Union Mills, trying to dry his leg by alternately beating it or rubbing it against the cabin wall. 'Once begin wrong with that kind of snipe and you drag everybody down with you.'

This vague conclusion was received with dead silence. Everybody had become interested in the speaker's peculiar method of drying his leg, to the exclusion of the previous topic. A few offered criticism, no one assistance.

'Who did the grocery man say that to?' asked the Right Bower, finally returning to the question.

'The Old Man,' answered the Judge.

'Of course,' ejaculated the Right Bower sarcastically.

'Of course,' echoed the other partners together. 'That's like him. The Old Man all over!'

It did not appear exactly what was like the Old Man, or why it was like him, but generally that he alone was responsible for the grocery man's defection. It was put more concisely by Union Mills.

'That comes of letting him go there! It's just a fair provocation to any man to have the Old Man sent to him. They can't, sorter, restrain themselves at him. He's enough to spoil the credit of the Rothschilds.'

'That's so,' chimed in the Judge. 'And look at his prospecting. Why, he was out two nights last week, all night, prospecting in the moonlight for blind leads, just out of sheer foolishness.'

'It was quite enough for me,' broke in the Left Bower, 'when the other day, you remember when, he proposed to us white men to settle down to plain ground sluicing, making "grub" wages just like any Chinaman. It just showed his idea of the Lone Star claim.'

'Well, I never said it afore,' added Union Mills, 'but when that one of the Mattison boys came over here to examine the claim with an eye to purchasin', it was the Old Man that took the conceit out of him. He just as good as admitted that a lot of work had got to be done afore any pay ore could be realised. Never even asked him over to the shanty here to jine us in a friendly game; just kept him, so to speak, to himself. And naturally the Mattisons didn't see it.'

A silence followed, broken only by the rain monotonously falling on the roof, and occasionally through the broad adobe chimney, where it provoked a retaliating hiss and splutter from the dying embers of the hearth. The Right Bower, with a sudden access of energy, drew the empty barrel before him, and taking a pack of well-worn cards from his pocket, began to make a 'solitaire' upon the lid. The others gazed at him with languid interest.

'Makin' it for anythin'?' asked Mills.

The Right Bower nodded.

The Judge and Left Bower, who were partly lying in their respective bunks, sat up to get a better view of the game. Union Mills slowly disengaged himself from the wall and leaned over the 'solitaire' player. The Right Bower turned the last card in a pause of almost thrilling suspense, and clapped it down on the lid with fateful emphasis.

'It went!' said the Judge in a voice of hushed respect. 'What did you make it for?' he almost whispered.

'To know if we'd make the break we talked about and vamoose the ranch. It's the *fifth* time today,' continued the Right Bower in a voice of gloomy significance. 'And it went agin bad cards too.'

'I ain't superstitious,' said the Judge, with awe and fatuity beaming from every line of his credulous face, 'but it's flyin' in the face of Providence to go agin such signs as that.'

'Make it again, to see if the Old Man must go,' suggested the Left Bower.

The suggestion was received with favour, the three men gathering breathlessly around the player. Again the fateful cards were shuffled deliberately, placed in their mysterious combination, with the same ominous result. Yet everybody seemed to breathe more freely, as if relieved from some responsibility, the Judge accepting this manifest expression of Providence with resigned self-righteousness.

'Yes, gentlemen,' resumed the Left Bower, serenely, as if a calm legal decision had just been recorded, 'we must not let any foolishness or sentiment get mixed up with this thing, but look at it like businessmen. The only sensible move is to get up and get out of the camp.'

'And the Old Man?' queried the Judge.

'The Old Man – hush! he's coming.'

The doorway was darkened by a slight lissome shadow. It was the absent partner, otherwise known as 'the Old Man'. Need it be added that he was a *boy* of nineteen, with a slight down just clothing his upper lip!

'The creek is up over the ford, and I had to shin up a willow on the bank and swing myself across,' he said, with a quick, frank laugh; 'but all the same, boys, it's going to clear up in about an hour, you bet. It's breaking away over Bald Mountain, and there's a sun flash on a bit of snow on Lone Peak. Look! you can see it from here. It's for all the world like Noah's dove just landed on Mount Ararat. It's a good omen.'

From sheer force of habit the men had momentarily brightened up at the Old Man's entrance. But the unblushing exhibition of degrading superstition shown in the last sentence recalled their just severity. They exchanged meaning glances. Union Mills uttered hopelessly to himself: 'Hell's full of such omens.'

Too occupied with his subject to notice this ominous reception, the Old Man continued: 'I reckon I struck a fresh lead in the new grocery man at the Crossing. He says he'll let the Judge have a pair of boots on credit, but he can't send them over here; and considering that the Judge has got to try them anyway, it don't seem to be asking too much for the Judge to go over there. He says he'll give us a barrel of pork and a bag of flour if we'll give him the right of using our tail-race and clean out the lower end of it.'

'It's the work of a Chinaman, and a four days' job,' broke in the Left Bower.

'It took one white man only two hours to clean out a third of it,' retorted the Old Man triumphantly, 'for *I* pitched in at once with a pick he let me have on credit, and did that amount of work this morning, and told him the rest of you boys would finish it this afternoon.'

A slight gesture from the Right Bower checked an angry exclamation from the Left. The Old Man did not notice either, but, knitting his smooth young brow in a paternally reflective fashion, went on: 'You'll have to get a new pair of trousers, Mills, but as he doesn't keep clothing, we'll have to get some canvas and cut you out a pair. I traded off the beans he let me have for some tobacco for the Right Bower at the other shop, and got them to throw in a new pack of cards. These are about played out. We'll be wanting some brushwood for the fire; there's a heap in the hollow. Who's going to bring it in? It's the Judge's turn, isn't it? Why, what's the matter with you all?'

The restraint and evident uneasiness of his companions had at last touched him. He turned his frank young eyes upon them; they glanced helplessly at each other. Yet his first concern was for them, his first instinct paternal and protecting. He ran his eyes quickly over them; they were all there and apparently in their usual condition. 'Anything wrong with the claim?' he suggested.

Without looking at him the Right Bower rose, leaned against the open door with his hands behind him and his face towards the landscape, and said, apparently to the distant prospect: 'The claim's played out, the partnership's played out, and the sooner we skedaddle out of this the better. If,' he added, turning to the Old Man, 'if *you* want to stay, if you want to do Chinaman's work at Chinaman's wages, if you want to hang on to the charity of the traders at the Crossing, you can do it, and enjoy the prospects and the Noah's doves alone. But we're calculatin' to step out of it.'

'But I haven't said I wanted to do it *alone*,' protested the Old Man with a gesture of bewilderment.

'If these are your general ideas of the partnership,' continued the Right Bower, clinging to the established hypothesis of the other partners for support, 'it ain't ours, and the only way we can prove it is to stop the foolishness right here. We calculated to dissolve the partnership and strike out for ourselves elsewhere. You're no longer responsible for us, nor we for you. And we reckon it's the square thing to leave you the claim and the cabin and all it contains. To prevent any trouble with the traders, we've drawn up a paper here' –

'With a bonus of fifty thousand dollars each down, and the rest to be settled on my children,' interrupted the Old Man, with a half uneasy laugh. 'Of course. But' – he stopped suddenly, the blood dropped from his fresh cheek, and he again glanced quickly round the group. 'I don't think – I – I quite *sabe*, boys,' he added, with a slight tremor of voice and lip. 'If it's a conundrum, ask me an easier one.'

Any lingering doubt he might have had of their meaning was dispelled by the Judge. 'It's about the softest thing you kin drop into, Old Man,' he said confidentially; 'if *I* hadn't promised the other boys to go with them, and if I didn't need the best medical advice in Sacramento for my lungs, I'd just enjoy staying with you.'

'It gives a sorter freedom to a young fellow like you, Old Man, like goin' into the world on your own capital, that every Californian boy hasn't got,' said Union Mills, patronisingly.

'Of course it's rather hard papers on us, you know, givin' up everything, so to speak; but it's for your good, and we ain't goin' back on you,' said the Left Bower, 'are we, boys?'

The colour had returned to the Old Man's face a little more quickly and freely than usual. He picked up the hat he had cast down, put it on carefully over his brown curls, drew the flap down on the side towards his companions, and put his hands in his pockets. 'All right,' he said, in a slightly altered voice. 'When do you go?'

'Today,' answered the Left Bower. 'We calculate to take a moonlight *pasear* over to the Cross Roads and meet the down stage at about twelve tonight. There's plenty of time yet,' he added, with a slight laugh; 'it's only three o'clock now.'

There was a dead silence. Even the rain withheld its continuous patter, a dumb, grey film covered the ashes of the hushed hearth. For the first time the Right Bower exhibited some slight embarrassment.

'I reckon it's held up for a spell,' he said, ostentatiously examining the weather, 'and we might as well take a run round the claim to see if we've forgotten nothing. Of course, we'll be back again,' he added hastily, without looking at the Old Man, 'before we go, you know.'

The others began to look for their hats, but so awkwardly and with such evident preoccupation of mind that it was not at first discovered that the Judge had his already on. This raised a laugh, as did also a clumsy stumble of Union Mills against the pork barrel, although that gentleman took refuge from his confusion and secured a decent retreat by a gross exaggeration of his lameness, as he limped after the Right Bower. The Judge whistled feebly. The Left Bower, in a more ambitious effort to impart a certain gaiety to his exit, stopped on the threshold and said, as if in arch confidence, to his companions, 'Darned if the Old Man don't look two inches higher since he became a proprietor,' laughed patronisingly, and vanished.

If the newly made proprietor had increased in stature, he had not otherwise changed his demeanour. He remained in the same attitude until the last figure disappeared behind the fringe of buckeye that hid the distant highway. Then he walked slowly to the fireplace, and, leaning against the chimney, kicked the dying embers together with his foot. Something dropped and spattered in the film of hot ashes. Surely the rain had not yet ceased!

His high colour had already fled except for a spot on either cheekbone that lent a brightness to his eyes. He glanced around the cabin. It looked familiar and yet strange. Rather, it looked strange *because* still familiar, and therefore incongruous with the new atmosphere that surrounded it – discordant with the echo of their last meeting, and painfully accenting the change. There were the four 'bunks', or sleeping berths, of his companions, each still bearing some traces of the individuality of its late occupant with a dumb loyalty that seemed to make their light-hearted defection monstrous. In the dead ashes of the Judge's pipe, scattered on his shelf, still lived his old fire; in the whittled and carved edges of the Left Bower's bunk still were the memories of bygone days of delicious indolence; in the bullet-holes clustered round a knot of one of the beams there was still the record of the Right Bower's old-time skill and practice; in the few engravings of female loveliness stuck upon each headboard there were the proofs of their old extravagant devotion – all a mute protest to the change.

He remembered how, a fatherless, truant schoolboy, he had drifted into their adventurous, nomadic life, itself a life of grown-up truancy like his own, and become one of that gypsy family. How they had taken the place of relations and household in his boyish fancy, filling it with the unsubstantial pageantry of a child's play at grown-up existence, he knew only too well. But how, from being a pet and *protégé*, he had gradually and unconsciously asserted his own individuality and taken upon his younger shoulders not only a poet's keen appreciation of that life, but its actual responsibilities and half-childish burdens, he never suspected. He had fondly believed that he was a neophyte in their ways, a novice in their charming faith and indolent creed, and they had encouraged it; now their renunciation of that faith could only be an excuse for a renunciation of *him*. The poetry that had for two years invested the material and some-times even mean details of their existence was too much a part of himself to be lightly dispelled. The lesson of those ingenuous moralists failed, as such lessons are apt to fail; their discipline provoked but did not subdue; a rising indignation, stirred by a sense of injury, mounted to his cheek and eyes. It was slow to come, but was none the less violent that it had been preceded by the benumbing shock of shame and pride.

I hope I shall not prejudice the reader's sympathies if my duty as a simple chronicler compels me to state, therefore, that the sober second thought of this gentle poet was to burn down the cabin on the spot with all its contents. This yielded to a milder counsel – waiting for the return of the party, challenging the Right Bower, a duel to the death, perhaps himself the victim, with the crushing explanation *in extremis*, 'It seems we are *one* too many. No matter; it is settled now. Farewell!' Dimly remembering, however, that there was something of this in the last well-worn novel they had read together, and that his antagonist might recognise it, or even worse, anticipate it himself, the idea was quickly rejected. Besides, the opportunity for an apotheosis of self-sacrifice was past. Nothing remained now but to refuse the proffered bribe of claim and cabin by letter, for he must not wait their return. He tore a leaf from a blotted diary, begun and abandoned long since, and essayed to write. Scrawl after scrawl was torn up, until his fury had cooled down to a frigid third personality. 'Mr John Ford regrets to inform his late partners that their tender of house, of furniture,' however, seemed too inconsistent with the pork-barrel table he was writing on; a more eloquent renunciation of their offer became frivolous and idiotic from a caricature of Union Mills, label and all, that appeared suddenly on the other side of the leaf; and when he at last indited a satisfactory and impassioned exposition of his feelings, the legible *addendum* of 'Oh, ain't you glad you're out of the wilderness!' – the forgotten first line of a popular song, which no scratching would erase – seemed too like an ironical postscript to be thought of for a moment. He threw aside his pen and cast the discordant record of past foolish pastime into the dead ashes of the hearth.

How quiet it was! With the cessation of the rain the wind too had gone down, and scarcely a breath of air came through the open door. He walked to the threshold and gazed on the hushed prospect. In this listless attitude he was faintly conscious of a distant reverberation, a mere phantom of sound – perhaps the explosion of a distant blast in the hills – that left the silence more marked and oppressive. As he turned again into the cabin a change seemed to have come over it. It already looked old and decayed. The loneliness of years of desertion seemed to have taken possession of it; the atmosphere of dry rot was in the beams and rafters. To his excited fancy the few disordered blankets and articles of clothing seemed dropping to pieces; in one of the bunks there was a hideous resemblance in the longitudinal heap of clothing to a withered and mummied corpse. So it might look in after-years when some passing stranger – but he stopped. A dread of the place was beginning to creep over him; a dread of the days to come, when the monotonous sunshine should lay bare the loneliness of these walls; the long, long days of endless blue and cloudless, overhanging solitude; summer days when the wearying, incessant trade winds should sing around that empty shell and voice its desolation. He gathered together hastily a few articles that were especially his own – rather that the free communion of the camp, from indifference or accident, had left wholly to him. He hesitated for a moment over his rifle, but, scrupulous in his wounded pride, turned away and left the familiar weapon that in the dark days had so often provided the dinner or breakfast of the little household. Candour compels me to state that his equipment was not large nor eminently practical. His scant pack was a light weight for even his young shoulders, but I fear he thought more of getting away from the Past than providing for the Future.

With this vague but sole purpose he left the cabin, and almost mechanically turned his steps towards the creek he had crossed that morning. He knew that by this route he would avoid meeting his companions; its difficulties and circuitousness would exercise his feverish limbs and give him time for reflection. He had determined to leave the claim, but whence he had not yet considered. He reached the bank of the creek where he had stood two hours before; it seemed to him two years. He looked curiously at his reflection in one of the broad pools of overflow, and fancied he looked older. He watched the rush and outset of the turbid current hurrying to meet the South Fork, and to eventually lose itself in the yellow Sacramento. Even in his preoccupation he was impressed with a likeness to himself and his companions in this flood that had burst its peaceful boundaries. In the drifting fragments of one of their forgotten flumes washed from the bank, he fancied he saw an omen of the disintegration and decay of the Lone Star claim.

The strange hush in the air that he had noticed before – a calm so inconsistent with that hour and the season as to seem portentous – became more marked in contrast to the feverish rush of the turbulent watercourse. A few clouds lazily huddled in the west apparently had gone to rest with the sun on beds of somnolent poppies. There was a gleam as of golden water everywhere along the horizon, washing out the cold snow-peaks, and drowning even the rising moon. The creek caught it here and there, until, in grim irony, it seemed to bear their broken sluice-boxes and useless engines on the very Pactolian stream they had been hopefully created to direct and carry. But by some peculiar trick of the atmosphere the perfect plenitude of that golden sunset glory was lavished on the rugged sides and tangled crest of the Lone Star Mountain. That isolated peak, the landmark of their claim, the gaunt monument of their folly, transfigured in the evening splendour, kept its radiance unquenched long after the glow had fallen from the encompassing skies, and when at last the rising moon, step by step, put out the fires along the winding valley and plains, and crept up the bosky sides of the cañon, the vanishing sunset was lost only to reappear as a golden crown.

The eyes of the young man were fixed upon it with more than a momentary picturesque interest. It had been the favourite ground of his prospecting exploits, its lowest flank had been scarred in the old enthusiastic days with hydraulic engines, or pierced with shafts, but its central position in the claim and its superior height had always given it a commanding view of the extent of their valley and its approaches, and it was this practical pre-eminence that alone attracted him at that moment. He knew that from its crest he would be able to distinguish the figures of his companions, as they crossed the valley near the cabin, in the growing moonlight. Thus he could avoid encountering them on his way to the highroad, and yet see them, perhaps, for the last time. Even in his sense of injury there was a strange satisfaction in the thought.

The ascent was toilsome, but familiar. All along the dim trail he was accompanied by gentler memories of the past, that seemed, like the faint odour of spiced leaves and fragrant grasses wet with the rain and crushed beneath his ascending tread, to exhale the sweeter perfume in his effort to subdue or rise above them. There was the thicket of manzanita, where they had broken noonday bread together; here was the rock beside their maiden shafts, where they had poured a wild libation in boyish enthusiasm of success; and here the ledge where their first flag, a red shirt heroically sacrificed, was displayed from a long-handled shovel to the gaze of admirers below. When he at last reached the summit, the mysterious hush was still in the air, as if in breathless sympathy with his expedition. In the west, the plain was faintly illuminated, but disclosed no moving figures. He turned towards the rising moon, and moved slowly to the eastern edge. Suddenly he stopped. Another step would have been his last! He stood upon the crumbling edge of a precipice. A landslip had taken place on the eastern flank, leaving the gaunt ribs and fleshless bones of Lone Star Mountain bare in the moonlight. He understood now the strange rumble and reverberation he had heard; he understood now the strange hush of bird and beast in brake and thicket!

Although a single rapid glance convinced him that the slide had taken place in an unfrequented part of the mountain, above an inaccessible canon, and reflection assured him his companions could not have reached that distance when it took place, a feverish impulse led him to descend a few rods in the track of the avalanche. The frequent recurrence of outcrop and angle made this comparatively easy. Here he called aloud; the feeble echo of his own voice seemed only a dull impertinence to the significant silence. He turned to reascend; the furrowed flank of the mountain before him lay full in the moonlight. To his excited fancy a dozen luminous star-like points in the rocky crevices started into life as he faced them. Throwing his arm over the ledge above him, he supported himself for a moment by what appeared to be a projection of the solid rock. It trembled slightly. As he raised himself to its level, his heart stopped beating. It was simply a fragment detached from the outcrop, lying loosely on the ledge but upholding him by *its own weight only*. He examined it with trembling fingers; the encumbering soil fell from its sides and left its smoothed and worn protuberances glistening in the moonlight. It was virgin gold!

Looking back upon that moment afterwards, he remembered that he was not dazed, dazzled or startled. It did not come to him as a discovery or an accident, a stroke of chance or a caprice of fortune. He saw it all in that supreme moment; Nature had worked out their poor deduction. What their feeble engines had essayed spasmodically and helplessly against the curtain of soil that hid the treasure, the elements had achieved with mightier but more patient forces. The slow sapping of the winter rains had loosened the soil from the auriferous rock, even while the swollen stream was carrying their impotent and shattered engines to the sea. What mattered that his single arm could not lift the treasure he had found; what mattered that to unfix those glittering stars would still tax both skill and patience! The work was done, the goal was reached! even his boyish impatience was content with that. He rose slowly to his feet, unstrapped his long-handled shovel from his back, secured it in the crevice, and quietly regained the summit.

It was all his own! His own by right of discovery under the law of the land, and without accepting a favour from *them*. He recalled even the fact that it was *his* prospecting on the mountain that first suggested the existence of gold in the outcrop and the use of the hydraulic. *He* had never abandoned that belief, whatever the others had done. He dwelt somewhat indignantly to himself on this circumstance, and half unconsciously faced defiantly towards the plain below. But it was sleeping peacefully in the full sight of the moon, without life or motion. He looked at the stars; it was still far from midnight. His companions had no doubt long since returned to the cabin to prepare for their midnight journey. They were discussing him, perhaps laughing at him, or worse, pitying him and his bargain. Yet here was his bargain! A slight laugh he gave vent to here startled him a little, it sounded so hard and so unmirthful, and so unlike, as he oddly fancied, what he really *thought*. But *what* did he think?

Nothing mean or revengeful; no, they never would say *that*. When he had taken out all the surface gold and put the mine in working order, he would send them each a draft for a thousand dollars. Of course, if they were ever ill or poor he would do more. One of the first, the very first things he should do would be to send them each a handsome gun and tell them that he only asked in return the old-fashioned rifle that once was his. Looking back at the moment in after-years, he wondered that, with this exception, he made no plans for his own future, or the way he should dispose of his newly acquired wealth. This was the more singular as it had been the custom of the five partners to lie awake at night, audibly comparing with each other what they would do in case they made a strike. He remembered how, Alnaschar-like, they nearly separated once over a difference in the disposal of a hundred thousand dollars that they never had, nor expected to have. He remembered how Union Mills always began his career as a millionaire by a 'square meal' at Delmonico's; how the Right Bower's initial step was always a trip home 'to see his mother'; how the Left Bower would immediately placate the parents of his beloved with priceless gifts (it may be parenthetically remarked that the parents and the beloved one were as hypothetical as the fortune); and how the Judge would make his first start as a capitalist by breaking a certain faro bank in Sacramento. He himself had been equally eloquent in extravagant fancy in those penniless days, he who now was quite cold and impassive beside the more extravagant reality.

How different it might have been! If they had only waited a day longer! if they had only broken their resolves to him kindly and parted in goodwill! How he would long ere this have rushed to greet them with the joyful news! How they would have danced around it, sung themselves hoarse, laughed down their enemies, and run up the flag triumphantly on the summit of the Lone Star Mountain! How they would have crowned him, 'the Old Man', 'the hero of the camp'! How he would have told them the whole story; how some strange instinct had impelled him to ascend the summit, and how another step on that summit would have precipitated him into the cañon! And how – but what if somebody else, Union Mills or the Judge, had been the first discoverer? Might they not have meanly kept the secret from him; have selfishly helped themselves and done –

'What *you* are doing now.'

The hot blood rushed to his cheek, as if a strange voice were at his ear. For a moment he could not believe that it came from his own pale lips until he found himself speaking. He rose to his feet, tingling with shame, and began hurriedly to descend the mountain.

He would go to them, tell them of his discovery, let them give him his share, and leave them for ever. It was the only thing to be done; strange that he had not thought of it at once. Yet it was hard, very hard and cruel, to be forced to meet them again. What had he done to suffer this mortification? For a moment he actually hated this vulgar treasure that had forever buried under its gross ponderability the light and careless past, and utterly crushed out the poetry of their old, indolent, happy existence.

He was sure to find them waiting at the Cross Roads where the coach came past. It was three miles away, yet he could get there in time if he hastened. It was a wise and practical conclusion of his evening's work, a lame and impotent conclusion to his evening's indignation.

No matter. They would perhaps at first think he had come weakly to follow them, perhaps they would at first doubt his story. No matter. He bit his lips to keep down the foolish rising tears, but still went blindly forward.

He saw not the beautiful night, cradled in the dark hills, swathed in luminous mists and hushed in the awe of its own loveliness! Here and there the moon had laid her calm face on lake and overflow, and gone to sleep embracing them, until the whole plain seemed to be lifted into infinite quiet. Walking on as in a dream, the black, impenetrable barriers of skirting thickets opened and gave way to vague distances that it appeared impossible to reach, dim vistas that seemed unapproachable. Gradually he seemed himself to become a part of the mysterious night. He was becoming as pulseless, as calm, as passionless.

What was that? A shot in the direction of the cabin! yet so faint, so echoless, so ineffective in the vast silence, that he would have thought it his fancy but for the strange instinctive jar upon his sensitive nerves. Was it an accident, or was it an intentional signal to him? He stopped; it was not repeated, the silence reasserted itself, but this time with an ominous deathlike suggestion. A sudden and terrible thought crossed his mind. He cast aside his pack and all encumbering weight, took a deep breath, lowered his head, and darted like a deer in the direction of the challenge.

THE OUTCASTS OF POKER FLAT

BRET HARTE

As MR JOHN OAKHURST, gambler, stepped into the main street
of Poker Flat on the morning of the twenty-third of November
1850, he was conscious of a change in its moral atmoshere since
the preceding night. Two or three men, conversing earnestly together,
ceased as he approached, and exchanged significant glances. There was a
Sabbath lull in the air which, in a settlement unused to Sabbath influences,
looked ominous.

Mr Oakhurst's calm, handsome face betrayed small concern with these
indications. Whether he was conscious of any predisposing cause was
another question. 'I reckon they're after somebody,' he reflected; 'likely
it's me.' He returned to his pocket the handkerchief with which he had
been whipping away the red dust of Poker Flat from his neat boots, and
quietly discharged his mind of any further conjecture.

In point of fact, Poker Flat was 'after somebody'. It had lately suffered
the loss of several thousand dollars, two valuable horses and a prominent
citizen. It was experiencing a spasm of virtuous reaction, quite as lawless
and ungovernable as any of the acts that had provoked it. A secret
committee had determined to rid the town of all improper persons.
This was done permanently in regard of two men who were then
hanging from the boughs of a sycamore in the gulch, and temporarily in
the banishment of certain other objectionable characters. I regret to say
that some of these were ladies. It is but due to the sex, however, to state
that their impropriety was professional, and it was only in such easily
established standards of evil that Poker Flat ventured to sit in judgement.

Mr Oakhurst was right in supposing that he was included in this
category. A few of the committee had urged hanging him as a possible
example, and a sure method of reimbursing themselves from his pockets
of the sums he had won from them. 'It's agin justice,' said Jim Wheeler,
'to let this yer young man from Roaring Camp – an entire stranger –
carry away our money.' But a crude sentiment of equity residing in the
breasts of those who had been fortunate enough to win from Mr Oakhurst
overruled this narrower local prejudice.

Mr Oakhurst received his sentence with philosophic calmness, none
the less coolly that he was aware of the hesitation of his judges. He was
too much of a gambler not to accept Fate. With him life was at best an

uncertain game, and he recognised the usual percentage in favour of the dealer.

A body of armed men accompanied the deported wickedness of Poker Flat to the outskirts of the settlement. Besides Mr Oakhurst, who was known to be a coolly desperate man, and for whose intimidation the armed escort was intended, the expatriated party consisted of a young woman familiarly known as the 'Duchess'; another, who had won the title of 'Mother Shipton'; and 'Uncle Billy', a suspected sluice-robber and confirmed drunkard. The cavalcade provoked no comments from the spectators, nor was any word uttered by the escort. Only, when the gulch which marked the uttermost limit of Poker Flat was reached, the leader spoke briefly and to the point. The exiles were forbidden to return at the peril of their lives.

As the escort disappeared, their pent-up feelings found vent in a few hysterical tears from the Duchess, some bad language from Mother Shipton and a Parthian volley of expletives from Uncle Billy. The philosophic Oakhurst alone remained silent. He listened calmly to Mother Shipton's desire to cut somebody's heart out, to the repeated statements of the Duchess that she would die in the road and to the alarming oaths that seemed to be bumped out of Uncle Billy as he rode forward. With the easy good humour characteristic of his class, he insisted upon exchanging his own riding horse, 'Five Spot', for the sorry mule which the Duchess rode. But even this act did not draw the party into any closer sympathy. The young woman readjusted her somewhat draggled plumes with a feeble, faded coquetry; Mother Shipton eyed the possessor of 'Five Spot' with malevolence and Uncle Billy included the whole party in one sweeping anathema.

The road to Sandy Bar – a camp that, not having as yet experienced the regenerating influences of Poker Flat, consequently seemed to offer some invitation to the emigrants – lay over a steep mountain range. It was distant a day's severe travel. In that advanced season, the party soon passed out of the moist, temperate regions of the foothills into the dry, cold, bracing air of the Sierras. The trail was narrow and difficult. At noon the Duchess, rolling out of her saddle upon the ground, declared her intention of going no farther, and the party halted.

The spot was singularly wild and impressive. A wooded amphitheatre, surrounded on three sides by precipitous cliffs of naked granite, sloped gently towards the crest of another precipice that overlooked the valley. It was, undoubtedly, the most suitable spot for a camp, had camping been advisable. But Mr Oakhurst knew that scarcely half the journey to Sandy Bar was accomplished, and the party were not equipped or provisioned for delay. This fact he pointed out to his companions curtly, with a philosophic commentary on the folly of 'throwing up their hand before the game was played out'. But they were furnished with liquor, which in this emergency stood them in place of food, fuel, rest and prescience. In spite of his remonstrances, it was not long before they were more or less under its influence. Uncle Billy passed rapidly from a bellicose state into one of stupor, the Duchess became maudlin and Mother Shipton snored. Mr Oakhurst alone remained erect, leaning against a rock, calmly surveying them.

Mr Oakhurst did not drink. It interfered with a profession which required coolness, impassiveness, and presence of mind and, in his own language, he 'couldn't afford it'. As he gazed at his recumbent fellow exiles, the loneliness begotten of his pariah trade, his habits of life, his very vices, for the first time seriously oppressed him. He bestirred himself in dusting his black clothes, washing his hands and face and other acts characteristic of his studiously neat habits, and for a moment forgot his annoyance. The thought of deserting his weaker and more pitiable companions never perhaps occurred to him. Yet he could not help feeling the want of that excitement which, singularly enough, was most conducive to that calm equanimity for which he was notorious. He looked at the gloomy walls that rose a thousand feet sheer above the circling pines around him; at the sky, ominously clouded; at the valley below, already deepening into shadow. And, doing so, suddenly he heard his own name called.

A horseman slowly ascended the trail. In the fresh, open face of the newcomer Mr Oakhurst recognised Tom Simson, otherwise known as the 'Innocent' of Sandy Bar. He had met him some months before over a 'little game', and had, with perfect equanimity, won the entire fortune – amounting to some forty dollars – of that guileless youth. After the game was finished, Mr Oakhurst drew the youthful speculator behind the door and thus addressed him: 'Tommy, you're a good little man, but you can't gamble worth a cent. Don't try it over again.' He then handed him his money back, pushed him gently from the room, and so made a devoted slave of Tom Simson.

There was a remembrance of this in his boyish and enthusiastic greeting of Mr Oakhurst. He had started, he said, to go to Poker Flat to seek his fortune. 'Alone?' No, not exactly alone; in fact (a giggle), he had run away with Piney Woods. Didn't Mr Oakhurst remember Piney? She that used to wait on the table at the Temperance House? They had been engaged a long time, but old Jake Woods had objected, and so they had run away, and were going to Poker Flat to be married, and here they were. And they were tired out, and how lucky it was they had found a place to camp and company. All this the Innocent delivered rapidly, while Piney, a stout, comely damsel of fifteen, emerged from behind the pine tree, where she had been blushing unseen, and rode to the side of her lover.

Mr Oakhurst seldom troubled himself with sentiment, still less with propriety; but he had a vague idea that the situation was not fortunate. He retained, however, his presence of mind sufficiently to kick Uncle Billy, who was about to say something, and Uncle Billy was sober enough to recognise in Mr Oakhurst's kick a superior power that would not bear trifling. He then endeavoured to dissuade Tom Simson from delaying further, but in vain. He even pointed out the fact that there was no provision, nor means of making a camp. But, unluckily, the Innocent met this objection by assuring the party that he was provided with an extra mule loaded with provisions and by the discovery of a rude attempt at a log house near the trail. 'Piney can stay with Mrs Oakhurst,' said the Innocent, pointing to the Duchess, 'and I can shift for myself.'

Nothing but Mr Oakhurst's admonishing foot saved Uncle Billy from bursting into a roar of laughter. As it was, he felt compelled to retire up the canyon until he could recover his gravity. There he confided the joke to the tall pine trees, with many slaps of his leg, contortions of his face, and the usual profanity. But when he returned to the party, he found them seated by a fire – for the air had grown strangely chill and the sky overcast – in apparently amicable conversation. Piney was actually talking in an impulsive, girlish fashion to the Duchess, who was listening with an interest and animation she had not shown for many days. The Innocent was holding forth, apparently with equal effect, to Mr Oakhurst and Mother Shipton, who was actually relaxing into amiability. 'Is this yer a damned picnic?' said Uncle Billy with inward scorn as he surveyed the sylvan group, the glancing firelight, and the tethered animals in the foreground. Suddenly an idea mingled with the alcoholic fumes that disturbed his brain. It was apparently of a jocular nature, for he felt impelled to slap his leg again and cram his fist into his mouth.

As the shadows crept slowly up the mountain, a slight breeze rocked the tops of the pine trees, and moaned through their long and gloomy aisles. The ruined cabin, patched and covered with pine boughs, was set apart for the ladies. As the lovers parted, they unaffectedly exchanged a kiss, so honest and sincere that it might have been heard above the swaying pines. The frail Duchess and the malevolent Mother Shipton were probably too stunned to remark upon this last evidence of simplicity, and so turned without a word to the hut. The fire was replenished, the men lay down before the door, and in a few minutes were asleep.

Mr Oakhurst was a light sleeper. Towards morning he awoke benumbed and cold. As he stirred the dying fire, the wind, which was now blowing strongly, brought to his cheek that which caused the blood to leave it – snow!

He started to his feet with the intention of awakening the sleepers, for there was no time to lose. But turning to where Uncle Billy had been lying, he found him gone. A suspicion leaped to his brain and a curse to his lips. He ran to the spot where the mules had been tethered; they were no longer there. The tracks were already rapidly disappearing in the snow.

The momentary excitement brought Mr Oakhurst back to the fire with his usual calm. He did not waken the sleepers. The Innocent slumbered peacefully, with a smile on his good-humoured, freckled face; the virgin Piney slept beside her frailer sisters as sweetly as though attended by celestial guardians; and Mr Oakhurst, drawing his blanket over his shoulders, stroked his moustaches and waited for the dawn. It came slowly in a whirling mist of snowflakes that dazzled and confused the eye. What could be seen of the landscape appeared magically changed. He looked over the valley, and summed up the present and future in two words – 'snowed in!'

A careful inventory of the provisions, which, fortunately for the party, had been stored within the hut and so escaped the felonious fingers of Uncle Billy, disclosed the fact that with care and prudence they might last ten days longer. 'That is,' said Mr Oakhurst, sotto voce to the Innocent, 'if you're willing to board us. If you ain't – and perhaps you'd better not – you can wait till Uncle Billy gets back with provisions.' For some occult reason, Mr Oakhurst could not bring himself to disclose Uncle Billy's rascality, and so offered the hypothesis that he had wandered from the camp and had accidentally stampeded the animals. He dropped a warning to the Duchess and Mother Shipton, who of course knew the facts of their associate's defection. 'They'll find out the truth about us all when they find out anything,' he added, significantly, 'and there's no good frightening them now.'

Tom Simson not only put all his worldly store at the disposal of Mr

Oakhurst, but seemed to enjoy the prospect of their enforced seclusion. 'We'll have a good camp for a week, and then the snow'll melt, and we'll all go back together.' The cheerful gaiety of the young man, and Mr Oakhurst's calm, infected the others. The Innocent with the aid of pine boughs extemporised a thatch for the roofless cabin, and the Duchess directed Piney in the rearrangement of the interior with a taste and tact that opened the blue eyes of that provincial maiden to their fullest extent. 'I reckon now you're used to fine things at Poker Flat,' said Piney. The Duchess turned away sharply to conceal something that reddened her cheeks through its professional tint, and Mother Shipton requested Piney not to 'chatter'. But when Mr Oakhurst returned from a weary search for the trail, he heard the sound of happy laughter echoed from the rocks. He stopped in some alarm, and his thoughts first naturally reverted to the whiskey, which he had prudently cached. 'And yet it don't somehow sound like whiskey,' said the gambler. It was not until he caught sight of the blazing fire through the still-blinding storm and the group around it that he settled to the conviction that it was 'square fun'.

Whether Mr Oakhurst had cached his cards with the whiskey as something debarred the free access of the community, I cannot say. It was certain that, in Mother Shipton's words, he 'didn't say cards once' during that evening. Haply the time was beguiled by an accordion, produced somewhat ostentatiously by Tom Simson from his pack. Notwithstanding some difficulties attending the manipulation of this instrument, Piney Woods managed to pluck several reluctant melodies from its keys, to an accompaniment by the Innocent on a pair of bone castanets. But the crowning festivity of the evening was reached in a rude camp-meeting hymn, which the lovers, joining hands, sang with great earnestness and vociferation. I fear that a certain defiant tone and Covenanter's swing to its chorus, rather than any devotional quality, caused it speedily to infect the others, who at last joined in the refrain:

'I'm proud to live in the service of the Lord,
And I'm bound to die in His army.'

The pines rocked, the storm eddied and whirled above the miserable group, and the flames of their altar leaped heavenward as if in token of the vow.

At midnight the storm abated, the rolling clouds parted, and the stars glittered keenly above the sleeping camp. Mr Oakhurst, whose professional habits had enabled him to live on the smallest possible amount of sleep, in dividing the watch with Tom Simson somehow managed to take upon himself the greater part of that duty. He excused himself to the Innocent by saying that he had 'often been a week without sleep'. 'Doing what?' asked Tom. 'Poker!' replied Oakhurst, sententiously; 'when a man gets a streak of luck, he don't get tired. The luck gives in first. Luck,' continued the gambler, reflectively, 'is a mighty queer thing. All you know about it for certain is that it's bound to change. And it's finding out when it's going to change that makes you. We've had a streak of bad luck since we left Poker Flat – you come along, and slap you get into it, too. If you can hold your cards right along you're all right. For,' added the gambler, with cheerful irrelevance,

' "I'm proud to live in the service of the Lord,
And I'm bound to die in His army." '

The third day came, and the sun, looking through the white-curtained valley, saw the outcasts divide their slowly decreasing store of provisions for the morning meal. It was one of the peculiarities of that mountain climate that its rays diffused a kindly warmth over the wintry landscape, as if in regretful commiseration of the past. But it revealed drift on drift of snow piled high around the hut – a hopeless, uncharted, trackless sea of white lying below the rocky shores to which the castaways still clung. Through the marvellously clear air the smoke of the pastoral village of Poker Flat rose miles away. Mother Shipton saw it, and from a remote pinnacle of her rocky fastness hurled in that direction a final malediction. It was her last vituperative attempt, and perhaps for that reason was invested with a certain degree of sublimity. It did her good, she privately informed the Duchess. 'Just you go out there and cuss, and see.' She then set herself to the task of amusing 'the child', as she and the Duchess were pleased to call Piney. Piney was no chicken, but it was a soothing and original theory of the pair thus to account for the fact that she didn't swear and wasn't improper.

When night crept up again through the gorges, the reedy notes of the accordion rose and fell in fitful spasms and long-drawn gasps by the flickering campfire. But music failed to fill entirely the aching void left by insufficient food, and a new diversion was proposed by Piney – story-telling. Neither Mr Oakhurst nor his female companions caring to relate their personal experiences, this plan would have failed too but for the Innocent. Some months before he had chanced upon a stray copy of Mr Pope's ingenious translation of the *Iliad*. He now proposed to narrate the principal incidents of that poem – having thoroughly mastered the argument and fairly forgotten the words – in the current vernacular of

Sandy Bar. And so for the rest of that night the Homeric demigods again walked the earth. Trojan bully and wily Greek wrestled in the winds, and the great pines in the canyon seemed to bow to the wrath of the son of Peleus. Mr Oakhurst listened with quiet satisfaction. Most especially was he interested in the fate of 'Ash-heels', as the Innocent persisted in denominating the 'swift-footed Achilles'.

So with small food and much of Homer and the accordion, a week passed over the heads of the outcasts. The sun again forsook them, and again from leaden skies the snowflakes were sifted over the land. Day by day closer around them drew the snowy circle, until at last they looked from their prison over drifted walls of dazzling white that towered twenty feet above their heads. It became more and more difficult to replenish their fires, even from the fallen trees beside them, now half-hidden in the drifts. And yet no one complained. The lovers turned from the dreary prospect and looked into each other's eyes, and were happy. Mr Oakhurst settled himself coolly to the losing game before him. The Duchess, more cheerful than she had been, assumed the care of Piney. Only Mother Shipton – once the strongest of the party – seemed to sicken and fade. At midnight on the tenth day she called Oakhurst to her side. 'I'm going,' she said, in a voice of querulous weakness, 'but don't say anything about it. Don't waken the kids. Take the bundle from under my head and open it.' Mr Oakhurst did so. It contained Mother Shipton's rations for the last week, untouched. 'Give 'em to the child,' she said, pointing to the sleeping Piney. 'You've starved yourself,' said the gambler. 'That's what they call it,' said the woman, querulously, as she lay down again and, turning her face to the wall, passed quietly away.

The accordion and the bones were put aside that day, and Homer was forgotten. When the body of Mother Shipton had been committed to the snow, Mr Oakhurst took the Innocent aside and showed him a pair of snowshoes which he had fashioned from the old pack saddle. 'There's one chance in a hundred to save her yet,' he said, pointing to Piney; 'but it's there,' he added, pointing towards Poker Flat. 'If you can reach there in two days she's safe.' 'And you?' asked Tom Simson. 'I'll stay here,' was the curt reply.

The lovers parted with a long embrace. 'You are not going, too?' said the Duchess as she saw Mr Oakhurst apparently waiting to accompany him. 'As far as the canyon,' he replied. He turned suddenly, and kissed the Duchess, leaving her pallid face aflame and her trembling limbs rigid with amazement.

Night came, but not Mr Oakhurst. It brought the storm again and the whirling snow. Then the Duchess, feeding the fire, found that someone had quietly piled beside the hut enough fuel to last a few days longer. The tears rose to her eyes, but she hid them from Piney.

The women slept but little. In the morning, looking into each other's faces, they read their fate. Neither spoke; but Piney, accepting the position of the stronger, drew near and placed her arm around the Duchess's waist. They kept this attitude for the rest of the day. That night the storm reached its greatest fury and, rending asunder the protecting pines, invaded the very hut.

Toward morning they found themselves unable to feed the fire, which gradually died away. As the embers slowly blackened, the Duchess crept closer to Piney, and broke the silence of many hours: 'Piney, can you pray?' 'No, dear,' said Piney, simply. The Duchess, without knowing exactly why, felt relieved, and, putting her head upon Piney's shoulder, spoke no more. And so reclining, the younger and purer pillowing the head of her soiled sister upon her virgin breast, they fell asleep.

The wind lulled as if it feared to waken them. Feathery drifts of snow, shaken from the long pine boughs, flew like white-winged birds, and settled about them as they slept. The moon through the rifted clouds looked down upon what had been the camp. But all human stain, all trace of earthly travail, was hidden beneath the spotless mantle mercifully flung from above.

They slept all that day and the next, nor did they waken when voices and footsteps broke the silence of the camp. And when pitying fingers brushed the snow from their wan faces, you could scarcely have told from the equal peace that dwelt upon them which was she that had sinned. Even the law of Poker Flat recognised this, and turned away, leaving them still locked in each other's arms.

But at the head of the gulch, on one of the largest pine trees, they found the deuce of clubs pinned to the bark with a bowie knife. It bore the following, written in pencil, in a firm hand:

BENEATH THIS TREE LIES THE BODY OF
JOHN OAKHURST
WHO STRUCK A STREAK OF BAD LUCK
ON THE 23RD NOVEMBER 1850
AND HANDED IN HIS CHECKS
ON THE 7TH DECEMBER 1850.

JOHNSON'S 'OLD WOMAN'

BRET HARTE

I T WAS GROWING DARK, and the Sonora trail was becoming more indistinct before me at every step. The difficulty had increased over the grassy slope, where the overflow from some smaller water course above had worn a number of diverging gullies so like the trail as to be undistinguishable from it. Unable to determine which was the right one, I threw the reins over the mule's neck and resolved to trust to that superior animal's sagacity, of which I had heard so much. But I had not taken into account the equally well-known weaknesses of sex and species, and Chu Chu had already shown uncontrollable signs of wanting her own way. Without a moment's hesitation, feeling the relaxed bridle, she lay down and rolled over.

In this perplexity the sound of horse's hoofs ringing out of the rocky canyon beyond was a relief, even if momentarily embarrassing. An instant afterwards a horse and rider appeared cantering round the hill on what was evidently the lost trail, and pulled up as I succeeded in forcing Chu Chu to her legs again.

'Is that the trail from Sonora?' I asked.

'Yes;' but with a critical glance at the mule, 'I reckon you ain't going thar tonight.'

'Why not?'

'It's a matter of eighteen miles, and most of it a blind trail through the woods after you take the valley.'

'Is it worse than this?'

'What's the matter with this trail? Ye ain't expecting a racecourse or a shell road over the foothills – are ye?'

'No. Is there any hotel where I can stop?'

'Nary.'

'Nor any house?'

'No.'

'Thank you. Good-night.'

He had already passed on, when he halted again and turned in his saddle. 'Look yer. Just a spell over yon canyon ye'll find a patch o' buckeyes; turn to the right and ye'll see a trail. That'll take ye to a shanty. You ask if it's Johnson's.'

'Who's Johnson?'

'I am. You ain't lookin' for Vanderbilt or God Almighty up here, are you? Well, then, you hark to me, will you? You say to my old woman to give you supper and a shakedown somewhar tonight. Say I sent you. So long.'

He was gone before I could accept or decline. An extraordinary noise proceeded from Chu Chu, not unlike a suppressed chuckle. I looked sharply at her; she coughed affectedly, and with her head and neck stretched to their greatest length, appeared to contemplate her neat little off-fore shoe with admiring abstraction. But as soon as I had mounted she set off abruptly, crossed the rocky canyon, apparently sighted the patch of buckeyes of her own volition, and without the slightest hesitation found the trail to the right and in half an hour stood before the shanty.

It was a log cabin with an additional 'lean-to' of the same material, roofed with bark, and on the other side a larger and more ambitious 'extension' built of rough, unplaned and unpainted redwood boards, lightly shingled. The 'lean-to' was evidently used as a kitchen, and the central cabin as a living-room. The barking of a dog as I approached called four children of different sizes to the open door, where already an enterprising baby was feebly essaying to crawl over a bar of wood laid across the threshold to restrain it.

'Is this Johnson's house?'

My remark was really addressed to the eldest, a boy of apparently nine or ten, but I felt that my attention was unduly fascinated by the baby, who at that moment had toppled over the bar, and was calmly eyeing me upside down, while silently and heroically suffocating in its petticoats. The boy disappeared without replying, but presently returned with a taller girl of fourteen or fifteen. I was struck with the way that, as she reached the door, she passed her hands rapidly over the heads of the others as if counting them, picked up the baby, reversed it, shook out its clothes, and returned it to the inside, without even looking at it. The act was evidently automatic and habitual.

I repeated my question timidly.

Yes, it *was* Johnson's, but he had just gone to King's Mills. I replied, hurriedly, that I knew it, – that I had met him beyond the canyon. As I had lost my way and couldn't get to Sonora tonight, he had been good enough to say that I might stay there until morning. My voice was slightly raised for the benefit of Mr Johnson's 'old woman', who, I had no doubt, was inspecting me furtively from some corner.

The girl drew the children away, except the boy. To him she said simply, 'Show the stranger whar to stake out his mule, 'Dolphus', and disappeared into the 'extension' without another word. I followed my little guide, who was perhaps more actively curious, but equally unresponsive. To my various questions he simply returned a smile of exasperating vacuity. But he never took his eager eyes from me, and I was satisfied that not a detail of my appearance escaped him. Leading the way behind the house to a little wood, whose only 'clearing' had been effected by decay or storm, he stood silently apart while I picketed Chu Chu, neither offering to assist me nor opposing any interruption to my survey of the locality. There was no trace of human cultivation in the surroundings of the cabin; the wilderness still trod sharply on the heels of the pioneer's fresh footprints, and even seemed to obliterate them. For a few yards around the actual dwelling there was an unsavoury fringe of civilisation in the shape of cast-off clothes, empty bottles and tin cans, and the adjacent thorn and elder bushes blossomed unwholesomely with bits of torn white paper and bleaching dishcloths. This hideous circle never widened; Nature always appeared to roll back the intruding debris; no bird nor beast carried it away; no animal ever forced the uncleanly barrier; civilisation remained grimly trenched in its own exuviae. The old terrifying girdle of fire around the hunter's camp was not more deterring to curious night prowlers than this coarse and accidental outwork.

When I regained the cabin I found it empty, the doors of the lean-to and extension closed, but there was a stool set before a rude table, upon which smoked a tin cup of coffee, a tin dish of hot saleratus biscuit and a plate of fried beef. There was something odd and depressing in this silent exclusion of my presence. Had Johnson's 'old woman' from some dark post of observation taken a dislike to my appearance, or was this churlish withdrawal a peculiarity of Sierran hospitality? Or was Mrs Johnson young and pretty, and hidden under the restricting ban of Johnson's jealousy, or was she a deformed cripple, or even a bedridden crone? From the extension at times came a murmur of voices, but never the accents of adult womanhood. The gathering darkness, relieved only by a dull glow from the smouldering logs in the adobe chimney, added to my loneliness. In the circumstances I knew I ought to have put aside the repast and given myself up to gloomy and pessimistic reflection; but Nature is often inconsistent, and in that keen mountain air, I grieve to say, my physical and moral condition was not in that perfect accord always indicated by romancers. I had an appetite and I gratified it;

dyspepsia and ethical reflections might come later. I ate the saleratus biscuit cheerfully, and was meditatively finishing my coffee when a gurgling sound from the rafters above attracted my attention. I looked up; under the overhang of the bark roof three pairs of round eyes were fixed upon me. They belonged to the children I had previously seen, who, in the attitude of Raphael's cherubs, had evidently been deeply interested spectators of my repast. As our eyes met an inarticulate giggle escaped the lips of the youngest.

I never could understand why the shy amusement of children over their elders is not accepted as philosophically by its object as when it proceeds from an equal. We fondly believe that when Jones or Brown laughs at us it is from malice, ignorance or a desire to show his superiority, but there is always a haunting suspicion in our minds that these little critics *really* see something in us to laugh at. I, however, smiled affably in return, ignoring any possible grotesqueness in my manner of eating in private.

'Come here, Johnny,' I said blandly.

The two elder ones, a girl and a boy, disappeared instantly, as if the crowning joke of this remark was too much for them. From a scraping and kicking against the log wall I judged that they had quickly dropped to the ground outside. The younger one, the giggler, remained fascinated, but ready to fly at a moment's warning.

'Come here, Johnny, boy,' I repeated gently. 'I want you to go to your mother, please, and tell her' –

But here the child, who had been working its face convulsively, suddenly uttered a lugubrious howl and disappeared also. I ran to the front door and looked out in time to see the tallest girl, who had received me, walking away with it under her arm, pushing the boy ahead of her and looking back over her shoulder, not unlike a youthful she-bear conducting her cubs from danger. She disappeared at the end of the extension, where there was evidently another door.

It was very extraordinary. It was not strange that I turned back to the cabin with a chagrin and mortification which for a moment made me entertain the wild idea of saddling Chu Chu, and shaking the dust of that taciturn house from my feet. But the ridiculousness of such an act, to say nothing of its ingratitude, as quickly presented itself to me. Johnson had offered me only food and shelter; I could have claimed no more from the inn I had asked him to direct me to. I did not re-enter the house, but, lighting my last cigar, began to walk gloomily up and down the trail.

With the outcoming of the stars it had grown lighter; through a wind opening in the trees I could see the heavy bulk of the opposite mountain, and beyond it a superior crest defined by a red line of forest fire, which, however, cast no reflection on the surrounding earth or sky. Faint woodland currents of air, still warm from the afternoon sun, stirred the leaves around me with long-drawn aromatic breaths. But these in time gave way to the steady Sierran night wind sweeping down from the higher summits, and rocking the tops of the tallest pines, yet leaving the tranquillity of the dark lower aisles unshaken. It was very quiet; there was no cry nor call of beast or bird in the darkness; the long rustle of the tree-tops sounded as faint as the far-off wash of distant seas. Nor did the resemblance cease there; the close-set files of the pines and cedars, stretching in illimitable ranks to the horizon, were filled with the im-measurable loneliness of an ocean shore. In this vast silence I began to think I understood the taciturnity of the dwellers in the solitary cabin.

When I returned, however, I was surprised to find the tallest girl standing by the door. As I approached she retreated before me, and pointing to the corner where a common cot bed had been evidently just put up, said, 'Ye can turn in thar, only ye'll have to rouse out early when 'Dolphus does the chores,' and was turning towards the extension again, when I stopped her almost appealingly.

'One moment, please. Can I see your mother?'

She paused and looked at me with a singular expression. Then she said sharply: 'You know, fust rate, she's dead.'

She was turning away again, but I think she must have seen my concern in my face, for she hesitated.

'But,' I said quickly, 'I certainly understood your father, that is, Mr Johnson,' I added, interrogatively, 'to say that – that I was to speak to' – I didn't like to repeat the exact phrase – 'his *wife*.'

'I don't know what he was playin' ye for,' she said shortly. 'Mar has been dead mor'n a year.'

'But,' I persisted, 'is there no grown-up woman here?'

'No.'

'Then who takes care of you and the children?'

'I do.'

'Yourself and your father – eh?'

'Dad ain't here two days running, and then on'y to sleep.'

'And you take the entire charge of the house?'

'Yes, and the log tallies.'

'The log tallies?'

'Yes; keep count and measure the logs that go by the slide.'

It flashed upon me that I had passed the slide or declivity on the hillside, where logs were slipped down into the valley, and I inferred that Johnson's business was cutting timber for the mill.

'But you're rather young for all this work,' I suggested.

'I'm goin' on sixteen,' she said gravely.

Indeed, for the matter of that, she might have been any age. Her face, on which sunburn took the place of complexion, was already hard and set. But on a nearer view I was struck with the fact that her eyes, which were not large, were almost indistinguishable from the presence of the most singular eyelashes I had ever seen. Intensely black, intensely thick, and even tangled in their profusion, they bristled rather than fringed her eyelids, obliterating everything but the shining black pupils beneath, which were like certain lustrous hairy mountain berries. It was this woodland suggestion that seemed uncannily to connect her with the locality.

I went on playfully, 'That's not *very* old – but tell me – does your father, or *did* your father, ever speak of you as his "old woman"?'

She nodded. 'Then you thought I was mar?' she said, smiling.

It was such a relief to see her worn face relax its expression of pathetic gravity – although this operation quite buried her eyes in their black thickset hedge again – that I continued cheerfully: 'It wasn't much of a mistake, considering all you do for the house and family.'

'Then you didn't tell Billy "to go and be dead in the ground with mar", as he 'lows you did?' she said half suspiciously, yet trembling on the edge of a smile.

No, I had not, but I admitted that my asking him to go to his mother might have been open to this dismal construction by a sensitive infant mind. She seemed mollified, and again turned to go.

'Good-night, miss – you know, your father didn't tell me your real name,' I said.

'Karline!'

'Good-night, Miss Karline.'

I held out my hand.

She looked at it and then at me through her intricate eyelashes. Then she struck it aside briskly, but not unkindly, said, 'Quit foolin', now,' as she might have said to one of the children, and disappeared through the inner door. Not knowing whether to be amused or indignant, I remained silent a moment. Then I took a turn outside in the increasing darkness, listened to the now hurrying wind over the tree-tops, re-entered the cabin, closed the door, and went to bed.

But not to sleep. Perhaps the responsibility towards these solitary children, which Johnson had so lightly shaken off, devolved upon me as I lay there, for I found myself imagining a dozen emergencies of their unprotected state, with which the elder girl could scarcely grapple. There was little to fear from depredatory man or beast – desperadoes of the mountain trail never stooped to ignoble burglary, bear or panther seldom approached a cabin – but there was the chance of sudden illness, fire, the accidents that beset childhood, to say nothing of the narrowing moral and mental effect of their isolation at that tender age. It was scandalous in Johnson to leave them alone.

In the silence I found I could hear quite distinctly the sound of their voices in the extension, and it was evident that Caroline was putting them to bed. Suddenly a voice was uplifted – her own! She began to sing and the others to join her. It was the repetition of a single verse of a well-known lugubrious Negro melody. 'All the world am sad and dreary,' wailed Caroline, in a high head-note, 'everywhere I roam.' 'Oh, darkieth,' lisped the younger girl in response, 'how my heart growth weary, far from the old folkth at h-o-o-me.' This was repeated two or three times before the others seemed to get the full swing of it, and then the lines rose and fell sadly and monotonously in the darkness. I don't know why, but I at once got the impression that those motherless little creatures were under a vague belief that their performance was devotional, and was really filling the place of an evening hymn. A brief and indistinct kind of recitation, followed by a dead silence, broken only by the slow creaking of new timber, as if the house were stretching itself to sleep too, confirmed my impression. Then all became quiet again.

But I was more wide awake than before. Finally I rose, dressed myself, and dragging my stool to the fire, took a book from my knapsack, and by the light of a guttering candle, which I discovered in a bottle in the corner of the hearth, began to read. Presently I fell into a doze. How long I slept I could not tell, for it seemed to me that a dreamy consciousness of a dog barking at last forced itself upon me so strongly that I awoke. The barking appeared to come from behind the cabin in the direction of the clearing where I had tethered Chu Chu. I opened the door hurriedly, ran round the cabin towards the hollow, and was almost at once met by the bulk of the frightened Chu Chu, plunging out of the darkness towards me, kept only in check by her reata in the hand of a blanketed shape slowly advancing with a gun over its shoulder out of the hollow. Before I had time to recover from my astonishment I was thrown into greater confusion by recognising the shape as none other than Caroline!

Without the least embarrassment or even self-consciousness of her appearance, she tossed the end of the reata to me with the curtest explanation as she passed by. Some prowling bear or catamount had frightened the mule. I had better tether it before the cabin away from the wind.

'But I thought wild beasts never came so near,' I said quickly.

'Mule meat's mighty temptin',' said the girl sententiously and passed on. I wanted to thank her; I wanted to say how sorry I was that she had been disturbed; I wanted to compliment her on her quiet midnight courage, and yet warn her against recklessness; I wanted to know whether she had been accustomed to such alarms; and if the gun she carried was really a necessity. But I could only respect her reticence, and I was turning away when I was struck by a more inexplicable spectacle. As she neared the end of the extension I distinctly saw the tall figure of a man, moving with a certain diffidence and hesitation that did not, however, suggest any intention of concealment, among the trees; the girl apparently saw him at the same moment and slightly slackened her pace. Not more than a dozen feet separated them. He said something that was inaudible to my ears – but which from his hesitation or the distance I could not determine. There was no such uncertainty in her reply, however, which was given in her usual curt fashion: 'All right. You can traipse along home now and turn in.'

She turned the corner of the extension and disappeared. The tall figure of the man wavered hesitatingly for a moment, and then vanished also. But I was too much excited by curiosity to accept this unsatisfactory conclusion, and, hastily picketing Chu Chu a few rods from the front door, I ran after him, with an instinctive feeling that he had not gone far. I was right. A few paces distant he had halted in the same dubious, lingering way.

'Hallo!' I said.

He turned towards me in the like awkward fashion, but with neither astonishment nor concern.

'Come up and take a drink with me before you go,' I said, 'if you're not in a hurry. I'm alone here, and since I *have* turned out I don't see why we mightn't have a smoke and a talk together.'

'I dursn't.'

I looked up at the six feet of strength before me and repeated wonderingly, 'Dare not?'

'*She* wouldn't like it.' He made a movement with his right shoulder towards the extension.

'Who?'

'Miss Karline.'

'Nonsense!' I said. 'She isn't in the cabin – you won't see *her*. Come along.' He hesitated, although from what I could discern of his bearded face it was weakly smiling. 'Come.'

He obeyed, following me not unlike Chu Chu, I fancied, with the same sense of superior size and strength and a slight whitening of the eye, as if ready to shy at any moment. At the door he 'backed'. Then he entered sideways. I noticed that he cleared the doorway at the top and the sides only by a hair's breadth.

By the light of the fire I could see that, in spite of his full first growth of beard, he was young – even younger than myself – and that he was by no means bad-looking. As he still showed signs of retreating at any moment, I took my flask and tobacco from my saddle-bags, handed them to him, pointed to the stool and sat down myself upon the bed.

'You live near here?'

'Yes,' he said a little abstractedly, as if listening for some interruption, 'at Ten Mile Crossing.'

'Why, that's two miles away.'

'I reckon.'

'Then you don't live here – on the clearing?'

'No. I b'long to the mill at Ten Mile. '

'You were on your way home?'

'No,' he hesitated, looking at his pipe; 'I kinder meander round here at this time, when Johnson's away, to see if everything's goin' straight.'

'I see – you're a friend of the family.'

' 'Deed no!' He stopped, laughed, looked confused, and added, apparently to his pipe, 'That is, a sorter friend. Not much. *She*' – he lowered his voice as if that potential personality filled the whole cabin – 'wouldn't like it.'

'Then at night, when Johnson's away, you do sentry duty round the house?'

'Yes, "sentry dooty", that's it' – he seemed impressed with the suggestion – 'that's it! Sentry dooty. You've struck it, pardner.'

'And how often is Johnson away?'

' 'Bout two or three times a week on an average.'

'But Miss Caroline appears to be able to take care of herself. She has no fear.'

'Fear! Fear wasn't hangin' round when *she* was born!' He paused. 'No, sir. Did ye ever look into them eyes?'

I hadn't, on account of the lashes. But I didn't care to say this, and only nodded.

'There ain't the created thing livin' or dead that she can't stand straight up to and look at.'

I wondered if he had fancied she experienced any difficulty in standing up before that innocently good-humoured face, but I could not resist saying, 'Then I don't see the use of your walking four miles to look after her.'

I was sorry for it the next minute, for he seemed to have awkwardly broken his pipe, and had to bend down for a long time afterwards to laboriously pick up the smallest fragments of it. At last he said, cautiously:

'Ye noticed them bits o' flannin' round the chillern's throats?'

I remembered that I had, but was uncertain whether it was intended as a preventive of cold or a child's idea of decoration. I nodded.

'That's their trouble. One night, when old Johnson had been off for three days to Coulterville, I was prowling round here and I didn't git to see no one, though there was a light burnin' in the shanty all night. The next night I was here again – the same light twinklin', but no one about. I reckoned that was mighty queer, and I jess crep' up to the house an' listened. I heard suthin' like a little cough oncet in a while, and at times suthin' like a little moan. I didn't durst to sing out for I knew *she* wouldn't like it, but whistled keerless like, to let the chillern know I was there. But it didn't seem to take. I was jess goin' off, when – darn my skin! – if I didn't come across the bucket of water I'd fetched up from the spring *that mornin'*, standin' there full, and *never taken in*! When I saw that I reckoned I'd jess wade in, anyhow, and I knocked. Pooty soon the door was half opened, and I saw her eyes blazin' at me like them coals. Then she 'lowed I'd better "git up and git", and shet the door to! Then I 'lowed she might tell me what was up – through the door. Then she said, through the door, as how the chillern lay all sick with that hoss-distemper, diphthery. Then she 'lowed she'd use a doctor ef I'd fetch him. Then she 'lowed again I'd better take the baby that hadn't ketched it yet along with me, and leave it where it was safe. Then she passed out the baby through the door all wrapped up in a blankit like a papoose, and you bet I made tracks with it. I knowed thar wasn't no good going to the mill, so I lit out for White's, four miles beyond, whar there was White's old mother. I told her how things were pointin', and she lent me a hoss, and I jess rounded on Doctor Green at Mountain Jim's, and had him back here afore sun-up! And then I heard she wilted – regularly played out, you see – for she had it all along wuss than the lot, and never let on or whimpered!'

'It was well you persisted in seeing her that night,' I said, watching the rapt expression of his face.

He looked up quickly, became conscious of my scrutiny and dropped his eyes again, smiled feebly and, drawing a circle in the ashes with the broken pipe-stem, said, 'But *she* didn't like it, though.'

I suggested, a little warmly, that if she allowed her father to leave her alone at night with delicate children, she had no right to choose *who* should assist her in an emergency. It struck me afterwards that this was not very complimentary to him, and I added hastily that I wondered if she expected some young lady to be passing along the trail at midnight! But this reminded me of Johnson's style of argument, and I stopped.

'Yes,' he said meekly, 'and ef she didn't keer enough for herself and her brothers and sisters, she orter remember them Beazeley chillern.'

'Beazeley children?' I repeated wonderingly.

'Yes; them two little ones, the size of Mirandy; they're Beazeley's.'

'Who is Beazeley, and what are his children doing here?'

'Beazeley up and died at the mill, and she bedevilled her father to let her take his two young 'uns here.'

'You don't mean to say that with her other work she's taking care of other people's children too?'

'Yes, and eddicatin' them.'

'Educating them?'

'Yes; teachin' them to read and write and do sums. One of our loggers ketched her at it when she was keepin' tally.'

We were both silent for some moments.

'I suppose you know Johnson?' I said finally.

'Not much.'

'But you call here at other times than when you're helping her?'

'Never been in the house before.'

He looked slowly around him as he spoke, raising his eyes to the bare rafters above, and drawing a few long breaths, as if he were inhaling the aura of some unseen presence. He appeared so perfectly gratified and contented, and I was so impressed with this humble and silent absorption of the sacred interior, that I felt vaguely conscious that any interruption of it was a profanation, and I sat still, gazing at the dying fire. Presently he arose, stretched out his hand, shook mine warmly, said, 'I reckon I'll meander along,' took another long breath, this time secretly, as if conscious of my eyes, and then slouched sideways out of the house into the darkness again, where he seemed suddenly to attain his full height, and so looming, disappeared. I shut the door, went to bed, and slept soundly.

So soundly that when I awoke the sun was streaming on my bed from the open door. On the table before me my breakfast was already laid. When I had dressed and eaten it, struck by the silence, I went to the door and looked out. 'Dolphus was holding Chu Chu by the reata a few paces from the cabin.

'Where's Caroline?' I asked.

He pointed to the woods and said: 'Over yon: keeping tally.'

'Did she leave any message?'

'Said I was to git your mule for you.'

'Anything else?'

'Yes; said you was to go.'

I went, but not until I had scrawled a few words of thanks on a leaf of my notebook, which I wrapped about my last Spanish dollar, addressed it to 'Miss Johnson', and laid it upon the table.

*　　*　　*

It was more than a year later that in the bar-room of the Mariposa Hotel a hand was laid upon my sleeve. I looked up. It was Johnson.

He drew from his pocket a Spanish dollar. 'I reckoned,' he said, cheerfully, 'I'd run agin ye somewhar sometime. My old woman told me to give ye that when I did, and say that she "didn't keep no hotel". But she allowed she'd keep the letter, and has spelled it out to the chillern.'

Here was the opportunity I had longed for to touch Johnson's pride and affection in the brave but unprotected girl. 'I want to talk to you about Miss Johnson,' I said, eagerly.

'I reckon so,' he said, with an exasperating smile. 'Most fellers do. But she ain't Miss Johnson no more. She's married.'

'Not to that big chap over from Ten Mile Mills?' I said breathlessly.

'What's the matter with *him*,' said Johnson. 'Ye didn't expect her to marry a nobleman, did ye?'

I said I didn't see why she shouldn't – and believed that she *had*.

THE REFORMATION OF CALLIOPE

O. HENRY

CALLIOPE CATESBY was in his humours again. Ennui was upon him. This goodly promontory, the earth – particularly that portion of it known as Quicksand – was to him no more than a pestilent congregation of vapours. Overtaken by the megrims, the philosopher may seek relief in soliloquy; my lady find solace in tears; the flaccid Easterner scold at the millinery bills of his womenfolk. Such recourse was insufficient to the denizens of Quicksand. Calliope, especially, was wont to express his ennui according to his lights.

Overnight Calliope had hung out signals of approaching low spirits. He had kicked his own dog on the porch of the Occidental Hotel, and refused to apologise. He had become capricious and fault-finding in conversation. While strolling about he reached often for twigs of mesquite and chewed the leaves fiercely. That was always an ominous act. Another symptom alarming to those who were familiar with the different stages of his doldrums was his increasing politeness and a tendency to use formal phrases. A husky softness succeeded the usual penetrating drawl in his tones. A dangerous courtesy marked his manners. Later, his smile became crooked, the left side of his mouth slanting upwards, and Quicksand got ready to stand from under.

At this stage Calliope generally began to drink. Finally, about midnight, he was seen going homeward, saluting those whom he met with exaggerated but inoffensive courtesy. Not yet was Calliope's melancholy at the danger point. He would seat himself at the window of the room he occupied over Silvester's tonsorial parlours and there chant lugubrious and tuneless ballads until morning, accompanying the noises by appropriate maltreatment of a jangling guitar. More magnanimous than Nero, he would thus give musical warning of the forthcoming municipal upheaval that Quicksand was scheduled to endure.

A quiet, amiable man was Calliope Catesby at other times – quiet to indolence, and amiable to worthlessness. At best he was a loafer and a nuisance; at worst he was the Terror of Quicksand. His ostensible occupation was something subordinate in the real-estate line; he drove the beguiled Easterner in buckboards out to look over lots and ranch property. Originally he came from one of the Gulf states, his lank six feet, slurring rhythm of speech and sectional idioms giving evidence of his birthplace.

And yet, after taking on Western adjustments, this languid pine-box whittler, cracker-barrel hugger, shady-corner lounger of the cotton fields and sumac hills of the South became famed as a bad man among men who had made a lifelong study of the art of truculence.

At nine the next morning Calliope was fit. Inspired by his own barbarous melodies and the contents of his jug, he was ready primed to gather fresh laurels from the diffident brow of Quicksand. Encircled and criss-crossed with cartridge belts, abundantly garnished with revolvers, and copiously drunk, he poured forth into Quicksand's main street. Too chivalrous to surprise and capture a town by silent sortie, he paused at the nearest corner and emitted his slogan – that fearful, brassy yell, so reminiscent of the steam piano, that had gained for him the classic appellation that had superseded his own baptismal name. Following close upon his vociferation came three shots from his ·45 by way of limbering up the guns and testing his aim. A yellow dog, the personal property of Colonel Swazey, the proprietor of the Occidental, fell feet upward in the dust with one farewell yelp. A Mexican who was crossing the street from the Blue Front grocery carrying in his hand a bottle of kerosene, was stimulated to a sudden and admirable burst of speed, still grasping the neck of the shattered bottle. The new gilt weathercock on Judge Riley's lemon and ultramarine two-storey residence shivered, flapped, and hung by a splinter, the sport of the wanton breezes.

The artillery was in trim. Calliope's hand was steady. The high, calm ecstasy of habitual battle was upon him, though slightly embittered by the sadness of Alexander in that his conquests were limited to the small world of Quicksand.

Down the street went Calliope, shooting right and left. Glass fell like hail; dogs vamoosed; chickens flew, squawking; feminine voices shrieked concernedly to youngsters at large. The din was perforated at intervals by the staccato of the Terror's guns, and was drowned periodically by the brazen screech that Quicksand knew so well. The occasions of Calliope's low spirits were legal holidays in Quicksand. All along the main street in advance of his coming clerks were putting up shutters and closing doors. Business would languish for a space. The right of way was Calliope's, and as he advanced, observing the dearth of opposition and the few opportunities for distraction, his ennui perceptibly increased.

But, some four squares farther down, lively preparations were being made to minister to Mr Catesby's love for interchange of compliments and repartee. On the previous night numerous messengers had hastened to advise Buck Patterson, the city marshal, of Calliope's impending eruption. The patience of that official, often strained in extending leniency toward the disturber's misdeeds, had been overtaxed. In Quicksand some indulgence was accorded the natural ebullition of human nature. Providing that the lives of the more useful citizens were not recklessly squandered, or too much property needlessly laid waste, the community sentiment was against a too strict enforcement of the law. But Calliope had raised the limit. His outbursts had been too frequent and too violent to come within the classification of a normal and sanitary relaxation of spirit.

Buck Patterson had been expecting and awaiting in his little ten-by-twelve frame office that preliminary yell announcing that Calliope was feeling blue. When the signal came the city marshal rose to his feet and buckled on his guns. Two deputy sheriffs and three citizens who had proven the edible qualities of fire also stood up, ready to bandy with Calliope's leaden jocularities.

'Gather that fellow in,' said Buck Patterson, setting forth the lines of the campaign. 'Don't have no talk, but shoot as soon as you can get a show. Keep behind cover and bring him down. He's a nogood 'un. It's up to Calliope to turn up his toes this time, I reckon. Go to him all spraddled out, boys. And don't git too reckless, for what Calliope shoots at he hits.'

Buck Patterson, tall, muscular, and solemn-faced, with his bright 'City Marshal' badge shining on the breast of his blue flannel shirt, gave his posse directions for the onslaught upon Calliope. The plan was to accomplish the downfall of the Quicksand Terror without loss to the attacking party, if possible.

The splenetic Calliope, unconscious of retributive plots, was steaming down the channel, cannonading on either side, when he suddenly became aware of breakers ahead. The city marshal and one of the deputies rose up behind some dry-goods boxes half a square to the front and opened fire. At the same time the rest of the posse, divided, shelled him from two side streets up which they were cautiously manoeuvring from a well-executed detour.

The first volley broke the lock of one of Calliope's guns, cut a neat underbite in his right ear and exploded a cartridge in his crossbelt, scorching his ribs as it burst. Feeling braced up by this unexpected tonic to his spiritual depression, Calliope executed a fortissimo note from his upper register, and returned the fire like an echo. The upholders of the law dodged at his flash, but a trifle too late to save one of the deputies a bullet just above the elbow, and the marshal a bleeding cheek from a splinter that a ball tore from the box he had ducked behind.

And now Calliope met the enemy's tactics in kind. Choosing with a rapid eye the street from which the weakest and least accurate fire had come, he invaded it at a double-quick, abandoning the unprotected middle of the street. With rare cunning the opposing force in that direction – one of the deputies and two of the valorous volunteers – waited, concealed by beer barrels, until Calliope had passed their retreat, and then peppered him from the rear. In another moment they were reinforced by the marshal and his other men, and then Calliope felt that in order successfully to prolong the delights of the controversy he must find some means of reducing the great odds against him. His eye fell upon a structure that seemed to hold out this promise, providing he could reach it.

Not far away was the little railroad station, its building a strong box house, ten by twenty feet, resting upon a platform four feet above ground. Windows were in each of its walls. Something like a fort it might become to a man thus sorely pressed by superior numbers.

Calliope made a bold and rapid spurt for it, the marshal's crowd 'smoking' him as he ran. He reached the haven in safety, the station agent leaving the building by a window, like a flying squirrel, as the garrison entered the door.

Patterson and his supporters halted under protection of a pile of lumber and held consultations. In the station was an unterrified desperado who was an excellent shot and carried an abundance of ammunition. For thirty yards on either side of the besieged was a stretch of bare, open ground. It was a sure thing that the man who attempted to enter that unprotected area would be stopped by one of Calliope's bullets.

The city marshal was resolved. He had decided that Calliope Catesby should no more wake the echoes of Quicksand with his strident whoop. He had so announced. Officially and personally he felt imperatively bound to put the soft pedal on that instrument of discord. It played bad tunes.

Standing near was a hand truck used in the manipulation of small freight. It stood by a shed full of sacked wool, a consignment from one of the sheep ranches. On this truck the marshal and his men piled three heavy sacks of wool. Stooping low, Buck Patterson started for Calliope's fort, slowly pushing this loaded truck before him for protection. The posse, scattering broadly, stood ready to nip the besieged in case he should show himself in an effort to repel the juggernaut of justice that was creeping upon him. Only once did Calliope make demonstration.

He fired from a window, and some tufts of wool spurted from the marshal's trustworthy bulwark. The return shots from the posse pattered against the window frame of the fort. No loss resulted on either side.

The marshal was too deeply engrossed in steering his protected battle-ship to be aware of the approach of the morning train until he was within a few feet of the platform. The train was coming up on the other side of it. It stopped only one minute at Quicksand. What an opportunity it would offer to Calliope! He had only to step out the other door, mount the train, and away.

Abandoning his breastwork, Buck, with his gun ready, dashed up the steps and into the room, driving open the closed door with one heave of his weighty shoulder. The members of the posse heard one shot fired inside, and then there was silence.

*   *   *

At length the wounded man opened his eyes. After a blank space he again could see and hear and feel and think. Turning his eyes about, he found himself lying on a wooden bench. A tall man with a perplexed coun-tenance, wearing a big badge with 'City Marshal' engraved upon it, stood over him. A little old woman in black, with a wrinkled face and sparkling black eyes, was holding a wet handkerchief against one of his temples. He was trying to get these facts fixed in his mind and connected with past events, when the old woman began to talk.

'There now, great, big, strong man! That bullet never tetched ye! Jest skeeted along the side of your head and sort of paralysed ye for a spell. I've heerd of sech things afore; cun–cussion is what they names it. Abel Wadkins used to kill squirrels that way – barkin' 'em, Abe called it. You jest been barked, sir, and you'll be all right in a little bit. Feel lots better already, don't ye! You just lay still a while longer and let me bathe your head. You don't know me, I reckon, and 'tain't surprisin' that you shouldn't. I come in on that train from Alabama to see my son. Big son, ain't he? Lands! you wouldn't hardly think he'd ever been a baby, would ye? This is my son, sir.'

Half turning, the old woman looked up at the standing man, her worn face lighting with a proud and wonderful smile. She reached out one veined and calloused hand and took one of her son's. Then, smiling cheerily down at the prostrate man, she continued to dip the handkerchief in the waiting-room tin washbasin and gently apply it to his temple. She had the benevolent garrulity of old age.

'I ain't seen my son before,' she continued, 'in eight years. One of my nephews, Elkanah Price, he's a conductor on one of them railroads and he got me a pass to come out here. I can stay a whole week on it, and then it'll take me back again. Jest think, now, that little boy of mine has got to be a officer – a city marshal of a whole town! That's somethin' like a constable, ain't it? I never knowed he was a officer; he didn't say nothin' about it in his letters. I reckon he thought his old mother'd be skeered about the danger he was in. But, laws! I never was much of a hand to git skeered. 'Tain't no use. I heard them guns a-shootin' while I was gettin' off them cars, and I see smoke a-comin' out of the depot, but I jest walked right along. Then I see my son's face lookin' out through the window. I knowed him at oncet. He met me at the door, and squeezes me 'most to death. And there you was, sir, a-lyin' there jest like you was dead, and I 'lowed we'd see what might be done to help sot you up.'

'I think I'll sit up now,' said the concussion patient. 'I'm feeling pretty fair by this time.'

He sat, somewhat weakly yet, leaning against the wall. He was a rugged man, big-boned and straight. His eyes, steady and keen, seemed to linger upon the face of the man standing so still above him. His look wandered often from the face he studied to the marshal's badge upon the other's breast.

'Yes, yes, you'll be all right,' said the old woman, patting his arm, 'if you don't get to cuttin' up agin, and havin' folks shooting at you. Son told me about you, sir, while you was layin' senseless on the floor. Don't you take it as meddlesome fer an old woman with a son as big as you to talk about it. And you mustn't hold no grudge ag'in' my son for havin' to shoot at ye. A officer has got to take up for the law – it's his duty – and them that acts bad and lives wrong has to suffer. Don't blame my son any, sir – 'tain't his fault. He's always been a good boy – good when he was growin' up, and kind and 'bedient and well behaved. Won't you let me advise you, sir, not to do so no more? Be a good man, and leave liquor alone and live peaceably and goodly. Keep away from bad company and work honest and sleep sweet.'

The black-mitted hand of the old pleader gently touched the breast of the man she addressed. Very earnest and candid her old, worn face looked. In her rusty black dress and antique bonnet she sat, near the close of a long life, and epitomised the experience of the world. Still the man to whom she spoke gazed above her head, contemplating the silent son of the old mother.

'What does the marshal say?' he asked. 'Does he believe the advice is good? Suppose the marshal speaks up and says if the talk's all right?'

The tall man moved uneasily. He fingered the badge on his breast for a moment, and then he put an arm around the old woman and drew her close to him. She smiled the unchanging mother smile of three-score years, and patted his big brown hand with her crooked, mittened fingers while her son spoke.

'I says this,' he said, looking squarely into the eyes of the other man, 'that if I was in your place I'd follow it. If I was a drunken, desp'rate character, without shame or hope, I'd follow it. If I was in your place and you was in mine I'd say: "Marshal, I'm willin' to swear if you'll give me the chance I'll quit the racket. I'll drop the tanglefoot and the gun play, and won't play hoss no more. I'll be a good citizen and go to work and quit my foolishness. So help me God!" That's what I'd say to you if you was marshal and I was in your place.'

'Hear my son talkin',' said the old woman softly. 'Hear him, sir. You promise to be good and he won't do you no harm. Forty-one year ago his heart first beat ag'in' mine, and it's beat true ever since.'

The other man rose to his feet, trying his limbs and stretching his muscles.

'Then,' said he, 'if you was in my place and said that, and I was marshal, I'd say: "Go free, and do your best to keep your promise."'

'Lawsy!' exclaimed the old woman, in a sudden flutter, 'ef I didn't clear forget that trunk of mine! I see a man settin' it on the platform jest as I seen my son's face in the window, and it went plum out of my head. There's eight jars of home-made quince jam in that trunk that I made myself. I wouldn't have nothin' happen to them jars for a red apple.'

Away to the door she trotted, spry and anxious, and then Calliope Catesby spoke out to Buck Patterson: 'I just couldn't help it, Buck. I seen her through the window a-comin' in. She never had heard a word 'bout my tough ways. I didn't have the nerve to let her know I was a worthless cuss bein' hunted down by the community. There you was lyin' where my shot laid you, like you was dead. The idea struck me sudden, and I just took your badge off and fastened it on to myself, and I fastened my reputation on to you. I told her I was the marshal and you was a holy terror. You can take your badge back now, Buck.'

With shaking fingers Calliope began to unfasten the disc of metal from his shirt.

'Easy there!' said Buck Patterson. 'You keep that badge right where it

is, Calliope Catesby. Don't you dare to take it off till the day your mother
leaves this town. You'll be city marshal of Quicksand as long as she's here
to know it. After I stir around town a bit and put 'em on I'll guarantee
that nobody won't give the thing away to her. And say, you leather-
headed, rip-roarin', low-down son of a locoed cyclone, you follow that
advice she give me! I'm goin' to take some of it myself, too.'

'Buck,' said Calliope feelingly, 'ef I don't I hope I may –'

'Shut up,' said Buck. 'She's a-comin' back.'

THE HIGHER ABDICATION

O. HENRY

CURLY THE TRAMP sidled toward the free-lunch counter. He caught a fleeting glance from the bartender's eye, and stood still, trying to look like a businessman who had just dined at the Menger and was waiting for a friend who had promised to pick him up in his motor car. Curly's histrionic powers were equal to the impersonation; but his make-up was wanting.

The bartender rounded the bar in a casual way, looking up at the ceiling as though he was pondering some intricate problem of interior decoration, and then fell upon Curly so suddenly that the roadster had no excuses ready. Irresistibly, but so composedly that it seemed almost absent-mindedness on his part, the dispenser of drinks pushed Curly to the swinging doors and kicked him out, with a nonchalance that almost amounted to sadness. That was the way of the Southwest.

Curly arose from the gutter leisurely. He felt no anger or resentment toward his ejector. Fifteen years of tramp-hood spent out of the twenty-two years of his life had hardened the fibres of his spirit. The slings and arrows of outrageous fortune fell blunted from the buckler of his armoured pride. With especial resignation did he suffer contumely and injury at the hands of bartenders. Naturally, they were his enemies; and unnaturally, they were often his friends. He had to take his chances with them. But he had not yet learned to estimate these cool, languid, Southwestern knights of the bungstarter, who had the manners of an Earl of Pawtucket, and who, when they disapproved of your presence, moved you with the silence and despatch of a chess automaton advancing a pawn.

Curly stood for a few moments in the narrow, mesquite-paved street. San Antonio puzzled and disturbed him. Three days he had been a non-paying guest of the town, having dropped off there from a box car of an International & Great Northern Railroad freight, because Greaser Johnny had told him in Des Moines that the Alamo City was manna fallen, gathered, cooked, and served free with cream and sugar. Curly had found the tip partly a good one. There was hospitality in plenty of a careless, liberal, irregular sort. But the town itself was a weight upon his spirits after his experience with the rushing, businesslike, systematised cities of the North and East. Here he was often flung a dollar, but too frequently a good-natured kick would follow it. Once a band of hilarious cowboys had roped him on Military Plaza and dragged him across the black soil until no respectable rag-bag would have stood sponsor for his clothes. The winding, doubling streets, leading nowhere, bewildered him. And then there was a little river, crooked as a pot-hook, that crawled through the middle of the town, crossed by a hundred little bridges so nearly alike that they got on Curly's nerves. And the last bartender wore a number nine shoe.

The saloon stood on a corner. The hour was eight o'clock. Homefarers and outgoers jostled Curly on the narrow stone sidewalk. Between the buildings to his left he looked down a cleft that proclaimed itself another thoroughfare. The alley was dark except for one patch of light. Where there was light there were sure to be human beings. Where there were human beings after nightfall in San Antonio there might be food, and there was sure to be drink. So Curly headed for the light.

The illumination came from Schwegel's Cafe. On the sidewalk in front of it Curly picked up an old envelope. It might have contained a check for a million. It was empty; but the wanderer read the address, 'Mr Otto Schwegel', and the name of the town and State. The postmark was Detroit.

Curly entered the saloon. And now in the light it could be perceived that he bore the stamp of many years of vagabondage. He had none of the tidiness of the calculating and shrewd professional tramp. His wardrobe represented the cast-off specimens of half a dozen fashions and eras. Two factories had combined their efforts in providing shoes for his feet. As you gazed at him there passed through your mind vague impressions of mummies, wax figures, Russian exiles, and men lost on desert islands. His face was covered almost to his eyes with a curly brown beard that he kept trimmed short with a pocket-knife, and that had furnished him with his nicknmae. Light-blue eyes, full of sullenness, fear, cunning, impudence and fawning, witnessed the stress that had been laid upon his soul.

The saloon was small, and in its atmosphere the odours of meat and drink struggled for the ascendancy. The pig and the cabbage wrestled with hydrogen and oxygen. Behind the bar Schwegel laboured with an assistant whose epidermal pores showed no signs of being obstructed. Hot weinerwurst and sauerkraut were being served to purchasers of beer. Curly shuffled to the end of the bar, coughed hollowly, and told Schwegel that he was a Detroit cabinet-maker out of a job.

It followed as the night the day that he got his schooner and lunch.

'Was you acquainted maybe with Heinrich Strauss in Detroit?' asked Schwegel.

'Did I know Heinrich Strauss?' repeated Curly, affectionately. 'Why, say, I wish I had a dollar for every game of pinochle me and Heine has played on Sunday afternoons.'

More beer and a second plate of steaming food was set before the diplomat. And then Curly, knowing to a fluid-drachm how far a 'con' game would go, shuffled out into the unpromising street.

And now he began to perceive the inconveniences of this stony Southern town. There was none of the outdoor gaiety and brilliancy and music that provided distraction even to the poorest in the cities of the North. Here, even so early, the gloomy, rock-walled houses were closed and barred against the murky dampness of the night. The streets were mere fissures through which flowed grey wreaths of river mist. As he walked he heard laughter and the chink of coin and chips behind darkened windows, and music coming from every chink of wood and stone. But the diversions were selfish; the day of popular pastimes had not yet come to San Antonio.

But at length Curly, as he strayed, turned the sharp angle of another lost street and came upon a rollicking band of stockmen from the outlying ranches celebrating in the open in front of an ancient wooden hotel. One great roisterer from the sheep country who had just instigated a movement toward the bar, swept Curly in like a stray goat with the rest of his flock. The princes of kine and wool hailed him as a new zoological discovery, and uproariously strove to preserve him in the diluted alcohol of their compliments and regards.

An hour afterward Curly staggered from the hotel bar-room dismissed by his fickle friends, whose interest in him had subsided as quickly as it had risen. Full – stoked with alcoholic fuel and cargoed with food, the only question remaining to disturb him was that of shelter and bed.

A drizzling, cold Texas rain had begun to fall – an endless, lazy, unintermittent downfall that lowered the spirits of men and raised a reluctant steam from the warm stones of the streets and houses. Thus comes the 'norther', dousing gentle spring and amiable autumn with the chilling salutes and adieux of coming and departing winter.

Curly followed his nose down the first tortuous street into which his irresponsible feet conducted him. At the lower end of it, on the bank of the serpentine stream, he perceived an open gate in a cemented rock wall. Inside he saw camp fires and a row of low wooden sheds built against three sides of the enclosing wall. He entered the enclosure. Under the sheds many horses were champing at their oats and corn. Many wagons and buckboards stood about with their teams' harness thrown carelessly upon the shafts and doubletrees. Curly recognised the place as a wagon-yard, such as is provided by merchants for their out-of-town friends and customers. No one was in sight. No doubt the drivers of these wagons were scattered about the town 'seeing the elephant and hearing the owl'. In their haste to become patrons of the town's dispensaries of mirth and good cheer, the last ones to depart must have left the great wooden gate swinging open.

Curly had satisfied the hunger of an anaconda and the thirst of a camel, so he was neither in the mood nor the condition of an explorer. He zigzagged his way to the first wagon that his eyesight distinguished in the semi-darkness under the shed. It was a two-horse wagon with a top of white canvas. The wagon was half filled with loose piles of wool sacks, two or three great bundles of grey blankets, and a number of bales, bundles and boxes. A reasoning eye would have estimated the load at once as ranch supplies, bound on the morrow for some outlying hacienda. But to the drowsy intelligence of Curly they represented only warmth and softness and protection against the cold humidity of the night. After several unlucky efforts, at last he conquered gravity so far as to climb over a wheel and pitch forward upon the best and warmest bed he had fallen upon in many a day. Then he became instinctively a burrowing animal, and dug his way like a prairie-dog down among the sacks and blankets, hiding himself from the cold air as snug and safe as a bear in his den. For three nights sleep had visited Curly only in broken and shivering doses. So now, when Morpheus condescended to pay him a call, Curly got such a stranglehold on the mythological old gentleman that it was a wonder that anyone else in the whole world got a wink of sleep that night.

* * *

Six cowpunchers of the Cibolo Ranch were waiting around the door of the ranch store. Their ponies cropped grass near by, tied in the Texas fashion – which is not tied at all. Their bridle reins had been dropped to the earth, which is a more effectual way of securing them (such is the power of habit and imagination) than you could devise out of a half-inch rope and a live-oak tree.

These guardians of the cow lounged about, each with a brown cigarette paper in his hand, and gently but unceasingly cursed Sam Revell, the storekeeper. Sam stood in the door, snapping the red elastic bands on his pink madras shirtsleeves and looking down affectionately at the only pair of tan shoes within a forty-mile radius. His offence had been serious, and he was divided between humble apology and admiration for the beauty of his raiment. He had allowed the ranch stock of 'smoking' to become exhausted.

'I thought sure there was another case of it under the counter, boys,' he explained. 'But it happened to be catterdges.'

'You've sure got a case of happenedicitis,' said Poky Rodgers, fancy rider of the Largo Verde . 'Somebody ought to happen to give you a knock on the head with the butt end of a quirt. I've rode in nine miles for some tobacco; and it don't appear natural and seemly that you ought to be allowed to live.'

'The boys was smokin' cut plug and dried mesquite leaves mixed when I left,' sighed Mustang Taylor, horse wrangler of the Three Elm camp. 'They'll be lookin' for me back by nine. They'll be settin' up, with their papers ready to roll a whiff of the real thing before bedtime. And I've got to tell 'em that this pink-eyed, sheep-headed, sulphur-footed, shirt-waisted son of a calico broncho, Sam Revell, hasn't got no tobacco on hand.'

Gregorio Falcon, Mexican vaquero and best thrower of the rope on the Cibolo, pushed his heavy, silver-embroidered straw sombrero back upon his thicket of jet-black curls and scraped the bottoms of his pockets for a few crumbs of the precious weed.

'Ah, Don Samuel,' he said, reproachfully, but with his touch of Castilian manners, 'escuse me. Dthey say dthe jackrabbeet and dthe sheep have dthe most leetle – how you call dthem – brain-es? Ah don't believe dthat, Don Samuel – escuse me. Ah dthink people w'at don't keep esmokin' tobacco, dthey – bot you weel escuse me, Don Samuel.'

'Now, what's the use of chewin' the rag, boys,' said the untroubled Sam, stooping over to rub the toes of his shoes with a red-and-yellow handkerchief. 'Ranse took the order for some more smokin' to San Antone with him Tuesday. Pancho rode Ranse's hoss back yesterday; and Ranse is goin' to drive the wagon back himself. There wa'n't much of a load – just some woolsacks and blankets and nails and canned peaches and a few things we was out of. I look for Ranse to roll in today sure. He's an early starter and a hell-to-split driver, and he ought to be here not far from sundown.'

'What plugs is he drivin'?' asked Mustang Taylor, with a smack of hope in his tone.

'The buckboard greys,' said Sam.

'I'll wait a spell, then,' said the wrangler. 'Them plugs eat up a trail like a road-runner swallowin' a whip snake. And you may bust me open a can of greengage plums, Sam, while I'm waitin' for somethin' better.'

'Open me some yellow clings,' ordered Poky Rodgers. 'I'll wait, too.'

The tobaccoless punchers arranged themselves comfortably on the steps of the store. Inside Sam chopped open with a hatchet the tops of the cans of fruit.

The store, a big white wooden building like a barn, stood fifty yards from the ranch-house. Beyond it were the horse corrals; and still farther the wool sheds and the brush-topped shearing pens – for the Rancho Cibolo raised both cattle and sheep. Behind the store, at a little distance, were the grass-thatched *jacal* of the Mexicans who bestowed their allegiance upon the Cibolo.

The ranch-house was composed of four large rooms, with plastered adobe walls, and a two-room wooden ell. A twenty-feet-wide 'gallery' circumvented the structure. It was set in a grove of immense live-oaks and water-elms near a lake – a long, not very wide and tremendously deep lake in which, at nightfall, great gars leaped to the surface and plunged with the noise of hippopotamuses frolicking at their bath. From the trees hung garlands and massive pendants of the melancholy grey moss of the South. Indeed, the Cibolo ranch-house seemed more of the South than of the West. It looked as if old 'Kiowa' Truesdell might have brought it with him from the lowlands of Mississippi when he came to Texas with his rifle in the hollow of his arm in '55.

But, though he did not bring the family mansion, Truesdell did bring something in the way of a family inheritance that was more lasting than brick or stone. He brought one end of the Truesdell-Curtis family feud. And when a Curtis bought the Rancho de Los Olmos, sixteen miles from the Cibolo, there were lively times on the pear flats and in the chaparral thickets off the Southwest. In those days Truesdell cleaned the brush of many a wolf and tiger cat and Mexican lion; and one or two Curtises fell heirs to notches on his rifle stock. Also he buried a brother with a Curtis bullet in him on the bank of the lake at Cibolo. And then the Kiowa Indians made their last raid upon the ranches between the Frio and the Rio Grande, and Truesdell at the head of his rangers rid the earth of them to the last brave, earning his sobriquet. Then came prosperity in the form of waxing herds and broadening lands. And then old age and bitterness, when he sat, with his great mane of hair as white as the Spanish-dagger blossoms and his fierce, pale-blue eyes, on the shaded gallery at Cibolo, growling like the pumas that he had slain. He snapped his fingers at old age; the bitter taste to life did not come from that. The cup that stuck at his lips was that his only son Ransom wanted to marry a Curtis, the last youthful survivor of the other end of the feud.

*　　*　　*

For a while the only sounds to be heard at the store were the rattling of the tin spoons and the gurgling intake of the juicy fruits by the cowpunchers, the stamping of the grazing ponies and the singing of a doleful song by Sam as he contentedly brushed his stiff auburn hair for the twentieth time that day before a crinkly mirror.

From the door of the store could be seen the irregular, sloping stretch of prairie to the south, with its reaches of light-green, billowy mesquite flats in the lower places, and its rises crowned with nearly black masses of short chaparral. Through the mesquite flat wound the ranch road that, five miles away, flowed into the old government trail to San Antonio. The sun was so low that the gentlest elevation cast its grey shadow miles into the green-gold sea of sunshine.

That evening ears were quicker than eyes.

The Mexican held up a tawny finger to still the scraping of tin against tin.

'One waggeen,' said he, 'cross dthe Arroyo Hondo. Ah heard the wheel. Verree rockee place, dthe Hondo.'

'You've got good ears, Gregorio,' said Mustang Taylor. 'I never heard nothin' but the songbird in the bush and the zephyr skallyhootin' across the peaceful dell.'

In ten minutes Taylor remarked: 'I see the dust of a wagon risin' right above the fur end of the flat.'

'You have verree good eyes, señor,' said Gregorio, smiling.

Two miles away they saw a faint cloud dimming the green ripples of the mesquites. In twenty minutes they heard the clatter of the horses' hoofs: in five minutes more the grey plugs dashed out of the thicket, whickering for oats and drawing the light wagon behind them like a toy.

From the *jacal* came a cry of: 'El Amo! El Amo!' Four Mexican youths raced to unharness the greys. The cowpunchers gave a yell of greeting and delight.

Ranse Truesdell, driving, threw the reins to the ground and laughed.

'It's under the wagon sheet, boys,' he said. 'I know what you're waiting for. If Sam lets it run out again we'll use those yellow shoes of his for a target. There's two cases. Pull 'em out and light up. I know you all want a smoke.'

After striking dry country Ranse had removed the wagon sheet from the bows and thrown it over the goods in the wagon. Six pair of hasty hands dragged it off and grabbled beneath the sacks and blankets for the cases of tobacco.

Long Collins, tobacco messenger from the San Gabriel outfit, who rode with the longest stirrups west of the Mississippi, delved with an arm like the tongue of a wagon. He caught something harder than a blanket and pulled out a fearful thing – a shapeless, muddy bunch of leather tied together with wire and twine. From its ragged end, like the head and claws of a disturbed turtle, protruded human toes.

'Who-ee!' yelled Long Collins. 'Ranse, are you a-packin' around of corpuses? Here's a – howlin' grasshoppers!'

Up from his long slumber popped Curly, like some vile worm from its burrow. He clawed his way out and sat blinking like a disreputable, drunken owl. His face was as bluish-red and puffed and seamed and cross-lined as the cheapest round steak of the butcher. His eyes were swollen slits; his nose a pickled beet; his hair would have made the wildest thatch of a Jack-in-the-box look like the satin poll of a Cleo de Merode. The rest of him was scarecrow done to the life.

Ranse jumped down from his seat and looked at his strange cargo with wide-open eyes.

'Here, you maverick, what are you doing in my wagon? How did you get in there?'

The punchers gathered around in delight. For the time they had forgotten tobacco.

Curly looked around him slowly in every direction. He snarled like a Scotch terrier through his ragged beard.

'Where is this?' he rasped through his parched throat. 'It's a damn farm in an old field. What'd you bring me here for – say? Did I say I wanted to come here? What are you Reubs rubberin' at – hey? G'wan or I'll punch some of yer faces.'

'Drag him out, Collins,' said Ranse.

Curly took a slide and felt the ground rise up and collide with his shoulder blades. He got up and sat on the steps of the store shivering from outraged nerves, hugging his knees and sneering. Taylor lifted out a case of tobacco and wrenched off its top. Six cigarettes began to glow, bringing peace and forgiveness to Sam.

'How'd you come in my wagon?' repeated Ranse, this time in a voice that drew a reply.

Curly recognised the tone. He had heard it used by freight brakemen and large persons in blue carrying clubs.

'Me?' he growled. 'Oh, was you talkin' to me? Why, I was on my way to the Menger, but my valet had forgot to pack my pyjamas. So I crawled into that wagon in the wagon-yard – see? I never told you to bring me out to this bloomin' farm – see?'

'What is it, Mustang?' asked Poky Rodgers, almost forgetting to smoke in his ecstasy. 'What do it live on?'

'It's a galliwampus, Poky,' said Mustang. 'It's the thing that hollers "willi-walloo" up in ellum trees in the low grounds of nights. I don't know if it bites.'

'No, it ain't, Mustang,' volunteered Long Collins. 'Them galliwampuses has fins on their backs and eighteen toes. This here is a hicklesnifter. It lives under the ground and eats cherries. Don't stand so close to it. It wipes out villages with one stroke of its prehensile tail.'

Sam, the cosmopolite, who called bartenders in San Antone by their first name, stood in the door. He was a better zoologist.

'Well, ain't that a Willie for your whiskers?' he commented. 'Where'd you dig up the hobo, Ranse? Goin' to make an auditorium for inbreviates out of the ranch?'

'Say,' said Curly, from whose panoplied breast all shafts of wit fell blunted. 'Any of you kiddin' guys got a drink on you? Have your fun. Say, I've been hittin' the stuff till I don't know straight up.'

He turned to Ranse. 'Say, you shanghaied me on your damned old prairie schooner – did I tell you to drive me to a farm? I want a drink. I'm goin' all to little pieces. What's doin'?'

Ranse saw that the tramp's nerves were racking him. He despatched one of the Mexican boys to the ranch-house for a glass of whiskey. Curly gulped it down; and into his eyes came a brief, grateful glow – as human as the expression in the eye of a faithful setter dog.

'Thanky, boss,' he said, quietly.

'You're thirty miles from a railroad, and forty miles from a saloon,' said Ranse.

Curly fell back weakly against the steps.

'Since you are here,' continued the ranchman, 'come along with me. We can't turn you out on the prairie. A rabbit might tear you to pieces.'

He conducted Curly to a large shed where the ranch vehicles were kept. There he spread out a canvas cot and brought blankets.

'I don't suppose you can sleep,' said Ranse, 'since you've been pounding your ear for twenty-four hours. But you can camp here till morning. I'll have Pedro fetch you up some grub.'

'Sleep!' said Curly. 'I can sleep a week. Say, sport, have you got a coffin nail on you?'

* * *

Fifty miles had Ransom Truesdell driven that day. And yet this is what he did.

Old 'Kiowa' Truesdell sat in his great wicker chair reading by the light of an immense oil lamp. Ranse laid a bundle of newspapers fresh from town at his elbow.

'Back, Ranse?' said the old man, looking up. 'Son,' old 'Kiowa' continued, 'I've been thinking all day about a certain matter that we have talked about. I want you to tell me again. I've lived for you. I've fought wolves and Indians and worse white men to protect you. You never had any mother that you can remember. I've taught you to shoot straight, ride hard and live clean. Later on I've worked to pile up dollars that'll be yours. You'll be a rich man, Ranse, when my chunk goes out. I've made you. I've licked you into shape like a leopard cat licks its cubs. You don't belong to yourself – you've got to be a Truesdell first. Now, is there to be any more nonsense about this Curtis girl?'

'I'll tell you once more,' said Ranse, slowly. 'As I am a Truesdell and as you are my father, I'll never marry a Curtis.'

'Good boy,' said old 'Kiowa'. 'You'd better go get some supper.'

Ranse went to the kitchen at the rear of the house. Pedro, the Mexican cook, sprang up to bring the food he was keeping warm in the stove.

'Just a cup of coffee, Pedro,' he said, and drank it standing. And then:

'There's a tramp on a cot in the wagon-shed. Take him something to eat. Better make it enough for two.'

Ranse walked out toward the . A boy came running.

'Manuel, can you catch Vaminos, in the little pasture, for me?'

'Why not, señor? I saw him near the *puerto* but two hours past. He bears a drag-rope.'

'Get him and saddle him as quick as you can.'

'*Prontito, señor.*'

Soon, mounted on Vaminos, Ranse leaned in the saddle, pressed with his knees, and galloped eastward past the store, where sat Sam trying his guitar in the moonlight.

Vaminos shall have a word – Vaminos the good dun horse. The Mexicans, who have a hundred names for the colours of a horse, called him *gruyo*. He was a mouse-coloured, slate-coloured, flea-bitten roan-dun, if you can conceive it. Down his back from his mane to his tail went a line of black. He would live for ever; and surveyors have not laid off as many miles in the world as he could travel in a day.

Eight miles east of the Cibolo ranch-house Ranse loosened the pressure of his knees, and Vaminos stopped under a big ratama tree. The yellow ratama blossoms showered fragrance that would have undone the roses of France. The moon made the earth a great concave bowl with a crystal sky for a lid. In a glade five jack-rabbits leaped and played together like kittens. Eight miles farther east shone a faint star that appeared to have dropped below the horizon. Night riders, who often steered their course by it, knew it to be the light in the Rancho de Los Olmos.

In ten minutes Yenna Curtis galloped to the tree on her sorrel pony Dancer. The two leaned and clasped hands heartily.

'I ought to have ridden nearer your home,' said Ranse. 'But you never will let me.'

Yenna laughed. And in the soft light you could see her strong white teeth and fearless eyes. No sentimentality there, in spite of the moonlight, the odour of the ratamas and the admirable figure of Ranse Truesdell, the lover. But she was there, eight miles from her home, to meet him.

'How often have I told you, Ranse,' she said, 'that I am your halfway girl? Always halfway.'

'Well?' said Ranse, with a question in his tones.

'I did,' said Yenna, with almost a sigh. 'I told him after dinner when I thought he would be in a good humour. Did you ever wake up a lion, Ranse, with the mistaken idea that he would be a kitten? He almost tore the ranch to pieces. It's all up. I love my daddy, Ranse, and I'm afraid – I'm afraid of him too. He ordered me to promise that I'd never marry a Truesdell. I promised. That's all. What luck did you have?'

'The same,' said Ranse, slowly. 'I promised him that his son would never marry a Curtis. Somehow I couldn't go against him. He's mighty old. I'm sorry, Yenna.'

The girl leaned in her saddle and laid one hand on Ranse's, on the horn of his saddle.

'I never thought I'd like you better for giving me up,' she said ardently, 'but I do. I must ride back now, Ranse. I slipped out of the house and saddled Dancer myself. Good-night, neighbour.'

'Good-night,' said Ranse. 'Ride carefully over them badger holes.'

They wheeled and rode away in opposite directions. Yenna turned in her saddle and called clearly:

'Don't forget I'm your halfway girl, Ranse.'

'Damn all family feuds and inherited scraps,' muttered Ranse vindictively to the breeze as he rode back to the Cibolo.

Ranse turned his horse into the small pasture and went to his own room. He opened the lowest drawer of an old bureau to get out the packet of letters that Yenna had written him one summer when she had gone to Mississippi for a visit. The drawer stuck, and he yanked at it savagely – as a man will. It came out of the bureau, and bruised both his shins – as a drawer will. An old, folded yellow letter without an envelope fell from somewhere – probably from where it had lodged in one of the upper drawers. Ranse took it to the lamp and read it curiously.

Then he took his hat and walked to one of the Mexican *jacals*.

'Tia Juana,' he said, 'I would like to talk with you a while.'

An old, old Mexican woman, white-haired and wonderfully wrinkled, rose from a stool.

'Sit down,' said Ranse, removing his hat and taking the one chair in the *jacal*. 'Who am I, Tia Juana?' he asked, speaking Spanish.

'Don Ransom, our good friend and employer. Why do you ask?' answered the old woman wonderingly.

'Tia Juana, who am I?' he repeated, with his stern eyes looking into hers.

A frightened look came into the old woman's face. She fumbled with her black shawl.

'Who am I, Tia Juana?' said Ranse once more.

'Thirty-two years I have lived on the Rancho Cibolo,' said Tia Juana. 'I thought to be buried under the coma mott beyond the garden before these things should be known. Close the door, Don Ransom, and I will speak. I see in your face that you know.'

An hour Ranse spent behind Tia Juana's closed door. As he was on his way back to the house Curly called to him from the wagon-shed.

The tramp sat on his cot, swinging his feet and smoking.

'Say, sport,' he grumbled. 'This is no way to treat a man after kid-nappin' him. I went up to the store and borrowed a razor from that fresh guy and had a shave. But that ain't all a man needs. Say – can't you loosen up for about three fingers more of that booze? I never asked you to bring me to your damned farm.'

'Stand up out here in the light,' said Ranse, looking at him closely.

Curly got up sullenly and took a step or two.

His face, now shaven smooth, seemed transformed. His hair had been combed, and it fell back from the right side of his forehead with a peculiar wave. The moonlight charitably softened the ravages of drink; and his aquiline, well-shaped nose and small, square cleft chin almost gave distinction to his looks.

Ranse sat on the foot of the cot and looked at him curiously.

'Where did you come from – have you got any home or folks any-where?'

'Me? Why, I'm a dook,' said Curly. 'I'm Sir Reginald – oh, cheese it. No; I don't know anything about my ancestors. I've been a tramp ever since I can remember. Say, old pal, are you going to set 'em up again tonight or not?'

'You answer my questions and maybe I will. How did you come to be a tramp?'

'Me?' answered Curly. 'Why, I adopted that profession when I was an infant. Case of had to. First thing I can remember, I belonged to a big, lazy hobo called Beefsteak Charley. He sent me around to houses to beg. I wasn't hardly big enough to reach the latch of a gate.'

'Did he ever tell you how he got you?' asked Ranse.

'Once when he was sober he said he bought me for an old six-shooter and six bits from a band of drunken Mexican sheep-shearers. But what's the diff? That's all I know.'

'All right,' said Ranse. 'I reckon you're a maverick for certain. I'm going to put the Rancho Cibolo brand on you. I'll start you to work in one of the camps tomorrow.'

'Work!' sniffed Curly, disdainfully. 'What do you take me for? Do you think I'd chase cows and hop-skip-and-jump around after crazy sheep like that pink and yellow guy at the store says these Reubs do? Forget it.'

'Oh, you'll like it when you get used to it,' said Ranse. 'Yes, I'll send you up one more drink by Pedro. I think you'll make a first-class cow-puncher before I get through with you.'

'Me?' said Curly. 'I pity the cows you set me to chaperon. They can go chase themselves. Don't forget my nightcap, please, boss.'

Ranse paid a visit to the store before going to the house. Sam Revell was taking off his tan shoes regretfully and preparing for bed.

'Any of the boys from the San Gabriel camp riding in early in the morning?' asked Ranse.

'Long Collins,' said Sam briefly. 'For the mail.'

'Tell him,' said Ranse, 'to take that tramp out to camp with him and keep him till I get there.'

* * *

Curly was sitting on his blankets in the San Gabriel camp cursing talentedly when Ranse Truesdell rode up and dismounted on the next afternoon. The cowpunchers were ignoring the stray. He was grimy with dust and black dirt. His clothes were making their last stand in favour of the conventions.

Ranse went up to Buck Rabb, the camp boss, and spoke briefly.

'He's a plumb buzzard,' said Buck. 'He won't work, and he's the low-downest passel of inhumanity I ever see. I didn't know what you wanted done with him, Ranse, so I just let him set. That seems to suit him. He's been condemned to death by the boys a dozen times, but I told 'em maybe you was savin' him for the torture.'

Ranse took off his coat.

'I've got a hard job before me, Buck, I reckon, but it has to be done. I've got to make a man out of that thing. That's what I've come to camp for.'

He went up to Curly.

'Brother,' he said, 'don't you think if you had a bath it would allow you to take a seat in the company of your fellow-man with less injustice to the atmosphere.'

'Run away, farmer,' said Curly, sardonically. 'Willie will send for nursey when he feels like having his tub.'

The *charco*, or water hole, was twelve yards away. Ranse took one of Curly's ankles and dragged him like a sack of potatoes to the brink. Then with the strength and sleight of a hammer-throw he hurled the offending member of society far into the lake.

Curly crawled out and up the bank spluttering like a porpoise.

Ranse met him with a piece of soap and a coarse towel in his hands.

'Go to the other end of the lake and use this,' he said. 'Buck will give you some dry clothes at the wagon.'

The tramp obeyed without protest. By the time supper was ready he had returned to camp. He was hardly to be recognised in his new shirt and brown duck clothes. Ranse observed him out of the corner of his eye.

'Lordy, I hope he ain't a coward,' he was saying to himself. 'I hope he won't turn out to be a coward.'

His doubts were soon allayed. Curly walked straight to where he stood. His light-blue eyes were blazing.

'Now I'm clean,' he said meaningly, 'maybe you'll talk to me. Think you've got a picnic here, do you? You clodhoppers think you can run over a man because you know he can't get away. All right. Now, what do you think of that?'

Curly planted a stinging slap against Ranse's left cheek. The print of his hand stood out a dull red against the tan.

Ranse smiled happily.

The cowpunchers talk to this day of the battle that followed.

Somewhere in his restless tour of the cities, Curly had acquired the art of self-defence. The ranchman was equipped only with the splendid strength and equilibrium of perfect health and the endurance conferred by decent living. The two attributes nearly matched. There were no formal rounds. At last the fibre of the clean liver prevailed. The last time Curly went down from one of the ranchman's awkward but powerful blows he remained on the grass, but looking up with an unquenched eye.

Ranse went to the water barrel and washed the red from a cut on his chin in the stream from the faucet.

On his face was a grin of satisfaction.

Much benefit might accrue to educators and moralists if they could know the details of the curriculum of reclamation through which Ranse put his waif during the month that he spent in the San Gabriel camp. The ranchman had no fine theories to work out – perhaps his whole stock of pedagogy embraced only a knowledge of horse-breaking and a belief in heredity.

The cowpunchers saw that their boss was trying to make a man out of the strange animal that he had sent among them, and they tacitly organised themselves into a faculty of assistants. But their system was their own.

Curly's first lesson stuck. He became on friendly and then on intimate terms with soap and water. And the thing that pleased Ranse most was that his 'subject' held his ground at each successive higher step. But the steps were sometimes far apart.

Once he got at the quart bottle of whiskey kept sacredly in the grub tent for rattlesnake bites, and spent sixteen hours on the grass, magnificently drunk. But when he staggered to his feet his first move was to find his soap and towel and start for the *charco*. And once, when a treat came from the ranch in the form of a basket of fresh tomatoes and young onions, Curly devoured the entire consignment before the punchers reached the camp at suppertime.

And then the punchers punished him in their own way. For three days they did not speak to him, except to reply to his own questions or remarks. And they spoke with absolute and unfailing politeness. They played tricks on one another; they pounded one another hurtfully and affectionately; they heaped upon one another's heads friendly curses and obloquy; but they were polite to Curly. He saw it, and it stung him as much as Ranse hoped it would.

Then came a night that brought a cold, wet norther. Wilson, the youngest of the outfit, had lain in camp two days, ill with fever. When Joe got up at daylight to begin breakfast he found Curly sitting asleep against a wheel of the grub wagon with only a saddle blanket around him, while Curly's blankets were stretched over Wilson to protect him from the rain and wind.

Three nights after that Curly rolled himself in his blanket and went to sleep. Then the other punchers rose up softly and began to make preparations. Ranse saw Long Collins tie a rope to the horn of a saddle. Others were getting out their six-shooters.

'Boys,' said Ranse, 'I'm much obliged. I was hoping you would. But I didn't like to ask.'

Half a dozen six-shooters began to pop – awful yells rent the air – Long Collins galloped wildly across Curly's bed, dragging the saddle after him. That was merely their way of gently awaking their victim. Then they hazed him for an hour, carefully and ridiculously, after the code of cow camps. Whenever he uttered protest they held him stretched over a roll of blankets and thrashed him woefully with a pair of leather leggings.

And all this meant that Curly had won his spurs, that he was receiving the puncher's accolade. Nevermore would they be polite to him. But he would be their 'pardner' and stirrup-brother, foot to foot.

When the fooling was ended all hands made a raid on Joe's big coffee-pot by the fire for a Java nightcap. Ranse watched the new knight carefully to see if he understood and was worthy. Curly limped with his cup of coffee to a log and sat upon it. Long Collins followed and sat by his side. Buck Rabb went and sat at the other. Curly – grinned.

And then Ranse furnished Curly with mounts and saddle and equipment, and turned him over to Buck Rabb, instructing him to finish the job.

Three weeks later Ranse rode from the ranch into Rabb's camp, which was then in Snake Valley. The boys were saddling for the day's ride. He sought out Long Collins among them.

'How about that bronco?' he asked.

Long Collins grinned.

'Reach out your hand, Ranse Truesdell,' he said, 'and you'll touch him. And you can shake his'n, too, if you like, for he's plumb white and there's none better in no camp.'

Ranse looked again at the clear-faced, bronzed, smiling cowpuncher who stood at Collins's side. Could that be Curly? He held out his hand, and Curly grasped it with the muscles of a bronco-buster.

'I want you at the ranch,' said Ranse.

'All right, sport,' said Curly, heartily. 'But I want to come back again. Say, pal, this is a dandy farm. And I don't want any better fun than hustlin' cows with this bunch of guys. They're all to the merry-merry.'

At the Cibolo ranch-house they dismounted. Ranse bade Curly wait at the door of the living-room. He walked inside. Old 'Kiowa' Truesdell was reading at a table.

'Good-morning, Mr Truesdell,' said Ranse.

The old man turned his white head quickly.

'How is this?' he began. 'Why do you call me "Mr" – ?'

When he looked at Ranse's face he stopped, and the hand that held his newspaper shook slightly.

'Boy,' he said slowly, 'how did you find it out?'

'It's all right,' said Ranse, with a smile. 'I made Tia Juana tell me. It was kind of by accident, but it's all right.'

'You've been like a son to me,' said old 'Kiowa', trembling.

'Tia Juana told me all about it,' said Ranse. 'She told me how you adopted me when I was knee-high to a puddle duck out of a wagon train of prospectors that was bound West. And she told me how the kid – your own kid, you know – got lost or was run away with. And she said it was the same day that the sheep-shearers got on a bender and left the ranch.'

'Our boy strayed from the house when he was two years old,' said the old man. 'And then along came those emigrant wagons with a youngster they didn't want; and we took you. I never intended you to know, Ranse. We never heard of our boy again.'

'He's right outside, unless I'm mighty mistaken,' said Ranse, opening the door and beckoning.

Curly walked in.

No one could have doubted. The old man and the young had the same sweep of hair, the same nose, chin, line of face and prominent light-blue eyes.

Old 'Kiowa' rose eagerly.

Curly looked about the room curiously. A puzzled expression came over his face. He pointed to the wall opposite.

'Where's the tick-tock?' he asked, absent-mindedly.

'The clock,' cried old 'Kiowa' loudly. 'The eight-day clock used to stand there. Why – '

He turned to Ranse, but Ranse was not there.

Already a hundred yards away, Vaminos, the good flea-bitten dun, was bearing him eastward like a racer through dust and chaparral towards the Rancho de Los Olmos.

THE CABALLERO'S WAY

O. HENRY

THE CISCO KID had killed six men in more or less fair scrimmages, had murdered twice as many (mostly Mexicans), and had winged a larger number whom he modestly forbore to count. Therefore a woman loved him.

The Kid was twenty-five, looked twenty; and a careful insurance company would have estimated the probable time of his demise at, say, twenty-six. His habitat was anywhere between the Frio and the Rio Grande. He killed for the love of it, because he was quick-tempered, to avoid arrest, for his own amusement – any reason that came to his mind would suffice. He had escaped capture because he could shoot five-sixths of a second sooner than any sheriff or ranger in the service, and because he rode a speckled roan horse that knew every cow-path in the mesquite and pear thickets from San Antonio to Matamoras.

Tonia Perez, the girl who loved the Cisco Kid, was half Carmen, half Madonna, and the rest – oh, yes, a woman who is half Carmen and half Madonna can always be something more – the rest, let us say, was humming-bird. She lived in a grass-roofed *jacal* near a little Mexican settlement at the Lone Wolf Crossing of the Frio. With her lived a father or grandfather, a lineal Aztec, somewhat less than a thousand years old, who herded a hundred goats and lived in a continuous drunken dream from drinking *mescal*. Back of the *jacal* a tremendous forest of bristling pear, twenty feet high at its worst, crowded almost to its door. It was along the bewildering maze of this spinous thicket that the speckled roan would bring the Kid to see his girl. And once, clinging like a lizard to the ridge-pole, high up under the peaked grass roof, he had heard Tonia, with her Madonna face and Carmen beauty and humming-bird soul, parley with the sheriff's posse, denying knowledge of her man in her soft *mélange* of Spanish and English.

One day the adjutant-general of the State, who is, *ex offico*, commander of the ranger forces, wrote some sarcastic lines to Captain Duval of Company X, stationed at Laredo, relative to the serene and undisturbed existence led by murderers and desperadoes in the said captain's territory.

The captain turned the colour of brick dust under his tan, and forwarded the letter, after adding a few comments, per ranger Private Bill

Adamson, to ranger Lieutenant Sandridge, camped at a water hole on the Nueces with a squad of five men in preservation of law and order.

Lieutenant Sandridge turned a beautiful *couleur de rose* through his ordinary strawberry complexion, tucked the letter in his hip pocket, and chewed off the ends of his gamboge moustache.

The next morning he saddled his horse and rode alone to the Mexican settlement at the Lone Wolf Crossing of the Frio, twenty miles away.

Six feet two, blond as a Viking, quiet as a deacon, dangerous as a machine gun, Sandridge moved among the *jacales*, patiently seeking news of the Cisco Kid.

Far more than the law, the Mexicans dreaded the cold and certain vengeance of the lone rider that the ranger sought. It had been one of the Kid's pastimes to shoot Mexicans 'to see them kick': if he demanded from them moribund Terpsichorean feats, simply that he might be entertained, what terrible and extreme penalties would be certain to follow should they anger him! One and all they lounged with upturned palms and shrugging shoulders, filling the air with '*quien sabes*' and denials of the Kid's acquaintance.

But there was a man named Fink who kept a store at the Crossing – a man of many nationalities, tongues, interests and ways of thinking.

'No use to ask them Mexicans,' he said to Sandridge. 'They're afraid to tell. This *hombre* they call the Kid – Goodall is his name, ain't it? – he's been in my store once or twice. I have an idea you might run across him at – but I guess I don't keer to say, myself. I'm two seconds later in pulling a gun than I used to be, and the difference is worth thinking about. But this Kid's got a half-Mexican girl at the Crossing that he comes to see. She lives in that *jacal* a hundred yards down the arroyo at the edge of the pear. Maybe she – no, I don't suppose she would, but that *jacal* would be a good place to watch, anyway.'

Sandridge rode down to the *jacal* of Perez. The sun was low, and the broad shade of the great pear thicket already covered the grass-thatched hut. The goats were enclosed for the night in a brush corral near by. A few kids walked the top of it, nibbling the chaparral leaves. The old Mexican lay upon a blanket on the grass, already in a stupor from his *mescal*, and dreaming, perhaps, of the nights when he and Pizarro touched glasses to their New World fortunes – so old his wrinkled face seemed to proclaim him to be. And in the door of the *jacal* stood Tonia. And Lieutenant Sandridge sat in his saddle staring at her like a gannet agape at a sailorman.

The Cisco Kid was a vain person, as all eminent and successful assassins are, and his bosom would have been ruffled had he known that at a simple exchange of glances two persons, in whose minds he had been looming large, suddenly abandoned (at least for the time) all thought of him.

Never before had Tonia seen such a man as this. He seemed to be made of sunshine and blood-red tissue and clear weather. He seemed to illuminate the shadow of the pear when he smiled, as though the sun were rising again. The men she had known had been small and dark. Even the Kid, in spite of his achievements, was a stripling no larger than herself, with black, straight hair and a cold, marble face that chilled the noonday.

As for Tonia, though she sends description to the poorhouse, let her make a millionaire of your fancy. Her blue-black hair, smoothly divided in the middle and bound close to her head, and her large eyes full of the Latin melancholy, gave her the Madonna touch. Her motions and air spoke of the concealed fire and the desire to charm that she had inherited from the *gitanas* of the Basque province. As for the humming-bird part of her, that dwelt in her heart; you could not perceive it unless her bright-red skirt and dark-blue blouse gave you a symbolic hint of the vagarious bird.

The newly lighted sun-god asked for a drink of water. Tonia brought it from the red jar hanging under the brush shelter. Sandridge considered it necessary to dismount so as to lessen the trouble of her ministrations.

I play no spy; nor do I assume to master the thoughts of any human heart; but I assert, by the chronicler's right, that before a quarter of an hour had sped, Sandridge was teaching her how to plait a six-strand rawhide stake-rope, and Tonia had explained to him that were it not for her little English book that the peripatetic *padre* had given her and the little crippled *chivo*, that she fed from a bottle, she would be very, very lonely indeed.

Which leads to a suspicion that the Kid's fences needed repairing, and that the adjutant-general's sarcasm had fallen upon unproductive soil.

In his camp by the water hole Lieutenant Sandridge announced and reiterated his intention of either causing the Cisco Kid to nibble the black loam of the Frio country prairies or of hauling him before a judge and jury. That sounded businesslike. Twice a week he rode over to the Lone Wolf Crossing of the Frio, and directed Tonia's slim, slightly lemon-tinted fingers among the intricacies of the slowly growing lariata. A six-strand plait is hard to learn and easy to teach.

The ranger knew that he might find the Kid there at any visit. He kept his armament ready, and had a frequent eye for the pear thicket at the rear of the *jacal*. Thus he might bring down the kite and the humming-bird with one stone.

While the sunny-haired ornithologist was pursuing his studies the Cisco Kid was also attending to his professional duties. He moodily shot up a saloon in a small cow village on Quintana Creek, killed the town marshal (plugging him neatly in the centre of his tin badge), and then rode away, morose and unsatisfied. No true artist is uplifted by shooting an aged man carrying an old-style .38 bulldog.

On his way the Kid suddenly experienced the yearning that all men feel when wrongdoing loses its keen edge of delight. He yearned for the woman he loved to reassure him that she was his in spite of it. He wanted her to call his bloodthirstiness bravery and his cruelty devotion. He wanted Tonia to bring him water from the red jar under the brush shelter, and tell him how the *chivo* was thriving on the bottle.

The Kid turned the speckled roan's head up the ten-mile pear flat that stretches along the Arroyo Hondo until it ends at the Lone Wolf Crossing of the Frio. The roan whickered; for he had a sense of locality and direction equal to that of a belt-line street-car horse; and he knew he would soon be nibbling the rich mesquite grass at the end of a forty-foot stake-rope while Ulysses rested his head in Circe's straw-roofed hut.

More weird and lonesome than the journey of an Amazonian explorer is the ride of one through a Texas pear flat. With dismal monotony and startling variety the uncanny and multiform shapes of the cacti lift their twisted trunks and fat, bristly hands to encumber the way. The demon plant, appearing to live without soil or rain, seems to taunt the parched traveller with its lush grey greenness. It warps itself a thousand times about what look to be open and inviting paths, only to lure the rider into blind and impassable spine-defended 'bottoms of the bag', leaving him to retreat, if he can, with the points of the compass whirling in his head.

To be lost in the pear is to die almost the death of the thief on the cross, pierced by nails and with grotesque shapes of all the fiends hovering about.

But it was not so with the Kid and his mount. Winding, twisting, circling, tracing the most fantastic and bewildering trail ever picked out, the good roan lessened the distance to the Lone Wolf Crossing with every coil and turn that he made.

While they fared the Kid sang. He knew but one tune and sang it, as he knew but one code and lived it, and but one girl and loved her. He was a single-minded man of conventional ideas. He had a voice like a coyote with bronchitis, but whenever he chose to sing his song he sang it. It was a conventional song of the camps and trail, running at its beginning as near as may be to these words:

'Don't you monkey with my Lulu girl
Or I'll tell you what I'll do – '

and so on. The roan was inured to it, and did not mind.

But even the poorest singer will, after a certain time, gain his own consent to refrain from contributing to the world's noises. So the Kid, by the time he was within a mile or two of Tonia's *jacal*, had reluctantly allowed his song to die away – not because his vocal performance had become less charming to his own ears, but because his laryngeal muscles were aweary.

As though he were in a circus-ring the speckled roan wheeled and danced through the labyrinth of pear until at length his rider knew by certain landmarks that the Lone Wolf Crossing was close at hand. Then, where the pear was thinner, he caught sight of the grass roof of the *jacal* and the hackberry tree on the edge of the arroyo. A few yards farther the Kid stopped the roan and gazed intently through the prickly openings. Then he dismounted, dropped the roan's reins, and proceeded on foot, stooping and silent, like an Indian. The roan, knowing his part, stood still, making no sound.

The Kid crept noiselessly to the very edge of the pear thicket and reconnoitred between the leaves of a clump of cactus.

Ten yards from his hiding-place, in the shade of the *jacal*, sat his Tonia calmly plaiting a rawhide lariat. So far she might surely escape condemnation; women have been known, from time to time, to engage in more mischievous occupations. But if all must be told, there is to be added that her head reposed against the broad and comfortable chest of a tall red-and-yellow man, and that his arm was about her, guiding her nimble fingers that required so many lessons at the intricate six-strand plait.

Sandridge glanced quickly at the dark mass of pear when he heard a slight squeaking sound that was not altogether unfamiliar. A gun-scabbard will make that sound when one grasps the handle of a six-shooter suddenly. But the sound was not repeated; and Tonia's fingers needed close attention.

And then, in the shadow of death, they began to talk of their love; and in the still July afternoon every word they uttered reached the ears of the Kid.

'Remember, then,' said Tonia, 'you must not come again until I send for you. Soon he will be here. A vaquero at the *tienda* said today he saw him on the Guadalupe three days ago. When he is that near he always comes. If he comes and finds you here he will kill you. So, for my sake, you must come no more until I send you the word.'

'All right,' said the stranger. 'And then what?'

'And then,' said the girl, 'you must bring your men here and kill him. If not, he will kill you.'

'He ain't a man to surrender, that's sure,' said Sandridge. 'It's kill or be killed for the officer that goes up against Mr Cisco Kid.'

'He must die,' said the girl. 'Otherwise there will not be any peace in the world for thee and me. He has killed many. Let him so die. Bring your men, and give him no chance to escape.'

'You used to think right much of him,' said Sandridge.

Tonia dropped the lariat, twisted herself around, and curved a lemon-tinted arm over the ranger's shoulder.

'But then,' she murmured in liquid Spanish, 'I had not beheld thee, thou great red mountain of a man! And thou art kind and good, as well as strong. Could one choose him, knowing thee? Let him die; for then I will not be filled with fear by day and night lest he hurt thee or me.'

'How can I know when he comes?' asked Sandridge.

'When he comes,' said Tonia, 'he remains two days, sometimes three. Gregorio, the small son of old Luisa, the *lavendera*, has a swift pony. I will write a letter to thee and send it by him, saying how it will be best to come upon him. By Gregorio will the letter come. And bring many men with thee, and have much care, oh, dear red one, for the rattlesnake is not quicker to strike than is *El Chivato*, as they call him, to send a ball from his *pistola*.'

'The Kid's handy with his gun, sure enough,' admitted Sandridge, 'but when I come for him I shall come alone. I'll get him by myself or not at all. The Cap wrote one or two things to me that make me want to do the trick without any help. You let me know when Mr Kid arrives, and I'll do the rest.'

'I will send you the message by the boy Gregorio,' said the girl. 'I knew you were braver than that small slayer of men who never smiles. How could I ever have thought I cared for him?'

It was time for the ranger to ride back to his camp on the water hole.

Before he mounted his horse he raised the slight form of Tonia with one arm high from the earth for a parting salute. The drowsy stillness of the torpid summer air still lay thick upon the dreaming afternoon. The smoke from the fire in the *jacal*, where the *frijoles* blubbered in the iron pot, rose straight as a plumb-line above the clay-daubed chimney. No sound or movement disturbed the serenity of the dense pear thicket ten yards away.

When the form of Sandridge had disappeared, loping his big dun down the steep banks of the Frio crossing, the Kid crept back to his own horse, mounted him, and rode back along the tortuous trail he had come.

But not far. He stopped and waited in the silent depths of the pear until half an hour had passed. And then Tonia heard the high, untrue notes of his unmusical singing coming nearer and nearer; and she ran to the edge of the pear to meet him.

The Kid seldom smiled; but he smiled and waved his hat when he saw her. He dismounted, and his girl sprang into his arms. The Kid looked at her fondly. His thick, black hair clung to his head like a wrinkled mat. The meeting brought a slight ripple of some undercurrent of feeling to his smooth, dark face that was usually as motionless as a clay mask.

'How's my girl?' he asked, holding her close.

'Sick of waiting so long for you, dear one,' she answered. 'My eyes are dim with always gazing into that devil's pincushion through which you come. And I can see into it such a little way, too. But you are here, beloved one, and I will not scold. *Que mal muchacho!* not to come to see your *alma* more often. Go in and rest, and let me water your horse and stake him with the long rope. There is cool water in the jar for you.'

The Kid kissed her affectionately.

'Not if the court knows itself do I let a lady stake my horse for me,' said he. 'But if you'll run in, *chica*, and throw a pot of coffee together while I attend to the *caballo*, I'll be a good deal obliged.'

Besides his marksmanship the Kid had another attribute for which he admired himself greatly. He was muy caballero, as the Mexicans express it, where the ladies were concerned. For them he had always gentle words and consideration. He could not have spoken a harsh word to a woman. He might ruthlessly slay their husbands and brothers, but he could not have laid the weight of a finger in anger upon a woman. Wherefore many of that interesting division of humanity who had come under the spell of his politeness declared their disbelief in the stories circulated about Mr Kid. One shouldn't believe everything one heard, they said. When confronted by their indignant menfolk with proof of the *caballero's* deeds of infamy, they said maybe he had been driven to it – and that he knew how to treat a lady, anyhow.

Considering this extremely courteous idiosyncrasy of the Kid and the pride he took in it, one can perceive that the solution of the problem that was presented to him by what he saw and heard from his hiding-place in the pear that afternoon (at least as to one of the actors) must have been obscured by difficulties. And yet one could not think of the Kid over-looking little matters of that kind.

At the end of the short twilight they gathered around a supper of *frijoles*, goat steaks, canned peaches and coffee by the light of a lantern in the *jacal*. Afterward, the ancestor, his flock corralled, smoked a cigarette and became a mummy in a grey blanket. Tonia washed the few dishes while the Kid dried them with the flour-sacking towel. Her eyes shone; she chatted volubly of the inconsequent happenings of her small world since the Kid's last visit; it was as all his other homecomings had been.

Then outside Tonia swung in a grass hammock with her guitar and sang sad *canciones de amor*.

'Do you love me just the same, old girl?' asked the Kid, hunting for his cigarette papers.

'Always the same, little one,' said Tonia, her dark eyes lingering upon him.

'I must go over to Fink's,' said the Kid, rising, 'for some tobacco. I thought I had another sack in my coat. I'll be back in a quarter of an hour.'

'Hasten,' said Tonia, 'and tell me – how long shall I call you my own this time? Will you be gone again tomorrow, leaving me to grieve, or will you be longer with your Tonia?'

'Oh, I might stay two or three days this trip,' said the Kid, yawning. 'I've been on the dodge for a month, and I'd like to rest up.'

He was gone half an hour for his tobacco. When he returned Tonia was still lying in the hammock.

'It's funny,' said the Kid, 'how I feel. I feel like there was somebody lying behind every bush and tree waiting to shoot me. I never had mullygrubs like them before. Maybe it's one of them presumptions. I've got half a notion to light out in the morning before day. The Guadalupe country is burning up about that old Dutchman I plugged down there.'

'You are not afraid – no one could make my brave little one fear.'

'Well, I haven't been usually regarded as a jack-rabbit when it comes to scrapping; but I don't want a posse smoking me out when I'm in your *jacal*. Somebody might get hurt that oughtn't to.'

'Remain with your Tonia; no one will find you here.'

The Kid looked keenly into the shadows up and down the arroyo and toward the dim lights of the Mexican village.

'I'll see how it looks later on,' was his decision.

* * *

At midnight a horseman rode into the rangers' camp, blazing his way by noisy 'halloes' to indicate a pacific mission. Sandridge and one or two others turned out to investigate the row. The rider announced himself to be Domingo Sales, from the Lone Wolf Crossing. He bore a letter for Señor Sandridge. Old Luisa, the *lavendera*, had persuaded him to bring it, he said, her son Gregorio being too ill of a fever to ride.

Sandridge lighted the camp lantern and read the letter:

DEAR ONE – He has come. Hardly had you ridden away when he came out of the pear. When he first talked he said he would stay three days or more. Then as it grew later he was like a wolf or a fox, and walked about without rest, looking and listening. Soon he said he must leave before daylight when it is dark and stillest. And then he seemed to suspect that I be not true to him. He looked at me so strange that I am frightened. I swear to him that I love him, his own Tonia. Last of all he said I must prove to him I am true. He thinks that even now men are waiting to kill him as he rides from my house. To escape he says he will dress in my clothes, my red skirt and the blue waist I wear and the brown mantilla over the head, and thus ride away. But before that he says that I must put on his clothes, his *pantalones* and *camisa* and hat, and ride away on his horse from the *jacal* as far as the big road beyond the Crossing and back again. This before he goes, so he can tell if I am true and if men are hidden to shoot him. It is a terrible thing. An hour before daybreak this is to be. Come, my dear one, and kill this man and take me for your Tonia. Do not try to take hold of him alive, but kill him quickly. Knowing all, you should do that. You must come long before the time and hide yourself in the little shed near the *jacal* where the wagon and saddles are kept. It is dark in there. He will wear my red skirt and blue waist and brown mantilla. I send you a hundred kisses. Come surely and shoot quickly and straight.

Thine Own TONIA

Sandridge quickly explained to his men the official part of the missive. The rangers protested against his going alone.

'I'll get him easy enough,' said the lieutenant. 'The girl's got him trapped. And don't even think he'll get the drop on me.'

Sandridge saddled his horse and rode to the Lone Wolf Crossing. He tied his big dun in a clump of brush on the arroyo, took his Winchester from its scabbard, and carefully approached the Perez *jacal*. There was only the half of a high moon drifted over by ragged, milk-white gulf clouds.

The wagon-shed was an excellent place for ambush; and the ranger got inside it safely. In the black shadow of the brush shelter in front of the *jacal* he could see a horse tied and hear him impatiently pawing the hard-trodden earth.

He waited almost an hour before two figures came out of the *jacal*. One, in man's clothes, quickly mounted the horse and galloped past the wagon-shed toward the crossing and village. And then the other figure, in skirt, waist and mantilla over its head, stepped out into the faint moonlight, gazing after the rider. Sandridge thought he would take his chance then before Tonia rode back. He fancied she might not care to see it.

'Throw up your hands,' he ordered loudly, stepping out of the wagon-shed with his Winchester at his shoulder.

There was a quick turn of the figure, but no movement to obey, so the ranger pumped in the bullets – one – two – three – and then twice more; for you never could be too sure of bringing down the Cisco Kid. There was no danger of missing at ten paces, even in that half moonlight.

The old ancestor, asleep on his blanket, was awakened by the shots. Listening further, he heard a great cry from some man in mortal distress or anguish, and rose up grumbling at the disturbing ways of moderns.

The tall, red ghost of a man burst into the *jacal*, reaching one hand, shaking like a *tule* reed, for the lantern hanging on its nail. The other spread a letter on the table.

'Look at this letter, Perez,' cried the man. 'Who wrote it?'

'*Ah, Dios*! it is Señor Sandridge,' mumbled the old man, approaching. '*Pues, señor*, that letter was written by *El Chivato*, as he is called – by the man of Tonia. They say he is a bad man; I do not know. While Tonia slept he wrote the letter and sent it by this old hand of mine to Domingo Sales to be brought to you. Is there anything wrong in the letter? I am very old; and I did not know. *Valgame Dios*! it is a very foolish world; and there is nothing in the house to drink – nothing to drink.'

Just then all that Sandridge could think of to do was to go outside and throw himself face downward in the dust by the side of his humming-bird, of whom not a feather fluttered. He was not a *caballero* by instinct, and he could not understand the niceties of revenge.

A mile away the rider who had ridden past the wagon-shed struck up a harsh, untuneful song, the words of which began:

> 'Don't you monkey with my Lulu girl
> Or I'll tell you what I'll do – '

A CHAPARRAL PRINCE

O. HENRY

NINE O'CLOCK AT LAST, and the drudging toil of the day was ended. Lena climbed to her room in the third half-storey of the Quarrymen's Hotel. Since daylight she had slaved, doing the work of a full-grown woman, scrubbing the floors, washing the heavy ironstone plates and cups, making the beds and supplying the insatiate demands for wood and water in that turbulent and depressing hostelry.

The din of the day's quarrying was over – the blasting and drilling, the creaking of the great cranes, the shouts of the foremen, the backing and shifting of the flat-cars hauling the heavy blocks of limestone. Down in the hotel office three or four of the labourers were growling and swearing over a belated game of checkers. Heavy odours of stewed meat, hot grease and cheap coffee hung like a depressing fog about the house.

Lena lit the stump of a candle and sat limply upon her wooden chair. She was eleven years old, thin and ill-nourished. Her back and limbs were sore and aching. But the ache in her heart made the biggest trouble. The last straw had been added to the burden upon her small shoulders. They had taken away *Grimm*. Always at night, however tired she might be, she had turned to *Grimm* for comfort and hope. Each time had *Grimm* whispered to her that the prince or the fairy would come and deliver her out of the wicked enchantment. Every night she had taken fresh courage and strength from *Grimm*.

To whatever tale she read she found an analogy in her own condition. The woodcutter's lost child, the unhappy goose girl, the persecuted stepdaughter, the little maiden imprisoned in the witch's hut – all these were but transparent disguises for Lena, the overworked kitchenmaid in the Quarrymen's Hotel. And always when the extremity was direst came the good fairy or the gallant prince to the rescue.

So, here in the ogre's castle, enslaved by a wicked spell, Lena had leaned upon *Grimm* and waited, longing for the powers of goodness to prevail. But on the day before Mrs Maloney had found the book in her room and had carried it away, declaring sharply that it would not do for servants to read at night; they lost sleep and did not work briskly the next day. Can one only eleven years old, living away from one's mamma, and never having any time to play, live entirely deprived of *Grimm*? Just try it once and you will see what a difficult thing it is.

Lena's home was in Texas, away up among the little mountains on the Pedernales River, in a little town called Fredericksburg. They are all German people who live in Fredericksburg. Of evenings they sit at little tables along the sidewalk and drink beer and play pinochle and scat. They are very thrifty people.

Thriftiest among them was Peter Hildesmüller, Lena's father. And that is why Lena was sent to work in the hotel at the quarries, thirty miles away. She earned three dollars every week there, and Peter added her wages to his well-guarded store. Peter had an ambition to become as rich as his neighbour, Hugo Heffelbauer, who smoked a meerschaum pipe three feet long and had wiener schnitzel and hassenpffeffer for dinner every day in the week. And now Lena was quite old enough to work and assist in the accumulation of riches. But conjecture, if you can, what it means to be sentenced at eleven years of age from a home in the pleasant little Rhine village to hard labour in the ogre's castle, where you must fly to serve the ogres, while they devour cattle and sheep, growling fiercely as they stamp white limestone dust from their great shoes for you to sweep and scour with your weak, aching fingers. And then – to have *Grimm* taken away from you!

Lena raised the lid of an old empty case that had once contained canned corn and got out a sheet of paper and a piece of pencil. She was going to write a letter to her mamma. Tommy Ryan was going to post it for her at Ballinger's. Tommy was seventeen, worked in the quarries, went home to Ballinger's every night, and was now waiting in the shadows under Lena's window for her to throw the letter out to him. That was the only way she could send a letter to Fredericksburg. Mrs Maloney did not like for her to write letters.

The stump of the candle was burning low, so Lena hastily bit the wood from around the lead of her pencil and began. This is the letter she wrote:

DEAREST MAMMA – I want so much to see you. And Gretel and Claus and Heinrich and little Adolf. I am so tired. I want to see you. Today I was slapped by Mrs Maloney and had no supper. I could not bring in enough wood, for my hand hurt. She took my book yesterday. I mean *Grimm's Fairy Tales*, which Uncle Leo gave me. It did not hurt anyone for me to read the book. I try to work as well as I can, but there is so much to do. I read only a little bit every night. Dear mamma, I shall tell you what I am going to do. Unless you send for me tomorrow to bring me home I shall go to a deep place I know in the river and drown. It is wicked to drown, I suppose, but I wanted to see you, and there is no one else. I am very tired, and Tommy is waiting for the letter. You will excuse me, mamma, if I do it.

Your respectful and loving daughter,
LENA

Tommy was still waiting faithfully when the letter was concluded, and when Lena dropped it out she saw him pick it up and start up the steep hillside. Without undressing she blew out the candle and curled herself upon the mattress on the floor.

At ten-thirty old man Ballinger came out of his house in his stocking feet and leaned over the gate, smoking his pipe. He looked down the big road, white in the moonshine, and rubbed one ankle with the toe of his other foot. It was time for the Fredericksburg mail to come pattering up the road.

Old man Ballinger had waited only a few minutes when he heard the lively hoofbeats of Fritz's team of little black mules, and very soon afterward his covered spring wagon stood in front of the gate. Fritz's big spectacles flashed in the moonlight and his tremendous voice shouted a greeting to the postmaster of Ballinger's. The mail-carrier jumped out and took the bridles from the mules, for he always fed them oats at Ballinger's.

While the mules were eating from their feed bags old man Ballinger brought out the mail sack and threw it into the wagon.

Fritz Bergmann was a man of three sentiments – or to be more accurate – four, the pair of mules deserving to be reckoned individually. Those mules were the chief interest and joy of his existence. Next came the Emperor of Germany and Lena Hildesmüller.

'Tell me,' said Fritz, when he was ready to start, 'contains the sack a letter to Frau Hildesmüller from the little Lena at the quarries? One came in the last mail to say that she is a little sick, already. Her mamma is very anxious to hear again.'

'Yes,' said old man Ballinger, 'thar's a letter for Mrs Helterskelter, or some sich name. Tommy Ryan brung it over when he come. Her little gal workin' over thar, you say?'

'In the hotel,' shouted Fritz, as he gathered up the lines; 'eleven years old and not bigger as a frankfurter. The close-fist of a Peter Hildesmüller! – someday I shall with a big club pound that man's dummkopf – all in and out the town. Perhaps in this letter Lena will say that she is yet feeling better. So, her mamma will be glad. *Auf wiedersehen*, Herr Ballinger – your feets will take cold out in the night air.'

'So long, Fritzy,' said old man Ballinger. 'You got a nice cool night for your drive.'

Up the road went the little black mules at their steady trot, while Fritz thundered at them occasional words of endearment and cheer.

These fancies occupied the mind of the mail-carrier until he reached the big post-oak forest, eight miles from Ballinger's. Here his ruminations were scattered by the sudden flash and report of pistols and a whooping as if from a whole tribe of Indians. A band of galloping centaurs closed in around the mail wagon. One of them leaned over the front wheel, covered the driver with his revolver, and ordered him to stop. Others caught at the bridles of Donder and Blitzen.

'Donnerwetter!' shouted Fritz, with all his tremendous voice – 'wass ist? Release your hands from dose mules. Ve vas der United States mail!'

'Hurry up, Dutch!' drawled a melancholy voice. 'Don't you know when you're in a stick-up? Reverse your mules and climb out of the cart.'

It is due to the breadth of Hondo Bill's demerit and the largeness of his achievements to state that the holding up of the Fredericksburg mail was not perpetrated by way of an exploit. As the lion while in the pursuit of prey commensurate to his prowess might set a frivolous foot upon a casual rabbit in his path, so Hondo Bill and his gang had swooped sportively upon the pacific transport of Meinherr Fritz.

The real work of their sinister night ride was over. Fritz and his mailbag and his mules came as gentle relaxation, grateful after the arduous duties of their profession. Twenty miles to the southeast stood a train with a killed engine, hysterical passengers and a looted express and mail car. That represented the serious occupation of Hondo Bill and his gang. With a fairly rich prize of currency and silver the robbers were making a wide detour to the west through the less populous country, intending to seek safety in Mexico by means of some fordable spot on the Rio Grande. The booty from the train had melted the desperate bushrangers to jovial and happy skylarkers.

Trembling with outraged dignity and no little personal apprehension, Fritz climbed out to the road after replacing his suddenly removed spectacles. The band had dismounted and were singing, capering and whooping, thus expressing their satisfied delight in the life of a jolly outlaw. Rattlesnake Rogers, who stood at the heads of the mules, jerked a little too vigorously at the rein of the tender-mouthed Donder, who reared and emitted a loud, protesting snort of pain. Instantly Fritz, with a scream of anger, flew at the bulky Rogers and began assiduously to pummel that surprised freebooter with his fists.

'Villain!' shouted Fritz, 'dog, bigstiff! Dot mule he has a soreness by his mouth. I vill knock off your shoulders mit your head – robbermans!'

'Yi-yi!' howled Rattlesnake, roaring with laughter and ducking his head, 'somebody git this here sour-krout off 'n me!'

One of the band yanked Fritz back by the coat-tail, and the woods rang with Rattlesnake's vociferous comments.

'The doggoned little wienerwurst,' he yelled, amiably. 'He's not so much of a skunk, for a Dutchman. Took up for his animile plum quick, didn't he? I like to see a man like his hoss, even if it is a mule. The dad-blamed little Limburger he went for me, didn't he! Whoa, now, muley – I ain't a-goin' to hurt your mouth agin any more.'

Perhaps the mail would not have been tampered with had not Ben Moody, the lieutenant, possessed certain wisdom that seemed to promise more spoils.

'Say, Cap,' he said, addressing Hondo Bill, 'there's likely to be good pickings in these mail sacks. I've done some hoss tradin' with these Dutchmen around Fredericksburg, and I know the style of the varmints. There's big money goes through the mails to that town. Them Dutch risk a thousand dollars sent wrapped in a piece of paper before they'd pay the banks to handle the money.'

Hondo Bill, six feet two, gentle of voice and impulsive in action, was dragging the sacks from the rear of the wagon before Moody had finished his speech. A knife shone in his hand, and they heard the ripping sound as it bit through the tough canvas. The outlaws crowded around and began tearing open letters and packages, enlivening their labours by swearing affably at the writers, who seemed to have conspired to confute the prediction of Ben Moody. Not a dollar was found in the Fredericksburg mail.

'You ought to be ashamed of yourself,' said Hondo Bill to the mail-carrier in solemn tones, 'to be packing around such a lot of old, trashy paper as this. What d'you mean by it, anyhow? Where do you Dutchers keep your money at?'

The Ballinger mail sack opened like a cocoon under Hondo's knife. It contained but a handful of mail. Fritz had been fuming with terror and excitement until this sack was reached. He now remembered Lena's letter. He addressed the leader of the band, asking for that particular missive be spared.

'Much obliged, Dutch,' Hondo said to the disturbed carrier. 'I guess that's the letter we want. Got spondulicks in it, ain't it? Here she is. Make a light, boys.'

Hondo found and tore open the letter to Mrs Hildesmüller. The others stood about, lighting twisted-up letters one from another. Hondo gazed with mute disapproval at the single sheet of paper covered with the angular German script.

'Whatever is this you've humbugged us with, Dutchy? You call this here a valuable letter? That's a mighty low-down trick to play on your friends what come along to help you distribute your mail.'

'That's Chiny writin',' said Sandy Grundy, peering over Hondo's shoulder.

'You're off your kazip,' declared another of the gang, an effective youth, covered with silk handkerchiefs and nickel plating. 'That's short-hand. I see 'em do it once in court.'

'Ach, no, no, no – dot is German,' said Fritz. 'It is no more as a little girl writing a letter to her mamma. One poor little girl, sick and vorking hard avay from home. Ach! it is a shame. Good Mr Robberman, you vill please let me have dot letter?'

'What the devil do you take us for, old pretzels?' said Hondo with sudden and surprising severity. 'You ain't presumin' to insinuate that we gents ain't possessed of sufficient politeness for to take an interest in the miss's health, are you? Now, you go on, and you read that scratchin' out loud and in plain United States language to this here company of educated society.'

Hondo twirled his six-shooter by its trigger guard and stood towering above the little German, who at once began to read the letter, translating the simple words into English. The gang of rovers stood in absolute silence, listening intently. 'How old is that kid?' he asked when the letter was done.

'Eleven,' said Fritz.

'And where is she at?'

'At dose rock quarries – working. Ach, mein Gott – little Lena, she speak of drowning. I do not know if she vill do it, but if she shall I schwear I vill dot Peter Hildesmüller shoot mit a gun.'

'You Dutchers,' said Hondo Bill, his voice swelling with fine contempt, 'make me plenty tired. Hirin' out your kids to work when they ought to be playin' dolls in the sand. You're a hell of a sect of people. I reckon we'll fix your clock for a while just to show what we think of your old cheesy nation. Here, boys!'

Hondo Bill parleyed aside briefly with his band, and then they seized Fritz and conveyed him off the road to one side. Here they bound him fast to a tree with a couple of lariats. His team they tied to another tree near by.

'We ain't going to hurt you bad,' said Hondo reassuringly. ' 'Twon't hurt you to be tied up for a while. We will now pass you the time of day, as it is up to us to depart. Ausgespielt – nixcumrous, Dutchy. Don't get any more impatience.'

Fritz heard a great squeaking of saddles as the men mounted their horses. Then a loud yell and a great clatter of hoofs as they galloped pell-mell back along the Fredericksburg road the way Fritz had come.

For more than two hours Fritz sat against his tree, tightly but not painfully bound. Then from the reaction after his exciting adventure he sank into slumber. How long he slept he knew not, but he was at last awakened by a rough shake. Hands were untying his ropes. He was lifted to his feet, dazed, confused in mind and weary of body. Rubbing his eyes, he looked and saw that he was again in the midst of the same band of terrible bandits. They shoved him up to the seat of his wagon and placed the lines in his hands.

'Hit it out for home, Dutch,' said Hondo Bill's voice commandingly. 'You've given us lots of trouble and we're pleased to see the back of your neck. Spiel! Zwei bier! Vamoose!'

Hondo reached out and gave Blitzen a smart cut with his quirt.

The little mules sprang ahead, glad to be moving again. Fritz urged them along, himself dizzy and muddled over his fearful adventure.

According to schedule time, he should have reached Fredericksburg at daylight. As it was, he drove down the long street of the town at eleven o'clock A. M. He had to pass Peter Hildesmüller's house on his way to the post-office. He stopped his team at the gate and called. But Frau Hildesmüller was watching for him. Out rushed the whole family of Hildesmüllers.

Frau Hildesmüller, fat and flushed, enquired if he had a letter from Lena, and then Fritz raised his voice and told the tale of his adventure. He told the contents of that letter that the robber had made him read, and then Frau Hildesmüller broke into wild weeping. Her little Lena drown herself! Why had they sent her from home? What could be done? Perhaps it would be too late by the time they could send for her now. Peter Hildesmüller dropped his meerschaum on the walk and it shivered into pieces.

'Woman!' he roared at his wife, 'why did you let that child go away? It is your fault if she comes home to us no more.'

Everyone knew that it was Peter Hildesmüller's fault, so they paid no attention to his words.

A moment afterward a strange, faint voice was heard to call: 'Mamma!' Frau Hildesmüller at first thought it was Lena's spirit calling, and then she rushed to the rear of Fritz's covered wagon, and with a loud shriek of joy, caught up Lena herself, covering her pale little face with kisses and smothering her with hugs. Lena's eyes were heavy with the deep slumber of exhaustion, but she smiled and lay close to the one she had longed to see. There among the mail sacks, covered in a nest of strange blankets and comforters, she had lain asleep until wakened by the voices around her.

Fritz stared at her with eyes that bulged behind his spectacles.

'Gott in Himmel!' he shouted. 'How did you get in that wagon? Am I going crazy as well as to be murdered and hanged by robbers this day?'

'You brought her to us, Fritz,' cried Frau Hildesmüller. 'How can we ever thank you enough?'

'Tell mamma how you came in Fritz's wagon,' said Frau Hildesmüller.

'I don't know,' said Lena. 'But I know how I got away from the hotel. The Prince brought me.'

'By the Emperor's crown!' shouted Fritz, 'we are all going crazy.'

'I always knew he would come,' said Lena, sitting down on her bundle of bedclothes on the sidewalk. 'Last night he came with his armed knights and captured the ogre's castle. They broke the dishes and kicked down the doors. They pitched Mr Maloney into a barrel of rainwater and threw flour all over Mrs Maloney. The workmen in the hotel jumped out of the windows and ran into the woods when the knights began firing their guns. They wakened me up and I peeped down the stair. And then the Prince came up and wrapped me in the bedclothes and carried me out. He was so tall and strong and fine. His face was as rough as a scrubbing brush, and he talked soft and kind and smelled of schnapps. He took me on his horse before him and we rode away among the knights. He held me close and I went to sleep that way, and didn't wake up till I got home.'

'Rubbish!' cried Fritz Bergmann. 'Fairy tales! How did you come from the quarries to my wagon?'

'The Prince brought me,' said Lena, confidently.

And to this day the good people of Fredericksburg haven't been able to make her give any other explanation.

SCIENCE AT HEART'S DESIRE

EMERSON HOUGH

'THAT OLD RAILROAD'LL shore bust me up a heap if it ever does git in here,' remarked Tom Osby one morning in the forum of Whiteman's corral, where the accustomed group was sitting in the sun, waiting for someone to volunteer as Homer for the day.

There was little to do but listen to storytelling, for Tom Osby dwelt in the tents of Kedar, delaying departure on his accustomed trip to Vegas.

'A feller down there to Sky Top,' he went on, arousing only the most indolent interest, 'one of them spy-glass ingineers – tenderfoot, with his six-shooter belt buckled so tight he couldn't get his feet to the ground – he says to me I might as well trade my old greys for a nice new checker-board, or a deck of author cards, for I won't have nothing to do but just amuse myself when the railroad cars gets here.'

No one spoke. All present were trying to imagine how Heart's Desire would seem with a railroad train each day.

'Things'll be some different in them days, mebbe so.' Tom recrossed his legs with well-considered deliberation.

'There's a heap of things different already from what they used to be when I first hit the cow range,' said Curly. 'The whole country's changed, and it ain't changed for the better, either. Grass is longer, and horns is shorter, and men is triflin'er. Since the Yankees has got west of the Missouri River a ranch foreman ain't allowed to run his own brandin' iron any more, and that takes more'n half the poetry out of the cow business, don't it, Mac?' This to McKinney, who was nearly asleep.

'Everything else is changing too,' Curly continued, gathering fluency as memories began to crowd upon him. 'Look at the lawyers and doctors there is in the Territory now – and this country used to be respectable. Why, when I first come here there wasn't a doctor within a thousand miles, and no need for one. If one of the boys got shot up much, we always found some way to laundry him and sew him together again without no need of a diplomy. No one ever got sick; and, of course, no one ever did die of his own accord, the way they do back in the States.'

'What's it all about, Curly?' drawled Dan Anderson. 'You can't tell a story worth a cent.' Curly paid no attention to him.

'The first doctor that ever come out here for to alleviate us fellers,' he went on, 'why, he settled over on the Sweetwater. He was a allopath from

Bitter Creek. What medicine that feller did give! He gradual drifted into the vet'inary line.

'Then there come a homeopath – that was after a good many women-folk had settled in along the railroad over west. Still, there wasn't much sickness, and I don't reckon the homeopath ever did winter through. I was livin' with the Bar T outfit on the Oscura range, at that time.

'Next doctor that come along was a ostypath.' Curly took a chew of tobacco, and paused a moment reflectively.

'I said the first feller drifted into vet'inary lines, didn't I?' he resumed. 'Well, the ostypath did, too. Didn't you never hear about that? Why, he ostypathed a horse!'

'Did *what?*' asked Tom Osby sitting up; for hitherto there had seemed no need to listen attentively.

'Yes, sir,' he went on, 'he ostypathed a horse for us. The boys they gambled about two thousand dollars on that horse over at Socorro. It was a cross-eyed horse, too.'

'What's that?' Doc Tomlinson objected. 'There never was such a thing as a cross-eyed horse.'

'Oh, there wasn't, wasn't there?' said Curly. 'Well, now, my friend, when you talk that-a-way, you simply show me how much you don't know about horses. This here Bar T horse was as cross-eyed as a saw-horse, until we got him ostypathed. But, of course, if you don't believe what I say, there's no use tellin' you this story at all.'

'Oh, go on, go on,' McKinney spoke up, 'don't pay no attention to Doc.'

'Well,' Curly resumed, 'that there horse was knowed constant on this range for over three years. He was a outlaw, with cream mane and tail, and a pinto map of Europe, Asia and Africa wrote all over his ribs. Run? Why, that horse could run down a coyote as a moral pastime. We used him to catch jack rabbits with between meals. It wasn't no trouble for him to *run*. The trouble was to tell when he was goin' to *stop* runnin'. Sometimes it was a good while before the feller ridin' him could get him around to where he begun to run. He run in curves natural, and he handed out a right curve or a left one, just as he happened to feel, same as the feller dealin' faro, and just as easy.

'Tom Redmond, on the Bar T, he got this horse from a feller by the name of Hasenberg that brought in a bunch of has-beens and outlaws and commenced to distribute 'em in this country. Hasenberg was a foreign gent that looked a good deal like Whiteman, our distinguished feller-citizen here. He was cross-eyed hisself, body and soul. There wasn't a straight thing about him. We allowed that maybe this pinto *caballo* got cross-eyed from associatin' with old Hasenberg, who was strictly on the bias, any way you figured.'

'You ain't so bad, after all, Curly,' said Dan Andersen, sitting up. 'You're beginning now to hit the human-interest part. You ought to be a reg'lar contributor.'

'Shut up!' said Curly. 'Now Tom Redmond, he took to this here pinto horse from havin' seen him jump the corral fence several times, and start floatin' off across the country for a eight- or ten-mile sashay without no special encouragement. He hired three Castilian busters to operate on Pinto, and he got so he could be rode occasional, but everyone allowed they never did see any horse just like him. He was the most aggravatinest thing we ever did have on this range. He had a sort of odd-lookin' white eye, but a heap of them pintos has got glass eyes, and so no one thought to examine his lookers very close, though it was noticed early in the game that Pinto might be lookin' one way and goin' the other, at the same time. He'd be goin' on a keen lope, and then something or other might get on his mind, and he'd stop and untangle hisself from all kinds of ridin'. Sometimes he'd jump and snort like he was seein' ghosts. A feller on that horse could have roped antelopes as easy as yearlin' calves, if he could just have told which way Mr Pinto was goin'; but he was a shore hard one to estermate.

'At last Tom, why, he suspected somethin' wasn't right with Pinto's lamps. If you stuck out a bunch of hay at him, he couldn't bite it by about five feet. When you led him down to water, you had to go sideways; and if you wanted to get him in through the corral gate, you had to push him in backwards. We discovered right soon that he was born with his parallax or something out of gear. His graduated scale of seein' things was different from our'n. I don't reckon anybody ever will know what all Pinto saw with them glass lamps of his, but all the time we knowed that if we could ever onct get his lookin' outfit tuned up proper, we had the whole country skinned in a horse race; for he could shore run copious.

'That was why he had the whole Bar T outfit guessin' all the time. We all wanted to bet on him, and we was all scared to. Sometimes we'd make up a purse among us, and we'd go over to some social getherin' or other, and win a thousand dollars. Old Pinto could run all day; he can yet, for that matter. Didn't make no difference to him how often we raced him;

and natural, after we'd won one hatful of money with him, we'd want to win another. That was where our judgement was weak.

'You never could tell whether Pinto was goin' to finish under the wire, or out in the landscape. His eyes seemed to be sort of moverble, but like enough they'd get sot when he went to runnin'. Then he'd run whichever way he was lookin' at the time, or happened to think he was lookin'; and dependin' additional on what he thought he saw. And law! A whole board of supervisors and school commissioners couldn't have looked that horse in the face, and guessed on their sacred honour whether he was goin' to jump the fence to the left, or take to the high sage on the outside of the track.

'Onct in a while we'd git Pinto's left eye set at a angle, and he'd come around the track and under the wire before she wobbled out of place. On them occasions we made money a heap easier than I ever did a-gettin' it from home. But, owin' to the looseness of them eyes, I don't reckon there never was no horse racin' as uncertain as this here; and like enough you may have observed it's uncertain enough even when things is fixed in the most comf'terble way possible.'

A deep sigh greeted this, which showed that Curly's audience was in full sympathy.

'You always felt like puttin' the saddle on to Pinto hind end to, he was so cross-eyed,' he resumed ruminatingly, 'but still you couldn't help feelin' sorry for him, neither. Now, he had a right pained and grieved look in his face all the time. I reckon he thought this was a hard sort of a world to get along in. It is. A cross-eyed man has a hard enough time, but a cross-eyed *horse* – well, you don't know how much trouble he can be for hisself, and everyone else around him.

'Now, here we was, fixed up like I told you. Mr Allopath is over on Sweetwater creek, Mr Homeopath is maybe in the last stages of starvation. Old Pinto looks plumb hopeless, and all us fellers is mostly hopeless too, owin' to his uncertain habits in a horse race, yet knowin' that it ain't perfessional for us not to back a Bar T horse that can run as fast as this one can.

'About then along comes Mr Ostypath. This was just about thirty days before the county fair at Socorro, and there was money hung up for horse races over there that made us feel sick to think of. We knew we could go out of the cow-punchin' business for good if we could just only onct get Pinto over there, and get him to run the right way for a few brief moments.

'Was he game? I don't know. There never was no horse ever got clost enough to him in a horse race to tell whether he was game or not. He might not get back home in time for supper, but he would shore run industrious. Say, I talked in a telyphome onct. The book hung on the box said the telyphome was instantaneous. It ain't. But now this Pinto, he was a heap more instantaneous than a telyphome.

'As I was sayin', it was long about now Mr Ostypath comes in. He talks with the boss about locatin' around in here. Boss studies him over a while, and as there ain't been anybody sick for over ten years he tries to break it to Mr Ostypath gentle that the Bar T ain't a good place for a doctor. They have some conversation along in there, that-a-way, and Mr Ostypath before long gets the boss interested deep and plenty. He says there ain't no such a thing as gettin' sick. We all knew that before; but he certainly floors the lot when he allows that the reason a feller don't feel good, so as he can eat tenpenny nails, and make a million dollars a year, is always because there is something wrong with his osshus structure.

'He says the only thing that makes a feller have rheumatism, or dyspepsia, or headache, or nosebleed, or red hair, or any other sickness, is that something is wrong with his nervous system. Now, it's this-a-way. He allows them nerves is like a bunch of garden hose. If you put your foot on the hose, the water can't run right free. If you take it off, everything's lovely. "Now," says Mr Ostypath, "if, owin' to some luxation, some leeshun, some temporary mechanical disarrangement of your osshus structure, due to a oversight of a All-wise Providence, or maybe a fall off 'n a buckin' horse, one of them bones of yours gets to pressin' on a nerve, why, it ain't natural you *ought* to feel good. Now, *is* it?" says he.

'He goes on and shows how all up and down a feller's backbone there is plenty of soft spots, and he shows likewise that there is scattered around in different parts of a feller's territory something like two hundred and four and a half bones, any one of which is likely any minute to jar loose and go to pressin' on a soft spot; "In which case," says he, "there is need of a ostypath immediate."

'For instance,' he says to me, 'I could make quite a man out of you in a couple of years if I had the chanct.' I ast him what his price would be for that, and he said he was willin' to tackle it for about fifty dollars a month. That bein' just five dollars a month more than the boss was allowing me at the time, and me seein' I'd have to go about two years without anything to wear or eat – let alone anything to drink – I had to let this chanct go by. I been strugglin' along, as you know, ever since, just like this, some shopworn, but so's to set up. There was one while, I admit, when the doc made me some nervous, when I thought of all them soft spots in my spine, and all them bones liable to get loose any minute and go to pressin' on them. But I had to take my chances, like any other cow puncher at forty-five a month.'

'You ought to raise his wages, Mac,' said Doc Tomlinson to McKinney, the ranch foreman, but the latter only grunted.

'Mr Ostypath, he stayed around the Bar T quite a while,' began Curly again, 'and we got to talkin' to him a heap about modern science. Says he, one evenin', this-a-way to us fellers, says he, "Why, a great many things goes wrong because the nervous system is interfered with, along of your osshus structure. You think your stomach is out of whack," says he. "It ain't. All it needs is more nerve supply. I git that by loosenin' up the bones in your back. Why, I've cured a heap of rheumatism, and paralysis, and cross eyes, and – "

' "What's that?" says Tom Redmond, right sudden.

' "You heard me, sir," says the doc, severe.

'Tom, he couldn't hardly wait, he was so bad struck with the idea he had. "Come here, doc," says he. And then him and the doc walked off a little ways and begun to talk. When they come up towards us again, we heard the doc sayin': "Of course I could cure him. Straybismus is dead easy. I never did operate on no horse, but I've got to eat, and if this here is the only patient in this whole blamed country, why I'll have to go to, if it's only for the sake of science," says he.

Then we all bunched in together and drifted off towards the corral, where old Pinto was standin', lookin' hopeless and thoughtful.

"Is this the patient?" says the doc, sort of sighin'.

' "It are," says Tom Redmond.

'The doc he walks up to old Pinto, and has a look at him, frontways, sideways, and all around. Pinto raises his head up, snorts, and looks the doc full in the face; leastwise, if he'd 'a' been any other horse, he'd 'a' been lookin' him full in the face. The doc he stands thoughtful for quite a while, and then he goes and kind of runs his hand up and down along Pinto's spine. He growed plumb enthusiastic then, "Beautiful subject," says he. "Be-yoo-tiful ostypathic subject! Whole osshus structure exposed!" And Pinto shore was a dream if bones was needful in the game.'

Curly paused for another chew of tobacco, then went on again.

'Well, it's like this, you see; the backbone of a man or a horse is full of little humps – you can see that easy in the springtime. Now old Pinto's back, it looked like a topygraphical survey of the whole Rocky Mountain range.

'The doc he runs his hand up and down along this high divide, and says he, "Just like I thought," says he. "The patient has suffered a distinct leeshun in the immediate vicinity of his vaseline motor centres." '

'You mean the vaso-motor centres,' suggested Dan Anderson.

'That's what I said,' said Curly, aggressively.

'Now, when we all heard the doc say them words we knowed he was shore scientific, and we come up clost while the examination was progressin'.

' "Most extraordinary," says the doc, feelin' some more. "Now, here is a distant luxation in the lumber regions." He talked like Pinto had a wooden leg.

' "I should diagnose great cerebral excitation, along with pernounced ocular hesitation," says the doc at last.

' "Now look here, doc," says Tom Redmond to him then. "You go careful. We all know there's something strange about this here horse; but now, if he's got any bone pressin' on him anywhere that makes him *run* the way he does, why, you be blamed careful not to monkey with that there particular bone. Don't you touch his *runnin'* bone, because *that's* all right the way it is."

' "Don't you worry any," says the doc. "All I should do would only be to increase his nerve supply. In time I could remedy his ocular defecks, too," says he. He allows that if we will give him time, he can make Pinto's eyes straighten out so's he'll look like a new rockin' horse Christmas mornin' at a church festerval. Incidentally he suggests that we get a tall leather blinder and run it down Pinto's nose, right between his eyes.

'This last was what caught us most of all. "This here blinder idea," says Tom Redmond, 'is plumb scientific. The trouble with us cowpunchers is we ain't got no brains – or we wouldn't be cowpunchers! Now look here, Pinto's right eye looks off to the left, and his left eye looks off to the right. Like enough he sees all sorts of things on both sides of him, and gets 'em mixed. Now, you put this here harness leather between his eyes, and his right eye looks plumb into it on one side, and his left eye looks into it on the other. Result is, he can't see nothing at *all*! Now, if he'll only run when he's *blind*, why, we can skin them Socorro people till it seems like a shame.'

'Well, right then we all felt money in our pockets. We seemed most too good to be out ridin' sign, or pullin' old cows out of mudholes. "You leave all that to me," says the doc. "By the time I've worked on this patient's nerve centres for a while, I'll make a new horse out of him. You watch me," says he. That made us all feel cheerful. We thought this wasn't such a bad world, after all.

'We passed the hat in the interest of modern science, and we fenced off a place in the corral and set up a school of ostypathy in our midst. The doc, he done some things that seemed to us right strange at first. He gets Pinto up in one corner and takes him by the ear, and tries to break his neck, with his foot in the middle of his back. Then he goes around on the other side and does the same thing. He hammers him up one side and down the other, and works him and wiggles him till us cowpunchers thought he was goin' to scatter him around worse than Cassybianca on the burnin' deck after the exploshun. My experience, though, is that it's right hard to shake a horse to pieces. Pinto, he stood it all right. And say, he got so gentle, with that tall blinder between his eyes, that he'd 'a' followed off a sheepherder.

'All this time we was throwin' oats a-plenty into Pinto, rubbin' his legs down, and gettin' him used to a saddle a little bit lighter than a regular cow saddle. The doc, he allows he can see his eyes straightenin' out every day. "I ought to have a year on this job," says he; "but these here is urgent times."

'I should say they was urgent. The time for the county fair at Socorro was comin' right clost.

'At last we takes the old Hasenberg Pinto over to Socorro to the fair, and there we enters him in everything from the front to the back of the racin' book. My friends, you would 'a' shed tears of pity to see them folks fall down over theirselves tryin' to hand us their money against old Pinto. There was horses there from Montanny to Arizony, all kinds of fancy riders, and money – oh, law! Us Bar T fellers, we took everything offered – put up everything we had, down to our spurs. Then we'd go off by ourselves and look at each other solemn. We was gettin' rich so quick we felt almost scared.

'There come nigh to bein' a little shootin' just before the horses was gettin' ready for the first race, which was for a mile and a half. We led old Pinto out, and some feller standin' by, he says, sarcastic like, "What's that I see comin'; a snow-plough?" Him alludin' to the single blinder on Pinto's nose.

' "I reckon you'll think it's been snowin' when we get through," says Tom Redmond to him, scornful. "The best thing you can do is to shut up, unless you've got a little money you want to contribute to the Bar T festerval." But about then they hollered for the horses to go to the post, and there wasn't no more talk.

'Pinto he acted meek and humble, just like a glass-eyed angel, and the starter didn't have no trouble with him at all. At last he got them all off, so clost together one saddle blanket would have done for the whole bunch. Say, man, that was a fine start.

'Along with oats and ostypathy, old Pinto he'd come out on the track that day just standin' on the edges of his feet, he was feelin' that fine. We put José Santa Maria Trujillo, one of our lightest boys, up on Pinto for to ride him. Now a greaser ain't got no sense. It was that fool boy José that busted up modern science on the Bar T.

'I was tellin' you that there horse was ostypathed, so to speak, plumb to a razor edge, and I was sayin' that he went off on an even start. Then what did he do? Run? No, he didn't *run*. He just sort of passed *away* from the place where he started at. Our greaser, he sees the race is all over, and like any fool cowpuncher, he must get frisky. Comin' down the homestretch, only needin' about one more jump – for it ain't above a quarter of a mile – José , he stands up in his stirrups and pulls off his hat, and just whangs old Pinto over the head with it, friendly like, to show him there ain't no coldness.

'We never did rightly know what happened at that time. The greaser admits he may have busted off the fastenin' of that single blinder down Pinto's nose. Anyhow, Pinto runs a few short jumps, and then stops, lookin' troubled. The next minute he hides his face on the greaser and there is a glimpse of bright, glad sunlight on the bottom of José's moccasins. Next minute after that Pinto is up in the grandstand among the ladies, and there he sits down in the lap of the governor's wife, which was among them present.

'There was time, even then, to lead him down and over the line, but before we could think of that he falls to buckin' sincere and conscientious, up there among the benches, and if he didn't jar his osshus structure a heap *then*, it wasn't no fault of his'n. We all run up in front of the grandstand, and stood lookin' up at Pinto, and him the maddest, scaredest, cross-eyedest horse I ever did see in all my life. His single blinder was swingin' loose under his neck. His eyes was right mean and white, and the Mexican saints only knows which way he *was* a-lookin'.

'So there we was,' went on Curly, with another sigh, 'all Socorro sayin' bright and cheerful things to the Bar T, and us plumb broke, and far, far from home.

'We roped Pinto, and led him home behind the wagon, forty miles over the sand, by the soft, silver light of the moon. There wasn't a horse or saddle left in our rodeo, and we had to ride on the grub wagon, which you know is a disgrace to any gentleman that wears spurs. Pinto, he was the gayest one in the lot. I reckon he allowed he'd been Queen of the May. Every time he saw a jack rabbit or a bunch of sage brush, he'd snort and take a *pasear* sideways as far as the rope would let him go.

' "The patient seems to be still labourin' under great cerebral excitation," says the doc, which was likewise on the wagon. "I ought to have had a year on him," says he, despondent like.

' "Shut up," says Tom Redmond to the doc. "I'd shoot up your own osshus structure plenty," says he, "if I hadn't bet my gun on that horse race."

'Well, we got home, the wagon-load of us, in the mornin' sometime, every one of us ashamed to look the cook in the face, and hopin' the boss was away from home. But he wasn't. He looks at us, and says he: ' "Is this a sheep outfit I see before me, or is it the remnants of the former cow camp on the Bar T?" He was right sarcastic. "Doc," says he, "explain this here to me." But the doc, he couldn't. Says the boss to him at last, "The *right* time to do the explainin' is before the hoss race is over, and not after," says he. "That's the only kind of science that goes hereafter on the Bar T," says he.

'I reckon the boss was feelin' a little riled, because he had two hundred on Pinto hisself. A cross-eyed horse shore can make a sight of trouble,' Curly sighed in conclusion; 'yet I bought Pinto for four dollars, and – sometimes, anyway – he's the best horse in my string down at Carrizosy, ain't he, Mac?'

In the thoughtful silence following this tale, Tom Osby knocked his pipe reflectively against a cedar log. 'That's the way with the railroad,' he said. 'It's goin' to come in here with one eye on the gold mines and the other on the town – and there won't be no blind-bridle up in front of old Mr Ingine, neither. If we got as much sense as the Bar T feller, we'll do our explainin' before, and not after the hoss race is over. Before I leave for Vegas, I want to see one of you ostypothetic lawyers about that there railroad outfit.'

ALL GOLD CANYON

JACK LONDON

I T WAS THE GREEN HEART of the canyon, where the walls
swerved back from the rigid plan and relieved their harshness of line
by making a little sheltered nook and filling it to the brim with sweetness and roundness and softness. Here all things rested. Even the narrow
stream ceased its turbulent down-rush long enough to form a quiet pool.
Knee-deep in the water, with drooping head and half-shut eyes, drowsed
a red-coated, many-antlered buck.

On one side, beginning at the very lip of the pool, was a tiny meadow,
a cool, resilient surface of green that extended to the base of the frowning
wall. Beyond the pool a gentle slope of earth ran up and up to meet the
opposing wall. Fine grass covered the slope – grass that was spangled
with flowers, with here and there patches of colour, orange and purple
and golden. Below, the canyon was shut in. There was no view. The walls
leaned together abruptly and the canyon ended in a chaos of rocks, moss-
covered and hidden by a green screen of vines and creepers and boughs
of trees. Up the canyon rose far hills and peaks, the big foothills, pine-
covered and remote. And far beyond, like clouds upon the border of the
sky, towered minarets of white, where the Sierra's eternal snows flashed
austerely the blazes of the sun.

There was no dust in the canyon. The leaves and flowers were clean
and virginal. The grass was young velvet. Over the pool three cottonwoods sent their snowy fluffs fluttering down the quiet air. On the slope
the blossoms of the wine-wooded manzanita filled the air with springtime
odours, while the leaves, wise with experience, were already beginning
their vertical twist against the coming aridity of summer. In the open
spaces on the slope, beyond the farthest shadow-reach of the manzanita,
poised the mariposa lilies, like so many flights of jewelled moths suddenly
arrested and on the verge of trembling into flight again. Here and there
that woods harlequin, the madrone, permitting itself to be caught in the
act of changing its pea-green trunk to madder-red, breathed its fragrance
into the air from great clusters of waxen bells. Creamy white were these
bells, shaped like lilies-of-the-valley, with the sweetness of perfume that
is of the springtime.

There was not a sigh of wind. The air was drowsy with its weight of
perfume. It was a sweetness that would have been cloying had the air

been heavy and humid. But the air was sharp and thin. It was as starlight transmuted into atmosphere, shot through and warmed by sunshine, and flower-drenched with sweetness.

An occasional butterfly drifted in and out through the patches of light and shade. And from all about rose the low and sleepy hum of mountain bees – feasting Sybarites that jostled one another good-naturedly at the board, nor found time for rough discourtesy. So quietly did the little stream drip and ripple its way through the canyon that it spoke only in faint and occasional gurgles. The voice of the stream was as a drowsy whisper, ever interrupted by dozings and silences, ever lifted again in the awakenings.

The motion of all things was a drifting in the heart of the canyon. Sunshine and butterflies drifted in and out among the trees. The hum of the bees and the whisper of the stream were a drifting of sound. And the drifting sound and drifting colour seemed to weave together in the making of a delicate and intangible fabric which was the spirit of the place. It was a spirit of peace that was not of death but of smooth-pulsing life, of quietude that was not silence, of movement that was not action, of repose that was quick with existence without being violent with struggle and travail. The spirit of the place was the spirit of the peace of the living, somnolent with the easement and content of prosperity and undisturbed by rumours of far wars.

The red-coated, many-antlered buck acknowledged the lordship of the spirit of the place and dozed knee-deep in the cool, shaded pool. There seemed no flies to vex him and he was languid with rest. Sometimes his ears moved when the stream awoke and whispered; but they moved lazily, with foreknowledge that it was merely the stream grown garrulous at discovery that it had slept.

But there came a time when the buck's ears lifted and tensed with swift eagerness for sound. His head was turned down the canyon. His sensitive, quivering nostrils scented the air. His eyes could not pierce the green screen through which the stream rippled away, but to his ears came the voice of a man. It was a steady, monotonous, singsong voice. Once the buck heard the harsh clash of metal upon rock. At the sound he snorted with a sudden start that jerked him through the air from water to meadow, and his feet sank into the young velvet, while he pricked his ears and again scented the air. Then he stole across the tiny meadow, pausing once and again to listen, and faded away out of the canyon like a wraith, soft-footed and without sound.

The clash of steel-shod soles against the rocks began to be heard, and the man's voice grew louder. It was raised in a sort of chant and became distinct with nearness, so that the words could be heard:

'Tu'n around an' tu'n yo' face
Untoe them sweet hills of grace
  (D' pow'rs of sin yo' am scornin'!).
Look about an' look aroun',
Fling yo' sin-pack on d' groun'
  (Yo' will meet wid d' Lord in d' mornin'!).'

A sound of scrambling accompanied the song, and the spirit of the place fled away on the heels of the red-coated buck. The green screen was burst asunder, and a man peered out at the meadow and the pool and the sloping side-hill. He was a deliberate sort of man. He took in the scene with one embracing glance, then ran his eyes over the details to verify the general impression. Then, and not until then, did he open his mouth in vivid and solemn approval: 'Smoke of life an' snakes of purgatory! Will you just look at that! Wood an' water an' grass an' a side-hill! A pocket-hunter's delight an' a cayuse's paradise! Cool green for tired eyes! Pink pills for pale people ain't in it. A secret pasture for prospectors and a resting-place for tired burros. It's just booful!'

He was a sandy-complexioned man in whose face geniality and humour seemed the salient characteristics. It was a mobile face, quick-changing to inward mood and thought. Thinking was in him a visible process. Ideas chased across his face like wind-flaws across the surface of a lake. His hair, sparse and unkempt of growth, was as indeterminate and colourless as his complexion. It would seem that all the colour of his frame had gone into his eyes, for they were startlingly blue. Also, they were laughing and merry eyes, within them much of the naivety and wonder of the child; and yet, in an unassertive way, they contained much of calm self-reliance and strength of purpose founded upon self-experience and experience of the world.

From out the screen of vines and creepers he flung ahead of him a miner's pick and shovel and gold-pan. Then he crawled out himself into the open. He was clad in faded overalls and black cotton shirt, with hobnailed brogans on his feet, and on his head a hat whose shapelessness and stains advertised the rough usage of wind and rain and sun and camp-smoke. He stood erect, seeing wide-eyed the secrecy of the scene and sensuously inhaling the warm, sweet breath of the canyon-garden through nostrils that dilated and quivered with delight. His eyes narrowed to laughing slits of blue, his face wreathed itself in joy, and his mouth curled in a smile as he cried aloud: 'Jumping dandelions and happy hollyhocks, but that smells good to me! Talk about your attar o' roses an' cologne factories! They ain't in it!'

He had the habit of soliloquy. His quick-changing facial expressions might tell every thought and mood, but the tongue, perforce, ran hard after, repeating, like a second Boswell.

The man lay down on the lip of the pool and drank long and deep of its water. 'Tastes good to me,' he murmured, lifting his head and gazing across the pool at the side-hill, while he wiped his mouth with the back of his hand. The side-hill attracted his attention. Still lying on his stomach, he studied the hill formation long and carefully. It was a practised eye that travelled up the slope to the crumbling canyon-wall and back and down again to the edge of the pool. He scrambled to his feet and favoured the side-hill with a second survey.

'Looks good to me,' he concluded, picking up his pick and shovel and gold-pan.

He crossed the stream below the pool, stepping agilely from stone to stone. Where the side-hill touched the water he dug up a shovelful of dirt and put it into the gold-pan. He squatted down, holding the pan in his two hands, and partly immersing it in the stream. Then he imparted to the pan a deft circular motion that sent the water sluicing in and out through the dirt and gravel. The larger and the lighter particles worked to the surface, and these, by a skilful dipping movement of the pan, he spilled out and over the edge. Occasionally, to expedite matters, he rested the pan and with his fingers raked out the large pebbles and pieces of rock.

The contents of the pan diminished rapidly until only fine dirt and the smallest bits of gravel remained. At this stage he began to work very deliberately and carefully. It was fine washing, and he washed fine and finer, with a keen scrutiny and delicate and fastidious touch. At last the pan seemed empty of everything but water; but with a quick semicircular flirt that sent the water flying over the shallow rim into the stream, he disclosed a layer of black sand on the bottom of the pan. So thin was this layer that it was like a streak of paint. He examined it closely. In the midst of it was a tiny golden speck. He dribbled a little water in over the depressed edge of the pan. With a quick flirt he sent the water sluicing across the bottom, turning the grains of black sand over and over. A second tiny golden speck rewarded his effort.

The washing had now become very fine – fine beyond all need of ordinary placer-mining. He worked the black sand, a small portion at a time, up the shallow rim of the pan. Each small portion he examined sharply, so that his eyes saw every grain of it before he allowed it to slide over the edge and away. Jealously, bit by bit, he let the black sand slip away. A golden speck, no larger than a pin-point, appeared on the rim, and by his manipulation of the water it returned to the bottom of the pan. And in such fashion another speck was disclosed, and another. Great was his care of them. Like a shepherd he herded his flock of golden specks so that not one should be lost. At last, of the pan of dirt nothing remained but his golden herd. He counted it, and then, after all his labour, sent it flying out of the pan with one final swirl of water.

But his blue eyes were shining with desire as he rose to his feet. 'Seven,' he muttered aloud, asserting the sum of the specks for which he had toiled so hard and which he had so wantonly thrown away. 'Seven,' he repeated, with the emphasis of one trying to impress a number on his memory.

He stood still a long while, surveying the hillside. In his eyes was a curiosity, new-aroused and burning. There was an exultance about his bearing and a keenness like that of a hunting animal catching the fresh scent of game.

He moved down the stream a few steps and took a second panful of dirt.

Again came the careful washing, the jealous herding of the golden specks, and the wantonness with which he sent them flying into the stream.

'Five,' he muttered, and repeated, 'five.'

He could not forbear another survey of the hill before filling the pan farther down the stream. His golden herds diminished. 'Four, three, two, two, one,' were his memory tabulations as he moved down the stream. When but one speck of gold rewarded his washing, he stopped and built a fire of dry twigs. Into this he thrust the gold-pan and burned it till it was blue-black. He held up the pan and examined it critically. Then he nodded approbation. Against such a colour-background he could defy the tiniest yellow speck to elude him.

Still moving down the stream, he panned again. A single speck was his reward. A third pan contained no gold at all. Not satisfied with this, he panned three times again, taking his shovels of dirt within a foot of one another. Each pan proved empty of gold, and the fact, instead of discouraging him, seemed to give him satisfaction. His elation increased with each barren washing, until he arose, exclaiming jubilantly: 'If it ain't the real thing, may God knock off my head with sour apples!'

Returning to where he had started operations, he began to pan up the stream. At first his golden herds increased – increased prodigiously. 'Fourteen, eighteen, twenty-one, twenty-six,' ran his memory tabulations. Just above the pool he struck his richest pan – thirty-five colours.

'Almost enough to save,' he remarked regretfully as he allowed the water to sweep them away.

The sun climbed to the top of the sky. The man worked on. Pan by pan, he went up the stream, the tally of results steadily decreasing.

'It's just booful, the way it peters out,' he exulted when a shovelful of dirt contained no more than a single speck of gold. And when no specks at all were found in several pans, he straightened up and favoured the hillside with a confident glance.

'Ah, ha! Mr Pocket!' he cried out, as though to an auditor hidden somewhere above him beneath the surface of the slope. 'Ah, ha! Mr Pocket! I'm a-comin', I'm a-comin', an' I'm shorely gwine to get yer! You heah me, Mr Pocket? I'm gwine to get yer as shore as punkins ain't cauliflowers!'

He turned and flung a measuring glance at the sun poised above him in the azure of the cloudless sky. Then he went down the canyon, following the line of shovel-holes he had made in filling the pans. He crossed the stream below the pool and disappeared through the green screen. There was little opportunity for the spirit of the place to return with its quietude and repose, for the man's voice, raised in ragtime song, still dominated the canyon with possession.

After a time, with a greater clashing of steel-shod feet on rock, he returned. The green screen was tremendously agitated. It surged back and forth in the throes of a struggle. There was a loud grating and clanging of metal. The man's voice leaped to a higher pitch and was sharp with imperativeness. A large body plunged and panted. There was a snapping and ripping and rending, and amid a shower of falling leaves a horse burst through the screen. On its back was a pack, and from this trailed broken vines and torn creepers. The animal gazed with astonished eyes at the scene into which it had been precipitated, then dropped its head to the grass and began contentedly to graze. A second horse scrambled into view, slipping once on the mossy rocks and regaining equilibrium when its hoofs sank into the yielding surface of the meadow.

It was riderless, though on its back was a high-horned Mexican saddle, scarred and discoloured by long usage.

The man brought up the rear. He threw off pack and saddle, with an eye to camp location, and gave the animals their freedom to graze. He unpacked his food and got out frying-pan and coffee-pot. He gathered an armful of dry wood, and with a few stones made a place for his fire.

'My!' he said, 'but I've got an appetite. I could scoff iron-filings an' horseshoe nails an' thank you kindly, ma'am, for a second helpin'.'

He straightened up, and, while he reached for matches in the pocket of his overalls, his eyes travelled across the pool to the side-hill. His fingers had clutched the matchbox, but they relaxed their hold and the hand came out empty. The man wavered perceptibly. He looked at his preparations for cooking and he looked at the hill.

'Guess I'll take another whack at her,' he concluded, starting to cross the stream. 'They ain't no sense in it, I know,' he mumbled apologetically. 'But keepin' grub back an hour ain't go in' to hurt none, I reckon.'

A few feet back from his first line of test-pans he started a second line. The sun dropped down the western sky, the shadows lengthened, but the man worked on. He began a third line of test-pans. He was cross-cutting the hillside, line by line, as he ascended. The centre of each line produced the richest pans, while the ends came where no colours showed in the pan. And as he ascended the hillside the lines grew perceptibly shorter. The regularity with which their length diminished served to indicate that somewhere up the slope the last line would be so short as to have scarcely length at all, and that beyond could come only a point. The design was growing into an inverted V. The converging sides of this V marked the boundaries of the gold-bearing dirt.

The apex of the V was evidently the man's goal. Often he ran his eye along the converging sides and on up the hill, trying to divine the apex, the point where the gold-bearing dirt must cease. Here resided 'Mr Pocket' – for so the man familiarly addressed the imaginary point above him on the slope, crying out: 'Come down out o' that, Mr Pocket! Be right smart an' agreeable, an' come down!'

'All right,' he would add later, in a voice resigned to determination. 'All right, Mr Pocket. It's plain to me I got to come right up an' snatch you out bald-headed. An' I'll do it! I'll do it!' he would threaten still later.

Each pan he carried down to the water to wash, and as he went higher up the hill the pans grew richer, until he began to save the gold in an empty baking-powder can which he carried carelessly in his hip-pocket.

So engrossed was he in his toil that he did not notice the long twilight of oncoming night. It was not until he tried vainly to see the gold colours in the bottom of the pan that he realised the passage of time. He straightened up abruptly. An expression of whimsical wonderment and awe overspread his face as he drawled: 'Gosh darn my buttons! If I didn't plumb forget dinner!'

He stumbled across the stream in the darkness and lighted his long-delayed fire. Flapjacks and bacon and warmed-over beans constituted his supper. Then he smoked a pipe by the smouldering coals, listening to the night noises and watching the moonlight stream through the canyon. After that he unrolled his bed, took off his heavy shoes, and pulled the blankets up to his chin. His face showed white in the moonlight, like the face of a corpse. But it was a corpse that knew its resurrection, for the man rose suddenly on one elbow and gazed across at his hillside.

'Good-night, Mr Pocket,' he called sleepily. 'Good-night.'

He slept through the early grey of morning until the direct rays of the sun smote his closed eyelids, when he awoke with a start and looked about him until he had established the continuity of his existence and identified his present self with the days previously lived.

To dress, he had merely to buckle on his shoes. He glanced at his fireplace and at his hillside, wavered, but fought down the temptation and started the fire.

'Keep yer shirt on, Bill; keep yer shirt on,' he admonished himself. 'What's the good of rushin'? No use in gettin' all het up an' sweaty. Mr Pocket'll wait for you. He ain't a-runnin' away before you can get your breakfast. Now, what you want, Bill, is something fresh in yer bill o' fare. So it's up to you to go an' get it.'

He cut a short pole at the water's edge and drew from one of his pockets a bit of line and a draggled fly that had once been a royal coachman.

'Mebbe they'll bite in the early morning,' he muttered, as he made his first cast into the pool. And a moment later he was gleefully crying: 'What'd I tell you, eh? What'd I tell you?'

He had no reel, nor any inclination to waste time, so by main strength, and swiftly, he drew out of the water a flashing ten-inch trout. Three more, caught in rapid succession, furnished his breakfast. When he came to the stepping-stones on his way to his hillside, he was struck by a sudden thought, and paused.

'I'd just better take a hike downstream a ways,' he said. 'There's no tellin' who may be snoopin' around.'

But he crossed over on the stones, and with a, 'I really oughter take that hike,' the need of the precaution passed out of his mind and he fell to work.

At nightfall he straightened up. The small of his back was stiff from stooping toil, and as he put his hand behind him to soothe the protesting muscles, he said: 'Now what d'ye think of that? I clean forgot my dinner again! If I don't watch out, I'll sure be degeneratin' into a two-meal-a-day crank.'

'Pockets is the hangedest things I ever see for makin' a man absent-minded,' he communed that night, as he crawled into his blankets. Nor did he forget to call up the hillside, 'Good-night, Mr Pocket! Good-night!'

Rising with the sun, and snatching a hasty breakfast, he was early at work. A fever seemed to be growing in him, nor did the increasing richness of the test-pans allay this fever. There was a flush in his cheek other than that made by the heat of the sun, and he was oblivious to fatigue and the passage of time. When he filled a pan with dirt, he ran down the hill to wash it; nor could he forbear running up the hill again, panting and stumbling profanely, to refill the pan.

He was now a hundred yards from the water, and the inverted V was assuming definite proportions. The width of the pay-dirt steadily decreased, and the man extended in his mind's eye the sides of the V to their meeting place far up the hill. This was his goal, the apex of the V, and he panned many times to locate it.

'Just about two yards above that manzanita bush an' a yard to the right,' he finally concluded.

Then the temptation seized him. 'As plain as the nose on your face,' he said, as he abandoned his laborious cross-cutting and climbed to the indicated apex. He filled a pan and carried it down the hill to wash. It contained no trace of gold. He dug deep, and he dug shallow, filling and washing a dozen pans, and was unrewarded even by the tiniest golden speck. He was enraged at having yielded to the temptation, and berated himself blasphemously and pridelessly. Then he went down the hill and took up the cross-cutting.

'Slow an' certain, Bill; slow an' certain,' he crooned. 'Short-cuts to fortune ain't in your line, an' it's about time you knew it. Get wise, Bill; get wise. Slow an' certain's the only hand you can play; so go to it, an' keep to it, too.'

As the cross-cuts decreased, showing that the sides of the V were converging, the depth of the V increased. The gold-trace was dipping into the hill. It was only at thirty inches beneath the surface that he could get colours in his pan. The dirt he found at twenty-five inches from the surface, and at thirty-five inches yielded barren pans. At the base of the V, by the water's edge, he had found the gold colours at the grass roots. The higher he went up the hill, the deeper the gold dipped. To dig a hole three feet deep in order to get one test-pan was a task of no mean magnitude; while between the man and the apex intervened an untold number of such holes to be dug. 'An' there's no tellin' how much deeper it'll pitch,' he sighed, in a moment's pause, while his fingers soothed his aching back.

Feverish with desire, with aching back and stiffening muscles, with pick and shovel gouging and mauling the soft brown earth, the man toiled up the hill. Before him was the smooth slope, spangled with flowers and made sweet with their breath. Behind him was devastation. It looked like some terrible eruption breaking out on the smooth skin of the hill. His slow progress was like that of a slug, befouling beauty with a monstrous trail.

Though the dipping gold-trace increased the man's work, he found consolation in the increasing richness of the pans. Twenty cents, thirty cents, fifty cents, sixty cents, were the values of the gold found in the pans, and at nightfall he washed his banner pan, which gave him a dollar's worth of gold-dust from a shovelful of dirt.

'I'll just bet it's my luck to have some inquisitive one come buttin' in here on my pasture,' he mumbled sleepily that night as he pulled the blankets up to his chin.

Suddenly he sat upright. 'Bill!' he called sharply. 'Now, listen to me, Bill; d'ye hear! It's up to you, tomorrow mornin', to mosey round an' see what you can see. Understand? Tomorrow morning, an' don't you forget it!'

He yawned and glanced across at his side-hill. 'Good-night, Mr Pocket,' he called.

In the morning he stole a march on the sun, for he had finished breakfast when its first rays caught him, and he was climbing the wall of the canyon where it crumbled away and gave footing. From the outlook at the top he found himself in the midst of loneliness. As far as he could see, chain after chain of mountains heaved themselves into his vision. To the east his eyes, leaping the miles between range and range and between many ranges, brought up at last against the white-peaked Sierras – the main crest, where the backbone of the Western world reared itself against the sky. To the north and south he could see more distinctly the cross-systems that broke through the main trend of the sea of mountains. To the west the ranges fell away, one behind the other, diminishing and fading into the gentle foothills that, in turn, descended into the great valley which he could not see.

And in all that mighty sweep of earth he saw no sign of man nor of the handiwork of man – save only the torn bosom of the hillside at his feet. The man looked long and carefully. Once, far down his own canyon, he thought he saw in the air a faint hint of smoke. He looked again and decided that it was the purple haze of the hills made dark by a convolution of the canyon wall at its back.

'Hey, you, Mr Pocket!' he called down into the canyon. 'Stand out from under! I'm a-comin', Mr Pocket! I'm a-comin'!'

The heavy brogans on the man's feet made him appear clumsy-footed, but he swung down from the giddy height as lightly and airily as a mountain goat. A rock, turning under his foot on the edge of the precipice, did not disconcert him. He seemed to know the precise time required for the turn to culminate in disaster, and in the meantime he utilised the false footing itself for the momentary earth-contact necessary to carry him on into safety. Where the earth sloped so steeply that it was impossible to stand for a second upright, the man did not hesitate. His foot pressed the impossible surface for but a fraction of the fatal second and gave him the bound that carried him onward. Again, where even the fraction of a second's footing was out of the question, he would swing his body past by a moment's hand-grip on a jutting knob of rock, a crevice, or a precariously rooted shrub. At last, with a wild leap and yell, he exchanged the face of the wall for an earth-slide and finished the descent in the midst of several tons of sliding earth and gravel.

His first pan of the morning washed out over two dollars in coarse gold. It was from the centre of the V. To either side the diminution in the values of the pans was swift. His lines of cross-cutting holes were growing very short. The converging sides of the inverted V were only a few yards apart. Their meeting-point was only a few yards above him. But the pay-streak was dipping deeper and deeper into the earth. By early afternoon he was sinking the test-holes five feet before the pans could show the gold-trace.

For that matter, the gold-trace had become something more than a trace; it was a placer mine in itself, and the man resolved to come back after he had found the pocket and work over the ground. But the increasing richness of the pans began to worry him. By late afternoon the worth of the pans had grown to three and four dollars. The man scratched his head perplexedly and looked a few feet up the hill at the manzanita bush that marked approximately the apex of the V. He nodded his head and said oracularly: 'It's one o' two things, Bill: one o' two things. Either Mr Pocket's spilled himself all out an' down the hill, or else Mr Pocket's so rich you maybe won't be able to carry him all away with you. And that'd be an awful shame, wouldn't it, now?' He chuckled at contemplation of so pleasant a dilemma.

Nightfall found him by the edge of the stream, his eyes wrestling with the gathering darkness over the washing of a five-dollar pan.

'Wisht I had an electric light to go on working,' he said.

He found sleep difficult that night. Many times he composed himself and closed his eyes for slumber to overtake him; but his blood pounded with too strong desire, and as many times his eyes opened and he murmured wearily, 'Wisht it was sun-up.'

Sleep came to him in the end, but his eyes were open with the first paling of the stars, and the grey of dawn caught him with breakfast finished and climbing the hillside in the direction of the secret abiding-place of Mr Pocket.

The first cross-cut the man made, there was space for only three holes, so narrow had become the pay-streak and so close was he to the fountainhead of the golden stream he had been following for four days.

'Be ca'm, Bill; be ca'm,' he admonished himself, as he broke ground for the final hole where the sides of the V had at last come together in a point.

'I've got the almighty cinch on you, Mr Pocket, an' you can't lose me,' he said many times as he sank the hole deeper and deeper.

Four feet, five feet, six feet, he dug his way down into the earth. The digging grew harder. His pick grated on broken rock. He examined the rock. 'Rotten quartz,' was his conclusion as, with the shovel, he cleared the bottom of the hole of loose dirt. He attacked the crumbling quartz with the pick, bursting the disintegrating rock asunder with every stroke.

He thrust his shovel into the loose mass. His eye caught a gleam of yellow. He dropped the shovel and squatted suddenly on his heels. As a farmer rubs the clinging earth from fresh-dug potatoes, so the man, a piece of rotten quartz held in both hands, rubbed the dirt away.

'Sufferin' Sardanopolis!' he cried. 'Lumps an' chunks of it! Lumps an' chunks of it!'

It was only half rock he held in his hand. The other half was virgin gold. He dropped it into his pan and examined another piece. Little yellow was to be seen, but with his strong fingers he crumbled the rotten quartz away till both hands were filled with glowing yellow. He rubbed the dirt away from fragment after fragment, tossing them into the gold-pan. It was a treasure-hole. So much had the quartz rotted away that there was less of it than there was of gold. Now and again he found a piece to which no rock clung – a piece that was all gold. A chunk, where the pick had laid open the heart of the gold, glittered like a handful of yellow jewels, and he cocked his head at it and slowly turned it around and over to observe the rich play of the light upon it.

'Talk about yer too-much-gold diggin's!' the man snorted contemptuously. 'Why, this diggin' 'd make it look like thirty cents. This diggin' is All Gold. An' right here an' now I name this yere canyon "All Gold Canyon", b' gosh!'

Still squatting on his heels, he continued examining the fragments and tossing them into the pan. Suddenly there came to him a premonition of danger. It seemed a shadow had fallen upon him. But there was no shadow. His heart had given a great jump up into his throat and was choking him. Then his blood slowly chilled and he felt the sweat of his shirt cold against his flesh.

He did not spring up nor look around. He did not move. He was considering the nature of the premonition he had received, trying to locate the source of the mysterious force that had warned him, striving to sense the imperative presence of the unseen thing that threatened him. There is an aura of things hostile, made manifest by messengers too refined for the senses to know; and this aura he felt, but knew not how he felt it. His was the feeling as when a cloud passes over the sun. It seemed that between him and life had passed something dark and smothering and menacing; a gloom, as it were, that swallowed up life and made for death – his death.

Every force of his being impelled him to spring up and confront the unseen danger, but his soul dominated the panic, and he remained squatting on his heels, in his hands a chunk of gold. He did not dare to look around, but he knew by now that there was something behind him and above him. He made believe to be interested in the gold in his hand. He examined it critically, turned it over and over, and rubbed the dirt from it. And all the time he knew that something behind him was looking at the gold over his shoulder.

Still feigning interest in the chunk of gold in his hand, he listened intently and he heard the breathing of the thing behind him. His eyes searched the ground in front of him for a weapon, but they saw only the uprooted gold, worthless to him now in his extremity. There was his pick, a handy weapon on occasion; but this was not such an occasion. The man realised his predicament. He was in a narrow hole that was seven feet deep. His head did not come to the surface of the ground. He was in a trap.

He remained squatting on his heels. He was quite cool and collected; but his mind, considering every factor, showed him only his helplessness. He continued rubbing the dirt from the quartz fragments and throwing the gold into the pan. There was nothing else for him to do. Yet he knew that he would have to rise up, sooner or later, and face the danger that breathed at his back. The minutes passed, and with the passage of each minute he knew that by so much he was nearer the time when he must stand up, or else – and his wet shirt went cold against his flesh again at the thought – or else he might receive death as he stooped there over his treasure.

Still he squatted on his heels, rubbing dirt from gold and debating in just what manner he should rise up. He might rise up with a rush and claw his way out of the hole to meet whatever threatened on the even footing above ground. Or he might rise up slowly and carelessly, and feign casually to discover the thing that breathed at his back. His instinct and every fighting fibre of his body favoured the mad, clawing rush to the surface. His intellect, and the craft thereof, favoured the slow and cautious meeting with the thing that menaced and which he could not see. And while he debated, a loud, crashing noise burst on his ear. At the same instant he received a stunning blow on the left side of the back, and from the point of impact felt a rush of flame through his flesh. He sprang up in the air, but halfway to his feet collapsed. His body crumpled in like a leaf withered in sudden heat, and he came down, his chest across his pan of gold, his face in the dirt and rock, his legs tangled and twisted because of the restricted space at the bottom of the hole. His legs twitched convulsively several times. His body was shaken as with a mighty ague. There was a slow expansion of the lungs, accompanied by a deep sigh. Then the air was slowly, very slowly, exhaled, and his body as slowly flattened itself down into inertness.

Above, revolver in hand, a man was peering down over the edge of the hole. He peered for a long time at the prone and motionless body beneath him. After a while the stranger sat down on the edge of the hole so that he could see into it, and rested the revolver on his knee. Reaching his hand into a pocket, he drew out a wisp of brown paper. Into this he dropped a few crumbs of tobacco. The combination became a cigarette, brown and squat, with the ends turned in. Not once did he take his eyes from the body at the bottom of the hole. He lighted the cigarette and drew its smoke into his lungs with a caressing intake of the breath. He smoked slowly. Once the cigarette went out and he relighted it. And all the while he studied the body beneath him.

In the end he tossed the cigarette stub away and rose to his feet. He moved to the edge of the hole. Spanning it, a hand resting on each edge, and with the revolver still in the right hand, he muscled his body down into the hole. While his feet were yet a yard from the bottom he released his hands and dropped down.

At the instant his feet struck bottom he saw the pocket-miner's arm leap out, and his own legs knew a swift, jerking grip that overthrew him. In the nature of the jump his revolver hand was above his head. Swiftly as the grip had flashed about his legs, just as swiftly he brought the revolver down. He was still in the air, his fall in process of completion, when he pulled the trigger. The explosion was deafening in the confined space. The smoke filled the hole so that he could see nothing. He struck the bottom on his back, and like a cat's the pocket-miner's body was on top of him. Even as the miner's body passed on top, the stranger crooked in his right arm to fire; and even in that instant the miner, with a quick thrust of elbow, struck his wrist. The muzzle was thrown up and the bullet thudded into the dirt of the side of the hole.

The next instant the stranger felt the miner's hand grip his wrist. The struggle was now for the revolver. Each man strove to turn it against the other's body. The smoke in the hole was clearing. The stranger, lying on his back, was beginning to see dimly. But suddenly he was blinded by a handful of dirt deliberately flung into his eyes by his antagonist. In that moment of shock his grip on the revolver was broken. In the next moment he felt a smashing darkness descend upon his brain, and in the midst of the darkness even the darkness ceased.

But the pocket-miner fired again and again, until the revolver was empty. Then he tossed it from him and, breathing heavily, sat down on the dead man's legs.

The miner was sobbing and struggling for breath. 'Measly skunk!' he panted; 'a-campin' on my trail an' lettin' me do the work, an' then shootin' me in the back!'

He was half crying from anger and exhaustion. He peered at the face of the dead man. It was sprinkled with loose dirt and gravel, and it was difficult to distinguish the features.

'Never laid eyes on him before,' the miner concluded his scrutiny. 'Just a common an' ordinary thief, hang him! An' he shot me in the back! He shot me in the back!'

He opened his shirt and felt himself, front and back, on his left side.

'Went clean through, and no harm done!' he cried jubilantly. 'I'll bet he aimed all right; but he drew the gun over when he pulled the trigger – the cur! But I fixed 'm! Oh, I fixed 'm!'

His fingers were investigating the bullet-hole in his side, and a shade of regret passed over his face. 'It's goin' to be stiffer 'n hell,' he said. 'An' it's up to me to get mended an' get out o' here.'

He crawled out of the hole and went down the hill to his camp. Half an hour later he returned, leading his packhorse. His open shirt disclosed the rude bandages with which he had dressed his wound. He was slow and awkward with his left-hand movements, but that did not prevent his using the arm.

The bight of the pack-rope under the dead man's shoulders enabled him to heave the body out of the hole. Then he set to work gathering up his gold. He worked steadily for several hours, pausing often to rest his stiffening shoulder and to exclaim: 'He shot me in the back, the measly skunk! He shot me in the back!'

When his treasure was quite cleaned up and wrapped securely into a number of blanket-covered parcels, he made an estimate of its value.

'Four hundred pounds, or I'm a Hottentot,' he concluded. 'Say two hundred in quartz an' dirt – that leaves two hundred pounds of gold. Bill! Wake up! Two hundred pounds of gold! Forty thousand dollars! An' it's yourn – all yourn!'

He scratched his head delightedly and his fingers blundered into an unfamiliar groove. They quested along it for several inches. It was a crease through his scalp where the second bullet had ploughed.

He walked angrily over to the dead man.

'You would, would you!' he bullied. 'You would, eh? Well, I fixed you good an' plenty, an' I'll give you decent burial, too. That's more 'n you'd have done for me.'

He dragged the body to the edge of the hole and toppled it in. It struck the bottom with a dull crash, on its side, the face twisted up to the light. The miner peered down at it.

'An' you shot me in the back!' he said accusingly.

With pick and shovel he filled the hole. Then he loaded the gold on his horse. It was too great a load for the animal, and when he had gained his camp he transferred part of it to his saddle-horse. Even so, he was compelled to abandon a portion of his outfit – pick and shovel and gold-pan, extra food and cooking utensils, and divers odds and ends.

The sun was at the zenith when the man forced the horses at the screen of vines and creepers. To climb the huge boulders the animals were compelled to uprear and struggle blindly through the tangled mass of vegetation. Once the saddle-horse fell heavily and the man removed the pack to get the animal on its feet. After it started on its way again the man thrust his head out from among the leaves and peered up at the hillside.

'The measly skunk!' he said, and disappeared.

There was a ripping and tearing of vines and boughs. The trees surged back and forth, marking the passage of the animals through the midst of them. There was a clashing of steel-shod hoofs on stone, and now and again a sharp cry of command. Then the voice of the man was raised in song:

> 'Tu'n around an' tu'n yo' face
> Untoe them sweet hills of grace
>   (D' pow'rs of sin yo' am scornin'!).
> Look about an' look aroun',
> Fling yo' sin-pack on d' groun'
>   (Yo' will meet wid d' Lord in d' mornin'!).'

The song grew faint and fainter, and through the silence crept back the spirit of the place. The stream once more drowsed and whispered; the hum of the mountain bees rose sleepily. Down through the perfume-weighted air fluttered the snowy fluffs of the cottonwoods. The butterflies drifted in and out among the trees, and over all blazed the quiet sunshine. Only remained the hoof-marks in the meadow and the torn hillside to mark the boisterous trail of the life that had broken the peace of the place and passed on.

TO BUILD A FIRE

JACK LONDON

DAY HAD BROKEN COLD AND GREY, exceedingly cold and grey, when the man turned aside from the main Yukon trail and climbed the high earth-bank, where a dim and little travelled trail led eastward through the fat spruce timberland. It was a steep bank, and he paused for breath at the top, excusing the act to himself by looking at his watch. It was nine o'clock. There was no sun nor hint of sun, though there was not a cloud in the sky. It was a clear day, and yet there seemed an intangible pall over the face of things, a subtle gloom that made the day dark, and that was due to the absence of sun. This fact did not worry the man. He was used to the lack of sun. It had been days since he had seen the sun, and he knew that a few more days must pass before that cheerful orb, due south, would just peep above the skyline and dip immediately from view.

The man flung a look back along the way he had come. The Yukon lay a mile wide and hidden under three feet of ice. On top of this ice were as many feet of snow. It was all pure white, rolling in gentle undulations where the ice-jams of the freeze-up had formed. North and south, as far as his eye could see, it was unbroken white, save for a dark hair-line that curved and twisted from around the spruce-covered island to the south, and that curved and twisted away into the north, where it disappeared behind another spruce-covered island. This dark hair-line was the trail – the main trail – that led south five hundred miles to the Chilcoot Pass, Dyea, and salt water; and that led north seventy miles to Dawson, and still on to the north a thousand miles to Nulato, and finally to St Michael on the Bering Sea, a thousand miles and half a thousand more.

But all this – the mysterious, far-reaching hairline trail, the absence of sun from the sky, the tremendous cold and the strangeness and weirdness of it all – made no impression on the man. It was not because he was long used to it. He was a newcomer in the land, a *chechaquo*, and this was his first winter. The trouble with him was that he was without imagination. He was quick and alert in the things of life, but only in the things and not in the significances. Fifty degrees below zero meant eighty odd degrees of frost. Such fact impressed him as being cold and uncomfortable, and that was all. It did not lead him to meditate upon his frailty as a creature of temperature, and upon man's frailty in general, able only to live within certain narrow limits of heat and cold; and from there on it did not lead him to the conjectural field of immortality and man's place in the universe. Fifty degrees below zero stood for a bite of frost that hurt and that must be guarded against by the use of mittens, ear-flaps, warm moccasins and thick socks. Fifty degrees below zero was to him just precisely fifty degrees below zero. That there should be anything more to it than that was a thought that never entered his head.

As he turned to go on, he spat speculatively. There was a sharp, explosive crackle that startled him. He spat again. And again, in the air, before it could fall to the snow, the spittle crackled. He knew that at fifty below spittle crackled on the snow, but this spittle had crackled in the air. Undoubtedly it was colder than fifty below – how much colder he did not know. But the temperature did not matter. He was bound for the old claim on the left fork of Henderson Creek, where the boys were already. They had come over across the divide from the Indian Creek country, while he had come the roundabout way to take a look at the possibilities of getting out logs in the spring from the islands in the Yukon. He would be in to camp by six o'clock; a bit after dark, it was true, but the boys would be there, a fire would be going, and a hot supper would be ready. As for lunch, he pressed his hand against the protruding bundle under his jacket. It was also under his shirt, wrapped up in a handkerchief and lying against the naked skin. It was the only way to keep the biscuits from freezing. He smiled agreeably to himself as he thought of those biscuits, each cut open and sopped in bacon grease, and each enclosing a generous slice of fried bacon.

He plunged in among the big spruce trees. The trail was faint. A foot of snow had fallen since the last sled had passed over, and he was glad he was without a sled, travelling light. In fact, he carried nothing but the lunch wrapped in the handkerchief. He was surprised, however, at the cold. It certainly was cold, he concluded, as he rubbed his numbed nose and cheek-bones with his mittened hand. He was a warm-whiskered man, but the hair on his face did not protect the high cheek-bones and the eager nose that thrust itself aggressively into the frosty air.

At the man's heels trotted a dog, a big native husky, the proper wolf-dog, grey-coated and without any visible or temperamental difference from its brother, the wild wolf. The animal was depressed by the tremendous cold. It knew that it was no time for travelling. Its instinct told it a truer tale than was told to the man by the man's judgement. In reality, it was not merely colder than fifty below zero; it was colder than sixty below, than seventy below. It was seventy-five below zero. Since the freezing-point is thirty-two above zero, it meant that one hundred and seven degrees of frost obtained. The dog did not know anything about thermometers. Possibly in its brain there was no sharp consciousness of a condition of very cold such as was in the man's brain. But the brute had its instinct. It experienced a vague but menacing apprehension that subdued it and made it slink along at the man's heels, and that made it question eagerly every unwonted movement of the man as if expecting him to go into camp or to seek shelter somewhere and build a fire. The dog had learned fire, and it wanted fire, or else to burrow under the snow and cuddle its warmth away from the air.

The frozen moisture of its breathing had settled on its fur in a fine powder of frost, and especially were its jowls, muzzle and eyelashes whitened by its crystalled breath. The man's red beard and moustache were likewise frosted, but more solidly, the deposit taking the form of ice and increasing with every warm, moist breath he exhaled. Also, the man was chewing tobacco, and the muzzle of ice held his lips so rigidly that he was unable to clear his chin when he expelled the juice. The result was that a crystal beard of the colour and solidity of amber was increasing its length on his chin. If he fell down it would shatter itself, like glass, into brittle fragments. But he did not mind the appendage. It was the penalty all tobacco-chewers paid in that country, and he had been out before in two cold snaps. They had not been so cold as this, he knew, but by the spirit thermometer at Sixty Mile he knew they had been registered at fifty below and at fifty-five.

He held on through the level stretch of woods for several miles, crossed a wide flat of nigger-heads, and dropped down a bank to the frozen bed of a small stream. This was Henderson Creek, and he knew he was ten miles from the forks. He looked at his watch. It was ten o'clock. He was making four miles an hour, and he calculated that he would arrive at the forks at half-past twelve. He decided to celebrate that event by eating his lunch there.

The dog dropped in again at his heels, with a tail drooping dis-couragement, as the man swung along the creek-bed. The furrow of the old sled-trail was plainly visible, but a dozen inches of snow covered the marks of the last runners. In a month no man had come up or down that silent creek. The man held steadily on. He was not much given to thinking, and just then particularly he had nothing to think about save that he would eat lunch at the forks and that at six o'clock he would be in camp with the boys. There was nobody to talk to and, had there been, speech would have been impossible because of the ice-muzzle on his mouth. So he continued monotonously to chew tobacco and to increase the length of his amber beard.

Once in a while the thought reiterated itself that it was very cold and that he had never experienced such cold. As he walked along he rubbed his cheek-bones and nose with the back of his mittened hand. He did this automatically, now and again changing hands. But rub as he would, the instant he stopped his cheek-bones went numb, and the following instant the end of his nose went numb. He was sure to frost his cheeks; he knew that, and experienced a pang of regret that he had not devised a nose-strap of the sort Bud wore in cold snaps. Such a strap passed across the cheeks, as well, and saved them. But it didn't matter much, after all. What were frosted cheeks? A bit painful, that was all; they were never serious.

Empty as the man's mind was of thoughts, he was keenly observant, and he noticed the changes in the creek, the curves and bends and timber-jams, and always he sharply noted where he placed his feet. Once, coming around a bend, he shied abruptly, like a startled horse, curved away from the place where he had been walking, and retreated several paces back along the trail. The creek he knew was frozen clear to the bottom – no creek could contain water in that arctic winter – but he knew also that there were springs that bubbled out from the hillsides and ran along under the snow and on top of the ice of the creek. He knew that the coldest snaps never froze these springs, and he knew likewise their danger. They were traps. They hid pools of water under the snow that might be three inches deep, or three feet. Sometimes a skin of ice half an inch thick covered them, and in turn was covered by the snow. Sometimes there were alternate layers of water and ice-skin, so that when a man broke through he kept on breaking through for a while, sometimes wetting himself to the waist.

That was why he had shied in such panic. He had felt the give under his feet and heard the crackle of a snow-hidden ice-skin. And to get his feet wet in such a temperature meant trouble and danger. At the very least it meant delay, for he would be forced to stop and build a fire, and under its protection to bare his feet while he dried his socks and moccasins. He stood and studied the creek-bed and its banks, and decided that the flow of water came from the right. He reflected awhile, rubbing his nose and cheeks, then skirted to the left, stepping gingerly and testing the footing for each step. Once clear of the danger, he took a fresh chew of tobacco and swung along at his four-mile gait.

In the course of the next two hours he came upon several similar traps. Usually the snow above the hidden pools had a sunken, candied appearance that advertised the danger. Once again, however, he had a close call; and once, suspecting danger, he compelled the dog to go on in front. The dog did not want to go. It hung back until the man shoved it forward, and then it went quickly across the white, unbroken surface. Suddenly it broke through, floundered to one side, and got away to firmer footing. It had wet its forefeet and legs, and almost immediately the water that clung to them turned to ice. It made quick efforts to lick the ice off its legs, then dropped down in the snow and began to bite out the ice that had formed between the toes. This was a matter of instinct. To permit the ice to remain would mean sore feet. It did not know this. It merely obeyed the mysterious prompting that arose from the deep crypts of its being. But the man knew, having achieved a judgement on the subject, and he removed the mitten from his right hand and helped tear out the ice-particles. He did not expose his fingers more than a minute, and was astonished at the swift numbness that smote them. It certainly was cold. He pulled on the mitten hastily, and beat the hand savagely across his chest.

At twelve o'clock the day was at its brightest. Yet the sun was too far south on its winter journey to clear the horizon. The bulge of the earth intervened between it and Henderson Creek, where the man walked under a clear sky at noon and cast no shadow. At half-past twelve, to the minute, he arrived at the forks of the creek. He was pleased at the speed he had made. If he kept it up, he would certainly be with the boys by six. He unbuttoned his jacket and shirt and drew forth his lunch. The action consumed no more than a quarter of a minute, yet in that brief moment the numbness laid hold of the exposed fingers. He did not put the mitten on, but, instead, struck the fingers a dozen sharp smashes against his leg. Then he sat down on a snow-covered log to eat. The sting that followed upon the striking of his fingers against his leg ceased so quickly that he was startled, he had had no chance to take a bite of biscuit. He struck the fingers repeatedly and returned them to the mitten, baring the other hand for the purpose of eating. He tried to take a mouthful, but the ice-muzzle prevented it. He had forgotten to build a fire and thaw out. He chuckled at his foolishness, and as he chuckled he noted the numbness creeping into the exposed fingers. Also, he noted that the stinging which had first come to his toes when he sat down was already passing away. He wondered whether the toes were warm or numbed. He moved them inside the moccasins and decided that they were numbed.

He pulled the mitten on hurriedly and stood up. He was a bit frightened. He stamped up and down until the stinging returned into the feet. It certainly was cold, was his thought. That man from Sulphur Creek had spoken the truth when telling how cold it sometimes got in the country. And he had laughed at him at the time! That showed one must not be too sure of things. There was no mistake about it, it was cold. He strode up and down, stamping his feet and threshing his arms, until reassured by the returning warmth. Then he got out matches and proceeded to make a fire. From the undergrowth, where high water of the previous spring had lodged a supply of seasoned twigs, he got his firewood. Working carefully from a small beginning, he soon had a roaring fire, over which he thawed the ice from his face and in the protection of which he ate his biscuits. For the moment the cold of space was outwitted. The dog took satisfaction in the fire, stretching out close enough for warmth and far enough away to escape being singed.

When the man had finished, he filled his pipe and took his comfortable time over a smoke. Then he pulled on his mittens, settled the ear-flaps of his cap firmly about his ears, and took the creek trail up the left fork. The dog was disappointed and yearned back toward the fire. This man did not know cold. Possibly all the generations of his ancestry had been ignorant of cold, of real cold, of cold one hundred and seven degrees below freezing-point. But the dog knew; all its ancestry knew, and it had inherited the knowledge. And it knew that it was not good to walk abroad in such fearful cold. It was the time to lie snug in a hole in the snow and wait for a curtain of cloud to be drawn across the face of outer space whence this cold came. On the other hand, there was keen intimacy between the dog and the man. The one was the toil-slave of the other, and the only caresses it had ever received were the caresses of the whiplash and of harsh and menacing throat-sounds that threatened the whiplash. So the dog made no effort to communicate its apprehension to the man. It was not concerned in the welfare of the man; it was for its own sake that it yearned back toward the fire. But the man whistled, and spoke to it with the sound of whiplashes, and the dog swung in at the man's heels and followed after.

The man took a chew of tobacco and proceeded to start a new amber beard. Also, his moist breath quickly powdered with white his moustache, eyebrows and lashes. There did not seem to be so many springs on the left fork of the Henderson, and for half an hour the man saw no signs of any. And then it happened. At a place where there were no signs, where the soft, unbroken snow seemed to advertise solidity beneath, the man broke through. It was not deep. He wetted himself halfway to the knees before he floundered out to the firm crust.

He was angry, and cursed his luck aloud. He had hoped to get into camp with the boys at six o'clock, and this would delay him an hour, for he would have to build a fire and dry out his foot-gear. This was imperative at that low temperature – he knew that much; and he turned aside to the bank, which he climbed. On top, tangled in the underbrush about the trunks of several small spruce trees, was a high-water deposit of dry firewood – sticks and twigs principally, but also larger portions of seasoned branches and fine, dry, last-year's grasses. He threw down several large pieces on top of the snow. This served for a foundation and prevented the young flame from drowning itself in the snow it otherwise would melt. The flame he got by touching a match to a small shred of birch-bark that he took from his pocket. This burned even more readily than paper. Placing it on the foundation, he fed the young flame with wisps of dry grass and with the tiniest dry twigs.

He worked slowly and carefully, keenly aware of his danger. Gradually, as the flame grew stronger, he increased the size of the twigs with which he fed it. He squatted in the snow, pulling the twigs out from their entanglement in the brush and feeding directly to the flame. He knew there must be no failure. When it is seventy-five below zero, a man must not fail in his first attempt to build a fire – that is, if his feet are wet. If his feet are dry, and he fails, he can run along the trail for half a mile and restore his circulation. But the circulation of wet and freezing feet cannot be restored by running when it is seventy-five below. No matter how fast he runs, the wet feet will freeze the harder.

All this the man knew. The old-timer on Sulphur Creek had told him about it the previous fall, and now he was appreciating the advice. Already all sensation had gone out of his feet. To build the fire he had been forced to remove his mittens, and the fingers had quickly gone numb. His pace of four miles an hour had kept his heart pumping blood to the surface of his body and to all the extremities. But the instant he stopped, the action of the pump eased down. The cold of space smote the unprotected tip of the planet, and he, being on that unprotected tip, received the full force of the blow. The blood of his body recoiled before it. The blood was alive, like the dog, and like the dog it wanted to hide away and cover itself up from the fearful cold. So long as he walked four miles an hour, he pumped that blood, willy-nilly, to the surface; but now it ebbed away and sank down into the recesses of his body. The extremities were the first to feel its absence. His wet feet froze the faster, and his exposed fingers numbed the faster, though they had not yet begun to freeze. Nose and cheeks were already freezing, while the skin of all his body chilled as it lost its blood.

But he was safe. Toes and nose and cheeks would be only touched by the frost, for the fire was beginning to burn with strength. He was feeding it with twigs the size of his finger. In another minute he would be able to feed it with branches the size of his wrist, and then he could remove his wet foot-gear, and, while it dried, he could keep his naked feet warm by the fire, rubbing them at first, of course, with snow. The fire was a success. He was safe. He remembered the advice of the old-timer on Sulphur Creek, and smiled. The old-timer had been very serious in laying down the law that no man must travel alone in the Klondike after fifty below. Well, here he was; he had had the accident; he was alone; and he had saved himself. Those old-timers were rather womanish, some of them, he thought. All a man had to do was to keep his head, and he was all right. Any man who was a man could travel alone. But it was surprising, the rapidity with which his cheeks and nose were freezing. And he had not thought his fingers could go lifeless in so short a time. Lifeless they were, for he could scarcely make them move together to grip a twig, and they seemed remote from his body and from him. When he touched a twig, he had to look and see whether or not he had hold of it. The wires were pretty well down between him and his finger-ends.

All of which counted for little. There was the fire, snapping and crackling and promising life with every dancing flame. He started to untie his moccasins. They were coated with ice; the thick German socks were like sheaths of iron halfway to the knees; and the moccasin strings were like rods of steel all twisted and knotted as by some conflagration. For a moment he tugged with his numbed fingers, then, realising the folly of it, he drew his sheath-knife.

But before he could cut the strings, it happened. It was his own fault or, rather, his mistake. He should not have built the fire under the spruce tree. He should have built it in the open. But it had been easier to pull the twigs from the brush and drop them directly on the fire. Now the tree under which he had done this carried a weight of snow on its boughs. No wind had blown for weeks, and each bough was fully freighted. Each time he had pulled a twig he had communicated a slight agitation to the tree – an imperceptible agitation, so far as he was concerned, but an agitation sufficient to bring about the disaster. High up in the tree one bough capsized its load of snow. This fell on the boughs beneath, capsizing them. This process continued, spreading out and involving the whole tree. It grew like an avalanche, and it descended without warning upon the man and the fire, and the fire was blotted out! Where it had burned was a mantle of fresh and disordered snow.

The man was shocked. It was as though he had just heard his own sentence of death. For a moment he sat and stared at the spot where the fire had been. Then he grew very calm. Perhaps the old-timer on Sulphur Creek was right. If he had only had a trail-mate he would have been in no danger now. The trail-mate could have built the fire. Well, it was up to him to build the fire over again, and this second time there must be no failure. Even if he succeeded, he would most likely lose some toes. His feet must be badly frozen by now, and there would be some time before the second fire was ready.

Such were his thoughts, but he did not sit and think them. He was busy all the time they were passing through his mind; he made a new foundation for a fire, this time in the open, where no treacherous tree could blot it out. Next, he gathered dry grasses and tiny twigs from the high-water flotsam. He could not bring his fingers together to pull them out, but he was able to gather them by the handful. In this way he got many rotten twigs and bits of green moss that were undesirable, but it was the best he could do. He worked methodically, even collecting an armful of the larger branches to be used later when the fire gathered strength. And all the while the dog sat and watched him, a certain yearning wistfulness in its eyes, for it looked upon him as the fire-provider, and the fire was slow in coming.

When all was ready, the man reached in his pocket for a second piece of birch-bark. He knew the bark was there, and, though he could not feel it with his fingers, he could hear its crisp rustling as he fumbled for it. Try as he would, he could not clutch hold of it. And all the time, in his consciousness, was the knowledge that each instant his feet were freezing. This thought tended to put him in a panic, but he fought against it and kept calm. He pulled on his mittens with his teeth, and threshed his arms back and forth, beating his hands with all his might against his sides. He did this sitting down, and he stood up to do it; and all the while the dog sat in the snow, its wolf-brush of a tail curled around warmly over its forefeet, its sharp wolf-ears pricked forward intently as it watched the man. And the man as he beat and threshed with his arms and hands, felt a great surge of envy as he regarded the creature that was warm and secure in its natural covering.

After a time he was aware of the first far-away signals of sensation in his beaten fingers. The faint tingling grew stronger till it evolved into a stinging ache that was excruciating, but which the man hailed with satisfaction. He stripped the mitten from his right hand and fetched forth the birch-bark. The exposed fingers were quickly going numb again. Next he brought out his bunch of sulphur matches. But the tremendous cold had already driven the life out of his fingers. In his effort to separate one match from the others, the whole bunch fell in the snow. He tried to pick it out of the snow, but failed. The dead fingers could neither touch nor clutch. He was very careful. He drove the thought of his freezing feet, and nose, and cheeks, out of his mind, devoting his whole soul to the matches. He watched, using the sense of vision in place of that of touch, and when he saw his fingers on each side the bunch, he closed them – that is, he willed to close them, for the wires were drawn, and the fingers did not obey. He pulled the mitten on the right hand, and beat it fiercely against his knee. Then, with both mittened hands, he scooped the bunch of matches, along with much snow, into his lap. Yet he was no better off.

After some manipulation he managed to get the bunch between the heels of his mittened hands. In this fashion he carried it to his mouth. The ice crackled and snapped when by a violent effort he opened his mouth. He drew the lower jaw in, curled the upper lip out of the way, and scraped the bunch with his upper teeth in order to separate a match. He succeeded in getting one, which he dropped on his lap. He was no better off. He could not pick it up. Then he devised a way. He picked it up in his teeth and scratched it on his leg. Twenty times he scratched before he succeeded in lighting it. As it flamed he held it with his teeth to the birch-bark. But the burning brimstone went up his nostrils and into his lungs, causing him to cough spasmodically. The match fell into the snow and went out.

The old-timer on Sulphur Creek was right, he thought in the moment of controlled despair that ensued: after fifty below, a man should travel with a partner. He beat his hands, but failed in exciting any sensation. Suddenly he bared both hands, removing the mittens with his teeth. He caught the whole bunch between the heels of his hands. His arm-muscles not being frozen enabled him to press the hand-heels tightly against the matches. Then he scratched the bunch along his leg. It flared into flame, seventy sulphur matches at once! There was no wind to blow them out. He kept his head to one side to escape the strangling fumes, and held the blazing bunch to the birch-bark. As he so held it, he became aware of sensation in his hand. His flesh was burning. He could smell it. Deep down below the surface he could feel it. The sensation developed into pain that grew acute. And still he endured it, holding the flame of the matches clumsily to the bark that would not light readily because his own burning hands were in the way, absorbing most of the flame.

At last, when he could endure no more, he jerked his hands apart. The blazing matches fell sizzling into the snow, but the birch-bark was alight. He began laying dry grasses and the tiniest twigs on the flame. He could not pick and choose, for he had to lift the fuel between the heels of his hands. Small pieces of rotten wood and green moss clung to the twigs, and he bit them off as well as he could with his teeth. He cherished the flame carefully and awkwardly. It meant life, and it must not perish. The withdrawal of blood from the surface of his body now made him begin to shiver, and he grew more awkward. A large piece of green moss fell squarely on the little fire. He tried to poke it out with his fingers, but his shivering frame made him poke too far, and he disrupted the nucleus of the little fire, the burning grasses and tiny twigs separating and scattering. He tried to poke them together again, but in spite of the tenseness of the effort, his shivering got away with him, and the twigs were hopelessly scattered. Each twig gushed a puff of smoke and went out. The fire-provider had failed. As he looked apathetically about him, his eyes chanced on the dog, sitting across the ruins of the fire from him, in the snow, making restless, hunching movements, slightly lifting one forefoot and then the other, shifting its weight back and forth on them with wistful eagerness.

The sight of the dog put a wild idea into his head. He remembered the tale of the man, caught in a blizzard, who killed a steer and crawled inside the carcass, and so was saved. He would kill the dog and bury his hands in the warm body until the numbness went out of them. Then he could build another fire. He spoke to the dog, calling it to him; but in his voice was a strange note of fear that frightened the animal, who had never known the man to speak in such way before. Something was the matter, and its suspicious nature sensed danger – it knew not what danger, but somewhere, somehow, in its brain arose an apprehension of the man. It flattened its ears down at the sound of the man's voice, and its restless, hunching movements and the liftings and shiftings of its forefeet became more pronounced but it would not come to the man. He got on his hands and knees and crawled toward the dog. This unusual posture again excited suspicion, and the animal sidled mincingly away.

The man sat up in the snow for a moment and struggled for calmness. Then he pulled on his mittens, by means of his teeth, and got upon his feet. He glanced down at first in order to assure himself that he was really standing up, for the absence of sensation in his feet left him unrelated to the earth. His erect position in itself started to drive the webs of suspicion from the dog's mind; and when he spoke peremptorily, with the sound of whiplashes in his voice, the dog rendered its customary allegiance and came to him. As it came within reaching distance, the man lost his control. His arms flashed out to the dog, and he experienced genuine surprise when he discovered that his hands could not clutch, that there was neither bend nor feeling in the fingers. He had forgotten for the moment that they were frozen and that they were freezing more and more. All this happened quickly, and before the animal could get away, he encircled its body with his arms. He sat down in the snow, and in this fashion held the dog, while it snarled and whined and struggled.

But it was all he could do, hold its body encircled in his arms and sit there. He realised that he could not kill the dog. There was no way to do it. With his helpless hands he could neither draw nor hold his sheath-knife nor throttle the animal. He released it, and it plunged wildly away, with tail between its legs, and still snarling. It halted forty feet away and surveyed him curiously, with ears sharply pricked forward. The man looked down at his hands in order to locate them, and found them hanging on the ends of his arms. It struck him as curious that he should have to use his eyes in order to find out where his hands were. He began threshing his arms back and forth, beating the mittened hands against his sides. He did this for five minutes, violently, and his heart pumped enough blood up to the surface to put a stop to his shivering. But no sensation was aroused in the hands. He had an impression that they hung like weights on the ends of his arms, but when he tried to run the impression down, he could not find it.

A certain fear of death, dull and oppressive, came to him. This fear quickly became poignant as he realised that it was no longer a mere matter of freezing his fingers and toes, even losing his hands and feet, but that it was a matter of life and death with the chances against him. This threw him into a panic, and he turned and ran up the creek-bed along the old, dim trail. The dog joined in behind and kept up with him. He ran blindly, without intention, in fear such as he had never known in his life.

Slowly, as he ploughed and floundered through the snow, he began to see things again – the banks of the creek, the old timber-jams, the leafless aspens and the sky. The running made him feel better. He did not shiver. Maybe, if he ran on, his feet would thaw out; and, anyway, if he ran far enough, he would reach camp and the boys. Without doubt he would lose some fingers and toes and some of his face; but the boys would take care of him, and save the rest of him when he got there. And at the same time there was another thought in his mind that said he would never get to the camp and the boys; that it was too many miles away, that the freezing had too great a start on him, and that he would soon be stiff and dead. This thought he kept in the background and refused to consider. Sometimes it pushed itself forward and demanded to be heard, but he thrust it back and strove to think of other things.

It struck him as curious that he could run at all on feet so frozen that he could not feel them when they struck the earth and took the weight of his body. He seemed to himself to skim along above the surface and to have no connection with the earth. Somewhere he had once seen a winged Mercury, and he wondered if Mercury felt as he felt when skimming over the earth.

His theory of running until he reached camp and the boys had one flaw in it: he lacked the endurance. Several times he stumbled, and finally he tottered, crumpled up and fell. When he tried to rise, he failed. He must sit and rest, he decided, and next time he would merely walk and keep on going. As he sat and regained his breath, he noted that he was feeling quite warm and comfortable. He was not shivering, and it even seemed that a warm glow had come to his chest and trunk. And yet, when he touched his nose or cheeks, there was no sensation. Running would not thaw them out. Nor would it thaw out his hands and feet. Then the thought came to him that the frozen portions of his body must be extending. He tried to keep this thought down, to forget it, to think of something else; he was aware of the panicky feeling that it caused, and he was afraid of the panic. But the thought asserted itself, and persisted, until it produced a vision of his body totally frozen. This was too much, and he made another wild run along the trail. Once he slowed down to a walk, but the thought of the freezing extending itself made him run again.

And all the time the dog ran with him, at his heels. When he fell down a second time, it curled its tail over its forefeet and sat in front of him, facing him, curiously eager and intent. The warmth and security of the animal angered him, and he cursed it till it flattened down its ears appeasingly. This time the shivering came more quickly upon the man. He was losing in his battle with the frost. It was creeping into his body from all sides. The thought of it drove him on, but he ran no more than a hundred feet before he staggered and pitched headlong. It was his last panic. When he had recovered his breath and control, he sat up and entertained in his mind the conception of meeting death with dignity. However, the conception did not come to him in such terms. His idea of it was that he had been making a fool of himself, running around like a chicken with its head cut off – such was the simile that occurred to him. Well, he was bound to freeze anyway, and he might as well take it decently. With this new-found peace of mind came the first glimmerings of drowsiness. A good idea, he thought, to sleep off to death. It was like taking an anaesthetic. Freezing was not so bad as people thought. There were lots worse ways to die.

He pictured the boys finding his body next day. Suddenly he found himself with them, coming along the trail and looking for himself. And, still with them, he came around a turn in the trail and found himself lying in the snow. He did not belong with himself any more, for even then he was out of himself, standing with the boys and looking at himself in the snow. It certainly was cold, was his thought. When he got back to the States he could tell the folks what real cold was. He drifted on from this to a vision of the old-timer on Sulphur Creek. He could see him quite clearly, warm and comfortable, and smoking a pipe.

'You were right, old hoss; you were right,' the man mumbled to the old-timer of Sulphur Creek.

Then the man drowsed off into what seemed to him the most comfortable and satisfying sleep he had ever known. The dog sat facing him and waiting. The brief day drew to a close in a long, slow twilight. There were no signs of a fire to be made, and, besides, never in the dog's experience had it known a man to sit like that in the snow and make no fire. As the twilight drew on, its eager yearning for the fire mastered it, and with a great lifting and shifting of forefeet, it whined softly, then flattened its ears down in anticipation of being chidden by the man. But the man remained silent. Later, the dog whined loudly. And still later it crept close to the man and caught the scent of death. This made the animal bristle and back away. A little longer it delayed, howling under the stars that leaped and danced and shone brightly in the cold sky. Then it turned and trotted up the trail in the direction of the camp it knew, where were the other food-providers and fire-providers.

IN A FAR COUNTRY

JACK LONDON

W HEN A MAN JOURNEYS into a far country, he must be prepared to forget many of the things he has learned, and to acquire such customs as are inherent with existence in the new land; he must abandon the old ideals and the old gods, and oftentimes he must reverse the very codes by which his conduct has hitherto been shaped. To those who have the protean faculty of adaptability, the novelty of such change may even be a source of pleasure; but to those who happen to be hardened to the ruts in which they were created, the pressure of the altered environment is unbearable, and they chafe in body and in spirit under the new restrictions which they do not understand. This chafing is bound to act and react, producing divers evils and leading to various misfortunes. It were better for the man who cannot fit himself to the new groove to return to his own country; if he delay too long, he will surely die.

The man who turns his back upon the comforts of an elder civilisation to face the savage youth, the primordial simplicity of the North, may estimate success at an inverse ratio to the quantity and quality of his hopelessly fixed habits. He will soon discover, if he be a fit candidate, that the material habits are the less important. The exchange of such things as a dainty menu for rough fare, of the stiff leather shoe for the soft, shapeless moccasin, of the feather bed for a couch in the snow, is after all a very easy matter. But his pinch will come in learning properly to shape his mind's attitude toward all things, and especially toward his fellow man. For the courtesies of ordinary life, he must substitute unselfishness, forbearance and tolerance. Thus, and thus only, can he gain that pearl of great price – true comradeship. He must not say "thank you"; he must mean it without opening his mouth, and prove it by responding in kind. In short, he must substitute the deed for the word, the spirit for the letter.

When the world rang with the tale of Arctic gold, and the lure of the North gripped the heartstrings of men, Carter Weatherbee threw up his snug clerkship, turned the half of his savings over to his wife, and with the remainder bought an outfit. There was no romance in his nature – the bondage of commerce had crushed all that; he was simply tired of the ceaseless grind, and wished to risk great hazards in view of corresponding returns. Like many another fool, disdaining the old trails used by the Northland pioneers for a score of years, he hurried to Edmonton in the spring of the year; and there, unluckily for his soul's welfare, he allied himself with a party of men.

There was nothing unusual about this party, except its plans. Even its goal, like that of all the other parties, was the Klondike. But the route it had mapped out to attain that goal took away the breath of the hardiest native, born and bred to the vicissitudes of the Northwest. Even Jacques Baptiste, born of a Chippewa woman and a renegade voyageur (having raised his first whimpers in a deerskin lodge north of the sixty-fifth parallel and had the same hushed by blissful sucks of raw tallow), was surprised. Though he sold his services to them and agreed to travel even to the never-opening ice, he shook his head ominously whenever his advice was asked.

Percy Cuthfert's evil star must have been in the ascendant, for he, too, joined this company of argonauts. He was an ordinary man, with a bank account as deep as his culture, which is saying a good deal. He had no reason to embark on such a venture – no reason in the world save that he suffered from an abnormal development of sentimentality. He mistook this for the true spirit of romance and adventure. Many another man has done the like, and made as fatal a mistake.

The first break-up of spring found the party following the ice-run of Elk River. It was an imposing fleet, for the outfit was large, and they were accompanied by a disreputable contingent of half-breed voyageurs with their women and children. Day in and day out, they laboured with the bateaux and canoes, fought mosquitoes and other kindred pests, or sweated and swore at the portages. Severe toil like this lays a man naked to the very roots of his soul, and ere Lake Athabasca was lost in the south, each member of the party had hoisted his true colours.

The two shirks and chronic grumblers were Carter Weatherbee and Percy Cuthfert. The whole party complained less of its aches and pains than did either of them. Not once did they volunteer for the thousand and one petty duties of the camp. A bucket of water to be brought, an extra armful of wood to be chopped, the dishes to be washed and wiped, a search to be made through the outfit for some suddenly indispensable article – and these two effete scions of civilisation discovered sprains or blisters requiring instant attention.

They were the first to turn in at night, with score of tasks yet undone; the last to turn out in the morning, when the start should be in readiness before the breakfast was begun. They were the first to fall to at mealtime, the last to have a hand in the cooking; the first to dive for a slim delicacy, the last to discover they had added to their own another man's share. If they toiled at the oars, they slyly cut the water at each stroke and allowed the boat's momentum to float up the blade. They thought nobody noticed; but their comrades swore under their breaths and grew to hate them, while Jacques Baptiste sneered openly and damned them from morning till night. But Jacques Baptiste was no gentleman.

At the Great Slave, Hudson Bay dogs were purchased, and the fleet sank to the guards with its added burden of dried fish and pemican. Then canoe and bateau answered to the swift current of the Mackenzie, and they plunged into the Great Barren Ground. Every likely-looking 'feeder' was prospected, but the elusive 'pay-dirt' danced ever to the north. At the Great Bear, overcome by the common dread of the Unknown Lands, their voyageurs began to desert, and Fort of Good Hope saw the last and bravest bending to the towlines as they bucked the current down which they had so treacherously glided.

Jacques Baptiste alone remained. Had he not sworn to travel even to the never-opening ice? The lying charts, compiled in main from hearsay, were now constantly consulted.

And they felt the need of hurry, for the sun had already passed its northern solstice and was leading the winter south again. Skirting the shores of the bay where the Mackenzie disembogues into the Arctic Ocean, they entered the mouth of the Little Peel River. Then began the arduous upstream toil, and the two Incapables fared worse than ever. Towline and pole, paddle and tumpline, rapids and portages – such tortures served to give the one a deep disgust for great hazards, and printed for the other a fiery text on the true romance of adventure. One day they waxed mutinous, and being vilely cursed by Jacques Baptiste, turned, as worms sometimes will. But the half-breed thrashed the twain, and sent them, bruised and bleeding, about their work. It was the first time either had been manhandled.

Abandoning their river craft at the headwaters of the Little Peel, they consumed the rest of the summer in the great portage over the Mackenzie watershed to the West Rat. This little stream fed the Porcupine, which in turn joined the Yukon where that mighty highway of the North counter-marches on the Arctic Circle.

But they had lost in the race with winter, and one day they tied their rafts to the thick eddy-ice and hurried their goods ashore. That night the river jammed and broke several times; the following morning it had fallen asleep for good. 'We can't be more'n four hundred miles from the Yukon,' concluded Sloper, multiplying his thumb nails by the scale of the map. The council, in which the two Incapables had whined to excellent disadvantage, was drawing to a close.

'Hudson Bay Post, long time ago. No use um now.' Jacques Baptiste's father had made the trip for the Fur Company in the old days, incidentally marking the trail with a couple of frozen toes.

'Sufferin' cracky!' cried another of the party. 'No whites?'

'Nary white,' Sloper sententiously affirmed; 'but it's only five hundred more up the Yukon to Dawson. Call it a rough thousand from here.'

Weatherbee and Cuthfert groaned in chorus.

'How long'll that take, Baptiste?'

The half-breed figured for a moment. 'Workum like hell, no man play out, ten – twenty – forty – fifty days. Um babies come' (designating the Incapables), 'no can tell. Mebbe when hell freeze over; mebbe not then.' The manufacture of snowshoes and moccasins ceased. Somebody called the name of an absent member, who came out of an ancient cabin at the edge of the campfire and joined them. The cabin was one of the many mysteries which lurk in the vast recesses of the North. Built when and by whom, no man could tell.

Two graves in the open, piled high with stones, perhaps contained the secret of those early wanderers. But whose hand had piled the stones? The moment had come. Jacques Baptiste paused in the fitting of a harness and pinned the struggling dog in the snow. The cook made mute protest for delay, threw a handful of bacon into a noisy pot of beans, then came to attention. Sloper rose to his feet. His body was a ludicrous contrast to the healthy physiques of the Incapables. Yellow and weak, fleeing from a South American fever-hole, he had not broken his flight across the zones, and was still able to toil with men. His weight was probably ninety pounds, with the heavy hunting knife thrown in, and his grizzled hair told of a prime which had ceased to be. The fresh young muscles of either Weatherbee or Cuthfert were equal to ten times the endeavour of his; yet he could walk them into the earth in a day's journey. And all this day he had whipped his stronger comrades into venturing a thousand miles of the stiffest hardship man can conceive. He was the incarnation of the unrest of his race, and the old Teutonic stubbornness, dashed with the quick grasp and action of the Yankee, held the flesh in the bondage of the spirit.

'All those in favour of going on with the dogs as soon as the ice sets, say ay.'

'Ay!' rang out eight voices – voices destined to string a trail of oaths along many a hundred miles of pain.

'Contrary minded?'

'No!' For the first time the Incapables were united without some compromise of personal interests.

'And what are you going to do about it?' Weatherbee added belligerently.

'Majority rule! Majority rule!' clamoured the rest of the party.

'I know the expedition is liable to fall through if you don't come,' Sloper replied sweetly; 'but I guess, if we try real hard, we can manage to do without you. What do you say, boys?' The sentiment was cheered to the echo.

'But I say, you know,' Cuthfert ventured apprehensively; 'what's a chap like me to do?'

'Ain't you coming with us.'

'No–o.'

'Then do as you damn well please. We won't have nothing to say.'

'Kind o' calkilate yuh might settle it with that canoodlin' pardner of yourn,' suggested a heavy-going Westerner from the Dakotas, at the same time pointing out Weatherbee. 'He'll be shore to ask yuh what yur a-goin' to do when it comes to cookin' an' gatherin' the wood.'

'Then we'll consider it all arranged,' concluded Sloper. 'We'll pull out tomorrow, if we camp within five miles – just to get everything in running order and remember if we've forgotten anything.'

The sleds groaned by on their steel-shod runners, and the dogs strained low in the harnesses in which they were born to die.

Jacques Baptiste paused by the side of Sloper to get a last glimpse of the cabin. The smoke curled up pathetically from the Yukon stovepipe. The two Incapables were watching them from the doorway.

Sloper laid his hand on the other's shoulder.

'Jacques Baptiste, did you ever hear of the Kilkenny cats?' The half-breed shook his head.

'Well, my friend and good comrade, the Kilkenny cats fought till neither hide, nor hair, nor yowl, was left. You understand? – till nothing was left. Very good. Now, these two men don't like work. They'll be all alone in that cabin all winter – a mighty long, dark winter. Kilkenny cats – well?'

The Frenchman in Baptiste shrugged his shoulders, but the Indian in him was silent. Nevertheless, it was an eloquent shrug, pregnant with prophecy.

* * *

Things prospered in the little cabin at first. The rough badinage of their comrades had made Weatherbee and Cuthfert conscious of the mutual responsibility which had devolved upon them; besides, there was not so much work after all for two healthy men. And the removal of the cruel whiphand, or in other words the bulldozing half-breed, had brought with it a joyous reaction. At first, each strove to outdo the other, and they performed petty tasks with an unction which would have opened the eyes of their comrades who were now wearing out bodies and souls on the Long Trail.

All care was banished. The forest, which shouldered in upon them from three sides, was an inexhaustible woodyard. A few yards from their door slept the Porcupine, and a hole through its winter robe formed a bubbling spring of water, crystal clear and painfully cold. But they soon grew to find fault with even that. The hole would persist in freezing up, and thus gave them many a miserable hour of ice-chopping. The unknown builders of the cabin had extended the sidelogs so as to support a cache at the rear. In this was stored the bulk of the party's provisions.

Food there was, without stint, for three times the men who were fated to live upon it. But the most of it was the kind which built up brawn and sinew, but did not tickle the palate.

True, there was sugar in plenty for two ordinary men; but these two were little else than children. They early discovered the virtues of hot water judiciously saturated with sugar, and they prodigally swam their flapjacks and soaked their crusts in the rich, white syrup. Then coffee and tea, and especially the dried fruits, made disastrous inroads upon it. The first words they had were over the sugar question. And it is a really serious thing when two men, wholly dependent upon each other for company, begin to quarrel.

Weatherbee loved to discourse blatantly on politics, while Cuthfert, who had been prone to clip his coupons and let the commonwealth jog on as best it might, either ignored the subject or delivered himself of startling epigrams. But the clerk was too obtuse to appreciate the clever shaping of thought, and this waste of ammunition irritated Cuthfert. He had been used to blinding people by his brilliancy, and it worked him quite a hardship, this loss of an audience. He felt personally aggrieved and unconsciously held his muttonhead companion responsible for it.

Save existence, they had nothing in common – came in touch on no single point.

Weatherbee was a clerk who had known naught but clerking all his life; Cuthfert was a master of arts, a dabbler in oils, and had written not a little. The one was a lower-class man who considered himself a gentleman, and the other was a gentleman who knew himself to be such. From this it may be remarked that a man can be a gentleman without possessing the first instinct of true comradeship. The clerk was as sensuous as the other was aesthetic, and his love adventures, told at great length and chiefly coined from his imagination, affected the super-sensitive master of arts in the same way as so many whiffs of sewer gas. He deemed the clerk a filthy, uncultured brute, whose place was in the muck with the swine, and told him so; and he was reciprocally informed that he was a milk-and-water sissy and a cad. Weatherbee could not have defined 'cad' for his life; but it satisfied its purpose, which after all seems the main point in life.

Weatherbee flatted every third note and sang such songs as 'The Boston Burglar' and 'The Handsome Cabin Boy' for hours at a time, while Cuthfert wept with rage, till he could stand it no longer and fled into the outer cold. But there was no escape. The intense frost could not be endured for long at a time, and the little cabin crowded them – beds, stove, table and all – into a space of ten by twelve. The very presence of either became a personal affront to the other, and they lapsed into sullen silences which increased in length and strength as the days went by. Occasionally, the flash of an eye or the curl of a lip got the better of them, though they strove wholly to ignore each other during these mute periods.

And a great wonder sprang up in the breast of each as to how God had ever come to create the other.

With little to do, time became an intolerable burden to them. This naturally made them still lazier. They sank into a physical lethargy which there was no escaping, and which made them rebel at the performance of the smallest chore. One morning when it was his turn to cook the common breakfast, Weatherbee rolled out of his blankets, and to the snoring of his companion, lighted first the slush lamp and then the fire. The kettles were frozen hard, and there was no water in the cabin with which to wash. But he did not mind that. Waiting for it to thaw, he sliced the bacon and plunged into the hateful task of bread-making. Cuthfert had been slyly watching through his half-closed lids.

Consequently there was a scene, in which they fervently blessed each other, and agreed, henceforth, that each do his own cooking. A week later, Cuthfert neglected his morning ablutions, but none the less complacently ate the meal which he had cooked. Weatherbee grinned. After that the foolish custom of washing passed out of their lives.

As the sugar-pile and other little luxuries dwindled, they began to be afraid they were not getting their proper shares, and in order that they might not be robbed, they fell to gorging themselves. The luxuries suffered in this gluttonous contest, as did also the men.

In the absence of fresh vegetables and exercise, their blood became impoverished, and a loathsome, purplish rash crept over their bodies. Yet they refused to heed the warning.

Next, their muscles and joints began to swell, the flesh turning black, while their mouths, gums and lips took on the colour of rich cream. Instead of being drawn together by their misery, each gloated over the other's symptoms as the scurvy took its course.

They lost all regard for personal appearance, and for that matter, common decency. The cabin became a pigpen, and never once were the beds made or fresh pine boughs laid underneath. Yet they could not keep to their blankets, as they would have wished, for the frost was inexorable, and the fire box consumed much fuel. The hair of their heads and faces grew long and shaggy, while their garments would have disgusted a ragpicker. But they did not care. They were sick, and there was no one to see; besides, it was very painful to move about.

To all this was added a new trouble – the Fear of the North. This Fear was the joint child of the Great Cold and the Great Silence, and was born in the darkness of December, when the sun dipped below the horizon for good. It affected them according to their natures.

Weatherbee fell prey to the grosser superstitions and did his best to resurrect the spirits which slept in the forgotten graves. It was a fascinating thing, and in his dreams they came to him from out of the cold, and snuggled into his blankets, and told him of their toils and troubles ere they died. He shrank away from the clammy contact as they drew closer and twined their frozen limbs about him, and when they whispered in his ear of things to come, the cabin rang with his frightened shrieks. Cuthfert did not understand – for they no longer spoke – and when thus awakened he invariably grabbed for his revolver. Then he would sit up in bed, shivering nervously, with the weapon trained on the unconscious dreamer. Cuthfert deemed the man going mad, and so came to fear for his life.

His own malady assumed a less concrete form. The mysterious artisan who had laid the cabin, log by log, had pegged a wind-vane to the ridgepole. Cuthfert noticed it always pointed south, and one day, irritated by its steadfastness of purpose, he turned it toward the east. He watched eagerly, but never a breath came by to disturb it. Then he turned the vane to the north, swearing never again to touch it till the wind did blow. But the air frightened him with its unearthly calm, and he often rose in the middle of the night to see if the vane had veered – ten degrees would have satisfied him. But no, it poised above him as unchangeable as fate.

His imagination ran riot, till it became to him a fetish. Sometimes he followed the path it pointed across the dismal dominions, and allowed his soul to become saturated with the Fear. He dwelt upon the unseen and the unknown till the burden of eternity appeared to be crushing him. Everything in the Northland had that crushing effect – the absence of life and motion; the darkness; the infinite peace of the brooding land; the ghastly silence, which made the echo of each heartbeat a sacrilege; the solemn forest which seemed to guard an awful, inexpressible something, which neither word nor thought could compass.

The world he had so recently left, with its busy nations and great enterprises, seemed very far away. Recollections occasionally obtruded – recollections of marts and galleries and crowded thoroughfares, of evening dress and social functions, of good men and dear women he had known – but they were dim memories of a life he had lived long centuries agone, on some other planet. This phantasm was the Reality. Standing beneath the wind-vane, his eyes fixed on the polar skies, he could not bring himself to realise that the Southland really existed, that at that very moment it was a-roar with life and action.

There was no Southland, no men being born of women, no giving and taking in marriage.

Beyond his bleak skyline there stretched vast solitudes, and beyond these still vaster solitudes.

There were no lands of sunshine, heavy with the perfume of flowers. Such things were only old dreams of paradise. The sunlands of the West and the spicelands of the East, the smiling Arcadias and blissful Islands of the Blest – ha! ha! His laughter split the void and shocked him with its unwonted sound. There was no sun.

This was the Universe, dead and cold and dark, and he its only citizen. Weatherbee? At such moments, Weatherbee did not count. He was a Caliban, a monstrous phantom, fettered to him for untold ages, the penalty of some forgotten crime.

He lived with Death among the dead, emasculated by the sense of his own insignificance, crushed by the passive mastery of the slumbering ages. The magnitude of all things appalled him. Everything partook of the superlative save himself – the perfect cessation of wind and motion, the immensity of the snow-covered wildness, the height of the sky and the depth of the silence. That wind-vane – if it would only move. If a thunderbolt would fall, or the forest flare up in flame. The rolling up of the heavens as a scroll, the crash of Doom – anything, anything! But no, nothing moved; the Silence crowded in, and the Fear of the North laid icy fingers on his heart.

Once, like another Crusoe, by the edge of the river he came upon a track – the faint tracery of a snowshoe rabbit on the delicate snow-crust. It was a revelation. There was life in the Northland. He would follow it, look upon it, gloat over it.

He forgot his swollen muscles, plunging through the deep snow in an ecstasy of anticipation. The forest swallowed him up, and the brief midday twilight vanished; but he pursued his quest till exhausted nature asserted itself and laid him helpless in the snow.

There he groaned and cursed his folly, and knew the track to be the fancy of his brain; and late that night he dragged himself into the cabin on hands and knees, his cheeks frozen and a strange numbness about his feet. Weatherbee grinned malevolently, but made no offer to help him. He thrust needles into his toes and thawed them out by the stove. A week later mortification set in.

But the clerk had his own troubles. The dead men came out of their graves more frequently now, and rarely left him, waking or sleeping. He grew to wait and dread their coming, never passing the twin cairns without a shudder. One night they came to him in his sleep and led him forth to an appointed task. Frightened into inarticulate horror, he awoke between the heaps of stones and fled wildly to the cabin. But he had lain there for some time, for his feet and cheeks were also frozen.

Sometimes he became frantic at their insistent presence, and danced about the cabin, cutting the empty air with an axe, and smashing everything within reach. During these ghostly encounters, Cuthfert huddled into his blankets and followed the madman about with a cocked revolver, ready to shoot him if he came too near.

But, recovering from one of these spells, the clerk noticed the weapon trained upon him. His suspicions were aroused, and thenceforth he, too, lived in fear of his life. They watched each other closely after that, and faced about in startled fright whenever either passed behind the other's back. The apprehensiveness became a mania which controlled them even in their sleep. Through mutual fear they tacitly let the slush-lamp burn all night, and saw to a plentiful supply of bacon-grease before retiring. The slightest movement on the part of one was sufficient to arouse the other, and many a still watch their gazes countered as they shook beneath their blankets with fingers on the trigger-guards.

What with the Fear of the North, the mental strain and the ravages of the disease, they lost all semblance of humanity, taking on the appearance of wild beasts, hunted and desperate. Their cheeks and noses, as an aftermath of the freezing, had turned black.

Their frozen toes had begun to drop away at the first and second joints. Every movement brought pain, but the fire box was insatiable, wringing a ransom of torture from their miserable bodies. Day in, day out, it demanded its food – a veritable pound of flesh – and they dragged themselves into the forest to chop wood on their knees. Once, crawling thus in search of dry sticks, unknown to each other they entered a thicket from opposite sides.

Suddenly, without warning, two peering death's-heads confronted each other. Suffering had so transformed them that recognition was impossible. They sprang to their feet, shrieking with terror, and dashed away on their mangled stumps; and falling at the cabin's door, they clawed and scratched like demons till they discovered their mistake.

Occasionally they lapsed normal, and during one of these sane intervals, the chief bone of contention, the sugar, had been divided equally between them. They guarded their separate sacks, stored up in the cache, with jealous eyes; for there were but a few cupfuls left, and they were totally devoid of faith in each other.

But one day Cuthfert made a mistake. Hardly able to move, sick with pain, with his head swimming and eyes blinded, he crept into the cache, sugar canister in hand, and mistook Weatherbee's sack for his own.

January had been born but a few days when this occurred. The sun had some time since passed its lowest southern declination, and at meridian now threw flaunting streaks of yellow light upon the northern sky. On the day following his mistake with the sugar-bag, Cuthfert found himself feeling better, both in body and in spirit. As noontime drew near and the day brightened, he dragged himself outside to feast on the evanescent glow, which was to him an earnest of the sun's future intentions. Weatherbee was also feeling somewhat better, and crawled out beside him. They propped themselves in the snow beneath the moveless wind-vane, and waited.

The stillness of death was about them. In other climes, when nature falls into such moods, there is a subdued air of expectancy, a waiting for some small voice to take up the broken strain. Not so in the North. The two men had lived seeming aeons in this ghostly peace.

They could remember no song of the past; they could conjure no song of the future. This unearthly calm had always been – the tranquil silence of eternity.

Their eyes were fixed upon the north. Unseen, behind their backs, behind the towering mountains to the south, the sun swept toward the zenith of another sky than theirs. Sole spectators of the mighty canvas, they watched the false dawn slowly grow. A faint flame began to glow and smoulder. It deepened in intensity, ringing the changes of reddish-yellow, purple and saffron. So bright did it become that Cuthfert thought the sun must surely be behind it – a miracle, the sun rising in the north! Suddenly, without warning and without fading, the canvas was swept clean. There was no colour in the sky. The light had gone out of the day.

They caught their breaths in half-sobs. But lo! the air was aglint with particles of scintillating frost, and there, to the north, the wind-vane lay in vague outline on the snow.

A shadow! A shadow! It was exactly midday. They jerked their heads hurriedly to the south. A golden rim peeped over the mountain's snowy shoulder, smiled upon them an instant, then dipped from sight again.

There were tears in their eyes as they sought each other. A strange softening came over them. They felt irresistibly drawn toward each other. The sun was coming back again. It would be with them tomorrow, and the next day, and the next. And it would stay longer every visit, and a time would come when it would ride their heaven day and night, never once dropping below the skyline. There would be no night. The ice-locked winter would be broken; the winds would blow and the forests answer; the land would bathe in the blessed sunshine, and life renew.

Hand in hand, they would quit this horrid dream and journey back to the Southland. They lurched blindly forward, and their hands met – their poor maimed hands, swollen and distorted beneath their mittens.

But the promise was destined to remain unfulfilled. The Northland is the Northland, and men work out their souls by strange rules, which other men, who have not journeyed into far countries, cannot come to understand.

An hour later, Cuthfert put a pan of bread into the oven, and fell to speculating on what the surgeons could do with his feet when he got back.

Home did not seem so very far away now. Weatherbee was rummaging in the cache. Of a sudden, he raised a whirlwind of blasphemy, which in turn ceased with startling abruptness. The other man had robbed his sugar-sack. Still, things might have happened differently had not the two dead men come out from under the stones and hushed the hot words in his throat. They led him quite gently from the cache, which he forgot to close. That consummation was reached; that something they had whispered to him in his dreams was about to happen. They guided him gently, very gently, to the woodpile, where they put the axe in his hands.

Then they helped him shove open the cabin door, and he felt sure they shut it after him – at least he heard it slam and the latch fall sharply into place. And he knew they were waiting just without, waiting for him to do his task.

'Carter! I say, Carter!' Percy Cuthfert was frightened at the look on the clerk's face, and he made haste to put the table between them.

Carter Weatherbee followed, without haste and without enthusiasm. There was neither pity nor passion in his face, but rather the patient, stolid look of one who has certain work to do and goes about it methodically.

'I say, what's the matter?'

The clerk dodged back, cutting off his retreat to the door, but never opening his mouth.

'I say, Carter, I say; let's talk. There's a good chap.' The master of arts was thinking rapidly, now, shaping a skilful flank movement on the bed where his Smith & Wesson lay. Keeping his eyes on the madman, he rolled backward on the bunk, at the same time clutching the pistol.

'Carter!' The powder flashed full in Weatherbee's face, but he swung his weapon and leaped forward. The axe bit deeply at the base of the spine, and Percy Cuthfert felt all consciousness of his lower limbs leave him. Then the clerk fell heavily upon him, clutching him by the throat with feeble fingers. The sharp bite of the axe had caused Cuthfert to drop the pistol, and as his lungs panted for release, he fumbled aimlessly for it among the blankets. Then he remembered. He slid a hand up the clerk's belt to the sheath-knife, and they drew very close to each other in that last clinch.

Percy Cuthfert felt his strength leave him. The lower portion of his body was useless. The inert weight of Weatherbee crushed him – crushed him and pinned him there like a bear under a trap. The cabin became filled with a familiar odour, and he knew the bread to be burning. Yet what did it matter? He would never need it. And there were all of six cupfuls of sugar in the cache – if he had foreseen this he would not have been so saving the last several days. Would the wind-vane ever move? Why not? Had he not seen the sun today? He would go and see. No; it was impossible to move. He had not thought the clerk so heavy a man.

How quickly the cabin cooled! The fire must be out. The cold was forcing in. It must be below zero already, and the ice creeping up the inside of the door. He could not see it, but his past experience enabled him to gauge its progress by the cabin's temperature. The lower hinge must be white ere now. Would the tale of this ever reach the world? How would his friends take it? They would read it over their coffee, most likely, and talk it over at the clubs. He could see them very clearly. 'Poor Old Cuthfert,' they murmured; 'not such a bad sort of a chap, after all.' He smiled at their eulogies, and passed on in search of a Turkish bath. It was the same old crowd upon the streets.

Strange, they did not notice his moosehide moccasins and tattered German socks! He would take a cab. And after the bath a shave would not be bad. No; he would eat first.

Steak, and potatoes, and green things – how fresh it all was! And what was that? Squares of honey, streaming liquid amber! But why did they bring so much? Ha! ha! he could never eat it all.

Shine! Why certainly. He put his foot on the box. The bootblack looked curiously up at him, and he remembered his moosehide moccasins and went away hastily.

Hark! The wind-vane must be surely spinning. No; a mere singing in his ears. That was all – a mere singing. The ice must have passed the latch by now. More likely the upper hinge was covered. Between the moss-chinked roof-poles, little points of frost began to appear. How slowly they grew! No; not so slowly. There was a new one, and there another. Two – three – four; they were coming too fast to count. There were two growing together. And there, a third had joined them. Why, there were no more spots! They had run together and formed a sheet.

Well, he would have company. If Gabriel ever broke the silence of the North, they would stand together, hand in hand, before the great White Throne. And God would judge them, God would judge them!

Then Percy Cuthfert closed his eyes and dropped off to sleep.

BUCK FANSHAW'S FUNERAL

MARK TWAIN

SOMEBODY HAS SAID that in order to know a community, one must observe the style of its funerals and know what manner of men they bury with most ceremony. I cannot say which class we buried with most éclat in our 'flush times', the distinguished public benefactor or the distinguished rough – possibly the two chief grades or grand divisions of society honoured their illustrious dead about equally; and hence, no doubt the philosopher I have quoted from would have needed to see two representative funerals in Virginia before forming his estimate of the people.

There was a grand time over Buck Fanshaw when he died. He was a representative citizen. He had 'killed his man' – not in his own quarrel, it is true, but in defence of a stranger unfairly beset by numbers. He had kept a sumptuous saloon. He had been the proprietor of a dashing helpmeet whom he could have discarded without the formality of a divorce. He had held a high position in the fire department and been a very Warwick in politics. When he died there was great lamentation throughout the town, but especially in the vast bottom-stratum of society.

On the inquest it was shown that Buck Fanshaw, in the delirium of a wasting typhoid fever, had taken arsenic, shot himself through the body, cut his throat, and jumped out of a four-storey window and broken his neck – and after due deliberation, the jury, sad and tearful, but with intelligence unblinded by its sorrow, brought in a verdict of death 'by the visitation of God'. What could the world do without juries?

Prodigious preparations were made for the funeral. All the vehicles in town were hired, all the saloons put in mourning, all the municipal and fire-company flags hung at half-mast, and all the firemen ordered to muster in uniform and bring their machines duly draped in black. Now – let us remark in parenthesis – as all the peoples of the earth had representative adventurers in the Silverland, and as each adventurer had brought the slang of his nation or his locality with him, the combination made the slang of Nevada the richest and the most infinitely varied and copious that had ever existed anywhere in the world, perhaps, except in the mines of California in the 'early days'. Slang was the language of Nevada. It was hard to preach a sermon without it, and be understood. Such phrases as 'You bet!' 'Oh, no, I reckon not!' 'No Irish need apply,' and a hundred others, became so common as to fall from the lips of a speaker unconsciously – and very often when they did not touch the subject under discussion and consequently failed to mean anything.

After Buck Fanshaw's inquest, a meeting of the short-haired brotherhood was held, for nothing can be done on the Pacific coast without a public meeting and an expression of sentiment. Regretful resolutions were passed and various committees appointed; among others, a committee of one was deputed to call on the minister, a fragile, gentle, spiritual new fledgling from an Eastern theological seminary, and as yet unacquainted with the ways of the mines. The committeeman, 'Scotty' Briggs, made his visit; and in after days it was worth something to hear the minister tell about it. Scotty was a stalwart rough, whose customary suit, when on weighty official business, like committee work, was a fire helmet, flaming red flannel shirt, patent-leather belt with spanner and revolver attached, coat hung over arm, and pants stuffed into boot tops. He formed something of a contrast to the pale theological student. It is fair to say of Scotty, however, in passing, that he had a warm heart, and a strong love for his friends, and never entered into a quarrel when he could reasonably keep out of it. Indeed, it was commonly said that whenever one of Scotty's fights was investigated, it always turned out that it had originally been no affair of his, but that out of native goodheartedness he had dropped in of his own accord to help the man who was getting the worst of it. He and Buck Fanshaw were bosom friends, for years, and had often taken adventurous 'pot-luck' together. On one occasion, they had thrown off their coats and taken the weaker side in a fight among strangers, and after gaining a hard-earned victory, turned and found that the men they were helping had deserted early, and not only that, but had stolen their coats and made off with them! But to return to Scotty's visit to the minister. He was on a sorrowful mission, now, and his face was the picture of woe. Being admitted to the presence he sat down before the clergyman, placed his fire-hat on an unfinished manuscript sermon under the minister's nose, took from it a red silk handkerchief, wiped his brow and heaved a sigh of dismal impressiveness, explanatory of his business.

He choked, and even shed tears; but with an effort he mastered his voice and said in lugubrious tones: 'Are you the duck that runs the gospel-mill next door?'

'Am I the – pardon me, I believe I do not understand?'

With another sigh and a half-sob, Scotty rejoined: 'Why you see we are in a bit of trouble, and the boys thought maybe you would give us a lift, if we'd tackle you – that is, if I've got the rights of it and you are the head clerk of the doxology-works next door.'

'I am the shepherd in charge of the flock whose fold is next door.'

'The which?'

'The spiritual adviser of the little company of believers whose sanctuary adjoins these premises.'

Scotty scratched his head, reflected a moment, and then said: 'You ruther hold over me, pard. I reckon I can't call that hand. Ante and pass the buck.'

'How? I beg pardon. What did I understand you to say?'

'Well, you've ruther got the bulge on me. Or maybe we've both got the bulge, somehow. You don't smoke me and I don't smoke you. You see, one of the boys has passed in his checks and we want to give him a good send-off, and so the thing I'm on now is to roust out somebody to jerk a little chin-music for us and waltz him through handsome.'

'My friend, I seem to grow more and more bewildered. Your observations are wholly incomprehensible to me. Cannot you simplify them in some way? At first I thought perhaps I understood you, but I grope now. Would it not expedite matters if you restricted yourself to categorical statements of fact unencumbered with obstructing accumulations of metaphor and allegory?'

Another pause, and more reflection. Then, said Scotty: 'I'll have to pass, I judge.'

'How?'

'You've raised me out, pard.'

'I still fail to catch your meaning.'

'Why, that last lead of yourn is too many for me – that's the idea. I can't neither trump nor follow suit.'

The clergyman sank back in his chair perplexed. Scotty leaned his head on his hand and gave himself up to thought.

Presently his face came up, sorrowful but confident.

'I've got it now, so's you can savvy,' he said. 'What we want is a gospel-sharp. See?'

'A what?'

'Gospel-sharp. Parson.'

'Oh! Why did you not say so before? I am a clergyman – a parson.'

'Now you talk! You see my blind and straddle it like a man. Put it there!' – extending a brawny paw, which closed over the minister's small hand and gave it a shake indicative of fraternal sympathy and fervent gratification.

'Now we're all right, pard. Let's start fresh. Don't you mind my snuffling a little – becuz we're in a power of trouble. You see, one of the boys has gone up the flume – '

'Gone where?'

'Up the flume – throwed up the sponge, you understand.'

'Thrown up the sponge?'

'Yes – kicked the bucket – '

'Ah – has departed to that mysterious country from whose bourne no traveller returns.'

'Return! I reckon not. Why pard, he's *dead*!'

'Yes, I understand.'

'Oh, you do? Well I thought maybe you might be getting tangled some more. Yes, you see he's dead again – '

'Again? Why, has he ever been dead before?'

'Dead before? No! Do you reckon a man has got as many lives as a cat? But you bet you he's awful dead now, poor old boy, and I wish I'd never seen this day. I don't want no better friend than Buck Fanshaw. I knowed him by the back; and when I know a man and like him, I freeze to him – you hear me. Take him all round, pard, there never was a bullier man in the mines. No man ever knowed Buck Fanshaw to go back on a friend. But it's all up, you know, it's all up. It ain't no use. They've scooped him.'

'Scooped him?'

'Yes – death has. Well, well, well, we've got to give him up. Yes indeed. It's a kind of a hard world, after all, *ain't* it? But pard, he was a rustler! You ought to seen him get started once. He was a bully boy with a glass eye! Just spit in his face and give him room according to his strength, and it was just beautiful to see him peel and go in. He was the worst son of a thief that ever drawed breath. Pard, he was *on* it! He was on it bigger than an Injun!'

'On it? On what?'

'On the shoot. On the shoulder. On the fight, you understand. *He* didn't give a continental for *any*body. *Beg* your pardon, friend, for coming so near saying a cuss-word – but you see I'm on an awful strain, in this palaver, on account of having to cramp down and draw everything so mild. But we've got to give him up. There ain't any getting around that, I don't reckon. Now if we can get you to help plant him – '

'Preach the funeral discourse? Assist at the obsequies?'

'Obs'quies is good. Yes. That's it – that's our little game. We are going to get the thing up regardless, you know. He was always nifty himself, and so you bet you his funeral ain't going to be no slouch – solid silver door-plate on his coffin, six plumes on the hearse, and a nigger on the box in a biled shirt and a plug hat – how's that for high? And we'll take care of *you*, pard. We'll fix you all right. There'll be a kerridge for you; and whatever you want, you just 'scape out and we'll 'tend to it. We've got a shebang fixed up for you to stand behind, in No. 1's house, and don't you be afraid. Just go in and toot your horn, if you don't sell a clam. Put Buck through as bully as you can, pard, for anybody that knowed him will tell you that he was one of the whitest men that was ever in the mines. You can't draw it too strong. He never could stand it to see things going wrong. He's done more to make this town quiet and peaceable than any man in it. I've seen him lick four greasers in eleven minutes, myself. If a thing wanted regulating, *he* warn't a man to go browsing around after somebody to do it, but he would prance in and regulate it himself. He warn't a Catholic. Scasely. He was down on 'em. His word was, "No Irish need apply!" But it didn't make no difference about that when it came down to what a man's rights was – and so, when some roughs jumped the Catholic bone-yard and started in to stake out town-lots in it he went for 'em! And he *cleaned* 'em, too! I was there, pard, and I seen it myself.'

'That was very well indeed – at least the impulse was – whether the act was strictly defensible or not. Had deceased any religious convictions? That is to say, did he feel a dependence upon, or acknowledge allegiance to a higher power?'

More reflection.

'I reckon you've stumped me again, pard. Could you say it over once more, and say it slow?'

'Well, to simplify it somewhat, was he, or rather had he ever been connected with any organisation sequestered from secular concerns and devoted to self-sacrifice in the interests of morality?'

'All down but nine – set 'em up on the other alley, pard.'

'What did I understand you to say?'

'Why, you're most too many for me, you know. When you get in with your left I hunt grass every time. Every time you draw, you fill; but I don't seem to have any luck. Let's have a new deal.'

'How? Begin again?'

'That's it.'

'Very well. Was he a good man, and – '

'There – I see that; don't put up another chip till I look at my hand. A good man, says you? Pard, it ain't no name for it. He was the best man that ever – pard, you would have doted on that man. He could lam any galoot of his inches in America. It was him that put down the riot last election before it got a start; and everybody said he was the only man that could have done it. He waltzed in with a spanner in one hand and a trumpet in the other, and sent fourteen men home on a shutter in less than three minutes. He had that riot all broke up and prevented nice before anybody ever got a chance to strike a blow. He was always for peace, and he would *have* peace – he could not stand disturbances. Pard, he was a great loss to this town. It would please the boys if you could chip in something like that and do him justice. Here once when the Micks got to throwing stones through the Methodis' Sunday-school windows, Buck Fanshaw, all of his own notion, shut up his saloon and took a couple of six-shooters and mounted guard over the Sunday school. Says he, "No Irish need apply!" And they didn't. He was the bulliest man in the mountains, pard! He could run faster, jump higher, hit harder, and hold more tangle-foot whiskey without spilling it than any man in seventeen counties. Put that in, pard – it'll please the boys more than anything you could say. And you can say, pard, that he never shook his mother.'

'Never shook his mother?'

'That's it – any of the boys will tell you so.'

'Well, but why *should* he shake her?'

'That's what *I* say – but some people does.'

'Not people of any repute?'

'Well, some that averages pretty so-so.'

'In my opinion the man that would offer personal violence to his own mother, ought to – '

'Cheese it, pard; you've banked your ball clean outside the string. What I was a drivin' at was that he never *throwed off* on his mother – don't you see? No indeedy. He give her a house to live in, and town lots, and plenty of money; and he looked after her and took care of her all the time; and when she was down with the small-pox I'm damned if he didn't set up nights and nuss her himself! *Beg* your pardon for saying it, but it hopped out too quick for yours truly.

'You've treated me like a gentleman, pard, and I ain't the man to hurt your feelings intentional. I think you're white. I think you're a square man, pard. I like you, and I'll lick any man that don't. I'll lick him till he can't tell himself from a last year's corpse! Put it *there*!' (Another fraternal hand-shake – and exit.)

The obsequies were all that 'the boys' could desire. Such a marvel of funeral pomp had never been seen in Virginia. The plumed hearse, the dirge-breathing brass bands, the closed marts of business, the flags drooping at half mast, the long, plodding procession of uniformed secret societies, military battalions and fire companies, draped engines, carriages of officials and citizens in vehicles and on foot attracted multitudes of spectators to the sidewalks, roofs and windows; and for years afterwards, the degree of grandeur attained by any civic display in Virginia was determined by comparison with Buck Fanshaw's funeral.

Scotty Briggs, as a pall-bearer and a mourner, occupied a prominent place at the funeral, and when the sermon was finished and the last sentence of the prayer for the dead man's soul ascended, he responded, in a low voice, but with feeling: '*Amen*. No Irish need apply.'

As the bulk of the response was without apparent relevancy, it was probably nothing more than a humble tribute to the memory of the friend that was gone; for, as Scotty had once said, it was 'his word'.

Scotty Briggs, in after days, achieved the distinction of becoming the only convert to religion that was ever gathered from the Virginia roughs; and it transpired that the man who had it in him to espouse the quarrel of the weak out of inborn nobility of spirit was no mean timber whereof to construct a Christian. The making him one did not warp his generosity or diminish his courage; on the contrary it gave intelligent direction to the one and a broader field to the other.

If his Sunday-school class progressed faster than the other classes, was it matter for wonder? I think not. He talked to his pioneer small-fry in a language they understood! It was my large privilege, a month before he died, to hear him tell the beautiful story of Joseph and his brethren to his class 'without looking at the book'. I leave it to the reader to fancy what it was like, as it fell, riddled with slang, from the lips of that grave, earnest teacher, and was listened to by his little learners with a consuming interest that showed that they were as unconscious as he was that any violence was being done to the sacred proprieties!

THE HONK-HONK BREED

STEWART EDWARD WHITE

I T WAS SUNDAY AT THE RANCH. For a wonder the weather had been favourable; the windmills were all working, the bogs had dried up, the beef had lasted over, the *remuda* had not strayed – in short, there was nothing to do. Sang had given us a baked bread-pudding with raisins in it. We filled it in – a wash basin full of it – on top of a few incidental pounds of chile con, baked beans, soda biscuits, 'air tights', and other delicacies. Then we adjourned with our pipes to the shady side of the blacksmith's shop where we could watch the ravens on top the adobe wall of the corral. Somebody told a story about ravens. This led to road-runners. This suggested rattlesnakes. They started Windy Bill.

'Speakin' of snakes,' said Windy, 'I mind when they catched the great-granddaddy of all the bullsnakes up at Lead in the Black Hills. I was only a kid then. This wasn't no such tur'ble long a snake, but he was more'n a foot thick. Looked just like a sahuaro stalk. Man name of Terwilliger Smith catched it. He named this yere bullsnake Clarence, and got it so plumb gentle it followed him everywhere. One day old P. T. Barnum come along and wanted to buy this Clarence snake – offered Terwilliger a thousand cold – but Smith wouldn't part with the snake nohow. So finally they fixed up a deal so Smith could go along with the show. They shoved Clarence in a box in the baggage car, but after a while Mr Snake gets so lonesome he gnaws out and starts to crawl back to find his master. Just as he is halfway between the baggage car and the smoker, the couplin' give way – right on that heavy grade between Custer and Rocky Point. Well, sir, Clarence wound his head 'round one brake wheel and his tail around the other, and held that train together to the bottom of the grade. But it stretched him twenty-eight feet so they had to advertise him as a boa-constrictor.'

Windy Bill's story of the faithful bullsnake aroused to reminiscence the grizzled stranger, who thereupon held forth as follows:

Wall, I've see things and I've heerd things, some of them ornery, and some you'd love to believe, they was that gorgeous and improbable. Nat'ral history was always my hobby and sportin' events my special pleasure and this yarn of Windy's reminds me of the only chanst I ever had to ring in business and pleasure and hobby all in one grand merry-go-round of joy. It come about like this: One day, a few year back, I was sittin' on the beach at Santa Barbara watchin' the sky stay up, and wonderin' what to do with my year's wages, when a little squinch-eye round-face with big bow spectacles came and plumped down beside me.

'Did you ever stop to think,' says he, shovin' back his hat, 'that if the horsepower delivered by them waves on this beach in one single hour could be concentrated behind washin' machines, it would be enough to wash all the shirts for a city of four hundred and fifty-one thousand one hundred and thirty-six people?'

'Can't say I ever did,' says I, squintin' at him sideways.

'Fact,' says he; 'and did it ever occur to you that if all the food a man eats in the course of a natural life could be gathered together at one time, it would fill a wagon-train twelve miles long?'

'You make me hungry,' says I.

'And ain't it interestin' to reflect,' he goes on, 'that if all the fingernail parin's of the human race for one year was to be collected and subjected to hydraulic pressure it would equal in size the pyramid of Cheops?'

'Look yere,' says I, sittin' up, 'did *you* ever pause to excogitate that if all the hot air you is dispensin' was to be collected together it would fill a balloon big enough to waft you and me over that Bullyvard of Palms to yonder gin mill on the corner?'

He didn't say nothin' to that – just yanked me to my feet, faced me towards the gin mill above mentioned, and exerted considerable pressure on my arm in urgin' of me forward.

'You ain't so much of a dreamer, after all,' thinks I. 'In important matters you are plumb decisive.'

We sat down at little tables, and my friend ordered a beer and a chicken sandwich.

'Chickens,' says he, gazin' at the sandwich, 'is a dollar apiece in this country, and plumb scarce. Did you ever pause to ponder over the returns chickens would give on a small investment? Say you start with ten hens. Each hatches out thirteen aigs, of which allow a loss of say six for childish accidents. At the end of the year you has eighty chickens. At the end of two years that flock has increased to six hundred and twenty. At the end of the third year – '

He had the medicine tongue! Ten days later him and me was occupyin' of an old ranch fifty mile from anywhere. When they run stagecoaches this joint used to be a roadhouse. The outlook was on about a thousand little brown foothills. A road two miles four rods two foot eleven inches in sight run by in front of us. It come over one foothill and disappeared over another. I know just how long it was, for later in the game I measured it.

Out back was about a hundred little wire chicken corrals filled with chickens. We had two kinds. That was the doin's of Tuscarora. My pardner called himself Tuscarora Maxillary. I asked him once if that was his real name.

'It's the realest little old name you ever heerd tell of,' says he. 'I know, for I made it myself – liked the sound of her. Parents ain't got no rights to name their children. Parents don't have to be called them names.'

Well, these chickens, as I said, was of two kinds. The first was these low-set, heavyweight propositions with feathers on their laigs, and not much laigs at that, called Cochin Chinys. The other was a tall ridiculous outfit made up entire of bulgin' breast and gangle laigs. They stood about two foot and a half tall, and when they went to peck the ground their tail feathers stuck straight up to the sky. Tusky called 'em Japanese Games.

'Which the chief advantage of them chickens is,' says he, 'that in weight about ninety per cent of 'em is breast meat. Now my idee is, that if we can cross 'em with these Cochin Chiny fowls we'll have a low-hung, heavyweight chicken runnin' strong on breast meat. These Jap Games is too small, but if we can bring 'em up in size and shorten their laigs, we'll shore have a winner.'

That looked good to me, so we started in on that idee. The theery was bully, but she didn't work out. The first broods we hatched growed up with big husky Cochin Chiny bodies and little short necks, perched up on laigs three foot long. Them chickens couldn't reach ground nohow. We had to build a table for 'em to eat off, and when they went out rustlin' for themselves they had to confine themselves to side-hills or flyin' insects. Their breasts was all right, though – 'And think of them drumsticks for the boardinghouse trade!' says Tusky.

So far things wasn't so bad. We had a good grubstake. Tusky and me used to feed them chickens twict a day, and then used to set around watchin' the playful critters chase grasshoppers up an' down the wire corrals, while Tusky figgered out what'd happen if somebody was dum-fool enough to gather up somethin' and fix it in baskets or wagons or such. That was where we showed our ignorance of chickens.

One day in the spring I hitched up, rustled a dozen of the youngsters into coops, and druv over to the railroad to make our first sale. I couldn't fold them chickens up into them coops at first, but then I stuck the coops up on aidge and they worked all right, though I will admit they was a comical sight. At the railroad one of them towerist trains had just slowed down to a halt as I come up, and the towerists was paradin' up and down allowin' they was particular enjoyin' of the warm Californy sunshine. One old terrapin, with grey chin whiskers, projected over, with his wife, and took a peek through the slats of my coop. He straightened up like someone had touched him off with a red-hot poker.

'Stranger,' said he, in a scared kind of whisper, 'what's them?'

'Them's chickens,' says I.

He took another long look.

'Marthy,' says he to the old woman, 'this will be about all! We come out from Ioway to see the Wonders of Californy, but I can't go nothin' stronger than this. If these is chickens, I don't want to see no Big Trees.'

Well, I sold them chickens all right for a dollar and two bits, which was better than I expected, and got an order for more. About ten days later I got a letter from the commission house.

'We are returnin' a sample of your Arts and Crafts chickens with the lovin' marks of the teeth still on to him,' says they. 'Don't send any more till they stops pursuin' of the nimble grasshopper. Dentist bill will foller.'

With the letter came the remains of one of the chickens. Tusky and I, very indignant, cooked her for supper. She was tough, all right. We thought she might do better biled, so we put her in the pot over night. Nary bit. Well, then we got interested. Tusky kep' the fire goin' and I rustled greasewood. We cooked her three days and three nights. At the end of that time she was sort of pale and frazzled, but still givin' points to three-year-old jerky on cohesion and other uncompromisin' forces of nature. We buried her then, and went out back to recuperate.

There we could gaze on the smilin' landscape, dotted by about four hundred long-laigged chickens swoopin' here and there after grasshoppers.

'We got to stop that,' says I.

'We can't,' murmured Tusky, inspired. 'We can't. It's born in 'em; it's a primal instinct, like the love of a mother for her young, and it can't be eradicated! Them chickens is constructed by a divine providence for the express purpose of chasin' grasshoppers, jest as the beaver is made for buildin' dams, and the cow-puncher is made for whiskey and faro-games. We can't keep 'em from it. If we was to shut 'em in a dark cellar, they'd flop after imaginary grasshoppers in their dreams, and die emaciated in the midst of plenty. Jimmy, we're up agin the Cosmos, the oversoul – ' Oh, he had the medicine tongue, Tusky had, and risin' on the wings of eloquence that way, he had me faded in ten minutes. In fifteen I was wedded solid to the notion that the bottom had dropped out of the chicken business. I think now that if we'd shut them hens up, we might have – still, I don't know; they was a good deal in what Tusky said.

'Tuscarora Maxillary,' says I, 'did you ever stop to entertain that beautiful thought that if all the dumfoolishness possessed now by the human race could be gathered together, and lined up alongside of us, the first feller to come along would say to it, "Why, hello, Solomon!" '

We quit the notion of chickens for profit right then and there, but we couldn't quit the place. We hadn't much money, for one thing, and then we kind of liked loafin' around and raisin' a little garden truck, and – oh, well, I might as well say so, we had a notion about placers in the dry wash back of the house – you know how it is. So we stayed on, and kept a-raisin' these long-laigs for the fun of it. I used to like to watch 'em projectin' around, and I fed 'em twice a day about as usual.

So Tusky and I lived alone there together, happy as ducks in Arizona. About onc't in a month somebody'd pike along the road. She wasn't much of a road, generally more chuck-holes than bumps, though some-times it was the other way around. Unless it happened to be a man on horseback or maybe a freighter without the fear of God in his soul, we didn't have no words with them; they was too busy cussin' the highways and generally too mad for social discourses.

One day early in the year, when the 'dobe mud made ruts to add to the bumps, one of these automobeels went past. It was the first Tusky and me had seen in them parts, so we run out to view her. Owin' to the high spots on the road, she looked like one of these movin' picters, as to blur and wobble; sounded like a cyclone mingled with cuss-words, and smelt like hell on housecleanin' day.

'Which them folks don't seem to be enjoyin' of the scenery,' says I to Tusky. 'Do you reckon that there blue trail is smoke from the machine or remarks from the inhabitants thereof?'

Tusky raised his head and sniffed long and enquirin'.

'It's langwidge,' says he. 'Did you ever stop to think that all the words in the dictionary stretched end to end would reach – '

But at that minute I catched sight of somethin' brass lyin' in the road. It proved to be a curled-up sort of horn with a rubber bulb on the end. I squoze the bulb and jumped twenty foot over the remark she made.

'Jarred off the machine,' says Tusky.

'Oh, did it?' says I, my nerves still wrong. 'I thought maybe it had growed up from the soil like a toadstool.'

About this time we abolished the wire chicken corrals, because we needed some of the wire. Them long-laigs thereupon scattered all over the flat searchin' out their prey. When feed time come I had to screech my lungs out gettin' of 'em in, and then sometimes they didn't all hear. It was plumb discouragin', and I mighty nigh made up my mind to quit 'em, but they had come to be sort of pets, and I hated to turn 'em down. It used to tickle Tusky almost to death to see me out there hollerin' away like an old bull-frog. He used to come out reg'lar, with his pipe lit, just to enjoy me. Finally I got mad and opened up on him.

'Oh,' he explains, 'it just plumb amuses me to see the dumfool at his childish work. Why don't you teach 'em to come to that brass horn, and save your voice?'

'Tusky,' says I, with feelin', 'sometimes you do seem to get a glimmer of real sense.'

Well, first off them chickens used to throw back-sommersets over that horn. You have no idee how slow chickens is to learn things. I could tell you things about chickens – say, this yere bluff about roosters bein' gallant is all wrong. I've watched 'em. When one finds a nice feed he gobbles it so fast that the pieces foller down his throat like yearlin's through a hole in the fence. It's only when he scratches up a measly one-grain quick-lunch that he calls up the hens and stands noble and self-sacrificin' to one side. That ain't the point, which is that after two months I had them long-laigs so they'd drop everythin' and come kitin' at the *honk-honk* of that horn. It was a purty sight to see 'em, sailin' in from all directions twenty foot at a stride. I was proud of 'em, and named 'em the Honk-Honk Breed. We didn't have no others, for by now the coyotes and bob-cats had nailed the straight-breds. There wasn't no wild cat or coyote could catch one of my Honk-Honks, no, sir!

We made a little on our placer – just enough to keep interested. Then the supervisors decided to fix our road, and what's more, *they done it*! That's the only part in this yarn that's hard to believe, but, boys, you'll have to take it on faith. They ploughed her, and crowned her, and scraped her, and rolled her, and when they moved on we had the fanciest highway in the State of Californy.

That noon – the day they called her a job – Tusky and I sat smokin' our pipes as per usual, when way over the foothills we seen a cloud of dust and faint to our ears was bore a whizzin' sound. The chickens was gathered under the cottonwood for the heat of the day, but they didn't pay no attention. Then faint, but clear, we heard another of them brass horns: 'Honk! honk!' says it, and every one of them chickens woke up, and stood at attention.

'Honk! honk!' it hollered clearer and nearer.

Then over the hill come an automobeel, blowin' vigorous at every jump.

'My God!' I yells to Tusky, kickin' over my chair as I springs to my feet. 'Stop 'em! Stop 'em!'

But it was too late. Out the gate sprinted them poor devoted chickens, and up the road they trailed in vain pursuit. The last we seen of 'em was a mingling of dust and dim figgers goin' thirty mile an hour after a disappearin' automobeel.

That was all we seen for the moment. About three o'clock the first straggler came limpin' in, his wings hangin', his mouth open, his eyes glazed with the heat. By sundown fourteen had returned. All the rest had disappeared utter; we never seen 'em again. I reckon they just naturally run themselves into a sunstroke and died on the road.

It takes a long time to learn a chicken a thing, but a heap longer to unlearn him. After that two or three of these yere automobeels went by every day, all a-blowin' of their horns, all kickin' up a hell of a dust. And every time them fourteen Honk-Honks of mine took along after 'em, just as I'd taught 'em to do, layin' to get to their corn when they caught up. No more of 'em died, but that fourteen did get into elegant trainin'. After a while they got plumb to enjoyin' it. When you come right down to it, a chicken don't have many amusements and relaxations in this life. Searchin' for worms, chasin' grasshoppers, and wallerin' in the dust is about the limits of joys for chickens.

It was sure a fine sight to see 'em after they got well into the game. About nine o'clock every mornin' they would saunter down to the rise of the road where they would wait patient until a machine came along. Then it would warm your heart to see the enthusiasm of them. With exultant cackles of joy they'd trail in, reachin' out like quarter-horses, their wings half spread out, their eyes beamin' with delight. At the lower turn they'd quit. Then, after talkin' it over excited-like for a few minutes, they'd calm down and wait for another.

After a few months of this sort of trainin' they got purty good at it. I had one two-year-old rooster that made fifty-four mile an hour behind one of those sixty-horsepower Panhandles. When cars didn't come along often enough, they'd all turn out and chase jack-rabbits. They wasn't much fun in that. After a short, brief sprint the rabbit would crouch down plumb terrified, while the Honk-Honks pulled off triumphal dances around his shrinkin' form.

Our ranch got to be purty well known them days among automobee-lists. The strength of their cars was horse-power, of course, but the speed of them they got to ratin' by chicken-power. Some of them used to come way up from Los Angeles just to try out a new car along our road with the Honk-Honks for pace-makers. We charged them a little somethin', and then, too, we opened up the road-house and the bar, so we did purty well. It wasn't necessary to work any longer at that bogus placer. Evenin's we sat around outside and swapped yarns, and I bragged on my chickens. The chickens would gather round close to listen.

They liked to hear their praises sung, all right. You bet they *sabe*! The only reason a chicken, or any other critter, isn't intelligent is because he hasn't no chance to expand.

Why, we used to run races with 'em. Some of us would hold two or more chickens back of a chalk line, and the starter'd blow the horn from a hundred yards to a mile away, dependin' on whether it was a sprint or for distance. We had pools on the results, gave odds, made books and kept records. After the thing got knowed we made money hand over fist.

* * *

The stranger broke off abruptly and began to roll a cigarette.

'What did you quit it for, then?' ventured Charley, out of the hushed silence.

'Pride,' replied the stranger solemnly. 'Haughtiness of spirit.'

'How so?' urged Charley, after a pause.

'Them chickens,' continued the stranger, after a moment, 'stood around listenin' to me a-braggin' of what superior fowls they was until they got all puffed up. They wouldn't have nothin' whatever to do with the ordinary chickens we brought in for eatin' purposes, but stood around lookin' bored when there wasn't no sport doin'. They got to be just like that Four Hundred you read about in the papers. It was one continual round of grasshopper balls, race meets and afternoon hen-parties. They got idle and haughty, just like folks. Then come race suicide. They got to feelin' so aristocratic the hens wouldn't have no eggs.'

Nobody dared say a word.

'Windy Bill's snake – ' began the narrator genially.

'Stranger,' broke in Windy Bill, with great emphasis, 'as to that snake, I want you to understand this: yereafter in my estimation that snake is nothin' but an ornery angleworm!'

THE LONG STORIES

THE LOG OF A COWBOY

ANDY ADAMS

Contents

CHAPTER 1

Up the Trail

JUST WHY MY FATHER MOVED, at the close of the Civil War, from Georgia to Texas, is to this good hour a mystery to me. While we did not exactly belong to the poor whites, we classed with them in poverty, being renters; but I am inclined to think my parents were intellectually superior to that common type of the South. Both were foreign born, my mother being Scotch and my father a North of Ireland man – as I remember him now, impulsive, hasty in action and slow to confess a fault. It was his impulsiveness that led him to volunteer and serve four years in the Confederate army – trying years to my mother, with a brood of seven children to feed, garb and house. The war brought me my initiation as a cowboy, of which I have now, after the long lapse of years, the greater portion of which were spent with cattle, a distinct recollection. Sherman's army, in its march to the sea, passed through our county, devastating that section for miles in its passing.

Foraging parties scoured the country on either side of its path. My mother had warning in time and set her house in order. Our work stock consisted of two yoke of oxen, while our cattle numbered three cows – and for saving them from the foragers, credit must be given to my mother's generalship. There was a wild canebrake, in which the cattle fed, several hundred acres in extent, about a mile from our little farm, and it was necessary to bell them in order to locate them when wanted. But the cows were in the habit of coming up to be milked, and a soldier can hear a bell as well as anyone. I was a lad of eight at the time, and while my two older brothers worked our few fields, I was sent into the canebrake to herd the cattle. We had removed the bells from the oxen and cows, but one ox was belled after darkness each evening, to be unbelled again at daybreak. I always carried the bell with me, stuffed with grass, in order to have it at hand when wanted.

During the first few days of the raid, a number of mounted foraging parties passed our house, but its poverty was all too apparent, and nothing was molested. Several of these parties were driving herds of cattle and work stock of every description, while by day and by night gins and plantation houses were being given to the flames. Our one-roomed log cabin was spared, due to the ingenious tale told by my mother as to the whereabouts of my father; and yet she taught her children to fear God and tell the truth. My vigil was trying to one of my years, for the days seemed like weeks, but the importance of hiding our cattle was thoroughly impressed upon my mind. Food was secretly brought to me, and, under cover of darkness, my mother and eldest brother would come and milk the cows, when we would all return home together. Then, before daybreak, we would be in the cane listening for the first tinkle, to find the cattle and remove the bell. And my day's work commenced anew.

Only once did I come near betraying my trust. About the middle of the third day I grew very hungry, and as the cattle were lying down, I crept to the edge of the canebrake to see if my dinner was not forthcoming. Soldiers were in sight, which explained everything. Concealed in the rank cane I stood and watched them. Suddenly a squad of five or six turned a point of the brake and rode within fifty feet of me. I stood like a stone statue, my concealment being perfect. After they had passed, I took a step forward, the better to watch them as they rode away, when the grass dropped out of the bell and it clattered. A red-whiskered soldier heard the tinkle, and wheeling his horse, rode back. I grasped the clapper and lay flat on the ground, my heart beating like a trip-hammer. He rode within twenty feet of me, peering into the thicket of cane, and not seeing anything unusual, turned and galloped away after his companions. Then the lesson taught me by my mother of being 'faithful over a few things' flashed through my mind, and though our cattle were spared to us, I felt very guilty.

Another vivid recollection of those boyhood days in Georgia was the return of my father from the army. The news of Lee's surrender had reached us, and all of us watched for his coming. Though he was long delayed, when at last he did come riding home on a swallow-marked brown mule, he was a conquering hero to us children. We had never owned a horse, and he assured us that the animal was his own, and by turns set us on the tired mule's back. He explained to mother and us children how, though he was an infantryman, he came into possession of the animal. Now, however, with my mature years and knowledge of brands, I regret to state that the mule had not been condemned and was in the 'US' brand. A story which Priest, 'The Rebel', once told me throws some light on the matter; he asserted that all good soldiers would steal. 'Can you take the city of St Louis?' was asked of General Price. 'I don't know as I can take it,' replied the general to his consulting superiors, 'but if you will give me Louisiana troops, I'll agree to steal it.'

Though my father had lost nothing by the war, he was impatient to go to a new country. Many of his former comrades were going to Texas, and, as our worldly possessions were movable, to Texas we started. Our four oxen were yoked to the wagon, in which our few household effects were loaded and in which mother and the smaller children rode, and with the cows, dogs and elder boys bringing up the rear, our caravan started, my father riding the mule and driving the oxen. It was an entire summer's trip, full of incident, privation and hardship. The stock fared well, but several times we were compelled to halt and secure work in order to supply our limited larder. Through certain sections, however, fish and game were abundant. I remember the enthusiasm we all felt when we reached the Sabine River, and for the first time viewed the promised land. It was at a ferry, and the sluggish river was deep. When my father informed the ferryman that he had no money with which to pay the ferriage, the latter turned on him, remarking sarcastically: 'What, no money? My dear sir, it certainly can't make much difference to a man which side of the river he's on, when he has no money.'

Nothing daunted by this rebuff, my father argued the point at some length, when the ferryman relented so far as to inform him that ten miles higher up, the river was fordable. We arrived at the ford the next day. My father rode across and back, testing the stage of the water and the river's bottom before driving the wagon in. Then taking one of the older boys behind him on the mule in order to lighten the wagon, he drove the oxen into the river. Near the middle the water was deep enough to reach the wagon box, but with shoutings and a free application of the gad, we hurried through in safety. One of the wheel oxen, a black steer which we called 'Pop-eye', could be ridden, and I straddled him in fording, laving my sunburned feet in the cool water. The cows were driven over next, the dogs swimming, and at last, bag and baggage, we were in Texas.

We reached the Colorado River early in the fall, where we stopped and picked cotton for several months, making quite a bit of money, and near Christmas reached our final destination on the San Antonio River, where we took up land and built a house. That was a happy home; the country was new and supplied our simple wants; we had milk and honey, and, though the fig tree was absent, along the river grew endless quantities of mustang grapes. At that time the San Antonio valley was principally a cattle country, and as the boys of our family grew old enough the fascination of a horse and saddle was too strong to be resisted. My two older brothers went first, but my father and mother made strenuous efforts to keep me at home, and did so until I was sixteen. I suppose it is natural for every country boy to be fascinated with some other occupation than the one to which he is bred. In my early teens, I always thought I should like either to drive six horses to a stage or clerk in a store, and if I could have attained either of those lofty heights, at that age, I would have asked no more. So my father, rather than see me follow in the footsteps of my older brothers, secured me a situation in a village store some twenty miles distant. The storekeeper was a fellow countryman of my father – from the same county in Ireland, in fact – and I was duly elated on getting away from home to the life of the village.

But my elation was short-lived. I was to receive no wages for the first six months. My father counselled the merchant to work me hard, and, if possible, cure me of the 'foolish notion', as he termed it. The storekeeper cured me. The first week I was with him he kept me in a back warehouse shelling corn. The second week started out no better. I was given a shovel and put on the street to work out the poll-tax, not only of the merchant but of two other clerks in the store. Here was two weeks' work in sight, but the third morning I took breakfast at home. My mercantile career had ended, and forthwith I took to the range as a preacher's son takes to vice. By the time I was twenty there was no better cow-hand in the entire country. I could, besides, speak Spanish and play the fiddle, and thought nothing of riding thirty miles to a dance. The vagabond temperament of the range I easily assimilated.

Christmas in the South is always a season of festivity, and the magnet of mother and home yearly drew us to the family hearthstone. There we brothers met and exchanged stories of our experiences. But one year both my brothers brought home a new experience. They had been up the trail, and the wondrous stories they told about the northern country set my blood on fire. Until then I thought I had had adventures, but mine paled into insignificance beside theirs. The following summer, my eldest brother, Robert, himself was to boss a herd up the trail, and I pleaded with him to give me a berth, but he refused me, saying: 'No, Tommy; the trail is one place where a foreman can have no favourites. Hardship and privation must be met, and the men must throw themselves equally into the collar. I don't doubt but you're a good hand; still the fact that you're my brother might cause other boys to think I would favour you. A trail outfit has to work as a unit, and dissensions would be ruinous.' I had seen favouritism shown on ranches, and understood his position to be right. Still I felt that I must make that trip if it were possible. Finally Robert, seeing that I was over-anxious to go, came to me and said: 'I've been thinking that if I recommended you to Jim Flood, my old foreman, he might take you with him next year. He is to have a herd that will take five months from start to delivery, and that will be the chance of your life. I'll see him next week and make a strong talk for you.'

True to his word, he bespoke me a job with Flood the next time he met him, and a week later a letter from Flood reached me, terse and pointed, engaging my services as a trail hand for the coming summer. The outfit would pass near our home on its way to receive the cattle which were to make up the trail herd. Time and place were appointed where I was to meet them in the middle of March, and I felt as if I were made. I remember my mother and sisters twitted me about the swagger that came into my walk, after the receipt of Flood's letter, and even asserted that I sat my horse as straight as a poker. Possibly! but wasn't I going up the trail with Jim Flood, the boss foreman of Don Lovell, the cowman and drover?

Our little ranch was near Cibollo Ford on the river, and as the outfit passed down the country, they crossed at that ford and picked me up. Flood was not with them, which was a disappointment to me, 'Quince' Forrest acting as *segundo* at the time. They had four mules to the 'chuck' wagon under Barney McCann as cook, while the *remuda*, under Billy Honeyman as horse wrangler, numbered a hundred and forty-two, ten horses to the man, with two extra for the foreman. Then, for the first time, I learned that we were going down to the mouth of the Rio Grande to receive the herd from across the river in Old Mexico; and that they were contracted for delivery on the Blackfoot Indian Reservation in the northwest corner of Montana. Lovell had several contracts with the Indian Department of the government that year, and had been granted the privilege of bringing in, free of duty, any cattle to be used in filling Indian contracts.

My worst trouble was getting away from home on the morning of starting. Mother and my sisters, of course, shed a few tears; but my father, stern and unbending in his manner, gave me his benediction in these words: 'Thomas Moore, you're the third son to leave our roof, but your father's blessing goes with you. I left my own home beyond the sea before I was your age.' And as they all stood at the gate, I climbed into my saddle and rode away, with a lump in my throat which left me speechless to reply.

CHAPTER 2

Receiving

It was a nice ten days' trip from the San Antonio to the Rio Grande River. We made twenty-five to thirty miles a day, giving the saddle horses all the advantage of grazing on the way. Rather than hobble, Forrest night-herded them, using five guards, two men to the watch of two hours each. 'As I have little hope of ever rising to the dignity of foreman,' said our *segundo*, while arranging the guards, 'I'll take this occasion to show you varmints what an iron will I possess. With the amount of help I have, I don't propose even to catch a night horse; and I'll give the cook orders to bring me a cup of coffee and a cigarette before I arise in the morning. I've been up the trail before and realise that this authority is short-lived, so I propose to make the most of it while it lasts. Now you all know your places, and see you don't incur your foreman's displeasure.'

The outfit reached Brownsville on March 25th, where we picked up Flood and Lovell, and dropping down the river about six miles below Fort Brown, went into camp at a cattle ford known as Paso Ganado. The Rio Grande was two hundred yards wide at this point, and at its then stage was almost swimming from bank to bank. It had very little current, and when winds were favourable the tide from the Gulf ran in above the ford. Flood had spent the past two weeks across the river, receiving and road-branding the herd, so when the cattle should reach the river on the Mexican side we were in honour bound to accept everything bearing the 'circle dot' on the left hip. The contract called for a thousand she cattle, three and four years of age, and two thousand four- and five-year-old beeves, estimated as sufficient to fill a million-pound beef contract. For fear of losses on the trail, our foreman had accepted fifty extra head of each class, and our herd at starting would number thirty-one hundred head. They were coming up from ranches in the interior, and we expected to cross them the first favourable day after their arrival. A number of different rancheros had turned in cattle in making up the herd, and Flood reported them in good, strong condition.

Lovell and Flood were a good team of cowmen. The former, as a youth, had carried a musket in the ranks of the Union army, and at the end of that struggle, cast his fortune with Texas; where others had seen nothing but the desolation of war, Lovell saw opportunities of business, and had yearly forged ahead as a drover and beef contractor. He was well calculated to manage the cattle business, but was irritable and inclined to borrow trouble, therefore unqualified personally to oversee the actual management of a cow herd. In repose, Don Lovell was slow, almost dull, but in an emergency was astonishingly quick-witted and alert. He never insisted on temperance among his men, and though usually of a placid temperament, when out of tobacco – Lord!

Jim Flood, on the other hand, was in a hundred respects the antithesis of his employer. Born to the soil of Texas, he knew nothing but cattle, but he knew them thoroughly. Yet in their calling, the pair were a harmonious unit. He never crossed a bridge till he reached it, was indulgent with his men, and would overlook any fault, so long as they rendered faithful service. Priest told me this incident: Flood had hired a man at Red River the year before, when a self-appointed guardian present called Flood to one side and said – 'Don't you know that that man you've just hired is the worst drunkard in this country?'

'No, I didn't know it,' replied Flood, 'but I'm glad to hear he is. I don't want to ruin an innocent man, and a trail outfit is not supposed to have any morals. Just so the herd don't count out shy on the day of delivery, I don't mind how many drinks the outfit takes.'

The next morning after going into camp, the first thing was the allotment of our mounts for the trip. Flood had the first pick, and cut twelve bays and browns. His preference for solid colours, though they were not the largest in the *remuda*, showed his practical sense of horses. When it came the boys' turn to cut, we were only allowed to cut one at a time by turns, even casting lots for first choice. We had ridden the horses enough to have a fair idea as to their merits, and every lad was his own judge. There were, as it happened, only three pinto horses in the entire saddle stock, and these three were the last left of the entire bunch. Now a little boy or girl, and many an older person, thinks that a spotted horse is the real thing, but practical cattlemen know that this freak of colour in range-bred horses is the result of in-and-in breeding, with consequent physical and mental deterioration. It was my good fortune that morning to get a good mount of horses – three sorrels, two greys, two coyotes, a black, a brown and a *grulla*. The black was my second pick, and though the colour is not a hardy one, his 'breadbasket' indicated that he could carry food for a long ride, and ought to be a good swimmer. My judgement of him was confirmed throughout the trip, as I used him for my night horse and when we had swimming rivers to ford. I gave this black the name of 'Nigger Boy.'

For the trip each man was expected to furnish his own accoutrements. In saddles, we had the ordinary Texas make, the housings of which covered our mounts from withers to hips, and would weigh from thirty to forty pounds, bedecked with the latest in the way of trimmings and trappings.

Our bridles were in keeping with the saddles, the reins as long as plough lines, while the bit was frequently ornamental and costly. The indispensable slicker, a greatcoat of oiled canvas, was ever at hand, securely tied to our cantle strings. Spurs were a matter of taste. If a rider carried a quirt, he usually dispensed with spurs, though, when used, those with large, dull rowels were the make commonly chosen. In the matter of leggings, not over half our outfit had any, as a trail herd always kept in the open, and except for night herding they were too warm in summer. Our craft never used a cattle whip, but if emergency required, the loose end of a rope served instead, and was more humane.

Either Flood or Lovell went into town every afternoon with some of the boys, expecting to hear from the cattle. On one trip they took along the wagon, laying in a month's supplies. The rest of us amused ourselves in various ways. One afternoon when the tide was in, we tried our swimming horses in the river, stripping to our underclothing, and, with nothing but a bridle on our horses, plunged into tidewater. My Nigger Boy swam from bank to bank like a duck. On the return I slid off behind, and taking his tail, let him tow me to our own side, where he arrived snorting like a tugboat.

One evening, on their return from Brownsville, Flood brought word that the herd would camp that night within fifteen miles of the river. At daybreak Lovell and the foreman, with 'Fox' Quarternight and myself, started to meet the herd. The nearest ferry was at Brownsville, and it was eleven o'clock when we reached the cattle. Flood had dispensed with an interpreter and had taken Quarternight and me along to do the interpreting. The cattle were well shed and in good flesh for such an early season of the year, and in receiving, our foreman had been careful and had accepted only such as had strength for a long voyage. They were the long-legged, long-horned Southern cattle, pale-coloured as a rule, possessed the running powers of a deer, and in an ordinary walk could travel with a horse. They had about thirty vaqueros under a corporal driving the herd, and the cattle were strung out in regular trailing manner. We rode with them until the noon hour, when, with the understanding that they were to bring the herd to Paso Ganado by ten o'clock the following day, we rode for Matamoros. Lovell had other herds to start on the trail that year, and was very anxious to cross the cattle the following day, so as to get the weekly steamer – the only mode of travel – which left Point Isabel for Galveston on the first of April.

The next morning was bright and clear, with an east wind, which ensured a flood tide in the river. On first sighting the herd that morning, we made ready to cross them as soon as they reached the river. The wagon was moved up within a hundred yards of the ford, and a substantial corral of ropes was stretched. Then the entire saddle stock was driven in, so as to be at hand in case a hasty change of mounts was required. By this time Honeyman knew the horses of each man's mount, so all we had to do was to sing out our horse, and Billy would have a rope on one and have him at hand before you could unsaddle a tired one. On account of our linguistic accomplishments, Quarternight and I were to be sent across the river to put the cattle in and otherwise assume control. On the Mexican side there was a single string of high brush fence on the lower side of the ford, commencing well out in the water and running back about two hundred yards, thus giving us a half chute in forcing the cattle to take swimming water. This ford had been in use for years in crossing cattle, but I believe this was the first herd ever crossed that was intended for the trail, or for beyond the bounds of Texas.

When the herd was within a mile of the river, Fox and I shed our saddles, boots, and surplus clothing and started to meet it. The water was chilly, but we struck it with a shout, and with the cheers of our outfit behind us, swam like smugglers. A swimming horse needs freedom, and we scarcely touched the reins, but with one hand buried in a mane hold, and giving gentle slaps on the neck with the other, we guided our horses for the other shore. I was proving out my black, Fox had a grey of equal barrel displacement – both good swimmers; and on reaching the Mexican shore, we dismounted and allowed them to roll in the warm sand.

Flood had given us general instructions, and we halted the herd about half a mile from the river. The Mexican corporal was only too glad to have us assume charge, and assured us that he and his outfit were ours to command. I at once proclaimed Fox Quarternight, whose years and experience outranked mine, the *gringo* corporal for the day, at which the vaqueros smiled, but I noticed they never used the word. On Fox's suggestion the Mexican corporal brought up his wagon and corralled his horses as we had done, when his cook, to our delight, invited all to have coffee before starting. That cook won our everlasting regard, for his coffee was delicious. We praised it highly, whereupon the corporal ordered the cook to have it at hand for the men in the intervals between crossing the different bunches of cattle. A March day on the Rio Grande with wet clothing is not summer, and the vaqueros hesitated a bit before following the example of Quarternight and myself and dispensing with saddles and boots. Five men were then detailed to hold the herd as compact as possible, and the remainder, twenty-seven all told, cut off about three hundred head and started for the river. I took the lead, for though cattle are less gregarious by nature than other animals, under pressure of excitement they will follow a leader. It was about noon and the herd were thirsty, so when we reached the brush chute, all hands started them on a run for the water. When the cattle were once inside the wing we went rapidly, four vaqueros riding outside the fence to keep the cattle from turning the chute on reaching swimming water. The leaders were crowding me close when Nigger breasted the water, and closely followed by several lead cattle, I struck straight for the American shore. The vaqueros forced every hoof into the river, following and shouting as far as the midstream, when they were swimming so nicely, Quarternight called off the men and all turned their horses back to the Mexican side. On landing opposite the exit from the ford, our men held the cattle as they came out, in order to bait the next bunch.

I rested my horse only a few minutes before taking the water again, but Lovell urged me to take an extra horse across, so as to have a change in case my black became fagged in swimming. Quarternight was a harsh *segundo*, for no sooner had I reached the other bank than he cut off the second bunch of about four hundred and started them. Turning Nigger Boy loose behind the brush fence, so as to be out of the way, I galloped out on my second horse, and meeting the cattle, turned and again took the lead for the river. My substitute did not swim with the freedom and ease of the black, and several times cattle swam so near me that I could lay my hand on their backs. When about halfway over, I heard shoutings behind me in English, and on looking back saw Nigger Boy swimming after us. A number of vaqueros attempted to catch him, but he outswam them and came out with the cattle; the excitement was too much for him to miss.

Each trip was a repetition of the former, with varying incident. Every hoof was over in less than two hours. On the last trip, in which there were about seven hundred head, the horse of one of the Mexican vaqueros took cramps, it was supposed, at about the middle of the river, and sank without a moment's warning. A number of us heard the man's terrified cry, only in time to see horse and rider sink. Every man within reach turned to the rescue, and a moment later the man rose to the surface. Fox caught him by the shirt, and, shaking the water out of him, turned him over to one of the other vaqueros, who towed him back to their own side. Strange as it may appear, the horse never came to the surface again, which supported the supposition of cramps.

After a change of clothes for Quarternight and myself, and rather late dinner for all hands, there yet remained the counting of the herd. The Mexican corporal and two of his men had come over for the purpose, and though Lovell and several wealthy rancheros, the sellers of the cattle, were present, it remained for Flood and the corporal to make the final count, as between buyer and seller. There was also present a river guard – sent out by the United States Custom House, as a matter of form in the entry papers – who also insisted on counting. In order to have a second count on the herd, Lovell ordered The Rebel to count opposite the government's man. We strung the cattle out, now logy with water, and after making quite a circle, brought the herd around where there was quite a bluff bank of the river. The herd handled well, and for a quarter of an hour we lined them between our four mounted counters. The only difference in the manner of counting between Flood and the Mexican corporal was that the American used a tally string tied to the pommel of his saddle, on which were ten knots, keeping count by slipping a knot on each even hundred, while the Mexican used ten small pebbles, shifting a pebble from one hand to the other on hundreds. 'Just a mere difference in nationality,' Lovell had me interpret to the selling dons.

When the count ended only two of the men agreed on numbers, The Rebel and the corporal making the same thirty-one hundred and five – Flood being one under and the Custom House man one over. Lovell at once accepted the count of Priest and the corporal; and the delivery, which, as I learned during the interpreting that followed, was to be sealed with a supper that night in Brownsville, was consummated. Lovell was compelled to leave us, to make the final payment for the herd, and we would not see him again for some time. They were all seated in the vehicle ready to start for town, when the cowman said to his foreman, 'Now, Jim, I can't give you any pointers on handling a herd, but you have until the 10th day of September to reach the Blackfoot Agency. An average of fifteen miles a day will put you there on time, so don't hurry. I'll try and see you at Dodge and Ogalalla on the way. Now, live well, for I like your outfit of men. Your credit letter is good anywhere you need supplies, and if you want more horses on the trail, buy them and draft on me through your letter of credit. If any of your men meet with an accident or get sick, look out for them the same as you would for yourself, and I'll honour all bills. And don't be stingy over your expense account, for if that herd don't make money, you and I had better quit cows.'

I had been detained to do any interpreting needful, and at parting Lovell beckoned to me. When I rode alongside the carriage, he gave me his hand and said, 'Flood tells me today that you're a brother of Bob Quirk. Bob is to be foreman of my herd that I'm putting up in Nueces County. I'm glad you're here with Jim, though, for it's a longer trip. Yes, you'll get all the circus there is, and stay for the concert besides. They say God is good to the poor and the Irish; and if that's so, you'll pull through all right. Goodbye, son.' And as he gave me a hearty, ringing grip of the hand, I couldn't help feeling friendly towards him, Yankee that he was.

After Lovell and the dons had gone, Flood ordered McCann to move his wagon back from the river about a mile. It was now too late in the day to start the herd, and we wanted to graze them well, as it was our first night with them. About half our outfit grazed them around on a large circle, preparatory to bringing them up to the bed ground as it grew dusk. In the untrammelled freedom of the native range, a cow or steer will pick old dry grass on which to lie down, and if it is summer, will prefer an elevation sufficient to catch any passing breeze. Flood was familiar with the habits of cattle, and selected a nice elevation on which the old dry grass of the previous summer's growth lay matted like a carpet.

Our saddle horses by this time were fairly well broken to camp life, and, with the cattle on hand, night herding them had to be abandoned. Billy Honeyman, however, had noticed several horses that were inclined to stray on day herd, and these few leaders were so well marked in his memory that, as a matter of precaution, he insisted on putting a rope hobble on them. At every noon and night camp we strung a rope from the hind wheel of our wagon and another from the end of the wagon tongue back to stakes driven in the ground or held by a man, forming a triangular corral. Thus in a few minutes, under any conditions, we could construct a temporary corral for catching a change of mounts, or for the wrangler to hobble untrustworthy horses. On the trail all horses are free at night, except the regular night ones, which are used constantly during the entire trip, and under ordinary conditions keep strong and improve in flesh.

Before the herd was brought in for the night, and during the supper hour, Flood announced the guards for the trip. As the men usually bunked in pairs, the foreman chose them as they slept, but was under the necessity of splitting two berths of bedfellows. 'Rod' Wheat, Joe Stallings and Ash Borrowstone were assigned to the first guard, from eight to ten-thirty p.m. Bob Blades, 'Bull' Durham and Fox Quarternight were given second guard, from ten-thirty to one. Paul Priest, John Officer and myself made up the third watch, from one to three-thirty. The Rebel and I were bunkies, and this choice of guards, while not ideal, was much better than splitting bedfellows and having them annoy each other by going out and returning from guard separately. The only fault I ever found with Priest was that he could use the poorest judgement in selecting a bed ground for our blankets, and always talked and told stories to me until I fell asleep. He was a light sleeper himself, while I, being much younger, was the reverse. The fourth and last guard, from three-thirty until relieved after daybreak, fell to Wyatt Roundtree, Quince Forrest and 'Moss' Strayhorn. Thus the only men in the outfit not on night duty were Honeyman, our horse wrangler, Barney McCann, our cook, and Flood, the foreman. The latter, however, made up by riding almost double as much as any man in his outfit. He never left the herd until it was bedded down for the night, and we could always hear him quietly arousing the cook and horse wrangler an hour before daybreak. He always kept a horse on picket for the night, and often took the herd as it left the bed ground at clear dawn.

A half-hour before dark, Flood and all the herd men turned out to bed down the cattle for our first night. They had been well grazed after counting, and as they came up to the bed ground there was not a hungry or thirsty animal in the lot. All seemed anxious to lie down, and by circling around slowly, while gradually closing in, in the course of half an hour all were bedded nicely on possibly five or six acres. I remember there were a number of muleys among the cattle, and these would not venture into the compact herd until the others had lain down. Being hornless, instinct taught them to be on the defensive, and it was noticeable that they were the first to arise in the morning, in advance of their horned kin. When all had lain down, Flood and the first guard remained, the others returning to the wagon.

The guards ride in a circle about four rods outside the sleeping cattle, and by riding in opposite directions make it impossible for any animal to make its escape without being noticed by the riders. The guards usually sing or whistle continuously, so that the sleeping herd may know that a friend and not an enemy is keeping vigil over their dreams. A sleeping herd of cattle make a pretty picture on a clear moonlight night, chewing their cud and grunting and blowing over contented stomachs. The night horses soon learn their duty, and a rider may fall asleep or doze along in the saddle, but the horses will maintain their distance in their leisurely, sentinel rounds.

On returning to the wagon, Priest and I picketed our horses, saddled, where we could easily find them in the darkness, and unrolled our bed. We had two pairs of blankets each, which, with an ordinary wagon sheet doubled for a tarpaulin, and coats and boots for pillows, completed our couch. We slept otherwise in our clothing worn during the day, and if smooth, sandy ground was available on which to spread our bed, we had no trouble in sleeping the sleep that long hours in the saddle were certain to bring. With all his pardonable faults, The Rebel was a good bunkie and a hail companion, this being his sixth trip over the trail. He had been with Lovell over a year before the two made the discovery that they had been on opposite sides during the 'late unpleasantness'. On making this discovery, Lovell at once rechristened Priest 'The Rebel', and that name he always bore. He was fifteen years my senior at this time, a wonderfully complex nature, hardened by unusual experiences into a character the gamut of whose moods ran from that of a good-natured fellow to a man of unrelenting severity in anger.

We were sleeping a nine-knot gale when Fox Quarternight of the second guard called us on our watch. It was a clear, starry night, and our guard soon passed, the cattle sleeping like tired soldiers. When the last relief came on guard and we had returned to our blankets, I remember Priest telling me this little incident as I fell asleep.

'I was at a dance once in Live Oak County, and there was a stuttering fellow there by the name of Lem Todhunter. The girls, it seems, didn't care to dance with him, and pretended they couldn't understand him. He had asked every girl at the party, and received the same answer from each – they couldn't understand him. "W–w–w–ell, g–g–g–go to hell, then. C–c–c–can y–y–you understand that?" he said to the last girl, and her brother threatened to mangle him horribly if he didn't apologise, to which he finally agreed. He went back into the house and said to the girl, "Y–y–you n–n–n–needn't g–g–g–go to hell; y–y–your b–b–b–brother and I have m–m–made other 'r–r–r–rangements."'

CHAPTER 3

The Start

On the morning of April 1, 1882, our Circle Dot herd started on its long tramp to the Blackfoot Agency in Montana. With six men on each side, and the herd strung out for three quarters of a mile, it could only be compared to some mythical serpent or Chinese dragon, as it moved forward on its sinuous, snail-like course. Two riders, known as point men, rode out and well back from the lead cattle, and by riding forward and closing in as occasion required, directed the course of the herd. The main body of the herd trailed along behind the leaders like an army in loose marching order, guarded by outriders, known as swing men, who rode well out from the advancing column, warding off range cattle and seeing that none of the herd wandered away or dropped out. There was no driving to do; the cattle moved of their own free will as in ordinary travel.

Flood seldom gave orders; but, as a number of us had never worked on the trail before, at breakfast on the morning of our start he gave in substance these general directions: 'Boys, the secret of trailing cattle is never to let your herd know that they are under restraint. Let everything that is done be done voluntarily by the cattle. From the moment you let them off the bed ground in the morning until they are bedded at night, never let a cow take a step, except in the direction of its destination. In this manner you can loaf away the day, and cover from fifteen to twenty miles, and the herd in the meantime will enjoy all the freedom of an open range. Of course, it's long, tiresome hours to the men; but the condition of the herd and saddle stock demands sacrifices on our part, if any have to be made. And I want to caution you younger boys about your horses; there is such a thing as having ten horses in your string, and at the same time being afoot. You are all well mounted, and on the condition of the *remuda* depends the success and safety of the herd. Accidents will happen to horses, but don't let it be your fault; keep your saddle blankets dry and clean, for no better word can be spoken of a man than that he is careful of his horses. Ordinarily a man might get along with six or eight horses, but in such emergencies as we are liable to meet, we have not a horse to spare, and a man afoot is useless.'

And as all of us younger boys learned afterward, there was plenty of good, solid, horse-sense in Flood's advice; for before the trip ended there were men in our outfit who were as good as afoot, while others had their original mounts, every one fit for the saddle. Flood had insisted on a good mount of horses, and Lovell was cowman enough to know that what the mule is to the army the cow-horse is to the herd.

The first and second day out there was no incident worth mentioning. We travelled slowly, hardly making an average day's drive. The third morning Flood left us, to look out a crossing on the Arroyo Colorado. On coming down to receive the herd, we had crossed this sluggish bayou about thirty-six miles north of Brownsville. It was a deceptive-looking stream, being over fifty feet deep and between bluff banks. We ferried our wagon and saddle horses over, swimming the loose ones. But the herd was keeping near the coast line for the sake of open country, and it was a question if there was a ford for the wagon as near the coast as our course was carrying us. The murmurings of the Gulf had often reached our ears the day before, and herds had been known, in former years, to cross from the mainland over to Padre Island, the intervening Laguna Madre being fordable.

We were nooning when Flood returned with the news that it would be impossible to cross our wagon at any point on the bayou, and that we would have to ford around the mouth of the stream. Where the fresh and salt water met in the laguna, there had formed a delta, or shallow bar, and by following its contour we would not have over twelve to fourteen inches of water, though the half circle was nearly two miles in length. As we would barely have time to cross that day, the herd was at once started, veering for the mouth of the Arroyo Colorado. On reaching it, about the middle of the afternoon, the foreman led the way, having crossed in the morning and learned the ford. The wagon followed, the saddle horses came next, while the herd brought up the rear. It proved good footing on the sandbar, but the water in the laguna was too salty for the cattle, though the loose horses lay down and wallowed in it. We were about an hour in crossing, and on reaching the mainland met a vaquero, who directed us to a large freshwater lake a few miles inland, where we camped for the night.

It proved an ideal camp, with wood, water and grass in abundance, and very little range stock to annoy us. We had watered the herd just before noon, and before throwing them upon the bed ground for the night, watered them a second time. We had a splendid campfire that night, of dry live oak logs, and after supper was over and the first guard had taken the herd, smoking and storytelling were the order of the evening. The campfire is to all outdoor life what the evening fireside is to domestic life. After the labours of the day are over, the men gather around the fire, and the social hour of the day is spent in yarning. The stories told may run from the sublime to the ridiculous, from a true incident to a base fabrication, or from a touching bit of pathos to the most vulgar vulgarity.

'Have I ever told this outfit my experience with the vigilantes when I was a kid?' enquired Bull Durham. There was a general negative response, and he proceeded. 'Well, our folks were living on the Frio at the time, and there was a man in our neighbourhood who had an outfit of four men out beyond Nueces Canon hunting wild cattle for their hides. It was necessary to take them out supplies about every so often, and on one trip he begged my folks to let me go along for company. I was a slim slip of a colt about fourteen at the time, and as this man was a friend of ours, my folks consented to let me go along. We each had a good saddle horse, and two pack mules with provisions and ammunition for the hunting camp. The first night we made camp, a boy overtook us with the news that the brother of my companion had been accidentally killed by a horse, and of course he would have to return. Well, we were twenty miles on our way, and as it would take some little time to go back and return with the loaded mules, I volunteered, like a fool kid, to go on and take the packs through.

'The only question was, could I pack and unpack. I had helped him at this work, double-handed, but now that I was to try it alone, he showed me what he called a squaw hitch, with which you can lash a pack single-handed. After putting me through it once or twice, and satisfying himself that I could do the packing, he consented to let me go on, he and the messenger returning home during the night. The next morning I packed without any trouble and started on my way. It would take me two days yet, poking along with heavy packs, to reach the hunters. Well, I hadn't made over eight or ten miles the first morning, when, as I rounded a turn in the trail, a man stepped out from behind a rock, threw a gun in my face, and ordered me to hold up my hands. Then another appeared from the opposite side with his gun levelled on me. Inside of half a minute a dozen men galloped up from every quarter, all armed to the teeth. The man on leaving had given me his gun for company, one of these old smoke-pole, cap-and-ball six-shooters, but I must have forgotten what guns were for, for I elevated my little hands nicely. The leader of the party questioned me as to who I was, and what I was doing there, and what I had in those packs. That once, at least, I told the truth. Every mother's son of them was cursing and cross-questioning me in the same breath. They ordered me off my horse, took my gun, and proceeded to verify my tale by unpacking the mules. So much ammunition aroused their suspicions, but my story was as good as it was true, and they never shook me from the truth of it. I soon learned that robbery was not their motive, and the leader explained the situation.

'A vigilance committee had been in force in that county for some time, trying to rid the country of lawless characters. But lawlessness got into the saddle, and had bench warrants issued and served on every member of this vigilance committee. As the vigilantes numbered several hundred, there was no jail large enough to hold such a number, so they were released on parole for appearance at court. When court met, every man served with a capias – '

'Hold on! hold your horses just a minute,' interrupted Quince Forrest, 'I want to get that word. I want to make a memorandum of it, for I may want to use it myself sometime. Capias? Now I have it; go ahead.'

'When court met, every man served with a bench warrant from the judge presiding was present, and as soon as court was called to order, a squad of men arose in the courtroom, and the next moment the judge fell riddled with lead. Then the factions scattered to fight it out, and I was passing through the county while matters were active.

'They confiscated my gun and all the ammunition in the packs, but helped me to repack and started me on my way. A happy thought struck one of the men to give me a letter, which would carry me through without further trouble, but the leader stopped him, saying, "Let the boy alone. Your letter would hang him as sure as hell's hot, before he went ten miles farther." I declined the letter. Even then I didn't have sense enough to turn back, and inside of two hours I was rounded up by the other faction. I had learned my story perfectly by this time, but those packs had to come off again for everything to be examined. There was nothing in them now but flour and salt and such things – nothing that they might consider suspicious. One fellow in this second party took a fancy to my horse, and offered to help hang me on general principles, but kinder counsels prevailed. They also helped me to repack, and I started on once more. Before I reached my destination the following evening, I was held up seven different times. I got so used to it that I was happily disappointed every shelter I passed if some man did not step out and throw a gun in my face.

'I had trouble to convince the cattle hunters of my experiences, but the absence of any ammunition, which they needed worst, at last led them to give credit to my tale. I was expected home within a week, as I was to go down on the Nueces on a cow hunt which was making up, and I only rested one day at the hunters' camp. On their advice, I took a different route on my way home, leaving the mules behind me. I never saw a man the next day returning, and was feeling quite gala on my good fortune. When evening came on, I sighted a little ranch house some distance off the trail, and concluded to ride to it and stay overnight. As I approached, I saw that someone lived there, as there were chickens and dogs about, but not a person in sight. I dismounted and knocked on the door, when, without a word, the door was thrown wide open and a half dozen guns were poked into my face. I was ordered into the house and given a chance to tell my story again. Whether my story was true or not, they took no chances on me, but kept me all night. One of the men took my horse to the stable and cared for him, and I was well fed and given a place to sleep, but not a man offered a word of explanation, from which I took it they did not belong to the vigilance faction. When it came time to go to bed, one man said to me, "Now, sonny, don't make any attempt to get away, and don't move out of your bed without warning us, for you'll be shot as sure as you do. We won't harm a hair on your head if you're telling us the truth; only do as you're told, for we'll watch you."

'By this time I had learned to obey orders while in that county, and got a fair night's sleep, though there were men going and coming all night. The next morning I was given my breakfast; my horse, well cuffed and saddled, was brought to the door, and with this parting advice I was given permission to go: "Son, if you've told us the truth, don't look back when you ride away. You'll be watched for the first ten miles after leaving here, and if you've lied to us it will go hard with you. Now, remember, don't look back, for these are times when no one cares to be identified." I never questioned that man's advice; it was "die dog or eat the hatchet" with me. I mounted my horse, waved the usual parting courtesies, and rode away. As I turned into the trail about a quarter mile from the house, I noticed two men ride out from behind the stable and follow me. I remembered the story about Lot's wife looking back, though it was lead and not miracles that I was afraid of that morning.

'For the first hour I could hear the men talking and the hoofbeats of their horses, as they rode along always the same distance behind me. After about two hours of this one-sided joke, as I rode over a little hill, I

looked out of the corner of my eye back at my escort, still about a quarter
of a mile behind me. One of them noticed me and raised his gun, but I
instantly changed my view, and the moment the hill hid me, put spurs to
my horse, so that when they reached the brow of the hill, I was half a mile
in the lead, burning the earth like a canned dog. They threw lead close
around me, but my horse lengthened the distance between us for the next
five miles, when they dropped entirely out of sight. By noon I came into
the old stage road, and by the middle of the afternoon reached home
after over sixty miles in the saddle without a halt.'

Just at the conclusion of Bull's story, Flood rode in from the herd, and
after picketing his horse, joined the circle. In reply to an enquiry from
one of the boys as to how the cattle were resting, he replied, 'This herd is
breaking into trail life nicely. If we'll just be careful with them now for
the first month, and no bad storms strike us in the night, we may never
have a run the entire trip. That last drink of water they had this evening
gave them a nightcap that'll last them until morning. No, there's no
danger of any trouble tonight.'

For fully an hour after the return of our foreman, we lounged around
the fire, during which there was a full and free discussion of stampedes.
But finally, Flood, suiting the action to the word by arising, suggested
that all hands hunt their blankets and turn in for the night. A quiet wink
from Bull to several of the boys held us for the time being, and innocently
turning to Forrest, Durham enquired, 'Where was – when was – was it
you that was telling someone about a run you were in last summer? I
never heard you tell it. Where was it?'

'You mean on the Cimarron last year when we mixed two herds,' said
Quince, who had taken the bait like a bass and was now fully embarked
on a yarn. 'We were in rather close quarters, herds ahead and behind us,
when one night here came a cow herd like a cyclone and swept right
through our camp. We tumbled out of our blankets and ran for our
horses, but before we could bridle – '

Bull had given us the wink, and every man in the outfit fell back, and
the snoring that checked the storyteller was like a chorus of rip saws
running through pine knots. Forrest took in the situation at a glance, and
as he arose to leave, looked back and remarked, 'You must all think that's
smart.'

Before he was out of hearing, Durham said to the rest of us. 'A few
doses like that will cure him of sucking eggs and acting smart, interrupting
folks.'

CHAPTER 4

The Atascosa

For the next few days we paralleled the coast, except when forced inland by various arms of the Laguna Madre. When about a week out from the Arroyo Colorado, we encountered the Salt Lagoon, which threw us at least fifty miles in from the coast. Here we had our last view of salt water, and the murmurings of the Gulf were heard no more. Our route now led northward through what were then the two largest ranches in Texas, the 'Running W' and Laurel Leaf, which sent more cattle up the trail, bred in their own brand, than any other four ranches in the Lone Star State. We were nearly a week passing through their ranges, and on reaching Santa Gertruda Ranch learned that three trail herds, of over three thousand head each, had already started in these two brands, while four more were to follow.

So far we had been having splendid luck in securing water for the herd, once a day at least, and often twice and three times. Our herd was becoming well trail-broken by this time, and for range cattle had quieted down and were docile and easy to handle. Flood's years of experience on the trail made him a believer in the theory that stampedes were generally due to negligence in not having the herd full of grass and water on reaching the bed ground at night. Barring accidents, which will happen, his view is the correct one, if care has been used for the first few weeks in properly breaking the herd to the trail. But though hunger and thirst are probably responsible for more stampedes than all other causes combined, it is the unexpected which cannot be guarded against. A stampede is the natural result of fear, and at night or in an uncertain light, this timidity might be imparted to an entire herd by a flash of lightning or a peal of thunder, while the stumbling of a night horse, or the scent of some wild animal, would in a moment's time, from frightening a few head, so infect a herd as to throw them into the wildest panic. Among the thousands of herds like ours which were driven over the trail during its brief existence, none ever made the trip without encountering more or less trouble from runs. Frequently a herd became so spoiled in this manner that it grew into a mania with them, so that they would stampede on the slightest provocation – or no provocation at all.

A few days after leaving Santa Gertruda Ranch, we crossed the Nueces River, which we followed up for several days, keeping in touch with it for water for the herd. But the Nueces, after passing Oakville, makes an abrupt turn, doubling back to the southwest; and the Atascosa, one of its tributaries, became our source of water supply. We were beginning to feel a degree of over-confidence in the good behaviour of our herd, when one night during the third week out, an incident occurred in which they displayed their running qualities to our complete satisfaction.

It occurred during our guard, and about two o'clock in the morning. The night was an unusually dark one and the atmosphere was very humid. After we had been on guard possibly an hour, John Officer and I riding in one direction on opposite sides of the herd, and The Rebel circling in the other, Officer's horse suddenly struck a gopher burrow with his front feet, and in a moment horse and rider were sprawling on the ground. The accident happened but a few rods from the sleeping herd, which instantly came to their feet as one steer, and were off like a flash. I was riding my Nigger Boy, and as the cattle headed towards me, away from the cause of their fright, I had to use both quirt and rowel to keep clear of the onrush. Fortunately we had a clear country near the bed ground, and while the terrified cattle pressed me close, my horse kept the lead. In the rumbling which ensued, all sounds were submerged by the general din; and I was only brought to the consciousness that I was not alone by seeing several distinct flashes from six-shooters on my left, and, realising that I also had a gun, fired several times in the air in reply. I was soon joined by Priest and Officer, the latter having lost no time in regaining his seat in the saddle, and the three of us held together some little distance, for it would have been useless to attempt to check or turn this onslaught of cattle in their first mad rush.

The wagon was camped about two hundred yards from the bed ground, and the herd had given ample warning to the boys asleep, so that if we three could hold our position in the lead, help would come to us as soon as the men in camp could reach their horses. Realising the wide front of the running cattle, Priest sent Officer to the left and myself to the right, to point in the leaders in order to keep the herd from splitting or scattering, while he remained in the centre and led the herd. I soon gained the outside of the leaders, and by dropping back and coming up the line, pointed them in to the best of my ability. I had repeated this a number of times, even quirting some cattle along the outside, or burning a little powder in the face of some obstinate leader, when across the herd and to the rear I saw a succession of flashes like fireflies, which told me the boys were coming to our assistance.

Running is not a natural gait with cattle, and if we could only hold them together and prevent splitting up, in time they would tire, while the rear cattle could be depended on to follow the leaders. All we could hope to do was to force them to run straight, and in this respect we were succeeding splendidly, though to a certain extent it was a guess in the dark. When they had run possibly a mile, I noticed a horseman overtake Priest. After they had ridden together a moment, one of them came over to my point, and the next minute our foreman was racing along by my side. In his impatience to check the run, he took me with him, and circling the leaders we reached the left point, by which time the remainder of the outfit had come up. Now massing our numbers, we fell on the left point, and amid the flash of guns deflected their course for a few moments. A dozen men, however, can cover but a small space, and we soon realised that we had turned only a few hundred head, for the momentum of the main body bore steadily ahead. Abandoning what few cattle we had turned, which, owing to their running ability, soon resumed their places in the lead, we attempted to turn them to the left. Stretching out our line until there was a man about every twenty feet, we threw our force against the right point and lead in the hope of gradually deviating their course. For a few minutes the attempt promised to be successful, but our cordon was too weak and the cattle went through between the riders, and we soon found a portion of our forces on either side of the herd, while a few of the boys were riding out of the rush in the lead.

On finding our forces thus divided, the five or six of us who remained on the right contented ourselves by pointing in the leaders, for the cattle, so far as we could tell, were running compactly. Our foreman, however, was determined to turn the run, and after a few minutes' time rejoined us on the right, when under his leadership we circled the front of the herd and collected on the left point, when, for a third time, we repeated the same tactics in our efforts to turn the stampede. But in this, which was our final effort, we were attempting to turn them slowly and on a much larger circle, and with a promise of success. Suddenly in the dark we encountered a mesquite thicket into which the lead cattle tore with a crashing of brush and a rattle of horns that sent a chill up and down my spine. But there was no time to hesitate, for our horses were in the thicket, and with the herd closing in on us there was no alternative but to go through it, every man for himself. I gave Nigger a free rein, shutting my eyes and clutching both cantle and pommel to hold my seat; the black responded to the rowel and tore through the thicket, in places higher than my head, and came out in an open space considerably in the lead of the cattle.

This thicket must have been eight or ten rods wide, and checked the run to a slight extent; but as they emerged from it, they came out like scattering flies and resumed their running. Being alone, and not knowing which way to turn, I rode to the right and front and soon found myself in the lead of quite a string of cattle. Nigger and I were piloting them where they listed, when Joe Stallings, hatless himself and his horse heaving, overtook me, and the two of us gave those lead cattle all the trouble we knew how. But we did not attempt to turn them, for they had caught their wind in forcing the thicket, and were running an easy stroke. Several times we worried the leaders into a trot, but as other cattle in the rear came up, we were compelled to loosen out and allow them to resume their running, or they would have scattered on us like partridges. At this stage of the run, we had no idea where the rest of the outfit were, but both of us were satisfied the herd had scattered on leaving the mesquite thicket, and were possibly then running in half a dozen bunches like the one we were with.

Stallings's horse was badly winded, and on my suggestion, he dropped out on one side to try to get some idea how many cattle we were leading. He was gone some little time, and as Nigger cantered along easily in the lead, I managed to eject the shells from my six-shooter and refill the cylinder. On Joe's overtaking me again, he reported that there was a slender column of cattle, half a mile in length, following. As one man could easily lead this string of the herd until daybreak, I left Stallings with them and rode out to the left nearly a quarter of a mile, listening to hear if there were any cattle running to the left of those we were leading. It took me but a few minutes to satisfy myself that ours was the outside band on the left, and after I rejoined Joe, we made an effort to check our holding.

There were about fifty or sixty big steers in the lead of our bunch, and after worrying them into a trot, we opened in their front with our six-shooters, shooting into the ground in their very faces, and were rewarded by having them turn tail and head the other way. Taking advantage of the moment, we jumped our horses on the retreating leaders, and as fast as the rear cattle forged forward, easily turned them. Leaving Joe to turn the rear as they came up, I rode to the lead, unfastening my slicker as I went, and on reaching the turned leaders, who were running on an angle from their former course, flaunted my 'fish' in their faces until they re-entered the rear guard of our string, and we soon had a mill going which kept them busy, and rested our horses. Once we had them milling, our trouble, as far as running was concerned, was over, for all two of us could hope to do was to let them exhaust themselves in this endless circle.

It then lacked an hour of daybreak, and all we could do was to ride around and wait for daylight. In the darkness preceding dawn, we had no idea of the number of our bunch, except as we could judge from the size and compactness of the milling cattle, which must have covered an acre or more. The humidity of the atmosphere, which had prevailed during the night, by dawn had changed until a heavy fog, cutting off our view on every hand, left us as much at sea as we had been previously. But with the break of day we rode through our holding a number of times, splitting and scattering the milling cattle, and as the light of day brightened, we saw them quiet down and go to grazing as though they had just arisen from the bed ground. It was over an hour before the fog lifted sufficiently to give us any idea as to our whereabouts, and during the interim both Stallings and myself rode to the nearest elevation, firing a number of shots in the hope of getting an answer from the outfit, but we had no response.

When the sun was sufficiently high to scatter the mists which hung in clouds, there was not an object in sight by which we could determine our location. Whether we had run east, west, or south during the night neither of us knew, though both Stallings and myself were satisfied that we had never crossed the trail, and all we did know for a certainty was that we had between six and seven hundred head of cattle. Stallings had lost his hat, and I had one sleeve missing and both outside pockets torn out of my coat, while the mesquite thorns had left their marks on the faces of both of us, one particularly ugly cut marking Joe's right temple. 'I've worn leggin's for the last ten years,' said Stallings to me, as we took an inventory of our disfigurements, 'and for about ten seconds in forcing that mesquite thicket was the only time I ever drew interest on my investment. They're a heap like a six-shooter – wear them all your life and never have any use for them.'

With a cigarette for breakfast, I left Joe to look after our bunch, and after riding several miles to the right, cut the trail of quite a band of cattle. In following up this trail I could easily see that someone was in their lead, as they failed to hold their course in any one direction for any distance, as free cattle would. After following this trail about three miles, I sighted the band of cattle, and on overtaking them, found two of our boys holding about half as many as Stallings had. They reported that The Rebel and Bob Blades had been with them until daybreak, but having the freshest horses had left them with the dawn and ridden away to the right, where it was supposed the main body of the herd had run. As Stallings's bunch was some three or four miles to the rear and left of this band, Wyatt Roundtree suggested that he go and pilot in Joe's cattle, as he felt positive that the main body were somewhere to our right. On getting directions from me as to where he would find our holding, he rode away, and I again rode off to the right, leaving Rod Wheat with their catch.

The sun was now several hours high, and as my black's strength was standing the test bravely, I cross-cut the country and was soon on another trail of our stampeded cattle. But in following this trail, I soon noticed two other horsemen preceding me. Knowing that my services would be too late, I only followed far enough to satisfy myself of the fact. The signs left by the running cattle were as easy to follow as a public road, and in places where the ground was sandy, the sod was cut up as if a regiment of cavalry had charged across it. On again bearing off to the right, I rode for an elevation which ought to give me a good view of the country. Slight as this elevation was, on reaching it, I made out a large band of cattle under herd, and as I was on the point of riding to them, saw our wagon and saddle horses heave in sight from a northwest quarter. Supposing they were following up the largest trail, I rode for the herd, where Flood and two of the boys had about twelve hundred cattle. From a comparison of notes, our foreman was able to account for all the men with the exception of two, and as these proved to be Blades and Priest, I could give him a satisfactory explanation as to their probable whereabouts. On my report of having sighted the wagon and *remuda*, Flood at once ordered me to meet and hurry them in, as not only he, but Strayhorn and Officer, were badly in need of a change of mounts.

I learned from McCann, who was doing the trailing from the wagon, that the regular trail was to the west, the herd having crossed it within a quarter of a mile after leaving the bed ground. Joining Honeyman, I took the first horse which came within reach of my rope, and with a fresh mount under me, we rushed the saddle horses past the wagon and shortly came up with our foreman. There we rounded in the horses as best we could without the aid of the wagon, and before McCann arrived, all had fresh mounts and were ready for orders. This was my first trip on the trail, and I was hungry and thirsty enough to hope something would be said about eating, but that seemed to be the last idea in our foreman's mind. Instead, he ordered me to take the two other boys with me, and after putting them on the trail of the bunch which The Rebel and Blades were following, to drift in what cattle we had held on our left. But as we went, we managed to encounter the wagon and get a drink and a canteen of water from McCann before we galloped away on our mission. After riding a mile or so together, we separated, and on my arrival at the nearest bunch, I found Roundtree and Stallings coming up with the larger holding. Throwing the two hunches together, we drifted them a free clip towards camp. We soon sighted the main herd, and saw across to our right and about five miles distant two of our men bringing in another bunch. As soon as we turned our cattle into the herd, Flood ordered me, on account of my light weight, to meet this bunch, find out where the last cattle were, and go to their assistance.

With a hungry look in the direction of our wagon, I obeyed, and on meeting Durham and Borrowstone, learned that the outside bunch on the right, which had got into the regular trail, had not been checked until daybreak. All they knew about their location was that the upstage from Oakville had seen two men with Circle Dot cattle about five miles below, and had sent up word by the driver that they had something like four hundred head. With this meagre information, I rode away in the direction where one would naturally expect to find our absent men, and after scouring the country for an hour, sighted a single horseman on an elevation whom from the grey mount I knew for Quince Forrest. He was evidently on the lookout for some one to pilot them in. They had been drifting like lost sheep ever since dawn, but we soon had their cattle pointed in the right direction, and Forrest taking the lead, Quarternight and I put the necessary push behind them. Both of them cursed me roundly for not bringing them a canteen of water, though they were well aware that in an emergency, like the present, our foreman would never give a thought to anything but the recovery of the herd. Our comfort was nothing; men were cheap, but cattle cost money.

We reached the camp about two o'clock, and found the outfit cutting out range cattle which had been absorbed into the herd during the run. Throwing in our contingent, we joined in the work, and though Forrest and Quarternight were as good as afoot, there were no orders for a change of mounts, to say nothing of food and drink. Several hundred mixed cattle were in the herd, and after they had been cut out, we lined our cattle out for a count. In the absence of Priest, Flood and John Officer did the counting, and as the hour of the day made the cattle sluggish, they lined through between the counters as though they had never done anything but walk in their lives. The count showed sixteen short of twenty-eight hundred, which left us yet over three hundred out. But good men were on their trail, and leaving two men on herd, the rest of us obeyed the most welcome orders of the day when Flood intimated that we would 'eat a bite and go after the rest'.

As we had been in our saddles since one or two o'clock the morning before, it is needless to add that our appetites were equal to the spread which our cook had waiting for us. Our foreman, as though fearful of the loss of a moment's time, sent Honeyman to rustle in the horses before we had finished our dinners. Once the *remuda* was corralled, under the rush of a tireless foreman, dinner was quickly over, and fresh horses became the order of the moment. The Atascosa, our nearest water, lay beyond the regular trail to the west, and leaving orders for the outfit to drift the herd into it and water, Flood and myself started in search of our absent men, not forgetting to take along two extra horses as a remount for Blades and Priest. The leading of these extra horses fell to me, but with the loose end of a rope in Jim Flood's hand as he followed, it took fast riding to keep clear of them.

After reaching the trail of the missing cattle, our foreman set a pace for five or six miles which would have carried us across the Nueces by nightfall, and we were only checked by Moss Strayhorn riding in on an angle and intercepting us in our headlong gait. The missing cattle were within a mile of us to the right, and we turned and rode to them. Strayhorn explained to us that the cattle had struck some recent fencing on their course, and after following down the fence several miles had encountered an offset, and the angle had held the squad until The Rebel and Blades overtook them. When Officer and he reached them, they were unable to make any accurate count, because of the range cattle among them, and they had considered it advisable to save horseflesh, and not cut them until more help was available. When we came up with the cattle, my bunkie and Blades looked wistfully at our saddles, and anticipating their want, I untied my slicker, well remembering the reproof of Quarternight and Forrest, and produced a full canteen of water – warm of course, but no less welcome.

No sooner were saddles shifted than we held up the bunch, cut out the range cattle, counted, and found we had some three hundred and thirty odd Circle Dots – our number more than complete. With nothing now missing, Flood took the loose horses and two of the boys with him and returned to the herd, leaving three of us behind to bring in this last contingent of our stampeded cattle. This squad were nearly all large steers, and had run fully twenty miles, before, thanks to an angle in a fence, they had been checked. As our foreman galloped away, leaving us behind, Bob Blades said, 'Hasn't the boss got a wiggle on himself today! If he'd made this old world, he'd have made it in half a day, and gone fishing in the afternoon – if his horses had held out.'

We reached the Atascosa shortly after the arrival of the herd, and after holding the cattle on the water for an hour, grazed them the remainder of the evening, for if there was any virtue in their having full stomachs, we wanted to benefit from it. While grazing that evening, we recrossed the trail on an angle, and camped in the most open country we could find, about ten miles below our camp of the night before. Every precaution was taken to prevent a repetition of the run; our best horses were chosen for night duty, as our regular ones were too exhausted; every advantage of elevation for a bed ground was secured, and thus fortified against accident, we went into camp for the night. But the expected never happens on the trail, and the sun arose the next morning over our herd grazing in peace and contentment on the flowery prairies which border on the Atascosa.

CHAPTER 5

A Dry Drive

Our cattle quieted down nicely after this run, and the next few weeks brought not an incident worth recording. There was no regular trail through the lower counties, so we simply kept to the open country. Spring had advanced until the prairies were swarded with grass and flowers, while water, though scarcer, was to be had at least once daily. We passed to the west of San Antonio – an outfitting point which all herds touched in passing northward – and Flood and our cook took the wagon and went in for supplies. But the outfit with the herd kept on, now launched on a broad, well-defined trail, in places seventy-five yards wide, where all local trails blended into the one common pathway, known in those days as the Old Western Trail. It is not in the province of this narrative to deal with the cause or origin of this cattle trail, though it marked the passage of many hundred thousand cattle which preceded our Circle Dots, and was destined to afford an outlet to several millions more to follow. The trail proper consisted of many scores of irregular cow paths, united into one broad passageway, narrowing and widening as conditions permitted, yet ever leading northward. After a few years of continued use, it became as well defined as the course of a river.

Several herds which had started farther up country were ahead of ours, and this we considered an advantage, for wherever one herd could go, it was reasonable that others could follow. Flood knew the trail as well as any of the other foremen, but there was one thing he had not taken into consideration: the drought of the preceding summer. True, there had been local spring showers, sufficient to start the grass nicely, but water in such quantities as we needed was growing daily more difficult to find. The first week after leaving San Antonio, our foreman scouted in quest of water a full day in advance of the herd. One evening he returned to us with the news that we were in for a dry drive, for after passing the nearby chain of lakes it was sixty miles to the next water, and reports regarding the water supply even after crossing this arid stretch were very conflicting.

'While I know every foot of this trail through here,' said the foreman, 'there's several things that look scaly. There are only five herds ahead of us, and the first three went through the old route, but the last two, after passing Indian Lakes, for some reason or other turned and went westward. These last herds may be stock cattle, pushing out west to new ranges; but I don't like the outlook. It would take me two days to ride across and back, and by that time we could be two thirds of the way through. I've made this drive before without a drop of water on the way, and wouldn't dread it now, if there was any certainty of water at the other end. I reckon there's nothing to do but tackle her; but isn't this a hell of a country? I've ridden fifty miles today and never saw a soul.'

The Indian Lakes, some seven in number, were natural reservoirs with rocky bottoms, and about a mile apart. We watered at ten o'clock the next day, and by night camped fifteen miles on our way. There was plenty of good grazing for the cattle and horses, and no trouble was experienced the first night. McCann had filled an extra twenty-gallon keg for this trip. Water was too precious an article to be lavish with, so we shook the dust from our clothing and went unwashed. This was no serious deprivation, and no one could be critical of another, for we were all equally dusty and dirty.

The next morning by daybreak the cattle were thrown off the bed ground and started grazing before the sun could dry out what little moisture the grass had absorbed during the night. The heat of the past week had been very oppressive, and in order to avoid it as much as possible, we made late and early drives. Before the wagon passed the herd during the morning drive, what few canteens we had were filled with water for the men. The *remuda* was kept with the herd, and four changes of mounts were made during the day, in order not to exhaust any one horse. Several times for an hour or more, the herd was allowed to lie down and rest; but by the middle of the afternoon thirst made them impatient and restless, and the point men were compelled to ride steadily in the lead in order to hold the cattle to a walk. A number of times during the afternoon we attempted to graze them, but not until the twilight of evening was it possible.

After the fourth change of horses was made, Honeyman pushed on ahead with the saddle stock and overtook the wagon. Under Flood's orders he was to tie up all the night horses, for if the cattle could be induced to graze, we would not bed them down before ten that night, and all hands would be required with the herd. McCann had instructions to make camp on the divide, which was known to be twenty-five miles from our camp of the night before, or forty miles from the Indian Lakes. As we expected, the cattle grazed willingly after nightfall, and with a fair moon, we allowed them to scatter freely while grazing forward. The beacon of McCann's fire on the divide was in sight over an hour before the herd grazed up to camp, all hands remaining to bed the thirsty cattle. The herd was given triple the amount of space usually required for bedding, and even then for nearly an hour scarcely half of them lay down.

We were handling the cattle as humanely as possible under the circumstances. The guards for the night were doubled, six men on the first half and the same on the latter, Bob Blades being detailed to assist Honeyman in night-herding the saddle horses. If any of us got more than an hour's sleep that night, he was lucky. Flood, McCann, and the horse wranglers did not even try to rest. To those of us who could find time to eat, our cook kept open house. Our foreman knew that a well-fed man can stand an incredible amount of hardship, and appreciated the fact that on the trail a good cook is a valuable asset. Our outfit therefore was cheerful to a man, and jokes and songs helped to while away the weary hours of the night.

The second guard, under Flood, pushed the cattle off their beds an hour before dawn, and before they were relieved had urged the herd more than five miles on the third day's drive over this waterless mesa. In spite of our economy of water, after breakfast on this third morning there was scarcely enough left to fill the canteens for the day. In view of this, we could promise ourselves no midday meal – except a can of tomatoes to the man; so the wagon was ordered to drive through to the expected water ahead, while the saddle horses were held available as on the day before for frequent changing of mounts. The day turned out to be one of torrid heat, and before the middle of the forenoon, the cattle lolled their tongues in despair, while their sullen lowing surged through from rear to lead and back again in piteous yet ominous appeal. The only relief we could offer was to travel them slowly, as they spurned every opportunity offered them either to graze or to lie down.

It was nearly noon when we reached the last divide, and sighted the scattering timber of the expected watercourse. The enforced order of the day before – to hold the herd in a walk and prevent exertion and heating – now required four men in the lead, while the rear followed over a mile behind, dogged and sullen. Near the middle of the afternoon, McCann returned on one of his mules with the word that it was a question if there was water enough to water even the horse stock. The preceding outfit, so he reported, had dug a shallow well in the bed of the creek, from which he had filled his kegs, but the stock water was a mere loblolly. On receipt of this news, we changed mounts for the fifth time that day; and Flood, taking Forrest, the cook, and the horse wrangler, pushed on ahead with the *remuda* to the waterless stream.

The outlook was anything but encouraging. Flood and Forrest scouted the creek up and down for ten miles in a fruitless search for water. The outfit held the herd back until the twilight of evening, when Flood returned and confirmed McCann's report. It was twenty miles yet to the next water ahead, and if the horse stock could only be watered thoroughly, Flood was determined to make the attempt to nurse the herd through to water. McCann was digging an extra well, and he expressed the belief that by hollowing out a number of holes, enough water could be secured for the saddle stock. Honeyman had corralled the horses and was letting only a few go to the water at a time, while the night horses were being thoroughly watered as fast as the water rose in the well.

Holding the herd this third night required all hands. Only a few men at a time were allowed to go into camp and eat, for the herd refused even to lie down. What few cattle attempted to rest were prevented by the more restless ones. By spells they would mill, until riders were sent through the herd at a breakneck pace to break up the groups. During these milling efforts of the herd, we drifted over a mile from camp; but by the light of moon and stars and the number of riders, scattering was prevented. As the horses were loose for the night, we could not start them on the trail until daybreak gave us a change of mounts, so we lost the early start of the morning before.

Good cloudy weather would have saved us, but in its stead was a sultry morning without a breath of air, which bespoke another day of sizzling heat. We had not been on the trail over two hours before the heat became almost unbearable to man and beast. Had it not been for the condition of the herd, all might yet have gone well; but over three days had now elapsed without water for the cattle, and they became feverish and ungovernable. The lead cattle turned back several times, wandering aimlessly in any direction, and it was with considerable difficulty that the herd could be held on the trail. The rear overtook the lead, and the cattle gradually lost all semblance of a trail herd. Our horses were fresh, how-ever, and after about two hours' work, we once more got the herd strung out in trailing fashion; but before a mile had been covered, the leaders again turned, and the cattle congregated into a mass of unmanageable animals, milling and lowing in their fever and thirst. The milling only intensified their sufferings from the heat, and the outfit split and quartered them again and again, in the hope that this unfortunate outbreak might be checked. No sooner was the milling stopped than they would surge hither and yon, sometimes half a mile, as ungovernable as the waves of an ocean. After wasting several hours in this manner, they finally turned back over the trail, and the utmost efforts of every man in the outfit failed to check them. We threw our ropes in their faces, and when this failed, we resorted to shooting; but in defiance of the fusillade and the smoke they walked sullenly through the line of horsemen across their front. Six-shooters were discharged so close to the leaders' faces as to singe their hair, yet, under a noonday sun, they disregarded this and every other device to turn them, and passed wholly out of our control. In a number of instances wild steers deliberately walked against our horses, and then for the first time a fact dawned on us that chilled the marrow in our bones – *the herd was going blind*.

The bones of men and animals that lie bleaching along the trails abundantly testify that this was not the first instance in which the plain had baffled the determination of man. It was now evident that nothing short of water would stop the herd, and we rode aside and let them pass.

As the outfit turned back to the wagon, our foreman seemed dazed by the sudden and unexpected turn of affairs, but rallied and met the emergency.

'There's but one thing left to do,' said he, as we rode along, 'and that is to hurry the outfit back to Indian Lakes. The herd will travel day and night, and instinct can be depended on to carry them to the only water they know. It's too late to be of any use now, but it's plain why those last two herds turned off at the lakes; some one had gone back and warned them of the very thing we've met. We must beat them to the lakes, for water is the only thing that will check them now. It's a good thing that they are strong, and five or six days without water will hardly kill any. It was no vague statement of the man who said if he owned hell and Texas, he'd rent Texas and live in hell, for if this isn't Billy hell, I'd like to know what you call it.'

We spent an hour watering the horses from the wells of our camp of the night before, and about two o'clock started back over the trail for Indian Lakes. We overtook the abandoned herd during the afternoon. They were strung out nearly five miles in length, and were walking about a three-mile gait. Four men were given two extra horses apiece and left to throw in the stragglers in the rear, with instructions to follow them well into the night, and again in the morning as long as their canteens lasted. The remainder of the outfit pushed on without a halt, except to change mounts, and reached the lakes shortly after midnight. There we secured the first good sleep of any consequence for three days.

It was fortunate for us that there were no range cattle at these lakes, and we had only to cover a front of about six miles to catch the drifting herd. It was nearly noon the next day before the cattle began to arrive at the water holes in squads of from twenty to fifty. Pitiful objects as they were, it was a novelty to see them reach the water and slake their thirst. Wading out into the lakes until their sides were half covered, they would stand and low in a soft moaning voice, often for half an hour before attempting to drink. Contrary to our expectation, they drank very little at first, but stood in the water for hours. After coming out, they would lie down and rest for hours longer, and then drink again before attempting to graze, their thirst overpowering hunger. That they were blind there was no question, but with the causes that produced it once removed, it was probable their eyesight would gradually return.

By early evening, the rear guard of our outfit returned and reported the tail end of the herd some twenty miles behind when they left them. During the day not over a thousand head reached the lakes, and towards evening we put these under herd and easily held them during the night. All four of the men who constituted the rear guard were sent back the next morning to prod up the rear again, and during the night at least a thousand more came into the lakes, which held them better than a hundred men. With the recovery of the cattle our hopes grew, and with the gradual accessions to the herd, confidence was again completely restored. Our saddle stock, not having suffered as had the cattle, were in a serviceable condition, and while a few men were all that were necessary to hold the herd, the others scoured the country for miles in search of any possible stragglers which might have missed the water.

During the forenoon of the third day at the lakes, Nat Straw, the foreman of Ellison's first herd on the trail, rode up to our camp. He was scouting for water for his herd and, when our situation was explained and he had been interrogated regarding loose cattle, gave us the good news that no stragglers in our road brand had been met by their outfit. This was welcome news, for we had made no count yet, and feared some of them, in their locoed condition, might have passed the water during the night. Our misfortune was an ill wind by which Straw profited, for he had fully expected to keep on by the old route, but with our disaster staring him in the face, a similar experience was to be avoided. His herd reached the lakes during the middle of the afternoon, and after watering, turned and went westward over the new route taken by the two herds which preceded us. He had a herd of about three thousand steers, and was driving to the Dodge market. After the experience we had just gone through, his herd and outfit were a welcome sight. Flood made enquiries after Lovell's second herd, under my brother Bob as foreman, but Straw had seen or heard nothing of them, having come from Goliad County with his cattle.

After the Ellison herd had passed on and out of sight, our squad which had been working the country to the northward, over the route by which the abandoned herd had returned, came in with the information that that section was clear of cattle, and that they had only found three head dead from thirst. On the fourth morning, as the herd left the bed ground, a count was ordered, and to our surprise we counted out twenty-six head more than we had received on the banks of the Rio Grande a month before. As there had been but one previous occasion to count, the number of strays absorbed into our herd was easily accounted for by Priest: 'If a steer herd could increase on the trail, why shouldn't ours, that had over a thousand cows in it?' The observation was hardly borne out when the ages of our herd were taken into consideration. But 1882 in Texas was a liberal day and generation, and 'cattle stealing' was too drastic a term to use for the chance gain of a few cattle, when the foundations of princely fortunes were being laid with a rope and a branding iron.

In order to give the Ellison herd a good start of us, we only moved our wagon to the farthest lake and went into camp for the day. The herd had recovered its normal condition by this time, and of the troubles of the past week not a trace remained. Instead, our herd grazed in leisurely content over a thousand acres, while with the exception of a few men on herd, the outfit lounged around the wagon and beguiled the time with cards.

We had undergone an experience which my bunkie, The Rebel, termed 'an interesting incident in his checkered career', but which not even he would have cared to repeat. That night while on night herd together – the cattle resting in all contentment – we rode one round together, and as he rolled a cigarette he gave me an old war story.

'They used to tell the story in the army, that during one of the winter retreats, a cavalryman, riding along in the wake of the column at night, saw a hat apparently floating in the mud and water. In the hope that it might be a better hat than the one he was wearing, he dismounted to get it. Feeling his way carefully through the ooze until he reached the hat, he was surprised to find a man underneath and wearing it. "Hello, comrade," he sang out, "can I lend you a hand?"

' "No, no," replied the fellow, "I'm all right; I've got a good mule yet under me." '

CHAPTER 6

A Reminiscent Night

On the ninth morning we made our second start from the Indian Lakes. An amusing incident occurred during the last night of our camp at these water holes. Coyotes had been hanging around our camp for several days, and during the quiet hours of the night these scavengers of the plain had often ventured in near the wagon in search of scraps of meat or anything edible. Rod Wheat and Ash Borrowstone had made their beds down some distance from the wagon; the coyotes as they circled round the camp came near their bed, and in sniffing about awoke Borrowstone. There was no more danger of attack from these cowards than from field mice, but their presence annoyed Ash, and as he dared not shoot, he threw his boots at the varmints. Imagine his chagrin the next morning to find that one boot had landed among the banked embers of the campfire, and was burned to a crisp. It was looked upon as a capital joke by the outfit, as there was no telling when we would reach a store where he could secure another pair.

The new trail, after bearing to the westward for several days, turned northward, paralleling the old one, and a week later we came into the old trail over a hundred miles north of the Indian Lakes. With the exception of one thirty-mile drive without water, no fault could be found with the new trail. A few days after coming into the old trail, we passed Mason, a point where trail herds usually put in for supplies. As we passed during the middle of the afternoon, the wagon and a number of the boys went into the burg. Quince Forrest and Billy Honeyman were the only two in the outfit for whom there were any letters, with the exception of a letter from Lovell, which was common property. Never having been over the trail before, and not even knowing that it was possible to hear from home, I wasn't expecting any letter; but I felt a little twinge of homesickness that night when Honeyman read us certain portions of his letter, which was from his sister. Forrest's letter was from a sweetheart, and after reading it a few times, he burnt it, and that was all we ever knew of its contents, for he was too foxy to say anything, even if it had not been unfavourable. Borrowstone swaggered around camp that evening in a new pair of boots, which had the Lone Star set in filigree-work in their red tops.

At our last camp at the lakes, The Rebel and I, as partners, had been shamefully beaten in a game of seven-up by Bull Durham and John Officer, and had demanded satisfaction in another trial around the fire that night. We borrowed McCann's lantern, and by the aid of it and the campfire, had an abundance of light for our game. In the absence of a table, we unrolled a bed and sat down Indian fashion over a game of cards in which all friendship ceased.

The outfit, with the exception of myself, had come from the same neighbourhood, and an item in Honeyman's letter causing considerable comment was a wedding which had occurred since the outfit had left. It seemed that a number of the boys had sparked the bride in times past, and now that she was married, their minds naturally became reminiscent over old sweethearts.

'The way I make it out,' said Honeyman, in commenting on the news, 'is that the girl had met this fellow over in the next county while visiting her cousins the year before. My sister gives it as a horseback opinion that she'd been engaged to this fellow nearly eight months; girls, you know, sabe each other that way. Well, it won't affect my appetite any if all the girls I know get married while I'm gone.'

'You certainly have never experienced the tender passion,' said Fox Quarternight to our horse wrangler, as he lighted his pipe with a brand from the fire. 'Now I have. That's the reason why I sympathise with these old beaus of the bride. Of course I was too old to stand any show on her string, and I reckon the fellow who got her ain't so powerful much, except his veneering and being a stranger, which was a big advantage. To be sure, if she took a smile to this stranger, no other fellow could check her with a three-quarter rope and a snubbing post. I've seen girls walk right by a dozen good fellows and fawn over some scrub. My experience teaches me that when there's a woman in it, it's haphazard pot luck with no telling which way the cat will hop. You can't play any system, and merit cuts little figure in general results.'

'Fox,' said Durham, while Officer was shuffling the cards, 'your auger seems well oiled and working keen tonight. Suppose you give us that little experience of yours in love affairs. It will be a treat to those of us who have never been in love, and won't interrupt the game a particle. Cut loose, won't you?'

'It's a long time back,' said Quarternight, meditatively, 'and the scars have all healed, so I don't mind telling it. I was born and raised on the border of the Blue Grass region in Kentucky. I had the misfortune to be born of poor but honest parents, as they do in stories; no hero ever had the advantage of me in that respect. In love affairs, however, it's a high card in your hand to be born rich. The country around my old home had good schools, so we had the advantage of a good education. When I was about nineteen, I went away from home one winter to teach school – a little country school about fifteen miles from home. But in the old States fifteen miles from home makes you a dead rank stranger. The trustee of the township was shucking corn when I went to apply for the school. I simply whipped out my peg and helped him shuck out a shock or two while we talked over school matters. The dinner bell rang, and he insisted on my staying for dinner with him. Well, he gave me a better school than I had asked for – better neighbourhood, he said – and told me to board with a certain family who had no children; he gave his reasons, but that's immaterial. They were friends of his, so I learned afterwards. They proved to be fine people. The woman was one of those kindly souls who never know where to stop. She planned and schemed to marry me off in spite of myself. The first month that I was with them she told me all about the girls in that immediate neighbourhood. In fact, she rather got me unduly excited, being a youth and somewhat verdant. She dwelt powerful heavy on a girl who lived in a big brick house which stood back of the road some distance. This girl had gone to school at a seminary for young ladies near Lexington – studied music and painting and was way up on everything. She described her to me as black-eyed with raven tresses, just like you read about in novels.

'Things were rocking along nicely, when a few days before Christmas a little girl who belonged to the family who lived in the brick house brought me a note one morning. It was an invitation to take supper with them the following evening. The note was written in a pretty hand, and the name signed to it – I'm satisfied now it was a forgery. My landlady agreed with me on that point; in fact, she may have mentioned it first. I never ought to have taken her into my confidence like I did. But I wanted to consult her, showed her the invitation, and asked her advice. She was in the seventh heaven of delight; had me answer it at once, accept the invitation with pleasure and a lot of stuff that I never used before – she had been young once herself. I used up five or six sheets of paper in writing the answer, spoilt one after another, and the one I did send was a flat failure compared to the one I received. Well, the next evening when it was time to start, I was nervous and uneasy. It was nearly dark when I reached the house, but I wanted it that way. Say, but when I knocked on the front door of that house it was with fear and trembling. "Is this Mr Quarternight?" enquired a very affable lady who received me. I knew I was one of old man Quarternight's seven boys, and admitted that that was my name, though it was the first time anyone had ever called me *mister*. I was welcomed, ushered in, and introduced all around. There were a few small children whom I knew, so I managed to talk to them. The girl whom I was being braced against was not a particle overrated, but sustained the Kentucky reputation for beauty. She made herself so pleasant and agreeable that my fears soon subsided. When the man of the house came in I was cured entirely. He was gruff and hearty, opened his mouth and laughed deep. I built right up to him. We talked about cattle and horses until supper was announced. He was really sorry I hadn't come earlier, so as to look at a three-year-old colt that he set a heap of store by. He showed him to me after supper with a lantern. Fine colt, too. I don't remember much about the supper, except that it was fine and I came near spilling my coffee several times, my hands were so large and my coat sleeves so short. When we returned from looking at the colt, we went into the parlour. Say, fellows, it was by far the nicest thing that ever I went against. Carpet that made you think you were going to bog down every step, springy like marshland, and I was glad I came. Then the younger children were ordered to retire, and shortly afterwards the man and his wife followed suit.

'When I heard the old man throw his heavy boots on the floor in the next room, I realised that I was left all alone with their charming daughter. All my fears of the early part of the evening tried to crowd on me again, but were calmed by the girl, who sang and played on the piano with no audience but me. Then she interested me by telling her school experiences, and how glad she was that they were over. Finally she lugged out a great big family album, and sat down aside of me on one of these horsehair sofas. That album had a clasp on it, a buckle of pure silver, same as these eighteen-dollar bridles. While we were looking at the pictures – some of the old varmints had fought in the Revolutionary war, so she said – I noticed how close we were sitting together. Then we sat farther apart after we had gone through the album, one on each end of the sofa, and talked about the neighbourhood, until I suddenly remembered that I had to go. While she was getting my hat and I was getting away, somehow she had me promise to take dinner with them on Christmas.

'For the next two or three months it was hard to tell if I lived at my boarding house or at the brick. If I failed to go, my landlady would hatch up some errand and send me over. If she hadn't been such a good woman, I'd never forgive her for leading me to the sacrifice like she did. Well, about two weeks before school was out, I went home over Saturday and Sunday. Those were fatal days in my life. When I returned on Monday morning, there was a letter waiting for me. It was from the girl's mamma. There had been a quilting in the neighbourhood on Saturday, and at this meet of the local gossips, someone had hinted that there was liable to be a wedding as soon as school was out. Mamma was present, and neither admitted nor denied the charge. But there was a woman at this quilting who had once lived over in our neighbourhood and felt it her duty to enlighten the company as to who I was. I got all this later from my landlady. "Law me," said this woman, "folks round here in this section think our teacher is the son of that big farmer who raises so many cattle and horses. Why, I've known both families of those Quarternights for nigh on to thirty year. Our teacher is one of old John Fox's boys, the Irish

Quarternights, who live up near the salt licks on Doe Run. They were always so poor that the children never had enough to eat and hardly half enough to wear."

'This plain statement of facts fell like a bombshell on mamma. She started a private investigation of her own, and her verdict was in that letter. It was a centre shot. That evening when I locked the schoolhouse door it was for the last time, for I never unlocked it again. My landlady, dear old womanly soul, tried hard to have me teach the school out at least, but I didn't see it that way. The cause of education in Kentucky might have gone straight to eternal hell before I'd have stayed another day in that neighbourhood. I had money enough to get to Texas with, and here I am. When a fellow gets it burnt into him like a brand that way once, it lasts him quite a while. He'll feel his way next time.'

'That was rather a raw deal to give a fellow,' said Officer, who had been listening while playing cards. 'Didn't you never see the girl again?'

'No, nor you wouldn't want to either if that letter had been written to you. And some folks claim that seven is a lucky number; there were seven boys in our family and nary one ever married.'

'That experience of Fox's,' remarked Honeyman, after a short silence, 'is almost similar to one I had. Before Lovell and Flood adopted me, I worked for a horse man down on the Nueces. Every year he drove up the trail a large herd of horse stock. We drove to the same point on the trail each year, and I happened to get acquainted up there with a family that had several girls in it. The youngest girl in the family and I seemed to understand each other fairly well. I had to stay at the horse camp most of the time, and in one way and another did not get to see her as much as I would have liked. When we sold out the herd, I hung around for a week or so, and spent a month's wages showing her the cloud with the silver lining. She stood it all easy, too. When the outfit went home, of course I went with them. I was banking plenty strong, however, that next year, if there was a good market in horses, I'd take her home with me. I had saved my wages and rustled around, and when we started up the trail next year, I had forty horses of my own in the herd. I had figured they would bring me a thousand dollars, and there was my wages besides.

'When we reached this place, we held the herd out twenty miles, so it was some time before I got into town to see the girl. But the first time I did get to see her I learned that an older sister of hers, who had run away with some renegade from Texas a year or so before, had drifted back home lately with tears in her eyes and a big fat baby boy in her arms. She warned me to keep away from the house, for men from Texas were at a slight discount right then in that family. The girl seemed to regret it and talked reasonable, and I thought I could see encouragement. I didn't crowd matters, nor did her folks forget me when they heard that Byler had come in with a horse herd from the Nueces. I met the girl away from home several times during the summer, and learned that they kept hot water on tap to scald me if I ever dared to show up. One son-in-law from Texas had simply surfeited that family – there was no other vacancy. About the time we closed out and were again ready to go home, there was a cattleman's ball given in this little trail town. We stayed over several days to take in this ball, as I had some plans of my own. My girl was at the ball all easy enough, but she warned me that her brother was watching me. I paid no attention to him, and danced with her right along, begging her to run away with me. It was obviously the only play to make. But the more I'd 'suade her the more she'd 'fuse. The family was on the prod bigger than a wolf, and there was no use reasoning with them. After I had had every dance with her for an hour or so, her brother coolly stepped in and took her home. The next morning he felt it his duty, as his sister's protector, to hunt me up and inform me that if I even spoke to his sister again, he'd shoot me like a dog.

' "Is that a bluff, or do you mean it for a real play?" I enquired, politely.

' "You'll find that it will be real enough," he answered, angrily.

' "Well, now, that's too bad," I answered; "I'm really sorry that I can't promise to respect your request. But this much I can assure you: any time that you have the leisure and want to shoot me, just cut loose your dog. But remember this one thing – that it will be my second shot." '

'Are you sure you wasn't running a blazer yourself, or is the wind merely rising?' enquired Durham, while I was shuffling the cards for the next deal.

'Well, if I was, I hung up my gentle honk before his eyes and ears and gave him free licence to call it. The truth is, I didn't pay any more attention to him than I would to an empty bottle. I reckon the girl was all right, but the family were these razor-backed, barnyard savages. It makes me hot under the collar yet when I think of it. They'd have lawed me if I had, but I ought to have shot him and checked the breed.'

'Why didn't you run off with her?' enquired Fox, dryly.

'Well, of course a man of your nerve is always capable of advising others. But you see, I'm strong on the breed. Now a girl can't show her true colours like the girl's brother did, but get her in the harness once, and then she'll show you the white of her eye, balk, and possibly kick over the wagon tongue. No, I believe in the breed – blood'll tell.'

'I worked for a cowman once,' said Bull, irrelevantly, 'and they told it on him that he lost twenty thousand dollars the night he was married.'

'How, gambling?' I enquired.

'No. The woman he married claimed to be worth twenty thousand dollars and she never had a cent. Spades trump?'

'No; hearts,' replied The Rebel. 'I used to know a foreman up in DeWitt County – 'Honest' John Glen they called him. He claimed the only chance he ever had to marry was a widow, and the reason he didn't marry her was he was too honest to take advantage of a dead man.'

While we paid little attention to wind or weather, this was an ideal night, and we were laggard in seeking our blankets. Yarn followed yarn; for nearly every one of us, either from observation or from practical experience, had a slight acquaintance with the great mastering passion. But the poetical had not been developed in us to an appreciative degree, so we discussed the topic under consideration much as we would have done horses or cattle.

Finally the game ended. A general yawn went the round of the loungers about the fire. The second guard had gone on, and when the first rode in, Joe Stallings, halting his horse in passing the fire, called out sociably, 'That muley steer, the white four-year-old, didn't like to bed down among the others, so I let him come out and lay down by himself. You'll find him over on the far side of the herd. You all remember how wild he was when we first started? Well, you can ride within three feet of him tonight, and he'll grunt and act sociable and never offer to get up. I promised him that he might sleep alone as long as he was good; I just love a good steer. Make down our bed, pardner; I'll be back as soon as I picket my horse.'

CHAPTER 7

The Colorado

The month of May found our Circle Dot herd, in spite of all drawbacks, nearly five hundred miles on its way. For the past week we had been travelling over that immense tableland which skirts the arid portion of western Texas. A few days before, while passing the blue mountains which stand as a southern sentinel in the chain marking the headwaters of the Concho River, we had our first glimpse of the hills. In its almost primitive condition, the country was generous, supplying every want for sustenance of horses and cattle. The grass at this stage of the season was well matured, the herd taking on flesh in a very gratifying manner, and, while we had crossed some rocky country, lame and sore-footed cattle had as yet caused us no serious trouble.

One morning when within one day's drive of the Colorado River, as our herd was leaving the bed ground, the last guard encountered a bunch of cattle drifting back down the trail. There were nearly fifty head of the stragglers; and as one of our men on guard turned them to throw them away from our herd, the road brand caught his eye, and he recognised the strays as belonging to the Ellison herd which had passed us at the Indian Lakes some ten days before. Flood's attention once drawn to the brand, he ordered them thrown into our herd. It was evident that some trouble had occurred with the Ellison cattle, possibly a stampede; and it was but a neighbourly act to lend any assistance in our power. As soon as the outfit could breakfast, mount, and take the herd, Flood sent Priest and me to scout the country to the westward of the trail, while Bob Blades and Ash Borrowstone started on a similar errand to the eastward, with orders to throw in any drifting cattle in the Ellison road brand. Within an hour after starting, the herd encountered several straggling bands, and as Priest and I were on the point of returning to the herd, we almost overrode a bunch of eighty odd head lying down in some broken country. They were gaunt and tired, and The Rebel at once pronounced their stiffened movements the result of a stampede.

We were drifting them bask towards the trail, when Nat Straw and two of his men rode out from our herd and met us. 'I always did claim that it was better to be born lucky than handsome,' said Straw as he rode up. 'One week Flood saves me from a dry drive, and the very next one, he's just the right distance behind to catch my drift from a nasty stampede. Not only that, but my peelers and I are riding Circle Dot horses, as well as reaching the wagon in time for breakfast and lining our flues with Lovell's good chuck. It's too good luck to last, I'm afraid.

'I'm not hankering for the dramatic in life, but we had a run last night that would curl your hair. Just about midnight a bunch of range cattle ran into us, and before you could say Jack Robinson, our dogies had vamoosed the ranch and were running in half a dozen different directions. We rounded them up the best we could in the dark, and then I took a couple of men and came back down the trail about twenty miles to catch any drift when day dawned. But you see there's nothing like being lucky and having good neighbours – cattle caught, fresh horses, and a warm breakfast all waiting for you. I'm such a lucky dog, it's a wonder someone didn't steal me when I was little. I can't help it, but someday I'll marry a banker's daughter, or fall heir to a ranch as big as old McCulloch County.'

Before meeting us, Straw had confided to our foreman that he could assign no other plausible excuse for the stampede than that it was the work of cattle rustlers. He claimed to know the country along the Colorado, and unless it had changed recently, those hills to the westward harboured a good many of the worst rustlers in the State. He admitted it might have been wolves chasing the range cattle, but thought it had the earmarks of being done by human wolves. He maintained that few herds had ever passed that river without loss of cattle, unless the rustlers were too busy elsewhere to give the passing herd their attention. Straw had ordered his herd to drop back down the trail about ten miles from their camp of the night previous, and about noon the two herds met on a branch of Brady Creek. By that time our herd had nearly three hundred head of the Ellison cattle, so we held it up and cut theirs out. Straw urged our foreman, whatever he did, not to make camp in the Colorado bottoms or anywhere near the river, if he didn't want a repetition of his experience. After starting our herd in the afternoon, about half a dozen of us turned back and lent a hand in counting Straw's herd, which proved to be over a hundred head short, and nearly half his outfit were still out hunting cattle. Acting on Straw's advice, we camped that night some five or six miles back from the river on the last divide. From the time the second guard went on until the third was relieved, we took the precaution of keeping a scout outriding from a half to three quarters of a mile distant from the herd, Flood and Honeyman serving in that capacity. Every precaution was taken to prevent a surprise; and in case anything did happen, our night horses tied to the wagon wheels stood ready saddled and bridled for any emergency. But the night passed without incident.

An hour or two after the herd had started the next morning, four well-mounted, strange men rode up from the westward, and representing themselves as trail cutters, asked for our foreman. Flood met them, in his usual quiet manner, and after admitting that we had been troubled more or less with range cattle, assured our callers that if there was anything in the herd in the brands they represented, he would gladly hold it up and give them every opportunity to cut their cattle out. As he was anxious to cross the river before noon, he invited the visitors to stay for dinner, assuring them that before starting the herd in the afternoon, he would throw the cattle together for their inspection. Flood made himself very agreeable, enquiring into cattle and range matters in general as well as the stage of water in the river ahead. The spokesman of the trail cutters met Flood's invitation to dinner with excuses about the pressing demands on his time, and urged, if it did not seriously interfere with our plans, that he be allowed to inspect the herd before crossing the river. His reasons seemed trivial and our foreman was not convinced.

'You see, gentlemen,' he said, 'in handling these southern cattle, we must take advantage of occasions. We have timed our morning's drive so as to reach the river during the warmest hour of the day, or as near noon as possible. You can hardly imagine what a difference there is, in fording this herd, between a cool, cloudy day and a clear, hot one. You see the herd is strung out nearly a mile in length now, and to hold them up and waste an hour or more for your inspection would seriously disturb our plans. And then our wagon and *remuda* have gone on with orders to noon at the first good camp beyond the river. I perfectly understand your reasons, and you equally understand mine; but I will send a man or two back to help you recross any cattle you may find in our herd. Now, if a couple of you gentlemen will ride around on the far side with me, and the others will ride up near the lead, we will trail the cattle across when we reach the river without cutting the herd into blocks.'

Flood's affability, coupled with the fact that the lead cattle were nearly up to the river, won his point. Our visitors could only yield, and rode forward with our lead swing men to assist in forcing the lead cattle into the river. It was swift water, but otherwise an easy crossing, and we allowed the herd, after coming out on the farther side, to spread out and graze forward at its pleasure. The wagon and saddle stock were in sight about a mile ahead, and leaving two men on herd to drift the cattle in the right direction, the rest of us rode leisurely on to the wagon, where dinner was waiting. Flood treated our callers with marked courtesy during dinner, and casually enquired if any of their number had seen any cattle that day or the day previous in the Ellison road brand. They had not, they said, explaining that their range lay on both sides of the Concho, and that during the trail season they kept all their cattle between that river and the main Colorado. Their work had kept them on their own range recently, except when trail herds were passing and needed to be looked through for strays. It sounded as though our trail cutters could also use diplomacy on occasion.

When dinner was over and we had caught horses for the afternoon and were ready to mount, Flood asked our guests for their credentials as duly authorised trail cutters. They replied that they had none, but offered in explanation the statement that they were merely cutting in the interest of the immediate locality, which required no written authority.

Then the previous affability of our foreman turned to iron. 'Well, men,' said he, 'if you have no authority to cut this trail, then you don't cut this herd. I must have inspection papers before I can move a brand out of the county in which it is bred, and I'll certainly let no other man, local or duly appointed, cut an animal out of this herd without written and certified authority. You know that without being told, or ought to. I respect the rights of every man posted on a trail to cut it. If you want to see my inspection papers, you have a right to demand them, and in turn I demand of you your credentials, showing who you work for and the list of brands you represent; otherwise no harm's done; nor do you cut any herd that I'm driving.'

'Well,' said one of the men, 'I saw a couple of head in my own individual brand as we rode up the herd. I'd like to see the man who says that I haven't the right to claim my own brand, anywhere I find it.'

'If there's anything in our herd in your individual brand,' said Flood, 'all you have to do is to give me the brand, and I'll cut it for you. What's your brand?'

'The "Window Sash".'

'Have any of you boys seen such a brand in our herd?' enquired Flood, turning to us as we all stood by our horses ready to start.

'I didn't recognise it by that name,' replied Quince Forrest, who rode in the swing on the branded side of the cattle and belonged to the last guard, 'but I remember seeing such a brand, though I would have given it a different name. Yes, come to think, I'm sure I saw it, and I'll tell you where: yesterday morning when I rode out to throw those drifting cattle away from our herd, I saw that brand among the Ellison cattle which had stampeded the night before. When Straw's outfit cut theirs out yesterday, they must have left the "Window Sash" cattle with us; those were the range cattle which stampeded his herd. It looked to me a little blotched, but if I'd been called on to name it, I'd have called it a thief's brand. If these gentlemen claim them, though, it'll only take a minute to cut them out.'

'This outfit needn't get personal and fling out their insults,' retorted the claimant of the 'Window Sash' brand, 'for I'll claim my own if there were a hundred of you. And you can depend that any animal I claim, I'll take, if I have to go back to the ranch and bring twenty men to help me do it.'

'You won't need any help to get all that's coming to you,' replied our foreman, as he mounted his horse. 'Let's throw the herd together, boys, and cut these "Window Sash" cattle out. We don't want any cattle in our herd that stampede on an open range at midnight; they must certainly be terrible wild.'

As we rode out together, our trail cutters dropped behind and kept a respectable distance from the herd while we threw the cattle together. When the herd had closed to the required compactness, Flood called our trail cutters up and said, 'Now, men, each one of you can take one of my outfit with you and inspect this herd to your satisfaction. If you see anything there you claim, we'll cut it out for you, but don't attempt to cut anything yourselves.'

We rode in by pairs, a man of ours with each stranger, and after riding leisurely through the herd for half an hour, cut out three head in the blotched brand called the 'Window Sash'. Before leaving the herd, one of the strangers laid claim to a red cow, but Fox Quarternight refused to cut the animal.

When the pair rode out the stranger accosted Flood. 'I notice a cow of mine in there,' said he, 'not in your road brand, which I claim. Your man here refuses to cut her for me, so I appeal to you.'

'What's her brand, Fox?' asked Flood.

'She's a "Q" cow, but the colonel here thinks it's an "O". I happen to know the cow and the brand both; she came into the herd four hundred miles south of here while we were watering the herd in the Nueces River. The "Q" is a little dim, but it's plenty plain to hold her for the present.'

'If she's a "Q" cow I have no claim on her,' protested the stranger, 'but if the brand is an "O", then I claim her as a stray from our range, and I don't care if she came into your herd when you were watering in the San Fernando River in Old Mexico, I'll claim her just the same. I'm going to ask you to throw her.'

'I'll throw her for you,' coolly replied Fox, 'and bet you my saddle and six-shooter on the side that it isn't an "O", and even if it was, you and all the thieves on the Concho can't take her. I know a few of the simple principles of rustling myself. Do you want her thrown?'

'That's what I asked for.'

'Throw her, then,' said Flood, 'and don't let's parley.'

Fox rode back into the herd, and after some little delay, located the cow and worked her out to the edge of the cattle. Dropping his rope, he cut her out clear of the herd, and as she circled around in an endeavour to re-enter, he rode close and made an easy cast of the rope about her horns. As he threw his horse back to check the cow, I rode to his assistance, my rope in hand, and as the cow turned ends, I heeled her. A number of the outfit rode up and dismounted, and one of the boys taking her by the tail, we threw the animal as humanely as possible. In order to get at the brand, which was on the side, we turned the cow over, when Flood took out his knife and cut the hair away, leaving the brand easily traceable.

'What is she, Jim?' enquired Fox, as he sat his horse holding the rope taut.

'I'll let this man who claims her answer that question,' replied Flood, as her claimant critically examined the brand to his satisfaction.

'I claim her as an "O" cow,' said the stranger, facing Flood.

'Well, you claim more than you'll ever get,' replied our foreman. 'Turn her loose, boys.'

The cow was freed and turned back into the herd, but the claimant tried to argue the matter with Flood, claiming the branding iron had simply slipped, giving it the appearance of a 'Q' instead of an 'O', as it was intended to be. Our foreman paid little attention to the stranger, but when his persistence became annoying checked his argument by saying, 'My Christian friend, there's no use arguing this matter. You asked to have the cow thrown, and we threw her. You might as well try to tell me that the cow is white as to claim her in any other brand than a "Q". You may read brands as well as I do, but you're wasting time arguing against the facts. You'd better take your "Window Sash" cattle and ride on, for you've cut all you're going to cut here today. But before you go, for fear I may never see you again, I'll take this occasion to say that I think you're common cow thieves.'

By his straight talk, our foreman stood several inches higher in our estimation as we sat our horses, grinning at the discomfiture of the trail cutters, while a dozen six-shooters slouched languidly at our hips to give emphasis to his words.

'Before going, I'll take this occasion to say to you that you will see me again,' replied the leader, riding up and confronting Flood. 'You haven't got near enough men to bluff me. As to calling me a cow thief, that's altogether too common a name to offend anyone; and from what I can gather, the name wouldn't miss you or your outfit over a thousand miles. Now, in taking my leave, I want to tell you that you'll see me before another day passes, and what's more, I'll bring an outfit with me and we'll cut your herd clean to your road brand, if for no better reasons, just to learn you not to be so insolent.'

After hanging up this threat, Flood said to him as he turned to ride away, 'Well, now, my young friend, you're bargaining for a whole lot of fun. I notice you carry a gun and quite naturally suppose you shoot a little as occasion requires. Suppose when you and your outfit come back, you come a-shooting, so we'll know who you are; for I'll promise you there's liable to be some powder burnt when you cut this herd.'

Amid jeers of derision from our outfit, the trail cutters drove off their three lonely 'Window Sash' cattle. We had gained the point we wanted, and now in case of any trouble, during inspection or at night, we had the river behind us to catch our herd. We paid little attention to the threat of our disappointed callers, but several times Straw's remarks as to the character of the residents of those hills to the westward recurred to my mind. I was young, but knew enough, instead of asking foolish questions, to keep mum, though my eyes and ears drank in everything. Before we had been on the trail over an hour, we met two men riding down the trail towards the river. Meeting us, they turned and rode along with our foreman, some distance apart from the herd, for nearly an hour, and curiosity ran freely among us boys around the herd as to who they might be. Finally Flood rode forward to the point men and gave the order to throw off the trail and make a short drive that afternoon. Then in company with the two strangers, he rode forward to overtake our wagon, and we saw nothing more of him until we reached camp that evening. This much, however, our point man was able to get from our foreman: that the two men were members of a detachment of Rangers who had been sent as a result of information given by the first herd over the trail that year. This herd, which had passed some twenty days ahead of us, had met with a stampede below the river, and on reaching Abilene had reported the presence of rustlers preying on through herds at the crossing of the Colorado.

On reaching camp that evening with the herd, we found ten of the Rangers as our guests for the night. The detachment was under a corporal named Joe Hames, who had detailed the two men we had met during the afternoon to scout this crossing. Upon the information afforded by our foreman about the would-be trail cutters, these scouts, accompanied by Flood, had turned back to advise the Ranger squad, encamped in a secluded spot about ten miles northeast of the Colorado crossing. They had only arrived late the day before, and this was their first meeting with any trail herd to secure any definite information.

Hames at once assumed charge of the herd, Flood gladly rendering every assistance possible. We night herded as usual, but during the two middle guards, Hames sent out four of his Rangers to scout the immediate outlying country, though, as we expected, they met with no adventure. At daybreak the Rangers threw their packs into our wagon and their loose stock into our *remuda*, and riding up the trail a mile or more, left us, keeping well out of sight. We were all hopeful now that the trail cutters of the day before would make good their word and return. In this hope we killed time for several hours that morning, grazing the cattle and holding the wagon in the rear. Sending the wagon ahead of the herd had been agreed on as the signal between our foreman and the Ranger corporal, at first sight of any posse behind us. We were beginning to despair of their coming, when a dust cloud appeared several miles back down the trail. We at once hurried the wagon and *remuda* ahead to warn the Rangers, and allowed the cattle to string out nearly a mile in length.

A fortunate rise in the trail gave us a glimpse of the cavalcade in our rear, which was entirely too large to be any portion of Straw's outfit; and shortly we were overtaken by our trail cutters of the day before, now increased to twenty-two mounted men. Flood was intentionally in the lead of the herd, and the entire outfit galloped forward to stop the cattle. When they had nearly reached the lead, Flood turned back and met the rustlers.

'Well, I'm as good as my word,' said the leader, 'and I'm here to trim your herd as I promised you I would. Throw off and hold up your cattle, or I'll do it for you.'

Several of our outfit rode up at this juncture in time to hear Flood's reply: 'If you think you're equal to the occasion, hold them up yourself. If I had as big an outfit as you have, I wouldn't ask any man to help me. I want to watch a Colorado River outfit work a herd – I might learn something. My outfit will take a rest, or perhaps hold the cut or otherwise clerk for you. But be careful and don't claim anything that you are not certain is your own, for I reserve the right to look over your cut before you drive it away.'

The rustlers rode in a body to the lead, and when they had thrown the herd off the trail, about half of them rode back and drifted forward the rear cattle. Flood called our outfit to one side and gave us our instructions, the herd being entirely turned over to the rustlers. After they began cutting, we rode around and pretended to assist in holding the cut as the strays in our herd were being cut out. When the red 'Q' cow came out, Fox cut her back, which nearly precipitated a row, for she was promptly recut to the strays by the man who claimed her the day before. Not a man of us even cast a glance up the trail, or in the direction of the Rangers; but when the work was over, Flood protested with the leader of the rustlers over some five or six head of dim-branded cattle which actually belonged to our herd. But he was exultant and would listen to no protests, and attempted to drive away the cut, now numbering nearly fifty head. Then we rode across their front and stopped them.

In the parley which ensued, harsh words were passing, when one of our outfit blurted out in well-feigned surprise; 'Hello, who's that, coming over there?'

A squad of men were riding leisurely through our abandoned herd, coming over to where the two outfits were disputing.

'What's the trouble here, gents?' enquired Hames as he rode up.

'Who are you and what might be your business, may I ask?' enquired the leader of the rustlers.

'Personally I'm nobody, but officially I'm Corporal in Company B, Texas Rangers – well, if there isn't smiling Ed Winters, the biggest cattle thief ever born in Medina County. Why, I've got papers for you; for altering the brands on over fifty head of "C" cattle into a "G" brand. Come here, dear, and give me that gun of yours. Come on, and no false moves or funny work or I'll shoot the white out of your eye. Surround this layout, lads, and let's examine them more closely.'

At this command, every man in our outfit whipped out his six-shooter, the Rangers levelled their carbines on the rustlers, and in less than a minute's time they were disarmed and as crestfallen a group of men as ever walked into a trap of their own setting. Hames got out a 'black book', and after looking the crowd over concluded to hold the entire covey, as the descriptions of the 'wanted' seemed to include most of them. Some of the rustlers attempted to explain their presence, but Hames decided to hold the entire party, 'just to learn them to be more careful of their company the next time', as he put it.

The cut had drifted away into the herd again during the arrest, and about half our outfit took the cattle on to where the wagon was camped for noon. McCann had anticipated an extra crowd for dinner and was prepared for the emergency. When dinner was over and the Rangers had packed and were ready to leave, Hames said to Flood, 'Well, Flood, I'm powerful glad I met you and your outfit. This has been one of the biggest round-ups for me in a long time. You don't know how proud I am over this bunch of beauties. Why, there's liable to be enough rewards out for this crowd to buy my girl a new pair of shoes. And say, when your wagon comes into Abilene, if I ain't there, just drive around to the sheriff's office and leave those captured guns. I'm sorry to load your wagon down that way, but I'm short on pack mules and it will be a great favour to me; besides, these fellows are not liable to need any guns for some little time. I like your company and your chuck, Flood, but you see how it is; the best of friends must part; and then I have an invitation to take dinner in Abilene by tomorrow noon, so I must be a-riding. Adios, everybody.'

CHAPTER 8

On the Brazos and Wichita

As we neared Buffalo Gap a few days later, a deputy sheriff of Taylor County, who resided at the Gap, rode out and met us. He brought an urgent request from Hames to Flood to appear as a witness against the rustlers, who were to be given a preliminary trial at Abilene the following day. Much as he regretted to leave the herd for even a single night, our foreman finally consented to go. To further his convenience we made a long evening drive, camping for the night well above Buffalo Gap, which at that time was little more than a landmark on the trail. The next day we made an easy drive and passed Abilene early in the afternoon, where Flood rejoined us, but refused anyone permission to go into town, with the exception of McCann with the wagon, which was a matter of necessity. It was probably for the best, for this cow town had the reputation of setting a pace that left the wayfarer purseless and breathless, to say nothing about headaches. Though our foreman had not reached those mature years in life when the pleasures and frivolities of dissipation no longer allure, yet it was but natural that he should wish to keep his men from the temptation of the cup that cheers and the wiles of the siren. But when the wagon returned that evening, it was evident that our foreman was human, for with a box of cigars which were promised us were several bottles of Old Crow.

After crossing the Clear Fork of the Brazos a few days later, we entered a well-watered, open country, through which the herd made splendid progress. At Abilene, we were surprised to learn that our herd was the twentieth that had passed that point. The weather so far on our trip had been exceptionally good; only a few showers had fallen, and those during the daytime. But we were now nearing a country in which rain was more frequent, and the swollen condition of several small streams which have their headwaters in the Staked Plains was an intimation to us of recent rains to the westward of our route. Before reaching the main Brazos, we passed two other herds of yearling cattle, and were warned of the impassable condition of that river for the past week. Nothing daunted, we made our usual drive; and when the herd camped that night, Flood, after scouting ahead to the river, returned with the word that the Brazos had been unfordable for over a week, five herds being waterbound.

As we were then nearly twenty miles south of the river, the next morning we threw off the trail and turned the herd to the northeast, hoping to strike the Brazos a few miles above Round Timber ferry. Once the herd was started and their course for the day outlined to our point men by definite landmarks, Flood and Quince Forrest set out to locate the ferry and look up a crossing. Had it not been for our wagon, we would have kept the trail, but as there was no ferry on the Brazos at the crossing of the western trail, it was a question either of waiting or of making this detour. Then all the grazing for several miles about the crossing was already taken by the waterbound herds, and to crowd up and trespass on range already occupied would have been a violation of an unwritten law. Again, no herd took kindly to another attempting to pass them when in travelling condition the herds were on an equality. Our foreman had conceived the scheme of getting past these waterbound herds, if possible, which would give us a clear field until the next large watercourse was reached.

Flood and Forrest returned during the noon hour, the former having found, by swimming, a passable ford near the mouth of Monday Creek, while the latter reported the ferry in 'apple-pie order'. No sooner, then, was dinner over than the wagon set out for the ferry under Forrest as pilot, though we were to return to the herd once the ferry was sighted. The mouth of Monday Creek was not over ten miles below the regular trail crossing on the Brazos, and much nearer our noon camp than the regular one; but the wagon was compelled to make a direct elbow, first turning to the eastward, then doubling back after the river was crossed. We held the cattle off water during the day, so as to have them thirsty when they reached the river. Flood had swum it during the morning, and warned us to be prepared for fifty or sixty yards of swimming water in crossing. When within a mile, we held up the herd and changed horses, every man picking out one with a tested ability to swim. Those of us who were expected to take the water as the herd entered the river divested ourselves of boots and clothing, which we entrusted to riders in the rear. The approach to crossing was gradual, but the opposite bank was abrupt, with only a narrow passageway leading out from the channel. As the current was certain to carry the swimming cattle downstream, we must, to make due allowance, take the water nearly a hundred yards above the outlet on the other shore. All this was planned out in advance by our foreman, who now took the position of point man on the right hand or down the riverside; and with our saddle horses in the immediate lead, we breasted the angry Brazos.

The water was shallow as we entered, and we reached nearly the middle of the river before the loose saddle horses struck swimming water. Honeyman was on their lee, and with the cattle crowding in their rear, there was no alternative but to swim. A loose horse swims easily, however, and our *remuda* readily faced the current, though it was swift enough to carry them below the passageway on the opposite side. By this time the lead cattle were adrift, and half a dozen of us were on their lower side, for the footing under the cutbank was narrow, and should the cattle become congested on landing, some were likely to drown. For a quarter of an hour it required cool heads to keep the trail of cattle moving into the water and the passageway clear on the opposite landing. While they were crossing, the herd represented a large letter 'U', caused by the force of the current drifting the cattle downstream, or until a foothold was secured on the farther side. Those of us fortunate enough to have good swimming horses swam the river a dozen times, and then after the herd was safely over, swam back to get our clothing. It was a thrilling experience to us younger lads of the outfit, and rather attractive; but the elder and more experienced men always dreaded swimming rivers. Their reasons were made clear enough when, a fortnight later, we crossed Red River, where a newly made grave was pointed out to us, among others of men who had lost their lives while swimming cattle.

Once the bulk of the cattle were safely over, with no danger of congestion on the farther bank, they were allowed to loiter along under the cutbank and drink to their hearts' content. Quite a number strayed above the passageway, and in order to rout them out, Bob Blades, Moss Strayhorn and I rode out through the outlet and up the river, where we found some of them in a passageway down a dry arroyo. The steers had found a soft, damp place in the bank, and were so busy horning the waxy, red mud, that they hardly noticed our approach until we were within a rod of them. We halted our horses and watched their antics. The kneeling cattle were cutting the bank viciously with their horns and matting their heads with the red mud, but on discovering our presence, they curved their tails and stampeded out as playfully as young lambs on a hillside.

'Can you sabe where the fun comes in to a steer, to get down on his knees in the mud and dirt, and horn the bank and muss up his curls and enjoy it like that?' enquired Strayhorn of Blades and me.

'Because it's healthy and funny besides,' replied Bob, giving me a cautious wink. 'Did you never hear of people taking mud baths? You've seen dogs eat grass, haven't you? Well, it's something on the same order. Now, if I was a student of the nature of animals, like you are, I'd get off my horse and imagine I had horns, and scar and otherwise mangle that mud bank shamefully. I'll hold your horse if you want to try it – some of the secrets of the humour of cattle might be revealed to you.'

The banter, though given in jest, was too much for this member of a craft that can always be depended on to do foolish things; and when we rejoined the outfit, Strayhorn presented a sight no sane man save a member of our tribe ever would have conceived of.

The herd had scattered over several thousand acres after leaving the river, grazing freely, and so remained during the rest of the evening. Forrest changed horses and set out down the river to find the wagon and pilot it in, for with the long distance that McCann had to cover, it was a question if he would reach us before dark. Flood selected a bed ground and camp about a mile out from the river, and those of the outfit not on herd dragged up an abundance of wood for the night, and built a roaring fire as a beacon to our absent commissary. Darkness soon settled over camp, and the prospect of a supperless night was confronting us; the first guard had taken the herd, and yet there was no sign of the wagon. Several of us youngsters then mounted our night horses and rode down the river a mile or over in the hope of meeting McCann. We came to a steep bank, caused by the shifting of the first bottom of the river across to the north bank, rode up this bluff some little distance, dismounted, and fired several shots; then with our ears to the earth patiently awaited a response. It did not come, and we rode back again. 'Hell's fire and little fishes!' said Joe Stallings, as we clambered into our saddles to return, 'it's not supper or breakfast that's troubling me, but will we get any dinner tomorrow? That's a more pregnant question.'

It must have been after midnight when I was awakened, by the braying of mules and the rattle of the wagon, to hear the voices of Forrest and McCann, mingled with the rattle of chains as they unharnessed, condemning to eternal perdition the broken country on the north side of the Brazos, between Round Timber ferry and the mouth of Monday Creek.

'I think that when the Almighty made this country on the north side of the Brazos,' said McCann the next morning at breakfast, 'the Creator must have grown careless or else made it out of odds and ends. There's just a hundred and one of these dry arroyos that you can't see until you are right on to them. They wouldn't bother a man on horseback, but with a loaded wagon it's different. And I'll promise you all right now that if Forrest hadn't come out and piloted me in, you might have tightened up your belts for breakfast and drank out of cow tracks and smoked cigarettes for nourishment. Well, it'll do you good; this high living was liable to spoil some of you, but I notice that you are all on your feed this morning. The black strap? Honeyman, get that molasses jug out of the wagon – it sits right in front of the chuck box. It does me good to see this outfit's tastes once more going back to the good old staples of life.'

We made our usual early start, keeping well out from the river on a course almost due northward. The next river on our way was the Wichita, still several days' drive from the mouth of Monday Creek. Flood's intention was to parallel the old trail until near the river, when, if its stage of water was not fordable, we would again seek a lower crossing in the hope of avoiding any waterbound herds on that watercourse. The second day out from the Brazos it rained heavily during the day and drizzled during the entire night. Not a hoof would bed down, requiring the guards to be doubled into two watches for the night. The next morning, as was usual when off the trail, Flood scouted in advance, and near the middle of the afternoon's drive we came into the old trail. The weather in the meantime had faired off, which revived life and spirit in the outfit, for in trail work there is nothing that depresses the spirits of men like falling weather. On coming into the trail, we noticed that no herds had passed since the rain began. Shortly afterwards our rear guard was overtaken by a horseman who belonged to a mixed herd which was encamped some four or five miles below the point where we came into the old trail. He reported the Wichita as having been unfordable for the past week, but at that time falling; and said that if the rain of the past few days had not extended as far west as the Staked Plains, the river would be fordable in a day or two.

Before the stranger left us, Flood returned and confirmed this information, and reported further that there were two herds lying over at the Wichita ford expecting to cross the following day. With this outlook, we grazed our herd up to within five miles of the river and camped for the night, and our visitor returned to his outfit with Flood's report of our expectation of crossing on the morrow. But with the fair weather and the prospects of an easy night, we encamped entirely too close to the trail, as we experienced to our sorrow. The grazing was good everywhere, the recent rains having washed away the dust, and we should have camped farther away. We were all sleepy that night, and no sooner was supper over than every mother's son of us was in his blankets. We slept so soundly that the guards were compelled to dismount when calling the relief, and shake the next guards on duty out of their slumber and see that they got up, for men would unconsciously answer in their sleep. The cattle were likewise tired, and slept as willingly as the men.

About midnight, however, Fox Quarternight dashed into camp, firing his six-shooter and yelling like a demon. We tumbled out of our blankets in a dazed condition to hear that one of the herds camped near the river had stampeded, the heavy rumbling of the running herd and the shooting of their outfit now being distinctly audible. We lost no time getting our horses, and in less than a minute were riding for our cattle, which had already got up and were timidly listening to the approaching noise. Although we were a good quarter mile from the trail, before we could drift our herd to a point of safety, the stampeding cattle swept down the trail like a cyclone and our herd was absorbed into the maelstrom of the onrush like leaves in a whirlwind. It was then that our long-legged Mexican steers set us a pace that required a good horse to equal, for they easily took the lead, the other herd having run between three and four miles before striking us, and being already well winded. The other herd were Central Texas cattle, and numbered over thirty-five hundred, but in running capacity were never any match for ours.

Before they had run a mile past our camp, our outfit, bunched well together on the left point, made the first effort to throw them out and off the trail, and try to turn them. But the waves of an angry ocean could as easily have been brought under subjection as our terrorised herd during this first mad dash. Once we turned a few hundred of the leaders, but about the time we thought success was in reach, another contingent of double the number had taken the lead; then we had to abandon what few we had, and again ride to the front. When we reached the lead, there, within half a mile ahead, burned the campfire of the herd of mixed cattle which had moved up the trail that evening. They had had ample warning of impending trouble, just as we had; and before the running cattle reached them about half a dozen of their outfit rode to our assistance, when we made another effort to turn or hold the herds from mixing. None of the outfit of the first herd had kept in the lead with us, their horses fagging, and when the foreman of this mixed herd met us, not knowing that we were as innocent of the trouble as himself, he made some slighting remarks about our outfit and cattle. But it was no time to be sensitive, and with his outfit to help we threw our whole weight against the left point a second time, but only turned a few hundred; and before we could get into the lead again their campfire had been passed and their herd of over three thousand cattle more were in the run. As cows and calves predominated in this mixed herd, our own southerners were still leaders in the stampede.

It is questionable if we would have turned this stampede before day-break, had not the nature of the country come to our assistance. Some-thing over two miles below the camp of the last herd was a deep creek, the banks of which were steep and the passages few and narrow. Here we succeeded in turning the leaders, and about half the outfit of the mixed herd remained, guarding the crossing and turning the lagging cattle in the run as they came up. With the leaders once turned and no chance for the others to take a new lead, we had the entire run of cattle turned back within an hour and safely under control. The first outfit joined us during the interim, and when day broke we had over forty men drifting about ten thousand cattle back up the trail. The different outfits were unfortunately at loggerheads, no one being willing to assume any blame. Flood hunted up the foreman of the mixed herd and demanded an apology for his remarks on our abrupt meeting with him the night before; and while it was granted, it was plain that it was begrudged. The first herd disclaimed all responsibility, holding that the stampede was due to an unavoidable accident, their cattle having grown restless during their enforced lay-over. The indifferent attitude of their foreman, whose name was Wilson, won the friendly regard of our outfit, and before the wagon of the mixed cattle was reached, there was a compact, at least tacit, between their outfit and ours. Our foreman was not blameless, for had we taken the usual precaution and camped at least a mile off the trail, which was our custom when in close proximity to other herds, we might and probably would have missed this mix-up, for our herd was inclined to be very tractable. Flood, with all his experience, well knew that if stampeded cattle ever got into a known trail, they were certain to turn backward over their course; and we were now paying the fiddler for lack of proper precaution.

Within an hour after daybreak, and before the cattle had reached the camp of the mixed herd, our saddle horses were sighted coming over a slight divide about two miles up the trail, and a minute later McCann's mules hove in sight, bringing up the rear. They had made a start with the first dawn, rightly reasoning, as there was no time to leave orders on our departure, that it was advisable for Mohammed to go to the mountain. Flood complimented our cook and horse wrangler on their foresight, for the wagon was our base of sustenance; and there was little loss of time before Barney McCann was calling us to a hastily prepared breakfast. Flood asked Wilson to bring his outfit to our wagon for breakfast, and as fast as they were relieved from herd, they also did ample justice to McCann's cooking. During breakfast, I remember Wilson explaining to Flood what he believed was the cause of the stampede. It seems that there were a few remaining buffalo ranging north of the Wichita, and at night when they came into the river to drink they had scented the cattle on the south side. The bellowing of buffalo bulls had been distinctly heard by his men on night herd for several nights past. The foreman stated it as his belief that a number of bulls had swum the river and had by stealth approached near the sleeping cattle – then, on discovering the presence of the herders, had themselves stampeded, throwing his herd into a panic.

We had got a change of mounts during the breakfast hour, and when all was ready Flood and Wilson rode over to the wagon of the mixed herd, the two outfits following, when Flood enquired of their foreman, 'Have you any suggestions to make in the cutting of these herds?'

'No suggestions,' was the reply, 'but I intend to cut mine first and cut them northward on the trail.'

'You intend to cut them northward, you mean, provided there are no objections, which I'm positive there will be,' said Flood. 'It takes me some little time to size a man up, and the more I see of you during our brief acquaintance, the more I think there's two or three things that you might learn to your advantage. I'll not enumerate them now, but when these herds are separated, if you insist, it will cost you nothing but the asking for my opinion of you. This much you can depend on: when the cutting's over, you'll occupy the same position on the trail that you did before this accident happened. Wilson, here, has nothing but jaded horses, and his outfit will hold the herd while yours and mine cut their cattle. And instead of you cutting north, you can either cut south where you belong on the trail or sulk in your camp, your own will and pleasure to govern. But if you are a cowman, willing to do your part, you'll have your outfit ready to work by the time we throw the cattle together.'

Not waiting for any reply, Flood turned away, and the double outfit circled around the grazing herd and began throwing the sea of cattle into a compact body ready to work. Rod Wheat and Ash Borrowstone were detailed to hold our cut, and the remainder of us, including Honeyman, entered the herd and began cutting. Shortly after we had commenced the work, the mixed outfit, finding themselves in a lonesome minority, joined us and began cutting out their cattle to the westward. When we had worked about half an hour, Flood called us out, and with the larger portion of Wilson's men, we rode over and drifted the mixed cut around to the southward, where they belonged. The mixed outfit pretended they meant no harm, and were politely informed that if they were sincere, they could show it more plainly. For nearly three hours we sent a steady stream of cattle out of the main herd into our cut, while our horses dripped with sweat. With our advantage in the start, as well as that of having the smallest herd, we finished our work first. While the mixed outfit were finishing their cutting, we changed mounts, and then were ready to work the separated herds. Wilson took about half his outfit, and after giving our herd a trimming, during which he recut about twenty, the mixed outfit were given a similar chance, and found about half a dozen of their brand. These cattle of Wilson's and the other herd among ours were not to be wondered at, for we cut by a liberal rule. Often we would find a number of ours on the outside of the main herd, when two men would cut the squad in a bunch, and if there was a wrong brand among them, it was no matter – we knew our herd would have to be retrimmed anyhow, and the other outfits might be disappointed if they found none of their cattle among ours.

The mixed outfit were yet working our herd when Wilson's wagon

CHAPTER 9

Doan's Crossing

It was a nice open country between the Wichita and Pease Rivers. On reaching the latter, we found an easy stage of water for crossing, though there was every evidence that the river had been on a recent rise, the debris of a late freshet littering the cutbank, while high-water mark could be easily noticed on the trees along the river bottom. Summer had advanced until the June freshets were to be expected, and for the next month we should be fortunate if our advance was not checked by floods and falling weather. The fortunate stage of the Pease encouraged us, however, to hope that possibly Red River, two days' drive ahead, would be fordable. The day on which we expected to reach it, Flood set out early to look up the ford which had then been in use but a few years, and which in later days was known as Doan's Crossing on Red River. Our foreman returned before noon and reported a favourable stage of water for the herd, and a new ferry that had been established for wagons. With this good news, we were determined to put that river behind us in as few hours as possible, for it was a common occurrence that a river which was fordable at night was the reverse by daybreak. McCann was sent ahead with the wagon, but we held the saddle horses with us to serve as leaders in taking the water at the ford.

The cattle were strung out in trailing manner nearly a mile, and on reaching the river near the middle of the afternoon, we took the water without a halt or even a change of horses. This boundary river on the northern border of Texas was a terror to trail drovers, but on our reaching it, it had shallowed down, the flow of water following several small channels. One of these was swimming, with shallow bars intervening between the channels. But the majestic grandeur of the river was apparent on every hand – with its red, bluff banks, the sediment of its red waters marking the timber along its course, while the driftwood, lodged in trees and high on the banks, indicated what might be expected when she became sportive or angry. That she was merciless was evident, for although this crossing had been in use only a year or two when we forded, yet five graves, one of which was less than ten days made, attested her disregard for human life. It can safely be asserted that at this and lower trail crossings on Red River, the lives of more trail men were lost by drowning than on all other rivers together. Just as we were nearing the river, an unknown horseman from the south overtook our herd. It was evident that he belonged to some through herd and was looking out the crossing. He made himself useful by lending a hand while our herd was fording, and in a brief conversation with Flood, informed him that he was one of the hands with a 'Running W' herd, gave the name of Bill Mann as their foreman, the number of cattle they were driving, and reported the herd as due to reach the river the next morning. He wasted little time with us, but recrossed the river, returning to his herd, while we grazed out four or five miles and camped for the night.

I shall never forget the impression left in my mind of that first morning after we crossed Red River into the Indian lands. The country was as primitive as in the first day of its creation. The trail led up a divide between the Salt and North forks of Red River. To the eastward of the latter stream lay the reservation of the Apaches, Kiowas and Comanches, the latter having been a terror to the inhabitants of western Texas. They were a warlike tribe, as the records of the Texas Rangers and government troops will verify, but their last effective dressing down was given them in a fight at Adobe Walls by a party of buffalo hunters whom they hoped to surprise. As we wormed our way up this narrow divide, there was revealed to us a panorama of green-swarded plain and timber-fringed watercourse, with not a visible evidence that it had ever been invaded by civilised man, save cattlemen with their herds. Antelope came up in bands and gratified their curiosity as to who these invaders might be, while old solitary buffalo bulls turned tail at our approach and lumbered away to points of safety. Very few herds had ever passed over this route, but buffalo trails leading downstream, deep worn by generations of travel, were to be seen by hundreds on every hand. We were not there for a change of scenery or for our health, so we may have overlooked some of the beauties of the landscape. But we had a keen eye for the things of our craft. We could see almost back to the river, and several times that morning noticed clouds of dust on the horizon. Flood noticed them first. After some little time the dust clouds arose clear and distinct, and we were satisfied that the 'Running W' herd had forded and were behind us, not more than ten or twelve miles away.

At dinner that noon, Flood said he had a notion to go back and pay Mann a visit. 'Why, I've not seen "Little-foot" Bill Mann,' said our foreman, as he helped himself to a third piece of 'fried chicken' (bacon), 'since we separated two years ago up at Ogalalla on the Platte. I'd just like the best in the world to drop back and sleep in his blankets one night and complain of his chuck. Then I'd like to tell him how we had passed them, starting ten days' drive farther south. He must have been among those herds laying over on the Brazos.'

'Why don't you go, then?' said Fox Quarternight. 'Half the outfit could hold the cattle now with the grass and water we're in at present.'

'I'll go you one for luck,' said our foreman. 'Wrangler, rustle in your horses the minute you're through eating. I'm going visiting.'

We all knew what horse he would ride, and when he dropped his rope on 'Alazanito', he had not only picked his own mount of twelve, but the top horse of the entire *remuda* – a chestnut sorrel, fifteen hands and an inch in height, that drew his first breath on the prairies of Texas. No man who sat him once could ever forget him. Now, when the trail is a lost occupation, and reverie and reminiscence carry the mind back to that day, there are friends and faces that may be forgotten, but there are horses that never will be. There were emergencies in which the horse was everything, his rider merely the accessory. But together, man and horse, they were the force that made it possible to move the millions of cattle which passed up and over the various trails of the West.

When we had caught our horses for the afternoon, and Flood had saddled and was ready to start, he said to us, 'You fellows just mosey along up the trail. I'll not be gone long, but when I get back I shall expect to find everything running smooth. An outfit that can't run itself without a boss ought to stay at home and do the milking. So long, fellows!'

The country was well watered, and when we rounded the cattle into the bed ground that night, they were actually suffering from stomachs gorged with grass and water. They went down and to sleep like tired children; one man could have held them that night. We all felt good, and McCann got up an extra spread for supper. We even had dried apples for dessert. McCann had talked the storekeeper at Doan's, where we got our last supplies, out of some extras as a *pelon*. Among them was a can of jam. He sprung this on us as a surprise. Bob Blades toyed with the empty can in mingled admiration and disgust over a picture on the paper label. It was a supper scene, every figure wearing full dress. 'Now, that's General Grant,' said he, pointing with his finger, 'and this is Tom Ochiltree. I can't quite make out this other duck, but I reckon he's some big auger – a senator or governor, maybe. Them old girls have got their gall with them. That style of dress is what you call *lo* and *behold*. The whole passel ought to be ashamed. And they seem to be enjoying themselves, too.'

Though it was a lovely summer night, we had a fire, and supper over, the conversation ranged wide and free. As the wagon on the trail is home, naturally the fire is the hearthstone, so we gathered and lounged around it.

'The only way to enjoy such a fine night as this,' remarked Ash, 'is to sit up smoking until you fall asleep with your boots on. Between too much sleep and just enough, there's a happy medium which suits me.'

'Officer,' enquired Wyatt Roundtree, trailing into the conversation very innocently, 'why is it that people who live up among those Yankees always say "be" the remainder of their lives?'

'What's the matter with the word?' countered Officer.

'Oh, nothing, I reckon, only it sounds a little odd, and there's a tale to it.'

'A story, you mean,' said Officer, reprovingly.

'Well, I'll tell it to you,' said Roundtree, 'and then you can call it to suit yourself. It was out in New Mexico where this happened. There was a fellow drifted into the ranch where I was working, dead broke. To make matters worse, he could do nothing; he wouldn't fit anywhere. Still, he was a nice fellow and we all liked him. Must have had a good education, for he had good letters from people up North. He had worked in stores and had once clerked in a bank, at least the letters said so. Well, we put up a job to get him a place in a little town out on the railroad. You all know how clannish Kentuckians are. Let two meet who never saw each other before, and inside of half an hour they'll be chewing tobacco from the same plug and trying to loan each other money.'

'That's just like them,' interposed Fox Quarternight.

'Well, there was an old man lived in this town, who was the genuine blend of blue grass and Bourbon. If another Kentuckian came within twenty miles of him, and he found it out, he'd hunt him up and they'd hold a two-handed reunion. We put up the job that this young man should play that he was a Kentuckian, hoping that the old man would take him to his bosom and give him something to do. So we took him into town one day, coached and fully posted how to act and play his part. We met the old man in front of his place of business, and, after the usual comment on the news over our way, weather, and other small talk, we were on the point of passing on, when one of our own crowd turned back and enquired, "Uncle Henry, have you met the young Kentuckian who's in the country?"

' "No," said the old man, brightening with interest, "who is he and where is he?"

' "He's in town somewhere," volunteered one of the boys. We pretended to survey the street from where we stood, when one of the boys blurted out, "Yonder he stands now. That fellow in front of the drugstore over there, with the hard-boiled hat on."

'The old man started for him, angling across the street, in disregard of sidewalks. We watched the meeting, thinking it was working all right. We were mistaken. We saw them shake hands – but then the old man turned and walked away very haughtily. Something had gone wrong. He took the sidewalk on his return, and when he came near enough to us, we could see that he was angry and on the prod. When he came near enough to speak, he said, "You think you're smart, don't you? He's a Kentuckian, is he? Hell's full of such Kentuckians!" And as he passed beyond hearing he was muttering imprecations on us. The young fellow joined us a minute later with the question, "What kind of a crank is that you ran me up against?"

' "He's as nice a man as there is in this country," said one of the crowd. "What did you say to him?"

' "Nothing; he came up to me, extended his hand, saying, 'My young friend, I understand that you're from Kentucky.' 'I be, sir,' I replied, when he looked me in the eye and said, 'You're a Goddamn liar,' and turned and walked away. Why, he must have wanted to insult me."

'And then we all knew why our little scheme had failed. There was food and raiment in it for him, but he *would* use that little word "be".'

'Did any of you notice my saddle horse lie down just after we crossed this last creek this afternoon?' enquired Rod Wheat.

'No; what made him lie down?' asked several of the boys.

'Oh, he just found a gopher hole and stuck his forefeet into it one at a time, and then tried to pull them both out at once, and when he couldn't do it, he simply shut his eyes like a dying sheep and lay down.'

'Then you've seen sheep die,' said the horse wrangler.

'Of course I have; a sheep can die any time he makes up his mind to by simply shutting both eyes – then he's a goner.'

Quince Forrest, who had brought in his horse to go out with the second watch, he and Bob Blades having taken advantage of the foreman's absence to change places on guard for the night, had been listening to the latter part of Wyatt's yarn very attentively. We all hoped that he would mount and ride out to the herd, for though he was a good storyteller and meaty with personal experiences, where he thought they would pass muster he was inclined to over colour his statements. We usually gave him respectful attention, but were frequently compelled to regard him as a cheerful, harmless liar. So when he showed no disposition to go, we knew we were in for one from him.

'When I was boss bull-whacker,' he began, 'for a big army sutler at Fort Concho, I used to make two round trips a month with my train. It was a hundred miles to wagon from the freight point where we got our supplies. I had ten teams, six and seven yoke to the team, and trail wagons to each. I was furnished a night herder and a cook, saddle horses for both night herder and myself. You hear me, it was a slam-up fine layout. We could handle three or four tons to the team, and with the whole train we could chamber two car loads of anything. One day we were nearing the fort with a mixed cargo of freight, when a messenger came out and met us with an order from the sutler. He wanted us to make the fort that night and unload. The mail buckboard had reported us to the sutler as camped out back on a little creek about ten miles. We were always entitled to a day to unload and drive back to camp, which gave us good grass for the oxen, but under the orders the whips popped merrily that afternoon, and when they all got well strung out, I rode in ahead, to see what was up. Well, it seems that four companies of infantry from Fort McKavett, which were out for field practice, were going to be brought into this post to be paid three months' wages. This, with the troops stationed at Concho, would turn loose quite a wad of money. The sutler called me into his office when I reached the fort, and when he had produced a black bottle used for cutting the alkali in your drinking water, he said, "Jack" – he called me Jack; my full name is John Quincy Forrest – "Jack, can you make the round trip, and bring in two cars of bottled beer that will be on the track waiting for you, and get back by pay day, the tenth?"

'I figured the time in my mind; it was twelve days.

' "There's five extra in it for each man for the trip, and I'll make it right with you," he added, as he noticed my hesitation, though I was only making a mental calculation.

' "Why, certainly, captain," I said. "What's that fable about the jack rabbit and the land tarrapin?" He didn't know and I didn't either, so I said to illustrate the point: "Put your freight on a bull train, and it always goes through on time. A race horse can't beat an ox on a hundred miles and repeat to a freight wagon." Well, we unloaded before night, and it was pitch dark before we made camp. I explained the situation to the men. We planned to go in empty in five days, which would give us seven to come back loaded. We made every camp on time like clockwork. The fifth morning we were anxious to get a daybreak start, so we could load at night. The night herder had his orders to bring in the oxen the first sign of day, and I called the cook an hour before light. When the oxen were brought in, the men were up and ready to go to yoking. But the nigh wheeler in Joe Jenk's team, a big brindle, muley ox, a regular pet steer, was missing. I saw him myself, Joe saw him, and the night herder swore he came in with the rest. Well, we looked high and low for that Mr Ox, but he had vanished. While the men were eating their breakfast, I got on my horse and the night herder and I scoured and circled that country for miles around, but no ox. The country was so bare and level that a jack rabbit needed to carry a fly for shade. I was worried, for we needed every ox and every moment of time. I ordered Joe to tie his mate behind the trail wagon and pull out one ox shy.

'Well, fellows, that thing worried me powerful. Half the teamsters, good, honest, truthful men as ever popped a whip, swore they saw that ox when they came in. Well, it served a strong argument that a man can be positive and yet be mistaken. We nooned ten miles from our night camp that day. Jerry Wilkens happened to mention it at dinner that he believed his trail needed greasing. "Why," said Jerry, "you'd think that I was loaded, the way my team kept their chains taut." I noticed Joe get up from dinner before he had finished, as if an idea had struck him. He went over and opened the sheet in Jerry's trail wagon, and a smile spread over his countenance. "Come here, fellows," was all he said.

'We ran over to the wagon and there – '

The boys turned their backs with indistinct mutterings of disgust.

'You all don't need to believe this if you don't want to, but there was the missing ox, coiled up and sleeping like a bear in the wagon. He even had Jerry's roll of bedding for a pillow. You see, the wagon sheet was open in front, and he had hopped up on the trail tongue and crept in there to steal a ride. Joe climbed into the wagon, and gave him a few swift kicks in the short ribs, whereupon he opened his eyes, yawned, got up, and jumped out.'

Bull was rolling a cigarette before starting, while Fox's night horse was hard to bridle, which hindered them. With this slight delay, Forrest turned his horse back and continued: 'That same ox on the next trip, one night when we had the wagons parked into a corral, got away from the herder, tip-toed over the men's beds in the gate, stood on his hind legs long enough to eat four fifty-pound sacks of flour out of the rear end of a wagon, got down on his side, and wormed his way under the wagon back into the herd, without being detected or waking a man.'

As they rode away to relieve the first guard, McCann said, 'Isn't he a muzzle-loading daisy? If I loved a liar I'd hug that man to death.'

The absence of our foreman made no difference. We all knew our places on guard. Experience told us there would be no trouble that night. After Wyatt Roundtree and Moss Strayhorn had made down their bed and got into it, Wyatt remarked: 'Did you ever notice, old sidey, how hard this ground is?'

'Oh, yes,' said Moss, as he turned over, hunting for a soft spot, 'it is hard, but we'll forget all that when this trip ends. Brother, dear, just think of those long slings with red cherries floating around in them that we'll be drinking, and picture us smoking cigars in a blaze. That thought alone ought to make a hard bed both soft and warm. Then to think we'll ride all the way home on the cars.'

McCann banked his fire, and the first guard, Wheat, Stallings and Borrowstone, rode in from the herd, all singing an old chorus that had been composed, with little regard for music or sense, about a hotel where they had stopped the year before:

> 'Sure it's one cent for coffee and two cents for bread,
> Three for a steak and five for a bed,
> Sea breeze from the gutter wafts a salt-water smell,
> To the festive cowboy in the Southwestern Hotel.'

CHAPTER 10

No Man's Land

Flood overtook us the next morning, and as a number of us gathered round him to hear the news, told us of a letter that Mann had got at Doan's, stating that the first herd to pass Camp Supply had been harassed by Indians. The 'Running W' people, Mann's employers, had a representative at Dodge, who was authority for the statement. Flood had read the letter, which intimated that an appeal would be made to the government to send troops from either Camp Supply or Fort Sill to give trail herds a safe escort in passing the western border of this Indian reservation. The letter, therefore, urged Mann, if he thought the Indians would give any trouble, to go up the south side of Red River as far as the Panhandle of Texas, and then turn north to the government trail at Fort Elliot.

'I told Mann,' said our foreman, 'that before I'd take one step backward, or go off on a wild-goose chase through that Panhandle country, I'd go back home and start over next year on the Chisholm trail. It's the easiest thing in the world for some big auger to sit in a hotel somewhere and direct the management of a herd. I don't look for no soldiers to furnish an escort; it would take the government six months to get a move on her, even in an emergency. I left Billy Mann in a quandary; he doesn't know what to do. That big auger at Dodge is troubling him, for if he don't act on his advice, and loses cattle as the result – well, he'll never boss any more herds for King and Kennedy. So, boys, if we're ever to see the Blackfoot Agency, there's but one course for us to take, and that's straight ahead. As old Oliver Loving, the first Texas cowman that ever drove a herd, used to say, "Never borrow trouble, or cross a river before you reach it." So when the cattle are through grazing, let them hit the trail north. It's entirely too late for us to veer away from any Indians.'

We were following the regular trail, which had been slightly used for a year or two, though none of our outfit had ever been over it, when late on the third afternoon, about forty miles out from Doan's, about a hundred mounted bucks and squaws sighted our herd and crossed the North Fork from their encampment. They did not ride direct to the herd, but came into the trail nearly a mile above the cattle, so it was some little time from our first sighting them before we met. We did not check the herd or turn out of the trail, but when the lead came within a few hundred yards of the Indians, one buck, evidently the chief of the band, rode forward a few rods and held up one hand, as if commanding a halt. At the sight of this gaudily bedecked apparition, the cattle turned out of the trail, and Flood and I rode up to the chief, extending our hands in friendly greeting. The chief could not speak a word of English, but made signs with his hands; when I turned loose on him in Spanish, however, he instantly turned his horse and signed back to his band. Two young bucks rode forward and greeted Flood and myself in good Spanish.

On thus opening up an intelligible conversation, I called Fox Quarternight, who spoke Spanish, and he rode up from his position of third man in the swing and joined in the council. The two young Indians through whom we carried on the conversation were Apaches, no doubt renegades of that tribe, and while we understood each other in Spanish, they spoke in a heavy guttural peculiar to the Indian. Flood opened the powwow by demanding to know the meaning of this visit. When the question had been properly interpreted to the chief, the latter dropped his blanket from his shoulders and dismounted from his horse. He was a fine specimen of the Plains Indian, fully six feet in height, perfectly proportioned, and in years well past middle life. He looked every inch a chief, and was a natural born orator. There was a certain easy grace to his gestures, only to be seen in people who use the sign language, and often when he was speaking to the Apache interpreters, I could anticipate his requests before they were translated to us, although I did not know a word of Comanche.

Before the powwow had progressed far it was evident that begging was its object. In his prelude, the chief laid claim to all the country in sight as the hunting grounds of the Comanche tribe – an intimation that we were intruders. He spoke of the great slaughter of the buffalo by the white hide-hunters, and the consequent hunger and poverty among his people. He dwelt on the fact that he had ever counselled peace with the whites, until now his band numbered but a few squaws and papooses, the younger men having deserted him for other chiefs of the tribe who advocated war on the palefaces. When he had fully stated his position, he offered to allow us to pass through his country in consideration of ten beeves. On receiving this proposition, all of us dismounted, including the two Apaches, the latter seating themselves in their own fashion, while we whites lounged on the ground in truly American laziness, rolling cigarettes. In dealing with people who know not the value of time, the civilised man is taken at a disadvantage, and unless he can show an equal composure in wasting time, results will be against him. Flood had had years of experience in dealing with Mexicans in the land of *manana*, where all maxims regarding the value of time are religiously discarded. So in dealing with this Indian chief he showed no desire to hasten matters, and carefully avoided all reference to the demand for beeves.

His first question, instead, was to know the distance to Fort Sill and Fort Elliot. The next was how many days it would take for cavalry to reach him. He then had us narrate the fact that when the first herd of cattle passed through the country less than a month before, some bad Indians had shown a very unfriendly spirit. They had taken many of the cattle and had killed and eaten them, and now the great white man's chief at Washington was very much displeased. If another single ox were taken and killed by bad Indians, he would send his soldiers from the forts to protect the cattle, even though their owners drove the herds through the reservation of the Indians – over the grass where their ponies grazed. He had us inform the chief that our entire herd was intended by the great white man's chief at Washington as a present to the Blackfeet Indians who lived in Montana, because they were good Indians, and welcomed priests and teachers among them to teach them the ways of the white man. At our foreman's request we then informed the chief that he was under no obligation to give him even a single beef for any privilege of passing through his country, but as the squaws and little papooses were hungry, he would give him two beeves.

The old chief seemed not the least disconcerted, but begged for five beeves, as many of the squaws were in the encampment across the North Fork, those present being not quite half of his village. It was now getting late in the day and the band seemed to be getting tired of the parleying, a number of squaws having already set out on their return to the village. After some further talk, Flood agreed to add another beef, on condition they be taken to the encampment before being killed. This was accepted, and at once the entire band set up a chattering in view of the coming feast. The cattle had in the meantime grazed off nearly a mile, the outfit, however, holding them under a close herd during the powwowing. All the bucks in the band, numbering about forty, now joined us, and we rode away to the herd. I noticed, by the way, that quite a number of the younger braves had arms, and no doubt they would have made a display of force had Flood's diplomacy been of a more warlike character. While drifting the herd back to the trail we cut out a big lame steer and two stray cows for the Indians, who now left us and followed the beeves which were being driven to their village.

Flood had instructed Quarternight and me to invite the two Apaches to our camp for the night, on the promise of sugar, coffee and tobacco. They consulted with the old chief, and gaining his consent came with us. We extended the hospitality of our wagon to our guests, and when supper was over, promised them an extra beef if they would give us particulars of the trail until it crossed the North Fork, after that river turned west towards the Panhandle. It was evident that they were familiar with the country, for one of them accepted our offer, and with his finger sketched a rude map on the ground where there had formerly been a campfire. He outlined the two rivers between which we were then encamped, and traced the trail until it crossed the North Fork or beyond the Indian reservation. We discussed the outline of the trail in detail for an hour, asking hundreds of unimportant questions, but occasionally getting in a leading one, always resulting in the information wanted. We learned that the big summer encampment of the Comanches and Kiowas was one day's ride for a pony or two days' with cattle up the trail, at the point where the divide between Salt and North Fork narrows to about ten miles in width. We leeched out of them very cautiously the information that the encampment was a large one, and that all herds this year had given up cattle, some as many as twenty-five head.

Having secured the information we wanted, Flood gave to each Apache a package of Arbuckle coffee, a small sack of sugar and both smoking and chewing tobacco. Quarternight informed them that as the cattle were bedded for the night, they had better remain until morning, when he would pick them out a nice fat beef. On their consenting, Fox stripped the wagon sheet off the wagon and made them a good bed, in which, with their body blankets, they were as comfortable as any of us. Neither of them was armed, so we felt no fear of them, and after they had lain down on their couch, Flood called Quarternight and me, and we strolled out into the darkness and reviewed the information. We agreed that the topography of the country they had given was most likely correct, because we could verify much of it by maps in our possession. Another thing on which we agreed was that there was some means of communication between this small and seemingly peaceable band and the main encampment of the tribe; and that more than likely our approach would be known in the large encampment before sunrise. In spite of the good opinion we entertained of our guests, we were also satisfied they had lied to us when they denied they had been in the large camp since the trail herds began to pass. This was the last question we had asked, and the artful manner in which they had parried it showed our guests to be no mean diplomats themselves.

Our camp was astir by daybreak, and after breakfast, as we were catching our mounts for the day, one of the Apaches offered to take a certain pinto horse in our *remuda* in lieu of the promised beef, but Flood declined the offer. On overtaking the herd after breakfast, Quarternight cut out a fat two-year-old stray heifer, and he and I assisted our guests to drive their beef several miles towards their village. Finally bidding them farewell, we returned to the herd, when the outfit informed us that Flood and The Rebel had ridden on ahead to look out a crossing on the Salt

Fork. From this move it was evident that if a passable ford could be found, our foreman intended to abandon the established route and avoid the big Indian encampment.

On the return of Priest and Flood about noon, they reported having found an easy ford of the Salt Fork, which, from the indications of their old trails centring from every quarter at this crossing, must have been used by buffalo for generations. After dinner we put our wagon in the lead, and following close at hand with the cattle, turned off the trail about a mile above our noon camp and struck to the westward for the crossing. This we reached and crossed early that evening, camping out nearly five miles to the west of the river. Rain was always to be dreaded in trail work, and when bedding down the herd that night, we had one of the heaviest downpours which we had experienced since leaving the Rio Grande. It lasted several hours, but we stood it uncomplainingly, for this fortunate drenching had obliterated every trace left by our wagon and herd since abandoning the trail, as well as the signs left at the old buffalo crossing on the Salt Fork. The rain ceased about ten o'clock, when the cattle bedded down easily, and the second guard took them for their watch. Wood was too scarce to afford a fire, and while our slickers had partially protected us from the rain, many of us went to bed in wet clothing that night. After another half day's drive to the west, we turned northward and travelled in that direction through a nice country, more or less broken with small hills, but well watered. On the morning of the first day after turning north, Honeyman reported a number of our saddle horses had strayed from camp. This gave Flood some little uneasiness, and a number of us got on our night horses without loss of time and turned out to look up the missing saddle stock. The Rebel and I set out together to the southward, while others of the outfit set off to the other points of the compass.

I was always a good trailer, was in fact acknowledged to be one of the best, with the exception of my brother Zack, on the San Antonio River, where we grew up as boys. In circling about that morning, I struck the trail of about twenty horses – the missing number – and at once signalled to Priest, who was about a mile distant, to join me. The ground was fortunately fresh from the recent rain and left an easy trail. We galloped along it easily for some little distance, when the trail suddenly turned and we could see that the horses had been running, having evidently received a sudden scare. On following up the trail nearly a mile, we noticed where they had quieted down and had evidently grazed for several hours, but in looking up the trail by which they had left these parts, Priest made the discovery of signs of cattle. We located the trail of the horses soon, and were again surprised to find that they had been running as before, though the trail was much fresher, having possibly been made about dawn. We ran the trail out until it passed over a slight divide, when there before us stood the missing horses. They never noticed us, but were standing at attention, cautiously sniffing the early morning air, on which was borne to them the scent of something they feared. On reaching them, their fear seemed not the least appeased, and my partner and I had our curiosity sufficiently aroused to ride forward to the cause of their alarm. As we rounded the spur of the hill, there in plain view grazed a band of about twenty buffalo. We were almost as excited as the horses over the discovery. By dropping back and keeping the hill between us and them, then dismounting and leaving our horses, we thought we could reach the apex of the hill. It was but a small elevation, and from its summit we secured a splendid view of the animals, now less than three hundred yards distant. Flattening ourselves out, we spent several minutes watching the shaggy animals as they grazed leisurely forward, while several calves in the bunch gambolled around their mothers. A buffalo calf, I had always heard, made delicious veal, and as we had had no fresh meat since we had started, I proposed to Priest that we get one. He suggested trying our ropes, for if we could ever get within effective six-shooter range, a rope was much the surest. Certainly such cumbrous, awkward looking animals, he said, could be no match for our Texas horses. We accordingly dropped back off the hill to our saddle stock, when Priest said that if he only had a certain horse of his out of the band we had been trailing he would promise me buffalo veal if he had to follow them to the Panhandle. It took us but a few minutes to return to our horses, round them in, and secure the particular horse he wanted. I was riding my Nigger Boy, my regular night horse, and as only one of my mount was in this bunch – a good horse, but sluggish – I concluded to give my black a trial, not depending on his speed so much as his staying qualities. It took but a minute for The Rebel to shift his saddle from one horse to another, when he started around to the south, while I turned to the north, so as to approach the buffalo simultaneously. I came in sight of the band first, my partner having a farther ride to make, but had only a few moments to wait, before I noticed the quarry take alarm, and the next instant Priest dashed out from behind a spur of the hill and was after them, I following suit. They turned westward, and when The Rebel and I came together on the angle of their course, we were several hundred yards in their rear. My bunkie had the best horse in speed by all odds, and was soon crowding the band so close that they began to scatter, and though I passed several old bulls and cows, it was all I could do to keep in sight of the calves. After the chase had continued over a mile, the staying qualities of my horse began to shine, but while I was nearing the lead, The Rebel tied to the largest calf in the bunch. The calf he had on his rope was a beauty, and on overtaking him, I reined in my horse, for to have killed a second one would have been sheer waste. Priest wanted me to shoot the calf, but I refused, so he shifted the rope to the pommel of my saddle, and, dismounting, dropped the calf at the first shot. We skinned him, cut off his head, and after disembowelling him, lashed the carcass across my saddle. Then both of us mounted Priest's horse, and started on our return.

On reaching the horse stock, we succeeded in catching a sleepy old horse belonging to Rod Wheat's mount, and I rode him bridleless and bareback to camp. We received an ovation on our arrival, the recovery of the saddle horses being a secondary matter compared to the buffalo veal. 'So it was buffalo that scared our horses, was it, and ran them out of camp?' said McCann, as he helped to unlash the calf. 'Well, it's an ill wind that blows nobody good.' There was no particular loss of time, for the herd had grazed away on our course several miles, and after changing our mounts we overtook the herd with the news that not only the horses had been found, but that there was fresh meat in camp – and buffalo veal at that! The other men out horse hunting, seeing the cattle strung out in travelling shape, soon returned to their places beside the trailing herd.

We held a due northward course, which we figured ought to carry us past and at least thirty miles to the westward of the big Indian encampment. The worst thing with which we had now to contend was the weather, it having rained more or less during the past day and night, or ever since we had crossed the Salt Fork. The weather had thrown the outfit into such a gloomy mood that they would scarcely speak to or answer each other. This gloomy feeling had been growing on us for several days, and it was even believed secretly that our foreman didn't know where he was; that the outfit was drifting and as good as lost. About noon of the third day, the weather continuing wet with cold nights, and with no abatement of the general gloom, our men on point noticed smoke arising directly ahead on our course, in a little valley through which ran a nice stream of water. When Flood's attention was directed to the smoke, he rode forward to ascertain the cause, and returned worse baffled than I ever saw him.

It was an Indian camp, and had evidently been abandoned only that morning, for the fires were still smouldering. Ordering the wagon to camp on the creek and the cattle to graze forward till noon, Flood returned to the Indian camp, taking two of the boys and myself with him. It had not been a permanent camp, yet showed evidence of having been occupied several days at least, and had contained nearly a hundred lean-tos, wickyups and tepees – altogether too large an encampment to suit our tastes. The foreman had us hunt up the trail leaving, and once we had found it, all four of us ran it out five or six miles, when, from the freshness of it, fearing that we might be seen, we turned back. The Indians had many ponies and possibly some cattle, though the sign of the latter was hard to distinguish from buffalo. Before quitting their trail, we concluded they were from one of the reservations, and were heading for their old stamping ground, the Panhandle country – peaceable probably; but whether peaceable or not, we had no desire to meet with them. We lost little time, then, in returning to the herd and making late and early drives until we were out of that section.

But one cannot foresee impending trouble on the cattle trail, any more than elsewhere, and although we encamped that night a long distance to the north of the abandoned Indian camp, the next morning we came near having a stampede. It happened just at dawn. Flood had called the cook an hour before daybreak, and he had started out with Honeyman to drive in the *remuda*, which had scattered badly the morning before. They had the horses rounded up and were driving them towards camp when, about half a mile from the wagon, four old buffalo bulls ran quartering past the horses. This was tinder among stubble, and in their panic the horses outstripped the wranglers and came thundering for camp. Luckily we had been called to breakfast, and those of us who could see what was up ran and secured our night horses. Before half of the horses were thus secured, however, one hundred and thirty loose saddle stock dashed through camp, and every horse on picket went with them, saddles and all, and dragging the picket ropes. Then the cattle jumped from the bed ground and were off like a shot, the fourth guard, who had them in charge, with them. Just for the time being it was an open question which way to ride, our saddle horses going in one direction and the herd in another. Priest was an early riser and had hustled me out early, so fortunately we reached our horses, though over half the outfit in camp could only look on and curse their luck at being left afoot. The Rebel was first in the saddle, and turned after the horses, but I rode for the herd.

The cattle were not badly scared, and as the morning grew clearer, five of us quieted them down before they had run more than a short mile.

The horses, however, gave us a long, hard run, and since a horse has a splendid memory, the effects of this scare were noticeable for nearly a month after. Honeyman at once urged our foreman to hobble at night, but Flood knew the importance of keeping the *remuda* strong, and refused. But his decision was forced, for just as it was growing dusk that evening, we heard the horses running, and all hands had to turn out to surround them and bring them into camp. We hobbled every horse and side-lined certain leaders, and for fully a week following, one scare or another seemed to hold our saddle stock in constant terror. During this week we turned out our night horses, and taking the worst of the leaders in their stead, tied them solidly to the wagon wheels all night, not being willing to trust to picket ropes. They would even run from a mounted man during the twilight of evening or early dawn, or from any object not distinguishable in uncertain light; but the wrangler now never went near them until after sunrise, and their nervousness gradually subsided. Trouble never comes singly, however, and when we struck the Salt Fork, we found it raging, and impassable nearly from bank to bank. But get across we must. The swimming of it was nothing, but it was necessary to get our wagon over, and there came the rub. We swam the cattle in twenty minutes' time, but it took us a full half day to get the wagon over. The river was at least a hundred yards wide, three quarters of which was swimming to a horse. But we hunted up and down the river until we found an eddy, where the banks had a gradual approach to deep water, and started to raft the wagon over – a thing none of the outfit had ever seen done, though we had often heard of it around campfires in Texas. The first thing was to get the necessary timber to make the raft. We scouted along the Salt Fork for a mile either way before we found sufficient dry, dead cottonwood to form our raft. Then we set about cutting it, but we had only one axe and were the poorest set of axemen that were ever called upon to perform a similar task; when we cut a tree it looked as though a beaver had gnawed it down. On horseback the Texan shines at the head of his class, but in any occupation which must be performed on foot he is never a competitor. There was scarcely a man in our outfit who could not swing a rope and tie down a steer in a given space of time, but when it came to swinging an axe to cut logs for the raft, our lustre faded. 'Cutting these logs,' said Joe Stallings, as he mopped the sweat from his brow, 'reminds me of what the Tennessee

THE LOG OF A COWBOY

girl who married a Texan wrote home to her sister. "Texas," so she wrote, "is a good place for men and dogs, but it's hell on women and oxen." '

Dragging the logs up to the place selected for the ford was an easy matter. They were light, and we did it with ropes from the pommels of our saddles, two to four horses being sufficient to handle any of the trees. When everything was ready, we ran the wagon out into two-foot water and built the raft under it. We had cut the dry logs from eighteen to twenty feet long, and now ran a tier of these under the wagon between the wheels. These we lashed securely to the axle and even lashed one large log on the underside of the hub on the outside of the wheel. Then we cross-timbered under these, lashing everything securely to this outside guard log. Before we had finished the cross-timbering, it was necessary to take an anchor rope ashore for fear our wagon would float away. By the time we had succeeded in getting twenty-five dry cottonwood logs under our wagon, it was afloat. Half a dozen of us then swam the river on our horses, taking across the heaviest rope we had for a tow line. We threw the wagon tongue back and lashed it, and making fast to the wagon with one end of the tow rope, fastened our lariats to the other. With the remainder of our unused rope, we took a guy line from the wagon and snubbed it to a tree on the south bank. Everything being in readiness, the word was given, and as those on the south bank eased away, those on horseback on the other side gave the rowel to their horses, and our commissary floated across. The wagon floated so easily that McCann was ordered on to the raft to trim the weight when it struck the current. The current carried it slightly downstream, and when it lodged on the other side, those on the south bank fastened lariats to the guy rope; and with them pulling from that side and us from ours, it was soon brought opposite the landing and hauled into shallow water. Once the raft timber was unlashed and removed, the tongue was lowered, and from the pommels of six saddles the wagon was set high and dry on the north bank. There now only remained to bring up the cattle and swim them, which was an easy task and soon accomplished.

After putting the Salt Fork behind us, our spirits were again dampened, for it rained all the latter part of the night and until noon the next day. It was with considerable difficulty that McCann could keep his fire from drowning out while he was getting breakfast, and several of the outfit refused to eat at all. Flood knew it was useless to rally the boys, for a wet, hungry man is not to be jollied or reasoned with. Five days had now elapsed since we turned off the established trail, and half the time rain had been falling. Besides, our doubt as to where we were had been growing, so before we started that morning, Bull Durham very good-naturedly asked Flood if he had any idea where he was.

'No, I haven't. No more than you have,' replied our foreman. 'But this much I do know, or will just as soon as the sun comes out: I know north from south. We have been travelling north by a little west, and if we hold that course we're bound to strike the North Fork, and within a day or two afterwards we will come into the government trail, running from Fort Elliot to Camp Supply, which will lead us into our own trail. Or, if we were certain that we had cleared the Indian reservation, we could bear to our right, and in time we would re-enter the trail that way. I can't help the weather, boys, and as long as I have chuck, I'd as lief be lost as found.'

If there was any recovery in the feelings of the outfit after this talk of Flood's, it was not noticeable, and it is safe to say that two thirds of the boys believed we were in the Panhandle of Texas. One man's opinion is as good as another's in a strange country, and while there wasn't a man in the outfit who cared to suggest it, I know the majority of us would have endorsed turning northeast. But the fates smiled on us at last. About the middle of the forenoon, on the following day, we cut an Indian trail, about three days old, of probably fifty horses. A number of us followed the trail several miles on its westward course, and among other things discovered that they had been driving a small bunch of cattle, evidently making for the sand hills which we could see about twenty miles to our left. How they had come by the cattle was a mystery – perhaps by forced levy, perhaps from a stampede. One thing was certain: the trail must have contributed them, for there were none but trail cattle in the country. This was reassuring and gave some hint of guidance. We were all tickled, therefore, after nooning that day and on starting the herd in the afternoon, to hear our foreman give orders to point the herd a little east of north. The next few days we made long drives, our saddle horses recovered from their scare, and the outfit fast regained its spirits.

On the morning of the tenth day after leaving the trail, we loitered up a long slope to a divide in our lead from which we sighted timber to the north. This we supposed from its size must be the North Fork. Our route lay up this divide some distance, and before we left it, someone in the rear sighted a dust cloud to the right and far behind us. As dust would hardly rise on a still morning without a cause, we turned the herd off the divide and pushed on, for we suspected Indians. Flood and Priest hung

back on the divide, watching the dust signals, and after the herd had left
them several miles in the rear, they turned and rode towards it – a move
which the outfit could hardly make out. It was nearly noon when we saw
them returning in a long lope, and when they came in sight of the herd,
Priest waved his hat in the air and gave the long yell. When he explained
that there was a herd of cattle on the trail in the rear and to our right, the
yell went around the herd, and was re-echoed by our wrangler and cook
in the rear. The spirits of the outfit instantly rose. We halted the herd
and camped for noon, and McCann set out his best in celebrating the
occasion. It was the most enjoyable meal we had had in the past ten days.
After a good noonday rest, we set out, and having entered the trail during
the afternoon, crossed the North Fork late that evening. As we were
going into camp, we noticed a horseman coming up the trail, who turned
out to be smiling Nat Straw, whom we had left on the Colorado River.
'Well, girls,' said Nat, dismounting, 'I didn't know who you were, but I
just thought I'd ride ahead and overtake whoever it was and stay all night.
Indians? Yes; I wouldn't drive on a trail that hadn't any excitement on it.
I gave the last big encampment ten strays, and won them all back and
four ponies besides on a horse race. Oh, yes, got some running stock with
us. How soon will supper be ready? Get up something extra, for you've
got company.'

CHAPTER 11

A Boggy Ford

That night we learned from Straw our location on the trail. We were far
above the Indian reservation, and instead of having been astray our
foreman had held a due northward course, and we were probably as far
on the trail as if we had followed the regular route. So in spite of all our
good maxims, we had been borrowing trouble; we were never over thirty
miles to the westward of what was then the new Western Cattle Trail.
We concluded that the 'Running W' herd had turned back, as Straw
brought the report that some herd had recrossed Red River the day
before his arrival, giving for reasons the wet season and the danger of
getting waterbound.

About noon of the second day after leaving the North Fork of Red
River, we crossed the Washita, a deep stream, the slippery banks of

which gave every indication of a recent rise. We had no trouble in crossing either wagon or herd, it being hardly a check in our onward course. The abandonment of the regular trail the past ten days had been a noticeable benefit to our herd, for the cattle had had an abundance of fresh country to graze over as well as plenty of rest. But now that we were back on the trail, we gave them their freedom and frequently covered twenty miles a day, until we reached the South Canadian, which proved to be the most delusive stream we had yet encountered. It also showed, like the Washita, every evidence of having been on a recent rampage. On our arrival there was no volume of water to interfere, but it had a quicksand bottom that would bog a saddle blanket. Our foreman had been on ahead and examined the regular crossing, and when he returned, freely expressed his opinion that we would be unable to trail the herd across, but might hope to effect it by cutting it into small bunches. When we came, therefore, within three miles of the river, we turned off the trail to a nearby creek and thoroughly watered the herd. This was contrary to our practice, for we usually wanted the herd thirsty when reaching a large river. But any cow brute that halted in fording the Canadian that day was doomed to sink into quicksands from which escape was doubtful.

We held the wagon and saddle horses in the rear, and when we were half a mile away from the trail ford, cut off about two hundred head of the leaders and started for the crossing, leaving only the horse wrangler and one man with the herd. On reaching the river we gave them an extra push, and the cattle plunged into the muddy water. Before the cattle had advanced fifty feet, instinct warned them of the treacherous footing, and the leaders tried to turn back; but by that time we had the entire bunch in the water and were urging them forward. They had halted but a moment and begun milling, when several heavy steers sank; then we gave way and allowed the rest to come back. We did not realise fully the treachery of this river until we saw that twenty cattle were caught in the merciless grasp of the quicksand. They sank slowly to the level of their bodies, which gave sufficient resistance to support their weight, but they were hopelessly bogged. We allowed the free cattle to return to the herd, and immediately turned our attention to those that were bogged, some of whom were nearly submerged by water. We dispatched some of the boys to the wagon for our heavy corral ropes and a bundle of horse-hobbles and the remainder of us, stripped to the belt, waded out and surveyed the situation at close quarters. We were all experienced in handling bogged cattle, though this quicksand was the most deceptive that I, at least, had ever witnessed. The bottom of the river as we waded through it was solid under our feet, and as long as we kept moving it felt so, but the moment we stopped we sank as in a quagmire. The 'pull' of this quicksand was so strong that four of us were unable to lift a steer's tail out, once it was embedded in the sand. And when we had released a tail by burrowing around it to arm's length and freed it, it would sink of its own weight in a minute's time until it would have to be burrowed out again. To avoid this we had to coil up the tails and tie them with a soft rope hobble.

Fortunately none of the cattle were over forty feet from the bank, and when our heavy rope arrived we divided into two gangs and began the work of rescue. We first took a heavy rope from the animal's horns to solid footing on the river bank, and tied to this five or six of our lariats. Meanwhile others rolled the steer over as far as possible and began burrowing with their hands down alongside a fore and hind leg simultaneously until they could pass a small rope around the pastern above the hoof, or better yet through the cloven in the hoof, when the leg could be readily lifted by two men. We could not stop burrowing, however, for a moment, or the space would fill and solidify. Once a leg was freed, we doubled it back short and securely tied it with a hobble, and when the fore and hind leg were thus secured, we turned the animal over on that side and released the other legs in a similar manner. Then we hastened out of the water and into our saddles, and wrapped the loose end of our ropes to the pommels, having already tied the lariats to the heavy corral rope from the animal's horns. When the word was given, we took a good swinging start, and unless something gave way there was one steer less in the bog. After we had landed the animal high and dry on the bank, it was but a minute's work to free the rope and untie the hobbles. Then it was advisable to get into the saddle with little loss of time and give him a wide berth, for he generally arose angry and sullen.

It was dark before we got the last of the bogged cattle out and retraced our way to camp from the first river on the trip that had turned us. But we were not the least discouraged, for we felt certain there was a ford that had a bottom somewhere within a few miles, and we could hunt it up on the morrow. The next one, however, we would try before we put the cattle in. There was no question that the treacherous condition of the river was due to the recent freshet, which had brought down new deposits of sediment and had agitated the old, even to changing the channel of the river, so that it had not as yet had sufficient time to settle and solidify.

The next morning after breakfast, Flood and two or three of the boys set out up the river, while an equal number of us started, under the leadership of The Rebel, down the river on a similar errand – to prospect for a crossing. Our party scouted for about five miles, and the only safe footing we could find was a swift, narrow channel between the bank and an island in the river, while beyond the island was a much wider channel with water deep enough in several places to swim our saddle horses. The footing seemed quite secure to our horses, but the cattle were much heavier; and if an animal ever bogged in the river, there was water enough to drown him before help could be rendered. We stopped our horses a number of times, however, to try the footing, and in none of our experiments was there any indication of quicksand, so we counted the crossing safe. On our return we found the herd already in motion, headed up the river where our foreman had located a crossing. As it was then useless to make any mention of the island crossing which we had located, at least until a trial had been given to the upper ford, we said nothing. When we came within half a mile of the new ford, we held up the herd and allowed them to graze, and brought up the *remuda* and crossed and recrossed them without bogging a single horse. Encouraged at this, we cut off about a hundred head of heavy lead cattle and started for the ford. We had a good push on them when we struck the water, for there were ten riders around them and Flood was in the lead. We called to him several times that the cattle were bogging, but he never halted until he pulled out on the opposite bank, leaving twelve of the heaviest steers in the quicksand.

'Well, in all my experience in trail work,' said Flood, as he gazed back at the dozen animals struggling in the quicksand, 'I never saw as deceptive a bottom in any river. We used to fear the Cimarron and Platte, but the old South Canadian is the girl that can lay it over them both. Still, there ain't any use crying over spilt milk, and we haven't got men enough to hold two herds, so surround them, boys, and we'll recross them if we leave twenty-four more in the river. Take them back a good quarter, fellows, and bring them up on a run, and I'll take the lead when they strike the water; and give them no show to halt until they get across.'

As the little bunch of cattle had already grazed out nearly a quarter, we rounded them into a compact body and started for the river to recross them. The nearer we came to the river, the faster we went, till we struck the water. In several places where there were channels, we could neither force the cattle nor ride ourselves faster than a walk on account of the depth of the water, but when we struck the shallows, which were the

349

really dangerous places, we forced the cattle with horse and quirt. Near the middle of the river, in shoal water, Rod Wheat was quirting up the cattle, when a big dun steer, trying to get out of his reach, sank in the quicksand, and Rod's horse stumbled across the animal and was thrown. He floundered in attempting to rise, and his hind feet sank to the haunches. His ineffectual struggles caused him to sink farther to the flanks in the loblolly which the tramping of the cattle had caused, and there horse and steer lay, side by side, like two in a bed. Wheat loosened the cinches of the saddle on either side, and stripping the bridle off, brought up the rear, carrying saddle, bridle, and blankets on his back. The river was at least three hundred yards wide, and when we got to the farther bank, our horses were so exhausted that we dismounted and let them blow. A survey showed we had left a total of fifteen cattle and the horse in the quicksands. But we congratulated ourselves that we had bogged down only three head in recrossing. Getting these cattle out was a much harder task than the twenty head gave us the day before, for many of these were bogged more than a hundred yards from the bank. But no time was to be lost; the wagon was brought up in a hurry, fresh horses were caught, and we stripped for the fray. While McCann got dinner we got out the horse, even saving the cinches that were abandoned in freeing him of the saddle.

During the afternoon we were compelled to adopt a new mode of procedure, for with the limited amount of rope at hand, we could only use one rope for drawing the cattle out to solid footing, after they were freed from the quagmire. But we had four good mules to our chuck wagon, and instead of dragging the cattle ashore from the pommels of saddles, we tied one end of the rope to the hind axle and used the mules in snaking the cattle out. This worked splendidly, but every time we freed a steer we had to drive the wagon well out of reach, for fear he might charge the wagon and team. But with three crews working in the water, tying up tails and legs, the work progressed more rapidly than it had done the day before, and two hours before sunset the last animal had been freed. We had several exciting incidents during the operation, for several steers showed fight, and when released went on the prod for the first thing in sight. The herd was grazing nearly a mile away during the afternoon, and as fast as a steer was pulled out, someone would take a horse and give the freed animal a start for the herd. One big black steer turned on Flood, who generally attended to this, and gave him a spirited chase. In getting out of the angry steer's way, he passed near the wagon, when the maddened beef turned from Flood and charged the commissary. McCann was riding the nigh wheel mule, and when he saw the steer coming, he poured the whip into the mules and circled around like a battery in field practice, trying to get out of the way. Flood made several attempts to cut off the steer from the wagon, but he followed it like a mover's dog, until a number of us, fearing our mules would be gored, ran out of the water, mounted our horses, and joined in the chase. When we came up with the circus, our foreman called to us to rope the beef, and Fox Quarternight, getting in the first cast, caught him by the two front feet and threw him heavily. Before he could rise, several of us had dismounted and were sitting on him like buzzards on carrion. McCann then drove the team around behind a sand dune, out of sight; we released the beef, and he was glad to return to the herd, quite sobered by the throwing.

Another incident occurred near the middle of the afternoon. From some cause or other, the hind leg of a steer, after having been tied up, became loosened. No one noticed this; but when, after several successive trials, during which Barney McCann exhausted a large vocabulary of profanity, the mule team was unable to move the steer, six of us fastened our lariats to the main rope, and dragged the beef ashore with great *éclat*. But when one of the boys dismounted to unloose the hobbles and rope, a sight met our eyes that sent a sickening sensation through us, for the steer had left one hind leg in the river, neatly disjointed at the knee. Then we knew why the mules had failed to move him, having previously supposed his size was the difficulty, for he was one of the largest steers in the herd. No doubt the steer's leg had been unjointed in swinging him around, but it had taken six extra horses to sever the ligaments and skin, while the merciless quicksands of the Canadian held the limb. A friendly shot ended the steer's sufferings, and before we finished our work for the day, a flight of buzzards were circling around in anticipation of the coming feast.

Another day had been lost, and still the South Canadian defied us. We drifted the cattle back to the previous night camp, using the same bed ground for our herd. It was then that The Rebel broached the subject of a crossing at the island which we had examined that morning, and offered to show it to our foreman by daybreak. We put two extra horses on picket that night, and the next morning, before the sun was half an hour high, the foreman and The Rebel had returned from the island down the river with word that we were to give the ford a trial, though we could not cross the wagon there. Accordingly we grazed the herd down the river and came opposite the island near the middle of the forenoon. As usual, we cut off about one hundred of the lead cattle, the leaders naturally being the heaviest, and started them into the water. We reached the island and scaled the farther bank without a single animal losing his footing. We brought up a second bunch of double, and a third of triple the number of the first, and crossed them with safety, but as yet the Canadian was dallying with us. As we crossed each successive bunch, the tramping of the cattle increasingly agitated the sands, and when we had the herd about half over, we bogged our first steer on the farther landing. As the water was so shallow that drowning was out of the question, we went back and trailed in the remainder of the herd, knowing the bogged steer would be there when we were ready for him, The island was about two hundred yards long by twenty wide, lying up and down the river, and in leaving it for the farther bank, we always pushed off at the upper end. But now, in trailing the remainder of the cattle over, we attempted to force them into the water at the lower end, as the footing at that point of this middle ground had not, as yet, been trampled up as had the upper end. Everything worked nicely until the rear guard of the last five or six hundred congested on the island, the outfit being scattered on both sides of the river as well as in the middle, leaving a scarcity of men at all points. When the final rear guard had reached the river the cattle were striking out for the farther shore from every quarter of the island at their own sweet will, stopping to drink and loitering on the farther side, for there was no one to hustle them out.

All were over at last, and we were on the point of congratulating our-selves – for, although the herd had scattered badly, we had less than a dozen bogged cattle, and those near the shore – when suddenly, up the river over a mile, there began a rapid shooting. Satisfied that it was by our own men, we separated, and, circling right and left, began to throw the herd together. Some of us rode up the river bank and soon located the trouble. We had not ridden a quarter of a mile before we passed a number of our herd bogged, these having re-entered the river for their noonday drink, and on coming up with the men who had done the shooting, we found them throwing the herd out from the water. They reported that a large number of cattle were bogged farther up the river.

All hands rounded in the herd, and drifting them out nearly a mile from the river, left them under two herders, when the remainder of us returned to the bogged cattle. There were by actual count, including those down at the crossing, over eighty bogged cattle that required our attention, extending over a space of a mile or more above the island ford.

The outlook was anything but pleasing. Flood was almost speechless over the situation, for it might have been guarded against. But realising the task before us, we recrossed the river for dinner, well knowing the inner man needed fortifying for the work before us. No sooner had we disposed of the meal and secured a change of mounts all round, than we sent two men to relieve the men on herd. When they were off, Flood divided up our forces for the afternoon work.

'It will never do,' said he, 'to get separated from our commissary. So, Priest, you take the wagon and *remuda* and go back up to the regular crossing and get our wagon over somehow. There will be the cook and wrangler besides yourself, and you may have two other men. You will have to lighten your load; and don't attempt to cross those mules hitched to the wagon; rely on your saddle horses for getting the wagon over. Forrest, you and Bull, with the two men on herd, take the cattle to the nearest creek and water them well. After watering, drift them back, so they will be within a mile of these bogged cattle. Then leave two men with them and return to the river. I'll take the remainder of the outfit and begin at the ford and work up the river. Get the ropes and hobbles, boys, and come on.'

John Officer and I were left with The Rebel to get the wagon across, and while waiting for the men on herd to get in, we hooked up the mules. Honeyman had the *remuda* in hand to start the minute our herders returned, their change of mounts being already tied to the wagon wheels. The need of haste was very imperative, for the river might rise without an hour's notice, and a two-foot rise would drown every hoof in the river as well as cut us off from our wagon. The South Canadian has its source in the Staked Plains and the mountains of New Mexico, and freshets there would cause a rise here, local conditions never affecting a river of such width. Several of us had seen these Plains rivers – when the mountain was sportive and dallying with the plain – under a clear sky and without any warning of falling weather, rise with a rush of water like a tidal wave or the stream from a broken dam. So when our men from herd galloped in, we stripped their saddles from tired horses and cinched them to fresh ones, while they, that there might be no loss of time, bolted their dinners. It took us less than an hour to reach the ford, where we unloaded the wagon of everything but the chuck-box, which was ironed fast. We had an extra saddle in the wagon, and McCann was mounted on a good horse, for he could ride as well as cook. Priest and I rode the river, selecting a route; and on our return, all five of us tied our lariats to the tongue and sides of the wagon. We took a running start, and until we struck the farther bank we gave the wagon no time to sink, but pulled it out of the river with a shout, our horses' flanks heaving. Then recrossing the river, we lashed all the bedding to four gentle saddle horses and led them over. But to get our provisions across was no easy matter, for we were heavily loaded, having taken on a supply at Doan's sufficient to last us until we reached Dodge, a good month's journey. Yet over it must go, and we kept a string of horsemen crossing and recrossing for an hour, carrying everything from pots and pans to axle grease, as well as the staples of life. When we had got the contents of the wagon finally over and reloaded, there remained nothing but crossing the saddle stock.

The wagon mules had been turned loose, harnessed, while we were crossing the wagon and other effects; and when we drove the *remuda* into the river, one of the wheel mules turned back, and in spite of every man, reached the bank again. Part of the boys hurried the others across, but McCann and I turned back after our wheeler. We caught him without any trouble, but our attempt to lead him across failed. In spite of all the profanity addressed personally to him, he proved a credit to his sire, and we lost ground in trying to force him into the river. The boys across the river watched a few minutes, when all recrossed to our assistance.

'Time's too valuable to monkey with a mule today,' said Priest, as he rode up; 'skin off that harness.'

It was off at once, and we blindfolded and backed him up to the river bank; then taking a rope around his forelegs, we threw him, hog-tied him, and rolled him into the water. With a rope around his forelegs and through the ring in the bridle bit, we asked no further favours, but snaked him ignominiously over to the farther side and reharnessed him into the team.

The afternoon was more than half spent when we reached the first bogged cattle, and by the time the wagon overtook us we had several tied up and ready for the mule team to give us a lift. The herd had been watered in the meantime and was grazing about in sight of the river, and as we occasionally drifted a freed animal out to the herd, we saw others being turned in down the river. About an hour before sunset, Flood rode up to us and reported having cleared the island ford, while a middle outfit under Forrest was working down towards it. During the twilight hours of evening, the wagon and saddle horses moved out to the herd and made ready to camp, but we remained until dark, and with but three horses released a number of light cows. We were the last outfit to reach the wagon, and as Honeyman had tied up our night horses, there was nothing for us to do but eat and go to bed, to which we required no coaxing, for we all knew that early morning would find us once more working with bogged cattle.

The night passed without incident, and the next morning in the division of the forces, Priest was again allowed the wagon to do the snaking out with, but only four men, counting McCann. The remainder of the outfit was divided into several gangs, working near enough each other to lend a hand in case an extra horse was needed on a pull. The third animal we struck in the river that morning was the black steer that had showed fight the day before. Knowing his temper would not be improved by soaking in the quicksand overnight, we changed our tactics. While we were tying up the steer's tail and legs, McCann secreted his team at a safe distance. Then he took a lariat, lashed the tongue of the wagon to a cottonwood tree, and jacking up a hind wheel, used it as a windlass. When all was ready, we tied the loose end of our cable rope to a spoke, and allowing the rope to coil on the hub, manned the windlass and drew him ashore. When the steer was freed, McCann, having no horse at hand, climbed into the wagon, while the rest of us sought safety in our saddles, and gave him a wide berth. When he came to his feet he was sullen with rage and refused to move out of his tracks. Priest rode out and baited him at a distance, and McCann, from his safe position, attempted to give him a scare, when he savagely charged the wagon. McCann reached down, and securing a handful of flour, dashed it into his eyes, which made him back away; and, kneeling, he fell to cutting the sand with his horns. Rising, he charged the wagon a second time, and catching the wagon sheet with his horns, tore two slits in it like slashes of a razor. By this time The Rebel ventured a little nearer, and attracted the steer's attention. He started for Priest, who gave the quirt to his horse, and for the first quarter mile had a close race. The steer, however, weakened by the severe treatment he had been subjected to, soon fell to the rear, and gave up the chase and continued on his way to the herd.

After this incident we worked down the river until the outfits met. We finished the work before noon, having lost three full days by the quicksands of the Canadian. As we pulled into the trail that afternoon near the first divide and looked back to take a parting glance at the river, we saw a dust cloud across the Canadian which we knew must be the Ellison herd under Nat Straw. Quince Forrest, noticing it at the same time as I did, rode forward and said to me, 'Well, old Nat will get it in the neck this time, if that old girl dallies with him as she did with us. I don't wish him any bad luck, but I do hope he'll bog enough cattle to keep his hand in practice. It will be just about his luck, though, to find it settled and solid enough to cross.' And the next morning we saw his signal in the sky about the same distance behind us, and knew he had forded without any serious trouble.

CHAPTER 12

The North Fork

There was never very much love lost between government soldiers and our tribe, so we swept past Camp Supply in contempt a few days later, and crossed the North Fork of the Canadian to camp for the night. Flood and McCann went into the post, as our supply of flour and navy beans was running rather low, and our foreman had hopes that he might be able to get enough of these staples from the sutler to last until we reached Dodge. He also hoped to receive some word from Lovell.

The rest of us had no lack of occupation, as a result of a chance find of mine that morning. Honeyman had stood my guard the night before, and in return, I had got up when he was called to help rustle the horses. We had every horse under hand before the sun peeped over the eastern horizon, and when returning to camp with the *remuda*, as I rode through a bunch of sumach bushes, I found a wild turkey's nest with sixteen fresh eggs in it. Honeyman rode up, when I dismounted, and putting them in my hat, handed them up to Billy until I could mount, for they were beauties and as precious to us as gold. There was an egg for each man in the outfit and one over, and McCann threw a heap of swagger into the enquiry, 'Gentlemen, how will you have your eggs this morning?' just as though it was an everyday affair. They were issued to us fried, and I naturally felt that the odd egg, by rights, ought to fall to me, but the opposing majority was formidable – fourteen to one – so I yielded. A number of ways were suggested to allot the odd egg, but the gambling fever in us being rabid, raffling or playing cards for it seemed to be the proper caper. Raffling had few advocates.

'It reflects on any man's raising,' said Quince Forrest, contemptuously, 'to suggest the idea of raffling, when we've got cards and all night to play for that egg. The very idea of raffling for it! I'd like to see myself pulling straws or drawing numbers from a hat, like some giggling girl at a church fair. Poker is a science; the highest court in Texas has said so, and I want some little show for my interest in that speckled egg. What have I spent twenty years learning the game for, will some of you tell me? Why, it lets me out if you raffle it.' The argument remained unanswered, and the play for it gave interest to that night.

As soon as supper was over and the first guard had taken the herd, the poker game opened, each man being given ten beans for chips. We had only one deck of cards, so one game was all that could be run at a time, but there were six players, and when one was frozen out another sat in and took his place. As wood was plentiful, we had a good fire, and this with the aid of the cook's lantern gave an abundance of light. We unrolled a bed to serve as a table, sat down on it Indian fashion, and as fast as one seat was vacated there was a man ready to fill it, for we were impatient for our turns in the game. The talk turned on an accident which had happened that afternoon. While we were crossing the North Fork of the Canadian, Bob Blades attempted to ride out of the river below the crossing, when his horse bogged down. He instantly dismounted, and his horse after floundering around scrambled out and up the bank, but with a broken leg. Our foreman had ridden up and ordered the horse unsaddled and shot, to put him out of his suffering.

While waiting our turns, the accident to the horse was referred to several times, and finally Blades, who was sitting in the game, turned to us who were lounging around the fire, and asked, 'Did you all notice that look he gave me as I was uncinching the saddle? If he had been human, he might have told what that look meant. Good thing he was a horse and couldn't realise.'

From then on, the yarning and conversation was strictly *horse*.

'It was always a mystery to me,' said Billy Honeyman, 'how a Mexican or Indian knows so much more about a horse than any of us. I have seen them trail a horse across a country for miles, riding in a long lope, with not a trace or sign visible to me. I was helping a horseman once to drive a herd of horses to San Antonio from the lower Rio Grande country. We were driving them to market, and as there were no railroads south then, we had to take along saddle horses to ride home on after disposing of the herd. We always took favourite horses which we didn't wish to sell, generally two apiece for that purpose. This time, when we were at least a hundred miles from the ranch, a Mexican, who had brought along a pet horse to ride home, thought he wouldn't hobble this pet one night, fancying the animal wouldn't leave the others. Well, next morning his pet was missing. We scoured the country around and the trail we had come over for ten miles, but no horse. As the country was all open, we felt positive he would go back to the ranch.

'Two days later and about forty miles higher up the road, the Mexican was riding in the lead of the herd, when suddenly he reined in his horse, throwing him back on his haunches, and waved for some of us to come to him, never taking his eyes off what he saw in the road. The owner was riding on one point of the herd and I on the other. We hurried around to him and both rode up at the same time, when the vaquero blurted out, "There's my horse's track."

' "What horse?" asked the owner.

' "My own; the horse we lost two days ago," replied the Mexican.

' "How do you know it's your horse's track from the thousands of others that fill the road?" demanded his employer.

' "Don Tomas," said the Aztec, lifting his hat, "how do I know your step or voice from a thousand others?"

'We laughed at him. He had been a peon, and that made him respect our opinions – at least he avoided differing with us. But as we drove on that afternoon, we could see him in the lead, watching for that horse's track. Several times he turned in his saddle and looked back, pointed to some track in the road, and lifted his hat to us. At camp that night we tried to draw him out, but he was silent.

'But when we were nearing San Antonio, we overtook a number of wagons loaded with wool, lying over, as it was Sunday, and there among their horses and mules was our Mexican's missing horse. The owner of the wagons explained how he came to have the horse. The animal had come to his camp one morning, back about twenty miles from where we had lost him, while he was feeding grain to his work stock, and being a pet insisted on being fed. Since then, I have always had a lot of respect for a greaser's opinion regarding a horse.'

'Turkey eggs is too rich for my blood,' said Bob Blades, rising from the game. 'I don't care a continental who wins the egg now, for whenever I get three queens pat beat by a four-card draw, I have misgivings about the deal. And old Quince thinks he can stack cards. He couldn't stack hay.'

'Speaking about Mexicans and Indians,' said Wyatt Roundtree, 'I've got more use for a good horse than I have for either of those grades of humanity. I had a little experience over east here, on the cut off from the Chisholm trail, a few years ago, that gave me all the Injun I want for some time to come. A band of renegade Cheyennes had hung along the trail for several years, scaring or begging passing herds into giving them a beef. Of course all the cattle herds had more or less strays among them, so it was easier to cut out one of these than to argue the matter. There was plenty of herds on the trail then, so this band of Indians got bolder than bandits. In the year I'm speaking of, I went up with a herd of horses belonging to a Texas man, who was in charge with us. When we came along with our horses – only six men all told – the chief of the band, called Running Bull Sheep, got on the bluff bigger than a wolf and demanded six horses. Well, that Texan wasn't looking for any particular Injun that day to give six of his own dear horses to. So we just drove on, paying no attention to Mr Bull Sheep. About half a mile farther up the trail, the chief overtook us with all his bucks, and they were an ugly looking lot. Well, this time he held up four fingers, meaning that four horses would be acceptable. But the Texan wasn't recognising the Indian levy of taxation that year. When he refused them, the Indians never parleyed a moment, but set up a "ki yi" and began circling round the herd on their ponies, Bull Sheep in the lead.

'As the chief passed the owner, his horse on a run, he gave a special shrill "ki yi", whipped a short carbine out of its scabbard, and shot twice into the rear of the herd. Never for a moment considering consequences, the Texan brought his six-shooter into action. It was a long, purty shot, and Mr Bull Sheep threw his hands in the air and came off his horse backwards, hard hit. This shooting in the rear of the horses gave them such a scare that we never checked them short of a mile. While the other Indians were holding a little powwow over their chief, we were making good time in the other direction, considering that we had over eight hundred loose horses. Fortunately our wagon and saddle horses had gone ahead that morning, but in the run we overtook them. As soon as we checked the herd from its scare, we turned them up the trail, stretched ropes from the wheels of the wagon, ran the saddle horses in, and changed mounts just a little quicker than I ever saw it done before or since. The cook had a saddle in the wagon, so we caught him up a horse, clapped leather on him, and tied him behind the wagon in case of an emergency. And you can just bet we changed to our best horses. When we overtook the herd, we were at least a mile and a half from where the shooting occurred, and there was no Indian in sight, but we felt that they hadn't given it up. We hadn't long to wait, though we would have waited willingly, before we heard their yells and saw the dust rising in clouds behind us. We quit the herd and wagon right there and rode for a swell of ground ahead that would give us a rear view of the scenery. The first view we caught of them was not very encouraging. They were riding after us like fiends and kicking up a dust like a wind storm. We had nothing but six-shooters, no good for long range. The owner of the horses admitted that it was useless to try to save the herd now, and if our scalps were worth saving it was high time to make ourselves scarce.

'Cantonment was a government post about twenty-five miles away, so we rode for it. Our horses were good Spanish stock, and the Indians' little bench-legged ponies were no match for them. But not satisfied with the wagon and herd falling into their hands, they followed us until we were within sight of the post. As hard luck would have it, the cavalry stationed at this post were off on some escort duty, and the infantry were useless in this case. When the cavalry returned a few days later, they tried to round up those Indians, and the Indian agent used his influence, but the horses were so divided up and scattered that they were never recovered.'

'And did the man lose his horses entirely?' asked Flood, who had anteed up his last bean and joined us.

'He did. There was, I remember, a tin-horn lawyer up about Dodge who thought he could recover their value, as these were agency Indians and the government owed them money. But all I got for three months' wages due me was the horse I got away on.'

McCann had been frozen out during Roundtree's yarn, and had joined the crowd of storytellers on the other side of the fire. Forrest was feeling quite gala, and took a special delight in taunting the vanquished as they dropped out.

'Is McCann there?' enquired he, well knowing he was. 'I just wanted to ask, would it be any trouble to poach that egg for my breakfast and serve it with a bit of toast; I'm feeling a little bit dainty. You'll poach it for me, won't you, please?'

McCann never moved a muscle as he replied, 'Will you please go to hell?'

The storytelling continued for some time, and while Fox Quarternight was regaling us with the history of a little black mare that a neighbour of theirs in Kentucky owned, a dispute arose in the card game regarding the rules of discard and draw.

'I'm too old a girl,' said The Rebel, angrily, to Forrest, 'to allow a pullet like you to teach me this game. When it's my deal, I'll discard just when I please, and it's none of your business so long as I keep within the rules of the game;' which sounded final, and the game continued.

Quarternight picked up the broken thread of his narrative, and the first warning we had of the lateness of the hour was Bull Durham calling to us from the game, 'One of you fellows can have my place, just as soon as we play this jackpot. I've got to saddle my horse and get ready for our guard. Oh, I'm on velvet, anyhow, and before this game ends, I'll make old Quince curl his tail; I've got him going south now.'

It took me only a few minutes to lose my chance at the turkey egg, and I sought my blankets. At 1 a.m., when our guard was called, the beans were almost equally divided among Priest, Stallings and Durham; and in view of the fact that Forrest, whom we all wanted to see beaten, had met defeat, they agreed to cut the cards for the egg, Stallings winning. We mounted our horses and rode out into the night, and the second guard rode back to our campfire.

CHAPTER 13

Dodge

At Camp Supply, Flood received a letter from Lovell, requesting him to come on into Dodge ahead of the cattle. So after the first night's camp above the Cimarron, Flood caught up a favourite horse, informed the outfit that he was going to quit us for a few days, and designated Quince Forrest as the *segundo* during his absence.

'You have a wide, open country from here into Dodge,' said he, when ready to start, 'and I'll make enquiry for you daily from men coming in, or from the buckboard which carries the mail to Supply. I'll try to meet you at Mulberry Creek, which is about ten miles south of Dodge. I'll make that town tonight, and you ought to make the Mulberry in two days. You will see the smoke of passing trains to the north of the Arkansaw, from the first divide south of Mulberry. When you reach that creek, in case I don't meet you, hold the herd there and three or four of you can come on into town. But I'm almost certain to meet you,' he called back as he rode away.

'Priest,' said Quince, when our foreman had gone, 'I reckon you didn't handle your herd to suit the old man when he left us that time at Buffalo

Gap. But I think he used rare judgement this time in selecting a *segundo*. The only thing that frets me is I'm afraid he'll meet us before we reach the Mulberry, and that won't give me any chance to go in ahead like a sure enough foreman. Fact is, I have business there; I deposited a few months' wages at the Long Branch gambling house last year when I was in Dodge, and failed to take a receipt. I just want to drop in and make enquiry if they gave me credit, and if the account is drawing interest. I think it's all right, for the man I deposited it with was a clever fellow and asked me to have a drink with him just as I was leaving. Still, I'd like to step in and see him again.'

Early in the afternoon of the second day after our foreman left us, we sighted the smoke of passing trains, though they were at least fifteen miles distant, and long before we reached the Mulberry, a livery rig came down the trail to meet us. To Forrest's chagrin, Flood, all dressed up and with a white collar on, was the driver, while on a back seat sat Don Lovell and another cowman by the name of McNulta. Every rascal of us gave old man Don the glad hand as they drove around the herd, while he, liberal and delighted as a bridegroom, passed out the cigars by the handful. The cattle were looking fine, which put the old man in high spirits, and he enquired of each of us if our health was good and if Flood had fed us well. They loitered around the herd the rest of the evening, until we threw off the trail to graze and camp for the night, when Lovell declared his intention of staying all night with the outfit.

While we were catching horses during the evening, Lovell came up to me where I was saddling my night horse, and recognising me gave me news of my brother Bob. 'I had a letter yesterday from him,' he said, 'written from Red Fork, which is just north of the Cimarron River over on the Chisholm route. He reports everything going along nicely, and I'm expecting him to show up here within a week. His herd are all beef steers, and are contracted for delivery at the Crow Indian Agency. He's not driving as fast as Flood, but we've got to have our beef for that delivery in better condition, as they have a new agent there this year, and he may be one of these knowing fellows. Sorry you couldn't see your brother, but if you have any word to send him, I'll deliver it.'

I thanked him for the interest he had taken in me, and assured him that I had no news for Robert; but took advantage of the opportunity to enquire if our middle brother, Zack Quirk, was on the trail with any of his herds. Lovell knew him, but felt positive he was not with any of his outfits.

We had an easy night with the cattle. Lovell insisted on standing a guard, so he took Rod Wheat's horse and stood the first watch, and after returning to the wagon, he and McNulta, to our great interest, argued the merits of the different trails until near midnight. McNulta had two herds coming in on the Chisholm trail, while Lovell had two herds on the Western and only one on the Chisholm.

The next morning Forrest, who was again in charge, received orders to cross the Arkansaw River shortly after noon, and then let half the outfit come into town. The old trail crossed the river about a mile above the present town of Dodge City, Kansas, so when we changed horses at noon, the first and second guards caught up their top horses, ransacked their war bags and donned their best toggery. We crossed the river about one o'clock in order to give the boys a good holiday, the stage of water making the river easily fordable. McCann, after dinner was over, drove down on the south side for the benefit of a bridge which spanned the river opposite the town. It was the first bridge he had been able to take advantage of in over a thousand miles of travel, and today he spurned the cattle ford as though he had never crossed at one. Once safely over the river, and with the understanding that the herd would camp for the night about six miles north on Duck Creek, six of our men quit us and rode for the town in a long gallop. Before the rig left us in the morning, McNulta, who was thoroughly familiar with Dodge, and an older man than Lovell, in a friendly and fatherly spirit, seeing that many of us were youngsters, had given us an earnest talk and plenty of good advice.

'I've been in Dodge every summer since '77,' said the old cowman, 'and I can give you boys some points. Dodge is one town where the average bad man of the West not only finds his equal, but finds himself badly handicapped. The buffalo hunters and range men have protested against the iron rule of Dodge's peace officers, and nearly every protest has cost human life. Don't ever get the impression that you can ride your horses into a saloon, or shoot out the lights in Dodge; it may go somewhere else, but it don't go there. So I want to warn you to behave yourselves. You can wear your six-shooters into town, but you'd better leave them at the first place you stop, hotel, livery or business house. And when you leave town, call for your pistols, but don't ride out shooting; omit that. Most cowboys think it's an infringement on their rights to give up shooting in town, and if it is, it stands, for your six-shooters are no match for Winchesters and buckshot; and Dodge's officers are as game a set of men as ever faced danger.'

Nearly a generation has passed since McNulta, the Texan cattle drover, gave our outfit this advice one June morning on the Mulberry, and in setting down this record, I have only to scan the roster of the peace officials of Dodge City to admit its correctness. Among the names that graced the official roster, during the brief span of the trail days, were the brothers Ed, Jim and 'Bat' Masterson, Wyatt Earp, Jack Bridges, 'Doc' Holliday, Charles Bassett, William Tillman, 'Shotgun' Collins, Joshua Webb, Mayor A. B. Webster and 'Mysterious' Dave Mather. The puppets of no romance ever written can compare with these officers in fearlessness. And let it be understood, there were plenty to protest against their rule; almost daily during the range season some equally fearless individual defied them.

'Throw up your hands and surrender,' said an officer to a Texas cowboy, who had spurred an excitable horse until it was rearing and plunging in the street, levelling meanwhile a double-barrelled shotgun at the horseman.

'Not to you, you white-livered son of a bitch,' was the instant reply, accompanied by a shot.

The officer staggered back mortally wounded, but recovered himself, and the next instant the cowboy reeled from his saddle, a load of buckshot through his breast.

After the boys left us for town, the remainder of us, belonging to the third and fourth guard, grazed the cattle forward leisurely during the afternoon. Through cattle herds were in sight both up and down the river on either side, and on crossing the Mulberry the day before, we learned that several herds were holding out as far south as that stream, while McNulta had reported over forty herds as having already passed northward on the trail. Dodge was the meeting point for buyers from every quarter. Often herds would sell at Dodge whose destination for delivery was beyond the Yellowstone in Montana. Herds frequently changed owners when the buyer never saw the cattle. A yearling was a yearling and a two-year-old was a two-year-old, and the seller's word, that they were 'as good or better than the string I sold you last year', was sufficient. Cattle were classified as northern, central and southern animals, and, except in case of severe drought in the preceding years, were pretty nearly uniform in size throughout each section. The prairie section of the State left its indelible imprint on the cattle bred in the open country, while the coast, as well as the piney woods and blackjack sections, did the same, thus making classification easy.

McCann overtook us early in the evening, and, being an obliging fellow, was induced by Forrest to stand the first guard with Honeyman so as to make up the proper number of watches, though with only two men on guard at a time, for it was hardly possible that any of the others would return before daybreak. There was much to be seen in Dodge, and as losing a night's sleep on duty was considered nothing, in hilarious recreation sleep would be entirely forgotten. McCann had not forgotten us, but had smuggled out a quart bottle to cut the alkali in our drinking water. But a quart among eight of us was not dangerous, so the night passed without incident, though we felt a growing impatience to get into town. As we expected, about sunrise the next morning our men off on holiday rode into camp, having never closed an eye during the entire night. They brought word from Flood that the herd would only graze over to Saw Log Creek that day, so as to let the remainder of us have a day and night in town. Lovell would only advance half a month's wages – twenty-five dollars – to each man. It was ample for any personal needs, though we had nearly three months' wages due, and no one protested, for the old man was generally right in his decisions. According to their report the boys had had a hog-killing time, old man Don having been out with them all night. It seems that McNulta stood in well with a class of practical jokers which included the officials of the town, and whenever there was anything on the tapis, he always got the word for himself and friends.

During breakfast Fox Quarternight told this incident of the evening. 'Some professor, a professor in the occult sciences I think he called himself, had written to the mayor to know what kind of a point Dodge would be for a lecture. The lecture was to be free, but he also intimated that he had a card or two on the side up his sleeve, by which he expected to graft on to some of the coin of the realm from the wayfaring man as well as the citizen. The mayor turned the letter over to Bat Masterson, the city marshal, who answered it, and invited the professor to come on, assuring him that he was deeply interested in the occult sciences, personally, and would take pleasure in securing him a hall and a date, besides announcing his coming through the papers.

'Well, he was billed to deliver his lecture last night. Those old long horns, McNulta and Lovell, got us in with the crowd, and while they didn't know exactly what was coming, they assured us that we couldn't afford to miss it. Well, at the appointed hour in the evening, the hall was packed, not over half being able to find seats. It is safe to say there were over five hundred men present, as it was announced for "men only". Every gambler in town was there, with a fair sprinkling of cowmen and our tribe. At the appointed hour, Masterson, as chairman, rapped for order, and in a neat little speech announced the object of the meeting. Bat mentioned the lack of interest in the West in the higher arts and sciences, and bespoke our careful attention to the subject under consideration for the evening. He said he felt it hardly necessary to urge the importance of good order, but if anyone had come out of idle curiosity or bent on mischief, as chairman of the meeting and a peace officer of the city, he would certainly brook no interruption. After a few other appropriate remarks, he introduced the speaker as Dr J. Graves-Brown, the noted scientist.

'The professor was an oily-tongued fellow, and led off on the prelude to his lecture, while the audience was as quiet as mice and as grave as owls. After he had spoken about five minutes and was getting warmed up to his subject, he made an assertion which sounded a little fishy, and someone back in the audience blurted out, "That's a damned lie." The speaker halted in his discourse and looked at Masterson, who arose, and, drawing two six-shooters, looked the audience over as if trying to locate the offender. Laying the guns down on the table, he informed the meeting that another interruption would cost the offender his life, if he had to follow him to the Rio Grande or the British possessions. He then asked the professor, as there would be no further interruptions, to proceed with his lecture. The professor hesitated about going on, until Masterson assured him that it was evident that his audience, with the exception of one skulking coyote, was deeply interested in the subject, but that no one man could interfere with the freedom of speech in Dodge as long as it was a free country and he was city marshal. After this little talk, the speaker braced up and launched out again on his lecture. When he was once more under good headway, he had occasion to relate an exhibition which he had witnessed while studying his profession in India. The incident related was a trifle rank for anyone to swallow raw, when the same party who had interrupted before sang out, "That's another damn lie."

'Masterson came to his feet like a flash, a gun in each hand, saying, "Stand up, you measly skunk, so I can see you." Half a dozen men rose in different parts of the house and cut loose at him, and as they did so the lights went out and the room filled with smoke. Masterson was blazing away with two guns, which so lighted up the rostrum that we could see the professor crouching under the table. Of course they were using blank cartridges, but the audience raised the long yell and poured out through the windows and doors, and the lecture was over. A couple of police came in later, so McNulta said, escorted the professor to his room in the hotel, and quietly advised him that Dodge was hardly capable of appreciating anything so advanced as a lecture on the occult sciences.'

Breakfast over, Honeyman ran in the *remuda*, and we caught the best horses in our mounts, on which to pay our respects to Dodge. Forrest detailed Rod Wheat to wrangle the horses, for we intended to take Honeyman with us. As it was only about six miles over to the Saw Log, Quince advised that they graze along Duck Creek until after dinner, and then graze over to the former stream during the afternoon. Before leaving, we rode over and looked out the trail after it left Duck, for it was quite possible that we might return during the night; and we requested McCann to hang out the lantern, elevated on the end of the wagon tongue, as a beacon. After taking our bearings, we reined southward over the divide to Dodge.

'The very first thing I do,' said Quince Forrest, as we rode leisurely along, 'after I get a shave and haircut and buy what few tricks I need, is to hunt up that gambler in the Long Branch, and ask him to take a drink with me – I took the parting one on him. Then I'll simply set in and win back every dollar I lost there last year. There's something in this northern air that I breathe in this morning that tells me that this is my lucky day. You other kids had better let the games alone and save your money to buy red silk handkerchiefs and soda water and such harmless jimcracks.' The fact that The Rebel was ten years his senior never entered his mind as he gave us this fatherly advice, though to be sure the majority of us were his juniors in years.

On reaching Dodge, we rode up to the Wright House, where Flood met us and directed our cavalcade across the railroad to a livery stable, the proprietor of which was a friend of Lovell's. We unsaddled and turned our horses into a large corral, and while we were in the office of the livery, surrendering our artillery, Flood came in and handed each of us twenty-five dollars in gold, warning us that when that was gone no more would be advanced. On receipt of the money, we scattered like partridges before a gunner. Within an hour or two, we began to return to the stable by ones and twos, and were stowing into our saddle pockets our purchases, which ran from needles and thread to .45 cartridges, every mother's son reflecting the art of the barber, while John Officer had his blond moustaches blackened, waxed and curled, like a French dancing master. 'If some of you boys will hold him,' said Moss Strayhorn, commenting on Officer's appearance, 'I'd like to take a good smell of him, just to see if he took oil up there where the end of his neck's haired over.' As Officer already had several drinks comfortably stowed away under his belt, and stood up strong six feet two, none of us volunteered.

After packing away our plunder, we sauntered around town, drinking moderately, and visiting the various saloons and gambling houses. I clung to my bunkie, The Rebel, during the rounds, for I had learned to like him, and had confidence he would lead me into no indiscretions. At the Long Branch, we found Quince Forrest and Wyatt Roundtree playing the faro bank, the former keeping cases. They never recognised us, but were answering a great many questions, asked by the dealer and lookout, regarding the possible volume of the cattle drive that year. Down at another gambling house, The Rebel met Ben Thompson, a faro dealer not on duty and an old cavalry comrade, and the two cronied around for over an hour like long-lost brothers, pledging anew their friendship over several social glasses, in which I was always included. There was no telling how long this reunion would have lasted, but happily for my sake, Lovell – who had been asleep all the morning – started out to round us up for dinner with him at the Wright House, which was at that day a famous hostelry, patronised almost exclusively by the Texas cowmen and cattle buyers.

We made the rounds of the gambling houses, looking for our crowd. We ran across three of the boys piking at a monte game, who came with us reluctantly; then, guided by Lovell, we started for the Long Branch, where we felt certain we would find Forrest and Roundtree, if they had any money left. Forrest was broke, which made him ready to come, and Roundtree, though quite a winner, out of deference to our employer's wishes, cashed in and joined us. Old man Don could hardly do enough for us; and before we could reach the Wright House, had lined us up against three different bars; and while I had confidence in my navigable capacity, I found they were coming just a little too fast and free, seeing I had scarcely drunk anything in three months but branch water. As we lined up at the Wright House bar for the final before dinner, The Rebel, who was standing next to me, entered a waiver and took a cigar, which I understood to be a hint, and I did likewise.

We had a splendid dinner. Our outfit, with McNulta, occupied a ten-chair table, while on the opposite side of the room was another large table, occupied principally by drovers who were waiting for their herds to arrive. Among those at the latter table, whom I now remember, was 'Uncle' Henry Stevens, Jesse Ellison, 'Lum' Slaughter, John Blocker, Ike Pryor, 'Dun' Houston and, last but not least, Colonel 'Shanghai' Pierce. The latter was possibly the most widely known cowman between the Rio Grande and the British possessions. He stood six feet four in his stockings, was gaunt and raw-boned, and the possessor of a voice which, even in ordinary conversation, could be distinctly heard across the street.

'No, I'll not ship any more cattle to your town,' said Pierce to a cattle solicitor during the dinner, his voice in righteous indignation resounding like a foghorn through the dining-room, 'until you adjust your yardage charges. Listen! I can go right up into the heart of your city and get a room for myself, with a nice clean bed in it, plenty of soap, water and towels, and I can occupy that room for twenty-four hours for two bits. And your stockyards, away out in the suburbs, want to charge me twenty cents a head and let my steer stand out in the weather.'

After dinner, all the boys, with the exception of Priest and myself, returned to the gambling houses as though anxious to work overtime. Before leaving the hotel, Forrest effected the loan of ten from Roundtree, and the two returned to the Long Branch, while the others as eagerly sought out a monte game. But I was fascinated with the conversation of these old cowmen, and sat around for several hours listening to their yarns and cattle talk.

'I was selling a thousand beef steers one time to some Yankee army contractors,' Pierce was narrating to a circle of listeners, 'and I got the idea that they were not up to snuff in receiving cattle out on the prairie. I was holding a herd of about three thousand, and they had agreed to take a running cut, which showed that they had the receiving agent fixed. Well, my foreman and I were counting the cattle as they came between us. But the steers were wild, long-legged coasters, and came through between us like scared wolves. I had lost the count several times, but guessed at them and started over, the cattle still coming like a whirlwind; and when I thought about nine hundred had passed us, I cut them off and sang out, "Here they come and there they go; just an even thousand, by gatlins! What do you make it, Bill?"

' "Just an even thousand, colonel," replied my foreman. Of course the contractors were counting at the same time, and I suppose didn't like to admit they couldn't count a thousand cattle where anybody else could, and never asked for a recount, but accepted and paid for them. They had hired an outfit, and held the cattle outside that night, but the next day, when they cut them into car lots and shipped them, they were a hundred and eighteen short. They wanted to come back on me to make them good, but, shucks! I wasn't responsible if their Jim Crow outfit lost the cattle.'

Along early in the evening, Flood advised us boys to return to the herd with him, but all the crowd wanted to stay in town and see the sights. Lovell interceded in our behalf, and promised to see that we left town in good time to be in camp before the herd was ready to move the next morning. On this assurance, Flood saddled up and started for the Saw Log, having ample time to make the ride before dark. By this time most of the boys had worn off the wire edge for gambling and were comparing notes. Three of them were broke, but Quince Forrest had turned the tables and was over a clean hundred winner for the day. Those who had no money fortunately had good credit with those of us who had, for there was yet much to be seen, and in Dodge in '82 it took money to see the elephant. There were several variety theatres, a number of dance halls, and other resorts which, like the wicked, flourish best under darkness. After supper, just about dusk, we went over to the stable, caught our horses, saddled them, and tied them up for the night. We fully expected to leave town by ten o'clock, for it was a good twelve mile ride to the Saw Log. In making the rounds of the variety theatres and dance halls, we hung together. Lovell excused himself early in the evening, and at parting we assured him that the outfit would leave for camp before midnight. We were enjoying ourselves immensely over at the Lone Star Dance Hall, when an incident occurred in which we entirely neglected the good advice of McNulta, and had the sensation of hearing lead whistle and cry around our ears before we got away from town.

Quince Forrest was spending his winnings as well as drinking freely, and at the end of a quadrille gave vent to his hilarity in an old-fashioned Comanche yell. The bouncer of the dance hall of course had his eye on our crowd, and at the end of a change, took Quince to task. He was a surly brute, and instead of couching his request in appropriate language, threatened to throw him out of the house. Forrest stood like one absent-minded and took the abuse, for physically he was no match for the bouncer, who was armed, moreover, and wore an officer's star. I was dancing in the same set with a red-headed, freckled-faced girl, who clutched my arm and wished to know if my friend was armed. I assured her that he was not, or we would have had notice of it before the bouncer's invective was ended. At the conclusion of the dance, Quince and The Rebel passed out, giving the rest of us the word to remain as though nothing was wrong. In the course of half an hour, Priest returned and asked us to take our leave one at a time without attracting any attention, and meet at the stable. I remained until the last, and noticed The Rebel and the bouncer taking a drink together at the bar – the former apparently in a most amiable mood. We passed out together shortly afterwards, and found the other boys mounted and awaiting our return, it being now about midnight. It took but a moment to secure our guns, and once in the saddle, we rode through the town in the direction of the herd. On the outskirts of the town, we halted. 'I'm going back to that dance hall,' said Forrest, 'and have one round at least with that whore-herder. No man who walks this old earth can insult me, as he did, not if he has a hundred stars on him. If any of you don't want to go along, ride right on to camp, but I'd like to have you all go. And when I take his measure, it will be the signal to the rest of you to put out the lights. All that's going, come on.' There were no dissenters to the programme. I saw at a glance that my bunkie was heart and soul in the play, and took my cue and kept my mouth shut. We circled round the town to a vacant lot within a block of the rear of the dance hall. Honey-man was left to hold the horses; then, taking off our belts and hanging them on the pommels of our saddles, we secreted our six-shooters inside the waistbands of our trousers. The hall was still crowded with the revellers when we entered, a few at a time, Forrest and Priest being the last to arrive. Forrest had changed hats with The Rebel, who always wore a black one, and as the bouncer circulated around, Quince stepped squarely in front of him. There was no waste of words, but a gun-barrel flashed in the lamplight, and the bouncer, struck with the six-shooter, fell like a beef. Before the bewildered spectators could raise a hand, five six-shooters were turned into the ceiling. The lights went out at the first fire, and amidst the rush of men and the screaming of women, we reached the outside, and within a minute were in our saddles. All would have gone well had we returned by the same route and avoided the town; but after crossing the railroad track, anger and pride having not been properly satisfied, we must ride through the town.

On entering the main street, leading north and opposite the bridge on the river, somebody of our party in the rear turned his gun loose into the air. The Rebel and I were riding in the lead, and at the clattering of hoofs and shooting behind us, our horses started on the run, the shooting by this time having become general. At the second street crossing, I noticed a rope of fire belching from a Winchester in the doorway of a store building. There was no doubt in my mind but we were the object of the manipulator of that carbine, and as we reached the next cross street, a man kneeling in the shadow of a building opened fire on us with a six-shooter. Priest reined in his horse, and not having wasted cartridges in the open-air shooting, returned the compliment until he emptied his gun. By this time every officer in the town was throwing lead after us, some of which cried a little too close for comfort. When there was no longer any shooting on our flanks, we turned into a cross street and soon left the lead behind us. At the outskirts of the town we slowed up our horses and took it leisurely for a mile or so, when Quince Forrest halted us and said, 'I'm going to drop out here and see if any one follows us. I want to be alone, so that if any officers try to follow us up, I can have it out with them.'

As there was no time to lose in parleying, and as he had a good horse, we rode away and left him. On reaching camp, we secured a few hours' sleep, but the next morning, to our surprise, Forrest failed to appear. We explained the situation to Flood, who said if he did not show up by noon, he would go back and look for him. We all felt positive that he would not dare to go back to town; and if he was lost, as soon as the sun arose he would be able to get his bearings. While we were nooning about seven miles north of the Saw Log, someone noticed a buggy coming up the trail. As it came nearer we saw that there were two other occupants of the rig besides the driver. When it drew up old Quince, still wearing The Rebel's hat, stepped out of the rig, dragged out his saddle from under the seat, and invited his companions to dinner. They both declined, when Forrest, taking out his purse, handed a twenty-dollar gold piece to the driver with an oath. He then asked the other man what he owed him, but the latter very haughtily declined any recompense, and the conveyance drove away.

'I suppose you fellows don't know what all this means,' said Quince, as he filled a plate and sat down in the shade of the wagon. 'Well, that horse of mine got a bullet plugged into him last night as we were leaving town, and before I could get him to Duck Creek, he died on me. I carried my saddle and blankets until daylight, when I hid in a draw and waited for something to turn up. I thought some of you would come back and look for me sometime, for I knew you wouldn't understand it, when all of a sudden here comes this livery rig along with that drummer – going out to Jetmore, I believe he said. I explained what I wanted, but he decided that his business was more important than mine, and refused me. I referred the matter to Judge Colt, and the judge decided that it was more important that I overtake this herd. I'd have made him take pay, too, only he acted so mean about it.'

After dinner, fearing arrest, Forrest took a horse and rode on ahead to the Solomon River. We were a glum outfit that afternoon, but after a good night's rest were again as fresh as daisies. When McCann started to get breakfast, he hung his coat on the end of the wagon rod, while he went for a bucket of water. During his absence, John Officer was noticed slipping something into Barney's coat pocket, and after breakfast when our cook went to his coat for his tobacco, he unearthed a lady's cambric handkerchief, nicely embroidered, and a silver mounted garter. He looked at the articles a moment, and, grasping the situation at a glance, ran his eye over the outfit for the culprit. But there was not a word or a smile. He walked over and threw the articles into the fire, remarking, 'Good whiskey and bad women will be the ruin of you varmints yet.'

CHAPTER 14

Slaughter's Bridge

Herds bound for points beyond the Yellowstone, in Montana, always considered Dodge as the halfway landmark on the trail, though we had hardly covered half the distance to the destination of our Circle Dots. But with Dodge in our rear, all felt that the backbone of the drive was broken, and it was only the middle of June. In order to divide the night work more equitably, for the remainder of the trip the first and fourth guards changed, the second and third remaining as they were. We had begun to feel the scarcity of wood for cooking purposes some time past, and while crossing the plains of western Kansas, we were frequently forced to resort to the old bed grounds of a year or two previous for cattle chips. These chips were a poor substitute, and we swung a cowskin under the reach of the wagon, so that when we encountered wood on creeks and rivers we could lay in a supply. Whenever our wagon was in the rear, the riders on either side of the herd were always on the skirmish for fuel, which they left alongside the wagon track, and our cook was sure to stow it away underneath on the cowskin.

In spite of any effort on our part, the length of the days made long drives the rule. The cattle could be depended on to leave the bed ground at dawn, and before the outfit could breakfast, secure mounts, and overtake the herd, they would often have grazed forward two or three miles. Often we never threw them on the trail at all, yet when it came time to bed them at night, we had covered twenty miles. They were long, monotonous days; for we were always sixteen to eighteen hours in the saddle, while in emergencies we got the benefit of the limit. We frequently saw mirages, though we were never led astray by shady groves of timber or tempting lakes of water, but always kept within a mile or two of the trail. The evening of the third day after Forrest left us, he returned as we were bedding down the cattle at dusk, and on being assured that no officers had followed us, resumed his place with the herd. He had not even reached the Solomon River, but had stopped with a herd of Millet's on Big Boggy. This creek he reported as bottomless, and the Millet herd as having lost between forty and fifty head of cattle in attempting to ford it at the regular crossing the day before his arrival. They had scouted the creek both up and down since without finding a safe crossing. It seemed that there had been unusually heavy June rains through that section, which accounted for Boggy being in its dangerous condition. Millet's foreman had not considered it necessary to test such an insignificant stream until he got a couple of hundred head of cattle floundering in the mire. They had saved the greater portion of the mired cattle, but quite a number were trampled to death by the others, and now the regular crossing was not approachable for the stench of dead cattle. Flood knew the stream, and so did a number of our outfit, but none of them had any idea that it could get into such an impassable condition as Forrest reported.

The next morning Flood started to the east and Priest to the west to look out a crossing, for we were then within half a day's drive of the creek. Big Boggy paralleled the Solomon River in our front, the two not being more than five miles apart. The confluence was far below in some settlements, and we must keep to the westward of all immigration, on account of the growing crops in the fertile valley of the Solomon. On the westward, had a favourable crossing been found, we would almost have had to turn our herd backward, for we were already within the half circle which this creek described in our front. So after the two men left us, we allowed the herd to graze forward, keeping several miles to the westward of the trail in order to get the benefit of the best grazing. Our herd, when left to itself, would graze from a mile to a mile and a half an hour, and by the middle of the forenoon the timber on Big Boggy and the Solomon beyond was sighted. On reaching this last divide, someone sighted a herd about five or six miles to the eastward and nearly parallel with us. As they were three or four miles beyond the trail, we could easily see that they were grazing along like ourselves, and Forrest was appealed to to know if it was the Millet herd. He said not, and pointed out to the northeast about the location of the Millet cattle, probably five miles in advance of the stranger on our right. When we overtook our wagon at noon, McCann, who had never left the trail, reported having seen the herd. They looked to him like heavy beef cattle, and had two yoke of oxen to their chuck wagon, which served further to proclaim them as strangers.

Neither Priest nor Flood returned during the noon hour, and when the herd refused to lie down and rest longer, we grazed them forward till the fringe of timber which grew along the stream loomed up not a mile distant in our front. From the course we were travelling, we would strike the creek several miles above the regular crossing, and as Forrest reported that Millet was holding below the old crossing on a small rivulet, all we could do was to hold our wagon in the rear, and await the return of our men out on scout for a ford. Priest was the first to return, with word that he had ridden the creek out for twenty-five miles and had found no crossing that would be safe for a mud turtle. On hearing this, we left two men with the herd, and the rest of the outfit took the wagon, went on to Boggy, and made camp. It was a deceptive-looking stream, not over fifty or sixty feet wide. In places the current barely moved, shallowing and deepening, from a few inches in places to several feet in others, with an occasional pool that would swim a horse. We probed it with poles until we were satisfied that we were up against a proposition different from anything we had yet encountered. While we were discussing the situation, a stranger rode up on a fine roan horse, and enquired for our foreman. Forrest informed him that our boss was away looking for a crossing, but we were expecting his return at any time; and invited the stranger to dismount. He did so, and threw himself down in the shade of our wagon. He was a small, boyish-looking fellow, of sandy complexion, not much, if any, over twenty years old, and smiling continuously.

'My name is Pete Slaughter,' said he, by way of introduction, 'and I've got a herd of twenty-eight hundred beef steers, beyond the trail and a few miles back. I've been riding since daybreak down the creek, and I'm prepared to state that the chance of crossing is as good right here as anywhere. I wanted to see your foreman, and if he'll help, we'll bridge her. I've been down to see this other outfit, but they ridicule the idea, though I think they'll come around all right. I borrowed their axe, and tomorrow morning you'll see me with my outfit cutting timber to bridge Big Boggy. That's right, boys; it's the only thing to do. The trouble is I've only got eight men all told. I don't aim to travel over eight or ten miles a day, so I don't need a big outfit. You say your foreman's name is Flood? Well, if he don't return before I go, some of you tell him that he's wasting good time looking for a ford, for there ain't none.'

In the conversation which followed, we learned that Slaughter was driving for his brother Lum, a widely known cowman and drover, whom we had seen in Dodge. He had started with the grass from north Texas, and by the time he reached the Platte, many of his herd would be fit to ship to market, and what were not would be in good demand as feeders in the corn belt of eastern Nebraska. He asked if we had seen his herd during the morning, and on hearing we had, got up and asked McCann to let him see our axe. This he gave a critical examination, before he mounted his horse to go, and on leaving said, 'If your foreman don't want to help build a bridge, I want to borrow that axe of yours. But you fellows talk to him. If any of you boys has ever been over on the Chisholm trail, you will remember the bridge on Rush Creek, south of the Washita River. I built that bridge in a day with an outfit of ten men. Why, shucks! if these outfits would pull together, we could cross tomorrow evening. Lots of these old foremen don't like to listen to a cub like me, but, holy snakes! I've been over the trail oftener than any of them. Why, when I wasn't big enough to make a hand with the herd – only ten years old – in the days when we drove to Abilene, they used to send me in the lead with an old cylinder gun to shoot at the buffalo and scare them off the trail. And I've made the trip every year since. So you tell Flood when he comes in, that Pete Slaughter was here, and that he's going to build a bridge, and would like to have him and his outfit help.'

Had it not been for his youth and perpetual smile, we might have taken young Slaughter more seriously, for both Quince Forrest and The Rebel remembered the bridge on Rush Creek over on the Chisholm. Still there was an air of confident assurance in the young fellow; and the fact that he was the trusted foreman of Lum Slaughter, in charge of a valuable herd of cattle, carried weight with those who knew that drover. The most unwelcome thought in the project was that it required the swinging of an axe to fell trees and to cut them into the necessary lengths, and, as I have said before, the Texan never took kindly to manual labour.

But Priest looked favourably on the suggestion, and so enlisted my support, and even pointed out a spot where timber was most abundant as a suitable place to build the bridge.

'Hell's fire,' said Joe Stallings, with infinite contempt, 'there's thousands of places to build a bridge, and the timber's there, but the idea is to cut it.' And his sentiments found a hearty approval in the majority of the outfit.

Flood returned late that evening, having ridden as far down the creek as the first settlement. The Rebel, somewhat antagonised by the attitude of the majority, reported the visit and message left for him by young Slaughter. Our foreman knew him by general reputation among trail bosses, and when Priest vouched for him as the builder of the Rush Creek bridge on the Chisholm trail, Flood said, 'Why, I crossed my herd four years ago on that Rush Creek bridge within a week after it was built, and wondered who it could be that had the nerve to undertake that task. Rush isn't over half as wide a bayou as Boggy, but she's a true little sister to this miry slough. So he's going to build a bridge anyhow, is he?'

The next morning young Slaughter was at our camp before sunrise, and never once mentioning his business or waiting for the formality of an invitation, proceeded to pour out a tin cup of coffee and otherwise provide himself with a substantial breakfast. There was something amusing in the audacity of the fellow which all of us liked, though he was fifteen years the junior of our foreman. McCann pointed out Flood to him, and taking his well-loaded plate, he went over and sat down by our foreman, and while he ate talked rapidly, to enlist our outfit in the building of the bridge. During breakfast, the outfit listened to the two bosses as they discussed the feasibility of the project – Slaughter enthusiastic, Flood reserved, and asking all sorts of questions as to the mode of procedure. Young Pete met every question with promptness, and assured our foreman that the building of bridges was his long suit. After breakfast, the two foremen rode off down the creek together, and within half an hour Slaughter's wagon and *remuda* pulled up within sight of the regular crossing, and shortly afterwards our foreman returned, and ordered our wagon to pull down to a clump of cotton woods which grew about half a mile below our camp. Two men were detailed to look after our herd during the day, and the remainder of us returned with our foreman to the site selected for the bridge. On our arrival three axes were swinging against as many cottonwoods, and there was no doubt in anyone's mind that we were going to be under a new foreman for that day at least. Slaughter had a big negro cook who swung an axe in a manner which bespoke him a job for the day, and McCann was instructed to provide dinner for the extra outfit.

The site chosen for the bridge was a miry bottom over which oozed three or four inches of water, where the width of the stream was about sixty feet, with solid banks on either side. To get a good foundation was the most important matter, but the brush from the trees would supply the material for that; and within an hour, brush began to arrive, dragged from the pommels of saddles, and was piled into the stream. About this time a call went out for a volunteer who could drive oxen, for the darky was too good an axeman to be recalled. As I had driven oxen as a boy, I was going to offer my services, when Joe Stallings eagerly volunteered in order to avoid using an axe. Slaughter had some extra chain, and our four mules were pressed into service as an extra team in snaking logs. As McCann was to provide for the inner man, the mule team fell to me; and putting my saddle on the nigh wheeler, I rode jauntily past Mr Stallings as he trudged alongside his two yoke of oxen.

About ten o'clock in the morning, George Jacklin, the foreman of the Millet herd, rode up with several of his men, and seeing the bridge taking shape, turned in and assisted in dragging brush for the foundation. By the time all hands knocked off for dinner, we had a foundation of brush twenty feet wide and four feet high, to say nothing about what had sunk in the mire. The logs were cut about fourteen feet long, and old Joe and I had snaked them up as fast as the axemen could get them ready. Jacklin returned to his wagon for dinner and a change of horses, though Slaughter, with plenty of assurance, had invited him to eat with us, and when he declined had remarked, with no less confidence, 'Well, then, you'll be back right after dinner. And say, bring all the men you can spare; and if you've got any gunny sacks or old tarpaulins, bring them; and by all means don't forget your spade.'

Pete Slaughter was a harsh master, considering he was working volunteer labour; but then we all felt a common interest in the bridge, for if Slaughter's beeves could cross, ours could, and so could Millet's. All the men dragging brush changed horses during dinner, for there was to be no pause in piling in a good foundation as long as the material was at hand. Jacklin and his outfit returned, ten strong, and with thirty men at work, the bridge grew. They began laying the logs on the brush after dinner, and the work of sodding the bridge went forward at the same time. The bridge stood about two feet above the water in the creek, but when near the middle of the stream was reached, the foundation gave way, and for an hour ten horses were kept busy dragging brush to fill that sink hole until it would bear the weight of the logs. We had used all the acceptable timber on our side of the stream for half a mile either way, and yet there were not enough logs to complete the bridge. When we lacked only some ten or twelve logs, Slaughter had the boys sod a narrow strip across the remaining brush, and the horsemen led their mounts across to the farther side. Then the axemen crossed, felled the nearest trees, and the last logs were dragged up from the pommels of our saddles.

It now only remained to sod over and dirt the bridge thoroughly. With only three spades the work was slow, but we cut sod with axes, and after several hours' work had it finished. The two yoke of oxen were driven across and back for a test, and the bridge stood it nobly. Slaughter then brought up his *remuda*, and while the work of dirting the bridge was still going on, crossed and recrossed his band of saddle horses twenty times. When the bridge looked completed to everyone else, young Pete advised laying stringers across on either side; so a number of small trees were felled and guard rails strung across the ends of the logs and staked. Then more dirt was carried in on tarpaulins and in gunny sacks, and every chink and crevice filled with sod and dirt. It was now getting rather late in the afternoon, but during the finishing touches, young Slaughter had dispatched his outfit to bring up his herd; and at the same time Flood had sent a number of our outfit to bring up our cattle. Now Slaughter and the rest of us took the oxen, which we had unyoked, and went out about a quarter of a mile to meet his herd coming up. Turning the oxen in the lead, young Pete took one point and Flood the other, and pointed in the lead cattle for the bridge. On reaching it the cattle hesitated for a moment, and it looked as though they were going to balk, but finally one of the oxen took the lead, and they began to cross in almost Indian file. They were big four- and five-year-old beeves, and too many of them on the bridge at one time might have sunk it, but Slaughter rode back down the line of cattle and called to the men to hold them back.

'Don't crowd the cattle,' he shouted. 'Give them all the time they want. We're in no hurry now; there's lots of time.'

They were a full half hour in crossing, the chain of cattle taking the bridge never for a moment being broken. Once all were over, his men rode to the lead and turned the herd up Boggy, in order to have it well out of the way of ours, which were then looming up in sight. Slaughter asked Flood if he wanted the oxen; and as our cattle had never seen a bridge in their lives, the foreman decided to use them; so we brought them back and met the herd, now strung out nearly a mile. Our cattle were naturally wild, but we turned the oxen in the lead, and the two bosses again taking the points, moved the herd up to the bridge. The oxen were again slow to lead out in crossing, and several hundred head of cattle had congested in front of the new bridge, making us all rather nervous, when a big white ox led off, his mate following, and the herd began timidly to follow. Our cattle required careful handling, and not a word was spoken as we nursed them forward, or rode through them to scatter large bunches. A number of times we cut the train of cattle off entirely, as they were congesting at the bridge entrance, and, in crossing, shied and crowded so that several were forced off the bridge into the mire. Our herd crossed in considerably less time than did Slaughter's beeves, but we had five head to pull out; this, however, was considered nothing, as they were light, and the mire was as thin as soup. Our wagon and saddle horses crossed while we were pulling out the bogged cattle, and about half the outfit, taking the herd, drifted them forward towards the Solomon. Since Millet intended crossing that evening, herds were likely to be too thick for safety at night. The sun was hardly an hour high when the last herd came up to cross. The oxen were put in the lead, as with ours, and all four of the oxen took the bridge, but when the cattle reached the bridge, they made a decided balk and refused to follow the oxen. Not a hoof of the herd would even set foot on the bridge. The oxen were brought back several times, but in spite of all coaxing and nursing, and our best endeavours and devices, they would not risk it. We worked with them until dusk, when all three of the foremen decided it was useless to try longer, but both Slaughter and Flood promised to bring back part of their outfits in the morning and make another effort.

McCann's campfire piloted us to our wagon, at least three miles from the bridge, for he had laid in a good supply of wood during the day; and on our arrival our night horses were tied up, and everything made ready for the night. The next morning we started the herd, but Flood took four of us with him and went back to Big Boggy. The Millet herd was nearly two miles back from the bridge, where we found Slaughter at Jacklin's wagon; and several more of his men were, we learned, coming over with the oxen at about ten o'clock. That hour was considered soon enough by the bosses, as the heat of the day would be on the herd by that time, which would make them lazy. When the oxen arrived at the bridge, we rode out twenty strong and lined the cattle up for another trial. They had grazed until they were full and sleepy, but the memory of some of them was too vivid of the hours they had spent in the slimy ooze of Big Boggy once on a time, and they began milling on sight of the stream. We took them back and brought them up a second time with the same results. We then brought them around in a circle a mile in diameter, and as the rear end of the herd was passing, we turned the last hundred, and throwing the oxen into their lead, started them for the bridge; but they too sulked and would have none of it. It was now high noon, so we turned the herd and allowed them to graze back while we went to dinner. Millet's foreman was rather discouraged with the outlook, but Slaughter said they must be crossed if he had to lay over a week and help. After dinner, Jacklin asked us if we wanted a change of horses, and as we could see a twenty-mile ride ahead of us in overtaking our herd, Flood accepted.

When all was ready to start, Slaughter made a suggestion. 'Let's go out,' he said, 'and bring them up slowly in a solid body, and when we get them opposite the bridge, round them in gradually as if we were going to bed them down. I'll take a long lariat to my white wheeler, and when they have quieted down perfectly, I'll lead old Blanco through them and across the bridge, and possibly they'll follow. There's no use crowding them, for that only excites them, and if you ever start them milling, the jig's up. They're nice, gentle cattle, but they've been balked once and they haven't forgotten it.'

What we needed right then was a leader, for we were all ready to catch at a straw, and Slaughter's suggestion was welcome, for he had established himself in our good graces until we preferred him to either of the other foremen as a leader. Riding out to the herd, which were lying down, we roused and started them back towards Boggy. While drifting them back, we covered a front a quarter of a mile in width, and as we neared the bridge we gave them perfect freedom. Slaughter had caught out his white ox, and we gradually worked them into a body, covering perhaps ten acres, in front of the bridge. Several small bunches attempted to mill, but some of us rode in and split them up, and after about half an hour's wait, they quieted down. Then Slaughter rode in whistling and leading his white ox at the end of a thirty-five foot lariat, and as he rode through them they were so logy that he had to quirt them out of the way. When he came to the bridge, he stopped the white wheeler until everything had quieted down; then he led old Blanco on again, but giving him all the time he needed and stopping every few feet. We held our breath as one or two of the herd started to follow him, but they shied and turned back, and our hopes of the moment were crushed. Slaughter detained the ox on the bridge for several minutes, but seeing it was useless, he dismounted and drove him back into the herd. Again and again he tried the same ruse, but it was of no avail. Then we threw the herd back about half a mile, and on Flood's suggestion cut off possibly two hundred head, a bunch which with our numbers we ought to handle readily in spite of their will, and by putting their *remuda* of over a hundred saddle horses in the immediate lead, made the experiment of forcing them. We took the saddle horses down and crossed and recrossed the bridge several times with them, and as the cattle came up turned the horses into the lead and headed for the bridge. With a cordon of twenty riders around them, no animal could turn back, and the horses crossed the bridge on a trot, but the cattle turned tail and positively refused to have anything to do with it. We held them like a block in a vice, so compactly that they could not even mill, but they would not cross the bridge.

When it became evident that it was a fruitless effort, Jacklin, usually a very quiet man, gave vent to a fit of profanity which would have put the army in Flanders to shame. Slaughter, somewhat to our amusement, reproved him: 'Don't fret, man; this is nothing – I balked a herd once in crossing a railroad track, and after trying for two days to cross them, had to drive ten miles and put them under a culvert. You want to cultivate patience, young fellow, when you're handling dumb brutes.'

If Slaughter's cook had been thereabouts then, and suggested a means of getting that herd to take the bridge, his suggestion would have been welcomed, for the bosses were at their wits' ends. Jacklin swore that he would bed that herd at the entrance, and hold them there until they starved to death or crossed, before he would let an animal turn back. But cooler heads were present, and The Rebel mentioned a certain adage, to the effect that when a bird or a girl, he didn't know which, could sing and wouldn't, she or it ought to be made to sing. He suggested that we hold the four oxen on the bridge, cut off fifteen head of cattle, and give them such a running start, they wouldn't know which end their heads were on when they reached the bridge. Millet's foreman approved of the idea, for he was nursing his wrath. The four oxen were accordingly cut out, and Slaughter and one of his men, taking them, started for the bridge with instructions to hold them on the middle. The rest of us took about a dozen head of light cattle, brought them within a hundred yards of the bridge, then with a yell started them on a run from which they could not turn back. They struck the entrance squarely, and we had our first cattle on the bridge. Two men held the entrance, and we brought up another bunch in the same manner, which filled the bridge. Now, we thought, if the herd could be brought up slowly, and this bridgeful let off in their lead, they might follow. To force a herd of cattle across in this manner would have been shameful, and the foreman of the herd knew it as well as anyone present; but no one protested, so we left men to hold the entrance securely and went back after the herd. When we got them within a quarter of a mile of the creek, we cut off about two hundred head of the leaders and brought them around to the rear, for among these leaders were certain to be the ones which had been bogged, and we wanted to have new leaders in this trial. Slaughter was on the farther end of the bridge, and could be depended on to let the oxen lead off at the opportune moment. We brought them up cautiously, and when the herd came within a few rods of the creek the cattle on the bridge lowed to their mates in the herd, and Slaughter, considering the time favourable, opened out and allowed them to leave the bridge on the farther side. As soon as the cattle started leaving on the farther side, we dropped back, and the leaders of the herd to the number of a dozen, after smelling the fresh dirt and seeing the others crossing, walked cautiously up on the bridge. It was a moment of extreme anxiety. None of us spoke a word, but the cattle crowding off the bridge at the farther end set it vibrating. That was enough: they turned as if panic-stricken and rushed back to the body of the herd. I was almost afraid to look at Jacklin. He could scarcely speak, but he rode over to me, ashen with rage, and kept repeating, 'Well, wouldn't that beat hell!'

Slaughter rode back across the bridge, and the men came up and gathered around Jacklin. We seemed to have run the full length of our rope. No one even had a suggestion to offer, and if anyone had had, it needed to be a plausible one to find approval, for hope seemed to have vanished. While discussing the situation, a one-eyed, pox-marked fellow belonging to Slaughter's outfit galloped up from the rear, and said almost breathlessly, 'Say, fellows, I see a cow and calf in the herd. Let's rope the calf, and the cow is sure to follow. Get the rope around the calf's neck, and when it chokes him, he's liable to bellow, and that will call the steers. And if you never let up on the choking till you get on the other side of the bridge, I think it'll work. Let's try it, anyhow.'

We all approved, for we knew that next to the smell of blood, nothing will stir range cattle like the bellowing of a calf. At the mere suggestion, Jacklin's men scattered into the herd, and within a few minutes we had a rope round the neck of the calf. As the roper came through the herd leading the calf, the frantic mother followed, with a train of excited steers at her heels. And as the calf was dragged bellowing across the bridge, it was followed by excited, struggling steers who never knew whether they were walking on a bridge or on *terra firma*. The excitement spread through the herd, and they thickened around the entrance until it was necessary to hold them back, and only let enough pass to keep the chain unbroken.

They were nearly a half-hour in crossing, for it was fully as large a herd as ours; and when the last animal had crossed, Pete Slaughter stood up in his stirrups and led the long yell. The sun went down that day on nobody's wrath, for Jacklin was so tickled that he offered to kill the fattest beef in his herd if we would stay overnight with him. All three of the herds were now over, but had not this herd balked on us the evening before, over nine thousand cattle would have crossed Slaughter's bridge the day it was built.

It was now late in the evening, and as we had to wait some little time to get our own horses, we stayed for supper. It was dark before we set out to overtake the herd, but the trail was plain, and letting our horses take their own time, we jollied along until after midnight. We might have missed the camp, but, by the merest chance, Priest sighted our campfire a mile off the trail, though it had burned to embers. On reaching camp, we changed saddles to our night horses, and, calling Officer, were ready for our watch. We were expecting the men on guard to call us any minute, and while Priest was explaining to Officer the trouble we had had in crossing the Millet herd, I dozed off to sleep there as I sat by the rekindled embers. In that minute's sleep my mind wandered in a dream to my home on the San Antonio River, but the next moment I was aroused to the demands of the hour by The Rebel shaking me and saying – 'Wake up, Tom, and take a new hold. They're calling us on guard. If you expect to follow the trail, son, you must learn to do your sleeping in the winter.'

CHAPTER 15

The Beaver

After leaving the country tributary to the Solomon River, we crossed a wide tableland for nearly a hundred miles, and with the exception of the Kansas Pacific Railroad, without a landmark worthy of a name. Western Kansas was then classified, worthily too, as belonging to the Great American Desert, and most of the country for the last five hundred miles of our course was entitled to a similar description. Once the freshness of spring had passed, the plain took on her natural sunburnt colour, and day after day, as far as the eye could reach, the monotony was unbroken, save by the variations of the mirages on every hand. Except at morning and evening, we were never out of sight of these optical illusions, sometimes miles away, and then again close up, when an antelope standing half a mile distant looked as tall as a giraffe. Frequently the lead of the herd would be in eclipse from these illusions, when to the men in the rear the horsemen and cattle in the lead would appear like giants in an old fairy story. If the monotony of the sea can be charged with dulling men's sensibilities until they become pirates, surely this desolate, arid plain might be equally charged with the wrongdoing of not a few of our craft.

On crossing the railroad at Grinnell, our foreman received a letter from Lovell, directing him to go to Culbertson, Nebraska, and there meet a man who was buying horses for a Montana ranch. Our employer had his business eye open for a possible purchaser for our *remuda*, and if the horses could be sold for delivery after the herd had reached its destination, the opportunity was not to be overlooked. Accordingly, on reaching Beaver Creek, where we encamped, Flood left us to ride through to the Republican River during the night. The trail crossed this river about twenty miles west of Culbertson, and if the Montana horse buyer were yet there, it would be no trouble to come up to the trail crossing and look at our horses.

So after supper, and while we were catching up our night horses, Flood said to us, 'Now, boys, I'm going to leave the outfit and herd under Joe Stallings as *segundo*. It's hardly necessary to leave you under anyone as foreman, for you all know your places. But someone must be made responsible, and one bad boss will do less harm than half a dozen that mightn't agree. So you can put Honeyman on guard in your place at night, Joe, if you don't want to stand your own watch. Now behave yourselves, and when I meet you on the Republican, I'll bring out a box of cigars and have it charged up as axle grease when we get supplies at Ogalalla. And don't sit up all night telling fool stories.'

'Now, that's what I call a good cow boss,' said Joe Stallings, as our foreman rode away in the twilight; 'besides, he used passable good judgement in selecting a *segundo*. Now, Honeyman, you heard what he said. Billy dear, I won't rob you of this chance to stand a guard. McCann, have you got on your next list of supplies any jam and jelly for Sundays? You have? That's right, son – that saves you from standing a guard tonight. Officer, when you come off guard at 3.30 in the morning, build the cook up a good fire. Let me see; yes, and I'll detail young Tom Quirk and The Rebel to grease the wagon and harness your mules before starting in the morning. I want to impress it on your mind, McCann, that I can appreciate a thoughtful cook. What's that, Honeyman? No, indeed, you can't ride my night horse. Love me, love my dog; my horse shares this snap. Now, I don't want to be under the necessity of speaking to any of you first guard, but flop into your saddles ready to take the herd. My turnip says it's eight o'clock now.'

'Why, you've missed your calling – you'd make a fine second mate on a river steamboat,' called back Quince Forrest, as the first guard rode away.

When our guard returned, Officer intentionally walked across Stallings's bed, and catching his spur in the tarpaulin, fell heavily across our *segundo*.

'Excuse me,' said John, rising, 'but I was just nosing around looking for the foreman. Oh, it's you, is it? I just wanted to ask if 4.30 wouldn't be plenty early to build up the fire. Wood's a little scarce, but I'll burn the prairies if you say so. That's all I wanted to know; you may lay down now and go to sleep.'

Our campfire that night was a good one, and in the absence of Flood, no one felt like going to bed until drowsiness compelled us. So we lounged around the fire smoking the hours away, and in spite of the admonition of our foreman, told stories far into the night. During the early portion of the evening, dog stories occupied the boards. As the evening wore on, the subject of revisiting the old States came up for discussion.

'You all talk about going back to the old States,' said Joe Stallings, 'but I don't take very friendly to the idea. I felt that way once and went home to Tennessee; but I want to tell you that after you live a few years in the sunny southwest and get on to her ways, you can't stand it back there like you think you can. Now, when I went back, and I reckon my relations will average up pretty well – fought in the Confederate army, vote the Democratic ticket, and belong to the Methodist church – they all seemed to be rapidly getting locoed. Why, my uncles, when they think of planting the old buck field or the widow's acre into any crop, they first go projecting around in the soil, and, as they say, analyse it, to see what kind of a fertiliser it will require to produce the best results. Back there if one man raises ten acres of corn and his neighbour raises twelve, the one raising twelve is sure to look upon the other as though he lacked enterprise or had modest ambitions. Now, up around that old cow town, Abilene, Kansas, it's a common sight to see the cornfields stretch out like an ocean.

'And then their stock – they are all locoed about that. Why, I know people who will pay a hundred dollars for siring a colt, and if there's one drop of mongrel blood in that sire's veins for ten generations back on either side of his ancestral tree, it condemns him, though he may be a good horse otherwise. They are strong on standard bred horses; but as for me, my mount is all right. I wouldn't trade with any man in this outfit, without it would be Flood, and there's none of them standard bred either. Why, shucks! if you had the pick of all the standard bred horses in Tennessee, you couldn't handle a herd of cattle like ours with them, without carrying a commissary with you to feed them. No; they would never fit here – it takes a range-raised horse to run cattle; one that can rustle and live on grass.'

'Another thing about those people back in those old States, not one in ten, I'll gamble, knows the teacher he sends his children to school to. But when he has a promising colt to be shod, the owner goes to the blacksmith shop himself, and he and the smith will sit on the back sill of the shop, and they will discuss how to shoe that filly so as to give her certain knee action which she seems to need. Probably, says one, a little weight on her toe would give her reach. And there they will sit and powwow and make medicine for an hour or two. And while the blacksmith is shoeing her, the owner will tell him in confidence what a wonderful burst of speed she developed yesterday, while he was speeding her on the back stretch. And then just as he turned her into the home stretch, she threw a shoe and he had to check her in; but if there'd been anyone to catch her time, he was certain it was better than a two-ten clip. And that same colt, you couldn't cut a lame cow out of the shade of a tree on her. A man back there – he's rich, too, though his father made it – gave a thousand dollars for a pair of dogs before they were born. The terms were one half cash and the balance when they were old enough to ship to him. And for fear they were not the proper mustard, he had that dog man sue him in court for the balance, so as to make him prove the pedigree. Now Bob, there, thinks that old hound of his is the real stuff, but he wouldn't do now; almost every year the style changes in dogs back in the old States. One year maybe it's a little white dog with red eyes, and the very next it's a long bench-legged, black dog with a Dutch name that right now I dis-remember. Common old pot hounds and everyday yellow dogs have gone out of style entirely. No, you can all go back that want to, but as long as I can hold a job with Lovell and Flood, I'll try and worry along in my own way.'

On finishing his little yarn, Stallings arose, saying, 'I must take a listen to my men on herd. It always frets me for fear my men will ride too near the cattle.'

A minute later he called us, and when several of us walked out to where he was listening, we recognised Roundtree's voice, singing:

> 'Little black bull came down the hillside,
> Down the hillside, down the hillside,
> Little black bull came down the hillside,
> Long time ago.'

'Whenever my men sing that song on guard, it tells me that everything is amply serene,' remarked our *segundo*, with the air of a field-marshal, as we walked back to the fire.

The evening had passed so rapidly it was now almost time for the second guard to be called, and when the lateness of the hour was announced, we skurried to our blankets like rabbits to their warrens. The second guard usually got an hour or two of sleep before being called, but in the absence of our regular foreman, the mice would play. When our guard was called at one o'clock, as usual, Officer delayed us several minutes looking for his spurs, and I took the chance to ask The Rebel why it was that he never wore spurs.

'It's because I'm superstitious, son,' he answered. 'I own a fine pair of silver-plated spurs that have a history, and if you're ever at Lovell's ranch I'll show them to you. They were given to me by a mortally wounded Federal officer the day the battle of Lookout Mountain was fought. I was an orderly, carrying dispatches, and in passing through a wood from which the Union army had been recently driven, this officer was sitting at the root of a tree, fatally wounded. He motioned me to him, and when I dismounted, he said, "Johnny Reb, please give a dying man a drink." I gave him my canteen, and after drinking from it he continued, "I want you to have my spurs. Take them off. Listen to their history: as you have taken them off me today, so I took them off a Mexican general the day the American army entered the capital of Mexico." '

CHAPTER 16

The Republican

The outfit were awakened out of sleep the next morning by shouts of, 'Whoa, *mula*! Whoa, you mongrel outcasts! Catch them blankety blank mules!' accompanied by a rattle of chain harness, and Quince Forrest dashed across our *segundo*'s bed, shaking a harness in each hand. We kicked the blankets off, and came to our feet in time to see the offender disappear behind the wagon, while Stallings sat up and yawningly enquired 'what other locoed fool had got funny'. But the camp was awake, for the cattle were leisurely leaving the bed ground, while Honeyman, who had been excused from the herd with the first sign of dawn, was rustling up the horses in the valley of the Beaver below camp. With the understanding that the Republican River was a short three days' drive from our present camp, the herd trailed out the first day with not an incident to break the monotony of eating and sleeping, grazing and guarding. But near noon of the second day, we were overtaken by an old, long-whiskered man and a boy of possibly fifteen. They were riding in a light, rickety vehicle, drawn by a small Spanish mule and a rough but clean-limbed bay mare. The strangers appealed to our sympathy, for they were guileless in appearance, and asked so many questions, indicating that ours might have been the first herd of trail cattle they had ever seen. The old man was a free talker, and innocently allowed us to inveigle it out of him that he had been down on the North Beaver, looking up land to homestead, and was then on his way up to take a look at the lands along the Republican. We invited him and the boy to remain for dinner, for in that monotonous waste, we would have been only too glad to entertain a bandit, or an angel for that matter, provided he would talk about something else than cattle. In our guest, however, we found a good conversationalist, meaty with stories not eligible for the retired list; and in return, the hospitality of our wagon was his and welcome. The travel-stained old rascal proved to be a good mixer, and before dinner was over he had won us to a man, though Stallings, in the capacity of foreman, felt it incumbent on him to act the host in behalf of the outfit. In the course of conversation, the old man managed to unearth the fact that our acting foreman was a native of Tennessee, and when he had got it down to town and county, claimed acquaintanceship with a family of men in that locality who were famed as breeders of racehorses. Our guest admitted that he himself was a native of that state, and in his younger days had been a devotee of the racecourse, with the name of every horseman in that commonwealth as well as the bluegrass regions of Kentucky on his tongue's end. But adversity had come upon him, and now he was looking out a new country in which to begin life over again.

After dinner, when our *remuda* was corralled to catch fresh mounts, our guest bubbled over with admiration of our horses, and pointed out several as promising speed and action. We took his praise of our horse-flesh as quite a compliment, never suspecting flattery at the hands of this nomadic patriarch. He innocently enquired which was considered the fastest horse in the *remuda*, when Stallings pointed out a brown, belonging to Flood's mount, as the best quarter horse in the band. He gave him a critical examination, and confessed he would never have picked him for a horse possessing speed, though he admitted that he was unfamiliar with range-raised horses, this being his first visit in the West. Stallings offered to loan him a horse out of his mount, and as the old man had no saddle, our *segundo* prevailed on McCann to loan his for the afternoon. I am inclined to think there was a little jealousy among us that afternoon, as to who was best entitled to entertain our company; and while he showed no partiality, Stallings seemed to monopolise his countryman to our disadvantage. The two jollied along from point to rear and back again, and as they passed us riders in the swing, Stallings ignored us entirely, though the old man always had a pleasant word as he rode by.

'If we don't do something to wean our *segundo* from that old man,' said Fox Quarternight, as he rode up and overtook me, 'he's liable to quit the herd and follow that old fossil back to Tennessee or some other port. Just look at the two now, will you? Old Joe's putting on as much dog as though he was asking the colonel for his daughter. Between me and you and the gatepost, Quirk, I'm a little dubious about the old varmint – he talks too much.'

But I had warmed up to our guest, and gave Fox's criticism very little weight, well knowing if any one of us had been left in charge, he would have shown the old man similar courtesies. In this view I was correct, for when Stallings had ridden on ahead to look up water that afternoon, the very man that entirely monopolised our guest for an hour was Mr John Fox Quarternight. Nor did he jar loose until we reached water, when Stallings cut him off by sending all the men on the right of the herd to hold the cattle from grazing away until every hoof had had ample time to drink. During this rest, the old man circulated around, asking questions as usual, and when I informed him that, with a half-mile of waterfront, it would take a full hour to water the herd properly, he expressed an innocent amazement which seemed as simple as sincere. When the wagon and *remuda* came up, I noticed the boy had tied his team behind our wagon, and was riding one of Honeyman's horses bareback, assisting the wrangler in driving the saddle stock. After the wagon had crossed the creek, and the kegs had been filled and the teams watered, Stallings took the old man with him and the two rode away in the lead of the wagon and *remuda* to select a camp and a bed ground for the night. The rest of us grazed the cattle, now thoroughly watered, forward until the wagon was sighted, when, leaving two men as usual to nurse them up to bed, the remainder of us struck out for camp. As I rode in, I sought out my bunkie to get his opinion regarding our guest. But The Rebel was reticent, as usual, of his opinions of people, so my enquiries remained unanswered, which only served to increase my confidence in the old man.

On arriving at camp we found Stallings and Honeyman entertaining our visitor in a little game of freeze-out for a dollar a corner, while McCann looked wistfully on, as if regretting that his culinary duties prevented his joining in. Our arrival should have been the signal to our wrangler for rounding in the *remuda* for night horses, but Stallings was too absorbed in the game even to notice the lateness of the hour and order in the saddle stock. Quarternight, however, had a few dollars burning holes in his pocket, and he called our horse rustler's attention to the approaching twilight; not that he was in any hurry, but if Honeyman vacated, he saw an opportunity to get into the game. The foreman gave the necessary order, and Quarternight at once bargained for the wrangler's remaining beans, and sat into the game. While we were catching up our night horses, Honeyman told us that the old man had been joking Stallings about the speed of Flood's brown, even going so far as to intimate that he didn't believe that the gelding could outrun that old bay harness mare which he was driving. He had confessed that he was too hard up to wager much on it, but he would risk a few dollars on his judgement on a running horse any day. He also said that Stallings had come back at him, more in earnest than in jest, that if he really thought his harness mare could outrun the brown, he could win every dollar the outfit had. They had codded one another until Joe had shown some spirit, when the old man suggested they play a little game of cards for fun, but Stallings had insisted on stakes to make it interesting, and on the old homesteader pleading poverty, they had agreed to make it for a dollar on the corner. After supper, our *segundo* wanted to renew the game; the old man protested that he was too unlucky and could not afford to lose, but was finally persuaded to play one more game, 'just to pass away the evening'. Well, the evening passed, and within the short space of two hours, there also passed to the supposed lean purse of our guest some twenty dollars from the feverish pockets of the outfit. Then the old man felt too sleepy to play any longer, but loitered around some time, and casually enquired of his boy if he had picketed their mare where she would get a good bait of grass. This naturally brought up the proposed race for discussion.

'If you really think that that old bay palfrey of yours can outrun any horse in our *remuda*,' said Stallings, tauntingly, 'you're missing the chance of your life not to pick up a few honest dollars as you journey along. You stay with us tomorrow, and when we meet our foreman at the Republican, if he'll loan me the horse, I'll give you a race for any sum you name, just to show you that I've got a few drops of sporting blood in me. And if your mare can outrun a cow, you stand an easy chance to win some money.'

Our visitor met Joe's bantering in a timid manner. Before turning in, however, he informed us that he appreciated our hospitality, but that he expected to make an early drive in the morning to the Republican, where he might camp several days. With this the old man and the boy unrolled their blankets, and both were soon sound asleep. Then our *segundo* quietly took Fox Quarternight off to one side, and I heard the latter agree to call him when the third guard was aroused. Having notified Honeyman that he would stand his own watch that night, Stallings, with the rest of the outfit, soon joined the old man in the land of dreams. Instead of the rough shaking which was customary on arousing a guard, when we of the third watch were called, we were awakened in a manner so cautious as to betoken something unusual in the air. The atmosphere of mystery soon cleared after reaching the herd, when Bob Blades informed us that it was the intention of Stallings and Quarternight to steal the old man's harness mare off the picket rope, and run her against their night horses in a trial race. Like love and war, everything is fair in horse racing, but the audacity of this proposition almost passed belief. Both Blades and Durham remained on guard with us, and before we had circled the herd half a dozen times, the two conspirators came riding up to the bed ground, leading the bay mare. There was a good moon that night; Quarternight exchanged mounts with John Officer, as the latter had a splendid night horse that had outstripped the outfit in every stampede so far, and our *segundo* and the second guard rode out of hearing of both herd and camp to try out the horses.

After an hour, the quartette returned, and under solemn pledges of secrecy Stallings said, 'Why, that old bay harness mare can't run fast enough to keep up with a funeral. I rode her myself, and if she's got any run in her, rowel and quirt won't bring it out. That chestnut of John's ran away from her as if she was hobbled and side-lined, while this coyote of mine threw dust in her face every jump in the road from the word go. If the old man isn't bluffing and will back his mare, we'll get back our freeze-out money with good interest. Mind you, now, we must keep it a dead secret from Flood – that we've tried the mare; he might get funny and tip the old man.'

We all swore great oaths that Flood should never hear a breath of it. The conspirators and their accomplices rode into camp, and we resumed our sentinel rounds. I had some money, and figured that betting in a cinch like this would be like finding money in the road.

But The Rebel, when we were returning from guard, said, 'Tom, you keep out of this race the boys are trying to jump up. I've met a good many innocent men in my life, and there's something about this old man that reminds me of people who have an axe to grind. Let the other fellows run on the rope if they want to, but you keep your money in your pocket. Take an older man's advice this once. And I'm going to round up John in the morning, and try and beat a little sense into his head, for he thinks it's a dead immortal cinch.'

I had made it a rule, during our brief acquaintance, never to argue matters with my bunkie, well knowing that his years and experience in the ways of the world entitled his advice to my earnest consideration. So I kept silent, though secretly wishing he had not taken the trouble to throw cold water on my hopes, for I had built several air castles with the money which seemed within my grasp. We had been out then over four months, and I, like many of the other boys, was getting ragged, and with Ogalalla within a week's drive, a town which it took money to see properly, I thought it a burning shame to let this opportunity pass. When I awoke the next morning the camp was astir, and my first look was in the direction of the harness mare, grazing peacefully on the picket rope where she had been tethered the night before.

Breakfast over, our venerable visitor harnessed in his team, preparatory to starting. Stallings had made it a point to return to the herd for a parting word.

'Well, if you must go on ahead,' said Joe to the old man, as the latter was ready to depart, 'remember that you can get action on your money, if you still think that your bay mare can outrun that brown cow horse which I pointed out to you yesterday. You needn't let your poverty interfere, for we'll run you to suit your purse, light or heavy. The herd will reach the river by the middle of the afternoon, or a little later, and you be sure and stay overnight there – stay with us if you want to – and we'll make up a little race for any sum you say, from marbles and chalk to a hundred dollars. I may be as badly deceived in your mare as I think you are in my horse; but if you're a Tennesseean, here's your chance.'

But beyond giving Stallings his word that he would see him again during the afternoon or evening, the old man would make no definite proposition, and drove away. There was a difference of opinion among the outfit, some asserting that we would never see him again, while the larger portion of us were at least hopeful that we would. After our guest was well out of sight, and before the wagon started, Stallings corralled the *remuda* a second time, and taking out Flood's brown and Officer's chestnut, tried the two horses for a short dash of about a hundred yards. The trial confirmed the general opinion of the outfit, for the brown outran the chestnut over four lengths, starting half a neck in the rear. A general canvass of the outfit was taken, and to my surprise there was over three hundred dollars among us. I had over forty dollars, but I only promised to loan mine if it was needed, while Priest refused flat-footed either to lend or bet his. I wanted to bet, and it would grieve me to the quick if there was any chance and I didn't take it – but I was young then.

Flood met us at noon about seven miles out from the Republican with the superintendent of a cattle company in Montana, and, before we started the herd after dinner, had sold our *remuda*, wagon and mules for delivery at the nearest railroad point to the Blackfoot Agency sometime during September. This cattle company, so we afterwards learned from

Flood, had headquarters at Helena, while their ranges were somewhere on the headwaters of the Missouri. But the sale of the horses seemed to us an insignificant matter, compared with the race which was on the tapis; and when Stallings had made the ablest talk of his life for the loan of the brown, Flood asked the new owner, a Texan himself, if he had any objections.

'Certainly not,' said he; 'let the boys have a little fun. I'm glad to know that the *remuda* has fast horses in it. Why didn't you tell me, Flood? – I might have paid you extra if I had known I was buying racehorses. Be sure and have the race come off this evening, for I want to see it.'

And he was not only good enough to give his consent, but added a word of advice. 'There's a deadfall down here on the river,' said he, 'that robs a man going and coming. They've got booze to sell you that would make a pet rabbit fight a wolf. And if you can't stand the whiskey, why, they have skin games running to fleece you as fast as you can get your money to the centre. Be sure, lads, and let both their whiskey and cards alone.'

While changing mounts after dinner, Stallings caught out the brown horse and tied him behind the wagon, while Flood and the horse buyer returned to the river in the conveyance, our foreman having left his horse at the ford. When we reached the Republican with the herd about two hours before sundown, and while we were crossing and watering, who should ride up on the Spanish mule but our Tennessee friend. If anything, he was a trifle more talkative and boastful than before, which was easily accounted for, as it was evident that he was drinking; and producing a large bottle which had but a few drinks left in it, insisted on everyone taking a drink with him. He said he was encamped half a mile down the river, and that he would race his mare against our horse for fifty dollars; that if we were in earnest, and would go back with him and post our money at the tent, he would cover it. Then Stallings in turn became crafty and diplomatic, and after asking a number of unimportant questions regarding conditions, returned to the joint with the old man, taking Fox Quarternight. To the rest of us it looked as though there was going to be no chance to bet a dollar even. But after the herd had been watered and we had grazed out some distance from the river, the two worthies returned. They had posted their money, and all the conditions were agreed upon; the race was to take place at sundown over at the saloon and gambling joint. In reply to an earnest enquiry by Bob Blades, the outfit were informed that we might get some side bets with the gamblers, but the money already posted was theirs, win or lose. T his selfishness was not looked upon very favourably, and some harsh comments were made, but Stallings and Quarternight were immovable.

We had an early supper, and pressing in McCann to assist The Rebel in grazing the herd until our return, the cavalcade set out, Flood and the horse buyer with us. My bunkie urged me to let him keep my money, but under the pretence of some of the outfit wanting to borrow it, I took it with me. The race was to be catch weights, and as Rod Wheat was the lightest in our outfit, the riding fell to him. On the way over I worked Bull Durham out to one side, and after explaining the jacketing I had got from Priest, and the partial promise I had made not to bet, gave him my forty dollars to wager for me if he got a chance. Bull and I were good friends, and on the understanding that it was to be a secret, I intimated that some of the velvet would line his purse. On reaching the tent, we found about half a dozen men loitering around, among them the old man, who promptly invited us all to have a drink with him. A number of us accepted and took a chance against the vintage of this canvas road-house, though the warnings of the Montana horse buyer were fully justified by the quality of the goods dispensed. While taking the drink, the old man was lamenting his poverty, which kept him from betting more money, and after we had gone outside, the saloon keeper came and said to him, in a burst of generous feeling, 'Old sport, you're a stranger to me, but I can see at a glance that you're a dead game man. Now, if you need any more money, just give me a bill of sale for your mare and mule, and I'll advance you a hundred. Of course I know nothing about the merits of the two horses, but I noticed your team as you drove up today, and if you can use any more money, just ask for it.'

The old man jumped at the proposition in delighted surprise; the two re-entered the tent, and after killing considerable time in writing out a bill of sale, the old grey-beard came out shaking a roll of bills at us. He was promptly accommodated, Bull Durham making the first bet of fifty; and as I caught his eye, I walked away, shaking hands with myself over my crafty scheme. When the old man's money was all taken, the hangers-on of the place became enthusiastic over the betting, and took every bet while there was a dollar in sight among our crowd, the horse buyer even making a wager. When we were out of money they offered to bet against our saddles, six-shooters and watches. Flood warned us not to bet our saddles, but Quarternight and Stallings had already wagered theirs, and were stripping them from their horses to turn them over to the saloon keeper as stakeholder. I managed to get a ten-dollar bet on my six-shooter, though it was worth double the money, and a similar amount on my watch. When the betting ended, every watch and six-shooter in the outfit was in the hands of the stakeholder, and had it not been for Flood our saddles would have been in the same hands.

It was to be a three-hundred-yard race, with an ask and answer start between the riders. Stallings and the old man stepped off the course parallel with the river, and laid a rope on the ground to mark the start and the finish. The sun had already set and twilight was deepening when the old man signalled to his boy in the distance to bring up the mare. Wheat was slowly walking the brown horse over the course, when the boy came up, cantering the mare, blanketed with an old government blanket, over the imaginary track also. These preliminaries thrilled us like the tuning of a fiddle for a dance. Stallings and the old homesteader went out to the starting point to give the riders the terms of the race, while the remainder of us congregated at the finish. It was getting dusk when the blanket was stripped from the mare and the riders began jockeying for a start. In that twilight stillness we could hear the question, 'Are you ready?' and the answer 'No,' as the two jockeys came up to the starting rope. But finally there was an affirmative answer, and the two horses were coming through like arrows in their flight. My heart stood still for the time being, and when the bay mare crossed the rope at the outcome an easy winner, I was speechless. Such a crestfallen-looking lot of men as we were would be hard to conceive. We had been beaten, and not only felt it but looked it. Flood brought us to our senses by calling our attention to the approaching darkness, and setting off at a gallop towards the herd. The rest of us trailed along silently after him in threes and fours. After the herd had been bedded and we had gone in to the wagon my spirits were slightly lightened at the sight of the two arch conspirators, Stallings and Quarter-night, meekly riding in bareback. I enjoyed the laughter of The Rebel and McCann at their plight; but when my bunkie noticed my six-shooter missing, and I admitted having bet it, he turned the laugh on me.

'That's right, son,' he said; 'don't you take anybody's advice. You're young yet, but you'll learn. And when you learn it for yourself, you'll remember it that much better.'

That night when we were on guard together, I eased my conscience by making a clean breast of the whole affair to my bunkie, which resulted in his loaning me ten dollars with which to redeem my six-shooter in the morning. But the other boys, with the exception of Officer, had no banker to call on as we had, and when Quarternight and Stallings asked the foreman what they were to do for saddles, the latter suggested that one of them could use the cook's, while the other could take it bareback or ride in the wagon. But the Montana man interceded in their behalf, and Flood finally gave in and advanced them enough to redeem their saddles. Our foreman had no great amount of money with him, but McCann and the horse buyer came to the rescue with what they had, and the guns were redeemed; not that they were needed, but we would have been so lonesome without them. I had worn one so long, I didn't trim well without it, but toppled forward and couldn't maintain my balance. But the most cruel exposure of the whole affair occurred when Nat Straw, riding in ahead of his herd, overtook us one day out from Ogalalla.

'I met old "Says I" Littlefield,' said Nat, 'back at the ford of the Republican, and he tells me that they won over five hundred dollars off this Circle Dot outfit on a horse race. He showed me a whole basketful of your watches. I used to meet old "Says I" over on the Chisholm trail, and he's a foxy old innocent. He told me that he put tar on his harness mare's back to see if you fellows had stolen the nag off the picket rope at night, and when he found you had, he robbed you to a finish. He knew you fool Texans would bet your last dollar on such a cinch. That's one of his tricks. You see the mare you tried wasn't the one you ran the race against. I've seen them both, and they look as much alike as two pint bottles. My, but you fellows are easy fish!'

And then Jim Flood lay down on the grass and laughed until the tears came into his eyes, and we understood that there were tricks in other trades than ours.

CHAPTER 17

Ogalalla

From the head of Stinking Water to the South Platte was a waterless stretch of forty miles, but by watering the herd about the middle of one forenoon, after grazing, we could get to water again the following evening. With the exception of the meeting with Nat Straw, the drive was featureless, but the night that Nat stayed with us, he regaled us with his experiences, in which he was as lucky as ever. Where we had lost three days on the Canadian with bogged cattle, he had crossed it within fifteen minutes after reaching it. His herd was sold before reaching Dodge, so that he lost no time there, and on reaching Slaughter's bridge, he was only two days behind our herd. His cattle were then *en route* for delivery on the Crazy Woman in Wyoming, and, as he put it, 'any herd was liable to travel faster when it had a new owner'.

Flood had heard from our employer at Culbertson, learning that he would not meet us at Ogalalla, as his last herd was due in Dodge about that time. My brother Bob's herd had crossed the Arkansaw a week behind us, and was then possibly a hundred and fifty miles in our rear.

We all regretted not being able to see old man Don, for he believed that nothing was too good for his men, and we all remembered the good time he had shown us in Dodge. The smoke of passing trains hung for hours in signal clouds in our front, during the afternoon of the second day's dry drive, but we finally scaled the last divide, and there, below us in the valley of the South Platte, nestled Ogalalla, the Gomorrah of the cattle trail. From among its half-hundred buildings, no church spire pointed upward, but instead three fourths of its business houses were dance halls, gambling houses and saloons. We all knew the town by reputation, while the larger part of our outfit had been in it before. It was there that Joel Collins and his outfit rendezvoused when they robbed the Union Pacific train in October, '77. Collins had driven a herd of cattle for his father and brother, and after selling them in the Black Hills, gambled away the proceeds. Some five or six of his outfit returned to Ogalalla with him, and being moneyless, concluded to recoup their losses at the expense of the railway company. Going eighteen miles up the river to Big Springs, seven of them robbed the express and passengers, the former yielding sixty thousand dollars in gold. The next morning they were in Ogalalla, paying debts and getting their horses shod. In Collins's outfit was Sam Bass, and under his leadership, until he met his death the following spring at the hands of Texas Rangers, the course of the outfit southward was marked by a series of daring bank and train robberies.

We reached the river late that evening, and after watering, grazed until dark and camped for the night. But it was not to be a night of rest and sleep, for the lights were twinkling across the river in town; and cook, horse wrangler, and all, with the exception of the first guard, rode across the river after the herd had been bedded. Flood had quit us while we were watering the herd and gone in ahead to get a draft cashed, for he was as moneyless as the rest of us. But his letter of credit was good anywhere on the trail where money was to be had, and on reaching town, he took us into a general outfitting store and paid us twenty-five dollars apiece. After warning us to be on hand at the wagon to stand our watches, he left us, and we scattered like lost sheep. Officer and I paid our loans to The Rebel, and the three of us wandered around for several hours in company with Nat Straw. When we were in Dodge, my bunkie had shown no inclination to gamble, but now he was the first one to suggest that we make up a 'cow', and let him try his luck at monte. Straw and Officer were both willing, and though in rags, I willingly consented and contributed my five to the general fund.

Every gambling house ran from two to three monte layouts, as it was a favourite game of cowmen, especially when they were from the far southern country. Priest soon found a game to his liking, and after watching his play through several deals, Officer and I left him with the understanding that he would start for camp promptly at midnight. There was much to be seen, though it was a small place, for the ends of the earth's iniquity had gathered in Ogalalla. We wandered through the various gambling houses, drinking moderately, meeting an occasional acquaintance from Texas, and in the course of our rounds landed in the Dew-Drop-In dance hall. Here might be seen the frailty of women in every grade and condition. From girls in their teens, launching out on a life of shame, to the adventuress who had once had youth and beauty in her favour, but was now discarded and ready for the final dose of opium and the coroner's verdict – all were there in tinsel and paint, practising a careless exposure of their charms. In a town which has no night, the hours pass rapidly; and before we were aware, midnight was upon us. Returning to the gambling house where we had left Priest, we found him over a hundred dollars winner, and, calling his attention to the hour, persuaded him to cash in and join us. We felt positively rich, as he counted out to each partner his share of the winnings! Straw was missing to receive his, but we knew he could be found on the morrow, and after a round of drinks, we forded the river. As we rode along, my bunkie said – 'I'm superstitious, and I can't help it. But I've felt for a day or so that I was in luck, and I wanted you lads in with me if my warning was true. I never was afraid to go into battle but once, and just as we were ordered into action, a shell killed my horse under me and I was left behind. I've had lots of such warnings, good and bad, and I'm influenced by them. If we get off tomorrow, and I'm in the mood, I'll go back there and make some monte bank look sick.'

We reached the wagon in good time to be called on our guard, and after it was over secured a few hours' sleep before the foreman aroused us in the morning. With herds above and below us, we would either have to graze contrary to our course or cross the river. The South Platte was a wide, sandy river with numerous channels, and as easily crossed as an alkali flat of equal width, so far as water was concerned. The sun was not an hour high when we crossed, passing within two hundred yards of the business section of the town, which lay under a hill. The valley on the north side of the river, and beyond the railroad, was not over half a mile wide, and as we angled across it, the town seemed as dead as those that slept in the graveyard on the first hill beside the trail.

Finding good grass about a mile farther on, we threw the herd off the trail, and leaving orders to graze until noon, the foreman with the first and second guard returned to town. It was only about ten miles over to the North Platte, where water was certain; and in the hope that we would be permitted to revisit the village during the afternoon, we who were on guard threw riders in the lead of the grazing cattle, in order not to be too far away should permission be granted us. That was a long morning for us of the third and fourth guards, with nothing to do but let the cattle feed, while easy money itched in our pockets. Behind us lay Ogalalla – and our craft did dearly love to break the monotony of our work by getting into town. But by the middle of the forenoon, the wagon and saddle horses overtook us, and ordering McCann into camp a scant mile in our lead, we allowed the cattle to lie down, they having grazed to contentment. Leaving two men on guard, the remainder of us rode in to the wagon, and lightened with an hour's sleep in its shade the time which hung heavy on our hands. We were aroused by our horse wrangler, who had sighted a cavalcade down the trail, which, from the colour of their horses, he knew to be our outfit returning. As they came nearer and their numbers could be made out, it was evident that our foreman was not with them, and our hopes rose. On coming up, they informed us that we were to have a half holiday, while they would take the herd over to the North River during the afternoon. Then emergency orders rang out to Honeyman and McCann, and as soon as a change of mounts could be secured, our dinners bolted, and the herders relieved, we were ready to go. Two of the six who returned had shed their rags and swaggered about in new, cheap suits; the rest, although they had money, simply had not had the time to buy clothes in a place with so many attractions.

When the herders came in deft hands transferred their saddles to waiting mounts while they swallowed a hasty dinner, and we set out for Ogalalla, happy as city urchins in an orchard. We were less than five miles from the burg, and struck a free gait in riding in, where we found several hundred of our craft holding high jinks. A number of herds had paid off their outfits and were sending them home, while from the herds for sale, holding along the river, every man not on day herd was paying his respects to the town. We had not been there five minutes when a horse race was run through the main street, Nat Straw and Jim Flood acting as judges on the outcome. The officers of Ogalalla were a different crowd from what we had encountered at Dodge, and everything went. The place suited us. Straw had entirely forgotten our 'cow' of the night before, and when The Rebel handed him his share of the winnings, he tucked it away in the watch pocket of his trousers without counting. But he had arranged a fiddling match between a darky cook of one of the returning outfits and a locoed white man, a mendicant of the place, and invited us to be present. Straw knew the foreman of the outfit to which the darky belonged, and the two had fixed it up to pit the two in a contest, under the pretence that a large wager had been made on which was the better fiddler. The contest was to take place at once in the corral of the Lone Star livery stable, and promised to be humorous if nothing more. So after the race was over, the next number on the programme was the fiddling match, and we followed the crowd. The Rebel had given us the slip during the race, though none of us cared, as we knew he was hungering for a monte game. It was a motley crowd which had gathered in the corral, and all seemed to know of the farce to be enacted, though the Texas outfit to which the darky belonged were flashing their money on their dusky cook, 'as the best fiddler that ever crossed Red River with a cow herd'.

'Oh, I don't know that your man is such an Ole Bull as all that,' said Nat Straw. 'I just got a hundred posted which says he can't even play a decent second to my man. And if we can get a competent set of judges to decide the contest, I'll wager a little more on the white against the black, though I know your man is a crackerjack.'

A canvass of the crowd was made for judges, but as nearly everyone claimed to be interested in the result, having made wagers, or was incompetent to sit in judgement on a musical contest, there was some little delay. Finally, Joe Stallings went to Nat Straw and told him that I was a fiddler, whereupon he instantly appointed me as judge, and the other side selected a red-headed fellow belonging to one of Dillard

Fant's herds. Between the two of us we selected as the third judge a bartender whom I had met the night before. The conditions governing the contest were given us, and two chuck wagons were drawn up alongside each other, in one of which were seated the contestants and in the other the judges. The gravity of the crowd was only broken as some enthusiast cheered his favourite or defiantly offered to wager on the man of his choice. Numerous sham bets were being made, when the red-headed judge arose and announced the conditions, and urged the crowd to remain quiet that the contestants might have equal justice. Each fiddler selected his own piece. The first number was a waltz, on the conclusion of which partisanship ran high, each faction cheering its favourite to the echo. The second number was a jig, and as the darky drew his bow several times across the strings tentatively, his foreman, who stood six inches taller than any man in a crowd of tall men, tapped himself on the breast with one forefinger, and with the other pointed at his dusky champion, saying, 'Keep your eye on me, Price. We're going home together, remember. You black rascal, you can make a mocking bird ashamed of itself if you try. You know I've swore by you through thick and thin; now win this money. Pay no attention to anyone else. Keep your eye on me.'

Straw, not to be outdone in encouragement, cheered his man with promises of reward, and his faction of supporters raised such a din that Fant's man arose, and demanded quiet so the contest could proceed. Though boisterous, the crowd was good-tempered, and after the second number was disposed of, the final test was announced, which was to be in sacred music. On this announcement, the tall foreman waded through the crowd, and drawing the darky to him, whispered something in his ear, and then fell back to his former position. The dusky artist's countenance brightened, and with a few preliminaries he struck into 'The Arkansaw Traveller', throwing so many contortions into its execution that it seemed as if life and liberty depended on his exertions. The usual applause greeted him on its conclusion, when Nat Straw climbed up on the wagon wheel and likewise whispered something to his champion. The little old wizened mendicant took his cue, and cut into 'The Irish Washerwoman' with a great flourish, and in the refrain chanted an unintelligible gibberish like the yelping of a coyote, which the audience so cheered that he repeated it several times. The crowd now gathered around the wagons and clamoured for the decision, and after consulting among ourselves some little time, and knowing that a neutral or indefinite verdict was desired, we delegated the bartender to announce our conclusions. Taking off his hat, he arose, and after requesting quietness, pretended to read our decision.

'Gentlemen,' he began, 'your judges feel a delicacy in passing on the merits of such distinguished artists, but in the first number the decision is unanimously in favour of the darky, while the second is clearly in favour of the white contestant. In regard to the last test, your judges cannot reach any decision, as the selections rendered fail to qualify under the head of –'

But two shots rang out in rapid succession across the street, and the crowd, including the judges and fiddlers, rushed away to witness the new excitement. The shooting had occurred in a restaurant, and quite a mob gathered around the door when the sheriff emerged from the building.

'It's nothing,' said he; 'just a couple of punchers, who had been drinking a little, were eating a snack, and one of them asked for a second dish of prunes, when the waiter got gay and told him that he couldn't have them – "that he was full of prunes now". So the lad took a couple of shots at him, just to learn him to be more courteous to strangers. There was no harm done, as the puncher was too unsteady.'

As the crowd dispersed from the restaurant, I returned to the livery stable, where Straw and several of our outfit were explaining to the old mendicant that he had simply outplayed his opponent, and it was too bad that they were not better posted in sacred music. Under Straw's leadership, a purse was being made up among them, and the old man's eyes brightened as he received several crisp bills and a handful of silver. Straw was urging the old fiddler to post himself in regard to sacred music, and he would get up another match for the next day, when Rod Wheat came up and breathlessly informed Officer and myself that The Rebel wanted us over at the Black Elephant gambling hall. As we turned to accompany him, we eagerly enquired if there were any trouble. Wheat informed us there was not, but that Priest was playing in one of the biggest streaks of luck that ever happened. 'Why, the old man is just wallowing in velvet,' said Rod, as we hurried along, 'and the dealer has lowered the limit from a hundred to fifty, for old Paul is playing them as high as a cat's tack. He isn't drinking a drop, and is as cool as a cucumber. I don't know what he wants with you fellows, but he begged me to hunt you up and send you to him.'

The Black Elephant was about a block from the livery, and as we entered, a large crowd of bystanders were watching the playing around one of the three monte games which were running. Elbowing our way through the crowd, we reached my bunkie, whom Officer slapped on the back and enquired what he wanted.

'Why, I want you and Quirk to bet a little money for me,' he replied. 'My luck is with me today, and when I try to crowd it, this layout gets foxy and pinches the limit down to fifty. Here, take this money and cover both those other games. Call out as they fall the layouts, and I'll pick the card to bet the money on. And bet her carelessly, boys, for she's velvet.'

As he spoke he gave Officer and myself each a handful of uncounted money, and we proceeded to carry out his instructions. I knew the game perfectly, having spent several years' earnings on my tuition, and was past master in the technical Spanish terms of the game, while Officer was equally informed. John took the table to the right, while I took the one on the left, and waiting for a new deal, called the cards as they fell. I enquired the limit of the dealer, and was politely informed that it was fifty today. At first our director ordered a number of small bets made, as though feeling his way, for cards will turn; but as he found the old luck was still with him, he gradually increased them to the limit. After the first few deals, I caught on to his favourite cards, which were the queen and seven, and on these we bet the limit. Aces and a 'face against an ace' were also favourite bets of The Rebel's, but for a smaller sum. During the first hour of my playing – to show the luck of cards – the queen won five consecutive times, once against a favourite at the conclusion of a deal. My judgement was to take up this bet, but Priest ordered otherwise, for it was one of his principles never to doubt a card as long as it won for you.

The play had run along some time, and as I was absorbed with watching, someone behind me laid a friendly hand on my shoulder. Having every card in the layout covered with a bet at the time, and supposing it to be some of our outfit, I never looked around, when there came a slap on my back which nearly loosened my teeth. Turning to see who was making so free with me when I was absorbed, my eye fell on my brother Zack, but I had not time even to shake hands with him, for two cards won in succession and the dealer was paying me, while the queen and seven were covered to the limit and were yet to be drawn for. When the deal ended and while the dealer was shuffling, I managed to get a few words with my brother, and learned that he had come through with a herd belonging to one-armed Jim Reed, and that they were holding about ten miles up the river. He had met Flood, who told him that I was in town; but as he was working on first guard with their herd, it was high time he was riding. The dealer was waiting for me to cut the cards, and stopping only to wring Zack's hand in farewell, I turned again to the monte layout.

Officer was not so fortunate as I was, partly by reason of delays, the dealer in his game changing decks on almost every deal, and under Priest's orders, we counted the cards with every change of the deck. A gambler would rather burn money than lose to a citizen, and every hoodoo which the superstition of the craft could invoke to turn the run of the cards was used to check us. Several hours passed and the lamps were lighted, but we constantly added to the good – to the discomfiture of the owners of the games. Dealers changed, but our vigilance never relaxed for a moment. Suddenly an altercation sprang up between Officer and the dealer of his game. The seven had proved the most lucky card to John, which fact was as plain to dealer as to player, but the dealer, by slipping one seven out of the pack after it had been counted, which was possible in the hands of an adept in spite of all vigilance, threw the percentage against the favourite card and in favour of the bank. Officer had suspected something wrong, for the seven had been loser during several deals, when with a seven-king layout, and two cards of each class yet in the pack, the dealer drew down until there were less than a dozen cards left, when the king came, which lost a fifty dollar bet on the seven. Officer laid his hand on the money, and, as was his privilege, said to the dealer, 'Let me look over the remainder of those cards. If there's two sevens there, you have won. If there isn't, don't offer to touch this bet.'

But the gambler declined the request, and Officer repeated his demand, laying a blue-barrelled six-shooter across the bet with the remark, 'Well, if you expect to rake in this bet you have my terms.'

Evidently the demand would not have stood the test, for the dealer bunched the deck among the passed cards, and Officer quietly raked in the money. 'When I want a skin game,' said John, as he arose, 'I'll come back and see you. You saw me take this money, did you? Well, if you've got anything to say, now's your time to spit it out.'

But his calling had made the gambler discreet, and he deigned no reply to the lank Texan, who, chafing under the attempt to cheat him, slowly returned his six-shooter to its holster. Although holding my own in my game, I was anxious to have it come to a close, but neither of us cared to suggest it to The Rebel; it was his money. But Officer passed outside the house shortly afterwards, and soon returned with Jim Flood and Nat Straw.

As our foreman approached the table at which Priest was playing, he laid his hand on The Rebel's shoulder and said, 'Come on, Paul, we're all ready to go to camp. Where's Quirk?'

Priest looked up in innocent amazement – as though he had been awakened out of a deep sleep, for, in the absorption of the game, he had taken no note of the passing hours and did not know that the lamps were burning. My bunkie obeyed as promptly as though the orders had been given by Don Lovell in person, and, delighted with the turn of affairs, I withdrew with him. Once in the street, Nat Straw threw an arm around The Rebel's neck and said to him, 'My dear sir, the secret of successful gambling is to quit when you're winner, and before luck turns. You may think this is a low-down trick, but we're your friends, and when we heard that you were a big winner, we were determined to get you out of there if we had to rope and drag you out. How much are you winner?'

Before the question could be correctly answered, we sat down on the sidewalk and the three of us disgorged our winnings so that Flood and Straw could count. Priest was the largest winner, Officer the smallest, while I never will know the amount of mine, as I had no idea what I started with. But the teller's report showed over fourteen hundred dollars among the three of us. My bunkie consented to allow Flood to keep it for him, and the latter attempted to hurrah us off to camp, but John Officer protested.

'Hold on a minute, Jim,' said Officer. 'We're in rags; we need some clothes. We've been in town long enough, and we've got the price, but it's been such a busy afternoon with us that we simply haven't had the time.'

Straw took our part, and Flood giving in, we entered a general out-fitting store, from which we emerged within a quarter of an hour, wearing cheap new suits, the colour of which we never knew until the next day. Then bidding Straw a hearty farewell, we rode for the North Platte, on which the herd would encamp. As we scaled the bluffs, we halted for our last glimpse of the lights of Ogalalla, and The Rebel remarked, 'Boys, I've travelled some in my life, but that little hole back there could give Natchez-under-the-hill cards and spades, and then outhold her as a tough town.'

CHAPTER 18

The North Platte

It was now July. We had taken on new supplies at Ogalalla, and a week afterwards the herd was snailing along the North Platte on its way to the land of the Blackfeet. It was always hard to get a herd past a supply point. We had the same trouble when we passed Dodge. Our long hours in the saddle, coupled with the monotony of our work, made these supply points of such interest to us that they were like oases in desert lands to devotees on pilgrimage to some consecrated shrine. We could have spent a week in Ogalalla and enjoyed our visit every blessed moment of the time. But now, a week later, most of the headaches had disappeared and we had settled down to our daily work.

At Horse Creek, the last stream of water before entering Wyoming, a lad who cut the trail at that point for some cattle companies, after trimming us up, rode along for half a day through their range, and told us of an accident which happened about a week before. The horse of some peeler, working with one of Shanghai Pierce's herds, acted up one morning, and fell backwards with him so that his gun accidentally discharged. The outfit lay over a day and gave him as decent a burial as they could. We would find the new-made grave ahead on Squaw Creek, beyond the crossing, to the right-hand side in a clump of cottonwoods. The next day, while watering the herd at this creek, we all rode over and looked at the grave. The outfit had fixed things up quite nicely. They had built a square pen of rough cottonwood logs around the grave, and had marked the head and foot with a big flat stone, edged up, heaping up quite a mound of stones to keep the animals away. In a tree his name was cut – sounded natural, too, though none of us knew him, as Pierce always drove from the east-coast country. There was nothing different about this grave from the hundreds of others which made landmarks on the Old Western Trail, except it was the latest.

That night around the campfire some of the boys were moved to tell their experiences. This accident might happen to any of us, and it seemed rather short notice to a man enjoying life, even though his calling was rough.

'As for myself,' said Rod Wheat, 'I'm not going to fret. You can't avoid it when it comes, and every now and then you miss it by a hair. I had an uncle who served four years in the Confederate army, went through thirty engagements, was wounded half a dozen times, and came home well and sound. Within a month after his return, a plough handle kicked him in the side and we buried him within a week.'

'Oh, well,' said Fox, commenting on the sudden call of the man whose grave we had seen, 'it won't make much difference to this fellow back here when the horn toots and the graves give up their dead. He might just as well start from there as anywhere. I don't envy him none, though; but if I had any pity to offer now, it would be for a mother or sister who might wish that he slept nearer home.'

This last remark carried our minds far away from their present surroundings to other graves which were not on the trail. There was a long silence. We lay around the campfire and gazed into its depths, while its flickering light threw our shadows out beyond the circle. Our reverie was finally broken by Ash Borrowstone, who was by all odds the most impressionable and emotional one in the outfit, a man who always argued the moral side of every question, yet could not be credited with possessing an iota of moral stamina. Gloomy as we were, he added to our depression by relating a pathetic incident which occurred at a child's funeral, when Flood reproved him, saying, 'Well, neither that one you mention, nor this one of Pierce's man is any of our funeral. We're on the trail with Lovell's cattle. You should keep nearer the earth.'

There was a long silence after this reproof of the foreman. It was evident there was a gloom settling over the outfit. Our thoughts were ranging wide. At last Rod Wheat spoke up and said that in order to get the benefit of all the variations, the blues were not a bad thing to have.

But the depression of our spirits was not so easily dismissed. In order to avoid listening to the gloomy tales that were being narrated around the campfire, a number of us got up and went out as if to look up the night horses on picket. The Rebel and I pulled our picket pins and changed our horses to fresh grazing, and after lying down among the horses, out of hearing of the camp, for over an hour, returned to the wagon expecting to retire. A number of the boys were making down their beds, as it was already late; but on our arrival at the fire one of the boys had just concluded a story, as gloomy as the others which had preceded it.

'These stories you are all telling tonight,' said Flood, 'remind me of what Lige Link said to the book agent when he was shearing sheep. "I reckon," said Lige, "that book of yours has a heap sight more poetry in it than there is in shearing sheep." I wish I had gone on guard tonight, so I could have missed these stories.'

At this juncture the first guard rode in, having been relieved, and John Officer, who had exchanged places on guard that night with Moss Strayhorn, remarked that the cattle were uneasy.

'This outfit,' said he, 'didn't half water the herd today. One third of them hasn't bedded down yet, and they don't act as if they aim to, either. There's no excuse for it in a well-watered country like this. I'll leave the saddle on my horse, anyhow.'

'Now that's the result,' said our foreman, 'of the hour we spent around that grave today, when we ought to have been tending to our job. This outfit,' he continued, when Officer returned from picketing his horse, 'have been trying to hold funeral services over that Pierce man's grave back there. You'd think so, anyway, from the tales they've been telling. I hope you won't get the sniffles and tell any.'

'This letting yourself get gloomy,' said Officer, 'reminds me of a time we once had at the "J. H." camp in the Cherokee Strip. It was near Christmas, and the work was all done up. The boys had blowed in their summer's wages and were feeling glum all over. One or two of the boys were lamenting that they hadn't gone home to see the old folks. This gloomy feeling kept spreading until they actually wouldn't speak to each other. One of them would go out and sit on the wood pile for hours, all by himself, and make a new set of good resolutions. Another would go out and sit on the ground, on the sunny side of the corrals, and dig holes in the frozen earth with his knife. They wouldn't come to meals when the cook called them.

'Now, Miller, the foreman, didn't have any sympathy for them; in fact he delighted to see them in that condition. He hadn't any use for a man who wasn't dead tough under any condition. I've known him to camp his outfit on alkali water, so the men would get out in the morning, and every rascal beg leave to ride on the outside circle on the morning round-up.

'Well, three days before Christmas, just when things were looking gloomiest, there drifted up from the Cheyenne country one of the old timers. None of them had seen him in four years, though he had worked on that range before, and with the exception of myself, they all knew him. He was riding the chuckline all right, but Miller gave him a welcome, as he was the real thing. He had been working out in the Panhandle country,

New Mexico, and the devil knows where, since he had left that range. He was meaty with news and scary stories. The boys would sit around and listen to him yarn, and now and then a smile would come on their faces. Miller was delighted with his guest. He had shown no signs of letting up at eleven o'clock the first night, when he happened to mention where he was the Christmas before.

' "There was a little woman at the ranch," said he, "wife of the owner, and I was helping her get up dinner, as we had quite a number of folks at the ranch. She asked me to make the bear sign – doughnuts, she called them – and I did, though she had to show me how some little. Well, fellows, you ought to have seen them – just sweet enough, browned to a turn, and enough to last a week. All the folks at dinner that day praised them. Since then, I've had a chance to try my hand several times, and you may not tumble to the diversity of all my accomplishments, but I'm an artist on bear sign."

'Miller arose, took him by the hand, and said, "That's straight, now, is it?"

' "That's straight. Making bear sign is my long suit."

' "Mouse," said Miller to one of the boys, "go out and bring in his saddle from the stable and put it under my bed. Throw his horse in the big pasture in the morning. He stays here until spring; and the first spear of green grass I see, his name goes on the pay roll. This outfit is shy on men who can make bear sign. Now, I was thinking that you could spread down your blankets on the hearth, but you can sleep with me tonight. You go to work on this specialty of yours right after breakfast in the morning, and show us what you can do in that line."

'They talked quite a while longer, and then turned in for the night. The next morning after breakfast was over, he got the needed articles together and went to work. But there was a surprise in store for him. There was nearly a dozen men lying around, all able eaters. By ten o'clock he began to turn them out as he said he could. When the regular cook had to have the stove to get dinner, the taste which we had had made us ravenous for more. Dinner over, he went at them again in earnest. A boy riding towards the railroad with an important letter dropped in, and as he claimed he could only stop for a moment, we stood aside until he had had a taste, though he filled himself like a poisoned pup. After eating a solid hour, he filled his pockets and rode away. One of our regular men called after him, "Don't tell anybody what we got."

'We didn't get any supper that night. Not a man could have eaten a bite. Miller made him knock off along in the shank of the evening, as he had done enough for any one day. The next morning after breakfast he fell to at the bear sign once more. Miller rolled a barrel of flour into the kitchen from the storehouse, and told him to fly at them. "About how many do you think you'll want?" asked our bear-sign man.

' "That big tub full won't be any too many," answered Miller. "Some of these fellows haven't had any of this kind of truck since they were little boys. If this gets out, I look for men from other camps."

'The fellow fell to his work like a thoroughbred, which he surely was. About ten o'clock two men rode up from a camp to the north, which the boy had passed the day before with the letter. They never went near the dug-out, but straight to the kitchen. That movement showed that they were on to the racket. An hour later old Tom Cave rode in, his horse all in a lather, all the way from Garretson's camp, twenty-five miles to the east. The old sinner said that he had been on the frontier some little time, and that there were the best bear sign he had tasted in forty years. He refused to take a stool and sit down like civilised folks, but stood up by the tub and picked out the ones which were a pale brown.

'After dinner our man threw off his overshirt, unbuttoned his red undershirt and turned it in until you could see the hair on his breast. Rolling up his sleeves, he flew at his job once more. He was getting his work reduced to a science by this time. He rolled his dough, cut his dough, and turned out the fine brown bear sign to the satisfaction of all.

'His capacity, however, was limited. About two o'clock Doc Langford and two of his peelers were seen riding up. When he came into the kitchen, Doc swore by all that was good and holy that he hadn't heard that our artist had come back to that country. But anyone that was noticing could see him edge around to the tub. It was easy to see that he was lying. This luck of ours was circulating faster than a secret among women. Our man, though, stood at his post like the boy on the burning deck. When night came on, he hadn't covered the bottom of the tub. When he knocked off, Doc Langford and his men gobbled up what was left. We gave them a mean look as they rode off, but they came back the next day, five strong. Our regular men around camp didn't like it, the way things were going. They tried to act polite to – '

'Calling bear sign doughnuts,' interrupted Quince Forrest, 'reminds me what – '

'Will you kindly hobble your lip,' said Officer; 'I have the floor at present. As I was saying, they tried to act polite to company that way, but we hadn't got a smell the second day. Our man showed no signs of fatigue, and told several good stories that night. He was tough. The next day was Christmas, but he had no respect for a holiday, and made up a large batch of dough before breakfast. It was a good thing he did, for early that morning "Original" John Smith and four of his peelers rode in from the west, their horses all covered with frost. They must have started at daybreak – it was a good twenty-two mile ride. They wanted us to believe that they had simply come over to spend Christmas with us. Company that way, you can't say anything. But the easy manner in which they gravitated around that tub – not even waiting to be invited – told a different tale. They were not nearly satisfied by noon.

'Then who should come drifting in as we were sitting down to dinner, but Billy Dunlap and Jim Hale from Quinlin's camp, thirty miles south on the Cimarron. Dunlap always holed up like a bear in the winter, and several of the boys spilled their coffee at sight of him. He put up a thin excuse just like the rest. Anyone could see through it. But there it was again – he was company. Lots of us had eaten at his camp and complained of his chuck; therefore, we were nice to him. Miller called our man out behind the kitchen and told him to knock off if he wanted to. But he wouldn't do it. He was keen as ever. Dunlap ate hardly any dinner, we noticed, and the very first batch of bear sign turned out, he loads up a tin plate and goes out and sits behind the storehouse in the sun, all alone in his glory. He satisfied himself out of the tub after that.

'He and Hale stayed all night, and Dunlap kept everyone awake with nightmares. Yes, kept fighting the demons all night. The next morning Miller told him that he was surprised that an old grey-haired man like him didn't know when he'd had enough, but must gorge himself like some silly kid. Miller told him that he was welcome to stay a week if he wanted to, but he would have to sleep in the stable. It was cruel to the horses, but the men were entitled to a little sleep, at least in the winter. Miller tempered his remarks with all kindness, and Dunlap acted as if he was sorry, and as good as admitted that his years were telling on him. That day our man filled his tub. He was simply an artist on bear sign.'

'Calling bear sign doughnuts,' cut in Quince Forrest again, as soon as he saw an opening, 'reminds me what the little boy said who went – '

But there came a rumbling of many hoofs from the bed ground. 'There's hell for you,' said half a dozen men in a chorus, and every man in camp ran for his horse but the cook, and he climbed into the wagon. The roar of the running cattle was like approaching thunder, but the flash from the six-shooters of the men on guard indicated they were quartering by camp, heading out towards the hills. Horses became so excited they were difficult to bridle. There was plenty of earnest and sincere swearing done that night. All the fine sentiment and melancholy of the hour previous vanished in a moment as the men threw themselves into their saddles, riding deep, for it was uncertain footing to horses.

Within two minutes from the time the herd left the bed ground, fourteen of us rode on their left point and across their front, firing our six-shooters in their faces. By the time the herd had covered a scant mile, we had thrown them into a mill. They had run so compactly that there were no stragglers, so we loosened out and gave them room; but it was a long time before they relaxed any; they continued going round and round like a water wheel or an endless chain. The foreman ordered three men on the heaviest horses to split them. The men rode out a short distance to get the required momentum, wheeled their horses, and, wedge-shaped, struck this sea of cattle and entered, but it instantly closed in their wake as though it had been water. For an hour they rode through the herd, back and forth, now from this quarter, now from that, and finally the mill was broken. After midnight, as luck would have it, heavy dark clouds banked in the northwest, and lightning flashed, and before a single animal had lain down, a drizzling rain set in. That settled it; it was an all-night job now. We drifted about hither and yon. Horses, men and cattle turned their backs to the wind and rain and waited for morning. We were so familiar with the signs of coming day that we turned them loose half an hour before dawn, leaving herders, and rode for camp.

As we groped our way in that dark hour before dawn, hungry, drenched and bedraggled, there was nothing gleeful about us, while Bob Blades expressed his disgust over our occupation. 'If ever I get home again,' said he, and the tones of his voice were an able second to his remarks, 'you all can go up the trail that want to, but here's one chicken that won't. There isn't a cowman in Texas who has money enough to hire me again.'

'Ah, hell, now,' said Bull, 'you oughtn't let a little rain ruffle your feathers that way. Cheer up, sonny; you may be rich some day yet and walk on brussels and velvet.'

CHAPTER 19

Forty Islands Ford

After securing a count on the herd that morning and finding nothing short, we trailed out up the North Platte River. It was an easy country in which to handle a herd; the trail in places would run back from the river as far as ten miles, and again follow close in near the river bottoms. There was an abundance of small creeks putting into this fork of the Platte from the south, which afforded water for the herd and good camp grounds at night. Only twice after leaving Ogalalla had we been compelled to go to the river for water for the herd, and with the exception of thunderstorms and occasional summer rains, the weather had been all one could wish. For the past week as we trailed up the North Platte, some one of us visited the river daily to note its stage of water, for we were due to cross at Forty Islands, about twelve miles south of old Fort Laramie. The North Platte was very similar to the South Canadian – a wide sandy stream without banks; and our experience with the latter was fresh in our memories. The stage of water had not been favourable, for this river also had its source in the mountains, and as now midsummer was upon us, the season of heavy rainfall in the mountains, augmented by the melting snows, the prospect of finding a fordable stage of water at Forty Islands was not very encouraging.

We reached this well-known crossing late in the afternoon the third day after leaving the Wyoming line, and found one of the Prairie Cattle Company's herds waterbound. This herd had been wintered on one of that company's ranges on the Arkansaw River in southern Colorado, and their destination was in the Bad Lands near the mouth of the Yellowstone, where the same company had a northern range. Flood knew the foreman, Wade Scholar, who reported having been waterbound over a week already with no prospect of crossing without swimming. Scholar knew the country thoroughly, and had decided to lie over until the river was fordable at Forty Islands, as it was much the easiest crossing on the North Platte, though there was a wagon ferry at Fort Laramie. He returned with Flood to our camp, and the two talked over the prospect of swimming it on the morrow.

'Let's send the wagons up to the ferry in the morning,' said Flood, 'and swim the herds. If you wait until this river falls, you are liable to have an experience like we had on the South Canadian – lost three days and bogged over a hundred cattle. When one of these sandy rivers has had a big freshet, look out for quicksands; but you know that as well as I do. Why, we've swum over half a dozen rivers already, and I'd much rather swim this one than attempt to ford it just after it has fallen. We can double our outfits and be safely across before noon. I've got nearly a thousand miles yet to make, and have just *got* to get over. Think it over tonight, and have your wagon ready to start with ours.'

Scholar rode away without giving our foreman any definite answer as to what he would do, though earlier in the evening he had offered to throw his herd well out of the way at the ford, and lend us any assistance at his command. But when it came to the question of crossing his own herd, he seemed to dread the idea of swimming the river, and could not be induced to say what he would do, but said that we were welcome to the lead. The next morning Flood and I accompanied our wagon up to his camp, when it was plainly evident that he did not intend to send his wagon with ours, and McCann started on alone, though our foreman renewed his efforts to convince Scholar of the feasibility of swimming the herds. Their cattle were thrown well away from the ford, and Scholar assured us that his outfit would be on hand whenever we were ready to cross, and even invited all hands of us to come to his wagon for dinner. When returning to our herd, Flood told me that Scholar was considered one of the best foremen on the trail, and why he should refuse to swim his cattle was unexplainable. He must have time to burn, but that didn't seem reasonable, for the earlier through cattle were turned loose on their winter range the better. We were in no hurry to cross, as our wagon would be gone all day, and it was nearly high noon when we trailed up to the ford.

With the addition to our force of Scholar and nine or ten of his men, we had an abundance of help, and put the cattle into the water opposite two islands, our saddle horses in the lead as usual. There was no swimming water between the south shore and the first island, though it wet our saddle skirts for some considerable distance, this channel being nearly two hundred yards wide. Most of our outfit took the water, while Scholar's men fed our herd in from the south bank, a number of their men coming over as far as the first island. The second island lay down the stream some little distance; and as we pushed the cattle off the first one we were in swimming water in no time, but the saddle horses were already landing on the second island, and our lead cattle struck out, and, breasting the water, swam as proudly as swans. The middle channel was nearly a hundred yards wide, the greater portion of which was swimming, though the last channel was much wider. But our saddle horses had already taken it, and when within fifty yards of the farther shore, struck solid footing. With our own outfit we crowded the leaders to keep the chain of cattle unbroken, and before Honeyman could hustle his horses out of the river, our lead cattle had caught a foothold, were heading upstream and edging out for the farther shore.

I had one of the best swimming horses in our outfit, and Flood put me in the lead on the point. As my horse came out on the farther bank, I am certain I never have seen a herd of cattle, before or since, which presented a prettier sight when swimming than ours did that day. There was fully four hundred yards of water on the angle by which we crossed, nearly half of which was swimming, but with the two islands which gave them a breathing spell, our Circle Dots were taking the water as steadily as a herd leaving their bed ground. Scholar and his men were feeding them in, while half a dozen of our men on each island were keeping them moving. Honeyman and I pointed them out of the river; and as they grazed away from the shore, they spread out fanlike, many of them kicking up their heels after they left the water in healthy enjoyment of their bath. Long before they were half over, the usual shouting had ceased, and we simply sat in our saddles and waited for the long train of cattle to come up and cross. Within less than half an hour from the time our saddle horses entered the North Platte, the tail end of our herd had landed safely on the farther bank.

As Honeyman and I were the only ones of our outfit on the north side of the river during the passage, Flood called to us from across the last channel to graze the herd until relieved, when the remainder of the outfit returned to the south side to recover their discarded effects and to get dinner with Scholar's wagon. I had imitated Honeyman, and tied my boots to my cantle strings, so that my effects were on the right side of the river; and as far as dinner was concerned – well, I'd much rather miss it than swim the Platte twice in its then stage of water. There is a difference in daring in one's duty and in daring out of pure venturesomeness, and if we missed our dinners it would not be the first time, so we were quite willing to make the sacrifice. If the Quirk family never achieve fame for daring by field and flood, until this one of the old man's boys brings the family name into prominence, it will be hopelessly lost to posterity.

We allowed the cattle to graze of their own free will, and merely turned in the sides and rear, but on reaching the second bottom of the river, where they caught a good breeze, they lay down for their noonday siesta, which relieved us of all work but keeping watch over them. The saddle horses were grazing about in plain view on the first bottom, so Honeyman and I dismounted on a little elevation overlooking our charges. We were expecting the outfit to return promptly after dinner was over, for it was early enough in the day to have trailed eight or ten miles farther. It would have been no trouble to send someone up the river to meet our wagon and pilot McCann to the herd, for the trail left on a line due north from the river. We had been lounging about for an hour while the cattle were resting, when our attention was attracted by our saddle horses in the bottom. They were looking at the ford, to which we supposed their attention had been attracted by the swimming of the outfit, but instead only two of the boys showed up, and on sighting us nearly a mile away, they rode forward very leisurely. Before their arrival we recognised them by their horses as Ash Borrowstone and Rod Wheat, and on their riding up the latter said as he dismounted, 'Well, they're going to cross the other herd, and they want you to come back and point the cattle with that famous swimming horse of yours. You'll learn after a while not to blow so much about your mount, and your cutting horses, and your night horses, and your swimming horses. I wish every horse of mine had a nigger brand on him and I had to ride in the wagon, when it comes to swimming these rivers. And I'm not the only one that has a distaste for a wet proposition, for I wouldn't have to guess twice as to what's the matter with Scholar. But Flood has pounded him on the back ever since he met him yesterday evening to swim his cattle, until it's either swim or say he's afraid to – it's "Shoot, Luke, or give up the gun" with him. Scholar's a nice fellow, but I'll bet my interest in goose heaven that I know what's the matter with him. And I'm not blaming him, either; but I can't understand why our boss should take such an interest in having him swim. It's none of his business if he swims now, or fords a month hence, or waits until the river freezes over in the winter and crosses on the ice. But let the big augers wrangle it out; you noticed, Ash, that not one of Scholar's outfit ever said a word one way or the other, but Flood poured it into him until he consented to swim. So fork that swimming horse of yours and wet your big toe again in the North Platte.'

As the orders had come from the foreman, there was nothing to do but obey. Honeyman rode as far as the river with me, where after shedding my boots and surplus clothing and secreting them, I rode up above the island and plunged in. I was riding the grey which I had tried in the Rio Grande the day we received the herd, and now that I understood handling him better, I preferred him to Nigger Boy, my night horse. We took the first and second islands with but a blowing spell between, and when I reached the farther shore, I turned in my saddle and saw Honeyman wave his hat to me in congratulation. On reaching their wagon, I found the herd was swinging around about a mile out from the river, in order to get a straight shoot for the entrance at the ford. I hurriedly swallowed my dinner, and as we rode out to meet the herd, asked Flood if Scholar were not going to send his wagon up to the ferry to cross, for there was as yet no indication of it. Flood replied that Scholar expected to go with the wagon, as he needed some supplies which he thought he could get from the sutler at Fort Laramie.

Flood ordered me to take the lower point again, and I rode across the trail and took my place when the herd came within a quarter of a mile of the river, while the remainder of the outfit took positions near the lead on the lower side. It was a slightly larger herd than ours – all steers, three-year-olds that reflected in their glossy coats the benefits of a northern winter. As we came up to the water's edge, it required two of their men to force their *remuda* into the water, though it was much smaller than ours – six horses to the man, but better ones than ours, being northern wintered. The cattle were well trail-broken, and followed the leadership of the saddle horses nicely to the first island, but they would have balked at the second channel, had it not been for the amount of help at hand. We lined them out, however, and they breasted the current, and landed on the second island. The saddle horses gave some little trouble on leaving for the farther shore, and before they were got off, several hundred head of cattle had landed on the island. But they handled obediently and were soon trailing out upon terra firma, the herd following across without a broken link in the chain. There was nothing now to do but keep the train moving into the water on the south bank, see that they did not congest on the islands, and that they left the river on reaching the farther shore. When the saddle horses reached the farther bank, they were thrown up the river and turned loose, so that the two men would be available to hold the herd after it left the water. I had crossed with the first lead cattle to the farther shore, and was turning them up the river as fast as they struck solid footing on that side. But several times I was compelled to swim back to the nearest island, and return with large bunches which had hesitated to take the last channel.

The two outfits were working promiscuously together, and I never knew who was the directing spirit in the work; but when the last two or three hundred of the tail-enders were leaving the first island for the second, and the men working in the rear started to swim the channel, amid the general hilarity I recognised a shout that was born of fear and terror. A hushed silence fell over the riotous riders in the river, and I saw those on the sand bar nearest my side rush down the narrow island and plunge back into the middle channel. Then it dawned on my mind in a flash that someone had lost his seat, and that terrified cry was for help. I plunged my grey into the river and swam to the first bar, and from thence to the scene of the trouble. Horses and men were drifting with the current down the channel, and as I appealed to the men I could get no answer but their blanched faces, though it was plain in every countenance that one of our number was under water if not drowned. There were not less than twenty horsemen drifting in the middle channel in the hope that whoever it was would come to the surface, and a hand could be stretched out in succour.

About two hundred yards down the river was an island near the middle of the stream. The current carried us near it, and, on landing, I learned that the unfortunate man was none other than Wade Scholar, the foreman of the herd. We scattered up and down this middle island and watched every ripple and floating bit of flotsam in the hope that he would come to the surface, but nothing but his hat was seen. In the disorder into which the outfits were thrown by this accident, Flood first regained his thinking faculties, and ordered a few of us to cross to either bank, and ride down the river and take up positions on the other islands, from which that part of the river took its name. A hundred conjectures were offered as to how it occurred; but no one saw either horse or rider after sinking. A free horse would be hard to drown, and on the nonappearance of Scholar's mount it was concluded that he must have become entangled in the reins or that Scholar had clutched them in his death grip, and horse and man thus met death together. It was believed by his own outfit that Scholar had no intention until the last moment to risk swimming the river, but when he saw all the others plunge into the channel, his better judgement was overcome, and rather than remain behind and cause comment, he had followed and lost his life.

We patrolled the river until darkness without result, the two herds in the meantime having been so neglected that they had mixed. Our wagon returned along the north bank early in the evening, and Flood ordered Priest to go in and make up a guard from the two outfits and hold the herd for the night. Someone of Scholar's outfit went back and moved their wagon up to the crossing, within hailing distance of ours. It was a night of muffled conversation, and every voice of the night or cry of waterfowl in the river sent creepy sensations over us. The long night passed, however, and the sun rose in Sabbath benediction, for it was Sunday, and found groups of men huddled around two wagons in silent contemplation of what the day before had brought. A more broken and disconsolate set of men than Scholar's would be hard to imagine.

Flood enquired of their outfit if there was any sub-foreman, or *segundo* as they were generally called. It seemed there was not, but their outfit was unanimous that the leadership should fall to a boyhood acquaintance of Scholar's by the name of Campbell, who was generally addressed as 'Black' Jim. Flood at once advised Campbell to send their wagon up to Laramie and cross it, promising that we would lie over that day and make an effort to recover the body of the drowned foreman. Campbell accordingly started his wagon up to the ferry, and all the remainder of the outfits, with the exception of a few men on herd, started out in search of the drowned man. Within a mile and a half below the ford, there were located over thirty of the forty islands, and at the lower end of this chain of sand bars we began and searched both shores, while three or four men swam to each island and made a vigorous search.

The water in the river was not very clear, which called for a close inspection; but with a force of twenty-five men in the hunt, we covered island and shore rapidly in our search. It was about eight in the morning, and we had already searched half of the islands, when Joe Stallings and two of Scholar's men swam to an island in the river which had a growth of small cottonwoods covering it, while on the upper end was a heavy lodgement of driftwood. John Officer, The Rebel and I had taken the next island above, and as we were riding the shallows surrounding it we heard a shot in our rear that told us the body had been found. As we turned in the direction of the signal, Stallings was standing on a large driftwood log, and signalling. We started back to him, partly wading and partly swimming, while from both sides of the river men were swimming their horses for the brushy island. Our squad, on nearing the lower bar, was compelled to swim around the driftwood, and some twelve or fifteen men from either shore reached the scene before us.

The body was lying face upward, in about eighteen inches of eddy water. Flood and Campbell waded out, and taking a lariat, fastened it around his chest under the arms. Then Flood, noticing I was riding my black, asked me to tow the body ashore. Forcing a passage through the driftwood, I took the loose end of the lariat and started for the north bank, the double outfit following. On reaching the shore, the body was carried out of the water by willing hands, and one of our outfit was sent to the wagon for a tarpaulin to be used as a stretcher.

Meanwhile, Campbell took possession of the drowned foreman's watch, six-shooter, purse and papers. The watch was as good as ruined, but the leather holster had shrunk and securely held the gun from being lost in the river. On the arrival of the tarpaulin, the body was laid upon it, and four mounted men, taking the four corners of the sheet, wrapped them on the pommels of their saddles and started for our wagon. When the corpse had been lowered to the ground at our camp, a look of enquiry passed from face to face which seemed to ask, 'What next?' But the enquiry was answered a moment later by Black Jim Campbell, the friend of the dead man. Memory may have dimmed the lesser details of that Sunday morning on the North Platte, for over two decades have since gone, but his words and manliness have lived, not only in my mind, but in the memory of every other survivor of those present. 'This accident,' said he in perfect composure, as he gazed into the calm, still face of his dead friend, 'will impose on me a very sad duty. I expect to meet his mother someday. She will want to know everything. I must tell her the truth, and I'd hate to tell her we buried him like a dog, for she's a Christian woman. And what makes it all the harder, I know that this is the third boy she has lost by drowning. Some of you may not have understood him, but among those papers which you saw me take from his pockets was a letter from his mother, in which she warned him to guard against just what has happened. Situated as we are, I'm going to ask you all to help me give him the best burial we can. No doubt it will be crude, but it will be some solace to her to know we did the best we could.'

Every one of us was eager to lend his assistance. Within five minutes Priest was galloping up the north bank of the river to intercept the wagon at the ferry, a well-filled purse in his pocket with which to secure a coffin at Fort Laramie. Flood and Campbell selected a burial place, and with our wagon spade a grave was being dug on a nearby grassy mound, where there were two other graves.

There was not a man among us who was hypocrite enough to attempt to conduct a Christian burial service, but when the subject came up, McCann said as he came down the river the evening before he noticed an emigrant train of about thirty wagons going into camp at a grove about five miles up the river. In a conversation which he had had with one of the party, he learned that they expected to rest over Sunday. Their respect for the Sabbath day caused Campbell to suggest that there might be someone in the emigrant camp who could conduct a Christian burial, and he at once mounted his horse and rode away to learn.

In preparing the body for its last resting-place we were badly handicapped, but by tearing a new wagon sheet into strips about a foot in width and wrapping the body, we gave it a humble bier in the shade of our wagon, pending the arrival of the coffin. The features were so ashened by having been submerged in the river for over eighteen hours, that we wrapped the face also, as we preferred to remember him as we had seen him the day before, strong, healthy and buoyant. During the interim, awaiting the return of Campbell from the emigrant camp and of the wagon, we sat around in groups and discussed the incident. There was a sense of guilt expressed by a number of our outfit over their hasty decision regarding the courage of the dead man. When we understood that two of his brothers had met a similar fate in Red River within the past five years, every guilty thought or hasty word spoken came back to us with tenfold weight. Priest and Campbell returned together; the former reported having secured a coffin which would arrive within an hour, while the latter had met in the emigrant camp a superannuated minister who gladly volunteered his services. He had given the old minister such data as he had, and two of the minister's granddaughters had expressed a willingness to assist by singing at the burial services. Campbell had set the hour for four, and several conveyances would be down from the emigrant camp. The wagon arriving shortly afterwards, we had barely time to lay the corpse in the coffin before the emigrants drove up. The minister was a tall, homely man, with a flowing beard, which the frosts of many a winter had whitened, and as he mingled among us in the final preparations, he had a kind word for everyone. There were ten in his party; and when the coffin had been carried out to the grave, the two granddaughters of the old man opened the simple service by singing very impressively the first three verses of the Portuguese Hymn. I had heard the old hymn sung often before, but the impression of the last verse rang in my ears for days afterwards.

'When through the deep waters I call thee to go,
The rivers of sorrow shall not overflow;
For I will be with thee thy troubles to bless,
And sanctify to thee thy deepest distress.'

As the notes of the hymn died away, there was for a few moments profound stillness, and not a move was made by anyone. The touching words of the old hymn expressed quite vividly the disaster of the previous day, and awakened in us many memories of home. For a time we were silent, while eyes unused to weeping filled with tears. I do not know how long we remained so. It may have been only for a moment, it probably was; but I do know the silence was not broken till the aged minister, who stood at the head of the coffin, began his discourse. We stood with uncovered heads during the service, and when the old minister addressed us he spoke as though he might have been holding family worship and we had been his children. He invoked Heaven to comfort and sustain the mother when the news of her son's death reached her, as she would need more than human aid in that hour; he prayed that her faith might not falter and that she might again meet and be with her loved ones for ever in the great beyond. He then took up the subject of life – spoke of its brevity, its many hopes that are never realised, and the disappointments from which no prudence or foresight can shield us. He dwelt at some length on the strange mingling of sunshine and shadow that seemed to belong to every life; on the mystery everywhere, and nowhere more impressively than in ourselves. With his long bony finger he pointed to the cold, mute form that lay in the coffin before us, and said, 'But this, my friends, is the mystery of all mysteries.' The fact that life terminated in death, he said, only emphasised its reality; that the death of our companion was not an accident, though it was sudden and unexpected; that the difficulties of life are such that it would be worse than folly in us to try to meet them in our own strength. Death, he said, might change, but it did not destroy; that the soul still lived and would live for ever; that death was simply the gateway out of time into eternity; and if we were to realise the high aim of our being, we could do so by casting our burdens on Him who was able and willing to carry them for us. He spoke feelingly of the Great Teacher, the lowly Nazarene, who also suffered and died, and he concluded with an eloquent description of the blessed life, the immortality of the soul and the resurrection of the body. After the discourse was ended and a brief and earnest prayer was covered, the two young girls sang the hymn, 'Shall we meet beyond the river?' The services being at an end, the coffin was lowered into the grave.

Campbell thanked the old minister and his two granddaughters, on their taking leave, for their presence and assistance; and a number of us boys also shook hands with the old man at parting.

CHAPTER 20

A Moonlight Drive

The two herds were held together a second night, but after they had grazed a few hours the next morning, the cattle were thrown together, and the work of cutting out ours commenced. With a double outfit of men available, about twenty men were turned into the herd to do the cutting, the remainder holding the main herd and looking after the cut. The morning was cool, everyone worked with a vim, and in about two hours the herds were again separated and ready for the final trimming. Campbell did not expect to move out until he could communicate with the head office of the company, and would go up to Fort Laramie for that purpose during the day, hoping to be able to get a message over the military wire. When his outfit had finished retrimming our herd, and we had looked over his cattle for the last time, the two outfits bade each other farewell, and our herd started on its journey.

The unfortunate accident at the ford had depressed our feelings to such an extent that there was an entire absence of hilarity by the way. This morning the farewell songs generally used in parting with a river which had defied us were omitted. The herd trailed out like an immense serpent, and was guided and controlled by our men as if by mutes. Long before the noon hour, we passed out of sight of Forty Islands, and in the next few days, with the change of scene, the gloom gradually lifted. We were bearing almost due north, and passing through a delightful country. To our left ran a range of mountains, while on the other hand sloped off the apparently limitless plain. The scarcity of water was beginning to be felt, for the streams which had not a source in the mountains on our left had dried up weeks before our arrival. There was a gradual change of air noticeable too, for we were rapidly gaining altitude, the heat of summer being now confined to a few hours at noonday, while the nights were almost too cool for our comfort.

When about three days out from the North Platte, the mountains disappeared on our left, while on the other hand appeared a rugged-looking country, which we knew must be the approaches of the Black Hills. Another day's drive brought us into the main stage road connecting the railroad to the south with the mining camps which nestled somewhere in those rocky hills to our right. The stage road followed the trail some ten or fifteen miles before we parted company with it on a dry fork of the Big Cheyenne River. There was a roadhouse and stage stand where these two thoroughfares separated, the one to the mining camp of Deadwood, while ours of the Montana cattle trail bore off for the Powder River to the northwest. At this stage stand we learned that some twenty herds had already passed by to the northern ranges, and that after passing the next fork of the Big Cheyenne we should find no water until we struck the Powder River – a stretch of eighty miles. The keeper of the roadhouse, a genial host, informed us that this drouthy stretch in our front was something unusual, this being one of the dryest summers that he had experienced since the discovery of gold in the Black Hills.

Here was a new situation to be met, an eighty-mile dry drive; and with our experience of a few months before at Indian Lakes fresh in our memories, we set our house in order for the undertaking before us. It was yet fifteen miles to the next and last water from the stage stand. There were several dry forks of the Cheyenne beyond, but as they had their source in the tablelands of Wyoming, we could not hope for water in their dry bottoms. The situation was serious, with only this encouragement: other herds had crossed this arid belt since the streams had dried up, and our Circle Dots could walk with any herd that ever left Texas. The wisdom of mounting us well for just such an emergency reflected the good cow sense of our employer; and we felt easy in regard to our mounts, though there was not a horse or a man too many. In summing up the situation, Flood said, 'We've got this advantage over the Indian Lake drive: there is a good moon, and the days are cool. We'll make twenty-five miles a day covering this stretch, as this herd has never been put to a test yet to see how far they could walk in a day. They'll have to do their sleeping at noon; at least cut it into two shifts, and if we get any sleep we'll have to do the same. Let her come as she will; every day's drive is a day nearer the Blackfoot agency.'

We made a dry camp that night on the divide between the roadhouse and the last water, and the next forenoon reached the South Fork of the Big Cheyenne. The water was not even running in it, but there were several long pools, and we held the cattle around them for over an hour, until every hoof had been thoroughly watered. McCann had filled every keg and canteen in advance of the arrival of the herd, and Flood had exercised sufficient caution, in view of what lay before us, to buy an extra keg and a bull's-eye lantern at the roadhouse. After watering, we trailed out some four or five miles and camped for noon, but the herd were allowed to graze forward until they lay down for their noonday rest. As the herd passed opposite the wagon, we cut a fat two-year-old stray heifer and killed her for beef, for the inner man must be fortified for the journey before us. After a two hours' siesta, we threw the herd on the trail and started on our way. The wagon and saddle horses were held in our immediate rear, for there was no telling when or where we would make our next halt of any consequence. We trailed and grazed the herd alternately until near evening, when the wagon was sent on ahead about three miles to get supper, while half the outfit went along to change mounts and catch up horses for those remaining behind with the herd. A half-hour before the usual bedding time, the relieved men returned and took the grazing herd, and the others rode in to the wagon for supper and a change of mounts. While we shifted our saddles, we smelled the savoury odour of fresh beef frying.

'Listen to that good old beef talking, will you?' said Joe Stallings, as he was bridling his horse. 'McCann, I'll take my *carne fresco* a trifle rare tonight, garnished with a sprig of parsley and a wee bit of lemon.'

Before we had finished supper, Honeyman had rehooked the mules to the wagon, while the *remuda* was at hand to follow. Before we left the wagon, a full moon was rising on the eastern horizon, and as we were starting out Flood gave us these general directions: 'I'm going to take the lead with the cook's lantern, and one of you rear men take the new bull's-eye. We'll throw the herd on the trail; and between the lead and rear light, you swing men want to ride well outside, and you point men want to hold the lead cattle so the rear will never be more than a half a mile behind. I'll admit that this is somewhat of an experiment with me, but I don't see any good reason why she won't work. After the moon gets another hour high we can see a quarter of a mile, and the cattle are so well trail broke they'll never try to scatter. If it works all right, we'll never bed them short of midnight, and that will put us ten miles farther. Let's ride, lads.'

By the time the herd was eased back on the trail, our evening campfire had been passed, while the cattle led out as if walking on a wager. After the first mile on the trail, the men on the point were compelled to ride in the lead if we were to hold them within the desired half mile. The men on the other side, or the swing, were gradually widening, until the herd must have reached fully a mile in length; yet we swing riders were never out of sight of each other, and it would have been impossible for any cattle to leave the herd unnoticed. In that moonlight the trail was as plain as day, and after an hour, Flood turned his lantern over to one of the point men, and rode back around the herd to the rear. From my position that first night near the middle of the swing, the lanterns both rear and forward being always in sight, I was as much at sea as anyone as to the length of the herd, knowing the deceitfulness of distance of campfires and other lights by night. The foreman appealed to me, as he rode down the column, to know the length of the herd, but I could give him no more than a simple guess. I could assure him, however, that the cattle had made no effort to drop out and leave the trail. But a short time after he passed me I noticed a horseman galloping up the column on the opposite side of the herd, and knew it must be the foreman. Within a short time, someone in the lead wig-wagged his lantern; it was answered by the light in the rear, and the next minute the old rear song:

> 'Ip–e–la–ago, go 'long little doggie,
> You'll make a beef-steer by and by,'

reached us riders in the swing, and we knew the rear guard of cattle was being pushed forward. The distance between the swing men gradually narrowed in our lead, from which we could tell the leaders were being held in, until several times cattle grazed out from the herd, due to the checking in front. At this juncture Flood galloped around the herd a second time, and as he passed us riding along our side, I appealed to him to let them go in front, as it now required constant riding to keep the cattle from leaving the trail to graze. When he passed up the opposite side, I could distinctly hear the men on that flank making a similar appeal, and shortly afterwards the herd loosened out and we struck our old gait for several hours.

Trailing by moonlight was a novelty to all of us, and in the stillness of those splendid July nights we could hear the point men chatting across the lead in front, while well in the rear, the rattling of our heavily loaded wagon and the whistling of the horse wrangler to his charges reached our ears. The swing men were scattered so far apart there was no chance for conversation among us, but every once in a while a song would be started, and as it surged up and down the line, every voice, good, bad and indifferent, joined in. Singing is supposed to have a soothing effect on cattle, though I will vouch for the fact that none of our Circle Dots stopped that night to listen to our vocal efforts. The herd was travelling so nicely that our foreman hardly noticed the passing hours, but along about midnight the singing ceased, and we were nodding in our saddles and wondering if they in the lead were never going to throw off the trail, when a great wig-wagging occurred in front, and presently we overtook The Rebel, holding the lantern and turning the herd out of the trail. It was then after midnight, and within another half hour we had the cattle bedded down within a few hundred yards of the trail. One-hour guards was the order of the night, and as soon as our wagon and saddle horses came up, we stretched ropes and caught out our night horses. These we either tied to the wagon wheels or picketed near at hand, and then we sought our blankets for a few hours' sleep. It was half-past three in the morning when our guard was called, and before the hour passed, the first signs of day were visible in the east. But even before our watch had ended, Flood and the last guard came to our relief, and we pushed the sleeping cattle off the bed ground and started them grazing forward.

Cattle will not graze freely in a heavy dew or too early in the morning, and before the sun was high enough to dry the grass, we had put several miles behind us. When the sun was about an hour high, the remainder of the outfit overtook us, and shortly afterwards the wagon and saddle horses passed on up the trail, from which it was evident that 'breakfast would be served in the dining-car ahead', as the travelled Priest aptly put it. After the sun was well up, the cattle grazed freely for several hours; but when we sighted the *remuda* and our commissary some two miles in our lead, Flood ordered the herd lined up for a count. The Rebel was always a reliable counter, and he and the foreman now rode forward and selected the crossing of a dry wash for the counting. On receiving their signal to come on, we allowed the herd to graze slowly forward, but gradually pointed them into an immense V, and as the point of the herd crossed the dry arroyo, we compelled them to pass in a narrow file between the two counters, when they again spread out fanlike and continued their feeding.

The count confirmed the success of our driving by night, and on its completion all but two men rode to the wagon for breakfast. By the time the morning meal was disposed of, the herd had come up parallel with the wagon but a mile to the westward, and as fast as fresh mounts could be saddled, we rode away in small squads to relieve the herders and to turn the cattle into the trail. It was but a little after eight o'clock in the morning when the herd was again trailing out on the Powder River trail, and we had already put over thirty miles of the dry drive behind us, while so far neither horses nor cattle had been put to any extra exertion. The wagon followed as usual, and for over three hours we held the trail without a break, when sighting a divide in our front, the foreman went back and sent the wagon around the herd with instructions to make the noon camp well up on the divide. We threw the herd off the trail, within a mile of this stopping place, and allowed them to graze, while two thirds of the outfit galloped away to the wagon.

We allowed the cattle to lie down and rest to their complete satisfaction until the middle of the afternoon; meanwhile all hands, with the exception of two men on herd, also lay down and slept in the shade of the wagon. When the cattle had had several hours' sleep, the want of water made them restless, and they began to rise and graze away. Then all hands were aroused and we threw them upon the trail. The heat of the day was already over, and until the twilight of the evening, we trailed a three-mile clip, and again threw the herd off to graze. By our travelling and grazing gaits, we could form an approximate idea as to the distance we had covered, and the consensus of opinion of all was that we had already killed over half the distance. The herd was beginning to show the want of water by evening, but among our saddle horses the lack of water was more noticeable, as a horse subsisting on grass alone weakens easily; and riding them made them all the more gaunt. When we caught up our mounts that evening, we had used eight horses to the man since we had left the South Fork, and another one would be required at midnight, or whenever we halted.

We made our drive the second night with more confidence than the one before, but there were times when the train of cattle must have been nearly two miles in length, yet there was never a halt as long as the man with the lead light could see the one in the rear. We bedded the herd about midnight; and at the first break of day, the fourth guard with the foreman joined us on our watch and we started the cattle again. There was a light dew the second night, and the cattle, hungered by their night walk, went to grazing at once on the damp grass, which would allay their thirst slightly. We allowed them to scatter over several thousand acres, for we were anxious to graze them well before the sun absorbed the moisture, but at the same time every step they took was one less to the coveted Powder River.

When we had grazed the herd forward several miles, and the sun was nearly an hour high, the wagon failed to come up, which caused our foreman some slight uneasiness. Nearly another hour passed, and still the wagon did not come up nor did the outfit put in an appearance. Soon afterwards, however, Moss Strayhorn overtook us, and reported that over forty of our saddle horses were missing, while the work mules had been overtaken nearly five miles back on the trail. On account of my ability as a trailer, Flood at once dispatched me to assist Honeyman in recovering the missing horses, instructing someone else to take the *remuda* and the wagon and horses to follow up the herd. By the time I arrived, most of the boys at camp had secured a change of horses, and I caught up my *grulla*, that I was saving for the last hard ride, for the horse hunt which confronted us. McCann, having no fire built, gave Honeyman and myself an impromptu breakfast and two canteens of water; but before we let the wagon get away, we rustled a couple of cans of tomatoes and buried them in a cache near the camp-ground, where we would have no trouble in finding them on our return. As the wagon pulled out, we mounted our horses and rode back down the trail.

Billy Honeyman understood horses, and at once volunteered the belief that we would have a long ride overtaking the missing saddle stock. The absent horses, he said, were principally the ones which had been under saddle the day before, and as we both knew, a tired, thirsty horse will go miles for water. He recalled, also, that while we were asleep at noon the day before, twenty miles back on the trail, the horses had found quite a patch of wild sorrel, and were foolish over leaving it. Both of us being satisfied that this would hold them for several hours at least, we struck a free gait for it. After we passed the point where the mules had been overtaken, the trail of the horses was distinct enough for us to follow in an easy canter. We saw frequent signs that they left the trail, no doubt to graze, but only for short distances, when they would enter it again, and keep it for miles. Shortly before noon, as we gained the divide above our noon camp of the day before, there about two miles distant we saw our missing horses, feeding over an alkali flat on which grew wild sorrel and other species of sour plants. We rounded them up, and finding none missing, we first secured a change of mounts. The only two horses of my mount in this portion of the *remuda* had both been under saddle the afternoon and night before, and were as gaunt as rails, and Honeyman had one unused horse of his mount in the hand. So when, taking down our ropes, we halted the horses and began riding slowly around them, forcing them into a compact body, I had my eye on a brown horse of Flood's that had not had a saddle on in a week, and told Billy to fasten to him if he got a chance. This was in violation of all custom, but if the foreman kicked, I had a good excuse to offer.

Honeyman was left-handed and threw a rope splendidly; and as we circled around the horses on opposite sides, on a signal from him we whirled our lariats and made casts simultaneously. The wrangler fastened to the brown I wanted, and my loop settled around the neck of his unridden horse. As the band broke away from our swinging ropes, a number of them ran afoul of my rope; but I gave the rowel to my *grulla*, and we shook them off. When I returned to Honeyman, and we had exchanged horses and were shifting our saddles, I complimented him on the long throw he had made in catching the brown, and incidentally mentioned that I had read of vaqueros in California who used a sixty-five-foot lariat. 'Hell,' said Billy, in ridicule of the idea, 'there isn't a man ever born who could throw a sixty-five-foot rope its full length – without he threw it down a well.'

The sun was straight overhead when we started back to overtake the herd. We struck into a little better than a five-mile gait on the return trip, and about two o'clock sighted a band of saddle horses and a wagon camped perhaps a mile forward and to the side of the trail. On coming near enough, we saw at a glance it was a cow outfit, and after driving our loose horses a good push beyond their camp, turned and rode back to their wagon.

'We'll give them a chance to ask us to eat,' said Billy to me, 'and if they don't, why, they'll miss a hell of a good chance to entertain hungry men.'

But the foreman with the stranger wagon proved to be a Bee County Texan, and our doubts did him an injustice, for, although dinner was over, he invited us to dismount and ordered his cook to set out something to eat. They had met our wagon, and McCann had insisted on their taking a quarter of our beef, so we fared well. The outfit was from a ranch near Miles City, Montana, and were going down to receive a herd of cattle at Cheyenne, Wyoming. The cattle had been bought at Ogalalla for delivery at the former point, and this wagon was going down with their ranch outfit to take the herd on its arrival. They had brought along about seventy-five saddle horses from the ranch, though in buying the herd they had taken its *remuda* of over a hundred saddle horses. The foreman informed us that they had met our cattle about the middle of the forenoon, nearly twenty-five miles out from Powder River. After we had satisfied the inner man, we lost no time getting off, as we could see a long ride ahead of us; but we had occasion as we rode away to go through their *remuda* to cut out a few of our horses which had mixed, and I found I knew over a dozen of their horses by the ranch brands, while Honeyman also recognised quite a few. Though we felt a pride in our mounts, we had to admit that theirs were better; for the effect of climate had transformed horses that we had once ridden on ranches in southern Texas. It does seem incredible, but it is a fact nevertheless, that a horse, having reached the years of maturity in a southern climate, will grow half a hand taller and carry two hundred pounds more flesh, when he has undergone the rigours of several northern winters.

We halted at our night camp to change horses and to unearth our cached tomatoes, and again set out. By then it was so late in the day that the sun had lost its force, and on this last leg in overtaking the herd we increased our gait steadily until the sun was scarcely an hour high, and yet we never sighted a dust-cloud in our front. About sundown we called a few minutes' halt, and after eating our tomatoes and drinking the last of our water, again pushed on. Twilight had faded into dusk before we reached a divide which we had had in sight for several hours, and which we had hoped to gain in time to sight the timber on Powder River before dark. But as we put mile after mile behind us, that divide seemed to move away like a mirage, and the evening star had been shining for an hour before we finally reached it, and sighted, instead of Powder's timber, the campfire of our outfit about five miles ahead. We fired several shots on seeing the light, in the hope that they might hear us in camp and wait; otherwise we knew they would start the herd with the rising of the moon.

When we finally reached camp, about nine o'clock at night, everything was in readiness to start, the moon having risen sufficiently. Our shooting, however, had been heard, and horses for a change were tied to the wagon wheels, while the remainder of the *remuda* was under herd in charge of Rod Wheat. The runaways were thrown into the horse herd while we bolted our suppers. Meantime, McCann informed us that Flood had ridden that afternoon to the Powder River, in order to get the lay of the land. He had found it to be ten or twelve miles distant from the present camp, and the water in the river barely knee deep to a saddle horse. Beyond it was a fine valley. Before we started, Flood rode in from the herd, and said to Honeyman, 'I'm going to send the horses and wagon ahead tonight, and you and McCann want to camp on this side of the river, under the hill and just a few hundred yards below the ford. Throw your saddle horses across the river, and build a fire before you go to sleep, so we will have a beacon light to pilot us in, in case the cattle break into a run on scenting the water. The herd will get in a little after midnight, and after crossing, we'll turn her loose just for luck.'

It did me good to hear the foreman say the herd was to be turned loose, for I had been in the saddle since three that morning, had ridden over eighty miles, and had now ten more in sight, while Honeyman would complete the day with over a hundred to his credit. We let the *remuda* take the lead in pulling out, so that the wagon mules could be spurred to their utmost in keeping up with the loose horses. Once they were clear of the herd, we let the cattle into the trail. They had refused to bed down, for they were uneasy with thirst, but the cool weather had saved them any serious suffering. We all felt gala as the herd strung out on the trail. Before we halted again there would be water for our dumb brutes and rest for ourselves. There was lots of singing that night. 'There's One more River to cross' and 'Roll, Powder, roll' were wafted out on the night air to the coyotes that howled on our flanks, or to the prairie dogs as they peeped from their burrows at this weird caravan of the night, and the lights which flickered in our front and rear must have been real Jack-o'-lanterns or Will-o'-the-wisps to these occupants of the plain. Before we had covered half the distance, the herd was strung-out over two miles, and as Flood rode back to the rear every half-hour or so, he showed no inclination to check the lead and give the sore-footed rear guard a chance to close up the column; but about an hour before midnight we saw a light low down in our front, which gradually increased until the treetops were distinctly visible, and we knew that our wagon had reached the river. On sighting this beacon, the long yell went up and down the column, and the herd walked as only long-legged, thirsty Texas cattle can walk when they scent water. Flood called all the swing men to the rear, and we threw out a half-circle skirmish line covering a mile in width, so far back that only an occasional glimmer of the lead light could be seen. The trail struck the Powder on an angle, and when within a mile of the river, the swing cattle left the deep-trodden paths and started for the nearest water.

The left flank of our skirmish line encountered the cattle as they reached the river, and prevented them from drifting up the stream. The point men abandoned the leaders when within a few hundred yards of the river. Then the rear guard of cripples and sore-footed cattle came up, and the two flanks of horsemen pushed them all across the river until they met, when we turned and galloped into camp, making the night hideous with our yelling. The longest dry drive of the trip had been successfully made, and we all felt jubilant. We stripped bridles and saddles from our tired horses, and unrolling our beds, were soon lost in well-earned sleep.

The stars may have twinkled overhead, and sundry voices of the night may have whispered to us as we lay down to sleep, but we were too tired for poetry or sentiment that night.

CHAPTER 21

The Yellowstone

The tramping of our *remuda* as they came trotting up to the wagon the next morning, and Honeyman's calling, 'Horses, horses,' brought us to the realisation that another day had dawned with its duty. McCann had stretched the ropes of our corral, for Flood was as dead to the world as any of us were, but the tramping of over a hundred and forty horses and mules, as they crowded inside the ropes, brought him into action as well as the rest of us. We had had a good five hours' sleep, while our mounts had been transformed from gaunt animals to round-barrelled saddle horses – that fought and struggled among themselves or artfully dodged the lariat loops which were being cast after them. Honeyman reported the herd quietly grazing across the river, and after securing our mounts for the morning, we breakfasted before looking after the cattle. It took us less than an hour to round up and count the cattle, and turn them loose again under herd to graze. Those of us not on herd returned to the wagon, and our foreman instructed McCann to make a two hours' drive down the river and camp for noon, as he proposed only to graze the herd that morning. After seeing the wagon safely beyond the rocky crossing, we hunted up a good bathing pool and disported ourselves for half an hour, taking a much needed bath. There were trails on either side of the Powder, and as our course was henceforth to the northwest, we remained on the west side and grazed or trailed down it. It was a beautiful stream of water, having its source in the Big Horn Mountains, frequently visible on our left. For the next four or five days we had easy work. There were range cattle through that section, but fearful of Texas fever, their owners gave the Powder River a wide berth. With the exception of holding the herd at night, our duties were light. We caught fish and killed grouse; and the respite seemed like a holiday after our experience of the past few days. During the evening of the second day after reaching the Powder, we crossed the Crazy Woman, a clear mountainous fork of the former river, and nearly as large as the parent stream. Once or twice we encountered range riders, and learned that the Crazy Woman was a stock country, a number of beef ranches being located on it, stocked with Texas cattle.

Somewhere near or about the Montana line, we took a left-hand trail. Flood had ridden it out until he had satisfied himself that it led over to the Tongue River and the country beyond. While large trails followed on down the Powder, their direction was wrong for us, as they led towards the Bad Lands and the lower Yellowstone country. On the second day out, after taking the left-hand trail, we encountered some rough country in passing across a saddle in a range of hills forming the divide between the Powder and Tongue Rivers. We were nearly a whole day crossing it, but had a well-used trail to follow, and down in the foothills made camp that night on a creek which emptied into the Tongue. The roughness of the trail was well compensated for, however, as it was a paradise of grass and water. We reached the Tongue River the next afternoon, and found it a similar stream to the Powder – clear as crystal, swift, and with a rocky bottom. As these were but minor rivers, we encountered no trouble in crossing them, the greatest danger being to our wagon. On the Tongue we met range riders again, and from them we learned that this trail, which crossed the Yellowstone at Frenchman's Ford, was the one in use by herds bound for the Musselshell and remoter points on the upper Missouri. From one rider we learned that the first herd of the present season which went through on this route were cattle, wintered on the Niobrara in western Nebraska, whose destination was Alberta in the British Possessions. This herd outclassed us in penetrating northward, though in distance they had not travelled half as far as our Circle Dots.

After following the Tongue River several days and coming out on that immense plain tributary to the Yellowstone, the trail turned to the northwest, gave us a short day's drive to the Rosebud River, and after following it a few miles, bore off again on the same quarter. In our rear hung the mountains with their sentinel peaks, while in our front stretched the valley tributary to the Yellowstone, in extent, itself, an inland empire. The month was August, and, with the exception of cool nights, no complaint could be made, for that rarefied atmosphere was a tonic to man and beast, and there was pleasure in the primitive freshness of the country which rolled away on every hand. On leaving the Rosebud, two days' travel brought us to the east fork of Sweet Grass, an insignificant stream, with a swift current and rocky crossings. In the first two hours after reaching it, we must have crossed it half a dozen times, following the grassy bottoms, which shifted from one bank to the other. When we were full forty miles distant from Frenchman's Ford on the Yellowstone, the wagon, in crossing Sweet Grass, went down a sidling bank into the bottom of the creek, the left hind wheel collided with a boulder in the water, dishing it, and every spoke in the wheel snapped off at the shoulder in the felloe. McCann never noticed it, but poured the whip into the mules, and when he pulled out on the opposite bank left the felloe of his wheel in the creek behind. The herd was in the lead at the time, and when Honeyman overtook us and reported the accident, we threw the herd off to graze, and over half the outfit returned to the wagon.

When we reached the scene, McCann had recovered the felloe, but every spoke in the hub was hopelessly ruined. Flood took in the situation at a glance. He ordered the wagon unloaded and the reach lengthened, took the axe, and, with The Rebel, went back about a mile to a thicket of lodge poles which we had passed higher up the creek. While the rest of us unloaded the wagon, McCann, who was swearing by both note and rhyme, unearthed his saddle from among the other plunder and cinched it on his nigh wheeler. We had the wagon unloaded and had reloaded some of the heaviest of the plunder in the front end of the wagon box by the time our foreman and Priest returned, dragging from their pommels a thirty-foot pole as perfect as the mast of a yacht. We knocked off all the spokes not already broken at the hub of the ruined wheel, and after jacking up the hind axle, attached the 'crutch'. By cutting a half-notch in the larger end of the pole, so that it fitted over the front axle, lashing it there securely, and allowing the other end to trail behind on the ground, we devised a support on which the hub of the broken wheel rested, almost at its normal height. There was sufficient spring to the pole to obviate any jolt or jar, while the rearrangement we had effected in distributing the load would relieve it of any serious burden. We took a rope from the coupling pole of the wagon and loosely noosed it over the crutch, which allowed leeway in turning, but prevented the hub from slipping off the support on a short turn to the left. Then we lashed the tyre and felloe to the front end of the wagon, and with the loss of but a couple of hours our commissary was again on the move.

The trail followed the Sweet Grass down to the Yellowstone; and until we reached it, whenever there were creeks to ford or extra pulls on hills, half a dozen of us would drop back and lend a hand from our saddle pommels. The gradual decline of the country to the river was in our favour at present, and we should reach the ford in two days at the farthest, where we hoped to find a wheelwright. In case we did not, our foreman thought he could effect a trade for a serviceable wagon, as ours was a new one and the best make in the market. The next day Flood rode on ahead to Frenchman's Ford, and late in the day returned with the information that the Ford was quite a pretentious frontier village of the squatter type. There was a blacksmith and a wheelwright in the town, but the prospect of an exchange was discouraging, as the wagons there were of the heavy freighting type, while ours was a wide tread – a serious objection, as wagons manufactured for southern trade were eight inches wider than those in use in the north, and therefore would not track on the same road. The wheelwright had assured Flood that the wheel could be filled in a day, with the exception of painting, and as paint was not important, he had decided to move up within three or four miles of the Ford and lie over a day for repairing the wagon, and at the same time have our mules reshod. Accordingly we moved up the next morning, and after unloading the wagon, both box and contents, over half the outfit – the first and second guards – accompanied the wagon into the Ford. They were to return by noon, when the remainder of us were to have our turn in seeing the sights of Frenchman's Ford. The horse wrangler remained behind with us, to accompany the other half of the outfit in the afternoon. The herd was no trouble to hold, and after watering about the middle of the forenoon, three of us went into camp and got dinner. As this was the first time since starting that our cook was absent, we rather enjoyed the opportunity to practise our culinary skill. Pride in our ability to cook was a weakness in our craft. The work was divided up between Joe Stallings, John Officer and myself, Honeyman being excused on agreeing to rustle the wood and water. Stallings prided himself on being an artist in making coffee, and while hunting for the coffee mill, found a bag of dried peaches.

'Say, fellows,' said Joe, 'I'll bet McCann has hauled this fruit a thousand miles and never knew he had it among all this plunder. I'm going to stew a saucepan full of it, just to show his royal nibs that he's been thoughtless of his boarders.'

Officer volunteered to cut and fry the meat, for we were eating stray beef now with great regularity; and the making of the biscuits fell to me. Honeyman soon had a fire so big that you could not have got near it without a wet blanket on; and when my biscuits were ready for the Dutch oven, Officer threw a bucket of water on the fire, remarking: 'Honeyman, if you was *cusi segundo* under me, and built up such a big fire for the chef, there would be trouble in camp. You may be a good enough horse wrangler for a through Texas outfit, but when it comes to playing second fiddle to a cook of my accomplishments – well, you simply don't know salt from wild honey. A man might as well try to cook on a burning haystack as on a fire of your building.'

When the fire had burned down sufficiently, the cooks got their respective utensils upon the fire; I had an ample supply of live coals for the Dutch oven, and dinner was shortly afterwards announced as ready. After dinner, Officer and I relieved the men on herd, but over an hour passed before we caught sight of the first and second guards returning from the Ford. They were men who could stay in town all day and enjoy themselves; but, as Flood had reminded them, there were others who were entitled to a holiday. When Bob Blades and Fox Quarternight came to our relief on herd, they attempted to detain us with a description of Frenchman's Ford, but we cut all conversation short by riding away to camp.

'We'll just save them the trouble, and go in and see it for ourselves,' said Officer to me, as we galloped along. We had left word with Honeyman what horses we wanted to ride that afternoon, and lost little time in changing mounts; then we all set out to pay our respects to the mushroom village on the Yellowstone. Most of us had money; and those of the outfit who had returned were clean shaven and brought the report that a shave was two-bits and a drink the same price. The town struck me as something new and novel, two thirds of the habitations being of canvas. Immense quantities of buffalo hides were drying or already baled, and waiting transportation as we afterward learned to navigable points on the Missouri. Large bull trains were encamped on the outskirts of the village, while many such outfits were in town, receiving cargoes or discharging freight. The drivers of these ox trains lounged in the streets and thronged the saloons and gambling resorts. The population was extremely mixed, and almost every language could be heard spoken on the streets. The men were fine types of the pioneer – buffalo hunters, freighters and other plainsmen, though hardly as picturesque in figure and costume as a modern artist would paint them. For native colouring, there were typical specimens of northern Indians, grunting their jargon amid the babel of other tongues; and groups of squaws wandered through the irregular streets in gaudy blankets and red calico. The only civilising element to be seen was the camp of engineers, running the survey of the Northern Pacific railroad.

Tying our horses in a group to a hitch-rack in the rear of a saloon called the Buffalo Bull, we entered by a rear door and lined up at the bar for our first drink since leaving Ogalalla. Games of chance were running in the rear for those who felt inclined to try their luck, while in front of the bar, against the farther wall, were a number of small tables, around which were seated the patrons of the place, playing for the drinks. One couldn't help being impressed with the unrestrained freedom of the village, whose sole product seemed to be buffalo hides. Every man in the place wore the regulation six-shooter in his belt, and quite a number wore two. The primitive law of nature known as self-preservation was very evident in August of '82 at Frenchman's Ford. It reminded me of the early days at home in Texas, where, on arising in the morning, a man buckled on his six-shooter as though it were part of his dress. After a second round of drinks, we strolled out into the front street to look up Flood and McCann, and incidentally get a shave. We soon located McCann, who had a hunk of dried buffalo meat, and was chipping it off and feeding it to some Indian children whose acquaintance he seemed to be cultivating. On sighting us, he gave the children the remainder of the jerked buffalo, and at once placed himself at our disposal as guide to Frenchman's Ford. He had been all over the town that morning; knew the name of every saloon and those of several bar keepers as well; pointed out the bullet holes in a log building where the last shooting scrape occurred, and otherwise showed us the sights in the village which we might have overlooked. A barber shop? Why, certainly; and he led the way, informing us that the wagon wheel would be filled by evening, that the mules were already shod and that Flood had ridden down to the crossing to look at the ford.

Two barbers turned us out rapidly, and as we left we continued to take in the town, strolling by pairs and drinking moderately as we went. Flood had returned in the meantime, and seemed rather convivial and quite willing to enjoy the enforced lay-over with us. While taking a drink in Yellowstone Bob's place, the foreman took occasion to call the attention of The Rebel to a cheap lithograph of General Grant which hung behind the bar. The two discussed the merits of the picture, and Priest, who was an admirer of the magnanimity as well as the military genius of Grant, spoke in reserved yet favourable terms of the general, when Flood flippantly chided him on his eulogistic remarks over an officer to whom he had once been surrendered. The Rebel took the chaffing in all good humour, and when our glasses were filled, Flood suggested to Priest that since he was such an admirer of Grant, possibly he wished to propose a toast to the general's health.

'You're young, Jim,' said The Rebel, 'and if you'd gone through what I have, your views of things might be different. My admiration for the generals on our side survived wounds, prisons and changes of fortune; but time has tempered my views on some things, and now I don't enthuse over generals when the men of the ranks who made them famous are forgotten. Through the fortunes of war, I saluted Grant when we were surrendered, but I wouldn't propose a toast or take off my hat now to any man that lives.'

During the comments of The Rebel, a stranger, who evidently over-heard them, rose from one of the tables in the place and sauntered over to the end of the bar, an attentive listener to the succeeding conversation. He was a younger man than Priest – with a head of heavy black hair reaching his shoulders, while his dress was largely of buckskin, profusely ornamented with beadwork and fringes. He was armed, as was everyone else, and from his languid demeanour as well as from his smart appearance, one would classify him at a passing glance as a frontier gambler. As we turned away from the bar to an unoccupied table and Priest waited for his change, and the stranger accosted him with an enquiry as to where he was from. In the conversation that ensued, the stranger, who had noticed the good-humoured manner in which The Rebel had taken the chiding of our foreman, pretended to take him to task for some of his remarks. But in this he made a mistake. What his friends might safely say to Priest would be treated as an insult from a stranger. Seeing that he would not stand his chiding, the other attempted to mollify him by proposing they have a drink together and part friendly, to which The Rebel assented. I was pleased with the favourable turn of affairs, for my bunkie had used some rather severe language in resenting the remarks of the stranger, which now had the promise of being dropped amicably.

I knew the temper of Priest, and so did Flood and Honeyman, and we were all anxious to get him away from the stranger. So I asked our foreman as soon as they had drunk together, to go over and tell Priest we were waiting for him to make up a game of cards. The two were standing at the bar in a most friendly attitude, but as they raised their glasses to drink, the stranger, holding his at arm's length, said: 'Here's a toast for you: To General Grant, the ablest – '

But the toast was never finished, for Priest dashed the contents of his glass in the stranger's face, and calmly replacing the glass on the bar, backed across the room towards us. When half-across, a sudden movement on the part of the stranger caused him to halt. But it seemed the picturesque gentleman beside the bar was only searching his pockets for a handkerchief.

'Don't get your hand on that gun you wear,' said The Rebel, whose blood was up, 'unless you intend to use it. But you can't shoot a minute too quick to suit me. What do you wear a gun for, anyhow? Let's see how straight you can shoot.'

As the stranger made no reply, Priest continued, 'The next time you have anything to rub in, pick your man better. The man who insults me'll get all that's due him for his trouble.' Still eliciting no response, The Rebel taunted him further, saying, 'Go on and finish your toast, you patriotic beauty. I'll give you another: Jeff Davis and the Southern Confederacy.'

We all rose from the table, and Flood, going over to Priest, said, 'Come along, Paul, we don't want to have any trouble here. Let's go across the street and have a game of California Jack.'

But The Rebel stood like a chiselled statue, ignoring the friendly counsel of our foreman, while the stranger, after wiping the liquor from his face and person, walked across the room and seated himself at the table from which he had risen. A stillness as of death pervaded the room, which was only broken by our foreman repeating his request to Priest to come away, but the latter replied, 'No; when I leave this place it will not be done in fear of any one. When any man goes out of his way to insult me he must take the consequences, and he can always find me if he wants satisfaction. We'll take another drink before we go. Everybody in the house, come up and take a drink with Paul Priest.'

The inmates of the place, to the number of possibly twenty, who had been witness to what had occurred, accepted the invitation, quitting their games and gathering around the bar. Priest took a position at the end of the bar, where he could notice any movement on the part of his adversary as well as the faces of his guests, and smiling on them, said in true hospitality, 'What will you have, gentlemen?' There was a forced effort on the part of the drinkers to appear indifferent to the situation, but with the stranger sitting sullenly in their rear and an iron-grey man standing at the farther end of the line, hungering for an opportunity to settle differences with six-shooters, their indifference was an empty mockery.

Some of the players returned to their games, while others sauntered into the street, yet Priest showed no disposition to go. After a while the stranger walked over to the bar and called for a glass of whiskey.

The Rebel stood at the end of the bar, calmly rolling a cigarette, and as the stranger seemed not to notice him, Priest attracted his attention and said, 'I'm just passing through here, and shall only be in town this afternoon; so if there's anything between us that demands settlement, don't hesitate to ask for it.'

The stranger drained his glass at a single gulp, and with admirable composure replied, 'If there's anything between us, we'll settle it in due time, and as men usually settle such differences in this country. I have a friend or two in town, and as soon as I see them, you will receive notice, or you may consider the matter dropped. That's all I care to say at present.'

He walked away to the rear of the room, Priest joined us, and we strolled out of the place. In the street, a grizzled, grey-bearded man, who had drunk with him inside, approached my bunkie and said, 'You want to watch that fellow. He claims to be from the Gallatin country, but he isn't, for I live there. There's a pal with him, and they've got some good horses, but I know every brand on the headwaters of the Missouri, and their horses were never bred on any of its three forks. Don't give him any the best of you. Keep an eye on him, comrade.' After this warning, the old man turned into the first open door, and we crossed over to the wheelwright's shop; and as the wheel would not be finished for several hours yet, we continued our survey of the town, and our next landing was at the Buffalo Bull. On entering we found four of our men in a game of cards at the very first table, while Officer was reported as being in the gambling room in the rear. The only vacant table in the bar-room was the last one in the far corner, and calling for a deck of cards, we occupied it. I sat with my back to the log wall of the low one-storey room, while on my left and fronting the door, Priest took a seat with Flood for his pardner, while Honeyman fell to me. After playing a few hands, Flood suggested that Billy go forward and exchange seats with some of our outfit, so as to be near the door, where he could see anyone that entered, while from his position the rear door would be similarly guarded. Under this change, Rod Wheat came back to our table and took Honeyman's place. We had been playing along for an hour, with people passing in and out of the gambling room, and expected shortly to start for camp, when Priest's long-haired adversary came in at the front door, and, walking through the room, passed into the gambling department.

John Officer, after winning a few dollars in the card room, was standing alongside watching our game; and as the stranger passed by, Priest gave him the wink, on which Officer followed the stranger and a heavy-set companion who was with him into the rear room. We had played only a few hands when the heavy-set man came back to the bar, took a drink, and walked over to watch a game of cards at the second table from the front door. Officer came back shortly afterward, and whispered to us that there were four of them to look out for, as he had seen them conferring together. Priest seemed the least concerned of any of us, but I noticed he eased the holster on his belt forward, where it would be ready to his hand. We had called for a round of drinks, Officer taking one with us, when two men came out of the gambling hell, and halting at the bar, pretended to divide some money which they wished to have it appear they had won in the card room. Their conversation was loud and intended to attract attention, but Officer gave us the wink, and their ruse was perfectly understood. After taking a drink and attracting as much attention as possible over the division of the money, they separated, but remained in the room.

I was dealing the cards a few minutes later, when the long-haired man emerged from the gambling hell, and imitating the maudlin, sauntered up to the bar and asked for a drink. After being served, he walked about halfway to the door, then whirling suddenly, stepped to the end of the bar, placed his hands upon it, sprang up and stood upright on it. He whipped out two six-shooters, let loose a yell which caused a commotion throughout the room, and walked very deliberately the length of the counter, his attention centred upon the occupants of our table. Not attracting the notice he expected in our quarter, he turned, and slowly repaced the bar, hurling anathemas on Texas and Texans in general.

I saw The Rebel's eyes, steeled to intensity, meet Flood's across the table, and in that glance of our foreman he evidently read approval, for he rose rigidly with the stealth of a tiger, and for the first time that day his hand went to the handle of his six-shooter. One of the two pretended winners at cards saw the movement in our quarter, and sang out as a warning, 'Cuidado, mucho.' The man on the bar whirled on the word of warning, and blazed away with his two guns into our corner. I had risen at the word and was pinned against the wall, where on the first fire a rain of dirt fell from the chinking in the wall over my head. As soon as the others sprang away from the table, I kicked it over in clearing myself, and came to my feet just as The Rebel fired his second shot. I had the satisfaction of seeing his long-haired adversary reel backwards, firing his guns into the ceiling as he went, and in falling crash heavily into the glassware on the back bar.

The smoke which filled the room left nothing visible for a few moments. Meantime Priest, satisfied that his aim had gone true, turned, passed through the rear room, gained his horse, and was galloping away to the herd before any semblance of order was restored. As the smoke cleared away and we passed forward through the room, John Officer had one of the three pardners standing with his hands to the wall, while his six-shooter lay on the floor under Officer's foot. He had made but one shot into our corner, when the muzzle of a gun was pushed against his ear with an imperative order to drop his arms, which he had promptly done. The two others, who had been under the surveillance of our men at the forward table, never made a move or offered to bring a gun into action, and after the killing of their picturesque pardner passed together out of the house. There had been five or six shots fired into our corner, but the first double shot, fired when three of us were still sitting, went too high for effect, while the remainder were scattering, though Rod Wheat got a bullet through his coat, close enough to burn the skin on his shoulder.

The dead man was laid out on the floor of the saloon; and through curiosity, for it could hardly have been much of a novelty to the inhabitants of Frenchman's Ford, hundreds came to gaze on the corpse and examine the wounds, one above the other through his vitals, either of which would have been fatal. Officer's prisoner admitted that the dead man was his pardner, and offered to remove the corpse if released. On turning his six-shooter over to the proprietor of the place, he was given his freedom to depart and look up his friends.

As it was after sundown, and our wheel was refilled and ready, we set out for camp, where we found that Priest had taken a fresh horse and started back over the trail. No one felt any uneasiness over his absence, for he had demonstrated his ability to protect himself; and truth compels me to say that the outfit to a man was proud of him. Honeyman was substituted on our guard in The Rebel's place, sleeping with me that night, and after we were in bed, Billy said in his enthusiasm: 'If that horse thief had not relied on pot shooting, and had been modest and only used one gun, he might have hurt some of you fellows. But when I saw old Paul raising his gun to a level as he shot, I knew he was cool and steady, and I'd rather died right there than see him fail to get his man.'

CHAPTER 22

Our Last Campfire

By early dawn the next morning we were astir at our last camp on Sweet Grass, and before the horses were brought in, we had put on the wagon box and reloaded our effects. The rainy season having ended in the mountain regions, the stage of water in the Yellowstone would present no difficulties in fording, and our foreman was anxious to make a long drive that day so as to make up for our enforced lay-over. We had breakfasted by the time the horses were corralled, and when we overtook the grazing herd, the cattle were within a mile of the river. Flood had looked over the ford the day before, and took one point of the herd as we went down into the crossing. The water was quite chilly to the cattle, though the horses in the lead paid little attention to it, the water in no place being over three feet deep. A number of spectators had come up from Frenchman's to watch the herd ford, the crossing being about half a mile above the village. No one made any enquiry for Priest, though ample opportunity was given them to see that the grey-haired man was missing. After the herd had crossed, a number of us lent a rope in assisting the wagon over, and when we reached the farther bank, we waved our hats to the group on the south side in farewell to them and to Frenchman's Ford.

The trail on leaving the river led up Many Berries, one of the tributaries of the Yellowstone putting in from the north side; and we paralleled it mile after mile. It was with difficulty that riders could be kept on the right hand side of the herd, for along it grew endless quantities of a species of upland huckleberry, and, breaking off branches, we feasted as we rode along. The grade up this creek was quite pronounced, for before night the channel of the creek had narrowed to several yards in width. On the second day out the wild fruit disappeared early in the morning, and after a continued gradual climb, we made camp that night on the summit of the divide within plain sight of the Musselshell River. From this divide there was a splendid view of the surrounding country as far as eye could see. To our right, as we neared the summit, we could see in that rarefied atmosphere the buttes, like sentinels on duty, as they dotted the immense tableland between the Yellowstone and the mother Missouri, while on

446

our left lay a thousand hills, untenanted save by the deer, elk and a remnant of buffalo. Another half-day's drive brought us to the shoals on the Musselshell, about twelve miles above the entrance of Flatwillow Creek. It was one of the easiest crossings we had encountered in many a day, considering the size of the river and the flow of water. Long before the advent of the white man, these shoals had been in use for generations by the immense herds of buffalo and elk migrating back and forth between their summer ranges and winter pasturage, as the converging game trails on either side indicated. It was also an old Indian ford. After crossing and resuming our afternoon drive, the cattle trail ran within a mile of the river, and had it not been for the herd of northern wintered cattle, and possibly others, which had passed along a month or more in advance of us, it would have been hard to determine which were cattle and which were game trails, the country being literally cut up with these pathways.

When within a few miles of the Flatwillow, the trail bore off to the northwest, and we camped that night some distance below the junction of the former creek with the Big Box Elder. Before our watch had been on guard twenty minutes that night, we heard someone whistling in the distance; and as whoever it was refused to come any nearer the herd, a thought struck me, and I rode out into the darkness and hailed him.

'Is that you, Tom?' came the question to my challenge, and the next minute I was wringing the hand of my old bunkie, The Rebel. I assured him that the coast was clear, and that no enquiry had been even made for him the following morning, when crossing the Yellowstone, by any of the inhabitants of Frenchman's Ford. He returned with me to the bed ground, and meeting Honeyman as he circled around, was almost unhorsed by the latter's warmth of reception, and Officer's delight on meeting my bunkie was none the less demonstrative. For nearly half an hour he rode around with one or the other of us, and as we knew he had had little if any sleep for the last three nights, all of us begged him to go on into camp and go to sleep. But the old rascal loafed around with us on guard, seemingly delighted with our company and reluctant to leave. Finally Honeyman and I prevailed on him to go to the wagon, but before leaving us he said, 'Why, I've been in sight of the herd for the last day and night, but I'm getting a little tired of lying out with the dry cattle these cool nights, and living on huckleberries and grouse, so I thought I'd just ride in and get a fresh horse and a square meal once more. And if Flood says stay, you'll see me at my old place on the point tomorrow.'

Had the owner of the herd suddenly appeared in camp, he could not have received such an ovation as was extended Priest the next morning when his presence became known. From the cook to the foreman, they gathered around our bed, where The Rebel sat up in the blankets and held an informal reception; and two hours afterwards he was riding on the right point of the herd as if nothing had happened. We had a fair trail up Big Box Elder, and for the following few days, or until the source of that creek was reached, met nothing to check our course. Our foreman had been riding in advance of the herd, and after returning to us at noon one day, reported that the trail turned a due northward course towards the Missouri, and all herds had seemingly taken it. As we had to touch at Fort Benton, which was almost due westward, he had concluded to quit the trail and try to intercept the military road running from Fort Maginnis to Benton. Maginnis lay to the south of us, and our foreman hoped to strike the military road at an angle on as near a westward course as possible.

Accordingly after dinner he set out to look out the country, and took me with him. We bore off towards the Missouri, and within half an hour's ride after leaving the trail we saw some loose horses about three miles distant, down in a little valley through which flowed a creek towards the Musselshell. We reined in and watched the horses several minutes, when we both agreed from their movements that they were hobbled. We scouted out some five or six miles, finding the country somewhat rough, but passable for a herd and wagon. Flood was anxious to investigate those hobbled horses, for it bespoke the camp of someone in the immediate vicinity. On our return, the horses were still in view, and with no little difficulty, we descended from the mesa into the valley and reached them. To our agreeable surprise, one of them was wearing a bell, while nearly half of them were hobbled, there being twelve head, the greater portion of which looked like pack horses. Supposing the camp, if there was one, must be up in the hills, we followed a bridle path upstream in search of it, and soon came upon four men, placer mining on the banks of the creek.

When we made our errand known, one of these placer miners, an elderly man who seemed familiar with the country, expressed some doubts about our leaving the trail, though he said there was a bridle path with which he was acquainted across to the military road. Flood at once offered to pay him well if he would pilot us across to the road, or near enough so that we could find our way. The old placerman hesitated, and after consulting among his partners, asked how we were fixed for provisions, explaining that they wished to remain a month or so longer, and that game had been scared away from the immediate vicinity, until it had become hard to secure meat. But he found Flood ready in that quarter, for he immediately offered to kill a beef and load down any two pack horses they had, if he would consent to pilot us over to within striking distance of the Fort Benton road. The offer was immediately accepted, and I was dispatched to drive in their horses. Two of the placer miners accompanied us back to the trail, both riding good saddle horses and leading two others under pack saddles. We overtook the herd within a mile of the point where the trail was to be abandoned, and after sending the wagon ahead, our foreman asked our guests to pick out any cow or steer in the herd. When they declined, he cut out a fat stray cow which had come into the herd down on the North Platte, had her driven in after the wagon, killed and quartered. When we had laid the quarters on convenient rocks to cool and harden during the night, our future pilot timidly enquired what we proposed to do with the hide, and on being informed that he was welcome to it, seemed delighted, remarking, as I helped him to stake it out where it would dry, that 'rawhide was mighty handy repairing pack saddles'.

Our visitors interested us, for it is probable that not a man in our outfit had ever seen a miner before, though we had read of the life and were deeply interested in everything they did or said. They were very plain men and of simple manners, but we had great difficulty in getting them to talk. After supper, while idling away a couple of hours around our campfire, the outfit told stories, in the hope that our guests would become reminiscent and give us some insight into their experiences, Bob Blades leading off.

'I was in a cow town once up on the head of the Chisholm trail at a time when a church fair was being pulled off. There were lots of old long-horn cowmen living in the town, who owned cattle in that Cherokee Strip that Officer is always talking about. Well, there's lots of folks up there that think a nigger is as good as anybody else, and when you find such people set in their ways, it's best not to argue matters with them, but lay low and let on you think that way too. That's the way those old Texas cowmen acted about it.

'Well, at this church fair there was to be voted a prize of a nice baby wagon, which had been donated by some merchant, to the prettiest baby under a year old. Colonel Bob Zellers was in town at the time, stopping at a hotel where the darky cook was a man who had once worked for him on the trail. "Frog", the darky, had married when he quit the colonel's service, and at the time of this fair there was a pickaninny in his family about a year old, and nearly the colour of a new saddle. A few of these old cowmen got funny and thought it would be a good joke to have Frog enter his baby at the fair, and Colonel Bob being the leader in the movement, he had no trouble convincing the darky that that baby wagon was his, if he would only enter his youngster. Frog thought the world of the old colonel, and the latter assured him that he would vote for his baby while he had a dollar or a cow left. The result was, Frog gave his enthusiastic consent, and the colonel agreed to enter the pickaninny in the contest.

'Well, the colonel attended to the entering of the baby's name, and then on the dead quiet went around and rustled up every cowman and puncher in town, and had them promise to be on hand, to vote for the prettiest baby at ten cents a throw. The fair was being held in the largest hall in town, and at the appointed hour we were all on hand, as well as Frog and his wife and baby. There were about a dozen entries, and only one blackbird in the covey. The list of contestants was read by the minister, and as each name was announced, there was a vigorous clapping of hands all over the house by the friends of each baby. But when the name of Miss Precilla June Jones was announced, the Texas contingent made their presence known by such a deafening outburst of applause that old Frog grinned from ear to ear – he saw himself right then pushing that baby wagon.

'Well, on the first heat we voted sparingly, and as the vote was read out about every quarter hour, Precilla June Jones on the first turn was fourth in the race. On the second report, our favourite had moved up to third place, after which the weaker ones were deserted, and all the voting blood was centred on the two white leaders, with our blackbird a close third. We were behaving ourselves nicely, and our money was welcome if we weren't. When the third vote was announced, Frog's pickaninny was second in the race, with her nose lapped on the flank of the leader. Then those who thought a darky was as good as anyone else got on the prod in a mild form, and you could hear them voicing their opinions all over the hall. We heard it all, but sat as nice as pie and never said a word.

'When the final vote was called for, we knew it was the home stretch, and every rascal of us got his weasel skin out and sweetened the voting on Miss Precilla June Jones. Some of those old long-horns didn't think any more of a twenty-dollar gold piece than I do of a white chip, especially when there was a chance to give those good people a dose of their own medicine. I don't know how many votes we cast on the last whirl, but we swamped all opposition, and our favourite cantered under the wire an easy winner. Then you should have heard the kicking, but we kept still and inwardly chuckled. The minister announced the winner, and some of those good people didn't have any better manners than to hiss and cut up ugly. We stayed until Frog got the new baby wagon in his clutches, when we dropped out casually and met at the Ranch saloon, where Colonel Zellers had taken possession behind the bar and was dispensing hospitality in proper celebration of his victory.'

Much to our disappointment, our guests remained silent and showed no disposition to talk, except to answer civil questions which Flood asked regarding the trail crossing on the Missouri, and what that river was like in the vicinity of old Fort Benton. When the questions had been answered, they again relapsed into silence. The fire was replenished, and after the conversation had touched on several subjects, Joe Stallings took his turn with a yarn.

'When my folks first came to Texas,' said Joe, 'they settled in Ellis County, near Waxahachie. My father was one of the pioneers in that county at a time when his nearest neighbour lived ten miles from his front gate. But after the war, when the country had settled up, these old pioneers naturally hung together and visited and chummed with one another in preference to the new settlers. One spring when I was about fifteen years old, one of those old pioneer neighbours of ours died, and my father decided that he would go to the funeral or burst a hamstring. If any of you know anything about that black-waxy, hog-wallow land in Ellis County, you know that when it gets muddy in the spring a wagon wheel will fill solid with waxy mud. So at the time of this funeral it was impossible to go on the road with any kind of a vehicle, and my father had to go on horseback. He was an old man at the time and didn't like the idea, but it was either go on horseback or stay at home, and go he would.

'They raise good horses in Ellis County, and my father had raised some of the best of them – brought the stock from Tennessee. He liked good blood in a horse, and was always opposed to racing, but he raised some boys who weren't. I had a number of brothers older than myself, and they took a special pride in trying every colt we raised, to see what he amounted to in speed. Of course this had to be done away from home; but that was easy, for these older brothers thought nothing of riding twenty miles to a tournament, barbecue or round-up, and when away from home they always tried their horses with the best in the country. At the time of this funeral, we had a crackerjack five-year-old-chestnut sorrel gelding that could show his heels to any horse in the country. He was a peach – you could turn him on a saddle blanket and jump him fifteen feet, and that cow never lived that he couldn't cut.

'So the day of the funeral my father was in a quandary as to which horse to ride, but when he appealed to his boys, they recommended the best on the ranch, which was the chestnut gelding. My old man had some doubts as to his ability to ride the horse, for he hadn't been on a horse's back for years; but my brothers assured him that the chestnut was as obedient as a kitten, and that before he had been on the road an hour the mud would take all the frisk and frolic out of him. There was nearly fifteen miles to go, and they assured him that he would never get there if he rode any other horse. Well, at last he consented to ride the gelding, and the horse was made ready, properly groomed, his tail tied up, and saddled and led up to the block. It took every member of the family to get my father rigged to start, but at last he announced himself as ready. Two of my brothers held the horse until he found the off stirrup, and then they turned him loose. The chestnut danced off a few rods, and settled down into a steady clip that was good for five or six miles an hour.

'My father reached the house in good time for the funeral service, but when the procession started for the burial ground, the horse was some-what restless and impatient from the cold. There was quite a string of wagons and other vehicles from the immediate neighbourhood which had braved the mud, and the line was nearly half a mile in length between the house and the graveyard. There were also possibly a hundred men on horseback bringing up the rear of the procession; and the chestnut, not understanding the solemnity of the occasion, was right on his mettle. Surrounded as he was by other horses, he kept his weather eye open for a race, for in coming home from dances and picnics with my brothers, he had often been tried in short dashes of half a mile or so. In order to get him out of the crowd of horses, my father dropped back with another pioneer to the extreme rear of the funeral line.

'When the procession was nearing the cemetery, a number of horse-men, who were late, galloped up in the rear. The chestnut, supposing a race was on, took the bit in his teeth and tore down past the procession as though it was a free-for-all Texas sweepstake, the old man's white beard whipping the breeze in his endeavour to hold in the horse. Nor did he check him until the head of the procession had been passed. When my father returned home that night, there was a family round-up, for he was smoking under the collar. Of course, my brothers denied having ever run the horse, and my mother took their part; but the old gent knew a thing or two about horses, and shortly afterwards he got even with his boys by selling the chestnut, which broke their hearts properly.'

The elder of the two placer miners, a long-whiskered, pock-marked man, arose, and after walking out from the fire some distance, returned and called our attention to signs in the sky, which he assured us were a sure indication of a change in the weather. But we were more anxious that he should talk about something else, for we were in the habit of taking the weather just as it came. When neither one showed any disposition to talk, Flood said to them, 'It's bedtime with us, and one of you can sleep with me, while I've fixed up an extra bed for the other. I generally get out about daybreak, but if that's too early for you, don't let my getting up disturb you. And you fourth-guard men, let the cattle off the bed ground on a due westerly course and point them up the divide. Now get to bed, everybody, for we want to make a big drive tomorrow.'

CHAPTER 23

Delivery

I shall never forget the next morning – August 26, 1882. As we of the third guard were relieved, about two hours before dawn, the wind veered around to the northwest, and a mist which had been falling during the fore part of our watch changed to soft flakes of snow. As soon as we were relieved, we skurried back to our blankets, drew the tarpaulin over our heads, and slept until dawn, when on being awakened by the foreman, we found a wet, slushy snow some two inches in depth on the ground. Several of the boys in the outfit declared it was the first snowfall they had ever seen, and I had but a slight recollection of having witnessed one in early boyhood in our old Georgia home. We gathered around the fire like a lot of frozen children, and our only solace was that our drive was nearing an end. The two placermen paid little heed to the raw morning, and our pilot assured us that this was but the squaw winter which always preceded Indian summer.

We made our customary early start, and while saddling up that morning, Flood and the two placer miners packed the beef on their two pack horses, first cutting off enough to last us several days. The cattle, when we overtook them, presented a sorry spectacle, apparently being as cold as we were, although we had our last stitch of clothing on, including our slickers, belted with a horse hobble. But when Flood and our guide rode past the herd, I noticed our pilot's coat was not even buttoned, nor was the thin cotton shirt which he wore, but his chest was exposed to that raw morning air which chilled the very marrow in our bones. Our foreman and guide kept in sight in the lead, the herd travelling briskly up the long mountain divide, and about the middle of the forenoon the sun came out warm and the snow began to melt. Within an hour after starting that morning, Quince Forrest, who was riding in front of me in the swing, dismounted, and picking out of the snow a brave little flower which looked something like a pansy, dropped back to me and said, 'My weather gauge says it's eighty-eight degrees below freezo. But I want you to smell this posy, Quirk, and tell me on the dead thieving, do you ever expect to see your sunny southern home again? And did you notice the pock-marked colonel, baring his brisket to the morning breeze?'

Two hours after the sun came out, the snow had disappeared, and the cattle fell to and grazed until long after the noon hour. Our pilot led us up the divide between the Missouri and the headwaters of the Musselshell during the afternoon, weaving in and out around the heads of creeks putting into either river; and towards evening we crossed quite a creek running towards the Missouri, where we secured ample water for the herd. We made a late camp that night, and our guide assured us that another half-day's drive would put us on the Judith River, where we would intercept the Fort Benton road.

The following morning our guide led us for several hours up a gradual ascent to the plateau, till we reached the tableland, when he left us to return to his own camp. Flood again took the lead, and within a mile we turned on our regular course, which by early noon had descended into the valley of the Judith River, and entered the Fort Maginnis to Fort Benton military road. Our route was now clearly defined, and about noon on the last day of the month we sighted, beyond the Missouri River, the flag floating over Fort Benton. We made a crossing that afternoon below the fort, and Flood went into the post, expecting either to meet Lovell or to receive our final instructions regarding the delivery.

After crossing the Missouri, we grazed the herd over to the Teton River, a stream which paralleled the former watercourse – the military post being located between the two. We had encamped for the night when Flood returned with word of a letter he had received from our employer and an interview he had had with the commanding officer of Fort Benton, who, it seemed, was to have a hand in the delivery of the herd. Lovell had been detained in the final settlement of my brother Bob's herd at the Crow Agency by some differences regarding weights. Under our present instructions, we were to proceed slowly to the Blackfoot Agency, and immediately on the arrival of Lovell at Benton, he and the commandant would follow by ambulance and overtake us. The distance from Fort Benton to the agency was variously reported to be from one hundred and twenty to one hundred and thirty miles, six or seven days' travel for the herd at the farthest, and then goodbye, Circle Dots!

A number of officers and troopers from the post overtook us the next morning and spent several hours with us as the herd trailed out up the Teton. They were riding fine horses, which made our through saddle stock look insignificant in comparison, though had they covered twenty-four hundred miles and lived on grass as had our mounts, some of the lustre of their glossy coats would have been absent. They looked well, but it would have been impossible to use them or any domestic-bred horses in trail work like ours, unless a supply of grain could be carried with us. The range country produced a horse suitable to range needs, hardy and a good forager, which, when not overworked under the saddle, met every requirement of his calling, as well as being self-sustaining. Our horses, in fact, were in better flesh when we crossed the Missouri than they were the day we received the herd on the Rio Grande. The spectators from the fort quitted us near the middle of the forenoon, and we snailed on westward at our leisurely gait.

There was a fair road up the Teton, which we followed for several days without incident, to the forks of that river, where we turned up Muddy Creek, the north fork of the Teton. That noon, while catching saddle horses, dinner not being quite ready, we noticed a flurry among the cattle, then almost a mile in our rear. Two men were on herd with them as usual, grazing them forward up the creek and watering as they came, when suddenly the cattle in the lead came tearing out of the creek, and on reaching open ground turned at bay. After several bunches had seemingly taken fright at the same object, we noticed Bull Durham, who was on herd, ride through the cattle to the scene of disturbance. We saw him, on nearing the spot, lie down on the neck of his horse, watch intently for several minutes, then quietly drop back to the rear, circle the herd, and

455

ride for the wagon. We had been observing the proceedings closely, though from a distance, for some time. Daylight was evidently all that saved us from a stampede, and as Bull Durham galloped up he was almost breathless. He informed us that an old cinnamon bear and two cubs were berrying along the creek, and had taken the right of way. Then there was a hustling and borrowing of cartridges, while saddles were cinched on to horses as though human life depended on alacrity. We were all feeling quite gala anyhow, and this looked like a chance for some sport. It was hard to hold the impulsive ones in check until the others were ready. The cattle pointed us to the location of the quarry as we rode forward. When within a quarter of a mile, we separated into two squads, in order to gain the rear of the bears, cut them off from the creek, and force them into the open. The cattle held the attention of the bears until we had gained their rear, and as we came up between them and the creek, the old one reared up on her haunches and took a most astonished and innocent look at us.

A single 'woof' brought one of the cubs to her side, and she dropped on all fours and lumbered off, a half-dozen shots hastening her pace in an effort to circle the horsemen who were gradually closing in. In making this circle to gain the protection of some thickets which skirted the creek, she was compelled to cross quite an open space, and before she had covered the distance of fifty yards, a rain of ropes came down on her, and she was thrown backward with no less than four lariats fastened over her neck and fore parts. Then ensued a lively scene, for the horses snorted and in spite of rowels refused to face the bear. But ropes securely snubbed to pommels held them to the quarry. Two minor circuses were meantime in progress with the two cubs, but pressure of duty held those of us who had fastened on to the old cinnamon. The ropes were taut and several of them were about her throat; the horses were pulling in as many different directions, yet the strain of all the lariats failed to choke her as we expected. At this juncture, four of the loose men came to our rescue, and proposed shooting the brute. We were willing enough, for though we had better than a tail hold, we were very ready to let go. But while there were plenty of good shots among us, our horses had now become wary, and could not, when free from ropes, be induced to approach within twenty yards of the bear, and they were so fidgety that accurate aim was impossible. We who had ropes on the old bear begged the boys to get down and take it afoot, but they were not disposed to listen to our reasons, and blazed away from rearing horses, not one shot in ten taking effect. There was no telling how long this random shooting would have lasted; but one shot cut my rope two feet from the noose, and with one rope less on her the old bear made some ugly surges, and had not Joe Stallings had a wheeler of a horse on the rope, she would have done somebody damage.

The Rebel was on the opposite side from Stallings and myself, and as soon as I was freed, he called me around to him, and shifting his rope to me, borrowed my six-shooter and joined those who were shooting. Dismounting, he gave the reins of his horse to Flood, walked up to within fifteen steps of mother bruin, and kneeling, emptied both six-shooters with telling accuracy. The old bear winced at nearly every shot, and once she made an ugly surge on the ropes, but the three guy lines held her up to Priest's deliberate aim. The vitality of that cinnamon almost staggers belief, for after both six-shooters had been emptied into her body, she floundered on the ropes with all her former strength, although the blood was dripping and gushing from her numerous wounds. Borrowing a third gun, Priest returned to the fight, and as we slacked the ropes slightly, the old bear reared, facing her antagonist. The Rebel emptied his third gun into her before she sank, choked, bleeding and exhausted, to the ground; and even then no one dared to approach her, for she struck out wildly with all fours as she slowly succumbed to the inevitable.

One of the cubs had been roped and afterwards shot at close quarters, while the other had reached the creek and climbed a sapling which grew on the bank, when a few shots brought him to the ground. The two cubs were about the size of a small black bear, though the mother was a large specimen of her species. The cubs had nice coats of soft fur, and their hides were taken as trophies of the fight, but the robe of the mother was a summer one and worthless. While we were skinning the cubs, the foreman called our attention to the fact that the herd had drifted up the creek nearly opposite the wagon. During the encounter with the bears he was the most excited one in the outfit, and was the man who cut my rope with his random shooting from horseback. But now the herd recovered his attention, and he dispatched some of us to ride around the cattle. When we met at the wagon for dinner, the excitement was still on us, and the hunt was unanimously voted the most exciting bit of sport and powder burning we had experienced on our trip.

Late that afternoon a forage wagon from Fort Benton passed us with four loose ambulance mules in charge of five troopers, who were going on ahead to establish a relay station in anticipation of the trip of the post commandant to the Blackfoot Agency. There were to be two relay stations between the post and the agency, and this detachment expected to go into camp that night within forty miles of our destination, there to await the arrival of the commanding officer and the owner of the herd at Benton. These soldiers were out two days from the post when they passed us, and they assured us that the ambulance would go through from Benton to Blackfoot without a halt, except for the changing of relay teams. The next forenoon we passed the last relay camp, well up the Muddy, and shortly afterwards the road left that creek, turning north by a little west, and we entered on the last tack of our long drive. On the evening of the 6th of September, as we were going into camp on Two Medicine Creek, within ten miles of the agency, the ambulance overtook us, under escort of the troopers whom we had passed at the last relay station. We had not seen Don Lovell since June, when we passed Dodge, and it goes without saying that we were glad to meet him again. On the arrival of the party, the cattle had not yet been bedded, so Lovell borrowed a horse, and with Flood took a look over the herd before darkness set in, having previously prevailed on the commanding officer to rest an hour and have supper before proceeding to the agency.

When they returned from inspecting the cattle, the commandant and Lovell agreed to make the final delivery on the 8th, if it were agreeable to the agent, and with this understanding continued their journey. The next morning Flood rode into the agency, borrowing McCann's saddle and taking an extra horse with him, having left us instructions to graze the herd all day and have them in good shape with grass and water, in case they were inspected that evening on their condition. Near the middle of the afternoon quite a cavalcade rode out from the agency, including part of a company of cavalry temporarily encamped there. The Indian agent and the commanding officer from Benton were the authorised representatives of the government, it seemed, as Lovell took extra pains in showing them over the herd, frequently consulting the contract which he held, regarding sex, age and flesh of the cattle.

The only hitch in the inspection was over a number of sore-footed cattle, which was unavoidable after such a long journey. But the condition of these tender-footed animals being otherwise satisfactory, Lovell urged the agent and commandant to call up the men for explanations. The agent was no doubt a very nice man, and there may have been other things that he understood better than cattle, for he did ask a great many simple, innocent questions. Our replies, however, might have been condensed into a few simple statements. We had, we related, been over five months on the trail; after the first month, tender-footed cattle began to appear from time to time in the herd, as stony or gravelly portions of the trail were encountered – the number so affected at any one time varying from ten to forty head. Frequently well-known lead cattle became tender in their feet and would drop back to the rear, and on striking soft or sandy footing recover and resume their position in the lead; that since starting, it was safe to say, fully ten per cent of the entire herd had been so affected, yet we had not lost a single head from this cause; that the general health of the animal was never affected, and that during enforced layovers nearly all so affected recovered. As there were not over twenty-five sore-footed animals in the herd on our arrival, our explanation was sufficient and the herd was accepted. There yet remained the counting and classification, but as this would require time, it went over until the following day. The cows had been contracted for by the head, while the steers went on their estimated weight in dressed beef, the contract calling for a million pounds with a ten-per-cent leeway over that amount.

I was among the first to be interviewed by the Indian agent, and on being excused, I made the acquaintance of one of two priests who were with the party. He was a rosy-cheeked, well-fed old padre, who informed me that he had been stationed among the Blackfeet for over twenty years, and that he had laboured long with the government to assist these Indians. The cows in our herd, which were to be distributed among the Indian families for domestic purposes, were there at his earnest solicitation. I asked him if these cows would not perish during the long winter – my recollection was still vivid of the touch of squaw winter we had experienced some two weeks previous. But he assured me that the winters were dry, if cold, and his people had made some progress in the ways of civilisation, and had provided shelter and forage against the wintry weather. He informed me that previous to his labours among the Blackfeet their ponies wintered without loss on the native grasses, though he had since taught them to make hay, and in anticipation of receiving these cows, such families as were entitled to share in the division had amply provided for the animals' sustenance.

Lovell returned with the party to the agency, and we were to bring up the herd for classification early in the morning. Flood informed us that a beef pasture had been built that summer for the steers, while the cows would be held under herd by the military, pending their distribution. We spent our last night with the herd singing songs, until the first guard called the relief, when, realising the lateness of the hour, we burrowed into our blankets.

'I don't know how you fellows feel about it,' said Quince Forrest, when the first guard were relieved and they had returned to camp, 'but I bade those cows goodbye on their beds tonight without a regret or a tear. The novelty of night-herding loses its charm with me when it's drawn out over five months. I might be fool enough to make another such trip, but I'd rather be the Indian and let the other fellow drive the cows to me – there's a heap more comfort in it.'

The next morning, before we reached the agency, a number of gaudily bedecked bucks and squaws rode out to meet us. The arrival of the herd had been expected for several weeks, and our approach was a delight to the Indians, who were flocking to the agency from the nearest villages. Physically, they were fine specimens of the aborigines. But our Spanish, which Quarternight and I tried on them, was as unintelligible to them as their guttural gibberish was to us.

Lovell and the agent, with a detachment of the cavalry, met us about a mile from the agency buildings, and we were ordered to cut out the cows. The herd had been grazed to contentment, and were accordingly rounded in, and the task begun at once. Our entire outfit were turned into the herd to do the work, while an abundance of troopers held the herd and looked after the cut. It took about an hour and a half, during which time we worked like Trojans. Cavalrymen several times attempted to assist us, but their horses were no match for ours in the work. A cow can turn on much less space than a cavalry horse, and except for the amusement they afforded, the military were of very little effect.

After we had retrimmed the cut, the beeves were started for their pasture, and nothing now remained but the counting to complete the receiving. Four of us remained behind with the cows, but for over two hours the steers were in plain sight, while the two parties were endeavouring to make a count. How many times they recounted them before agreeing on the numbers I do not know, for the four of us left with the cows became occupied by a controversy over the gender of a young Indian – a Blackfoot – riding a cream-coloured pony. The controversy originated between Fox Quarternight and Bob Blades, who had discovered this swell among a band who had just ridden in from the west, and John Officer and myself were appealed to for our opinions. The Indian was pointed out to us across the herd, easily distinguished by beads and beaver fur trimmings in the hair, so we rode around to pass our judgement as experts on the beauty. The young Indian was not over sixteen years of age, with remarkable features, from which every trace of the aborigine seemed to be eliminated. Officer and myself were in a quandary, for we felt perfectly competent when appealed to for our opinions on such a delicate subject, and we made every endeavour to open a conversation by signs and speech. But the young Blackfoot paid no attention to us, being intent upon watching the cows. The neatly moccasined feet and the shapely hand, however, indicated the feminine, and when Blades and Quarternight rode up, we rendered our decision accordingly. Blades took exception to the decision and rode alongside the young Indian, pretending to admire the long plaits of hair, toyed with the beads, pinched and patted the young Blackfoot, and finally, although the rest of us, for fear the Indian might take offence and raise trouble, pleaded with him to desist, he called the youth his 'squaw', when the young blood, evidently understanding the appellation, relaxed into a broad smile, and in fair English said, 'Me buck.'

Blades burst into a loud laugh at his success, at which the Indian smiled but accepted a cigarette, and the two cronied together, while we rode away to look after our cows. The outfit returned shortly afterward, when The Rebel rode up to me and expressed himself rather profanely at the inability of the government's representatives to count cattle in Texas fashion. On the arrival of the agent and others, the cows were brought around; and these being much more gentle, and being under Lovell's instruction fed between the counters in the narrowest file possible, a satisfactory count was agreed upon at the first trial. The troopers took charge of the cows after counting, and, our work over, we galloped away to the wagon, hilarious and care free.

McCann had camped on the nearest water to the agency, and after dinner we caught out the top horses, and, dressed in our best, rode into the agency proper. There was quite a group of houses for the attachés, one large general warehouse, and several school and chapel buildings. I again met the old padre, who showed us over the place. One could not help being favourably impressed with the general neatness and cleanliness of the place. In answer to our questions, the priest informed us that he had mastered the Indian language early in his work, and had adopted it in his ministry, the better to effect the object of his mission. There was something touching in the zeal of this devoted padre in his work among the tribe, and the recognition of the government had come as a fitting climax to his work and devotion.

As we rode away from the agency, the cows being in sight under herd of a dozen soldiers, several of us rode out to them, and learned that they intended to corral the cows at night, and within a week distribute them to Indian families, when the troop expected to return to Fort Benton. Lovell and Flood appeared at the camp about dusk – Lovell in high spirits. This, he said, was the easiest delivery of the three herds which he had driven that year. He was justified in feeling well over the year's drive, for he had in his possession a voucher for our Circle Dots which would crowd six figures closely. It was a gay night with us, for man and horse were free, and as we made down our beds, old man Don insisted that Flood and he should make theirs down alongside ours. He and The Rebel had been joking each other during the evening, and as we went to bed were taking an occasional fling at one another as opportunity offered.

'It's a strange thing to me,' said Lovell, as he was pulling off his boots, 'that this herd counted out a hundred and twelve head more than we started with, while Bob Quirk's herd was only eighty-one long at the final count.'

'Well, you see,' replied The Rebel, 'Quirk's was a steer herd, while ours had over a thousand cows in it, and you must make allowance for some of them to calve on the way. That ought to be easy figuring for a foxy, long-headed Yank like you.'

CHAPTER 24

Back to Texas

The nearest railroad point from the Blackfoot Agency was Silver Bow, about a hundred and seventy-five miles due south, and at that time the terminal of the Utah Northern Railroad. Everything connected with the delivery having been completed the previous day, our camp was astir with the dawn in preparation for departure on our last ride together. As we expected to make not less than forty miles a day on the way to the railroad, our wagon was lightened to the least possible weight. The chuck-box, water kegs, and such superfluities were dropped, and the supplies reduced to one week's allowance, while beds were overhauled and extra wearing apparel of the outfit was discarded. Who cared if we did sleep cold and hadn't a change to our backs? We were going home and would have money in our pockets.

'The first thing I do when we strike that town of Silver Bow,' said Bull Durham, as he was putting on his last shirt, 'is to discard to the skin and get me new togs to a finish. I'll commence on my little pattering feet, which will require fifteen-dollar moccasins, and then about a six-dollar checked cottonade suit, and top off with a seven-dollar brown Stetson. Then with a few drinks under my belt and a rim-fire cigar in my mouth, I'd admire to meet the governor of Montana if convenient.'

Before the sun was an hour high, we bade farewell to the Blackfoot Agency and were doubling back over the trail, with Lovell in our company. Our first night's camp was on the Muddy and the second on the Sun River. We were sweeping across the tablelands adjoining the main divide of the Rocky Mountains like the chinook winds which sweep that majestic range on its western slope. We were a free outfit; even the cook and wrangler were relieved; their little duties were divided among the crowd and almost disappeared. There was a keen rivalry over driving the wagon, and McCann was transferred to the hurricane deck of a cow horse, which he sat with ease and grace, having served an apprenticeship in the saddle in other days. There were always half a dozen wranglers available in the morning, and we travelled as if under forced marching orders. The third night we camped in the narrows between the Missouri River and the Rocky Mountains, and on the evening of the fourth day camped several miles to the eastward of Helena, the capital of the territory.

Don Lovell had taken the stage for the capital the night before; and on making camp that evening, Flood took a fresh horse and rode into town. The next morning he and Lovell returned with the super-intendent of the cattle company which had contracted for our horses and outfit on the Republican. We corralled the horses for him, and, after roping out about a dozen which, as having sore backs or being lame, he proposed to treat as damaged and take at half price, the *remuda* was counted out, a hundred and forty saddle horses, four mules and a wagon constituting the transfer. Even with the loss of two horses and the concessions on a dozen others, there was a nice profit on the entire outfit over its cost in the lower country, due to the foresight of Don Lovell in mounting us well. Two of our fellows who had borrowed from the superintendent money to redeem their six-shooters after the horse race on the Republican, authorised Lovell to return him the loans and thanked him for the favour. Everything being satisfactory between buyer and seller, they returned to town together for a settlement, while we moved on south towards Silver Bow, where the outfit was to be delivered.

Another day's easy travel brought us to within a mile of the railroad terminus; but it also brought us to one of the hardest experiences of our trip, for each of us knew, as we unsaddled our horses, that we were doing it for the last time. Although we were in the best of spirits over the successful conclusion of the drive; although we were glad to be free from herd duty and looked forward eagerly to the journey home, there was still a feeling of regret in our hearts which we could not dispel. In the days of my boyhood I have shed tears when a favourite horse was sold from our little ranch on the San Antonio, and have frequently witnessed Mexican children unable to hide their grief when need of bread had compelled the sale of some favourite horse to a passing drover. But at no time in my life, before or since, have I felt so keenly the parting between man and horse as I did that September evening in Montana. For on the trail an affection springs up between a man and his mount which is almost human. Every privation which he endures his horse endures with him – carrying him through falling weather, swimming rivers by day and riding in the lead of stampedes by night, always faithful, always willing and always patiently enduring every hardship, from exhausting hours under saddle to the sufferings of a dry drive. And on this drive, covering nearly three thousand miles, all the ties which can exist between man and beast had not only become cemented, but our *remuda* as a whole had won the affection of both men and employer for carrying without serious mishap a valuable herd all the way from the Rio Grande to the Blackfoot Agency. Their bones may be bleaching in some coulee by now, but the men who knew them then can never forget them or the part they played in that long drive.

Three men from the ranch rode into our camp that evening, and the next morning we counted over our horses to them and they passed into strangers' hands. That there might be no delay, Flood had ridden into town the evening before and secured a wagon and gunny bags in which to sack our saddles; for while we willingly discarded all other effects, our saddles were of sufficient value to return and could be checked home as baggage. Our foreman reported that Lovell had arrived by stage and was awaiting us in town, having already arranged for our transportation as far as Omaha, and would accompany us to that city, where other transportation would have to be secured to our destination. In our impatience to get into town, we were trudging in by twos and threes before the wagon arrived for our saddles, and had not Flood remained behind to look after them, they might have been abandoned.

There was something about Silver Bow that reminded me of Frenchman's Ford on the Yellowstone. Being the terminal of the first railroad into Montana, it became the distributing point for all the western portion of that territory, and immense ox trains were in sight for the transportation of goods to remoter points in the north and west. The population too was very much the same as at Frenchman's, though the town in general was an improvement over the former, there being some stability to its buildings. As we were to leave on an eleven o'clock train, we had little opportunity to see the town, and for the short time at our disposal, barber shops and clothing stores claimed our first attention. Most of us had some remnants of money, while my bunkie was positively rich, and Lovell advanced us fifty dollars apiece, pending a final settlement on reaching our destination.

Within an hour after receiving the money, we blossomed out in new suits from head to heel. Our guard hung together as if we were still on night herd, and in the selection of clothing the opinion of the trio was equal to a purchase. The Rebel was very easily pleased in his selection, but John Officer and myself were rather fastidious. Officer was so tall it was with some little difficulty that a suit could be found to fit him, and when he had stuffed his pants in his boots and thrown away the vest, for he never wore either vest or suspenders, he emerged looking like an Alpine tourist, with his new pink shirt and nappy brown beaver slouch hat jauntily cocked over one ear. As we sauntered out into the street, Priest was dressed as became his years and mature good sense, while my costume rivalled Officer's in gaudiness, and it is safe to assert two thirds of our outlay had gone on boots and hats.

Flood overtook us in the street, and warned us to be on hand at the depot at least half an hour in advance of train time, informing us that he had checked our saddles and didn't want any of us to get left at the final moment. We all took a drink together, and Officer assured our foreman that he would be responsible for our appearance at the proper time, 'sober and sorry for it'. So we sauntered about the straggling village, drinking occasionally, and on the suggestion of The Rebel, made a cow by putting in five apiece and had Officer play it on faro, he claiming to be an expert on the game. Taking the purse thus made up, John sat into a game, while Priest and myself, after watching the play some minutes, strolled out again and met others of our outfit in the street, scarcely recognisable in their killing rigs. The Rebel was itching for a monte game, but this not being a cow town there was none, and we strolled next into a saloon, where a piano was being played by a venerable-looking individual – who proved quite amiable, taking a drink with us and favouring us with a number of selections of our choosing. We were enjoying this musical treat when our foreman came in and asked us to get the boys together. Priest and I at once started for Officer, whom we found quite a winner, but succeeded in choking him off on our employer's order, and after the checks had been cashed, took a parting drink, which made us the last in reaching the depot. When we were all assembled, our employer informed us that he only wished to keep us together until embarking, and invited us to accompany him across the street to Tom Robbins's saloon.

On entering the saloon, Lovell enquired of the young fellow behind the bar, 'Son, what will you take for the privilege of my entertaining this outfit for fifteen minutes?'

'The ranch is yours, sir, and you can name your own figures,' smilingly and somewhat shrewdly replied the young fellow, and promptly vacated his position.

'Now, two or three of you rascals get in behind there,' said old man Don, as a quartet of the boys picked him up and set him on one end of the bar, 'and let's see what this ranch has in the way of refreshment.'

McCann, Quarternight and myself obeyed the order, but the fastidious tastes of the line in front soon compelled us to call to our assistance both Robbins and the young man who had just vacated the bar in our favour.

'That's right, fellows,' roared Lovell from his commanding position, as he jingled a handful of gold coins, 'turn to and help wait on these thirsty Texans; and remember that nothing's too rich for our blood today. This outfit has made one of the longest cattle drives on record, and the best is none too good for them. So set out your best, for they can't cut much hole in the profits in the short time we have to stay. The train leaves in twenty minutes, and see that every rascal is provided with an extra bottle for the journey. And drop down this way when you get time, as I want a couple of boxes of your best cigars to smoke on the way. Montana has treated us well, and we want to leave some of our coin with you.'

SHOE-BAR STRATTON

JOSEPH BUSHNELL AMES

Contents

CHAPTER I

Back from the Dead

WESTWARD the little three-car train chugged its way fussily across the brown prairie towards distant mountains which, in that clear atmosphere, loomed so deceptively near. Standing motionless beside the weather-beaten station shed, the solitary passenger watched it absently, brows drawn into a single dark line above the bridge of his straight nose. Tall, lean, with legs spread apart a bit and shoulders slightly bent, he made a striking figure against that background of brilliant sky and drenching, golden sunlight. For a brief space he did not stir. Then of a sudden, when the train had dwindled to the size of a child's toy, he turned abruptly and drew a long, deep breath.

It was a curious transformation. A moment before his face – lined, brooding, sombre, oddly pale for that country of universal tan – looked almost old. At least one would have felt it the face of a man who had recently endured a great deal of mental or physical suffering. Now, as he turned with an unconscious straightening of broad shoulders and a characteristic uptilt of square, cleft chin, the lines smoothed away miraculously, a touch of red crept into his lean cheeks, an eager, boyish gleam of expectation flashed into the clear grey eyes that rested caressingly on the humdrum, sleepy picture before him.

Humdrum it was, in all conscience. A single street, wide enough, almost, for a plaza, paralleled the railroad tracks, the buildings, such as they were, all strung along the further side in an irregular line. One of these, ramshackle, weather-worn, labelled laconically 'The Store', stood directly opposite the station. The architecture of the 'Paloma Springs Hotel', next door, was very similar. On either side of these two structures a dozen or more discouraged-looking adobe houses were set down at uneven intervals. To the eastward the street ended in the corrals and shipping-pens; in the other direction it merged into a narrow dusty trail that curved northward from the twin steel rails and quickly lost itself in the encompassing prairie.

That was all. Paloma Springs in its entirety lay there in full view, drowsing in the torrid heat of mid-September. Not a human being was in sight. Only a brindled dog slept in a small patch of shade beside the store; and fastened to the hotel hitching-rack, two burros, motionless save for twitching tails and ears, were almost hidden beneath stupendous loads of firewood.

But to Buck Stratton the charm lay deeper than mere externals. As a matter of fact he had seen Paloma Springs only twice in his life, and then very briefly. But it was a typical little cow-town of the Southwest, and to the homesick cattleman the sight of it was like a refreshing draught of water in the desert. Pushing back his hat, Stratton drew another full breath, the beginnings of a smile curving the corners of his mouth.

'It sure is good to get back,' he murmured, picking up his bag. 'Someway the very air tastes different. Gosh almighty. It don't seem like two years, though.'

Abruptly the light went out of his eyes and his face clouded. No wonder the time seemed short when one of those years had vanished from his life as utterly and completely as if it had never been. Whenever Stratton thought of it, which was no oftener than he could help, he cringed mentally. There was something uncanny and even horrible in the realisation that for the better part of a twelve-month he had been eating, sleeping, walking about, making friends, even, like any normal person, without retaining a single atom of recollection of the entire period.

Frowning, Buck put up one hand and absently touched a freshly healed scar half-hidden by his thick hair. Even now there were moments when he felt the whole thing must be some wild nightmare. Vividly he remembered the sudden winking out of consciousness in the midst of that panting, uphill dash through Belleau Wood. He could recall perfectly the most trifling event leading up to it – the breaking down of his motorcycle in a strange sector just before the charge, his sudden determination to take part in it by hook or crook, even the thrill and tingle of that advance against heavy machine-gun fire.

The details of his awakening were equally clear. It was like closing his eyes one minute and opening them the next. He lay on a hospital bed, his head swathed in bandages. That seemed all right. He had been wounded in the charge against the Boche, and they had carried him to a field-hospital. He was darned lucky to have come out of it alive.

But little by little the conviction was forced upon him that it wasn't as simple as that. At length, when he was well on the way to recovery, he learned to his horror that the interval of mental blankness, instead of being a few hours, or at the most a day or two, had lasted for over a year!

Without fully understanding certain technical portions of the doctor's explanation, Stratton gathered that the bullet which had laid him low had produced a bone-pressure on the portion of his brain which was the seat of memory. The wound healing, he had recovered perfect physical health, but with a mind blank of anything previous to his awakening in the French hospital over a year ago. The recent operation, which was pronounced entirely successful, had been performed to relieve that pressure, and Stratton was informed that all he needed was a few weeks of convalescence to make him as good a man as he had ever been.

It took Buck all of that time to adjust himself to the situation. He was in America instead of France, without the slightest recollection of getting there. The war was over long ago. A thousand things had happened of which he had not the remotest knowledge. And because he was a very normal, ordinary young man with a horror of anything queer and eccentric, the thought of that mysterious year filled him with dismay and roused in him a passionate longing to escape at once from everything which would remind him of his uncanny lapse of memory. If he were only back where he belonged in the land of wide spaces, of clean, crisp air and blue, blue sky, he felt he would quickly forget this nightmare which haunted so many waking moments.

Unfortunately there were complications. To begin with he found himself in the extraordinary position of a man without identity. The record sent over from the hospital in France stated that he had been brought in from the field minus his tag and every other mark of identification. Buck was not surprised at this, nor at the failure of anyone in the strange sector to recognise him. Only a few hours before the battle the tape of his identification-disc had parted and he had thrust the thing carelessly into his pocket. He had seen too many wounded men brought into field-hospitals not to realise how easy it is to lose a blouse.

Recovering from the bullet-wound and unable to tell anything about himself, he had apparently passed under the name of Robert Green. Stratton wondered with a touch of grim amusement whether this christening was not the result of doughboy humour. He must have been green enough, in all conscience.

He was not even grimly amused by the ultimate discovery that the name of Roth Stratton had appeared months and months ago on one of the official lists of 'killed or missing'. It increased his discomfort over the whole hateful business and made him thankful for the first time that he was alone in the world. At least no mother or sister had been tortured by this strange prank of fate.

But at last the miles of red tape had been untied or cut, and the moment his discharge came Stratton took the first possible train out of New York. He did not even wire Bloss, his ranch-foreman, that he was coming. As a matter of fact he felt that doing so would only further complicate an already sufficiently difficult situation.

The Shoe-Bar outfit, in western Arizona, had been his property barely a week before he left it for the recruiting-office. Born and bred in the Texas Panhandle, he inherited his father's ranch when barely twenty-one. Even then many of the big outfits were being cut up into farms, public range-land had virtually ceased to exist, and one by one the cattlemen were driven westward before the slowly encroaching wave of civilisation.

Two years later Stratton decided to give up the fight and follow them. During the winter before the war he sold out for a handsome figure, spent several months looking over new ground, and finally located and bought the Shoe-Bar outfit.

The deal was hurried through because of his determination to enlist. Indeed, he would probably not have purchased at all had not the new outfit, even to his hasty inspection, seemed to be so unusual a bargain and so exactly what he wanted. But buy he did, placed Joe Bloss, a reliable and experienced cattleman who had been with him for years, in charge, and departed.

From that moment he had never once set eyes on the Shoe-Bar. Bloss wrote frequent and painstaking reports which seemed to indicate that everything was going well. But all through the long and tedious journey ending at the little Arizona way-station, Stratton fumed and fretted and wondered. Even if Joe had failed to see his name amongst the missing, what must he have thought of his interminable silence? All through Buck's brief training and the longer interval overseas, the foreman's letters had come with fair regularity and been answered promptly and in detail. What had Bloss done when the break came? What had he been doing ever since?

A fresh wave of troubled curiosity sent Stratton swinging briskly across the street. Keeping inside the long hitching-rack, he crossed the sagging porch and stepped through the open door into the store. For a moment he thought it empty. Then a chair scraped, and over in one corner a short, stout, grizzled man dropped his feet from the window-sill and shuffled forward, yawning.

'Wal! Wal!' he mumbled, his faded, sleep-dazed eyes taking in Buck's bag. 'Train come in? Reckon I must of been dozin' a mite.'

'Looks to me like the whole place was taking an afternoon nap,' smiled Stratton. 'Not much doing this time of day, I expect.'

'You said it,' yawned the stout man, supporting himself against the rough pine counter. 'Things is liable to brisk up in a hour or two, though, when the boys begin to drift in. Stranger around these parts, ain't yuh?' he added curiously.

For a tiny space Buck hesitated. Then, moved by an involuntary impulse he did not even pause to analyse, he shrugged his shoulders slightly.

'I was out at the Shoe-Bar a couple of times about two years ago,' he answered. 'Haven't been around here since.'

'The Shoe-Bar? Huh?' Pop Daggett looked interested. 'You don't say so! Funny I don't recollect yore face.'

'Not so very. I only passed through here to take the train.'

'That was it, eh? Two years ago must of been about the time the outfit was bought by that Stratton feller from Texas. Yuh know him well?'

'Joe Bloss, the foreman, was a friend of mine,' evaded Stratton. 'He's the one I stopped off now to see.'

Pop Daggett's jaw sagged, betraying a cavernous expanse of sparsely toothed gums. 'Joe Bloss!' he ejaculated. 'My land! I hope you ain't travelled far fur that. If so, yuh sure got yore trouble for yore pains. Why, man alive! Joe Bloss ain't been nigh the Shoe-Bar for close on to a year.'

Stratton's eyes narrowed. 'A year?' he repeated curtly. 'Where's he gone?'

'You got me. I did hear he'd signed up with the Flying-Vs over to New Mexico, but that might have been jest talk.' He sniffed disapprovingly. 'There ain't no doubt about it; the old Shoe-Bar's changed powerful these two years. I dunno what we're comin' to with wimmin buttin' into the cattle business.'

Buck stared at him in frank amazement. 'Women?' he repeated. 'What the dickens are you talking about, anyway?'

'I sh'd think I was plain enough,' retorted Pop Daggett with some asperity. 'Mebbe female ranchers ain't no novelty to yuh, but this is the first time I ever run up ag'in one m'self, an' I ain't much in love with the idear.'

Stratton's teeth dug into his under lip, and one hand gripped the edge of the counter with a force that brought out a row of white dots across the knuckles.

'You mean to tell me there's a – a – woman at the Shoe-Bar?' he asked incredulously.

'At it?' snorted the old man. 'Why, by cripes, she *owns* it! Not only that, but folks say she's goin' to run the outfit herself like as if she was a man.' He paused to spit accurately and with volume into the empty stove. 'Her name's Thorne,' he added curtly. 'Mary Thorne.'

CHAPTER 2

Crooked Work

Stratton suddenly turned his back and stared blankly through the open door. With the same unconscious instinct which had moved him to conceal his face from the old man, he fumbled in one pocket and drew forth papers and tobacco sack. It spoke well for his self-control that his fingers were almost steady as he deliberately fashioned a cigarette and thrust it between his lips. When he had lighted it and inhaled a puff or two, he turned slowly to Pop Daggett again.

'You sure know how to shoot a surprise into a fellow, old-timer,' he drawled. 'A woman rancher, eh? That's going some around this country, I'll say. How long has she – er – owned the Shoe-Bar?'

'Only since her pa died about four months back.' Pop Daggett assumed an easier pose; his tone had softened to one of garrulous satisfaction at having a new listener to a tale he had worn threadbare. 'It's consid'able of a story, but if yuh ain't pressed for time – '

'Go to it,' invited Buck, leaning back against the counter. 'I've got all the time there is.'

Daggett's small, faded blue eyes regarded him curiously.

'Did yuh ever meet up with this here Stratton?' he asked abruptly.

'I – a – know what he looks like.'

'It's more'n I do,' grumbled Pop regretfully. 'The only two times he was here I was laid up with a mean attack of rheumatis, an' never sot eyes on him. Still an' all, there ain't hardly anybody else around Paloma that more 'n glimpsed him passin' through. He bought the outfit in a terrible hurry, an' I thinks to m'self at the time he must be awful trustin', or else a mighty right smart jedge uh land an' cattle. He couldn't of hardly rid over it even once real thorough before he plunks down his money, gets him a proper title, an' hikes off to the war, leavin' Joe Bloss in charge.'

He paused, fished in his pocket, and, producing a plug, carefully bit off one corner. Stratton watched him impatiently, a faint flush staining his clear, curiously white skin.

'Well?' he prodded presently. 'What happened then? From what I know of Joe, I'll say he made good all right.'

'Sure he did.' Pop spoke with emphasis, though somewhat thickly. 'There ain't nobody can tell Joe Bloss much about cattle. He whirled in right capable and got things runnin' good. For a while he was so danged busy he'd hardly ever get to town, but come winter the work eased up an' I used to see him right frequent. He'd set there alongside the stove evenings an' tell me what he was doin', or how he'd jest had a letter from Stratton, who was by now in France, an' all the rest of it. Wal, to make a long story short, a year last month the letters stopped comin'. Joe begun to get worried, but I told him likely Stratton was too busy fightin' to write, or he might even of got wounded. Yuh could have knocked me down with a wisp uh bunch-grass when one uh the boys come in one night with a Phoenix paper, an' showed me Stratton's name on a list uh killed or missin'!'

'When was that?' asked Buck briefly, seeing that Daggett evidently expected some comment. If only the man would get on!

' 'Round the middle of September. Joe was jest naturally shot to pieces, him knowin' young Stratton from a kid an' likin' him fine, besides bein' consid'able worried about what was goin' to happen to the ranch an' him. Still an' all, there wasn't nothin' he could do but go on holdin' down his job, which he done until the big bust along the end of October.'

He paused again expectantly. Buck ground the butt of his cigarette under one heel and reached for the makings. He had an almost irresistible desire to take the garrulous old man by the shoulders and shake him till his teeth rattled.

'It was this here Thorne from Chicago,' resumed Daggett, a trifle disappointed. Usually at this point of the story, his listener broke in with exclamation or interested question. 'He showed up one morning with the sheriff an' claimed the ranch was his. Said Stratton had sold it to him an' produced the deed, signed, sealed, an' witnessed all right an' proper.'

Match in one hand and cigarette in the other, Buck stared at him, the picture of arrested motion. For a moment or two his brain whirled. Could he possibly have done such a thing and not remember? With a ghastly sinking of his heart he realised that anything might have been possible during that hateful vanished year. Mechanically he lit his cigarette and of a sudden he grew calmer. According to the hospital records he had not left France until well into November of the preceding year. Tossing the match into the stove, he met Pop Daggett's glance.

'How could that be?' he asked briefly. 'Didn't you say this Stratton was in France for months before he was killed?'

Pop nodded hearty agreement. 'That's jest what I said, an' so did Bloss. But according to Thorne this here transfer was made a couple uh weeks before Stratton went over to France.'

'But that's impossible!' exclaimed Buck hotly. 'How could he have – '

He ceased abruptly and bit his lip. Daggett chuckled.

'Gettin' kinda interested, ain't yuh?' he remarked in a satisfied tone. 'I thought you would 'fore I was done. I don't say as it's impossible, but it shore looked queer to me. As Joe says, why would he go an' sell the outfit jest after buyin' it without a word to him. Not only that but he kept on writin' about how Joe was to do this an' that an' the other thing like he was mighty interested in havin' it run good. Joe, he even got suspicions uh somethin' crooked an' hired a lawyer to look into it, Stratton not havin' any folks. But that's all the good it done him. He couldn't pick no flaw in it at all. Seems Stratton was in Chicago on one of these here furloughs jest before he took ship. One uh the witnesses had gone to war, but they hunted out the other one an' he swore he'd seen the deed signed.'

'Did this Thorne – What did you say his name was?'

'I don't recolleck sayin', but it was Andrew J.'

Buck's lids narrowed; a curious gleam flashed for an instant in his grey eyes and was gone.

'Well, did Thorne explain why he let it go so long before making his claim?'

'Oh, shore! He was right there when it come to explainin'. Seems he had some important war business on his hands an' wanted to get shed uh that before he took up ranchin'. Knowed it was in good hands, 'count uh Bloss bein' on the job, an' Stratton havin' promised to write frequent an' keep Joe toein' the mark. Stratton, it seems, had sold out because he didn't know what might happen to him across the water. Oh, Andrew J. was a right smooth talker, believe me, but still an' all he didn't make no great hit with folks around the country even after he settled down on the Shoe-Bar and brung his daughter there to live. There weren't no tears shed, neither, when an ornery paint horse throwed him last May an' broke his neck.'

'What about Bloss?' Stratton asked briefly.

'Oh, he got his time along with all the other cowmen. There shore was a clean sweep when Thorne whirled in an' took hold. Joe hung around here a week or two an' then drifted down to Phoenix. Last I heard he was goin' to try the Flyin'-V, but that was six months or more ago.'

Buck's shoulders straightened and his chin went up with a sudden touch of swift decision.

'Got a horse I can hire?' he asked abruptly.

Pop hesitated, his shrewd gaze travelling swiftly over Stratton's straight, tall figure to rest reflectively on the lean, square-jawed, level-eyed young face.

'I dunno but I have,' he answered slowly. 'Uh course I don't know yore name even, an' a man's got to be careful how he – '

'Oh, that'll be all right,' interrupted Stratton, his white teeth showing briefly in a smile. 'I'll leave you a deposit. My name's Bob Green, though folks mostly call me Buck. I've got a notion to ride over to the Shoe-Bar and see if they know anything about – Joe.'

' 'T ain't likely they will,' shrugged Daggett. 'Still, it won't do no harm to try. Yuh can't ride in them things, though,' he added, surveying Stratton's well-cut suit of grey.

'I don't specially want to, but they're all I've got,' smiled Buck. 'When I quit ranching to show 'em how to run the war, I left my outfit behind, and I haven't been back yet to get it.'

'Cowman eh?' Pop nodded approvingly. 'I thought so; yuh got the look, someway. Wal, yore welcome to some duds I bought off 'n Dick Sanders about a month ago. He quit the Rockin'-R to go railroadin' or somethin', an' sold his outfit, saddle an' all. I reckon they'll suit.'

Stepping behind the counter, he poked around amongst a mass of miscellaneous merchandise and finally drew forth a pair of much-worn leather chaps, high-heeled boots almost new, and a cartridge-belt from which dangled an empty holster.

'There yuh are,' he said triumphantly, spreading them out on the counter. 'Gun's the only thing missin'. He kep' that, but likely yuh got one of yore own. Saddle's hangin' out in the stable.'

Without delay Stratton took off his coat and vest and sat down on an empty box to try the boots, which proved a trifle large but still wearable. He already had on a dark flannel shirt and a new Stetson, which he had bought in New York; and when he pulled on the chaps and buckled the cartridge-belt around his slim waist Pop Daggett surveyed him with distinct approval.

'All yuh need is a good coat uh tan to look like the genuine article,' he remarked. 'How come yuh to be so white?'

'Haven't been out of the hospital long enough to get browned up.' Buck opened his bag and, fumbling for a moment, produced a forty-five army automatic. 'This don't go very well with the outfit,' he shrugged. 'Happen to have a regular six-gun around the place you'll sell me?'

Pop had, this being part of his stock in trade. Buck looked the lot over carefully, finally picking out a thirty-eight Colt with a good heft. When he had paid for this and a supply of ammunition, Pop led the way out to a shed back of the store and pointed out a Fraser saddle, worn but in excellent condition, hanging from a hook.

'It's a wonder to me any cowman is ever fool enough to sell his saddle,' commented Stratton as he took it down. 'They never get much for 'em, and new ones are so darn ornery to break in.'

'Yuh said it,' agreed Daggett. 'I'd ruther buy one second-hand than new any day. There's the bridle. Yuh take that roan in the near stall. He ain't much to look at, but he'll travel all day.'

Fifteen minutes later the roan, saddled and bridled, pawed the dust beside the hitching rack in front of the store, while Buck Stratton made a small bundle of his coat, vest, and a few necessaries from his bag and fastened it behind the saddle. The remainder of his belongings had been left with Pop Daggett, who lounged in the doorway fingering a roll of bills in his trousers pocket and watching his new acquaintance with smiling amiability.

'Well, I'll be going,' said Stratton, tying the last knot securely. 'I'll bring your cayuse back tomorrow or the day after at the latest.'

Pop looked surprised. 'The day after?' he repeated. 'What's goin' to keep yuh that long?'

'Will you be needing the horse sooner?'

'No, I dunno's I will. But seems like yuh ought to be back by noon tomorrow. It ain't more 'n eighteen miles.' He straightened abruptly and his blue eyes widened. 'Say, young feller! Yuh ain't thinkin' of gettin a job out there, are yuh?'

Stratton hesitated for an instant. 'Well, I don't know,' he shrugged presently. 'I've got to get to work right soon at something.'

Daggett took a swift step or two across the sagging porch, his face grown oddly serious. 'Wal, I wouldn't try the Shoe-Bar, nohow. There's the Rockin'-R. They're short a man or two. Yuh go see Jim Tenny an' tell him – '

'What's the matter with the Shoe-Bar?' persisted Buck.

Pop's glance avoided Stratton's. 'Yuh – wouldn't like it,' he mumbled, glancing down the trail. 'It – it ain't like it was in Joe's time. That there Tex Lynch – he – he don't get on with the boys.'

'Who's he? The foreman?'

'Yeah. Beauty Lynch, some calls him 'count uh his looks. I ain't denyin' he's han'some, with them black eyes an' red cheeks uh his, but somethin' queer – Like I said, there ain't nobody stays long at the Shoe-Bar. Yuh take my advice, Buck, an' try the Rockin'-R. They's a nice bunch there.'

Buck swung himself easily into the saddle; 'I'll think about it,' he smiled, gathering up the reins. 'Well, so-long; see you in a day or so, anyway. Thanks for helping me out, old-timer.'

He loosened the reins, and the roan took the trail at a canter. Well beyond the last adobe house, Stratton glanced back to see old Pop Daggett still standing on the store porch and staring after him. Buck flung up one arm in a careless gesture of farewell; then a gentle downward slope in the prairie carried him out of sight of the little settlement.

'Acts to me like he was holding back something,' he thought as he rode briskly on through the wide, rolling solitudes. 'Now, I wonder what sort of a guy is this Tex Lynch, and what's going on at the Shoe-Bar that an old he-gossip like Pop Daggett is afraid to talk about?'

CHAPTER 3

Mistress Mary Quite Contrary

But Stratton's mind was too full of the amazing information he had gleaned from the old storekeeper to leave much room for minor reflections. He had been stunned at first – so completely floored that anyone save the garrulous old man intent on making the most of his shop-worn story could not have helped seeing that something was seriously wrong. Then anger came – a hot, raging fury against the authors of this barefaced, impudent attempt at swindle. From motives of policy he had done his best to conceal that, too, from Pop Daggett; but now that he was alone it surged up again within him, dyeing his face a deep crimson and etching hard lines on his forehead and about his straight-lipped mouth.

'Thought they'd put it over easy,' he growled behind set teeth, one clenched, gloved hand thumping the saddle-horn. 'Saw the notice in the papers, of course, and decided it would be a cinch to rob a dead man. Well, there's a surprise coming to somebody that'll make mine look like thirty cents.'

His lips relaxed in a grim smile, which presently merged into an expression of puzzled wonder. Thorne, of all people, to try and put across a crooked deal like this! Stratton had never known the man really intimately, but during the several years of their business relationship the Chicago lawyer struck him as being scrupulously honest and upright. Indeed, when Buck came to enlist, it seemed a perfectly safe and natural thing to leave his deeds and other important papers in Andrew Thorne's keeping.

'Shows how you can be fooled in a man,' murmured Stratton, as he followed the trail down into a shallow draw. 'I sure played into his hands nice. He had the deeds and everything, and it would be simple enough to fake a transfer when he thought I was dead and knew I hadn't any kin to make trouble. I wonder what the daughter's like. A holy terror, I'll bet, and tarred with the same brush. Well, she'll get hers in about two hours' time, and get it good.'

The grim smile flickered again on his lips for a moment, to vanish as he saw the head and shoulders of a horseman appear over the further edge of the draw. An instant later the bulk of a big sorrel flashed into view and thudded towards him.

On the open range men usually stop for a word or two when they meet, but this one did not. As he approached Stratton at a rapid speed there was a brief, involuntary movement as if he meant to pull up and then changed his mind. The next moment he had whirled past with a careless, negligent gesture of one hand and a keen, penetrating, questioning stare from a pair of hard black eyes.

Buck glanced over one shoulder at the flying dust-cloud and pursed his lips.

'Wonder if that's the mysterious Tex?' he pondered, urging his horse forward. 'Black eyes and red cheeks, all right. He's a good-looking scoundrel – too darn good-looking for a man. All the same, I can't say it was a case of love at first sight.'

Unconsciously his right hand dropped to the holster at his side, the fingers caressing for an instant the butt of his Colt. He had set out on his errand of exposure with an angry impulsiveness which gave no thought to details or possibilities. But in some subtle fashion that searching glance from the passing stranger brought him up with a little mental jerk. For the first time he remembered that he was playing a lone hand, that the very nature of his business was likely to rouse the most desperate and unscrupulous opposition. Considering the value of the stake and the penalties involved, the present occupant of the Shoe-Bar was likely to use every means in her power to prevent his accusations from becoming public. If the fellow who had just passed really was Tex Lynch, Buck had a strong intuition that he was the sort of a man who could be counted on to take a prominent hand in the game, and also that he wouldn't be any too particular as to how he played it.

A mile beyond the draw the trail forked, and Stratton took the left-hand branch. The grazing hereabouts was poor, and at this time of year particularly the Shoe-Bar cattle were more likely to be confined to the richer fenced-in pastures belonging to the ranch. The scenery thus presenting no points of interest, Buck's thoughts turned to the interview ahead of him. Marshalling his facts, he planned briefly how he would make use of them, and finally began to draw scrappy mental pen-pictures of the usurping Mary Thorne.

She would be tall, probably, and rawboned – that domineering, 'bossy' type he always associated with women who assumed men's jobs – harsh-voiced and more than a trifle hard. He dwelt particularly on her hard-ness, for surely no other sort of woman could possibly have helped to engineer the crooked deal which Andrew Thorne and his daughter had so successfully put across. She would be painfully plain, of course, and doubtless also would wear knickerbockers like a certain woman farmer he had once met in Texas, smoke cigarettes constantly, and pack a gun. Having endowed the lady with a few other disagreeable qualities which pleased him mightily, Buck awoke to the realisation that he was approaching the eastern extremity of the Shoe-Bar ranch. His eyes brightened, and, dismissing all thoughts of Miss Thorne, he began to cast interested, appraising glances to right and left as he rode.

There is little that escapes the eye of the professional ranchman, especially when he has been absent from his property for more than two years. Buck Stratton observed quite as much as the average man, and it presently became evident that what he saw did not please him. His keen eyes sought out sagging fence-wire where staples, drawn or fallen out, had never been replaced. Here and there a rotting post leaned at a precarious angle, or gates between pastures needed repairing badly. What cattle were in sight seemed in good condition but their number was much less than he expected. Only once did he observe any signs of human activity, and then the loafing attitude of the two punchers riding leisurely through a field half a mile away was but too apparent. By the time he came within sight of the ranch-house, nestling pleasantly in a little grove of cotton-woods beyond the creek, his face was set in a hard scowl.

'Looks to me like they were letting the whole outfit go to pot,' he muttered angrily. 'It sure is time I whirled in and took a hand.'

Urging the roan forward, he rode splashing through the shallow stream, up the gentle slope, and swung out of his saddle close to the kitchen door. This stood open, and striding up to it Buck met the languid gaze of a swarthy middle-aged Mexican who lounged just within the portal.

'Miss Thorne around?' he asked curtly.

'Sure,' shrugged the Mexican. 'I t'ink she in fron' house. Yoh try aroun' other door, mebbe fin' her.'

In the old days the kitchen entrance had been the one most used, but Buck remembered that there was another at the opposite end of the building which opened directly into the ranch living-room. He sought it now, observing with preoccupied surprise that a small covered veranda had been built out from the house, found it ajar like the other, and knocked.

'Come in,' said a voice.

Stratton crossed the threshold, instinctively removing his hat. As he remembered it, the room, though of good size and comfortable enough, had been a clutter of purely masculine belongings. He was quite un-prepared for the colourful gleam of Navajo rugs, the curtained windows, the general air of swept and garnished tidiness which seemed almost luxury. Briefly his sweeping glance took in a bowl of flowers on the centre-table and then came to rest abruptly on a slight, girlish figure just risen from a chair beside it.

'I'd like to see Miss Thorne, please,' he said, stifling his momentary surprise.

The girl took a step forward, her slim, tanned, ringless fingers clasped loosely about a book she held.

'I'm Miss Thorne,' she answered in a low, pleasant voice.

Buck gasped and his eyes widened. Then he recovered himself swiftly.

'I mean Miss Mary Thorne,' he explained; 'the – er – owner of this outfit.'

The girl smiled faintly, a touch of veiled wistfulness in her eyes.

'I'm Mary Thorne,' she said quietly. 'There's only one, you know.'

CHAPTER 4

The Branding-Iron

Stratton was never sure just how long he stood staring at her in dumb, dazed bewilderment. After those mental pictures of the Mary Thorne he had expected to find, it was small wonder that the sight of this slip of a black-frocked girl, with her soft voice, her tawny-golden hair and wistful eyes, should stun him into temporary speechlessness. Even when he finally pulled himself together to feel a hot flush flaming in his face and find one gloved hand recklessly crumpling his new Stetson, he could not quite credit the evidence of his hearing.

'I – I beg pardon,' he said stiffly. 'But it doesn't seem possible that – '

He hesitated. The girl's smile deepened whimsically.

'I know,' she said ruefully. 'It never does. Nobody seems to think a girl can seriously attempt to run a cattle-ranch – even the way I'm trying to run it, with a capable foreman to look after things. Sometimes I wonder if – '

She paused, her glance falling on the book she held. Stratton saw that it was a shabby account-book, a stubby pencil thrust between the leaves.

'Yes?' he prompted, scarcely aware what made him ask the question.

She looked up at him, her eyes a little wider than before. They were a warm hazel, and for an instant in their depths Stratton glimpsed a troubled expression, so veiled and swiftly passing that a moment later he could not be sure he had read aright.

'It's nothing,' she shrugged. 'You probably know what a lot of nagging little worries a ranchman has, and sometimes it seems to me they all have to come at once. I suppose even a man gets a bit discouraged, now and then.'

'He sure does,' agreed Buck. 'What – er – particular sort of worry do you mean?'

He asked the question impulsively without realising how it might sound, coming from a total stranger. The girl's slim figure stiffened and her chin went up. Then – perhaps something in his expression told her he had not meant to be impertinent – her face cleared.

'The principal one is lack of help,' she explained readily enough, and yet Stratton got a curious impression, somehow, that this wasn't really the worst of her troubles. 'We're awfully short-handed.' She hesitated an instant and then went on frankly, 'To tell the truth, when you first came in I was hoping you might be looking for a job.'

For an instant Buck had all he could do to conceal his amazement at this extraordinary turn of events.

'You mean I'd stand a chance of being taken on?' he countered, sparring for time.

'Of course! That is – You are a cow-puncher, aren't you?'

Stratton's lips twitched slightly.

'I've worked around cattle all my life.'

'Then naturally it would be all right. I should be very glad to hire you. Tex Lynch usually looks after all that, but he's away this afternoon and there's no reason why I shouldn't – ' Her quaint air of dignity was marred by a sudden, amused twitch of the lips. 'I'm really awfully pleased you did come to me,' she smiled. 'He's been telling me for over two weeks that he couldn't hire a man for love or money; it'll be amusing to show him what I've done, sitting quietly here at home.'

'That's all settled, then?' Stratton had been doing some rapid thinking. 'You'd like me to start in right away, I suppose? That'll suit me fine. My name's Bob Green. If you'll just explain to Lynch that I'm hired, I'll go down to the bunk-house and he can put me to work when he comes back.'

With a slight bow, he was moving away when Miss Thorne stopped him.

'Wait!' she cried. 'Why, you haven't said a word about wages.'

Buck turned back, biting his lip and inwardly cursing himself for his carelessness.

'I s'posed it would be the usual forty dollars,' he explained.

'We pay that for new hands,' the girl informed him in some surprise. She sat down beside the table and opened her book. 'I can put you down for forty, I suppose, and then Tex will tell me what it ought to be after he's seen you work. Green, did you say?'

'Robert Green.'

'And the address?'

Buck scratched his head.

'I don't guess I've got any,' he returned. 'I used to punch cows in Texas, but I've been away two years and a half, and the last outfit I was with has sold out to farmers.'

'Oh!' She looked up swiftly and her gaze leaped unerringly to the scar which showed below his tumbled hair. 'Oh! I see. You – you've been through the war.'

Her voice broke a little, and to Buck's astonishment she turned quite white as her eyes sought the book again. A sudden fear smote him that she had guessed his real identity, but he dismissed the notion quickly. Such a thing was next to impossible when she had never set eyes upon him before today.

'That's all, I think,' she said presently in a low voice. 'You'll find the bunk-house, at the foot of the slope beside the creek. I'll speak to Tex as soon as he comes back.'

Outside the ranch-house, Buck paused for a moment or two, ostensibly to stare admiringly at a carefully tended flower-bed, but in reality to adjust his mind to the new and extraordinary situation. During the last two hours he had speculated a good deal on this interview, but not even his wildest imaginings had pictured the turn it had actually taken.

'Hired as a puncher on my own ranch by the girl whose father stole it from me!' he murmured under his breath. 'It's a scream! Darned if it wouldn't make a good vaudeville turn.'

But as he walked slowly back to where he had left his horse, Stratton's face grew thoughtful. He was trying to analyse the motives which had prompted him to accept such a position and found them a trifle mixed. Undeniably the girl's unexpected personality influenced him considerably. She did not strike him, even remotely, as the sort who would deliberately do anything dishonest. And though Buck knew there were women who might be able to assume that air of almost childlike innocence, he did not believe, somehow, that in her case it was assumed. At any rate a little delay would do no harm. By accepting the proffered job he would be able to study the lady and the situation at his leisure. Also – and this he told himself was even more important – he would have a chance of quietly investigating conditions on the ranch. Pop Daggett's vague hints, his own observations, and the intuition he had that Miss Thorne was worrying about something much more vital than the mere lack of hands, all combined to make him feel that things were not going right at the Shoe-Bar. Of course it might be simply a case of rotten management. But in the back of Buck's mind there lurked a curious notion that something deeper and more far-reaching was going on beneath the surface, though of what nature he could not even guess.

Leading the roan into a corral which ranged beyond the kitchen, Stratton unsaddled him and turned him loose. Having hung the saddle and bridle in the adjacent shed, he tucked his bundle under one arm and headed for the bunk-house. He was within a few yards of the entrance to the long, adobe structure when the door was suddenly flung open and a slim, slight figure, hatless and stripped to the waist, plunged out, closely pursued by three other men.

He ran blindly with head down, and Buck had just time to drop his bundle and extend both arms to prevent a collision. An instant later his tense muscles quivered under the impact of some hundred and thirty pounds of solid bone and muscle; the runner staggered and flung up his head, a gasp of terror jolted from his lips.

'Oh!' he said more quietly, his tone an equal blend of astonishment and relief. 'I thought – Don't let 'em – '

He broke off, flushing. He was a pleasant-faced youngster of not more than eighteen or nineteen, with a tangled mop of blonde hair and blue eyes, the pupils of which were curiously dilated. Stratton, whose extended arms had caught the boy just under the armpits, could feel his heart pounding furiously.

'What's the matter, kid?' he asked briefly.

'They were going to brand me – on the back,' the boy muttered.

Over the fellow's bare, muscular shoulders Buck's glance swept the trio who had pulled up just outside the bunk-house door. They seemed typical cow-punchers in dress and manner. Two of them were tall and well set up; the third was short and stocky and held a branding iron in one hand. Meeting Stratton's gaze, he laughed loudly.

'By cripes, Bud! Yuh shore are easy. I thought yuh had more guts than to be scared of an iron that's hardly had the chill took off.'

He guffawed again, the other two joining in. A flush crept up into the boy's face, but his lips were firm now, and as he turned to face the others his eyes narrowed slightly.

'If it's so cold as that mebbe you'd like me to try it on yuh,' he suggested significantly.

The short man haw-hawed again, but not quite so boisterously. Buck noticed that he held the branding iron carefully away from his leg.

'I shore wouldn't holler like you done 'fore I was touched,' he retorted. 'Wal, we got his goat good that time, didn't we, Butch? Better come in an' git yore shirt on 'fore the boss sees yuh half naked.'

He turned and disappeared into the bunk-house, followed by the two other punchers. Buck picked up his bundle and glanced at the boy.

'Seems like you've got a right sociable, amusing bunch around here,' he drawled.

The youngster's lips parted impulsively, to close as swiftly over his white teeth.

'Oh, they're a great lot of jokers,' he returned non-committally, moving towards the door. 'Coming in?'

The room they entered was long and rather narrow, with built-in bunks occupying most of the wall space, while the usual assemblage of bridles, ropes, old hats, and garments, hanging from pegs, crowded the remainder. Opposite the door stood a rusty, potbellied stove which gave forth a heat that seemed rather superfluous on such a warm evening. The stocky fellow, having leaned his branding iron against the adobe chimney, was occupied in closing the drafts. His two companions, both rolling cigarettes, stood beside him, while lounging at a rough table to the left of the door sat two other men, one of them idly shuffling a pack of dirty cards. As he entered, Stratton was conscious of the intent scrutiny of all five, and an easy, careless smile curved his lips.

'Reckon this is the bunk-house, all right,' he drawled. 'The lady told me it was down this way. My name's Bob Green – Buck for short. I've just been hired to show you guys how to punch cows proper.'

There was a barely perceptible silence, broken by one of the men at the table.

'Hired?' he repeated curtly. 'Why, I thought Tex went to town.'

'Tex?' queried Stratton. 'Oh, you mean the foreman. The lady did say something about that when she signed me up. Said she'd tell him about it when he came back.'

He was aware of a swift exchange of glances between several of the men. The stocky fellow suddenly abandoned his manipulation of the stove-dampers and came forward.

'Oh, that's it?' he remarked with an amiable grin. 'Tex most always does the hirin', yuh see. Glad to know yuh. My name's McCabe – Slim, they calls me, 'count uh my sylphlike figger. These here guys is Bill Joyce an' his sidekick, Butch Siegrist; likewise Flint Kreeger an' Doc Peters over to the table. Bud Jessup yuh already met.'

He chuckled, and Buck glancing towards the corner where the youngster was tucking in the tails of his flannel shirt, smiled slightly.

'Got acquainted kinda sudden, didn't we?' he grinned. 'Glad to meet you gents. Whereabouts is a bunk I can stake my claim to?'

'This here's vacant,' spoke up Bud Jessup quickly, indicating one next to his own.

Buck stepped over and tossed his bundle into it. As he did so the raucous clanging of a bell sounded from the direction of the ranch-house, accompanied by a stentorian shout: 'Grub-pile!' which galvanised the punchers into action.

Stratton and the boy were the last to leave the room, and as he reached the door Buck noticed a tiny wisp of smoke curling up from the floor to one side of the stove. Looking closer he saw that it was caused by the branding iron, one corner of which rested on the end of a board where the rough flooring came in contact with the square of hard-packed earth beneath the stove. Bud Jessup saw it, too, and without comment he stepped over and moved the iron to a safer position.

Still without words, the two left the bunk-house. But as they headed for the kitchen Buck's eyes narrowed slightly and he flashed a momentary glance at his companion which was full of curiosity and thoughtful speculation.

CHAPTER 5

Tex Lynch

Supper, which was served in the ranch-house kitchen by Pedro, the Mexican cook, was not enlivened by much conversation. The food was plentiful and of good quality, and the punchers addressed themselves to its consumption with the single-hearted purpose of hungry men whose appetites have been sharpened by a long day in the saddle. Now and then someone mumbled a request to 'pass the sugar', or desired more steak or coffee from the shuffling Pedro; but for the most part the serious business of eating occupied them exclusively.

There was no sign of Miss Thorne. Buck decided that she took her meals elsewhere and approved the isolation. It must be pretty hard, he thought, for a girl like that to be living her young life in this out-of-the-way corner of the world with no women companions to keep her company. Then he remembered that for all he knew she might not be the only one of her sex on the Shoe-Bar, and when the meal was over and the men were straggling back towards the bunk-house, he put the question to Bud Jessup, who walked beside him.

'Huh?' grunted the youngster, with a sharp, enquiring glance at his face. 'What d'yuh want to know that for?'

Stratton shrugged his shoulders. 'No particular reason,' he smiled. 'I only thought she'd find it mighty dull alone on the ranch with a bunch of punchers.'

Bud continued to eye him intently. 'Well, she ain't alone,' he said briefly. 'Mrs Archer lives with her; an' uh course there's Pedro's Maria.'

'Who's Mrs Archer?'

'Her aunt. Kinda nice old lady, but she ain't got much pep. Maria's jest the other way. When she's got a grouch on she's some cat, believe me!'

For some reason the subject appeared to be distasteful to Jessup, and Buck asked no more questions. Instead of following the others into the bunk-house they strolled on along the bank of the creek, which was lined with fair-sized cottonwoods. The sun had set, but the glow of it still lingered in the west. Glinting like a flame on the windows of the ranch-house, it even dappled the placid waters of the little stream with red-gold splotches, which mingled effectively with the mirrored reflections of the overhanging trees. From the kitchen chimney a wisp of smoke rose straight into the still clear air. In a corner of the corral half a dozen horses were bunched, lazily switching their tails at intervals. Through one of the pastures across the stream some cattle drifted, idly feeding their way to water.

It was a peaceful picture, yet Stratton could not rid his mind of the curious feeling that the peacefulness was all on the surface. He had not missed that swift exchange of glances that heralded his first appearance in the bunk-house; and though Slim McCabe particularly had been almost effusively affable, Buck was none the less convinced that his presence here was unwelcome. That business of the branding iron, too, was puzzling. Was it merely a bit of rough but harmless horseplay or had it a deeper meaning? Bud did not look like a fellow to lose his nerve easily, and the iron had certainly been hot enough to brand even the tough hide of a three-year-old steer.

Buck glanced sidewise at his companion to find the blue eyes studying his face with a keen, questioning scrutiny. They were hastily withdrawn, and a faint colour crept up, darkening the youngster's tan.

'Trying to size me up,' thought Stratton interestedly. 'He's got something on his chest, too.'

But he gave no sign of what was in his mind. A moment or two later he paused and, leaning indolently against a tree, let his gaze sweep idly over the cattle in the nearby pasture.

'Looks to me like a pretty good bunch of steers,' he commented, and then added carelessly: 'What sort of a guy is this Tex Lynch, anyhow?'

Bud hesitated briefly, sending a swift, momentary glance towards the bunk-house.

'Oh, he's all right, I guess,' he answered slowly.

Stratton grinned. 'If you don't look out you'll be overpraising him, kid,' he chuckled.

Jessup shrugged his shoulders. 'I didn't say I liked him,' he defended. 'He knows his business all right.'

'Oh, sure. Otherwise, I s'pose he wouldn't hold down his job. But what I want to know is the kind of boss he is. Does he treat the fellows white, or is he a sneak?'

Bud's face darkened. 'He treats some of 'em white enough,' he snapped.

'That so? Favourites, eh? I've met up with that kind before. Is he hard to get on the right side of?'

'Dunno,' growled the youngster. 'I never tried.'

Buck chuckled again. 'Well, kid, so long as you don't seem to think it's worth while, I dunno why I should take the trouble. Who else is on the outs with him?'

Jessup flashed a startled glance at him. 'How in blazes do you know – '

'Oh, gosh! That's easy. That open-faced countenance of yours would give you away even if your tongue didn't. I'd say you weren't a bit in love with Lynch, or any of the rest of the bunch, either. Likely you got a good reason, an' of course it ain't any of my business; but if that stunt with the red-hot branding iron is a sample of their playfulness, I should think you'd drift. There must be plenty of peaceful jobs open in the neighbourhood.'

'But that's just what they want me to do,' snapped Jessup hotly. 'They're doin' their best to drive me – '

His jaws clamped shut and a sudden suspicion flashed into his eyes, which caused Buck promptly to relinquish all hope of getting any further information from the boy. Evidently he had said the wrong thing and got the fellow's back up, though he could not imagine how. And so, when Jessup curtly proposed that they return to the bunk-house, Stratton readily acquiesced.

They found the five punchers gathered around the table playing draw-poker under the light of a flaring oil lamp. McCabe extended a breezy invitation to Buck to join them, which he accepted promptly, drawing up an empty box to a space made for him between Slim and Butch Siegrist. With scarcely a glance at the group, Jessup selected a tattered magazine from a pile in one corner and sprawled out on his bunk, first lighting a small hand lamp and placing it on the floor beside him.

Stratton liked poker and played a good game, but he soon discovered that he was up against a pretty stiff proposition. The limit was the sky, and Kreeger and McCabe especially seemed to have a run of phenomenal luck. Buck didn't believe there was anything crooked about their playing; at least he could detect no sign of it, though he kept a sharp lookout as he always did when sitting in with strangers. But he was rather uncomfortably in a hole and was just beginning to realise rather whimsically that for a while at least he had only a cowman's pay to depend on for spending-money, when the door was suddenly jerked open and a tall, broad-shouldered figure loomed in the opening.

'Well, it's all right, fellows,' said the newcomer, blinking a little at the light. 'I saw – '

He caught himself up abruptly and glowered at Stratton.

'Who the devil are yuh?' he enquired harshly, stepping into the room.

Buck met his hard glance with smiling amiability.

'Name of Buck Green,' he drawled. 'Passed you on the trail this afternoon, didn't I? You must be Tex Lynch.'

With a scarcely perceptible movement he shifted his cards to his left hand. His right, the palm half open, rested on the edge of the table just above his thigh. He didn't really believe the foreman would start anything, but one never knew, especially with a man of such evidently uncertain temper.

'Huh!' grunted Lynch. 'Why didn't yuh stop me then? Yuh might have saved yourself a ride.' He continued to stare at Stratton, a veiled speculation in his smouldering eyes. 'Well?' he went on impatiently. 'What can I do for yuh now I'm here?'

Buck raised his eyebrows. 'Do for me? Why, I don't know as there's anything right this minute. I s'pose you'll be wanting to put me to work in the morning.'

'You've sure got nerve a-plenty,' rasped the foreman. 'I ain't hirin' anybody that comes along just because he wears chaps.'

'That so?' drawled Buck. 'Funny the lady didn't mention that when she signed me up this afternoon.'

Lynch's face darkened. 'Yuh mean to say – '

He paused abruptly, his angry eyes sweeping past Stratton, to rest for an instant on Flint Kreeger, who sat just beyond McCabe. What he saw there Buck did not know, but it must have been something of warning or information. When his eyes returned to Stratton their expression was veiled under drooping lids; his lithe figure relaxed into an easier position against the door-casing, both hands resting lightly on slim hips.

'Miss Thorne hired yuh, then?' he remarked in a non-committal voice which yet held no touch of friendliness. 'Well, that's different. Where've yuh worked?'

'The last outfit was the Three-Circles in Texas.' Buck named at random an outfit in the southern part of the state with which he was slightly acquainted. 'Been in the army over two years, and just got my discharge.'

'Texas?' repeated Lynch curtly. 'How the devil do yuh happen to be lookin' for work here?'

'I'd heard Joe Bloss was foreman,' explained Buck calmly. 'We used to work together on the Three-Circles, and I knew he'd give me a job. When I found out in Paloma he'd gone, I took a chance an' rode out anyhow.'

He bore the foreman's searching scrutiny very well, without a change of colour or the quiver of an eyelash. Nevertheless he was not a little relieved when Lynch, with a brief comment about trying him out in the morning, moved around the table and sat down on a bunk to pull off his chaps. That sudden and complete bottling up of emotion had shown Buck how much more dangerous the man was than he had supposed, and he was pleased enough to come out of their first encounter so well.

With a barely perceptible sense of relaxing tension, the poker game was resumed, for which Buck was devoutly thankful. Throughout the interruption he had not forgotten his hand, which was by far the best he had held that evening. He played it and the succeeding ones so well that when the game ended he had managed to break even.

Ten minutes later the lights were out, and the silence of the bunk-house was broken only by the regular breathing of eight men, or the occasional creak of some one shifting his position in the narrow bunk. Having no blankets – a deficiency he meant to remedy if he could get off long enough tomorrow to ride to Paloma Springs – Buck removed merely chaps and boots and stretched his long form on the corn-husk tick with a little sigh of weariness. Until this moment he had not realised how tired he was. But he had slept poorly on the train, and this, coupled with the heady air and the somewhat stirring events of the last few hours, dragged his eyelids shut almost as soon as his head struck the improvised pillow.

It seemed as if scarcely a moment had passed before he opened them again. But he knew that it must be several hours later, for it had been pitch-dark when he went to sleep, and now a square of moonlight lay across the floor under the southern window, bringing into faint relief the outlines of the long room.

Just what had roused him he did not know; some noise, no doubt, either inside the bunk-house or without. Nerves attuned to battlefront conditions are likely to become sharp as razor-edges, and Buck, starting from deep slumber to complete wakefulness, was almost instantly aware of a sense of strangeness in his surroundings.

In a moment he knew what it was. Even though they may not snore, the breathing of seven sleeping men is unmistakable. Buck did not have to strain his ears to realise that not a sound came from any of the other bunks, and swiftly the utter, unnatural stillness became oppressive.

Quietly he swung his stockinged feet to the floor and was reaching for the holster and cartridge-belt he had laid beside him, when, from the adjoining bunk, Bud Jessup's voice came in a cautious whisper.

'They're gone. The whole bunch of 'em just rode off.'

CHAPTER 6

The Blood-Stained Saddle

'Hello, kid!' said Stratton quietly. 'You awake? What's up, anyhow?'

There was a rustle in the adjoining bunk, the thud of bare feet on the floor, and Jessup's face loomed, wedge-shaped and oddly white, through the shadows.

'They're gone,' he repeated, with a curious, nervous hesitancy of manner.

'I know. You said that before. What the devil are they doing out this time of night?'

In drawing his weapon to him, Buck's eyes had fallen on his wristwatch, the radiolite hands of which indicated twenty minutes after twelve. He awaited Jessup's reply with interest, and it struck him as unnaturally long in coming.

'I don't rightly know,' the youngster said at length. 'I s'pose they must have gone out after – the rustlers.'

Buck straightened abruptly. 'What!' he exclaimed. 'You mean to say there's been rustling on the Shoe-Bar?'

Again Jessup hesitated, but more briefly. 'I don't know why I shouldn't tell yuh. Everybody's wise to it, or suspects somethin'. They've got away

495

with quite a bunch – mostly from the pastures around Las Vegas, over near the hills. Tex says they're greasers, but I think – ' He broke off to add a moment later in a troubled tone, 'I wish to thunder he hadn't gone an' left Rick out there all alone.'

Stratton remembered Las Vegas as the name of a camp down at the southwesterly extremity of the ranch. It consisted of a one-room adobe shack, which was occupied at certain seasons of the year by one or two punchers, who from there could more easily look after the nearby cattle, or ride fence, than by going back and forth every day from the ranch headquarters.

'Who's Rick?' he asked briefly.

'Rick Bemis. He – he's one dandy fellow. We've worked together over two years.'

'H'm. How long's this rustling been going on?'

'Three or four months.'

'Lost many head, have they?'

'Quite a bunch, I'd say, but I don't know. They never tell me or Rick anythin'.'

Bud's tone was bitter, and Stratton noticed it in spite of his pre-occupation. Rustling! That would account for several of the things that had puzzled him. Rustling was possible, too, with the borderline comparatively near, and that stretch of rough, hilly country which touched the lower extremity of the ranch. But for the stealing to go on for three or four months, without something drastic being done to stop it, seemed peculiar, to say the least.

'What's been done about it?' Buck asked briefly.

'Oh, they've gone out at night a few times, but they never caught anybody that I heard. Seems like the thieves were too slick, or else – '

He paused; Buck regarded him curiously through the faintly luminous shadows.

'Well?' he prodded

Bud moved uneasily. 'It ain't anythin' special,' he returned evasively. 'All this time they never left anybody down to Las Vegas till Rick was sent day before yesterday. I up an' told Tex straight out there'd oughta be another fellow with him, but all he done was to bawl me out an' tell me to mind my own business. It ain't safe, an' now they've gone out – '

Again he broke off, his voice a trifle husky with emotion. He was evidently growing more and more worked up and alarmed for the safety of his friend. It was plain, too, that the recent departure of the punchers for the scene of action, instead of reassuring Bud, had greatly increased his anxiety. Buck decided that the situation wasn't as simple as it looked, and promptly determined on a little action.

'Would it ease your mind any if we saddled up an' followed the bunch?' he asked.

Jessup drew a quick breath and half rose from the bunk. 'By cripes, yes!' he exclaimed. 'Yuh mean you'd – '

'Sure,' said Stratton, reaching for his boots. 'Why not? If there's going to be any excitement I'd like to be on hand. Pile into your clothes, kid, and let's go.'

Jessup began to dress rapidly. 'I don't s'pose Tex'll be awful pleased,' he murmured, dragging on his shirt.

'I don't see he'll have any kick coming,' returned Buck easily. 'If he's laying for rustlers, seems like he'd ought to have routed out the two of us in the beginning to have as big a crowd as possible. You never know what you're up against with those slippery cusses.'

Bud made no further comment, and a few minutes later they left the bunk-house and went up to the corral. The bright moonlight illumined everything clearly and made it easy to rope and saddle two of the three horses remaining in the enclosure. Then, swinging into the saddle, they rode down the slope, splashed through the creek, and entering the further pasture by a gate, headed south at a brisk lope.

The land comprising the Shoe-Bar ranch was a roughly rectangular strip, much longer than it was wide, which skirted the foothills of the Escalante Mountains. As the crow flies it was roughly seven miles from the ranch-house to Las Vegas camp, and for the better part of that distance there was little conversation between the two riders. Buck would have liked to question his companion about a number of things that puzzled him, but having sized up Jessup and come to the conclusion that the youngster was the sort whose confidence must be given uninvited or not at all, he held his peace. Apparently Bud had not yet made up his mind whether to class Stratton as an enemy or a friend, and Buck felt he could not do better than endeavour unobtrusively to impress the latter fact upon him. That done, he was sure the boy would open up freely.

The wisdom of this policy became evident sooner than he expected. From time to time as they rode, Stratton commented casually, as a new hand would be likely to do, on some feature or other connected with the ranch or their fellow-punchers. To these remarks Jessup replied readily enough, but in a preoccupied manner, until all at once, moved either by

497

something Buck had said, or possibly by a mind burdened to the point where self-restraint was no longer possible, he burst into sudden surprising speech.

'That wasn't no foolin' with that iron this afternoon. If yuh hadn't come along jest then they'd of branded me on the back.'

Astonished, Buck glanced at him sharply. They had travelled more than two-thirds of the distance to Las Vegas camp, and he had quite given up hope of Jessup's opening up during the ride.

'Oh, say!' he protested. 'Are you trying to throw a load into me? Why would they want to do that?'

Jessup gave a short brittle laugh.

'They want me to quit,' he retorted curtly.

'Quit?' repeated Stratton, his eyes widening. 'But – '

'Tex don't want me here,' broke in the youngster. 'For the last three months he's tried all kinds of ways to make me an' Rick take our time; but it won't work.' His lips pressed together firmly. 'I promised Miss – '

His words clipped off abruptly, as a single shot, sharp and distinct, shattered the still serenity of the night. It came from the south, from the direction of Las Vegas. Buck flung up his head and pulled instinctively on the reins. Jessup caught his breath with an odd, whistling intake.

'There!' he gasped unevenly.

For a moment or two they sat motionless, listening intently, Buck's face a curious mixture of alertness and surprise. Up to this moment he had taken the whole business rather casually, with small expectation that anything would come of it, but the sound of that shot changed everything. Something was happening, then, after all – something sinister, perhaps, and certainly not far away. His eyes narrowed, and when no other sound followed that single report, he loosed his reins and urged the roan to a gallop.

For perhaps half a mile the two plunged forward amidst a silence that was broken only by the dull thudding of their horses' hoofs and their own rapid breathing. Then all at once Buck jerked his roan to a standstill.

'Some one's coming,' he warned briefly.

Straight ahead of them the moonlight lay across the flat, rolling prairie almost like a pathway of molten silver. On either side of the brilliant stretch the light merged gradually and imperceptibly into shadows – shadows which yet held a curious, half-luminous quality, giving a sense of shifting horizons and lending a touch of mystery to the vague distances which seemed to be revealed.

From somewhere in that illusive shadow land came the faint beat of a horse's hoofs, growing steadily louder. Eyes narrowed to mere slits, Stratton stared ahead intently until of a sudden his gaze focused on a faintly visible moving shape.

He straightened, his right hand falling to the butt of his Colt. But presently his grip relaxed and he reached out slowly for his rope.

'There's no one on him,' he murmured in surprise.

Without turning his head, Jessup made an odd, throaty sound of acquiescence.

'He's saddled, though,' he muttered a moment later, and also began taking down his rope.

Straight towards them along that moonlit pathway came the flying horse, head down, stirrups of the empty saddle flapping. Buck held his rope ready, and when the animal was about a hundred feet away he spurred suddenly to the right, whirling the widening loop above his head. As it fell accurately about the horse's neck the animal stopped short with the mechanical abruptness of the well-trained range mount and stood still, panting.

Slipping to the ground, Bud ran towards him, with Stratton close behind. The strange cayuse, a sorrel of medium size, was covered with foam and lather, and as Jessup came close to him he rolled his eyes in a frightened manner.

'It's Rick's saddle,' said Bud in an agitated tone, after he had made a hasty examination. 'I'd know it anywhere from – that – cut – in – '

His voice trailed off into silence and he gazed with wide-eyed, growing horror at the hand that had rested on the saddle-skirt. It was stained bright crimson, and Buck, staring over his shoulder, noticed that the leather surface glistened darkly ominous in the bright moonlight.

Slowly the boy turned his head and looked at Stratton. His face was lint-white, and the pupils of his eyes were curiously dilated.

'It's Rick's saddle,' he repeated dully, and shuddered as he stared again at his blood-stained hand.

Buck's own fingers caught the youngster's shoulder in a reassuring grip, and his lips parted. But before he had time to speak a sudden volley of shots rang out ahead of them, so crisp and distinct and clear that instinctively he stiffened, his ears attuned for the familiar, vibrant hum of flying bullets.

CHAPTER 7

Rustlers

Swiftly the echoes of the shots died away, leaving the still serenity of the night again unruffled. For a moment or two Stratton waited expectantly; then his shoulders squared decisively.

'I reckon it's up to us to find out what's going on down there,' he said, turning towards his horse.

Jessup nodded curt agreement. 'Better take the sorrel along, hadn't we?' he asked.

'Sure.' Buck swung himself lightly into the saddle, shortening the lead rope and fastening it to the horn. 'I was thinking of that.'

Five minutes later they pulled up in front of a small adobe shack nestling against a background of cottonwoods that told of the near presence of the creek. The door stood open, framing a black rectangle which proclaimed the emptiness of the hut, and with scarcely a pause the two rode slowly on, searching the moonlit vistas with keen alertness.

On their right the country had grown noticeably rougher. Here and there low spurs from the nearby western hills thrust out into the flat prairie, and deep shadows which marked the opening of draw or gully loomed up frequently. It was from one of these, about half a mile south of the hut, that a voice issued suddenly, halting the two riders abruptly by the curtness of its snarling menace.

'Hands up!'

Buck obeyed promptly, having learned from experience the futility of trying to draw on a person whose very outlines are invisible. Jessup's hands went up, too, and then dropped quickly to his sides again.

'Why, it's Slim!' he cried, and spurred swiftly towards the mouth of the gully. 'What the deuce is the matter?' he asked anxiously. 'What's happened to Rick?'

There was a momentary pause, and then McCabe stepped out of the shadows, six-gun in one hand.

'What the devil are yuh doin' here?' he demanded with a harshness which struck Buck in curious contrast to his usual air of good humour. 'Who's that with yuh?'

'Only Green. We – we got worried, an' saddled up an' – followed yuh.

500

When we heard the shots – What *did* happen to Rick, Slim? We caught his horse out there, the saddle all – '

'Since yuh gotta know,' snapped the puncher, 'he got a hole drilled through one leg. He's right here behind me.'

As Bud flung himself out of the saddle and hurried over to the man lying just inside the gully, McCabe stepped swiftly to the side of Stratton's horse. There was a mingling of doubt and sharp suspicion in the upturned face.

'Yuh sure are up an' doin' for a new hand,' he commented swiftly. 'Was it yuh put it into his head to come out here?'

'I reckon maybe it was,' returned Buck easily. 'When we woke up an' found you all gone, the kid got fretting considerable about his friend here, and I didn't see why we shouldn't ride out and join you. According to my mind, when you're out after rustlers, the more the merrier.'

'Huh! He told yuh we was after rustlers?'

'Sure. Why not? It ain't any secret, is it? Leastwise, I didn't gather that from Bud.'

McCabe's face relaxed. 'Wal, I dunno as 't is,' he shrugged. 'Tex likes to run things his own way, though. Still, I dunno as there's any harm done. Truth is, we didn't get started soon enough. We was half a mile off when we heard the shot, an' rid up to find Rick drilled through the leg an' the thieves beatin' it for the mountains. The rest of the bunch lit out after 'em while I stayed with Rick. I dunno as they caught any of 'em, but I reckon they didn't have time to run off no cattle.'

Stratton slid out of the saddle and threw the reins over the roan's head. He had not failed to notice the slight discrepancy in McCabe's statement as to the length of time it took the punchers to ride from the bunk-house to this spot, but he made no comment.

'Bemis hurt bad?' he asked.

'Not serious. It's a clean wound in his thigh. I got it tied up with his neckerchief.'

Buck nodded and walked over to where Bud was squatting beside the wounded cow-puncher. By this time his eyes were accustomed to the half-darkness, and he could easily distinguish the long length of the fellow, and even noted that the dark eyes were regarding him questioningly out of a white, rather strained face.

'Want me to look you over?' he asked, bending down. 'I've had considerable experience with this sort of thing, and maybe I can make you easier.'

'Go to it,' nodded the young chap briefly. 'It ain't bleedin' like it was, but it could be a whole lot more comfortable.'

With the aid of Jessup and McCabe, Bemis was moved out into the moonlight, where Stratton made a careful examination of his wound. He found that the bullet had ploughed through the fleshy part of the thigh, just missing the bone, and, barring chances of infection, it was not likely to be dangerous. He was readjusting Slim's crude bandaging when he heard the beat of hoofs and out of the corner of one eye saw McCabe walk swiftly out to meet the returning punchers.

These halted about fifty feet away, and there was a brief exchange of words of which Buck could distinguish nothing. Presently two of the men dashed off in the direction of the ranch-house, while Lynch rode slowly forward and dismounted.

'How yuh feelin'?' he asked Bemis, adding with a touch of sarcasm in his voice, 'I hear yuh got a reg'lar professional sawbones to look after yuh.'

'He acts like he knew what he was about,' returned Bemis briefly. 'How yuh goin' to get me home?'

'I've sent Butch an' Flint after the wagon,' explained Lynch. 'They'll hustle all they can.'

'Did you catch sight of the rustlers?' asked Stratton suddenly.

The foreman flashed him a sudden not over-friendly glance.

'No,' he returned curtly, and turning on his heel led his horse over to where the others had gathered in the shadow of a rocky butte.

It was nearly an hour before the lumbering farm-wagon appeared. During the interval Buck sat beside the wounded man, smoking and exchanging occasional brief comments with Bud, who stayed close by. One or two of the others strolled up to ask about Bemis, but for the most part they remained in their little group, the intermittent glow of their cigarettes flickering in the darkness, and the constant low murmur of their conversation wafted indistinguishably across the intervening space.

Their behaviour piqued Buck's curiosity tremendously. What were they talking about so continually? Where had the outlaws gone, and why hadn't they been pursued further? Had the whole pursuit been merely in the nature of a bluff? And if so, whom had it been intended to deceive? These and a score of other questions passed through his mind as he sat there waiting, but when the dull rumble of the wagon started them all into activity, he had not succeeded in finding any really plausible answers.

The return trip was necessarily slow, and dawn was just breaking as they forded the creek and drove up to the bunk-house. They had barely come to a standstill when, to Buck's surprise, the slim figure of Mary Thorne, bareheaded and clad in riding-clothes, appeared suddenly around the corner of the ranch-house and came swiftly towards them.

'Pedro told me,' she said briefly, pausing beside the wagon. 'How is he?'

'Doin' fine,' responded Lynch promptly. 'It's a clean wound an' ought to heal in no time. Our new hand Green tied him up like a regular professional.'

His manner was almost fulsomely pleasant; Miss Thorne's expression of anxiety relaxed.

'I'm so glad. You'd better bring him right up to the house; he'll be more comfortable there.'

'That ain't hardly necessary,' objected Lynch. 'He'll do all right here. We don't want him to be a bother to yuh.'

'He won't be,' retorted Miss Thorne with unexpected decision. 'We've plenty of room, and Maria has a bed all ready. The bunk-house is no place for a sick man.'

During the brief colloquy Bemis, though perfectly conscious, made no comment whatever. But Buck, glancing towards him as he lay on the husk mattress behind the driver, surprised a fleeting but unmistakable expression of relief in his tanned face.

'He don't want to stay in the bunk-house,' thought Stratton. 'I don't know as I blame him, neither. I wonder, though, if it's because he figures on being more comfortable up there, or – '

The unvoiced question ended with a shrug as Lynch, somewhat curt of manner, gave the order to move.

'Yuh don't all of yuh have to come, neither,' he added quickly. 'Butch an' Slim an' me can carry him in.'

Miss Thorne, who had already started towards the house, glanced over one shoulder. 'If Green knows something about first aid, as you say, he'd better come too, I think.'

Buck glanced questioningly at the foreman, received a surly nod and dismounted, smiling inwardly. It amused him exceedingly to see the dictatorial Tex forced to take orders from this slip of a girl. Evidently she was not quite so pathetically helpless as he had supposed the afternoon before. He began to wonder how she did it, for Lynch struck him as a far from easy person to manage. He was still turning the question over in his mind when he received a shock which for the moment banished every other thought.

The wagon was backed up to the porch, and the four punchers, each taking a corner of the mattress, lifted Bemis out and carried him across the living-room and through a door on the further side which Miss Thorne held open. The room was light and airy, and Buck was conscious of a vague sense of familiarity, which he set down to his rather brief acquaintance with the place two years ago. But when Bemis had been undressed and put to bed and his wound thoroughly cleansed with antiseptic and freshly bandaged, Stratton, really looking about him for the first time, made an odd discovery.

It was his own room! He remembered perfectly choosing it and moving in his belongings the day before he left; and as he stared curiously around he could not see that a single one of them had been touched. There were his trunks just as they had come from Texas. His bureau stood between the windows, and on it lay a pair of brushes and the few odds and ends he had left there when he enlisted. A pair of chaps and a well-worn Stetson hung near the door, and he had just stepped over to make sure they were actually the ones he had left behind when Miss Thorne, who had been talking in the living-room with Lynch, appeared suddenly on the threshold.

As their glances met she drew herself up a little, and a curious expression came into her eyes. Her lips parted impulsively, but when, after a momentary hesitation, she spoke, Buck had an impression that something quite different had been on the tip of her tongue an instant before.

'He'd better have the doctor at once, don't you think?' she said briefly.

Buck nodded. 'Yes, ma'am, he ought. I've done the best I could, and the chances are he'll get along all right; but a regular doctor ought to look him over as soon as possible.'

'I thought so. I've just told Tex to send a man to town at once and wire Dr Blanchard, who lives about twelve miles up the line. It'll take him three or four hours to ride over, but there's no one nearer.'

'I wish you'd let me go,' said Stratton impulsively. 'I've got to return the horse I borrowed and get blankets and some things I left at the store. There's really nothing more I can do for Bemis by hanging around.'

Her brows crinkled doubtfully. 'Well, if you're sure – I suppose there's no reason why you shouldn't. Tell Tex I said you were to go. He'll give you the directions. Only you'll have to hurry.'

With a murmured word of thanks, Buck snatched up his hat and hastened into the living-room. As he passed the big table he was aware of a door at the farther end opening, but he did not turn his head. An instant later, as he was in the act of springing off the porch, he heard a woman's voice behind him, soft, low, and a little shaken.

'What is it, Mary? What's happened? You don't mean to tell me that – that another man's been shot.'

Buck's eyes widened, but he did not pause. 'That's the aunt, I reckon,' he muttered, as he sped down the slope. His lips straightened. 'Another! Holy cats! What the devil am I up against, anyhow? A murder syndicate?'

CHAPTER 8

The Hoodoo Outfit

Pop Daggett hesitated and glanced uneasily towards the door.

'I warned yuh, didn't I, the Shoe-Bar was a hoodoo outfit?' he evaded.

Stratton shook some tobacco into a cigarette-paper and jerked the drawstring with his teeth.

'Sure you did, but that's not the question,' he persisted. 'I asked you if any other punchers had met up with – accidents out there lately.'

The old man continued to cock an eye on the store entrance.

'Since yuh gotta know,' he answered in a lowered tone, 'there was two. About three months ago Jed Terry was scoutin' around back in the mountains, Lord knows what fur, an' fell into a canyon an' broke his skull. Four or five weeks arter that Sam Bennett was plugged through the chest down below Las Vegas.'

'Did Lynch happen to be with either of them?'

'No, sir-ee,' returned Daggett hastily. 'An' don't yuh go blattin' around I told yuh anythin' about it. I ain't one to gossip about my neighbours, more especially Tex Lynch. Them two deaths – Say, Tex ain't in town with yuh, is he?'

'Not that I know of. He certainly didn't come with me.'

'Huh! Wal, yuh never c'n tell with him. As I was sayin', Terry's death was pernounced a accident, an' they allowed Bennett was plugged by one of them greaser rustlers I hear tell of. I ain't sayin' nothing to the contrary. All I'm tellin' yuh is the Shoe-Bar ain't a healthy outfit to work for, an' this business about Rick Bemis proves it. I wouldn't sign on with 'em, not for a hundred a month.'

Buck thrust the cigarette between his lips and felt for a match. 'Still I've got a mind to stick it out a while,' he drawled. 'Accidents come in threes, they say, so there won't likely be another right soon. Well, I reckon I'd better be travelling. How long will it take that doctor man to get over?'

'Not much longer than 't will yuh, if he was home when yuh tele-phoned,' answered Daggett. 'The railroad takes a bend, an' Harpswell ain't more than a mile or two further from the Shoe-Bar than Paloma.'

Evidently Dr Blanchard must have been at home, for Buck had just finished unsaddling and was coming away from the corral when he rode up. Stratton took his horse and answered his brief questions as to the accident, and then walked down to the bunk-house with his blankets, tarp, and other belongings. The place was empty, for it was after one o'clock and evidently the men had gone off somewhere directly after dinner. Indeed, Buck learned as much from Pedro when he went back to forage for something to eat.

'They go to move herd some place,' shrugged the Mexican. 'W'ere, I don' know.'

Stratton ate his meal of beef, bread, and warmed-over coffee in silence and then returned to the bunk-house, vaguely dissatisfied at the idle afternoon which stretched before him. Of course, Lynch had no way of knowing when he would get back from town, but it seemed to Buck that an up-and-doing foreman would have left word for him to join them when he did return.

'Unless, of course, he don't want me around,' murmured Stratton. 'Though for the life of me I can't see what he gains by keeping me idle.'

Presently it occurred to him that this might be a good chance of pursuing some of the investigations he had planned. Since noticing the disreputable condition of the fence the afternoon of his arrival, he had kept his eyes open, and a number of other little signs had confirmed his suspicion that the ranch had very much gone to seed. Of course this might be merely the result of careless, slovenly methods on the part of the foreman, and possibly it did not extend to anything really radical. It would need a much wider, more general inspection to justify a definite con-clusion, and Stratton decided he might as well do some of it this afternoon. On the plea of seeking Lynch and the other men, he could ride almost anywhere without exciting suspicion, and he at once left the bunk-house to carry out his plan. Just outside the door he met Dr Blanchard.

'You made a good job of that dressing,' remarked the older man briefly. He was tall with a slight stoop, bearded, a little slovenly in dress, but with clear, level eyes and a capable manner. 'Where'd you learn how?'

Stratton smiled. 'Overseas. I was in the Transportation, and we had to know a little of everything, including first aid.'

'Hum,' grunted the doctor. 'Well, the kid's doing all right. I won't have to come over again unless fever develops.'

As they walked back to the hitching-rack, he gave Buck a few directions about the care of the invalid. There followed a slight pause.

'You're new here,' commented the doctor, untying his bridle-reins.

'Just came yesterday,' answered Stratton.

'Friend of Lynch?'

Buck's lips twitched. 'Not exactly,' he shrugged. 'Miss Thorne hired me while he was in Paloma. I got a notion he was rather peevish about it. Reckon he prefers to pick his own hands.'

As the doctor swung into the saddle, his face momentarily lightened.

'Don't let that worry you,' he said, a faint little twinkle in his eyes. 'It isn't good for anybody to have their own way all the time. Well, you know what to do about Bemis. If he shows any signs of fever, get hold of me right away.'

With a wave of his hand he rode off. Stratton's glance followed him curiously. Had he really been pleased to find that the new hand was not a friend of Tex Lynch, or was the idea merely a product of Buck's imagination?

Still pondering, he turned abruptly to find Pedro regarding him intently from the kitchen door. As their glances met, the Mexican's lids drooped and his face smoothed swiftly into its usual indolent indifference; but he was not quite quick enough to hide entirely that first look of searching speculation mingled with not a little venom.

Stratton's own expression was the perfection of studied self-control. He half smiled, and yawned in a realistically bored manner.

'You sure you don't know where the bunch went?' he asked. 'I'm getting dead sick of hanging around doing nothing.'

'They don' say,' shrugged the Mexican. 'I wash dishes an' don' see 'em go. Mebbe back soon.'

'Not if they're moving a herd – I don't think!' retorted Buck. 'Guess I'll ask Miss Thorne,' he added, struck by a sudden inspiration.

Without waiting for a reply, he walked briskly along the front of the house towards the further entrance. As he turned the corner he met the girl, booted, spurred, her face shaded becomingly by a wide-brimmed Stetson.

'I was just going to find you,' she said. 'Rick wants to see you a minute.'

Stratton followed her into the living-room, where she paused and glanced back at him.

'You haven't met my aunt, Mrs Archer,' she said in her low, pleasant voice. 'Auntie, this is Buck Green, our new hand.'

From a chair beside one of the west windows, there rose a little old lady at the sight of whom Buck's eyes widened in astonishment. Just what he had expected Mrs Archer to be he hardly knew, but certainly it wasn't this dainty, delicate, Dresden-China person who came forward to greet him. Tiny she was, from her old-fashioned lace cap to the tips of her small, trim shoes. Her gown, of some soft grey stuff, with touches of old lace here and there, was modishly cut yet without any traces of exaggeration. Her abundant white hair was beautifully arranged, and her cheeks, amazingly soft and smooth, with scarcely a line in them, were faintly pink. A more utterly incongruous figure to find on an outlying Arizona ranch would be impossible to imagine, and Buck was hard put to refrain from showing his surprise.

'How do you do, Mr Green?' she said in a soft agreeable voice, which Stratton recognised at once as the one he had overheard that morning. 'My niece has told me how helpful you've been already.'

Buck took her outstretched hand gingerly, and looked down into her upturned face. Her eyes were blue, and very bright and eager, with scarcely a hint of age in them. For a brief moment they gazed steadily into his, searching, appraising, an underlying touch of wistful anxiety in their clear depths. Then a twinkle flashed into them and of a sudden Stratton felt that he liked her very much indeed.

'I'm mighty glad to meet you,' he said impulsively.

The smile spread from eyes to lips. 'Thank you,' she replied. 'I think I may say the same thing. I hope you'll like it here well enough to stay.'

There was a faint accent on the last word. Buck noticed it, and after she had left them, saying she was going to rest a little, he wondered. Did she want him to remain merely because of the short-handed condition of the ranch, or was there a deeper reason? He glanced at Miss Thorne to find her regarding him with something of the same anxious scrutiny he had noticed in her aunt. Her gaze was instantly averted, and a faint flush tinged her cheeks, to be reflected an instant later in Stratton's face.

'By the way,' he said hurriedly, annoyed at his embarrassment, 'do you happen to know where the men are? I thought I'd hunt them up. There's no sense in my hanging around all afternoon doing nothing.'

* * *

'They're down at the south pasture,' she answered readily. 'Tex thinks it will be better to move the cattle to where it won't be so easy for those rustlers to get at them. I'm just going down there and we can ride together, if you like.' She turned towards the door. 'When you're through with Rick you'll find me out at the corral.'

'Don't you want me to saddle up for you?'

'Pedro will do that, thank you. Tell Rick if he wants anything while I'm gone all he has to do is to ring the bell beside his bed and Maria will answer it.'

She departed, and Buck walked briskly into the bedroom. Bemis lay in bed propped up with pillows and looking much better physically than he had done that morning. But his face was still strained, with that harassed, worried expression about the eyes which Stratton had noted before.

'Yuh saw Doc Blanchard, didn't yuh?' he asked, as Buck sat down on the side of his bed. 'What'd he say?'

'Why, that you were doing fine. Not a chance in a hundred, he said, of your having any trouble with the wound.'

'Oh, I know that. But when'd he say I'd be on my feet?'

Buck shrugged his shoulders. 'He didn't mention any particular time for that. I should think it would be two or three weeks, at least.'

'Hell!' The young fellow's fingers twisted the coverlet nervously. 'Don't yuh believe I could – er – ride before that?' he added, almost pleadingly.

Stratton's eyes widened. 'Ride!' he repeated. 'Where the deuce do you want to ride to?'

Bemis hesitated, a slow flush creeping into his tanned face. The glance he bent on Stratton was somewhat shamefaced.

'Anywhere,' he answered curtly, a touch of defiance in his tone. 'You'll say I've lost my nerve, an' maybe I have. But after what's happened around this joint lately, and especially last night – '

He paused, glancing nervously towards the door. Buck's expression had grown suddenly keen and eager.

'Well?' he urged. 'What did happen, anyhow? I had my suspicions there was something queer about that business, but – You can trust me, old man.'

Bemis nodded, his dark eyes searching Stratton's face. 'I'll take a chance,' he answered. 'I got to. There ain't nobody else. They've kept Bud away, and Miss Mary – Well, she's all right, uh course, but Tex has got her buffaloed. She won't believe nothin' ag'in him. I told Bud I'd stay as long as he did, but – A man's got to look after himself some. They ain't likely to miss twice runnin'.'

'You mean to say – '

Bemis stopped him with a cautious gesture. 'Where's that sneaking greaser?' he asked in a low tone, his eyes shifting nervously to the open door.

'Out saddling her horse.'

'Oh! Well, listen.' The young puncher's voice sank almost to a whisper. 'That sendin' me down to Las Vegas was a plant; I'm shore of it. My orders was to sleep days an' patrol around nights to get a line on who was after the cattle. I wasn't awful keen about it, but still an' all, I didn't think they'd dare do what they tried to.'

'You mean there weren't any rustlers at all?' put in Stratton impulsively.

'Shore there was, but they didn't fire that shot that winged me. I'd just got sight of 'em four or five hundred yards away an' was ridin' along in the shadow tryin' to edge close enough to size 'em up an' mebbe pick off a couple. My cayuse was headin' south, with the rustlers pretty near dead ahead, when I come to a patch of moonlight I had to cross. I pulled out considerable to ride around a spur just beyond, so when that shot came I was facin' pretty near due east. The bullet hit me in the left leg, yuh recollect.'

Stratton's eyes narrowed. 'Then it must have been fired from the north – from the direction of the – '

He broke off abruptly as Rick's fingers gripped his wrist.

'Look!' breathed Bemis, in a voice that was scarcely audible.

He was staring over the low footboard of the bed straight at the open door, and Buck swiftly followed the direction of his glance. For an instant he saw nothing. The doorway was quite empty, and he could not hear a sound. Then, of a sudden, his gaze swept on across the living-room and he caught his breath.

On the further wall, directly opposite the bedroom door, hung a long mirror in a tarnished gilded frame. It reflected not only the other side of the doorway but a portion of the wall on either side of it – reflected clearly, among other things, the stooping figure of a woman, her limp calico skirts dragged cautiously back in one skinny hand, her sharp, swarthy face bent slightly forward in an unmistakable attitude of listening.

CHAPTER 9

Revelations

It was the Mexican woman, Maria. As Buck recognised her he rose quietly and moved swiftly towards the door. But if he had hoped to catch her unawares, he was disappointed. He had scarcely taken a step when, through the telltale mirror, he saw her straighten like a flash and move back with catlike swiftness towards the passage leading to the kitchen. When he reached the living-room she stood there calm and casual, with quite the air of one entering for the first time.

'Mees T'orne, she ask me see if Reek, he wan' somet'ing,' she explained, with a flash of her white teeth.

'He doesn't,' returned Buck shortly, eyeing the woman intently. 'If he does, he'll ring the bell.'

'Ver' good,' she nodded. 'I leave the door open to 'ear.'

With a nod and another smile she departed, and Buck heard her moving away along the passage. For a moment he was tempted to close and lock the door. Then he realised that even if she dared return to her eavesdropping, he would have ample warning by keeping an eye on the mirror, and so returned to Bemis.

'I hate that woman,' said Rick, when informed of her departure. 'She's always snoopin' around, an' so is her greaser husband. Down at the bunk-house it's the same way, with Slim, an' Flint Kreeger an' the rest. I tell yuh, I'm dead sick of being spied on, an' plotted against, an' never knowin' when yuh may get a knife in the back, or stop a bullet. I hate to leave Bud, but he's so plumb set on – '

'But what's it all about?' put in Buck impatiently. 'Can't you tell a fellow, or don't you know?'

Bemis flushed slightly at his tone. 'I can tell yuh this much,' he retorted. 'Tex don't want them rustlers caught. He throws a clever bluff, an' he's pulled the wool over Miss Mary's eyes, but for all that, he's workin' on their side. What kind of a foreman is it who'll lose over a thousand head without stoppin' the stealin'? It ain't lack of brains, neither; Tex has got them a-plenty.'

'But Miss Thorne – ' protested Stratton, half-incredulously.

'I tell yuh, he's got her buffaloed. She won't believe a word against him. He was here in her dad's time, an' he's played his cards mighty slick since then. She's told yuh he can't get men, mebbe? All rot, of course. He could get plenty of hands, but he don't want 'em. What's more, he's done his best to get rid of me an' Bud, an' would of long ago, only Miss Mary won't let him fire us.'

'But what in thunder's his object?'

'So's to have the place to himself, I reckon. He an' those greasers in the kitchen, and the rest of the bunch, are as thick as thieves.'

'You mean he'd find it easier to get away with cattle if there wasn't anybody around to keep tabs on him?'

Bemis hesitated. 'I – I'm not sure,' he replied slowly. 'Partly that, mebbe, but there's somethin' else. I've overheard things now an' then I couldn't make head or tail of, but they're up to somethin' – Yuh ain't goin', are yuh?'

Buck had risen. 'Got to,' he shrugged. 'Miss Thorne's waiting for me to go down to the south pasture.'

Bemis raised up on his pillows. 'Well, listen; keep what I said under yore hat, will yuh?'

'Sure,' nodded Stratton reassuringly. 'You needn't worry about that. Anything else you want before I go?'

'Yes. Jest reach me my six-gun outer the holster there in the chair. If I'm goin' to be left alone with that greaser, Pedro, I'd feel more comfortable, someway, with that under my pillow.'

Buck did as he requested and then departed. Something else! That was the very feeling which had assailed him vaguely at times, that some deviltry which he couldn't understand was going on beneath the surface. As he made for the corral, a sudden possibility flashed into his mind. With her title so precarious, might not Mary Thorne be at the bottom of a systematic attempt to loot the Shoe-Bar of its movable value against the time of discovery? But when he met her face to face the idea vanished and he even felt ashamed of having considered it for a moment. Whatever crookedness was going on, this sweet-faced, clear-eyed girl was much more likely to be a victim than one of the perpetrators. The feeling was vastly strengthened when he had saddled up and they rode off together.

'There's something I've been meaning to – to tell you,' the girl said suddenly, breaking a brief silence.

Buck glanced at her to find her eyes fixed on the ears of her horse and a faint flush staining her cheeks.

'That room – ' she went on determinedly, but with an evident effort.

'A man's room – You must have thought it strange. Indeed, I saw you thought it strange –'

Again she paused, and in his turn Buck felt a sudden rush of embarrassment.

'I didn't mean to –' he began awkwardly. 'It just seemed funny to find a regular man's room in a household of women. I suppose it was your – your father's,' he added.

'No, it wasn't,' she returned briefly. She glanced at him for an instant and then looked away again. 'You probably don't know the history of the Shoe-Bar,' she went on more firmly. 'Two years ago it was bought by a young man named Stratton. I never met him, but he was a business acquaintance of my father's and naturally I heard a good deal of him from time to time. He was a ranchman all his life and very keen about it, and the moment he saw the Shoe-Bar he fell in love with it. But the war came, and he had scarcely taken title to the place before he went off and enlisted. Just before he sailed for France he sold the ranch to my father, with the understanding that if he came back safely, Dad would turn it over to him again. He felt, I suppose, how uncertain it all was and that money in the bank would be easier for his – his heirs, than property.'

She paused for an instant, her lips pressed tightly together. 'He never came back,' she went on in a lower, slightly unsteady voice. 'He – gave up his life for those of us who stayed behind. After a little we left Chicago and came here. I loved the place at once, and I've gone on caring for it increasingly ever since. But back of everything there's always been a sense of the tragedy, the injustice of it all. They never even found his body. He was just – missing. And yet, when I came into that room, with his things about just as he had left them when he went away, he seemed so *real*, – I – I couldn't touch it. Somehow, it was all that was left of him. And even though I'd never seen him, I felt as if I wanted to keep it that way always in memory of a – a brave soldier, and a – man.'

Her low voice ceased. With face averted, she stared in silence across the brown, scorched prairie. Stratton, his eyes fixed straight ahead, and his cheeks tinged with unwonted colour, found it quite impossible to speak, and for a space the stillness was broken only by the creak of saddle-leather and the dull thud of horses' hoofs.

'It's mighty fine of you to feel like that,' he said at length. 'I'm sorry if I gave you the idea I – I was – curious.'

'But you would be, naturally. You see, the other boys all know.' She turned her head and looked at him. 'I think we're all curious at times about things which really don't concern us. I've even wondered once or twice about you. You know you don't talk like the regulation cow-puncher – quite.'

Stratton laughed. 'Oh, but I am,' he assured her. 'I suppose the war rubbed off some of the accents, and of course I had a pretty good education to start with. But I'm too keen about the country and the life to ever want to do anything else.'

Her face glowed. 'It is wonderful,' she agreed. 'When I think of the years I've wasted in cities! I couldn't ever go back. Even with all the worries, this is a thousand times better. Ah! There they are ahead. They're turning the herd into this pasture, you see.'

Half a mile or more to the southward a spreading dust-cloud hugged the earth, through which, indistinctly, Stratton could make out the moving figures of men and cattle. The two spurred forward, reaching the wide opening in the fence ahead of the vanguard of steers. Passing through, they circled to the right to avoid turning back any of the cattle, and joined the sweating, hard-worked cow-punchers.

As they rode up together, Buck found Lynch's eyes fixed on him with an expression of angry surprise, which was suppressed with evident difficulty.

'How'd yuh get back so quick?' he enquired curtly.

'Nothing more to keep me,' shrugged Stratton. 'I waited for the doctor to look Rick over, and then thought I'd come out and see if you needed me.'

'Huh! Well, since you're here, yuh might as well whirl in. Get over on the far side of the herd an' help Flint. Don't let any of 'em break away, but don't crowd 'em too much.'

As Buck rode off he heard Miss Thorne ask if there wasn't something she could do. Lynch's reply was indistinct, but the tone of his voice, deferential, yet with a faint undercurrent of honey-sweetness, irritated him inexplicably. With a scowl, he spurred forward, exchanged a brief greeting with Bud Jessup as he passed, and finally joined Kreeger, who was having considerable difficulty in keeping the herd together at that point.

During the succeeding two hours or so, Buck forgot his irritation in the interest and excitement of the work. Strenuous as it was, he found a distinct pleasure in the discovery that two years' absence from the range had not lessened his ability to hold his own. His horse was well trained, and he thoroughly enjoyed the frequent sharp dashes after some refractory steer, who stubbornly opposed being driven. Before the last animal had passed through the fence-gap into the further pasture, he was drenched from head to foot with perspiration and his muscles ached from the unaccustomed labour, but all that was discounted by the satisfaction of doing his chosen work again, and doing it well.

Then, in the lull which followed, his thoughts returned to Miss Thorne and he wondered whether there would be any chance for further conversation with her on the way back to the ranch-house? The question was quickly answered in a manner he did not in the least enjoy. After giving instructions about nailing up the fence, Tex Lynch joined the girl, who sat her horse at a little distance, and the two rode off together.

For a moment or two Stratton's frowning glance followed them. Then of a sudden he realised that Slim McCabe's shrewd eyes were fixed curiously on him, and the discovery brought him abruptly to his senses. For a space he had forgotten what his position was at the Shoe-Bar. He must keep a better guard over himself, or he would certainly arouse suspicion. Averting his eyes, but still continuing to frown a little as if lack of tobacco was responsible for his annoyance, he searched through his pockets.

'Got the makin's?' he asked McCabe. 'Darned if I haven't left mine in the bunk-house.'

Slim readily produced a sack, and when Buck had rolled a cigarette, he returned it with a jesting remark, and swung himself rather stiffly out of his saddle.

'Haven't any hammer, but I can help tighten wires,' he commented.

He had intended joining Bud Jessup and trying while helping him to get a chance to discuss some of the things he had learned from Bemis. But somehow he found himself working beside McCabe, and when the fence had been put up again and they started home, it was Slim who rode beside him, chatting volubly and amusingly, but sticking like a leach.

It 'gave one to think', Stratton decided grimly, remembering the expressive French phrase he had heard so often overseas. He could not quite make up his mind whether the action was deliberate or the result of accident, but after supper he had no doubt whatever.

During the meal Lynch showed himself in quite a new light. He chatted and joked with a careless good humour which was a revelation to Stratton, whom he treated with special favour. Afterward he asked Buck if he didn't want to look his patient over, and accompanied him into Bemis's room, remaining while the wound was inspected and freshly dressed. Later, in the bunk-house, he announced that they would start a round-up next morning to pick out some three-year-olds for shipment.

'Got a rush order for twelve hundred head,' he explained. 'We'll all have to get busy early except Bud, who'll stay here to look after things. If any of yuh have saddles or anythin' else to look after, yuh'd better do it tonight, so's we can get goin' by daybreak.'

Like a flash Stratton realised the other's game, and his eyes narrowed ever so little. So that was it! By this most simple of expedients, he was to be kept away from the ranch-house and incidentally from any communication with Bemis or Bud, or Mary Thorne, unless accompanied by Lynch or one of his satellites. And the worst of it was he was quite helpless. He was merely a common, ordinary hand, and at the first sign of disobedience, or even evasion of orders, Lynch would have a perfectly good excuse to discharge him – an excuse he was doubtless itching to create.

CHAPTER 10

Buck Finds Out Something

When the fact is chronicled that no less than three times in the succeeding eight days Buck Stratton was strongly tempted to put an end to the whole puzzling business by the simple expedient of declaring his identity and taking possession of the Shoe-Bar as his own, something may be guessed of the ingenuity of Tex Lynch in making life unpleasant for the new hand.

Buck told himself more than once that if he had really been a new hand and nothing more, he wouldn't have lasted forty-eight hours. Any self-respecting cowman would have promptly demanded his time and betaken himself to another outfit, and Stratton sometimes wondered whether his mere acceptance of the persecution might not rouse the foreman's suspicion that he had motives for staying which did not appear on the surface.

He had to admit that Lynch's whole course of action was rather cleverly worked out. It consisted mainly in giving Stratton the most difficult and arduous work to do, and keeping him at it longer than anyone else, not only on the round-up, but while driving the herd to Paloma Springs and right up to the point where the steers were loaded on cattle-cars and the job was over.

That, broadly speaking, was the scheme; but there were delicate touches of refinement and ingenuity in the process which wrung from Stratton, in rare intervals when he was not too furious to judge calmly, a grudging measure of admiration for the wily foreman. Frequently, for instance, Stratton would be assigned to night-herd duty with promise of relief at a certain hour. Almost always that relief failed to materialise, and Buck, unable to leave the herd, reeling with fatigue and cursing impotently, had to keep at it till daybreak. The erring puncher generally had an excellent excuse, which might have passed muster once, but which grew threadbare with repetition.

Then, after an hour or two of sleep, the victim was more likely than not to be dragged out of bed and ordered to take the place of Peters, Kreeger, or one of the others, who had been sent to the ranch or elsewhere on so-called necessary business. More than once the others got started on a meal ahead of him, and what food remained was cold, unappetising, and scant in quantity. There were other little things Lynch thought of from time to time to make Buck's life miserable, and he quite succeeded, though it must be said that Stratton's hard-won self-control prevented the foreman from enjoying the full measure of his triumph.

What chiefly influenced Buck in holding back his big card and scoring against them all was the feeling that Mary Thorne would be the one to suffer most. He would be putting an abrupt finish to Lynch's game, whatever that was, but his action would also involve the girl in deep and bitter humiliation, if not something worse. Moreover, he was not quite ready to stop Lynch's scheming. He wanted to find out first what it was all about, and he felt he had a better chance of success by continuing to play his present part, hedged in and handicapped though he was, than by coming out suddenly in his own proper person.

So he stuck it out to the end, successfully suppressing all evidence of the smouldering rage that grew steadily within him against the whole crowd. Returning to the ranch for the first time in more than a week, he went to bed directly after supper and slept like a log until breakfast. Rising, refreshed and fit, he decided that the time had come to abandon his former haphazard methods of getting information, and to launch a campaign of active detective work without further delay.

Since the night of Bemis's accident, Buck had scarcely had a word with Bud Jessup, who he felt could give him some information, though he was not counting much on the importance of what the youngster was likely to know. Through the day there was no chance of getting the fellow apart. But Buck kept his eyes and ears open, and at supper-time Bud's casual remark to Lynch that he 's'posed he'd have to fix that busted saddle-girth before he hit the hay' did not escape him.

The meal over, Stratton left the kitchen and headed for the bunk-house with a purposeful air, soon leaving the others well in the rear. Presently one of them snickered.

'Looks like the poor rube's goin' to tear off some more sleep,' commented Kreeger in a suppressed tone, evidently not thinking Stratton was near enough to hear.

But Buck's ears were sharp, and his lips twitched in a grim smile as he moved steadily on, shoulders purposely sagging. When he had passed through the doorway his head went up abruptly and his whole manner changed. Darting to his bunk, he snatched the blankets out and unrolled them with a jerk. Scrambling his clothes and other belongings into a rough mound, he swiftly spread the blankets over them, patted down a place or two to increase the likeness to a human body, dropped his hat on the floor beside the bunk, and then made a lightning exit through a window at the rear.

It was all accomplished with such celerity that before the dawdling punchers had entered the bunk-house, Buck was out of sight among the bushes which thickly lined the creek. From here he had no difficulty in making his way unseen around to the back of the barns and other out-buildings, one of which he entered through a rear door. A moment or two later he found Jessup, as he expected, squatting on the floor of the harness-room, busily mending his broken saddle-girth.

'Hello, Bud,' he grinned, as the youngster looked up in surprise. 'Thought I'd come up and have a chin with you.'

'But how the deuce – I thought they – yuh – '

'You thought right,' replied Stratton, as Jessup hesitated. 'Tex and his friends have been sticking around pretty close for the past week or so, but I gave 'em the slip just now.'

Briefly he explained what he had done, and then paused, eyeing the young fellow speculatively.

'There's something queer going on here, old man,' he began presently. 'You'll say it's none of my business, maybe, and I reckon it isn't. But unless I've sized 'em up wrong, Lynch and his gang are a bunch of crooks, and I'm not the sort to sit back quietly and leave a lady like Miss Thorne to their mercy.'

Jessup's eyes widened. 'What do yuh know?' he demanded. 'What have yuh found out?'

Buck shrugged his shoulders. 'Found out? Why, nothing, really. But I've seen enough to know that bunch is up to some deviltry, and naturally the owner of the outfit is the one who'll suffer, in pocket, if not something worse. It's a dirty deal, taking advantage of a girl's ignorance and inexperience, as that gang sure is doing some way – specially a girl who's as decent and white as she is. I thought maybe you and me might get together and work out something. You don't act like you were for 'em any more than I am.'

'I'll tell a man I ain't!' declared Jessup emphatically. 'They're a rotten bunch. Yuh can go as far's you like, an' I'll stick with yuh. Have yuh got anything on 'em?'

'Not exactly, but we may have if we put our heads together and talk it over.' He glanced questioningly around the dusty room. 'They'll likely find out the trick I played on 'em, and come snooping around here before long. Suppose we slip out and go down by the creek where we can talk without being interrupted.'

Jessup agreed readily and followed Buck into the barn and out through the back door, where they sought a secluded spot down by the stream, well shielded by bushes.

'You've been here longer than I have and noticed a lot more,' Stratton remarked when they were settled. 'I wish you'd tell me what you think that bunch is up to. They haven't let me out of their sight for over a week. What's the idea, anyhow?'

'They don't want yuh should find out anythin',' returned Bud promptly.

'That's what I s'posed, but what's there to find out? That's what I can't seem to get at. Bemis says they're in with the rustlers, but even he seems to think there's something else in the wind besides that.'

Jessup snorted contemptuously. 'Bemis – huh! I'm through with him. He's a quitter. I was in chinnin' with him last night an' he's lost his nerve. Says he's through, an' is goin' to take his time the minute he's fit to back a horse. Still an' all,' he added, forehead wrinkling thoughtfully, 'he's right in a way. There is somethin' doin' beside rustling, but I'm hanged if I can find out what. The only thing I'm dead sure of is that it's crooked. Look at the way they're tryin' to get rid of us – Rick an' me an' you. Whatever they're up to they want the ranch to themselves before they go any further. Now Rick's out of the way, I s'pose I'll be next. They're tryin' their best to make me quit, but when they find out that won't work, I reckon they'll try somethin' – worse.'

'Why don't Lynch just up an' fire you?' Buck asked curiously. 'He's foreman.'

Bud's young jaw tightened stubbornly. 'He can't get nothin' on me,' he stated. 'It's this way. When help begun to get shy a couple of months ago – that's when he started his business of gittin' rid of the men one way or another – Tex must of hinted around to Miss Mary that I was goin' to quit, for she up an' asked me one day if it was true, an' said she hoped me an' Rick wasn't goin' to leave like the rest of 'em.'

He paused, a faint flush darkening his tan. 'I dunno as you've noticed it,' he went on, plucking a long spear of grass and twisting it between his brown fingers, 'but Miss Mary's got a way about her that – that sort of gets a man. She's so awful young, an' – an' – earnest, an' though she don't know one thing hardly about ranchin', she's dead crazy about this place, an' mighty anxious to make it pay. When she asks yuh to do somethin', yuh jest natu'ally feel like yuh wanted to oblige. I felt like that, anyhow, an' I was hot under the collar at Tex for lyin' about me like he must of done. So I tells her straight off I wasn't thinkin' of anythin' of the sort. "Fu'thermore," I says, "I'll stick to the job as long as yuh like if you'll do one thing." She asks what's that, an' I told her that some folks, namin' no names, was tryin' to make out to her I wasn't doin' my work good, an' doin' their best to get me in bad.

' "Oh, but I think you're mistaken," she says, catchin' on right away who I meant. "Tex wouldn't do anythin' like that. He needs help too bad, for one thing."

' "Well," I says, "let it go at that. Only, if yuh hear anythin' against me, I'd like for yuh not to take anybody else's word for it. It's got to be proved I ain't capable, or I've done somethin' I oughta be fired for. An' if things gets so I got to go, I'll come to yuh an' ask for my time myself. Fu'thermore, I'll get Rick to promise the same thing."

'Well, to make a long story short, she said she'd do it, though I could see she was still thinkin' me mistaken about Tex doin' anythin' out of the way. He's a rotten skunk, but you'd better believe he don't let her see it. He's got her so she believes every darn word he says is gospel.'

He finished in an angry key. Stratton's face was thoughtful.

'How long has he been here?' he asked.

'Who? Tex? Oh, long before I come. The old man made him foreman pretty near a year ago in place of Bloss, who run the outfit for Stratton, that fellow who was killed in the war that old Thorne bought the ranch off of.'

'What sort of a man was this Thorne?' Buck presently enquired.

'Pretty decent, though kinda stand-offish with us fellows. He was awful thick with Tex, though, an' mebbe that's the reason Miss Mary thinks so much of him. She took his death mighty hard, believe me!'

With a mind groping after hidden clues, Stratton subconsciously disentangled the various 'hes' and 'hims' of Jessup's slightly involved remark.

'Pop Daggett told me about his being thrown and breaking his neck,' he said presently. 'You were here then, weren't you? Was there anything queer about it? I mean, like the two punchers who were killed later on?'

Jessup's eyes widened. 'Queer?' he repeated. 'Why, I – I never thought about it that way. I wasn't around when it happened. Nobody was with him but – but – Tex.' He stared at Buck. 'Yuh don't mean to say – '

'I don't say anything,' returned Stratton, as he paused. 'How can I, without knowing the facts? Was the horse a bad one?'

'He was new – jest been put in the *remuda*. I never saw him rid except by Doc Peters, who's a shark. I did notice, afterward, he was sorta mean, though I've seen worse. We was on the spring round-up, jest startin' to brand over in the middle pasture.' Bud spoke slowly with thoughtfully wrinkled brows. 'It was right after dinner when the old man rode up on Socks, the horse he gen'ally used. He seemed pretty excited for him. He got hold of Tex right away, an' the two of them went off to one side an' chinned consid'able. Then they changed the saddle onto this here paint horse, Socks bein' sorta tuckered out, an' rode off together. It was near three hours before Tex came gallopin' back alone with word that the old man's horse had stepped in a hole an' throwed him, breakin' his neck.'

'Was that part of it true?' asked Buck, who had been listening intently.

'About his neck? Sure. They had Doc Blanchard over right away. He'd been throwed, all right, too, from the scratches on his face.'

'Where did it happen?'

'Yuh got me. I wasn't one of the bunch that brought him in. I never thought to ask afterwards, neither. It must of been somewhere up to the north end of the ranch, though, if they kep' on goin' the way they started.'

For a moment or two Stratton sat silent, staring absently at the sloping bank below him. Was there anything back of the ranch-owner's tragic death save simple accident? The story was plausible enough. Holes were plentiful, and it wouldn't be the first time a horse's stumble had resulted fatally to the rider. On the other hand, it is quite possible, by an abrupt though seemingly accidental thrust or collision, to stir a horse of uncertain temper into sudden, vehement action. At length Buck sighed and abandoned his cogitations as fruitless. Short of a miracle, that phase of the problem was never likely to be answered.

'I wonder what took him off like that?' he pondered aloud. 'Have you any notion? Is there anything particular up that way?'

'Why, no. Nobody hardly ever goes there. They call it the north pasture, but it's never used. There's nothin' there but sand an' cactus an' all that; a goat couldn't hardly keep body an' soul together. Except once lookin' for strays that got through the fence, I never set foot in it myself.'

Down in the shallow gully where they sat, the shadows were gathering, showing that dusk was rapidly approaching. With a shake of his head and a movement of his wide shoulders, Buck mentally dismissed that subject.

'It's getting dark,' he said briskly. 'We'll have to hustle, or there'll be a searching party out after us. Have you noticed anything else particularly – about Lynch, I mean, or any of the others?'

'Nothin' I can make sense of,' returned Jessup. 'Tex has been off the ranch a lot. Two or three times he's stayed away over night. It might of been reg'lar business, I s'pose, but once Bill Harris, over to the Rockin'- R, said he'd seen him in Tucson with some guys in a big automobile. That rustlin', of course, yuh know about. On the evidence, I dunno as yuh could swear he was in it, but it's a sure thing that any foreman worth his salt would of stopped the business before now, or else get the sheriff on the job if he couldn't handle it himself.'

'That's one thing I've wondered,' commented Buck. 'Why doesn't he? What's his excuse for holding off?'

Bud gave a short, brittle laugh. 'I'll tell yuh. He says the sheriff's a crook! What do you know about that? I heard him tellin' it to Miss Mary the other day when he come in from Paloma about dinner-time. She was askin' him the same question, an' he up an' tells her it wouldn't be worth while; tells her the man is a half-breed an' always plays in with the greasers, so he wouldn't be no use. I never met up with Jim Hardenberg, but he sure ain't a breed, an' he's got a darn good rep as sheriff.' He groaned. 'Wimmin sure is queer. Think of anybody believin' that sort of rot.'

'Did Lynch know you were listening?'

Jessup reddened a little. 'No. They were talkin' in the big room, an' I was standin' to one side of the open window. I don't call it sneakin' to try an' get the drop on a coyote like him.'

'I don't either,' smiled Stratton, getting on his feet. The swift, southern darkness had fallen so quickly that they could barely see each other's faces. 'It's one of their own little tricks, and turn about is fair play. Our job, I reckon, is to keep our eyes open every minute and not let anything slip. We'll find a way to get together again if anything should turn up. I'll be going back.'

He turned away and took a few steps along the bank. Then all at once he stopped and walked back.

'Say, Bud, how big is that north pasture place you were telling about?' he asked. 'I don't seem to remember going over it when I was – '

He broke off abruptly, and a sudden flush burned into his cheeks at the realisation that he had almost betrayed himself. Fortunately Jessup did not seem to notice the slip.

'I don't know exactly,' replied the youngster. 'About two miles square, maybe. Why?'

'Oh, I just wondered,' shrugged Stratton. 'Well, so-long.'

Again they parted, Bud returning to the harness-room, where he would have to finish his work by lantern-light.

'Gee, but that was close!' murmured Bud, feeling his way through the darkness. 'Just about one more word and I'd have given away the show completely.'

He paused under a cottonwood as a gleam of light from the open bunk-house door showed through the leaves.

'I wonder?' he mused thoughtfully.

A waste of sand, cactus, and scanty desert growth! In Arizona nothing is more ordinary or commonplace, more utterly lacking in interest and significance. Yet Stratton's mind returned to it persistently as he considered one by one the scanty details of Jessup's brief narrative.

What was there about a spot like that to rouse excitement in the breast of the usually phlegmatic Andrew Thorne? Why had he been in such haste to drag Lynch thither, and what had passed between the two before the older man came to his sudden and tragic end? Was it possible that somewhere within that four square miles of desolate wilderness might lie the key to the puzzling mystery Buck had set himself to solve?

'I wonder?' he murmured again, and leaving the margin of the creek, he moved slowly towards the open bunk-house door.

CHAPTER 11

Danger

As Buck appeared in the doorway, blinking a little at the lamplight, the five card-players stared at him in astonishment.

'Where the devil have you been?' enquired Kreeger, surprised out of his accustomed taciturnity.

'I thought yuh was asleep,' added Peters, casting a bewildered glance at the shadowy bunk.

Buck, who had scarcely hoped his little stratagem would succeed so well, refrained with difficulty from showing the pleasure he felt.

'So I have,' he drawled.

'But I thought yuh was in yore bunk,' commented McCabe, his light-blue eyes narrowing slightly.

'No, I was outside,' explained Stratton carelessly. 'It was too hot in here, so I went out and sat down by the creek. I must have dropped off pretty soon, and when I came to it was dark.'

As he spoke he glanced casually at Tex Lynch, and despite himself a little shiver flickered on his spine. The foreman, who had not spoken, sat motionless on the further side of the table regarding Stratton steadily. His lids drooped slightly and his face was almost expressionless. But in spite of that Buck got a momentary impression of baffled fury and a deadly, murderous hate, the more startling because of its very repression. Coupling it with what he knew or suspected of the man, Stratton felt there was some excuse for that momentary mental shrinking.

'He'd as soon put me out of the way as shoot a coyote,' he said to himself, as he walked over to his bunk. 'All he wants is a chance to do it without getting caught.'

But with ordinary care and caution he did not see just how Tex was going to get the chance. Buck never went anywhere without his gun, and he flattered himself he was as quick on the draw as the average. Besides, he knew better now than to trust himself alone with Lynch or any of the others on some outlying part of the range where a fatal accident could plausibly be laid to marauding greasers, or to some similar agency.

'I'm not saying any one of 'em couldn't pick me off a dozen times a day and make an easy getaway across the border,' he thought, stretching himself out on the husk mattress. 'But Lynch don't want to have to make a getaway. There's something right here on the Shoe-Bar that interests him a whole lot too much.'

Presently Bud came in, parried with some success the half-questioning comments of the men, and went to bed. Buck lay awake a while longer, trying to patch together into some semblance of pattern the isolated scraps of information he had gained, but without any measure of success.

There followed four surprising days of calm, during which the Shoe-Bar, to every outward seeming, might have been the most ordinary and humdrum of outfits, with not a hint of anything sinister or mysterious beneath the surface.

Each morning the men sallied forth to work, returned for noon dinner, and rode off again soon afterward. Lynch was neither grouchy nor over-jovial. He seemed the typical ranch-boss, whose chief thought is to get the work done, and his berating was entirely impartial. Bud had spent most of his time around the ranch, but once or twice he rode out with the others, and there was no attempt on their part to keep him and Buck from talking together as privately as they pleased. Only where Miss Thorne was concerned was Stratton conscious of the old unobtrusive surveillance. He saw her several times during his brief visits to Bemis, who was improving daily and fretting to be gone, but always Lynch, McCabe, or some one just 'happened' to be along.

The effect of this unexpected peace and quiet on Stratton, however, was precisely opposite from the one he presumed was intended. He had a feeling that it was a calm before the storm, and became more alert than ever. The unnatural placidity weighed on him, and as day followed day serenely his nerves grew edgy.

After supper on the fourth day Lynch went up to the ranch-house and was closeted for more than an hour with Miss Thorne. On his return to the bunk-house, Stratton, who had now come to speculate on his every move, studied him covertly but found his manner quite as usual.

In the morning they started off for the middle pasture, where they were engaged in repairing a fence which had all but fallen flat. Quite by accident, and without any inkling of what was to come of his carelessness, Buck left his hammer and pliers beside the corral gate instead of sticking them into his saddle-pockets. Before they had gone a quarter of a mile he discovered the omission and pulled up, explaining what had happened.

'It won't take me five minutes to go back for them,' he added, gathering up his reins.

'I'll go with yuh,' said McCabe promptly. 'With a little hustlin', we can easy catch up with the gang before they get to the pasture.'

'Well, speed up, both of yuh,' admonished Lynch. 'We want to finish that job today.'

Slightly amused and wondering whether they thought for an instant he was too blind to see through their game, Stratton put spurs to his horse and the two rode back together, McCabe apparently making a special effort to be amusing. The tools were found where Buck had left them, and the latter was on the point of remounting, when Mary Thorne came suddenly around the corner of the house.

'Good morning,' she greeted them both pleasantly, but with a slight undercurrent of preoccupation in her manner. 'I was afraid you'd gone.' Her eyes met Stratton's. 'Could I speak to you a moment?' she asked.

'Certainly, ma'am.'

Buck dropped his bridle-reins and moved forward. For an instant McCabe sat motionless; then he swung himself out of the saddle.

'If it's anythin' I can help about – ' he began, awkwardly, yet ingratiatingly.

'Thank you very much, Slim, but it isn't,' the girl answered quietly.

'We ain't got much time,' protested McCabe uneasily. 'We jest came back to get them tools Buck forgot. Tex is in a hurry to finish up the job.'

'I don't believe five minutes' delay will matter very much,' returned Miss Thorne, with a touch of that unexpected decision Stratton had noticed once or twice before. 'I sha'n't be any longer.'

She moved away from the corral and Buck, walking beside her, was conscious of a curious tension in the air. For a moment he thought McCabe meant to persist and force his presence on them. But evidently the stocky cow-puncher found the situation too difficult for him to cope with, for he remained standing beside his horse, though his glance followed them intently, and throughout the brief interview his eyes searched their faces, as if he strove to read from their expression or the movement of their lips some inkling of what it was all about.

'I won't keep you but a moment,' the girl began, her colour slightly heightened. 'I only thought that perhaps I might persuade you to – to change your mind, and – and stay. If the work's too hard, we might be able to – '

She paused. Buck stared at her in astonishment. 'I don't understand,' he said briefly.

Her flush deepened. 'I meant about your going. I understood you weren't satisfied, and wanted to – to leave.'

'Who told you that?'

'Why – Tex. Isn't it – '

Buck frowned, and then, conscious of the watching McCabe, his face cleared and he laughed.

'He must have got me wrong, Miss Ma – er – Thorne,' he returned lightly. 'Perhaps he's heard me grumbling a bit; cowmen do that from force of habit sometimes, you know. But I've nothing to complain of about the work, and certainly I had no idea of quitting.'

Her face cleared amazingly. 'I'm so glad,' she said in a relieved tone. 'I suppose I seem fussy, but now and then the problem of help gets to be a regular nightmare. Once or twice lately I've been afraid I was making a terrible mess of things, and might, after all, have to accept one of the offers I've had for the ranch. I should hate dreadfully to leave here, but if I can't make it pay – '

She finished with a shrug. Stratton regarded her thoughtfully. 'You've had several offers?' he asked hesitatingly, wondering whether she would think the question an impertinence.

Apparently she didn't. 'Two; really most awfully good ones. Indeed, Tex strongly advised me to sell out and buy another outfit if I still wanted to ranch. But I don't want another one. It's the Shoe-Bar I'm so keen about because of – But I really mustn't keep you. Thank you so much for relieving my mind. When Tex comes in I'll tell him he was mistaken.'

Buck hesitated for an instant. 'It might be better not to say anything about it,' he suggested. 'Some foremen don't like the least bit of inter-ference, you know. Suppose we just let it go, and if he brings up the subject to me, I'll tell him he got me wrong.'

'Very well. It doesn't make any difference so long as you're staying. Goodbye.'

With a little gesture of farewell, she walked away towards the ranch-house, leaving Stratton to return to where McCabe fidgeted beside the horses. There was no time for deliberate reasoning or planning. Buck only felt sure that Lynch was up to something underhand, and when Slim, with almost too great a casualness, enquired what it was all about, he obeyed a strong impulse and lied.

'Oh, it's Bemis,' he shrugged, as they rode off together. 'He's fretting to get away. Lost his nerve, I reckon, and wants to pull out. She wanted to know how long I thought it would be before he could back a horse. I s'pose he might chance it in about a week, but I'm hanged if I can see why he's in such a rush. He's sure got it soft enough here.'

While he talked he was busy rolling a cigarette, but this did not prevent him from being aware of Slim's intent, sidelong scrutiny. He could not be quite certain whether or not he succeeded in deceiving the fellow, but from the character of McCabe's comments, he rather thought he had. Certainly he hoped so. Slim was sure to tell Lynch about the incident, but if he himself believed it harmless, the foreman was likely to take the same point of view, and continue to carry out the scheme he had in mind. Whatever this was, Stratton, in his present frame of mind, preferred that it should be brought to a head rather than continue any longer in suspense.

Throughout the day he could get no hint of what was going on. Once the thought occurred to him that it might be a variation of the trick Lynch had tried to play on Bud. By preparing Miss Thorne beforehand for the departure of the new hand, he could discharge Stratton and then represent to the girl that he had quit of his own accord. But somehow this didn't altogether fit. It assumed that Buck would take his dismissal quietly without attempting a personal appeal to the ranch-owner; also it took no account of Bud Jessup. By this time Tex must realise that there had been more or less intimate communication between the two, and Bud was not the sort to stand by quietly and see his friend turned out without stirring vehemently in his behalf.

Considering all this, Buck could not see that there was much to fear in Lynch's present manoeuvring; and it was something of a shock to find Bud absent from the supper-table.

'Gone to Paloma to fetch those wagon-bolts,' explained Tex, who had come in about an hour ahead of the others, in answer to Peters's query. 'They'd ought to of come in by mail yesterday or the day before, an' we need 'em bad. He'll get supper in town an' be back before dark.'

Somewhat thoughtful, Buck accompanied the others to the bunk-house, where he was cordially invited to join the evening game of draw, but declined on the plea of having a couple of letters to write. It was a subterfuge, of course; he had nobody to write to. But in his mind had risen a strong preference for being in a position where he could overlook the whole group, rather than be seated in their very midst.

There had come to him a sudden, vivid conviction that he had under-estimated the foreman's resources and his own possible danger. As he sat there mechanically scribbling random sentences, it was brought home to him for the first time how unpleasantly alone he was. Save for a helpless girl and an even more helpless old woman, there wasn't a soul within a dozen miles on whom he could count for help in an emergency. Of course when Bud returned –

But Bud didn't return. Nine o'clock brought no sign of him. Another hour passed and still he failed to show up. It began to look very much as if the youngster had met with some accident or was being purposely kept out of the way.

When the men finished their game and began to turn in, Stratton reluctantly followed their example. As long as there was any light he felt perfectly able to take care of himself. It was the darkness he feared – that inky, suffocating darkness which masks everything like a pall. He dreaded, too, the increased chances bed would bring of yielding for a single fatal instant to treacherous sleep; but he couldn't well sit up all night, so he undressed leisurely with the rest and stretched his long length between the blankets.

When the lamp was out, he cautiously flung aside his coverings, drew himself into a reclining position, and with gun in one hand and some matches close beside the other, began his vigil.

For a long time – it must have been an hour at least – there was no need to fight off sleep. His mind was far too active. But his thoughts were not altogether cheering, for he began to see clearly how Lynch might hope to accomplish the impossible.

So far there had been reassurance in the feeling that the foreman would not dare proceed to open violence because of the almost certain consequences to himself. Buck realised now that, under the conditions of the moment, those consequences might become almost negligible. Suppose, for instance, that by next morning Stratton had disappeared. Lynch and his confederates would tell a plausible story of his having demanded his time the night before and ridden off early in the morning. It was a story Tex had carefully prepared Miss Thorne to hear, and whether or not, after Buck's talk with her during the morning, she might be suspicious, that would make no difference in the foreman's actions now. He would see that a horse was gone, and attend to all the other necessary details. He had the better part of the night and miles of desert waste in which to dispose of every trace of Stratton and his belongings. Bud would be suspicious, but between suspicion and proof there is a great gulf fixed. And though Lynch might not know it, one of his strongest cards was the fact that if Stratton should vanish off the earth, there was not a soul who would ever come around asking awkward questions.

'But I'm not going to be bumped off just now, thank you,' Buck said to himself with a grim straightening of the lips. 'They won't dare fire a gun, and they don't know I'm ready for them and waiting.'

Another hour passed, a tortured, harrowing hour in which he fought sleep desperately with all the limited resources at his command. In spite of his determination to keep his eyes open at any cost, his lids drooped and lifted, drooped and lifted, drooped and were dragged open by sheer will-power. Each time it was more difficult. Just as the water laps inexorably at length over the face of an exhausted swimmer, so these waves of sleep, smothering, clutching, dulled his senses and strove to wrap him in their soft, treacherous embrace.

There came at last a complete wiping out of consciousness, how long or short he never knew, from which he was jarred into sudden wakefulness by a sound. He had no idea what it was nor whence it came. He merely found himself abruptly in full possession of his senses, nerves tingling, moisture dewing his forehead, his whole being concentrated in the one act of – listening!

For what seemed an eternity he could hear nothing save the heavy breathing of sleeping men. Then it came again, a slow, faint, dragging sound that ceased almost as soon as it began.

Some one was creeping stealthily towards him across the cabin floor!

CHAPTER 12

Thwarted

Instantly a sense of elation, tingling as an electric shock, surged over Stratton, and his grip on the Colt tightened. At last he was face to face with something definite and concrete, and in a moment all the little doubts and nagging nervous qualms which had assailed him from time to time during his long vigil were swept away. Cautiously drawing his gun into position, he felt for a match with the other hand and prepared to scratch it against the side of the bunk.

Slowly, stealthily, with many a cautious pause, the crawling body drew steadily nearer. Though the intense darkness prevented him from seeing anything, Buck felt at last that he had correctly gauged the position of the unknown plotter. Trying to continue that easy, steady breathing, which had been no easy matter, he slightly raised his weapon and then, with a sudden, lightning movement, he drew the match firmly across the rough board.

To his anger and chagrin the head broke off. Before he could snatch up another and strike it viciously, there came from close at hand a sudden rustle, a creak, the clatter of something on the floor, followed by dead silence. When the light flared up, illumining dimly almost the whole length of the room, there was nothing in the least suspicious to be seen.

Nevertheless, with inward cursing, Stratton sprang up and lit the lamp he had used early in the evening and which he had purposely left within reach. With this added illumination he made a discovery that brought his lips together in a grim line.

Someone lay stretched out in the bunk next to his own – Jessup's bunk, which had been empty when he went to bed.

For a fleeting instant Buck wondered whether Bud could possibly have returned and crawled in there unheard. Then, as the wick flared up, he not only realised that this couldn't have happened, but recognised lying on the youngster's rolled-up blankets the stout figure and round, unshaven face of – Slim McCabe.

As he stood staring at the fellow, there was a stir from further down the room and a sleepy voice growled:

'What's the matter? It ain't time to get up yet, is it?'

Buck, who had just caught a glint of steel on the floor at the edge of the bunk, pulled himself together.

'No; I – I must have had a – nightmare,' he returned in a realistically dazed tone. 'I was dreaming about – rustlers, and thought I heard some-body walking around.'

Still watching McCabe surreptitiously, he saw the fellow's lids lift sleepily.

'W'a's matter?' murmured Slim, blinking at the lamp.

'Nothing. I was dreaming. What the devil are you doing in that bunk?'

McCabe appeared to rouse himself with an effort and partly sat up, yawning prodigiously.

'It was hot in my own, so I come over here to get the air from the window,' he mumbled. 'What's the idea of waking a guy up in the middle of the night?'

Buck did not answer for a moment but, stepping back, trod as if by accident on the end of his trailing blanket. As he intended, the move-ment sent his holster and belt tumbling to the floor, and with perfect naturalness he stooped to pick them up. When he straightened, his face betrayed nothing of the grim satisfaction he felt at having proved his point. The bit of steel was a hunting-knife with a seven-inch blade, sharp as a razor, and with a distinctive stag-horn handle, which Tex Lynch had used only a few evenings before to remove the skin from a coyote he had brought down.

'Sorry, but I was dreaming,' drawled Stratton. 'No harm done, though, is there? You ain't likely to stay awake long.'

Without further comment he blew out the light and crawled into bed again. He found no difficulty now in keeping awake for the remainder of the night; there was too much to think about and decide. Now that he had measured the lengths to which Lynch seemed willing to go, he realised that a continuance of present conditions was impossible. An exact repetition of this particular attempt was unlikely, but there were plenty of variations against which no single individual could hope to guard. He must bring things to a head at once, either by quitting the ranch, by playing the important card of his own identity he had so far held back, or else by finding some other way of tying Lynch's hands effectually. He was equally reluctant to take either of the two former steps, and so it pleased him greatly when at last he began to see his way towards working things out in another fashion.

'I'm blessed if that won't put a spoke in his wheel,' he thought jubilantly, considering details. 'He won't dare to touch me.'

When dawn came filtering through the windows, and one thing after another slowly emerged from the obscurity, Buck's eyes swiftly sought the floor below Bud's bunk. But though McCabe lay there snoring loudly, the knife had disappeared.

Though outwardly everything seemed normal, Buck noticed a slight restlessness and laxing tension about the men that morning. There was delay in getting to work, which might have been accounted for by the cessation of one job and the starting of another. But knowing what he did, Stratton felt that the flat failure of their plot had much to do with it.

He himself took advantage of the lull to slip away to the harness-room on the plea of mending a rip in the stitching of his chaps. Pulling a box over by the window where he could see anyone approaching, he produced pencil and paper and proceeded to write out a rather voluminous document, which he afterward read over and corrected carefully. He sealed it up in an envelope, wrote a much briefer note, and enclosed both in a second envelope which he addressed to Sheriff J. Hardenberg. Finally he felt around in his pocket and pulled forth the scrawl he had composed the night before.

'They look about the same,' he murmured, comparing them. 'Nobody will notice the difference.'

Buck was on the point of sealing the envelope containing the scrawl when it occurred to him to read the contents over and see what he had written.

The letter was headed 'Dear Friend', and proved to be a curious composition. With a mind intent on other things, Stratton had written almost mechanically, intending merely to give an air of reality to his occupation. In the beginning the scrawl read very much as if the 'friend' were masculine. Bits of ranch happenings and descriptions were jotted down as one would in writing to a cowboy friend located on a distant outfit. But gradually, imperceptibly almost, the tone shifted. Buck himself had been totally unaware of any change until he read over the last few pages. And then, as he took in the subtle undercurrent of meaning which lay beneath the pencilled lines, a slow flush crept up into his face, and he frowned.

It was all rot, of course! He had merely written for the sake of writing something – anything. She was a nice little thing, of course, with an attractive feminine manner and an unexpected lot of nerve. He was sorry for her, naturally, and would like to help her out of what he felt to be a most disagreeable, if not hazardous situation. But as for anything further –

Still frowning, he thrust the sheets back into the envelope and licked the flap. He was on the point of stubbornly scrawling a man's name on the outside when he realised how foolish he would be not to carry out his first and much more sensible intention.

He wanted an excuse for asking permission to ride to town to post a letter. This, in itself, was an extremely nervy request and under ordinary conditions almost certain to be profanely refused. But Buck had a shrewd notion that after the failure of Lynch's plans, the foreman might welcome the chance of talking things over with his confederates without danger of being observed or overheard. On the other hand, if there should be the least suspicion that his letter was not of the most innocent and harmless sort, he would never in the world be allowed to get away with it.

The result was that when he strolled out of the harness-room a little later the envelope bearing the name of Sheriff Hardenberg reposed within his shirt, while the other, addressed now to a mythical 'Miss Florence

Denby', at an equally mythical street number in Dallas, Texas, protruded from a pocket of his chaps.

'I don't s'pose you've got a stamp you'll sell me,' he enquired of Lynch, whom he found in the bunk-house with McCabe. 'I'd like to get this letter off as soon as I can.'

Balancing the envelope in his hand, he held it so that the foreman could easily read the address.

'I might have,' returned Lynch briefly. 'Looks like that letter was heavy enough to need two.'

Buck allowed him to weigh it in his hand for an instant, and then, in simulated confusion, he snatched it back.

'Must be writin' to yore girl,' grinned McCabe, who had also been regarding the address curiously.

Stratton retorted in a convincingly embarrassed fashion, received his stamps and then proffered his request, which was finally granted with an air of reluctance and much grumbling.

'I wouldn't let yuh go, only I don't know what the devil's keepin' that fool Bud,' growled Lynch. 'Yuh tell the son-of-a-gun I ain't expectin' him to stop in town the rest of his natural life. If them wagon-bolts ain't come, we'll have to do without 'em. Yuh bring him back with yuh, an' see yuh both get here by dinner time without fail.'

Buck gave the desired promise and, hastily saddling up, departed. About three miles from the ranch, he rode off to the side of the trail and dismounted beside a stunted mesquite. Under its twisting branches, he dug a hole with the toe of his boot and interred therein Miss Florence Denby's letter, torn into small fragments.

This done he swung himself into the saddle and headed again for Paloma Springs, and as he rode he began to whistle blithely.

CHAPTER 13

Counterplot

'The low-down, ornery liar!' sputtered Bud Jessup, face flushed and eyes snapping. 'He told me to wait for them bolts if I had to stay here all day. I thought it was kinda funny he'd let me waste all this time, but I didn't have no idea at all he'd got me out of the way a-purpose to put across that dirty deal. Why, the rotten son-of-a – '

'Easy, kid,' cautioned Buck, glancing at the open door of the store. 'You'll have Pop comin' out to see what all the excitement's about, and that isn't our game – yet.'

He had found Bud alone on the rickety porch, kicking his heels against the railing and fretting at his enforced idleness; and having hitched his horse, he lost no time in giving the youngster a brief account of the happenings of the night before.

'Not him,' shrugged Jessup, though he did lower his voice a trifle. 'The up train's due in less than half an hour, an' Pop's gettin' the mailbag ready. That means readin' all the postcards twice at least, an' makin' out all he can through the envelopes, if the paper's thin enough. I often wondered why he didn't go the whole hog an' have a kettle ready to steam the flaps open, he seems to get so much pleasure out of other people's business.'

Stratton chuckled. This suited him perfectly up to a certain point. He pulled the letter out of his shirt and was pleased to see that none of the writing was visible. Then he displayed the face of the envelope to his companion.

Bud's eyes widened. 'Whew!' he whistled. 'That sure looks like business. What's up, Buck? Can't yuh tell a man?'

'I will on the way back; no time just now. Let's go in.'

He led the way into the store and walked down to where Daggett was slowly sorting a small pile of letters and postcards.

'Hello, Pop!' he greeted. 'Looks like I was just in time.'

The old man peered over the tops of his spectacles. 'Yuh be, if yuh want to catch the up-mail,' he nodded. 'Where's it to?'

He took the letter from Stratton's extended hand and studied it with frank interest.

'Jim Hardenberg!' he commented. 'Wal! Wal! Friend of yores, eh?'

'Oh, I don't know as you'd hardly call him that,' evaded Stratton. 'Haven't seen him in over two years, I reckon.'

Pop waited expectantly, but no further information was forthcoming. He eyed the letter curiously, manoeuvring as if by accident to hold it up against the light. He even tried, by obvious methods, to get rid of the two punchers, but they persisted in hanging around until at length the near approach of the train-hour forced the old man to drop the letter into the mailbag with the others and snap the lock. On the plea of seeing whether their package had come, both Stratton and Jessup escorted him over to the station platform and did not quit his side until the train had departed, carrying the mail-sack with it.

There were a few odds and ends of mail for the Shoe-Bar, but no parcel. When this became certain, Bud got his horse and the two mounted in front of the store.

'By gee!' exclaimed Pop suddenly as they were on the point of riding off. 'I clean forgot to tell yuh. They got blackleg over to the T-T's.'

Both men turned abruptly in their saddles and stared at him in dismay. To the bred-in-the-bone rancher the mention of blackleg, that deadly contagious and most fatal of cattle diseases, is almost as startling as bubonic plague would be to the average human.

'Hell!' ejaculated Bud forcefully. 'Yuh sure about that, Pop?'

'Sartain sure,' nodded the old man. 'One of their men, Bronc Tippets, was over here last night an' told me. Said their yearlings is dyin' off like flies.'

'That sure is mighty hard luck,' remarked Jessup as they rode out of town. 'I'm glad this outfit ain't any nearer.'

'Somewhere off to the west of the Shoe-Bar, isn't it?' asked Stratton.

'Yeah. 'Way the other side of the mountains. There's a short cut through the hills that comes out around the north end of middle pasture, but there ain't one steer in a thousand could find his way through. Well, let's hear what you're up to, old man. I'm plumb interested.'

Buck's serious expression relaxed and he promptly launched into a detailed explanation of his scheme. When he had made everything clear Bud's face lit up and he regarded his friend admiringly.

'By cripes, Buck!' he exclaimed delightedly. 'That sure oughta work. When are yuh goin' to spring it on 'em?'

'First good chance I get,' returned Buck. 'The sooner the better, so they won't have time to try any more dirty work.'

The opportunity was not long in coming. They reached the ranch just before dinner and when the meal was over learned that the afternoon was to be devoted to repairing the telephone leading from the ranch-house to Las Vegas camp, which had been out of order for several weeks. As certain fence wires were utilised for line purposes, this meant considerable work, if Stratton could judge by the ruinous condition of most of those he had seen. He wondered not a little at the meaning of the move, but did not allow his curiosity to interfere with the project he had in mind.

They had left the ranch in a bunch, Kreeger and Siegrist alone remaining behind for some other purpose. They had not gone more than two miles when a remark of McCabe's on mining claims gave Buck his cue.

'A fellow who goes into that game with a bunch takes a lot of chances,' he commented. 'I knew a chap once who came mighty near being croaked, to say nothing of losing a valuable claim, by being too confiding with a gang he thought could be trusted.'

'How was that?' enquired Slim amiably, as Stratton paused.

'They wanted the whole hog instead of being contented with their share, and tried two or three times to get this fellow – er – Brown. When Brown wised up to what was going on he thought at first he'd have to pull out to save his hide. But just in time he doped out a scheme to stop their dirty work, and it sure was a slick one, all right.'

Buck chuckled retrospectively. Though the pause was unbroken by any questions, he saw that he had the complete and undivided attention of his audience.

'What he did,' resumed Stratton, 'was to write out a detailed account of all the things they'd tried to put across, one of which was an attempt to – a – shoot him in his bunk while he was asleep. He sealed that up in an envelope and sent it to the sheriff with a note asking him to keep it safe, but not to open it unless the writer, Brown, got bumped off in some violent way or disappeared, in which case the sheriff was to act on the information in it and nab the crooks. After he'd got word of its receipt, he up and told the others what he'd done. Pretty cute, wasn't it?'

The brief pause that followed was tense and fraught with suppressed emotion.

'Did it work?' McCabe at length enquired, with elaborate casualness.

'Sure. The gang didn't dare raise a finger to him. They might have put a bullet through him any time, or a knife, and made a safe getaway, but then they'd have had to desert the claims, which wasn't their game at all. Darn good stunt to remember, ain't it, if a person ever got up against that sort of thing?'

There was no direct reply to the half-question, and Buck shot a glance at his companions. Lynch rode slightly behind him and was out of the line of vision. McCabe, with face averted, bent over fussing with his saddle-strings. The sight of Doc Peters's face, however, pale, strained, with wide, frightened eyes and sagging jaw, told Stratton that his thrust had penetrated as deeply as he could have hoped.

'We'll start here.'

It was Lynch's voice, curt and harsh, that broke the odd silence as he jerked his horse up and dismounted. 'Get yore tools out an' don't waste any time.'

There was no mistaking his mood, and in the hours that followed he was a far from agreeable taskmaster. He snapped and growled and swore at them impartially, acting generally like a bear with a sore ear whom nothing can please. If he could be said to be less disagreeable to anyone, it was, curiously enough, Bud Jessup, whom he kept down at one end of the line most of the afternoon. Later Stratton discovered the reason.

'It worked fine,' Bud whispered to him jubilantly, when they were alone together for a few minutes after supper. 'Did yuh see him hangin' around me this afternoon? He was grouchin' around and pretendin' to be mad because he'd let yuh go to town this mornin' just to mail a letter to some fool girl.'

'Of course I pulled the baby stare an' told him I didn't see no letter to no girl. Yuh sure didn't mail one while I was with yuh, I says.

' "Didn't mail no letter at all?" he wants to know, scowlin'.

' "Sure," I says. "Only it went to Jim Hardenberg over to Perilla. I seen him hand it to old Pop Daggett, who was peevish as a wet hen 'cause he couldn't find out nothin' about what was in it, 'count of Buck hangin' around till it got on the train. That's the only letter I seen."

'He didn't have no more to say, but walked off, scowlin' fierce. I'll bet yuh my new Stetson to a two-bit piece, Buck, he rides in to town mighty quick to find out what Pop knows about it.'

Stratton did not take him up, for it had already occurred to him that such a move on Lynch's part was almost certain. As a matter of fact the foreman did leave the ranch early the next morning, driving a pair of blacks harnessed to the buckboard. Buck and Jessup were both surprised at this unwonted method of locomotion, which usually indicated a passenger to be brought back, or, more rarely, a piece of freight or express, too large or heavy to be carried on horseback, yet not bulky enough for the lumbering freight-wagon.

'An' if it was freight, he'd have sent one of us,' commented Bud, as they saddled up preparatory to resuming operations on the fences. 'Still an' all, I reckon he wants to see Pop himself and get a line on what that old he-gossip knows. He'll have his ear full, all right,' he finished in a tone of vindictive satisfaction.

To make up for the day before, the whole gang took life very easily, and knocked off work rather earlier than usual. They had loafed ten or fifteen minutes in the bunk-house and were straggling up the slope in answer to Pedro's summons to dinner when, with a clatter of hoofs, the blacks whirled through the further gate and galloped towards the house.

Buck, among the others, glanced curiously in that direction and observed with much interest that a woman occupied the front seat of the buckboard with Tex, while a young man and two small trunks more than filled the rear.

'Some dame!' he heard Bud mutter under his breath.

A moment later Lynch pulled up the snorting team and called Jessup to hold them. Buck was just turning away from a lightning appraisal of the new-comers, when, to his amazement, the young woman smiled at him from her seat.

'Why, Mr Green!' she called out in surprise. 'To think of finding you here!'

Buck stared at her, wide-eyed and bewildered. With her crisp, dark hair, fresh colour, and regular features, she was very good to look at. But he had never consciously set eyes on her before in all his life!

CHAPTER 14

The Lady from the Past

Stratton's first feeling was that the girl must have made a mistake. In a dazed fashion he stepped forward and helped her out of the buckboard, but this was a more or less mechanical action and because she so evidently expected it. As he took her hand she pressed it warmly and did not at once relinquish it after she had reached the ground.

'I'm awfully glad to see you again,' she said, her colour heightened a little. 'But how on earth do you come to be away off here?'

With an effort Buck pulled himself together. He could see that the men were regarding him curiously, and felt that he must say something.

'That's simple enough,' he answered briefly. 'I've got a job on this ranch.'

She looked slightly puzzled. 'Really? But I thought – I had no idea you knew – Mary.'

'I didn't. I needed a job and drifted in here thinking I'd find a friend of mine who used to work on the same outfit in Texas. He was gone, but Miss Thorne took me on.'

'You mean you're a regular cowboy?' the girl asked in surprise. 'Why, you never told me that aboard ship.'

A sudden chill swept over Stratton, and for a moment he was stricken speechless. Aboard ship! Was it possible that this girl had been part of that uncanny, vanished year, the very thought of which troubled and oppressed him. His glance desperately evaded her charming, questioning eyes and rested suddenly with a curious cool sense of relief on the face of Mary Thorne, who had come up unperceived from behind.

But as their eyes met Buck was conscious of an odd veiled expression in their clear depths which vaguely troubled him. It vanished quickly as Miss Thorne moved quickly forward to embrace her friend.

'Stella!' she cried. 'I'm so awfully glad to see you.'

There were kisses and renewed embracings; the young man was greeted more decorously but with almost equal warmth, and then suddenly Miss Thorne turned to Stratton, who stood back a little, struggling between a longing to escape and an equally strong desire to find out a little more about this attractive but startling reminder of his unknown past.

'I had no idea you knew Miss Manning,' she said, with the faintest hint of stiffness in her manner.

Buck swallowed hard but was saved from further embarrassment by the girl.

'Oh, yes!' she said brightly. 'We came home on the same ship. Mr Green had been wounded, you know, and was under my care. We got to be – great friends.'

Was there a touch of meaning in the last two words? Stratton preferred to lay it to his imagination, and was glad of the diversion caused by the introduction of the young man, who proved to be Miss Manning's brother. Buck was not at all impressed by the fellow's handsome face, athletic figure, and immaculate clothes. The clothes especially seemed ridiculously out of place for even a visitor on a ranch, and he had always detested those dinky half-shaved moustaches.

Meanwhile the trunks had been carried in and the team led away, and Pedro was peevishly complaining from the kitchen door that dinner was getting cold. Buck learned that the visitors were from Chicago, where they had been close friends of the Thorne family for years, and then he managed to break away and join the fellows in the kitchen.

During the meal there was a lot of more or less quiet joking on the subject of Stratton's acquaintance with the lady, which he managed to parry rather cleverly. As a matter of fact the acute horror he felt at the very thought of the truth about himself getting out, quickened his wits and kept him constantly on his guard. He kept his temper and his head, explaining calmly that Miss Manning had been one of the nurses detailed to look after the batch of wounded men of whom he had been one. Naturally he had seen considerable of her during the long and tedious voyage, but there were one or two others he liked equally well.

His careless manner seemed to convince the men that there was no particular amusement to be extracted from the situation, and to Buck's relief they passed on to a general discussion of strangers on a ranch, the bother they were, and the extra amount of work they made.

'Always wantin' to ride around with yuh an' see what's goin' on,' declared Butch Siegrist sourly. 'If they're wimmin, yuh can't even give a cuss without lookin' first to see if they're near enough to hear.'

Stratton made a mental resolution that if anything of that sort came up, he would do his best to duck the job of playing cicerone to Miss Stella Manning, attractive as she was. So far his bluff seemed to have worked, but with a mind so entirely blank of the slightest detail of their acquaintance, he knew that at any moment the most casual remark might serve to rouse her suspicion.

Fortunately, his desire to remain in the background was abetted by Tex Lynch. Whether or not the foreman wanted to keep him away from the ranch-owner's friends as well as from Miss Thorne herself, Buck could not quite determine. But while the fence-repairing progressed, Stratton was never by any chance detailed to other duties which might keep him in the neighbourhood of the ranch-house, and on the one occasion when Miss Thorne and her guests rode out to where the men were working, Lynch saw to it that there was no opportunity for anything like private conversation between them and the object of his solicitude.

Buck watched his manoeuvring with secret amusement.

'Wouldn't he be wild if he knew he was playing right into my hands?' he thought.

His face darkened as he glanced thoughtfully at the departing figure of Miss Manning. She had greeted him warmly and betrayed a very evident inclination to linger in his vicinity. There had been a slight touch of pique in her treatment of Lynch, who hung around so persistently.

'I wish to thunder I had an idea of how much she knows,' he muttered. 'Did I act like a brainless idiot when I was – was that way, or not?'

He had asked the same question of the hospital surgeon and got an unsatisfactory answer. It all depended, the doctor told him non-committally. He might easily have shown evidences of lost memory; on the other hand, it was quite possible, especially with chance acquaintances, that his manner had been entirely normal.

There was nothing to be gained, however, by racking his brain for something that wasn't there, and Buck soon gave up the attempt. He could only trust to luck and his own inventiveness, and hope that Lynch's delightfully unconscious easing of the situation would continue.

The work was finished towards noon on the third day after the arrival of the Mannings, and all the connections hooked up. There remained nothing to do but test the line, and Tex, after making sure everything was in order, glanced over his men, who lounged in front of the Las Vegas shack.

'Yuh may as well stay down at this end,' he remarked, looking at Buck, 'while the rest of us go back. Stick around where yuh can hear the bell, an' if it don't ring in, say, an hour, try to get the house yourself. If that don't work, come along in an' report. I reckon everything's all right, though.'

Stratton was conscious of a sudden sense of alertness. He had grown so used to suspecting and analysing everything the foreman said or did that for a moment he forgot the precautions he had taken and wondered whether Lynch was up to some new crooked work. Then he remembered and relaxed mentally. Considering the consequences, Tex would hardly dare try any fresh violence against him, especially quite so soon. Besides, in broad daylight and in this open country, Buck couldn't imagine any form of danger he wouldn't be able to meet successfully alone.

So he acquiesced indifferently, and from the open doorway of the hut watched the others mount and ride away. There were only four of them, for Kreeger and Butch Siegrist had been dispatched early that morning to ride fence on the other side of the ranch-house. When they were well on their way, Buck untied his lunch from the saddle and went into the shack to eat it.

In spite of the feeling that he had nothing to fear, he took a position which gave him a good outlook from both door and window, and saw that his gun was loose in the holster. After he had eaten, he went down and got a drink from the creek. He had not been back in the shack a great while before the telephone bell jangled, and taking down the receiver he heard Lynch's voice at the other end.

Owing to the rather crude nature of the contrivance there was a good deal of buzzing on the line. But this was to be expected, and when Tex had talked a few minutes and decided that the system was working as well as could be hoped, he told Stratton to come in to the ranch, and hung up.

Buck had not ridden more than a quarter of a mile across the prairie, when all at once he pulled his horse to a standstill. The thought had suddenly come to him that this was the chance he had wanted so long to take a look at that mysterious stretch of desert known as the north pasture. He would be delayed, of course, but explanations were easy and that did not disturb him. It was too good an opportunity to miss, and without delay he turned his horse and spurred forward.

An instinct of caution made him keep as close as possible to the rough, broken country that edged the western extremity of the ranch, where he would run less chance of being seen than on the flat, open plain. He pushed his horse as much as was wise, and presently observed with satisfaction – though it was still a good way off – the line of fence that marked the northern boundary of middle pasture.

A few hundred yards ahead lay a shallow draw, and beyond it a weather-worn ridge thrust its blunt nose out into the plain considerably further than any Buck had yet passed. He turned the horse out, intending to ride around it, but a couple of minutes later jerked him to a standstill and sat motionless in the saddle, eyes narrowing with a sudden, keen surprise.

He had reached a point where, for the first time, he could make out, over the obstruction ahead, the extreme northwest corner of the pasture. Almost at the spot where the two lines of fence made a right angle were two horsemen in the typical cowman attire. At first they stood close together, but as Stratton stared intently, rising a little in his stirrups to get a clearer view through the scanty fringe of vegetation that topped the ridge, one of them rode forward and, dismounting, began to manipulate the fence wires with quick, jerky movements of his hands.

CHAPTER 15

'Blackleg'

More than once during the next ten minutes Buck cursed himself inwardly for not having brought along the small but powerful pair of field-glasses that were tucked away in his bag. He had picked them up at the Divisional Headquarters only a week or two before the Belleau Woods business, and how they had stuck to him until his arrival in America remained one of the minor mysteries of that vanished year. He would have given anything for them now, for though he could make out fairly well the movements of the two men, he was too far away to distinguish their faces.

Watching closely, he saw that the first fellow was taking down a short section of the fence, either by cutting or by pulling out the staples. When this lay flat he remounted and, joining his companion, the two proceeded to drive through the gap nothing more significant than a solitary steer.

It was a yearling, Buck could easily see even at that distance, and he almost laughed aloud at the sudden let-down of suspense. By this time a little individual trick of carriage made him suspect that the foremost puncher was Butch Siegrist, and when the men came into clearer view, he recognised scarcely without question the big sorrel with white trimmings on which Kreeger had ridden off that morning. The two men had found a Shoe-Bar stray; that was all. And yet, on second thought, how did they come to be here when they were supposed to be working at the very opposite extremity of the ranch?

It was this query which made Stratton refrain from showing himself. With considerable annoyance, for time was passing, he waited where he was until the two men had gone back through the gap in the fence and restored the wires. He watched them turn northward and ride rapidly across the sandy waste until at length their diminishing figures disappeared into the distance. Even then it was ten or fifteen minutes before he emerged from his seclusion, and when he finally did he headed straight for the young steer, who had been the cause of so much exertion on the part of the two men who ordinarily shirked work whenever they could.

Under the lash of a rope, the animal had lumbered across the pasture for several hundred yards, where he paused languidly to crunch some bunch-grass. There was an air of lassitude and weakness about the creature which made Buck, as he approached, eye it with anxious intentness. A dozen feet or so away he jerked his horse to a standstill and caught his breath with an odd whistling sound.

'Great Godfrey!' he breathed.

Bending slightly forward in the saddle, he stared at the creature's badly swollen off hind leg, but there was no need whatever for a prolonged inspection. Having been through one blackleg epidemic back in Texas, he knew the signs only too well.

'That's it, sure enough,' he muttered, straightening up.

His gaze swept across the prairie to where, half a mile away, a bunch of Shoe-Bar cattle grazed peacefully. If this sick beast should get amongst them, the yearlings at least, to whom the disease is fatal, would be dying like flies in twenty-four hours. Buck glanced back at the steer again, and as he noted the T-T brand, his face hardened and he began taking down his rope.

'The hellions!' he grated, an angry flush darkening his tan. 'They ought to be strung up.'

The animal started to move away, and Buck lost no time in roping him. Then he turned his horse and urged him towards the fence, dragging the reluctant brute behind. Fortunately he had his pliers in the saddle-pocket, and, taking down the wires, he forced the creature through and headed for a deep gully the mouth of which lay a few hundred yards to the left. Penetrating into this as far as he was able, he took out his Colt and deliberately shot the steer through the head. And if Kreeger or Siegrist had been present at that moment, he was furious enough to treat either of them in the same way without a particle of compunction.

'Hanging would be too good for them, the dirty beasts!' he grated.

The thing had been so fiendishly cold-blooded and calculating that it made his blood boil, for it was perfectly evident now to Buck that he had thwarted a deliberate plot to introduce the blackleg scourge among the Shoe-Bar cattle. Instead of riding fence, the two punchers must have made their roundabout way immediately to the stricken T-T ranch, secured in some manner an infected yearling and brought it back through the twisting mountain trail Bud had spoken of a few days before.

Lynch's was the directing spirit, of course; for none of the others would dare act save under his orders. But what was his object? What could he possibly hope to gain by such a thing? Buck could understand a man allowing rustlers to loot a ranch, if the same individual were in with them secretly and shared the plunder. But there was no profit in this for anyone – only an infinite amount of trouble and worry and extra work for them all, to say nothing of great financial loss to – Mary Thorne.

When Stratton had secured his rope and rode back to the Shoe-Bar pasture, his face was thoughtful. He was thinking of those excellent offers for the outfit Miss Thorne had lately spoken of, which Lynch was so anxious for her to accept. Could the foreman's plotting be for the purpose of forcing her to sell? From something she had let fall, Buck guessed that she was more or less dependent on the income from the ranch, and if this failed she might no longer be able to hold the property.

But even supposing this was true, it all still failed to make sense. The land itself was good enough, as Stratton knew from his former careful inspections, but it would be of little use for any purpose save ranching; and since the value of a cattle-ranch consists largely in the cattle themselves, it followed logically that by reducing the number, by theft, by disease, or any other means, the value would be very much less to a prospective purchaser.

Unable to make head or tail of the problem, Buck finally gave it up for the time being. He put back the fence with care and then headed straight for the ranch. There was no time left for the desired inspection of the north pasture. To undertake it now would mean a much longer delay than he could plausibly explain, and he was particularly anxious to avoid the need of any explanation which might arouse suspicion that the criminal action of the two men had been overseen.

'If they guessed, they'd be likely to try it again,' he thought, 'and another time they might succeed.'

Stratton managed his route so that for the last two miles it took exactly the course he would have followed in returning directly from Las Vegas camp. His plan was further favoured by the discovery that none of the men save Bud were anywhere about the ranch-house.

'Gone off to ride fence along with Flint an' Butch,' Jessup informed him, when Buck located him in the wagon-shed. 'Wonder why he's so awful interested in fences all of a sudden,' he went on thoughtfully. 'They've been let go all over the ranch till they're plumb fallin' to pieces.'

'You've got me,' shrugged Stratton. He had been cogitating whether or not to confide in Bud, and finally decided in the negative. It would do no particular good, and the youngster might impulsively let out something to the others. 'Why didn't they take you along, too?'

'I sure wish they had,' Bud answered shortly. 'Then I wouldn't of had to be lookin' at that all afternoon.'

He straightened from the wagon-body he was tinkering and waved a wrench towards the window behind Stratton. Turning quickly, the latter saw that it looked out on the rear of the ranch-house, where there were a few stunted trees and a not altogether successful attempt at a small flower-garden. On a rough, rustic bench under one of the trees sat young Manning and Mary Thorne, in earnest conversation.

'Sickening, ain't it?' commented Bud, taking encouragement from Stratton's involuntary frown. 'I been expectin' 'em to hold hands any minute.'

Buck laughed, mainly because he was annoyed with himself for feeling any emotion whatever. 'You don't seem to like Mr Alfred Manning,' he remarked.

'Who would?' snorted Jessup. 'He sure gets my goat, with them dude clothes, an' that misplaced piece of eyebrow on his lip, an' his superior airs. I wouldn't of thought Miss Mary was the kind to – '

'Where's – er – Miss Manning?' broke in Buck, reluctant to continue the discussion.

'Gone in with Mrs Archer,' Bud explained. 'They was both out there a while ago, but I reckon they got tired hangin' around.'

Stratton turned his back on the dingy window and fell to work on the wagon with Bud.

'Seen Bemis lately?' he asked presently, realising of a sudden that he had not visited the invalid for several days.

Bud sniffed. 'Sure. I was in there this mornin'. He's outa bed now moochin' around the room an' countin' the hours till he can back a horse.'

'Still got that notion the outfit isn't safe?'

'I'll tell the world! He says life's too short to take any more chances of bein' bumped off. Tried to make me believe my turn'll come next.'

Stratton shrugged his shoulders. 'I reckon there isn't much chance of that. They're not keen to get the sheriff down on their trail. Well, if he feels like that he wouldn't be much use here even if we could persuade him to stick.'

About half-past five they decided to call it a day and went down to the bunk-house, through the open door of which Buck presently observed the arrival of the remainder of the outfit. They came from the east, and Kreeger and Siegrist were with them. As Buck expected, the former rode the sorrel with distinctive white markings, while the latter bestrode a nondescript bay. The second of the two riders he had watched that afternoon had been mounted on just such a bay, and if there had been a lingering touch of doubt in Stratton's mind as to the identity of the two criminals, it remained no longer.

CHAPTER 16

The Unexpected

More than once during the following few days, Stratton was forced to a grudging admiration of Tex Lynch's cleverness. Even knowing what he did, he failed to detect the slightest sign in either the foreman or his men that they were waiting expectantly for something to happen. The only significant feature was their marked avoidance of the middle pasture. This might readily be accounted for by the fact that the work now lay on the other side of the outfit, but Buck was convinced that their real purpose was to allow the blackleg scourge to gain as great a hold as possible on Shoe-Bar cattle before its discovery.

The cold-blooded brutality of that quiescence made Stratton furious, but it also brought home more effectually than ever the nature of the men he had to deal with. They were evidently the sort to stop at nothing, and Buck had moments of wondering whether or not he was proceeding in the right way to uncover the mystery of their motive.

So far he had really accomplished very little. The unabated watchfulness of the crowd so hedged in and hampered him that it was quite impossible to do any extended investigating. He still had the power of ending the whole affair at any moment and clearing the ranch of the entire gang. But aside from his unwillingness to humiliate Mary Thorne, he realised that this would not necessarily accomplish what he wanted.

'It would stop their deviltry all right,' he thought 'but I might never find out what they're after. About the only way is to give 'em enough rope to hang themselves, and I'm blowed if I don't believe I could do that better by leaving the outfit and doing a little sleuthing on my own.'

Yet somehow that did not altogether appeal to him, either. The presence of handsome Alf Manning may have had something to do with Buck's reluctance to quit the ranch just now, but he would never have admitted it, even to himself. He simply made up his mind to wait a while, at least until he could see what happened when Lynch discovered the failure of his latest plot, and then be governed by circumstances.

In the meantime the situation, so far as Miss Manning was concerned, grew daily more complicated. She showed a decided inclination for Stratton's society, and when he came to know her better he found her frank, breezy, and delightfully companionable. He knew perfectly well that unless he wanted to take a chance of making some tremendous blunder he ought to avoid any prolonged conversation with the lady. But she was so charming that every now and then he flung prudence to the winds – and usually regretted it.

It was not that she said anything definitely disconcerting, but there were occasional hints and innuendoes, and now and then a question which seemed innocent enough but which Stratton found difficult to parry. He couldn't quite make up his mind whether or not she suspected the truth about his former mental condition, but he had an uncomfortable notion that she sensed a difference and was trying to find out just where it lay.

Time and again he told himself that at the worst there was nothing disgraceful in that vanished past. But he had the ordinary healthy man's horror for the abnormal, and the very fact that it had vanished so utterly beyond recall made him willing, in order to avoid having it dragged back into the light and made public property, to do almost anything, even to being almost rude to a pretty girl.

Thus between escaping Miss Manning and trying to keep an eye on Lynch, Stratton had his work cut out for him. He knew that sooner or later some one would be sent out to take a look through the middle pasture, and he wanted very much to be on hand when the report came back to Lynch that his plot had miscarried. It was consequently with very bad grace that Buck received an order to ride in to Paloma one morning for the long-delayed wagon-bolts and a few necessary supplies from the store.

He felt at once that it was a put-up job to get him out of the way. Only yesterday Rick Bemis, able at length to ride that distance, had quit the ranch escorted by Slim McCabe. If anything was really needed the latter could have brought it back and saved the expense of sending another man twenty-four hours later.

But there was no reasonable excuse for Buck's protesting, and he held his tongue. He wished that he had taken Jessup into his confidence about the blackleg plot, but there was no time for that now. He did manage, on his way to the corral, to whisper a word or two in passing, urging the youngster to take particular note of anything that went on during his absence, but he would have much preferred giving Bud some definite idea of what to look for, and his humour, as he saddled up and left the ranch, was far from amiable.

But gradually, as he rode rapidly along the trail, the crisp, clean air brushing his face and the early morning sun caressing him with a pleasant warmth, his mood changed. After all, it was really of very little moment whether or not he was present when Lynch first learned that things had failed to go his way. At best he might have had a momentary vindictive thrill at glimpsing the fellow's thwarted rage; perhaps not even that, for Tex was uncommonly good at hiding his emotions. It was much more important for him to decide definitely and soon about his own future plans, and this solitary ride over an easy, familiar trail gave him as good a chance as he was ever likely to have.

A little straight thinking made him realise – with a half-guilty feeling of having deliberately shut his eyes to it before – that he could not hope to get much further under present conditions. Tied down as he was, a dozen promising clues might pop up, which he would have no chance whatever of investigating. Indeed, looking at the situation in this light, he felt a wonder that Lynch should ever have tried to oust him from the ranch, where he could be kept under constant observation and followed up in every move. Working from the outside, with freedom to come and go as he liked, he could accomplish a vast deal more than in this present hampered fashion. There still remained traces of his vague, underlying reluctance to leave the place at this particular time, but Buck crushed it down firmly, even a little angrily.

'It's up to me to quit,' he muttered. 'I'd be a blooming jackass to waste any more time here. I'll have to work it naturally, though, or Lynch will smell a rat.'

At that moment the trail dipped down into a gully – the very one, in fact, where he had passed Tex that first day he had ridden out to the ranch. Thinking of the encounter, Buck recalled his own emotions with a curious feeling of remoteness. The grotesque mental picture he had formed of Mary Thorne contrasted so amusingly with the reality that he grinned and might have broken into a laugh had he not caught sight at that moment of a figure riding towards him from the other end of the gully.

The high-crowned sombrero, abnormally broad of brim, the gaudy saddle-trappings and touches of bright colour about the stranger's equipment, brought a slight frown to Stratton's face. Apart even from his recent unpleasant associations with them, he had never had any great fondness for Mexicans, whom he considered slick and slippery beyond the average. He watched this one's approach warily, and when the fellow pulled up with a glistening smile and a polite '*Buenas tardes*', Stratton responded with some curtness.

'Fine day, señor,' remarked the stranger pleasantly.

'You've said it,' returned Buck drily. 'We haven't had rain in as much as three weeks.'

'Tha's right,' agreed the other. His glance strayed to the brand on Buck's cayuse, and his swarthy face took on an expression of pleased surprise. 'You come from Shoe-Bar?' he questioned.

'You're some mind-reader,' commented Stratton briefly. 'What of it?'

'Mebbe yo' do me favour,' pursued the Mexican eagerly. 'Save me plenty hot ride.' He pulled an envelope from the pocket of his elaborately silver-conched chaps. 'Rocking-R boss, he tell me take thees to Mister Leench at Shoe-Bar. Eef yo' take heem, I am save mooch trouble, eh?'

Buck eyed the extended envelope doubtfully. Then, ashamed of his momentary hesitation to perform this simple service, he took it and tucked it away in one pocket.

'All right,' he agreed. 'I'll take it over for you. I've got to go in to town first, though.'

'No matter,' shrugged the Mexican. 'There is no hurry.'

With reiterated and profuse thanks, he pulled his horse around and rode back with Stratton as far as the Rocking-R trail, where he turned off.

'He'll find some corner where he can curl up and snooze for the couple of hours he's saved,' thought Buck, watching the departing figure. 'Those fellows are so doggone lazy they'd sit and let grasshoppers eat holes in their breeches.'

As he rode on he wondered a little what Jim Tenny, the Rocking-R foreman, could have to do with Lynch, who seemed to be on the outs with everybody, but presently he dismissed the subject with a shrug.

'I'll be getting as bad as Pop if I'm not careful,' he thought. 'Likely it's some perfectly ordinary range business.'

He found Daggett in a garrulous mood but was in no humour to waste time listening to his flood of talk and questions. The bolts had come at last, and when he had secured them and the other things from the store, Buck promptly mounted and set out on his return.

Tex met him just outside the corral and received the letter without comment, thrusting it into his pocket unread. He seemed much more interested in the arrival of the bolts, and after dinner set Stratton and McCabe to work in the wagon-shed replacing the broken ones. It was not until late in the afternoon that Buck managed a few words in private with Jessup, and was surprised to learn that the gang had been working all day to the southeast of the ranch. Tex himself had been absent from the party for an hour or two in the morning, but when he joined them he came from the direction of the Paloma trail, and Stratton did not believe he could have had time thoroughly to inspect the middle pasture and return so soon by so roundabout a course.

'He'll do it tomorrow, sure,' decided Buck. 'It isn't human nature to hold off much longer.'

He was right. After breakfast Stratton and McCabe were ordered to resume work on the wagons, while the others sallied forth with Lynch, ostensibly to ride fence along the southern side of middle pasture. Buck awaited their return with interest and curiosity. He thought he might possibly detect some signs of glumness in the faces of the foreman and his confederates, but he was quite unprepared for the open anger and excitement which stamped every face, Bud Jessup's included.

'Rustlers were out again last night,' Bud explained, the moment he had a chance.

Buck stared at him in amazement, the totally unexpected nature of the thing taking him completely by surprise.

'Why I thought – '

'So did I,' interrupted Bud curtly. 'I didn't believe they'd dare break into middle pasture, but they have. There's a gap a hundred yards wide in the fence, and they've got away with a couple of hundred head at least.'

'You're sure it happened last night?'

'Dead certain. The tracks are too fresh. Buck, if Tex Lynch don't get Hardenberg on the job now, we'll *know* he's crooked.'

'We'd pretty near decided that anyhow, hadn't we?' returned Stratton absently.

He was wondering how this new move had been managed and what it meant. If it had been merely part of a scheme to loot the Shoe-Bar for his own benefit, Tex would never have allowed his rustler accomplices to touch a steer from that middle pasture herd, which he must feel by this time to be thoroughly and completely infected. Even if he had managed during his brief absence yesterday to make a hurried inspection, and suspected that the blackleg plot had failed, he couldn't be certain enough to take a chance like this.

The foreman's manner gave Buck no clue. At dinner he was unusually silent and morose, taking no part in the discussion of this latest outrage, which the others kept up with such a convincing semblance of indignation. To Stratton he acted like a man who has come to some new and not altogether agreeable decision, which in any other person would probably mean that he had at last made up his mind to call in the sheriff. But Buck was convinced that this was the last thing Lynch intended to do, and gradually there grew up in his mind, fostered by one or two trifling particulars in Tex's manner towards himself, a curious, instinctive feeling of premonitory caution.

This increased during the afternoon, when the men were sent out to repair the broken fence, while Lynch remained behind. It fed on little details, such as a chance side glance from one of the men, or the sight of two of them in low-voiced conversation when he was not supposed to be looking – details he would scarcely have noticed ordinarily. Towards the end of the day Buck had grown almost certain that some fresh move was being directed against himself, and when the blow fell only its nature came as a surprise.

The foreman was standing near the corral when they returned, and as soon as Stratton had unsaddled and turned his horse loose, Lynch drew him to one side.

'Here's your time up to tonight,' he said curtly, holding out a handful of crumpled bills and silver. 'Miss Thorne's decided she don't want yuh on the outfit any longer.'

For a moment Stratton regarded the foreman in silence, observing the glint of veiled triumph in his eyes and the malicious curve of the full red lips. The thought flashed through his mind that Lynch would hardly be quite so pleased if he knew how much time Buck himself had given lately to thinking up some scheme of plausibly bringing about this very situation.

'*Is* that so?' he drawled presently. 'How did you work it?' he added, in the casual tone of one seeking to gratify a trifling curiosity.

Lynch scowled. 'Work it?' he snapped. 'I didn't have to work it. Yuh know damn well why you're sacked. Why should I waste time tellin' yuh?'

Stratton smiled blandly. 'In that case I reckon I'll have to ask Miss Thorne,' he remarked, standing with legs slightly apart and thumbs hooked loosely in his chap-belt. 'I'm rather curious, you know.'

'Like hell yuh will!' rasped Lynch, as Buck took a step or two towards the house.

Impulsively Lynch's right hand dropped to his gun but as his fingers touched the stock he found himself staring at the uptilted end of Stratton's holster frayed a little at the end so that the glint of a blued steel barrel showed through the leather.

'Just move your hand a mite,' Buck suggested in a quiet, level tone, which was nevertheless obeyed promptly. 'Now, listen here. I want you to get this. I ain't longing to stick around any outfit when the boss don't want me. If the lady says I'm to go, I'll get out *pronto*; but I don't trust you, and she's got to tell me that face to face before I move a step. *Sabe?*'

His eyes narrowed slightly, and Lynch, crumpling the unheeded money in his hand, stepped aside with an expression of baffled fury and watched him stride along the side of the house and disappear around the corner.

He was far from lacking nerve, but he had suddenly remembered that letter to Sheriff Hardenberg, regarding which he had long ago obtained confirmation from Pop Daggett. If he could rely on the meaning of Stratton's little anecdote – and he had an uncomfortable conviction that he could – the letter would be opened in case Buck met his death by violence. And once it was opened by the sheriff, only Tex Lynch knew how very much the fat would be in the fire.

So, though his fingers twitched, he held his hand, and presently, hearing voices in the living-room, he crept over to an open window and, standing close to one side of it, bent his head to listen.

CHAPTER 17

The Primeval Instinct

On the other side of the house Buck found the mistress of the ranch and her two guests standing in a little group beside one of the dusty, discouraged-looking flower-beds. As he appeared they all glanced towards him, and a troubled, almost frightened expression flashed across Mary Thorne's face.

'Could I speak to you a moment, ma'am?' asked Stratton, doffing his Stetson.

That expression, and her marked hesitation in coming forward, were both significant, and Buck felt a sudden little stab of anger. Was she afraid of him? he wondered; and tried to imagine what beastly lies Lynch must have told her to bring about such an extraordinary state of mind.

But as she moved slowly towards him, the anger ebbed as swiftly as it had come. She looked so slight and frail and girlish, and he observed that her lips were pressed almost as tightly together as the fingers of those small, brown hands hanging straight at her sides. At the edge of the porch she paused and looked up at him, and though the startled look had gone, he could see that she was still nervous and apprehensive.

'Should you rather go inside?' she murmured.

Buck flashed a glance at the two Mannings, still within hearing. 'If you don't mind,' he answered briefly.

In the living-room she turned and faced him, her back against the table, on which she rested the tips of her outspread fingers. She was so evidently nerving herself for an interview she dreaded that Buck almost regretted having forced it.

'I won't keep you a minute,' he began hurriedly. 'Tex tells me you have no more use for me here.'

'I'm – sorry,' fell almost mechanically from her set lips.

'But he didn't tell me why.'

Her eyes, which from the first had scarcely left his face, widened, and a puzzled look came into them.

'But you must know,' she returned a trifle stiffly.

'I'm sorry, but I don't,' he assured her.

'Oh – duties!' She spoke with a touch of soft impatience. 'It's what you've done, not what you haven't done that – . But surely this is a waste of time? It's not particularly – pleasant; and I don't see what will be gained by going into all the – the details.'

Something in her tone stung him. 'Still, it doesn't seem quite fair to condemn even a common cow-puncher unheard,' he retorted with a touch of sarcasm.

She stiffened, and a faint flush crept into her face. Then her chin went up determinedly.

'You rode to Paloma yesterday morning.' It was more of a statement than a question.

'Yes.'

'In the gully this side of the Rocking-R trail you met a Mexican on a sorrel horse?'

Again Buck acquiesced, but inwardly he wondered. So far as he knew there had been no witness to that meeting.

'He handed you a letter?'

Buck nodded, a sudden feeling of puzzled wariness surging over him. For an instant the girl hesitated. Then she went on in a soft rush of indignation:

'And so last night those Mexican thieves, warned that the middle pasture would be unguarded, broke in there and carried off nearly two hundred head of cattle!'

As he caught her meaning, which he did almost instantly, Buck flushed crimson and his eyes flashed. For a moment or so he was too furious to speak; and though most of his rage was directed against the man who, with such brazen effrontery, had sought to shift the blame of his own criminal plotting, he could not help feeling resentment that the girl should so readily believe the worst against him. A vehement denial trembled on his lips, but in time he remembered that he could not utter it without giving away more than he was willing to at the present moment. With an effort he got a grip on himself, but though his voice was quiet enough, his eyes still smouldered and his lips were hard.

'I see,' he commented briefly. 'You believe it all, of course?'

She had been watching him closely, and now a touch of troubled uncertainty crept into her face.

'What else can I do?' she countered. 'You admit getting the letter from that Mexican, and I saw Tex take it out of your bag.'

This information brought Buck's lips tightly together and he frowned. 'Could I see it – the letter, I mean?' he asked.

She hesitated a moment, and then, reaching across the table, took up the shabby account-book he had seen before and drew from it a single sheet of paper. The note was short and written in Spanish. It was headed '*Amigo Green*', and as Buck swiftly translated the few lines in which the writer gave thanks for information purported to have been given about the middle pasture and stated that the raid would take place that night according to arrangement, his lips curled. From his point of view it seemed incredible that anyone could be deceived by such a clumsy fraud. But he was forced to admit that up to a few weeks ago the girl had never set eyes on him, and knew nothing of his antecedents, whereas she trusted Lynch implicitly. So he refrained from any comment as he handed back the letter.

'You don't – deny it?' asked the girl, an undertone of disappointment in her voice.

'What's the use?' shrugged Stratton. 'You evidently believe Lynch.'

She did not answer at once, but stood silent, searching his face with a troubled, wistful scrutiny.

'I don't know quite what to believe,' she told him presently. 'You – you don't seem like a person who would – who would – And yet some one must have given information.' Her chin suddenly tilted and her lips grew firm. 'If you'll tell me straight out that you're nothing but an ordinary cow-puncher, that you have no special object in being here on the ranch, that you're exactly what you seem and nothing more, then I – I'll believe you.'

Her words banished the last part of resentment lingering in Stratton's mind. She was a good sort, after all. He found himself of a sudden regarding her with a feeling that was almost tenderness, and wishing very much that he might tell her everything. But that, of course, was impossible.

'I can't quite do that,' he answered slowly.

The hopeful gleam died out of her eyes, and she made an eloquent, discouraged gesture with both hands.

'You see? What else can I do but let you go? Unless I take every possible precaution I'll be ruined by these dreadful thieves.'

Buck moved his shoulders slightly. 'I understand. I'm not kicking. Well, I won't keep you any longer. Thank you very much for telling me what you have.'

Abruptly he turned away and in the doorway came face to face with Alfred Manning, who seemed to expect the cow-puncher to step obsequiously aside and let him pass. But Buck was in no humour to step aside for any one, and for a silent instant their glances clashed. In the end it was Manning, flushed and looking daggers, who gave way, and as Stratton passed the open window a moment later he heard the other's voice raised in an angry pitch.

'Perfectly intolerable! I tell you, Mary, you ought to have that fellow arrested.'

'I don't mean to do anything of the sort,' retorted Miss Thorne.

'But it's your duty. He'll get clean away, and go right on stealing – '

'Please, Alf!' There was a tired break in the girl's voice. 'I don't want to talk any more about it. I've had enough – '

Stratton's lips tightened and he passed on out of hearing. The encounter with Manning had irritated him, and a glimpse of Lynch he caught through the kitchen door fanned into a fresh glow his smouldering anger against the foreman. It was not that he minded in the least the result of the fellow's plotting. But the method of it, the effrontery of that cowardly, insolent attempt to blacken and besmirch him with Mary Thorne, made him more furious each time he thought of it. When he reached the bunk-house his rage was white hot.

He found Jessup the sole occupant. It was still rather early for quitting, and Tex must have set the other men to doing odd jobs around the barns and nearby places.

'What's happened?' demanded Bud, as Buck appeared. 'Tex put me to work oiling harness, but I sneaked off as soon as he was out of sight. I heard Slim say yuh were fired.'

Flinging his belongings together as he talked, Stratton briefly retailed the essentials of the situation.

'I'm going to saddle up and start for town right away,' he concluded. 'If I hang around here much longer I don't know as I can keep my hands off that double-faced crook.'

He added some more man-sized adjectives, to which Bud listened with complete approval.

'Yuh ain't said half enough,' he growled, from where he stood to the left of the closed door. 'I wish yuh would stay an' give him one almighty good beating up. He thinks there ain't a man on the range can stand up against him.'

Buck's eyes narrowed. 'I'd sure like to try,' he said regretfully. 'I don't say I could knock him out, but I'd guarantee to give him something to think about. Trouble is, there's nothing gained by starting a mess like that except letting off steam, and there might be a whole lot – '

He broke off abruptly as the door swung open to admit Lynch and McCabe. The foreman, pausing just inside the room, eyed Stratton's preparations for departure with curling lips. As a matter of fact, what he had overheard of the interview between Buck and Mary Thorne had given him the impression that Stratton was an easy mark, whose courage and ability had been greatly overestimated. A more sagacious person would have been content to let well enough alone. But Tex had a disposition which impelled him to rub things in.

'There's yore dough,' he said sneeringly, flinging the little handful of money on the table with such force that several coins fell to the floor and rolled into remote corners. 'Yuh better put it away safe, 'cause after this there ain't nobody around these parts'll hire yuh, I'll tell a man!'

His tone was indescribably taunting, and of a sudden Buck saw red. Dominated by the single-minded impulse of primeval man to use the weapons nature gave him, he forgot momentarily that he carried a gun. When the two men entered, he had been bending over, rolling his blankets. Since then, save to raise his head, he had scarcely altered his position, and yet, as he poised there motionless, fists clenched, muscles tense, eyes narrowed to mere slits, Lynch suddenly realised that he had blundered, and reached swiftly for his Colt.

But another hand was ahead of his. Standing just behind him, Bud Jessup had sized up the situation a fraction of a second before Tex, and like a flash he bent forward and snatched the foreman's weapon from its holster.

'Cut that out, Slim!' he shrilled, forestalling a sudden downward jerk of McCabe's right hand. 'No horning in, now. Give it here.'

An instant later he had slammed the door and shot the bolt, and stood with back against it, a Colt in each hand. His freckled face was flushed and his eyes gleamed with excitement.

'Go to it, Buck!' he yelled jubilantly. 'My money's up on yuh, old man. Give him hell!'

Lynch darted out into the middle of the room, thrusting aside the table with a single powerful sweep of one arm. There was no hint of reluctance in his manner, nor lack of efficiency in the lowering droop of his big shoulders or the way his fists fell automatically into position. His face had hardened into a fierce mask, out of which savage eyes blazed fearlessly.

An instant later, like the spring of a panther, Stratton's lean, lithe body launched forward.

CHAPTER 18

A Change of Base

Stratton staggered back against the wall and leaned there, panting. All his strength had gone out in that last terrific blow, and for a space he seemed incapable of movement. At length, conscious of a warm, moist trickle on his chin, he raised one hand mechanically to his face and brought it away, dabbled with bright crimson. For a moment or two he regarded the stiff, crooked fingers and bruised knuckles in a dazed, impersonal fashion as if the hand belonged to some one else. Then he became aware that Bud was speaking.

'Sure,' he mumbled, when the meaning of the reiterated question penetrated to his consciousness. 'I'm – all – right.'

Then his head began to clear, and, slowly straightening his sagging shoulders, he glanced down at the hulking figure sprawling motionless amidst the debris of the wrecked table.

'Is – he – ' he began slowly.

'He's out, that's all,' stated Jessup crisply. 'Golly, Buck! That was some punch.' He paused, regarding his friend eagerly. 'What are yuh goin' to do now?' he asked.

A tiny trickle of blood from Stratton's cut lip ran down his chin and splashed on the front of his torn, disordered shirt.

'Wash, I reckon,' he answered, with a twisted twitch of his stiff lips that was meant to be a smile. 'I sure need it bad.'

'But I mean after that,' explained Bud. 'Don't yuh want me to saddle up while you're gettin' ready? There ain't no point in hangin' around till he comes to.'

Buck took a step or two away from the wall and regarded the prostrate Lynch briefly, his glance also taking in McCabe, who bent over him.

'I reckon not,' he agreed briefly. 'Likewise, if I don't get astride a cayuse mighty soon, I won't be able to climb onto him at all. Go ahead and saddle up, kid, and I'll be with you *pronto*. You'd better ride to town with me and bring back the horse.'

Bud nodded and, breaking the Colts one after another, pocketed the shells and dropped the weapons into a nearby bunk.

'Yuh needn't bother to do that,' commented McCabe sourly. 'Nobody ain't goin' to drill no holes in yuh; we're only too tickled to see yuh get out. If you're wise, kid, you'll stay away, likewise. I wouldn't be in yore shoes for no money when Tex comes around an' remembers what yuh done.'

'I reckon I can take care of m'self,' retorted Jessup. 'It ain't Tex's game to be took up for no murder yet awhile.'

Without further comment he gathered up most of Stratton's belongings and departed for the corral. Buck took his handbag and, leaving the cabin, limped slowly down to the creek. He was surprised to note that the encounter seemed to have attracted no attention up at the ranch-house. Then he realised that with the door and windows closed, what little noise there had been might well have passed unnoticed, especially as the men were at work back in the barns.

At the creek he washed the blood from his face and hands, changed his shirt, put a strip of plaster on his cut lip, and decided that any further repairs could wait until he reached Paloma.

When he arrived at the corral Bud had just finished saddling the second horse, and they lost no time making fast Buck's belongings. The animals were then led out, and Stratton was on the point of mounting when the sound of light footsteps made him turn quickly to find Miss Manning almost at his elbow.

'But you're not leaving now, without waiting to say goodbye?' she expostulated.

Buck's lips straightened grimly, with a grotesque twisted effect caused by the plaster at the corner.

'After what's happened I hardly supposed anybody'd want any farewell words,' he commented with a touch of sarcasm.

Miss Manning stamped her shapely, well-shod foot petulantly. 'Rubbish!' she exclaimed. 'You don't suppose I believe that nonsense, do you?'

'I reckon you're about the only one who doesn't, then.'

'I'm not. Mrs Archer agrees with me. She says you couldn't be a – a thief if you tried. And down in her heart even Mary – But whatever has happened to your face?'

Stratton flushed faintly. 'Oh, I just – cut myself against something,' he shrugged. 'It's nothing serious.'

'I'm glad of that,' she commented, dimpling a little. 'It certainly doesn't add to your beauty.'

She was bareheaded, and the slanting sunlight, caressing the crisp waves of hair, revealed an unsuspected reddish glint amongst the dark tresses. As he looked down into her clear, friendly eyes, Buck realised, and not for the first time, how very attractive she really was. If things had only been different, if only the barrier of that hateful mental lapse of his had not existed, he had a feeling that they might have been very good friends indeed.

His lips had parted for a farewell word or two when suddenly he caught the flutter of skirts over by the corner of the ranch-house. It was Mary Thorne, and Buck wondered with an odd, unexpected little thrill, whether by any chance she too might be coming to say goodbye. Whatever may have been her intention, however, it changed abruptly. Catching sight of the group beside the corral fence, she stopped short, hesitated an instant, and then, turning square about, disappeared in the direction she had come. As he glanced back to Stella Manning, Buck's face was a little clouded.

'We'll have to be getting started, I reckon,' he said briefly. 'Thank you very much for – for seeing me off.'

'But where are you going?'

'Paloma for tonight; after that I'll be hunting another job.'

The girl put out her hand and Stratton took it, hoping that she wouldn't notice his raw, bruised knuckles. He might have spared himself the momentary anxiety. She wasn't looking at his fingers.

'Well, it's goodbye, then,' she said, a note of regret underlying the surface brightness of her tone. 'But when you're settled you must send me a line. We were such good pals aboard ship, and I haven't enough friends to want to lose even one of them. Send a letter here to the ranch, and if we're gone, Mary will forward it.'

Buck promised, and swung himself stiffly into the saddle. As he and Bud rode briskly down the slope, he turned and glanced back for an instant. Miss Manning stood where they had left her, handkerchief fluttering from her upraised hand, but Stratton scarcely saw her. His gaze swept the front of the ranch-house, scrutinising each gaping, empty window and the deserted porch. Finally, with a faint sigh and a little shrug of his shoulders, he mentally dismissed the past and fell to considering the future.

There was a good deal yet to be talked over and decided, and when he had briefly detailed to Bud the various happenings he was still ignorant of, Buck went on to outline his plans.

'There are several things I want to look into, and to do it I've got to be on the loose,' he explained. 'At the same time I don't want Lynch to get the idea I'm snooping around. What sort of a fellow is this Tenny, over at the Rocking-R?'

'He's white,' returned Bud promptly. 'No squarer ranch-boss around the country. I'd of gone there instead of the Shoe-Bar, only they was full up. What was yuh thinkin' of – bracin' him for a job?'

'Not exactly, though I'd like Lynch to think I'd been taken on there. Do you suppose, if I put Tenny wise to what I was after, that he'd let me have a cayuse and packhorse, and stake me to enough grub to keep me a week or two in the mountains back of the Shoe-Bar?'

'He might, especially when he knows you're buckin' Tex; he never was much in love with Lynch.' Jessup paused, eyeing his companion curiously. 'Say, Buck,' he went on quickly, 'what makes yuh so keen about this, anyhow? Yuh ain't no deputy sheriff, or anythin' like that, are yuh?'

For a moment Stratton was taken aback by the unexpectedness of the question. He had come to regard Jessup and himself so completely at one in their desire to penetrate the mystery of Lynch's shady doings that it had never occurred to him that his intense absorption in the situation might strike Bud as peculiar. It was one thing to behave as Bud was doing, especially as he frankly had the interest of Mary Thorne at heart, and quite another to throw up a job and plan to carry on an unproductive investigation from a theoretical desire to bring to justice a crooked foreman whom he had never seen until a few weeks ago.

'Why, of course not,' parried Buck. 'What gave you that notion?'

'I dunno exactly. I s'pose mebbe it's the way you're plannin' to give yore time to it without pay or nothin'. There won't be a darn cent in it for yuh, even if yuh do land Tex in the pen.'

'I know that,' and Buck smiled; 'but I'm a stubborn cuss when I get started on anything. Besides, I love Tex Lynch well enough to want to see him get every mite that's comin' to him. I've got a little money saved up, and I'll get more fun spending it this way than any other I can think of.'

'There's somethin' in that,' agreed Jessup. 'Golly, Buck! I wisht I could go along with yuh. I never was much on savin', but I could manage a couple of weeks without a job.'

Stratton hesitated. 'I'd sure like it, kid,' he answered. 'It would be a whole lot pleasanter for me, but I'm wondering if you wouldn't do more good there on the Shoe-Bar. With nobody at all to cross him, there's no tellin' what Lynch might try and pull off. Besides, it seems to me somebody ought to be there to sort of look after Miss – ' He broke off, struck by a sudden possibility. 'You don't suppose he'll get really nasty about what you – '

'Hell!' broke in Bud sharply. 'I wasn't thinking about that. He'll be nasty, of course, but he can't go more than so far. I reckon you're right, Buck. Miss Mary oughtn't to be left there by herself.'

'Of course, there's Manning – '

Bud disposed of the aristocratic Alfred with a forceable epithet which ought to have made his ears burn. 'Besides, that bird ain't goin' to stay forever, I hope,' he added.

This settled, they passed on to other details, and by the time they reached Paloma, everything had been threshed out and decided, including a possible means of communication in case of emergency.

Ravenously hungry, they sought the ramshackle hotel at once, and though it was long after the regular supper hour, they succeeded in getting a fair meal cooked and served. Concluding that it would be pleasanter all around to give Lynch as much time as possible to recover from his spleen, Bud decided to defer his return to the ranch until early morning. So when they had finished eating, they walked down to the store to arrange for hiring one of Daggett's horses again. Here they were forced to spend half an hour listening to old Pop's garrulous comments and the repeated 'I told you so', which greeted the news of Stratton's move before they could tear themselves away and turn in.

They were up at dawn, ate a hurried breakfast, and then set out along the trail. Where the Rocking-R track branched off they paused for a few casual words of farewell, and then each went his way. A few hundred yards beyond, Buck turned in his saddle just in time to see Jessup, leading Stratton's old mount, ride briskly into a shallow draw and disappear.

He had a feeling that he was going to miss the youngster, with his cheerful optimism and dependable ways; but he felt that at the most a few weeks would see them together again. Fortunately for his peace of mind, he had not the least suspicion of the circumstances which were to bring about their next meeting.

CHAPTER 19

The Mysterious Motorcar

Buck took to Jim Tenny at once. There was something about this long, lean, brown-faced foreman of the Rocking-R, with his clear grey eyes and that half-humorous twist to his thin lips, which inspired not only confidence but liking as well. He listened without comment to Buck's story, which included practically everything save the revelation of his own identity; but once or twice, especially at the brief mention of the fight in the bunk-house, his eyes gleamed with momentary approval. When Buck told about the blackleg incident his face darkened and he spoke for the first time.

'Seems like yuh had him there,' he said briefly. 'That job alone ought to land him in the pen.'

Buck nodded. 'I know; but I'm afraid he couldn't be convicted on my evidence alone. Kreeger and Siegrist fixed up a pretty decent alibi, you see, and it would only be my word against theirs. Even the carcass of the beast wouldn't help much. They'd say it wandered through the pass by itself, and I suppose there's one chance in a thousand it could have.'

'Damned unlikely, though,' shrugged Tenny.

'Sure; but the law's that way. You've got to be dead certain. Besides, if he was pulled in for that we might never find out just what's at the bottom of it all. That's the important thing, and if I can only get a line on what he's up to, we'll land him swift enough, believe me!'

Warned by Bud's unexpected question the evening before that he must have a more plausible motive for following up the case, Buck had coolly appointed himself one of Jim Hardenberg's deputies. He hinted that rumours of the cattle-stealing had reached the sheriff, who, debarred from taking up the matter openly by the absence of any complaint from the owner of the Shoe-Bar, had dispatched Stratton on a secret investigation. The process of that investigation having disclosed evidences of rascality of which the rustling was but a minor feature, Stratton's desire to probe the mystery to the bottom seemed perfectly natural, and the need for secrecy was also accounted for. The only risk Buck ran was of Tenny's mentioning the matter to Hardenberg himself, and that seemed slight enough. At the worst it would merely mean anticipating a little; for if he did succeed in solving the problem of Tex Lynch's motives, the next and final step would naturally be up to the sheriff.

'I get yuh,' said Tenny, nodding. 'That's true enough. Well, what do you want me to do?'

Buck told him briefly, and the foreman's eyes twinkled.

'That's some order,' he commented.

'I'd pay you for the stock and grub, of course,' Stratton assured him; 'and at least put up a deposit for the cayuses.'

'Oh, that part ain't frettin' me none. I reckon I can trust yuh. I was thinkin' about how I could stall off Lynch in case he comes around askin' questions. Yuh want he should get the idea I hired yuh?'

'I thought it would ease his mind and give him the notion I was safe for a while,' smiled Stratton. 'Of course you could say I tried for a job but you were full up.'

'That would be easier,' agreed Tenny. 'I could keep my mouth shut, but I couldn't guarantee about the boys. They wouldn't say nothin' a-purpose, but like as not if they should meet up with one of that slick crowd at the Shoe-Bar they'd let somethin' slip without thinkin'. On the other hand, it sure would make him a mite careless if he thought yuh was tied down here on a reg'lar job.'

He paused reflectively; then suddenly his eyes brightened.

'I got it,' he chuckled. 'I'll send you down to help Gabby Smith at Red Butte camp. That's 'way to hell and gone down at the south end of the outfit, where nobody goes from here more'n about once in six months. Gabby's one of these here solitary guys that's sorta soured on the world in gen'al, an' don't hardly open his face except to take in grub, but yuh can trust him. Jest tell him what yuh want and he'll do it, providin' yuh don't hang around the camp too long. Gabby does hate company worse'n a dose of poison.'

Tenny lost no time in carrying out his plans. He hunted out a few simple cooking-utensils and enough canned goods and other stores to last two weeks, picked a pack-animal and a riding horse, and by dinner-time had everything ready for Buck to start immediately afterward.

The six or seven cow-punchers who responded to the gong presented a marked and pleasant contrast to the Shoe-Bar outfit. They greeted Stratton with some brevity, but after the first pangs of hunger had been assuaged and they learned where he was bound for, they expanded, and Buck was the object of much joking commiseration on the prospect before him.

'You'll sure have one wild time,' grinned a dark-haired, blue-eyed youngster called Broncho. 'Gabby's about as sociable as a rattler. I wouldn't change places with yuh for no money.'

No one seemed to suspect any ulterior motive beneath the plan, and when Buck rode off about one o'clock, leading his packhorse, his spirits rose insensibly at the ease with which things seemed to be working out.

He reached Red Butte camp in a little more than three hours and found the adobe shack deserted. It was similar in size and construction to Las Vegas, but there all likeness ceased, for the interior was surprisingly comfortable and as spick-and-span as the Shoe-Bar line camp was cluttered and dirty. Everything was so immaculate, in fact, that Buck had a moment of hesitation about flicking his cigarette ashes on the floor, and banished his scruples mainly because he had never heard of a cow-man dropping them anywhere else.

Gabby appeared about an hour later, a tall, stooping man of uncertain middle age, with a cold eye and a perpetual, sour droop to his lids. At the sight of Buck the sourness became accentuated and increased still more when he observed the ashes on the floor. His only reply to Stratton's introduction of himself was a grunt and Buck lost no time in easing the fellow's mind of any fear of a prolonged spell of company.

Even then Gabby's gloom scarcely lightened. He listened, however, to Stratton's brief explanation and in a few gruff words agreed that in the unlikely event of any enquiry he would say that the new hand was off riding fence or something of the sort. Then he swept out the offending ashes and proceeded methodically to get supper, declining any assistance from his visitor.

His manner was so dispiriting that Buck was thankful when the silent meal was over, and even more so an hour later to spread his blankets in one of the spare bunks and turn in. His relief at getting away early the next morning was almost as great as Gabby's could be to see him go.

It was late in the afternoon, after a careful circuit of the southern end of the Shoe-Bar, that Buck reached the foothills. Bud had told him of a spring to the northwest of Las Vegas camp, but the rough travelling decided him to camp that night on the further side of the creek. In the morning he went on through a wilderness of arroyos, canyons, and gullies that twisted endlessly between the barren hills, and made him realise how simple it would be for any number of men and cattle to evade pursuit in this wild country.

Fortunately Jessup's directions had been explicit, and towards noon Buck found the spring at the bottom of a small canyon and proceeded to unpack and settle down. Bud himself had discovered the place by accident, and as far as Stratton could judge it was not a likely spot to be visited either by the Shoe-Bar hands or their Mexican confederates. A wide, overhanging ledge provided shelter for himself, and there was plenty of forage in sight for the two horses. Taken all in all, it was as snug a retreat as any one could wish, and Buck congratulated himself on having such safe and secluded headquarters from which to carry on his investigations.

These first took him southward, and for five days he rode through the hills, traversing gullies and canyons, and spying out the whole country generally, in a systematic effort to find the route taken by the rustlers in driving off their booty.

Once he found the spot where they had taken to the hills, the rest was comparatively simple. There were a number of signs to guide him, including the bodies of two animals bearing the familiar brand, and he succeeded in tracing the thieves to a point on the edge of a stretch of desert twenty miles or more below the Shoe-Bar land. About twelve miles beyond lay another range of hills, which would give them cover until they were within a short distance of the border.

'A dozen good fellows stationed here,' thought Stratton, critically surveying the gully behind him, 'would catch them without any trouble. There's no other way I've seen of getting out with a bunch of cattle.'

Having settled this point to his satisfaction, Buck's mind veered swiftly – with an odd sense of relief that now at last he could investigate the matter seriously – to the other problem which had stirred his curiosity so long.

When his attention was first attracted to the north pasture by Bud's account of Andrew Thorne's tragic death, its connection with the mystery of the ranch seemed trivial. But for some reason the thing stuck in his mind, returning again and again with a teasing persistence and gaining each time in significance. From much thinking about it, Buck could almost reconstruct the scene, with its familiar, humdrum background of bawling calves, lowing mothers, dust, hot irons, swearing, sweating men, and all the other accompaniments of the spring branding. That was the picture into which Thorne had suddenly ridden, his face stamped with an excitement in marked contrast to his usual phlegmatic calm. In his mind's eye Stratton could see him clutch Tex Lynch and draw him hastily to one side, could imagine vividly the low-voiced conversation that followed, the hurried saddling of a fresh horse, and the swift departure of the two northward – to what?

Buck had asked himself that question a hundred times. Three hours had passed before the return of Lynch alone, with the shocking news – time enough to ride twice the distance to north pasture and back again. Where had the interval been passed, and how?

Stratton realised that they might easily have changed their direction, once they were out of sight of the men. They might have gone eastward towards the ranch-house – which they had not – or westward into the mountains. Once or twice Buck considered the possibility of the old man's having stumbled on a rich lode of precious metal. But as far as he knew no trace of gold had ever been found in these mountains. Moreover, though Lynch was perfectly capable of murdering his employer for that knowledge, his next logical move would have been an immediate taking up of the claims, instead of which he remained quietly on the ranch to carry on his slow and secret plotting.

Stratton long ago dismissed that possibility. There remained only the north pasture, and the longer he considered it the more he became convinced that Thorne had met his death there, and that the chances were strong that somewhere in those wastes of worthless desert land lay the key to the whole enthralling mystery.

Buck was so eager to start his investigations that it irked him to have to spend the few remaining hours of the afternoon in idleness. But as he knew that the undertaking would take a full day or even longer, he possessed his soul with patience and made arrangements for an early start next morning.

The dawn was just breaking when he left camp mounted on Pete, the Rocking-R horse that he had found so reliable in the rough country. The simplest and most direct way would have been to descend to level ground and ride along the edge of the Shoe-Bar land. But he dared not take any chances of being observed by Lynch or his gang, and was forced to make a long detour through the hills.

The way was difficult and roundabout. Frequently he was turned back by blind canyons or gullies which had no outlet, and there were few places where the horse could go faster than a walk. To Buck's impatient spirit it was all tiresome and exasperating, and he had moments of wondering whether he was ever going to get anywhere.

Finally, about the middle of the afternoon, he was cheered for the first time by an unexpected glimpse of his goal. For several miles he had been following a rough trail which wound around the side of a steep, irregular hill. Coming out abruptly on a little plateau, with the tumbled rocks rising at his back, there spread out suddenly before him to the east a wide, extended sweep of level country.

At first he could scarcely believe that the sandy stretch below him was the north pasture he was seeking. But swiftly he realised that the thread-like line a little to the south must be the fence dividing the desert from the fertile portions of the Shoe-Bar, and he even thought he recognised the corner where the infected steer had been driven through. With an exclamation of satisfaction he was reaching for his field-glasses when of a sudden a strange, slowly moving shape out in the desert caught his attention and riveted it instantly.

For a few seconds Buck thought his eyes were playing tricks. Amazed, incredulous, forgetting for an instant the field-glasses in his hand, he stared blankly from under squinting lids at the incredible object that crawled lurchingly through the shimmering, glittering desert atmosphere.

'I'm dotty!' he muttered at length. 'It can't be!'

Then, remembering the glasses, he raised them hastily to his eyes and focused them with a twist or two of practised fingers.

He was neither crazy nor mistaken. Drawn suddenly out of its blurred obscurity by the powerful lenses, there sprang up before Buck's eyes, sharp and clear in every detail, a big grey motorcar that moved slowly but steadily, with many a bump and sidewise lurch, diagonally across the cactus-sprinkled desert below him.

CHAPTER 20

Catastrophe

The discovery galvanised Stratton into instant, alert attention. Motorcars were rare in this remote range country and confined almost solely to the sort of 'flivver' which is not entirely dependent on roads. The presence in the north pasture of this powerful grey machine, which certainly did not belong in the neighbourhood, was more than significant, and Buck tried at once to get a view of the occupants.

In this he was not successful. There were three of them, one in the driver's seat and two others in the tonneau. But the top prevented more than a glimpse of the latter, while the cap and goggles of the chauffeur left visible only a wedge of brick-red, dust-coated skin, a thin, prominent nose and a wisp of wiry black moustache.

One thing was certain – the fellow knew his job. Under his masterly guidance the big car ploughed steadily through the clogging sand, avoiding obstructions or surmounting them with the least possible expenditure of power, never once stalled, and, except for a necessary slight divergence now and then, held closely to its northwesterly course across the desert.

Buck, who had driven under the worst possible battlefront conditions, fully appreciated the coaxing, the general manoeuvring, the constant delicate manipulation of brake and throttle necessary to produce this result. But his admiration of the fellow's skill was swiftly swallowed up in eager curiosity and speculation.

Who were they? What were they doing here? Where were they going? At first he had a momentary fear lest they should see him perched up here on his point of vantage. Then he realised that the backing of rocks prevented his figure from showing against the skyline, which, together with the distance and the clouds of dust stirred up by the car itself, made the danger almost negligible. So he merely dismounted and, leaning against his horse, kept the glasses riveted on the slowly moving machine.

The car advanced steadily until it reached a point about a quarter of a mile from the rough ground and a little distance north of where Buck stood. Then it stopped, and a capped and goggled head was thrust out of the tonneau. Buck could make out nothing definite about the face save that it was smooth-shaven and rather heavy-jowled. He was hoping that the fellow would alight from the car and show himself more plainly but to his disappointment the head was presently drawn back and the machine crept on, swerving a little so that it headed almost due north.

Ten minutes later it halted again, and this time the two men got out and walked slowly over the sand. Both were clad in long dust-coats, and one seemed stouter and heavier than the other. Unfortunately they were too far beyond the carrying power of the binoculars to get anything more clearly, and Buck swore and fretted and strained his eyes in vain. After a delay of nearly an hour, he saw the car start again, and followed its blurred image until it finally disappeared beyond an out-thrust spur well to the northward.

Stratton lowered his glasses and stood for a moment or two rubbing his cramped arm absently. His face was thoughtful, with a glint of excitement in his eyes. Presently his shoulders straightened resolutely.

'Anyhow, I can follow the tracks of the tyres and find out what they've been up to,' he muttered.

The difficulty was to descend from his rocky perch, and it proved to be no small one. He might have clambered down the face of the cliff, but that would mean abandoning his horse. In the end he was forced to retrace his steps along the twisting ledge by which he had come.

From his knowledge of the country to the south, Buck had started out with the idea that it would be simple enough to reach the flats through one of the many gullies and canyons that fringed the margin of the hills further down. He had not counted on the fact that as the range widened it split into two distinct ridges, steep and declivitous on the outer edges, with the space between them broken up into a network of waterworn gullies and arroyos.

'I ought to have known from the look of the north pasture that all the water goes the other way,' he grumbled. 'Best thing I can do is to head for that trail Bud spoke of that cuts through to the T-T ranch. It can't be so very far north.'

It wasn't, as the crow flies, but Buck was no aviator. He was forced to take a most tortuous, roundabout route, and when he finally emerged on the first passable track heading approximately in the right direction, the sun was low and there seemed little chance of his accomplishing his purpose in the few hours of daylight remaining.

Still, he kept on. At least he was mapping out a route which would be easily and swiftly followed another time. And if darkness threatened, he could return to his little camp through the open Shoe-Bar pastures, where neither Lynch nor his men were at all likely to linger after dusk.

The trail followed a natural break in the hills and, though not especially difficult under foot, was twisting and irregular, full of sharp descents and equally steep upward slopes. Buck had covered about two miles and was growing impatient when he came to the hardest climb he had yet encountered and swung himself out of the saddle.

'No use killing you, Pete, to save a little time,' he commented, giving the horse's sweaty neck a slap. 'I'd like to know how the devil those two ever drove a steer through here.'

It did seem as if this must have been uncommonly difficult. The trail curved steeply around the side of a hill, following a ledge similar to the one Buck had taken earlier in the afternoon with such interesting results. There was width enough for safety, but on one side the rocks rose sharply to the summit of the hill, while on the other there was a sheer drop into a gulch below, which, at the crown of the slope, must have been fifty or sixty feet at least.

Leading the horse, Buck plodded on in a rather discouraged fashion until he had covered about three-quarters of the distance to the top. Then of a sudden his pace quickened, as a bend in the trail revealed hopeful glimpses of open spaces ahead. It was nothing really definite – merely a falling away of the hills on either side and a wide expanse of unobstructed sky beyond, but it made him feel that he was at last coming out of this rocky wilderness. A moment or two later he gained the summit of the slope and his eyes brightened as they rested on the section of sandy, cactus-dotted country spread out below him.

A dozen feet ahead the trail curved sharply around a rocky buttress, which hid the remainder of it from view. In his eagerness to see what lay beyond, Stratton did not mount but led his horse over the short stretch of level rock. But as he turned the corner, he caught his breath and jerked back on Pete's reins.

By one of those freaks of nature that are often so surprising, the trail led straight down to level ground with almost the regularity of some work of engineering. At the foot of it stood the grey motorcar – empty!

The sight of it, and especially that unnatural air of complete desertion, instantly aroused in Buck a sense of acute danger. He turned swiftly to retreat, and caught a glimpse of a figure crouching in a little rocky niche almost at his elbow.

There was no time to leap back or forward; no time even to stir.

Already the man's arm was lifted, and though Stratton's hand jerked automatically to his gun, he was too late.

An instant later something struck his head with crushing force and crumpled him to the ground.

*   *   *

When Buck began to struggle out of that black, bottomless abyss of complete oblivion, he thought at first – as soon as he could think at all – that he was lying in his bunk back at the Shoe-Bar. What gave him the idea he could not tell. His head throbbed painfully, and his brain seemed to swim in a vague, uncertain mist. A deadly lassitude gripped him, making all movement, even to the lifting of his eyelids, an exertion too great to be considered.

But presently, when his brain had cleared a little, he became aware of voices. One in particular seemed, even in his dreamlike state, to sting into his consciousness with a peculiar, bitter instinct of hatred. When at length he realised that it was the voice of Tex Lynch, the discovery had a curiously reviving effect upon his dazed senses. He could not yet remember what had happened, but intuitively he associated his helplessness with the foreman's presence, and that same instinct caused him to make a desperate attempt to understand what the man was saying. At first the fellow's words seemed blurred and broken, but little by little their meaning grew clearer to the injured man.

' … ain't safe … suspects somethin' … snoopin' around ever since … thought he was up to somethin' … saw him up on that ledge watchin' yuh … dead sure. I had a notion he'd ride around to this trail, 'cause it's the only way down to north pasture. I tell yuh, Paul, he's wise, an' he'll spill the beans sure. We got to do it.'

'I don't like it, I tell you!' protested a shrill, high-pitched voice querulously. 'I can't stand blood.'

'Wal, all yuh got to do is go back to the car an' wait,' retorted Lynch. 'I ain't so partic'lar. Besides,' his tone changed subtly, 'his head's smashed in an' he's sure to croak, anyhow. It would be an act of kindness, yuh might say.'

'I don't like it,' came again in the shrill voice. 'I'd – hear the shot. I'd know what you were doing. It would be on my – my conscience. I'd dream – If he's going to – to die, as you say, why not just – leave him here?'

An involuntary shudder passed over Stratton. It had all come back, and with a thrill of horror he realised that they were talking about him. They

573

were discussing his fate as calmly and callously as if he had been a steer with a broken leg. A feeble protest trembled on his lips, but was choked back unuttered. He knew how futile any protest would be with Tex Lynch.

'Yeah!' the latter snarled. 'An' have somebody come along an' find him! Like as not he'd hang on long enough to blab all he knows, an' then where would we be? Where would we be even if somebody run acrost his body? I ain't takin' no chances like that, I'll tell the world!'

'But isn't there some other way?' faltered the high-pitched voice.

In the brief pause that followed, Stratton dragged his lids open. He was lying where he had fallen at the curve in the trail. Tex Lynch stood close beside him. A little beyond, leaning against the rocky cliff, was a bulky figure in a long dust-coat. He had pushed up his motor-goggles and was wiping his forehead with a limp handkerchief. His round, fat face, with pursed-up lips and wide-open light-blue eyes, bore the expression of a fretful child. On his left was a lean, thin-faced fellow with a black moustache who looked scared and nervous. There was no sign of the third person who had been in the car, and even at this crucial moment Buck found time to observe the absence of his horse, Pete, and wondered momentarily what had become of him.

'Yuh an' Hurd go back to the car.' Lynch broke the silence in a tone of sudden decision. 'I'll tend to this business, an' there won't be no shootin' neither. Hustle, now! We ain't got any time to lose.'

Again Buck shuddered, and there pulsed through him that tremendous and passionate instinct for self-preservation which comes to every man at such a time. What Tex meant to do he could not guess, but he knew that if he were left alone with the fellow he might as well give up all hope. He was weak as a cat, and felt sure that no appeal from him would move Lynch a particle. His only chance lay with the fat man and his companion, and as the two turned away, Buck tried his best to call out after them.

The only result was an inarticulate croak. Lynch heard it, and instantly dropping on his knees, he clapped one hand over Stratton's mouth. In spite of Buck's futile struggles, he held it there firmly while the two men moved out of sight down the trail. His face, which still bore the fading marks of Buck's fists, was a trifle pale, but hard and determined, and in his eyes triumph and a curious, nervous shrinking struggled for mastery.

But as the moments dragged on leaden wings, not a word passed his tight lips. Presently he glanced swiftly over one shoulder. An instant later Buck's lips were freed, and he felt the foreman's hands slipping under his body.

'You hellion!' he gasped, as Lynch's purpose flashed on him in all its horror. 'You damned cowardly hound!'

As he felt himself thrust helplessly towards the precipice, Buck made a tremendous, despairing effort and managed to catch Lynch by the belt and clung there for a moment. When one hand was torn loose, he even struck Tex wildly in the face. But there was no strength in his arm, and Lynch, with a growl of rage, jerked himself free and sprang to his feet.

For an instant he towered over his helpless enemy, white-faced and hesitating. Then Stratton caught the hard impact of his boot against his side, and felt the edge of the rock slipping horribly beneath him. Powerless to help himself, his clutching fingers slid despairingly across the smooth surface. A blinding ray of sunlight dazzled him for an instant and vanished; the mountain trail flashed out of sight. His heart leaped, then sank, with a tremendous, poignant agony that seemed to tear him into shreds. Then blackness seemed to rush out of the gulch to enfold him in an impenetrable cloud of merciful oblivion.

CHAPTER 21

What Mary Thorne Found

A few hundred yards away from the fence strung along the western side of middle pasture, Mary Thorne pulled her horse down to a walk and straightened her hat mechanically. Her cheeks were flushed becomingly and her eyes shone, but at the end of that sharp little canter much of the brightness faded and her face clouded.

For the last week or more it had grown increasingly difficult to keep up a cheerful front and prevent the doubts and troubles which harassed her from causing comment. This morning she had reached the limit of suppression. Stella got on her nerves more than usual; Alf annoyed her with his superior air and those frequent little intimate mannerisms which, though unnoticed during all the years of their friendship, had lately grown curiously irksome to the girl. Even Mrs Archer's calm placidity weighed on her spirits, and when that happened Mary knew that it was high time for her to get away by herself for a few hours and make a vigorous effort to recover her wonted serenity of mind.

She told herself that she was tired and jaded, and that a solitary ride would soothe her ragged nerves. And so, at the first opportunity after breakfast, she slipped quietly away, saddled her favourite horse, Freckles, and leaving word with Pedro that she would be back by dinner-time, departed hastily.

It was rather curious behaviour in a girl usually so frank and open, and free from even a suspicion of guile, but she deliberately gave the Mexican an impression that she was going to join the men down in south pasture, and as long as she remained within sight of the ranch-house she kept her horse headed in that direction. Furthermore, before abruptly changing her course to the northwest, she pulled up and glanced sharply around to make certain she was not observed.

As a matter of fact one of the things which had lately puzzled and troubled her was a growing impression of surveillance. Several times she had surprised Pedro or his wife in attitudes which seemed suspiciously as if they had been spying. McCabe, too, and some of the other men were inclined to pop up when she least expected them. Indeed, looking back on the last two weeks she realised how very little she had been alone except in the close confines of the ranch-house. If she rode forth to inspect the work or merely to take a little canter, Tex or one of the punchers was almost sure to join her. They always had a good excuse, but equally always they were there; and though Mary Thorne had not the remotest notion of the meaning of it all, she had grown convinced that there must be some hidden motive beneath their actions, and the thought troubled her.

Tex Lynch's altered manner gave her even greater cause for anxiety. It would have been difficult to put into words exactly where the change lay, but she was sure that there was a difference. Up to a short time ago she had regarded him impersonally as merely an efficient foreman whom she had inherited from her father along with the ranch. She did so still, but she could not remain blind to the fact that the man himself was deliberately striving to inject a more intimate note into their intercourse. His methods were subtle enough, but Mary Thorne was far from dull, and the alteration in his manner made her at once indignant and a little frightened.

'I suppose it's silly to feel that way, especially with Alf here,' she murmured as she reached the fence and swung herself out of the saddle. 'But I do wish I hadn't taken his word about – Buck Green.'

She took a small pair of pliers from her saddle-pocket and deftly untwisted the strands of wire from one of the posts, while Freckles looked on with an expression of intelligent interest. When the gap was opened in the fence, he walked through and waited quietly on the other side until the wire had been replaced. It was not the first time he had done this trick, for the trail through the mountains was a favourite retreat of the girl's. She had discovered it long ago, and returned to it frequently, through her own private break in the fence, especially on occasions like this when she wanted to get away from everybody and be quite alone.

Having remounted and headed northward along the edge of the hills, her thoughts flashed back to the discharged cow-puncher, and her brow puckered. The whole subject affected her in a curiously complicated fashion. From the first she had been conscious of having done the young man an injustice. And yet, as often as she went over their final interview in her mind – which was not seldom – she did not see how she could have done otherwise. Her woman's intuition told her over and over again that he could not possibly be a common thief; but if this was so, why had he refused her the simple assurance she asked for?

That was the stumbling-block. If he had only been frank and open, she felt that she would have believed him, even in the face of Lynch's conviction of his guilt, though she was frank enough to admit that the foreman's attitude would probably have influenced her much more strongly a week ago than it did at present. It was this thought which brought her mind around to another of her worries.

Not only did she intensely dislike Lynch's present manner towards herself, but there had lately grown up in her mind a vague distrust of the man generally. She could not put her finger on anything really definite. There were moments, indeed, when she wondered if she was not a silly little fool making bogies out of shadows. But the feeling persisted, growing on unconsidered trifles, that Tex was playing at some subtle, secret game, of the character of which she had not even the most remote conception.

'But if that's so – if he can't be trusted any longer,' she said aloud, stung by a sudden, sharp realisation of the gravity of such a situation, 'what am I to do?'

Of his own accord Freckles had turned aside into the little curved depression in the cliffs and was plodding slowly up the trail. Staring blindly at the rough, ragged cliffs and peaks ahead of her, the girl was suddenly overwhelmed by a feeling of helplessness. If Lynch failed her, what could she do? Whom could she turn to for help or even for counsel? There was Alf Manning, but Alf knew nothing whatever of range conditions, and besides neither he nor Stella expected to stay on indefinitely. Her mind ranged swiftly over other more or less remote possibilities, but save for a few distant cousins with whom they had never been on intimate terms, she could think of no one. She even considered for a moment Jim Tenny of the Rocking-R, whom she had met and liked, or Dr Blanchard, but a sudden reviving burst of spirit caused her quickly to dismiss the thought.

'They'd think I was a silly, hysterical idiot,' she murmured. 'Why, I couldn't even tell them what I was afraid of. I wonder if it can possibly be just nerves? It doesn't seem as if – '

She broke off abruptly and tightened on her reins. Freckles had carried her over the summit of the trail and had almost reached the hollow on the other side, formed by the bottom of a gully that crossed the path. Mary had once explored it and knew that to the left it deepened into a gloomy gulch that hugged the cliff for some distance and then curved abruptly to the south. So far as she knew, it led nowhere, and yet, to her astonishment, not a hundred feet away a saddled horse, with bridle-reins trailing, stood cropping the leaves of a stunted mesquite.

'That's funny,' she said aloud in a low tone.

As she spoke the horse threw up his head and stared at her, ears pointed enquiringly. When Freckles nickered, the strange animal gave an answering whinny, but did not move.

Puzzled and a little nervous, Mary glanced sharply to right and left amongst the scattered rocks. In her experience a saddled horse meant that the owner was not far away; but she could see no signs of any one, and at length, taking courage from the silence, she rode slowly forward.

As she came closer the horse backed away a foot or two and half turned, exposing a brand on his shoulder. The girl stared at it with a puckered frown, wondering what on earth any one from the Rocking-R was doing here. Then her glance strayed to the saddle, flittered indifferently over cantle and skirts, to pause abruptly, with a sudden keen attention, on the flap of the right-hand pocket, which bore the initials 'R. S.' cut with some skill on the smooth leather.

With eyes widening, the girl bent forward, studying the flap intently. She was not mistaken; the initials *were* R. S., and in a flash there came back to her a memory of that afternoon, which seemed so long ago, when she and Buck Green rode out together to the south pasture. She had noticed those initials then on his saddle-pocket, and knowing how unusual it was for a cowman to touch his precious saddle with a knife, she made some casual comment, and learned how it had come into Buck's possession.

What did it mean? What was *he* doing here on a Rocking-R horse? Above all, where was he?

Suddenly her heart began to beat unevenly and her frightened eyes stared down the gulch to where an out-thrust buttress provokingly hid the greater part of it from view. Her glance shifted again to the horse, who stood motionless, regarding her with liquid, intelligent eyes, and for the first time she noticed that the ends of the trailing reins were scratched and torn and ragged.

How still the place was! She fumbled in her blouse, and drawing forth a handkerchief, passed it mechanically over her damp forehead. Then abruptly her slight figure straightened, and tightening the reins she urged Freckles along the rock-strewn bottom of the gulch.

The distance to the rocky buttress seemed at once interminable and incredibly short. As she reached it she held her breath and her teeth dug into her colourless lips. But when another section of the winding gorge lay before her, silent, empty save for scattered boulders and a few scanty bits of stunted vegetation, one small, gloved hand fluttered to her breast, then dropped, clenched, against the saddle-horn.

A rounded mass of rock, fallen in ages past from the cliffs above, blocked her path, and mechanically the girl reined Freckles around it. An instant later the horse stopped of his own accord, and the girl found herself staring down with horror-stricken eyes at the body of a man stretched out on the further side of the boulders. Motionless he lay there, a long length of brown chaps and torn, disordered shirt. His face was hidden in his crooked arms; the tumbled mass of brown hair was matted with ominous dark clots. But in that single, stricken second Mary Thorne knew whom she had found.

'Oh!' she choked, fighting desperately against a wave of faintness that threatened to overwhelm her. 'Oh!'

Slowly the man's face lifted, and two bloodshot eyes regarded her dully through a matted lock of hair that lay stiffly plastered against his forehead. With a curious, stealthy movement, one hand twisted back to his side and fumbled there for an instant. Then the man groaned softly.

'I forgot,' he mumbled. 'It's gone. You – you've got me this time, I reckon.'

Face drained to paper-white and lips quivering, Mary Thorne slid out of her saddle, steadied herself against the horse for a second, and then dropped on her knees beside him.

'Buck!' she cried in a shaking voice. 'You – you're hurt! What – what is it?'

A puzzled look came into his face, and as he stared into the wide, frightened hazel eyes so close to his, recognition slowly dawned.

'You!' he muttered. 'What – How –'

She twined her fingers together to stop their trembling. 'I was riding through the pass,' she told him briefly. 'I saw your horse and I – I was – afraid –'

A faint gleam came into the bloodshot eyes. 'My – my horse? You mean a – a Rocking-R cayuse?'

'Yes.'

He tried to sit up, but the effort turned him so white that the girl cried out protestingly.

'You mustn't. You're badly hurt. I – I'll ride back for help.' She sprang to her feet. 'But first I must get you water.'

He stared at her as one regards a desert mirage. 'Water!' he repeated unbelievingly. 'You know where – If you could –'

A sudden moisture dimmed her eyes, but she winked it resolutely back. 'There's a little spring the other side of the trail,' she explained. 'You lie quietly and I'll be back in just a minute.'

Stumbling in her haste, she turned and ran past the buttress and on towards the trail. Not a hundred feet beyond, a tiny spring bubbled up in the rocks, and dropping down beside it, the girl jerked the pins from her hat and let the cool water trickle into the capacious crown of the Stetson. It seemed to take an eternity to fill, but at length the water ran over the brim, and carefully guarding her precious burden, she hurried back again.

The man was watching for her – eagerly, longingly, with an underlying touch of apprehensive doubt, as if he half feared to find her merely one of those dreamlike phantoms that had haunted him through the long, painful hours. As the girl sank down beside him, there was a look in his eyes that sent a strange thrill through her and caused her hands to tremble, sending a little stream of water trickling over the soggy hat-brim to the ground.

She steadied herself resolutely and bending forward held the hat against Buck's lips. As he plunged his face into it and began to suck up the water in great, famished gulps, the girl's lips quivered, and her eyes, resting on the matted tangle of dark hair, filled with sudden tears.

CHAPTER 22

Nerve

With a deep sigh, Buck lifted his face from the water and regarded her gratefully.

'That just about saved my life,' he murmured.

Mary Thorne carefully set down the improvised water-bucket, its contents much depleted, and taking out her handkerchief, soaked it thoroughly.

'I'm awfully stupid about first aid,' she said. 'But your head must be badly cut, and – '

'Don't,' he protested, as the moist bit of cambric touched his hair. 'You'll spoil it.'

'As if that mattered!' she retorted. 'Just rest your head on your arms; it'll be easier.'

With deft, gentle touches, she cleaned away the blood and grime, parting his thick hair now and then with delicate care. Her hands were steady now, and having steeled herself for anything, the sight of a jagged, ugly-looking cut on his scalp did not make her flinch. She even bent forward a little to examine it more closely, and saw that a ridge of clotted blood had temporarily stopped its oozing.

'I think I'd better let it alone,' she said aloud. 'I might start it bleeding again. How – how did it happen?'

Buck raised his head and regarded her with a slow, thoughtful stare.

'I fell off the cliff back there,' he replied at length.

Her eyes widened. 'You – fell off the cliff!' she gasped. 'It's a wonder – But is this the only place you're hurt?'

His lips twisted in a grim smile. 'Oh, no! I've got a sprained ankle and what feels like a broken rib, though it may be only bruises. But as you're thinking, I'm darned lucky to get off alive. I must have struck a ledge or something part way down, but how I managed from there I haven't the least idea.'

Hands clenched together in her lap, she stared at him in dismay.

'I thought perhaps you might be strong enough in a little while to ride back with me to the ranch. I – I could help you mount, and we could go very slowly. But of course that's impossible. I'd better start at once and bring back some of the men.'

She made a move to rise, but he stopped her with a quick, imperative gesture. 'No, you mustn't,' he said firmly. 'That won't do at all. I can't go to the ranch.' He paused, his forehead wrinkled thoughtfully. 'You may not have guessed it, but Lynch and I don't pull together at all,' he finished, with a whimsical intonation.

'But surely that wouldn't make any difference – now!' she protested.

'Only the difference that he'd have me just where he wanted me,' he retorted. He was regarding her with a steady, questioning stare, and presently he gave a little sigh. 'I'll have to tell you something I didn't mean to,' he said. 'In my opinion Tex Lynch is pretty much of a scoundrel. He knows I know it, and there isn't anything he wouldn't do to shut my mouth – for good.'

To his amazement, instead of showing the indignation he expected, the girl merely stared at him in surprise.

'What!' she cried. 'You believe that, too?'

'I'm sure of it. But I thought you trusted – '

'I don't any longer.' She was surprised at the immensity of the relief that surged over her at this chance to unburden her soul of the load of perplexity and trouble which harassed her. 'For a long time I haven't – There've been a number of things. I still haven't an idea of what it's all about, but – '

'I'm mighty glad you feel that way,' Buck said, as she paused. 'I'm not quite sure myself just what he's up to, but I believe I'm on the right trail.' Very briefly he told her of the steps he had taken since leaving the Shoe-Bar. 'You see how impossible it would be to trust myself in his power again,' he concluded.

For a moment or two Mary Thorne sat silent, regarding him with a curious expression.

'So that was the reason,' she murmured at length.

His eyes questioned her mutely, and a slow flush crept into her face.

'The reason you – you couldn't say you had no – special object in being on the Shoe-Bar,' she explained haltingly. 'I'm – sorry I didn't understand.'

'I couldn't very well tell you without running the risk of Lynch's finding out. As it happened, I was trying my best to think up a reasonable excuse for leaving the outfit to do some investigating from this end, so you really did me a good turn.'

'Investigating what? Haven't you any idea what he's up to?'

Buck hesitated. 'A very little, but it's too indefinite to put into words just yet. I've a feeling I'll get at the bottom of it soon, though, and then I'll tell you. In the meantime, when you go back, don't breathe a word of having seen me, and on no account let any one persuade you to – sell the outfit.'

She stared at him with crinkled brows. 'But what are you going to do now?' she asked suddenly, her mind flashing back to the present difficulty.

He dragged himself into a sitting posture. He was evidently feeling stronger and looked much more like himself.

'Try and get back to that camp of mine I told you of,' he explained. 'I reckon I'll have to lay up there a while, but there's food a-plenty, and a good spring, so – '

'But I don't believe you can even stand,' she protested. 'And if your ribs are broken – '

'Likely it's only one and I can strap that good and tight with a piece of my shirt or something. Then if you could catch Pete and bring him over here, I'll manage to climb into the saddle some way. It's only three or four miles, and the going's not so very bad.'

She made no further protest, but her lips straightened firmly and there was a look of decision in her girlish face as she set about helping him with his preparations.

It was she who tore a broad band from his flannel shirt, roughly fringed the ends with Buck's knife and tied it so tightly about his body that he had hard work to keep from wincing. She insisted on bandaging his head, and while he rested in the shade went back into the gulch to look for his hat and the Colt that had fallen from his holster.

She finally found them both under a narrow ledge that thrust out a dozen feet below the edge of the trail. A stunted bush, rooted deep in some hidden crevice, grew up before it, and, staring upward at it, the girl guessed that to this little bush alone Buck owed his life. He had been able to give her no further details of his descent, but she saw that it would be possible for a man to crawl along the narrow ledge to where another crossed it at a descending angle, and thence gain the bottom of the gulch.

'I wonder how he ever came to fall,' she murmured, remembering how wide the trail was at the summit.

Returning, however, she asked no questions. In the face of what lay before her, the matter seemed trivial and unimportant. She caught the Rocking-R horse without much trouble and led him back to a broad, flat boulder on which Buck had managed to crawl. Obliged to hold the animal, whose slightest movement might prove disastrous, she could give no further aid, but was forced to stand helpless, watching with troubled, sympathetic eyes the man's painful struggles to gain the saddle. When at last he succeeded and slumped there, mouth twisted and face bathed in perspiration, her knees were shaking and she felt limp and nerveless.

'We'll stop at the spring first for more water,' she said, pulling herself together with an effort.

Too exhausted for speech, Buck merely nodded, and the girl, gathering up Freckles's bridle in her other hand, led the two horses slowly towards the trail. At the spring Buck drank deeply of the water she handed him, and seemed much refreshed.

'That's good,' he murmured, with an effort to straighten his bent body. 'Well, I reckon I'd better be starting. I – I can't thank you enough for all you've done, Miss – Thorne. It was mighty plucky – '

'You mustn't waste your strength talking,' she interrupted quietly. 'Just tell me which way to go, and we'll start.'

'We?' he repeated sharply. 'But you're not going.'

'Of course I am. Did you think for a moment I'd let you take that ride alone?' She smiled faintly with a brave attempt at lightness. 'You'd be falling off and breaking another rib. Please don't make difficulties. I'm going with you, and that's an end of it.'

Perhaps the firmness of her manner made Buck realise the futility of further protest, or possibly he was in no condition to argue. At all events he gave in, and when the girl swung herself into the saddle, the slow journey began.

To Mary Thorne the memory of it remained ever afterward in her mind a chaotic medley of strange emotions and impressions, vague yet vivid. At first, where the width of the trail permitted it, she rode beside him, making an effort to talk casually and lightly, yet not too constantly, but continually keeping a watchful eye on the drooping figure at her right, whose hands presently sought and gripped the saddle-horn.

When they left the trail for rougher ground, she dismounted in spite of Buck's protest, and walked beside him, and it was well she did. Once when the horse slipped or stumbled on a loose stone and the man's body swayed perilously in the saddle, she put up both hands swiftly and held him there.

Before they had gone a mile her boots began to hurt her, but the pain was so trifling in comparison with what Buck must be suffering that she scarcely noticed it. He was putting up a brave front, but there were signs that were difficult to conceal, and towards the end of that toilsome journey it was evident that he could not possibly have kept his seat much longer. Indeed, when they had ridden the short length of the little canyon and stopped before the overhanging shelf of rocks, he toppled suddenly sidewise, and only the girl's frail body prevented him from crashing roughly to the ground.

She brought him water from the spring, and searching through his belongings found a flask of brandy and forced some between his teeth. When he had recovered from his momentary faintness, she managed somehow to get him over to the blankets spread beneath the ledge. Then she built a fire and set some coffee on it to boil, unsaddled Pete, fed and watered the three horses, finally returning with a cup of steaming liquid to where Buck lay exhausted with closed eyes.

His face was drawn and haggard, and his lashes, long and soft and thick, lay against a skin drained of every particle of colour. A sudden choking sob rose to the girl's lips, but she managed to force it back, and when the man's lids slowly lifted, she smiled tremulously.

'Here's some coffee,' she said, kneeling down and holding the rim of the cup to his lips.

Buck drank obediently in slow gulps.

'You're all nerve,' he murmured when the cup was empty. He lay silent for a few moments. 'Don't you think you'd better be starting back?' he asked at length.

'How can I go and leave you like this?' she protested. 'You're so weak. You might get fever. Anything might happen.'

'But you certainly can't stay,' he retorted with unexpected decision. 'Let alone a whole lot of other reasons,' he went on, watching her mutinous face, 'if you did, Tex would have a posse out hunting for you in no time. Sooner or later they'd find this place, and you know what that would mean. I'm feeling better every minute – honest. By tomorrow I'll be able to hobble around and look after myself fine.'

His logic was irresistible, and for a time she sat silent, torn by a conflict of emotions. Then all at once her face brightened.

'I've got it!' she cried. 'Why can't I send Bud out? He's to be trusted, surely?'

Buck's eyes lit up in a way that brought to the girl a curious, jealous pang.

'Bud? Sure, he's all right. That's one fine idea. You'll have to be careful Lynch doesn't know where he's going, though.'

'I'll manage that all right.'

Reluctant to go, yet feeling that she ought to make haste, the girl got out some crackers and placed them, with a pail of water, within his reach. Then she listened while Stratton told her of a short cut out to the middle pasture.

'I understand,' she nodded. 'You'll promise to be careful, won't you? Bud ought to be here in a couple of hours, though he may be delayed a little longer. You'd better not try and move until he comes.'

'I won't,' Buck answered. 'I'm too darn comfortable.'

'Well, goodbye, then,' she said briefly, moving over to her horse.

'Goodbye; and – thank you a thousand times!'

She made no answer, but a faint, enigmatic smile quivered for an instant on her lips as she turned the stirrup and swung herself into the saddle. When Freckles had reached a little distance, she glanced back and waved her hand. From where he lay Stratton could see almost the whole length of the little canyon, and as long as the slight figure on the big grey horse remained in sight, his eyes followed her intently, a sort of wistful hunger in their depths. But when she disappeared, the man's head fell back limply on the blankets and his eyes closed.

CHAPTER 23

Where the Wheel Tracks Led

Bud Jessup removed a battered stew-pan from the fire and set it aside to cool a little.

'Well, by this time I reckon friend Tex is all worked up over what's become of me,' he remarked in a tone of satisfaction, deftly shifting the coffeepot to a bed of deeper coals. 'He's sure tried often enough to get rid of me, but I don't guess he quite relishes my droppin' out of sight like this.'

Buck Stratton, his back resting comfortably against a rock a little way from the fire, nodded absently.

'You're sure you didn't leave any trace they could pick up?' he asked with a touch of anxiety.

'Certain sure,' returned Jessup confidently. 'When Miss Mary came in around four, I was in the wagon-shed, the rest of the crowd bein' down in south pasture. Like I told yuh before, she had a good-sized package all done up nice in her hand, an' it didn't take her long to tell me what was up. Then we walks out together an' stops by the kitchen door.

' "Yuh better get yore supper at the hotel," she says, "an' ride back afterwards. I meant to send in right after dinner to mail the package, but I got held up out on the range."

'Then she seems to catch sight of the greaser for the first time jest inside the door, though I noticed him snoopin' there when we first come up.

' "I hope yuh got somethin' left from dinner, Pedro," she says, with one of them careless natural smiles of hers, like as if she hadn't a care on her mind except food. "I'm half starved." '

Bud sighed and finished with a note of admiration. 'Some girl, all right!'

'You've said it,' agreed Buck fervently.

His appearance had improved surprisingly in the ten days that had passed since his accident. The head-bandage was gone, and his swollen ankle, though still tender at times, had been reduced to almost normal size by constant applications of cold water. His body was still tightly strapped up with yards and yards of bandage, which Mary Thorne had thoughtfully packed, with a number of other first-aid necessities, in the parcel which was Bud's excuse for making a trip to town.

Stratton was not certain that a rib had been broken after all. When Jessup came to examine him he found the flesh terribly bruised and refrained from any unnecessary prodding. It was still somewhat painful to the touch, but from the ease with which he could get about, Buck had a notion that at the worst the bone was merely cracked.

'They wouldn't be likely to notice where you left the Paloma trail, would they?' Buck asked, after a brief retrospective silence.

'Not unless they're a whole lot better trackers than I think for,' Jessup assured him. 'I picked a rocky place this side of the gully, an' cut around the north end of middle pasture, where the land slopes down a bit, an' yuh can't be seen from the south more 'n a quarter of a mile. I kept my eyes peeled, believe me! an' didn't glimpse a soul all the way. I wouldn't fret none about their followin' me here.'

'I reckon it is foolish,' admitted Stratton. 'But lying around not able to do anything makes a fellow think up all kinds of trouble. Lynch isn't a fool, and there's no doubt when you didn't come back that night he'd begin to smell a rat right off.'

'Sure. An' next day he likely sent in to town, where he'd find out from old Pop that I never showed up there at all. After that, accordin' to my figgerin', he'd be up against it hard. Yuh can bank on Miss Mary playin' the game, an' registerin' surprise an' worry an' all the rest of it. There ain't a chance in the world of his thinkin' to look for me here.'

'I reckon that's true. Of course we've got to remember that so far as he knows I'm out of the way for good.'

Bud took up coffeepot and stew-pan and set them down beside Stratton, where the rest of the meal was spread.

'Sure,' he chuckled, dropping down against the ledge. 'Officially, you're a corpse. That's yore strong point, old-timer. By golly!' he added, with a sudden, fierce revulsion of spirit. 'I only hope I'll be on hand when he gets what's comin' to him, the damn', cowardly skunk!'

'Maybe you will,' commented Buck grimly. 'Well, let's eat. Seems like I do nothing but eat and sleep and loaf around. I've a good notion to bust up the monotony,' he added, after a few minutes had passed in the silent consumption of food, 'and take that trip to north pasture tomorrow.'

'Don't be loco,' Bud told him hastily. 'Yuh ain't fit for nothin' like that yet.'

'I did it a few days ago,' Stratton reminded him, 'and I'm feeling a hundred per cent better now.'

'Mebbe so; but what's the use in takin' chances? We got plenty of time.'

'I'm not so sure of that,' Buck said seriously. 'You say that Lynch thinks I'm dead and out of the way. Well, maybe he does; but unless he's a lot bigger fool than I think for, he's not going to leave a body around in plain sight for anybody to find. He'll be slipping down into that gulch one of these days to get rid of it, and when he finds there ain't any body – then what?'

'He'll begin to see he's got into one hell of a mess, I reckon,' commented Jessup.

'Right. And he'll be willing to do anything on earth to crawl out safe. Like enough he'll connect your disappearance with the business, and that would worry him more than ever. He might even get scared enough to throw up the whole game and beat it; and believe me, that wouldn't suit me at all.'

'Yuh said a mouthful!' snarled Jessup. 'If that hellion should get away – Say, Buck, why couldn't yuh get him for attempted murder?'

'I might, but the witnesses are all on his side, and there'd be a good chance of his slipping out. Besides, I'm set on finding out first what his game is. I'm dead certain now it's connected somehow with the north pasture, and I've an idea it's something big. That car I told you about, and everything – Well, there's no sense guessing any longer when we can make a stab at finding out. We'll start the first thing tomorrow.'

Bud made no further protest, and at dawn next morning they left camp and set out northward through the hills. It was a slow journey, and towards the end of it Buck felt rather seedy. But this was only natural, he told himself, after lying around and doing nothing; and he even wished he had made the move sooner.

Both he and Jessup were conscious of a growing excitement as they neared the goal from which circumstances had held them back so long. Were they going to find out something definite at last? Or would fate thrust another unexpected obstacle in their way? Above all, if fortune proved kind, what would be the character of their discovery?

Immensely intrigued and curious, Bud chattered constantly through-out the ride, suggesting all sorts of solutions of the problem, some of which were rather far-fetched. Gold was his favourite – as it has been the favourite lure for adventurers all down the ages – and he drew an entrancing picture of desert sands sprinkled with the yellow dust. He thought of other precious metals, too, and even gave a passing con-sideration to a deposit of diamonds or some other precious or semi-precious stones. Once he switched off oddly on the subject of prehistoric remains, and Stratton's surprised enquiry revealed the fact that three years ago he had worked for a party of scientific excavators in Montana.

'Them bones and skeletons as big as houses bring a pile of money, believe me!' he assured his companion. 'The country up there ain't a mite different from this, neither.'

Buck himself was unusually silent and abstracted. During the last ten days of enforced idleness he had considered the subject for hours at a time and from every conceivable angle, with the result that a certain possibility occurred to him and persisted in lingering in his mind, in spite of its seeming improbability. It was so vague and unlikely that he said nothing about it to Bud; but now, mounting the steep trail, the thought of it came back with gathering strength, and he wondered whether it could possibly be true.

Advancing with every possible precaution, they gained the summit and passed on down the other side. Before them lay the desert, glittering and glowing in the morning sun, without a sign of alien presence. Keeping a sharp lookout, they reached the little, half-circular recess in the cliffs that formed the end of the trail, and paused.

No rain had fallen in the last ten days and the print of motor-tyres was almost as clear and unmistakable as the day it had been made. They could make out easily where the car had been driven in, the footprints about it, and the marks left by its turning; and with equal lack of difficulty they picked out the track made as it departed.

The latter headed north, but Stratton was not interested in it. Without hesitation he selected the incoming trail, and the two followed it out into the desert. For a few hundred yards they rode almost due east. Then the wheel-marks turned abruptly to the south, and a little further on Buck noted the prints of a galloping horse beside them.

'Lynch, I reckon,' he commented, pointing them out to his companion. 'When he saw me up on the cliffs down yonder, he must have hustled to catch up with the car.'

Neither of them spoke again until they reached the spot where Buck had seen the car stop and the men get out and walk about. Here they dismounted and followed the footprints with careful scrutiny. Bud saw nothing significant, and when they had covered the ground thoroughly, he expressed his disappointment freely. Stratton merely shrugged his shoulders.

'We'll follow the back track and see where else they stopped,' he said curtly.

His voice was a little hoarse, and there was an odd gleam in his eyes. When they were in the saddle again, he urged his horse forward at a speed which presently brought a protest from Jessup.

'Yuh better take it easy, old man,' he cautioned. 'If that cayuse steps in a hole, you're apt to get a jolt that'll put you out of business.'

'I don't guess it'll hurt me,' returned Stratton with preoccupied brevity.

Bud gave a resigned shrug, and for ten minutes the silence remained unbroken. Then all at once Buck gave a muttered exclamation and pulled his horse up with a jerk.

They were on the rim of a wide, shallow depression in the sand. There was nothing remarkable about it at first sight, save, perhaps, the total absence of desert vegetation for some distance all around. But Stratton slid hastily out of his saddle, flung the reins over Pete's head, and walked swiftly forward. Thrilled with a sudden excitement and suspense, Bud followed.

'What is it?' he questioned eagerly, as Buck bent down to scoop up a handful of the trampled sand. 'What have yuh – '

He broke off abruptly as Stratton turned suddenly on him, eyes dilated and a spot of vivid colour glowing on each cheekbone.

'Don't you see?' he demanded, thrusting his hand towards the boy. 'Don't you understand?'

Staring at the open palm, Jessup's eyes widened and his jaw dropped.

'Good Lord!' he gasped. 'You don't mean that it – it's – '

He paused incredulously, and Buck nodded.

'I'm sure of it,' he stated crisply.

CHAPTER 24

The Secret of North Pasture

Jessup swallowed hard. 'But – but – ' he faltered, 'there ain't never been any found around here. The nearest fields are hundreds of miles away, ain't they?'

Stratton dropped the lump of sand. A number of particles still clung to his palm, and over the skin there spread an oily, slightly iridescent film. His manner had suddenly grown composed, though his eyes still shone with suppressed excitement.

'Just the same, it's – oil!' he returned quietly. 'There's no doubt at all about it. Look at the ground there.'

Mechanically Bud's glance shifted to the wide, shallow depression in the desert. The sand was noticeably darker, and here and there under the sun's rays, it held that faintly iridescent glint that was unmistakable. At a distance he would have said there was a spring somewhere beneath the surface. But no water ever had that look, and now that he was prepared for it he even noticed a faint, distinctive odour in the air.

'By golly!' he cried excitedly. 'You mean to say the whole pasture's full of it?'

'Not likely, but it looks to me as if there was a-plenty. There were traces back there where we stopped, and there's no telling how many more – '

'But I didn't see nothin',' interrupted Bud in surprise.

'You weren't looking for it, that's why,' shrugged Stratton. 'I was. Thinking it all over this past week, I got to wondering if oil might not just possibly be what we ought to look for. I was so doubtful I didn't say anything about it. Like you said, nobody's ever struck it anywhere around these parts, but I reckon you never can tell.'

'Wough!' Bud suddenly exploded in a tremendous exhalation of breath.

'I can't seem to get it through my nut. Why, it means a fortune for Miss Mary! No wonder that skunk tried his best to do her out of it.'

Buck stared at him oddly. A fortune for Mary Thorne! Somehow, until this moment he had not realised that this must seem to every one to be the object of his efforts – to rid Mary Thorne of all her cares and troubles and bring her measureless prosperity. Ignorant of Stratton's identity and of all the circumstances of her father's treachery and double-dealing, she must hold that view herself. The thought disturbed Buck, and he wondered uncomfortably what her feelings would be when she learned the truth.

'What's the matter?' enquired Bud suddenly. 'What yuh scowlin' that way for?'

'Nothing special,' evaded Buck. 'I was just thinking.' After all, there was no use crossing bridges until one came to them. 'We'd better get started,' he added briskly. 'We've found out all we want here, and there's no sense in taking chances of running up against the gang.'

'What's the next move?' asked Bud, when they had mounted and started back over their trail.

'Look up Hardenberg and put him wise to what we know,' answered Stratton promptly. 'We've done about all we can; the rest of it's up to him.'

'I reckon so,' agreed Jessup. 'I never met up with him, but they say he's a good skate. Perilla's some little jaunt from here, though. Yuh thinkin' of riding all the way?'

'Why not? It'll be quicker in the end than going to Harpswell and taking the train. We'll likely need the cayuses, too, when we get there. I've done forty miles at a stretch plenty of times.'

'So've I, but not with a bad ankle and a bunged-up side,' returned Bud dryly. 'How yuh feelin'?'

'Fine! I've hardly had a twinge all day. That bandage stuff is great dope for keeping a fellow strapped up comfortable.'

'Well, if you're up to it, I reckon that would be better than the train,' Bud admitted. 'For one thing, if we take the trail around south of the Rocking-R we ain't likely to meet up with anybody who'll put Lynch wise, an' I take it that's important.'

'I'll say so!' agreed Buck emphatically. 'The chances are that even if he got wind of you and me being together, he'd realise the game was up, and probably beat it for the border. As long as we can manage to keep out of the spotlight, he may suspect a lot of things, but considering the size of the stake, he's likely to take a chance and hang on.'

'Let's hope he don't take it into his head to ride up here this morning,' remarked Jessup, glancing apprehensively across the desert wastes towards the south. 'That would spill the beans for fair.'

The very possibility made them urge the horses to an even greater speed, and neither of them really breathed freely until they had gained the little sheltered depression in the cliffs, from which the trail led over the shoulder of the mountain.

'I reckon we're safe enough now,' commented Stratton, drawing rein. 'I didn't see a sign of anybody as we came along.'

Halting for ten minutes to rest the horses, they started up the trail in single file, Bud going first. For a greater part of the distance the rocky spurs shielded them from any save a very limited field of observation. But at the summit there was an almost level stretch of twenty feet or more from which an extended view could be had, not only of a wide sweep of desert country, but of a section of the northern end of middle pasture as well. Reaching this point, Buck glanced back searchingly. An instant later he was out of the saddle and crouching against the rocky wall.

'Lead Pete around the corner,' he urged Jessup sharply. 'Get out of sight as quick as you can.'

Bud obeyed without question, and Stratton hastily took out his field-glasses and focused them on the three figures he had glimpsed riding along the northern extremity of the Shoe-Bar pasture. He recognised them instantly, pausing only long enough to make out that they did not seem to be in haste, and that so far as he could tell they were not looking in the direction of the trail. Then he thrust the glasses back into the case, and slipping around the buttress rejoined his companion.

'Lynch, with McCabe and Kreeger,' he explained curtly, gathering up the reins and swinging himself into the saddle.

'Did they see yuh?'

'I don't think so. They seemed to be taking things easy, and weren't looking this way at all. I wonder what they're up to?'

'Couldn't we stick around here for a while and watch them?' Bud asked eagerly.

Buck hesitated an instant. 'I guess we'd better not take a chance,' he replied at length. 'Such a whale of a lot depends on his not knowing that I'm alive and kicking; I'd hate like the devil to spoil everything now by his getting a glimpse of me. Besides, for all we know they may be coming through here to meet somebody – the rest of the gang, perhaps, or – '

'That's right,' interrupted Bud hastily. 'Let's go. Sooner we're off this here trail the better.'

Without further delay they rode on down the slope, paused for a moment or two at the spring in the hollow to water the horses, and then pushed on again. Passing the entrance to the gulch, Jessup glanced that way curiously.

'Mebbe they're on their way to dispose of yore corpse, Buck,' he chuckled.

Stratton grinned. 'I thought of that, and I rather hope it's so. They'd be puzzled and suspicious, maybe, but they couldn't be really sure of anything. It would be a whole lot better than to have them run across our tracks in the sand back there. That would give away the show completely.'

Twenty minutes or so later they reached the gully through which they had come out on the trail. Though there had been no further signs of the Shoe-Bar men, their vigilance did not relax. Pushing on with all possible speed, they covered the distance to the little camp in very much less time than it had taken in the morning.

Here the horses had a brief rest while the two men collected their few belongings and loaded them on the packhorse, for they had decided to go on at once. Both felt that no time should be lost in finding the sheriff and setting the machinery of the law in motion. Moreover, they were down to the last scrap of food and unless they stirred themselves they were likely to go hungry that night.

An hour later found them riding southward, following the route through the mountains used by the cattle-rustlers. Making the same cautious circuit Buck had taken around the southern end of the Shoe-Bar, they reached Rocking-R land without adventure and pulled up before the door of Red Butte camp about six o'clock.

Gabby Smith was cooking supper and greeted them with his customary lack of enthusiasm. Bud, who had never seen him before, was much diverted by his manner, and during the meal kept up a constant chatter of comment and question for the purpose, as he afterward confessed, of making the taciturn puncher go the limit in the matter of loquacity. His effort, though it could scarcely be termed successful, evidently got on Gabby's nerves, for afterward he turned both men out of the cabin while he cleared up, a process lasting until nearly bedtime.

It was not until then that Stratton, by a chance remark, learned that three or four days after his departure from the camp two weeks earlier, a stranger had been there making enquiries about him. Gabby's stenographic brevity made it difficult to extract details, but apparently the fellow had passed himself off as an old friend of Buck's from Texas, desirous of looking him up. He was a stranger to Gabby, slight, dark, with eyes set rather closely together, and he rode a Shoe-Bar horse. Apparently he had hung around camp until nearly dusk, and then departed only when Gabby got rid of him by suggesting that his man had probably ridden in to spend the night at the Rocking-R ranch-house.

Stratton and Jessup discussed the incident while making brief preparation for bed. So far as Bud knew there had been no stranger on the Shoe-Bar at that time; but it seemed certain that the fellow must have been sent by Lynch to spy around and find out where Buck was.

'I s'pose he went to the ranch-house first and Tenny sent him down here, knowing he wouldn't get much out of Gabby,' remarked Stratton. 'Well, as far as I can see he had his trouble for his pains. Unless he hung around for two or three days he couldn't very well be certain I wasn't somewhere on the ranch.'

Save as a matter of curiosity, however, the whole affair lay too far in the past to be of the least importance now, and it was soon dismissed. Having removed boots and outer clothing, and spread their blankets in one of the pair of double-decked bunks, the two men lost no time crawling between them, and fell almost instantly asleep.

CHAPTER 25

The Trap

'Yuh out last night?' brusquely enquired Gabby, as they were dressing next morning.

A direct question from the eccentric individual was so novel that Buck paused in buckling on his cartridge-belt, and stared at him in frank surprise.

'Why, no,' he returned promptly. 'Were you, Bud?'

'I sure wasn't. I didn't budge after my head hit the mattress. What gave yuh the notion, old-timer?'

'Door unlatched,' growled Gabby, continuing his preparations for breakfast.

'Is that all?' shrugged Bud. 'Likely nobody thought to close it tight.'

Gabby made no answer, but his expression, as he went silently about his work, failed to show conviction.

'Ain't he a scream?' enquired Bud an hour later, when they had saddled up and were on their way. 'I don't wonder Tenny can't get nobody to stay in camp with him. It would be about as cheerful as a morgue.'

'Must have got soured in his youth,' remarked Stratton. 'I had to put up a regular fight to get him to look after the packhorse till somebody can take it back to the ranch-house. Where do we hit this trail you were telling me about?'

'About a mile and a half further on. It ain't much to boast of, but chances are we won't meet up with a soul till we run into the main road a mile or so this side of Perilla.'

Bud's prediction proved accurate. They encountered no one through-out the entire length of the twisting, narrow, little-used trail, and even when they reached the main road early in the afternoon there was very little passing.

'Reckon they're all taking their siesta,' commented Bud. 'Perilla's a great place for greasers, yuh know, bein' so near the border. There's a heap sight more of 'em than whites.'

Presently they began to pass small, detached adobe huts, some of them the merest hovels. A few dark-faced children were in sight here and there, but the older persons were all evidently comfortably indoors, slumbering through the noonday heat.

Further on the houses were closer together, and at length Bud announced that they were nearing the main street, one end of which crossed the road they were on at right angles.

'That rickety old shack there is just on the corner,' he explained. 'It's a Mexican eating-house, as I remember. Most of the stores an' decent places are up further.'

'Wonder where Hardenberg hangs out?' remarked Stratton.

'Yuh got me. I never had no professional use for him before. Reckon most anybody can tell us, though. That looks like a cowman over there. Let's ask him.'

A moment or two later they stopped before the dingy, weather-beaten building on the corner. Two horses fretted at the hitching-rack, and on the steps lounged a man in regulation cowboy garb. A cigarette dangled from one corner of his mouth, and as the two halted he glanced up from the newspaper he was reading. 'Hardenberg?' he repeated in answer to the question. 'Yuh mean the sheriff? Why, he's inside there.'

Bud looked surprised and somewhat incredulous. 'What the devil's he doin' in that greaser eatin'-house?'

The stranger squinted one eye as the cigarette smoke curled up into his face. 'Oh, he ain't patronisin' the joint,' he explained with a touch of dry amusement. 'He's after old Jose Maria for sellin' licker, I reckon. Him an' one of his deputies rode up about five minutes ago.'

After a momentary hesitation Stratton and Jessup dismounted and tied their horses to the rack. Buck realised that the sheriff might not care to be interrupted while on business of this sort, but their own case was so urgent that he decided to take a chance. At least he could find out when Hardenberg would be at leisure.

Pushing through the swinging door, they found themselves in a single, long room, excessively dingy and rather dark, the only light coming from two unshuttered windows on the north side. To Buck's surprise at least a score of Mexicans were seated around five or six bare wooden tables eating and drinking. Certainly if a raid was on they were taking it very calmly. The next moment he was struck by two things; the sudden hush which greeted their appearance, and the absence of any one who could possibly be the man they sought.

'Looks like that fellow must have given us the wrong tip,' he said, glancing at Jessup. 'I don't see any one here who – '

He paused as a wizened, middle-aged Mexican got up from the other end of the room and came towards them.

'Yo' wish zee table, señors?' he enquired. 'P'raps like zee *chile con carne*, or zee – '

'We don't want anything to eat,' interrupted Stratton. 'I understand Sheriff Hardenberg is here. Could I see him a minute?'

'Oh, zee shereef!' shrugged the Mexican, with a characteristic gesture of his hands. 'He in zee back room with Jose Maria. Yo' please come zis way.'

He turned and walked towards a door at the further end of the long room, the two men following him between the tables. But Buck had not taken more than half a dozen steps before he stopped abruptly. That curious silence seemed to him too long continued to be natural; there was a hint of tension, of suspense in it. And something about the attitude of the seated Mexicans – a vague sense of watchful, stealthy scrutiny, of tense, quivering muscles – confirmed his sudden suspicion.

'Hold up, Bud!' he warned impulsively. 'There's something wrong here.'

As if the words were a signal, the crowd about them surged up suddenly, with the harsh scrape of many chair-legs and an odd, sibilant sound, caused by a multitude of quick-drawn breaths. Like a flash Buck pulled his gun and levelled it on the nearest greaser.

'Get out of the way,' he ordered, taking a step towards the outer door.

The fellow shrank back instinctively, but to Buck's surprise – the average Mexican is not noted for daredevil bravery – several others behind pushed themselves forward. Suddenly Jessup's voice rose in shrill warning.

'Look out, Buck! Behind yuh – quick! That guy's got a knife.'

Stratton whirled swiftly to catch a flashing vision of a tall Mexican creeping towards him, a long, slim knife glittering in his upraised hand. The fellow was so close that another step would bring him within striking distance, and without hesitation Buck's finger pressed the trigger.

The hammer fell with an ominous, metallic click. Amazed, Buck hastily pulled the trigger twice again without results. As he realised that in some mysterious manner the weapon had been tampered with, his teeth grated, but with no perceptible pause in the swiftness of his action he drew back his arm and hurled the pistol straight into the greaser's face.

His aim was deadly. The heavy Colt struck the fellow square on the mouth, and with a smothered cry he dropped the knife and staggered back, flinging up both hands to his face. But others leaped forward to take his place, a dozen knives flashing in as many hands. The ring closed swiftly, and from behind him Stratton heard Bud cry out with an oath that his gun was useless.

There was no time for conscious planning. It was instinct alone – that primitive instinct of every man sore pressed to get his back against something solid – that made Buck lunge forward suddenly, seize a Mexican around the waist, and hurl him bodily at one side of the closing circle.

This parted abruptly and two men went sprawling. One of them Buck kicked out of the way, feeling a savage satisfaction at the impact of his boot against soft flesh and at the yell of pain that followed. Catching Jessup by an arm he swept him towards one of the tables, snatched up a chair, and with his back against the heavy piece of furniture he faced the mob. His hat was gone, and as he stood there, big body braced, mouth set, and hair crested above his smouldering eyes, he made a splendid picture of force and strength which seemed for an instant to awe the Mexicans into inactivity.

But the pause was momentary. Urged on by a voice in the rear, they surged forward again, two of the foremost hurling their knives with deadly aim. One Stratton avoided by a swift duck of his head; the other he caught dexterously on the chair-bottom. Then, over the heads of the crowd, another chair came hurtling with unexpected force and precision. It struck Buck's crude weapon squarely, splintering the legs and leaving him only the back and precariously wobbling seat.

He flung this at one of the advancing men and floored him. But another, slipping agilely in from the side, rushed at him with upraised knife. He was the same greaser who, weeks before, had played that trick about the letter; and Buck's lips twitched grimly as he recognised him.

As the knife flashed downward, Stratton squirmed his body sidewise so that the blade merely grazed one shoulder. Grasping the slim wrist, he twisted it with brutal force, and the weapon clattered to the floor. An instant later he had gripped the fellow about the body and, exerting all his strength, hurled him across the table and straight through the nearby window.

The sound of a shrill scream and the crash of shattered glass came simultaneously. In the momentary, dead silence that followed, one could have almost heard a pin drop.

CHAPTER 26

Sheriff Hardenberg Intervenes

During that brief lull Buck found time to wonder why no one had sense enough to use a gun to bring them down. But almost as swiftly the answer came to him; they dared not risk the sound of a shot bringing interference from without. He flashed a glance at Bud, who sagged panting against the table, the fragments of a chair in his hands and a trickle of blood running down his face. Somehow the sight of that blood turned Buck into a raging savage.

'Come on, you damned coyotes!' he snarled. 'Come and get yours.'

For a brief space it looked as if no one had nerve enough to accept his challenge, and Buck shot a sudden appraising glance towards the outer door, between which and them their assailants crowded thickest. But before he could plan a way to rush the throng, that same sharp voice sounded from the rear which before had stirred the greasers into action, and six or seven of them began to creep warily forward. Their movements were plainly reluctant, however, and of a sudden Stratton gave a spring which carried him within reaching distance of the two foremost. Gripping each by a collar, he cracked their heads together thrice in swift succession, hurled their limp bodies from him, grabbed another chair from the floor, and was back beside Jessup before any of their startled companions had time to stir.

'Now's the time to rush 'em, kid,' he panted in Jessup's ear. 'When I give the word – '

He broke off abruptly as the front door was flung suddenly open and a sharp, incisive, dominant voice rang through the room.

'What in hell 's doing here?'

For a fraction of a second the silence was intense. Then like a flash a man leaped up and flung himself through the window, while three others plunged out of the rear door and disappeared. Others were crowding after them when there came a sudden spurt of flame, the sharp sound of a pistol-shot, and a bullet buried itself in the casing of the rear door.

'Stand still, every damn' one of you,' ordered the new-comer.

He strode down the room through the light powder-haze and paused before Stratton, tall, wide-shouldered, and lean of flank, with a thin, hawklike face and penetrating grey eyes.

'Well?' he questioned curtly. 'What's it all about? That scoundrel been selling licker again?'

'Not to us,' snapped Buck. 'Are you Hardenberg?' he added, with sudden inspiration.

'I am.'

'Well, you're the cause of our being in here.'

The grey eyes studied him narrowly. 'How come?'

'I came to town to see you specially and was told by a man outside that you were making a raid on this joint. We hadn't been inside three minutes before we found it was a plant to get us here and knife us.'

'I don't get you,' remarked the sheriff in a slightly puzzled tone.

By this time Buck's momentary irritation at the hint that it was all merely a drunken quarrel was dying away.

'I don't wonder,' he returned in a more amiable tone. 'It's a long story – too long to tell just now. I can only say that we were attacked without cause by the whole gang here, and if you hadn't shown up just now, it's a question whether we'd have gotten away alive.'

The sheriff's glance swept over the disordered room, taking in the shattered window, the bodies on the floor, the Mexican who crouched moaning in a corner, and returned to Stratton's face.

'I'm not so sure about that last,' he commented, with a momentary grim smile. 'What's your name?'

'Buck Green.'

'Oh! You wrote me a letter – '

'Sure. I'll explain about that later. Meanwhile – '

He broke off and, bending swiftly, pulled his Colt from under the table. Breaking the weapon, he ejected a little shower of empty brass shells, at the sight of which his lips tightened. Still without comment, he rapidly filled it from his belt, Hardenberg watching him intently the while.

'Meanwhile, you'd like a little action, eh?' drawled the sheriff. 'You're right. Either of you hurt?'

He glanced enquiringly at Jessup, who was just wiping the blood from his cut face.

'Not me,' snapped Bud. 'This don't amount to nothin'. Say, was there a guy hangin' around outside when yuh came in – short, with black hair an' eyes set close together?'

Buck gave a slight start; the sheriff shook his head.

'I might have known he'd beat it,' snorted Bud. 'But I'll get the lyin' son-of-a-gun yet; it was him told us yuh were in here.'

Hardenberg's grey eyes narrowed slightly. 'That'll come later. We'll round up this bunch first. If you two will ride around to Main Street and get hold of half a dozen of my deputies, I'll stay here and hold this bunch.'

Rapidly he mentioned the names of the men he wanted and where they could be found, and Stratton and Jessup hastily departed. Outside they found three horses, their own, tied to the hitching-rack as they had left them, and a big, powerful black, who stood squarely facing the door, reins merely trailing and ears pricked forward. The two that had been there when they first rode up were gone.

'Just like I thought,' said Jessup, as they mounted and swung around the corner. 'That guy was planted there a-purpose to get us into the eatin'-house. What's more, I'll bet my saddle he was the same one who came snoopin' around Red Butte camp two weeks ago. Recollect, Gabby said he was small, with black hair an' eyes close together?'

Buck nodded. 'It's a mighty sure thing he was there again last night and pulled our loads,' he added in a tone of chagrin. 'We're a pretty dumb pair, kid. Next time we'll believe Gabby when he says his door was opened in the night.'

'I'll say so. But I thought the old bird was just fussing. Never even looked at my gun. But why the devil should we have suspected anythin'? Why, Lynch don't even know yore alive!'

'He must have found out someway,' shrugged Stratton, 'though I can't imagine how. No use shedding tears over it, though. What we've got to do is get Hardenberg moving double-quick. Here's George Harley; I'll take him, and you go on to the next one.'

Rapidly the deputies were gathered together and hurried back to the eating-house to find Hardenberg holding the Mexicans without difficulty. Half an hour later these were safely lodged in the jail, and the sheriff began a rigorous examination, which lasted until late in the afternoon.

The boldness of the affair angered him and made him determined to get at the bottom of it; but this proved no easy matter. To begin with, Jose Maria, the proprietor of the restaurant, was missing. Either he had merely rented his place to the instigator of the plot, and was prudently absenting himself for a while, or else he was one of those who had escaped through the rear door. Most of the Mexicans were natives of Perilla, and one and all swore that they were as innocent of evil intent as unborn children. They had merely happened to be there getting a meal when the fracas started. The miscreants who had drawn knives on the two whites were quite unknown to them, and must be the ones who had escaped.

Hardenberg knew perfectly well that they were lying, but for the moment he let it pass. He had an idea that Stratton could throw some light on the situation, and leaving the prisoners to digest a few pithy truths, he took the cow-puncher into his private room to hear his story.

Though Buck tried to make this as brief as possible, it took some time, especially as the sheriff showed an absorbing interest from the start and persisted in asking frequent questions and requesting fuller details. When he had finally heard everything, he leaned back in his chair, regarding Stratton thoughtfully.

'Mighty interesting dope,' he remarked, lighting a cigarette. 'I've had my eyes on Tex Lynch for some time, but I had no idea he was up to anything like this. You're dead sure about that oil?'

Buck nodded. 'Of course, you can't ever be certain about the quantity until you bore, but I went over some of the Oklahoma fields a few years ago, and this sure looks like something big.'

'Pretty soft for the lady,' commented Hardenberg. He paused, regarding Stratton curiously. 'Just whereabouts do you come off?' he asked frankly.

'I've been wondering about that all along, and you can see I've got to be dead sure of my facts before I get busy on this seriously.'

Though Buck had been expecting the question, he hesitated for an instant before replying.

'I'll tell you,' he replied slowly at length, 'but for the present I'd like to have you keep it under your hat. My name isn't Green at all, but – Stratton.'

'Stratton?' repeated the sheriff in a puzzled tone. 'Stratton?' A sudden look of incredulity flashed into his eyes. 'You're not trying to make out that you're the Buck Stratton who owned the Shoe-Bar?'

Buck flushed a little. 'I was afraid you'd find it hard to swallow, but it's true,' he said quietly. 'You see, the papers got it wrong. I wasn't killed at all, but only wounded in the head. For – for over a year I hadn't any memory.'

Briefly he narrated the circumstances of the unusual case, and Hardenberg listened with absorbed attention, watching him closely, weighing every word, and noting critically the most trifling gesture or change of expression. For a while his natural scepticism struggled with a growing conviction that the man before him was telling the truth. It was an extraordinary experience, to be sure, but he quickly realised that Stratton had nothing to gain by a deliberate imposture.

'You can prove all that, of course?' he asked when Buck had finished.

'Of course. I haven't any close relatives, but there are plenty of men who'll swear to my identity.'

The sheriff sat silent for a moment. 'Some experience,' he mused presently. 'Rotten hard luck, too, I'll say. Of course you never had a suspicion of oil when you sold the outfit to old man Thorne.'

Again Buck hesitated. Somehow he found this part of the affair extraordinarily hard to put into words. But he knew that it must be done.

'I didn't sell it,' he said curtly at length. 'That transfer of Thorne's was a forgery. He was a man I'd had a number of business dealings with, and when I went to France I left all my papers in his charge. I suppose when he saw my name on the list of missing, he thought he could take a chance. But his daughter knew nothing whatever about it. She's white all through and thinks the ranch is honestly hers. That's the reason why I want you to keep quiet about this for a while. You can see how she'd feel if this came out.'

A faint, fleeting smile curved the corners of Jim Hardenberg's straight mouth. Accustomed by his profession to think the worst of people, and to probe deeply and callously for hidden evil motives, it amused and rather pleased him to meet a man whose extraordinary story roused not the faintest doubt in his critical mind.

'Some dirty business,' he commented at length. 'Still, it's come out all right, and at that you're ahead of the game. That oil might have laid there for years without your getting wise to it. Well, let's get down to cases. It's going to take some planning to get that scoundrel Lynch, to say nothing of the men higher up. Tell me about those fellows in the car again.'

Buck readily went over that part of his story, describing the fat man and his driver as accurately as he was able. The sheriff's eyes narrowed thoughtfully as he listened.

'Think you know him?' Buck asked curiously.

'I'm not sure. Description sounds a bit familiar, but descriptions are apt to fool you. I wish you'd managed to get the number of the car.'

'That would likely be a fake one,' Stratton reminded him.

'Maybe. Well, I'll make a few enquiries.' He stood up stretching. 'I'd like mighty well to start for the Shoe-Bar tonight, but I'm afraid I can't get a posse together soon enough. We'll need some bunch to round up that gang. You'll be at the United States Hotel, I suppose? Well, I'll get busy now, and after supper I'll drop around to let you know how things are going. With what you've told me I'll see if I can't squeeze some information out of those greasers. It may help.'

They left the room together, the sheriff pausing outside to give some instructions to his assistant. Buck gathered in Jessup, who had been waiting, and the two left the building and walked towards the hotel, where they had left their horses.

Perilla was a town of some size, and at this hour the main street was fairly well crowded with a picturesque throng of cowboys, Mexicans, and Indians from the nearby reservation, with the usual mingling of more prosaic-looking business men. Not a few motorcars mingled with horsemen and wagons of various sorts in the roadway, but as Buck's glance fell on a big, shiny, black touring-car standing at the kerb, he was struck by a sudden feeling of familiarity.

Mechanically he noted the licence-number. Then his eyes narrowed as he saw the pudgy, heavily built figure in the tan dust-coat on the point of descending from the tonneau.

An instant later they were face to face. For a second the fat man glanced at him indifferently with that same pouting droop to the small lips which Stratton knew he never could forget. Then, like a flash, the round eyes widened and filled with horror, the jaw dropped, the fat face turned to a pale, sickly green. A choking gurgle burst from the man's lips, and he seemed on the point of collapse when a hand reached out and dragged him back into the car, which, at a hasty word from the occupant of the back seat, shot from the kerb and hummed rapidly away.

Thinking to stop them by shooting up the tyres, Buck's hand dropped instinctively to his gun. But he realised in time that such drastic methods were neither expedient nor necessary. Instead, he turned and halted a man of about forty who was passing.

'Any idea who that fellow is?' he asked, motioning towards the car, just whirling around the next corner. 'He's short and fat, in a big black Hammond car.'

'Short and fat in a Hammond car?' repeated the man, staring down the street. 'Hum! Must be Paul Draper from Amarillo. He's the only one I know around these parts who owns a Hammond. Come to think, though, his car is grey.'

'He's probably had it painted lately,' suggested Stratton quietly. 'Much obliged. I thought I'd seen him before some place.'

CHAPTER 27

An Hour Too Late

'I had an idea that's who it was when you described him,' said Sheriff Hardenberg, to whom Stratton returned at once with the news. 'There's only one "Paul" around here who fits the bill, and he sure does to perfection.'

'Who is he?' asked Buck curiously.

Hardenberg's eyes narrowed. 'The slickest piece of goods in the State of Arizona, I'd say. He's been mixed up in more crooked deals than any man I ever ran up against; but he's so gol-darn cute nobody's ever been able to catch him with the goods.'

'He sure don't look it,' commented Stratton. 'With that baby stare of his and –'

'I know,' interrupted the sheriff. 'That's part of his stock in trade; it's pulled many a sucker. He's got a mighty convincing way about him, believe me! He can tell the damnedest bunch of lies, looking you straight in the eyes all the time, till you'd swear everything he said was gospel. But his big speciality is egging somebody else on to do the dirty work, and when the dangerous part is over, he steps in and hogs most of the profits. He's organised fake mining companies and stock companies. Last year he got up a big cattle-raising combine, persuaded three or four men over in the next county to pool their outfits, and issued stock for about three times what it was worth. It busted up, of course, but not before he'd sold a big block to some Eastern suckers and got away with the proceeds.'

'I'd think that would have been enough to land him.'

'You would, wouldn't you?' returned Hardenberg with a shrug. 'But the law's a tricky business sometimes, and he managed to shave the line just close enough to be safe. Well, it looks as if we had a chance of bagging him at last,' he added in a tone of heartfelt satisfaction.

'Going to arrest him before we start for the Shoe-Bar?' asked Buck.

Hardenberg laughed shortly. 'Hell, no! You don't know Paul Draper if you think he could be convicted on your statement, unsupported by witnesses. Believe me, by this time he's doped out an ironclad alibi, or something, and we wouldn't have a chance. But if one of the Shoe-Bar gang should turn State's evidence, that's another matter.'

'Aren't you afraid he may beat it if you let him go that long?'

'I'll see to that. One of my men will start for Amarillo right away and keep him in sight till we come back. By the way, we've got Jose Maria, and that guy you fired through the window. Caught the old fox sneaking back of those shacks along the north road.'

'Going to warn Lynch, I reckon,' suggested Buck crisply.

'That's what I thought, so I strung some men along at likely points to pick up any more that may try the same trick. I haven't got anything out of Jose yet, but a little thumbscrewing may produce results. I'll tell you about it tonight.'

It was late when he finally appeared at the hotel lobby, and he had no very favourable news to impart. Jose Maria, it appeared, had stuck to the story of being engaged by an alleged Federal official to apprehend two outlaws, whose descriptions fitted Buck and his companion perfectly. He admitted having engaged the other Mexicans to help him, but swore that he had never intended any harm to the two men. Their instructions were merely to capture and hold them until the arrival of the supposed official.

'All rot, of course,' Hardenberg stated in conclusion. 'But it hangs together a bit too well for any greaser to have thought out by himself. I reckon that cowman who got you into the joint was responsible for the yarn and told Jose to give it out in case things should go wrong. Well, I won't waste any more time on the bunch. You two be around about seven tomorrow. I'd like to start sooner, but some of the boys have to come in from a distance.'

Buck and Jessup were there ahead of time, but it was more than an hour later when the posse left Perilla. There were about twenty men in all, for Hardenberg planned to send a portion of them across country to guard the outlet of that secret trail through the mountains of which Buck had told him. If Lynch and his men had any warning of their coming, or happened to be out on the range, the chances were all in favour of their making for the mountains and trying to escape by the cattle-rustlers' route.

During the ride the thought of Mary Thorne was often in Buck's mind. He did not fear for her personal safety. Alf Manning was there, and though Stratton did not like him he had never doubted the fellow's courage or his ability to act as a protector to the three women, should the need arise. But that such a need would arise seemed most unlikely, for Lynch had nothing to gain by treating the girl save with respect and consideration. He had no compunction about robbing her, but she could scarcely be expected to enter further into his schemes and calculations, especially at a time when his whole mind must be a turmoil of doubt and fear and uncertainty as to the future.

Nevertheless, Buck wished more than once that he had been able to get in touch with her since that memorable afternoon when he had watched her ride out of sight down the little canyon, if only to prepare her for what was going on. It must have been very hard for her to go about day after day, knowing nothing, suspecting a thousand things, fretting, worrying, with not a soul to confide in, yet forced continually to present an untroubled countenance to those about her.

'Thank the Lord it'll soon be over and she'll be relieved,' he thought, when they finally came in sight of the ranch-house.

As the posse swept through the lower gate and up the slope, Buck's eyes searched the building keenly. Not a soul was in sight, either there or about the corrals. He had seen it thus apparently deserted more than once before, and told himself now that his uneasiness was absurd. But when the girl suddenly appeared on the veranda and stood staring at the approaching horsemen, Buck's heart leaped with a sudden spasm of intense relief, and unconsciously he spurred his horse ahead of the others.

As he swung himself out of the saddle, she came swiftly forward, her face glowing with surprise and pleasure.

'Oh, I'm so glad you've come,' she said in a low, quick voice, clasping his outstretched hand. 'We've been worrying – You – you're quite all right now?'

'Fine and dandy,' Buck assured her. 'Thanks to you, and Bud, I'm perfectly whole again.'

She greeted Jessup, who came up smiling, and then Sheriff Hardenberg was presented.

'Very glad to meet you, Miss Thorne,' he said. There was a faint twinkle in his eyes as he glanced towards Stratton for an instant, his belief confirmed as to the principal reason for Buck's desire to keep the secret of the Shoe-Bar ownership. Then he became businesslike.

'Where's Lynch and the rest of 'em?' he asked briskly.

The girl's face grew suddenly serious. 'I don't know,' she answered quickly. 'They were all working about the barns until a strange cowboy rode in about two hours ago. I saw him pass the window but didn't think much about it. About half an hour or so later I went out to give some orders to Pedro; he's the cook, you know. But he wasn't there and neither was Maria, and when I went out to the barns the men were gone. Of course something urgent might easily have taken them out on the range, but neither Maria nor Pedro has been off the place for weeks. Besides, when I peeped into the bunk-house everything was tossed about in confusion, as if – Well, I was afraid something – had happened.'

'Something has,' stated the sheriff grimly. 'The truth is, that scoundrel Lynch has got to the end of his rope, and we're after him.'

The girl's face paled, then flushed deeply. 'What – what is it?' she asked in a low, troubled voice. 'What has he –'

'It's rather a long story, and I'm afraid there isn't time to stop and tell you now,' explained the sheriff as she paused. 'We've got to make every minute count. You have no idea which way they went?'

'It must have been west or south,' the girl answered promptly. 'If they'd gone any other way I should have seen them.'

'Fine,' said Hardenberg, wheeling his horse. 'Don't you worry about anything,' he added over one shoulder. 'We'll be back in a jiffy.'

As he and his men spurred down the slope towards the entrance to middle pasture, the girl's eyes sought Stratton's.

'You –'

'I must.' He quickly answered her unspoken question. 'They'll need us to show them the way. We'll be back, though, as soon as we possibly can. You're not nervous, are you? You're perfectly safe, of course, with –'

'Of course,' she assured him promptly. 'Lynch has gone. There'll be nothing for us to worry about here. Goodbye, then, for a while. And do be careful – both of you.'

Her face was a trifle pale, and about her mouth and chin were traced a few faint lines which hinted vaguely of forced composure. As Buck hastened to overtake the posse, he recalled her expression, and wondered with a troubled qualm whether she wasn't really more nervous than she let herself appear. Perhaps she might have been more comfortable if he or Bud had remained at the ranch-house.

'Probably it's all my imagination,' he decided at length. 'With Manning there, she's perfectly safe, especially as we've got the whole gang on the run. The ranch-house would be the very last place they'd head for.'

CHAPTER 28

Forebodings

Almost at once they struck a fresh trail, made by a number of horsemen riding in a bunch, which led diagonally across middle pasture. It was easy to follow, and Hardenberg pushed his men hard to make up for delays which were likely to come later on. For a time Buck rode beside the sheriff, discussing their plans and explaining the lay of the land. Then he fell back a little to chat with Jessup.

'I'm sure glad of one thing,' Bud said emphatically, after a few desultory remarks. 'Miss Mary won't be bothered no more now with that son-of-a-gun hangin' around an' makin' eyes.'

Stratton turned on him suddenly. 'Who the devil do you mean?' he demanded sharply.

'Why, Tex, of course,' shrugged Jessup. 'He used to put in considerable time soft-soapin' around her. A hell of a nerve, I'll say, makin' up to such as her.'

Buck scowled. 'I never saw anything like that,' he said brusquely, 'except maybe once,' he added, with a sudden recollection of that after-noon they moved the herd out of south pasture.

'Likely not,' returned Bud. 'He wasn't so bad till after yuh went. I got the notion he took to courtin' her, yuh might say, as a kind of last hope. If he could figger on gettin' her to marry him, he'd have the ranch an' everythin' on it without no more trouble at all. You'd think even a scoundrel like him would see she wouldn't look at him.'

'Did he – Was he – '

'Oh, no! Nothin' raw a-tall,' returned Bud, divining the thought in Stratton's mind. 'He just hung around the ranch-house a lot, an' was awful sweet, an' used them black eyes of his consid'able. Sorta preparing the way, I reckon. But he didn't get far.' He chuckled reminiscently. 'I'll tell the world, she didn't waste no time sendin' him about his business.'

For a time Buck rode on in frowning silence. The very thought enraged him and added deeply to the score that was piling up so rapidly against the scoundrel.

Presently Bud's voice broke in upon his savage reverie.

'Funny we didn't see nothin' of the Mannings back there,' he commented. 'The lady couldn't of known yuh was around.' He glanced slyly at Buck. 'Besides,' he added, seeing that his friend's expression did not lighten, 'with somethin' like this doin', you'd think his lordship would want to strut around in them baggy pants an' yellow boots, an' air his views on how to go about to catch the gang.'

Stratton turned his head abruptly. 'But they must be there!' he said sharply. 'They surely can't have gone away.'

'There wasn't no talk of it when I left,' shrugged Bud. 'Still, an' all, me an' his nibs wasn't on exactly confidential terms, an' he might have forgot to tell me about his plans. Yuh got to remember, too, I've been gone over a week.'

A worried wrinkle dodged into Buck's forehead. All along he had taken the presence of the Mannings so entirely for granted that the possibility of their having left the ranch never once occurred to him. But now, in a flash, he realised that by this time, for all he knew, they might be back in Chicago. As Bud said, it certainly seemed odd that neither of them had appeared when the posse rode up to the ranch-house. What a fool he had been not to make sure about it. Why hadn't he asked the question outright?

'But I did mention it while we were talking,' he thought, trying to reconstruct that brief interview with Mary Thorne. 'Hang it all! No, I didn't. I was going to, but she interrupted. But she must have known what I referred to.'

Suddenly there came back the vivid recollection of the girl's face as she said goodbye. Outwardly cheerful and composed, that faint pallor and the few lines of strain etched about her mouth and chin struck him now with a tremendous significance. She had known what was in his mind, but purposely refrained from revealing the truth for fear of becoming a drag and hamper to him. She was game through and through.

The realisation brought a wave of tenderness surging over the man, followed swiftly by a deepening sense of trouble and uneasiness.

'I don't like it at all, Bud,' he burst out abruptly. 'I wish to thunder we'd found out for sure about those Mannings. If they have gone, one of us at least ought to have stayed.'

'Well, of course I'm only guessin'. Quite likely they're there yet, only it just seemed funny not to see them. But even if she is left alone with only Mrs Archer, yuh ain't worryin' about anythin' really happenin' to her, are yuh? It'll be darn lonesome, an' all that, but Lynch an' the whole gang has beat it – '

'How do we know where they have gone?' cut in Stratton curtly. 'They had a good hour's start, and more. It'll be getting dusk pretty quick. What's to prevent one or more of 'em circling back by the southeast? Lynch is capable of anything, and after what you've just told me – '

Bud's eyes widened. 'But what would he have to gain – '

'Gain?' repeated Buck irritably. 'How the devil do I know what's in that polecat's mind? He's quite capable of hiding behind a woman's skirts. He's even capable of carrying her off and trying to force her to marry him, or something like that. I've half a mind to – '

He broke off, frowning. Bud, now thoroughly alarmed, stared at him uneasily. 'You'd better let me go back,' he said quickly. 'They'll need yuh more.'

'I don't give a damn whether they need me or not,' retorted Buck swiftly. 'I've got a better idea, though. We'll hit Las Vegas inside of ten minutes. The 'phone's still working, isn't it?'

'It was the last I knew.'

'I'll take a chance. There's been nothing to put it out of business. By calling up we'll know how things stand a whole lot quicker. If she and Mrs Archer are alone, I'll chase back at once and you can show Hardenberg the way into the mountains.'

Though Bud's face showed no particular pleasure in the plan, he made no comment, and they rode on in silence. Presently the sheriff turned and called to Stratton. The trail was spreading out, he said, and growing more and more difficult to follow in the waning light.

'I don't understand why they rode so far apart,' he said, 'unless it was to make it hard for any one to track them. Looks to me, though, as if they were heading straight for that cut into the mountains you told me about. Is it much further off?'

'About a quarter of a mile below the little 'dobe shack we're coming to,' Stratton answered. 'The creek takes a sharp turn to the southeast, and right at the bend you cross and ride straight west into a narrow draw that doesn't look like it went anywhere. Further on it twists around and leads into a short canyon that brings you through to a sort of valley lying between the hills. After that everything's plain sailing. It's almost as plain as a regular trail.'

'Good,' nodded Hardenberg. 'Anything to mark the draw?'

Buck thought a minute. 'As I remember, there's a low ridge on the north side, and a big clump of mesquite on the right just before you leave the flats.'

'Well, you'll be with us to act as guide. I wish we'd had an hour's earlier start, though. It won't be any cinch travelling through these mountains in the dark. Still, at the worst, we can count on Dick Jordan's bunch to nab them as they come out.'

Buck nodded. 'I'm not sure I can stick along with you much longer,' he added briefly. 'But Jessup can show you the way quite as well. There seems to be some doubt now about those people I spoke of being still at the ranch.'

'Humph! That would mean that Miss Thorne would be there alone?'

'Yes, except for her aunt. I may be worrying unnecessarily, but with a scoundrel like Lynch – '

'You never can tell,' finished the sheriff as he hesitated. 'That's true enough. We mustn't take any chances. But how – '

'Telephone. There's a line from the ranch-house to Las Vegas camp just ahead.' Buck pointed where, through the gathering dusk, the outlines of the adobe shack showed dimly. 'If I find there's no one with her, I'll ride back.'

'Go to it,' nodded the sheriff. 'If you don't show up I'll understand. At a pinch I reckon we could find the trail ourselves from your directions.'

As Stratton pulled off to the right, he waved his hand and swept onward with the posse. Buck reached the door and swung out of the saddle, flinging the reins over Pete's head. Then he found that Bud had followed him.

'I'm goin' to wait an' hear what yuh find out,' the youngster stated resolutely. 'I can catch up with 'em easy enough.'

'All right.'

Buck hastily entered the shack, which was almost pitch-dark. A faint glint of metal came from the telephone, hanging beside one window; and as he swiftly crossed the room and fumbled for the bell, there stirred within him a sudden sense of apprehension that was almost dread.

CHAPTER 29

Creeping Shadows

With her back against the veranda pillar, Mary Thorne watched the group of mounted men canter down the slope, splash across the creek, and file briskly through the gate leading to middle pasture. Perhaps it would be more accurate to say that, for the most part, her glance followed one of them, and when the erect, jaunty, broad-shouldered figure on the big roan had disappeared, she gave a little sigh.

'He looks better – much better,' she murmured.

Her eyes grew dreamy, and in her mind she saw again that little hidden canyon with its overhanging ledge beneath which the man lay stretched out on his blankets. Somehow, the anxiety and suspense, the heart-breaking worry and weariness of that strange experience had faded utterly. There remained only a very vivid recollection of the touch of her hand against his damp forehead, the feeling of his crisp, dark hair as she pushed it gently back, the look of those long, thick lashes lying so still against his pallid face.

Not seldom she had wished those fleeting moments might have been prolonged. Once or twice she was even a little jealous of Bud Jessup's ministrations; just as, thinking of him now, she was jealous of his constant nearness to Buck and the manner in which he seemed so intently to share all the other's plans and projects, and even thoughts.

'Well, anyway,' she said suddenly aloud, 'I'm glad Stella's not here.'

Then, realising that she had spoken aloud, she blushed and looked hastily around. No one was in sight, but a moment or two later Mrs Archer appeared on the veranda.

'I thought I heard voices a little while ago,' she said, glancing around. 'Have the men come back?'

Mary turned to meet her. 'No, dear. That was the – the sheriff and some of his men.'

'The sheriff!' An expression of anxiety came into Mrs Archer's pretty, faded face. 'But what has happened? What – ?'

'I'm not quite sure; they had no time to explain.' The girl put an arm reassuringly around the older woman's shoulder. 'But they're after Tex and the other hands. They've done something – '

'Ha!' In any other person the sound would have seemed suspiciously like a crow of undisguised satisfaction. 'Well, I'm thankful that at last somebody's shown some common sense.'

'Why, auntie!' Astonished, the girl held her off at arm's length and stared into her face. 'You don't mean to say you've suspected – ?'

Mrs Archer sniffed. 'Suspected! Why, for weeks and weeks I've been perfectly certain the creature was up to no good. You know I never trusted him.'

'Yes; but – '

'The last straw was his bringing that ridiculous charge against Buck Green,' Mrs Archer interrupted with unexpected spirit. 'That stamped him for what he was; because a nicer, cleaner, better-mannered young man I've seldom seen. He could no more have stolen cattle than – than I could.'

A mental picture of her tiny, delicate, fragile-looking aunt engaged in that strenuous and illicit operation brought a momentary smile to Mary Thorne's lips. Then her face grew serious.

'But you know I didn't believe it – really,' she protested. 'I offered to keep him on if he'd only assure me he wasn't here for any – any secret reason. But he wouldn't, and at the time there seemed nothing to do but let him go.'

'I suppose he might have had some other private reason than stealing cattle,' commented Mrs Archer.

'He had,' returned Mary, suppressing a momentary sense of annoyance that her aunt had shown the greater faith. 'As nearly as I can make out, he was here to shadow Tex. As a matter of fact he really wanted to leave the ranch and work from a different direction, so it turned out all right in the end. He thinks it was Tex himself who secretly instigated the cattle-stealing.'

'The villain!' ejaculated Mrs Archer energetically. 'But where has – er – Buck been all this time? Where is he now?'

The girl smiled faintly. 'He was here a little while ago. He and Bud are both with the sheriff's posse. They believe the men are heading for the mountains and have gone after them.'

Mrs Archer glanced sharply at her niece, noted a faint flush on the girl's face, and pursed her lips.

'When are they coming back?' she asked, after a little pause.

Mary shrugged her shoulders. 'Not until they catch them, I suppose.'

'Which certainly won't be tonight. I'm rather surprised at Buck. It seems to me that he ought to have stayed here to look after things, instead of rushing off to chase outlaws.'

'It wasn't his fault,' defended Mary quickly. 'He thought Alf and Stella were here.'

'Alf and Stella! Good gracious, child! How could he, when they left four days ago?'

'He didn't know that. He took it for granted they were still here, and I let him think so. They needed him to guide the posse, and I knew if I told him, he'd insist on staying behind. After all, dear, there's nothing for us to worry about. It'll be a bit lonesome tonight, but – '

'Worry! I'm not worrying – about myself.' Mrs Archer regarded her niece with a curiously keen expression that seemed oddly incongruous in that delicate fragile-looking face. 'I'm not blind,' she went on quickly. 'I've noticed what's been going on – the wretch! You're afraid of him, too, I can see, and no wonder. I wish somebody had stayed – Still, we must make the best of it. What are you going to do about the stock?'

'Feed them,' said Mary laconically, quelling a little shiver that went over her. 'Let's go and do it now.'

Together they walked around to the corral, where Mary forked down some hay for the three horses, and filled the sunken water-barrel from the tank. Already shadows were creeping up from the hollows, and the place seemed very still and deserted.

In the kitchen the sense of silent emptiness was even greater, accustomed as they were to the constant presence of Pedro and his wife. The two women did not linger longer than was necessary to fill a tray with supper, which they carried into the living-room. Here Mary closed the door, lit two lamps, and touched a match to the wood piled up in the big fireplace.

'It'll make things more cheerful,' she remarked with an attempt at casualness which was not altogether successful. 'I don't see why we shouldn't heat some water here and make tea,' she added with sudden inspiration.

Mrs Archer, who liked her cup of tea, made no objections, and Mary sprang up and went back to the kitchen. Filling a saucepan from the pump, she got the tea-caddy out of a cupboard, and then paused in the middle of the room, staring out into the gathering dusk.

Neither doors nor windows in the ranch-house were ever locked, and, save on really cold nights, they were rarely even closed. But now, of a sudden, the girl felt she would be much more comfortable if everything were shut up tight, and setting down the pan and caddy on the table, she went over to the nearest window.

It looked out on the various barns and sheds clustered at the back of the ranch-house. The harness-room occupied the ground floor of the nearest shed, with a low, seldom-entered loft above, containing a single, narrow window without glass or shutters.

As Mary approached the open kitchen window, herself invisible in the shadows of the room, a slight sense of movement in that little square under the eaves of the shed roof drew her glance swiftly upward. To her horror she caught a momentary glimpse of a face framed in the narrow opening. It vanished swiftly – far too swiftly to be recognised. But recognition was not necessary. The mere knowledge that some one was hidden in the loft – had probably been hidden there all along – turned the girl cold and instantly awakened her worst fears.

CHAPTER 30

Lynch Scores

How long she stood there staring fearfully at the empty window of the shed, Mary Thorne had no idea. She seemed frozen and incapable of movement. But at last, with a shiver, she came to herself, and bending out, drew in the heavy wooden, shutters and fumbled with the catch. The bolt was stiff from disuse, and her hands shook so that she was scarcely able to thrust it into the socket. Still trembling, she closed and bolted the door and made fast the other windows. Then she paused in the middle of the room, slim fingers clenched tightly together, and heart beating loudly and unevenly.

'What shall I do?' she said aloud in a strained whisper. 'What shall I do?'

Her glance sought the short passage, and, through it, the cosy brightness of the living-room.

'I mustn't let her know,' she murmured.

After a moment more of indecision she stepped into the small room opening off the kitchen, which had been occupied by Pedro and his wife. Having bolted the shutters of the single window, she came back into the kitchen and stood beside the table, making a determined effort for self-control. Suddenly the sound of her aunt's voice came from the living-room.

'What are you doing, Mary? Can I help you?'

For a second the girl hesitated, nails digging painfully into her palms. Then she managed to find her voice.

'No thanks, dear. I'll be there in just a minute.' Resolutely she took up the saucepan and caddy and walked slowly towards the lighted doorway. She felt that a glance at her face would probably tell Mrs Archer that something was wrong, and so, entering the living-room, she went straight over to the fireplace. Kneeling on the hearth, she took the poker and made a little hollow amongst the burning sticks in which she placed the covered saucepan. When she stood up the heat had burned a convincingly rosy flush into her cheeks.

'I was closing the shutters,' she explained in a natural tone. 'While the water's boiling I think I'll do the same in the other rooms. Then we'll feel quite safe and snug.'

Mrs Archer, who was arranging their supper on one end of the big table, agreed briefly but made no other comment. When Mary had secured the living-room door and windows, she took the four bedrooms in turn, ending in the one whose incongruously masculine appointments had once aroused the curiosity of Buck Green.

How long ago that seemed! She set her candle on the dresser and stared around the room. If only she wasn't such a helpless little ninny!

'And I'm such a fool I wouldn't know how to use a revolver if I had it,' thought the girl forlornly. 'I don't even know what I did with Dad's.'

Then, of a sudden, her glance fell upon the cartridge-belt hanging on the wall, from whose pendant holster protruded the butt of an efficient-looking six-shooter – Stratton's weapon, which, like everything else in the room, she had left religiously as she found it.

Stepping forward, she took hold of it gingerly and managed to draw it forth – a heavy, thirty-eight Colt, the barrel rust-pitted in a few places, but otherwise in excellent condition. She had no idea how to load it, but presently discovered by peering into the magazine that the shells seemed to be already in place. Then all at once her eyes filled and a choking little sob rose in her throat.

'Oh, if you were only here!' she whispered unevenly.

It would be hard to determine whether she was thinking of Stratton, that dreamlike hero of hers, whose tragic death she had felt so keenly, or of another man who was very much alive indeed. Perhaps she scarcely knew herself. At all events it was only a momentary little breakdown. Pulling herself together, she returned to the living-room, carrying the big six-shooter half hidden by her skirts, and managed to slip it, apparently unseen, on a little stand above which hung the telephone to Las Vegas camp. By this time the water was boiling, and having made tea, she carried the pot back to the big table and sat down opposite Mrs Archer.

For a minute or two she was busy with the cups and had no occasion to observe her aunt's expression. Then, chancing to glance across the table, she was dismayed to find the older woman regarding her with searching scrutiny.

'Well?' questioned Mrs Archer briefly. 'What is it?'

Mary stared at her guiltily. 'What's – what?' she managed to parry.

'Why beat about the bush?' retorted her aunt. 'Something's happened to frighten you. I can see that perfectly well. You know how I detest being kept in the dark, so you may as well tell me at once.'

Mary hesitated. 'But it – it may not – come to anything,' she stammered. 'I didn't want to – to frighten you – '

'Rubbish!' An odd, delicately grim expression came into the little old lady's face. 'I'd rather be frightened unnecessarily than have something drop on me out of a clear sky. Out with it!'

Then Mary gave in and was conscious of a distinct relief in having a confidante.

'It's only this,' she said briefly. 'When I went to close the back kitchen window a little while ago, I saw a – a face looking out of that little window above the harness-room. Some one's – hiding there.'

For an instant Mrs Archer's delicately pretty, faded face turned quite pale. Then she rallied bravely.

'Who – who was it?' she asked in a voice not altogether steady.

'I – don't know. It disappeared at once. But I'm sure it wasn't imagination.'

For a moment or two her aunt sat thinking. Then she glanced quickly across the room. 'Is that gun loaded?' she asked.

The girl nodded; she had ceased to be surprised at anything. For a space Mrs Archer regarded her untouched cup of tea thoughtfully. When she looked up a bright spot of pink was glowing in each wrinkled cheek.

'It's not pleasant, but we must face it,' she said. 'It may be Pedro, or even Maria. Both of them are cowards. On the other hand it may be Lynch. There's no use shutting one's eyes to possibilities.'

Abruptly she rose and walked quickly into her bedroom, returning in a moment or two with a little chamois case from which she drew a tiny twenty-two-calibre revolver, beautifully etched and silver-mounted, with a mother-of-pearl stock.

'Your uncle gave it to me many years ago and showed me how to use it,' she explained, laying it beside her plate. 'I've never shot it off, but I see no reason why – '

She broke off with a gasp, and both women started and turned pale, as a harsh, metallic rattle rang through the room.

'What is it?' whispered Mary, half rising.

'The telephone! I can't get used to that strange rattle. Answer it, quickly!'

Springing up, Mary flew across the room and took down the receiver.

'Hello,' she said tremulously. 'Who is – *Oh, Buck!*' Her eyes widened and the blood rushed into her face. 'I'm so glad! But where are you? ... I see. No, they're not here ... I know I did, but I thought – I wish now I'd told you. We – we're frightened ... What? ... No, not yet; but – but there's some one hiding in the loft over the harness-room ... I don't know, but I saw a face at the window ... Yes, everything's locked up, but – '

Abruptly she broke off and turned her head a little, the blood draining slowly from her face. A sound had come to her which struck terror to her heart. Yet it was a sound familiar enough on the range-land – merely the beat of a horse's hoofs, faint and far away, but growing rapidly nearer.

'Wait!' she called into the receiver, 'Just a – minute.'

Her frightened eyes sought Mrs Archer and read confirmation in the elder woman's strained attitude of listening.

'Some one's coming,' the girl breathed. Suddenly she flung herself desperately at the telephone. 'Buck!' she cried. 'There's some one riding up ... I don't know, but I'm – afraid ... Yes, do come quickly ... What's that?'

With a little cry she rattled the hook and repeatedly pressed the round button which operated the bell. 'Buck! Buck!' she cried into the receiver.

The thud of hoofs came clearly to her now; it was as if the horse was galloping up the slope from the lower gate.

'What's the matter?' demanded Mrs Archer, in a hoarse, dry voice.

With a despairing gesture the girl dropped the receiver and turned a face drained of every particle of colour.

'The wire's – dead,' she said hopelessly.

Mrs Archer caught her breath sharply, but made no other sound. In the silence that followed they could hear the horse pull up just beyond the veranda, and the sound of a man dropping lightly to the ground. Then came very faintly the murmur of voices.

To the two women, standing motionless, with eyes riveted on the door, the pause that followed lengthened interminably. It seemed as if that low, stealthy, sibilant whispering was going on forever. Mrs Archer held her little pearl-handled toy with a spasmodic grip which brought out a row of dots across her delicate knuckles, rivalling her face in whiteness. Mary Thorne's grey eyes, dilated with emotion, stood out against her pallor like deep wells of black. One clenched hand hung straight at her side; the other rested on the butt of the Colt, lying on the stand below the useless instrument.

Suddenly the tension snapped as the heavy tread of feet sounded across the porch and a hand rattled the latch.

'Open up!' called a harsh, familiar voice.

There was no answer. Mrs Archer reached out to steady herself against the table. Mary's grip on the Colt tightened convulsively.

'Open up, I tell yuh,' repeated the voice. 'I ain't aimin' to – hurt yuh.'

Then apparently a heavy shoulder thrust against the door, which shook and creaked ominously. Suddenly the girl's slim figure straightened and she brought her weapon around in front of her, holding it with both hands.

'If – if you try to force that door, I – I'll shoot,' she called out.

The only answer was an incredulous laugh, and an instant later the man's shoulder struck the panels with a crash that cracked one of them and partly tore the bolt from its insecure fastenings.

Promptly the girl cocked her weapon, shut both eyes, and pulled the trigger. The recoil jerked the barrel up, and the bullet lodged in the ceiling. Before she could recover from the shock, there came another crash, the shattered door swung inward, and Tex Lynch sprang across the threshold.

Again Mary lifted the heavy weapon and tried to nerve herself to fire. But somehow this was different from shooting through a solid wooden door, and she could not bring herself to do it. Mrs Archer had no such scruples. Her small, delicately chiselled face was no longer soft and gentle. It had frozen into a white mask of horror, out of which the once-soft eyes blazed with fierce determination. Bending across the table, she levelled her toylike weapon at the advancing outlaw, and by the merest chance sent a bullet flying so close to his head that he ducked instinctively. An instant later Pedro darted through the passage from the kitchen, snatched the weapon from her hand, and flung her roughly into a chair.

Her aunt's half-stifled cry stung Mary like a lash and roused her from the almost hypnotic state in which, wide-eyed and terrified, she had been watching Lynch's swift advance.

'Oh!' she cried furiously. 'You – you beast!'

He was within a few feet of her now, and moved by the double impulse of fear and anger, her finger pressed the trigger. But there was no response, and too late the girl realised that she had failed to cock the weapon. In another moment Lynch had wrenched it from her hand.

CHAPTER 31

Gone

Motionless in his saddle, save for an occasional restless stamp of his horse, Bud Jessup waited patiently in front of the adobe shack at Las Vegas camp. His face was serious and thoughtful, and his glance was fixed on the open door through which came the broken, indistinguishable murmur of Buck Stratton's voice. Once, thinking he heard an unusual sound, the youngster turned his head alertly and stared westward through the shadows. But a moment later his eyes flashed back to that narrow, black oblong, and he resumed his uneasy pondering as to what Buck might possibly be finding out.

Suddenly he gave a start as Stratton's voice, harsh, startled, came to him distinctly.

'Mary! Mary! Why don't you answer? What's happened?'

The words were punctuated by a continuous rattle, and ended abruptly with the clatter of metal against metal.

'Hell!' rasped Buck, in a hoarse, furious voice with an undercurrent of keen apprehension that made Bud's nerves tingle. 'The wire's been cut!'

An instant later he appeared, running. Snatching the reins, he gained the saddle in a single bound, jerked his horse around, and was off across the pasture.

'Come on!' he shouted back over one shoulder. 'There's trouble at the ranch.'

Bud dug spurs into his cayuse and followed, but it was some minutes before he managed to catch up with his friend.

'What is it?' he cried anxiously. 'What's wrong? Have the Mannings – '

'They've gone, as I thought,' snapped Stratton. 'The two women are alone. But that isn't the worst.' A sudden spasm of uncontrolled fury rose in his throat and choked him momentarily. 'There's some one hidden in the loft over the harness-room,' he managed to finish hoarsely.

Bud stared at him in dismay. 'Who the devil – '

'I don't know. She just got a glimpse of a – a face in the window while she was closing up the kitchen.'

'Do you suppose it's – Tex?'

'I don't know,' retorted Buck through his clenched teeth. 'What difference does it make, anyhow? Some one hid there for a – a purpose. By God! What fools we were not to make a search!'

'It seemed so darn sure they'd all beat it,' faltered Bud. 'Besides, I don't guess any of us would of thought to look in that loft.'

'Maybe not. It doesn't matter. We didn't.' Stratton's voice was brittle. 'But if anything happens – '

'Have they locked up the whole house?' Jessup asked as Stratton paused.

'Yes, but what good'll that do with two able-bodied men set on getting in? There isn't a door or shutter that wouldn't – '

'Two!' gasped Bud. 'You didn't say – '

'Didn't I? It was just at the end. She was telling me about seeing the face and locking up the house. Then all at once she broke off.' Buck's tone was calmer now, but it was the hard-won calm of determined will, and every now and then there quivered through it a faint, momentary note that told eloquently of the mingled dread and fury that were tearing his nerves to pieces. 'I asked what was the matter and she said to wait a minute. It seemed like she stopped to listen for something. Then all of a sudden she cried out that some one was riding up.'

'It – it might not have been any of the gang,' murmured Bud, voicing a hope he did not feel.

'Who else would be likely to come at this time of night?' demanded Stratton. 'Lynch is on the outs with everybody around Perilla. They don't go near the ranch unless they have to. It couldn't have been one of Hardenberg's men; he's not expecting any one.'

'Did – did she say anything else?' asked Jessup, after a brief pause.

Buck hesitated. 'Only that she – was afraid, and wanted us to – come quickly. Then the wire went dead as if it had been cut.'

Silence fell, broken only by the thud of hoofs and the heavy breathing of the two horses. Bud's slim, lithe figure had slumped a little in the saddle, and his eyes were fixed unseeingly on the wide, flat sweep of prairie unfolding before them, dim and mysterious under the brilliant stars.

In his mind anxiety, rage, and apprehension contended with a dull, dead hopelessness which lay upon his heart like lead. For something in Buck's tone made him realise in a flash a situation which, strangely, he had never even suspected. He wondered dully why he hadn't ever thought of it before; perhaps because Buck was a new-comer who had seemed to see so little of Mary Thorne. Probably, also, the very friendly manner of Stella Manning had something to do with Jessup's blindness. But his eyes were opened now, thoroughly and effectually, and for a space, how long or short he never knew, he fought out his silent battle.

It ended in a victory. Down in his heart he knew that he had never really had any hope of winning Mary Thorne himself. He had cherished aspirations, of course, and dreamed wonderful dreams; but when it came down to hard actualities, romance did not blind him to the fact that she looked on him merely as a friend and nothing more. Indeed, though they were virtually of the same age, he had been aware at times of an oddly maternal note in her attitude towards him which was discouraging. Still, it was not easy definitely to relinquish all hope and bring himself to write 'finis' to the end of the chapter. Indeed, he did not reach that state of mind until, glancing sidewise at his friend, there came to him a sudden, faintly bitter realisation of the wide contrast between them, and of how much more Buck had to offer than himself.

Stratton's erect, broad shoulders, the lean length of him, the way he held his head, gave Jessup a curious, unexpected impression of strength and ability and power. Buck's eyes were set straight ahead and his clean-cut profile, clearly visible in the luminous starlight, had a look of sensitive-ness and refinement, despite the strength of his jaw and chin and the sombreness of his eyes. Bud turned away with a little sigh.

'I never had no chance at all,' he thought. 'Someway he don't look like a cow-puncher, nor talk quite like one. I wonder why?'

Half a mile further on Buck suddenly broke the prolonged silence.

'I've been thinking it over,' he said briefly. 'The man on the horse was probably Lynch. He could easily have started off with the rest and then made a circuit around below the ranch-house. If he picked his ground, we'd never notice where he left the others, especially as we weren't looking for anything of the sort.'

'Who do you s'pose hid over the harness-room?'

'It might have been Slim, or Kreeger, or even Pedro. The whole thing was certainly a put-up job – damn them!' His voice shook with sudden passion. 'Well, we'll soon know,' he finished, and his mouth clamped shut.

Already the row of cottonwoods that lined the creek was faintly visible ahead, a low, vague mass, darker a little than the background of blue-black sky. Both spurred their jaded horses and a moment or two later pulled up with a jerk at the gate. Before his mount had come to a standstill, Bud was out of his saddle fumbling with the catch. When he swung it open, Stratton dashed through, swiftly crossed the shallow creek, and galloped up the long, easy slope beyond.

A chill struck him as the ranch-house loomed up, ominously black and desolate as any long-deserted dwelling. He had forgotten for an instant the heavy, wooden shutters, and when, with teeth clenched and heart thudding in his throat, he reached the veranda corner, the sight of that yellow glow streaming from the open door gave him a momentary shock of supreme relief.

An instant later he saw the shattered door, and the colour left his face. In two strides he crossed the porch and, with fingers tightening about the butt of his Colt, he stared searchingly around the big, brightly lighted, strangely empty-looking room.

It held but a single occupant. Huddled in a chair on the further side of the long table was Mrs Archer. Both hands rested on the polished oak, and clutched in her small, wrinkled hands was a heavy, cumbrous revolver, pointed directly at the door. Her white, strained face, stamped with an expression of hopeless tragedy, looked ten years older than when Buck had last seen it. As she recognised him she dropped the gun and tottered to her feet.

'Oh!' she cried, in a sharp, wailing voice. 'You! You!'

In a moment Buck had her in his arms, holding her tight as one holds a hurt or frightened child. Mechanically he soothed her as she clung to him, that amazing self-control, which had upheld her for so long, snapping like a taut rope when the strain becomes too great. But all the while his eyes – wide, smouldering eyes, filled with a mingling of pity, of dread questioning and furious passion – swept the room searchingly.

Over the little lady's bowed grey head his glance took in swiftly a score of details – the dead fire, the dangling receiver of the useless telephone, a little pearl-handled revolver lying in a far corner as if it had been flung there, an upset chair. Suddenly his gaze halted at the edge of the shattered door and a faint tremor shook his big body. A comb lay on the floor there – a single comb of tortoiseshell made for a woman's hair. But it was a comb he knew well. And as his eyes met Bud's, staring from the doorway at the strange scene, they were the eyes of a man tortured.

CHAPTER 32

Buck Rides

Presently Mrs Archer released her spasmodic grip on Stratton's flannel shirt and fumbled for her handkerchief.

'I'm a fool to – to waste time like this,' she faltered, dabbing her eyes with the crumpled square of cambric.

'I think you're rather wonderful,' returned Buck gently. He helped her to a chair. 'Sit down here, and when you're able, tell us just what – happened.'

Her hands dropped suddenly to her lap and she looked up at him with wide, blazing eyes. Bud had approached and stood on the other side of the chair, listening intently.

'It was that creature Lynch,' she said in a voice that trembled a little with anger and indignation. 'He was the one who rode up on horseback. It was Pedro who was hidden in the loft. Mary told you about that before the telephone went dead.'

'The wire was cut,' muttered Stratton. 'That must have been the greaser's work.'

She gave a quick nod. 'Very likely. He's equal to anything. They met just outside the door and talked together. It seemed as if they'd never leave off whispering. Mary was over by the telephone and I stood here. She had that revolver, which she'd found in the other room.' Her eyes indicated the weapon on the table, and Buck was conscious of a queer thrill as he recognised it as his own. 'We waited. At last the – the beast pounded at the door and called to us to open. We didn't stir. Then he threw himself against the door, which cracked. Mary cried out that if he tried to force it, she'd shoot. The creature only laughed, and when she did fire, the bullet went wild.'

She paused an instant, her fingers twitching at the handkerchief clasped in her lap.

'And then he broke in?' questioned Buck, in a hard voice.

She nodded. 'Yes. I fired once, but it did no good. Before I could shoot again, Pedro came up from behind and snatched the revolver away. He must have forced his way into the kitchen. He threw me into a chair, while Lynch went after Mary.'

Buck's lips were pressed tightly together; his face was hard as stone. 'Didn't she fire again?'

'No, I don't know why. I couldn't see very well. Something may have gone wrong with the revolver; perhaps she had scruples. I should have had none.' Mrs Archer's small, delicate face looked almost savage. 'I'd have gloried in shooting the brute. At any rate, she didn't, and he took the weapon away from her and flung it on the table.'

Again she hesitated briefly, overcome by her emotions. Stratton's face was stony, save for a momentary ripple of the muscles about his mouth.

'And then?' he questioned.

'I – I tried to go to her, but Pedro held me in the chair.' Mrs Archer drew a long, quivering breath. 'Lynch had her by the wrist; I heard him say something about not hurting her; and then he said, quite plainly, that since she'd got him in this mess, she'd have to get him out. I couldn't understand, but all at once I realised that if they did – take her away, they'd probably tie me up, or something, to prevent my giving the alarm, and so I pretended to faint.'

She lifted her handkerchief to her lips and let it fall again. 'It wasn't easy to lie still in that chair and see the dear child – being dragged away. But I knew I'd be quite helpless against those two villains. She – she didn't struggle much; perhaps she hadn't the strength.' The old lady's voice shook, and she began again plucking nervously at her handkerchief. 'The minute they were out of the door, I got up and followed them. I thought perhaps I might be able to see which way they went. It was pitch-dark, and I crept along beside the house to the corner. I could just see their outlines over by the corral. Pedro was saddling two horses. When he had done, that creature, Lynch, made Mary mount and got on his own horse, which he had been leading. Then the two men began to talk. I couldn't hear everything, but it sounded as if they were arranging to meet somewhere. They gave the name of a place.'

Her eyes searched Buck's face with a troubled, anxious scrutiny. 'So many Arizona towns have a foreign sound, but somehow I – I've never even heard of Santa Clara.'

'Santa Clara!' burst out Bud. 'Why, that's over in Sonora. If he should get her across the border –'

Mrs Archer sprang to her feet and caught Stratton by one arm.

'Mexico!' she cried hysterically. 'Oh, Buck! You must save her from that creature! You mustn't let him – '

'He sha'n't. Don't worry,' interrupted Stratton harshly. 'Tell me as quickly as you can what else you heard. Was there anything said about the way he meant to take?'

Mrs Archer clenched her small hands and fought bravely for self-control. 'He said he – he might be delayed. He didn't dare take the road through Perilla, and the trail through the mountains was probably blocked by the sheriff.' Her forehead wrinkled thoughtfully. 'He said the only way was to – to go through the pass and turn south along the edge of the T-T land. That – that was all.'

Buck's face lighted with sombre satisfaction. 'It's a good bit,' he said briefly. 'When they started off did you notice which way they went?'

'Pedro rode past the house towards the lower gate. Lynch went straight down the slope towards the bunk-house. He was leading Mary's horse. I ran a little way after them and saw them cross the creek this side of the middle pasture gate.'

Buck shot a glance at Jessup. 'The north pasture!' he muttered. 'He knows there'll be no one around there, and it'll be the safest way to reach the T-T trail. I'll saddle a fresh cayuse and be off.' He turned to Mrs Archer. 'Don't you worry,' he said, with a momentary touch on her shoulder that was at once a caress and an assurance. 'I'll bring her back.'

'You must!' she cried. 'They said something – It isn't possible that he can – force her to – to marry him?'

'A lot of things are possible, but he won't have the chance,' replied Stratton grimly. 'Bud, you stay here with Mrs Archer, and I'll – '

'Oh, no!' protested the old lady. 'You must both go. I don't need any one. I'm not afraid of being here alone. No one will come – now.'

'Why couldn't I go after Hardenberg and get him to take a bunch around the south end of the hills,' suggested Jessup quickly. 'They might be able to head him off.'

'All right,' nodded Stratton curtly. 'Go to it.'

Inaction had suddenly grown intolerable. He would have agreed to anything save the suggestion that he delay his start even for another sixty seconds. With a hurried goodbye to Mrs Archer, he hastened from the room, swung into his saddle, and rode swiftly around to the corral. A brief search through the darkness showed him that only a single horse remained there. He lost not a moment in roping the animal, and was transferring his saddle from Pete, when Bud appeared.

'You'll have to catch a horse from the *remuda*,' he said briefly. 'I've taken the last one. Turn Pete into the corral, will you, and give him a little feed.' Straightening up, he turned the stirrup, mounted swiftly, and spurred his horse forward. 'So-long,' he called back over one shoulder.

The thud of hoofs drowned Bud's reply, and as the night closed about him, Buck gave a faint sigh of relief. There was a brief delay at the gate, and then, heading northwest, he urged the horse to a canter.

He was taking a chance in following this short cut through the middle pasture, but he felt he had no choice. To attempt to trail Lynch would be futile, and if he waited until dawn, the scoundrel would be hopelessly in the lead. He knew of only one pass through the mountains to T-T ground, and for this he headed, convinced that it was also Lynch's goal, and praying fervently that the scoundrel might not change his mind.

He was under no delusions as to the task which lay before him. Lynch would be somewhat handicapped by the presence of the girl, especially if he continued to lead her horse. But he had a good hour's start, and once in the mountains the handicap would vanish. The chase was likely to be prolonged, particularly as Lynch knew every foot of the mountain trail and the country beyond, which Stratton had never seen.

But the presence of difficulties only strengthened Buck's resolution and confidence. As he sped on through the luminous darkness, the cool night wind brushing his face, a seething rage against Tex Lynch dominated him. Now and then the thought of Mary Thorne came to torture him. Vividly he pictured the scene at the ranch-house which Mrs Archer had described, imagining the girl's fear and horror and despair, then and afterward, with a realism which made him wince. But always his mind flashed back to the man who was to blame for it all, and with savage curses he pledged himself to a reckoning.

And so, with mind divided between alternating spasms of tenderness and fury, he came at last to the further side of middle pasture and dismounted to let down the fence. It was characteristic of the born and bred ranchman that instead of riding swiftly on and letting the cut wires dangle, he automatically obeyed one of the hard and fast rules of the range and fastened them behind him. He did not pause again until he reached the little sheltered nook in the face of the high cliffs, out of which led the trail.

Had those two passed yet, or were they still out there somewhere in the sandy wastes of north pasture? He wondered as he reined in his horse. He scarcely dared hope that already he could have forestalled the crafty Lynch, but it was important to make sure. And so, slipping out of the saddle, he flung the reins over the roan's head and, walking forward a few steps, lit a match and searched the ground carefully for any signs.

Three matches had been consumed before he found what he was looking for – the fresh prints of two horses leading towards the trail. Hastily returning to his cayuse, he swung into the saddle and headed the roan towards the grade. They were ahead of him, then; but how far?

It was impossible to make any speed along the rough uncertainties of this rocky trail, but Buck wasted no time. Down in the further hollow he turned aside to the spring, not knowing when he would again find water for his horse. He did not dismount, and as the roan plunged velvet nozzle into the spring, a picture rose in Buck's mind of that other day – how long ago it seemed! – when he himself, sagging painfully in the saddle, had sucked the water with as great an eagerness out of a woman's soggy Stetson, and then, over the limp brim, gazed gratefully into a pair of tender hazel eyes which tried in vain to mask anxiety beneath a surface of lightness.

He bit his lips and struck the saddle-horn fiercely with one clenched fist. When the horse had finished drinking, he turned him swiftly and, regaining the trail, pushed on feverishly at reckless speed.

About an hour later the first pale signs of dawn began to lighten the darkness. Slowly, gradually, almost imperceptibly, a cold grey crept into the sky, blotting out the stars. Little by little the light strengthened, searching out shadowy nooks and corners, revealing this peak or that, widening the horizon, until at length the whole, wide, tumbled mass of peak and precipice, of canyon, valley, and tortuous, twisted mountain trail lay revealed in all its grim, lifeless, forbidding desolation.

From his point of vantage at the summit of a steep grade, Buck halted and stared ahead with a restless, keen eagerness. He could see the trail curving over the next rise, and farther still he glimpsed a tiny patch of it rounding the shoulder of a hill. But it was empty, lifeless; and as he loosed the reins and touched the roan lightly with a spur, Stratton's face grew blank and hard again.

From somewhere amongst the rocks the long-drawn, quavering howl of a coyote sounded mournfully.

CHAPTER 33

Carried Away

The same dawn unrolled before the eyes of a man and a girl, riding southward along the ragged margin of the T-T ranch. Westward stretched the wide, rolling range-land, empty at the moment of any signs of life. And somehow, for the very reason that one expected something living there, it seemed even more desolate than the rough, broken country bordering the mountains on the other side.

That, at least, was Mary Thorne's thought. Emerging from the mountain trail just as dawn broke, her eyes brightened as she took in the flat, familiar country, even noting a distant line of wire fence, and for the first time in many hours despair gave place to sudden hope. Where there was range-land there must be cattle and men to tend them, and her experience with Western cowmen had not been confined to those of Lynch's type. Him she knew now, to her regret and sorrow, to be the great exception. The majority were clean-cut, brave, courteous, slow of speech, perhaps, but swift in action; simple of mind and heart – the sort of man, in short, to whom a woman in distress might confidently turn for help.

But presently, as the rising sun, gilding the peaks that towered above her, emphasised the utter emptiness of those sweeping pastures, the light died out of her eyes and she remembered with a sinking heart the blackleg scourge which had so recently afflicted the T-T outfit. There had been much discussion of it at the Shoe-Bar, and now she recalled vaguely hearing that it had first broken out in these very pastures. Doubtless, as a method of prevention, the surviving stock had been moved elsewhere, and her chances for help would be as likely in the midst of a trackless desert as here.

The reaction made her lips quiver and there swept over her with renewed force that wave of despair which had been gaining strength all through those interminable black hours. She had done her best to combat it. Over and over again she told herself that the situation was far from hopeless. Something must happen. Some one – mostly she thought of Buck, though she did not name him even to herself – would come to her aid. It was incredible that in this day and generation a person could be successfully carried off even by one as crafty, resourceful, and unscrupulous as Tex Lynch. But in spite of all her reasoning there remained in the back of Mary's mind a feeling of cold horror, born of those few sentences she had overheard while Pedro was saddling the horses. Like a poisonous serpent, it reared its ugly head persistently, to demolish in an instant her most specious arguments. The very thought of it now filled her with the same fear and dread that had overwhelmed her when the incredible words first burned into her consciousness, and made her glance with a sudden, sharp terror at the man beside her. She met a stare from his bold, heavy-lidded eyes that sent the blood flaming into her cheeks.

'Well?' queried Lynch, smiling. 'Feelin' better, now it's mornin'?'

The girl made no answer. Hastily averting her eyes, she rode on in silence, lips pressed together and chin a little tilted.

'Sulking, eh?' drawled Lynch. 'What's the good? Yuh can't keep that sort of thing up forever. After we're – married – '

He paused significantly. The girl's lip quivered but she set her teeth into it determinedly. Presently, with an effort, she forced herself to speak.

'Aren't you rather wasting time trying to – to frighten me with that sort of rubbish?' she asked coldly. 'In these days marriage isn't something that can be forced.'

The man's laugh was not agreeable. 'Oh, is that so?' he enquired. 'You're likely to learn a thing or two before long, I'll say.'

His tone was so carelessly confident, so entirely assured, that in an instant her pitiful little pretence of courage was swept away.

'It isn't so!' she cried, turning on him with wide eyes and quivering lips. 'You couldn't – There isn't a – real clergyman who'd do – do such a thing. No one could force me to – to – Why, I'd rather die than – '

She paused, choking. Lynch shrugged his shoulders.

'Oh, no, yuh wouldn't,' he drawled. 'Dyin' is mighty easy to talk about, but when yuh get right down to it, I reckon you'd change yore mind. I don't see why yore so dead set against me,' he added. 'I ain't so hard to look at, am I? An' with me as yore husband, things will – will be mighty different on the ranch. You'll never have to pinch an' worry like yuh do now.'

Tears blinded her, and, turning away quickly, she stared unseeing through a blurring haze, fighting desperately for at least a semblance of self-control. He was so confident, so terribly sure of himself! What if he could do the thing he said? She did not see how such a ghastly horror could be possible; but then, what did she know of conditions in the place to which he was taking her?

Suddenly, as she struggled against that overpowering weight of misery and despair, her thoughts flew longingly to another man, and for an instant she seemed to look into his eyes – whimsical, a little tender, with a faint touch of suppressed longing in their clear grey depths.

'Buck! Oh, Buck!' she yearned under her breath.

Then of a sudden she felt a hand on her bridle and became aware that Lynch was speaking.

'We'll stop here for a bit,' he informed her briefly. 'You'd better get down and stretch yoreself.'

She looked at him, a little puzzled. 'I'm quite comfortable as I am,' she returned stiffly.

'I expect yuh are,' he said meaningly. 'But I ain't takin' any chances.' With a wave of his hand he indicated a steepish knoll that rose up on their left. 'I'm goin' up there to look around an' see what the country looks like ahead,' he explained. 'I'll take both cayuses along, jest in case yuh should take the notion to go for a little canter. *Sabe?*'

Without a word she slipped out of the saddle and, moving to one side, listlessly watched him gather up the reins of her horse and ride towards the foot of the hill. Its lower levels sloped easily, and in spite of the handicap of the led horse, who pulled back and seemed reluctant to follow, Lynch took it with scarcely a pause.

There came a point, however, about halfway to the summit, from which he would have to proceed on foot. Lynch dismounted briskly enough and tied both horses to a low bush. Then, instead of starting directly on the brief upward climb, he turned and glanced back to where Mary stood.

That glance, indicating doubt and suspicion, set the girl suddenly to wondering. Ever so little her slim figure straightened, losing its discouraged droop. Was it possible? He seemed to think so, or why had he looked back so searchingly? Guardedly her glance swept to right and left. A hundred feet or so to the south a spur of the little hill thrust out, hiding what lay beyond. If she could reach it, might there not possibly be some spot in all that jumble of rocks and gullies where she at least might hide?

Filled with a new wild hope; realising that nothing she might do could make her situation worse, Mary's eyes returned to the climbing man, and she watched him narrowly. Little by little, when his back was towards her, she edged towards the spur. She told herself that when he reached the top she would make a dash, but in the end her tense, raw nerves played her false. Quivering with eagerness, she held herself together until he was within twenty feet or more of the summit, and then her self-control snapped abruptly.

She had covered scarcely a dozen yards over the rough ground when a hoarse shout of surprise came from Lynch, followed by the clatter of rolling stones as he plunged back down the hill. But she did not turn her head; there was no time or need. Running as she had never run before, she rounded the spur and with a gasp of dismay saw that the cliffs curved back abruptly, forming an intervening open space that seemed to extend for miles, but which, in reality, was only a few hundred yards across.

Still she did not halt, but sped on gamely, heading for the mouth of the nearest gully. Presently the thud of hoofs terrified her, but stung her to even greater effort. Nearer the hoof-beats came, and nearer still. Breathless, panting, she knew now she could never reach the gully. The realisation sent her heart sinking like a lead plummet, but fear drove her blindly on. Suddenly the bulk of a horse loomed beside her and a man's easy, sneering laugh bit into her soul like vitriol. An instant later Lynch leaped from his saddle and caught her around the waist.

'Yuh would, would yuh?' he cried, gazing down into her flushed, frightened face. 'Tried to shake me, eh?'

For a moment he held her thus, devouring her with his eyes, holding the bridles of both horses in his free hand. Then all at once he laughed again, hatefully, and crushing her to him, he kissed her, roughly, savagely – kissed her repeatedly on the lips and cheeks and throat.

Mary cried out once and tried to struggle. Then of a sudden her muscles relaxed and she lay limply in his arms, eyes closed, wishing that she might die, or, better yet, that some supreme force would suddenly strike the creature dead.

How long she lay there shuddering with disgust and loathing, she did not know. It seemed an eternity before she realised that his lips no longer touched her, and opening her eyes she was startled at the sight of his face.

It was partly turned away from her as he stared southward across the flats. His eyes were wide, incredulous, and filled with a mingling of anger and dismay. In another moment he jerked her roughly to her feet, dragged her around to the side of her horse, and fairly flung her into the saddle. Vaulting into his own, he spurred the beast savagely and rode back towards the out-thrust spur at a gallop, dragging the unwilling Freckles with him.

Gripping the saddle-horn to keep her precarious seat, Mary yet found time for a hurried backward glance before she was whisked out of sight of that wide stretch of open country to the south. But that glance was enough to make her heart leap. Dots – moving dots which she had no difficulty in recognising as horsemen – were sweeping northward along the edge of the breaks. Who they were she neither knew nor cared. It was enough that they were men. Her eyes sparkled, and a wild new hope flamed up within her, even though she was being carried swiftly away from them.

Once in the shelter of the spur, Lynch did not halt but rode on at full speed, heading northward. For half a mile or so the thudding hoof-beats of the two horses alone broke the silence. Then, as their advance opened up a fresh sweep of country, Lynch jerked his mount to a standstill with a suddenness that raised a cloud of dust about them.

'Hell!' he rasped, staring from under narrowing lids.

For full half a minute he sat motionless, his face distorted with baffled fury and swiftly growing fear. Then his eyes flashed towards the hills on the right and swept them searchingly. A second later he had turned his cayuse and was speeding towards a narrow break between two spurs, keeping a tight hold on the girl's bridle.

'You try any monkey tricks,' he flung back over one shoulder, 'and I'll – kill yuh.'

Mary made no answer, but the savage ferocity of his tone made her shiver, and she instantly abandoned the plan she had formed of trying, by little touches of hand and heel, to make Freckles still further hamper Lynch's actions. Through the settling dust-haze she had seen the cause of his perturbation – a single horseman less than a mile away galloping straight towards them – and felt that her enemy was cornered. But the very strength of her exultation gave her a passionate longing for life and happiness, and she realised vividly the truth of Lynch's callous, sneering words, that when one actually got down to it, it was not an easy thing to die. She must take no chances. Surely it could be only a question of a little time now before she would be free.

But presently her high confidence began to fade. With the manner of one on perfectly familiar ground, Lynch rode straight into the break between the rocks, which proved to be the entrance to a gully that widened and then turned sharply to the right. Here he stopped and ordered Mary to ride in front of him.

'You go ahead,' he growled, flinging her the reins. 'Don't lose any time, neither.'

Without question she obeyed, choosing the way from his occasional, tersely flung directions. This led them upward, slowly, steadily with many a twist and turn, until at length, passing through a narrow opening in the rocks, Mary came out suddenly on a ledge scarcely a dozen feet in width. On one side the cliffs rose in irregular, cluttered masses, too steep to climb. On the other was a precipitous drop into a canyon of unknown depth.

'Get down,' ordered Lynch, swinging out of his saddle.

As she slid to the ground he handed her his bridle-reins.

'Take the horses a ways back an' hold 'em,' he told her curtly. 'An' remember this: Not a peep out of yuh, or it'll be yore last. Nobody yet's double-crossed me an' got away with it, an' nobody ain't goin' to – not even a woman. That canyon's pretty deep, an' there's sharp stones a-plenty at the bottom.'

White-faced and tight-lipped, she turned away from him without a word and led the two horses back to the point he indicated. The ledge, which sloped sharply upward, was cluttered with loose stones, and she moved slowly, avoiding these with instinctive caution and trying not to glance towards the precipice. A dozen feet away she paused, holding the horses tightly by their bridles and pressing herself against the lathered neck of Freckles, who she knew was steady. Then she glanced back and caught her breath with a swift, sudden intake.

Kneeling close to the opening, but a little to one side, Lynch was whirling the cylinder of his Colt. Watching him with fascinated horror, Mary saw him break the weapon, closely inspect the shells, close it again, and test the trigger. Then, revolver gripped in right hand, he settled himself into a slightly easier position, eyes fixed on the opening and head thrust a little forward in an attitude of listening.

Only too well she guessed his purpose. He was waiting in ambush to 'get' that solitary horseman they had seen riding from the north. Whether or not he had come here for the sole purpose of luring the other to his death, Mary had no notion. But she could see clearly that once this stranger was out of the way, Lynch would at least have a chance to penetrate into the mountains before the others from the south arrived to halt him.

Slowly, interminably the minutes ticked away as the girl stood motionless, striving desperately to think of something she might do to prevent the catastrophe. If only she had some way of knowing when the stranger was near she might cry out a warning, even at the risk of Lynch's violence.

But thrust here in the background as she was, the unknown was likely to come within range of Lynch's gun before she even knew of his approach.

Suddenly, out of the dead silence, the clatter of a pebble struck on the girl's raw nerves and made her wince. She saw the muscles of Lynch's back stiffen and the barrel of his Colt flash up to cover the narrow entrance to the ledge. For an instant she hesitated, choked by the beating of her heart. Should she cry out? Was it the man really coming? Her dry lips parted, and then all at once a curious, slowly moving object barely visible above the rocky shoulder that sheltered Lynch, startled her and kept her silent.

In that first flash she had no idea what it was. Then abruptly the truth came to her. It was the top of a man's Stetson. The ledge sloped upward, and where she stood it was a good two feet higher than at the entrance. A man was riding up the outer slope and, remembering the steepness of it, Mary knew that, in a moment, more of him would come into view before he became visible to Lynch.

White-faced, dry-lipped, she waited breathlessly. Now she could see the entire hat. A second later she glimpsed the top of an ear, a bit of forehead, a sweeping lock of dark-brown hair – and her heart died suddenly within her.

The man was Buck Green!

CHAPTER 34

The Fight on the Ledge

In that instant of supreme horror, Mary Thorne found time to be thankful that terror struck her momentarily dumb. For now, with lips parted and a cry of warning trembling there, she saw that it was too late. Like a pointer freezing to the scent, Lynch's whole body had stiffened; one hand gripped the levelled Colt, a finger caressed the trigger. At this juncture a cry would almost surely bring that tiny, muscular contraction which might be fatal.

From behind the ledge Buck's hat had disappeared, and a faint creak of saddle-leather told the girl that he had dismounted and by so doing must have moved a trifle out of range.

Sick with horror and desperation, the girl's eye fell upon a stone lying at her feet – a jagged piece of granite perhaps twice the size of a baseball.

In a flash she dropped the bridle-reins and, bending, caught it up stealthily. Freckles pricked his ears forward, but with a fleeting, imploring touch of one hand against his sweaty neck, Mary steadied herself for a moment, slowly drew back her arm, and, with a fervent, silent prayer for strength, she hurled the stone.

It grazed Lynch's face and struck his wrist with a force that jerked up the barrel of the revolver. The spurt of flame, the sharp crack of the shot, the clatter of the Colt striking the edge of the precipice, all seemed to the girl to come simultaneously. A belated second afterward Lynch's furious curses came to her. With dilated eyes she saw him snatch frantically at the sliding weapon, and as it toppled out of sight into the canyon barely an inch ahead of his clutching, striving fingers, she thrilled with sudden fierce joy.

'Curse you!' he frothed, springing up and rushing at her. 'You – '

'Buck!' she screamed. 'Quick! His gun's gone! He – '

A blow from his fist struck her mouth and flung her backward against the horse. Half fainting, she saw Freckles lunge over her shoulder and heard the vicious click of his teeth snapping together. But Lynch, ducking out of reach of the angry horse, caught Mary about the waist and dragged her towards the precipice.

Involuntarily she closed her eyes. When she opened them again, stirred by the curious silence and the sudden cessation of all movement, she found herself staring dazedly into the face of Buck Green.

He stood very quietly just inside the narrow entrance to the ledge, not more than ten feet from her. In one hand was a six-shooter; the other hung straight at his side, the fingers tightly clenched. As he met her bewildered glance, his eyes softened tenderly and the corners of his lips curved in a momentary, reassuring smile. Then abruptly his face froze again.

'Yuh take another step an' down she'll go,' said a hoarse voice close to the girl's ear.

It was Lynch; and Mary, her senses clearing, knew whose hands gripped her so tightly that she could scarcely breathe. Glancing sidewise, she hastily averted her eyes. She was standing within six inches of the edge of the precipice. For the first time she could look down into those sheer depths, and even that hurried glimpse made her shiver.

'Well, I admit you've got the bulge on me, as it were.' Buck's voice suddenly broke the silence. 'Still, I don't see how you're going to get out of this hole. You can't stand like this forever.'

Mary stared at him, amazed at his cool, drawling, matter-of-fact tone. She was still more puzzled to note that he seemed to be juggling with his revolver in a manner which seemed, to say the least, extraordinarily careless.

'I can stand here till I get tired,' retorted Lynch. 'After that – Well, I'd as soon end up down there as get a bullet through my ribs. One thing, I wouldn't go alone.'

'Suppose I offered to let you go free if you give up Miss Thorne?' Stratton asked with sudden earnestness.

'Offer? Hell! Yuh can't fool me with that kind of talk. Not unless yuh hand over yore gun, that is. Do that, an' I might consider the proposition – not otherwise.'

Buck hesitated, his eyes flashing from the weapon he whirled so carelessly between his fingers to Lynch, whose eyes regarded him intently over the girl's shoulder.

'That would be putting an awful lot of trust in you,' he commented. 'Once you had the gun, what's to prevent you from drilling me – Oh, damn!'

He made a sudden, ineffectual grab at the gun, which had slipped from his fingers, and missed. As the weapon clattered against the rocks, Lynch's covetous glance followed it involuntarily. What happened next was a bewildering whirl of violent, unexpected action.

To Mary it seemed as if Buck cleared the space between them in a single amazing leap. He landed with one foot slipping on the ragged edge of the precipice, and apparently threw his whole weight sidewise against Lynch and the girl he held. Just how it happened she did not know, but in another moment Mary found herself freed from those hateful, gripping hands and flung back against her horse, while at her feet the two men grappled savagely.

Over and over on the narrow confines of the sloping ledge they struggled fiercely, heaving, panting, with muscles cracking, each seemingly possessed with a grim determination to thrust the other into the abyss. Now Buck was uppermost; again Lynch, by some clever trick, tore himself from Stratton's hold to gain a momentary advantage.

Like one meshed in the thralls of some hateful nightmare, the girl crouched against her horse, her face so still and white and ghastly that it might well have been some clever sculptor's bizarre conception of 'Horror' done in marble. Only her eyes seemed to live. Wide, dilated, glittering with an unnatural light, they shifted constantly, following the progress of those two writhing bodies.

Once, when Lynch's horse snorted and moved uneasily, she caught his bridle and quieted him with a soothing word, her voice so choked and hoarse that she scarcely knew it. Again, as the men rolled towards the outer side of the ledge and seemed for a moment almost to overhang the precipice, she gave a smothered cry and darted forward, moved by some wild impulse to fling her puny strength into the scale against the outlaw.

But with a heave of his big body, Buck saved himself as he had done more than once before, and the struggle was resumed. Back and forth they fought, over and over around that narrow space, until Mary was filled with the dazed feeling that it had been going on forever, that it would never end.

But not for an instant did she cease to follow every tiny variation of the fray, and of a sudden she gave another cry. Gripped in a fierce embrace, the two men rolled towards the entrance to the ledge, and all at once Mary saw one of Lynch's hands close over and instantly seize the revolver Buck had dropped there.

Instantly she darted forward and tried to wrest it from his grasp. Finding his strength too great, she straightened swiftly and lifting one foot, brought her riding boot down fiercely with all her strength on Lynch's hand. With a smothered grunt his fingers laxed, and she caught up the weapon and stepped quickly back, wondering, if Lynch came uppermost, whether she would dare to try to shoot him.

No scruples now deterred her. These had vanished utterly, and with them fear, nervousness, fatigue, and every thought of self. For the moment she was like the primitive savage, willing to do anything on earth to save – her man! But so closely were the two men entwined that she was afraid if she shot at Lynch the bullet might injure Buck.

Once more the fight veered close to the precipice. Lynch was again uppermost; and, whether by his greater strength, or from some injury Buck had sustained against the rocks, the girl was seized by a horrible conviction that he had the upper hand. Knees gripping Stratton about the body, hands circling his throat, Lynch, apparently oblivious to the blows rained on his chest and neck, was slowly but surely forcing his opponent over the ragged margin of the ledge. It was at this instant that the frantic girl discovered that her weapon had suffered some damage when it fell and was quite useless.

Already Buck's head overhung the precipice, his face a dark, strangled red. Flinging the revolver from her, Mary rushed forward and began to beat Lynch wildly with her small, clenched fists.

But she might as effectually have tried to move a rooted tree, and with a strangled cry, she wound her fingers in his coarse black hair and strove with all her strength to drag Lynch back.

CHAPTER 35

The Dead Heart

Vaguely, as of a sound coming from far distances, the crack of a revolver-shot penetrated to the girl's numbed brain. It did not surprise her. Indeed, it roused only a feeling of the mildest curiosity in one whose nerves had been strained almost to the breaking-point. When Lynch, with a hoarse cry, toppled back against her, she merely stepped quickly to one side, and an instant later she was on her knees beside Stratton.

'Buck!' she sobbed. 'Oh, Buck!' clutching at him as if from some wild fear that he would topple into the abyss.

Hands suddenly put her gently to one side, and some one dragged Stratton from his dangerous position and supported him against an upraised knee. It was Bud Jessup, and behind him loomed the figures of Sheriff Hardenberg and several of his men.

Mary's glance noted them briefly, incuriously, returning anxiously to the man beside her. His eyes were open now, and he was sucking in the air in deep, panting gulps.

'How yuh feelin'?' asked Bud briefly.

'All right – get my breath,' mumbled Buck.

'Yuh hurt any place?' Jessup continued, after a brief pause.

'Not to speak of,' returned Stratton in a stronger tone. 'When I first jumped for the cuss, I hit my head the devil of a crack, and – pretty near went out. But that don't matter – now.'

His eyes sought the girl's and dwelt there, longingly, caressingly. There was tribute in their depths, appreciation, and something stronger, more abiding which brought a faint flush into her tired face and made her heart beat faster. Presently, when he staggered to his feet and took a step or two towards her, she felt no shame in meeting him halfway. Quite as naturally as his arm slipped around her shoulders, her lifted hands rested against the front of his flannel shirt, torn into ribbons and stained with grime.

'For a little one,' he murmured, looking down into her eyes, 'you're some spunky fighter, believe me!'

She flushed deeper and her lids drooped. Of a sudden Sheriff Hardenberg spoke up briskly:

'That was a right nice shot, kid. You got him good.'

He was standing beside the body sprawling on the ground, and the
words had scarcely left his lips when Lynch's eyes opened slowly.

'Yes – yuh got me,' he mumbled.

Slowly his glance swept the circle of faces until it rested finally on the
man and girl standing close together. For a long moment he stared at
them silently, his pale lips twitching. Then all at once a look of cunning
satisfaction swept the baffled fury from his smouldering eyes.

'Yuh got me,' he repeated in a stronger voice. 'Looks like yuh got her,
too. Maybe yuh think you've gobbled up the ranch, likewise, an' – an'
everything. That's where yuh get stung.'

He fell to coughing suddenly, and for a few minutes his great body was
racked with violent paroxysms that brought a bright crimson stain to the
sleeve he flung across his mouth. But all the while his eyes, full of strange
venomous triumph, never once left Stratton's face.

'Yuh see,' he choked out finally, 'the ranch – ain't – hers.'

He paused, speechless; and Mary, looking down on him, felt merely
that his brain was wandering and found room in her heart to be a little
sorry.

'Why ain't it hers?' demanded Bud with youthful impetuosity. 'Her
father left it to her, an' – '

'It wasn't his to – to leave. He stole it.' Lynch's voice was weaker, but
his eyes still glowed with hateful triumph. 'He forged the deed – from –
from papers – Stratton left with him – when he went – to war.' He
moistened his dry lips with his tongue. 'When Stratton was – killed – he
didn't leave – no kin – to make trouble, an' Thorne – took a chance.'

His voice faltered, ceased. Mary stared at him dumbly, a slow, oppressive
dread creeping into her heart. Little forgotten things flashed back into her
mind. Her father's financial reverses, his reticence about the acquisition of
the Shoe-Bar, the strange hold Lynch had seemed to have on him, rose up
to torment her. Suddenly she glanced quickly at Buck for reassurance.

'It isn't so!' she cried. 'It can't be. My father – '

Slowly the words died on her lips. There was love, tenderness, pity in
the man's eyes, but no – denial!

'Ain't it, though?' Lynch spoke in a laboured whisper; his eyes were
glazing. 'Yuh thinks – I'm – loco. I – ain't. It's – gospel truth. Yuh find
Quinlan, the – the witness. No, Quinlan's dead. It's – it's – Kaylor. Kaylor

got – got – What was I sayin'.' He plucked feebly at his chap-belt. 'I know. Kaylor got – a clean thousand for – for swearin' – the signature – was – Stratton's. Yuh find Kaylor. Hardenberg … thumbscrew … the truth … '

The low, uneven whisper merged into a murmur; then silence fell, broken only by the laboured breathing of the dying man. Dazed, bewildered, conscious of a horrible conviction that he spoke the truth, Mary stood frozen, struggling against a wave of utter weariness and despair that surged over her. She felt the arm about her tighten, but for some strange reason the realisation brought her little comfort.

Suddenly Hardenberg broke the silence. He had been watching the girl, and could no longer bear the misery in her white, strained face.

'You think you've turned a smart trick, don't you?' he snapped with angry impulsiveness. 'As a matter of fact the ranch belongs to him already. The man you've known as Green is Buck Stratton himself.'

Lynch's lids flashed up. 'Yuh – lie!' he murmured. 'Stratton's – dead!'

'Nothing like it,' retorted the sheriff. 'The papers got it wrong. He was only badly wounded. This fellow here is Buck Stratton, and he can prove it.'

A spasm quivered over Lynch's face. He tried to speak, but only a faint gurgle came from his blood-flecked lips. Too late Hardenberg, catching an angry glance from Buck, realised and regretted his impulsive indiscretion. For Mary Thorne, turning slowly like a person in a dream, stared into the face of the man beside her, lips quivering and eyes full of a great horror.

'You!' she faltered, in a pitiful, small voice. 'You – '

Stratton held her closer, a troubled tenderness sweeping the anger from his eyes.

'But – but, Mary – ' he stammered – 'what difference does – '

Suddenly her nerves snapped under the culminating strain of the past few hours.

'Difference!' she cried hysterically. 'Difference!' Her heart lay like a cold, dead thing within her; she felt utterly miserable and alone. 'You – My father! Oh, God!'

She made a weak effort to escape from his embrace. Then, abruptly, her slim, girlish figure grew limp, her head fell back against Stratton's shoulder, her eyes closed.

CHAPTER 36

Two Trails Converge

Mrs Archer sat alone in the ranch-house living-room, doing absolutely nothing. As a matter of fact, she had little use for those minor solaces of knitting or crocheting which soothe the waking hours of so many elderly women. More than once, indeed, she had been heard to state with mild emphasis that when she was no longer able to entertain herself with human nature, or, at the worst, with an interesting book, it would be high time to retire into a nunnery, or its modern equivalent.

Sitting there beside one of the sunny southern windows, her small, faintly wrinkled hands lying reposefully in her lap, she made a dainty, attractive picture of age which was yet not old. Her hair was frankly grey, but luxuriant and crisply waving. No one would have mistaken the soft, faded pink of her complexion, well preserved though it was, for that of a young woman. But her eyes, bright, eager, humorous, changing with every mood, were full of the fire of eternal youth.

Just now there was a thoughtful retrospection in their clear depths. Occasionally she glanced interestedly out of the window, or turned her head questioningly towards the closed door of her niece's bedroom. But for the most part she sat quietly thinking, and the tolerant, humorous curve of her lips showed that her thoughts were far from disagreeable.

'Astonishing!' she murmured presently. 'Really quite amazing! And yet things could scarcely have turned out more – ' She paused, a faint wrinkle marring the smoothness of her forehead. 'Really, I must guard against this habit of talking to myself,' she went on with mild vexation. 'They say it's one of the surest signs of age. Come in!'

The outer door opened and Buck Stratton entered. Pausing for an instant on the threshold, he glanced eagerly about the room, his face falling a little as he walked over to where Mrs Archer sat.

She looked up at him for a moment in silence, surveying with frank approval his long length, his wide chest and lean flanks, the clean-cut face which showed such few signs of fatigue or strain. Then her glance grew quizzical.

'You give yourself away too quickly,' she smiled. 'Even an old woman scarcely feels complimented when a man looks downcast at the sight of her.'

'Rubbish!' retorted Buck. 'You know it wasn't that.' Bending swiftly, he put an arm about her shoulders and kissed her. 'You brought it on yourself,' he told her, grinning, as he straightened up. 'You've no business to look so – pretty.'

The pink in Mrs Archer's cheeks deepened faintly. 'Aren't you rather lavish this morning?' she murmured teasingly. 'Hadn't you better save those for – ' Suddenly her face grew serious. 'I do understand, of course. She hasn't come out yet, but she's dressing. I made her eat her breakfast in bed.'

'Good business,' approved Buck. 'How is she?'

'Very much better, physically. Her nerves are practically all right again; but of course she's very much depressed.'

Stratton's face clouded. 'She still persists – '

Mrs Archer nodded. 'Oh, dear me, yes! That is, she thinks she does. But there's no need to look as if all hope were lost. Indeed, I'm quite certain that a little pressure at the right moment – ' She broke off, glancing at the bedroom door. 'I've an idea it would be better for me to do a little missionary work first. Suppose you go now and come back later. Come back,' she finished briskly, 'when you see my handkerchief lying here on the window-ledge.'

He nodded and was halfway across the room when she called to him guardedly:

'Oh, Buck! There's a phrase I noticed in that rather lurid magazine Bud brought me two or three weeks ago.' Her eyes twinkled. ' "Caveman stuff", I think it was.' Coming from her lips the words had an oddly bizarre sound. 'It seemed descriptive. Of course one would want to use refinements.'

'I get you!' Stratton grinned as he departed.

His head had scarcely passed the window before the inner door opened and Mary Thorne appeared.

Her face was pale, with deep shadows under the eyes, and her slim, girlish figure drooped listlessly. She walked slowly over to the table, took up a book, fluttered the pages, and laid it down again. Then a pile of mail caught her eyes, and picking up the topmost letter, she tore it open and glanced through it indifferently.

'From Stella,' she commented aloud, dropping it on the table. 'They got home all right. She says she had a wonderful time, and asks after – '

'After me, I suppose,' said Mrs Archer, as Mary paused. 'Give her my love when you write.' She hesitated, glancing shrewdly at the girl. 'Don't you want to hear the news, dear?' she asked.

Mary turned abruptly, her eyes widening with sudden interest. 'News? What news?'

'Why, about everything that's happened. They caught all of the men except that wretch, Pedro. The sheriff's taken them to Perilla for trial. He says they'll surely be convicted. Better yet, one of them has turned State's evidence and implicated a swindler named Draper, who was at the bottom of everything.'

'Everything?' repeated the girl in a slightly puzzled tone, as she dropped listlessly into a chair beside her aunt. 'What do you mean, dear, by – everything?'

'How dull I am!' exclaimed Mrs Archer. 'I hope that isn't another sign of encroaching age. I quite forgot you hadn't heard what it was all about. It seems there's oil in the north pasture. Lynch found it and told this man Draper, and ever since then they've been trying to force you to sell the ranch so they could gobble it up themselves.'

'Oil?' questioned Mary. 'You mean oil wells, and that sort of thing?'

'There'll be wells in time, I presume; just now it's merely in the ground. I understand it's quite valuable.'

She went on to explain in detail all she knew. Mary listened silently, head bent and hands absently plucking at the plaiting of her gown. When Mrs Archer finally ceased speaking, the girl made no comment for a time, but sat quite motionless, with drooping face and nervously moving fingers.

'Did you hear about – about – ' she began in an uncertain voice, and then stopped, unable to go on.

'Yes, dear,' returned Mrs Archer simply. 'Bud told me. It's a – a terrible thing, of course, but I think – ' She paused, choosing her words. 'You mustn't spoil your life, my dear, by taking it – too seriously.'

Mary turned suddenly and stared at her, surprise battling with the misery in her face.

'Too seriously!' she cried. 'How can I possibly help taking it seriously? It's too dreadful and – and horrible, almost, to think of.'

'It's dreadful, I admit,' returned the old lady composedly. 'But after all, it's your father's doings. You are not to blame.'

The girl made a swift, dissenting gesture with both hands. 'Perhaps not, in the way you mean. I didn't do the – stealing.' Her voice was bitter.

'I didn't even know about it. But I – profited. Oh, how could Dad ever have done such an awful thing? When I think of his – his deliberately robbing this man who – who had given his life bravely for his country, I could die of shame!'

Her lips quivered and she buried her face in her hands. Mrs Archer reached out and patted her shoulder consolingly.

'But he didn't die for his country,' she reminded her niece practically. 'He's very much alive, and here. He's got his ranch back, with the addition of valuable oil deposits, or whatever you call them, which, Bud tells me, might not have been discovered for years but for this.' She paused, her eyes fixed intently on the girl. 'Do you – love him, Mary?' she asked abruptly.

The girl looked up at her, a slow flush creeping into her face. 'What difference does that make?' she protested. 'I could never make up to him for – for what – father did.'

'It makes every difference in the world,' retorted Mrs Archer positively. 'As for making up – Why, don't you know that you're more to him than ranches, or oil wells, or – anything on earth? You must realise that in your heart.'

Placing her handkerchief on the window-ledge, she rose briskly.

'I really must go and change my shoes,' she said in quite a different tone. 'These slippers seem to – er – pinch a bit.'

If they really did pinch, there was no sign of it as she crossed the room and disappeared through a door at the farther end. Mary stared after her, puzzled and a little hurt at the apparent lack of sympathy in one to whom she had always turned for comfort and understanding. Then her mind flashed back to her aunt's farewell words, and her brow wrinkled thoughtfully.

A knock at the door made her start nervously, and for a long moment she hesitated before replying. At the sight of Buck Stratton standing on the threshold, she flushed painfully and sprang to her feet.

'Good morning,' he said gently, as he came quickly over to her. 'I hope you're feeling a lot better.'

'Oh, yes,' she answered briefly. 'I'm really quite all right now.'

He had taken her hand and still held it, and somehow the mere pressure of his fingers embarrassed her oddly and seemed to weaken her resolution.

'You don't quite look it,' he commented. 'I reckon it'll take some time to get rid of those – those shadows and hollows and all.'

He was looking down at her with that same tender, whimsical smile that quirked the corners of his mouth unevenly, and the expression in his eyes set Mary's heart to fluttering. She could not bear it, somehow! To give him up was even harder than she had expected, and suddenly her lids drooped defensively to hide the bright glitter that smarted in her eyes.

Suddenly he broke the brief silence. 'When are you going to marry me, dear?' he asked quietly.

Her lids flew up and she stared at him through a blurring haze of tears. 'Oh!' she cried unsteadily. 'I can't! I – can't. You – you don't know how I feel. It's all too – dreadful! It doesn't seem as if I could ever – look you in the face again.'

Swiftly his arms slid about her, and she was drawn gently but irresistibly to him.

'Don't try just now, dear, if you'd rather not,' he murmured, smiling down into her tear-streaked face. 'You'll have a long time to get used to it, you know.'

Instinctively she tried to struggle. Then all at once a wave of incredible happiness swept over her. Abruptly nothing seemed to matter – nothing on earth save this one thing. With a little sigh like that of a tired child, her arm stole up about his neck, her head fell gently back against his shoulder.

*   *   *

'Oh!' Mary said abruptly, struck by a sudden recollection. It was an hour later, and they sat together on the sofa. 'I had a letter from Stella today.' A faintly mischievous light sparkled in her eyes. 'She sent her love – to you.'

Buck flushed a little under his tan. 'Some little kidder, isn't she, on short acquaintance?' he commented.

'Short!' Mary's eyes widened. 'Why, she knew you before I did!'

'Maybe so, but I didn't know her.'

Buck had rather dreaded the moment when he would have to tell her of that beastly, vanished year, but somehow he did not find it hard.

'As long as you don't ever let it happen again, I sha'n't mind,' she smiled, when he had finished. 'I simply couldn't bear it, though, if you should lose your memory – now.'

'No danger,' he assured her, with a look that deepened the colour in her radiant face.

For a moment she did not speak. Then all at once her smile faded and she turned quickly to him.

'The – the ranch, dear,' she said abruptly. 'There's something, isn't there, I should do about – about turning it over – to you?'

He drew her head down against his shoulder. 'No use bothering about that now,' he shrugged. 'We're going to be made one so soon that – How about riding to Perilla tomorrow and – '

'Oh, Buck!' she protested. 'I – I couldn't.'

His arm tightened about her. 'Well, say the day after,' he suggested. 'I'm afraid we'll have to spend our honeymoon right here getting things to rights, so you won't have to get a lot of new clothes and all that. There's nothing unlucky about Thursday, is there?'

She hid her face against his coat. 'No–o; but I don't see how – I can – so soon. Well, maybe – perhaps – '

RIDERS OF THE PURPLE SAGE

ZANE GREY

Contents

CHAPTER 1

Lassiter

A SHARP CLIP-CLOP OF IRON-SHOD HOOFS deadened and died away, and clouds of yellow dust drifted from under the cottonwoods out over the sage.

Jane Withersteen gazed down the wide purple slope with dreamy and troubled eyes. A rider had just left her and it was his message that held her thoughtful and almost sad, awaiting the churchmen who were coming to resent and attack her right to befriend a Gentile.

She wondered if the unrest and strife that had lately come to the little village of Cottonwoods was to involve her. And then she sighed, remembering that her father had founded this remotest border settlement of southern Utah and that he had left it to her. She owned all the ground and many of the cottages. Withersteen House was hers, and the great ranch, with its thousands of cattle, and the swiftest horses of the sage. To her belonged Amber Spring, the water which gave verdure and beauty to the village and made living possible on that wild purple upland waste. She could not escape being involved by whatever befell Cottonwoods.

That year, 1871, had marked a change which had been gradually coming in the lives of the peace-loving Mormons of the border. Glaze – Stone Bridge – Sterling, villages to the north, had risen against the invasion of Gentile settlers and the forays of rustlers. There had been opposition to the one and fighting with the other. And now Cottonwoods had begun to wake and bestir itself and grow hard.

Jane prayed that the tranquillity and sweetness of her life would not be permanently disrupted. She meant to do so much more for her people than she had done. She wanted the sleepy quiet pastoral days to last always. Trouble between the Mormons and the Gentiles of the community would make her unhappy. She was Mormon-born, and she was a friend to poor and unfortunate Gentiles. She wished only to go on doing good and being happy. And she thought of what that great ranch meant to her. She loved it all – the grove of cottonwoods, the old stone house, the amber-tinted water, and the droves of shaggy, dusty horses and mustangs, the sleek, clean-limbed, blooded racers, and the browsing herds of cattle and the lean, sun-browned riders of the sage.

While she waited there she forgot the prospect of untoward change. The bray of a lazy burro broke the afternoon quiet, and it was comfortingly suggestive of the drowsy farmyard, and the open corrals, and the green alfalfa fields. Her clear sight intensified the purple sage-slope as it rolled before her. Low swells of prairie-like ground sloped up to the west. Dark, lonely cedar trees, few and far between, stood out strikingly, and at long distances ruins of red rocks. Farther on, up the gradual slope, rose a broken wall, a huge monument, looming dark purple and stretching its solitary, mystic way, a wavering line that faded in the north. Here to the westward was the light and colour and beauty. Northward the slope descended to a dim line of canyons from which rose an up-flinging of the earth, not mountainous, but a vast heave of purple uplands, with ribbed and fan-shaped walls, castle-crowned cliffs, and grey escarpments. Over it all crept the lengthening, waning afternoon shadows.

The rapid beat of hoofs recalled Jane Withersteen to the question at hand. A group of riders cantered up the lane, dismounted, and threw their bridles. They were seven in number, and Tull, the leader, a tall, dark man, was an elder of Jane's church.

'Did you get my message?' he asked, curtly.

'Yes,' replied Jane.

'I sent word I'd give that rider Venters half an hour to come down to the village. He didn't come.'

'He knows nothing of it,' said Jane. 'I didn't tell him. I've been waiting here for you.'

'Where is Venters?'

'I left him in the courtyard.'

'Here, Jerry,' called Tull, turning to his men, 'take the gang and fetch Venters out here if you have to rope him.'

The dusty-booted and long-spurred riders clanked noisily into the grove of cottonwoods and disappeared in the shade.

'Elder Tull, what do you mean by this?' demanded Jane. 'If you must arrest Venters you might have the courtesy to wait till he leaves my home. And if you do arrest him it will be adding insult to injury. It's absurd to accuse Venters of being mixed up in that shooting fray in the village last night. He was with me at the time. Besides, he let me take charge of his guns. You're only using this as a pretext. What do you mean to do to Venters?'

'I'll tell you presently,' replied Tull. 'But first tell me why you defend this worthless rider?'

'Worthless!' exclaimed Jane, indignantly. 'He's nothing of the kind. He was the best rider I ever had. There's not a reason why I shouldn't champion him and every reason why I should. It's no little shame to me, Elder Tull, that through my friendship he has roused the enmity of my people and become an outcast. Besides, I owe him eternal gratitude for saving the life of little Fay.'

'I've heard of your love for Fay Larkin and that you intend to adopt her. But – Jane Withersteen, the child is a Gentile!'

'Yes. But, Elder, I don't love the Mormon children any less because I love a Gentile child. I shall adopt Fay if her mother will give her to me.'

'I'm not so much against that. You can give the child Mormon teaching,' said Tull. 'But I'm sick of seeing this fellow Venters hang around you. I'm going to put a stop to it. You've so much love to throw away on these beggars of Gentiles that I've an idea you might love Venters.'

Tull spoke with the arrogance of a Mormon whose power could not be brooked and with the passion of a man in whom jealousy had kindled a consuming fire.

'Maybe I do love him,' said Jane. She felt both fear and anger stir her heart. 'I'd never thought of that. Poor fellow! he certainly needs someone to love him.'

'This'll be a bad day for Venters unless you deny that,' returned Tull, grimly.

Tull's men appeared under the cottonwoods and led a young man out into the lane. His ragged clothes were those of an outcast. But he stood tall and straight, his wide shoulders flung back, with the muscles of his bound arms rippling and a blue flame of defiance in the gaze he bent on Tull.

For the first time Jane Withersteen felt Venters's real spirit. She wondered if she would love this splendid youth. Then her emotion cooled to the sobering sense of the issue at stake.

'Venters, will you leave Cottonwoods at once and forever?' asked Tull, tensely.

'Why?' rejoined the rider.

'Because I order it.'

Venters laughed in cool disdain.

The red leaped to Tull's dark cheek.

'If you don't go it means your ruin,' he said, sharply.

'Ruin!' exclaimed Venters, passionately. 'Haven't you already ruined me? What do you call ruin? A year ago I was a rider. I had horses and cattle of my own. I had a good name in Cottonwoods. And now when I come into the village to see this woman you set your men on me. You hound me. You trail me as if I were a rustler. I've no more to lose – except my life.'

'Will you leave Utah?'

'Oh! I know,' went on Venters, tauntingly, 'it galls you, the idea of beautiful Jane Withersteen being friendly to a poor Gentile. You want her all yourself. You're a wiving Mormon. You have use for her – and Withersteen House and Amber Spring and seven thousand head of cattle!'

Tull's hard jaw protruded, and rioting blood corded the veins of his neck.

'Once more. Will you go?'

'*No!*'

'Then I'll have you whipped within an inch of your life,' replied Tull, harshly. 'I'll turn you out in the sage. And if you ever come back you'll get worse.'

Venters's agitated face grew coldly set and the bronze changed to grey.

Jane impulsively stepped forward. 'Oh! Elder Tull!' she cried. 'You won't do that!'

Tull lifted a shaking finger towards her.

'That'll do from you. Understand, you'll not be allowed to hold this boy to a friendship that's offensive to your Bishop. Jane Withersteen, your father left you wealth and power. It has turned your head. You haven't yet come to see the place of Mormon women. We've reasoned with you, borne with you. We've patiently waited. We've let you have your fling, which is more than I ever saw granted to a Mormon woman. But you haven't come to your senses. Now, once for all, you can't have any further friendship with Venters. He's going to be whipped, and he's got to leave Utah!'

'Oh! Don't whip him! It would be dastardly!' implored Jane, with slow certainty of her failing courage.

Tull always blunted her spirit, and she grew conscious that she had feigned a boldness which she did not possess. He loomed up now in different guise, not as a jealous suitor, but embodying the mysterious despotism she had known from childhood – the power of her creed.

'Venters, will you take your whipping here or would you rather go out in the sage?' asked Tull. He smiled a flinty smile that was more than inhuman, yet seemed to give out of its dark aloofness a gleam of righteousness.

'I'll take it here – if I must,' said Venters. 'But by God! – Tull, you'd better kill me outright. That'll be a dear whipping for you and your praying Mormons. You'll make me another Lassiter!'

The strange glow, the austere light which radiated from Tull's face, might have been a holy joy at the spiritual conception of exalted duty. But there was something more in him, barely hidden, a something personal and sinister, a deep of himself, an engulfing abyss. As his religious mood was fanatical and inexorable, so would his physical hate be merciless.

'Elder, I – I repent my words,' Jane faltered. The religion in her, the long habit of obedience, of humility, as well as agony of fear, spoke in her voice. 'Spare the boy!' she whispered.

'You can't save him now,' replied Tull, stridently.

Her head was bowing to the inevitable. She was grasping the truth, when suddenly there came, in inward constriction, a hardening of gentle forces within her breast. Like a steel bar it was, stiffening all that had been soft and weak in her. She felt a birth in her of something new and unintelligible. Once more her strained gaze sought the sage-slopes. Jane Withersteen loved that wild and purple wilderness. In times of sorrow it had been her strength, in happiness its beauty was her continual delight. In her extremity she found herself murmuring 'Whence cometh my help!' It was a prayer, as if forth from those lonely purple reaches and walls of red and clefts of blue might ride a fearless man, neither creed-bound nor creed-mad, who would hold up a restraining hand in the faces of her ruthless people.

The restless movements of Tull's men suddenly quieted down. Then followed a low whisper, a rustle, a sharp exclamation.

'Look!' said one, pointing to the west.

'A rider!'

Jane Withersteen wheeled and saw a horseman, silhouetted against the western sky, coming riding out of the sage. He had ridden down from the left, in the golden glare of the sun, and had been unobserved till close at hand. An answer to her prayer!

'Do you know him? Does anyone know him?' questioned Tull, hurriedly.

His men looked and looked, and one by one shook their heads.

'He's come from far,' said one.

'Thet's a fine hoss,' said another.

'A strange rider.'

'Huh! he wears black leather,' added a fourth.

With a waving of his hand, enjoining silence, Tull stepped forward in such a way that he concealed Venters.

The rider reined in his mount, and with a lithe forward-slipping action appeared to reach the ground in one long step. It was a peculiar movement in its quickness and inasmuch that while performing it the rider did not swerve in the slightest from a square front to the group before him.

'Look!' hoarsely whispered one of Tull's companions. 'He packs two black-butted guns – low down – they're hard to see – black agin them black chaps.'

'A gunman!' whispered another. 'Fellers, careful now about movin' your hands.'

The stranger's slow approach might have been a mere leisurely manner of gait or the cramped short steps of a rider unused to walking; yet, as well, it could have been the guarded advance of one who took no chances with men.

'Hello, stranger!' called Tull. No welcome was in this greeting, only a gruff curiosity.

The rider responded with a curt nod. The wide brim of a black sombrero cast a dark shade over his face. For a moment he closely regarded Tull and his comrades, and then, halting in his slow walk, he seemed to relax.

'Evenin', ma'am,' he said to Jane, and removed his sombrero with quaint grace.

Jane, greeting him, looked up into a face that she trusted instinctively and which riveted her attention. It had all the characteristics of the range rider's – the leanness, the red burn of the sun, and the set changelessness that came from years of silence and solitude. But it was not these which held her; rather the intensity of his gaze, a strained weariness, a piercing wistfulness of keen, grey sight, as if the man was forever looking for that which he never found. Jane's subtle woman's intuition, even in that brief instant, felt a sadness, a hungering, a secret.

'Jane Withersteen, ma'am?' he enquired.

'Yes,' she replied.

'The water here is yours?'

'Yes.'

'May I water my horse?'

'Certainly. There's the trough.'

'But mebbe if you knew who I was – ' He hesitated, with his glance on the listening men. 'Mebbe you wouldn't let me water him – though I ain't askin' none for myself.'

'Stranger, it doesn't matter who you are. Water your horse. And if you are thirsty and hungry come into my house.'

'Thanks, ma'am. I can't accept for myself – but for my tired horse – '

Trampling of hoofs interrupted the rider. More restless movements on the part of Tull's men broke up the little circle, exposing the prisoner Venters.

'Mebbe I've kind of hindered somethin' – for a few moments, perhaps?' enquired the rider.

'Yes,' replied Jane Withersteen, with a throb in her voice.

She felt the drawing power of his eyes; and then she saw him look at the bound Venters, and at the men who held him, and their leader.

'In this here country all the rustlers an' thieves an' cutthroats an' gun-throwers an' all-round no-good men jest happen to be Gentiles. Ma'am, which of the no-good class does that young feller belong to?'

'He belongs to none of them. He's an honest boy.'

'You *know* that, ma'am?'

'Yes – yes.'

'Then what has he done to get tied up that way?'

His clear and distinct question, meant for Tull as well as for Jane Withersteen, stilled the restlessness and brought a momentary silence.

'Ask him,' replied Jane, her voice rising high.

The rider stepped away from her, moving out with the same slow, measured stride in which he had approached; and the fact that his action placed her wholly to one side, and him no nearer to Tull and his men, had a penetrating significance.

'Young feller, speak up,' he said to Venters.

'Here, stranger, this's none of your mix,' began Tull. 'Don't try any interference. You've been asked to drink and eat. That's more than you'd have got in any other village on the Utah border. Water your horse and be on your way.'

'Easy – easy – I ain't interferin' yet,' replied the rider. The tone of his voice had undergone a change. A different man had spoken. Where, in addressing Jane, he had been mild and gentle, now, with his first speech to Tull, he was dry, cool, biting. 'I've jest stumbled on to a queer deal. Seven Mormons all packin' guns, an' a Gentile tied with a rope, an' a woman who swears by his honesty! Queer, ain't that?'

'Queer or not, it's none of your business,' retorted Tull.

'Where I was raised a woman's word was law. I ain't quite outgrowed that yet.'

Tull fumed between amaze and anger.

'Meddler, we have a law here something different from woman's whim – Mormon law! . . . Take care you don't transgress it.'

'To hell with your Mormon law!'

The deliberate speech marked the rider's further change, this time from kindly interest to an awakening menace. It produced a transformation in Tull and his companions. The leader gasped and staggered backwards at a blasphemous affront to an institution he held most sacred. The man Jerry, holding the horses, dropped the bridles and froze in his tracks. Like posts the other men stood, watchful-eyed, arms hanging rigid, all waiting.

'Speak up now, young man. What have you done to be roped that way?'

'It's a damned outrage!' burst out Venters. 'I've done no wrong. I've offended this Mormon Elder by being a friend to that woman.'

'Ma'am, is it true – what he says?' asked the rider of Jane; but his quiveringly alert eyes never left the little knot of quiet men.

'True? Yes, perfectly true,' she answered.

'Well, young man, it seems to me that bein' a friend to such a woman would be what you wouldn't want to help an' couldn't help . . . What's to be done to you for it?'

'They intend to whip me. You know what that means – in Utah!'

'I reckon,' replied the rider, slowly.

With his grey glance cold on the Mormons, with the restive bit-champing of the horses, with Jane failing to repress her mounting agitation, with Venters standing pale and still, the tension of the moment tightened. Tull broke the spell with a laugh, a laugh without mirth, a laugh that was only a sound betraying fear.

'Come on, men!' he called.

Jane Withersteen turned again to the rider.

'Stranger, can you do nothing to save Venters?'

'Ma'am, you ask me to save him – from your own people?'

'Ask you? I beg of you!'

'But you don't dream who you're askin'.'

'Oh, sir, I pray you – save him!'

'These are Mormons, an' I . . .'

'At – at any cost – save him. For I – I care for him!'

Tull snarled. 'You lovesick fool! Tell your secrets. There'll be a way to teach you what you've never learned . . . Come men, out of here!'

'Mormon, the young man stays,' said the rider.

Like a shot his voice halted Tull.

'What!'

'He stays.'

'Who'll keep him? He's my prisoner!' cried Tull, hotly. 'Stranger, again I tell you – don't mix here. You've meddled enough. Go your way now or – '

'Listen! . . . He stays.'

Absolute certainty, beyond any shadow of doubt, breathed in the rider's low voice.

'Who are you? We are seven here.'

The rider dropped his sombrero and made a rapid movement, singular in that it left him somewhat crouched, arms bent and stiff, with the big black gun-sheaths swung round to the fore.

'*Lassiter!*'

It was Venters's wondering, thrilling cry that bridged the fateful connection between the rider's singular position and the dreaded name.

Tull put out a groping hand. The life of his eyes dulled to the gloom with which men of his fear saw the approach of death. But death, while it hovered over him, did not descend for the rider waited for the twitching fingers, the downward flash of hand that did not come. Tull, gathering himself together, turned to the horses, attended by his pale comrades.

CHAPTER 2

Cottonwoods

Venters appeared too deeply moved to speak the gratitude his face expressed. And Jane turned upon the rescuer and gripped his hands. Her smiles and tears seemingly dazed him. Presently, as something like calmness returned, she went to Lassiter's weary horse.

'I will water him myself,' she said, and she led the horse to a trough under a huge old cottonwood. With nimble fingers she loosened the bridle and removed the bit. The horse snorted and bent his head. The trough was of solid stone, hollowed out, moss-covered and green and wet and cool, and the clear brown water that fed it spouted and splashed from a wooden pipe.

'He has brought you far today?'

'Yes, ma'am, a matter of over sixty miles, mebbe seventy.'

'A long ride – a ride that – Ah, he is blind!'

'Yes, ma'am,' replied Lassiter.

'What blinded him?'

'Some men once roped an' tied him, an' then held white-iron close to his eyes.'

'Oh! Men? You mean devils . . . Were they your enemies – Mormons?'

'Yes, ma'am.'

'To take revenge on a horse! Lassiter, the men of my creed are unnaturally cruel. To my everlasting sorrow I confess it. They have been driven, hated, scourged till their hearts have hardened. But we women hope and pray for the time when our men will soften.'

'Beggin' your pardon, ma'am – that time will never come.'

'Oh, it will! . . . Lassiter, do you think Mormon women wicked? Has your hand been against them, too?'

'No. I believe Mormon women are the best and noblest, the most long-sufferin', and the blindest, unhappiest women on earth.'

'Ah!' She gave him a grave, thoughtful look. 'Then you will break bread with me?'

Lassiter had no ready response, and he uneasily shifted his weight from one leg to another, and turned his sombrero round and round in his hands. 'Ma'am,' he began, presently, 'I reckon your kindness of heart makes you overlook things. Perhaps I ain't well known hereabouts, but back up North there's Mormons who'd rest oneasy in their graves at the idea of me sittin' to table with you.'

'I dare say. But – will you do it, anyway?' she asked.

'Mebbe you have a brother or relative who might drop in an' be offended, an' I wouldn't want to – '

'I've not a relative in Utah that I know of. There's no one with a right to question my actions.' She turned smilingly to Venters. 'You will come in, Bern, and Lassiter will come in. We'll eat and be merry while we may.'

'I'm only wonderin' if Tull an' his men'll raise a storm down in the village,' said Lassiter, in his last weakening stand.

'Yes, he'll raise the storm – after he has prayed,' replied Jane. 'Come.'

She led the way, with the bridle of Lassiter's horse over her arm. They entered a grove and walked down a wide path shaded by great low-branching cottonwoods. The last rays of the setting sun sent golden bars through the leaves. The grass was deep and rich, welcome contrast to sage-tired eyes. Twittering quail darted across the path, and from a tree-top somewhere a robin sang its evening song, and on the still air floated the freshness and murmur of flowing water.

The home of Jane Withersteen stood in a circle of cottonwoods, and was a flat, long, red-stone structure with a covered court in the centre through which flowed a lively stream of amber-coloured water. In the massive blocks of stone and heavy timbers and solid doors and shutters showed the hand of a man who had builded against pillage and time; and in the flowers and mosses lining the stone-bedded stream, in the bright colours of rugs and blankets on the court floor, and the cosy corner with hammock and books, and the clean-linened table, showed the grace of a daughter who lived for happiness and the day at hand.

Jane turned Lassiter's horse loose in the thick grass. 'You will want him to be near you,' she said, 'or I'd have him taken to the alfalfa fields.' At her call appeared women who began at once to bustle about, hurrying to and fro, setting the table. Then Jane, excusing herself, went within.

She passed through a huge low-ceiled chamber, like the inside of a fort, and into a smaller one where a bright wood-fire blazed in an old open fireplace, and from this into her own room. It had the same comfort as was manifested in the homelike outer court; moreover, it was warm and rich in soft hues.

Seldom did Jane Withersteen enter her room without looking into her mirror. She knew she loved the reflection of that beauty which since early childhood she had never been allowed to forget. Her relatives and friends, and later a horde of Mormon and Gentile suitors, had fanned the flame of natural vanity in her. So that at twenty-eight she scarcely thought at all of her wonderful influence for good in the little community where her father had left her practically its beneficent landlord; but cared most for the dream and the assurance and the allurement of her beauty. This time, however, she gazed into her glass with more than the usual happy motive, without the usual slight conscious smile. For she was thinking of more than the desire to be fair in her own eyes, in those of her friend; she wondered if she were to seem fair in the eyes of this Lassiter, this man whose name had crossed the long, wild brakes of stone and plains of sage, this gentle-voiced, sad-faced man who was a hater and a killer of Mormons. It was not now her usual half-conscious vain obsession that actuated her as she hurriedly changed her riding-dress to one of white, and then looked long at the stately form with its gracious contours, at the fair face with its strong chin and full firm lips, at the dark-blue, proud, and passionate eyes.

'If by some means I can keep him here a few days, a week – he will never kill another Mormon,' she mused. 'Lassiter! . . . I shudder when I think of that name, of him. But when I look at the man I forget who he is – I almost like him. I remember only that he saved Bern. He has suffered. I wonder what it was – did he love a Mormon woman once? How splendidly he championed us poor misunderstood souls! Somehow he knows – much.'

Jane Withersteen joined her guests and bade them to her board. Dismissing her woman, she waited upon them with her own hands. It was a bountiful supper and a strange company. On her right sat the ragged and half-starved Venters; and though blind eyes could have seen what he counted for in the sum of her happiness, yet he looked the gloomy outcast his allegiance had made him, and about him there was the shadow of the ruin presaged by Tull. On her left sat the black-leather-garbed Lassiter looking like a man in a dream. Hunger was not with him, nor composure, nor speech, and when he twisted in frequent unquiet movements the heavy guns that he had not removed knocked against the table-legs. If it had been otherwise possible to forget the presence of Lassiter those telling little jars would have rendered it unlikely. And Jane Withersteen talked and smiled and laughed with all the dazzling play of lips and eyes that a beautiful, daring woman could summon to her purpose.

When the meal ended, and the men pushed back their chairs, she leaned closer to Lassiter and looked square into his eyes.

'Why did you come to Cottonwoods?'

Her question seemed to break a spell. The rider arose as if he had just remembered himself and had tarried longer than his wont.

'Ma'am, I have hunted all over Southern Utah and Nevada for – somethin'. An' through your name I learned where to find it – here in Cottonwoods.'

'My name! Oh, I remember. You did know my name when you spoke first. Well, tell me where you heard it and from whom?'

'At the little village – Glaze, I think it's called – some fifty miles or more west of here. An' I heard it from a Gentile, a rider who said you'd know where to tell me to find – '

'What?' she demanded, imperiously, as Lassiter broke off.

'Milly Erne's grave,' he answered low, and the words came with a wrench.

Venters wheeled in his chair to regard Lassiter in amazement, and Jane slowly raised herself in white, still wonder.

'Milly Erne's grave?' she echoed, in a whisper. 'What do you know of Milly Erne, my best-beloved friend – who died in my arms? What were you to her?'

'Did I claim to be anythin'?' he enquired. 'I know people – relatives – who have long wanted to know where she's buried. That's all.'

'Relatives? She never spoke of relatives, except a brother who was shot in Texas. Lassiter, Milly Erne's grave is in a secret burying-ground on my property.'

'Will you take me there? . . . You'll be offendin' Mormons worse than by breakin' bread with me.'

'Indeed yes, but I'll do it. Only we must go unseen. Tomorrow, perhaps.'

'Thank you, Jane Withersteen,' replied the rider, and he bowed to her and stepped backward out of the court.

'Will you not stay – sleep under my roof?' she asked.

'No, ma'am, an' thanks again. I never sleep indoors. An' even if I did there's that gatherin' storm in the village below. No, no. I'll go to the sage. I hope you won't suffer none for your kindness to me.'

'Lassiter,' said Venters, with a half-bitter laugh, 'my bed, too, is the sage. Perhaps we may meet out there.'

'Mebbe so. But the sage is wide an' I won't be near. Good-night.'

At Lassiter's low whistle the black horse whinnied, and carefully picked his blind way out of the grove. The rider did not bridle him, but walked beside him, leading him by touch of hand, and together they passed slowly into the shade of the cottonwoods.

'Jane, I must be off soon,' said Venters. 'Give me my guns. If I'd had my guns – '

'Either my friend or the Elder of my church would be lying dead,' she interposed.

'Tull would be – surely.'

'Oh, you fierce-blooded, savage youth! Can't I teach you forbearance, mercy? Bern, it's divine to forgive your enemies. "Let not the sun go down upon thy wrath." '

'Hush! Talk to me no more of mercy or religion – after today. Today this strange coming of Lassiter left me still a man, and now I'll die a man! . . . Give me my guns.'

Silently she went into the house, to return with a heavy cartridge-belt and gun-filled sheath and a long rifle; these she handed to him, and as he buckled on the belt she stood before him in silent eloquence.

'Jane,' he said, in gentler voice, 'don't look so. I'm not going out to murder your churchman. I'll try to avoid him and all his men. But can't you see I've reached the end of my rope? Jane, you're a wonderful woman. Never was there a woman so unselfish and good. Only you're blind in one way . . . Listen!'

From behind the grove came the clicking sound of horses in a rapid trot.

'Some of your riders,' he continued. 'It's getting time for the night shift. Let us go out to the bench in the grove and talk there.'

It was still daylight in the open, but under the spreading cottonwoods shadows were obscuring the lanes. Venters drew Jane off from one of these into a shrub-lined trail, just wide enough for the two to walk abreast, and in a roundabout way led her far from the house to a knoll on the edge of the grove. Here in a secluded nook was a bench from which, through an opening in the tree-tops, could be seen the sage-slope and the wall of rock and the dim lines of canyons. Jane had not spoken since Venters had shocked her with his first harsh speech; but all the way she had clung to his arm, and now, as he stopped and laid his rifle against the bench, she still clung to him.

'Jane, I'm afraid I must leave you.'

'Bern!' she cried.

'Yes, it looks that way. My position is not a happy one – I can't feel right – I've lost all – '

'I'll give you anything you – '

'Listen, please. When I say loss I don't mean what you think. I mean loss of goodwill, good name – that which would have enabled me to stand up in this village without bitterness. Well, it's too late . . . Now, as to the future, I think you'd do best to give me up. Tull is implacable. You ought to see from his intention today that that – But you can't see. Your blindness – your damned religion! . . . Jane, forgive me – I'm sore within and something rankles. Well, I fear that invisible hand will turn its hidden work to your ruin.'

'Invisible hand? Bern!'

'I mean your Bishop.' Venters said it deliberately and would not release her as she started back. 'He's the law. The edict went forth to ruin me. Well, look at me! It'll now go forth to compel you to the will of the Church.'

'You wrong Bishop Dyer. Tull is hard, I know. But then he has been in love with me for years.'

'Oh, your faith and your excuses! You can't see what I know – and if you did see it you'd not admit it to save your life. That's the Mormon of you. These elders and bishops will do absolutely any deed to go on building up the power and wealth of their church, their empire. Think of what they done to the Gentiles here, to me – think of Milly Erne's fate!'

'What do you know of her story?'

'I know enough – all, perhaps, except the name of the Mormon who brought her here. But I must stop this kind of talk.'

She pressed his hand in response. He helped her to a seat beside him on the bench. And he respected a silence that he divined was full of woman's deep emotion, beyond his understanding.

It was the moment when the last ruddy rays of the sunset brightened momentarily before yielding to twilight. And for Venters the outlook before him was in some sense similar to a feeling of his future, and with searching eyes he studied the beautiful purple, barren waste of sage. Here was the unknown and the perilous. The whole scene impressed Venters as a wild, austere, and mighty manifestation of nature. And as it somehow reminded him of his prospect in life, so it suddenly resembled the woman near him, only in her there were greater beauty and peril, a mystery more unsolvable, and something nameless that numbed his heart and dimmed his eye.

'Look! A rider!' exclaimed Jane, breaking the silence. 'Can that be Lassiter?'

Venters moved his glance once more to the west. A horseman showed dark on the skyline, then merged into the colour of the sage.

'It might be. But I think not – that fellow was coming in. One of your riders, more likely. Yes, I see him clearly now. And there's another.'

'I see them, too.'

'Jane, your riders seem as many as the bunches of sage. I ran into five yesterday 'way down near the trail to Deception Pass. They were with the white herd.'

'You still go to that canyon? Bern, I wish you wouldn't. Oldring and his rustlers live somewhere down there.'

'Well, what of that?'

'Tull has already hinted of your frequent trips into Deception Pass.'

'I know.' Venters uttered a short laugh. 'He'll make a rustler of me next. But, Jane, there's no water for fifty miles after I leave here, and that nearest is in the canyon. I must drink and water my horse. There! I see more riders. They are going out.'

'The red herd is on the slope, towards the Pass.'

Twilight was fast falling. A group of horsemen crossed the dark line of low ground to become more distinct as they climbed the slope. The silence broke to a clear call from an incoming rider, and, almost like the peal of a hunting-horn, floated back the answer. The outgoing riders moved swiftly, came sharply into sight as they topped a ridge to show wild and black above the horizon, and then passed down, dimming into the purple of the sage.

'I hope they don't meet Lassiter,' said Jane.

'So do I,' replied Venters. 'By this time the riders of the night shift know what happened today. But Lassiter will likely keep out of their way.'

'Bern, who is Lassiter? He's only a name to me – a terrible name.'

'Who is he? I don't know, Jane. Nobody I ever met knows him. He talks a little like a Texan, like Milly Erne. Did you note that?'

'Yes. How strange of him to know of her! And she lived here ten years and has been dead two. Bern, what do you know of Lassiter? Tell me what he has done – why you spoke of him to Tull – threatening to become another Lassiter yourself?'

'Jane, I only heard things, rumours, stories, most of which I disbelieved. At Glaze his name was known, but none of the riders or ranchers I knew there ever met him. At Stone Bridge I never heard him mentioned. But at Sterling and villages north of there he was spoken of often. I've never been in a village which he had been known to visit. There were many conflicting stories about him and his doings. Some said he had shot up this and that Mormon village, and others denied it. I'm inclined to believe he has, and you know how Mormons hide the truth. But here was one feature about Lassiter upon which all agree – that he was what riders in this country call a gunman. He's a man with marvellous quickness and accuracy in the use of a Colt. And now that I've seen him I know more. Lassiter was born without fear. I watched him with eyes which saw him my friend. I'll never forget the moment I recognised him from what had been told me of his crouch before the draw. It was then I yelled his name.

I believe that yell saved Tull's life. At any rate, I know this, between Tull and death then there was not the breadth of the littlest hair. If he or any of his men had moved a finger downward . . . '

Venters left his meaning unspoken, but at the suggestion Jane shuddered.

The pale afterglow in the west darkened with the merging of twilight into night. The sage now spread out black and gloomy. One dim star glimmered in the south-west sky. The sound of trotting horses had ceased, and there was silence broken only by a faint, dry pattering of cottonwood leaves in the soft night wind.

Into this peace and calm suddenly broke the high-keyed yelp of a coyote, and from far off in the darkness came the faint answering note of a trailing mate.

'Hello! the sage-dogs are barking,' said Venters.

'I don't like to hear them,' replied Jane. 'At night, sometimes, when I lie awake, listening to the long mourn or breaking bark or wild howl, I think of you asleep somewhere in the sage, and my heart aches.'

'Jane, you couldn't listen to sweeter music, nor could I have a better bed.'

'Just think! Men like Lassiter and you have no home, no comfort, no rest, no place to lay your weary heads. Well! . . . Let us be patient. Tull's anger may cool, and time may help us. You might do some service to the village – who can tell! Suppose you discovered the long-unknown hiding-place of Oldring and his band, and told it to my riders? That would disarm Tull's ugly hints and put you in favour. For years my riders have trailed the tracks of stolen cattle. You know as well as I how dearly we've paid for our ranges in this wild country. Oldring drives our cattle down into that network of deceiving canyons, and somewhere far to the north or east he drives them up and out to Utah markets. If you will spend time in Deception Pass try to find the trails.'

'Jane, I've thought of that. I'll try.'

'I must go now. And it hurts, for now I'll never be sure of seeing you again. But tomorrow, Bern?'

'Tomorrow surely. I'll watch for Lassiter and ride in with him.'

'Good-night.'

Then she left him and moved away, a white, gliding shape that soon vanished in the shadows.

Venters waited until the faint slam of a door assured him she had reached the house; and then, taking up his rifle, he noiselessly slipped through the bushes, down the knoll, and on under the dark trees to the edge of the grove. The sky was now turning from grey to blue; stars had begun to lighten the earlier blackness; and from the wide flat sweep before him blew a cool wind, fragrant with the breath of sage. Keeping close to the edge of the cottonwoods, he went swiftly and silently westward. The grove was long, and he had not reached the end when he heard something that brought him to a halt. Low padded thuds told him horses were coming his way. He sank down in the gloom, waiting, listening. Much before he had expected, judging from sound, to his amazement he descried horsemen near at hand. They were riding along the border of the sage, and instantly he knew the hoofs of the horses were muffled. Then the pale starlight afforded him indistinct sight of the riders. But his eyes were keen and used to the dark, and by peering closely he recognised the huge bulk and black-bearded visage of Oldring and the lithe, supple form of the rustler's lieutenant, a masked rider. They passed on; the darkness swallowed them. Then, farther out on the sage, a dark, compact body of horsemen went by, almost without sound, almost like spectres, and they, too, melted into the night.

CHAPTER 3

Amber Spring

No unusual circumstance was it for Oldring and some of his men to visit Cottonwoods in the broad light of day, but for him to prowl about in the dark with the hoofs of his horses muffled meant that mischief was brewing. Moreover, to Venters the presence of the masked rider with Oldring seemed especially ominous. For about this man there was mystery; he seldom rode through the village, and when he did ride through it was swiftly; riders seldom met him by day on the sage; but wherever he rode there always followed deeds as dark and mysterious as the mask he wore. Oldring's band did not confine themselves to the rustling of cattle.

Venters lay low in the shade of the cottonwoods, pondering this chance meeting, and not for many moments did he consider it safe to move on. Then, with sudden impulse, he turned the other way and went back along the grove. When he reached the path leading to Jane's home he decided to go down to the village. So he hurried onwards, with quick soft steps. Once beyond the grove he entered the one and only street. It was wide, lined with tall poplars, and under each row of trees, inside the footpath, were ditches where ran the water from Jane Withersteen's spring.

Between the trees twinkled lights of cottage candles, and far down flared bright windows of the village stores. When Venters got closer to these he saw knots of men standing together in earnest conversation. The usual lounging on the corners and benches and steps was not in evidence. Keeping in the shadow, Venters went closer and closer until he could hear voices. But he could not distinguish what was said. He recognised many Mormons, and looked hard for Tull and his men but looked in vain. Venters concluded that the rustlers had not passed along the village street. No doubt these earnest men were discussing Lassiter's coming. But Venters felt positive that Tull's intention towards himself that day had not been and would not be revealed.

So Venters, seeing there was little for him to learn, began retracing his steps. The church was dark, Bishop Dyer's home next to it was also dark, and likewise Tull's cottage. Upon almost any night at this hour there would be lights here, and Venters marked the unusual omission.

As he was about to pass out of the street to skirt the grove, he once more slunk down at the sound of trotting horses. Presently he descried two mounted men riding towards him. He hugged the shadow of a tree. Again the starlight, brighter now, aided him, and he made out Tull's stalwart figure, and beside him the short, frog-like shape of the rider Jerry. They were silent, and they rode on to disappear.

Venters went his way with busy, gloomy mind, revolving events of the day, trying to reckon those brooding in the night. His thoughts overwhelmed him. Up in that dark grove dwelt a woman who had been his friend. And he skulked about her home, gripping a gun stealthily as an Indian, a man without place or people or purpose. Above her hovered the shadow of grim, hidden, secret power. No queen could have given more royally out of a bounteous store than Jane Withersteen gave her people, and likewise to those unfortunates whom her people hated. She asked only the divine right of all women – freedom; to love and to live as her heart willed. And yet prayer and her hope were vain.

'For years I've seen a storm clouding over her and the village of Cottonwoods,' muttered Venters, as he strode on. 'Soon it'll burst. I don't like the prospect.' That night the villagers whispered in the street – and night-riding rustlers muffled horses – and Tull was at work in secret – and out there in the sage hid a man who meant something terrible – Lassiter!

Venters passed the black cottonwoods, and, entering the sage, climbed the gradual slope. He kept his direction in line with a western star. From time to time he stopped to listen and heard only the usual familiar bark of coyote and sweep of wind and rustle of sage. Presently a low jumble of rocks loomed up darkly somewhat to his right, and, turning that way, he whistled softly. Out of the rocks glided a dog that leaped and whined about him. He climbed over rough, broken rock, picking his way carefully, and then went down. Here it was darker, and sheltered from the wind. A white object guided him. It was another dog, and this one was asleep, curled up between a saddle and a pack. The animal awoke and thumped his tail in greeting. Venters placed the saddle for a pillow, rolled in his blankets, with his face upward to the stars. The white dog snuggled close to him. The other whined and pattered a few yards to the rise of ground and there crouched on guard. And in that wild covert Venters shut his eyes under the great white stars and intense vaulted blue, bitterly comparing their loneliness to his own, and fell asleep.

When he awoke, day had dawned and all about him was bright steel-grey. The air had a cold tang. Arising, he greeted the fawning dogs and stretched his cramped body, and then, gathering together bunches of dead sage sticks, he lighted a fire. Strips of dried beef held to the blaze for a moment served him and the dogs. He drank from a canteen. There was nothing else in his outfit; he had grown used to a scant fare. Then he sat over the fire, palms outspread, and waited. Waiting had been his chief occupation for months, and he scarcely knew what he waited for, unless it was the passing of the hours. But now he sensed action in the immediate present; the day promised another meeting with Lassiter and Jane, perhaps news of the rustlers; on the morrow he meant to take the trail to Deception Pass.

And while he waited he talked to his dogs. He called them Ring and Whitie; they were sheep-dogs, half collie, half deer-hound, superb in build, perfectly trained. It seemed that in his fallen fortunes these dogs understood the nature of their value to him, and governed their affection and faithfulness accordingly. Whitie watched him with sombre eyes of love, and Ring, crouched on the little rise of ground above, kept tireless guard. When the sun rose, the white dog took the place of the other, and Ring went to sleep at his master's feet.

By and by Venters rolled up his blankets and tied them and his meagre pack together, then climbed out to look for his horse. He saw him, presently, a little way off in the sage, and went to fetch him. In that country, where every rider boasted of a fine mount and was eager for a race, where thoroughbreds dotted the wonderful grazing ranges, Venters rode a horse that was sad proof of his misfortunes.

Then, with his back against a stone, Venters faced the east, and, stick in hand and idle blade, he waited. The glorious sunlight filled the valley with purple fire. Before him, to left, to right, waving, rolling, sinking, rising, like low swells of a purple sea, stretched the sage. Out of the grove of cottonwoods, a green patch on the purple, gleamed the dull red of Jane Withersteen's old stone house. And from there extended the wide green of the village gardens and orchards marked by the graceful poplars; and farther down shone the deep, dark richness of the alfalfa fields. Numberless red and black and white dots speckled the sage, and these were cattle and horses.

So, watching and waiting, Venters let the time wear away. At length he saw a horse rise above a ridge, and he knew it to be Lassiter's black. Climbing to the highest rock, so that he would show against the skyline, he stood and waved his hat. The almost instant turning of Lassiter's horse attested to the quickness of that rider's eye. Then Venters climbed down, saddled his horse, tied on his pack, and, with a word to his dogs, was about to ride out to meet Lassiter, when he concluded to wait for him there, on higher ground, where the outlook was commanding.

It had been long since Venters had experienced friendly greeting from a man. Lassiter's warmed in him something that had grown cold from neglect. And when he had returned it, with a strong grip of the iron hand that held his, and met the grey eyes, he knew that Lassiter and he were to be friends.

'Venters, let's talk awhile before we go down there,' said Lassiter, slipping his bridle. 'I ain't in no hurry. Them's sure fine dogs you've got.' With a rider's eye he took in the points of Venters's horse, but did not speak his thoughts. 'Well, did anything come off after I left you last night?'

Venters told him about the rustlers.

'I was snug hid in the sage,' replied Lassiter, 'an' didn't see or hear no one. Oldrin's got a high hand here, I reckon. It's no news up in Utah how he holes in canyons an' leaves no track.' Lassiter was silent a moment. 'Me an' Oldrin' wasn't exactly strangers some years back when he drove cattle into Bostil's Ford, at the head of the Rio Virgin. But he got harassed there an' now he drives some place else.'

'Lassiter, you knew him? Tell me, is he Mormon or Gentile?'

'I can't say. I've knowed Mormons who pretended to be Gentiles.'

'No Mormon ever pretended that unless he was a rustler,' declared Venters.

'Mebbe so.'

'It's a hard country for anyone, but hardest for Gentiles. Did you ever know or hear of a Gentile prospering in a Mormon community?'

'I never did.'

'Well, I want to get out of Utah. I've a mother living in Illinois. I want to go home. It's eight years now.'

The older man's sympathy moved Venters to tell his story. He had left Quincy, run off to seek his fortune in the gold fields, had never got any farther than Salt Lake City, wandered here and there as helper, teamster, shepherd, and drifted southward over the divide and across the barrens and up the rugged plateau through the passes to the last border settlements. Here he became a rider of the sage, had stock of his own, and for a time prospered, until chance threw him in the employ of Jane Withersteen.

'Lassiter, I needn't tell you the rest.'

'Well, it'd be no news to me. I know Mormons. I've seen their women's strange love an' patience an' sacrifice an' silence an' what I call madness for their idea of God. An' over against that I've seen the tricks of the men. They work hand in hand, all together, an' in the dark. No man can hold out against them, unless he takes to packin' guns. For Mormons are slow to kill. That's the only good I ever seen in their religion. Venters, take this from me, these Mormons ain't just right in their minds. Else could a Mormon marry one woman when he already had a wife, an' call it duty?'

'Lassiter, you think as I think,' returned Venters.

'How'd it come then that you never throwed a gun on Tull or some of them?' enquired the rider, curiously.

'Jane pleaded with me, begged me to be patient, to overlook. She even took my guns from me. I lost all before I knew it,' replied Venters, with the red colour in his face. 'But, Lassiter, listen. Out of the wreck I saved a Winchester, two Colts, and plenty of shells. I packed these down into Deception Pass. There, almost every day for six months, I have practised with my rifle till the barrel burnt my hands. Practised the draw – the firing of a Colt, hour after hour!'

'Now that's interestin' to me,' said Lassiter, with a quick uplift of his head and a concentration of his grey gaze on Venters. 'Could you throw a gun before you began that practisin'?'

'Yes. And now . . . ' Venters made a lightning-swift movement.

Lassiter smiled, and then his bronzed eyelids narrowed till his eyes seemed mere grey slits. 'You'll kill Tull!' He did not question; he affirmed.

'I promised Jane Withersteen I'd try to avoid Tull. I'll keep my word. But sooner or later Tull and I will meet. As I feel now, if he even looks at me I'll draw!'

'I reckon so. There'll be hell down there, presently.' He paused a moment and flicked a sage-brush with his quirt. 'Venters, seein' as you're considerable worked up, tell me Milly Erne's story.'

Venters's agitation stilled to the trace of suppressed eagerness in Lassiter's query.

'Milly Erne's story? Well, Lassiter, I'll tell you what I know. Milly Erne had been in Cottonwoods years when I first arrived there, and most of what I tell you happened before my arrival. I got to know her pretty well. She was a slip of a woman, and crazy on religion. I conceived an idea that I never mentioned – I thought she was at heart more Gentile than Mormon. But she passed as a Mormon, and certainly she had the Mormon woman's locked lips. You know, in every Mormon village there are women who seem mysterious to us, but about Milly there was more than the ordinary mystery. When she came to Cottonwoods she had a beautiful little girl whom she loved passionately. Milly was not known openly in Cottonwoods as a Mormon wife. That she really was a Mormon wife I have no doubt. Perhaps the Mormon's other wife or wives would not acknowledge Milly. Such things happen in these villages. Mormon wives wear yokes, but they get jealous. Well, whatever had brought Milly to this country – love or madness of religion – she repented of it. She gave up teaching the village school. She quit the church. And she began to fight Mormon upbringing for her baby girl. Then the Mormons put on the screws – slowly, as is their way. At last the child disappeared. Lost, was the report. The child was stolen, I know that. So do you. That wrecked Milly Erne. But she lived on in hope. She became a slave. She worked her heart and soul and life out to get back her child. She never heard of it again. Then she sank . . . I can see her now, a frail thing, so transparent you could almost look through her – white like ashes – and her eyes! . . . Her eyes have always haunted me. She had one real friend – Jane Withersteen. But Jane couldn't mend a broken heart, and Milly died.'

For moments Lassiter did not speak, or turn his head.

'The man!' he exclaimed, presently, in husky accents.

'I haven't the slightest idea who the Mormon was,' replied Venters; 'nor has any Gentile in Cottonwoods.'

'Does Jane Withersteen know?'

'Yes. But a red-hot running-iron couldn't burn that name out of her!'

Without further speech Lassister started off, walking his horse, and Venters followed with his dogs. Half a mile down the slope they entered a luxuriant growth of willows and soon came into an open space carpeted with grass like deep green velvet. The rushing of water and singing of birds filled their ears. Venters led his comrade to a shady bower and showed him Amber Spring. It was a magnificent outburst of clear, amber water pouring from a dark, stone-lined hole. Lassiter knelt and drank, lingered there to drink again. He made no comment, but Venters did not need words. Next to his horse a rider of the sage loved a spring. And this spring was the most beautiful and remarkable known to the upland riders of southern Utah. It was the spring that made old Withersteen a feudal lord and now enabled his daughter to return the toll which her father had exacted from the toilers of the sage.

The spring gushed forth in a swirling torrent, and leaped down joyously to make its swift way along a willow-skirted channel. Moss and ferns and lilies overhung its green banks. Except for the rough-hewn stones that held and directed the water, this willow thicket and glade had been left as nature had made it.

Below were artificial lakes, three in number, one above the other in banks of raised earth; and round about them rose the lofty green-foliaged shafts of poplar trees. Ducks dotted the glassy surface of the lakes; a blue heron stood motionless on a water-gate; kingfishers darted with shrieking flight along the shady banks; a white hawk sailed above; and from the trees and shrubs came the song of robins and cat-birds. It was all in strange contrast to the endless slopes of lonely sage and the wild rock environs beyond. Venters thought of the woman who loved the birds and the green of the leaves and the murmur of water.

Next on the slope, just below the third and largest lake, were corrals and a wide stone barn and open sheds and coops and pens. Here were clouds of dust, and cracking sounds of hoofs, and romping colts and hee-hawing burros. Neighing horses trampled to the corral fences. And from the little windows of the barn projected bobbing heads of bays and blacks and sorrels. When the two men entered the immense barnyard, from all around the din increased. This welcome, however, was not seconded by the several men and boys who vanished on sight.

Venters and Lassiter were turning towards the house when Jane appeared in the lane leading a horse. In riding-skirt and blouse she seemed to have lost some of her statuesque proportions, and looked more like a girl-rider than the mistress of Withersteen. She was bright, smiling, and her greeting was warmly cordial.

'Good news,' she announced. 'I've been to the village. All is quiet. I expected – I don't know what. But there's no excitement. And Tull has ridden out on his way to Glaze.'

'Tull gone?' enquired Venters, with surprise. He was wondering what could have taken Tull away. Was it to avoid another meeting with Lassiter that he went? Could it have any connection with the probable nearness of Oldring and his gang?

'Gone, yes, thank goodness,' replied Jane. 'Now I'll have peace for a while. Lassiter, I want you to see my horses. You are a rider, and you must be a judge of horseflesh. Some of mine have Arabian blood. My father got his best strain in Nevada from Indians who claimed their horses were bred down from the original stock left by the Spaniards.'

'Well, ma'am, the one you've been ridin' takes my eye,' said Lassiter, as he walked round the racy, clean-limbed, and fine-pointed roan.

'Where are the boys?' she asked, looking about. 'Jerd, Paul, where are you? Here, bring out the horses.'

The sound of dropping bars inside the barn was the signal for the horses to jerk their heads in the windows, to snort and stamp. Then they came pounding out of the door, a file of thoroughbreds, to plunge about the barnyard, heads and tails up, manes flying. They halted afar off, squared away to look, came slowly forward with whinnies for their mistress, and doubtful snorts for the strangers and their horses.

'Come – come – come,' called Jane, holding out her hands. 'Why Bells – Wrangle, where are your manners? Come, Black Star – come, Night. Ah, you beauties! My racers of the sage!'

Only two came up to her; those she called Night and Black Star. Venters never looked at them without delight. The first was soft dead black, the other glittering black, and they were perfectly matched in size, both being high and long-bodied, wide through the shoulders, with lithe, powerful legs. That they were a woman's pets showed in the gloss of skin, the fineness of mane. It showed, too, in the light of big eyes and the gentle reach of eagerness.

'I never seen their like,' was Lassiter's encomium, 'an' in my day I've seen a sight of horses. Now, ma'am, if you was wantin' to make a long an' fast ride across the sage – say to elope – '

Lassiter ended there with dry humour, yet behind that was meaning.

677

Jane blushed and made arch eyes at him.

'Take care, Lassiter, I might think that a proposal,' she replied, gaily. 'It's dangerous to propose elopement to a Mormon woman. Well, I was expecting you. Now will be a good hour to show you Milly Erne's grave. The day-riders have gone, and the night-riders haven't come in. Bern, what do you make of that? Need I worry? You know I have to be made worry.'

'Well, it's not usual for the night shift to ride in so late,' replied Venters, slowly, and his glance sought Lassiter's. 'Cattle are usually quiet after dark. Still, I've known even a coyote to stampede your white herd.'

'I refuse to borrow trouble. Come,' said Jane.

They mounted, and, with Jane in the lead, rode down the lane, and, turning off into a cattle trail, proceeded westward. Venters's dogs trotted behind them. On this side of the ranch the outlook was different from that on the other; the immediate foreground was rough and the sage more rugged and less colourful; there were no dark-blue lines of canyons to hold the eye, nor any up-rearing rock walls. It was a long roll and slope into grey obscurity. Soon Jane left the trail and rode into the sage, and presently she dismounted and threw her bridle. The men did likewise. Then, on foot, they followed her, coming out at length on the rim of a low escarpment. She passed by several little ridges of earth to halt before a faintly defined mound. It lay in the shade of a sweeping sage-brush close to the edge of the promontory; and a rider could have jumped his horse over it without recognising a grave.

'Here!'

She looked sad as she spoke, but she offered no explanation for the neglect of an unmarked, uncared-for grave. There was a little bunch of pale, sweet lavender daisies, doubtless planted there by Jane.

'I only come here to remember and to pray,' she said. 'But I leave no trail!'

A grave in the sage! How lonely this resting-place of Milly Erne! The cottonwoods or the alfalfa fields were not in sight, nor was there any rock or ridge or cedar to lend contrast to the monotony. Grey slopes, tinging the purple, barren and wild, with the wind waving the sage, swept away to the dim horizon.

Lassiter looked at the grave and then out into space. At that moment he seemed a figure of bronze.

Jane touched Venters's arm and led him back to the horses.

'Bern!' cried Jane, when they were out of hearing. 'Suppose Lassiter were Milly's husband – the father of that little girl lost so long ago!'

'It might be, Jane. Let us ride on. If he wants to see us again he'll come.'

So they mounted and rode out to the cattle trail and began to climb. From the height of the ridge, where they had started down, Venters looked back. He did not see Lassiter, but his glance, drawn irresistibly farther out on the gradual slope, caught sight of a moving cloud of dust.

'Hello, a rider!'

'Yes, I see,' said Jane.

'That fellow's riding hard. Jane, there's something wrong.'

'Oh yes, there must be . . . How he rides!'

The horse disappeared in the sage, and then puffs of dust marked his course.

'He's short-cut on us – he's making straight for the corrals.'

Venters and Jane galloped their steeds and reined in at the turning of the lane. This lane led down to the right of the grove. Suddenly into its lower entrance flashed a bay horse. Then Venters caught the fast rhythmic beat of pounding hoofs. Soon his keen eye recognised the swing of the rider in his saddle.

'It's Judkins, your Gentile rider!' he cried. 'Jane, when Judkins rides like that it means hell!'

CHAPTER 4

Deception Pass

The rider thundered up and almost threw his foam-flecked horse in the sudden stop. He was of giant form, and with fearless eyes.

'Judkins, you're all bloody!' cried Jane, in affright. 'Oh, you've been shot!'

'Nothin' much, Miss Withersteen. I got a nick in the shoulder. I'm some wet an' the hoss's been throwin' lather, so all this aint blood.'

'What's up?' queried Venters, sharply.

'Rustlers sloped off with the red herd.'

'Where are my riders?' demanded Jane.

'Miss Withersteen, I was alone all night with the herd. At daylight this mornin' the rustlers rode down. They began to shoot at me on sight. They chased me hard an' far, burnin' powder all the time, but I got away.'

'Jud, they meant to kill you,' declared Venters.

'Now I wonder,' returned Judkins. 'They wanted me bad. An' it ain't regular for rustlers to waste time chasin' one rider.'

'Thank Heaven you got away,' said Jane. 'But my riders – where are they?'

'I don't know. The night-riders weren't there last night when I rode down, an' this mornin' I met no day-riders.'

'Judkins! Bern! they've been set upon – killed by Oldring's men!'

'I don't think so,' replied Venters, decidedly. 'Jane, your riders haven't gone out in the sage.'

'Bern, what do you mean?' Jane Withersteen turned deathly pale.

'You remember what I said about the unseen hand?'

'Oh! . . . Impossible!'

'I hope so. But I fear – ' Venters finished, with a shake of his head.

'Bern, you're bitter; but that's only natural. We'll wait to see what's happened to my riders. Judkins, come to the house with me. Your wound must be attended to.'

'Jane, I'll find out where Oldring drives the herd,' vowed Venters.

'No, no! Bern, don't risk it now – when the rustlers are in such shooting mood.'

'I'm going. Jud, how many cattle in that red herd?'

'Twenty-five hundred head.'

'Whew! What on earth can Oldring do with so many cattle? Why, a hundred head is a big steal. I've got to find out.'

'Don't go,' implored Jane.

'Bern, you want a hoss thet can run. Miss Withersteen, if it's not too bold of me to advise, make him take a fast hoss or don't let him go.'

'Yes, yes, Judkins. He must ride a horse that can't be caught. Which one – Black Star – Night?'

'Jane, I won't take either,' said Venters, emphatically. 'I wouldn't risk losing one of your favourites.'

'Wrangle, then?'

'Thet's the hoss,' replied Judkins. 'Wrangle can outrun Black Star an' Night. You'd never believe it, Miss Withersteen, but I know. Wrangle's the biggest an' fastest hoss on the sage.'

'Oh, no Wrangle can't beat Black Star. But, Bern, take Wrangle, if you will go. Ask Jerd for anything you need. Oh, be watchful, careful . . . God speed you!'

She clasped his hand, turned quickly away, and went down the lane with the rider.

Venters rode to the barn, and, leaping off, shouted for Jerd. The boy came running. Venters sent him for meat, bread, and dried fruits, to be packed in saddle-bags. His own horse he turned loose into the nearest corral. Then he went for Wrangle. The giant sorrel had earned his name for a trait the opposite of amiability. He came readily out of the barn, but once in the yard he broke from Venters, and plunged about with ears laid back. Venters had to rope him, and then he kicked down a section of fence, stood on his hind legs, crashed down and fought the rope. Jerd returned to lend a hand.

'Wrangle don't git enough work,' said Jerd, as the big saddle went on. 'He's unruly when he's corralled, an' wants to run. Wait till he smells the sage!'

'Jerd, this horse is an iron-jawed devil. I never straddled him but once. Run? Say, he's swift as wind!'

When Venters's boot touched the stirrup the sorrel bolted, giving him the rider's flying mount. The swing of this fiery horse recalled to Venters days that were not really long past, when he rode into the sage as the leader of Jane Withersteen's riders. Wrangle pulled hard on a tight rein. He galloped out of the lane, down the shady border of the grove, and hauled up at the watering-trough, where he pranced and champed his bit. Venters got off and filled his canteen while the horse drank. The dogs, Ring and Whitie, came trotting up for their drink. Then Venters remounted and turned Wrangle towards the sage.

A wide, white trail wound away down the slope. One keen, sweeping glance told Venters that there was neither man nor horse nor steer within the limit of his vision, unless they were lying down in the sage. Ring loped in the lead and Whitie loped in the rear. Wrangle settled gradually into an easy swinging canter, and Venters's thoughts, now that the rush and flurry of the start were past, and the long miles stretched before him, reverted to a calm reckoning of late singular coincidences.

There was the night ride of Tull's, which, viewed in the light of subsequent events, had a look of his covert machinations; Oldring and his Masked Rider and his rustlers riding muffled horses; the report that Tull had ridden out that moment with his man Jerry on the trail to Glaze, the strange disappearance of Jane Withersteen's riders, the unusually determined attempt to kill the one Gentile still in her employ, an intention frustrated, no doubt, only by Judkins's magnificent riding of her racer, and lastly the driving of the red herd. These events, to Venters's colour of mind, had a dark relationship. Remembering Jane's accusation of bitterness, he tried hard to put aside his rancour in judging Tull. But it was bitter knowledge that made him see the truth. He had felt the shadow of an unseen hand; he had watched till he saw its dim outline, and then he had traced it to a man's hate, to the rivalry of a Mormon Elder, to the power of a Bishop, to the long, far-reaching arm of a terrible creed. That unseen hand had made its first move against Jane Withersteen. Her riders had been called in, leaving her without help to drive seven thousand head of cattle. But to Venters it seemed extraordinary that the power which had called in these riders had left so many cattle to be driven by rustlers and harried by wolves. For hand in glove with that power was an insatiate greed; they were one and the same.

'What can Oldring do with twenty-five hundred head of cattle?' muttered Venters. 'Is he a Mormon? Did he meet Tull last night? It looks like a black plot to me. But Tull and his churchmen wouldn't ruin Jane Withersteen unless the Church was to profit by that ruin. Where does Oldring come in? I'm going to find out about these things.'

Wrangle did twenty-five miles in three hours and walked little of the way. When he had got warmed up he had been allowed to choose his own gait. The afternoon had well advanced when Venters struck the trail of the red herd and found where it had grazed the night before. Then Venters rested the horse and used his eyes. Near at hand were a cow and a calf and several yearlings, and farther out in the sage some straggling steers. He caught a glimpse of coyotes skulking near the cattle. The slow, sweeping gaze of the rider failed to find other living things within the field of sight. The sage about him was breast-high to his horse, oversweet with its warm, fragrant breath, grey where it waved to the light, darker where the wind left it still, and beyond the wonderful haze-purple lent by distance. Far across that wide waste came the slow lift of uplands through which Deception Pass cut its tortuous many canyoned way.

Venters raised the bridle of his horse and followed the broad cattle trail. The crushed sage resembled the path of a monster snake. In a few miles of travel he passed several cows and calves that had escaped the drive. Then he stood on the last high bench of the slope with the floor of the valley beneath. The opening of the canyon showed in a break of the sage, and the cattle trail paralleled it as far as he could see. That trail led to an undiscovered point where Oldring drove cattle into the pass, and many a rider who had followed it had never returned. Venters satisfied himself that the rustlers had not deviated from their usual course, and then he turned at right angles off the cattle trail and made for the head of the pass.

The sun lost its heat and wore down to the western horizon, where it changed from white to gold and rested like a huge ball about to roll on its golden shadows down the slope. Venters watched the lengthening of the rays and bars, and marvelled at his own league-long shadow. The sun sank. There was instant shading of brightness about him, and he saw a kind of cold purple bloom creep ahead of him to cross the canyon, to mount the opposite slope and chase and darken and bury the last golden flare of sunlight.

Venters rode into a trail that he always took to get down into the canyon. He dismounted and found no tracks but his own made several days previous. Nevertheless he sent the dog Ring ahead and waited. In a little while Ring returned. Whereupon Venters led his horse on to the break in the ground.

The opening into Deception Pass was one of the remarkable natural phenomena in a country remarkable for vast slopes of sage, uplands insulated by gigantic red walls, and deep canyons of mysterious source and outlet. Here the valley floor was level, and here opened a narrow chasm, a ragged vent in yellow walls of stone. The trail down the five hundred feet of sheer depth always tested Venters's nerve. It was bad going for even a burro. But Wrangle, as Venters led him, snorted defiance or disgust rather than fear, and, like a hobbled horse on the jump, lifted his ponderous iron-shod fore hoofs and crashed down over the first rough step. Venters warmed to greater admiration of the sorrel; and, giving him a loose bridle, he stepped down foot by foot. Oftentimes the stones and shale started by Wrangle buried Venters to his knees; again he was hard put to it to dodge a rolling boulder; there were times when he could not see Wrangle for dust, and once he and the horse rode a sliding shelf of yellow, weathered cliff. It was a trail on which there could be no stops, and, therefore, if perilous, it was at least one that did not take long in the descent.

Venters breathed lighter when that was over, and felt a sudden assurance in the success of his enterprise. For at first it had been a reckless determination to achieve something at any cost, and now it resolved itself into an adventure worthy of all his reason and cunning, and keenness of eye and ear.

Pinyon pines clustered in little clumps along the level floor of the pass. Twilight had gathered under the walls. Venters rode into the trail and up the canyon. Gradually the trees and caves and objects low down turned black, and this blackness moved up the walls till night enfolded the pass, while day still lingered above. The sky darkened; and stars began to show, at first pale and then bright. Sharp notches of the rim-wall, biting like teeth into the blue, were landmarks by which Venters knew where his camping site lay. He had to feel his way through a thicket of slender oaks to a spring where he watered Wrangle and drank himself. Here he unsaddled and turned Wrangle loose, having no fear that the horse would leave the thick, cool grass adjacent to the spring. Next he satisfied his own hunger, fed Ring and Whitie, and, with them curled beside him, composed himself to await sleep.

There had been a time when night in the high altitude of these Utah uplands had been satisfying to Venters. But that was before the oppression of enemies had made the change in his mind. As a rider guarding the herd he had never thought of the night's wildness and loneliness; as an outcast, now when the full silence set in, and the deep darkness, and trains of radiant stars shone cold and calm, he lay with an ache in his heart. For a year he had lived as a black fox, driven from his kind. He longed for the sound of a voice, the touch of a hand. In the daytime there was riding from place to place, and the gun practice to which something drove him, and other tasks that at least necessitated action; at night, before he won sleep there was strife in his soul. He yearned to leave the endless sage slopes, the wilderness of canyons; and it was in the lonely night that this yearning grew unbearable. It was then that he reached forth to feel Ring or Whitie, immeasurably grateful for the love and companionship of two dogs.

On this night the same old loneliness beset Venters, the old habit of sad thought and burning unquiet had its way. But from it evolved a conviction that his useless life had undergone a subtle change. He had sensed it first when Wrangle swung him up to the high saddle, he knew it now when he lay in the gateway of Deception Pass. He had no thrill of adventure, rather a gloomy perception of great hazard, perhaps death. He meant to find Oldring's retreat. The rustlers had fast horses, but none that could catch Wrangle. Venters knew no rustler could creep upon him at night when Ring and Whitie guarded his hiding-place. For the rest, he had eyes and ears, and a long rifle and an unerring aim, which he meant to use. Strangely his foreshadowing of change did not hold a thought of the killing of Tull. It related only to what was to happen to him in Deception Pass; and he could no more lift the veil of that mystery than tell where the trails led to in that unexplored canyon. Moreover, he did not care. And at length, tired out by stress of thought, he fell asleep.

When his eyes unclosed, day had come again, and he saw the rim of the opposite wall tipped with the gold of sunrise. A few moments sufficed for the morning's simple camp duties. Near at hand he found Wrangle, and to his surprise the horse came to him. Wrangle was one of the horses that left his viciousness in the home corral. What he wanted was to be free of mules and burros and steers, to roll in dust-patches, and then to run down the wide, open, windy sage-plains, and at night browse and sleep in the cool wet grass of a spring-hole. Jerd knew the sorrel when he said of him, 'Wait till he smells the sage!'

Venters saddled and led him out of the oak thicket, and, leaping astride, rode up the canyon, with Ring and Whitie trotting behind. An old grass-grown trail followed the course of a shallow wash where flowed a thin stream of water. The canyon was a hundred rods wide; its yellow walls were perpendicular; it had abundant sage and a scant growth of oak and Pinyon. For five miles it held to a comparatively straight bearing, and then began a heightening of rugged walls and a deepening of the floor. Beyond this point of sudden change in the character of the canyon Venters had never explored, and here was the real door to the intricacies of Deception Pass.

He reined Wrangle to a walk, halted now and then to listen, and then proceeded cautiously with shifting and alert gaze. The canyon assumed proportions that dwarfed those of its first ten miles. Venters rode on and on, not losing in the interest of his wide surroundings any of his caution or keen search for tracks or sight of living thing. If there ever had been a trail here, he could not find it. He rode through sage and clumps of pinyon trees and grassy plots where long petalled purple lilies bloomed. He rode though a dark constriction of the pass no wider than the lane in the grove at Cottonwoods. And he came out into a great amphitheatre in which jutted huge towering corners of a confluence of intersecting canyons.

Venters sat his horse, and, with a rider's eye, studied this wild cross-cut of huge stone gullies. Then he went on, guided by the course of running water. If it had not been for the main stream of water flowing north he would never have been able to tell which of those many openings was a continuation of the pass. In crossing this amphitheatre he went by the mouths of five canyons, fording little streams that flowed into the larger one. Gaining the outlet which he took to be the pass, he rode on again under overhanging walls. One side was dark in shade, the other light in sun. This narrow passageway turned and twisted and opened into a valley that amazed Venters.

Here again was a sweep of purple sage, richer than upon the higher levels. The valley was miles long, several wide, and enclosed by unscalable walls. But it was the background of this valley that so forcibly struck him. Across the sage-flat rose a strange up-flinging of yellow rocks. He could not tell which were close and which were distant. Scrawled mounds of stone, like mountain waves, seemed to roll up to steep bare slopes and towers.

In this plain of sage Venters flushed birds and rabbits, and when he had proceeded about a mile he caught sight of the bobbing white tails of a herd of running antelope. He rode along the edge of the stream which wound towards the western end of the slowly looming mounds of stone. The high slope retreated out of sight behind the nearer projection. To Venters the valley appeared to have been filled in by a mountain of melted stone that had hardened in strange shapes of rounded outline. He followed the stream till he lost it in a deep cut. Therefore Venters quit the dark slit which baffled further search in that direction, and rode out along the curved edge of stone where it met the sage. It was not long before he came to a low place, and here Wrangle readily climbed up.

All about him was ridgy roll of wind-smoothed, rain-washed rock. Not a tuft of grass or a bunch of sage coloured the dull rust-yellow. He saw where, to the right, this uneven flow of stone ended in a blunt wall. Leftward, from the hollow that lay at his feet, mounted a gradual slow-swelling slope to a great height topped by leaning, cracked, and ruined crags. Not for some time did he grasp the wonder of that acclivity. It was no less than a mountain-side, glistening in the sun like polished granite, with cedar trees springing as if by magic out of the denuded surface. Winds had swept it clear of weathered shale, and rains had washed it free of dust. Far up the curved slope its beautiful lines broke to meet the vertical rim-wall, to lose its grace in a different order and colour of rock, a stained yellow cliff of cracks and caves and seamed crags. And straight before Venters was a scene less striking but more significant to his keen survey. For beyond a mile of the bare, hummocky rock began the valley of sage, and the mouths of canyons, one of which surely was another gateway into the pass.

*   *   *

686

He got off his horse, and, giving the bridle to Ring to hold, he commenced a search for the cleft where the stream ran. He was not successful and concluded the water dropped into an underground passage. Then he returned to where he had left Wrangle, and led him down off the stone to the sage. It was a short ride to the opening canyons. There was no reason for a choice of which one to enter. The one he rode into was a clear, sharp shaft in yellow stone a thousand feet deep, with wonderful wind-worn caves low down and high above buttressed and turreted ramparts. Farther on Venters came into a region where deep indentations marked the line of canyon walls. These were huge, cove-like blind pockets extending back to a sharp corner with a dense growth of underbrush and trees.

Venters penetrated into one of these offshoots, and, as he had hoped, he found abundant grass. He had to bend the oak saplings to get his horse through. Deciding to make this a hiding-place if he could find water, he worked back to the limit of the shelving walls. In a little cluster of silver spruces he found a spring. This enclosed nook seemed an ideal place to leave his horse and to camp at night, and from which to make stealthy trips on foot. The thick grass hid his trail; the dense growth of oaks in the opening would serve as a barrier to keep Wrangle in, if, indeed, the luxuriant browse would not suffice for that. So Venters, leaving Whitie with the horse, called Ring to his side, and, rifle in hand, worked his way out to the open. A careful photographing in mind of the formation or the bold outlines of rim-rock assured him he would be able to return to his retreat, even in the dark.

Bunches of scattered sage covered the centre of the canyon, and among these Venters threaded his way with the step of an Indian. At intervals he put his hand on the dog and stopped to listen. There was a drowsy hum of insects, but no other sound disturbed the warm midday stillness. Venters saw ahead a turn, more abrupt than any yet. Warily he rounded this corner, once again to halt bewildered.

The canyon opened fan-shaped into a great oval of green and grey growths. It was the hub of an oblong wheel, and from it, at regular distances, like spokes, ran the outgoing canyons. Here a dull red colour predominated over the fading yellow. The corners of wall bluntly rose, scarred and scrawled, to taper into towers and serrated peaks and pinnacled domes.

Venters pushed on more heedfully than ever. Towards the centre of this circle the sage-brush grew smaller and farther apart. He was about to sheer off to the right, where thickets and jumbles of fallen rock would afford him cover, when he ran right upon a broad cattle trail. Like a road it was, more than a trail; and the cattle tracks were fresh. What surprised him more, they were wet! He pondered over this feature. It had not rained. The only solution to his puzzle was that the cattle had been driven through water, and water deep enough to wet their legs.

Suddenly Ring growled low. Venters rose cautiously and looked over the sage. A band of straggling horsemen were riding across the oval. He sank down, startled and trembling. 'Rustlers!' he muttered. Hurried he glanced about for a place to hide. Near at hand there was nothing but sage-brush. He dared not risk crossing the open patches to reach the rocks. Again he peeped over the sage. The rustlers – four – five – seven – eight in all, were approaching, but not directly in line with him. That was relief for a cold deadness which seemed to be creeping inward along his veins. He crouched down with bated breath and held the bristling dog.

He heard the click of iron-shod hoofs on stone, the coarse laughter of men, and then voices gradually dying away. Long moments passed. Then he rose. The rustlers were riding into a canyon. Their horses were tired, and they had several pack animals; evidently they had travelled far. Venters doubted that they were the rustlers who had driven the red herd. Oldring's band had split. Venters watched these horsemen disappear under a bold canyon wall.

The rustlers had come from the northwest side of the oval. Venters kept a steady gaze in that direction, hoping, if there were more, to see from what canyon they rode. A quarter of an hour went by. Reward for his vigilance came when he descried three more mounted men, far over to the north. But out of what canyon they had ridden it was too late to tell. He watched the three ride across the oval and round the jutting red corner where the others had gone.

'Up that canyon!' exclaimed Venters. 'Oldring's den! I've found it!'

A knotty point for Venters was the fact that the cattle tracks all pointed west. The broad trail came from the direction of the canyon into which the rustlers had ridden, and undoubtedly the cattle had been driven out of it across the oval. There were no tracks pointing the other way. It had been in his mind that Oldring had driven the red herd towards the rendezvous, and not from it. Where did that broad trail come down into the pass, and where did it lead? Venters knew he wasted time in pondering the question, but it held a fascination not easily dispelled. For many years Oldring's mysterious entrance and exit to Deception Pass had been all-absorbing topics to sage-riders.

All at once the dog put an end to Venters's pondering. Ring sniffed the air, turned slowly in his tracks with a whine, and then growled. Venters wheeled. Two horsemen were within a hundred yards, coming straight at him. One, lagging behind the other, was Oldring's Masked Rider.

Venters cunningly sank, slowly trying to merge into sage-brush. But, guarded as his action was, the first horse detected it. He stopped short, snorted, and shot up his ears. The rustler bent forward, as if keenly peering ahead. Then, with a swift sweep, he jerked a gun from its sheath and fired.

The bullet zipped through the sage-brush. Flying bits of wood struck Venters, and the hot, stinging pain seemed to lift him in one leap. Like a flash the blue barrel of his rifle gleamed level and he shot once – twice.

The foremost rustler dropped his weapon and toppled from his saddle, to fall with his foot catching in a stirrup. The horse snorted wildly and plunged away, dragging the rustler through the sage.

The Masked Rider huddled over his pommel, slowly swaying to one side, and then, with a faint, strange cry slipped out of the saddle.

CHAPTER 5

The Masked Rider

Venters looked quickly from the fallen rustlers to the canyon where the others had disappeared. He calculated on the time needed for running horses to return to the open, if their riders heard shots. He waited breathlessly. But the estimated time dragged by and no riders appeared. Venters began presently to believe that the rifle reports had not penetrated into the recesses of the canyon, and felt safe for the immediate present.

He hurried to the spot where the first rustler had been dragged by his horse. The man lay in deep grass, dead, jaw fallen, eyes protruding – a sight that sickened Venters. The first man at whom he had ever aimed a weapon he had shot through the heart. With the clammy sweat oozing from every pore Venters dragged the rustler in among some boulders and covered him with slabs of rock. Then he smoothed out the crushed trail in grass and sage. The rustler's horse had stopped a quarter of a mile off and was grazing.

When Venters rapidly strode towards the Masked Rider not even the cold nausea that gripped him could wholly banish curiosity. For he had shot Oldring's infamous lieutenant, whose face had never been seen. Venters experienced a grim pride in the feat. What would Tull say to this achievement of the outcast who rode too often to Deception Pass?

Venters's curious eagerness and expectation had not prepared him for the shock he received when he stood over a slight, dark figure. The rustler wore the black mask that had given him his name, but he had no weapons. Venters glanced at the drooping horse; there were no gun-sheaths on the saddle.

'A rustler who didn't pack guns!' muttered Venters. 'He wears no belt. He couldn't pack guns in that rig . . . Strange!'

A low, gasping intake of breath and a sudden twitching of body told Venters the rider still lived.

'He's alive! . . . I've got to stand here and watch him die. And I shot an unarmed man.'

Shrinkingly Venters removed the rider's wide sombrero and the black cloth mask. This action disclosed bright chestnut hair, inclined to curl, and a white, youthful face. Along the lower line of cheek and jaw was a clear demarcation, where the brown of tanned skin met the white that had been hidden from the sun.

'Oh, he's only a boy! . . . What! Can he be Oldring's Masked Rider?'

The boy showed signs of returning consciousness. He stirred; his lips moved; a small brown hand clenched in his blouse.

Venters knelt with a gathering horror of his deed. His bullet had entered the rider's right breast, high up to the shoulder. With hands that shook, Venter's untied a black scarf and ripped open the blood-wet blouse.

First he saw a gaping hole, dark red against a whiteness of skin, from which welled a slender red stream. Then the graceful, beautiful swell of a woman's breast!

'A woman!' he cried. 'A girl! . . . I've killed a girl!'

She suddenly opened eyes that transfixed Venters. They were fathom-less blue. Consciousness of death was there, a blended terror and pain, but no consciousness of sight. She did not see Venters. She stared into the unknown.

Then came a spasm of vitality. She writhed in a torture of reviving strength, and in her convulsions she almost tore from Venters's grasp. Slowly she relaxed and sank partly back. The ungloved hand sought the wound, and pressed so hard her wrist half buried itself in her bosom. Blood trickled between her spread fingers. And she looked at Venters with eyes that saw him.

He cursed himself and the unerring aim of which he had been so proud. He had seen that look in the eyes of a crippled antelope which he was about to finish with his knife. But in her it had infinitely more – a revelation of mortal spirit. The instinctive clinging to life was there, and the divining helplessness and the terrible accusation of the stricken.

'Forgive me! I didn't know!' burst out Venters.

'You shot me – you've killed me!' she whispered, in panting gasps. Upon her lips appeared a fluttering, bloody froth. By that Venters knew the air in her lungs was mixing with blood. 'Oh, I knew – it would – come – someday! . . . Oh, the burn! . . . Hold me – I'm sinking – it's all dark . . . Ah, God! . . . Mercy – '

Her rigidity loosened in one long quiver and she lay back limp, still, white as snow, with closed eyes.

Venters thought then that she died. But the faint pulsation of her breast assured him that life yet lingered. Death seemed only a matter of moments, for the bullet had gone clear through her. Nevertheless, he tore sage-leaves from a bush, and, pressing them tightly over her wounds, he bound the black scarf round her shoulder, tying it securely under her arm. Then he closed the blouse, hiding from his sight that blood-stained, accusing breast.

'What – now?' he questioned, with flying mind. 'I must get out of here. She's dying – but I can't leave her.'

He rapidly surveyed the sage to the north and made out no animate object. Then he picked up the girl's sombrero and the mask. This time the mask gave him as great a shock as when he first removed it from her face. For in the woman he had forgotten the rustler, and this black strip of felt-cloth established the identity of Oldring's Masked Rider. Venters had solved the mystery. He slipped his rifle under her, and, lifting her carefully upon it, he began to retrace his steps. The dog trailed in his shadow. And the horse, that had stood drooping by, followed without a call. Venters chose the deepest tufts of grass and clumps of sage on his return. From time to time he glanced over his shoulder. He did not rest. His concern was to avoid jarring the girl and to hide his trail. Gaining the narrow canyon, he turned and held close to the wall till he reached his hiding-place. When he entered the dense thicket of oaks he was hard put to it to force a way through. But he held his burden almost upright, and by slipping sidewise and bending the saplings he got in. Through sage and grass he hurried to the grove of silver spruces.

He laid the girl down, almost fearing to look at her. Though marble pale and cold, she was living. Venters then appreciated the tax that long carry had been to his strength. He sat down to rest. Whitie sniffed at the pale girl and whined and crept to Venters's feet. Ring lapped the water in the runway of the spring.

Presently Venters went out to the opening, caught the horse, and, leading him through the thicket, unsaddled him and tied him with a long halter. Wrangle left his browsing long enough to whinny and toss his head. Venters felt that he could not rest easily till he had secured the other rustler's horse; so, taking his rifle and calling for Ring, he set out. Swiftly yet watchfully he made his way through the canyon to the oval and out to the cattle trail. What few tracks might have betrayed him he obliterated, so only an expert tracker could have trailed him. Then, with many a wary backward glance across the sage, he started to round up the rustler's horse. This was unexpectedly easy. He led the horse to lower ground, out of sight from the opposite side of the oval, along the shadowy western wall, and so on into his canyon and secluded camp.

The girl's eyes were open; a feverish spot burned in her cheeks; she moaned something unintelligible to Venters, but he took the movement of her lips to mean that she wanted water. Lifting her head, he tipped the canteen to her lips. After that she again lapsed into unconsciousness or a weakness which was its counterpart. Venters noted, however, that the burning flush had faded into the former pallor.

The sun set behind the high canyon rim, and a cool shade darkened the walls. Venters fed the dogs and put a halter on the dead rustler's horse. He allowed Wrangle to browse free. This done, he cut spruce boughs and made a lean-to for the girl. Then, gently lifting her upon a blanket, he folded the sides over her. The other blanket he wrapped about his shoulders and found a comfortable seat against a spruce tree that upheld the little shack. Ring and Whitie lay near at hand, one asleep, the other watchful.

Venters dreaded the night's vigil. At night his mind was active, and this time he had to watch and think and feel beside a dying girl whom he had all but murdered. A thousand excuses he invented for himself, yet not one made any difference in his act or his self-reproach.

It seemed to him that when night fell black he could see her white face so much more plainly.

'She'll go, presently,' he said, 'and be out of agony – thank God!'

Every little while certainty of her death came to him with a shock; and then he would bend over and lay his ear on her breast. Her heart still beat.

The early night blackness cleared to the cold starlight. The horses were not moving, and no sound disturbed the deathly silence of the canyon.

'I'll bury her here,' thought Venters, 'and let her grave be as much a mystery as her life was.'

For the girl's few words, the look of her eyes, the prayer, had strangely touched Venters.

'She was only a girl,' he soliloquised. 'What was she to Oldring? Rustlers don't have wives nor sisters nor daughters. She was bad – that's all. But somehow . . . well, she may not have willingly become the companion of rustlers. That prayer of hers to God for mercy! . . . Life is strange and cruel. I wonder if other members of Oldring's gang are women? Likely enough. But what was his game? Oldring's Masked Rider! A name to make villagers hide and lock their doors. A name credited with a dozen murders, a hundred forays, and a thousand stealings of cattle. What part did the girl have in this? It may have served Oldring to create mystery.'

Hours passed. The white stars moved across the narrow strip of dark-blue sky above. The silence awoke to the low hum of insects. Venters watched the immovable white face, and as he watched, hour by hour waiting for death, the infamy of her passed from his mind. He thought only of the sadness, the truth of the moment. Whoever she was – whatever she had done – she was young and she was dying.

The after-part of the night wore on interminably. The starlight failed and the gloom blackened to the darkest hour. 'She'll die at the grey of dawn,' muttered Venters, remembering some old woman's fancy. The blackness paled to grey, and the grey lightened and day peeped over the eastern rim. Venters listened at the breast of the girl. She still lived. Did he only imagine that her heart beat stronger, ever so slightly, but stronger? He pressed his ear closer to her breast. And he rose with his own pulse quickening.

'If she doesn't die soon – she's got a chance – the barest chance – to live,' he said.

He wondered if the internal bleeding had ceased. There was no more film of blood upon her lips. But no corpse could have been whiter. Opening her blouse, he untied the scarf, and carefully picked away the sage-leaves from the wound in her shoulder. It had closed. Lifting her lightly, he ascertained that the same was true of the hole where the bullet had come out. He reflected on the fact that clean wounds closed quickly in the healing upland air. He recalled instances of riders who had been cut and shot, apparently to fatal issues; yet the blood had clotted, the wounds closed, and they had recovered. He had no way to tell if internal haemorrhage still went on, but he believed that it had stopped. Otherwise she would surely not have lived so long. He marked the entrance of the bullet, and concluded that it had just touched the upper lobe of her lung. Perhaps the wound in the lung had also closed. As he began to wash the blood stains from her breast and carefully rebandage the wound, he was vaguely conscious of a strange, grave happiness in the thought that she might live.

Broad daylight and a hint of sunshine high on the cliff-rim to the west brought him to consideration of what he had better do. And while busy with his few camp tasks he revolved the thing in his mind. It would not be wise for him to remain long in his present hiding-place. And if he intended to follow the cattle trail and try to find the rustlers he had better make a move at once. For he knew that rustlers, being riders, would not make much of a day's or night's absence from camp for one or two of their number; but when the missing ones failed to show up in reasonable time there would be a search. And Venters was afraid of that.

'A good tracker could trail me,' he muttered. 'And I'd be cornered here. Let's see. Rustlers are a lazy set when they're not on the ride. I'll risk it. Then I'll change my hiding-place.'

He carefully cleaned and reloaded his guns. When he rose to go he bent a long glance down upon the unconscious girl. Then, ordering Whitie and Ring to keep guard, he left the camp.

The safest cover lay close under the wall of the canyon, and here through the dense thickets Venters made his slow, listening advance towards the oval. Upon gaining the wide opening he decided to cross it and follow the left wall till he came to the cattle trail. He scanned the oval as keenly as if hunting for antelope. Then, stooping, he stole from one cover to another, taking advantage of rocks and bunches of sage, until he had reached the thickets under the opposite wall. Once there, he exercised extreme caution in his surveys of the ground ahead, but increased his speed when moving. Dodging from bush to bush, he passed the mouths of two canyons, and in the entrance of a third canyon he crossed a wash of swift, clear water, to come abruptly upon the cattle trail.

It followed the low bank of the wash, and, keeping it in sight, Venters hugged the line of sage and thicket. Like the curves of a serpent the canyon wound for a mile or more and then opened into a valley. Patches of red showed clear against the purple of sage, and farther out on the level dotted strings of red led away to the wall of rock.

'Ha, the red herd!' exclaimed Venters.

Then dots of white and black told him there were cattle of other colours in this enclosed valley. Oldring, the rustler, was also a rancher. Venters's calculating eye took count of stock that outnumbered the red herd.

'What a range!' went on Venters. 'Water and grass enough for fifty thousand head, and no riders needed!'

After his first burst of surprise and rapid calculation Venters lost no time there, but slunk again into the sage on his back trail. With the discovery of Oldring's hidden cattle-range had come enlightenment on several problems. Here the rustler kept his stock; here was Jane Withersteen's red herd; here were the few cattle that had disappeared from the Cottonwoods slopes during the last two years. Until Oldring had driven the red herd his thefts of cattle for that time had not been more than enough to supply meat for his men. Of late no drives had been reported from Sterling or the villages north. And Venters knew that the riders had wondered at Oldring's inactivity in that particular field. He and his band had been active enough in their visits to Glaze and Cottonwoods; they always had gold; but of late the amount gambled away and drunk and thrown away in the villages had given rise to much conjecture. Oldring's more frequent visits had resulted in new saloons, and where there had formerly been one raid or shooting fray in the little hamlets there were now many. Perhaps Oldring had another range farther on up the pass, and from there drove the cattle to distant Utah towns where he was little known. But Venters came finally to doubt this. And, from what he had learned in the last few days, a belief began to form in Venters's mind that Oldring's intimidations of the villages and the mystery of the Masked Rider, with his alleged evil deeds, and the fierce resistance offered any trailing riders, and the rustling of cattle – these things were only the craft of the rustler-chief to conceal his real life and purpose and work in Deception Pass.

And like a scouting Indian Venters crawled through the sage of the oval valley, crossed trail after trail on the north side, and at last entered the canyon out of which headed the cattle trail, and into which he had watched the rustlers disappear.

If he had used caution before, now he strained every nerve to force himself to creeping stealth and to sensitiveness of ear. He crawled along so hidden that he could not use his eyes except to aid himself in the toilsome progress through the brakes and ruins of cliff-wall. Yet from time to time, as he rested, he saw the massive red walls growing higher and wilder, more looming and broken. He made note of the fact that he was turning and climbing. The sage and thickets of oak and brakes of alder gave place to pinyon pine growing out of rocky soil. Suddenly a low, dull murmur assailed his ears. At first he thought it was thunder, then the slipping of a weathered slope of rock. But it was incessant, and as he progressed it filled out deeper and from a murmur changed into a soft roar.

'Falling water,' he said. 'There's volume to that. I wonder if it's the stream I lost.'

The roar bothered him, for he could hear nothing else. Likewise, however, no rustlers could hear him. Emboldened by this, and sure that nothing but a bird could see him, he arose from his hands and knees to hurry on. An opening in the pinyons warned him that he was nearing the height of slope.

He gained it, and dropped low with a burst of astonishment. Before him stretched a short canyon with rounded stone floor bare of grass or sage or tree, and with curved, shelving walls. A broad rippling stream flowed towards him, and at the back of the canyon a waterfall burst from a wide rent in the cliff, and, bounding down in two green steps, spread into a long white sheet.

If Venters had not been indubitably certain that he had entered the right canyon his astonishment would not have been so great. There had been no breaks in the walls, no side canyons entering this one where the rustlers tracks and the cattle trail had guided him, and, therefore, he could not be wrong. But here the canyon ended, and presumably the trails also.

'That cattle trail headed out of here,' Venters kept saying to himself. 'It headed out. Now what I want to know is how on earth did cattle ever get in there?'

If he could be sure of anything it was of the careful scrutiny he had given that cattle track, every hoof-mark of which headed straight west. He was now looking east at an immense round boxed corner of canyon down which tumbled a thin, white veil of water, scarcely twenty yards wide. Somehow, somewhere, his calculations had gone wrong. For the first time in years he found himself doubting his rider's skill in finding tracks, and his memory of what he had actually seen. In his anxiety to keep under cover he must have lost himself in this offshoot of Deception Pass, and thereby, in some unaccountable manner, missed the canyon with the trails. There was nothing else for him to think. Rustlers could not fly, nor cattle jump down thousand-foot precipices. He was only proving what the sage-riders had long said of this labyrinthine system of deceitful canyons and valleys – trails led down into Deception Pass, but no rider had ever followed them.

On a sudden he heard above the soft roar of the waterfall an unusual sound that he could not define. He dropped flat behind a stone and listened. From the direction he had come swelled something that resembled a strange muffled pounding and splashing and ringing. Despite his nerve the chill sweat began to dampen his forehead. What might not be possible in this stonewalled maze of mystery? The unnatural sound passed beyond him as he lay gripping his rifle and fighting for coolness. Then from the open came the sound, now distinct and different. Venters recognised a hobble-bell of a horse, and the cracking of iron on submerged stones, and the hollow splash of hoofs in water.

Relief surged over him. His mind caught again at realities, and curiosity prompted him to peep from behind the rock.

In the middle of the stream waded a long string of packed burros driven by three superbly mounted men. Had Venters met these dark-clothed, dark-visaged, heavily armed men anywhere in Utah, let alone in this robbers' retreat, he would have recognised them as rustlers. The discerning eye of a rider saw the signs of a long, arduous trip. These men were packing in supplies from one of the northern villages. They were tired, and their horses were almost played out, and the burros plodded on, after the manner of their kind when exhausted, faithful and patient, but as if every weary, splashing, slipping step would be their last.

All this Venters noted in one glance. After that he watched with a thrilling eagerness. Straight at the waterfall the rustlers drove the burrows, and straight through the middle where the water spread into a fleecy, thin film like dissolving smoke. Following closely, the rustlers rode into this white mist, showing in bold black relief for an instant, and then they vanished.

Venters drew a full breath that rushed out in brief and sudden utterance.

'Good Heaven! Of all the holes for a rustler! . . . There's a cavern under that waterfall, and a passageway leading out to a canyon beyond. Oldring hides in there. He needs only to guard a trail leading down from

the sage-flat above. Little danger of this outlet to the pass being discovered. I stumbled on it by luck, after I had given up. And now I know
the truth of what puzzled me most – why that cattle trail was wet!'

He wheeled and ran down the slope, and out to the level of the sagebrush. Returning, he had no time to spare, only now and then, between
dashes, a moment when he stopped to cast sharp eyes ahead. The
abundant grass left no trace of his trail. Short work he made of the
distance to the circle of canyons. He doubted that he would ever see it
again; he knew he never wanted to; yet he looked at the red corners and
towers with the eyes of a rider picturing landmarks never to be forgotten.

Here he spent a panting moment in a slow-circling gaze of the sage-
oval and the gaps between the bluffs. Nothing stirred except the gentle
wave of the tips of the brush. Then he pressed on past the mouths of
several canyons and over ground new to him, now close under the eastern
wall. This latter part proved to be easy travelling, well screened from
possible observation from the north and west, and he soon covered it and
felt safer in the deepening shade of his own canyon. Then the huge,
notched bulge of red rim loomed over him, a mark by which he knew
again the deep cove where his camp lay hidden. As he penetrated the
thicket, safe again for the present, his thoughts reverted to the girl he had
left there. The afternoon had far advanced. How would he find her? He
ran into camp, frightening the dogs.

The girl lay with wide-open, dark eyes, and they dilated when he knelt
beside her. The flush of fever shone in her cheeks. He lifted her and held
water to her dry lips, and felt an inexplicable sense of lightness as he saw
her swallow in a slow, choking gulp. Gently he laid her back.

'Who – are – you?' she whispered, haltingly.

'I'm the man who shot you,' he replied.

'You'll – not – kill me – now?'

'No, no.'

'What – will – you – do – with me?'

'When you get better – strong enough – I'll take you back to the
canyon where the rustlers ride through the waterfall.'

As with a faint shadow from a flitting wing overhead, the marble
whiteness of her face seemed to change.

'Don't – take – me – back – there!'

CHAPTER 6

The Mill-Wheel of Steers

Meantime, at the ranch, when Judkins's news had sent Venters on the trail of the rustlers, Jane Withersteen led the injured man to her house and with skilled fingers dressed the gunshot wound in his arm.

'Judkins, what do you think happened to my riders?'

'I – I'd rather not say,' he replied.

'Tell me. Whatever you'll tell me I'll keep to myself. I'm beginning to worry about more than the loss of a herd of cattle. Venters hinted of – but tell me, Judkins.'

'Well, Miss Withersteen, I think as Venters thinks – your riders have been called in.'

'Judkins! . . . By whom?'

'You know who handles the reins of your Mormon riders.'

'Do you dare insinuate that my churchmen have ordered in my riders?'

'I ain't insinuatin' nothin', Miss Withersteen,' answered Judkins, with spirit. 'I know what I'm talking about. I didn't want to tell you.'

'Oh, I can't believe that! I'll not believe it! Would Tull leave my herds at the mercy of rustlers and wolves just because – because – ? No, no! It's unbelievable.'

'Yes, thet particular thing's onheard of around Cottonwoods. But, beggin' pardon, Miss Withersteen, there never was any other rich Mormon woman here on the border, let alone one thet's taken the bit between her teeth.'

That was a bold thing for the reserved Judkins to say, but it did not anger her. This rider's crude hint of her spirit gave her a glimpse of what others might think. Humility and obedience had been hers always. But had she taken the bit between her teeth? Still she wavered. And then, with a quick spurt of warm blood along her veins, she thought of Black Star when he got the bit fast between his iron jaws and ran wild in the sage. If she ever started to run! Jane smothered the glow and burn within her, ashamed of a passion for freedom that opposed her duty.

'Judkins, go to the village,' she said, 'and when you have learned anything definite about my riders please come to me at once.'

When he had gone Jane resolutely applied her mind to a number of tasks that of late had been neglected. Her father had trained her in the management of a hundred employees and the working of gardens and fields; and to keep record of the movements of cattle and riders. And beside the many duties she had added to this work was one of extreme delicacy, such as required all her tact and ingenuity. It was an unobtrusive, almost secret aid which she rendered to the Gentile families of the village. Though Jane Withersteen never admitted so to herself, it amounted to no less than a system of charity. But for her invention of numberless kinds of employment, for which there was no actual need, these families of Gentiles, who had failed in a Mormon community, would have starved.

In aiding these poor people Jane thought she deceived her keen churchmen, but it was a kind of deceit for which she did not pray to be forgiven. Equally as difficult was the task of deceiving the Gentiles, for they were as proud as they were poor. It had been a great grief to her to discover how these people hated her people; and it had been a source of great joy that through her they had come to soften in hatred. At any time this work called for a clearness of mind that precluded anxiety and worry; but under the present circumstances it required all her vigour and obstinate tenacity to pin her attention upon her task.

Sunset came, bringing with the end of her labour a patient calmness and power to wait that had not been hers earlier in the day. She expected Judkins, but he did not appear. Her house was always quiet; tonight, however, it seemed unusually so. At supper her women served her with a silent assiduity; it spoke what their sealed lips could not utter – the sympathy of Mormon women. Jerd came to her with the key of the great door of the stone stable, and to make his daily report about the horses. One of his daily duties was to give Black Star and Night and the other racers a ten-mile run. This day it had been omitted, and the boy grew confused in explanations that she had not asked for. She did enquire if he would return on the morrow, and Jerd, in mingled surprise and relief, assured her he would always work for her. Jane missed the rattle and trot, canter and gallop of the incoming riders on the hard trails. Dusk shaded the grove where she walked; the birds ceased singing; the wind sighed through the leaves of the cottonwoods, and the running water murmured down its stone-bedded channel. The glimmering of the first star was like the peace and beauty of the night. Her faith welled up in her heart and said that all would soon be right in her little world. She pictured Venters about his lonely camp-fire sitting between his faithful dogs. She prayed for his safety, for the success of his undertaking.

Early the next morning one of Jane's women brought in word that Judkins wished to speak to her. She hurried out, and in her surprise to see him armed with rifle and revolver, she forgot her intention to enquire about his wound.

'Judkins! Those guns? You never carried guns.'

'It's high time, Miss Withersteen,' he replied. 'Will you come into the grove? It ain't jest exactly safe for me to be seen here.'

She walked with him into the shade of the cottonwoods.

'What do you mean?'

'Miss Withersteen, I went to my mother's house last night. While there, someone knocked, an' a man asked for me. I went to the door. He wore a mask. He said I'd better not ride any more for Jane Withersteen. His voice was hoarse an' strange, disguised, I reckon, like his face. He said no more, an' ran off in the dark.'

'Did you know who he was?' asked Jane, in a low voice.

'Yes.'

Jane did not ask to know; she did not want to know; she feared to know. All her calmness fled at a single thought.

'Thet's why I'm packin' guns,' went on Judkins. 'For I'll never quit ridin' for you, Miss Withersteen, till you let me go.'

'Judkins, do you want to leave me?'

'Do I look thet way? Give me a hoss – a fast hoss, an' send me out on the sage.'

'Oh, thank you, Judkins! You're more faithful than my own people. I ought not accept your loyalty – you might suffer more through it. But what in the world can I do? My head whirls. The wrong to Venters – the stolen herd – these masks, threats, this coil in the dark! I can't understand! But I feel something dark and terrible closing in around me.'

'Miss Withersteen, it's all simple enough,' said Judkins, earnestly. 'Now please listen – an' beggin' your pardon – jest turn thet deaf Mormon ear aside, an' let me talk clear an' plain in the other. I went around to the saloons an' the stores an' the loafin' places yesterday. All your riders are in. There's talk of a vigilance band organised to hunt down rustlers. They call themselves 'The Riders.' Thet's the report – thet's the reason given for your riders leavin' you. Strange thet only a few riders of other ranchers joined the band! An' Tull's man, Jerry Card – he's the leader. I seen him an' his hoss. He ain't been to Glaze. I'm not easy to fool on the looks of a hoss thet's travelled the sage. Tull an' Jerry didn't ride to Glaze! . . . Well, I met Blake an' Dorn, both good friends of mine, usually, as far as their Mormon lights will let 'em go. But these fellers couldn't fool me, an' they didn't try very hard. I asked them straight out like a man, why they left you like thet. I didn't forget to mention how you nursed Blake's poor old mother when she was sick, an' how good you was to Dorn's kids. They looked ashamed, Miss Withersteen. An' they jest froze up – thet dark set look thet makes them strange an' different to me. But I could tell the difference between thet first natural twinge of conscience an' the later look of some secret thing. An' the difference I caught was thet they couldn't help themselves. They hadn't no say in the matter. They looked as if their bein' unfaithful to you was bein' faithful to a higher duty. An' there's the secret. Why, it's as plain as – as sight of my gun here.'

'Plain! . . . My herds to wander in the sage – to be stolen! Jane Withersteen a poor woman! Her head to be brought low and her spirit broken! . . . Why, Judkins, it's plain enough.'

'Miss Withersteen, let me get what boys I can gather, an' hold the white herd. It's on the slope now, not ten miles out – three thousand head, an' all steers. They're wild, an' likely to stampede at the pop of a jack-rabbit's ears. We'll camp right with them, an' try to hold them.'

'Judkins, I'll reward you someday for your service, unless all is taken from me. Get the boys and tell Jerd to give you pick of my horses, except Black Star and Night. But – do not shed blood for my cattle nor heedlessly risk your lives.'

Jane Withersteen rushed to the silence and seclusion of her room, and there could not longer hold back the bursting of her wrath. She went stone-blind in the fury of a passion that had never before showed its power. Lying upon her bed, sightless, voiceless, she was a writhing, living flame. And she tossed there while her fury burned and burned, and finally burned itself out.

Then, weak and spent, she lay thinking, not of the oppression that would break her, but of this new revelation of self. Until the last few days there had been little in her life to rouse passions. Her forefathers had been Vikings, savage chieftains who bore no cross and brooked no hindrance to their will. Her father had inherited that temper; and at times, like antelope fleeing before fire on the slope, his people fled from his red rages. Jane Withersteen realised that the spirit of wrath and war had lain dormant in her. She shrank from black depths hitherto unsuspected. The one thing in man or woman that she scorned above all scorn, and which she could not forgive, was hate. Hate headed a flaming pathway straight to hell. All in a flash, beyond her control there had been in her a birth of fiery hate. And the man who had dragged her peaceful and loving spirit to this degradation was a minister of God's word, an Elder of her church, the counsellor of her beloved Bishop.

The loss of herds and ranges, even of Amber Spring and the Old Stone House, no longer concerned Jane Withersteen; she faced the foremost thought of her life, what she now considered the mightiest problem – the salvation of her soul.

She knelt by her bedside and prayed; she prayed as she had never prayed in all her life – prayed to be forgiven for her sin; to be immune from that dark, hot hate; to love Tull as her minister, though she could not love him as a man; to do her duty by her church and people and those dependent upon her bounty; to hold reverence of God and womanhood inviolate.

When Jane Withersteen rose from that storm of wrath and prayer for help she was serene, calm, sure – a changed woman. She would do her duty as she saw it, live her life as her own truth guided her. She might never be able to marry a man of her choice, but she certainly never would become the wife of Tull. Her churchmen might take her cattle and horses, ranges and fields, her corrals and stables, the house of Withersteen and the water that nourished the village of Cottonwoods; but they could not force her to marry Tull, they could not change her decision or break her spirit. Once resigned to further loss, and sure of herself, Jane Withersteen attained a peace of mind that had not been hers for a year. She forgave Tull, and felt a melancholy regret over what she knew he considered duty, irrespective of his personal feeling for her. First of all, Tull, as he was a man, wanted her for himself; and secondly, he hoped to save her and her riches for his church. She did not believe that Tull had been actuated solely by his minister's zeal to save her soul. She doubted her interpretation of one of his dark sayings – that if she were lost to him she might as well be lost to heaven. Jane Withersteen's common sense took arms against the binding limits of her religion; and she doubted that her Bishop, whom she had been taught had direct communication with God – would damn her soul for refusing to marry a Mormon. As for Tull and his churchmen, when they had harassed her, perhaps made her poor, they would find her unchangeable, and then she would get back most of what she had lost. So she reasoned, true at last to her faith in all men, and in their ultimate goodness.

The clank of iron hoofs upon the stone courtyard drew her hurriedly from her retirement. There, beside his horse, stood Lassiter, his dark apparel and the great black gun-sheaths contrasting singularly with his gentle smile. Jane's active mind took up her interest in him and her half-determined desire to use what charm she had to foil his evident design in visiting Cottonwoods. If she could mitigate his hatred of Mormons, or at least keep him from killing more of them, not only would she be saving her people, but also be leading back this blood-spiller to some semblance of the human.

'Mornin', ma'am,' he said, black sombrero in hand.

'Lassiter, I'm not an old woman, or even a madam,' she replied, with her bright smile. 'If you can't say Miss Withersteen – call me Jane.'

'I reckon Jane would be easier. First names are always handy for me.'

'Well, use mine, then. Lassiter, I'm glad to see you. I'm in trouble.'

Then she told him of Judkins's return, of the driving of the red herd, of Venters's departure on Wrangle, and the calling-in of her riders.

' 'Pears to me you're some smilin' an' pretty for a woman with so much trouble,' he remarked.

'Lassiter! Are you paying me compliments? But, seriously, I've made up my mind not to be miserable. I've lost much, and I'll lose more. Nevertheless, I won't be sour, and I hope I'll never be unhappy – again.'

Lassiter twisted his hat round and round, as was his way, and took his time in replying.

'Women are strange to me. I got to back-trailin' myself from them long ago. But I'd like a game woman. Might I ask, seein' as how you take this trouble, if you're goin' to fight?'

'Fight! How? Even if I would, I haven't a friend except that boy who doesn't dare stay in the village.'

'I make bold to say, ma'am – Jane – that there's another, if you want him.'

'Lassiter! . . . Thank you. But how can I accept you as a friend? Think! Why, you'd ride down into the village with those terrible guns and kill my enemies – who are also my churchmen.'

'I reckon I might be riled up to jest about that,' he replied, dryly.

She held out both hands to him.

'Lassiter! I'll accept your friendship – be proud of it – return it – if I may keep you from killing another Mormon.'

'I'll tell you one thing,' he said, bluntly, as the grey lightning formed in his eyes. 'You're too good a woman to be sacrificed as you're goin' to be . . . No, I reckon you an' me can't be friends on such terms.'

In her earnestness she stepped closer to him, repelled yet fascinated by the sudden transition of his moods. That he would fight for her was at once horrible and wonderful.

'You came here to kill a man – the man whom Milly Erne –'

'The man who dragged Milly Erne to hell – put it that way! . . . Jane Withersteen, yes, that's why I came here. I'd tell so much to no other livin' soul . . . There 're things such a woman as you'd never dream of – so don't mention her again. Not till you tell me the name of the man!'

'Tell you! I? Never!'

'I reckon you will. An' I'll never ask you. I'm a man of strange beliefs an' ways of thinkin', an' I seem to see into the future an' feel things hard to explain. The trail I've been followin' for so many years was twisted an' tangled, but it's straightenin' out now. An', Jane Withersteen, you crossed it long ago to ease poor Milly's agony. That, whether you want or not, makes Lassiter your friend. But you cross it now strangely to mean somethin' to me – God knows what! – unless by your noble blindness to incite me to greater hatred of Mormon men.'

Jane felt swayed by a strength that far exceeded her own. In a clash of wills with this man she would go to the wall. If she were to influence him it must be wholly through womanly allurement. There was that about Lassiter which commanded her respect; she had abhorred his name; face to face with him, she found she feared only his deeds. His mystic suggestion, his foreshadowing of something that she was to mean to him, pierced deep into her mind. She believed fate had thrown in her way the lover or husband of Milly Erne. She believed that through her an evil man might be reclaimed. His allusion to what he called her blindness terrified her. Such a mistaken idea of his might unleash the bitter, fatal mood she sensed in him. At any cost she must placate this man; she knew the die was cast, and that if Lassiter did not soften to a woman's grace and beauty and wiles, then it would be because she could not make him.

'I reckon you'll hear no more such talk from me,' Lassiter went on, presently. 'Now, Miss Jane, I rode in to tell you that your herd of white steers is down on the slope behind them big ridges. An' I seen somethin' goin' on that'd be mighty interestin' to you, if you could see it. Have you a field-glass?'

'Yes, I have two glasses. I'll get them and ride out with you. Wait, Lassiter, please,' she said, and hurried within. Sending word to Jerd to saddle Black Star and fetch him to the court, she then went to her room and changed to the riding-clothes she always donned when going into the sage. In this male attire her mirror showed her a jaunty, handsome rider. If she expected some little meed of admiration from Lassiter, she had no cause for disappointment. The gentle smile that she liked, which made of him another person, slowly overspread his face.

'If I didn't take you for a boy!' he exclaimed. 'It's powerful queer what difference clothes make. Now I've been some scared of your dignity, like when the other night you was all in white, but in this rig – '

Black Star came pounding into the court, dragging Jerd half off his feet, and he whistled at Lassiter's black. But at sight of Jane all his defiant lines seemed to soften, and with tosses of his beautiful head he whipped his bridle.

'Down, Black Star, down,' said Jane.

He dropped his head, and, slowly lengthening, he bent one foreleg, then the other, and sank to his knees. Jane slipped her left foot in the stirrup, swung lightly into the saddle, and Black Star rose with a ringing stamp. It was not easy for Jane to hold him to a canter through the grove, and like the wind he broke when he saw the sage. Jane let him have a couple of miles of free running on the open trail, and then she coaxed him in and waited for her companion. Lassiter was not long in catching up, and presently they were riding side by side. It reminded her how she used to ride with Venters. Where was he now? She gazed far down the slope to the curved purple lines of Deception Pass, and involuntarily shut her eyes with a trembling stir of nameless fear.

'We'll turn off here,' Lassiter said, 'an' take to the sage a mile or so. The white herd is behind them big ridges.'

'What are you going to show me?' asked Jane. 'I'm prepared – don't be afraid.'

He smiled as if he meant that bad news came swiftly enough without being presaged by speech.

When they reached the lee of a rolling ridge Lassiter dismounted, motioning to her to do likewise. They left the horses standing, bridles down. Then Lassiter, carrying the field-glasses, began to lead the way up the slow rise of ground. Upon nearing the summit he halted her with a gesture.

'I reckon we'd see more if we didn't show ourselves against the sky,' he said. 'I was here less than a hour ago. Then the herd was seven or eight miles south, an' if they ain't bolted yet – '

'Lassiter! . . . Bolted?'

'That's what I said. Now let's see.'

Jane climbed a few more paces behind him and then peeped over the ridge. Just beyond began a shallow swale that deepened and widened into a valley and then swung to the left. Following the undulating sweep of sage, Jane saw the straggling lines and then the great body of the white herd. She knew enough about steers, even at a distance of four or five miles, to realise that something was in the wind. Bringing her field-glass into use, she moved it slowly from left to right, which action swept the whole herd into range. The stragglers were restless; the more compactly massed steers were browsing. Jane brought the glass back to the big sentinels of the herd, and she saw them trot with quick steps, stop short and toss wide horns, look everywhere, and then trot in another direction.

'Judkins hasn't been able to get his boys together yet,' said Jane. 'But he'll be there soon. I hope not too late. Lassiter, what's frightening those big leaders?'

'Nothin' jest on the minute,' replied Lassiter. 'Them steers are quietin' down. They've been scared, but not bad yet. I reckon the whole herd has moved a few miles this way since I was here.'

'They didn't browse that distance – not in less than an hour. Cattle aren't sheep.'

'No, they jest run it, an' that looks bad.'

'Lassiter, what frightened them?' repeated Jane impatiently.

'Put down your glass. You'll see at first better with a naked eye. Now look along them ridges on the other side of the herd, the ridges where the sun shines bright on the sage ... That's right. Now look an' look hard an' wait.'

Long-drawn moments of straining sight rewarded Jane with nothing save the low, purple rim of ridge and the shimmering sage.

'It's begun again!' whispered Lassiter, and he gripped her arm. 'Watch ... There, did you see that?'

'No, no. Tell me what to look for?'

'A white flash – a kind of pin-point of quick light – a gleam as from sun shinin' on somethin' white.'

Suddenly Jane's concentrated gaze caught a fleeting glint. Quickly she brought her glass to bear on the spot. Again the purple sage, magnified in colour and size and wave, for long moments irritated her with its monotony. Then from out of the sage on the ridge flew up a broad, white object, flashed in the sunlight, and vanished. Like magic it was, and bewildered Jane.

'What on earth is that?'

'I reckon there's someone behind that ridge throwin' up a sheet or a white blanket to reflect the sunshine.'

'Why?' queried Jane, more bewildered than ever.

'To stampede the herd,' replied Lassiter, and his teeth clicked.

'Ah!' She made a fierce, passionate movement, clutched the glass tightly, shook as with the passing of a spasm, and then dropped her head. Presently she raised it to greet Lassiter with something like a smile. 'My righteous brethren are at work again,' she said, in scorn. She had stifled the leap of her wrath, but for perhaps the first time in her life a bitter derision curled her lips. Lassiter's cool grey eyes seemed to pierce her. 'I said I was prepared for anything; but that was hardly true. But why would they – anybody stampede my cattle?'

'That's a Mormon's godly way of bringin' a woman to her knees.'

'Lassiter, I'll die before I ever bend my knees. I might be led; I won't be driven. Do you expect the herd to bolt?'

'I don't like the looks of them big steers. But you can never tell. Cattle sometimes stampede as easily as buffalo. Any little flash or move will start them. A rider gettin down an' walkin' towards them sometimes will make them jump an' fly. Then again nothin' seems to scare them. But I reckon that white flare will do the biz. It's a new one on me, an' I've seen some ridin' an' rustlin'. It jest takes one of them God-fearin' Mormons to think of devilish tricks.'

'Lassiter, might not this trick be done by Oldring's men?' asked Jane, ever grasping at straws.

'It might be, but it ain't,' replied Lassiter. 'Oldrin's an honest thief. He don't skulk behind ridges to scatter your cattle to the four winds. He rides down on you, an' if you don't like it you can throw a gun.'

Jane bit her tongue to refrain from championing men who at the very moment were proving to her that they were little and mean compared even with rustlers.

'Look! . . . Jane, them leadin' steers have bolted! They're drawin' the stragglers, an' that'll pull the whole herd.'

Jane was not quick enough to catch the details called out by Lassiter, but she saw the line of cattle lengthening. Then, like a stream of white bees pouring from a huge swarm, the steers stretched out from the main body. In a few moments, with astonishing rapidity, the whole herd got into motion. A faint roar of trampling hoofs came to Jane's ears, and gradually swelled; low, rolling clouds of dust began to rise above the sage.

'It's a stampede, an' a hummer,' said Lassiter.

'Oh, Lassiter! The herd's running with the valley! It leads into the canyon! There's a straight jump-off!'

'I reckon they'll run into it, too. But that's a good many miles yet. An' Jane, this valley swings round almost north before it goes east. That stampede will pass within a mile of us.'

The long, white, bobbing line of steers streaked swiftly through the sage, and a funnel-shaped dust-cloud arose at a low angle. A dull rumbling filled Jane's ears.

'I'm thinkin' of millin' that herd,' said Lassiter. His grey glance swept up the slope to the west. 'There's some specks an' dust way off towards the village. Mebbe that's Judkins an' his boys. It ain't likely he'll get here in time to help. You'd better hold Black Star here on this high ridge.'

He ran to his horse and, throwing off saddle-bags and tightening the cinches, he leaped astride and galloped straight down across the valley.

Jane went for Black Star and, leading him to the summit of the ridge, she mounted and faced the valley with excitement and expectancy. She had heard of milling stampeded cattle, and knew it was a feat accomplished by only the most daring riders.

The white herd was now strung out in a line two miles long. The dull rumble of thousands of hoofs deepened into continuous low thunder, and as the steers swept swiftly closer the thunder became a heavy roll. Lassiter crossed in a few moments the level of the valley to the eastern rise of ground and there waited the coming of the herd. Presently, as the head of the white line reached a point opposite to where Jane stood, Lassiter spurred his black into a run.

Jane saw him take a position on the off side of the leaders of the stampede, and there he rode. It was like a race. They swept on down the valley, and when the end of the white line neared Lassiter's first stand the head had begun to swing round to the west. It swung slowly and stubbornly, yet surely, and gradually assumed a long, beautiful curve of moving white. To Jane's amaze she saw the leaders swinging, turning till they headed back towards her and up the valley. Out to the right of these wild, plunging steers ran Lassiter's black, and Jane's keen eye appreciated the fleet stride and sure-footedness of the blind horse. Then it seemed that the herd moved in a great curve, a huge half-moon, with the points of head and tail almost opposite, and a mile apart. But Lassiter relentlessly crowded the leaders, sheering them to the left, turning them little by little. And the dust-blinded wild followers plunged on madly in the tracks of their leaders. This ever-moving, ever-changing curve of steers rolled towards Jane, and when below her, scarce half a mile, it began to narrow and close into a circle. Lassiter had ridden parallel with her position, turned towards her, then aside, and now he was riding directly away from her, all the time pushing the head of that bobbing line inward.

It was then that Jane, suddenly understanding Lassiter's feat, stared and gasped at the riding of this intrepid man. His horse was fleet and tireless, but blind. He had pushed the leaders around and around till they were about to turn in on the inner side of the end of that line of steers. The leaders were already running in a circle; the end of the herd was still running almost straight. But soon they would be wheeling. Then, when Lassiter had the circle formed, how would he escape? With Jane Withersteen prayer was as ready as praise; and she prayed for this man's safety. A circle of dust began to collect. Dimly, as through a yellow veil, Jane saw Lassiter press the leaders inwards to close the gap in the sage. She lost sight of him in the dust; again she thought she saw the black, riderless now, rear and drag himself and fall. Lassiter had been thrown – lost! Then he reappeared running out of the dust into the sage. He had escaped, and she breathed again.

Spellbound, Jane Withersteen watched this stupendous mill-wheel of steers. Here was the milling of the herd. The white running circle closed in upon the open space of sage. And the dust circles closed above into a pall. The ground quaked and the incessant thunder of pounding hoofs rolled on. Jane felt deafened, yet she thrilled to a new sound. As the circle of sage lessened the steers began to bawl, and when it closed entirely there came a great upheaval in the centre, and a terrible thumping of heads and clicking of horns. Bawling, climbing, goring, the great mass of steers on the inside wrestled in a crashing din, heaved and groaned under the pressure. Then came a deadlock. The inner strife ceased, and the hideous roar and crash. Movement went on in the outer circle, and that, too, gradually stilled. The white herd had come to a stop, and the pall of yellow dust began to drift away on the wind.

Jane Withersteen waited on the ridge with full and grateful heart. Lassiter appeared, making his weary way towards her through the sage. And up on the slope Judkins rode into sight with his troop of boys. For the present, at least, the white herd would be looked after.

When Lassiter reached her and laid his hand on Black Star's mane, Jane could not find speech.

'Killed – my – hoss,' he panted.

'Oh! I'm sorry,' cried Jane. 'Lassiter! I know you can't replace him, but I'll give you any one of my racers – Bells, or Night, even Black Star.'

'I'll take a fast hoss, Jane, but not one of your favourites,' he replied. 'Only – will you let me have Black Star now an' ride him over there an' head off them fellers who stampeded the herd?'

He pointed to several moving specks of black and puffs of dust in the purple sage.

'I can head them off with this hoss, an' then – '

'Then, Lassiter?'

'They'll never stampede no more cattle.'

'Oh! No! No! . . . Lassiter, I won't let you go!'

But a flush of fire flamed in her cheeks, and her trembling hands shook Black Star's bridle, and her eyes fell before Lassiter's.

CHAPTER 7

The Daughter of Withersteen

'Lassiter, will you be my rider?' Jane had asked him.

'I reckon so,' he had replied.

Few as the words were, Jane knew how infinitely much they implied. She wanted him to take charge of her cattle and horses and ranges, and save them if that were possible. Yet, though she could not have spoken aloud all she meant, she was perfectly honest with herself. Whatever the price to be paid, she must keep Lassiter close to her; she must shield from him the man who had lured Milly Erne to Cottonwoods. In her fear she so controlled her mind that she did not whisper this Mormon's name to her own soul, she did not even think it. Besides, beyond this thing she regarded as a sacred obligation thrust upon her, was the need of a helper, of a friend, of a champion in this critical time. If she could rule this gunman, as Venters had called him, if she could even keep him from shedding blood, what strategy to play his name and his presence against the game of oppression her churchmen were waging against her? Never would she forget the effect upon Tull and his men when Venters shouted Lassiter's name. If she could not wholly control Lassiter, then what she could do might put off the fatal day.

One of her safe racers was a dark bay, and she called him Bells because of the way he struck his iron shoes on the stones. When Jerd led out this slender, beautifully built horse Lassiter suddenly became all eyes. A rider's love of a thoroughbred shone in them. Round and round Bells he walked, plainly weakening all the time in his determination not to take one of Jane's favourite racers.

'Lassiter, you're half horse, and Bells sees it already,' said Jane, laughing. 'Look at his eyes. He likes you. He'll love you, too. How can you resist him? Oh, Lassiter, but Bells can run! it's nip and tuck between him and Wrangle, and only Black Star can beat him. He's too spirited a horse for a woman. Take him. He's yours.'

'I jest am weak where a hoss's concerned,' said Lassiter. 'I'll take him, an' I'll take your orders, ma'am.'

'Well, I'm glad, but never mind the ma'am. Let it still be Jane.'

From that hour, it seemed, Lassiter was always in the saddle, riding early and late; and coincident with his part in Jane's affairs the days assumed their old tranquillity. Her intelligence told her this was only the lull before the storm, but her faith would not have it so.

She resumed her visits to the village, and upon one of these she encountered Tull. He greeted her as he had before any trouble came between them, and she, responsive to peace if not quick to forget, met him halfway with manner almost cheerful. He regretted the loss of her cattle; he assured her that the vigilantes which had been organised would soon rout the rustlers; when that had been accomplished her riders would likely return to her.

'You've done a headstrong thing to hire this man Lassiter,' Tull went on, severely. 'He came to Cottonwoods with evil intent.'

'I had to have somebody. And perhaps making him my rider may turn out best in the end for the Mormons of Cottonwoods.'

'You mean to stay his hand?'

'I do – if I can.'

'A woman like you can do anything with a man. That would be well, and would atone in some measure for the errors you have made.'

He bowed and passed on. Jane resumed her walk with conflicting thoughts. She resented Elder Tull's cold, impassive manner that looked down upon her as one who had incurred his just displeasure. Otherwise he would have been the same calm, dark-browed, impenetrable man she had known for ten years. In fact, except when he had revealed his passion in the matter of the seizing of Venters, she had never dreamed he could be other than the grave, reproving preacher. He stood out now a strange, secretive man. She would have thought better of him if he had picked up the threads of their quarrel where they had parted. Was Tull what he appeared to be? The question flung itself involuntarily over Jane Withersteen's inhibitive habit of faith without question. And she refused to answer it. Tull could not fight in the open. Venters had said, Lassiter had said, that her Elder shirked fight and worked in the dark. Just now in this meeting Tull had ignored the fact that he had sued, exhorted, demanded that she marry him. He made no mention of Venters. His manner was that of the minister who had been outraged, but who overlooked the frailties of a woman. Beyond question he seemed unutterably aloof from all knowledge of pressure being brought to bear upon her, absolutely guiltless of any connection with secret power over riders, with night journeys, with rustlers and stampedes of cattle. And that convinced her again of unjust suspicions. But it was convincement through an obstinate faith. She shuddered as she accepted it, and that shudder was the nucleus of a terrible revolt.

Jane turned into one of the wide lanes leading from the main street and entered a huge, shady yard. Here were sweet-smelling clover, alfalfa, flowers, and vegetables, all growing in happy confusion. And like these fresh green things were the dozens of babies, tots, toddlers, noisy urchins, laughing girls, a whole multitude of children of one family. For Collier Brandt, the father of all this numerous progeny, was a Mormon with four wives.

The big house where they lived was old, solid, picturesque, the lower part built of logs, the upper of rough clapboards, with vines growing up the outside stone chimneys. There were many wooden-shuttered windows, and one pretentious window of glass, proudly curtained in white. As this house had four mistresses, it likewise had four separate sections, not one of which communicated with another, and all had to be entered from the outside.

In the shade of a wide, low, vine-roofed porch Jane found Brandt's wives entertaining Bishop Dyer. They were motherly women, of comparatively similar ages, and plain-featured, and just at this moment anything but grave. The Bishop was rather tall, of stout build, with iron-grey hair and beard, and eyes of light blue. They were merry now; but Jane had seen them when they were not, and then she feared him as she had feared her father.

The women flocked around her in welcome.

'Daughter of Withersteen,' said the Bishop, gaily, as he took her hand, 'you have not been prodigal of your gracious self of late. A Sabbath without you at service! I shall reprove Elder Tull.'

'Bishop, the guilt is mine. I'll come to you and confess,' Jane replied, lightly; but she felt the undercurrent of her words.

'Mormon love-making!' exclaimed the Bishop, rubbing his hands. 'Tull keeps you all to himself.'

'No. He is not courting me.'

'What? The laggard! If he does not make haste I'll go a-courting myself up to Withersteen House.'

There was laughter and further bantering by the Bishop, and then mild talk of village affairs, after which he took his leave, and Jane was left with her friend, Mary Brandt.

'Jane, you're not yourself. Are you sad about the rustling of the cattle? But you have so many, you are so rich.'

Then Jane confided in her, telling much, yet holding back her doubts and fears.

'Oh, why don't you marry Tull and be one of us?'

'But, Mary, I don't love Tull,' said Jane, stubbornly.

'I don't blame you for that. But, Jane Withersteen, you've got to choose between the love of man and love of God. Often we Mormon women have to do that. It's not easy. The kind of happiness you want I wanted once. I never got it, nor will you, unless you throw away your soul. We've all watched your affair with Venters in fear and trembling. Some dreadful thing will come of it. You don't want him hanged or shot – or treated worse, as that Gentile boy was treated in Glaze for fooling round a Mormon woman. Marry Tull. It's your duty as a Mormon. You'll feel no rapture as his wife – but think of Heaven! Mormon women don't marry for what they expect on earth. Take up the cross, Jane. Remember your father found Amber Spring, built these old houses, brought Mormons here, and fathered them. You are the daughter of Withersteen!'

Jane left Mary Brandt and went to call upon other friends. They received her with the same glad welcome as had Mary, lavished upon her the pent-up affection of Mormon women, and let her go with her ears ringing of Tull, Venters, Lassiter, of duty to God and glory in Heaven.

'Verily,' murmured Jane, 'I don't know myself when, through all this, I remain unchanged – nay, more fixed of purpose.'

She returned to the main street and bent her thoughtful steps towards the centre of the village. A string of wagons drawn by oxen was lumbering along. These 'sage-freighters', as they were called, hauled grain and flour and merchandise from Sterling; and Jane laughed suddenly in the midst of her humility at the thought that they were her property, as was one of the three stores for which they freighted goods. The water that flowed along the path at her feet, and turned into each cottage-yard to nourish garden and orchard, also was hers, no less her private property because she chose to give it free. Yet in this village of Cottonwoods, which her father had founded and which she maintained, she was not her own mistress; she was not to abide by her own choice of a husband. She was the daughter of Witersteen. Suppose she proved it, imperiously! But she quelled that proud temptation at its birth.

Nothing could have replaced the affection which the village people had for her; no power could have made her happy as the pleasure her presence gave. As she went on down the street, past the stores with their rude platform entrances, and the saloons, where tired horses stood with bridles dragging, she was again assured of what was the bread and wine of life to her – that she was loved. Dirty boys playing in the ditch, clerks, teamsters, riders, loungers on the corners, ranchers on dusty horses, little girls running errands, and women hurrying to the stores all looked up at her coming with glad eyes.

Jane's various calls and wandering steps at length led her to the Gentile quarter of the village. This was at the extreme southern end, and here some thirty Gentile families lived in huts and shacks and log-cabins and several dilapidated cottages. The fortunes of these inhabitants of Cottonwoods could be read in their abodes. Water they had in abundance, and therefore grass and fruit trees and patches of alfalfa and vegetable gardens. Some of the men and boys had a few stray cattle, others obtained such intermittent employment as the Mormons reluctantly tendered them. But none of the families was prosperous, many were very poor, and some lived only by Jane Witersteen's beneficence.

As it made Jane happy to go among her own people, so it saddened her to come in contact with these Gentiles. Yet that was not because she was unwelcome; here she was gratefully received by the women, passionately by the children. But poverty and idleness, with their attendant wretchedness and sorrow, always hurt her. That she could alleviate this distress more now than ever before proved the adage that it was an ill wind that blew nobody good. While her Mormon riders were in her employ she had found few Gentiles who could stay with her, and now she was able to find employment for all the men and boys. No little shock was it to have man after man tell her that he dare not accept her kind offer.

'It won't do,' said one Carson, an intelligent man who had seen better days. 'We've had our warning. Plain and to the point! Now there's Judkins, he packs guns, and he can use them, and so can the daredevil boys he's hired. But they've little responsibility. Can we risk having our homes burned in our absence?'

Jane felt the stretching and chilling of the skin of her face as the blood left it.

'Carson, you and the others rent these houses?' she asked.

'You ought to know, Miss Withersteen. Some of them are yours.'

'I know? . . . Carson, I never in my life took a day's labour for rent or a yearling calf or a bunch of grass, let alone gold.'

'Bivens, your storekeeper, sees to that.'

'Look here, Carson,' went on Jane, hurriedly, and now her cheeks were burning. 'You and Black and Willet pack your goods and move your families up to my cabins in the grove. They're far more comfortable than these. Then go to work for me. And if aught happens to you there I'll give you money – gold enough to leave Utah!'

The man choked and stammered, and then, as tears welled into his eyes, he found the use of his tongue and cursed. No gentle speech could ever have equalled that curse in eloquent expression of what he felt for Jane Withersteen. How strangely his look and tone reminded her of Lassiter!

'No, it won't do,' he said, when he had somewhat recovered himself. 'Miss Withersteen, there are things that you don't know, and there's not a soul among us who can tell you.'

'I seem to be learning many things, Carson. Well, then, will you let me aid you – say till better times?'

'Yes, I will,' he replied, with his face lighting up. 'I see what it means to you, and you know what it means to me. Thank you! And if better times ever come I'll be only too happy to work for you.'

'Better times will come. I trust God and have faith in man. Good-day, Carson.'

The lane opened out upon the sage-enclosed alfalfa fields, and the last habitation, at the end of that lane of hovels, was the meanest. Formerly it had been a shed; now it was a home. The broad leaves of a wide-spreading cottonwood sheltered the sunken roof of weathered boards, like an Indian hut, it had one floor. Round about it were a few scanty rows of vegetables, such as the hand of a weak woman had time and strength to cultivate. This little dwelling-place was just outside the village limits, and the widow who lived there had to carry her water from the nearest irrigation ditch.

As Jane Withersteen entered the unfenced yard a child saw her, shrieked with joy, and came tearing towards her with curls flying. This child was a little girl of four called Fay. Her name suited her, for she was an elf, a sprite, a creature so fairy-like and beautiful that she seemed unearthly.

'Muvver sended for oo,' cried Fay, as Jane kissed her, 'an' oo never tome.'

'I didn't know, Fay; but I've come now.'

Fay was a child of outdoors, of the garden and ditch and field, and she was dirty and ragged. But rags and dirt did not hide her beauty. The one thin little bedraggled garment she wore half covered her fine, slim body. Red as cherries were her cheeks and lips; her eyes were violet blue, and the crown of her childish loveliness was the curling golden hair. All the children of Cottonwoods were Jane Withersteen's friends; she loved them all. But Fay was dearest to her. Fay had few playmates, for among the Gentile children there were none near her age, and the Mormon children were forbidden to play with her. So she was a shy, wild, lonely child.

'Muvver's sick,' said Fay, leading Jane towards the door of the hut.

Jane went in. There was only one room, rather dark and bare, but it was clean and neat. A woman lay upon a bed.

'Mrs Larkin, how are you?' asked Jane, anxiously.

'I've been pretty bad for a week, but I'm better now.'

'You haven't been here all alone – with no one to wait on you?'

'Oh no! My women neighbours are kind. They take turns coming in.'

'Did you send for me?'

'Yes, several times.'

'But I had no word – no messages ever got to me.'

'I sent the boys, and they left word with your women that I was ill and would you please come.'

A sudden deadly sickness seized Jane. She fought the weakness, as she fought to be above suspicious thoughts, and it passed, leaving her conscious of her utter impotence. That, too, passed as her spirit rebounded. But she had again caught a glimpse of dark underhand domination, running its secret lines this time into her own household. Like a spider in the blackness of night an unseen hand had begun to run these dark lines, to turn and twist them about her life, to plait and weave a web. Jane Withersteen knew it now, and in the realisation further coolness and sureness came to her, and the fighting courage of her ancestors.

'Mrs Larkin, you're better, and I'm so glad,' said Jane. 'But may I not do something for you – a turn at nursing, or send you things, or take care of Fay!'

'You're so good. Since my husband's been gone what would have become of Fay and me but for you? It was about Fay that I wanted to speak to you. This time I thought surely I'd die, and I was worried about Fay. Well, I'll be around all right shortly, but my strength's gone and I won't live long. So I may as well speak now. You remember you've been asking me to let you take Fay and bring her up as your daughter?'

'Indeed yes, I remember. I'll be happy to have her. But I hope the day – '

'Never mind that. The day'll come – sooner or later. I refused your offer, and now I'll tell you why.'

'I know why,' interposed Jane. 'It's because you don't want her brought up as a Mormon.'

'No, it wasn't altogether that,' Mrs Larkin raised her thin hand and laid it appealingly on Jane's. 'I don't like to tell you. But – it's this: I told all my friends what you wanted. They know you, care for you, and they said for me to trust Fay to you. Women will talk, you know. It got to the ears of Mormons – gossip of your love for Fay and your wanting her. And it came straight back to me, in jealousy, perhaps, that you wouldn't take Fay as much for love of her as because of your religious duty to bring up another girl for some Mormon to marry.'

'That's a damnable lie!' cried Jane Withersteen.

'It was what made me hesitate,' went on Mrs Larkin, 'but I never believed it at heart. And now I guess I'll let you – '

'Wait! Mrs Larkin, I may have told little white lies in my life, but never a lie that mattered, that hurt anyone. Now believe me. I love little Fay. If I had her near me I'd grow to worship her. When I asked for her I thought only of that love . . . Let me prove this. You and Fay come to live with me. I've such a big house, and I'm so lonely. I'll help nurse you, take care of you. When you're better you can work for me. I'll keep little Fay and bring her up – without Mormon teaching. When she's grown, if she should want to leave me, I'll send her, and not empty-handed, back to Illinois where you came from. I promise you.'

'I knew it was a lie,' replied the mother, and she sank back upon her pillow with something of peace in her white, worn face. 'Jane Withersteen, may Heaven bless you! I've been deeply grateful to you. But because you're a Mormon I never felt close to you till now. I don't know much about religion as religion, but your God and my God are the same.'

CHAPTER 8

Surprise Valley

Back in that strange canyon, which Venters had found indeed a valley of surprises, the wounded girl's whispered appeal, almost a prayer, not to take her back to the rustlers crowned the events of the last few days with a confounding climax. That she should not want to return to them staggered Venters. Presently, as logical thought returned, her appeal confirmed his first impression – that she was more unfortunate than bad – and he experienced a sensation of gladness. If he had known before that Oldring's Masked Rider was a woman his opinion would have been formed and he would have considered her abandoned. But his first knowledge had come when he lifted a white face quivering in a convulsion of agony; he had heard God's name whispered by blood-stained lips; through her solemn and awful eyes he had caught a glimpse of her soul. And just now had come the entreaty to him, 'Don't – take – me back – there!'

Once for all Venters's quick mind formed a permanent conception of this poor girl. He based it, not upon what the chances of life had made her, but upon the revelation of dark eyes that pierced the infinite, upon a few pitiful, halting words that betrayed failure and wrong and misery, yet breathed the truth of a tragic fate rather than a natural leaning to evil.

'What's your name?' he enquired.

'Bess,' she answered.

'Bess what?'

'That's enough – just Bess.'

The red that deepened in her cheeks was not all the flush of fever. Venters marvelled anew, and this time at the tint of shame in her face, at the momentary drooping of long lashes. She might be a rustler's girl, but she was still capable of shame; she might be dying, but she still clung to some little remnant of honour.

'Very well, Bess. It doesn't matter,' he said. 'But this matters – what shall I do with you?'

'Are – you – a rider?' she whispered.

'Not now. I was once. I drove the Withersteen herds. But I lost my place – lost all I owned – and now I'm – I'm a sort of outcast. My name's Bern Venters.'

'You won't – take me – to Cottonwoods – or Glaze? I'd be hanged.'

'No, indeed. But I must do something with you. For it's not safe for me here. I shot that rustler who was with you. Sooner or later he'll be found, and then my tracks. I must find a safer hiding-place where I can't be trailed.'

'Leave me – here.'

'Alone – to die!'

'Yes.'

'I will not.' Venters spoke shortly with a kind of ring in his voice.

'What – do you want – to do – with me?' Her whispering grew difficult, so low and faint that Venters had to stoop to hear her.

'Why, let's see,' he replied, slowly. 'I'd like to take you some place where I could watch by you, nurse you, till you're all right again.'

'And – then?'

'Well, it'll be time to think of that when you're cured of your wound. It's a bad one. And – Bess, if you don't want to live – if you don't fight for life – you'll never – '

'Oh! I want – to live! I'm afraid – to die. But I'd rather – die than go back – to – to – '

'To Oldring?' asked Venters, interrupting her in turn.

Her lips moved in an affirmative.

'I promise not to take you back to him or to Cottonwoods or to Glaze.'

The mournful earnestness of her gaze suddenly shone with unutterable gratitude and wonder. And as suddenly Venters found her eyes beautiful as he had never seen or felt beauty. They were as dark blue as the sky at night. Then the flashing changed to a long, thoughtful look, in which there was wistful, unconscious searching of his face, a look that trembled on the verge of hope and trust.

'I'll try – to live,' she said. The broken whisper just reached his ears. 'Do what – you want – with me.'

'Rest then – don't worry – sleep,' he replied.

Abruptly he arose, as if her words had been decision for him, and with a sharp command to the dogs he strode from the camp. Venters was conscious of an indefinite conflict of change within him. It seemed to be a vague passing of old moods, a dim coalescing of new forces, a moment of inexplicable transition. He was both cast down and uplifted. He wanted to think and think of the meaning, but he resolutely dispelled emotion. His imperative need at present was to find a safe retreat, and this called for action.

So he set out. It still wanted several hours before dark. This trip he turned to the left and wended his skulking way southward a mile or more to the opening of the valley, where lay the strange scrawled rocks. He did not, however, venture boldly out into the open sage, but clung to the right-hand wall and went along that till its perpendicular line broke into the long incline of bare stone.

Before proceeding farther he halted, studying the strange character of this slope and realising that a moving black object could be seen far against such background. Before him ascended a gradual swell of smooth stone. It was hard, polished, and full of pockets worn by centuries of eddying rain-water. A hundred yards up began a line of grotesque cedar trees, and they extended along the slope clear to its most southerly end. Beyond that end Venters wanted to get, and he concluded the cedars, few as they were, would afford some cover.

Therefore he climbed swiftly. The trees were farther up than he had estimated, though he had from long habit made allowance for the deceiving nature of distances in that country. When he gained the cover of cedars he paused to rest and look, and it was then he saw how the trees sprang from holes in the bare rock. Ages of rain had run down the slope, circling, eddying in depressions, wearing deep round holes. There had been dry seasons, accumulations of dust, wind-blown seeds, and cedars rose wonderfully out of solid rock. But these were not beautiful cedars. They were gnarled, twisted into weird contortions, as if growth were torture, dead at the tops, shrunken, grey and old. Theirs had been a bitter fight, and Venters felt a strange sympathy for them. This country was hard on trees – and men.

He slipped from cedar to cedar, keeping them between him and the open valley. As he progressed, the belt of trees widened, and he kept to its upper margin. He passed shady pockets half full of water, and, as he marked the location for possible future need, he reflected that there had been no rain since the winter snows. From one of these shady holes a rabbit hopped out and squatted down, laying its ears flat.

Venters wanted fresh meat now more than when he had only himself to think of. But it would not do to fire his rifle there. So he broke off a cedar branch and threw it. He crippled the rabbit, which started to flounder up the slope. Venters did not wish to lose the meat, and he never allowed crippled game to escape, to die lingeringly in some covert. So after a careful glance below, and back towards the canyon, he began to chase the rabbit.

The fact that rabbits generally ran uphill was not new to him. But it presently seemed singular why this rabbit, that might have escaped downward, chose to ascend the slope. Venters knew then that it had a burrow higher up. More than once he jerked over to seize it, only in vain, for the rabbit by renewed effort eluded his grasp. Thus the chase continued on up the bare slope. The farther Venters climbed the more determined he grew to catch his quarry. At last, panting and sweating, he captured the rabbit at the foot of a steeper grade. Laying his rifle on the bulge of rising stone, he killed the animal and slung it from his belt.

Before starting down he waited to catch his breath. He had climbed far up that wonderful smooth slope, and had almost reached the base of yellow cliff that rose skyward, a huge scarred and cracked bulk. It frowned down upon him as if to forbid further ascent. Venters bent over for his rifle, and, as he picked it up from where it leaned against the steeper grade, he saw several little nicks cut in the solid stone.

They were only a few inches deep and about a foot apart. Venters began to count them – one – two – three – four – on up to sixteen. That number carried his glance to the top of this first bulging bench of cliff-base. Above, after a more level offset, was still steeper slope, and the line of nicks kept on, to wind round a projecting corner of wall.

A casual glance would have passed by these little dents; if Venters had not known what they signified he would never have bestowed upon them the second glance. But he knew they had been cut there by hand, and, though age-worn, he recognised them as steps cut in the rock by the cliff-dwellers. With a pulse beginning to beat and hammer away his calmness, he eyed that indistinct line of steps, up to where the buttress of wall hid further sight of them. He knew that behind the corner of stone would be a cave or a crack which could never be suspected from below. Chance, that had sported with him of late, now directed him to a probable hiding-place. Again he laid aside his rifle, and, removing boots and belt, he began to walk up the steps. Like a mountain goat, he was agile, sure-footed, and he mounted the first bench without bending to use his hands. The next ascent took grip of fingers as well as toes, but he climbed steadily, swiftly, to reach the projecting corner, and slipped around it. Here he faced a notch in the cliff. At the apex he turned abruptly into a ragged vent that split the ponderous wall clear to the top, showing a narrow streak of blue sky.

At the base this vent was dark, cool, and smelled of dry, musty dust. It zigzagged so that he could not see ahead more than a few yards at a time.

He noticed tracks of wildcats and rabbits in the dusty floor. At every turn he expected to come upon a huge cavern full of little square stone houses, each with a small aperture like a staring dark eye. The passage lightened and widened, and opened at the foot of a narrow, steep, ascending chute.

Venters had a moment's notice of the rock, which was of the same smoothness and hardness as the slope below, before his gaze went irresistibly upward to the precipitous walls of this wide ladder of granite. These were ruined walls of yellow sandstone, and so split and splintered, so overhanging with great sections of balancing rim, so impending with tremendous crumbling crags, that Venters caught his breath sharply, and, appalled, he instinctively recoiled as if a step upward might jar the ponderous cliffs from their foundation. Indeed, it seemed that these ruined cliffs were but awaiting a breath of wind to collapse and come tumbling down. Venters hesitated. It would be a foolhardy man who risked his life under the leaning, waiting avalanches of rock in that gigantic split. Yet how many years had they leaned there without falling! At the bottom of the incline was an immense heap of weathered sandstone all crumbling to dust, but there were no huge rocks as large as houses, such as rested so lightly and frightfully above, waiting patiently and inevitably to crash down. Slowly split from the parent rock by the weathering process, and carved and sculptured by ages of wind and rain, they waited their moment. Venters felt how foolish it was for him to fear these broken walls; to fear that, after they had endured for thousands of years, the moment of his passing should be the one for them to slip. Yet he feared it.

'What a place to hide!' muttered Venters. 'I'll climb – I'll see where this thing goes. If only I can find water!'

With teeth tight shut he essayed the incline. And as he climbed he bent his eyes downward. This, however, after a little grew impossible; he had to look to obey his eager, curious mind. He raised his glance and saw light between row on row of shafts and pinnacles and crags that stood out from the main wall. Some leaned against the cliff, others against each other; many stood sheer and alone; all were crumbling, cracked, rotten. It was a place of yellow, ragged ruin. The passage narrowed as he went up; it became a slant, hard for him to stick on; it was smooth as marble. Finally he surmounted it, surprised to find the walls still several hundred feet high, and a narrow gorge leading down on the other side. This was a divide between two inclines about twenty yards wide. At one side stood an enormous rock. Venters gave it a second glance, because it rested on a pedestal. It attracted closer attention. It was like a colossal pear of stone standing on its stem. Around the bottom were thousands of little nicks just distinguishable to the eye. They were marks of stone hatchets. The cliff-dwellers had chipped and chipped away at this boulder till it rested its tremendous bulk upon a mere pin-point of its surface. Venters pondered. Why had the little stone-men hacked away at the big boulder? It bore no semblance to a statue or an idol or a godhead or a sphinx. Instinctively he put his hands on it and pushed; then his shoulder and heaved. The stone seemed to groan, to stir, to grate, and then to move. It tipped a little downward and hung balancing for a long instant, slowly returned, rocked slightly, groaned and settled back to its former position.

Venters divined its significance. It had been meant for defence. The cliff-dwellers, driven by dreaded enemies to this last stand, had cunningly cut the rock until it balanced perfectly, ready to be dislodged by strong hands. Just below it leaned a tottering crag that would have toppled, starting an avalanche on an acclivity where no sliding mass could stop. Crags and pinnacles, splintered cliffs, and leaning shafts and monuments, would have thundered down to block forever the outlet to Deception Pass.

'That was a narrow shave for me,' said Venters, soberly. 'A balancing rock! The cliff-dwellers never had to roll it. They died, vanished, and here the rock stands, probably little changed . . . But it might serve another lonely dweller of the cliffs. I'll hide up here somewhere, if I can only find water.'

He descended the gorge on the other side. The slope was gradual, the space narrow, the course straight for many rods. A gloom hung between the up-sweeping walls. In a turn the passage narrowed to scarce a dozen feet, and here was darkness of night. But light shone ahead; another abrupt turn brought day again, and then wide open space.

Above Venters loomed a wonderful arch of stone bridging the canyon rims, and through the enormous round portal gleamed and glistened a beautiful valley shining under sunset gold reflected by surrounding cliffs. He gave a start of surprise. The valley was a cove a mile long, half that wide, and its enclosing walls were smooth and stained, and curved inwards, forming great caves. He decided that its floor was far higher than the level of Deception Pass and the intersecting canyons. No purple sage coloured this valley floor. Instead there were the white of aspens, streaks of branch and slender trunk glistening from the green of leaves, and the darker green of oaks, and through the middle of this forest, from wall to wall, ran a winding line of brilliant green which marked the course of cottonwoods and willows.

'There's water here – and this is the place for me,' said Venters. 'Only birds can peep over those walls. I've gone Oldring one better.'

Venters waited no longer, and turned swiftly to retrace his steps. He named the canyon Surprise Valley and the huge boulder that guarded the outlet Balancing Rock. Going down he did not find himself attended by such fears as had beset him in the climb; still, he was not easy in mind and could not occupy himself with plans of moving the girl and his outfit until he had descended to the notch. There he rested a moment and looked about him. The pass was darkening with the approach of night. At the corner of the wall, where the stone steps turned, he saw a spur of rock that would serve to hold the noose of a lasso. He needed no more aid to scale that place. As he intended to make the move under cover of darkness, he wanted most to be able to tell where to climb up. So, taking several small stones with him, he stepped and slid down to the edge of the slope where he had left his rifle and boots. Here he placed the stones some yards apart. He left the rabbit lying upon the bench where the steps began. Then he addressed a keen-sighted, remembering gaze to the rim-wall above. It was serrated, and between two spears of rock, directly in line with his position, showed a zigzag crack that at night would let through the gleam of sky. This settled, he put on his belt and boots and prepared to descend. Some consideration was necessary to decide whether or not to leave his rifle there. On the return, carrying the girl and a pack, it would be added encumbrance; and after debating the matter he left the rifle leaning against the bench. As he went straight down the slope he halted every few rods to look up at his mark on the rim. It changed, but he fixed each change in his memory. When he reached the first cedar tree, he tied his scarf upon a dead branch, and then hurried towards camp, having no more concern about finding his trail upon the return trip.

Darkness soon emboldened and lent him greater speed. It occurred to him, as he glided into the grassy glade near camp and heard the whinny of a horse, that he had forgotten Wrangle. The big sorrel could not be got into Surprise Valley. He would have to be left here.

Venters determined at once to lead the other horses out through the thicket and turn them loose. The farther they wandered from this canyon the better it would suit him. He easily descried Wrangle through the gloom, but the others were not in sight. Venters whistled low for the dogs, and when they came trotting to him he sent them out to search for the horses, and followed. It soon developed that they were not in the glade nor the thicket. Venters grew cold and rigid at the thought of rustlers having entered his retreat. But the thought passed, for the demeanour of Ring and Whitie reassured him. The horses had wandered away.

Under the clump of silver spruces hung a denser mantle of darkness, yet not so thick that Venters's night-practised eyes could not catch the white oval of a still face. He bent over it with a slight suspension of breath that was both caution lest he frighten her and chill uncertainty of feeling lest he find her dead. But she slept, and he arose to renewed activity.

He packed his saddle-bags. The dogs were hungry, they whined about him and nosed his busy hands; but he took no time to feed them nor to satisfy his own hunger. He slung the saddle-bags over his shoulders and made them secure with his lasso. Then he wrapped the blankets closer about the girl and lifted her in his arms. Wrangle whinnied and thumped the ground as Venters passed him with the dogs. The sorrel knew he was being left behind, and was not sure whether he liked it or not. Venters went on and entered the thicket. Here he had to feel his way in pitch blackness and to wedge his progress between the close saplings. Time meant little to him now that he had started, and he edged along with slow side movement till he got clear of the thicket. Ring and Whitie stood waiting for him. Taking to the open aisles and patches of the sage, he walked guardedly, careful not to stumble or step in dust or strike against spreading sage-branches.

If he were burdened he did not feel it. From time to time, when he passed out of the black lines of shade into the wan starlight, he glanced at the white face of the girl lying in his arms. She had not awakened from her sleep or stupor. He did not rest until he cleared the black gate of the canyon. Then he leaned against a stone breast-high to him and gently released the girl from his hold. His brow and hair and the palms of his hands were wet, and there was a kind of nervous contraction of his muscles. They seemed to ripple and string tense. He had a desire to hurry and no sense of fatigue. A wind blew the scent of sage in his face. The first early blackness of night passed with the brightening of the stars. Somewhere back on his trail a coyote yelped, splitting the dead silence. Venters's faculties seemed singularly acute.

He lifted the girl again and pressed on. The valley afforded better travelling than the canyon. It was lighter, freer of sage, and there were no rocks. Soon, out of the pale gloom shone a still paler thing, and that was the low swell of slope. Venters mounted it, and his dogs walked beside him. Once upon the stone he slowed to snail pace, straining his sight to avoid the pockets and holes. Foot by foot he went up. The weird cedars, like great demons and witches chained to the rock and writhing in silent anguish, loomed up with wide and twisting naked arms. Venters crossed this belt of cedars, skirted the upper border, and recognised the tree he had marked, even before he saw his waving scarf.

Here he knelt and deposited the girl gently, feet first, and slowly laid her out full length. What he feared was to reopen one of her wounds. If he gave her a violent jar, or slipped and fell! But the supreme confidence so strangely felt that night admitted of no such blunders.

The slope before him seemed to swell into obscurity, to lose its definite outline in a misty, opaque cloud that shaded into the overshadowing wall. He scanned the rim where the serrated points speared the sky, and he found the zigzag crack. It was dim, only a shade lighter than the dark ramparts; but he distinguished it, and that served.

Lifting the girl, he stepped upwards, closely attending to the nature of the path under his feet. After a few steps he stopped to mark his line with the crack in the rim. The dogs clung closer to him. While chasing the rabbit this slope had appeared interminable to him; now, burdened as he was, he did not think of length or height or toil. He remembered only to avoid a misstep and to keep his direction. He climbed on, with frequent stops to watch the rim, and before he dreamed of gaining the bench he bumped his knees into it, and saw, in the dim grey light, his rifle and the rabbit. He had come straight up without mishap or swerving off his course, and his shut teeth unlocked.

As he laid the girl down in the shallow hollow of the little ridge, with her white face upturned, she opened her eyes. Wide, staring, black, at once like both the night and the stars, they made her face seem still whiter.

'Is – it – you?' she asked, faintly.

'Yes,' replied Venters.

'Oh! Where – are we?'

'I'm taking you to a safe place where no one will ever find you. I must climb a little here and call the dogs. Don't be afraid. I'll soon come for you.'

She said no more. Her eyes watched him steadily for a moment and then closed. Venters pulled off his boots and then felt for the little steps in the rock. The shade of the cliff above obscured the point he wanted to gain, but he could see dimly a few feet before him. What he had attempted with care he now went at with surpassing lightness. Buoyant, rapid, sure, he attained the corner of wall and slipped around it. Here he could not see a hand before his face, so he groped along, found a little flat space, and there removed the saddle-bags. The lasso he took back with him to the corner and looped the noose over the spur of rock.

'Ring – Whitie – come,' he called, softly.

Low whines came up from below.

'Here! Come, Whitie – Ring,' he repeated, this time sharply.

Then followed scraping of claws and pattering of feet; and out of the grey gloom below him swiftly climbed the dogs to reach his side and pass beyond.

Venters descended, holding to the lasso. He tested its strength by throwing all his weight upon it. Then he gathered the girl up, and, holding her securely in his left arm, he began to climb, at every few steps jerking his right hand upward along the lasso. It sagged at each forward movements he made, but he balanced himself lightly during the interval when he lacked the support of a taut rope. He climbed as if he had wings, the strength of a giant, and knew not the sense of fear. The sharp corner of cliff seemed to cut out of the darkness. He reached it and the protruding shelf, and then, entering the black shade of the notch, he moved blindly but surely to the place where he had left the saddle-bags. He heard the dogs, though he could not see them. Once more he carefully placed the girl at his feet. Then on hands and knees, he went over the little flat space, feeling for stones. He removed a number, and, scraping the deep dust into a heap, he unfolded the outer blanket from around the girl and laid her upon this bed. Then he went down the slope again for his boots, rifle, and the rabbit, and, bringing also his lasso with him, he made short work of that trip.

'Are – you – there?' The girl's voice came low from the blackness.

'Yes,' he replied, and was conscious that his labouring breast made speech difficult.

'Are we – in a cave?'

'Yes.'

'Oh, listen! . . . The waterfall! . . . I hear it! You've brought me back!'

Venters heard a murmuring moan that one moment swelled to a pitch almost softly shrill and the next lulled to a low, almost inaudible sigh.

'That's – wind blowing – in the – cliffs,' he panted. 'You're far – from Oldring's – canyon.'

The effort it cost him to speak made him conscious of extreme lassitude following upon great exertion. It seemed that when he lay down and drew his blanket over him the action was the last before utter prostration. He stretched inert, wet, hot, his body one great strife of throbbing, stinging nerves and bursting veins. And there he lay for a long while before he felt that he had begun to rest.

Rest came to him that night, but no sleep. Sleep he did not want. The hours of strained effort were now as if they had never been, and he wanted to think. Earlier in the day he had dismissed an inexplicable feeling of change; but now, when there was no longer demand on his cunning and strength and he had time to think, he could not catch the illusive thing that had sadly perplexed as well as elevated his spirit.

Above him, through a V-shaped cleft in the dark rim of the cliff, shone the lustrous stars that had been his lonely accusers for a long, long year. Tonight they were different. He studied them. Larger, whiter, more radiant they seemed; but that was not the difference he meant. Gradually it came to him that the distinction was not one he saw, but one he felt. In this he divined as much of the baffling change as he thought would be revealed to him then. And as he lay there, with the singing of the cliff-winds in his ears, the white stars above the dark, bold vent, the difference which he felt was that he was no longer alone.

CHAPTER 9

Silver Spruce and Aspens

The rest of that night seemed to Venters only a few moments of starlight, a dark overcasting of sky, an hour or so of grey gloom, and then the lighting of dawn.

When he had bestirred himself, feeding the hungry dogs and breaking his long fast, and had repacked his saddle-bags, it was clear daylight, though the sun had not tipped the yellow wall in the east. He concluded to make the climb and descent into Surprise Valley in one trip. To that end he tied his blanket upon Ring and gave Whitie the extra lasso and the rabbit to carry. Then, with the rifle and saddle-bags slung upon his back, he took up the girl. She did not awaken from heavy slumber.

That climb up under the rugged, menacing brows of the broken cliffs, in the face of a grim, leaning boulder that seemed to be weary of its age-

729

long wavering, was a tax on strength and nerve that Venters felt equally with something sweet and strangely exulting in its accomplishment. He did not pause until he gained the narrow divide and there he rested. Balancing Rock loomed huge, cold in the grey light of dawn, a thing without life, yet it spoke silently to Venters: 'I am waiting to plunge down, to shatter and crash, roar and boom, to bury your trail, and close forever the outlet to Deception Pass!'

On the descent of the other side Venters had easy going, but was somewhat concerned because Whitie appeared to have succumbed to temptation, and while carrying the rabbit was also chewing on it. And Ring evidently regarded this as an injury to himself, especially as he had carried the heavier load. Presently he snapped at one end of the rabbit and refused to let go. But his action prevented Whitie from further misdoing, and then the two dogs pattered down, carrying the rabbit between them.

Venters turned out of the gorge, and suddenly paused stock-still, astounded at the scene before him. The curve of the great stone bridge had caught the sunrise, and through the magnificent arch burst a glorious stream of gold that shone with a long slant down into the centre of Surprise Valley. Only through the arch did any sunlight pass, so that all the rest of the valley lay still asleep, dark green, mysterious, shadowy, merging its level into walls as misty and soft as morning clouds.

Venters then descended, passing through the arch, looking up at its tremendous height and sweep. It spanned the opening to Surprise Valley, stretching in almost perfect curve from rim to rim. Even in his hurry and concern Venters could not but feel its majesty, and the thought came to him that the cliff-dwellers must have regarded it as an object of worship.

Down, down, down Venters strode, more and more feeling the weight of his burden as he descended, and still the valley lay below him. As all other canyons and coves and valleys had deceived him, so had this deep, nestling oval. At length he passed beyond the slope of weathered stone that spread fan-shape from the arch, and encountered a grassy terrace running to the right and about on a level with the tips of the oaks and cottonwoods below. Scattered here and there upon this shelf were clumps of aspens, and he walked through them into a glade that surpassed, in beauty and adaptability for a wild home, any place he had ever seen. Silver spruces bordered the base of a precipitous wall that rose loftily. Caves indented its surface, and there were no detached ledges or weathered sections that might dislodge a stone. The level ground, beyond the spruces, dropped down into a little ravine. This was one dense line of slender aspens from which came the low splashing of water. And the terrace, lying open to the west, afforded unobstructed view of the valley of green tree-tops.

For his camp Venters chose a shady, grassy plot between the silver spruces and the cliff. Here, in the stone wall, had been wonderfully carved by wind or washed by water several deep caves above the level of the terrace. They were clean, dry, roomy. He cut spruce boughs and made a bed in the largest cave and laid the girl there. The first intimation that he had of her being aroused from sleep or lethargy was a low call for water.

He hurried down into the ravine with his canteen. It was a shallow, grass-green place with aspens growing up everywhere. To his delight he found a tiny brook of swift-running water. Its faint tinge of amber reminded him of the spring at Cottonwoods, and the thought gave him a little shock. The water was so cold it made his fingers tingle as he dipped the canteen. Having returned to the cave, he was glad to see the girl drink thirstily. This time he noted that she could raise her head slightly without his help.

'You were thirsty,' he said. 'It's good water. I've found a fine place. Tell me – how do you feel?'

'There's pain – here,' she replied, and moved her hand to her left side.

'Why, that's strange! Your wounds are on your right side. I believe you're hungry. Is the pain a kind of dull ache – a gnawing?'

'It's like – that.'

'Then it's hunger.' Venters laughed, and suddenly caught himself with a quick breath and felt again the little shock. When had he laughed? 'It's hunger,' he went on. 'I've had that gnaw many a time. I've got it now. But you mustn't eat. You can have all the water you want, but no food just yet.'

'Won't I – starve?'

'No, people don't starve easily. I've discovered that. You must lie perfectly still and rest and sleep – for days.'

'My hands – are dirty; my face feels – so hot and sticky; my boots hurt.' It was her longest speech as yet, and it trailed off in a whisper.

'Well, I'm a fine nurse!'

It annoyed him that he had never thought of these things. But then, awaiting her death and thinking of her comfort were vastly different matters. He unwrapped the blanket which covered her. What a slender girl she was! No wonder he had been able to carry her miles and pack her up that slippery ladder of stone. Her boots were of soft, fine leather, reaching clear to her knees. He recognised the make as one of a boot-maker in Sterling. Her spurs, that he had stupidly neglected to remove, consisted of silver frames and gold chains, and the rowels, large as silver dollars, were fancifully engraved. The boots slipped off rather hard. She wore heavy woollen rider's stockings, half length, and these were pulled up over the ends of her short trousers. Venters took off the stockings to note her little feet were red and swollen. He bathed them. Then he removed his scarf and bathed her face and hands.

'I must see your wounds now,' he said, gently.

She made no reply, but watched him steadily as he opened her blouse and untied the bandage. His strong fingers trembled a little as he removed it. If the wounds had reopened! A chill struck him as he saw the angry red bullet-mark, and a tiny stream of blood winding from it down her white breast. Very carefully he lifted her to see that the wound in her back had closed perfectly. Then he washed the blood from her breast, bathed the wound, and left it unbandaged, open to the air.

Her eyes thanked him.

'Listen,' he said, earnestly. 'I've had some wounds, and I've seen many. I know a little about them. The hole in your back has closed. If you lie still three days the one in your breast will close and you'll be safe. The danger from haemorrhage will be over.'

He had spoken with earnest sincerity, almost eagerness.

'Why – do you – want me – to get well?' she asked, wonderingly.

The simple question seemed unanswerable except on grounds of humanity. But the circumstances under which he had shot this strange girl, the shock and realisation, the waiting for death, the hope, had resulted in a condition of mind wherein Venters wanted her to live more than he had ever wanted anything. Yet he could not tell why. He believed the killing of the rustler and the subsequent excitement had disturbed him. For how else could he explain the throbbing of his brain, the heat of his blood, the undefined sense of full hours, charged, vibrant with pulsating mystery where once they had dragged in loneliness?

'I shot you,' he said, slowly, 'and I want you to get well, so I shall not have killed a woman. But – for your own sake, too – '

A terrible bitterness darkened her eyes, and her lips quivered.

'Hush,' said Venters. 'You've talked too much already.'

In her unutterable bitterness he saw a darkness of mood that could not have been caused by her present weak and feverish state. She hated the life she had led, that she probably had been compelled to lead. She had suffered some unforgivable wrong at the hands of Oldring. With that conviction Venters felt a flame throughout his body, and it marked the rekindling of fierce anger and ruthlessness. In the past long year he had nursed resentment. He had hated the wilderness – the loneliness of the uplands. He had waited for something to come to pass. It had come. Like an Indian stealing horses he had skulked into the recesses of the canyons. He had found Oldring's retreat; he had killed a rustler; he had shot an unfortunate girl, then had saved her from this unwitting act, and he meant to save her from the consequent wasting of blood, from fever and weakness. Starvation he had to fight for her and for himself. Where he had been sick at the letting of blood, now he remembered it in grim, cold calm. And as he lost that softness of nature, so he lost his fear of men. He would watch for Oldring, biding his time, and he would kill this great black-bearded rustler who had held a girl in bondage, who had used her to his infamous ends.

Venters surmised this much of the change in him – idleness had passed; keen, fierce vigour flooded his mind and body; all that had happened to him at Cottonwoods seemed remote and hard to recall; the difficulties and perils of the present absorbed him, held him in a kind of spell.

First, then, he fitted up the little cave adjoining the girl's room for his own comfort and use. His next work was to build a fireplace of stones and to gather a store of wood. That done, he spilled the contents of his saddle-bags upon the grass and took stock. His outfit consisted of a small-handled axe, a hunting-knife, a large number of cartridges for rifle or revolver, a tin plate, a cup, and a fork and spoon, a quantity of dried beef and dried fruits, and small canvas bags containing tea, sugar, salt, and pepper. For him alone this supply would have been bountiful to begin a sojourn in the wilderness, but he was no longer alone. Starvation in the uplands was not an unheard-of thing; he did not, however, worry at all on that score, and feared only his possible inability to supply the needs of a woman in a weakened and extremely delicate condition.

If there was no game in the valley – a contingency he doubted – it would not be a great task for him to go by night to Oldring's herd and pack out a calf. The exigency of the moment was to ascertain if there were game in Surprise Valley. Whitie still guarded the dilapidated rabbit, and Ring slept near by under a spruce. Venters called Ring and went to the edge of the terrace, and there halted to survey the valley.

He was prepared to find it larger than his unstudied glances had made it appear; for more than a casual idea of dimensions and a hasty conception of oval shape and singular beauty he had not had time. Again the felicity of the name he had given the valley struck him forcibly. Around the red perpendicular walls, except under the great arc of stone, ran a terrace fringed at the cliff-base by silver spruces; below that first terrace sloped another wider one densely overgrown with aspens, and the centre of the valley was a level circle of oaks and alders, with the glittering green line of willows and cottonwood dividing it in half. Venters saw a number and variety of birds flitting among the trees. To his left, facing the stone bridge, an enormous cavern opened in the wall; and low down, just above the tree-tops, he made out a long shelf of cliff-dwellings, with little black, staring windows or doors. Like eyes they were, and seemed to watch him. The few cliff-dwellings he had seen – all ruins – had left him with haunting memory of age and solitude and of something past. He had come, in a way, to be a cliff-dweller himself, and those silent eyes would look down upon him, as if in surprise that after thousands of years a man had invaded the valley. Venters felt sure that he was the only white man who had ever walked under the shadow of the wonderful stone bridge, down into that wonderful valley with its circle of caves and its terraced rings of silver spruce and aspens.

The dog growled below and rushed into the forest. Venters ran down the declivity to enter a zone of light shade streaked with sunshine. The oak trees were slender, none more than half a foot thick, and they grew close together, intermingling their branches. Ring came running back with a rabbit in his mouth. Venters took the rabbit and, holding the dog near him stole softly on. There were fluttering of wings among the branches and quick bird-notes, and rustling of dead leaves and rapid patterings. Venters crossed well-worn trails marked with fresh tracks; and when he had stolen on a little farther he saw many birds and running quail, and more rabbits than he could count. He had not penetrated the forest of oaks for a hundred yards, had not approached anywhere near the line of willows and cottonwoods which he knew grew along a stream. But he had seen enough to know that Surprise Valley was the home of many wild creatures.

Venters returned to camp. He skinned the rabbits, and gave the dogs the one they had quarrelled over, and the skin of this he dressed and hung up to dry, feeling that he would like to keep it. It was a particularly rich, furry pelt with a beautiful white tail. Venters remembered that but for the bobbing of that white tail catching his eye he would not have espied the rabbit, and he would never have discovered Surprise Valley. Little incidents of chance like this had turned him here and there in Deception Pass; and now they had assumed to him the significance and direction of destiny.

His good fortune in the matter of game at hand brought to his mind the necessity of keeping it in the valley. Therefore he took the axe and cut bundles of aspens and willows, and packed them up under the bridge to the narrow outlet of the gorge. Here he began fashioning a fence, by driving aspens into the ground and lacing them fast with willows. Trip after trip he made down for more building material, and the afternoon had passed when he finished the work to his satisfaction. Wildcats might scale the fence, but no coyote could come in to search for prey, and no rabbits or other small game could escape from the valley.

Upon returning to camp he set about getting his supper at ease, around a fine fire, without hurry or fear of discovery. After hard work that had definite purpose, this freedom and comfort gave him peculiar satisfaction. He caught himself often, as he kept busy round the camp-fire, stopping to glance at the quiet form in the cave, and at the dogs stretched cosily near him, and then out across the beautiful valley. The present was not yet real to him.

While he ate, the sun set beyond a dip in the rim of the curved wall. As the morning sun burst wondrously through a grand arch into this valley, in a golden, slanting shaft, so the evening sun, at the moment of setting, shone through a gap of cliffs, sending down a broad red burst to brighten the oval with a blaze of fire. To Venters both sunrise and sunset were unreal.

A cool wind blew across the oval, waving the tips of oaks, and, while the light lasted, fluttering the aspen leaves into millions of facets of red, and sweeping the graceful spruces. Then with the wind soon came a shade and a darkening, and suddenly the valley was grey. Night came there quickly after the sinking of the sun. Venters went softly to look at the girl. She slept, and her breathing was quiet and slow. He lifted Ring into the cave, with stern whisper for him to stay there on guard. Then he drew the blanket carefully over her and returned to the camp-fire.

Though exceedingly tired, he was yet loath to yield to lassitude, but this night it was not from listening, watchful vigilance; it was from a desire to realise his position. The details of his wild environment seemed the only substance of a strange dream. He saw the darkening rims, the grey oval turning black, the undulating surface of forest, like a rippling lake, and the spear-pointed spruces. He heard the flutter of aspen-leaves and the soft, continuous splash of falling water. The melancholy note of a canyon bird broke clear and lonely from the high cliffs. Venters had no name for this night singer, and he had never seen one; but the few notes, always pealing out just at darkness, were as familiar to him as the canyon silence. Then they ceased, and the rustle of leaves and the murmur of water hushed in a growing sound that Venters fancied was not of earth. Neither had he a name for this, only it was inexpressibly wild and sweet. The thought came that it might be a moan of the girl in her last outcry of life, and he felt a tremor shake him. But no! This sound was not human, though it was like despair. He began to doubt his sensitive perceptions, to believe that he half-dreamed what he thought he heard. Then the sound swelled with the strengthening of the breeze, and he realised it was the singing of the wind in the cliffs.

By and by a drowsiness overcame him, and Venters began to nod, half asleep, with his back against a spruce. Rousing himself and calling Whitie, he went to the cave. The girl lay barely visible in the dimness. Ring crouched beside her, and the patting of his tail on the stone assured Venters that the dog was awake and faithful to his duty. Venters sought his own bed of fragrant boughs; and as he lay back, somehow grateful for the comfort and safety, the night seemed to steal away from him and he sank softly into intangible space and rest and slumber.

Venters awakened to the sound of melody that he imagined was only the haunting echo of dream music. He opened his eyes to another surprise of this valley of beautiful surprises. Out of his cave he saw the exquisitely fine foliage of the silver spruces crossing a round space of blue morning sky; and in this lacy leafage fluttered a number of grey birds with black and white stripes and long tails. They were mocking-birds, and they were singing as if they wanted to burst their throats. Venters listened. One long, silver-tipped branch drooped almost to his cave, and upon it, within a few yards of him, sat one of the graceful birds. Venters saw the swelling and quivering of its throat in song. He arose, and when he slid down out of his cave the birds fluttered and flew farther away.

Venters stepped before the opening of the other cave and looked in. The girl was awake, with wide eyes and listening look, and she had a hand on Ring's neck.

'Mocking-birds!' she said.

'Yes,' replied Venters, 'and I believe they like our company.'

'Where are we?'

'Never mind now. After a little I'll tell you.'

'The birds woke me. When I heard them – and saw the shiny trees – and the blue sky – and then a blaze of gold dropping down – I wondered – '

She did not complete her fancy, but Venters imagined he understood her meaning. She appeared to be wandering in mind. Venters felt her face and hands and found them burning with fever. He went for water, and was glad to find it almost as cold as if flowing from ice. That water was the only medicine he had, and he put faith in it. She did not want to drink, but he made her swallow, and then he bathed her face and head and cooled her wrists.

The day began with a heightening of the fever. Venters spent the time reducing her temperature, cooling her hot cheeks and temples. He kept close watch over her, and at the least indication of restlessness, that he knew led to tossing and rolling of the body, he held her tightly, so no violent move could reopen her wounds. Hour after hour she babbled and laughed and cried and moaned in delirium; but whatever her secret was she did not reveal it. Attended by something sombre for Venters, the day passed. At night in the cool winds the fever abated and she slept.

The second day was a repetition of the first. On the third he seemed to see her wither and waste away before his eyes. That day he scarcely went from her side for a moment, except to run for fresh, cool water; and he did not eat. The fever broke on the fourth day and left her spent and shrunken, a slip of a girl with life only in her eyes. They hung upon Venters with a mute observance, and he found hope in that.

To rekindle the spark that had nearly flickered out, to nourish the little life and vitality that remained in her, was Venters's problem. But he had little resource other than the meat of the rabbits and quail; and from these he made broths and soups as best he could, and fed her with a spoon. It came to him that the human body, like the human soul, was a strange thing and capable of recovering from terrible shocks. For almost immediately she showed faint signs of gathering strength. There was one more waiting day, in which he doubted, and spent long hours by her side as she slept, and watched the gentle swell of her breast rise and fall in breathing, and the wind stir the tangled chestnut curls. On the next day he knew that she would live.

Upon realising it he abruptly left the cave and sought his accustomed seat against the trunk of a big spruce, where once more he let his glance stray along the sloping terraces. She would live, and the sombre gloom lifted out of the valley, and he felt relief that was pain. Then he roused to the call of action, to the many things he needed to do in the way of making camp fixtures and utensils, to the necessity of hunting food, and the desire to explore the valley.

But he decided to wait a few more days before going far from camp, because he fancied that the girl rested easier when she could see him near at hand. And on the first day her languor appeared to leave her in a renewed grip of life. She awoke stronger from each short slumber; she ate greedily, and she moved about in her bed of boughs; and always, it seemed to Venters, her eyes followed him. He knew now that her recovery would be rapid. She talked about the dogs, about the caves, the valley, about how hungry she was, till Venters silenced her, asking her to put off further talk till another time. She obeyed, but she sat up in her bed, and her eyes roved to and fro, and always back to him.

Upon the second morning she sat up when he wakened her, and would not permit him to bathe her face and feed her, which actions she performed for herself. She spoke little, however, and Venters was quick to catch in her the first intimations of thoughtfulness and curiosity and appreciation of her situation. He left camp and took Whitie out to hunt for rabbits. Upon his return he was amazed and somewhat anxiously concerned to see his invalid sitting with her back to a corner of the cave and her bare feet swinging out. Hurriedly he approached, intending to advise her to lie down again, to tell her that perhaps she might overtax her strength. The sun shone upon her, glinting on the little head with its tangle of bright hair and the small, oval face with its pallor, and dark-blue eyes underlined by dark-blue circles. She looked at him and he looked at her. In that exchange of glances he imagined each saw the other in some different guise. It seemed impossible to Venters that this frail girl could be Oldring's Masked Rider. It flashed over him that he had made a mistake which presently she would explain.

'Help me down,' she said.

'But – are you well enough?' he protested. 'Wait – a little longer.'

'I'm weak – dizzy. But I want to get down.'

He lifted her – what a light burden now! – and stood her upright beside him, and supported her as she essayed to walk with halting steps. She was like a stripling of a boy; the bright, small head scarcely reached his shoulder. But now, as she clung to his arm, the rider's costume she wore did not contradict, as it had done at first, his feeling of her femininity. She might be the famous Masked Rider of the uplands, she might resemble a boy; but her outline, her little hands and feet, her hair, her big eyes and tremulous lips, and especially a something that Venters felt as a subtle essence rather than what he saw, proclaimed her sex.

She soon tired. He arranged a comfortable seat for her under the spruce that overspread the camp-fire.

'Now tell me – everything,' she said.

He recounted all that had happened from the time of his discovery of the rustlers in the canyon up to the present moment.

'You shot me – and now you've saved my life?'

'Yes. After almost killing you I've pulled you through.'

'Are you glad?'

'I should say so!'

Her eyes were unusually expressive, and they regarded him steadily; she was unconscious of that mirroring of her emotions, and they shone with gratefulness and interest and wonder and sadness.

'Tell me – about yourself?' she asked.

He made this a briefer story, telling of his coming to Utah, his various occupations till he became a rider, and then how the Mormons had practically driven him out of Cottonwoods, an outcast.

Then, no longer able to withstand his own burning curiosity, he questioned her in turn.

'Are you Oldring's Masked Rider?'

'Yes,' she replied, and dropped her eyes.

'I knew it – I recognised your figure – and mask, for I saw you once. Yet I can't believe it! . . . But you never *were* really that rustler, as we riders knew him? A thief – a marauder – a kidnapper of women – a murderer of sleeping riders!'

'No! I never stole – or harmed anyone – in all my life. I only rode and rode – '

'But why – why?' he burst out. 'Why the name? I understand Oldring made you ride. But the black mask – the mystery – the things laid to your hands – the threats in your infamous name – the night-riding credited to you – the evil deeds deliberately blamed on you and acknowledged by rustlers – even Oldring himself! Why? Tell me why?'

'I never knew that,' she answered low. Her drooping head straightened, and the large eyes, larger now and darker, met Venters's with a clear, steadfast gaze in which he read truth. It verified his own conviction.

'Never knew? That's strange! Are you a Mormon?'

'No.'

'Is Oldring a Mormon?'

'No.'

'Do you – care for him?'

'Yes. I hate his men – his life – sometimes I almost hate him!'

Venters paused in his rapid-fire questioning, as if to brace himself to ask for a truth that would be abhorrent for him to confirm, but which he seemed driven to hear.

'What are – what *were* you to Oldring?'

Like some delicate thing suddenly exposed to blasting heat, the girl wilted; her head dropped, and into her white, wasted cheeks crept the red of shame.

Venters would have given anything to recall that question. It seemed so different – his thought when spoken. Yet her shame established in his mind something akin to the respect he had strangely been hungering to feel for her.

'Damn that question! – forget it!' he cried, in a passion of pain for her and anger at himself. 'But once and for all – tell me – I know it, yet I want to hear you say so – you couldn't help yourself?'

'Oh no.'

'Well, that makes it all right with me,' he went on, honestly. 'I – I want you to feel that . . . you see – we've been thrown together – and – and I want to help you – not hurt you. I thought life had been cruel to me, but when I think of yours I feel mean and little for my complaining. Anyway, I was a lonely outcast. And now! . . . I don't see very clearly what it all means. Only we are here – together. We've got to stay here, for long, surely till you are well. But you'll never go back to Oldring. And I'm sure helping you will help me, for I was sick in mind. There's something now for me to do. And if I can win back your strength – then get you away, out of this wild country – help you somehow to a happier life – just think how good that'll be for me.'

CHAPTER 10

Love

During all these waiting days Venters, with the exception of the afternoon when he had built the gate in the gorge, had scarcely gone out of sight of camp and never out of hearing. His desire to explore Surprise Valley was keen, and on the morning after his long talk with the girl he took his rifle and, calling Ring, made a move to start. The girl lay back in a rude chair of boughs he had put together for her. She had been watching him, and when he picked up the gun and called the dog Venters thought she gave a nervous start.

'I'm only going to look over the valley,' he said.

'Will you be gone long?'

'No,' he replied, and started off. The incident set him thinking of his former impression that, after her recovery from fever, she did not seem at ease unless he was close at hand. It was fear of being alone, due, he concluded, most likely to her weakened condition. He must not leave her much alone.

As he strode down the sloping terrace, rabbits scampered before him, and the beautiful valley quail, as purple in colour as the sage on the uplands, ran fleetly along the ground into the forest. It was pleasant under the trees, in the gold-flecked shade, with the whistle of quail and twittering of birds everywhere. Soon he had passed the limit of his former excursions and entered new territory. Here the woods began to show open glades and brooks running down from the slope, and presently he emerged from shade into the sunshine of a meadow. The shaking of the high grass told him of the running of animals, what species he could not tell, but from Ring's manifest desire to have a chase they were evidently some kind wilder than rabbits. Venters approached the willow and cottonwood belt that he had observed from the height of slope. He penetrated it to find a considerable stream of water and great half-submerged mounds of brush and sticks, and all about him were old and new gnawed circles at the base of the cottonwoods.

'Beaver!' he exclaimed. 'By all that's lucky! The meadow's full of beaver! How did they ever get here?'

Beaver had not found a way into the valley by the trail of the cliff-

741

dwellers, of that he was certain; and he began to have more than curiosity as to the outlet or inlet of the stream. When he passed some dead water, which he noted was held by a beaver-dam, there was a current in the stream, and it flowed west. Following its course, he soon entered the oak forest again, and passed through to find himself before massed and jumbled ruins of cliff-wall. There were tangled thickets of wild plum trees and other thorny growths that made passage extremely laboursome. He found innumerable tracks of wildcats and foxes. Rustlings in the thick undergrowth told him of stealthy movements of these animals. At length his further advance appeared futile, for the reason that the stream disappeared in a split at the base of immense rocks over which he could not climb. To his relief he concluded that though beaver might work their way up the narrow chasm where the water rushed, it would be impossible for men to enter the valley there.

This western curve was the only part of the valley where the walls had been split asunder, and it was a wildly rough and inaccessible corner. Going back a little way, he leaped the stream and headed towards the southern wall. Once out of the oaks he found again the low terrace of aspens, and above that the wide, open terrace fringed by silver spruces. This side of the valley contained the wind or water worn caves. As he pressed on, keeping to the upper terrace, cave after cave opened out of the cliff; now a large one, now a small one. Then yawned, quite suddenly and wonderfully above him, the great cavern of the cliff-dwellers.

It was still a goodly distance, and he tried to imagine, if it appeared so huge from where he stood, what it would be when he got there. He climbed the terrace and then faced a long, gradual ascent of weathered rock and dust, which made climbing too difficult for attention to anything else. At length he entered a zone of shade, and looked up. He stood just within the hollow of a cavern so immense that he had no conception of its real dimensions. The curved roof, stained by ages of leakage, with buff and black and rust-coloured streaks, swept up and loomed higher and seemed to soar to the rim of the cliff. Here again was a magnificent arch, such as formed the grand gateway to the valley, only in this instance it formed the dome of a cave instead of the span of a bridge.

Venters passed onward and upward. The stones he dislodged rolled down with strange, hollow crack and roar. He had climbed a hundred rods inward, and yet he had not reached the base of the shelf where the cliff-dwellings rested, a long half-circle of connected stone house, with little dark holes that he had fancied were eyes. At length he gained the base of the shelf, and here found steps cut in the rock. These facilitated climbing, and as he went up he thought how easily this vanished race of men might once have held that stronghold against an army. There was only one possible place to ascend, and this was narrow and steep.

Venters had visited cliff-dwellings before, and they had been in ruins, and of no great character or size but this place was of proportions that stunned him, and it had not been desecrated by the hand of man, nor had it been crumbled by the hand of time. It was a stupendous tomb. It had been a city. It was just as it had been left by its builders. The little houses were there, the smoke-blackened stains of fires, the pieces of pottery scattered about cold hearths, the stone hatchets; and stone pestles and mealing-stones lay beside round holes polished by years of grinding maize – lay there as if they had been carelessly dropped yesterday. But the cliff-dwellers were gone!

Dust! They were dust on the floor or at the foot of the shelf, and their habitations and utensils endured. Venters felt the sublimity of that marvellous vaulted arch, and it seemed to gleam with a glory of something that was gone. How many years had passed since the cliff-dwellers gazed out across the beautiful valley as he was gazing now? How long had it been since women ground grain in those polished holes? What time had rolled by since men of an unknown race lived, loved, fought, and died there? Had an enemy destroyed them? Had disease destroyed them, or only that greatest destroyer – time? Venters saw a long line of blood-red hands painted low down upon the yellow roof of stone. Here was strange portent, if not an answer to his queries. The place oppressed him. It was light, but full of a transparent gloom. It smelled of dust and musty stone, of age and disuse. It was sad. It was solemn. It had the look of a place where silence had become master and was now irrevocable and terrible and could not be broken. Yet, at the moment, from high up in the carved crevices of the arch, floated down the low, strange wail of wind – a knell indeed for all that had gone.

Venters, sighing, gathered up an armful of pottery, such pieces as he thought strong enough and suitable for his own use, and bent his steps towards camp. He mounted the terrace at an opposite point to which he had left. He saw the girl looking in the direction he had gone. His footsteps made no sound in the deep grass, and he approached close without her being aware of his presence. Whitie lay on the ground near where she sat, and he manifested the usual actions of welcome, but the girl did not notice them. She seemed to be oblivious to everything near at hand. She made a pathetic figure drooping there, with her sunny hair contrasting so markedly with her white, wasted cheeks and her hands listlessly clasped and her little bare feet propped in the framework of the rude seat. Venters could have sworn and laughed in one breath at the idea of the connection between this girl and Oldring's Masked Rider. She was the victim of more than accident of fate – a victim to some deep plot the mystery of which burned him. As he stepped forward with a half-formed thought that she was absorbed in watching for his return, she turned her head and saw him. A swift start, a change rather than rush of blood under her white cheeks, a flashing of big eyes that fixed their glance upon him, transformed her face in that single instant of turning; and he knew she had been watching for him, that his return was the one thing in her mind. She did not smile; she did not flush; she did not look glad. All these would have meant little compared to her indefinite expression. Venters grasped the peculiar, vivid, vital some-thing that leaped from her face. It was as if she had been in a dead, hopeless clamp of inaction and feeling, and had been suddenly shot through and through with quivering animation. Almost it was as if she had returned to life.

And Venters thought with lightning swiftness, 'I've saved her – I've unlinked her from that old life – she was watching as if I were all she had left on earth – she belongs to me!' The thought was startlingly new. Like a blow it was in an unprepared moment. The cheery salutation he had ready for her died unborn, and he tumbled the pieces of pottery awkwardly on the grass, while some unfamiliar, deep-seated emotion, mixed with pity and glad assurance of his power to succour her, held him dumb.

'What a load you had!' she said. 'Why, they're pots and crocks! Where did you get them?'

Venters laid down his rifle and, filling one of the pots from his canteen, he placed it on the smouldering camp-fire.

'Hope it'll hold water,' he said, presently. 'Why, there's an enormous cliff-dwelling just across there. I got the pottery there. Don't you think we needed something? That tin cup of mine has served to make tea, broth, soup – everything.'

'I noticed we hadn't a great deal to cook in.'

She laughed. It was the first time. He liked that laugh, and though he was tempted to look at her, he did not want to show his surprise or his pleasure.

'Will you take me over there, and all around in the valley – pretty soon when I'm well?' she added.

'Indeed I shall. It's a wonderful place. Rabbits so thick you can't step without kicking one out. And quail, beaver, foxes, wildcats. We're in a regular den. But – haven't you ever seen a cliff-dwelling?'

'No. I've heard about them, though. The – the men say the Pass is full of old houses and ruins.'

'Why, I should think you'd have run across one in all your riding around,' said Venters. He spoke slowly, choosing his words carefully, and he essayed a perfectly casual manner, and pretended to be busy assorting pieces of pottery. She must have no cause again to suffer shame for curiosity of his. Yet never in all his days had he been so eager to hear the details of anyone's life.

'When I rode – I rode like the wind,' she replied, 'and never had time to stop for anything.'

'I remember that day I – I met you in the Pass – how dusty you were, how tired your horse looked. Were you always riding?'

'Oh, no. Sometimes not for months, when I was shut up in the cabin.'

Venters tried to subdue a hot tingling.

'You were shut up, then?' he asked, carelessly.

'When Oldring went away on his long trips – he was gone for months sometimes – he shut me up in the cabin.'

'What for?'

'Perhaps to keep me from running away. I always threatened that. Mostly, though, because the men got drunk at the villages. But they were always good to me. I wasn't afraid.'

'A prisoner! That must have been hard on you?'

'I liked that. As long as I can remember I've been locked up there at times, and those times were the only happy ones I ever had. It's a big cabin, high up on a cliff, and I could look out. Then I had dogs and pets I had tamed, and books. There was a spring inside, and food stored, and the men brought me fresh meat. Once I was there one whole winter.'

It now required deliberation on Venters's part to persist in his unconcern and to keep at work. He wanted to look at her, to volley questions at her.

'As long as you can remember – you've lived in Deception Pass?' he went on.

'I've a dim memory of some other place, and women and children; but I can't make anything of it. Sometimes I think till I'm weary.'

'Then you can read – you have books?'

'Oh yes, I can read, and write, too, pretty well. Oldring is educated. He taught me, and years ago an old rustler lived with us, and he had been something different once. He was always teaching me.'

'So Oldring takes long trips,' mused Venters. 'Do you know where he goes?'

No. Every year he drives cattle north of Sterling – then does not return for months. I heard him accused once of living two lives – and he killed the man. That was at Stone Bridge.'

Venters dropped his apparent task and looked up with an eagerness he no longer strove to hide.

'Bess,' he said, using her name for the first time, 'I suspected Oldring was something besides a rustler. Tell me, what's his purpose here in the Pass? I believe much that he has done was to hide his real work here.'

'You're right. He's more than a rustler. In fact, as the men say, his rustling cattle is now only a bluff. There's gold in the canyons!'

'Ah!

'Yes, there's gold, not in great quantities, but gold enough for him and his men. They wash for gold week in and week out. Then they drive a few cattle and go into the villages to drink and shoot and kill – to bluff the riders.'

'Drive a few cattle! But, Bess, the Withersteen herd, the red herd – twenty-five hundred head! That's not a few. And I tracked them into a valley near here.'

'Oldring never stole the red herd. He made a deal with Mormons. The riders were to be called in, and Oldring was to drive the herd and keep it till a certain time – I don't know when – then drive it back to the range. What his share was I didn't hear.'

'Did you hear *why* that deal was made?' queried Venters.

'No. But it was a trick of Mormons. They're full of tricks. I've heard Oldring's men tell about Mormons. Maybe the Withersteen woman wasn't minding her halter! I saw the man who made the deal. He was a little, queer-shaped man, all humped up. He sat his horse well. I heard one of our men say afterwards there was no better rider on the sage than this fellow. What was the name? I forget.'

'Jerry Card?' suggested Venters.

'That's it. I remember – it's a name easy to remember – and Jerry Card appeared to be on fair terms with Oldring's men.'

'I shouldn't wonder,' replied Venters, thoughtfully. Verification of his suspicions in regard to Tull's underhand work – for the deal with Oldring made by Jerry Card assuredly had its inception in the Mormon Elder's brain, and had been accomplished through his orders – revived in Venters a memory of hatred that had been smothered by press of other emotions. Only a few days had elapsed since the hour of his encounter with Tull, yet they had been forgotten and now seemed far off, and the interval one that now appeared large and profound with incalculable change in his feelings. Hatred of Tull still existed in his heart; but it had lost its white heat. His affection for Jane Withersteen had not changed in the least; nevertheless, he seemed to view it from another angle and see it as another thing – what, he could not exactly define. The recalling of these two feelings was to Venters like getting glimpses into a self that was gone; and the wonder of them – perhaps the change which was too illusive for him – was the fact that a strange irritation accompanied the memory and a desire to dismiss it from mind. And straightway he did dismiss it, to return to thoughts of his significant present.

'Bess, tell me one more thing,' he said. 'Haven't you known any women – any young people?'

'Sometimes there were women with the men; but Oldring never let me know them. And all the young people I ever saw in my life was when I rode fast through the villages.'

Perhaps that was the most puzzling and thought-provoking thing she had yet said to Venters. He pondered, more curious the more he learned, but he curbed his inquisitive desires, for he saw her shrinking on the verge of that shame, the causing of which had occasioned him such self-reproach. He would ask no more. Still he had to think, and he found it difficult to think clearly. This sad-eyed girl was so utterly different from what it would have been reason to believe such a remarkable life would have made her. On this day he had found her simple and frank, as natural as any girl he had ever known. About her there was something sweet. Her voice was low and well modulated. He could not look into her face, meet her steady, unabashed, yet wistful eyes, and think of her as the woman she had confessed herself. Oldring's Masked Rider sat before him, a girl dressed as a man. She had been made to ride at the head of infamous forays and drives. She had been imprisoned for many months of her life in an obscure cabin. At times the most vicious of men had been her companions; and the vilest of women, if they had not been permitted to approach her, had, at least, cast their shadows over her. But – but in spite of all this – there thundered at Venters some truth that lifted its voice higher than the clamouring facts of dishonour, some truth that was the very life of her beautiful eyes; and it was innocence.

In the days that followed, Venters balanced perpetually in mind this haunting conception of innocence over against the cold and sickening fact of an unintentional yet actual gift. How could it be possible for the two things to be true? He believed the latter to be true, and he would not relinquish his conviction of the former; and these conflicting thoughts augmented the mystery that appeared to be a part of Bess. In those ensuing days, however, it became clear as clearest light that Bess was rapidly regaining strength; that, unless reminded of her long association with Oldring, she seemed to have forgotten it; that, like an Indian who lives solely from moment to moment, she was utterly absorbed in the present.

Day by day Venters watched the white of her face slowly change to brown, and the wasted cheeks fill out by imperceptible degrees. There came a time when he could just trace the line of demarcation between the part of her face once hidden by a mask and that left exposed to wind and sun. When that line disappeared in clear bronze tan it was as if she had been washed clean of the stigma of Oldring's Masked Rider. The suggestion of the mask always made Venters remember; now that it was gone he seldom thought of her past. Occasionally he tried to piece together the several stages of strange experience and to make a whole. He had shot a masked outlaw the very sight of whom had been ill omen to riders; he had carried off a wounded woman whose bloody lips quivered in prayer; he had nursed what seemed a frail, shrunken boy; and now he watched a girl whose face had become strangely sweet, whose dark-blue eyes were ever upon him without boldness, without shyness, but with a steady, grave, and growing light. Many times Venters found the clear gaze embarrassing to him, yet, like wine, it had an exhilarating effect. What did she think when she looked at him so? Almost he believed she had no thought at all. All about her and the present there in Surprise Valley, and the dim yet subtly impending future, fascinated Venters and made him thoughtful as all his lonely vigils in the sage had not.

Chiefly it was the present that he wished to dwell upon; but it was the call of the future which stirred him to action. No idea had he of what that future had in store for Bess and him. He began to think of improving Surprise Valley as a place to live in, for there was no telling how long they would be compelled to stay there. Venters stubbornly resisted the entering into his mind of an insistent thought that, clearly realised, might have made it plain to him that he did not want to leave Surprise Valley at all. But it was imperative that he consider practical matters; and whether or not he was destined to stay long there, he felt the immediate need of a change of diet. It would be necessary for him to go farther afield for a variety of meat, and also that he soon visit Cottonwoods for a supply of food.

It occurred again to Venters that he could go to the canyon where Oldring kept his cattle, and at little risk he could pack out some beef. He wished to do this, however, without letting Bess know of it till after he had made the trip. Presently he hit upon the plan of going while she was asleep.

That very night he stole out of camp, climbed up under the stone bridge, and entered the outlet to the Pass. The gorge was full of luminous gloom. Balancing Rock loomed dark and leaned over the pale descent. Transformed in the shadowy light, it took shape and dimensions of a spectral god waiting – waiting for the moment to hurl himself down upon the tottering walls and close forever the outlet to Deception Pass. At night more than by day Venters felt something fearful and fateful in that rock, and that it had leaned and waited through a thousand years to have somehow to deal with his destiny.

'Old man, if you must roll, wait till I get back to the girl, and then roll!' he said, aloud, as if the stones were indeed a god.

And those spoken words, in their grim note to his ear, as well as contents to his mind, told Venters that he was all but drifting on a current which he had not power nor wish to stem.

Venters exercised his usual care in the matter of hiding tracks from the outlet, yet it took him scarcely an hour to reach Oldring's cattle. Here sight of many calves changed his original intention, and instead of packing out meat he decided to take a calf out alive. He roped one, securely tied its feet, and swung it up over his shoulder. Here was an exceedingly heavy burden, but Venters was powerful – he could take up a sack of grain and with ease pitch it over a pack-saddle – and he made long distance without resting. The hardest work came in the climb up to the outlet and on through to the valley. When he had accomplished it, he became fired with another idea that again changed his intention. He would not kill the calf, but keep it alive. He would go back to Oldring's herd and pack out more calves. Thereupon he secured the calf in the best available spot for the moment and turned to make a second trip.

When Venters got back to the valley with another calf, it was close upon daybreak. He crawled into his cave and slept late. Bess had no inkling that he had been absent from camp nearly all night, and only remarked solicitously that he appeared to be more tired than usual, and more in the need of sleep. In the afternoon Venters built a gate across a small ravine near camp, and here corralled the calves; and he succeeded in completing his task without Bess being any the wiser.

That night he made two more trips to Oldring's range, and again on the following night, and yet another on the next. With eight calves in his corral, he concluded that he had enough; but it dawned upon him then that he did not want to kill one. 'I've rustled Oldring's cattle,' he said, and laughed. He noted then that all the calves were red. 'Red!' he exclaimed. 'From the red herd. I've stolen Jane Withersteen's cattle! . . . That's about the strangest thing yet.'

One more trip he undertook to Oldring's valley, and this time he roped a yearling steer and killed it and cut out a small quarter of beef. The howling of coyotes told him he need have no apprehension that the work of his knife would be discovered. He packed the beef back to camp and hung it upon a spruce tree. Then he sought his bed.

On the morrow he was up bright and early, glad that he had a surprise for Bess. He could hardly wait for her to come out. Presently she appeared and walked under the spruce. Then she approached the camp-fire. There was a tinge of healthy red in the bronze of her cheeks, and her slender form had begun to round out in graceful lines.

'Bess, didn't you say you were tired of rabbit?' enquired Venters. 'And quail and beaver?'

'Indeed I did.'

'What would you like?'

'I'm tired of meat, but if we have to live on it I'd like some beef.'

'Well, how does that strike you?' Venters pointed to the quarter hanging from the spruce tree. 'We'll have fresh beef for a few days, then we'll cut the rest into strips and dry it.'

'Where did you get that?' asked Bess, slowly.

'I stole that from Oldring.'

'You went back to the canyon – you risked – ' While she hesitated the tinge of bloom faded out of her cheeks.

'It wasn't any risk, but it was hard work.'

'I'm sorry I said I was tired of rabbit. Why! How – When did you get that beef?'

'Last night.'

'While I was asleep?'

'Yes.'

'I woke last night sometime – but I didn't know.'

Her eyes were widening, darkening with thought, and whenever they did so the steady, watchful, seeing gaze gave place to the wistful light. In the former she saw as the primitive woman without thought; in the latter she looked inward, her gaze was the reflection of a troubled mind. For long Venters had not seen that dark change, that deepening of blue, which he thought was beautiful and sad. But now he wanted to make her think.

'I've done more than pack in that beef,' he said. 'For five nights I've been working while you slept. I've got eight calves corralled near a ravine. Eight calves, all alive, and doing fine!'

'You went five nights!'

All that Venters could make of the dilation of her eyes, her slow pallor, and her exclamation, was fear – fear for herself or for him.

'Yes. I didn't tell you, because I knew you were afraid to be left alone.'

'Alone?' She echoed his word, but the meaning of it was nothing to her. She had not even thought of being left alone. It was not, then, fear for herself, but for him. This girl, always slow of speech and action, now seemed almost stupid. She put forth a hand that might have indicated the groping of her mind. Suddenly she stepped swiftly to him, with a look and touch that drove from him any doubt of her quick intelligence or feeling.

'Oldring has men watch the herds – they would kill you. You must never go again!'

When she had spoken, the strength and the blaze of her died, and she swayed towards Venters.

'*Bess, I'll not go again*,' he said, catching her.

She leaned against him, and her body was limp and vibrated to a long, wavering tremble. Her face was upturned to his. Woman's face, woman's eyes, woman's lips – all acutely and blindly and sweetly and terribly truthful in their betrayal! But as her fear was instinctive, so was her clinging to this one and only friend.

Venters gently put her from him and steadied her upon her feet; and all the while his blood raced wild, and a thrilling tingle unsteadied his nerve, and something – that he had seen and felt in her – that he could not understand – seemed very close to him, warm and rich as a fragrant breath, sweet as nothing had ever before been sweet to him.

With all his will Venters strove for calmness and thought and judgement unbiased by pity, and reality unswayed by sentiment. Bess's eyes were still fixed upon him with all her soul bright in that wistful light. Swiftly, resolutely he put out of mind all of her life except what had been spent with him. He scorned himself for the intelligence that made him still doubt. He meant to judge her as she had judged him. He was face to face with the inevitableness of life itself. He saw destiny in the dark, straight path of her wonderful eyes. Here was the simplicity, the sweetness of a girl contending with new and strange and enthralling emotions; here the living truth of innocence; here the blind terror of a woman confronted with the thought of death to her saviour and protector. All this Venters saw, but, besides, there was in Bess's eyes a slow-dawning consciousness that seemed about to break out in glorious radiance.

'Bess, are you thinking?' he asked.

'Yes – oh yes!'

'Do you realise we are here alone – man and woman?'

'Yes.'

'Have you thought that we may make our way out to civilisation, or we may have to stay here – alone – hidden from the world all our lives?'

'I never thought – till now.'

'Well, what's your choice – to go – or to stay here – alone with me?'

'Stay!' New-born thought of self, ringing vibrantly in her voice, gave her answer singular power.

Venters trembled, and then swiftly turned his gaze from her face – from her eyes. He knew what she had only half divined – that she loved him.

CHAPTER 11

Faith and Unfaith

At Jane Withersteen's home the promise made to Mrs Larkin to care for little Fay had begun to be fulfilled. Like a gleam of sunlight through the cottonwoods was the coming of the child to the gloomy house of Withersteen. The big, silent halls echoed with childish laughter. In the shady court, where Jane spent many of the hot July days, Fay's tiny feet pattered over the stone flags and splashed in the amber stream. She prattled incessantly. What difference, Jane thought, a child made in her home! It

had never been a real home, she discovered. Even the tidiness and
neatness she had so observed, and upon which she had insisted to her
women, became, in the light of Fay's smile, habits that now lost their
importance. Fay littered the court with Jane's books and papers, and
other toys her fancy improvised, and many a strange craft went floating
down the little brook.

And it was owing to Fay's presence that Jane Withersteen came to see
more of Lassiter. The rider had for the most part kept to the sage. He
rode for her, but he did not seek her except on business; and Jane had to
acknowledge in pique that her overtures had been made in vain. Fay,
however, captured Lassiter the moment he first laid eyes on her.

Jane was present at the meeting, and there was something about it
which dimmed her sight and softened her towards this foe of her people.
The rider had clanked into the court, a tired yet wary man, always looking
for the attack upon him that was inevitable and might come from any
quarter; and he had walked right upon little Fay. The child had been
beautiful even in her rags and amid the surroundings of the hovel in the
sage, but now, in a pretty white dress, with her shining curls brushed and
her face clean and rosy, she was lovely. She left her play and looked up at
Lassiter.

If there was not an instinct for all three of them in that meeting, an
unreasoning tendency towards a closer intimacy, then Jane Withersteen
believed she had been subject to a queer fancy. She imagined any child
would have feared Lassiter. And Fay Larkin had been a lonely, a solitary
elf of the sage, not at all an ordinary child, and exquisitely shy with
strangers. She watched Lassiter with great, round, grave eyes, but showed
no fear. The rider gave Jane a favourable report of cattle and horses; and
as he took the seat to which she invited him, little Fay edged as much as
half an inch nearer. Jane replied to his look of enquiry and told Fay's
story. The rider's grey, earnest gaze troubled her. Then he turned to Fay
and smiled in a way that made Jane doubt her sense of the true relation of
things. How could Lassiter smile so at a child when he had made so many
children fatherless? But he did smile, and to the gentleness she had seen
a few times he added something that was infinitely sad and sweet. Jane's
intuition told her that Lassiter had never been a father; but if life ever so
blessed him he would be a good one. Fay, also, must have found that
smile singularly winning. For she edged closer and closer, and then, by
way of feminine capitulation, went to Jane, from whose side she bent a
beautiful glance upon the rider.

Lassiter only smiled at her.

Jane watched them, and realised that now was the moment she should seize, if she was ever to win this man from his hatred. But the step was not easy to take. The more she saw of Lassiter the more she respected him, and the greater her respect the harder it became to lend herself to mere coquetry. Yet as she thought of her great motive, of Tull, and of that other whose name she had schooled herself never to think of in connection with Milly Erne's avenger, she suddenly found she had no choice. And her creed gave her boldness far beyond the limit to which vanity would have led her.

'Lassiter, I see so little of you now,' she said, and was conscious of heat in her cheeks.

'I've been ridin' hard,' he replied.

'But you can't live in the saddle. You come in sometimes. Won't you come here to see me – oftener?'

'Is that an order?'

'Nonsense! I simply ask you to come to see me when you find time.'

'Why?'

The query once heard was not so embarrassing to Jane as she might have imagined. Moreover, it established in her mind a fact that there existed actually other than selfish reasons for her wanting to see him. And as she had been bold, so she determined to be both honest and brave.

'I've reasons – only one of which I need mention,' she answered. 'If it's possible I want to change you towards my people. And on the moment I can conceive of little I wouldn't do to gain that end.'

How much better and freer Jane felt after that confession! She meant to show him that there was one Mormon who could play a game or wage a fight in the open.

'I reckon,' said Lassiter, and he laughed.

It was the best in her, if the most irritating, that Lassiter always aroused.

'Will you come?' She looked into his eyes, and for the life of her could not quite subdue an imperiousness that rose with her spirit. 'I never asked so much of any man – except Bern Venters.'

' 'Pears to me that you'd run no risk, or Venters, either. But mebbe that doesn't hold good for me.'

'You mean it wouldn't be safe for you to be often here? You look for ambush in the cottonwoods?'

'Not that so much.'

At this juncture little Fay sidled over to Lassiter.

'Has oo a little dirl?' she enquired.

'No, lassie,' replied the rider.

Whatever Fay seemed to be searching for in Lassiter's sun-reddened face and quiet eyes she evidently found. 'Oo tan tum to see me,' she added, and with that, shyness gave place to friendly curiosity. First his sombrero with its leather band and silver ornaments commanded her attention; next his quirt, and then the clinking, silver spurs. These held her for some time, but presently, true to childish fickleness, she left off playing with them to look for something else. She laughed in glee as she ran her little hands down the slippery, shiny surface of Lassiter's leather chaps. Soon she discovered one of the hanging gun-sheaths, and she dragged it up and began tugging at the huge black handle of the gun. Jane Withersteen repressed an exclamation. What significance there was to her in the little girl's efforts to dislodge that heavy weapon! Jane Withersteen saw Fay's play and her beauty and her love as most powerful allies to her own woman's part in a game that suddenly had acquired a strange zest and a hint of danger. And as for the rider, he appeared to have forgotten Jane in the wonder of this lovely child playing about him. At first he was much the shyer of the two. Gradually her confidence overcame his backwardness, and he had the temerity to stroke her golden curls with a great hand. Fay rewarded his boldness with a smile, and when he had gone to the extreme of closing that great hand over her little brown one, she said, simply, 'I like oo!'

Sight of his face then made Jane oblivious for the time to his character as a hater of Mormons. Out of the mother longing that swelled her breast she divined the child hunger in Lassiter.

He returned the next day, and the next; and upon the following he came both at morning and at night. Upon the evening of this fourth day Jane seemed to feel the breaking of a brooding struggle in Lassiter. During all these visits he had scarcely a word to say, though he watched her and played absent-mindedly with Fay. Jane had contented herself with silence. Soon little Fay substituted for the expression of regard, 'I like oo,' a warmer and more generous one, 'I love oo.'

Thereafter Lassiter came oftener to see Jane and her little protégée. Daily he grew more gentle and kind, and gradually developed a quaintly merry mood. In the morning he lifted Fay upon his horse and let her ride as he walked beside her to the edge of the sage. In the evening he played with the child at an infinite variety of games she invented, and then, oftener than not, he accepted Jane's invitation to supper. No other visitor came to Withersteen House during those days. So that in spite of watchfulness he never forgot, Lassiter began to show he felt at home there. After the meal they walked into the grove of cottonwoods or up by the lakes, and little Fay held Lassiter's hand as much as she held Jane's. Thus a strange relationship was established, and Jane liked it. At twilight they always returned to the house, where Fay kissed them and went in to her mother. Lassiter and Jane were left alone.

Then, if there were anything that a good woman could do to win a man and still preserve her self-respect, it was something which escaped the natural subtlety of a woman determined to allure. Jane's vanity, that after all was not great, was soon satisfied with Lassiter's silent admiration. And her honest desire to lead him from his dark, blood-stained path would never have blinded her to what she owed herself. But the driving passion of her religion, and its call to save Mormons' lives, one life in particular, bore Jane Withersteen close to an infringement of her woman-hood. In the beginning she had reasoned that her appeal to Lassiter must be through the senses. With whatever means she possessed in the way of adornment she enhanced her beauty. And she stooped to artifices that she knew were unworthy of her, but which she deliberately chose to employ. She made of herself a girl in every variable mood wherein a girl might be desirable. In those moods she was not above the methods of an inexperienced though natural flirt. She kept close to him whenever opportunity afforded; and she was forever playfully, yet passionately underneath the surface, fighting him for possession of the great black guns. These he would never yield to her. And so in that manner their hands were often and long in contact. The more of simplicity that she sensed in him the greater the advantage she took.

She had a trick of changing – and it was not altogether voluntary – from this gay, thoughtless, girlish coquettishness to the silence and the brooding, burning mystery of a woman's mood. The strength and passion and fire of her were in her eyes, and she so used them that Lassiter had to see this depth in her, this haunting promise more fitted to her years than to the flaunting guise of a wilful girl.

The July days flew by. Jane reasoned that if it were possible for her to be happy during such a time, then she was happy. Little Fay completely filled a long aching void in her heart. In fettering the hands of this Lassiter she was accomplishing the greatest good of her life, and to do good even in a small way rendered happiness to Jane Withersteen. She had attended the regular Sunday services of her church; otherwise she had not gone to the village for weeks. It was unusual that none of her churchmen or friends had called upon her of late; but it was neglect for which she was glad. Judkins and his boy riders had experienced no difficulty in driving the white herd. So these warm July days were free of worry, and soon Jane hoped she had passed the crisis; and for her to hope was presently to trust, and then to believe. She thought often of Venters, but in a dreamy, abstract way. She spent hours teaching and playing with little Fay. And the activity of her mind centred around Lassiter. The direction she had given her will seemed to blunt any branching off of thought from that straight line. The mood came to obsess her.

In the end, when her awakening came, she learned that she had builded better than she knew. Lassiter, though kinder and gentler than ever, had parted with his quaint humour and his coldness and his tranquillity to become a restless and unhappy man. Whatever the power of his deadly intent towards Mormons, that passion now had a rival, and one equally burning and consuming. Jane Withersteen had one moment of exultation before the dawn of a strange uneasiness. What if she had made of herself a lure, at tremendous cost to him and to her and all in vain!

That night in the moonlit grove she summoned all her courage and, turning suddenly in the path, she faced Lassiter, and leaned close to him, so that she touched him and her eyes looked up to his.

'Lassiter! . . . Will you do anything for me?'

In the moonlight she saw his dark, worn face change, and by that change she seemed to feel him immovable as a wall of stone.

Jane slipped her hands down to the swinging gun-sheaths, and when she had locked her fingers around the huge, cold handles of the guns, she trembled as with a chilling ripple over all her body.

'May I take your guns?'

'Why?' he asked, and for the first time to her his voice carried a harsh note. Jane felt his hard, strong hands close round her wrists. It was not wholly with intent that she leaned towards him, for the look of his eyes and the feel of his hands made her weak.

'It's no trifle – no woman's whim – it's deep – as my heart. Let me take them?'

'Why?'

'I want to keep you from killing more men – Mormons. You must let me save you from more wickedness – more wanton bloodshed – ' Then the truth forced itself falteringly from her lips. 'You must – let – me – help me to keep my vow to Milly Erne. I swore to her – as she lay dying – that if ever anyone came here to avenge her – I swore I would stay his hand. Perhaps – I alone can save the – the man who – who – Oh, Lassiter! . . . I feel that if I can't change you – then soon you'll go out to kill – and you'll kill by instinct – and among the Mormons you kill will be the one – who . . . Lassiter, if you care a little for me – let me – for my sake – let me take your guns!'

As if her hands had been those of a child, he unclasped their clinging grip from the handles of his guns, and, pushing her away, he turned his grey face to her in one look of terrible realisation and then strode off into the shadows of the cottonwoods.

When the first shock of her futile appeal to Lassiter had passed, Jane took his cold, silent condemnation and abrupt departure not so much as a refusal to her entreaty as a hurt and stunned bitterness for her attempt at his betrayal. Upon further thought and slow consideration of Lassiter's past actions, she believed he would return and forgive her. The man could not be hard to a woman, and she doubted that he could stay away from her. But at the point where she had hoped to find him vulnerable she now began to fear he was proof against all persuasion. The iron and stone quality that she had early suspected in him had actually cropped out as an impregnable barrier. Nevertheless, if Lassiter remained in Cottonwoods she would never give up her hope and desire to change him. She would change him if she had to sacrifice everything dear to her except hope of heaven. Passionately devoted as she was to her religion, she had yet refused to marry a Mormon. But a situation had developed wherein self paled in the great white light of religious duty of the highest order. That was the leading motive, the divinely spiritual one; but there were other motives, which, like tentacles, aided in drawing her will to the acceptance of a possible abnegation. And through the watches of that sleepless night Jane Withersteen, in fear and sorrow and doubt, came finally to believe that if she must throw herself into Lassiter's arms to make him abide by 'Thou shalt not kill!' she would yet do well.

In the morning she expected Lassiter at the usual hour, but she was not able to go at once to the court, so she sent little Fay. Mrs Larkin was ill and required attention. It appeared that the mother, from the time of her arrival at Withersteen House, had relaxed and was slowly losing her hold on life. Jane had believed that absence of worry and responsibility coupled with good nursing and comfort would mend Mrs Larkin's broken health. Such, however, was not the case.

When Jane did get out to the court, Fay was there alone, and at the moment embarking on a dubious voyage down the stone-lined amber stream upon a craft of two brooms and a pillow. Fay was as delightfully wet as she could possibly wish to get.

Clatter of hoofs distracted Fay and interrupted the scolding she was gleefully receiving from Jane. The sound was not the light-spirited trot that Bells made when Lassiter rode him into the outer court. This was slower and heavier, and Jane did not recognise in it any of her other horses. The appearance of Bishop Dyer startled Jane. He dismounted with his rapid, jerky motion, flung the bridle, and, as he turned towards the inner court and stalked up on the stone flags, his boots rang. In his authoritative front, and in the red anger unmistakably flaming in his face, he reminded Jane of her father.

'Is that the Larkin pauper?' he asked, brusquely, without any greeting to Jane.

'It's Mrs Larkin's little girl,' replied Jane, slowly.

'I hear you intend to raise the child?'

'Yes,'

'Of course you mean to give her Mormon bringing-up?'

'No!'

His questions had been swift. She was amazed at a feeling that someone else was replying for her.

'I've come to say a few things to you.' He stopped to measure her with stern, speculative eye.

Jane Withersteen loved this man. From earliest childhood she had been taught to revere and love bishops of her church. And for ten years Bishop Dyer had been the closest friend and counsellor of her father, and for the greater part of that period her own friend and Scriptural teacher. Her interpretation of her creed and her religious activity in fidelity to it, her acceptance of mysterious and holy Mormon truths, were all invested in this Bishop. Bishop Dyer as an entity was next to God. He was God's mouthpiece to the little Mormon community at Cottonwoods. God revealed himself in secret to this mortal.

And Jane Withersteen suddenly suffered a paralysing affront to her consciousness of reverence by some strange, irresistible twist of thought wherein she saw this Bishop as a man. And the train of thought hurdled the rising, crying protests of that other self whose poise she had lost. It was not her Bishop who eyed her in curious measurement. It was a man who tramped into her presence without removing his hat, who had no greeting for her, who had no semblance of courtesy. In looks, as in action, he made her think of a bull stamping cross-grained into a corral. She had heard of Bishop Dyer forgetting the minister in the fury of a common man, and now she was to feel it. The glance by which she measured him in turn momentarily veiled the divine in the ordinary. He looked a rancher; he was booted, spurred and covered with dust; he carried a gun at his hip, and she remembered that he had been known to use it. But during the long moment while he watched her there was nothing commonplace in the slow-gathering might of his wrath.

'Brother Tull has talked to me,' he began. 'It was your father's wish that you marry Tull, and my order. You refused him?'

'Yes.'

'You would not give up your friendship with that tramp Venters?'

'No.'

'But you'll do as *I* order!' he thundered. 'Why, Jane Withersteen, you are in danger of becoming a heretic! You can thank your Gentile friends for that. You face the damning of your soul to perdition.'

In the flux and reflux of the whirling torture of Jane's mind, that new, daring spirit of hers vanished in the old habitual order of her life. She was a Mormon, and the Bishop regained ascendance.

'It's well I got you in time, Jane Withersteen. What would your father have said to these goings-on of yours? He would have put you in a stone cage on bread and water. He would have taught you something about Mormonism. Remember, you're a *born* Mormon. There have been Mormons who turned heretic – damn their souls! – but no born Mormon ever left us yet. Ah, I see your shame. Your faith is not shaken. You are only a wild girl.' The Bishop's tone softened. 'Well, it's enough that I got to you in time . . . Now tell me about this Lassiter. I hear strange things.'

'What do you wish to know?' queried Jane.

'About this man. You hired him?'

'Yes, he's riding for me. When my riders left me I had to have anyone I could get.'

'Is it true what I hear – that he's a gunman, a Mormon-hater, steeped in blood?'

'True – terribly true, I fear.'

'But what's he doing here in Cottonwoods? This place isn't notorious enough for such a man. Sterling and the villages north, where there's universal gunpacking and fights every day – where there are more men like him, it seems to me they would attract him most. We're only a wild, lonely border settlement. It's only recently that the rustlers have made killings here. Nor have there been saloons till lately, nor the drifting in of outcasts. Has not this gunman some special mission here?'

Jane maintained silence.

'Tell me,' ordered Bishop Dyer, sharply.

'Yes,' she replied.

'Do you know what it is?'

'Yes.'

'Tell me that.'

'Bishop Dyer, I don't want to tell.'

He waved his hand in an imperative gesture of command. The red once more leaped to his face, and in his steel-blue eyes glinted a pinpoint of curiosity.

'That first day,' whispered Jane, 'Lassiter said he came here to find – Milly Erne's grave!'

With downcast eyes Jane watched the swift flow of the amber water. She saw it and tried to think of it, of the stones, of the ferns; but, like her body, her mind was in a leaden vice. Only the Bishop's voice could release her. Seemingly there was silence of longer duration than all her former life.

'For what – else?' When Bishop Dyer's voice did cleave the silence it was high, curiously shrill, and on the point of breaking. It released Jane's tongue, but she could not lift her eyes.

'To kill the man who persuaded Milly Erne to abandon her home and her husband – and her God!'

With wonderful distinctness Jane Withersteen heard her own clear voice. She heard the water murmur at her feet and flow on to the sea; she heard the rushing of all the waters in the world. They filled her ears with low, unreal murmurings – these sounds that deadened her brain and yet could not break the long and terrible silence. Then, from somewhere – from an immeasurable distance – came a slow, guarded, clinking, clanking step. Into her it shot electrifying life. It released the weight upon her numbed eyelids. Lifting her eyes she saw – ashen, shaken, stricken – not the Bishop but the man! And beyond him, from round the corner came that soft, silvery step. A long black boot with a gleaming spur swept into sight – and then Lassiter! Bishop Dyer did not see, did not hear: he stared at Jane in the throes of sudden revelation.

'Ah, I understand!' he cried, in hoarse accents. 'That's why you made love to this Lassiter – to bind his hands!'

It was Jane's gaze riveted upon the rider that made Bishop Dyer turn. Then clear sight failed her. Dizzily, in a blur, she saw the Bishop's hand jerk to his hip. She saw gleam of blue and spout of red. In her ears burst a thundering report. The court floated in darkening circles around her, and she fell into utter blackness.

The darkness lightened, turned to slow-drifting haze, and lifted. Through a thin film of blue smoke she saw the rough-hewn timbers of the court roof. A cool, damp touch moved across her brow. She smelled powder, and it was that which galvanised her suspended thought. She moved, to see that she lay prone upon the stone flags with her head on Lassiter's knee, and he was bathing her brow with water from the stream. The same swift glance, shifting low, brought into range of her sight a smoking gun and splashes of blood.

'*Ah-h!*' she moaned, and was drifting, sinking again into darkness, when Lassiter's voice arrested her.

'It's all right, Jane. It's all right.'

'Did – you – kill – him?' she whispered.

'Who? That fat party who was here? No. I didn't kill him.'

'Oh! . . . Lassiter!'

'Say! It was queer for you to faint. I thought you were such a strong woman, not faintish like that. You're all right now – only some pale. I thought you'd never come to. But I'm awkward round women folks. I couldn't think of anythin'.'

'Lassiter! . . . the gun there! . . . the blood!'

'So that's troublin' you. I reckon it needn't. You see it was this way. I come round the house an' seen that fat party an' heard him talkin' loud. Then he seen me, an' very impolite goes straight for his gun. He oughtn't have tried to throw a gun on me – whatever his reason was. For that's meetin' me on my own grounds. I've seen runnin' molasses that was quicker 'n him. Now I didn't know who he was, visitor or friend or relation of yours, though I see he was a Mormon all over, an' I couldn't get serious about shootin'. So I winged him – put a bullet through his arm as he was pullin' at his gun. An' he dropped the gun there, an' a little blood. I told him he'd introduced himself sufficient, an' to please move out of my vicinity. An' he went.'

Lassiter spoke with slow, cool, soothing voice, in which there was a hint of levity, and his touch, as he continued to bathe her brow, was gentle and steady. His impassive face, and the kind, grey eyes, further stilled her agitation.

'He drew on you first, and you deliberately shot to cripple him – you wouldn't kill him – you – *Lassiter*?'

'That's about the size of it.'

Jane kissed his hand.

All that was calm and cool about Lassiter instantly vanished.

'Don't do that! I won't stand it! An' I don't care a damn who that fat party was.'

He helped Jane to her feet and to a chair. Then with the wet scarf he had used to bathe her face he wiped the blood from the stone flags and, picking up the gun, he threw it upon a couch. With that he began to pace the court, and his silver spurs jangled musically, and the great gun-sheaths softly brushed against his leather chaps.

'So – it's true – what I heard him say?' Lassiter asked, presently halting before her. 'You made love to me – to bind my hands?'

'Yes,' confessed Jane. It took all her woman's courage to meet the grey storm of his glance.

'All these days that you've been so friendly an' like a pardner – all these evenin's that have been so bewilderin' to me – your beauty – an' – an' the way you looked an' came close to me – they were woman's tricks to bind my hands?'

'Yes.'

'An' your sweetness that seemed so natural, an' your throwin' little Fay an' me so much together – to make me love the child – all that was for the same reason?'

'Yes.'

Lassiter flung his arms – a strange gesture for him.

'Mebbe it wasn't much in your Mormon thinkin', for you to play that game. But to ring the child in – that was hellish!'

Jane's passionate, unheeding zeal began to loom darkly.

'Lassiter, whatever my intention in the beginning, Fay loves you dearly – and I – I've grown to – to like you.'

'That's powerful kind of you, now,' he said. Sarcasm and scorn made his voice that of a stranger. 'An' you sit there an' look me straight in the eyes! You're a wonderful strange woman, Jane Withersteen.'

'I'm not ashamed, Lassiter. I told you I'd try to change you.'

'Would you mind tellin' me just what you tried?'

'I tried to make you see beauty in me and be softened by it. I wanted you to care for me so that I could influence you. It wasn't easy. At first you were stone-blind. Then I hoped you'd love little Fay, and through that come to feel the horror of making children fatherless.'

'Jane Withersteen, either you're a fool or noble beyond my understanding'. Mebbe you're both. I know you're blind. What you meant is one thing – what you *did* was to make me love you.'

'Lassiter!'

'I reckon I'm a human bein', though I never loved anyone but my sister, Milly Erne. That was long – '

'Oh, are you Milly's brother?'

'Yes, I was, an' I loved her. There never was anyone but her in my life till now. Didn't I tell you that long ago I back-trailed myself from women? I was a Texas ranger till – till Milly left home, an' then I became somethin' else – Lassiter! For years I've been a lonely man set on one thing. I came here an' met you. An' now I'm not the man I was. The change was gradual, an' I took no notice of it. I understand now that never-satisfied longin' to see you, listen to you, watch you, feel you near me. It's plain now why you were never out of my thoughts. I've had no thoughts but of you. I've lived an' breathed for you. An' now when I know what it means – what you've done – I'm burnin' up with hell's fire!'

'Oh, Lassiter – no – no – you don't love me that way!' Jane cried.

'If that's what love is, then I do.'

'Forgive me! I didn't mean to make you love me like that. Oh, what a tangle of our lives! You – Milly Erne's brother! And I – heedless, mad to melt your heart towards Mormons. Lassiter, I may be wicked, but not wicked enough to hate. If I couldn't hate Tull, could I hate you?'

'After all, Jane, mebbe you're only blind – Mormon blind. That only can explain what's close to selfishness – '

'I'm not selfish. I despise the very word. If I were free – '

'But you're not free. Not free of Mormonism. An' in playin' this game with me you've been unfaithful.'

'Un-faithful!' faltered Jane.

'Yes, I said unfaithful. You're faithful to your Bishop an' unfaithful to yourself. You're false to your womanhood an' true to your religion. But for a savin' innocence you'd have made yourself low an' vile – betrayin' yourself, betrayin' me – all to bind my hands an' keep me from snuffin' out Mormon life. It's your damned Mormon blindness.'

'Is it vile – is it blind – is it only Mormonism to save human life? No, Lassiter, that's God's law, divine, universal for all Christians.'

'The blindness I mean is blindness that keeps you from seein' the truth. I've known many good Mormons. But some are blacker than hell.

You won't see that even when you know it. Else, why all this blind passion to save the life of that – that . . .'

Jane shut out the light, and the hands she held over her eyes trembled and quivered against her face.

'Blind – yes, an' let me make it clear an' simple to you,' Lassiter went on, his voice losing its tone of anger. 'Take, for instance, that idea of yours last night when you wanted my guns. It was good an' beautiful, an' showed your heart – but – why, Jane, it was crazy. Mind I'm assumin' that life to me is as sweet as to any other man. An' to preserve that life is each man's first an' closest thought. Where would any man be on this border without guns? Where, especially, would Lassiter be? Well, I'd be under the sage with thousands of other men now livin' an' sure better men than me. Gun-packin' in the West since the Civil War has growed into a kind of moral law. An' out here on this border it's the difference between a man an' somethin' not a man. Look what your takin' Venters's guns from him all but made him! Why, your churchmen carry guns. Tull has killed a man an' drawed on others. Your Bishop has shot a half dozen men, an' it wasn't through prayers of his that they recovered. An' today he'd have shot me if he'd been quick enough on the draw. Could I walk or ride down into Cottonwoods without my guns? This is a wild time, Jane Withersteen, this year of our Lord eighteen seventy-one.'

'No time – for a woman!' exclaimed Jane, brokenly. 'Oh, Lassiter, I feel helpless – lost – and don't know where to turn. If I *am* blind – then – I need someone – a friend – you, Lassiter – more than ever!'

'Well, I didn't say nothin' about goin' back on you, did I?'

CHAPTER 12

The Invisible Hand

Jane received a letter from Bishop Dyer, not in his own handwriting, which stated that the abrupt termination of their interview had left him in some doubt as to her future conduct. A slight injury had incapacitated him from seeking another meeting at present, the letter went on to say, and ended with a request which was virtually a command, that she call upon him at once.

The reading of the letter acquainted Jane Withersteen with the fact that something within her had all but changed. She sent no reply to

Bishop Dyer nor did she go to see him. On Sunday she remained absent from the service – for the second time in years – and though she did not actually suffer there was a deadlock of feelings deep within her, and the waiting for a balance to fall on either side was almost as bad as suffering. She had a gloomy expectancy of untoward circumstances, and with it a keen-edged curiosity to watch developments. She had a half-formed conviction that her future conduct – as related to her churchmen – was beyond her control and would be governed by their attitude towards her. Something was changing in her, forming, waiting for decision to make it a real and fixed thing. She had told Lassiter that she felt helpless and lost in the fateful tangle of their lives; and now she feared that she was approaching the same chaotic condition of mind in regard to her religion. It appalled her to find that she questioned phases of that religion. Absolute faith had been her serenity. Though leaving her faith unshaken, her serenity had been disturbed, and now it was broken by open war between her and her ministers. That something within her – a whisper – which she had tried in vain to hush had become a ringing voice, and it called to her to wait. She had transgressed no laws of God. Her churchmen, however invested with the power and the glory of a wonderful creed, however they sat in inexorable judgement of her, must now practice towards her the simple, common Christian virtue they professed to preach, 'Do unto others as you would have others do unto you!'

Jane Withersteen, waiting in darkness of mind, remained faithful still. But it was darkness that must soon be pierced by light. If her faith were justified, if her churchmen were trying only to intimidate her, the fact would soon be manifest, as would their failure, and then she would redouble her zeal towards them and towards what had been the best work of her life – work for the welfare and happiness of those among whom she lived, Mormon and Gentile alike. If that secret, intangible power closed its coils round her again, if that great invisible hand moved here and there and everywhere, slowly paralysing her with its mystery and its inconceivable sway over her affairs, then she would know beyond doubt that it was not chance, nor jealousy, not intimidation, nor ministerial wrath at her revolt, but a cold and calculating policy thought out long before she was born, a dark, immutable will of whose empire she and all that was hers was but an atom.

Then might come her ruin. Then might come her fall into black storm. Yet she would rise again, and to the light. God would be merciful to a driven woman who had lost her way.

A week passed. Little Fay played and prattled and pulled at Lassiter's big black guns. The rider came to Withersteen House oftener than ever. Jane saw a change in him, though it did not relate to his kindness and gentleness. He was quieter and more thoughtful. While playing with Fay or conversing with Jane he seemed to be possessed of another self that watched with cool, roving eyes, that listened, listened always as if the murmuring amber stream brought messages, and the moving leaves whispered something. Lassiter never rode Bells into the court any more, nor did he come by the lane or the paths. When he appeared it was suddenly and noiselessly out of the dark shadow of the grove.

'I left Bells out in the sage,' he said, one day at the end of that week. 'I must carry water to him.'

'Why not let him drink at the trough or here?' asked Jane quickly.

'I reckon it'll be safer for me to slip through the grove. I've been watched when I rode in from the sage.'

'Watched? by whom?'

'By a man who thought he was well hid. But my eyes are pretty sharp. An', Jane,' he went on, almost in a whisper, 'I reckon it'd be a good idea for us to talk low. You're spied on here by your women.'

'Lassiter!' she whispered in turn. 'That's hard to believe. My women love me.'

'What of that?' he asked. 'Of course they love you. But they're Mormon women.'

Jane's old, rebellious loyalty clashed with her doubt.

'I won't believe it,' she replied, stubbornly.

'Well then, just act natural an' talk natural, an' pretty soon – give them time to hear us – pretend to go over there to the table, an' then quick-like make a move for the door an' open it.'

'I will,' said Jane, with heightened colour. Lassiter was right; he never made mistakes; he would not have told her unless he positively knew. Yet Jane was so tenacious of faith that she had to see with her own eyes, and so constituted that to employ even such small deceit towards her women made her ashamed, and angry for her shame as well as theirs. Then a singular thought confronted her that made her hold up this simple ruse – which hurt her, though it was well justified – against the deceit she had wittingly and eagerly used towards Lassiter. The difference was staggering in its suggestion of that blindness of which he had accused her. Fairness and justice and mercy, that she had imagined were anchor-cables to hold fast her soul to righteousness, had not been hers in the strange, biased duty that had so exalted and confounded her.

Presently Jane began to act her little part, to laugh and play with Fay, to talk of horses and cattle to Lassiter. Then she made deliberate mention of a book in which she kept records of all pertaining to her stock, and she walked slowly towards the table, and when near the door she suddenly whirled and thrust it open. Her sharp action nearly knocked down a woman who had undoubtedly been listening.

'Hester,' said Jane, sternly, 'you may go home, and you need not come back.'

Jane shut the door and returned to Lassiter. Standing unsteadily, she put her hand on his arm. She let him see that doubt had gone, and how this stab of disloyalty pained her.

'Spies! My own women! . . . Oh, miserable!' she cried, with flashing, tearful eyes.

'I hate to tell you,' he replied. By that she knew he had long spared her. 'It's begun again – that work in the dark.'

'Nay, Lassiter – it never stopped!'

So bitter certainty claimed her at last, and trust fled Withersteen House and fled forever. The women who owed much to Jane Withersteen changed not in love for her, nor in devotion to their household work, but they poisoned both by a thousand acts of stealth and cunning and duplicity. Jane broke out once and caught them in strange, stone-faced, unhesitating falsehood. Thereafter she broke out no more. She forgave them because they were driven. Poor, fettered, and sealed Hagars, how she pitied them! What terrible thing bound them and locked their lips when they showed neither consciousness of guilt towards their bene-factress nor distress at the slow wearing apart of long-established and dear ties?

'The blindness again!' cried Jane Withersteen. 'In my sisters as in me! . . . O God!'

There came a time when no words passed between Jane and her women. Silently they went about their household duties, and secretly they went about the underhand work to which they had been bidden. The gloom of the house and the gloom of its mistress, which darkened even the bright spirit of little Fay, did not pervade these women. Happiness was not among them, but they were aloof from gloom. They spied and listened; they received and sent secret messengers; and they stole Jane's books and records, and finally the papers that were deeds of her possessions. Through it all they were silent, rapt in a kind of trance. Then one by one, without leave or explanation or farewell, they left Withersteen House, and never returned.

Coincident with this disappearance, Jane's gardeners and workers in the alfalfa fields and stable men quit her, not even asking for their wages. Of all her Mormon employees about the great ranch only Jerd remained. He went on with his duty, but talked no more of the change than if it had never occurred.

'Jerd,' said Jane, 'what stock you can't take care of turn out in the sage. Let your first thought be for Black Star and Night. Keep them in perfect condition. Run them every day and watch them always.'

Though Jane Withersteen gave with such liberality, she loved her possessions. She loved the rich, green stretches of alfalfa, and the farms, and the grove, and the old stone house, and the beautiful, ever-faithful amber spring, and every one of a myriad of horses and colts and burrows and fowls down to the smallest rabbit that nipped her vegetables; but she loved best her noble Arabian steeds. In common with all riders of the upland sage Jane cherished two material things – the cold, sweet, brown water that made life possible in the wilderness and the horses which were a part of that life. When Lassiter asked her what Lassiter would be without his guns he was assuming that his horse was part of himself. So Jane loved Black Star and Night because it was her nature to love all beautiful creatures – perhaps all living things; and then she loved them because she herself was of the sage and in her had been born and bred the rider's instinct to rely on his four-footed brother. And when Jane gave Jerd the order to keep her favourites trained down to the day it was a half-conscious admission that presaged a time when she would need her fleet horses.

Jane had now, however, no leisure to brood over the coils that were closing round her. Mrs Larkin grew weaker as the August days began; she required constant care; there was little Fay to look after and such household work as was imperative. Lassiter put Bells in the stable with the other racers, and directed his efforts to a closer attendance upon Jane. She welcomed the change. He was always at hand to help, and it was her fortune to learn that his boast of being awkward around women had its root in humility and was not true.

His great, brown hands were skilled in a multiplicity of ways which a woman might have envied. He shared Jane's work, and was of especial help to her in nursing Mrs Larkin. The woman suffered most at night, and this often broke Jane's rest. So it came about that Lassiter would stay by Mrs Larkin during the day, when she needed care, and Jane would make up the sleep she lost in night-watches. Mrs Larkin at once took kindly to the gentle Lassiter, and, without ever asking who or what he was, praised him to Jane. 'He's a good man and loves children,' she said. How sad to hear this truth spoken of a man whom Jane thought lost beyond all redemption! Yet ever and ever Lassiter towered above her, and behind or through his black, sinister figure shone something luminous that strangely affected Jane. Good and evil began to seem incomprehensibly blended in her judgement. It was her belief that evil could not come forth from good; yet here was a murderer who dwarfed in gentleness, patience, and love any man she had ever known.

She had almost lost track of her more outside concerns when early one morning Judkins presented himself before her in the courtyard.

Thin, hard, burnt, bearded, with the dust and sage thick on him, with his leather wristbands shining from use, and his boots worn through on the stirrup side, he looked the rider of riders. He wore two guns and carried a Winchester.

Jane greeted him with surprise and warmth, set meat and bread and drink before him; and called Lassiter out to see him. The men exchanged glances, and the meaning of Lassiter's keen enquiry and Judkins's bold reply, both unspoken, was not lost upon Jane.

'Where's your hoss?' asked Lassiter, aloud.

'Left him down the slope,' answered Judkins. 'I footed it in a ways, an' slept last night in the sage. I went to the place you told me you 'most always slept, but didn't strike you.'

'I moved up some, near the spring, an' now I go there nights.'

'Judkins – the white herd?' queried Jane, hurriedly.

'Miss Withersteen, I made proud to say I've not lost a steer. Fer a good while after thet stampede Lassiter milled we hed no trouble. Why, even the sage dogs left us. But it's begun agin – thet flashin' of lights over ridge tips, an' queer puffin' of smoke, an' then at night strange whistles an' noises. But the herd's acted magnificent. An' my boys, say, Miss Withersteen, they're only kids, but I ask no better riders. I got the laugh in the village fer takin' them out. They're a wild lot, an' you know boys hev more nerve than grown men, because they don't know what danger is. I'm not denyin' there's danger. But they glory in it, an' mebbe I like it myself – anyway, we'll stick. We're goin' to drive the herd on the far side of the first break of Deception Pass. There's a great round valley over there, an' no ridges or piles of rocks to aid these stampeders. The rains are due. We'll hev plenty of water fer a while. An' we can hold thet herd from anybody except Oldrin'. I come in fer supplies. I'll pack a couple of burros an' drive out after dark tonight.'

'Judkins, take what you want from the store-room. Lassiter will help you. I – I can't thank you enough . . . but – wait.'

Jane went to the room that had once been her father's, and from a secret chamber in the thick stone wall she took a bag of gold, and, carrying it back to the court, she gave it to the rider.

'There, Judkins, and understand that I regard it as little for your loyalty. Give what is fair to your boys, and keep the rest. Hide it. Perhaps that would be wisest.'

'Oh . . . Miss Withersteen!' ejaculated the rider. 'I couldn't earn so much in – in ten years. It's not right – I oughtn't take it.'

'Judkins, you know I'm a rich woman. I tell you I've few faithful friends. I've fallen upon evil days. God only knows what will become of me and mine! So take the gold.'

She smiled in understanding of his speechless gratitude, and left him with Lassiter. Presently she heard him speaking low at first, then in louder accents emphasised by the thumping of his rifle on the stones. 'As infernal a job as even you, Lassiter, ever heerd of.'

'Why, son,' was Lassiter's reply, 'this breakin' of Miss Withersteen may seem bad to you, but it ain't bad – yet. Some of these wall-eyed fellers who look jest as if they was walkin' in the shadow of Christ himself, right down the sunny road, now they can think of things an' do things that are really hell-bent.'

Jane covered her ears and ran to her own room, and there like a caged lioness she paced to and fro till the coming of little Fay reversed her dark thoughts.

The following day, a warm and muggy one threatening rain, while Jane was resting in the court, a horseman clattered through the grove and up to the hitching-rack. He leaped off and approached Jane with the manner of a man determined to execute a difficult mission, yet fearful of its reception. In the gaunt, wiry figure and the lean, brown face Jane recognised one of her Mormon riders, Blake. It was he of whom Judkins had long since spoken. Of all the riders ever in her employ Blake owed her the most, and as he stepped before her, removing his hat and making manly efforts to subdue his emotion, he showed that he remembered.

'Miss Withersteen, mother's dead,' he said.

'Oh – Blake!' exclaimed Jane, and she could say no more.

'She died free from pain in the end, and she's buried – resting at last, thank God! . . . I've come to ride for you again, if you'll have me. Don't think I mentioned mother to get your sympathy. When she was living and your riders quit, I had to also. I was afraid of what might be done – said to her . . . Miss Withersteen, we can't talk of – of what's going on now – '

'Blake, do you know?'

'I know a great deal. You understand, my lips are shut. But without explanation or excuse I offer my services. I'm a Mormon – I hope a good one. But – there are some things! . . . It's no use, Miss Withersteen, I can't say any more – what I'd like to. But will you take me back?'

'Blake! . . . You know what it means?'

'I don't care. I'm sick of – of – I'll show you a Mormon who'll be true to you!'

'But, Blake – how terribly you might suffer for that!'

'Maybe. Aren't you suffering now?'

'God knows indeed I am!'

'Miss Withersteen, it's a liberty on my part to speak so, but I know you pretty well – know you'll never give in. I wouldn't if I were you. And I – I must – Something makes me tell you the worst is yet to come. That's all, I absolutely can't say more. Will you take me back – let me ride for you – show everybody what I mean?'

'Blake, it makes me happy to hear you. How my riders hurt me when they quit!' Jane felt the hot tears well to her eyes and splash down upon her hands. 'I thought so much of them – tried so hard to be good to them. And not one was true. You've made it easy to forgive. Perhaps many of them really feel as you do, but dare not return to me. Still, Blake, I hesitate to take you back. Yet I want you so much.'

'Do it, then. If you're going to make your life a lesson to Mormon women, let me make mine a lesson to the men. Right is right. I believe in you, and here's my life to prove it.'

'You hint it may mean your life!' said Jane, breathless and low.

'We won't speak of that. I want to come back. I want to do what every rider aches in his secret heart to do for you . . . Miss Withersteen, I hoped it'd not be necessary to tell you that my mother on her deathbed told me to have courage. She knew how the thing galled me – she told me to come back . . . Will you take me?'

'God bless you, Blake! Yes, I'll take you back. And will you – will you accept gold from me?'

'Miss Withersteen!'

'I just gave Judkins a bag of gold. I'll give you one. If you will not take it you must not come back. You might ride for me a few months – weeks – days till the storm breaks. Then you'd have nothing, and be in disgrace with your people. We'll forearm you against poverty, and me against endless regret. I'll give you gold which you can hide – till some future time.'

'Well, if it pleases you,' replied Blake. 'But you know I never thought of pay. Now, Miss Withersteen, one thing more. I want to see this man Lassiter. Is he here?'

'Yes, but, Blake – what – Need you see him? Why?' asked Jane, instantly worried. 'I can speak to him – tell him about you.'

'That won't do. I want to – I've got to tell him myself. Where is he?'

'Lassiter is with Mrs Larkin. She is ill. I'll call him,' answered Jane, and going to the door she softly called for the rider. A faint, musical jingle preceded his step – then his tall form crossed the threshold.

'Lassiter, here's Blake, an old rider of mine. He has come back to me and he wishes to speak to you.'

Blake's brown face turned exceedingly pale.

'Yes, I had to speak to you,' he said, swiftly. 'My name's Blake. I'm a Mormon and a rider. Lately I quit Miss Withersteen. I've come to beg her to take me back. Now I don't know you, but I know – what you are. So I've this to say to your face. It would never occur to this woman to imagine – let alone suspect me to be a spy. She couldn't think it might just be a low plot to come here and shoot you in the back. Jane Withersteen hasn't that kind of a mind . . . Well, I've not come for that. I want to help her – to pull a bridle along with Judkins and – and you. The thing is – do you believe me?'

'I reckon I do,' replied Lassiter. How this slow, cool speech contrasted with Blake's hot, impulsive words! 'You might have saved some of your breath. See here, Blake, cinch this in your mind. Lassiter has met some square Mormons! An' mebb – '

'Blake,' interrupted Jane, nervously anxious to terminate a colloquy that she perceived was an ordeal for him. 'Go at once and fetch me a report of my horses.'

'Miss Withersteen! . . . You mean the big drove – down in the sage-cleared fields?'

'Of course,' replied Jane. 'My horses are all there, except the blooded stock I keep here.'

'Haven't you heard – then?'

'Heard? No! What's happened to them?'

'They're gone, Miss Withersteen, gone these ten days past. Dorn told me, and I rode down to see for myself.'

'Lassiter – did you know?' asked Jane, whirling to him.

'I reckon so . . . But what was the use to tell you?'

It was Lassiter turning away his face and Blake studying the stone flags at his feet that brought Jane to the understanding of what she betrayed. She strove desperately, but she could not rise immediately from such a blow.

'My horses! My horses! What's become of them?'

'Dorn said the riders report another drive by Oldring . . . And I trailed the horses miles down the slope towards Deception Pass.'

'My red herd's gone! My horses gone! The white herd will go next. I can stand that. But if I lost Black Star and Night, it would be like parting with my own flesh and blood. Lassiter – Blake – am I in danger of losing my racers?'

'A rustler – or – or anybody stealin' hosses of yours would most of all want the blacks,' said Lassiter. His evasive reply was affirmative enough. The other rider nodded gloomy acquiescence.

'Oh! Oh!' Jane Withersteen choked, with violent utterance.

'Let me take charge of the blacks?' asked Blake. 'One more rider won't be any great help to Judkins. But I might hold Black Star and Night, if you put such store on their value.'

'Value! Blake, I love my racers. Besides, there's another reason why I mustn't lose them. You go to the stables. Go with Jerd every day when he runs the horses, and don't let them out of your sight. If you would please me – win my gratitude, guard my black racers.'

When Blake had mounted and ridden out of the court Lassiter regarded Jane with the smile that was becoming rarer as the days sped by.

' 'Pears to me, as Blake says, you do put some store on them hosses. Now I ain't gainsayin' that the Arabians are the handsomest hosses I ever seen. But Bells can beat Night, an' run neck an' neck with Black Star.'

'Lassiter, don't tease me now. I'm miserable – sick. Bells is fast, but he can't stay with the blacks, and you know it. Only Wrangle can do that.'

'I'll bet that big raw-boned brute can more'n show his heels to your black racers. Jane, out there in the sage, on a long chase, Wrangle could kill your favourites.'

'No, no,' replied Jane, impatiently. 'Lassiter, why do you say that so often? I know you've teased me at times, and I believe it's only kindness. You're always trying to keep my mind off worry. But you mean more by this repeated mention of my racers?'

'I reckon so.' Lassiter paused, and for the thousandth time in her presence moved his black sombrero round and round, as if counting the silver pieces on the band. 'Well, Jane, I've sort of read a little that's passin' in your mind.'

'You think I might fly from my home – from Cottonwoods – from the Utah border?'

'I reckon. An' if you ever do an' get away with the blacks I wouldn't like to see Wrangle left here on the sage. Wrangle could catch you. I know Venters had him. But you can never tell. Mebbe he hasn't got him now . . . Besides – things are happenin', an' somethin' of the same queer nature might have happened to Venters.'

'God knows you're right! . . . Poor Bern, how long he's gone! In my trouble I've been forgetting him. But, Lassiter, I've little fear for him. I've heard my riders say he's as keen as a wolf . . . As to your reading my thoughts – well, your suggestion makes an actual thought of what was only one of my dreams. I believe I dreamed of flying from this wild borderland, Lassiter. I've strange dreams. I'm not always practical and thinking of my many duties, as you said once. For instance – if I dared – if I dared I'd ask you to saddle the blacks and ride away with me – and hide me.'

'Jane!'

The rider's sunburnt face turned white. A few times Jane had seen Lassiter's cool calm broken – when he had met little Fay, when he had learned how and why he had come to love both child and mistress, when he had stood beside Milly Erne's grave. But one and all they could not be considered in the light of his present agitation. Not only did Lassiter turn white – not only did he grow tense, not only did he lose his coolness, but also he suddenly, violently, hungrily took her into his arms and crushed her to his breast.

'Lassiter!' cried Jane, trembling. It was an action for which she took sole blame. Instantly, as if dazed, weakened, he released her. 'Forgive me!' went on Jane. 'I'm always forgetting your – your feelings. I thought of you as my faithful friend. I'm always making you out more than human . . . only, let me say – I meant that – about riding away. I'm wretched, sick of this – this – Oh, something bitter and black grows on my heart!'

'Jane, the hell – of it,' he replied, with deep intake of breath, 'is you *can't* ride away. Mebbe realisin' it accounts for my grabbin' you – that way, as much as the crazy boy's rapture your words gave me. I don't understand myself . . . But the hell of this game is – you *can't* ride away.'

'Lassiter! . . . What on earth do you mean? I'm an absolutely free woman.'

'You ain't absolutely anythin' of the kind . . . I reckon I've got to tell you!'

'Tell me all. It's uncertainty that makes me a coward. It's faith and hope – blind love, if you will, that makes me miserable. Every day I awake believing – still believing. The day grows, and with it doubts, fears, and that black bat hate that bites hotter and hotter into my heart. Then comes night – I pray – I pray for all, and for myself – I sleep – and I awake free once more, trustful, faithful, to believe – to hope! Then, O my God! I grow and live a thousand years till night again! . . . But if you want to see me a woman, tell me why I can't ride away – tell me what more I'm to lose – tell me the worst.'

'Jane, you're watched. There's no single move of yours, except when you're hid in your house, that ain't seen by sharp eyes. The cottonwood grove's full of creepin', crawlin' men. Like Indians in the grass. When you rode, which wasn't often lately, the sage was full of sneakin' men. At night they crawl under your window, into the court, an' I reckon into the house. Jane Withersteen, you know, never locked a door! This here grove's a hummin' beehive of mysterious happenin's. Jane, it ain't so much that these spies keep out of my way as me keepin' out of theirs. They're goin' to try to kill me. That's plain. But mebbe I'm as hard to shoot in the back as in the face. So far I've seen fit to watch only. This all means, Jane, that you're a marked woman. You can't get away – not now. Mebbe later when you're broken, you might. But that's sure doubtful. Jane, you're to lose the cattle that's left – your home an' ranch – an' Amber Spring. You can't even hide a sack of gold! For it couldn't be slipped out of the house, day or night, an' hid or buried, let alone be rid off with. You may lose all. I'm tellin' you, Jane, hopin' to prepare you, if the worst does come. I told you once before about that strange power I've got to feel things.'

'Lassiter, what can I do?'

'Nothin', I reckon, except know what's comin' an' wait an' be game. If you'd let me make a call on Tull, an' a long deferred call on –'

'Hush! . . . Hush!' she whispered.

'Well, even that wouldn't help you any in the end.'

'What does it mean? Oh, what does it mean? I am my father's daughter – a Mormon, yet I can't see! I've not failed in religion – in duty. For years I've given with a free and full heart. When my father died I was rich. If I'm still rich it's because I couldn't find enough ways to become poor. What am I, what are my possessions to set in motion such intensity of secret oppression?'

'Jane, the mind behind it all is an empire builder.'

'But, Lassiter, I would give freely – all I own to avert this – this wretched thing. If I gave – that would leave me with faith still. Surely my – my churchmen think of my soul? If I lose my trust in them –'

'Child, be still!' said Lassiter, with a dark dignity that had in it something of pity. 'You are a woman, fine an' big an' strong, an' your heart matches your size. But in mind you're a child. I'll say a little more – then I'm done. I'll never mention this again. Among many thousands of women you're one who has bucked against your churchmen. They tried you out, an' failed of persuasion, an' finally of threats. You meet now the cold steel of a will as far from Christlike as the universe is wide. You're to be broken. Your body's to be held, given to some man, made, if possible, to bring children into the world. But your soul? . . . What do they care for your soul?'

CHAPTER 13

Solitude and Storm

In his hidden valley Venters awakened from sleep, and his ears rang with innumerable melodies from full-throated mockingbirds, and his eyes opened wide upon the glorious golden shaft of sunlight shining through the great stone bridge. The circle of cliffs surrounding Surprise Valley lay shrouded in morning mist, a dim blue low down along the terraces, a creamy, moving cloud along the ramparts. The oak forest in the centre was a plumed and tufted oval of gold.

He saw Bess under the spruces. Upon her complete recovery of strength she always rose with the dawn. At the moment she was feeding the quail she had tamed. And she had begun to tame the mocking-birds. They fluttered among the branches overhead, and some left off their songs to flit down and shyly hop near the twittering quail. Little grey and white rabbits crouched in the grass, now nibbling, now laying long ears flat and watching the dogs.

Venters's swift glance took in the brightening valley, and Bess and her pets, and Ring and Whitie. It swept over all to return again and rest upon the girl. She had changed. To the dark trousers and blouse she had added moccasins of her own make, but she no longer resembled a boy. No eye could have failed to mark the rounded contours of a woman. The change had been to grace and beauty. A glint of warm gold gleamed from her hair, and a tint of red shone in the clear dark brown of cheeks. The haunting sweetness of her lips and eyes, that earlier had been illusive, a promise, had become a living fact. She fitted harmoniously into that wonderful setting; she was like Surprise Valley – wild and beautiful.

Venters leaped out of his cave to begin the day.

He had postponed his journey to Cottonwoods until after the passing of the summer rains. The rains were due soon. But until their arrival and the necessity for his trip to the village he sequestered in a far corner of mind all thought of peril, of his past life, and almost that of the present. It was enough to live. He did not want to know what lay hidden in the dim and distant future. Surprise Valley had enchanted him. In this home of the cliff-dwellers there were peace and quiet and solitude, and another thing, wondrous as the golden morning shaft of sunlight, that he dared not ponder over long enough to understand.

The solitude he had hated when alone he had now come to love. He was assimilating something from this valley of gleams and shadows. From this strange girl he was assimilating more.

The day at hand resembled many days gone before. As Venters had no tools with which to build, or to till the terraces, he remained idle. Beyond the cooking of the simple fare there were no tasks. And as there were no tasks, there was no system. He and Bess began one thing, to leave it; to begin another, to leave that; and then do nothing but lie under the spruces and watch the great cloud-sails majestically move along the ramparts, and dream and dream. The valley was a golden, sunlit world. It was silent. The sighing wind and the twittering quail and the singing birds, even the rare and seldom-occurring hollow crack of a sliding weathered stone, only thickened and deepened that insulated silence.

Venters and Bess had vagrant minds.

'Bess, did I tell you about my horse Wrangle?' enquired Venters.

'A hundred times,' she replied.

'Oh, have I? I'd forgotten. I want you to see him. He'll carry us both.'

'I'd like to ride him. Can he run?'

'Run? He's a demon. Swiftest horse on the sage! I hope he'll stay in that canyon.'

'He'll stay.'

They left camp to wander along the terraces, into the aspen ravines, under the gleaming walls. Ring and Whitie wandered in the fore, often turning, often trotting back, open-mouthed and solemn-eyed and happy. Venters lifted his gaze to the grand archway over the entrance to the valley, and Bess lifted hers to follow his, and both were silent. Sometimes the bridge held their attention for a long time. Today a soaring eagle attracted them.

'How he sails!' exclaimed Bess. 'I wonder where his mate is?'

'She's at the nest. It's on the bridge in a crack near the top. I see her often. She's almost white.'

They wandered on down the terrace, into the shady, sun-flecked forest. A brown bird fluttered crying from a bush. Bess peeped into the leaves.

'Look! A nest and four little birds. They're not afraid of us. See how they open their mouths. They're hungry.'

Rabbits rustled the dead brush and pattered away. The forest was full of a drowsy hum of insects. Little darts of purple, that were running quail, crossed the glades. And a plaintive, sweet peeping came from the coverts. Bess's soft step disturbed a sleeping lizard that scampered away over the leaves. She gave chase and caught it, a slim creature of nameless colour but of exquisite beauty.

'Jewel eyes,' she said. 'It's like a rabbit – afraid. We won't eat you. There – go.'

Murmuring water drew their steps down into a shallow shaded ravine where a brown brook brawled softly over mossy stones. Multitudes of strange, grey frogs with white spots and black eyes lined the rock bank and leaped only at close approach. Then Venters's eye descried a very thin, very long green snake coiled round a sapling. They drew closer and closer till they could have touched it. The snake had no fear and watched them with scintillating eyes.

'It's pretty,' said Bess. 'How tame! I thought snakes always ran.'

'No. Even the rabbits didn't run here till the dogs chased them.'

On and on they wandered to the wild jumble of massed and broken fragments of cliff at the west end of the valley. The roar of the disappearing stream dinned in their ears. Into this maze of rocks they threaded a tortuous way, climbing, descending, halting to gather wild plums and great lavender lilies, and going on at the will of fancy. Idle and keen perceptions guided them equally.

'Oh, let us climb there!' cried Bess, pointing upward to a small space of terrace left green and shady between huge abutments of broken cliff. And they climbed to the nook and rested and looked out across the valley to the curling column of blue smoke from their camp-fire. But the cool shade and the rich grass and the fine view were not what they had climbed for. They could not have told, although whatever had drawn them was all-satisfying. Light, sure-footed as a mountain goat, Bess pattered down at Venters's heels; and they went on, calling the dogs, eyes dreamy and wide, listening to the wind and the bees and the crickets and the birds.

Part of the time Ring and Whitie led the way, then Venters, then Bess; and the direction was not an object. They left the sun-streaked shade of the oaks, brushed the long grass of the meadows, entered the green and fragrant swaying willows, to stop, at length, under the huge old cottonwoods where the beavers were busy.

Here they rested and watched. A dam of brush and logs and mud and stones backed the stream into a little lake. The round, rough beaver houses projected from the water. Like the rabbits the beavers had become shy. Gradually, however, as Venters and Bess knelt low, holding the dogs, the beavers emerged to swim with logs and gnaw at cottonwoods and pat mud walls with their paddle-like tails, and, glossy and shiny in the sun, to go on with their strange, persistent industry. They were the builders. The lake was a mud-hole, and the immediate environment a scarred and dead region, but it was a wonderful home of wonderful animals.

'Look at that one – he puddles in the mud,' said Bess. 'And there! See him dive! Hear them gnawing! I'd think they'd break their teeth. How's it they can stay out of the water and under the water?'

And she laughed.

Then Venters and Bess wandered farther, and, perhaps not all unconsciously this time, wended their slow steps to the cave of the cliff-dwellers, where she liked best to go.

The tangled thicket and the long slant of dust and little chips of weathered rock and the steep bench of stone and the worn steps, all were arduous work for Bess in the climbing. But she gained the shelf, gasping, hot of cheek, glad of eye with her hand in Venters's. Here they rested. The beautiful valley glittered below with its millions of wind-turned leaves bright-faced in the sun, and the mighty bridge towered heavenward, crowned with blue sky. Bess, however, never rested for long. Soon she was exploring, and Venters followed; she dragged forth from corners and shelves a multitude of crudely fashioned and painted pieces of pottery, and he carried them. They peeped down into the dark holes of the kivas, and Bess gleefully dropped a stone and waited for the long-coming hollow sound to rise. They peeped into the little globular houses, like mud-wasp nests, and wondered if these had been store-places for grain, or baby cribs, or what; and they crawled into the larger houses and laughed when they bumped their heads on the low roofs, and they dug in the dust of the floors. And they brought from dust and darkness arm loads of treasure which they carried to the light. Flints and stones and strange curved sticks and pottery they found; and twisted grass rope that crumbled in their hands, and bits of whitish stones which crushed to powder at a touch and seemed to vanish in the air.

'That white stuff was bone,' said Venters, slowly. 'Bones of a cliff-dweller.'

'No!' exclaimed Bess.

'Here's another piece. Look! . . . . Whew! dry, powdery smoke! That's bone.'

Then it was that Venters's primitive, childlike mood, like a savage's, seeing, yet unthinking, gave way to the encroachment of civilised thought. The world had not been made for a single day's play or fancy or idle watching. The world was old. Nowhere could be got a better idea of its age than in that gigantic silent tomb. The grey ashes in Venters's hand had once been bone of a human being like himself. The pale gloom of the cave had shadowed people long ago. He saw that Bess had received the same shock – could not in moments such as this escape her feeling, living, thinking destiny.

'Bern, people have *lived* here,' she said, with wide, thoughtful eyes.

'Yes,' he replied.

'How long ago?'

'A thousand years and more.'

'What were they?'

'Cliff-dwellers. Men who had enemies and made their homes high out of reach.'

'They had to fight?'

'Yes.'

'They fought for – what?'

'For life. For their homes, food, children, parents – for their women!'

'Has the world changed any in a thousand years?'

'I don't know – perhaps very little.'

'Have men?'

'I hope so – I think so.'

'Things crowd into my mind,' she went on, and the wistful light in her eyes told Venters the truth of her thoughts. 'I've ridden the border of Utah. I've seen people – know how they live – but they must be few of all who are living. I had my books and I studied them. But all that doesn't help me any more. I want to go out into the big world and see it. Yet I want to stay here more. What's to become of us? Are we cliff-dwellers? We're alone here. I'm happy when I don't think. These – these bones that fly into dust – they make me sick and a little afraid. Did the people who lived here once have the same feelings as we have? What was the good of their living at all? They're gone! What's the meaning of it all – of us?'

'Bess, you ask more than I can tell. It's beyond me. Only there was laughter here once – and now there's silence. There was life – and now there's death. Men cut these little steps, made these arrowheads and mealing-stones, plaited the ropes we found, and left their bones to crumble in our fingers. As far as time is concerned it might all have been yesterday. We're here today. Maybe we're higher in the scale of human beings – in intelligence. But who knows? We can't be any higher in the things for which life is lived at all.'

'What are they?'

'Why – I suppose relationship, friendship – love.'

'Love!'

'Yes. Love of man for woman – love of woman for man. That's the nature, the meaning, the best of life itself.'

She said no more. Wistfulness of glance deepened into sadness.

'Come, let us go,' said Venters.

Action brightened her. Beside him, holding his hand, she slipped down the shelf, ran down the long, steep slant of sliding stones, out of the cloud of dust, and likewise out of the pale gloom.

'We beat the slide,' she cried.

The miniature avalanche cracked and roared, and rattled itself into an inert mass at the base of the incline. Yellow dust like the gloom of the cave, but not so changeless, drifted away on the wind; the roar clapped in echo from the cliff, returned, went back, and came again to die in the hollowness. Down on the sunny terrace there was a different atmosphere. Ring and Whitie leaped around Bess. Once more she was smiling, gay, and thoughtless, with the dream-mood in the shadow of her eyes.

'Bess, I haven't seen that since last summer. Look!' said Venters, pointing to the scalloped edge of rolling purple clouds that peeped over the western wall. 'We're in for a storm.'

'Oh, I hope not. I'm afraid of storms.'

'Are you? Why?'

'Have you ever been down in one of these walled-up pockets in a bad storm?'

'No, now I think of it, I haven't.'

'Well, it's terrible. Every summer I get scared to death and hide somewhere in the dark. Storms up on the sage are bad, but nothing to what they are down here in the canyons. And in this little valley – why, echoes can rap back and forth so quick they'll split our ears.'

'We're perfectly safe here, Bess.'

'I know. But that hasn't anything to do with it. The truth is I'm afraid of lightning and thunder, and thunderclaps hurt my head. If we have a bad storm, will you stay close by me?'

'Yes.'

When they got back to camp the afternoon was closing, and it was exceedingly sultry. Not a breath of air stirred the aspen leaves, and when these did not quiver the air was indeed still. The dark-purple clouds moved almost imperceptibly out of the west.

'What have we for supper?' asked Bess.

'Rabbit.'

'Bern, can't you think of another new way to cook rabbit?' went on Bess, with earnestness.

'What do you think I am – a magician?' retorted Venters.

'I wouldn't dare tell you. But, Bern, do you want me to turn into a rabbit?'

There was a dark-blue, merry flashing of eyes and a parting of lips; then she laughed. In that moment she was naïve and wholesome.

'Rabbit seems to agree with you,' replied Venters. 'You are well and strong – and growing very pretty.'

Anything in the nature of compliment he had never before said to her, and just now he responded to a sudden curiosity to see its effect. Bess stared as if she had not heard aright, slowly blushed, and completely lost her poise in happy confusion.

'I'd better go right away,' he continued, 'and fetch supplies from Cottonwoods.'

A startlingly swift change in the nature of her agitation made him reproach himself for his abruptness.

'No, no, don't go!' she said. 'I didn't mean – that about the rabbit. I – I was only trying to be – funny. Don't leave me all alone!'

'Bess, I must go sometime.'

'Wait then. Wait till after the storms.'

The purple cloud-bank darkened the lower edge of the setting sun, crept up and up, obscuring its fiery red heart, and finally passed over the last ruddy crescent of its upper rim.

The intense dead silence awakened to a long, low, rumbling roll of thunder.

'Oh!' cried Bess, nervously.

'We've had big black clouds before this without rain,' said Venters. 'But there's no doubt about that thunder. The storms are coming. I'm glad. Every rider on the sage will hear that thunder with glad ears.'

Venters and Bess finished their simple meal and the few tasks around the camp, then faced the open terrace, the valley, and the west, to watch and await the approaching storm.

It required keen vision to see any movement whatever in the purple clouds. By infinitesimal degrees the dark cloud-line merged upwards into the golden-red haze of the afterglow of sunset. A shadow lengthened from under the western wall across the valley. As straight and rigid as steel rose the delicate spear-pointed silver spruces; the aspen leaves, by nature pendant and quivering, hung limp and heavy; no slender blade of grass moved. A gentle splashing of water came from the ravine. Then again from out of the west sounded the low, dull, and rumbling roll of thunder.

A wave, a ripple of light, a trembling and turning of the aspen leaves, like the approach of a breeze on the water, crossed the valley from the west; and the lull and the deadly stillness and the sultry air passed away on a cool wind.

The night bird of the canyon, with his clear and melancholy notes, announced the twilight. And from all along the cliffs rose the faint murmur and moan and mourn of the wind singing in the caves. The bank of clouds now swept hugely out of the western sky. Its front was purple and black, with grey between, a bulging, mushrooming, vast thing instinct with storm. It had a dark, angry, threatening aspect. As if all the power of the winds were pushing and piling behind, it rolled ponderously across the sky. A red flare burned out instantaneously, flashed from west to east, and died. Then from the deepest black of the purple cloud burst a boom. It was like the bowling of a huge boulder along the crags and ramparts, and seemed to roll on and fall into the valley to bound and bang and boom from cliff to cliff.

'Oh!' cried Bess, with her hands over her ears. 'What did I tell you?'

'Why, Bess, be reasonable!' said Venters.

'I'm a coward.'

'Not quite that, I hope. It's strange you're afraid. I love a storm.'

'I tell you a storm down in these canyons is an awful thing. I know Oldring hated storms. His men were afraid of them. There was one who went deaf in a bad storm, and never could hear again.'

'Maybe I've lots to learn, Bess. I'll lose my guess if this storm isn't bad enough. We're going to have heavy wind first, then lightning and thunder, then the rain. Let's stay out as long as we can.'

The tips of the cottonwoods and the oaks waved to the east, and the rings of aspens along the terraces twinkled their myriad of bright faces in fleet and glancing gleam. A low roar rose from the leaves of the forest, and the spruces swished in the rising wind. It came in gusts, with light breezes between. As it increased in strength the lulls shortened in length till there was a strong and steady blow all the time, and violent puffs at intervals, and sudden whirling currents. The clouds spread over the valley, rolling swiftly and low, and twilight faded into a sweeping darkness. Then the singing of the wind in the caves drowned the swift roar of rustling leaves; then the song swelled to a mourning, moaning wail; then with the gathering power of the wind the wail changed to a shriek. Steadily the wind strengthened and constantly the strange sound changed.

The last bit of blue sky yielded to the onsweep of clouds. Like angry surf the pale gleams of grey, amid the purple of that scudding front, swept beyond the eastern rampart of the valley. The purple deepened to black. Broad sheets of lightning flared over the western wall. There were not yet any ropes or zigzag streaks darting down through the gathering darkness. The storm centre was still beyond Surprise Valley.

'Listen! . . . Listen!' cried Bess, with her lips close to Venters's ear. 'You'll hear Oldring's knell!'

'What's that?'

'Oldring's knell. When the wind blows a gale in the caves it makes what the rustlers call Oldring's knell. They believe it bodes his death. I think he believes so, too. It's not like any sound on earth . . . It's beginning. Listen!'

The gale swooped down with a hollow unearthly howl. It yelled and pealed and shrilled and shrieked. It was made up of a thousand piercing cries. It was a rising and a moving sound. Beginning at the western break of the valley, it rushed along each gigantic cliff, whistling into the caves and cracks, to mount in power, to bellow a blast through the great stone bridge. Gone, as into an engulfing roar of surging waters, it seemed to shoot back and begin all over again.

It was only wind, thought Venters. Here sped and shrieked the sculptor that carved out the wonderful caves in the cliffs. It was only a gale, but as Venters listened, as his ears became accustomed to the fury and strife, out of it all or through it or above it pealed low and perfectly clear and persistently uniform a strange sound that had no counterpart in all the sounds of the elements. It was not of earth or of life. It was the grief and agony of the gale. A knell of all upon which it blew!

Black night enfolded the valley. Venters could not see his companion, and knew of her presence only through the tightening hold of her hand on his arm. He felt the dogs huddle closer to him. Suddenly the dense, black vault overhead split asunder to a blue-white, dazzling streak of lightning. The whole valley lay vividly clear and luminously bright in his sight. Up-reared, vast and magnificent, the stone bridge glimmered like some grand god of storm in the lightning's fire. Then all flashed black again – blacker than pitch – a thick, impenetrable coal-blackness. And there came a ripping, crashing report. Instantly an echo resounded with clapping crash. The initial report was nothing to the echo. It was a terrible, living, reverberating, detonating crash. The wall threw the sound across, and could have made no greater roar if it had slipped in avalanche. From cliff to cliff the echo went in crashing retort and banged in lessening power, and boomed in thinner volume, and clapped weaker and weaker till a final clap could not reach across to waiting cliff.

In the pitchy darkness Venters led Bess, and, groping his way, by feel of hand found the entrance to her cave and lifted her up. On the instant a blinding flash of lightning illumined the cave and all about him. He saw Bess's face white now, with dark, frightened eyes. He saw the dogs leap up, and he followed suit. The golden glare vanished; all was black; then came the splitting crack and the infernal din of echoes.

Bess shrank closer to him and closer, found his hands, and pressed them tightly over her ears, and dropped her face upon his shoulder, and hid her eyes.

Then the storm burst with a succession of ropes and streaks and shafts of lightning, playing continuously, filling the valley with a broken radiance; and the cracking shots followed each other swiftly till the echoes blended in one fearful, deafening crash.

Venters looked out upon the beautiful valley – beautiful now as never before – mystic in its transparent, luminous gloom, weird in the quivering, golden haze of lightning. The dark spruces were tipped with glimmering lights; the aspens bent low in the winds, as waves in a tempest at sea; the forest of oaks tossed wildly and shone with gleams of fire. Across the valley the huge cavern of the cliff-dwellers yawned in the glare; every little black window as clear as at noonday; but the night and the storm added to their tragedy. Flung arching to the black clouds, the great stone bridge seemed to bear the brunt of the storm. It caught the full fury of the rushing wind. It lifted its noble crown to meet the lightnings. Venters thought of the eagles and their lofty nest in a niche under the arch. A driving pall of rain, black as the clouds, came sweeping on to obscure the bridge and the gleaming walls and the shining valley. The lightning played incessantly, streaking down through opaque darkness of rain. The roar of the wind, with its strange knell and the recrashing echoes, mingled with the roar of the flooding rain, and all seemingly were deadened and drowned in a world of sound.

In the dimming pale light Venters looked down upon the girl. She had sunk into his arms, upon his breast, burying her face. She clung to him. He felt the softness of her, and the warmth, and the quick heave of her breast. He saw the dark, slender, graceful outline of her form. A woman lay in his arms! And he held her closer. He who had been alone in the sad, silent watches of the night was not now and never must be again alone. He who had yearned for the touch of a hand felt the long tremble and the heartbeat of a woman. By what strange chance had she come to love him! By what change – by what marvel had she grown into a treasure!

No more did he listen to the rush and roar of the thunderstorm. For with the touching of clinging hands and the throbbing bosom he grew conscious of an inward storm – the tingling of new chords of thought, strange music of unheard, joyous bells, sad dreams dawning to wakeful delight, dissolving doubt, resurging hope, force, fire, and freedom, unutterable sweetness of desire. A storm in his breast – a storm of real love.

CHAPTER 14

West Wind

When the storm abated Venters sought his own cave, and late in the night, as his blood cooled and the stir and throb and thrill subsided, he fell asleep.

With the breaking of dawn his eyes unclosed. The valley lay drenched and bathed, a burnished oval of glittering green. The rain-washed walls glistened in the morning light. Waterfalls of many forms poured over the rims. One, a broad, lacy sheet thin as smoke, slid over the western notch and struck a ledge in its downward fall, to bound into broader leap, to burst far below into white and gold and rosy mist.

Venters prepared for the day, knowing himself a different man.

'It's a glorious morning,' said Bess in greeting.

'Yes. After the storm the west wind,' he replied.

'Last night was I – very much of a baby?' she asked, watching him.

'Pretty much.'

'Oh, I couldn't help it!'

'I'm glad you were afraid.'

'Why?' she asked, in slow surprise.

'I'll tell you someday,' he answered, soberly. Then around the camp-fire and through the morning meal he was silent; afterwards he strolled thoughtfully off alone along the terrace. He climbed a great yellow rock raising its crest among the spruces, and there he sat down to face the valley and the west. 'I love her!'

Aloud he spoke – unburdened his heart – confessed his secret. For an instant the golden valley swam before his eyes, and the walls waved, and all about him whirled with tumult within.

'I love her! . . . I understand now.'

Reviving memory of Jane Withersteen and thought of the complications of the present amazed him with proof of how far he had drifted from his old life. He discovered that he hated to take up the broken threads, to delve into dark problems and difficulties. In this beautiful valley he had been living a beautiful dream. Tranquillity had come to him, and the joy of solitude, and interest in all the wild creatures and crannies of this incomparable valley – and love. Under the shadow of the great stone bridge God had revealed Himself to Venters.

'The world seems very far away,' he muttered, 'but it's there – and I'm not yet done with it. Perhaps I never shall be . . . Only – how glorious it would be to live here always and never think again!'

Whereupon the resurging reality of the present, as if in irony of his wish, steeped him instantly in contending thought. Out of it all he presently evolved these things: he must go to Cottonwoods; he must bring supplies back to Surprise Valley; he must cultivate the soil and raise corn and stock, and, most imperative of all, he must decide the future of the girl who loved him and whom he loved. The first of these things required tremendous effort, the last one, concerning Bess, seemed simply and naturally easy of accomplishment. He would marry her. Suddenly, as from roots of poisonous fire, flamed up the forgotten truth concerning her. It seemed to wither and shrivel up all his joy on its hot, tearing way to his heart. She had been Oldring's Masked Rider. To Venters's question, 'What were you to Oldring?' she had answered with scarlet shame and drooping head.

'What do I care who she is or what she was!' he cried, passionately. And he knew it was not his old self speaking. It was this softer, gentler man who had awakened to new thought in the quiet valley. Tenderness, masterful in him now, matched the absence of joy and blunted the knife-edge of entering jealousy. Strong and passionate effort of will, surprising to him, held back the poison from piercing his soul.

'Wait! . . . Wait!' he cried, as if calling. His hand pressed his breast, and he might have called to the pang there. 'Wait! It's all so strange – so wonderful. Anything can happen. Who am I to judge her'? I'll glory in my love for her. But I can't tell it – can't give up to it.'

Certainly he could not then decide her future. Marrying her was impossible in Surprise Valley and in any village south of Sterling. Even without the mask she had once worn she would easily have been recognised as Oldring's Rider. No man who had ever seen her would forget her, regardless of his ignorance as to her sex. Then more poignant than all other argument was the fact that he did not want to take her away from Surprise Valley. He resisted all thought of that. He had brought her to the most beautiful and wildest place of the uplands; he had saved her, nursed her back to strength, watched her bloom as one of the valley lilies; he knew her life there to be pure and sweet – she belonged to him, and he loved her. Still these were not all the reasons why he did not want to take her away. Where could they go? He feared the rustlers – he feared the riders – he feared the Mormons. And if he should ever succeed in getting Bess safely away from these immediate perils, he feared the sharp eyes of women and their tongues, the big outside world with its problems of existence. He must wait to decide her future, which, after all, was deciding his own. But between her future and his something hung impending. Like Balancing Rock, which waited darkly over the steep gorge, ready to close forever the outlet to Deception Pass, that nameless thing, as certain yet intangible as fate, must fall and close forever all doubts and fears of the future.

'I've dreamed,' muttered Venters, as he rose. 'Well, why not? . . . To dream is happiness! But let me just once see this clearly, wholly; then I can go on dreaming till the things falls. I've got to tell Jane Withersteen. I've dangerous trips to take. I've work here to make comfort for this girl. She's mine. I'll fight to keep her safe from that old life. I've already seen her forget it. I love her. And if a beast ever rises in me I'll burn my hand off before I lay it on her with shameful intent. And, by God! sooner or later I'll kill the man who hid her and kept her in Deception Pass!'

As he spoke the west wind softly blew in his face. It seemed to soothe his passion. That west wind was fresh, cool, fragrant, and it carried a sweet, strange burden of far-off things – tidings of life in other climes, of sunshine asleep on other walls – of other places where reigned peace. It carried, too, sad truth of human hearts and mystery – of promise and hope unquenchable. Surprise Valley was only a little niche in the wide world whence blew that burdened wind. Bess was only one of millions at the mercy of unknown motive in nature and life. Content had come to Venters in the valley; happiness had breathed in the slow, warm air; love as bright as light had hovered over the walls and descended to him; and now on the west wind came a whisper of the eternal triumph of faith over doubt.

'How much better I am for what has come to me!' he exclaimed. 'I'll let the future take care of itself. Whatever falls, I'll be ready.'

Venters retraced his steps along the terrace back to camp, and found Bess in the old familiar seat, waiting and watching for his return.

'I went off by myself to think a little,' he explained.

'You never looked that way before. What – what is it? Won't you tell me?'

'Well, Bess, the fact is I've been dreaming a lot. This valley makes a fellow dream. So I forced myself to think. We can't live this way much longer. Soon I'll simply have to go to Cottonwoods. We need a whole pack train of supplies. I can get – '

'Can you go safely?' she interrupted.

'Why, I'm sure of it. I'll ride through the Pass at night. I haven't any fear that Wrangle isn't where I left him. And once on him – Bess, just wait till you see that horse!'

'Oh, I want to see him – to ride him. But – but, Bern, this is what troubles me,' she said. 'Will – will you come back?'

'Give me four days. If I'm not back in four days you'll know I'm dead. For that only shall keep me.'

'Oh!'

'Bess, I'll come back. There's danger – I wouldn't lie to you – but I can take care of myself.'

'Bern, I'm sure – oh, I'm sure of it! All my life I've watched hunted men. I can tell what's in them. And I believe you can ride and shoot and see with any rider of the sage. It's not – not that I – fear.'

'Well, what is it, then?'

'Why – why – why should you come back at all?'

'I couldn't leave you here alone.'

'You might change your mind when you get to the village – among old friends – '

'I won't change my mind. As for old friends – ' He uttered a short, expressive laugh.

'Then – there – there must be a – a woman!' Dark red mantled the clear tan of temple and cheek and neck. Her eyes were eyes of shame, upheld a long moment by intense, straining search for the verification of her fear. Suddenly they drooped, her head fell to her knees, her hands flew to her hot cheeks.

'Bess – look here,' said Venters, with a sharpness due to the violence with which he checked his quick, surging emotion.

As if compelled against her will – answering to an irresistible voice – Bess raised her head, looked at him with sad, dark eyes, and tried to whisper with tremulous lips.

'There's no woman,' went on Venters, deliberately holding her glance with his. 'Nothing on earth, barring the chances of life, can keep me away.'

Her face flashed and flushed with the glow of a leaping joy; but like the vanishing of a gleam it disappeared to leave her as he had never beheld her.

'I am nothing – I am lost – I am nameless!'

'Do you *want* me to come back?' he asked, with sudden stern coldness. 'Maybe *you* want to go back to Oldring!'

That brought her erect, trembling and ashy pale, with dark, proud eyes and mute lips refuting his insinuation.

'Bess, I beg your pardon. I shouldn't have said that. But you angered me. I intend to work – to make a home for you here – to be a – a brother to you as long as ever you need me. And you must forget what you are – were – I mean, and be happy. When you remember that old life you are bitter, and it hurts me.'

'I was happy – I shall be very happy. Oh, you're so good that – that it kills me! If I think, I can't believe it. I grow sick with wondering *why*. I'm only a – *let me say it* – only a lost, nameless – girl of the rustlers. *Oldring's Girl*, they called me. That you should save me – be so good and kind – want to make me happy – why, it's beyond belief. No wonder I'm wretched at the thought of your leaving me. But I'll be wretched and bitter no more. I promise you. If only I could repay you even a little – '

'You've repaid me a hundredfold. Will you believe me?'

'Believe you! I couldn't do else.'

'Then listen! . . . Saving you, I saved myself. Living here in this valley with you, I've found myself. I've learned to think while I was dreaming. I never troubled myself about God. But God, or some wonderful spirit, has whispered to me here. I absolutely deny the truth of what you say about yourself. I can't explain it. There are things too deep to tell. Whatever the terrible wrongs you've suffered, God holds you blameless. I see that – feel that in you every moment you are near me. I've a mother and a sister 'way back in Illinois. If I could I'd take you to them – tomorrow.'

'*If it were true!* Oh, I might – I might lift my head!' she cried.

'Lift it then – you child. For I swear it's true.'

She did lift her head with the singular wild grace always a part of her actions, with that old unconscious intimation of innocence which always tortured Venters, but now with something more – a spirit rising from the depths that linked itself to his brave words.

'I've been thinking – too,' she cried, with quivering smile and swelling breast. 'I've discovered myself – too. I'm young – I'm alive – I'm so full – oh! I'm a woman!'

'Bess, I believe I can claim credit of that last discovery – before you,' Venters said, and laughed.

'Oh, there's more – there's something I must tell you.'

'Tell it, then.'

'When will you go to Cottonwoods?'

'As soon as the storms are past, or the worst of them.'

'I'll tell you before you go. I can't now. I don't know how I shall then. But it must be told. I'd never let you leave me without knowing. For in spite of what you say there's a chance you mightn't come back.'

Day after day the west wind blew across the valley. Day after day the clouds clustered grey and purple and black. The cliffs sang and the caves rang with Oldring's knell, and the lightning flashed, the thunder rolled, the echoes crashed and crashed, and the rains flooded the valley. Wild flowers sprang up everywhere, swaying with the lengthening grass on the terraces, smiling wanly from shady nooks, peeping wondrously from year-dry crevices of the walls. The valley bloomed into a paradise. Every single moment, from the breaking of the gold bar through the bridge at dawn on to the reddening of rays over the western wall, was one of colourful change. The valley swam in thick, transparent haze, golden at dawn, warm and white at noon, purple in the twilight. At the end of every storm a rainbow curved down into the leaf-bright forest to shine and fade and leave lingeringly some faint essence of its rosy iris in the air.

Venters walked with Bess, once more in a dream, and watched the lights change on the walls, and faced the wind from out of the west.

Always it brought softly to him strange, sweet tidings of far-off things. It blew from a place that was old and whispered of youth. It blew down the grooves of time. It brought a story of the passing hours. It breathed low of fighting men and praying women. It sang clearly the song of love. That ever was the burden of its tidings – youth in the shady woods, waders through the wet meadows, boy and girl at the hedgerow stile, bathers in the booming surf, sweet, idle hours on grassy, windy hills, long strolls down moonlit lanes – everywhere in far-off lands, fingers locked and bursting hearts and longing lips – from all the world tidings of unquenchable love.

Often, in these hours of dreams he watched the girl, and asked himself of what was she dreaming? For the changing light of the valley reflected its gleam and its colour and its meaning in the changing light of her eyes. He saw in them infinitely more than he saw in his dreams. He saw thought and soul and nature – strong vision of life. All tidings the west wind blew from distance and age he found deep in those dark-blue depths, and found them mysteries solved. Under their wistful shadow he softened, and in the softening felt himself grow a sadder, a wiser, and a better man.

While the west wind blew its tidings, filling his heart full, teaching him a man's part, the days passed, the purple clouds changed to white, and the storms were over for that summer.

'I must go now,' he said.

'When?' she asked.

'At once – tonight.'

'I'm glad the time has come. It dragged at me. Go – for you'll come back the sooner.'

Late in the afternoon, as the ruddy sun split its last flame in the ragged notch of the western wall, Bess walked with Venters along the eastern terrace, up the long, weathered slope, under the great stone bridge. They entered the narrow gorge to climb around the fence long before built there by Venters. Farther than this she had never been. Twilight had already fallen in the gorge. It brightened to waning shadow in the wider ascent. He showed her Balancing Rock, of which he had often told her, and explained its sinister leaning over the outlet. Shuddering she looked down the long, pale incline with its closed-in, toppling walls.

'What an awful trail! Did you carry me up here?'

'I did, surely,' replied he.

'It frightens me, somehow. Yet I never was afraid of trails. I'd ride anywhere a horse could go, and climb where he couldn't. But there's something fearful here. I feel as – as if the place was watching me.'

'Look at this rock. It's balance here – balanced perfectly. You know I told you the cliff-dwellers cut the rock, and why. But they're gone and the rock waits. Can't you see – feel how it waits here? I moved it once, and I'll never dare again. A strong heave would start it. Then it would fall and bang, and smash that crag, and jar the walls, and close forever the outlet to Deception Pass!'

'Ah! When you come back I'll steal up here and push and push with all my might to roll the rock and close forever the outlet to the Pass!' She said it lightly, but in the undercurrent of her voice was a heavier note, a ring deeper than any ever given mere play of words.

'Bess! . . . You can't dare me! Wait till I come back with supplies – then roll the stone.'

'I – was – in – fun.' Her voice now throbbed low. 'Always you must be free to go when you will. Go now . . . this place presses on me – stifles me.'

'I'm going – but you had something to tell me?'

'Yes . . . Will you – come back?'

'I'll come if I live.'

'But – but you mightn't come?'

'That's possible, of course. It'll take a good deal to kill me. A man couldn't have a faster horse or keener dog. And, Bess I've guns, and I'll use them if I'm pushed. But don't worry.'

'I've faith in you. I'll not worry until after four days. Only – because you mightn't come – I *must* tell you – '

She lost her voice. Her pale face, her great, glowing, earnest eyes, seemed to stand alone out of the gloom of the gorge. The dog whined, breaking the silence.

'I *must* tell you – because you mightn't come back,' she whispered. 'You *must* know what – what I think of your goodness – of you. Always I've been tongue-tied. I seemed not to be grateful. It was deep in my heart. Even now – if I were other than I am – I couldn't tell you. But I'm nothing – only a rustler's girl – nameless – infamous. You've saved me – and I'm – I'm yours to do with as you like . . . With all my heart and soul – I love you!'

CHAPTER 15

Shadows on the Sage-Slope

In the cloudy, threatening, waning summer days shadows lengthened down the sage-slope, and Jane Withersteen likened them to the shadows gathering and closing in around her life.

Mrs Larkin died, and little Fay was left an orphan with no known relative. Jane's love redoubled. It was the saving brightness of a darkening hour. Fay turned now to Jane in childish worship. And Jane at last found full expression for the mother-longing in her heart. Upon Lassiter, too, Mrs Larkin's death had some subtle reaction. Before, he had often, without explanation, advised Jane to send Fay back to any Gentile family that would take her in. Passionately and reproachfully and wonderingly Jane had refused even to entertain such an idea. And now Lassiter never advised it again, grew sadder and quieter in his contemplation of the child, and infinitely more gentle and loving. Sometimes Jane had a cold, inexplicable sensation of dread when she saw Lassiter watching Fay. What did the rider see in the future? Why did he, day by day, grow more silent, calmer, cooler, yet sadder in prophetic assurance of something to be?

No doubt, Jane thought, the rider, in his almost superhuman power of foresight, saw behind the horizon the dark, lengthening shadows that were soon to crowd and gloom over him and little Fay. Jane Withersteen awaited the long-deferred breaking of the storm with a courage and embittered calm that had come to her in her extremity. Hope had not died. Doubt and fear, subservient to her will, no longer gave her sleepless nights and tortured days. Love remained. All that she had loved she now loved the more. She seemed to feel that she was defiantly flinging the wealth of her love in the face of misfortune and of hate. No day passed but she prayed for all – and most fervently for her enemies. It troubled her that she had lost, or had never gained, the whole control of her mind. In some measure reason and wisdom and decision were locked in a chamber of her brain, awaiting a key. Power to think of some things was taken from her. Meanwhile, abiding a day of judgement, she fought ceaselessly to deny the bitter drops in her cup, to tear back the slow, the intangibly slow growth of a hot, corrosive lichen eating into her heart.

On the morning of August 10th, Jane, while waiting in the court for Lassiter, heard a clear, ringing report of a rifle. It came from the grove, somewhere towards the corrals. Jane glanced out in alarm. The day was dull, windless, soundless. The leaves of the cottonwoods drooped, as if they had foretold the doom of Withersteen House and were now ready to die and drop and decay. Never had Jane seen such shade. She pondered on the meaning of the report. Revolver shots had of late cracked from different parts of the grove – spies taking snapshots at Lassiter from a cowardly distance! But a rifle report meant more. Riders seldom used rifles. Judkins and Venters were the exceptions she called to mind. Had the men who hounded her hidden in her grove, taken to the rifle to rid her of Lassiter, her last friend? It was probable – it was likely. And she did not share his cool assumption that his death would never come at the hands of a Mormon. Long had she expected it. His constancy to her, his singular reluctance to use the fatal skill for which he was famed – both now plain to all Mormons – laid him open to inevitable assassination. Yet what charm against ambush and aim and enemy he seemed to bear about him! No, Jane reflected, it was not charm; only a wonderful training of eye and ear, and sense of impending peril. Nevertheless that could not forever avail against secret attack.

That moment a rustling of leaves attracted her attention; then the familiar clinking accompaniment of a slow, soft, measured step, and Lassiter walked into the court.

'Jane, there's a fellow out there with a long gun,' he said and, removing his sombrero, showed his head bound in a bloody scarf.

'I heard the shot; I knew it was meant for you. Let me see – you can't be badly injured?'

'I reckon not. But mebbe it wasn't a close call! . . . I'll sit here in this corner where nobody can see me from the grove.' He untied the scarf and removed it to show a long, bleeding furrow above his left temple.

'It's only a cut,' said Jane. 'But how it bleeds! Hold your scarf over it just a moment till I come back.'

She ran into the house and returned with bandages; and while she bathed and dressed the wound Lassiter talked.

'That fellow had a good chance to get me. But he must have flinched when he pulled the trigger. As I dodged down I saw him run through the trees. He had a rifle. I've been expectin' that kind of gun play. I reckon now I'll have to keep a little closer hid myself. These fellers all seem to get chilly or shaky when they draw a bead on me, but one of them might jest happen to hit me.'

'Won't you go away – leave Cottonwoods as I've begged you to – before someone does happen to hit you?' she appealed to him.

'I reckon I'll stay.'

'But, oh, Lassiter – your blood will be on my hands!'

'See here, lady, look at your hands now, right now. Aren't they fine, firm, white hands? Aren't they bloody now? Lassiter's blood! That's a queer thing to stain your beautiful hands. But if you could only see deeper you'd find a redder colour of blood. Heart colour, Jane!'

'Oh! . . . My friend!'

'No, Jane, I'm not one to quit when the game grows hot, no more than you. This game, though, is new to me, an' I don't know the moves yet, else I wouldn't have stepped in front of that bullet.'

'Have you no desire to hunt the man who fired at you – to find him – and – and kill him?'

'Well, I reckon I haven't any great hankerin' for that.'

'Oh, the wonder of it! . . . I knew – I prayed – I trusted. Lassiter, I almost gave – all myself to soften you to Mormons. Thank God, and thank you, my friend . . . But, selfish woman that I am, this is no great test. What's the life of one of those sneaking cowards to such a man as you? I think of your great hate towards him who – I think of your life's implacable purpose. Can it be – '

'Wait! . . . Listen!' he whispered. 'I hear a hoss.'

He rose noiselessly, with his ear to the breeze. Suddenly he pulled his sombrero down over his bandaged head and, swinging his gun-sheaths round in front, he stepped into the alcove.

'It's a hoss – comin' fast,' he added.

Jane's listening ear soon caught a faint, rapid, rhythmic beat of hoofs. It came from the sage. It gave her a thrill that she was at a loss to understand. The sound rose stronger, louder. Then came a clear, sharp difference when the horse passed from the sage trail to the hard-packed ground of the grove. It became a singing run – swift in its bell-like clatterings, yet singular in longer pause than usual between the hoofbeats of a horse.

'It's Wrangle! . . . It's Wrangle!' cried Jane Withersteen. 'I'd know him from a million horses!'

Excitement and thrilling expectancy flooded out all Jane Withersteen's calm. A tight band closed round her breast as she saw the giant sorrel flit in reddish-brown flashes across the openings in the green. Then he was pounding down the lane – thundering into the court – crashing his great iron-shod hoofs on the stone flags. Wrangle it was surely, but shaggy and wild-eyed, and sage-streaked, with dust-caked lather staining his flanks. He reared and crashed down and plunged. The rider leaped off, threw the bridle, and held hard on a lasso looped round Wrangle's head and neck. Jane's heart sank as she tried to recognise Venters in the rider. Something familiar struck her in the lofty stature, in the sweep of powerful shoulders. But this bearded, long-haired, unkempt man, who wore ragged clothes patched with pieces of skin, and boots that showed bare legs and feet – this dusty, dark, and wild rider could not possibly be Venters.

'Whoa, Wrangle, old boy! Come down. Easy now. So – so – so. You're home, old boy, and presently you can have a drink of water you'll remember.'

In the voice Jane knew the rider to be Venters. He tied Wrangle to the hitching-rack and turned to the court.

'Oh, Bern! . . . You wild man!' she exclaimed.

'Jane – Jane, it's good to see you! Hello, Lassiter! Yes, it's Venters.'

Like rough iron his hard hand crushed Jane's. In it she felt the difference she saw in him. Wild, rugged, unshorn, yet how splendid! He had gone away a boy – he had returned a man. He appeared taller, wider of shoulder, deeper-chested, more powerfully built. But was that only her fancy – he had always been a young giant – was the change one of spirit? He might have been absent for years, proven by fire and steel, grown like Lassiter, strong and cool and sure. His eyes – were they keener, more flashing than before? – met hers with clear, frank, warm regard, in which perplexity was not, nor discontent, nor pain.

'Look at me long as you like,' he said, with a laugh. 'I'm not much to look at. And, Jane, neither you nor Lassiter, can brag. You're paler than I ever saw you. Lassiter, here, he wears a bloody bandage under his hat. That reminds me. Someone took a flying shot at me down in the sage. It made Wrangle run some . . . Well, perhaps you've more to tell me than I've got to tell you.'

Briefly, in few words, Jane outlined the circumstances of her undoing in the few weeks of his absence.

Under his beard and bronze she saw his face whiten in terrible wrath. 'Lassiter – what held you back?'

No time in the long period of fiery moments and sudden shocks had Jane Withersteen ever beheld Lassiter as calm and serene and cool as then.

'Jane had gloom enough without my addin' to it by shootin' up the village,' he said.

As strange as Lassiter's coolness was Venters's curious, intent scrutiny of them both, and under it Jane felt a flaming tide wave from bosom to temples.

'Well – you're right,' he said, with slow pause. 'It surprises me a little, that's all.'

Jane sensed then a slight alteration in Venters, and what it was, in her own confusion, she could not tell. It had always been her intention to acquaint him with the deceit she had fallen to in her zeal to move Lassiter. She did not mean to spare herself. Yet now, at the moment, before these riders, it was an impossibility to explain.

Venters was speaking somewhat haltingly, without his former frankness. 'I found Oldring's hiding-place and your red herd. I learned – I know – I'm sure there was a deal between Tull and Oldring.' He paused and shifted his position and his gaze. He looked as if he wanted to say something that he found beyond him. Sorrow and pity and shame seemed to contend for mastery over him. Then he raised himself and spoke with effort. 'Jane, I've cost you too much. You've almost ruined yourself for me. It was wrong, for I'm not worth it. I never deserved such friendship. Well, maybe it's not too late. You must give me up. Mind, I haven't changed. I am just the same as ever. I'll see Tull while I'm here, and tell him to his face.'

'Bern, it's too late,' said Jane.

'I'll *make* him believe!' cried Venters, violently.

'You ask me to break our friendship?'

'Yes. If you don't, I shall!'

'Forever?'

'Forever!'

Jane sighed. Another shadow had lengthened down the sage-slope to cast further darkness upon her. A melancholy sweetness pervaded her resignation. The boy who had left her had returned a man, nobler, stronger, one in whom she divined something unbending as steel. There might come a moment later when she would wonder why she had not fought against his will, but just now she yielded to it. She liked him as well – nay, more, she thought, only her emotions were deadened by the long, menacing wait for the bursting storm.

Once before she had held out her hand to him – when she gave it; now she stretched it tremblingly forth in acceptance of the decree circumstance had laid upon them. Venters bowed over it, kissed it, pressed it hard, and half stifled a sound very like a sob. Certain it was that when he raised his head tears glistened in his eyes.

'Some – women – have a hard lot,' he said, huskily. Then he shook his powerful form, and his rags lashed about him. 'I'll say a few things to Tull – when I meet him.'

'Bern – you'll not draw on Tull? Oh, that must not be! Promise me –'

'I promise you this,' he interrupted, in stern passion that thrilled while it terrorised her. 'If you say one more word for that plotter I'll kill him as I would a mad coyote!'

Jane clasped her hands. Was this fire-eyed man the one whom she had once made as wax to her touch? Had Venters become Lassiter and Lassiter Venters?

'I'll – say no more,' she faltered.

'Jane, Lassiter once called you blind,' said Venters. 'It must be true. But I won't upbraid you. Only don't rouse the devil in me by praying for Tull! I'll try to keep cool when I meet him. That's all. Now there's one more thing I want to ask of you – the last. I've found a valley down in the Pass. It's a wonderful place. I intend to stay there. It's so hidden I believe no one can find it. There's good water, and browse, and game. I want to raise corn and stock. I need to take in supplies. Will you give them to me?'

'Assuredly. The more you take the better you'll please me – and perhaps the less my – my enemies will get.'

'Venters, I reckon you'll have trouble packin' anythin' away,' put in Lassiter.

'I'll go at night.'

'Mebbe that wouldn't be best. You'd sure be stopped. You'd better go early in the mornin' – say, just after dawn. That's the safest time to move round here.'

'Lassiter, I'll be hard to stop,' returned Venters, darkly.

'I reckon so.'

'Bern,' said Jane, 'go first to the riders' quarters and get yourself a complete outfit. You're a – a sight. Then help yourself to whatever else you need – burros, packs, grain, dried fruits, and meat. You must take coffee and sugar and flour – all kinds of supplies. Don't forget corn and seeds. I remember how you used to starve. Please – please take all you can pack away from here. I'll make a bundle for you, which you mustn't open till you're in your valley. How I'd like to see it! To judge by you and Wrangle, how wild it must be!'

Jane walked down into the outer court and approached the sorrel. Upstarting, he laid back his ears and eyed her.

'Wrangle – dear old Wrangle,' she said, and put a caressing hand on his matted mane. 'Oh, he's wild, but he knows me! Bern, can he run as fast as ever?'

'Run? Jane, he's done sixty miles since last night at dark, and I could make him kill Black Star right now in a ten-mile race.'

'He never could,' protested Jane. 'He couldn't even if he was fresh.'

'I reckon mebbe the best hoss'll prove himself yet,' said Lassiter, 'an', Jane, if it ever comes to that race I'd like you to be on Wrangle.'

'I'd like that, too,' rejoined Venters. 'But, Jane, maybe Lassiter's hint is extreme. Bad as your prospects are, you'll surely never come to the running point.'

'Who knows!' she replied, with mournful smile.

'No, no, Jane, it can't be so bad as all that. Soon as I see Tull there'll be a change in your fortunes. I'll hurry down to the village . . . Now don't worry.'

Jane retired to the seclusion of her room. Lassiter's subtle forecasting of disaster, Venters's forced optimism, neither remained in mind. Material loss weighed nothing in the balance with other losses she was sustaining. She wondered dully at her sitting there, hands folded listlessly, with a kind of numb deadness to the passing of time and the passing of her riches. She thought of Venters's friendship. She had not lost that, but she had lost him. Lassiter's friendship – that was more than love – it would endure, but soon he, too, would be gone. Little Fay slept dreamlessly upon the bed, her golden curls streaming over the pillow. Jane had the child's worship. Would she lose that, too? And if she did, what then would be left? Conscience thundered at her that there was left her religion. Conscience thundered that she should be grateful on her knees for this baptism of fire; that through misfortune, sacrifice, and suffering her soul might be fused pure gold. But the old, spontaneous, rapturous spirit no more exalted her. She wanted to be a woman not a martyr. Like the saint of old who mortified his flesh, Jane Withersteen had in her the temper for heroic martyrdom, if by sacrificing herself she could save the souls of others. But here the damnable verdict blistered her that the more she sacrificed herself the blacker grew the souls of her churchmen. There was something terribly wrong with her soul, something terribly wrong with her churchmen and her religion. In the whirling gulf of her thought there was yet one shining light to guide her, to sustain her in her hope; and it was that, despite her errors and her frailties and her blindness, she had one absolute and unfaltering hold on ultimate and supreme justice. That was love. 'Love your enemies as yourself!' was a divine word, entirely free from any church or creed.

Jane's meditations were disturbed by Lassiter's soft, tinkling step in the court. Always he wore the clinking spurs. Always he was in readiness to ride. She passed out and called him into the huge, dim hall.

'I think you'll be safer here. The court is too open,' she said.

'I reckon,' replied Lassiter. 'An' it's cooler here. The day's sure muggy. Well, I went down to the village with Venters.'

'Already! Where is he?' queried Jane, in quick amaze.

'He's at the corrals. Blake's helpin' him get the burros an' packs ready. That Blake is a good fellow.'

'Did – did Bern meet Tull?'

'I guess he did,' answered Lassiter, and he laughed dryly.

'Tell me! Oh, you exasperate me! You're so cool, so calm! For Heaven's sake, tell me what happened!'

'First time I've been in the village for weeks,' went on Lassiter, mildly. 'I reckon there ain't been more of a show for a long time. Me an' Venters walkin' down the road! It was funny. I ain't sayin' anybody was particular glad to see us. I'm not much thought of hereabouts, an' Venters he sure

looks like what you called him, a wild man. Well, there was some runnin'
of folks before we got to the stores. Then everybody vamoosed except
some surprised rustlers in front of a saloon. Venters went right in the
stores an' saloons, an' of course I went along. I don't know which tickled
me the most – the actions of many fellers we met, or Venters's nerve.
Jane I was downright glad to be along. You see *that* sort of thing is my
element, an' I've been away from it for a spell. But we didn't find Tull in
one of them places. Some Gentile feller at last told Venters he'd find Tull
in that long buildin' next to Parsons's store. It's a kind of meetin'-room;
and sure enough, when we peeped in, it was half full of men.

'Venters yelled: "Don't anybody pull guns! We ain't come for that!"
Then he tramped in, an' I was some put to keep alongside him. There
was a hard, scrapin' sound of feet, a loud cry, an' then some whisperin',
an' after that stillness you could cut with a knife. Tull was there, an' that
fat party who once tried to throw a gun on me, an' other important-
lookin' men, an' that little frog-legged feller who was with Tull the day I
rode in here. I wish you could have seen their faces, 'specially Tull's an'
the fat party's. But there ain't no use of my tryin' to tell you how they
looked.

'Well, Venters an' I stood there in the middle of the room, with that
batch of men all in front of us, an' not a blamed one of them winked an
eyelash or moved a finger. It was natural, of course, for me to notice
many of them packed guns. That's a way of mine, first noticin' them
things. Venters spoke up, an' his voice sort of chilled an' cut, an' he told
Tull he had a few things to say.'

Here Lassiter paused while he turned his sombrero round and round,
in his familiar habit, and his eyes had the look of a man seeing over again
some thrilling spectacle, and under his red bronze there was strange
animation.

'Like a shot, then, Venters told Tull that the friendship between you
an' him was all over, an' he was leaving your place. He said you'd both of
you broken off in the hope of propitiatin' your people, but you hadn't
changed your mind otherwise, an' never would.

'Next he spoke up for you. I ain't goin' to tell you what he said. Only –
no other woman who ever lived ever had such tribute! You had a champion,
Jane, an' never fear that those thick-skulled men don't know you now. It
couldn't be otherwise. He spoke the ringin', lightnin' truth . . . Then he
accused Tull of the underhand, miserable robbery of a helpless woman.
He told Tull where the red herd was, of a deal made with Oldrin', that

Jerry Card had made the deal. I thought Tull was goin' to drop, an' that little frog-legged cuss, he looked some limp an' white. But Venters's voice would have kept anybody's legs from bucklin'. I was stiff myself. He went on an' called Tull – called him every bad name ever known to a rider, an' then some. He cursed Tull. I never hear a man get such a cursin'. He laughed in scorn at the idea of Tull bein' a minister. He said Tull an' a few more dogs of hell builded their empire out of the hearts of such innocent an' God-fearing women as Jane Withersteen. He called Tull a binder of women, a callous beast who hid behind a mock mantle of righteousness – an' the last an' lowest coward on the face of the earth. To prey on weak women through their religion – that was the last unspeakable crime!

'Then he finished, an' by this time he'd almost lost his voice. But his whisper was enough. "Tull," he said, "*she* begged me not to draw on you today. *She* would pray for you if you burned her at the stake . . . But listen! . . . I swear if you and I ever come face to face again, I'll kill you!"

'We backed out of the door then, an' up the road. But nobody follered us.'

Jane found herself weeping passionately. She had not been conscious of it till Lassiter ended his story, and she experienced exquisite pain and relief in shedding tears. Long had her eyes been dry, her grief deep; long had her emotions been dumb. Lassiter's story put her on the rack; the appalling nature of Venters's act and speech had no parallel as an outrage; it was worse than bloodshed. Men like Tull had been shot, but had one ever been so terribly denounced in public? Overmounting her horror, an uncontrollable, quivering passion shook her very soul. It was sheer human glory in the deed of a fearless man. It was hot, primitive instinct to live – to fight. It was a kind of mad joy in Venters's chivalry. It was close to the wrath that had first shaken her in the beginning of this war waged upon her.

'Well, well, Jane, don't take it that way,' said Lassiter, in evident distress. 'I had to tell you. There's some things a feller jest can't keep. It's strange you give up on hearin' that, when all this long time you've been the gamest woman I ever seen. But I don't know women. Mebbe there's reason for you to cry. I know this – nothin' ever rang in my soul an' so filled it as what Venters did. I'd like to have done it, but – I'm only good for throwin' a gun, an' it seems you hate that . . . Well, I'll be goin' now.'

'Where?'

'Venters took Wrangle to the stable. The sorrel's shy a shoe, an' I've got to help hold the big devil an' put on another.'

'Tell Bern to come for the pack I want to give him – and – and to say goodbye,' called Jane, as Lassiter went out.

Jane passed the rest of that day in a vain endeavour to decide what and what not to put in the pack for Venters. This task was the last she would ever perform for him, and the gifts were the last she would ever make him. So she picked and chose and rejected, and chose again, and often paused in sad reverie, and began again, till at length she filled the pack.

It was about sunset, and she and Fay had finished supper and were sitting in the court, when Venters's quick steps rang on the stones. She scarcely knew him, for he had changed the tattered garments, and she missed the dark beard and long hair. Still he was not the Venters of old. As he came up the steps she felt herself pointing to the pack, and heard herself speaking words that were meaningless to her. He said goodbye; he kissed her, released her, and turned away. His tall figure blurred in her sight, grew dim through dark, streaked vision, and then he vanished.

Twilight fell around Withersteen House, and dusk and night. Little Fay slept; but Jane lay with strained, aching eyes. She heard the wind moaning in the cottonwoods and mice squeaking in the walls. The night was interminably long, yet she prayed to hold back the dawn. What would another day bring forth? The blackness of her room seemed blacker for the sad entering grey of morning light. She heard the chirp of awakening birds, and fancied she caught a faint clatter of hoofs. Then low, dull, distant, throbbed a heavy gunshot. She had expected it, was waiting for it; nevertheless, an electric shock checked her heart, froze the very living fibre of her bones. That vicelike hold on her faculties apparently did not relax for a long time, and it was a voice under her window that released her.

'Jane! . . . Jane!' softly called Lassiter.

She answered somehow.

'It's all right. Venters got away. I thought mebbe you'd heard that shot, an' I was worried some.'

'What was it – who fired?'

'Well – some fool feller tried to stop Venters out there in the sage – an' he only stopped lead! . . . I think it'll be all right. I haven't seen or heard of any other fellers round. Venters'll go through safe. An', Jane, I've got Bells saddled, an' I'm going to trail Venters. Mind, I won't show myself unless he falls foul of somebody an' needs me. I want to see if this place where he's goin' is safe for him. He says nobody can track him there. I never seen the place yet I couldn't track a man to. Now,

Jane you stay indoors while I'm gone, an' keep close watch on Fay. Will you?'

'Yes! Oh yes!'

'An' another thing, Jane,' he continued, then paused for long – 'another thing – if you ain't here when I come back – if you're *gone* – don't fear, I'll trail you – I'll find you.'

'My dear Lassiter, where could I be gone – as you put it?' asked Jane, in curious surprise.

'I reckon you might be somewhere. Mebbe tied in an old barn – or corralled in some gulch – or chained in a cave! *Milly Erne was* – till she give in! Mebbe that's news to you . . . Well, if you're gone I'll hunt for you.'

'No, Lassiter,' she replied, sadly and low. 'If I'm gone just forget the unhappy woman whose blinded selfish deceit you repaid with kindness and love.'

She heard a deep, muttering curse, under his breath, and then the silvery tingling of his spurs as he moved away.

Jane entered upon the duties of that day with a settled, gloomy calm. Disaster hung in the dark clouds, in the shade, in the humid west wind. Blake, when he reported, appeared without his usual cheer; and Jerd wore a harassed look of a worn and worried man. And when Judkins put in appearance, riding a lame horse, and dismounted with the cramp of a rider, his dust-covered figure and his darkly grim, almost dazed expression told Jane of dire calamity. She had no need of words.

'Miss Withersteen, I have to report – loss of the – white herd,' said Judkins, hoarsely.

'Come, sit down; you look played out,' replied Jane, solicitously. She brought him brandy and food, and while he partook of refreshments, of which he appeared badly in need, she asked no questions.

'No one rider – could hev done more – Miss Withersteen,' he went on, presently.

'Judkins, don't be distressed. You've done more than any other rider. I've long expected to lose the white herd. It's no surprise. It's in line with other things that are happening. I'm grateful for your service.'

'Miss Withersteen, I knew how you'd take it. But if anythin', that makes it harder to tell. You see, a feller wants to do so much fer you, an' I'd got fond of my job. We hed the herd a ways off to the north of the break in the valley. There was a big level an' pools of water an' tiptop browse. But the cattle was in a high nervous condition. Wild – as wild as antelope! You see, they'd been so scared they never slept. I ain't a-goin' to tell you of the many tricks that were pulled off out there in the sage. But there wasn't a day fer weeks thet the herd didn't get started to run. We allus managed to ride 'em close an' drive 'em back an' keep 'em bunched. Honest, Miss Withersteen, them steers was *thin*. They was *thin* when water and grass was everywhere. *Thin* at this season – thet'll tell you how your steers was pestered. Fer instance, one night a strange runnin' streak of fire run right through the herd. That streak was a coyote – *with an oiled an' blazin' tail*! Fer I shot it an' found out. We hed hell with the herd that night, an' if the sage an' grass hedn't been wet – we, hosses, steers, an' all would hev burned up. But I said I wasn't goin' to tell you any of the tricks . . . Strange now, Miss Withersteen, when the stampede did come it was from natural cause – jest a whirlin' devil of dust. You've seen the like often. An' this wasn't no big whirl, fer the dust was mostly settled. It had dried out in a little swale, an' ordinarily no steer would ever hev run fer it. But the herd was nervous an' wild. An' jest as Lassiter said, when that bunch of white steers got to movin' they was as bad as buffalo. I've seen some buffalo stampedes back in Nebraska, an' this bolt of the steers was the same kind.

'I tried to mill the herd jest as Lassiter did. But I wasn't equal to it, Miss Withersteen. I don't believe the rider lives who could hev turned thet herd. We kept along of the herd fer miles, an' more'n one of my boys tried to get the steers a-millin'. It wasn't no use. We got off level ground, goin' down, an' then the steers ran somethin' fierce. We left the little gullies an' washes level-full of dead steers. Finally I saw the herd was makin' to pass a kind of low pocket between ridges. There was a hog-back – as we used to call 'em – a pile of rocks stickin' up, an' I saw the herd was goin' to split round it, or swing out to the left. An' I wanted 'em to go to the right so mebbe we'd be able to drive 'em into the pocket. So, with all my boys except three, I rode hard to turn the herd a little to the right. We couldn't budge 'em. They went on an' split round the rocks, an' the most of 'em was turned sharp to the left by a deep wash we hedn't seen – hed no chance to see.

'The other three boys – Jimmy Vail, Joe Wills, an' thet little Cairns boy – a nervy kid! they, with Cairns leadin', tried to buck thet herd round to the pocket. It was a wild, fool idee. I couldn't do nothin'. The boys got hemmed in between the steers an' the wash – thet they hedn't no chance to see, either. Vail an' Wills was run down right before our eyes. An' Cairns, who rode a fine hoss, he did some ridin' I never seen equalled, an' would hev beat the steers if there'd been any room to run in. I was high up an' could see how the steers kept spillin' by twos an' threes over into the wash. Cairns put his hoss to a place thet was too wide fer any hoss, an' broke his neck an' the hoss's too. We found that out after, an' as fer Vail an' Wills – two thousand steers ran over the poor boys. There wasn't much left to pack home fer buryin'! . . . An', Miss Withersteen, thet all happened yesterday, an' I believe, if the white herd didn't run over the wall of the Pass, it's runnin' yet.'

On the morning of the second day after Judkins's recital, during which time Jane remained indoors a prey to regret and sorrow for the boy riders, and a new and now strangely insistent fear for her own person, she again heard what she had missed more than she dared honestly confess – the soft, jingling step of Lassiter. Almost overwhelming relief surged through her, a feeling as akin to joy as any she could have been capable of in those gloomy hours of shadow, and one that suddenly stunned her with the significance of what Lassiter had come to mean to her. She had begged him, for his own sake, to leave Cottonwoods. She might yet beg that, if her weakening courage permitted her to dare absolute loneliness and helplessness, but she realised now that if she were left alone her life would become one long, hideous nightmare.

When his soft steps clinked into the hall, in answer to her greeting, and his tall, black-garbed form filled the door, she felt an inexpressible sense of immediate safety. In his presence she lost her fear of the dim passageways of Withersteen House and of every sound. Always it had been that, when he entered the court or the hall, she had experienced a distinctly sickening but gradually lessening shock at sight of the huge black guns swinging at his sides. This time the sickening shock again visited her, it was, however, because a revealing flash of thought told her that it was not alone Lassiter who was thrillingly welcome, but also his fatal weapons. They meant so much. How she had fallen – how broken and spiritless must she be – to have still the same old horror of Lassiter's guns and his name, yet feel somehow a cold, shrinking protection in their law and might and use.

'Did you trail Venters – find his wonderful valley?' she asked eagerly.

'Yes, an' I reckon it's sure a wonderful place.'

'Is he safe there?'

'That's been botherin' me some. I tracked him an' part of the trail was the hardest I ever tackled. Mebbe there's a rustler or somebody in this country who's as good at trackin' as I am. If that's so Venters ain't safe.'

'Well – tell me all about Bern and his valley.'

To Jane's surprise Lassiter showed disinclination for further talk about his trip. He appeared to be extremely fatigued. Jane reflected that one hundred and twenty miles, with probably a great deal of climbing on foot, all in three days, was enough to tire any rider. Moreover, it presently developed that Lassiter had returned in a mood of singular sadness and preoccupation. She put it down to a moodiness over the loss of her white herd and the now precarious condition of her fortune.

Several days passed, and, as nothing happened, Jane's spirits began to brighten. Once in her musings she thought that this tendency of hers to rebound was as sad as it was futile. Meanwhile, she had resumed her walks through the grove with little Fay.

One morning she went as far as the sage. She had not seen the slope since the beginning of the rains, and now it bloomed a rich deep purple. There was a high wind blowing, and the sage tossed and waved and coloured beautifully from light to dark. Clouds scudded across the sky and their shadows sailed darkly down the sunny slope.

Upon her return towards the house she went by the lane to the stables, and she had scarcely entered the great open space with its corrals and sheds when she saw Lassiter hurriedly approaching. Fay broke from her and, running to a corral fence, began to pat and pull the long, hanging ears of a drowsy burro.

One look at Lassiter armed her for a blow.

Without a word he led her across the wide yard to the rise of the ground upon which the stable stood.

'Jane – look!' he said, and pointed to the ground.

Jane glanced down, and again, and upon steadier vision made out splotches of blood on the stones, and broad, smooth marks in the dust, leading out towards the sage.

'What made these?' she asked.

'I reckon somebody has dragged dead or wounded men out to where there was hosses in the sage.'

'Dead – or – wounded – men!'

'I reckon – Jane, are you strong? Can you bear up?'

His hands were gently holding hers, and his eyes – suddenly she could no longer look into them. 'Strong?' she echoed trembling. 'I – I will be.'

Up on the stone-flag drive, nicked with the marks made by the iron-shod hoofs of her racers, Lassiter led her, his grasp ever growing firmer.

'Where's Blake – and – and Jerd?' she asked, haltingly.

'I don't know where Jerd is. Bolted, most likely,' replied Lassiter, as he took her through the stone door. 'But Blake – poor Blake! He's gone forever! . . . Be prepared, Jane.'

With a cold prickling of her skin, with a queer thrumming in her ears, with fixed and staring eyes, Jane saw a gun lying at her feet with chamber swung and empty, and discharged shells scattered near.

Outstretched upon the stable floor lay Blake, ghastly white – dead – one hand clutching a gun and the other twisted in his bloody blouse.

'Whoever the thieves were, whether your people or rustlers – Blake killed some of them!' said Lassiter.

'Thieves?' whispered Jane.

'I reckon. Hoss-thieves! . . . Look!' Lassiter waved his hand towards the stalls.

The first stall – Bells's stall – was empty. All the stalls were empty. No racer whinnied and stamped greeting to her. Night was gone! Black Star was gone!

CHAPTER 16

Gold

As Lassiter had reported to Jane, Venters 'went through' safely, and after a toilsome journey reached the peaceful shelter of Surprise Valley. When finally he lay wearily down under the silver spruces, resting from the strain of dragging packs and burros up the slope and through the entrance to Surprise Valley, he had leisure to think, and a great deal of the time went in regretting that he had not been frank with his loyal friend, Jane Withersteen.

But, he kept continually recalling, when he had stood once more face to face with her and had been shocked at the change in her and had heard the details of her adversity, he had not had the heart to tell her of the closer interest which had entered his life. He had not lied; yet he had kept silence.

Bess was in transports over the stores of supplies and the outfit he had packed from Cottonwoods. He had certainly brought a hundred times more than he had gone for; enough, surely, for years, perhaps to make permanent home in the valley. He saw no reason why he need ever leave there again.

After a day of rest he recovered his strength and shared Bess's pleasure in rummaging over the endless packs, and began to plan for the future. And in this planning, his trip to Cottonwoods, with its revived hate of Tull and consequent unleashing of fierce passions, soon faded out of mind. By slower degrees his friendship for Jane Withersteen and his contrition drifted from the active preoccupation of his present thought to a place in memory, with more and more infrequent recalls.

And as far as the state of his mind was concerned, upon the second day after his return, the valley, with its golden hues and purple shades, the speaking west wind and the cool, silent night, and Bess's watching eyes with their wonderful light, so wrought upon Venters that he might never have left them at all.

That very afternoon he set to work. Only one thing hindered him upon beginning, though it in no wise checked his delight, and that was that in the multiplicity of tasks planned to make a paradise out of the valley he could not choose the one with which to begin. He had to grow into the habit of passing from one dreamy pleasure to another, like a bee going from flower to flower in the valley, and he found this wandering habit likely to extend to his labours. Nevertheless, he made a start.

At the outset he discovered Bess to be both a considerable help in some ways and a very great hindrance in others. Her excitement and joy were spurs, inspirations; but she was utterly impracticable in her ideas, and she flitted from one plan to another with bewildering vacillation. Moreover, he fancied that she grew more eager, youthful, and sweet; and he marked that it was far easier to watch her and listen to her than it was to work. Therefore he gave her tasks that necessitated her going often to the cave where he had stored his packs.

Upon the last of these trips, when he was some distance down the terrace and out of sight of camp, he heard a scream, and then the sharp barking of the dogs.

For an instant he straightened up, amazed. Danger for her had been absolutely out of his mind. She had seen a rattlesnake – or a wildcat. Still she would not have been likely to scream at sight of either; and the barking of the dogs was ominous. Dropping his work, he dashed back along the terrace. Upon breaking through a clump of aspens he saw the dark form of a man in the camp. Cold, then hot, Venters burst into frenzied speed to reach his guns. He was cursing himself for a thoughtless fool when the man's tall form became familiar and he recognised Lassiter. Then the reversal of emotions changed his run to a walk; he tried to call out, but his voice refused to carry; when he reached camp there was Lassiter staring at the white-faced girl. By that time Ring and Whitie had recognised him.

'Hello, Venters! I'm makin' you a visit,' said Lassiter, slowly. 'An' I'm some surprised to see you've a – a young feller for company.'

One glance had sufficed for the keen rider to read Bess's real sex, and for once his cool calm had deserted him. He stared till the white of Bess's cheeks flared into crimson. That, if it were needed, was the concluding evidence of her femininity; for it went fittingly with her sun-tinted hair and darkened, dilated eyes, the sweetness of her mouth, and the striking symmetry of her slender shape.

'Heavens! Lassiter!' panted Venters, when he caught his breath. 'What relief – it's only you! How – in the name of all – that's wonderful – did you ever get here?'

'I trailed you. We – I wanted to know where you was, if you had a safe place. So I trailed you.'

'Trailed me!' cried Venters, bluntly.

'I reckon. It was some of a job after I got to them smooth rocks. I was all day trackin' you up to them little cut steps in the rock. The rest was easy.'

'Where's your hoss? I hope you hid him.'

'I tied him in them queer cedars down on the slope. He can't be seen from the valley.'

'That's good. Well, well! I'm completely dumbfounded. It was my idea that no man could track me in here.'

'I reckon. But if there's a tracker in these uplands as good as me he can find you.'

'That's bad. That'll worry me. But, Lassiter, now you're here I'm glad to see you. And – and my companion here is not a young fellow! . . . Bess, this is a friend of mine. He saved my life once.'

The embarrassment of the moment did not extend to Lassiter. Almost at once his manner, as he shook hands with Bess, relieved Venters and put the girl at ease. After Venters's words and one quick look at Lassiter, her agitation stilled, and, though she was shy, if she were conscious of anything out of the ordinary in the situation, certainly she did not show it.

'I reckon I'll only stay a little while,' Lassiter was saying. 'An' if you don't mind troublin', I'm hungry. I fetched some biscuits along, but they're gone. Venters, this place is sure the wonderfullest ever seen.

Them cut steps on the slope! That outlet into the gorge! An' it's like climbin' up through hell into heaven to climb through that gorge into this valley! There's a queer-lookin' rock at the top of the passage. I didn't have time to stop. I'm wonderin' how you ever found this place. It's sure interestin'.'

During the preparation and eating of dinner Lassiter listened mostly, as was his wont, and occasionally he spoke in his quaint and dry way. Venters noted, however, that the rider showed an increasing interest in Bess. He asked her no questions, and only directed his attention to her while she was occupied and had no opportunity to observe his scrutiny. It seemed to Venters that Lassiter grew more and more absorbed in his study of Bess, and that he lost his coolness in some strange, softening sympathy. Then, quite abruptly, he arose and announced the necessity for his early departure. He said goodbye to Bess in a voice gentle and somewhat broken, and turned hurriedly away. Venters accompanied him, and they had traversed the terrace, climbed the weathered slope, and passed under the stone bridge before either spoke again.

Then Lassiter put a great hand on Venters's shoulder and wheeled him to meet a smouldering fire of grey eyes.

'Lassiter, I couldn't tell Jane! I couldn't,' burst out Venters, reading his friend's mind. 'I tried. But I couldn't. She wouldn't understand, and she has troubles enough. And I love the girl!'

'Venters, I reckon this beats me. I've seen some queer things in my time, too. This girl – who is she?'

'I don't know.'

'Don't know! What is she, then?'

'I don't know that, either. Oh, it's the strangest story you ever heard. I must tell you. But you'll never believe.'

'Venters, women were always puzzles to me. But for all that, if this girl ain't a child, an' as innocent, I'm no fit person to think of virtue an' goodness in anybody. Are you goin' to be square with her?'

'I am – so help me God!'

'I reckoned so. Mebbe my temper oughtn't led me to make sure. But, man, she's a woman in all but years. She's sweeter'n the sage.'

'Lassiter, I know, I know. And the *hell* of it is that in spite of her innocence and charm she's – she's not what she seems!'

'I wouldn't want to – of course, I couldn't call you a liar, Venters,' said the older man.

'What's more, she was Oldring's Masked Rider!'

Venters expected to floor his friend with that statement, but he was not in any way prepared for the shock his words gave. For an instant he was astounded to see Lassiter stunned; then his own passionate eagerness to unbosom himself, to tell the wonderful story, precluded any other thought.

'Son, tell me all about this,' presently said Lassiter as he seated himself on a stone and wiped his moist brow.

Thereupon Venters began his narrative at the point where he had shot the rustler and Oldring's Masked Rider, and he rushed through it, telling all, not holding back even Bess's unreserved avowal of her love or his deepest emotions.

'That's the story,' he said, concluding. 'I love her, though I've never told her. If I did tell her I'd be ready to marry her, and that seems impossible in this country. I'd be afraid to risk taking her anywhere. So I intend to do the best I can for her here.'

'The longer I live the stranger life is,' mused Lassiter, with downcast eyes. 'I'm reminded of somethin' you once said to Jane about hands in her game of life. There's that unseen hand of power, an' Tull's black hand, an' my red one, an' your indifferent one, an' the girl's little brown, helpless one. An', Venters, there's another one that's all-wise an' all-wonderful. *That's* the hand guidin' Jane Withersteen's game of life! ... Your story's one to daze a far clearer head than mine. I can't offer no advice, even if you asked for it. Mebbe I can help you. Anyway, I'll hold Oldrin' up when he comes to the village, an' find out about this girl. I knew the rustler years ago. He'll remember me.'

'Lassiter, if I ever meet Oldring I'll kill him!' cried Venters, with sudden intensity.

'I reckon that'd be perfectly natural,' replied the rider.

'Make him think Bess is dead – as she is to him and that old life.'

'Sure, sure, son. Cool down now. If you're goin' to begin pullin' guns on Tull an' Oldrin' you want to be cool. I reckon, though, you'd better keep hid here. Well, I must be leavin'.'

'One thing, Lassiter. You'll not tell Jane about Bess? Please don't!'

'I reckon not. But I would be afraid to bet that after she'd got over anger at your secrecy – Venters, she'd be furious once in her life! – she'd think more of you. I don't mind sayin' for myself that I think you're a good deal of a man.'

In the further ascent Venters halted several times with the intention of saying goodbye, yet he changed his mind and kept on climbing till they reached Balancing Rock. Lassiter examined the huge rock, listened to Venters's idea of its position and suggestion, and curiously placed a strong hand upon it.

'Hold on!' cried Venters. 'I heaved at it once and have never got over my scare.'

'Well, you do seem oncommon nervous,' replied Lassiter, much amused. 'Now, as for me, why I always had the funniest notion to roll stones! When I was a kid I did it an' the bigger I got the bigger stones I'd roll. Ain't that funny? Honest – even now I often get off my hoss just to tumble a big stone over a precipice, an' watch it drop, an' listen to it bang an' boom. I've started some slides in my time, an' don't you forget it. I never seen a rock I wanted to roll as bad as this one! Wouldn't there jest be roarin', crashin' hell down that trail?'

'You'd close the outlet forever!' exclaimed Venters. 'Well goodbye, Lassiter. Keep my secret and don't forget me. And be mighty careful how – you get out of the valley below. The rustlers' canyon isn't more than three miles up the Pass. Now you've tracked me here, I'll never feel safe again.'

In his descent to the valley, Venters's emotion, roused to stirring pitch by the recital of his love story, quieted gradually, and in its place came a sober, thoughtful mood. All at once he saw that he was serious, because he would never more regain his sense of security while in the valley. What Lassiter could do another skilful tracker might duplicate. Among the many riders with whom Venters had ridden he recalled no one who could have taken his trail at Cottonwoods and have followed it to the edge of the bare slope in the pass, let alone up that glistening smooth stone. Lassiter, however, was not an ordinary rider. Instead of hunting cattle tracks he had likely spent a goodly portion of his life tracking men. It was not improbable that among Oldring's rustlers there was one who shared Lassiter's gift for trailing. And the more Venters dwelt on this possibility the more perturbed he grew.

Lassiter's visit, moreover, had a disquieting effect upon Bess, and Venters fancied that she entertained the same thought as to future seclusion. The breaking of their solitude, though by a well-meaning friend, had not only dispelled all its dream and much of its charm, but had instilled a canker of fear. Both had seen the footprints in the sand.

Venters did no more work that day. Sunset and twilight gave way to night, and the canyon bird whistled its melancholy notes, and the wind sang softly in the cliffs, and the camp-fire blazed and burned down to red embers. To Venters a subtle difference was apparent in all of these, or else the shadowy change had been in him. He hoped that on the morrow this slight depression would have passed away.

In that measure, however, he was doomed to disappointment. Furthermore, Bess reverted to a wistful sadness that he had not observed in her since her recovery. His attempt to cheer her out of it resulted in dismal failure, and consequently in a darkening of his own mood. Hard work relieved him; still, when the day had passed, his unrest returned. Then he set to deliberate thinking, and there came to him the startling conviction that he must leave Surprise Valley and take Bess with him. As a rider he had taken many chances, and as an adventurer in Deception Pass he had unhesitatingly risked his life; but now he would run no preventable hazard of Bess's safety and happiness, and he was too keen not to see that hazard. It gave him a pang to think of leaving the beautiful valley just when he had the means to establish a permanent and delightful home there. One flashing thought tore in hot temptation through his mind – why not climb up into the gorge, roll Balancing Rock down the trail, and close forever the outlet to Deception Pass? 'That was the beast in me – showing his teeth!' muttered Venters, scornfully. 'I'll just kill him good and quick! I'll be fair to this girl, if it's the last thing I do on earth!'

Another day went by, in which he worked less and pondered more and all the time covertly watched Bess. Her wistfulness had deepened into downright unhappiness, and that made his task to tell her all the harder. He kept the secret another day, hoping by some chance she might grow less moody, and to his exceeding anxiety she fell into far deeper gloom. Out of his own secret and the torment of it he divined that she, too, had a secret and the keeping of it was torturing her. As yet he had no plan thought out in regard to how or when to leave the valley, but he decided to tell her the necessity of it and to persuade her to go. Furthermore, he hoped his speaking out would induce her to unburden her own mind.

'Bess, what's wrong with you?' he asked.

'Nothing,' she answered, with averted face.

Venters took hold of her and gently, though masterfully, forced her to meet his eyes.

'You can't look at me and lie,' he said. 'Now – what's wrong with you? You're keeping something from me. Well, I've got a secret, too, and I intend to tell it presently.'

'Oh – I *have* a secret. I was crazy to tell you when you came back. That's why I was so silly about everything. I kept holding my secret back – gloating over it. But when Lassiter came I got an idea – that changed my mind. Then I hated to tell you.'

'Are you going to now?'

'Yes – yes. I was coming to it. I tried yesterday, but you were so cold. I was afraid. I couldn't keep it much longer.'

'Very well, most mysterious lady, tell your wonderful secret.'

'You needn't laugh,' she retorted, with a first glimpse of reviving spirit. 'I can take the laugh out of you in one second.'

'It's a go.'

She ran through the spruces to the cave, and returned carrying something which was manifestly heavy. Upon nearer view he saw that whatever she held with such evident importance had been bound up in a black scarf he well remembered. That alone was sufficient to make him tingle with curiosity.

'Have you any idea what I did in your absence?' she asked.

'I imagine you lounged about, waiting and watching for me,' he replied, smiling. 'I've my share of conceit, you know.'

'You're wrong. I worked. Look at my hands.' She dropped on her knees close to where he sat, and, carefully depositing the black bundle, she held out her hands. The palms and inside of her fingers were white, puckered, and worn.

'Why, Bess, you've been fooling in the water,' he said.

'Fooling? Look here!' With deft fingers she spread open the black scarf, and the bright sun shone upon a dull, glittering heap of gold.

'Gold!' he ejaculated.

'Yes, gold! See, pounds of gold! I found it – washed it out of the stream – picked it out grain by grain, nugget by nugget!'

'Gold!' he cried.

'Yes. Now – now laugh at my secret!'

For a long minute Venters gazed. Then he stretched forth a hand to feel if the gold was real.

'*Gold!*' he almost shouted. 'Bess, there are hundreds – thousands of dollars' worth here!'

He leaned over to her, and put his hand, strong and clenching now, on hers.

'Is there more where this came from?' he whispered.

'Plenty of it, all the way up the stream to the cliff. You know I've often washed for gold. Then I've heard the men talk. Think there's no great quantity of gold here, but enough for – for a fortune for *you*.'

'That – was – your – secret!'

'Yes. I hate gold. For it makes men mad. I've seen them drunk with joy and dance and fling themselves around. I've seen them curse and rave. I've seen them fight like dogs and roll in the dust. I've seen them kill each other for gold.'

'Is that why you hated to tell me?'

'Not – not altogether.' Bess lowered her head. 'It was because I knew you'd never stay here long after you found gold.'

'You were afraid I'd leave you?'

'Yes.'

'Listen! . . . You great, simple child! Listen . . . You sweet, wonderful, wild, blue-eyed girl! I was tortured by my secret. It was that I knew we – *we* must leave the valley. We can't stay here much longer. I couldn't think how we'd get away – out of the country – or how we'd live, if we ever got out. I'm a beggar. That's why I kept my secret. I'm poor. It takes money to make way beyond Sterling. We couldn't ride horses or burros or walk forever. So while I knew we must go, I was distracted over how to go and what to do. *Now!* We've gold! Once beyond Sterling, we'll be safe from rustlers. We've no others to fear.

'Oh! Listen! Bess!' Venters now heard his voice ringing high and sweet, and he felt Bess's cold hands in his crushing grasp as she leaned towards him pale, breathless. 'This is how much I'd leave you! You made me live again! I'll take you away – far away from this wild country. You'll begin a new life. You'll be happy. You shall see cities, ships, people. You shall have anything your heart craves. All the shame and sorrow of your life shall be forgotten – as if they had never been. This is how much I'd leave you here alone – you sad-eyed girl. I love you! Didn't you know it? How could you fail to know it? I love you! I'm free! I'm a man – a man you've made – no more a beggar! . . . Kiss me! This is how much I'd leave you here alone – you beautiful, strange, unhappy girl. But I'll make you happy. What – what do I care for – your past! I love you! I'll take you home to Illinois – to my mother. Then I'll take you to far places. I'll make up all you've lost. Oh, I know you love me – knew it before you told me. And it changed my life. And you'll go with me, not as my companion as you are here, nor my sister, but, Bess, darling! . . . *As my wife!*'

CHAPTER 17

Wrangle's Race Run

The plan eventually decided upon by the lovers was for Venters to go to the village, secure a horse and some kind of a disguise for Bess, or at least less striking apparel than her present garb, and to return post-haste to the valley. Meanwhile, she would add to their store of gold. Then they would strike the long and perilous trail to ride out of Utah. In the event of his inability to fetch back a horse for her, they intended to make the giant sorrel carry double. The gold, a little food, saddle blankets, and Venters's guns were to compose the light outfit with which they would make the start.

'I love this beautiful place,' said Bess. 'It's hard to think of leaving it.'

'Hard! Well, I should think so,' replied Venters. 'Maybe – in years – ' But he did not complete in words his thought that it might be possible to return after many years of absence and change.

Once again Bess bade Venters farewell under the shadow of Balancing Rock, and this time it was with whispered hope and tenderness and passionate trust. Long after he had left her, all down through the outlet to the Pass, the clinging clasp of her arms, the sweetness of her lips, and the sense of a new and exquisite birth of character in her remained hauntingly and thrillingly in his mind. The girl who had sadly called herself nameless and nothing had been marvellously transformed in the moment of his avowal of love. It was something to think over, something to warm his heart, but for the present it had absolutely to be forgotten so that all his mind could be addressed to the trip so fraught with danger.

He carried only his rifle, revolver, and a small quantity of bread and meat; and thus lightly burdened, he made swift progress down the slope and out into the valley. Darkness was coming on, and he welcomed it. Stars were blinking when he reached his old hiding-place in the split of canyon wall, and by their aid he slipped through the dense thickets to the grassy enclosure. Wrangle stood in the centre of it with his head up, and he appeared black and of gigantic proportions in the dim light. Venters whistled softly, began a slow approach, and then called. The horse snorted and, plunging away with dull, heavy sound of hoofs, he disappeared in the gloom. 'Wilder than ever!' muttered Venters. He followed the sorrel into the narrowing split between the walls, and presently had to desist because he could not see a foot in advance. As he went back towards the open Wrangle jumped out of an ebony shadow of cliff and like a thunderbolt shot huge and black past him down into the starlit glade. Deciding that all attempts to catch Wrangle at night would be useless, Venters repaired to the shelving rock where he had hidden saddle and blanket, and there went to sleep.

The first peep of day found him stirring, and as soon as it was light enough to distinguish objects, he took his lasso off his saddle and went out to rope the sorrel. He espied Wrangle at the lower end of the cove and approached him in a perfectly natural manner. When he got near enough, Wrangle evidently recognised him, but was too wild to stand. He ran up the glade and on into the narrow lane between the walls. This favoured Venters's speedy capture of the horse, so, coiling his noose ready to throw, he hurried on. Wrangle let Venters get to within a hundred feet and then he broke. But as he plunged by, rapidly getting into his stride, Venters made a perfect throw with the rope. He had time to brace himself for the shock; nevertheless, Wrangle threw him and dragged him several yards before halting.

'You wild devil,' said Venters, as he slowly pulled Wrangle up. 'Don't you know me? Come now – old fellow – so – so – '

Wrangle yielded to the lasso and then to Venters's strong hand. He was as straggly and wild-looking as a horse left to roam free in the sage. He dropped his long ears and stood readily to be saddled and bridled. But he was exceedingly sensitive, and quivered at every touch and sound. Venters led him to the thicket, and, bending the close saplings to let him squeeze through, at length reached the open. Sharp survey in each direction assured him of the usual lonely nature of the canyon; then he was in the saddle, riding south.

Wrangle's long, swinging canter was a wonderful ground-gainer. His stride was almost twice that of an ordinary horse, and his endurance was equally remarkable. Venters pulled him in occasionally, and walked him up the stretches of rising ground and along the soft washes. Wrangle had never yet shown any indication of distress while Venters rode him. Nevertheless, there was now reason to save the horse; therefore Venters did not resort to the hurry that had characterised his former trip. He camped at the last water in the Pass. What distance that was to Cottonwoods he did not know; he calculated, however, that it was in the neighbourhood of fifty miles.

Early in the morning he proceeded on his way, and about the middle of the forenoon reached the constricted gap that marked the southerly end of the Pass, and through which led the trail up to the sage-level. He spied out Lassiter's tracks in the dust, but no others, and, dismounting, he straightened out Wrangle's bridle and began to lead him up the trail. The short climb, more severe on beast than on man, necessitated a rest on the level above, and during this he scanned the wide purple reaches of slope.

Wrangle whistled his pleasure at the smell of the sage. Remounting, Venters headed up the white trail with the fragrant wind in his face. He had proceeded for perhaps a couple of miles when Wrangle stopped with a suddenness that threw Venters heavily against the pommel.

'What's wrong, old boy?' called Venters, looking down for a loose shoe or a snake or a foot lamed by a picked-up stone. Unrewarded, he raised himself from his scrutiny. Wrangle stood stiff, head high, with his long ears erect. Thus guided, Venters swiftly gazed ahead to make out a dust-clouded, dark group of horsemen riding down the slope. If they had seen him, it apparently made no difference in their speed or direction.

'Wonder who they are!' exclaimed Venters. He was not disposed to run. His cool mood tightened under grip of excitement as he reflected that, whoever the approaching riders were, they could not be friends. He slipped out of the saddle and led Wrangle behind the tallest sage-brush. It might serve to conceal them until the riders were close enough for him to see who they were; after that he would be indifferent to how soon they discovered him.

After looking to his rifle and ascertaining that it was in working order, he watched, and as he watched, slowly the force of a bitter fierceness, long dormant, gathered ready to flame into life. If those riders were not rustlers he had forgotten how rustlers looked and rode. On they came, a small group, so compact and dark that he could not tell their number. How unusual that their horses did not see Wrangle! But such failure, Venters decided, was owing to the speed with which they were travelling. They moved at a swift canter affected more by rustlers than by riders. Venters grew concerned over the possibility that these horsemen would actually ride down on him before he had a chance to tell what to expect. When they were within three hundred yards he deliberately led Wrangle out into the trail.

Then he heard shouts, and the hard scrape of sliding hoofs, and saw horses rear and plunge back with up-flung heads and flying manes. Several little white puffs of smoke appeared sharply against the black background of riders and horses, and shots rang out. Bullets struck far in front of Venters, and whipped up the dust and then hummed low into the sage. The range was great for revolvers, but whether the shots were meant to kill or merely to check advance, they were enough to fire that waiting ferocity in Venters. Slipping his arm through the bridle, so that Wrangle could not get away, Venters lifted his rifle and pulled the trigger twice.

He saw the first horseman lean sideways and fall. He saw another lurch in his saddle and heard a cry of pain. Then Wrangle, plunging in fright, lifted Venters and nearly threw him. He jerked the horse down with a powerful hand and leaped into the saddle. Wrangle plunged again, dragging his bridle, that Venters had not had time to throw in place. Bending over with a swift movement, he secured it and dropped the loop over the pommel. Then, with grinding teeth, he looked to see what the issue would be.

The band had scattered so as not to afford such a broad mark for bullets. The riders faced Venters, some with red-belching guns. He heard a sharper report, and just as Wrangle plunged again he caught the whizz of a leaden missile that would have hit him but for Wrangle's sudden jump. A swift, hot wave, turning cold, passed over Venters. Deliberately he picked out the one rider with a carbine, and killed him. Wrangle snorted shrilly and bolted into the sage. Venters let him run a few rods, then with iron arm checked him.

Five riders, surely rustlers, were left. One leaped out of the saddle to secure his fallen comrade's carbine. A shot from Venters, which missed the man but sent the dust flying over him, made him run back to his horse. Then they separated. The crippled rider went one way; the one frustrated in his attempt to get the carbine rode another; Venters thought he made out a third rider, carrying a strange-appearing bundle and disappearing in the sage. But in the rapidity of action and vision he could not discern what it was. Two riders with three horses swung out to the right. Afraid of the long rifle – a burdensome weapon seldom carried by rustlers or riders – they had been put to rout.

Suddenly Venters discovered that one of the two men last noted was riding Jane Withersteen's horse Bells – the beautiful bay racer she had given to Lassiter. Venters uttered a savage outcry. Then the small, wiry, frog-like shape of the second rider, and the ease and grace of his seat in the saddle – things so strikingly incongruous – grew more and more familiar in Venters's sight.

'*Jerry Card!*' cried Venters.

It was indeed Tull's right-hand man. Such a white hot wrath inflamed Venters that he fought himself to see with clearer gaze.

'It's Jerry Card!' he exclaimed, instantly. '*And he's riding Black Star and leading Night!*'

The long-kindling, stormy fire in Venters's heart burst into flame. He spurred Wrangle, and as the horse lengthened his stride Venters slipped cartridges into the magazine of his rifle till it was once again full. Card and his companion were now half a mile or more in advance, riding easily down the slope. Venters marked the smooth gait, and understood it when Wrangle galloped out of the sage into the broad cattle trail, down which Venters had once tracked Jane Withersteen's red herd. This hard-packed trail, from years of use, was as clean and smooth as a road. Venters saw Jerry Card look back over his shoulder; the other rider did likewise. Then the three racers lengthened their stride to the point where the swinging canter was ready to break into a gallop.

'Wrangle, the race's on,' said Venters, grimly. 'We'll canter with them and gallop with them and run with them. We'll let them set the pace.'

Venters knew he bestrode the strongest, swiftest, most tireless horse ever ridden by any rider across the Utah uplands. Recalling Jane Wither-steen's devoted assurance that Night could run neck and neck with Wrangle, and Black Star could show his heels to him, Venters wished that Jane were there to see the race to recover her blacks and in the unqualified superiority of the giant sorrel. Then Venters found himself thankful that she was absent, for he meant that race to end in Jerry Card's death. The first flush, the raging of Venters's wrath, passed, to leave him in sullen, almost cold possession of his will. It was a deadly mood, utterly foreign to his nature, engendered, fostered, and released by the wild passions of wild men in a wild country. The strength in him then – the thing rife in him that was not hate, but something as remorseless – might have been the fiery fruition of a whole lifetime of vengeful quest. Nothing could have stopped him.

Venters thought out the race shrewdly. The rider on Bells would probably drop behind and take to the sage. What he did was of little moment to Venters. To stop Jerry Card, his evil, hidden career as well as his present flight, and then to catch the blacks – that was all that concerned Venters. The cattle trail wound for miles and miles down the slope. Venters saw with a rider's keen vision ten, fifteen, twenty miles of clear purple sage. There were no oncoming riders or rustlers to aid Card.

His only chance to escape lay in abandoning the stolen horses and creeping away in the sage to hide. In ten miles Wrangle could run Black Star and Night off their feet, and in fifteen he could kill them outright. So Venters held the sorrel in, letting Card make the running. It was a long race that would save the blacks.

In a few miles of that swinging canter Wrangle had crept appreciably closer to the three horses. Jerry Card turned again, and when he saw how the sorrel had gained, he put Black Star to a gallop. Night and Bells, on either side of him, swept into his stride.

Venters loosened the rein on Wrangle and let him break into a gallop. The sorrel saw the horses ahead and wanted to run. But Venters restrained him. And in the gallop he gained more than in the canter. Bells was fast in that gait, but Black Star and Night had been trained to run. Slowly Wrangle closed the gap down to a quarter of a mile, and crept closer and closer.

Jerry Card wheeled once more. Venters distinctly saw the red flash of his red face. This time he looked long. Venters laughed. He knew what passed in Card's mind. The rider was trying to make out what horse it happened to be that thus gained on Jane Withersteen's peerless racers. Wrangle had so long been away from the village that not improbably Jerry had forgotten. Besides, whatever Jerry's qualifications for his fame as the greatest rider of the sage, certain it was that his best point was not far-sightedness. He had not recognised Wrangle. After what must have been a searching gaze he got his comrade to face about. This action gave Venters amusement. It spoke so surely of the fact that neither Card nor the rustler actually knew their danger. Yet if they kept to the trail – and the last thing such men would do would be to leave it – they were both doomed.

This comrade of Card's whirled far around in his saddle, and he even shaded his eyes from the sun. He, too, looked long. Then, all at once, he faced ahead again and, bending lower in the saddle, began to fling his right arm up and down. That flinging Venters knew to be the lashing of Bells. Jerry also became active. And the three racers lengthened out into a run.

'Now, Wrangle!' cried Venters. 'Run, you big devil! Run!'

Venters laid the reins on Wrangle's neck and dropped the loop over the pommel. The sorrel needed no guiding on that smooth trail. He was surer-footed in a run than at any other fast gait, and his running gave the impression of something devilish. He might now have been actuated by

Venters's spirit; undoubtedly his savage running fitted the mood of his rider. Venters bent forward, swinging with the horse, and gripped his rifle. His eye measured the distance between him and Jerry Card.

In less than two miles of running Bells began to drop behind the blacks, and Wrangle began to overhaul him. Venters anticipated that the rustler would soon take to the sage. Yet he did not. Not improbably he reasoned that the powerful sorrel could more easily overtake Bells in the heavier going outside of the trail. Soon only a few hundred yards lay between Bells and Wrangle. Turning in his saddle, the rustler began to shoot, and the bullets beat up little whiffs of dust. Venters raised his rifle, ready to take snap shots, and waited for favourable opportunity when Bells was out of line with the forward horses. Venters had it in him to kill these men as if they were skunk-bitten coyotes, but also he had restraint enough to keep from shooting one of Jane's beloved Arabians.

No great distance was covered, however, before Bells swerved to the left, out of line with Black Star and Night. Then Venters, aiming high and waiting for the pause between Wrangle's great strides, began to take snap shots at the rustler. The fleeing rider presented a broad target for a rifle, but he was moving swiftly forward and bobbing up and down. Moreover, shooting from Wrangle's back was shooting from a thunderbolt. And added to that was the danger of a low-placed bullet taking effect on Bells. Yet, despite these considerations, making the shot exceedingly difficult, Venters's confidence, like his implacability, saw a speedy and fatal termination of that rustler's race. On the sixth shot the rustler threw up his arms and took a flying tumble off his horse. He rolled over and over, hunched himself to a half-erect position, fell, and then dragged himself into the sage. As Venters went thundering by he peered keenly into the sage, but caught no sign of the man. Bells ran a few hundred yards, slowed up, and had stopped when Wrangle passed him.

Again Venters began slipping fresh cartridges into the magazine of his rifle, and his hand was so sure and steady that he did not drop a single cartridge. With the eye of a rider and the judgement of a marksman he once more measured the distance between him and Jerry Card. Wrangle had gained, bringing him into rifle range. Venters was hard put to it now not to shoot, but thought it better to withhold his fire. Jerry, who, in anticipation of a running fusillade, had huddled himself into a little twisted ball on Black Star's neck, now surmising that this pursuer would make sure of not wounding one of the blacks, rose to his natural seat in the saddle.

In his mind perhaps, as certainly as in Venters's, this moment was the beginning of the real race.

Venters leaned forward to put his hand on Wrangle's neck; then backwards to put it on his flank. Under the shaggy, dusty hair trembled and vibrated and rippled a wonderful muscular activity. But Wrangle's flesh was still cold. What a cold-blooded brute, thought Venters, and felt in him a love for the horse he had never given to any other. It would not have been humanly possible for any rider, even though clutched by hate or revenge or a passion to save a loved one or fear of his own life, to be astride the sorrel, to swing with his swing, to see his magnificent stride and hear the rapid thunder of his hoofs, to ride him in that race and not glory in the ride.

So, with his passion to kill still keen and unabated, Venters lived out that ride, and drank a rider's sage-sweet cup of wildness to the dregs.

When Wrangle's long mane, lashing in the wind, stung Venters in the cheek, the sting added a beat to his flying pulse. He bent a downward glance to try to see Wrangle's actual stride, and saw only twinkling, darting streaks and the white rush of the trail. He watched the sorrel's savage head, pointed level, his mouth still closed and dry, but his nostrils distended as if he were snorting unseen fire. Wrangle was the horse for a race with death. Upon each side Venters saw the sage merged into a sailing, colourless wall. In front sloped the lay of ground with its purple breadth split by the white trail. The wind, blowing with heavy, steady blast into his face, sickened him with enduring, sweet odour, and filled his ears with a hollow, rushing roar.

Then for the hundredth time he measured the width of space separating him from Jerry Card. Wrangle had ceased to gain. The blacks were proving their fleetness. Venters watched Jerry Card, admiring the little rider's horsemanship. He had the incomparable seat of the upland rider, born in the saddle. It struck Venters that Card had changed his position, or the position of the horses. Presently Venters remembered positively that Jerry had been leading Night on the right-hand side of the trail. The racer was now on the side to the left. No – it was Black Star. But, Venters argued in amaze, Jerry had been mounted on Black Star. Another clearer, keener gaze assured Venters that Black Star was really riderless. Night now carried Jerry Card.

'He's changed from one to the other!' ejaculated Venters, realising the astounding feat with unstinted admiration. 'Changed at full speed! Jerry Card, that's what you've done unless I'm drunk on the smell of sage. But I've got to see the trick before I believe it.'

Thenceforth, while Wrangle sped on, Venters glued his eyes to the little rider. Jerry Card rode as only he could ride. Of all the daring horsemen of the uplands, Jerry was the one rider fitted to bring out the greatness of the blacks in that long race. He had them on a dead run, but not yet at the last strained and killing pace. From time to time he glanced backward, as a wise general in retreat calculating his chances and the power and speed of pursuers, and the moment for the last desperate burst. No doubt, Card, with his life at stake, gloried in that race, perhaps more wildly than Venters. For he had been born to the sage and the saddle and the wild. He was more than half horse. Not until the last call – the sudden up-flashing instinct of self-preservation – would he lose his skill and judgement and nerve and the spirit of that race. Venters seemed to read Jerry's mind. That little crime-stained rider was actually thinking of his horses, husbanding their speed, handling them with knowledge of years, glorying in their beautiful, swift, racing stride, and wanting them to win the race when his own life hung suspended in quivering balance. Again Jerry whirled in his saddle and the sun flashed red on his face. Turning, he drew Black Star closer and closer towards Night, till they ran side by side, as one horse. Then Card raised himself in the saddle, slipped out of the stirrups, and, somehow twisting himself, leaped upon Black Star. He did not even lose the swing of the horse. Like a leech he was there in the other saddle, and as the horse separated, his right foot, that had been apparently doubled under him, shot down to catch the stirrup. The grace and dexterity and daring of that rider's act won something more than admiration from Venters.

For the distance of a mile Jerry rode Black Star and then changed back to Night. But all Jerry's skill and the running of the blacks could avail little more against the sorrel.

Venters peered far ahead, studying the lay of the land. Straightaway for five miles the trail stretched, and then it disappeared in hummocky ground. To the right some few rods, Venters saw a break in the sage, and this was the rim of Deception Pass. Across the dark cleft gleamed the red of the opposite wall. Venters imagined that the trail went down into the Pass somewhere north of those ridges. And he realised that he must and would overtake Jerry Card in this straight course of five miles.

Cruelly he struck his spurs into Wrangle's flanks. A light touch of spur was sufficient to make Wrangle plunge. And now, with a ringing, wild snort, he seemed to double up in muscular convulsions and to shoot forward with an impetus that almost unseated Venters. The sage blurred by, the trail flashed by, and the wind robbed him of breath and hearing. Jerry Card turned once more. And the way he shifted to Black Star showed he had to make his last desperate running. Venters aimed to the side of the trail and sent a bullet puffing the dust beyond Jerry. Venters hoped to frighten the rider and get him to take to the sage. But Jerry returned the shot, and his ball struck dangerously close in the dust at Wrangle's flying feet. Venters held his fire then, while the rider emptied his revolver. For a mile, with Black Star leaving Night behind, and doing his utmost, Wrangle did not gain; for another mile he gained little, if at all. In the third he caught up with the now galloping Night and began to gain rapidly on the other black.

Only a hundred yards now stretched between Black Star and Wrangle. The giant sorrel thundered on – and on – and on. In every yard he gained a foot. He was whistling through his nostrils, wringing wet, flying lather, and as hot as fire. Savage as ever, strong as ever, fast as ever, but each tremendous stride jarred Venters out of the saddle! Wrangle's power and spirit and momentum had begun to run him off his legs. Wrangle's great race was nearly won – and run. Venters seemed to see the expanse before him as a vast, sheeted, purple plain sliding under him. Black Star moved in it as a blur. The rider, Jerry Card, appeared a mere dot bobbing dimly. Wrangle thundered on – on – on! Venters felt the increase in quivering, straining shock after every leap. Flecks of foam flew into Venters's eyes, burning him, making him see all the sage as red. But in that red haze he saw, or seemed to see, Black Star suddenly riderless and with broken gait. Wrangle thundered on to change his pace with a violent break. Then Venters pulled him hard. From run to gallop, gallop to canter, canter to trot, trot to walk, and walk to stop, the great sorrel ended his race.

Venters looked back. Black Star stood riderless in the trail. Jerry Card had taken to the sage. Far up the white trail Night came trotting faithfully down. Venters leaped off, still half blind, reeling dizzily. In a moment he had recovered sufficiently to have a care for Wrangle. Rapidly he took off the saddle and bridle. The sorrel was reeking, heaving, whistling, shaking. But he had still the strength to stand, and for him Venters had no fears.

As Venters ran back to Black Star he saw the horse stagger on shaking legs into the sage and go down in a heap. Upon reaching him Venters removed the saddle and bridle. Black Star had been killed on his legs, Venters thought. He had no hope for the stricken horse. Black Star lay flat, covered with bloody froth, mouth wide, tongue hanging, eyes glaring, and all his beautiful body in convulsions.

Unable to stay there to see Jane's favourite racer die, Venters hurried up the trail to meet the other black. On the way he kept a sharp lookout for Jerry Card. Venters imagined the rider would keep well out of range of the rifle, but, as he would be lost on the sage without a horse, not improbably he would linger in the vicinity on the chance of getting back one of the blacks. Night soon came trotting up, hot and wet and run out. Venters led him down near the others, and, unsaddling him, let him loose to rest. Night wearily lay down in the dust and rolled, proving himself not yet spent.

Then Venters sat down to rest and think. Whatever the risk, he was compelled to stay where he was, or comparatively near, for the night. The horses must rest and drink. He must find water. He was now seventy miles from Cottonwoods, and, he believed, close to the canyon where the cattle trail must surely turn off and go down into the Pass. After a while he rose to survey the valley.

He was very near to the ragged edge of a deep canyon into which the trail turned. The ground lay in uneven ridges divided by washes, and these sloped into the canyon. Following the canyon line, he saw where its rim was broken by other intersecting canyons, and farther down red walls and yellow cliffs leading towards a deep blue cleft that he made sure was Deception Pass. Walking out a few rods to a promontory, he found where the trail went down. The descent was gradual, along a stonewalled trail, and Venters felt sure that this was the place where Oldring drove cattle into the Pass. There was, however, no indication at all that he ever had driven cattle out at this point. Oldring had many holes to his burrow.

In searching round in the little hollows Venters, much to his relief, found water. He composed himself to rest and eat some bread and meat, while he waited for a sufficient time to elapse so that he could safely give the horses a drink. He judged the hour to be somewhere around noon. Wrangle lay down to rest and Night followed suit. So long as they were down Venters intended to make no move. The longer they rested the better, and the safer it would be to give them water. By and by he forced himself to go over to where Black Star lay, expecting to find him dead. Instead he found the racer partially if not wholly recovered. There was recognition, even fire, in his big black eyes. Venters was overjoyed. He sat by the black for a long time. Black Star presently laboured to his feet with a heave and a groan, shook himself, and snorted for water. Venters repaired to the little pool he had found, filled his sombrero, and gave the racer a drink. Black Star gulped it at one draught, as if it were but a drop, and pushed his nose into the hat and snorted for more. Venters now led Night down to drink, and after a further time Black Star also. Then the blacks began to graze.

The sorrel had wandered off down the sage between the trail and the canyon. Once or twice he disappeared in little swales. Finally Venters concluded Wrangle had grazed far enough, and, taking his lasso, he went to fetch him back. In crossing from one ridge to another he saw where the horse had made muddy a pool of water. It occurred to Venters then that Wrangle had drunk his fill, and did not seem the worse for it, and might be anything but easy to catch. And, true enough, he could not come within roping reach of the sorrel. He tried for an hour, and gave up in disgust. Wrangle did not seem so wild as simply perverse. In a quandary Venters returned to the other horses, hoping much, yet doubting more, that when Wrangle had grazed to suit himself he might be caught.

As the afternoon wore away Venters's concern diminished, yet he kept close watch on the blacks and the trail and the sage. There was no telling of what Jerry Card might be capable. Venters sullenly acquiesced to the idea that the rider had been too quick and too shrewd for him. Strangely and doggedly however, Venters clung to his foreboding of Card's downfall.

The wind died away; the red sun topped the far distant western rise of slope; and the long, creeping purple shadows lengthened. The rims of the canyons gleamed crimson and the deep clefts appeared to belch forth blue smoke. Silence enfolded the scene.

It was broken by a horrid, long-drawn scream of a horse and the thudding of heavy hoofs. Venters sprang erect and wheeled south. Along the canyon rim, near the edge, came Wrangle, once more in thundering flight.

Venters gasped in amazement. Had the wild sorrel gone mad? His head was high and twisted, in a most singular position for a running horse. Suddenly Venters descried a frog-like shape clinging to Wrangle's neck. Jerry Card! Somehow he had straddled Wrangle and now stuck like a huge burr. But it was his strange position and the sorrel's wild scream that shook Venters's nerves. Wrangle was pounding towards the turn where the trail went down. He plunged onwards like a blind horse. More than one of his leaps took him to the very edge of the precipice.

Jerry Card was bent forward with his teeth fast in the front of Wrangle's nose! Venters saw it, and there flashed over him a memory of this trick of a few desperate riders. He even thought of one rider who had worn off his teeth in this terrible hold to break or control desperate horses. Wrangle had indeed gone mad. The marvel was what guided him. Was it the half-brute, the more than half-horse instinct of Jerry Card? Whatever the mystery, it was true. And in a few more rods Jerry would have the sorrel turning into the trail leading down into the canyon.

'No – Jerry!' whispered Venters, stepping forward and throwing up the rifle. He tried to catch the little humped, froglike shape over the sights. It was moving too fast; it was too small. Yet Venters shot once . . . twice . . . the third time . . . four times . . . five! All wasted shots and precious seconds!

With a deep-muttered curse Venters caught Wrangle through the sights and pulled the trigger. Plainly he heard the bullet thus. Wrangle uttered a horrible strangling sound. In swift death action he whirled, and with one last splendid leap he cleared the canyon rim. And he whirled downward with the little frog-like shape clinging to his neck!

There was a pause which seemed never ending, a shock, and an instant's silence.

Then up rolled a heavy crash, a long roar of sliding rocks dying away in distant echo, then silence unbroken.

Wrangle's race was run.

CHAPTER 18

Oldring's Knell

Some forty hours or more later Venters created a commotion in Cotton-woods by riding down the main street on Black Star and leading Bells and Night. He had come upon Bells grazing near the body of a dead rustler, the only incident of his quick ride into the village.

Nothing was farther from Venters's mind than bravado. No thought came to him of the defiance and boldness of riding Jane Withersteen's racers straight into the arch-plotter's stronghold. He wanted men to see the famous Arabians; he wanted men to see them dirty and dusty, bearing all the signs of having been driven to their limit; he wanted men to see and to know that the thieves who had ridden them out into the sage had not ridden them back. Venters had come for that and for more – he wanted to meet Tull face to face; if not Tull, then Dyer; if not Dyer, then anyone in the secret of these master conspirators. Such was Venters's passion. The meeting with the rustlers, the unprovoked attack upon him, the spilling of blood, the recognition of Jerry Card and the horses, the race, and that last plunge of mad Wrangle – all these things, fuel on fuel to the smouldering fire, had kindled and swelled and leaped into living flame. He could have shot Dyer in the midst of his religious services at the altar; he could have killed Tull in front of wives and babes.

He walked the three racers down the broad, green-bordered village road. He heard the murmur of running water from Amber Spring. Bitter waters for Jane Withersteen! Men and women stopped to gaze at him and the horses. All knew him; all knew the blacks and the bay. As well as if it had been spoken, Venters read in the faces of men the intelligence that Jane Withersteen's Arabians had been known to have been stolen. Venters reined in and halted before Dyer's residence. It was a low, long, stone structure resembling Withersteen House. The spacious front yard was green and luxuriant with grass and flowers; gravel walks led to the high porch; a well-trimmed hedge of purple sage separated the yard from the church grounds; birds sang in the trees; water flowed musically along the walks; and there were glad, careless shouts of children. For Venters the beauty of this home, and the serenity and its apparent happiness, all turned red and black. For Venters a shade overspread the lawn, the flowers, the old vine-clad stone house. In the music of the singing birds, in the murmur of the running water, he heard an ominous sound. Quiet beauty – sweet music – innocent laughter! By what monstrous abortion of fate did these abide in the shadow of Dyer?

Venters rode on and stopped before Tull's cottage. Women stared at him with white faces and then flew from the porch. Tull himself appeared at the door, bent low, craning his neck. His dark face flashed out of sight; the door banged; a heavy bar dropped with a hollow sound.

Then Venters shook Black Star's bridle, and, sharply trotting, led the other horses to the centre of the village. Here at the intersecting streets and in front of the stores he halted once more. The usual lounging atmosphere of that prominent corner was not now in evidence. Riders and ranchers and villagers broke up what must have been absorbing conversation. There was a rush of many feet, and then the walk was lined with faces.

Venters's glance swept down the line of silent stone-faced men. He recognised many riders and villagers, but none of those he had hoped to meet. There was no expression in the faces turned towards him. All of them knew him, most were inimical, but there were few who were not burning with curiosity and wonder in regard to the return of Jane Withersteen's racers. Yet all were silent. Here were the familiar characteristics – masked feeling – strange secretiveness – expressionless expression of mystery and hidden power.

'Has anybody here seen Jerry Card?' queried Venters, in a loud voice.

In reply there came not a word, not a nod or shake of head, not so much as dropping eye or twitching lip – nothing but a quiet, stony stare.

'Been under the knife? You've a fine knife-wielder here – one Tull, I believe! . . . Maybe you've all had your tongues cut out?'

This passionate sarcasm of Venters brought no response, and the stony calm was as oil on the fire within him.

'I see some of you pack guns, too!' he added, in biting scorn. In the long, tense pause, strung keenly as a tight wire, he sat motionless on Black Star. 'All right,' he went on. 'Then let some of you take this message to Tull. Tell him I've seen Jerry Card! . . . Tell him Jerry Card *will never return!*'

Thereupon, in the same dead calm, Venters backed Black Star away from the kerb, into the street, and out of range. He was ready now to ride up to Withersteen House and turn the racers over to Jane.

'Hello, Venters!' a familiar voice cried, hoarsely, and he saw a man running towards him. It was the rider Judkins who came up and gripped Venters's hand. 'Venters, I could hev dropped when I seen them hosses. But thet sight ain't a marker to the looks of you. What's wrong? Hev you gone crazy? You must be crazy to ride in here this way – with them hosses – talkin' thet way about Tull an' Jerry Card.'

'Jud, I'm not crazy – only mad clean through,' replied Venters.

'Wal, now, Bern, I'm glad to hear some of your old self in your voice. Fer when you come up you looked like the corpse of a dead rider with fire fer eyes. You hed thet crowd too stiff fer throwin' guns. Come, we've got to hev a talk. Let's go up the lane. We ain't much safe here.'

Judkins mounted Bells and rode with Venters up to the cottonwood grove. Here they dismounted and went among the trees.

'Let's hear from you first,' said Judkins. 'You fetched back them hosses. Thet *is* the trick. An', of course, you got Jerry the same as you got Horne.'

'Horne!'

'Sure. He was found dead yesterday all chewed by coyotes, an' he'd been shot plumb centre.'

'Where was he found?'

'At the split down the trail – you know where Oldrin's cattle trail runs off north from the trail to the pass.'

'That's where I met Jerry and the rustlers. What was Horne doing with them? I thought Horne was an honest cattle-man.'

'Lord – Bern, don't ask me thet! I'm all muddled now tryin' to figure things.'

Venters told of the fight and the race with Jerry Card and its tragic conclusion.

'I knowed it! I knowed all along that Wrangle was the best hoss!' exclaimed Judkins, with his lean face working and his eyes lighting. 'Thet was a race! Lord, I'd like to hev seen Wrangle jump the cliff with Jerry. An' thet was goodbye to the grandest hoss an' rider ever on the sage! . . . But, Bern, after you got the hosses why'd you want to bolt right in Tull's face?'

'I want him to know. An' if I can get to him I'll – '

'You can't get near Tull,' interrupted Judkins. 'Thet vigilante bunch hev taken to bein' bodyguard for Tull an' Dyer, too.'

'Hasn't Lassiter made a break yet?' enquired Venters, curiously.

'Naw!' replied Judkins, scornfully. 'Jane turned his head. He's mad in love over her – follers her like a dog. He ain't no more Lassiter! He's lost his nerve; he doesn't look like the same feller. It's village talk. Everybody knows it. He hasn't thrown a gun, an' he won't!'

'Jud, I'll bet he does,' replied Venters, earnestly. 'Remember what I say. This Lassiter is something more than a gunman. Jud, he's big – he's great! . . . I feel that in him. God help Tull and Dyer when Lassiter does go after them. For horses and riders and stone walls won't save them.'

'Wal, hev it your way, Bern. I hope you're right. Nat'rully I've been some sore on Lassiter fer gittin' soft. But I ain't denyin' his nerve, or whatever's great in him thet sort of paralyses people. No later 'n this mornin' I seen him saunterin' down the lane, quiet an' slow. An' like his guns he comes black – *black*, thet's Lassiter. Wal, the crowd on the corner never batted an eye, an' I'll gamble my hoss thet there wasn't one who hed a heartbeat till Lassiter got by. He went in Snell's saloon, an' as there wasn't no gun play I had to go in, too. An' there, darn my pictures, if Lassiter wasn't standin' to the bar, drinkin' an' talkin' with Oldrin'.'

'*Oldring!*' whispered Venters. His voice, as all fire and pulse within him, seemed to freeze.

'Let go my arm!' exclaimed Judkins. 'Thet's my bad arm. Sure it was Oldrin'. What the hell's wrong with you, anyway? Venters, I tell you somethin's wrong. You're whiter 'n a sheet. You can't be *scared* of the rustler. I don't believe you've got a scare in you. Wal, now, jest let me talk. You know I like to talk, an' if I'm slow I allus git there sometime. As I said, Lassiter was talkin' chummy with Oldrin'. There wasn't no hard feelin's. An' the gang wasn't payin' no pertic'lar attention. But like a cat watchin' a mouse I hed my eyes on them two fellers. It was strange to me, thet confab. I'm gittin' to think a lot, fer a feller who doesn't know much. There's been some queer deals lately an' this seemed to me the queerest. These men stood to the bar alone, an' so close their big gun-hilts butted together. I seen Oldrin' was surprised at first, an' Lassiter was cool as ice. They talked, an' presently at somethin' Lassiter said the rustler bawled out a curse, an' then he jest fell up against the bar, an' sagged there. The gang in the saloon looked around an' laughed, an' thet's about all. Finally Oldrin' turned, and it was easy to see somethin' hed shook him. Yes, sir, thet big rustler – you know he's as broad as he is long, an' the powerfullest build of a man – yes, sir, the nerve had been taken out of him. Then, after a little, he began to talk an' said a lot to Lassiter, an' by an' by it didn't take much of an eye to see thet Lassiter was gittin' hit hard. I never seen him anyway but cooler 'n ice – till then. He seemed to be hit harder 'n Oldrin', only he didn't roar out thet way. He jest kind of sunk in, an' looked an' looked, an' he didn't see a livin' soul in thet saloon. Then he sort of come to, an' shakin' hands – mind you, *shakin hands* with Oldrin' – he went out. I couldn't help thinkin' how easy even a boy could hev dropped the great gunman then! . . . Wal, the rustler stood at the bar fer a long time, an' he was seein' things far off, too; then he come to an' roared fer whisky, an' gulped a drink thet was big enough to drown me.'

'Is Oldring here now?' whispered Venters. He could not speak above a whisper. Judkins's story had been meaningless to him.

'He's at Snell's yet. Bern, I hevn't told you yet thet the rustlers hev been raisin' hell. They shot up Stone Bridge an' Glaze, an' fer three days they've been here drinkin' an' gamblin' an' throwin' of gold. These rustlers hev a pile of gold. If it was gold dust or nugget gold I'd hev reason to think, but it's new coin gold, as if it had jest come from the United States treasury. An' the coin's genuine. Thet's all been proved. The truth is Oldrin's on a rampage. A while back he lost his Masked Rider, an' they say he's wild about thet. I'm wonderin' if Lassiter could hev told the rustler anythin' about thet little masked, hard-ridin' devil. Ride! He was most as good as Jerry Card. An', Bern, I've been wonderin' if you know – '

'Judkins, you're a good fellow,' interrupted Venters. 'Someday I'll tell you a story. I've no time now. Take the horses to Jane.'

Judkins stared, and then, muttering to himself, he mounted Bells, and stared again at Venters, and then, leading the other horses, he rode into the grove and disappeared.

Once, long before, on the night Venters had carried Bess through the canyon and up into Surprise Valley, he had experienced the strangeness of faculties singularly, tinglingly acute. And now the same sensation recurred. But it was different in that he felt cold, frozen, mechanical, incapable of free thought, and all about him seemed unreal, aloof, remote. He hid his rifle in the sage, marking its exact location with extreme care. Then he faced down the lane and strode towards the centre of the village. Perceptions flashed upon him, the faint, cold touch of the breeze, a cold, silvery tinkle of flowing water, a cold sun shining out of a cold sky, song of birds and laugh of children, coldly distant. Cold and intangible were all things in earth and heaven. Colder and tighter stretched the skin over his face; colder and harder grew the polished butts of his guns; colder and steadier became his hands as he wiped the clammy sweat from his face or reached low to his gun-sheaths. Men meeting him in the walk gave him wide berth. In front of Bevin's store a crowd melted apart for his passage, and their faces and whispers were faces and whispers of a dream. He turned a corner to meet Tull face to face, eye to eye. As once before he had seen this man pale to a ghastly, livid white, so again he saw the change. Tull stopped in his tracks, with right hand raised and shaking. Suddenly it dropped, and he seemed to glide aside, to pass out of Venters's sight. Next he saw many horses with bridles down – all clean-limbed, dark bays or blacks – rustlers' horses! Loud voices and boisterous laughter, rattle of dice and scrape of chair and clink of gold, burst in mingled din from an open doorway. He stepped inside.

With the sight of smoke-hazed room and drinking, cursing, gambling, dark-visaged men, reality once more dawned upon Venters.

His entrance had been unnoticed, and he bent his gaze upon the drinkers at the bar. Dark-clothed, dark-faced men they all were, burned by the sun, bow-legged as were most riders of the sage, but neither lean nor gaunt. Then Venters's gaze passed to the tables, and swiftly it swept over the hard-featured gamesters, to alight upon the huge, shaggy black head of the rustler chief.

'Oldring!' he cried, and to him his voice seemed to split a bell in his ears.

It stilled the din.

That silence suddenly broke to the scrape and crash of Oldring's chair as he rose; and then, while he passed, a great gloomy figure, again the thronged room stilled in silence yet deeper.

'Oldring, a word with you!' continued Venters.

'Ho! What's this?' boomed Oldring, in frowning scrutiny.

'Come outside, alone. A word for you – *from your Masked Rider!*'

Oldring kicked a chair out of his way and lunged forward with a stamp of heavy boot that jarred the floor. He waved down his muttering, rising men.

Venters backed out of the door and waited, hearing, as no sound had ever before struck into his soul, the rapid, heavy steps of the rustler.

Oldring appeared, and Venters had one glimpse of his great breadth and bulk, his gold-buckled belt with hanging guns, his high-top boots with gold spurs. In that moment Venters had a strange, unintelligible curiosity to see Oldring alive. The rustler's broad brow, his large black eyes, his sweeping beard, as dark as the wing of a raven, his enormous width of shoulder and depth of chest, his whole splendid presence so wonderfully charged with vitality and force and strength, seemed to afford Venters an unutterable fiendish joy because for that magnificent manhood and life he meant cold and sudden death.

'*Oldring, Bess is alive! But she's dead to you – dead to the life you made her lead – dead as you will be in one second!*'

Swift as lightning Venters's glance dropped from Oldring's rolling eyes to his hands. One of them, the right, swept out, then towards his gun – and Venters shot him through the heart.

Slowly Oldring sank to his knees, and the hand, dragging at the gun, fell away. Venters's strangely acute faculties grasped the meaning of that limp arm, of the swaying hulk, of the gasp and heave, of the quivering beard. But was that awful spirit in the black eyes only one of vitality?

'*Man – why – didn't – you – wait? Bess – was –* ' Oldring's whisper died under his beard, and with a heavy lurch he fell forward.

Bounding swiftly away, Venters fled around the corner, across the street, and, leaping a hedge, he ran through yard, orchard, and garden to the sage. Here, under cover of the tall brush, he turned west and ran on to the place where he had hidden his rifle. Securing that, he again set out into a run, and, circling through the sage, came up behind Jane Withersteen's stable and corrals. With labouring, dripping chest, and pain as of a knife thrust in his side, he stopped to regain his breath, and while resting his eyes roved around in search of a horse. Doors and windows of the stable were open wide and had a deserted look. One dejected, lonely burro stood in the near corral. Strange indeed was the silence brooding over the once happy, noisy home of Jane Withersteen's pets.

He went into the corral, exercising care to leave no tracks, and led the burro to the watering-trough. Venters, though not thirsty, drank till he could drink no more. Then, leading the burro over hard ground, he struck into the sage and down the slope.

He strode swiftly, turning from time to time to scan the slope for riders. His head just topped the level of sage-brush, and the burro could not have been seen at all. Slowly the green of Cottonwoods sank behind the slope, and at last a wavering line of purple sage met the blue of sky.

To avoid being seen, to get away, to hide his trail – these were the sole ideas in his mind as he headed for Deception Pass; and he directed all his acuteness of eye and ear, and the keenness of a rider's judgement for distance and ground, to stern accomplishment of the task. He kept to the sage far to the left of the trail leading into the Pass. He walked ten miles and looked back a thousand times. Always the graceful, purple wave of sage remained wide and lonely, a clear, undotted waste. Coming to a stretch of rocky ground, he took advantage of it to cross the trail and then continued down on the right. At length he persuaded himself that he would be able to see riders mounted on horses before they could see him on the little burro, and he rode bareback.

Hour by hour the tireless burro kept to his faithful, steady trot. The sun sank and the long shadows lengthened down the slope. Moving veils of purple twilight crept out of the hollows and, mustering and forming on the levels, soon merged and shaded into night. Venters guided the burro nearer to the trail, so that he could see its white line from the ridges, and rode on through the hours.

Once down in the Pass without leaving a trail, he would hold himself safe for the time being. When late in the night he reached the break in the sage, he sent the burro down ahead of him, and started an avalanche that all but buried the animal at the bottom of the trail. Bruised and battered as he was, he had a moment's elation, for he had hidden his tracks. Once more he mounted the burro and rode on. The hour was the blackest of the night when he made the thicket which enclosed his old camp. Here he turned the burro loose in the grass near the spring, and then lay down on his old bed of leaves.

He felt only vaguely, as outside things, the ache and burn and throb of the muscles of his body. But a dammed-up torrent of emotion at last burst its bounds, and the hour that saw his release from immediate action was one that confounded him in the reaction of his spirit. He suffered without understanding why. He caught glimpses into himself, into unlit darkness of soul. The fire that had blistered him and the cold which had frozen him now united in one torturing possession of his mind and heart, and like a fiery steed with ice-shod feet, ranged his being, ran rioting through his blood, trampling the resurging good, dragging ever at the evil.

Out of the subsiding chaos came a clear question. What had happened? He had left the valley to go to Cottonwoods. Why? It seemed that he had gone to kill a man – Oldring! The name riveted his consciousness upon the one man of all men upon earth whom he had wanted to meet. He had met the rustler. Venters recalled the smoky haze of the saloon, the dark-visaged men, the huge Oldring. He saw him step out of the door, a splendid specimen of manhood, a handsome giant with purple-black and sweeping beard. He remembered inquisitive gaze of falcon eyes. He heard himself repeating: '*Oldring, Bess is alive! But she's dead to you,*' and he felt himself jerk, and his ears throbbed to the thunder of a gun, and he saw the giant sink slowly to his knees. Was that only the vitality of him – that awful light in the eyes – only the hard-dying life of a tremendously powerful brute? A broken whisper, strange as death: '*Man – why – didn't – you – wait! Bess – was –* ' And Oldring plunged face forward, dead.

'I killed him,' cried Venters, in remembering shock. 'But it wasn't *that*. Ah, the look in his eyes and his whisper!'

Herein lay the secret that had clamoured to him through all the tumult and stress of his emotions. What a look in the eyes of a man shot through the heart! It had been neither hate nor ferocity nor fear of men nor fear of death. It had been no passionate, glinting spirit of a fearless foe, willing shot for shot, life for life, but lacking physical power. Distinctly recalled now, never to be forgotten, Venters saw in Oldring's magnificent eyes the rolling of great, glad surprise – softness – love! Then came a shadow and the terrible superhuman striving of his spirit to speak. Oldring, shot through the heart, had fought and forced back death, not for a moment in which to shoot or curse, but to whisper strange words.

What words for a dying man to whisper! Why had not Venters waited? For what? That was no plea for life. It was regret that there was not a moment of life left in which to speak. Bess was – Herein lay renewed torture for Venters. What had Bess been to Oldring? The old question, like a spectre, stalked from its grave to haunt him. He had overlooked, he had forgiven, he had loved, and he had forgotten; and now, out of the mystery of a dying man's whisper rose again that perverse, unsatisfied, jealous uncertainty. Bess had loved that splendid, black-crowned giant – by her own confession she had loved him; and in Venters's soul again flamed up the jealous hell. Then into the clamouring hell burst the shot that had killed Oldring, and it rang in a wild, fiendish gladness, a hateful, vengeful joy. That passed to the memory of the love and light in Oldring's eyes and the mystery in his whisper. So the changing, swaying emotions fluctuated in Venters's heart.

This was the climax of his year of suffering and the crucial struggle of his life. And when the grey dawn came he rose, a gloomy, almost heart-broken man, but victor over evil passions. He could not change the past; and, even if he had not loved Bess with all his soul, he had grown into a man who would not change the future he had planned for her. Only, and once for all, he must know the truth, know the worst, stifle all these insistent doubts and subtle hopes and jealous fancies, and kill the past by knowing truly what Bess had been to Oldring. For that matter he knew – he had always known, but he must hear it spoken. Then, when they had safely gotten out of that wild country to take up a new and an absorbing life, she would forget, she would be happy, and through that, in the years to come, he could not but find life worth living.

All day he rode slowly and cautiously up the Pass, taking time to peer around corners, to pick out hard ground and grassy patches, and to make sure there was no one in pursuit. In the night sometime he came to the smooth, crawled rocks dividing the valley, and here set the burro at liberty. He walked beyond, climbed the slope and the dim, starlit gorge. Then, weary to the point of exhaustion, he crept into a shallow cave and fell asleep.

In the morning, when he descended the trail, he found the sun was pouring a golden stream of light through the arch of the great stone bridge. Surprise Valley, like a valley of dreams, lay mystically soft and beautiful, awakening to the golden flood which was rolling away its slumberous bands of mist, brightening its walled faces.

While yet far off he discerned Bess moving under the silver spruces, and soon the barking of the dogs told him that they had seen him. He heard the mocking-birds singing in the trees, and then the twittering of the quail. Ring and Whitie came bounding towards him, and behind them ran Bess, her hands outstretched.

'Bern! You're back! You're back!' she cried, in a joy that rang of her loneliness.

'Yes, I'm back,' he said, as she rushed to meet him.

She had reached out for him when suddenly, as she saw him closely, something checked her, and as quickly all her joy fled, and with it her colour, leaving her pale and trembling.

'Oh! What's happened?'

'A good deal has happened, Bess. I don't need to tell you what. And I'm played out. Worn out in mind more than body.'

'Dear – you look strange to me!' faltered Bess.

'Never mind that. I'm all right. There's nothing for you to be scared about. Things are going to turn out just as we have planned. As soon as I'm rested we'll make a break to get out of the country. Only now, right now, I must know the truth about you.'

'Truth about me?' echoed Bess, shrinkingly. She seemed to be casting back into her mind for a forgotten key. Venters himself, as he saw her, received a pang.

'Yes – the truth. Bess, don't misunderstand. I haven't changed that way, I love you still. I'll love you more afterwards. Life will be just as sweet – sweeter to us. We'll be – be married as soon as ever we can. We'll be happy – but there's a devil in me. A perverse, jealous devil! Then I've queer fancies. I forgot for a long time. Now all those fiendish little whispers of doubt and faith and fear and hope come torturing me again. I've got to kill them with the truth.'

'I'll tell you anything you want to know,' she replied, frankly.

'Then, by Heaven! we'll have it over and done with! . . . Bess – did Oldring love you?'

'Certainly he did.'

'Did – did you love him?'

'Of course. I told you so.'

'How can you tell it so lightly?' cried Venters, passionately. 'Haven't you any sense of – of – ' He choked back speech. He felt the rush of pain and passion. He seized her in rude, strong hands and drew her close. He looked straight into her dark-blue eyes. They were shadowing with the old wistful light, but they were as clear as the limpid water of the spring. They were earnest, solemn in unutterable love and faith and abnegation. Venters shivered. He knew he was looking into her soul. He knew she could not lie in that moment; but that she might tell the truth, looking at him with those eyes, almost killed his belief in purity.

'What are – what were you to – to Oldring?' he panted, fiercely.

'I am his daughter,' she replied, instantly.

Venters slowly let go of her. There was a violent break in the force of his feeling – then creeping blankness.

'What – was it – you said?' he asked, in a kind of dull wonder.

'I am his daughter.'

'Oldring's daughter?' queried Venters, with life gathering in his voice.

'Yes.'

With a passionately awakening start he grasped her hands and drew her close.

'All the time – you've been Oldring's daughter?'

'Yes, of course all the time – always.'

'But, Bess, you told me – you let me think – I made out you were – a – so – so ashamed.'

'It is my shame,' she said, with voice deep and full, and now the scarlet fired her cheek. 'I told you – I'm nothing – nameless – just Bess, Oldring's girl!'

'I know – I remember. But I never thought – ' he went on, hurriedly, huskily. 'That time – when you lay dying – you prayed – you – somehow I got the idea you were bad.'

'Bad?' she asked, with a little laugh.

She looked up with a faint smile of bewilderment and the absolute unconsciousness of a child. Venters gasped in the gathering might of the truth. She did not understand his meaning.

'Bess! Bess!' He clasped her in his arms, hiding her eyes against his breast. She must not see his face in that moment. And he held her while he looked out across the valley. In his dim and blinded sight, in the blur of golden light and moving mist, he saw Oldring. She was the rustler's nameless daughter. Oldring had loved her. He had so guarded her, so kept her from women and men and knowledge of life that her mind was as a child's. That was part of the secret – part of the mystery. That was the wonderful truth. Not only was she not bad, but good, pure, innocent above all innocence in the world – the innocence of lonely girlhood.

He saw Oldring's magnificent eyes, inquisitive, searching – softening. He saw them flare in amaze, in gladness, with love, then suddenly strain in terrible effort of will. He heard Oldring whisper and saw him sway like a log and fall. Then a million bellowing, thundering voices – gunshots of conscience, thunderbolts of remorse – dinned horribly in his ears. He had killed Bess's father. Then a rushing wind filled his ears like the moan of wind in the cliffs, a knell indeed – Oldring's knell.

He dropped to his knees and hid his face against Bess, and grasped her with the hands of a drowning man.

'My God! . . . My God! . . . Oh, Bess! . . . Forgive me! Never mind what I've done – what I've thought. But forgive me. I'll give you my life. I'll live for you. I'll love you. Oh, I do love you as no man ever loved a woman. I want you to know – to remember that I fought a fight for you – however blind I was. I thought – I thought – never mind what I thought – but I loved you – I asked you to marry me. Let that – let me have that to hug to my heart. Oh, Bess, I was driven! And I might have known! I could not rest nor sleep till I had this mystery solved. God! how things work out!'

'Bern, you're weak – trembling – you talk wildly,' cried Bess. 'You've overdone your strength. There's nothing to forgive. There's no mystery except your love for me. You have come back to me!'

And she clasped his head tenderly in her arms and pressed it closely to her throbbing breast.

CHAPTER 19

Fay

At the home of Jane Withersteen Little Fay was climbing Lassiter's knee.

'Does oo love me?' she asked.

Lassiter, who was as serious with Fay as he was gentle and loving, assured her in earnest and elaborate speech that he was her devoted subject. Fay looked thoughtful and appeared to be debating the duplicity of men or searching for a supreme test to prove this cavalier.

'Does oo love my new muvver?' she asked, with bewildering suddenness.

Jane Withersteen laughed, and for the first time in many a day she felt a stir of her pulse and warmth in her cheek.

It was a still drowsy summer afternoon, and the three were sitting in the shade of the wooded knoll that faced the sage-slope. Little Fay's brief spell of unhappy longing for her mother – the childish, mystic gloom – had passed, and now where Fay was there were prattle and laughter and glee. She had emerged from sorrow to be the incarnation of joy and loveliness. She had grown supernaturally sweet and beautiful. For Jane Withersteen the child was an answer to prayer, a blessing, a possession infinitely more precious than all she had lost. For Lassiter, Jane divined that little Fay had become a religion.

'Does oo love my new muvver?' repeated Fay.

Lassiter's answer to this was a modest and sincere affirmative.

'Why don't oo marry my new muvver an' be my favver?'

Of the thousands of questions put by little Fay to Lassiter that was the first he had been unable to answer.

'Fay – Fay, don't ask questions like that,' said Jane.

'Why?'

'Because,' replied Jane. And she found it strangely embarrassing to meet the child's gaze. It seemed to her that Fay's violet eyes looked through her with piercing wisdom.

'Oo love him, don't oo?'

'Dear child – run and play,' said Jane, 'but don't go too far. Don't go from this little hill.'

Fay pranced off wildly, joyous over freedom that had not been granted her for weeks.

'Jane, why are children more sincere than grown-up persons?' asked Lassiter.

'Are they?'

'I reckon so. Little Fay there – she sees things as they appear on the face. An Indian does that. So does a dog. An' an Indian an' a dog are most of the time right in what they see. Mebbe a child is always right.'

'Well, what does Fay see?' asked Jane.

'I reckon you know. I wonder what goes on in Fay's mind when she sees part of the truth with the wise eyes of a child, an' wantin' to know more, meets with strange falseness from you? Wait! You are false in a way, though you're the best woman I ever knew. What I want to say is this. Fay has taken you're pretendin' to – to care for me for the thing it looks on the face. An' her little formin' mind asks questions. An' the answers she gets are different from the looks of things. So she'll grow up, gradually takin' on that falseness, an' be like the rest of women, an' men, too. An' the truth of this falseness to life is proved by your appearin' to love me when you don't. Things aren't what they seem.'

'Lassiter, you're right. A child should be told the absolute truth. But – is that possible? I haven't been able to do it, and all my life I've loved the truth, and I've prided myself upon being truthful. Maybe that was only egotism. I'm learning much, my friend. Some of those blinding scales have fallen from my eyes. And – and as to caring for you, I think I care a great deal. How much, how little, I couldn't say. My heart is almost broken, Lassiter. So now is not a good time to judge of affection. I can still play and be merry with Fay. I can still dream. But when I attempt serious thought I'm dazed. I don't think. I don't care any more. I don't pray! . . . Think of that, my friend! But in spite of my numb feeling I believe I'll rise out of all this dark agony a better woman, with greater love of man and God. I'm on the rack now; I'm senseless to all but pain, and growing dead to that. Sooner or later I shall rise out of this stupor. I'm waiting the hour.'

'It'll soon come, Jane,' replied Lassiter, soberly. 'Then I'm afraid for you. Years are terrible things, an' for years you've been bound. Habit of years is strong as life itself. Somehow, though, I believe as you – that you'll come out of it all a finer woman. I'm waitin', too. An' I'm wonderin' – I reckon, Jane, that marriage between us is out of all human reason?'

'Lassiter! . . . My dear friend! . . . It's impossible for us to marry.'

'Why – as Fay says?' enquired Lassiter, with gentle persistence.

'Why! I never thought why. But it's not possible. I am Jane, daughter of Withersteen. My father would rise out of his grave. I'm of Mormon birth. I'm being broken. But I'm still a Mormon woman. And you – you are Lassiter!'

'Mebbe I'm not so much Lassiter as I used to be.'

'What was it you said? Habit of years is strong as life itself! You can't change the one habit – the purpose of your life. For you still pack those black guns! You still nurse your passion for blood.'

A smile, like a shadow, flickered across his face.

'No.'

'Lassiter, I lied to you. But I beg of you – don't you lie to me. I've great respect for you. I believe you're softened towards most, perhaps all, my people except – . But when I speak of your purpose, your hate, your guns, I have only him in mind. I don't believe you've changed.'

For answer he unbuckled the heavy cartridge-belt, and laid it with the heavy, swing gun-sheaths in her lap.

'Lassiter!' Jane whispered, as she gazed from him to the black, cold guns. Without them he appeared shorn of strength, defenceless, a smaller man. Was she Delilah? Swiftly, conscious of only one motive – refusal to see this man called craven by his enemies – she rose, and with blundering fingers buckled the belt round his waist where it belonged.

'Lassiter, *I* am the coward.'

'Come with me out of Utah – where I can put away my guns an' be a man,' he said. 'I reckon I'll prove it to you then! Come! You've got Black Star back, an' Night an' Bells. Let's take the racers an' little Fay, an' ride out of Utah. The hosses an' the child are all you have left. Come!'

'No, no, Lassiter. I'll never leave Utah. What would I do in the world with my broken fortunes and my broken heart? I'll never leave these purple slopes I love so well.'

'I reckon I ought to 've knowed that. Presently you'll be livin' down here in a hovel, an' presently Jane Withersteen will be a memory. I only wanted to have a chance to show you how a man – *any* man – can be better 'n he was. If we left Utah I could prove – I reckon I could prove this thing you call love. It's strange, an' hell an' heaven at once, Jane Withersteen. 'Pears to me that you've thrown away your big heart on love – love of religion an' duty an' churchmen, an' riders an' poor families an' poor children! Yet you can't see what love is – how it changes a person! . . . Listen, an' in tellin' you Milly Erne's story I'll show you how love changed her.

'Milly an' me was children when our family moved from Missouri to Texas, an' we growed up in Texas ways same as if we'd been born there. We had been poor, an' there we prospered. In time the little village where we went became a town, an' strangers an' new families kept movin' in. Milly was the belle them days. I can see her now, a little girl no bigger 'n a bird, an' as pretty. She had the finest eyes, dark blue-black when she was excited, an' beautiful all the time. You remember Milly's eyes! An' she had light-brown hair with streaks of gold, an' a mouth that every feller wanted to kiss.

'An' about the time Milly was the prettiest an' the sweetest, along came a young minister who began to ride some of a race with the other fellers for Milly. An' he won. Milly had always been strong on religion, an' when she met Frank Erne she went in heart an' soul for the salvation of souls. Fact was, Milly, through study of the Bible an' attendin' church an' revivals, went a little out of her head. It didn't worry the old folks none, an' the only worry to me was Milly's everlastin' prayin' an' workin' to save my soul. She never converted me, but we was the best of comrades, an' I reckon no brother an' sister ever loved each other better. Well, Frank Erne an' me hit up a great friendship. He was a strappin' feller, good to look at, an' had the most pleasin' ways. His religion never bothered me, for he could hunt an' fish an' ride an' be a good feller. After buffalo once, he come pretty near to savin' my life. We got to be thick as brothers, an' he was the only man I ever seen who I thought was good enough for Milly. An' the day they were married I got drunk for the only time in my life.

'Soon after that I left home – it seems Milly was the only one who could keep me home – an' I went to the bad, as to prosperin'. I saw some pretty hard life in the Pan Handle, an' then I went North. In them days Kansas an' Nebraska was as bad, come to think of it, as these days right here on the border of Utah. I got to be pretty handy with guns. An' there wasn't many riders as could beat me ridin'. An' I can say all modest-like that I never seen the white man who could track a hoss or a steer or a man with me. Afore I knowed it two years slipped by an' all at once I got homesick, an' pulled a bridle south.

'Things at home had changed. I never got over that homecomin'. Mother was dead an' in her grave. Father was a silent, broken man, killed already on his feet. Frank Erne was a ghost of his old self, through with workin', through with preachin', almost through with livin', an' Milly was gone! . . . It was a long time before I got the story. Father had no mind left, an' Frank Erne was *afraid* to talk. So I had to pick up what'd happened from different people.

'It 'pears that soon after I left home another preacher come to the little town. An' he an' Frank become rivals. This feller was different from Frank. He preached some other kind of religion, and he was quick an' passionate, where Frank was slow an' mild. He went after people, women specially. In looks he couldn't compare to Frank Erne, but he had power over women. He had a voice, an' he talked an' talked an' preached an' preached. Milly fell under his influence. She became mightily interested in his religion. Frank had patience with her, as was his way, an' let her be as interested as she liked. All religions were devoted to one God, he said, an' it wouldn't hurt Milly none to study a different point of view. So the new preacher often called on Milly, an sometimes in Frank's absence. Frank was a cattle-man between Sundays.

'Along about this time an incident come off that I couldn't get much light on. A stranger come to town, an' was seen with the preacher. This stranger was a big man with an eye like blue ice, an' a beard of gold. He had money, an' he 'peared a man of mystery, an' the town went to buzzin' when he disappeared about the same time as a young woman known to be mightily interested in the new preacher's religion. Then presently, along comes a man from somewheres in Illinois, an' he up an' spots this preacher as a famous Mormon proselyter. That riled Frank Erne as nothin' ever before, an' from rivals they come to be bitter enemies. An' it ended in Frank goin' to the meetin'-house where Milly was listenin', an' before her an' everybody else he called that preacher – called him, well, almost as hard as Venters called Tull here sometime back. An' Frank followed up that call with a hoss-whippin', an' he drove the proselyter out of town.

'People noticed, so 'twas said, that Milly's sweet disposition changed. Some said it was because she would soon become a mother, an' others said she was pinin' after the new religion. An' there was women who said right out that she was pinin' after the Mormon. Anyway, one mornin' Frank rode in from one of his trips, to find Milly gone. He had no real near neighbours – livin' a little out of town – but those who was nearest said a wagon had gone by in the night, an' they thought it stopped at her door. Well, tracks always tell, an' there was the wagon tracks an' hoss tracks an' man tracks. The news spread like wildfire that Milly had run off from her husband. Everybody but Frank believed it, an' wasn't slow in tellin' why she run off. Mother had always hated that strange streak of Milly's, takin' up with the new religion as she had, an' she believed Milly ran off with the Mormon. That hastened mother's death, an' she died unforgivin'. Father wasn't the kind to bow down under disgrace or misfortune, but he had surpassin' love for Milly, an' the loss of her broke him.

'From the minute I heard of Milly's disappearance I never believed she went off of her own free will. I knew Milly, an' I knew she *couldn't* have done that. I stayed at home awhile, tryin' to make Frank Erne talk. But if he knowed anythin' then he wouldn't tell it. So I set out to find Milly. An' I tried to get on the trail of that proselyter. I knew if I ever struck a town he'd visited that I'd get a trail. I knew, too, that nothin' short of hell would stop his proselytin'. An' I rode from town to town. I had a blind faith that somethin' was guidin' me. An' as the weeks an' months went by I growed into a strange sort of a man, I guess. Anyway, people were afraid of me. Two years after that, way over in a corner of Texas, I struck a town where my man had been. He'd jest left. People said he came to that town *without* a woman. I back-trailed my man through Arkansas an' Mississippi, an' the old trail got hot again in Texas. I found the town where he first went after leavin' home. An' here I got track of Milly. I found a cabin where she had given birth to her baby. There was no way to tell whether she'd been kept a prisoner or not. The feller who owned the place was a mean, silent sort of a skunk, an' as I was leavin' I jest took a chance an' left my mark on him. Then I went home again.

'It was to find I hadn't any home, no more. Father had been dead a year. Frank Erne still lived in the house where Milly had left him. I stayed with him awhile, an' I grew old watchin' him. His farm had gone to weed, his cattle had strayed or been rustled, his house weathered till it wouldn't keep out rain nor wind. An' Frank set on the porch and whittled sticks, an' day by day wasted away. There was times when he ranted about like a crazy man, but mostly he was always sittin' an' starin' with eyes that made a man curse. I figured Frank had a secret fear that I needed to know. An' when I told him I'd trailed Milly for near three years an' had got trace of her, an' saw where she'd had her baby, I thought he would drop dead at my feet. An' when he'd come round more natural-like he begged me to *give up* the trail. But he wouldn't explain. So I let him alone, an' watched him day an' night.

'An' I found there was one thing still precious to him, an' it was a little drawer where he kept his papers. This was in the room where he slept. An' it 'peared he seldom slept. But after bein' patient I got the contents of that drawer an' found two letters from Milly. One was a long letter written a few months after her disappearance. She had been bound an' gagged an' dragged away from her home by three men, an' she named them – Hurd, Metzger, Slack. They was strangers to her. She was taken to the little town where I found trace of her two years after. But she didn't send the letter from that town. There she was penned in. 'Peared that the proselyter, who had, of course, come on the scene, was not runnin' any risks of losin' her. She went on to say that for a time she was out of her head, an' when she got right again all that kept her alive was the baby. It was a beautiful baby, she said, an' all she thought an' dreamed of was somehow to get baby back to its father, an' then she'd thankfully lay down and die. An' the letter ended abrupt, in the middle of a sentence, an' it wasn't signed.

'The second letter was written more than two years after the first. It was from Salt Lake City. It simply said that Milly had heard her brother was on her trail. She asked Frank to tell her brother to give up the search because if he didn't she would suffer in a way too horrible to tell. She didn't beg. She just stated a fact an' made the simple request. An' she ended that letter by sayin' she would soon leave Salt Lake City with the man she had come to love, an' would never be heard of again.

'I recognised Milly's handwritin', an' I recognised her way of puttin' things. But that second letter told me of some great change in her. Ponderin' over it, I felt at last she'd either come to love that feller an' his religion, or some terrible fear made her lie an' say so. I couldn't be sure which. But, of course, I meant to find out. I'll say here, if I'd known Mormons then as I do now I'd left Milly to her fate. For mebbe she was right about what she'd suffer if I kept on her trail. But I was young an' wild them days. First I went to the town where she'd first been taken, an' I went to the place where she'd been kept. I got that skunk who owned the place, an' took him out in the woods, an' made him tell all he knowed. That wasn't much as to length, but it was pure hell's-fire in substance. This time I left him some incapacitated for any more skunk work short of hell. Then I hit the trail for Utah.

'That was fourteen years ago. I saw the incomin' of most of the Mormons. It was a wild country an' a wild time. I rode from town to town, village to village, ranch to ranch, camp to camp. I never stayed long in one place. I never had but one idea. I never rested. Four years went by, an' I knowed every trail in northern Utah. I kept on an' as time went by, an' I'd begun to grow old in my search, I had firmer, blinder faith in whatever was guidin' me. Once I read about a feller who sailed the seven seas an' travelled the world, an' he had a story to tell, an' whenever he seen the man to whom he must tell that story he knowed him on sight. I was like that, only I had a question to ask. An' always I knew the man of whom I must ask. So I never really lost the trail, though for years it was the dimmest trail ever followed by any man.

'Then come a change in my luck. Along in Central Utah I rounded up Hurd, an' I whispered somethin' in his ear, an' watched his face, an' then throwed a gun against his bowels. An' he died with his teeth so tight shut I couldn't have pried them open with a knife. Slack an' Metzger that same year both heard me whisper the same question, an' neither would they speak a word when they lay dyin'. Long before I'd learned no man of this breed or class – or God knows what – would give up any secrets! I had to see in a man's fear of death the connections with Milly Erne's fate. An' as the years passed at long intervals I would find such a man.

'So as I drifted on the long trail down into southern Utah, my name preceded me, an' I had to meet a people prepared for me, an' ready with guns. They made me a gunman. An' that suited me. In all this time signs of the proselyter an' the giant with the blue-ice eyes an' the gold beard seemed to fade dimmer out of the trail. Only twice in ten years did I find a trace of that mysterious man who had visited the proselyter at my home

village. What he had to do with Milly's fate was beyond all hope for me
to learn, unless my guidin' spirit led me to him! As for the other man, I
knew, as sure as I breathed an' the stars shone an' the wind blew, that I'd
meet him someday.

'Eighteen years I've been on the trail. An' it led me to the last lonely
villages of the Utah border. Eighteen years! . . . I feel pretty old now. I
was only twenty when I hit that trail. Well, as I told you, back here a ways
a Gentile said Jane Withersteen could tell me about Milly Erne an' show
me her grave!'

The low voice ceased, and Lassiter slowly turned his sombrero round
and round, and appeared to be counting the silver ornaments on the
band. Jane, leaning towards him, sat as if petrified, listening intently,
waiting to hear more. She could have shrieked, but power of tongue and
lips were denied her. She saw only this sad, grey, passion-worn man, and
she heard only the faint rustling of the leaves.

'Well, I came to Cottonwoods,' went on Lassiter, 'an' you showed
me Milly's grave. An' though your teeth have been shut tighter'n them
of all the dead men lyin' back along that trail, jest the same you told me
the secret I've lived these eighteen years to hear! Jane, I said you'd tell
me without ever me askin'. I didn't need to ask my question here. The
day, you remember, when that fat party throwed a gun on me in your
court, an' – '

'Oh! Hush!' whispered Jane, blindly holding up her hands.

'*I seen in your face that Dyer, now a bishop, was the proselyter who ruined
Milly Erne!*'

For an instant Jane Withersteen's brain was a whirling chaos, and she
recovered to find herself grasping at Lassiter like one drowning. And as if
by a lightning stroke she sprang from her dull apathy into exquisite torture.

'*It's a lie!* Lassiter! No, no!' she moaned. 'I swear – you're wrong!'

'Stop! You'd perjure yourself! But I'll spare you that. You poor woman!
Still blind! Still faithful! . . . Listen. I *know*. Let that settle it. An' I give up
my purpose!'

'What is it – you say?'

'I give up my purpose. I've come to see an' feel differently. I can't help
poor Milly. An' I've out-growed revenge. I've come to see I can be no
judge for men. I can't kill a man jest for hate. Hate ain't the same with me
since I loved you and little Fay.'

'Lassiter! You mean you won't kill him?' Jane whispered.

'No.'

'For my sake?'

'I reckon. I can't understand, but I'll respect your feelin's.'

'Because you – oh, because you love me? . . . Eighteen years! You were that terrible Lassiter! And *now* – because you love me?'

'That's it, Jane.'

'Oh, you'll make me love you! How can I help but love you? My heart must be stone. But – oh, Lassiter, wait, wait! Give me time. I'm not what I was. Once it was so easy to love. Now it's easy to hate. Wait! My faith in God – *some* God – still lives. By it I see happier times for you, poor passion-swayed wanderer! For me – a miserable, broken woman. I loved your sister Milly. I *will* love you. I can't have fallen so low – I can't be so abandoned by God – that I've no love left to give you. Wait! Let us forget Milly's sad life. Ah, I knew it as no one else on earth! There's one thing I shall tell you – if you are at my deathbed, but I can't speak now.'

'I reckon I don't want to hear no more,' said Lassiter.

Jane leaned against him; as if some pent-up force had rent its way out, she fell into a paroxysm of weeping. Lassiter held her in silent sympathy. By degrees she regained composure, and she was rising, sensible of being relieved of a weighty burden, when a sudden start on Lassiter's part alarmed her.

'I heard hosses – hosses with muffled hoofs!' he said; and he got up guardedly.

'Where's Fay?' asked Jane, hurriedly glancing round the shady knoll. The bright-haired child, who had appeared to be close all the time, was not in sight.

'Fay!' called Jane.

No answering shout of glee. No patter of flying feet. Jane saw Lassiter stiffen.

'*Fay – oh – Fay!*' Jane almost screamed.

The leaves quivered and rustled; a lonesome cricket chirped in the grass; a bee hummed by. The silence of the waning afternoon breathed hateful portent. It terrified Jane. When had silence been so infernal!

'She's – only – strayed – out – of earshot,' faltered Jane, looking at Lassiter.

Pale, rigid as a statue, the rider stood, not in listening, searching posture, but in one of doomed certainty. Suddenly he grasped Jane with an iron hand, and, turning his face from her gaze, he strode with her from the knoll.

'See – Fay played here last – a house of stones an' sticks . . . An' here's a corral of pebbles with leaves for hosses,' said Lassiter, stridently, and pointed to the ground. 'Back an' forth she trailed here . . . See, she's buried somethin' – a dead grasshopper – there's a tombstone . . . here she went, chasin' a lizard – see the tiny streaked trail . . . she pulled bark off this cottonwood . . . look in the dust of the path – the letters you taught her – she's drawn pictures of birds an' hosses an' people . . . Look, a cross! Oh, Jane, *your* cross!'

Lassiter dragged Jane on, and as if from a book read the meaning of little Fay's trail. All the way down the knoll, through the shrubbery, round and round a cottonwood, Fay's vagrant fancy left records of her sweet musings and innocent play. Long had she lingered round a birdnest to leave therein the gaudy wing of a butterfly. Long had she played beside the running stream, sending adrift vessels freighted with pebbly cargo. Then she had wandered through the deep grass, her tiny feet scarcely turning a fragile blade, and she had dreamed beside some old faded flowers. Thus her steps led her into the broad lane. The little dimpled imprints of her bare feet showed clean-cut in the dust; they went a little way down the lane; and then, at a point where they stopped, the great tracks of a man led out from the shrubbery and returned.

CHAPTER 20

Lassiter's Way

Footprints told the story of little Fay's abduction.

In anguish Jane Withersteen turned speechlessly to Lassiter, and, confirming her fears, she saw him grey-faced, aged all in a moment, stricken as if by a mortal blow.

Then all her life seemed to fall about her in wreck and ruin.

'It's all over,' she heard her voice whisper. 'It's ended. I'm going – I'm going – '

'Where?' demanded Lassiter, suddenly looming darkly over her.

'To – to those cruel men – '

'Speak names!' thundered Lassiter.

'To Bishop Dyer – to Tull,' went on Jane, shocked into obedience.

'Well – what for?'

'I want little Fay. I can't live without her. They've stolen her as they stole Milly Erne's child. I must have little Fay. I want only her. I give up.

I'll go and tell Bishop Dyer – I'm broken. I'll tell him I'm ready for the yoke – only give me back Fay – and – and I'll marry Tull!'

'*Never!*' hissed Lassiter.

His long arm leaped at her. Almost running, he dragged her under the cottonwoods, across the court, into the huge hall of Withersteen House, and he shut the door with a force that jarred the heavy walls. Black Star and Night and Bells, since their return, had been locked in this hall, and now they stamped on the stone floor.

Lassiter released Jane and like a dizzy man swayed from her with a hoarse cry and leaned shaking against a table where he kept his rider's accoutrements. He began to fumble in his saddle-bags. His action brought a clinking, metallic sound – the rattling of gun-cartridges. His fingers trembled as he slipped cartridges into an extra belt. But as he buckled it over the one he habitually wore his hands became steady. This second belt contained two guns, smaller than the black ones swinging low, and he slipped them round so that his coat hid them. Then he fell to swift action. Jane Withersteen watched him, fascinated but uncomprehending; and she saw him rapidly saddle Black Star and Night. Then he drew her into the light of the huge window, standing over her, gripping her arm with fingers like cold steel.

'Yes, Jane, it's ended – but you're not goin' to Dyer! . . . *I'm goin' instead!*'

Looking at him – he was so terrible of aspect – she could not comprehend his words. Who was this man with the face grey as death, with eyes that would have made her shriek had she the strength, with the strange, ruthlessly bitter lips? Where was the gentle Lassiter? What was this presence in the hall, about him, about her – this cold, invisible presence?

'Yes, it's ended, Jane,' he was saying, so awfully quiet and cool and implacable, 'an' I'm goin' to make a little call. I'll lock you in here, an' when I get back have the saddle-bags full of meat an' bread. An' be ready to ride!'

'Lassiter!' cried Jane.

Desperately she tried to meet his grey eyes, in vain; desperately she tried again, fought herself as feeling and thought resurged in torment, and she succeeded; and then she knew.

'No – no – no!' she wailed. 'You said you'd foregone your vengeance. You promised not to kill Bishop Dyer.'

'If you want to talk to me about him – leave off the Bishop. I don't understand that name, or its use.'

'Oh, hadn't you foregone your vengeance on – on Dyer?'

'Yes.'

'But – your actions – your words – your guns – your terrible looks! . . . They don't seem foregoing vengeance?'

'Jane, now it's justice.'

'You'll – kill him?'

'If God lets me live another hour! If not God – then the devil who drives me!'

'You'll kill him – for yourself – for your vengeful hate?'

'No!'

'For Milly Erne's sake?'

'No.'

'For little Fay's?'

'No!'

'Oh – for whose?'

'*For yours!*'

'His blood on my soul!' whispered Jane, and she fell to her knees. This was the long-pending hour of fruition. And the habit of years – the religious passion of her life – leaped from lethargy, and the long months of gradual drifting to doubt were as if they had never been. 'If you spill his blood it'll be on my soul – and on my father's. Listen.' And she clasped his knees, and clung there as he tried to raise her. 'Listen. Am I nothing to you?'

'Woman – don't trifle at words! I love you! An' I'll soon prove it!'

'I'll give myself to you – I'll ride away with you – marry you, if only you'll spare him?'

His answer was a cold, ringing, terrible laugh.

'Lassiter – I'll love you. Spare him!'

'No!'

She sprang up in despairing, breaking spirit, and encircled his neck with her arms, and held him in an embrace that he strove vainly to loosen. 'Lassiter, would you kill me? I'm fighting my last fight for the principles of my youth – love of religion, love of father. You don't know – you can't guess the truth, and I can't speak it! I'm losing all. I'm changing. All I've gone through is nothing to this hour. Pity me – help me in my weakness. You're strong again – oh, so cruelly, coldly strong! You're killing me. I see you – feel you as some other Lassiter! My master, be merciful – spare him!'

His answer was a ruthless smile.

She clung the closer to him, and leaned her panting breast on him, and lifted her face to his. 'Lassiter, *I do love you!* It's leaped out of my agony. It comes suddenly with a terrible blow of truth. You are a man! I never knew it till now. Some wonderful change came to me when you buckled on these guns and showed that grey, awful face. I loved you then. All my life I've loved, but never as now. No woman can love like a broken woman. If it were not for one thing – just one thing – and yet! I *can't* speak it – I'd glory in your manhood – the lion in you that means to slay for me. Believe me – and spare Dyer. Be merciful – great as it's in you to be great . . . Oh, listen and believe – I have nothing, but I'm a woman – a beautiful woman, Lassiter – a passionate, loving woman – and I love you! Take me – hide me in some wild place – and love me and mend my broken heart. Spare him and take me away.'

She lifted her face closer and closer to his, until their lips nearly touched, and she hung upon his neck, and with strength almost spent pressed and still pressed her palpitating body to his.

'Kiss me!' she whispered, blindly.

'No – not at your price!' he answered. His voice had changed or she had lost clearness of hearing.

'Kiss me! . . . Are you a man? Kiss me and save me!'

'Jane, you never played fair with me. But now you're blisterin' your lips – blackenin' your soul with lies!'

'By the memory of my mother – by my Bible – no! No, I *have* no Bible! But by my hope of heaven I swear I love you!'

Lassiter's grey lips formed soundless words that meant even her love could not avail to bend his will. As if the hold of her arms was that of a child's he loosened it and stepped away.

'Wait! Don't go! Oh, hear a last word! . . . May a more just and merciful God than the God I was taught to worship judge me – forgive me – save me! For I can no longer keep silent! . . . Lassiter, in pleading for Dyer I've been pleading more for my father. My father was a Mormon master, close to the leaders of the church. It was my father who sent Dyer out to proselyte. It was my father who had the blue-ice eye and the beard of gold. It was my father you got trace of in the past years. Truly, Dyer ruined Milly Erne – dragged her from her home – to Utah – to Cottonwoods. *But it was for my father!* If Milly Erne was ever wife of a Mormon that Mormon was my father! I never knew – never will know whether or not she was a wife. Blind I may be, Lassiter – fanatically faithful to a false religion I may have been, but I know justice, and my father is beyond human justice. Surely he is meeting just punishment – somewhere. Always it has appalled me – the thought of your killing Dyer for my father's sins. So I have prayed!'

'Jane, the past is dead. In my love for you I forgot the past. This thing I'm about to do ain't for myself or Milly or Fay. It's not because of anythin' that ever happened in the past, but for what is happenin' right *now. It's for you!* . . . An' listen. Since I was a boy I've never thanked God for anythin'. If there is a God – an' I've come to believe it – I thank Him now for the years that made me Lassiter! . . . I can reach down an' feel these big guns, an' know what I can do with them. An', Jane, only one of the miracles Dyer professes to believe in can save him!'

Again for Jane Withersteen came the spinning of her brain in darkness, and as she whirled in endless chaos she seemed to be falling at the feet of a luminous figure – a man – Lassiter – who had saved her from herself, who could not be changed, who would slay rightfully. Then she slipped into utter blackness.

When she recovered from her faint she became aware that she was lying on a couch near the window in her sitting-room. Her brow felt damp and cold and wet; someone was chafing her hands; she recognised Judkins, and then saw that his lean, hard face wore the hue and look of excessive agitation.

'Judkins!' Her voice broke weakly.

'Aw, Miss Withersteen, you're comin' round fine. Now jest lay still a little. You're all right; everythin's all right.'

'Where is – he?'

'Who?'

'Lassiter!'

'You needn't worry none about him.'

'Where is he? Tell me – instantly.'

'Wal, he's in the other room patchin' up a few triflin' bullet-holes.'

'*Ah! . . . Bishop Dyer?*'

'When I seen him last – a matter of half an hour ago, he was on his knees. He was some busy, *but* he wasn't prayin'!'

'How strangely you talk! I'll sit up. I'm – well, strong again. Tell me. Dyer on his knees! What was he doing?'

'Wal, beggin' your pardon fer blunt talk, Miss Withersteen, Dyer was on his knees an' *not* prayin'. You remember his big, broad hands? You've seen 'em raised in blessin' over old grey men an' little curly-headed children like – like Fay Larkin! Come to think of thet, I disremember ever hearin' of his liftin' his big hands in blessin' over a *woman*. Wal, when I seen him last – jest a little while ago – he was on his knees, *not* prayin', as I remarked – an' he was pressin' his big hands over some bigger wounds.'

'Man, you drive me mad! Did Lassiter kill Dyer?'

'Yes.'

'Did he kill Tull?'

'No. Tull's out of the village with most of his riders. He's expected back before evenin'. Lassiter will hev to git away before Tull an' his riders come in. It's sure death fer him here. An' wuss fer you, too, Miss Withersteen. There'll be some of an uprisin' when Tull gits back.'

'I shall ride away with Lassiter. Judkins, tell me all you saw – all you know about this killing.' She realised, without wonder or amaze, how Judkins's one word, affirming the death of Dyer – that the catastrophe had fallen – had completed the change whereby she had been moulded or beaten or broken into another woman. She felt calm, slightly cold, strong as she had not been strong since the first shadow fell upon her.

'I jest saw about all of it, Miss Withersteen, an' I'll be glad to tell you if you'll only hev patience with me,' said Judkins, earnestly. 'You see, I've been pecooliarly interested an' nat'rully I'm some excited. An' I talk a lot thet mebbe ain't necessary, but I can't help thet.

'I was at the meetin'-house where Dyer was holdin' court. You know he allus acts as magistrate an' judge when Tull's away. An' the trial was fer tryin' what's left of my boy riders – thet helped me hold your cattle – fer a lot of hatched-up things the boys never did. We're used to thet, an' the boys wouldn't hev minded bein' locked up fer a while, or hevin' to dig ditches, or whatever the judge laid down. You see, I divided the gold you give me among all my boys, an' they all hid it, an' they all feel rich. Howsomever, court was adjourned before the judge passed sentence. Yes, ma'm, court was adjourned some strange an' quick, much as if lightnin' hed struck the meetin'-house.

'I hed trouble attendin' the trial, but I got in. There was a good many people there, all my boys, an' Judge Dyer with his several clerks. Also he hed with him the five riders who've been guardin' him pretty close of late. They was Carter, Wright, Jengessen, an' two new riders from Stone Bridge. I didn't hear their names, but I heard they was handy men with guns an' they looked more like rustlers than riders. Anyway, there they was, the five all in a row.

'Judge Dyer was tellin' Willie Kern, one of my best an' steadiest boys – Dyer was tellin' him how there was a ditch opened near Willie's home lettin' water through his lot, where it hadn't ought to go. An' Willie was tryin' to git a word in to prove he wasn't at home all the day it happened – which was true, as I know – but Willie couldn't git a word in, an' then Judge Dyer went on layin' down the law. An' all to onct he happened to look down the long room. An' if ever any man turned to stone he was thet man.

'Nat'rully I looked back to see what hed acted so powerful strange on the judge. An' there, halfway up the room, in the middle of the wide aisle, stood Lassiter! All white an' black he looked, an' I can't think of anythin' he resembled, onless it's death. Venters made thet same room some still an' chilly when he called Tull; but this was different. I give my word, Miss Withersteen, thet I went cold to my very marrow. I don't know why. But Lassiter has a way about him thet's awful. He spoke a word – a name – I couldn't understand it, though he spoke clear as a bell. I was too excited, mebbe. Judge Dyer must hev understood it, an' a lot more thet was mystery to me, fer he pitched forrard out of his chair right on to the platform.

'Then them five riders, Dyer's bodyguards, they jumped up, an' two of them thet I found out afterward were the strangers from Stone Bridge, they piled right out of a winder, so quick you couldn't catch your breath. It was plain they wasn't Mormons.

'Jengessen, Carter, an' Wright eyed Lassiter, for what must hev been a second an' seemed like an hour, an' they went white an' strung. But they didn't weaken nor lose their nerve.

'I hed a good look at Lassiter. He stood sort of stiff, bendin' a little, an' both his arms were crooked, an' his hands looked like a hawk's claws. But there ain't no tellin' how his eyes looked. I know this, though, an' thet is his eyes could read the mind of any man about to throw a gun. An' in watchin' him, of course, I couldn't see the three men go fer their guns. An' though I was lookin' right at Lassiter – lookin' hard – I couldn't see how he drawed. He was quicker 'n eyesight – thet's all. But I seen the red spurtin' of his guns, an' heard his shots jest the very littlest instant before I heard the shots of the riders. An' when I turned, Wright an' Carter was down, an' Jengessen, who's tough like a steer, was pullin' the trigger of a wabblin' gun. But it was plain he was shot through, plumb centre. An' sudden he fell with a crash, an' his gun clattered on the floor.

'Then there was a hell of a silence. Nobody breathed. Sartin I didn't, anyway. I saw Lassiter slip a smokin' gun back in a belt. But he hadn't throwed either of the big black guns, an' I thought thet strange. An' all this was happenin' quick – you can't imagine how quick.

'There come a scrapin' on the floor an' Dyer got up, his face like lead. I wanted to watch Lassiter, but Dyer's face, onct I seen it like thet, glued my eyes. I seen him go fer his gun – why, I could hev done better, quicker – an' then there was a thunderin' shot from Lassiter, an' it hit Dyer's right arm, an' his gun went off as it dropped. He looked at Lassiter like a cornered sage-wolf, an' sort of howled, an' reached down fer his gun. He'd jest picked it off the floor an' was raisin' it when another thunderin' shot almost tore thet arm off – so it seemed to me. The gun dropped again an' he went down on his knees, kind of flounderin' after it. It was some strange an' terrible to see his awful earnestness. Why would such a man cling so to life? Anyway, he got the gun with left hand an' was raisin' it, pullin' trigger in his madness, when the third thunderin' shot hit his left arm, an' he dropped the gun again. But thet left arm wasn't useless yet, fer he grabbed up the gun, an' with a shakin' aim thet would hev been pitiful to me – in any other man – he began to shoot. One wild bullet struck a man twenty feet from Lassiter. An' it killed thet man, as I seen afterward. Then come a bunch of thunderin' shots – nine I calkilated after, fer they come so quick I couldn't count them – an' I knew Lassiter hed turned the black guns loose on Dyer.

'I'm tellin' you straight, Miss Withersteen, fer I want you to know. Afterwards you'll git over it. I've seen some soul-rackin' scenes on this Utah border, but this was the awfullest. I remember I closed my eyes, an' fer a minute I thought of the strangest things, out of place there, such as you'd never dream would come to mind. I saw the sage, an' runnin' hosses – an' thet's the beautifullest sight to me – an' I saw dim things in the dark, an' there was a kind of hummin' in my ears. An' I remember distinctly – fer it was what made all these things whirl out of my mind an' opened my eyes – I remember distinctly it was the smell of gunpowder.

'The court had about adjourned fer thet judge. He was on his knees, an' he wasn't prayin'. He was gaspin' an' tryin' to press his big, floppin', crippled hands over his body. Lassiter had sent all those last thunderin' shots through his body. Thet was Lassiter's way.

'An' Lassiter spoke, an' if I ever forgit his words I'll never forgit the sound of his voice.

' "*Proselyter*, I reckon you'd better call quick on thet God who reveals Hisself to you on earth, because He won't be visitin' the place you're goin' to!"

'An' then I seen Dyer look at his big, hangin' hands thet wasn't big enough fer the last work he set them to. An' he looked up at Lassiter. An' then he stared horrible at somethin' thet wasn't Lassiter, nor anyone there, nor the room, nor the branches of purple sage peepin' into the winder. Whatever he seen, it was with the look of a man who *discovers* somethin' too late. Thet's a terrible look! . . . An' with a horrible *understandin'* cry he slid forrard on his face.'

Judkins paused in his narrative, breathing heavily while he wiped his perspiring brow.

'Thet's about all,' he concluded. 'Lassiter left the meetin' house an' I hurried to catch up with him. He was bleedin' from three gunshots, none of them much to bother him. An' we come right up here. I found you layin' in the hall, an' I hed to work some over you.'

Jane Withersteen offered up no prayer for Dyer's soul.

Lassiter's step sounded in the hall – the familiar soft, silver-clinking step – and she heard it with thrilling new emotions in which was a vague joy in her very fear of him. The door opened, and she saw him, the old Lassiter, slow, easy, gentle, cool, yet not exactly the same Lassiter. She rose, and for a moment her eyes blurred and swam in tears.

'Are you – all – all right?' she asked, tremulously.

'I reckon.'

'Lassiter, I'll ride away with you. Hide me till danger is past – till we are forgotten – then take me where you will. Your people shall be my people, and your God my God!'

He kissed her hand with the quaint grace and courtesy that came to him in rare moments.

'Black Star an' Night are ready,' he said, simply.

His quiet mention of the black racers spurred Jane to action. Hurrying to her room, she changed to her rider's suit, packed her jewellery, and the gold that was left, and all the woman's apparel for which there was space in the saddle-bags, and then returned to the hall. Black Star stamped his iron-shod hoofs and tossed his beautiful head, and eyed her with knowing eyes.

'Judkins, I give Bells to you,' said Jane. 'I hope you will always keep him and be good to him.'

Judkins mumbled thanks that he could not speak fluently, and his eyes flashed.

Lassiter strapped Jane's saddle-bags upon Black Star, and led the racers out into the court.

'Judkins, you ride with Jane out into the sage. If you see any riders comin' shout quick twice. An', Jane, *don't look back!* I'll catch up soon.

We'll get to the break into the Pass before midnight, an' then wait until mornin' to go down.'

Black Star bent his graceful neck and bowed his noble head, and his broad shoulders yielded as he knelt for Jane to mount.

She rose out of the court beside Judkins, through the grove, across the wide lane into the sage, and she realised that she was leaving Withersteen House forever, and she did not look back. A strange, dreamy, calm peace pervaded her soul. Her doom had fallen upon her, but, instead of finding life no longer worth living she found it doubly significant, full of sweetness as the western breeze, beautiful and unknown as the sage-slope stretching its purple sunset shadows before her. She became aware of Judkins's hand touching hers; she heard him speak a husky goodbye; then into the place of Bells shot the dead-black, keen, racy nose of Night, and she knew Lassiter rode beside her.

'Don't – look – back!' he said, and his voice, too, was not clear.

Facing straight ahead, seeing only the waving, shadowy sage, Jane held out her gauntleted hand, to feel it enclosed in strong clasp. So she rode on without a backward glance at the beautiful grove of Cottonwoods. She did not seem to think of the past, of what she left forever, but of the colour and mystery and wildness of the sage-slope leading down to Deception Pass, and of the future. She watched the shadows lengthen down the slope; she felt the cool west wind sweeping by from the rear; and she wondered at low, yellow clouds sailing swiftly over her and beyond.

'Don't – look – back!' said Lassiter.

Thick-driving belts of smoke travelled by on the wind, and with it came a strong, pungent odour of burning wood.

Lassiter had fired Withersteen House! But Jane did not look back.

A misty veil obscured the clear, searching gaze she had kept steadfastly upon the purple slope and the dim lines of canyons. It passed, as passed the rolling clouds of smoke, and she saw the valley deepening into the shades of twilight. Night came on, swift as the fleet racers, and stars peeped out to brighten and grow, and the huge, windy, eastern heave of sage-level paled under a rising moon and turned to silver. Blanched in moonlight, the sage yet seemed to hold its hue of purple and was infinitely more wild and lonely. So the night hours wore on, and Jane Withersteen never once looked back.

Black Star and Night

The time had come for Venters and Bess to leave their retreat. They were at great pains to choose the few things they would be able to carry with them on the journey out of Utah.

'Bern, whatever kind of a pack's this, anyhow?' questioned Bess, rising from her work with reddened face.

Venters, absorbed in his own task, did not look up at all, and in reply said he had brought so much from Cottonwoods that he did not recollect the half of it.

'A woman packed this!' Bess exclaimed.

He scarcely caught her meaning, but the peculiar tone of her voice caused him instantly to rise, and he saw Bess on her knees before an open pack which he recognised as the one given him by Jane.

'By George!' he ejaculated, guiltily, and then at sight of Bess's face he laughed outright.

'A woman packed this,' she repeated, fixing woeful, tragic eyes on him.

'Well, is that a crime?'

'There – there *is* a woman, after all!'

'Now, Bess – '

'You've lied to me!'

Then and there Venters found it imperative to postpone work for the present. All her life Bess had been isolated, but she had inherited certain elements of the eternal feminine.

'But there *was* a woman and you *did* lie to me,' she kept repeating, after he had explained.

'What of that? Bess, I'll get angry at you in a moment. Remember you've been pent up all your life. I venture to say that if you'd been out in the world you'd have had a dozen sweethearts and have told many a lie before this.'

'I wouldn't anything of the kind,' declared Bess, indignantly.

'Well – perhaps not lie. But you'd have had the sweethearts. You couldn't have helped that – being so pretty.'

This remark appeared to be a very clever and fortunate one; and the work of selecting and then of stowing all the packs in the cave went on without further interruption.

Venters closed up the opening of the cave with a thatch of willows and aspens, so that not even a bird or a rat could get in to the sacks of grain. And this work was in order with the precaution habitually observed by him. He might not be able to get out of Utah, and have to return to the valley. But he owed it to Bess to make the attempt, and in case they were compelled to turn back he wanted to find that fine store of food and grain intact. The outfit of implements and utensils he packed away in another cave.

'Bess, we have enough to live here all our lives,' he said once, dreamily.

'Shall I go roll Balancing Rock?' she asked, in light speech, but with deep-blue fire in her eyes.

'No – no.'

'Ah, you don't forget the gold and the world,' she sighed.

'Child, you forget the beautiful dresses and the travel – and everything.'

'Oh, I want to go. But I want to stay!'

'I feel the same way.'

They let the eight calves out of the corral, and kept only two of the burros Venters had brought from Cottonwoods. These they intended to hide. Bess freed all her pets – the quail and rabbits and foxes.

The last sunset and twilight and night were both the sweetest and saddest they had ever spent in Surprise Valley. Morning brought keen exhilaration and excitement. When Venters had saddled the two burros, strapped on the light packs and the two canteens, the sunlight was dispersing the lazy shadows from the valley. Taking a last look at the caves and the silver spruces, Venters and Bess made a reluctant start, leading the burros. Ring and Whitie looked keen and knowing. Something seemed to drag at Venters's feet and he noticed Bess lagged behind. Never had the climb from terrace to bridge appeared so long.

Not till they reached the opening of the gorge did they stop to rest and take one last look at the valley. The tremendous arch of stone curved clear and sharp in outline against the morning sky. And through it streaked the golden shaft. The valley seemed an enchanted circle of glorious veils of gold and wraiths of white and silver haze and dim, blue, moving shade – beautiful and wild and unreal as a dream.

'We – we can – th – think of it – always – re – remember,' sobbed Bess.

'Hush! Don't cry. Our valley has only fitted us for a better life somewhere. Come!'

They entered the gorge and he closed the willow gate. From rosy, golden morning light they passed into cool, dense gloom. The burros pattered up the trail with little hollow-cracking steps. And the gorge widened to narrow outlet and the gloom lightened to grey. At the divide they halted for another rest. Venters's keen, remembering gaze searched Balancing Rock, and the long incline, and the cracked toppling walls, but failed to note the slightest change.

The dogs led the descent; then came Bess leading her burro; then Venters leading his. Bess kept her eyes bent downward. Venters, however, had an irresistible desire to look upward at Balancing Rock. It had always haunted him, and now he wondered if he were really to get through the outlet before the huge stone thundered down. He fancied that would be a miracle. Every few steps he answered to the strange, nervous fear and turned to make sure the rock still stood like a giant statue. And, as he descended, it grew dimmer in his sight. It changed form; it swayed; it nodded darkly; and at last, in his heightened fancy, he saw it heave and roll. As in a dream when he felt himself falling yet knew he would never fall, so he saw this long-standing thunderbolt of the little stone-men plunge down to close forever the outlet to Deception Pass.

And while he was giving way to unaccountable dread imaginations the descent was accomplished without mishap.

'I'm glad that's over,' he said, breathing more freely. 'I hope I'm by that hanging rock for good and all. Since almost the moment I first saw it I've had an idea that it was waiting for me. Now, when it does fall, if I'm thousands of miles away, I'll hear it.'

With the first glimpses of the smooth slope leading down to the grotesque cedars and out to the Pass Venters's cool nerve returned. One long survey to the left, then one to the right satisfied his caution. Leading the burros down to the spur of rock, he halted at the steep incline.

'Bess, here's the bad place, the place I told you about, with the cut steps. You start down, leading your burro. Take your time and hold on to him if you slip. I've got a rope on him and a half-hitch on this point of rock, so I can let him down safely. Coming up here was a killing job. But it'll be easy going down.'

Both burros passed down the difficult stairs cut by the cliff-dwellers, and did it without a misstep. After that the descent down the slope and over the mile of scrawled, ribbed, and ridged rock required only careful guidance, and Venters got the burros to level ground in a condition that caused him to congratulate himself.

'Oh, if we only had Wrangle!' exclaimed Venters. 'But we're lucky. That's the worst of our trail passed. We've only men to fear now. If we get up in the sage we can hide and slip along like coyotes.'

They mounted and rode west through the valley and entered the canyon. From time to time Venters walked, leading his burro. When they got by all the canyons and gullies opening into the Pass they went faster and with fewer halts. Venters did not confide in Bess the alarming fact that he had seen horses and smoke less than a mile up one of the intersecting canyons. He did not talk at all. And long after he had passed this canyon and felt secure once more in the certainty that they had been unobserved he never relaxed his watchfulness. But he did not walk any more, and he kept the burros at a steady trot. Night fell before they reached the last water in the Pass and they made camp by starlight. Venters did not want the burros to stray, so he tied them with long halters in the grass near the spring. Bess, tired out and silent, laid her head in a saddle and went to sleep between the two dogs. Venters did not close his eyes. The canyon silence appeared full of the low, continuous hum of insects. He listened until the hum grew into a roar, and then, breaking the spell, once more he heard it low and clear. He watched the stars and the moving shadows, and always his glance returned to the girl's dimly pale face. And he remembered how white and still it had once looked in the starlight. And again stern thought fought his strange fancies. Would all his labour and his love be for naught? Would he lose her, after all? What did the dark shadow around her portend? Did calamity lurk on that long upland trail through the sage? Why should his heart swell and throb with nameless fear? He listened to the silence, and told himself that in the broad light of day he could dispel this leaden-weighted dread.

At the first hint of grey over the eastern rim he awoke Bess, saddled the burros, and began the day's travel. He wanted to get out of the Pass before there was any chance of riders coming down. They gained the break as the first red rays of the rising sun coloured the rim.

For once, so eager was he to get up to level ground, he did not send Ring or Whitie in advance. Encouraging Bess to hurry, pulling at his patient, plodding burro, he climbed the soft, steep trail.

Brighter and brighter grew the light. He mounted the last broken edge of rim to have the sun-fired, purple sage-slope burst upon him as a glory. Bess panted up to his side, tugging on the halter of her burro.

'We're up!' he cried, joyously. 'There's not a dot on the sage. We're safe. We'll not be seen! Oh, Bess – '

Ring growled and sniffed the keen air and bristled. Venters clutched at his rifle. Whitie sometimes made a mistake, but Ring never. The dull thud of hoofs almost deprived Venters of power to turn and see from where disaster threatened. He felt his eyes dilate as he stared at Lassiter leading Black Star and Night out of the sage, with Jane Withersteen, in rider's costume, close beside them.

For an instant Venters felt himself whirl dizzily in the centre of vast circles of sage. He recovered partially, enough to see Lassiter standing with a glad smile and Jane riveted in astonishment.

'Why, Bern!' she exclaimed. 'How good it is to see you! We're riding away, you see. The storm burst – and I'm a ruined woman! . . . I thought you were alone.'

Venters, unable to speak for consternation, and bewildered out of all sense of what he ought or ought not to do, simply stared at Jane.

'Son, where are you bound for?' asked Lassiter.

'Not safe – where I was. I'm – we're going out of Utah – back East,' he found tongue to say.

'I reckon this meetin's the luckiest thing that ever happened to you an' to me – an' to Jane – an' to Bess,' said Lassiter, coolly.

'*Bess!*' cried Jane, with a sudden leap of blood to her pale cheek.

It was entirely beyond Venters to see any luck in that meeting.

Jane Withersteen took one flashing, woman's glance at Bess's scarlet face, at her slender, shapely form.

'Venters! is this a girl – a woman?' she questioned, in a voice that stung.

'Yes.'

'Did you have her in that wonderful valley?'

'Yes, but Jane – '

'All the time you were gone?'

'Yes, but I couldn't tell – '

'Was it for *her* you asked me to give you supplies? Was it for *her* that you wanted to make your valley a paradise?'

'Oh – Jane – '

'Answer me.'

'Yes.'

'Oh, you liar!' And with these passionate words Jane Withersteen succumbed to fury. For the second time in her life she fell into the ungovernable rage that had been her father's weakness. And it was worse than his, for she was a jealous woman – jealous even of her friends.

As best he could, he bore the brunt of her anger. It was not only his deceit to her that she visited upon him, but her betrayal by religion, by life itself.

Her passion, like fire at white heat, consumed itself in little time. Her physical strength failed, and still her spirit attempted to go on in magnificent denunciation of those who had wronged her. Like a tree cut deep into its roots, she began to quiver and shake, and her anger weakened into despair. And her ringing voice sank into a broken, husky whisper. Then, spent and pitiable, upheld by Lassiter's arm, she turned and hid her face in Black Star's mane.

Numb as Venters was when at length Jane Withersteen lifted her head and looked at him, he yet suffered a pang.

'Jane, the girl is innocent!' he cried.

'Can you expect me to believe that?' she asked, with weary, bitter eyes.

'I'm not that kind of a liar. And you know it. If I lied – if I kept silent when honour should have made me speak, it was to spare you. I came to Cottonwoods to tell you. But I couldn't add to your pain. I intended to tell you I had come to love this girl. But, Jane, I hadn't forgotten how good you were to me. I haven't changed at all towards you. I prize your friendship as I always have. But, however it may look to you – don't be unjust. The girl is innocent. Ask Lassiter.'

'Jane, she's jest as sweet an' innocent as little Fay,' said Lassiter. There was a faint smile upon his face and a beautiful light.

Venters saw, and knew that Lassiter saw, how Jane Withersteen's tortured soul wrestled with hate and threw it – with scorn, doubt, suspicion, and overcame all.

'Bern, if in my misery I accused you unjustly, I crave forgiveness,' she said. 'I'm not what I once was. Tell me – who is this girl?'

'Jane, she is Oldring's daughter, and his Masked Rider. Lassiter will tell you how I shot her for a rustler, saved her life – all the story. It's a strange story, Jane, as wild as the sage. But it's true – true as her innocence. That you must believe!'

'Oldring's Masked Rider! Oldring's daughter!' exclaimed Jane. 'And she's innocent! You ask me to believe much. If this girl – is what you say, how could she be going away with the man who killed her father?'

'Why did you tell that?' cried Venters, passionately.

Jane's question had roused Bess out of stupefaction. Her eyes suddenly darkened and dilated. She stepped towards Venters and held up both hands as if to ward off a blow.

'Did – did you kill Oldring?'

'I did, Bess, and I hate myself for it. But you know I never dreamed he was your father. I thought he'd wronged you. I killed him when I was madly jealous.'

For a moment Bess was shocked into silence.

'But he was my father!' she broke out, at last. 'And now I must go back – I can't go with you. It's all over – that beautiful dream. Oh, I *knew* it couldn't come true. You can't take me now.'

'If you forgive me, Bess, it'll all come right in the end! implored Venters.

'It can't be right. I'll go back. After all, I loved him. He was good to me. I can't forget that.'

'If you go back to Oldring's men I'll follow you, and then they'll kill me,' said Venters, hoarsely.

'Oh no, Bern, you'll not come. Let me go. It's best for you to forget me. I've brought you only pain and dishonour.'

She did not weep. But the sweet bloom and life died out of her face. She looked haggard and sad, all at once stunted; and her hands dropped listlessly; and her head drooped in slow, final acceptance of a hopeless fate.

'Jane, look there!' cried Venters, in despairing grief. 'Need you have told her? Where was all your kindness of heart? This girl has had a wretched, lonely life. And I'd found a way to make her happy. You've killed it. You've killed something sweet and pure and hopeful, just as sure as you breathe.'

'Oh, Bern! It was a slip. I never thought – I never thought!' replied Jane. 'How could I tell she didn't know?'

Lassiter suddenly moved forward, and with the beautiful light on his face now strangely luminous, he looked at Jane and Venters and then let his soft, bright gaze rest on Bess.

'Well, I reckon you've all had your say, an' now it's Lassiter's turn. Why, I was jest prayin' for this meetin'. Bess, jest look here.'

Gently he touched her arm and turned her to face the others, and then outspread his great hand to disclose a shiny, battered gold locket.

'Open it,' he said, with a singularly rich voice.

Bess complied, but listlessly.

'Jane – Venters – come closer,' went on Lassiter. 'Take a look at the picture. Don't you know the woman?'

Jane, after one glance, drew back.

'Milly Erne!' she cried, wonderingly.

Venters, with tingling pulse, with something growing on him, recognised in the faded miniature portrait the eyes of Milly Erne.

'Yes, that's Milly,' said Lassiter, softly. 'Bess, did you ever see her face – look hard – with all your heart an' soul?'

'The eyes seem to haunt me,' whispered Bess. 'Oh, I can't remember – they're eyes of my dreams – but – but –'

Lassiter's strong arm went round her and he bent his head.

'Child, I thought you'd remember her eyes. They're the same beautiful eyes you'd see if you looked in a mirror or a clear spring. They're your mother's eyes. You are Milly Erne's child. Your name is Elizabeth Erne. You're not Oldring's daughter. You're the daughter of Frank Erne, a man once my best friend. Look! Here's his picture beside Milly's. He was handsome, an' as fine an' gallant a Southern gentleman as I ever seen. Frank come of an old family. You come of the best of blood, lass, an' blood tells.'

Bess slipped through his arm to her knees and hugged the locket to her bosom, and lifted wonderful, yearning eyes.

'It – can't – be – true!'

'Thank God, lass, it *is* true,' replied Lassiter. 'Jane an' Bern here – they both recognise Milly. They see Milly in you. They're so knocked out they can't tell you, that's all.'

'Who are you?' whispered Bess.

'I reckon I'm Milly's brother an' your uncle! . . . Uncle Jim! Ain't that fine?'

'Oh, I can't believe – Don't raise me! Bern, let me kneel. I see truth in your face – in Miss Withersteen's. But let me hear it all – all on my knees. Tell me *how* it's true!'

'Well, Elizabeth, listen,' said Lassiter. 'Before you was born your father made a mortal enemy of a Mormon named Dyer. They was both ministers an' come to be rivals. Dyer stole your mother away from her home. She gave birth to you in Texas eighteen years ago. Then she was taken to Utah, from place to place, an' finally to the last border settlement – Cottonwoods. You was about three years old when you was taken away from Milly. She never knew what had become of you. But she lived a good while hopin' and prayin' to have you again. Then she gave up an' died. An' I may as well put in here your father died ten years ago. Well, I spent my time tracin' Milly, an' some months back I landed in Cottonwoods. An' jest lately I learned all about you. I had a talk with

Oldrin' an' told him you was dead, an' he told me what I had so long been wantin' to know. It was Dyer, of course, who stole you from Milly. Part reason he was sore because Milly refused to give you Mormon teachin', but mostly he still hated Frank Erne so infernally that he made a deal with Oldrin' to take you an' bring you up as an infamous rustler an' rustler's girl. The idea was to break Frank Erne's heart if he ever came to Utah – to show him his daughter with a band of low rustlers. Well – Oldrin' took you, brought you up from childhood, an' then made you his Masked Rider. He made you infamous. He kept that part of the contract, but he learned to love you as a daughter an' never let any but his own men know you was a girl. I heard him say that with my own ears, an' I saw his big eyes grow dim. He told me how he had guarded you always, kept you locked up in his absence, was always at your side or near you on those rides that made you famous on the sage. He said he an' an old rustler whom he trusted had taught you how to read an' write. They selected the books for you. Dyer had wanted you brought up the vilest of the vile! An' Oldrin' brought you up the innocentest of the innocent. He said you didn't know what vileness was. I can hear his big voice tremble now as he said it. He told me how the men – rustlers an' outlaws – who from time to time tried to approach you familiarly – he told me how he shot them dead. I'm tellin' you this 'specially because you've showed such shame – sayin' you was nameless an' all that. Nothin' on earth can be wronger than that idea of yours. An' the truth of it is here. Oldrin' swore to me that if Dyer died, releasin' the contract, he intended to hunt up your father an' give you back to him. It seems Oldrin' wasn't all bad, an' he sure loved you.'

Venters leaned forward in passionate remorse.

'Oh, Bess! I know Lassiter speaks the truth. For when I shot Oldring he dropped to his knees and fought with unearthly power to speak. And he said: "Man – why – didn't – you – wait? Bess was – " Then he fell dead. And I've been haunted by his look and words. Oh, Bess, what a strange, splendid thing for Oldring to do! It all seems impossible. But, dear, you really are not what you thought.'

'Elizabeth Erne!' cried Jane Withersteen. 'I loved your mother and I see her in you!'

What had been incredible from the lips of men became, in the tone, look, and gesture of a woman, a wonderful truth for Bess. With little tremblings of all her slender body she rocked to and fro on her knees. The yearning wistfulness of her eyes changed to solemn splendour of joy. She believed. She was realising happiness. And as the process of thought was slow, so were the variations of her expression. Her eyes reflected the transformation of her soul. Dark, brooding, hopeless belief – clouds of gloom – drifted, paled, vanished in glorious light. An exquisite rose flush – a glow – shone from her face as she slowly began to rise from her knees. A great spirit uplifted her. All that she had held as base dropped from her.

Venters watched her in joy too deep for words. By it he divined something of what Lassiter's revelation meant to Bess, but he knew he could only faintly understand. That moment when she seemed to be lifted by some spiritual transfiguration was the most beautiful moment of his life. She stood with parted, quivering lips, with hands tightly clasping the locket to her heaving breast. A new conscious pride of worth dignified the old wild, free grace and poise.

'Uncle Jim!' she said, tremulously, with a different smile from any Venters had ever seen on her face.

Lassiter took her into his arms.

'I reckon. It's powerful fine to hear that,' replied Lassiter, unsteadily.

Venters, feeling his eyes grow hot and wet, turned away, and found himself looking at Jane Withersteen. He had almost forgotten her presence. Tenderness and sympathy were fast hiding traces of her agitation. Venters read her mind – felt the reaction of her noble heart – saw the joy she was beginning to feel at the happiness of others. And suddenly blinded, choked by his emotions, he turned from her also. He knew what she would do presently; she would make some magnificent amend for her anger; she would give some manifestation of her love; probably all in a moment, as she had loved Milly Erne, so would she love Elizabeth Erne.

' 'Pears to me, folks, that we'd better talk a little serious now,' remarked Lassiter, at length. 'Time flies.'

'You're right,' replied Venters, instantly. 'I'd forgotten time – place – danger. Lassiter, you're riding away. Jane's leaving Withersteen House?'

'Forever,' replied Jane.

'I fired Withersteen House,' said Lassiter

'Dyer?' questioned Venters, sharply.

'I reckon where Dyer's gone there won't be any kidnappin' of girls.'

'Ah! I knew it. I told Judkins – And Tull?' went on Venters, passionately.

'Tull wasn't around when I broke loose. By now he's likely on our trail with his riders.'

'Lassiter, you're going into the Pass to hide till all this storm blows over?'

'I reckon that's Jane's idea. I'm thinkin' the storm'll be a powerful long time blowin' over. I was comin' to join you in Surprise Valley. You'll go back now with me?'

'No. I want to take Bess out of Utah. Lassiter, Bess found gold in the valley. We've a saddle-bag full of gold. If we can reach Sterling – '

'Man! how're you ever goin' to do that? Sterlin' is a hundred miles.'

'My plan is to ride on, keeping sharp lookout. Somewhere up the trail we'll take to the sage and go round Cottonwoods and then hit the trail again.'

'It's a bad plan. You'll kill the burros in two days.'

'Then we'll walk.'

'That's more bad an' worse. Better go back down the Pass with me.'

'Lassiter, this girl has been hidden all her life in that lonely place,' went on Venters. 'Oldring's men are hunting me. We'd not be safe there any longer. Even if we would be I'd take this chance to get her out. I want to marry her. She shall have some of the pleasures of life – see cities and people. We've gold – we'll be rich. Why, life opens sweet for both of us. And, by Heaven! I'll get her out or lose my life in the attempt!'

'I reckon if you go on with them burros you'll lose your life all right. Tull will have riders all over this sage. You can't get out on them burros. It's a fool idea. That's not doin' best by the girl. Come with me an' take chances on the rustlers.'

Lassiter's cool argument made Venters waver, not in determination to go, but in hope of success.

'Bess, I want you to know. Lassiter says the trip's almost useless now. I'm afraid he's right. We've got about one chance in a hundred to go through. Shall we take it? Shall we go on?'

'We'll go on,' replied Bess.

'That settles it, Lassiter.'

Lassiter spread wide his hands, as if to signify he could do no more, and his face clouded.

Venters felt a touch on his elbow. Jane stood beside him with a hand on his arm. She was smiling. Something radiated from her, and like an electric current accelerated the motion of his blood.

'Bern, you'd be right to die rather than not take Elizabeth out of Utah – out of this wild country. You must do it. You'll show her the great world, with all its wonders. Think how little she has seen! Think what delight is in store for her! You have gold; you will be free; you will make her happy. What a glorious prospect! I share it with you – I'll think of you – dream of you – pray for you.'

'Thank you, Jane,' replied Venters, trying to steady his voice. 'It does look bright. Oh, if we were only across that wide, open waste of sage!'

'Bern, the trip's as good as made. It'll be safe – easy. It'll be a glorious ride,' she said, softly.

Venters stared. Had Jane's troubles made her insane? Lassiter, too, acted queerly, all at once beginning to turn his sombrero round with hands that actually shook.

'You are a rider. She is a rider. This will be the ride of your lives,' added Jane, in that same soft undertone, almost as if she were musing to herself.

'Jane!' he cried.

'I give you Black Star and Night!'

'*Black Star and Night!*' he echoed.

'It's done. Lassiter, put our saddle-bags on the burros.'

Only when Lassiter moved swiftly to execute her bidding did Venters's clogged brain grasp at literal meanings. He leaped to catch Lassiter's busy hands.

'No, no! What are you doing?' he demanded, in a kind of fury. 'I won't take her racers. What do you think I am? It'd be monstrous. Lassiter! stop it, I say! . . . You've got her to save. You've miles and miles to go. Tull is trailing you. There are rustlers in the Pass. Give me back that saddle-bag!'

'Son – cool down,' returned Lassiter, in a voice he might have used to a child. But the grip with which he tore away Venters's grasping hands was that of a giant. 'Listen – you fool boy! Jane's sized up the situation. The burros'll do for us. We'll sneak along an' hide. I'll take your dogs an' your rifle. Why, it's the trick. The blacks are yours, an' sure as I can throw a gun you're goin' to ride safe out of the sage.'

'Jane – stop him – please stop him,' gasped Venters. 'I've lost my strength. I can't do – anything. This 's hell for me! Can't you see that? I've ruined you – it was through me you lost all. You've only Black Star and Night left. You love these horses. Oh! I know how you must love them now! And – you're trying to give them to me. To help me out of Utah! To save the girl I love!'

'That will be my glory.'

Then in the white, rapt face in the unfathomable eyes, Venters saw Jane Withersteen in a supreme moment. This moment was one wherein she reached up to the height for which her noble soul had ever yearned. He, after disrupting the calm tenor of her peace, after bringing down on her head the implacable hostility of her churchmen, after teaching her a bitter lesson of life – he was to be her salvation. And he turned away again, this time shaken to the core of his soul. Jane Withersteen was the incarnation of selflessness. He experienced wonder and terror, exquisite pain and rapture. What were all the shocks life had dealt him compared to the thought of such loyal and generous friendship?

And instantly, as if by some divine insight, he knew himself in the remaking – tried, found wanting; but stronger, better, surer – and he wheeled to Jane Withersteen, eager, joyous, passionate, wild, exalted. He bent to her; he left tears and kisses on her hands.

'Jane, I – I can't find words – now,' he said. 'I'm beyond words. Only – I understand. And I'll take the blacks.'

'Don't be losin' no more time,' cut in Lassiter. 'I ain't certain, but I think I seen a speck up the sage-slope. Mebbe I was mistaken. But, anyway, we must all be movin'. I've shortened the stirrups on Black Star. Put Bess on him.'

Jane Withersteen held out her arms.

'Elizabeth Erne!' she cried, and Bess flew to her.

How inconceivably strange and beautiful it was for Venters to see Bess clasped to Jane Withersteen's breast!

Then he leaped astride Night.

'Venters, ride straight on up the slope,' Lassiter was saying, an' if you don't meet any riders keep on till you're a few miles from the village, then cut off in the sage an' go round to the trail. But you'll most likely meet riders with Tull. Jest keep right on till you're jest out of gunshot an' then make your cutoff into the sage. They'll ride after you, but it won't be no use. You can ride, an' Bess can ride. When you're out of reach turn on round to the west, an' hit the trail somewhere. Save the hosses all you can, but don't be afraid. Black Star and Night are good for a hundred miles before sundown, if you have to push them. You can get to Sterlin' by night if you want. But better make it along about tomorrow mornin'. When you get through the notch on the Glaze trail, swing to the right. You'll be able to see both Glaze an' Stone Bridge. Keep away from them villages. You won't run no risk of meetin' any of Oldrin's rustlers from Sterlin' on. You'll find water in them deep hollows north of the notch. There's an old trail there, not much used, an' it leads to Sterlin'. That's your trail. An' one thing more. If Tull pushes you – or keeps on persistent-like, for a few miles – jest let the blacks out an' lose him an' his riders.'

'Lassiter, may we meet again!' said Venters, in a deep voice.

'Son, it ain't likely – it ain't likely. Well, Bess Oldrin' – Masked Rider – Elizabeth Erne – now you climb on Black Star. I've heard you could ride. Well, every rider loves a good hoss. An', lass, there never was but one that could beat Black Star.'

'Ah, Lassiter, there never was any horse that could beat Black Star,' said Jane, with the old pride.

'I often wondered – mebbe Venters rode out that race when he brought back the blacks. Son, was Wrangle the best hoss?'

'No, Lassiter,' replied Venters. For this lie he had his reward in Jane's quick smile.

'Well, well, my hoss-sense ain't always right. An' here I'm talkin' a lot, wastin' time. It ain't so easy to find an' lose a pretty niece all in one hour! Elizabeth – goodbye!'

'Oh, Uncle Jim! . . . Goodbye!'

'Elizabeth Erne, be happy! Goodbye,' said Jane.

'Goodbye – oh – goodbye!'

In lithe, supple action Bess swung up to Black Star's saddle.

'Jane Withersteen! . . . Goodbye!' called Venters, hoarsely.

'Bern – Bess – riders of the purple sage – goodbye!'

CHAPTER 22

Riders of the Purple Sage

Black Star and Night, answering to spur, swept swiftly westward along the white, slow-rising, sage-bordered trail. Venters heard a mournful howl from Ring, but Whitie was silent. The blacks settled into their fleet, long-striding gallop. The wind sweetly fanned Venters's hot face. From the summit of the first low-swelling ridge he looked back. Lassiter waved his hand; Jane waved her scarf. Venters replied by standing in his stirrups and holding high his sombrero. Then the dip of the ridge hid them. From the height of the next he turned once more. Lassiter, Jane, and the burros had disappeared. They had gone down into the Pass. Venters felt a sensation of irreparable loss.

'Bern – look!' called Bess, pointing up the long slope.

A small, dark, moving dot split the line where purple sage met blue sky. That dot was a band of riders. 'Pull the black, Bess.'

They slowed from gallop to canter, then to trot. The fresh and eager horses did not like the check.

'Bern, Black Star has great eyesight.'

'I wonder if they're Tull's riders. They might be rustlers. But it's all the same to us.'

The black dot grew to a dark patch moving under low dust-clouds. It grew all the time, though very slowly. There were long periods when it was in plain sight, and intervals when it dropped behind the sage. The blacks trotted for half an hour, for another half-hour, and still the moving patch appeared to stay on the horizon line. Gradually, however, as time passed, it began to enlarge, to creep down the slope, to encroach upon the intervening distance.

'Bess, what do you make them out?' asked Venters. 'I don't think they're rustlers.'

'They're sage-riders,' replied Bess. 'I see a white horse and several greys. Rustlers seldom ride any horses but bays and blacks.'

'That white horse is Tull's. Pull the black, Bess. I'll get down and cinch up. We're in for some riding. Are you afraid?'

'Not now,' answered the girl, smiling.

'You needn't be. Bess, you don't weigh enough to make Black Star know you're on him. I won't be able to stay with you. You'll leave Tull and his riders as if they were standing still.'

'How about you?'

'Never fear. If I can't stay with you I can still laugh at Tull.'

'Look, Bern. They've stopped on the ridge. They see us.'

'Yes. But we're too far yet for them to make out who we are. They'll recognise the blacks first. We've passed most of the ridges and the thickest sage. Now, when I give the word, let Black Star go and ride!'

Venters calculated that a mile or more still intervened between them and the riders. They were approaching at a swift canter. Soon Venters recognised Tull's white horse, and concluded that the riders had likewise recognised Black Star and Night. But it would be impossible for Tull yet to see that the blacks were not ridden by Lassiter and Jane. Venters noted that Tull and the line of horsemen, perhaps ten or twelve in number, stopped several times and evidently looked hard down the slope. It must have been a puzzling circumstance for Tull. Venters laughed grimly at the thought of what Tull's rage would be when he finally discovered the trick. Venters meant to sheer out into the sage before Tull could possibly be sure who rode the blacks.

The gap closed to a distance of half a mile. Tull halted. His riders came up and formed a dark group around him. Venters thought he saw him wave his arms, and was certain of it when the riders dashed into the sage, to right and left of the trail. Tull had anticipated just the move held in mind by Venters.

'Now, Bess!' shouted Venters. 'Strike north. Go round those riders and turn west.'

Black Star sailed over the low sage, and in few leaps got into his stride and was running. Venters spurred Night after him. It was hard going in the sage. The horses could run as well there, but keen eyesight and judgement must constantly be used by the riders in choosing ground. And continuous swerving from aisle to aisle between the brush, and leaping little washes and mounds of the pack-rats, and breaking through sage, made rough riding. When Venters had turned into a long aisle he had time to look up at Tull's riders. They were now strung out into an extended line riding north-east. And, as Venters and Bess were holding due north, this meant, if the horses of Tull and his riders had the speed and the staying power, they would head the blacks and turn them back down the slope. Tull's men were not saving their mounts; they were driving them desperately. Venters feared only an accident to Black Star or Night, and skilful riding would mitigate possibility of that. One glance ahead served to show him that Bess could pick a course through the sage as well as he. She looked neither back nor at the running riders, and bent forward over Black Star's neck and studied the ground ahead.

It struck Venters, presently, after he had glanced up from time to time, that Bess was drawing away from him as he had expected. He had, however, only thought of the light weight Black Star was carrying and of his superior speed; he saw now that the black was being ridden as never before, except when Jerry Card lost the race to Wrangle. How easily, gracefully, naturally, Bess sat her saddle! She could ride! Suddenly Venters remembered she had said she could ride. But he had not dreamed she was capable of such superb horsemanship. Then all at once, flashing over him, thrilling him, came the recollection that Bess was Oldring's Masked Rider.

He forgot Tull – the running riders – the race. He let Night have a free rein and felt him lengthen out to suit himself, knowing he would keep to Black Star's course, knowing that he had been chosen by the best rider now on the upland sage. For Jerry Card was dead. And fame had rivalled him with only one rider, and that was the slender girl who now swung so easily with Black Star's stride. Venters had abhorred her notoriety, but now he took passionate pride in her skill, her daring, her power over a horse. And he delved into his memory, recalling famous rides which he had heard related in the villages and round the camp-fires. Oldring's Masked Rider! Many times this stranger, at once well known and unknown, had escaped pursuers by matchless riding. He had run the gauntlet of vigilantes down the main street of Stone Bridge, leaving dead horses and dead rustlers behind. He had jumped his horse over the Gerber Wash, a deep, wide ravine separating the fields of Glaze from the wild sage. He had been surrounded north of Sterling; and he had broken through the line. How often had been told the story of day stampedes, of night raids, of pursuit, and then how the Masked Rider, swift as the wind, was gone in the sage! A fleet, dark horse – a slender, dark form – a black mask – a driving run down the slope – a dot on the purple sage – a shadowy, muffled steed disappearing in the night!

And this Masked Rider of the uplands had been Elizabeth Erne!

The sweet sage wind rushed in Venters's face and sang a song in his ears. He heard the dull, rapid beat of Night's hoofs; he saw Black Star drawing away, farther and farther. He realised both horses were swinging to the west. Then gunshots in the rear reminded him of Tull. Venters looked back. Far to the side, dropping behind, trooped the riders. They were shooting. Venters saw no puffs of dust, heard no whistling bullets. He was out of range. When he looked back again Tull's riders had given up pursuit. The best they could do, no doubt, had been to get near enough to recognise who really rode the blacks. Venters saw Tull drooping in his saddle.

Then Venters pulled Night out of his running stride. Those few miles had scarcely warmed the black, but Venters wished to save him. Bess turned, and, though she was far away, Venters caught the white glint of her waving hand. He held Night to a trot and rode on, seeing Bess and Black Star, and the sloping upward stretch of sage, and from time to time the receding black riders behind. Soon they disappeared behind a ridge, and he turned no more. They would go back to Lassiter's trail and follow it, and follow in vain. So Venters rode on, with the wind growing sweeter to taste and smell, and the purple sage richer and the sky bluer in his sight; and the song in his ears ringing. By and by Bess halted to wait for him, and he knew she had come to the trail. When he reached her it was to smile at sight of her standing with arms round Black Star's neck. 'Oh, Bern! I love him!' she cried. 'He's beautiful; he knows; and how he can run! I've had fast horses. But Black Star! . . . Wrangle never beat him!'

'I'm wondering if I didn't dream that. Bess, the blacks are grand. What it must have cost Jane – ah! – well, when we get out of this wild country with Star and Night, back to my old home in Illinois, we'll buy a beautiful farm with meadows and springs and cool shade. There we'll turn the horses free – free to roam and browse and drink – never to feel a spur again – never to be ridden!'

'I would like that,' said Bess.

They rested. Then, mounting, they rode side by side up the white trail. The sun rose higher behind them. Far to the left a low line of green marked the site of Cottonwoods. Venters looked once and looked no more. Bess gazed only straight ahead. They put the blacks to the long, swinging rider's canter, and at times pulled them to a trot, and occasionally to a walk. The hours passed, the miles slipped behind, and the wall of rock loomed to the fore. The notch opened wide. It was a rugged, stony pass, but with level and open trail, and Venters and Bess ran the blacks through it. An old trail led off to the right, taking the line of the wall, and this Venters knew to be the trail mentioned by Lassiter.

The little hamlet, Glaze, a white and green patch in the vast waste of purple, lay miles down a slope much like the Cottonwoods slope, only this descended to the west. And miles farther west a faint green spot marked the location of Stone Bridge. All the rest of that world was seemingly smooth, undulating sage, with no ragged lines of canyons to accentuate its wildness.

'Bess, we're safe – we're free!' said Venters. 'We're alone on the sage. We're halfway to Sterling.'

'Ah! I wonder how it is with Lassiter and Miss Withersteen.'

'Never fear, Bess. He'll outwit Tull. He'll get away and hide her safely. He might climb into Surprise Valley, but I don't think he'll go so far.'

'Bern, will we ever find any place like our beautiful valley?'

'No. But, dear, listen. We'll go back someday, after years – ten years. Then we'll be forgotten. And our valley will be just as we left it.'

'What if Balancing Rock falls and closes the outlet to the Pass?'

'I've thought of that. I'll pack in ropes and ropes. And if the outlet's closed we'll climb up the cliffs and over them to the valley and go down on rope ladders. It could be done. I know just where to make the climb, and I'll never forget.'

'Oh yes, let us go back!'

'It's something sweet to look forward to. Bess, it's like all the future looks to me.'

'Call me – Elizabeth,' she said, shyly.

'Elizabeth Erne! It's a beautiful name. But I'll never forget Bess. Do you know – have you thought that very soon – by this time tomorrow – you will be Elizabeth Venters?'

So they rode on down the old trail. And the sun sloped to the west, and a golden sheen lay on the sage. The hours sped now; the afternoon waned. Often they rested the horses. The glisten of a pool of water in a hollow caught Venters's eye, and here he unsaddled the blacks and let them roll and drink and browse. When he and Bess rode up out of the hollow the sun was low, a crimson ball, and the valley seemed veiled in purple fire and smoke. It was that short time when the sun appeared to rest before setting, and silence, like a cloak of invisible life, lay heavy on all that shimmering world of sage.

They watched the sun begin to bury its red curve under the dark horizon.

'We'll ride on till late,' he said. 'Then you can sleep a little, while I watch and graze the horses. And we'll ride into Sterling early tomorrow. We'll be married! . . . We'll be in time to catch the stage. We'll tie Black Star and Night behind – and then – for a country not wild and terrible like this!'

'Oh, Bern! . . . But look! The sun is setting on the sage – the last time for us till we dare come again to the Utah border. Ten years! Oh, Bern, look, so you will never forget!'

Slumbering, fading purple fire burned over the undulating sage ridges. Long streaks and bars and shafts and spears fringed the far western slope. Drifting, golden veils mingled with low, purple shadows. Colours and shades changed in slow, wondrous transformation.

Suddenly Venters was startled by a low, rumbling roar – so low that it was like the roar in a sea-shell.

'Bess, did you hear anything?' he whispered.

'No.'

'Listen! . . . Maybe I only imagined – *Ah!*'

Out of the east or north, from remote distance, breathed an infinitely low, continuously long sound – deep, weird, detonating, thundering, deadening – dying.

CHAPTER 23

The Fall of Balancing Rock

Through tear-blurred sight Jane Withersteen watched Venters and Elizabeth Erne and the black racers disappear over the ridge of sage.

'They're gone!' said Lassiter. 'An' they're safe now. An' there'll never be a day of their comin' happy lives but what they'll remember Jane Withersteen an' – an' Uncle Jim! . . . I reckon, Jane, we'd better be on our way.'

The burros obediently wheeled and started down the break with little, cautious steps, but Lassiter had to leash the whining dogs and lead them. Jane felt herself bound in a feeling that was neither listlessness nor indifference, yet which rendered her incapable of interest. She was still strong in body, but emotionally tired. That hour at the entrance to Deception Pass had been the climax of her suffering – the flood of her wrath – the last of her sacrifice – the supremacy of her love – and the attainment of peace. She thought that if she had little Fay she would not ask any more of life.

Like an automaton she followed Lassiter down the steep trail of dust and bits of weathered stone; and when the little slides moved with her or piled around her knees she experienced no alarm. Vague relief came to her in the sense of being enclosed between dark stone walls, deep hidden from the glare of sun, from the glistening sage. Lassiter lengthened the stirrup straps on one of the burros and bade her mount and ride close to him. She was to keep the burro from cracking his little hard hoofs on stones. Then she was riding on between dark, gleaming walls. There were quiet and rest and coolness in this canyon. She noted indifferently that they passed close under shady, bulging shelves of cliff, through patches of grass and sage and thicket and groves of slender trees, and over white, pebbly washes, and around masses of broken rock. The burros trotted tirelessly; the dogs, once more free, pattered tirelessly; and Lassiter led on with never a stop, and at every open place he looked back. The shade under the walls gave place to sunlight. And presently they came to a dense thicket of slender trees, through which they passed to rich, green grass and water. Here Lassiter rested the burros for a little while, but he was restless, uneasy, silent, always listening, peering under the trees. She dully reflected that enemies were behind them – before them; still the thought awakened no dread or concern or interest.

At his bidding she mounted and rode on close to the heels of his burro. The canyon narrowed; the walls lifted their rugged rims higher; and the sun shone down hot from the centre of the blue stream of sky above. Lassiter travelled slower, with more exceeding care as to the ground he chose, and he kept speaking low to the dogs. They were now hunting-dogs – keen, alert, suspicious, sniffing the warm breeze. The monotony of the yellow walls broke in change of colour and smooth surface, and the rugged outline of rims grew craggy. Splits appeared in deep breaks, and gorges running at right angles, and then the Pass opened wide at a junction of intersecting canyons.

Lassiter dismounted, led his burro, called the dogs close, and proceeded at snail pace through dark masses of rock and dense thickets under the left wall. Long he watched and listened before venturing to cross the mouths of side canyons. At length he halted, tied his burro, lifted a warning hand to Jane, and then slipped away among the boulders, and, followed by the stealthy dogs, disappeared from sight. The time he remained absent was neither short nor long to Jane Withersteen.

When he reached her side again he was pale, and his lips were set in a hard line, and his grey eyes glittered coldly. Bidding her dismount, he led the burros into a covert of stones and cedars, and tied them.

'Jane, I've run into the fellers I've been lookin' for, an' I'm goin' after them,' he said.

'Why?' she asked.

'I reckon I won't take time to tell you.'

'Couldn't we slip by without being seen?'

'Likely enough. But that ain't my game. An' I'd like to know, in case I don't come back, what you'll do.'

'What can I do?'

'I reckon you can go back to Tull. Or stay in the Pass an' be taken off by rustlers. Which'll you do?'

'I don't know. I can't think very well. But I believe I'd rather be taken off by rustlers.'

Lassiter sat down, put his head in his hands, and remained for a few moments in what appeared to be deep and painful thought. When he lifted his face it was haggard, lined, cold as sculptured marble.

'I'll go. I only mentioned that chance of my not comin' back. I'm pretty sure to come.'

'Need you risk so much? Must you fight more? Haven't you shed enough blood?'

'I'd like to tell you why I'm goin',' he continued, in coldness he had seldom used to her. She remarked it, but it was the same to her as if he had spoken with his old gentle warmth. 'But I reckon I won't. Only, I'll say that mercy an' goodness, such as is in you, though they're the grand things in human nature, can't be lived up to on this Utah border. Life's hell out here. You think – or you used to think – that your religion made this life heaven. Mebbe them scales on your eyes has dropped now. Jane, I wouldn't have you no different, an' that's why I'm goin' to try to hide you somewhere in this Pass. I'd like to hide many more women, for I've come to see there are more like you among your people. An' I'd like you to see jest how hard an' cruel this border life is. It's bloody. You'd think churches an' churchmen would make it better. They make it worse. You give names to things – bishops, elders, ministers, Mormonism, duty, faith, glory. You dream – or you're driven mad. I'm a man, an' I know. I name fanatics, followers, blind women, oppressors, thieves, ranchers, rustlers, riders. An' we have – what you've lived through these last months. It can't be helped. But it can't last always. An' remember this – someday the border'll be better, cleaner, for the ways of men like Lassiter!'

She saw him shake his tall form erect, look at her strangely and steadfastly, and then, noiselessly, stealthily slip away amid the rocks and trees. Ring and Whitie, not being bidden to follow, remained with Jane. She felt extreme weariness, yet somehow it did not seem to be of her body. And she sat down in the shade and tried to think. She saw a creeping lizard, cactus flowers, the drooping burros, the resting dogs, an eagle high over a yellow crag. Once the meanest flower, a colour, the flight of a bee, or any living thing had given her deepest joy. Lassiter had gone off, yielding to his incurable blood lust, probably to his own death; and she was sorry, but there was no feeling in her sorrow.

Suddenly from the mouth of the canyon just beyond her rang out a clear, sharp report of a rifle. Echoes clapped. Then followed a piercingly high yell of anguish, quickly breaking. Again echoes clapped, in grim imitation. Dull revolver shots – hoarse yells – pound of hoofs – shrill neighs of horses – commingling of echoes – and again silence! Lassiter must be busily engaged, thought Jane, and no chill trembled over her, no blanching tightened her skin. Yes, the border was a bloody place. But life had always been bloody. Men were blood-spillers. Phases of the history of the world flashed through her mind – Greek and Roman wars, dark, medieval times, the crimes in the name of religion. On sea, on land, everywhere – shooting, stabbing, cursing, clashing, fighting men! Greed, power, oppression, fanaticism, love, hate, revenge, justice, freedom – for these, men killed one another.

She lay there under the cedars, gazing up through the delicate lace-like foliage at the blue sky, and she thought and wondered and did not care.

More rattling shots disturbed the noonday quiet. She heard a sliding of weathered rock, a hoarse shout of warning, a yell of alarm, again the clear, sharp crack of the rifle, and another cry that was a cry of death. Then rifle reports pierced a dull volley of revolver shots. Bullets whizzed over Jane's hiding-place; one struck a stone and whined away in the air. After that, for a time, succeeded desultory shots; and then they ceased under long, thundering fire from heavier guns.

Sooner or later, then, Jane heard the cracking of horses' hoofs on the stones, and the sound came nearer and nearer. Silence intervened until Lassiter's soft, jingling step assured her of his approach. When he appeared he was covered with blood.

'All right, Jane,' he said. 'I come back. An' don't worry.'

With water from a canteen he washed the blood from his face and hands.

'Jane, hurry now. Tear my scarf in two, an' tie up these places. That hole through my hand is some inconvenient, worse 'n this cut over my ear. There – you're doin' fine! Not a bit nervous – no tremblin'. I reckon I ain't done your courage justice. I'm glad you're brave jest now – you'll need to be. Well, I was hid pretty good, enough to keep them from shootin' me deep, but they was slingin' lead close all the time. I used up all the rifle shells, an' then I went after them. Mebbe you heard. It was then I got hit. I had to use up every shell in my own guns, an' they did, too, as I seen. Rustlers an' Mormons, Jane! An' now I'm packin' five bullet holes in my carcass, an' guns without shells. Hurry, now.'

He unstrapped the saddle-bags from the burros, slipped the saddles and let them lie, turned the burros loose, and, calling the dogs, led the way through stones and cedars to an open where two horses stood.

'Jane, are you strong?' he asked.

'I think so. I'm not tired,' Jane replied.

'I don't mean that way. Can you bear up?'

'I think I can bear anything.'

'I reckon you look a little cold an' thick. So I'm preparin' you.'

'For what?'

'I didn't tell you why I jest had to go after them fellers. I couldn't tell you. I believe you'd have died. But I can tell you now – if you'll bear up under a shock?'

'Go on, my friend.'

'*I've got little Fay!* Alive – bad hurt – but she'll live!'

Jane Withersteen's deadlocked feeling, rent by Lassiter's deep quivering voice, leaped into an agony of sensitive life.

'Here,' he added, and showed her where little Fay lay on the grass.

Unable to speak, unable to stand, Jane dropped on her knees. By that long, beautiful golden hair Jane recognised the beloved Fay. But Fay's loveliness was gone. Her face was drawn and looked old with grief. But she was not dead – her heart beat – and Jane Withersteen gathered strength and lived again.

'You see I jest had to go after Fay,' Lassiter was saying, as he knelt to bathe her little pale face. 'But I reckon I don't want no more choices like the one I had to make. There was a crippled feller in that bunch, Jane. Mebbe Venters crippled him. Anyway, that's why they were holdin' up here. I seen little Fay first thing, an' was hard put to it to figure out a way to get her. An' I wanted hosses, too. I had to take chances. So I crawled close to their camp. One feller jumped a hoss with little Fay, an' when I shot him, of course she dropped. She's stunned an' bruised – she fell right on her head. Jane, she's comin' to! She ain't bad hurt!'

Fay's long lashes fluttered; her eyes opened. At first they seemed glazed over. They looked dazed by pain. Then they quickened, darkened, to shine with intelligence – bewilderment – memory – and sudden wonderful joy.

'Muvver – Jane!' she whispered.

'Oh, little Fay, little Fay!' cried Jane, lifting, clasping the child to her.

'*Now*, we've got to rustle!' said Lassiter, in grim coolness. 'Jane, look down the Pass!'

Across the mounds of rock and sage Jane caught sight of a band of riders filing out of the narrow neck of the Pass; and in the lead was a white horse, which, even at a distance of a mile or more, she knew.

'Tull!' she almost screamed.

'I reckon. But, Jane, we've still got the game in our hands. They're ridin' tired hosses. Venters likely give them a chase. He wouldn't forget that. An' we've fresh hosses.'

Hurriedly he strapped on the saddle-bags, gave quick glance to girths and cinches and stirrups, then leaped astride.

'Lift little Fay up,' he said. With shaking arms Jane complied.

'Get back your nerve, woman! This's life or death now. Mind that. Climb up! Keep your wits. Stick close to me. Watch where your hoss's goin' an' ride!'

Somehow Jane mounted; somehow found strength to hold the reins, to spur, to cling on, to ride. A horrible quaking, craven fear possessed her soul. Lassiter led the swift flight across the wide space, over washes, through sage, into a narrow canyon where the rapid clatter of hoofs rapped sharply from the walls. The wind roared in her ears; the gleaming cliffs swept by; trail and sage and grass moved under her. Lassiter's bandaged, blood-stained face turned to her; he shouted encouragement; he looked back down the Pass; he spurred his horse. Jane clung on, spurring likewise. And the horses settled from hard, furious gallop into a long-striding, driving run. She had never ridden at anything like that pace; desperately she tried to get the swing of the horse, to be of some help to him in that race, to see the best of the ground and guide him into it. But she failed of everything except to keep her seat in the saddle, and to spur and spur. At times she closed her eyes, unable to bear sight of Fay's golden curls streaming in the wind. She could not pray; she could not rail; she no longer cared for herself. All of life, of good, of use in the world, of hope in heaven centred in Lassiter's ride with little Fay to safety. She would have tried to turn the iron-jawed brute she rode; she would have given herself to that relentless, dark-browed Tull. But she knew Lassiter would turn with her, so she rode on and on.

Whether that run was of moments or hours Jane Withersteen could not tell. Lassiter's horse covered her with froth that blew back in white streams. Both horses ran their limit, were allowed to slow down in time to save them, and went on dripping, heaving, staggering.

'Oh, Lassiter, we must run – we must run!'

He looked back, saying nothing. The bandage had blown from his head, and blood trickled down his face. He was bowing under the strain of injuries, of the ride, of his burden. Yet how cool and grey he looked – how intrepid!

The horses walked, trotted, galloped, ran, to fall again to walk. Hours sped or dragged. Time was an instant – an eternity. Jane Withersteen felt hell pursuing her, and dared not look back for fear she would fall from her horse.

'Oh, Lassiter! Is he coming?'

The grim rider looked over his shoulder, but said no word. Little Fay's golden hair floated on the breeze. The sun shone; the walls gleamed; the sage glistened. And then it seemed the sun vanished, the walls shaded, the sage paled. The horses walked – trotted – galloped – ran – to fall again to walk. Shadows gathered under shelving cliffs. The canyon turned, brightened, opened into long, wide, wall-enclosed valley. Again the sun, lowering in the west, reddened the sage. Far ahead round, scrawled stone appeared to block the Pass.

'Bear up, Jane, bear up!' called Lassiter. 'It's our game, if you don't weaken.'

'Lassiter! Go on – *alone*! Save little Fay!'

'Only with you!'

'Oh! – I'm a coward – a miserable coward! I can't fight or think or hope or pray! I'm lost! Oh, Lassiter, look back! Is he coming? I'll not – hold out –'

'Keep your breath, woman, an' ride not for yourself or for me, but for Fay!'

A last breaking run across the sage brought Lassiter's horse to a walk.

'He's done,' said the rider.

'Oh, no – no!' moaned Jane.

'Look back, Jane, look back. Three – four miles we've come across this valley, an' no Tull yet in sight. Only a few more miles!'

Jane looked back over the long stretch of sage, and found the narrow gap in the wall, out of which came a file of dark horses with a white horse in the lead. Sight of the riders acted upon Jane as a stimulant. The weight of cold, horrible terror lessened. And, gazing forward at the dogs, at Lassiter's limping horse, at the blood on his face, at the rocks growing nearer, last at Fay's golden hair, the ice left her veins, and slowly, strangely, she gained hold of strength that she believed would see her to the safety Lassiter promised. And, as she gazed, Lassiter's horse stumbled and fell.

He swung his leg and slipped from the saddle.

'Jane, take the child,' he said, and lifted Fay up. Jane clasped her with arms suddenly strong. 'They're gainin',' went on Lassiter, as he watched the pursuing riders. 'But we'll beat 'em yet.'

Turning with Jane's bridle in his hand, he was about to start when he saw the saddle-bag on the fallen horse.

'I've jest about got time,' he muttered, and with swift fingers that did not blunder or fumble he loosened the bag and threw it over his shoulder.

Then he started to run, leading Jane's horse, and he ran, and trotted, and walked, and ran again. Close ahead now Jane saw a rise of bare rock. Lassiter reached it, searched along the base, and, finding a low place, dragged the weary horse up and over round, smooth stone. Looking backward, Jane saw Tull's white horse not a mile distant, with riders strung out in a long line behind him. Looking forward, she saw more valley to the right, and to the left a towering cliff. Lassiter pulled the horse and kept on.

Little Fay lay in her arms with wide-open eyes – eyes which were still shadowed by pain, but no longer fixed, glazed in terror. The golden curls blew across Jane's lips; the little hands feebly clasped her arm; a ghost of a troubled, trustful smile hovered round the sweet lips. And Jane Withersteen awoke to the spirit of a lioness.

Lassiter was leading the horse up a smooth slope towards cedar trees of twisted and bleached appearance. Among these he halted.

'Jane, give me the girl an' get down,' he said. As if it wrenched him he unbuckled the empty black guns with a strange air of finality. He then received Fay in his arms and stood a moment looking backward. Tull's white horse mounted the ridge of round stone, and several bays or blacks followed. 'I wonder what he'll think when he sees them empty guns. Jane, bring your saddle-bag and climb after me.'

A glistening, wonderful bare slope, with little holes, swelled up and up to lose itself in a frowning yellow cliff. Jane closely watched her steps and climbed behind Lassiter. He moved slowly. Perhaps he was only husbanding his strength. But she saw drops of blood on the stone, and then she knew. They climbed and climbed without looking back. Her breast laboured; she began to feel as if little points of fiery steel were penetrating her side into her lungs. She heard the panting of Lassiter and the quicker panting of the dogs.

'Wait – here,' he said.

Before her rose a bulge of stone, nicked with little cut steps, and above that a corner of yellow wall, and overhanging that a vast, ponderous cliff.

The dogs pattered up, disappeared round the corner. Lassiter mounted the steps with Fay, and he swayed like a drunken man, and he too disappeared. But instantly he returned alone, and half ran, half slipped down to her.

Then from below pealed up hoarse shouts of angry men. Tull and several of his riders had reached the spot where Lassiter had parted with his guns.

'You'll need that breath – mebbe!' said Lassiter, facing downward, with glittering eyes.

'Now, Jane, the last pull,' he went on. 'Walk up them little steps. I'll follow an' steady you. Don't think. Jest go. Little Fay's above. Her eyes are open. She jest said to me, *"Where's muvver Jane?"* '

Without a fear or a tremor or a slip or a touch of Lassiter's hand Jane Withersteen walked up that ladder of cut steps.

He pushed her round the corner of wall. Fay lay, with wide staring eyes, in the shade of a gloomy wall. The dogs waited. Lassiter picked up the child and turned into a dark cleft. It zigzagged. It widened. It opened. Jane was amazed at a wonderfully smooth and steep incline leading up between ruined, splintered, toppling walls. A red haze from the setting sun filled this passage. Lassiter climbed with slow, measured steps, and blood dripped from him to make splotches on the white stone. Jane tried not to step in his blood, but was compelled, for she found no other footing. The saddle-bag began to drag her down; she gasped for breath; she thought her heart was bursting. Slower, slower yet the rider climbed, whistling as he breathed. The incline widened. Huge pinnacles and monuments of stone stood alone, leaning fearfully. Red sunset haze shone through cracks where the wall had split. Jane did not look high, but she felt the overshadowing of broken rims above. She felt that it was a fearful, menacing place. And she climbed on in heart-rending effort. And she fell beside Lassiter and Fay at the top of the incline in a narrow, smooth divide.

He staggered to his feet – staggered to a huge, leaning rock that rested on a small pedestal. He put his hand on it – the hand that had been shot through – and Jane saw blood drip from the ragged hole. Then he fell.

'Jane – I – can't – do – it!' he whispered.

'What?'

'Roll the – stone! . . . All my – life I've loved – to roll stones – an' now I – can't!'

'What of it? You talk strangely. Why roll that stone?'

'I planned to – fetch you here – to roll this stone. See! It'll smash the crags – loosen the walls – close the outlet!'

As Jane Withersteen gazed down that long incline, walled in by crumbling cliffs, awaiting only the slightest jar to make them fall asunder, she saw Tull appear at the bottom and begin to climb. A rider followed him – another – and another.

'See! Tull! The riders!'

'Yes – they'll get us – now.'

'Why? Haven't you strength left to roll the stone?'

'Jane – it ain't that – I've lost my nerve!'

'*You!* . . . Lassiter!'

'I wanted to roll it – meant to – but I – can't. Venters's valley is down behind here. We could – live there. But if I roll the stone – we're shut in for always. I don't dare. I'm thinkin' of you!'

'Lassiter! Roll the stone!' she cried.

He arose, tottering, but with set face, and again he placed the bloody hand on the Balancing Rock. Jane Withersteen gazed from him down the passageway. Tull was climbing. Almost, she thought, she saw his dark, relentless face. Behind him more riders climbed. What did they mean for Fay – for Lassiter – for herself?

'*Roll the stone! . . . Lassiter, I love you!*'

Under all his deathly pallor, and the blood, and the iron of seared cheek and lined brow, worked a great change. He placed both hands on the rock and then leaned his shoulder there and braced his powerful body.

'Roll the stone!'

It stirred, it groaned, it grated, it moved; and with a slow grinding, as of wrathful relief, began to lean. It had waited ages to fall, and now was slow in starting. Then, as if suddenly instinct with life, it leaped hurtlingly down to alight on the steep incline, to bound more swiftly into the air, to gather momentum, to plunge into the lofty leaning crag below. The crag thundered into atoms. A wave of air – a splitting shock! Dust shrouded the sunset red of shaking rims; dust shrouded Tull as he fell on his knees with uplifted arms. Shafts and monuments and sections of wall fell majestically.

From the depths there rose a long-drawn rumbling roar. The outlet to Deception Pass closed forever.

THE COVERED WAGON

EMERSON HOUGH

Contents

CHAPTER 1

Youth Marches

'LOOK AT 'EM COME, JESSE! More and more! Must be forty or fifty families.'

Molly Wingate, middle-aged, portly, dark browed and strong, stood at the door of the rude tent which for the time made her home. She was pointing down the road which lay like an ecru ribbon thrown down across the prairie grass, bordered beyond by the timber-grown bluffs of the Missouri.

Jesse Wingate allowed his team of harness-marked horses to continue their eager drinking at the watering hole of the little stream near which the camp was pitched, until, their thirst quenched, they began burying their muzzles and blowing into the water in sensuous enjoyment. He stood, a strong and tall man of perhaps forty-five years, of keen blue eye and short, close-matted, tawny beard. His garb was the loose dress of the outlying settler of the Western lands three-quarters of a century ago. A farmer he must have been back home.

Could this encampment, on the very front of the American civilisation, now be called a home? Beyond the prairie road could be seen a double furrow of jet-black glistening sod, framing the green grass and its spangling flowers, first browsing of the plough on virgin soil. It might have been the opening of a farm. But if so, why the crude bivouac? Why the gear of travellers? Why the massed arklike wagons, the scores of morning fires lifting lazy blue wreaths of smoke against the morning mists?

The truth was that Jesse Wingate, earlier and impatient on the front, out of the very suppression of energy, had been trying his plough in the first white furrows beyond the Missouri in the great year of 1848. Four hundred other nearby ploughs alike were avid for the soil of Oregon; as witness this long line of newcomers, late at the frontier rendezvous.

'It's the Liberty wagons from down river,' said the campmaster at length. 'Missouri movers and settlers from lower Illinois. It's time. We can't lie here much longer waiting for Missouri or Illinois, either. The grass is up.'

'Well, we'd have to wait for Molly to end her spring term, teaching in

897

Clay School, in Liberty,' rejoined his wife, 'else why'd we send her there to graduate? Twelve dollars a month, cash money, ain't to be sneezed at.'

'No; nor is two thousand miles of trail between here and Oregon, before snow, to be sneezed at, either. If Molly ain't with those wagons I'll send Jed over for her today. If I'm going to be captain I can't hold the people here on the river any longer, with May already begun.'

'She'll be here today,' asserted his wife. 'She said she would. Besides, I think that's her riding a little one side the road now. Not that I know who all is with her. One young man – two. Well' – with maternal pride – 'Molly ain't never lacked for beaus!

'But look at the wagons come!' she added. 'All the country's going West this spring, it certainly seems like.'

It was the spring gathering of the west-bound wagon-trains, stretching from old Independence to Westport Landing, the spot where that very year the new name of Kansas City was heard among the emigrants as the place of the jump-off. It was now an hour by sun, as these Western people would have said, and the low-lying valley mists had not yet fully risen, so that the atmosphere for a great picture was not lacking.

It was a great picture, a stirring panorama of an earlier day, which now unfolded. Slow, swaying, stately, the ox teams came on, as though impelled by and not compelling the fleet of white canvas sails. The teams did not hasten, did not abate their speed, but moved in an unagitated advance that gave the massed column something irresistibly epochal in look.

The train, foreshortened to the watchers at the rendezvous, had a well-spaced formation – twenty wagons, thirty, forty, forty-seven – as Jesse Wingate mentally counted them. There were outriders; there were clumps of driven cattle. Along the flanks walked tall men, who flung over the low-headed cattle an admonitory lash whose keen report presently could be heard, still faint and far off. A dull dust cloud arose, softening the outlines of the prairie ships. The broad gestures of arm and trunk, the monotonous soothing of commands to the sophisticated kine as yet remained vague, so that still it was properly a picture done on a vast canvas – that of the frontier in '48; a picture of might, of inevitableness. Even the sober souls of these waiters rose to it, felt some thrill they themselves had never analysed.

A boy of twenty, tall, blond, tousled, rode up from the grove back of the encampment of the Wingate family.

'You, Jed?' said his father. 'Ride on out and see if Molly's there.'

'Sure she is!' commented the youth, finding a plug in the pocket of his jeans. 'That's her. Two fellers, like usual.'

'Sam Woodhull, of course,' said the mother, still hand over eye. 'He hung around all winter, telling how him and Colonel Doniphan whipped all Mexico and won the war. If Molly ain't in a wagon of her own, it ain't his fault, anyways! I'll rest assured it's account of Molly's going out to Oregon that he's going too! Well!' And again, 'Well!'

'Who's the other fellow, though?' demanded Jed. 'I can't place him this far.'

Jesse Wingate handed over his team to his son and stepped out into the open road, moved his hat in an impatient signal, half of welcome, half of command. It apparently was observed.

To their surprise, it was the unidentified rider who now set spur to his horse and came on at a gallop ahead of the train. He rode carelessly well, a born horseman. In no more than a few minutes he could be seen as rather a gallant figure of the border cavalier – a border just then more martial than it had been before '46 and the days of 'Fifty-Four Forty or Fight'.

A shrewd man might have guessed this young man – he was no more than twenty-eight – to have got some military air on a border opposite to that of Oregon: the far Southwest, where Taylor and Scott and the less known Doniphan and many another fighting man had been adding certain thousands of leagues to the soil of this republic. He rode a compact, short-coupled, cat-hammed steed, coal black and with a dashing forelock reaching almost to his red nostrils – a horse never reared on the fat Missouri cornlands. Neither did his heavy embossed saddle with its silver concho decorations then seem familiar so far north; nor yet the thin braided-leather bridle with its hair frontlet band and its mighty bit; nor again the great spurs with jingling rowel bells. This rider's mount and trappings spoke the far and new Southwest, just then coming into our national ken.

The young man himself, however, was upon the face of his appearance nothing of the swashbuckler. True, in his close-cut leather trousers, his neat boots, his tidy gloves, his rather jaunty broad black hat of felted beaver, he made a somewhat raffish figure of a man as he rode up, weight on his under thigh, sidewise, and hand on his horse's quarters, carelessly; but his clean cut, unsmiling features, his direct and grave look out of dark eyes, spoke him a gentleman of his day and place, and no mere spectacular pretender assuming a virtue though he had it not.

He swung easily out of the saddle, his right hand on the tall, broad Spanish horn as easily as though rising from a chair at presence of a lady, and removed his beaver to this frontier woman before he accosted her husband. His bridle he flung down over his horse's head, which seemingly anchored the animal, spite of its loud whinnying challenge to these nearby stolid creatures which showed harness rubs and not whitened saddle hairs.

'Good morning, madam,' said he in a pleasant, quiet voice. 'Good-morning, sir. You are Mr and Mrs Jesse Wingate, I believe. Your daughter yonder told me so.'

'That's my name,' said Jesse Wingate, eyeing the newcomer suspiciously, but advancing with ungloved hand. 'You're from the Liberty train?'

'Yes, sir. My name is Banion – William Banion. You may not know me. My family were Kentuckians before my father came out to Franklin. I started up in the law at old Liberty town yonder not so long ago, but I've been away a great deal.'

'The law, eh?' Jesse Wingate again looked disapproval of the young man's rather pronouncedly neat turnout. 'Then you're not going West?'

'Oh, yes, I am, if you please, sir. I've done little else all my life. Two years ago I marched with all the others, with Doniphan, for Mexico. Well, the war's over, and the treaty's likely signed. I thought it high time to march back home. But you know how it is – the long trail's in my blood now. I can't settle down.'

Wingate nodded. The young man smilingly went on, 'I want to see how it is in Oregon. What with new titles and the like – and a lot of fighting men cast in together out yonder, too – there ought to be as much law out there as here, don't you think? So I'm going to seek my fortune in the Far West. It's too close and tame in here now. I'm' – he smiled just a bit more obviously and deprecatingly – 'I'm leading yonder *caballad* of our neighbours, with a bunch of Illinois and Indiana wagons. They call me Colonel William Banion. It's not right – I was no more than Will Banion, major, under Doniphan. I am not that now.'

A change, a shadow came over his face. He shook it off as though it were tangible.

'So I'm at your service, sir. They tell me you've been elected captain of the Oregon train. I wanted to throw in with you if I might, sir. I know we're late – we should have been in last night. I rode in to explain that. May we pull in just beside you, on this water?'

Molly Wingate, on whom the distinguished address of the stranger, his easy manner and his courtesy had not failed to leave their impression, answered before her husband.

'You certainly can, Major Banion.'

'Mr Banion, please.'

'Well then, Mr Banion. The water and grass is free. The day's young. Drive in and light down. You said you saw our daughter, Molly – I know you did, for that's her now.'

The young man coloured under his bronze of tan, suddenly shy.

'I did,' said he. 'The fact is, I met her earlier this spring at Clay Seminary, where she taught. She told me you-all were moving West this spring – said this was her last day. She asked if she might ride out with our wagons to the rendezvous. Well – '

'That's a fine horse you got there,' interrupted young Jed Wingate. 'Spanish?'

'Yes, sir.'

'Wild?'

'Oh, no, not now; only of rather good spirit. Ride him if you like. Gallop back, if you'd like to try him, and tell my people to come on and park in here. I'd like a word or so with Mr Wingate.'

With a certain difficulty, yet insistent, Jed swung into the deep saddle, sitting the restive, rearing horse well enough withal, and soon was off at a fast pace down the trail. They saw him pull up at the head of the caravan and motion, wide armed, to the riders, the train not halting at all.

He joined the two equestrian figures on ahead, the girl and the young man whom his mother had named as Sam Woodhull. They could see him shaking hands, then doing a curvet or so to show off his newly borrowed mount.

'He takes well to riding, your son,' said the newcomer approvingly.

'He's been crazy to get West,' assented the father. 'Wants to get among the buffalo.'

'We all do,' said Will Banion. 'None left in Kentucky this generation back; none now in Missouri. The Plains!' His eye gleamed.

'That's Sam Woodhull along,' resumed Molly Wingate. 'He was with Doniphan.'

'Yes.'

Banion spoke so shortly that the good dame, owner of a sought-for daughter, looked at him keenly.

'He lived at Liberty, too. I've known Molly to write of him.'

'Yes?' suddenly and with vigour. 'She knows him then?'

'Why, yes.'

'So do I,' said Banion simply. 'He was in our regiment – captain and adjutant, paymaster and quartermaster-chief, too, sometimes. The Army Regulations never meant much with Doniphan's column. We did as we liked – and did the best we could, even with paymasters and quarter-masters!'

He coloured suddenly, and checked, sensitive to a possible charge of jealousy before this keen-eyed mother of a girl whose beauty had been the talk of the settlement now for more than a year.

The rumours of the charm of Molly Wingate – Little Molly, as her father always called her to distinguish her from her mother – now soon were to have actual and undeniable verification to the eye of any sceptic who mayhap had doubted mere rumours of a woman's beauty. The three advance figures – the girl, Woodhull, her brother Jed – broke away and raced over the remaining few hundred yards, coming up abreast, laughing in the glee of youth exhilarated by the feel of good horseflesh under knee and the breath of a vital morning air.

As they flung off, Will Banion scarce gave a look to his own excited steed. He was first with a hand to Molly Wingate as she sprang lightly down, anticipating her other cavalier, Woodhull, who frowned, none too well pleased, as he dismounted.

Molly Wingate ran up and caught her mother in her strong young arms, kissing her roundly, her eyes shining, her cheeks flushed in the excitement of the hour, the additional excitement of the presence of these young men. She must kiss someone.

Yes, the rumours were true, and more than true. The young school-teacher could well carry her title as the belle of old Liberty town here on the far frontier. A lovely lass of eighteen years or so, she was, blue of eye and of abundant red-brown hair of that tint which ever has turned the eyes and heads of men. Her mouth, smiling to show white, even teeth, was wide enough for comfort in a kiss, and turned up strongly at the corners, so that her face would seem always sunny and carefree, were it not for the recurrent grave, almost sombre look of the wide-set eyes in moments of repose.

Above the middle height of woman's stature, she had none of the lank irregularity of the typical frontier woman of the early ague lands; but was round and well developed. Above the open collar of her brown riding costume stood the flawless column of a fair and tall white throat. New ripened into womanhood, wholly fit for love, gay of youth and its racing veins, what wonder Molly Wingate could have chosen not from two but twenty suitors of the best in all that countryside? Her conquests had been many since the time when, as a young girl, and fulfilling her parents' desire to educate their daughter, she had come all the way from the Sangamon country of Illinois to the best school then existent so far west – Clay Seminary, of quaint old Liberty.

The touch of dignity gained of the ancient traditions of the South, never lost in two generations west of the Appalachians, remained about the young girl now, so that she rather might have classed above her parents. They, moving from Kentucky into Indiana, from Indiana into Illinois, and now on to Oregon, never in all their toiling days had forgotten their reverence for the gentlemen and ladies who once were their ancestors east of the Blue Ridge. They valued education – felt that it belonged to them, at least through their children.

Education, betterment, progress, advance – those things perhaps lay in the vague ambitions of twice two hundred men who now lay in camp at the border of our unknown empire. They were all Americans – second, third, fourth generation Americans. Wild, uncouth, rude, unlettered, many or most of them, none the less there stood among them now and again some tall flower of that culture for which they ever hungered; for which they fought; for which they now adventured yet again.

Surely American also were these two young men whose eyes now unconsciously followed Molly Wingate in hot craving, even on a morning thus far breakfastless, for the young leader had ordered his wagons on to the rendezvous before crack of day. Of the two, young Woodhull, planter and man of means, mentioned by Molly's mother as open suitor, himself at first sight had not seemed so ill a figure, either. Tall, sinewy, well clad for the place and day, even more foppish than Banion in boot and glove, he would have passed well among the damsels of any courthouse day. The saddle and bridle of his mount also were a trace to the elegant, and the horse itself, a classy chestnut that showed bluegrass blood, even then had cost a pretty penny somewhere, that was sure.

Sam Woodhull, now moving with a half-dozen wagons of his own out to Oregon, was reputed well-to-do; reputed also to be well skilled at cards, at weapons and at women. Townsmen accorded him first place with Molly Wingate, the beauty from east of the river, until Will Banion came back from the wars. Since then had been another manner of war, that as ancient as male and female.

That Banion had known Woodhull in the field in Mexico he already had let slip. What had been the cause of his sudden pulling up of his starting tongue? Would he have spoken too much of that acquaintance? Perhaps a closer look at the loose lips, the high cheeks, the narrow, close-set eyes of young Woodhull, his rather assertive air, his slight, indefinable swagger, his slouch in standing, might have confirmed some sceptic disposed to analysis who would have guessed him less than strong of soul and character. For the most part, such sceptics were lacking.

By this time the last belated unit of the Oregon caravan was at hand. The feature of the dusty drivers could be seen. Unlike Wingate, the newly chosen master of the train, who had horses and mules about him, the young leader, Banion, captained only ox teams. They came now, slow footed, steady, low headed, irresistible, indomitable, the same locomotive power that carried the hordes of Asia into Eastern Europe long ago. And, as in the days of that invasion the conquerors carried their households, their flocks and herds with them, so now did these half-savage Saxon folk have with them their all.

Lean boys, brown, barefooted girls flanked the trail with driven stock. Chickens clucked in coops at wagonside. Uncounted children thrust out tousled heads from the openings of the canvas covers. Dogs beneath, jostling the tar buckets, barked in hostile salutation. Women in slatted sunbonnets turned impassive gaze from the high front seats, back of which, swung to the bows by leather loops, hung the inevitable family rifle in each wagon. And now, at the tail gate of every wagon, lashed fast for its last long journey, hung also the family plough.

It was '48, and the grass was up. On to Oregon! The ark of our covenant with progress was passing out. Almost it might have been said to have held every living thing, like that other ark of old.

Banion hastened to one side, where a grassy level beyond the little stream still offered stance. He raised a hand in gesture to the right. A sudden note of command came into his voice, lingering from late military days.

'By the right and left flank – wheel! March!'

With obvious training, the wagons broke apart, alternating right and left, until two long columns were formed. Each of these advanced, curving out, then drawing in, until a long ellipse, closed at front and rear, was formed methodically and without break or flaw. It was the barricade of the Plains, the moving fortresses of our soldiers of fortune, going West, across the Plains, across the Rockies, across the deserts that lay beyond.

They did not know all these dangers, but they thus were ready for any that might come.

'Look, mother!' Molly Wingate pointed with kindling eye to the wagon manoeuvre. 'We trained them all day yesterday, and long before. Perfect!'

Her gaze mayhap sought the tall figure of the young commander, chosen by older men above his fellow townsman, Sam Woodhull, as captain of the Liberty train. But he now had other duties in his own wagon group.

Ceased now the straining creak of gear and came rattle of yokes as the pins were loosed. Cattle guards appeared and drove the work animals apart to graze. Women clambered down from wagon seats. Sober-faced children gathered their little arms full of wood for the belated breakfast fires; boys came down for water at the stream.

The west-bound paused at the Missouri, as once they had paused at the Don.

A voice arose, of some young man back among the wagons busy at his work, paraphrasing an ante-bellum air:

> 'Oh, then, Susannah,
> Don't you cry fer me!
> I'm goin' out to Oregon,
> With my banjo on my knee!'

CHAPTER 2

The Edge of the World

More than two thousand men, women and children waited on the Missouri for the green fully to tinge the grasses of the prairies farther west. The waning town of Independence had quadrupled its population in thirty days. Boats discharged their customary western cargo at the newer landing on the river, not far above that town; but it all was not enough. Men of upper Missouri and lower Iowa had driven in herds of oxen, horses, mules; but there were not enough of these. Rumours came that a hundred wagons would take the Platte this year via the Council Bluffs, higher up the Missouri; others would join on from St Jo and Leavenworth.

March had come, when the wild turkey gobbled and strutted re-splendent in the forest lands. April had passed, and the wild fowl had gone north. May, and the upland plovers now were nesting all across the prairies. But daily had more wagons come, and neighbours had waited for neighbours, tardy at the great rendezvous. The encampment, scattered up and down the river front, had become more and more congested. Men began to know one another, families became acquainted, the gradual sifting and shifting in social values began. Knots and groups began to talk of some sort of accepted government for the common good.

They now were at the edge of the law. Organised society did not exist this side of the provisional government of Oregon, devised as a *modus vivendi* during the joint occupancy of that vast region with Great Britain – an arrangement terminated not longer than two years before. There must be some sort of law and leadership between the Missouri and the Columbia. Amid much bickering of petty politics, Jesse Wingate had some four days ago been chosen for the thankless task of train captain. Though that office had small authority and less means of enforcing its commands, none the less the train leader must be a man of courage, resource and decision. Those of the earlier arrivals who passed by his well-organised camp of forty-odd wagons from the Sangamon country of Illinois said that Wingate seemed to know the business of the trail. His affairs ran smoothly, he was well equipped and seemed a man of means. Some said he had three thousand in gold at the bottom of his cargo. Moreover – and this appeared important among the Northern element, at that time predominant in the rendezvous – he was not a Calhoun Secesh, or even a Benton Democrat, but an out-and-out, antislavery, free-soil man. And the provisional constitution of Oregon, devised by thinking men of two great nations, had said that Oregon should be free soil for ever.

Already there were mutterings in 1848 of the coming conflict which a certain lank young lawyer of Springfield, in the Sangamon country – Lincoln his name was – two years ago among his personal friends had predicted as inevitable. In a personnel made up of bold souls from both sides the Ohio, politics could not be avoided even on the trail; nor were these men the sort to avoid politics. Sometimes at their camp fire, after the caravan election, Wingate and his wife, and their son Jed, would compare notes, in a day when personal politics and national geography meant more than they do today.

'Listen, son,' Wingate one time concluded. 'All that talk of a railroad across this country to Oregon is silly, of course. But it's all going to be one country. The talk is that the treaty with Mexico must give us a slice of land from Texas to the Pacific, and a big one; all of it was taken for the sake of slavery. Not so Oregon – that's free for ever. This talk of splitting this country, North and South, don't go with me. The Alleghanies didn't divide it. Burr couldn't divide it. The Mississippi hasn't divided it, or the Missouri, so rest assured the Ohio can't. No, nor the Rockies can't! A railroad? No, of course not. But all the same, a practical wagon road from free soil to free soil – I reckon that was my platform, like enough. It made me captain.'

'No, 'twasn't that, Jesse,' said his wife. 'That ain't what put you in for train captain. It was your blamed impatience. Some of them lower Ioway men, them that first nominated you in the train meeting – town meeting – what you call it, they seen where you'd been ploughing along here just to keep your hand in. One of them says to me, "Ploughing, hey? Can't wait? Well, that's what we're going out for, ain't it – to plough?" says he. "That's the clean quill," says he. So they 'lected you, Jesse. And the Lord ha' mercy on your soul!'

Now the arrival of so large a new contingent as this of the Liberty train under young Banion made some sort of post-election ratification necessary, so that Wingate felt it incumbent to call the head men of the latecomers into consultation if for no better than reasons of courtesy. He dispatched his son Jed to the Banion park to ask the attendance of Banion, Woodhull and such of his associates as he liked to bring, at any suiting hour. Word came back that the Liberty men would join the Wingate conference around eleven of that morning, at which time the hour of the jump-off could be set.

CHAPTER 3

The Rendezvous

As to the start of the great wagon train, little time, indeed, remained. For days, in some instances for weeks, the units of the train had lain here on the border, and the men were growing restless. Some had come a thousand miles and now were keen to start out for more than two thousand miles additional. The grass was up. The men from Illinois, Indiana, Ohio, Iowa, Missouri, Kentucky, Arkansas fretted on the leash.

All along the crooked river front, on both sides from Independence to the river landing at Westport, the great spring caravan lay encamped, or housed in town. Now, on the last days of the rendezvous, a sort of hysteria seized the multitude. The sound of rifle fire was like that of a battle – every man was sighting-in his rifle. Singing and shouting went on everywhere. Someone fresh from the Mexican War had brought a drum, another a bugle. Without instructions, these began to sound their summons and continued all day long, at such times as the performers could spare from drink.

The Indians of the friendly tribes – Otos, Kaws, Osages – come in to trade, looked on in wonder at the revellings of the whites. The straggling street of each of the nearby river towns was full of massed wagons. The treble line of white tops, end to end, lay like a vast serpent, curving ahead to the West. Rivalry for the head of the column began. The sounds of the bugle set a thousand uncoordinated wheels spasmodically in motion. Organisation, system were as yet unknown in this rude and dominant democracy. Need was therefore for this final meeting in the interest of law, order and authority. Already some wagons had broken camp and moved on out into the main travelled road, which lay plain enough on westward, among the groves and glades of the valley of the Kaw. Each man wanted to be first to Oregon, no man wished to take the dust of his neighbour's wagon.

Wingate brought up all these matters at the train meeting of some three score men which assembled under the trees of his own encampment at eleven of the last morning. Most of the men he knew. Banion unobtrusively took a seat well to the rear of those who squatted on their heels or lolled full length on the grass.

After the fashion of the immemorial American town meeting, the beginning of all our government, Wingate called the meeting to order and stated its purposes. He then set forth his own ideas of the best manner for handling the trail work.

His plan, as he explained, was one long earlier perfected in the convoys of the old Santa Fe Trail. The wagons were to travel in close order. Four parallel columns, separated by not too great spaces, were to be maintained as much as possible, more especially towards nightfall. Of these, the outer two were to draw in together when camp was made, the other two to angle out, wagon lapping wagon, front and rear, thus making an oblong corral of the wagons, into which, through a gap, the work oxen were to be driven every night after they had fed. The tents and fires were to be outside of the corral unless in case of an Indian alarm, when the corral would represent a fortress.

The transport animals were to be hobbled each night. A guard, posted entirely around the corral and camp, was to be put out each night. Each man and each boy above fourteen was to be subject to guard duty under the ancient common law of the Plains, and from this duty no man might hope excuse unless actually too ill to walk; nor could any man offer to procure any substitute for himself. The watches were to be set as eight, each to stand guard one-fourth part of alternate nights, so that each man would get every other night undisturbed.

There were to be lieutenants, one for each of the four parallel divisions of the train; also eight sergeants of the guard, each of whom was to select and handle the men of the watch under him. No wagon might change its own place in the train after the start, dust or no dust.

When Wingate ended his exposition and looked around for approval it was obvious that many of these regulations met with disfavour at the start. The democracy of the train was one in which each man wanted his own way. Leaning head to head, speaking low, men grumbled at all this fuss and feathers and army stuff. Some of these were friends and backers in the late election. Nettled by their silence, or by their murmured comments, Wingate arose again.

'Well, you have heard my plan, men,' said he. 'The Santa Fe men worked it up, and used it for years, as you all know. They always got through. If there's anyone here knows a better way, and one that's got more experience back of it, I'd like to have him get up and say so.'

Silence for a time greeted this also. The Northern men, Wingate's partisans, looked uncomfortably one to the other. It was young Wood-hull, of the Liberty contingent, who rose at length.

'What Cap'n Wingate has said sounds all right to me,' said he. 'He's a new friend of mine – I never saw him till two-three hours ago – but I know about him. What he says about the Santa Fe fashion I know for true. As some of you know, I was out that way, up the Arkansas, with Doniphan, for the Stars and Stripes. Talk about wagon travel – you got to have a regular system or you have everything in a mess. This here, now, is a lot like so many volunteers enlisting for war. There's always a sort of preliminary election of officers; sort of shaking down and shaping up. I wasn't here when Cap'n Wingate was elected – our wagons were some late – but speaking for our men, I'd move to ratify his choosing, and that means to ratify his regulations. I'm wondering if I don't get a second for that?'

Some of the bewhiskered men who sat about him stirred, but cast their eyes towards their own captain, young Banion, whose function as their spokesman had thus been usurped by his defeated rival, Woodhull. Perhaps few of them suspected the *argumentum ad hominem* – or rather *ad feminam* – in Woodhull's speech.

Banion alone knew this favour-currying when he saw it, and knew well enough the real reason. It was Molly! Rivals indeed they were, these two, and in more ways than one. But Banion held his peace until one quiet father of a family spoke up.

'I reckon our own train captain, that we elected in case we didn't throw in with the big train, had ought to say what he thinks about it all.'

Will Banion now rose composedly and bowed to the leader.

'I'm glad to second Mr Woodhull's motion to throw our vote and our train for Captain Wingate and the big train,' said he. 'We'll ratify his captaincy, won't we?'

The nods of his associates now showed assent, and Wingate needed no more confirmation.

'In general, too, I would ratify Captain Wingate's scheme. But might I make a few suggestions?'

'Surely – go on.' Wingate half rose.

'Well then, I'd like to point out that we've got twice as far to go as the Santa Fe traders, and over a very different country – more dangerous, less known, harder to travel. We've many times more wagons than any Santa Fe train ever had, and we've hundreds of loose cattle along. That means a sweeping off of the grass at every stop, and grass we've got to have or the train stops.

'Besides our own call on grass, I know there'll be five thousand Mormons at least on the trail ahead of us this spring – they've crossed the river from here to the Bluffs, and they're out on the Platte right now. We take what grass they leave us.

'What I'm trying to get at, captain, is this: We might have to break into smaller detachments now and again. We could not possibly always keep alignment in four columns.'

'And then we'd be open to any Indian attack,' interrupted Woodhull.

'We might have to fight some of the time, yes,' rejoined Banion; 'but we'll have to travel all the time, and we'll have to graze our stock all the time. On that one basic condition our safety rests – grass and plenty of it. We're on a long journey.

'You see, gentlemen,' he added, smiling, 'I was with Doniphan also.

We learned a good many things. For instance, I'd rather see each horse on a thirty-foot picket rope, anchored safe each night, than to trust to any hobbles. A homesick horse can travel miles, hobbled, in a night. Horses are a lot of trouble.

'Now, I see that about a fourth of our people, including Captain Wingate, have horses and mules and not ox transport. I wish they all could trade for oxen before they start. Oxen last longer and fare better. They are easier to herd. They can be used for food in the hard first year out in Oregon. The Indians don't steal oxen – they like buffalo better – but they'll take any chance to run off horses or even mules. If they do, that means your women and children are on foot. You know the story of the Donner party, two years ago – on foot, in the snow. They died, and worse than died, just this side of California.'

Men of Iowa, of Illinois, Ohio, Indiana, began to nod to one another, approving the words of this young man.

'He talks sense,' said a voice aloud.

'Well, I'm talking a whole lot, I know,' said Banion gravely, 'but this is the time and place for our talking. I'm for throwing in with the Wingate train, as I've said. But will Captain Wingate let me add even just a few words more?

'For instance, I would suggest that we ought to have a record of all our personnel. Each man ought to be required to give his own name and late residence, and the names of all in his party. He should be obliged to show that his wagon is in good condition, with spare bolts, yokes, tyres, bows and axles, and extra shoes for the stock. Each wagon ought to be required to carry anyhow half a side of rawhide, and the usual tools of the farm and the trail, as well as proper weapons and abundance of ammunition.

'No man ought to be allowed to start with this caravan with less supplies, for each mouth of his wagon, than one hundred pounds of flour. One hundred and fifty or even two hundred would be much better – there is loss and shrinkage. At least half as much of bacon, twenty pounds of coffee, fifty of sugar would not be too much in my own belief. About double the pro rata of the Santa Fe caravans is little enough, and those whose transport power will let them carry more supplies ought to start full loaded, for no man can tell the actual duration of this journey, or what food may be needed before we get across. One may have to help another.'

Even Wingate joined in the outspoken approval of this, and Banion, encouraged, went on, 'Some other things, men, since you have asked each man to speak freely. We're not hunters, but homemakers. Each family, I suppose, has a plough and seed for the first crop. We ought, too, to find out all our blacksmiths, for I promise you we'll need them. We ought to have a half-dozen forges and as many anvils, and a lot of irons for the wagons.

'I suppose, too, you've located all your doctors; also all your preachers – you needn't camp them all together. Personally I believe in Sunday rest and Sunday services. We're taking church and state and home and law along with us, day by day, men, and we're not just trappers and adventurers. The fur trade's gone.

'I even think we ought to find out our musicians – it's good to have a bugler, if you can. And at night, when the people are tired and disheartened, music is good to help them pull together.'

The bearded men who listened nodded yet again.

'About schools, now – the other trains that went out, the Applegates in 1843, the Donners of 1846, each train, I believe, had regular schools along, with hours each day.

'Do you think I'm right about all this? I'm sure I don't want Captain Wingate to be offended. I'm not dividing his power. I'm only trying to stiffen it.'

Woodhull arose, a sneer on his face, but a hand pushed him down. A tall Missourian stood before him.

'Right ye air, Will!' said he. 'Ye've an old head, an' we kin trust hit. Ef hit wasn't Cap'n Wingate is more older than you, an' already done elected, I'd be for choosin' ye fer cap'n o' this here hull train right now. Seein' hit's the way hit is, I move we vote to do what Will Banion has said is fitten. An' I move we-uns throw in with the big train, with Jess Wingate for cap'n. An' I move we allow one more day to git in supplies an' fixin's, an' trade hosses an' mules an' oxens, an' then we start day atter tomorrow mornin' when the bugle blows. Then hooray fer Oregon!'

There were cheers and a general rising, as though after finished business, which greeted this. Jesse Wingate, somewhat crestfallen and chagrined over the forward ways of this young man, of whom he never had heard till that very morning, put a perfunctory motion or so, asked loyalty and allegiance, and so forth.

But what they remembered was that he appointed as his wagon-column captains Sam Woodhull, of Missouri; Caleb Price, an Ohio man of substance; Simon Hall, an Indiana merchant; and a farmer by name of Kelsey, from Kentucky. To Will Banion the trainmaster assigned the most difficult and thankless task of the train, the captaincy of the cow column; that is to say, the leadership of the boys and men whose families were obliged to drive the loose stock of the train.

There were sullen mutterings over this in the Liberty column. Men whispered they would not follow Woodhull. As for Banion, he made no complaint, but smiled and shook hands with Wingate and all his lieutenants and declared his own loyalty and that of his men; then left for his own little adventure of a half-dozen wagons which he was freighting out to Laramie – bacon, flour and sugar, for the most part; each wagon driven by a neighbour or a neighbour's son. Among these already arose open murmurs of discontent over the way their own contingent had been treated. Banion had to mend a potential split before the first wheel had rolled westward up the Kaw.

The men of the meeting passed back among their neighbours and families, and spoke with more seriousness than hitherto. The rifle firing ended, the hilarity lessened that afternoon. In the old times the keelboatmen bound west started out singing. The pack-train men of the fur trade went shouting and shooting, and the confident hilarity of the Santa Fe wagon caravans was a proverb. But now, here in the great Oregon train, matters were quite otherwise. There were women and children along. An unsmiling gravity marked them all. When the dusky velvet of the prairie night settled on almost the last day of the rendezvous it brought a general feeling of anxiety, dread, uneasiness, fear. Now, indeed, and at last, all these realised what was the thing that they had undertaken.

To add yet more to the natural apprehensions of men and women embarking on so stupendous an adventure, all manner of rumours now continually passed from one company to another. It was said that five thousand Mormons, armed to the teeth, had crossed the river at St Joseph and were lying in wait on the Platte, determined to take revenge for the persecutions they had suffered in Missouri and Illinois. Another story said that the Kaw Indians, hitherto friendly, had banded together for robbery and were only waiting for the train to appear. A still more popular story had it that a party of several Englishmen had hurried ahead on the trail to excite all the savages to waylay and destroy the caravans, thus to wreak the vengeance of England upon the Yankees for the loss of Oregon. Much unrest arose over reports, hard to trace, to the effect that it was all a mistake about Oregon; that in reality it was a truly horrible country, unfit for human occupancy, and sure to prove the grave of any lucky enough to survive the horrors of the trail, which never yet had been truthfully reported. Some returned travellers from the West beyond the Rockies, who were hanging about the landing at the river, made it all worse by relating what purported to be actual experiences.

'If you ever get through to Oregon,' they said, 'you'll be ten years older than you are now. Your hair will be white, but not by age.'

The Great Dipper showed clear and close that night, as if one might almost pick off by hand the familiar stars of the traveller's constellation. Overhead countless brilliant points of lesser light enamelled the night mantle, matching the many camp fires of the great gathering. The wind blew soft and low. Night on the prairie is always solemn, and tonight the tense anxiety, the strained anticipation of more than two thousand souls invoked a brooding melancholy which it seemed even the stars must feel.

A dog, ominous, lifted his voice in a long, mournful howl which made mothers put out their hands to their babes. In answer a coyote in the grass raised a high, quavering cry, wild and desolate, the voice of the Far West.

CHAPTER 4

Fever of New Fortunes

The notes of a bugle, high and clear, sang reveille at dawn. Now came hurried activities of those who had delayed. The streets of the two frontier settlements were packed with ox teams, horses, wagons, cattle driven through. The frontier stores were stripped of their last supplies. One more day, and then on to Oregon!

Wingate broke his own camp early in the morning and moved out to the open country west of the landing, making a last bivouac at what would be the head of the train. He had asked his four lieutenants to join him there. Hall, Price and Kelsey headed in with straggling wagons to form the nucleuses of their columns; but the morning wore on and the Missourians, now under Woodhull, had not yet broken park. Wingate waited moodily.

Now at the edge of affairs human apprehensions began to assert themselves, especially among the womenfolk. Even stout Molly Wingate gave way to doubt and fears. Her husband caught her, apron to eyes, sitting on the wagon tongue at ten in the morning, with her pots and pans unpacked.

'What?' he exclaimed. 'You're not weakening? Haven't you as much courage as those Mormon women on ahead? Some of them pushing carts, I've heard.'

'They've done it for religion, Jess. Oregon ain't no religion for me.'

'Yet it has music for a man's ears, Molly.'

'Hush! I've heard it all for the last two years. What happened to the Donners two years back? And four years ago it was the Applegates left home in old Missouri to move to Oregon. Who will ever know where their bones are laid? Look at our land we left – rich – black and rich as any in the world. What corn, what wheat – why, everything grew well in Illinois!'

'Yes, and cholera below us wiping out the people, and the trouble over slave-holding working up the river more and more, and the sun blazing in the summer, while in the wintertime we froze!'

'Well, as for food, we never saw any part of Kentucky with half so much grass. We had no turkeys at all there, and where we left you could kill one any gobbling time. The pigeons roosted not four miles from us. In the woods along the river even a woman could kill coons and squirrels, all we'd need – no need for us to eat rabbits like the Mormons. Our chicken yard was fifty miles across. The young ones'd be flying by roasting-ear time – and in fall the sloughs was black with ducks and geese. Enough and to spare we had; and our land opening; and Molly teaching the school, with twelve dollars a month cash for it, and Jed learning his blacksmith trade before he was eighteen. How could we ask more? What better will we do in Oregon?'

'You always throw the wet blanket on Oregon, Molly.'

'It is so far!'

'How do we know it is far? We know men and women have crossed, and we know the land is rich. Wheat grows fifty bushels to the acre, the trees are big as the spires on meeting houses, the fish run by millions in the streams. Yet the winters have little snow. A man can live there and not slave out a life.

'Besides' – and the frontier now spoke in him – 'this country is too old, too long settled. My father killed his elk and his buffalo, too, in Kentucky; but that was before my day. I want the buffalo. I crave to see the Plains, Molly. What real American does not?'

Mrs Wingate threw her apron over her face.

'The Oregon fever has witched you, Jesse!' she exclaimed between dry sobs.

Wingate was silent for a time.

'Corn ought to grow in Oregon,' he said at last.

'Yes, but does it?'

'I never heard it didn't. The soil is rich, and you can file on six hundred and forty acres. There's your donation claim, four times bigger than any land you can file on here. We sold out at ten dollars an acre – more'n our land really was worth, or ever is going to be worth. It's just the speculators says any different. Let 'em have it, and us move on. That's the way money's made, and always has been made, all across the United States.'

'Huh! You talk like a land speculator your own self!'

'Well, if it ain't the movers make a country, what does? If we don't settle Oregon, how long'll we hold it? The preachers went through to Oregon with horses. Like as not even the Applegates got their wagons across. Like enough they got through. I want to see the country before it gets too late for a good chance, Molly. First thing you know buffalo'll be getting scarce out West, too, like deer was getting scarcer on the Sangamon. We ought to give our children as good a chance as we had ourselves.'

'As good a chance! Haven't they had as good a chance as we ever had? Didn't our land more'n thribble, from a dollar and a quarter? It may thribble again, time they're old as we are now.'

'That's a long time to wait.'

'It's a long time to live a lifetime, but everybody's got to live it.'

She stood, looking at him.

'Look at all the good land right in here! Here we got walnut and hickory and oak – worlds of it. We got sassafras and pawpaw and hazel brush. We get all the hickory nuts and pecans we like any fall. The wild plums is better'n any in Kentucky; and as for grapes, they're big as your thumb, and thousands, on the river. Wait till you see the plum and grape jell I could make this fall!'

'Women – always thinking of jell!'

'But we got every herb here we need – boneset and sassafras and Injun physic and bark for the fever. There ain't nothing you can name we ain't got right here, or on the Sangamon, yet you talk of taking care of our children. Huh! We've moved five times since we was married. Now just as we got into a good country, where a woman could dry corn and put up jell, and where a man could raise some hogs, why, you wanted to move again – plumb out to Oregon! I tell you, Jesse Wingate, hogs is a blame sight better to tie to than buffalo! You talk like you had to settle Oregon!'

'Well, haven't I got to? Somehow it seems a man ain't making up his own mind when he moves West. Pap moved twice in Kentucky, once in Tennessee, and then over to Missouri, after you and me was married and moved up into Indiana, before we moved over into Illinois. He said to me – and I know it for the truth – he couldn't hardly tell who it was or what it was hitched up the team. But first thing he knew, there the old wagon stood, front of the house, cover all on, plough hanging on behind, tar bucket under the wagon, and dog and all. All he had to do, pap said, was just to climb up on the front seat and speak to the team. My maw, she climbed up on the seat with him. Then they moved – on West. You know, Molly. My maw, she climbed up on the front seat – '

His wife suddenly turned to him, the tears still in her eyes.

'Yes, and Jesse Wingate, and you know it, your wife's as good a woman as your maw! When the wagon was a-standing, cover on, and you on the front seat, I climbed up by you, Jess, same as I always have and always will. Haven't I always? You know that. But it's harder on women, moving is. They care more for a house that's rain-tight in a storm.'

'I know you did, Molly,' said her husband soberly.

'I suppose I can pack my jells in a box and put it in the wagon, anyways.' She was drying her eyes.

'Why, yes, I reckon so. And then a few sacks of dried corn will go mighty well on the road.'

'One thing' – she turned on him in wifely fury – 'you shan't keep me from taking my bureau and my six chairs all the way across! No, nor my garden seeds, all I saved. No, nor yet my rose roots that I'm taking along. We got to have a home, Jess – we got to have a home! There's Jed and Molly coming on.'

'Where's Molly now?' suddenly asked her husband. 'She'd ought to be helping you right now.'

'Oh, back at the camp, I s'pose – her and Jed, too. I told her to pick a mess of dandelion greens and bring it over. Larking around with them young fellows, like enough. Huh! She'll have less time. If Jed has to ride herd, Molly's got to take care of that team of big mules, and drive 'em all day in the light wagon too. I reckon if she does that, and teaches night school right along, she won't be feeling so gay.'

'They tell me folks has got married going across,' she added, 'not to mention buried. One book we had said, up on the Platte, two years back, there was a wedding and a birth and a burying in one train, all inside of one hour, and all inside of one mile. That's Oregon!'

'Well, I reckon it's life, ain't it?' rejoined her husband. 'One thing, I'm not keen to have Molly pay too much notice to that young fellow Banion – him they said was a leader of the Liberty wagons. Huh, he ain't leader now!'

'You like Sam Woodhull better for Molly, Jess?'

'Some ways. He falls in along with my ideas. He ain't so apt to make trouble on the road. He sided in with me right along at the last meeting.'

'He done that? Well, his father was a sheriff once, and his uncle, Judge Henry D. Showalter, he got into Congress. Politics! But some folks said the Banions was the best family. Kentucky, they was. Well, comes to siding in, Jess, I reckon it's Molly herself'll count more in that than either o' them or either o' us. She's eighteen past. Another year and she'll be an old maid. If there's a wedding going across – '

'There won't be,' said her husband shortly. 'If there is it won't be her and no William Banion, I'm saying that.'

CHAPTER 5

The Black Spaniard

Meantime the younger persons referred to in the frank discussion of Wingate and his wife were occupying themselves in their own fashion their last day in camp. Molly, her basket full of dandelion leaves, was reluctant to leave the shade of the grove by the stream, and Jed had business with the team of great mules that Molly was to drive on the trail.

As for the Liberty train, its oval remained unbroken, the men and women sitting in the shade of the wagons. Their outfitting had been done so carefully that little now remained for attention on the last day, but the substantial men of the contingent seemed far from eager to be on their way. Groups here and there spoke in monosyllables, sullenly. They wanted to join the great train, had voted to do so; but the cavalier deposing of their chosen man Banion – who before them all at the meeting had shown himself fit to lead – and the cool appointment of Woodhull in his place had on reflection seemed to them quite too high-handed a proposition. They said so now.

'Where's Woodhull now?' demanded the bearded man who had championed Banion. 'I see Will out rounding up his cows, but Sam Woodhull ain't turned a hand to hooking up to pull in west o' town with the others.'

'That's easy,' smiled another. 'Sam Woodhull is where he's always going to be – hanging around the Wingate girl. He's over at their camp now.'

'Well, I dunno's I blame him so much for that, neither. And he kin stay there fer all o' me. Fer one, I won't foller no Woodhull, least o' all Sam Woodhull, soldier or no soldier. I'll pull out when I git ready, and tomorrow mornin' is soon enough fer me. We kin jine on then, if so's we like.'

Someone turned on his elbow, nodded over his shoulder. They heard hoof beats. Banion came up, fresh from his new work on the herd. He asked for Woodhull, and learning his whereabouts trotted across the intervening glade.

'That's shore a hoss he rides,' said one man.

'An' a shore man a-ridin' of him,' nodded another. 'He may ride front o' the train an' not back o' hit, even yet.'

Molly Wingate sat on the grass in the little grove, curling a chain of dandelion stems. Near by Sam Woodhull, in his best, lay on the sward regarding her avidly, a dull fire in his dark eyes. He was so enamoured of the girl as to be almost unfit for aught else. For weeks he had kept close to her. Not that Molly seemed overmuch to notice or encourage him. Only, woman fashion, she ill liked to send away any attentive male. Just now she was uneasy. She guessed that if it were not for the presence of her brother Jed near by, this man would declare himself unmistakably.

If the safety of numbers was her main concern, perhaps that was what made Molly Wingate's eye light up when she heard the hoofs of Will Banion's horse splashing in the little stream. She sprang to her feet, waving a hand gayly.

'Oh, so there you are!' she exclaimed. 'I was wondering if you'd be over before Jed and I left for the prairie. Father and mother have moved on out west of town. We're all ready for the jump-off. Are you?'

'Yes, tomorrow by sun,' said Banion, swinging out of saddle and forgetting any errand he might have had. 'Then it's on to Oregon!'

He nodded to Woodhull, who little more than noticed him. Molly advanced to where Banion's horse stood, nodding and pawing restively as was his wont. She stroked his nose, patted his sweat-soaked neck.

'What a pretty horse you have, major,' she said. 'What's his name?'

'I call him Pronto,' smiled Banion. 'That means sudden.'

'He fits the name. May I ride him?'

'What? You ride him?'

'Yes, surely. I'd love to. I can ride anything. That funny saddle would do – see how big and high the horn is, good as the fork of a lady's saddle.'

'Yes, but the stirrup!'

'I'll put my foot in between the flaps above the stirrup. Help me up, sir?'

'I'd rather not.'

Molly pouted.

'Stingy!'

'But no woman ever rode that horse – not many men but me. I don't know what he'd do.'

'Only one way to find out.'

Jed, approaching, joined the conversation.

'I rid him,' said he. 'He's a goer all right, but he ain't mean.'

'I don't know whether he would be bad or not with a lady,' Banion still argued. 'These Spanish horses are always wild. They never do get over it. You've got to be a rider.'

'You think I'm not a rider? I'll ride him now to show you! I'm not afraid of horses.'

'That's right,' broke in Sam Woodhull. 'But, Miss Molly, I wouldn't tackle that horse if I was you. Take mine.'

'But I will! I've not been horseback for a month. We've all got to ride or drive or walk a thousand miles. I can ride him, man-saddle and all. Help me up, sir!'

Banion walked to the horse, which flung a head against him, rubbing a soft muzzle up and down.

'He seems gentle,' said he. 'I've pretty well topped him off this morning. If you're sure – '

'Help me up, one of you!'

It was Woodhull who sprang to her, caught her up under the arms and lifted her fully gracious weight to the saddle. Her left foot by fortune found the cleft in the stirrup fender, her right leg swung around the tall horn, hastily concealed by a clutch at her skirt even as she grasped the heavy knotted reins. It was then too late. She must ride.

Banion caught at a cheek strap as he saw Woodhull's act, and the horse was the safer for an instant. But in terror or anger at his unusual burden, with flapping skirt and no grip on his flanks, the animal reared and broke away from them all. An instant and he was plunging across the stream for the open glade, his head low.

He did not yet essay the short, stiff-legged action of the typical bucker, but made long, reaching, low-headed plunges, seeking his own freedom in that way, perhaps half in some equine wonder of his own. None the less the wrenching of the girl's back, the leverage on her flexed knee, unprotected, were unmistakable.

The horse reared again and yet again, high, striking out as she checked him. He was getting in a fury now, for his rider still was in place. Then with one savage sidewise shake of his head after another he plunged this way and that, rail-fencing it for the open prairie. It looked like a bolt, which with a horse of his spirit and stamina meant but one thing, no matter how long delayed.

It all happened in a flash. Banion caught at the rein too late, ran after – too slow, of course. The girl was silent, shaken, but still riding. No footman could aid her now.

With a leap, Banion was in the saddle of Woodhull's horse, which had been left at hand, its bridle down. He drove in the spurs and headed across the flat at the top speed of the fast and racy chestnut – no match, perhaps, for the black Spaniard, were the latter once extended, but favoured now by the angle of the two.

Molly had not uttered a word or cry, either to her mount or in appeal for aid. In sooth she was too frightened to do so. But she heard the rush of hoofs and the high call of Banion's voice back of her: 'Ho, Pronto! Pronto! *Vien' aqui!*'

Something of a marvel it was, and showing companionship of man and horse on the trail; but suddenly the mad black ceased his plunging. Turning, he trotted whinnying as though for aid, obedient to his master's command, 'Come here!' An instant and Banion had the cheek strap. Another and he was off, with Molly Wingate, in a white dead faint, in his arms.

By now others had seen the affair from their places in the wagon park. Men and women came hurrying. Banion laid the girl down, sought to raise her head, drove back the two horses, ran with his hat to the stream for water. By that time Woodhull had joined him, in advance of the people from the park.

'What do you mean, you damned fool, you, by riding my horse off without my consent!' he broke out. 'If she ain't dead – that damned wild horse – you had the gall – '

Will Banion's self-restraint at last was gone. He made one answer, voicing all his acquaintance with Sam Woodhull, all his opinion of him, all his future attitude in regard to him.

He dropped his hat to the ground, caught off one wet glove, and with a long backhanded sweep struck the cuff of it full and hard across Sam Woodhull's face.

CHAPTER 6

Issue Joined

There were dragoon revolvers in the holsters at Woodhull's saddle. He made a rush for a weapon – indeed, the crack of the blow had been so sharp that the nearest men thought a shot had been fired – but swift as was his leap, it was not swift enough. The long, lean hand of the bearded Missourian grasped his wrist even as he caught at a pistol grip. He turned a livid face to gaze into a cold and small blue eye.

'No, ye don't, Sam!' said the other, who was first of those who came up running.

Even as a lank woman stooped to raise the head of Molly Wingate, the sinewy arm back of the hand whirled Woodhull around so that he faced Banion, who had not made a move.

'Will ain't got no weapon, an' ye know it,' went on the same cool voice. 'What ye mean – a murder, besides that?'

He nodded towards the girl. By now the crowd surged between the two men, voices rose.

'He struck me!' broke out Woodhull. 'Let me go! He struck me!'

'I know he did,' said the intervener. 'I heard it. I don't know why. But whether it was over the girl or not, we ain't goin' to see this other feller shot down till we know more about hit. Ye can meet –'

'Of course, any time.'

Banion was drawing on his glove. The woman had lifted Molly, straightened her clothing.

'All blood!' said one. 'That saddle horn! What made her ride that critter?'

The Spanish horse stood facing them now, ears forward, his eyes showing through his forelock not so much in anger as in curiosity. The men hustled the two antagonists apart.

'Listen, Sam,' went on the tall Missourian, still with his grip on Wood- hull's wrist. 'We'll see ye both fair. Ye've got to fight now, in course – that's the law, an' I ain't learned it in the fur trade o' the Rockies fer nothin', ner have you people here in the settlements. But I'll tell ye one thing, Sam Woodhull, ef ye make one move afore we-uns tell ye how an' when to make hit, I'll drop ye, shore's my name's Bill Jackson. Ye got to

922

wait, both on ye. We're startin' out, an' we kain't start out like a mob. Take yer time.'

'Any time, any way,' said Banion simply. 'No man can abuse me.'

'How'd you gentlemen prefer fer to fight?' enquired the man who had described himself as Bill Jackson, one of the fur brigaders of the Rocky Mountain Company; a man with a reputation of his own in Plains and mountain adventures of hunting, trading and scouting. 'Hit's yore ch'ice o' weapons, I reckon, Will. I reckon he challenged you-all.'

'I don't care. He'd have no chance on an even break with me, with any sort of weapon, and he knows that.'

Jackson cast free his man and ruminated over a chew of plug.

'Hit's over a gal,' said he at length, judicially. 'Hit ain't usual; but seein' as a gal don't pick atween men because one's a quicker shot than another, but because he's maybe stronger, or something like that, why, how'd knuckle and skull suit you two roosters, best man win and us to see hit fair? Hit's one of ye fer the gal, like enough. But not right now. Wait till we're on the trail and clean o' the law. I heern there's a sheriff round yere some'rs.'

'I'll fight him any way he likes, or any way you say,' said Banion. 'It's not my seeking. I only slapped him because he abused me for doing what he ought to have done. Yes, I rode his horse. If I hadn't that girl would have been killed. It's not his fault she wasn't. I didn't want her to ride that horse.'

'I don't reckon hit's so much a matter about a hoss as hit is about a gal,' remarked Bill Jackson sagely. 'Ye'll hatter fight. Well then, seein' as hit's about a gal, knuckle an' skull, is that right?'

He cast a glance around this group of other fighting men of a border day. They nodded gravely, but with glittering eyes.

'Well then, gentlemen' – and now he stood free of Woodhull – 'ye both give word ye'll make no break till we tell ye? I'll say, two-three days out?'

'Suits me,' said Woodhull savagely. 'I'll break his neck for him.'

'Any time that suits the gentleman to break my neck will please me,' said Will Banion indifferently. 'Say when, friends. Just now I've got to look after my cows. It seems to me our wagon master might very well look after his wagons.'

'That sounds!' commented Jackson. 'That sounds! Sam, git on about yer business, er ye kain't travel in the Liberty train nohow! An' don't ye make no break, in the dark especial, fer we kin track ye anywhere's. Ye'll fight fair fer once – an' ye'll fight!'

By now the group massed about these scenes had begun to relax, to spread. Women had Molly in hand as her eyes opened. Jed came up at a run with the mule team and the light wagon from the grove, and they got the girl into the seat with him, neither of them fully cognisant of what had gone on in the group of tight-mouthed men who now broke apart and sauntered silently back, each to his own wagon.

CHAPTER 7

The Jump-Off

With the first thin line of pink, the coyotes hanging on the flanks of the great encampment raised their immemorial salutation to the dawn. Their clamourings were stilled by a new and sterner voice – the notes of the bugle summoning sleepers of the last night to the duties of the first day. Down the line from watch to watch passed the Plains command, 'Catch up! Catch up!' It was morning of the jump-off.

Little fires began at the wagon messes or family bivouacs. Men, boys, barefooted girls went out into the dew-wet grass to round up the transport stock. A vast confusion, a medley of unskilled endeavour marked the hour. But after an hour's wait, adjusted to the situation, the next order passed down the line, 'Roll out! Roll out!'

And now the march to Oregon was at last begun! The first dust cut by an ox hoof was set in motion by the whip crack of a barefooted boy in jeans, who had no dream that he one day would rank high in the councils of his state, at the edge of an ocean which no prairie boy ever had envisioned.

The compass finger of the trail, leading out from the timber groves, pointed into a sea of green along the valley of the Kaw. The grass, not yet tall enough fully to ripple as it would a half month later, stood waving over the black-burned ground which the semi-civilised Indians had left the fall before. Flowers dotted it, sometimes white like bits of old ivory on the vast rug of spindrift – the pink verbena, the wild indigo, the larkspur and the wild geranium – all woven into a wondrous spangled carpet. At times also appeared the shy buds of the sweet wild rose, loveliest flower of the prairie. Tall rosin weeds began to thrust up rankly, banks of sunflowers prepared to fling their yellow banners miles wide. The opulent, inviting land lay in a ceaseless succession of easy undulations, stretching away illimitably to far horizons, 'in such exchanging pictures of grace and charm as raised the admiration of even these simple folk to a pitch bordering upon exaltation'.

Here lay the West, barbaric, abounding, beautiful. Surely it could mean no harm to any man.

The men lacked experience in column travel, the animals were unruly. The train formation – clumsily trying to conform to the orders of Wingate to travel in four parallel columns – soon lost order. At times the wagons halted to re-form. The leaders galloped back and forth, exhorting, adjuring and restoring little by little a certain system. But they dealt with independent men. On ahead the landscape seemed so wholly free of danger that to most of these the road to the Far West offered no more than a pleasure jaunt. Wingate and his immediate aids were well worn when at mid afternoon they halted, fifteen miles out from Westport.

'What in hell you pulling up so soon for?' demanded Sam Woodhull surlily, riding up from his own column, far at the rear, and accosting the train leader. 'We can go five miles farther, anyhow, and maybe ten. We'll never get across in this way.'

'This is the very way we will get across,' rejoined Wingate. 'While I'm captain I'll say when to start and stop. But I've been counting on you, Woodhull, to throw in with me and help me get things shook down.'

'Well, hit looks to me ye're purty brash as usual,' commented another voice. Bill Jackson came and stood at the captain's side. He had not been far from Woodhull all day long. 'Ye're a nacherl damned fool, Sam Woodhull,' said he. 'Who 'lected ye fer train captain, an' when was it did? If ye don't like the way this train's run go on ahead an' make a train o' yer own, ef that's way ye feel. Pull on out tonight. What ye say, cap?'

'I can't really keep any man from going back or going ahead,' replied Wingate. 'But I've counted on Woodhull to hold those Liberty wagons together. Any plainsman knows that a little party takes big risks.'

'Since when did you come a plainsman?' scoffed the malcontent, for once forgetting his policy of favour-currying with Wingate in his own surly discontent. He had not been able to speak to Molly all day.

'Well, if he ain't a plainsman yit he will be, and I'm one right now, Sam Woodhull.' Jackson stood squarely in front of his superior. 'I say he's talkin' sense to a man that ain't got no sense. I was with Doniphan too. We found ways, huh?'

His straight gaze outfronted the other, who turned and rode back. But that very night eight men, covertly instigated or encouraged by Woodhull, their leader, came to the headquarters fire with a joint complaint. They demanded places at the head of the column, else would mutiny and go on ahead together. They said good mule teams ought not to take the dust of ox wagons.

'What do you say, men?' asked the train captain of his aids helplessly. 'I'm in favour of letting them go front.'

The others nodded silently, looking at one another significantly. Already cliques and factions were beginning.

Woodhull, however, had too much at stake to risk any open friction with the captain of the train. His own seat at the officers' fire was dear to him, for it brought him close to the Wingate wagons, and in sight – if nothing else – of Molly Wingate. That young lady did not speak to him all day, but drew close the tilt of her own wagon early after the evening meal and denied herself to all.

As for Banion, he was miles back, in camp with his own wagons, which Woodhull had abandoned, and on duty that night with the cattle guard – a herdsman and not a leader of men now. He himself was moody enough when he tied his cape behind his saddle and rode his black horse out into the shadows. He had no knowledge of the fact that the old mountain man, Jackson, wrapped in his blanket, that night instituted a solitary watch all his own.

The hundreds of camp fires of the scattered train, stretched out over five miles of grove and glade at the end of the first undisciplined day, lowered, glowed and faded. They were one day out to Oregon, and weary withal. Soon the individual encampments were silent save for the champ or cough of tethered animals, or the whining howl of coyotes, prowling in. At the Missouri encampment, last of the train, and that heading the great cattle drove, the hardy frontier settlers, as was their wont, soon followed the sun to rest.

The night wore on, incredibly slow to the novice watch for the first time now drafted under the prairie law. The sky was faint pink and the shadows lighter when suddenly the dark was streaked by a flash of fire and the silence broken by the crack of a border rifle. Then again and again came the heavier bark of a dragoon revolver, of the sort just then becoming known along the Western marches.

The camp went into confusion. Will Banion, just riding in to take his own belated turn in his blankets, almost ran over the tall form of Bill Jackson, rifle in hand.

'What was it, man?' demanded Banion. 'You shooting at a mule?'

'No, a man,' whispered the other. 'He ran this way. Reckon I must have missed. It's hard to draw down inter a hindsight in the dark, an' I jest chanced hit with the pistol. He was runnin' hard.'

'Who was he – some thief?'

'Like enough. He was crawlin' up towards yore wagon, I halted him an' he run.'

'You don't know who he was?'

'No. I'll see his tracks, come day. Go on to bed. I'll set out a whiles, boy.'

When dawn came, before he had broken his long vigil, Jackson was bending over footmarks in the moister portions of the soil.

'Tall man, young an' tracked clean,' he muttered to himself. 'Fancy boots, with rather little heels. Shame I done missed him!'

But he said nothing to Banion or anyone else. It was the twentieth time Bill Jackson, one of Sublette's men and a nephew of one of his partners, had crossed the Plains, and the lone hand pleased him best. He instituted his own government for the most part, and had thrown in with this train because that best suited his book, since the old pack trains of the fur trade were now no more. For himself, he planned settlement in eastern Oregon, a country he once had glimpsed in long-gone beaver days, a dozen years ago. The eastern settlements had held him long enough, the army life had been too dull, even with Doniphan.

'I must be gittin' old,' he muttered to himself as he turned to a breakfast fire. 'Missed – at seventy yard!'

CHAPTER 8

Man against Man

There were more than two thousand souls in the great caravan which reached over miles of springy turf and fat creek lands. There were more than a thousand children, more than a hundred babes in arm, more than fifty marriageable maids pursued by avid swains. There were bold souls and weak, strong teams and weak, heavy loads and light loads, neighbour groups and coteries of kindred blood or kindred spirits.

The rank and file had reasons enough for shifting. There were a score of Helens driving wagons – reasons in plenty for the futility of all attempts to enforce an arbitrary rule of march. Human equations, human elements would shake themselves down into place, willy-nilly. The great caravan therefore was scantily less than a rabble for the first three or four days out. The four columns were abandoned the first half-day. The loosely knit organisation rolled on in a broken-crested wave, ten, fifteen, twenty miles a day, the horse-and-mule men now at the front. Far to the rear, heading only the cow column, came the lank men of Liberty, trudging alongside their swaying ox teams, with many a monotonous 'Gee-whoa-haw! Git along thar, ye Buck an' Star!' So soon they passed the fork where the road to Oregon left the trail to Santa Fe; topped the divide that held them back from the greater valley of the Kaw.

Noon of the fifth day brought them to the swollen flood of the latter stream, at the crossing known as Papin's Ferry. Here the semi-civilised Indians and traders had a single rude ferryboat, a scow operated in part by setting poles, in part by the power of the stream against a cable. The noncommittal Indians would give no counsel as to fording. They had ferry hire to gain. Word passed that there were other fords a few miles higher up. A general indecision existed, and now the train began to pile up on the south bank of the river.

Late in the afternoon the scout, Jackson, came riding back to the herd where Banion was at work, jerking up his horse in no pleased frame of mind.

'Will,' said he, 'leave the boys ride now an' come on up ahead. We need ye.'

'What's up?' demanded Banion. 'Anything worse?'

'Yes. The old fool's had a row over the ferryboat. Hit'd take two weeks to git us all over that way, anyhow. He's declared fer fordin' the hull outfit, lock, stock an' barrel. To save a few dollars, he's a goin' to lose a lot o' loads an' drownd a lot o' womern an' babies – that's what he's goin' to do. Some o' us called a halt an' stood out fer a council. We want you to come on up.

'Woodhull's there,' he added. 'He sides with the old man, o' course. He rid on the same seat with that gal all day till now. Lord knows what he done or said. Ain't hit nigh about time now, major?'

'It's nigh about time,' said Will Banion quietly.

They rode side by side, past more than a mile of the covered wagons, now almost end to end, the columns continually closing up. At the bank of the river, at the ferry head, they found a group of fifty men. The ranks opened as Banion and Jackson approached, but Banion made no attempt to join a council to which he had not been bidden.

A half-dozen civilised Indians of the Kaws, owners or operators of the ferry, sat in a stolid line across the head of the scow at its landing stage, looking neither to the right nor the left and awaiting the white men's pleasure. Banion rode down to them.

'How deep?' he asked.

They understood but would not answer.

'Out of the way!' he cried, and rode straight at them. They scattered. He spurred his horse, the black Spaniard, over the stage and on the deck of the scow; drove him its full length, snorting; set the spurs hard at the farther end and plunged deliberately off into the swift, muddy stream.

The horse sank out of sight below the roily surface. They saw the rider go down to his armpits; saw him swing off saddle, upstream. The gallant horse headed for the centre of the heavy current, but his master soon turned him downstream and inshore. A hundred yards down they landed on a bar and scrambled up the bank.

Banion rode to the circle and sat dripping. He had brought not speech but action, not theory but facts, and he had not spoken a word.

His eyes covered the council rapidly, resting on the figure of Sam Woodhull, squatting on his heels. As though to answer the challenge of his gaze, the latter rose.

'Gentlemen,' said he, 'I'm not, myself, governed by any mere spirit of bravado. It's swimming water, yes – any fool knows that, outside of yon one. What I do say is that we can't afford to waste time here fooling with that boat. We've got to swim it. I agree with you, Wingate. This river's been forded by the trains for years, and I don't see as we need be any more chicken-hearted than those others that went through last year and earlier. This is the old fur-trader crossing, the Mormons crossed here, and so can we.'

Silence met his words. The older men looked at the swollen stream, turned to the horseman who had proved it.

'What does Major Banion say?' spoke up a voice.

'Nothing!' was Banion's reply. 'I'm not in your council, am I?'

'You are, as much as any man here,' spoke up Caleb Price, and Hall and Kelsey added yea to that. 'Get down. Come in.'

Banion threw his rein to Jackson and stepped into the ring, bowing to Jesse Wingate, who sat as presiding officer.

'Of course we want to hear what Mr Banion has to say,' said he. 'He's proved part of the question right now. I've always heard it's fording, part way, at Papin's Ferry. It don't look it now.'

'The river's high, Mr Wingate,' said Banion. 'If you ask me, I'd rather ferry than ford. I'd send the women and children over by this boat. We can make some more out of the wagon boxes. If they leak we can cover them with hides. The sawmill at the mission has some lumber. Let's knock together another boat or two. I'd rather be safe than sorry, gentlemen; and believe me, she's heavy water yonder.'

'I've never seed the Kaw so full,' asserted Jackson, 'an' I've crossed her twenty times in spring flood. Do what ye like, you-all – ole Missoury's goin' to take her slow an' keerful.'

'Half of you Liberty men are a bunch of damned cowards!' sneered Woodhull.

There was silence. An icy voice broke it.

'I take it, that means me?' said Will Banion.

'It does mean you, if you want to take it that way,' rejoined his enemy. 'I don't believe in one or two timid men holding up a whole train.'

'Never mind about holding up the train – we're not stopping any man from crossing right now. What I have in mind now is to ask you, do you classify me as a coward just because I counsel prudence here?'

'You're the one is holding back.'

'Answer me! Do you call that to me?'

'I do answer you, and I do call it to you then!' flared Woodhull.

'I tell you, you're a liar, and you know it, Sam Woodhull! And if it pleases your friends and mine, I'd like to have the order now made on unfinished business.'

Not all present knew what this meant, for only a few knew of the affair at the rendezvous, the Missourians having held their counsel in the broken and extended train, where men might travel for days and not meet. But Woodhull knew, and sprang to his feet, hand on revolver. Banion's hand was likewise employed at his wet saddle holster, to which he sprang, and perhaps then one man would have been killed but for Bill Jackson, who spurred between.

'Make one move an' I drop ye!' he called to Woodhull. 'Ye've give yer promise.'

'All right then, I'll keep it,' growled Woodhull.

'Ye'd better! Now listen! Do ye see that tall cottingwood tree a half-mile down – the one with the flat umbreller top, like a cypress? Ye kin? Well, in half a hour be thar with three o' yore friends, no more. I'll be thar with my man an' three o' his, no more, an' I'll be one o' them three. I allow our meanin' is to see hit fa'r. An' I allow that what has been unfinished business ain't goin' to be unfinished come sundown.

'Does this suit ye, Will?'

'It's our promise. Officers didn't usually fight that way, but you said it must be so, and we both agreed. I agree now.'

'You other folks all stay back,' said Bill Jackson grimly. 'This here is a little matter that us Missourians is goin' to settle in our own way an' in our own camp. Hit ain't none o' you-uns' business. Hit's plenty o' ourn.'

Men started to their feet over all the river front. The Indians rose, walked down the bank covertly.

'Fight!'

The word passed quickly. It was a day of personal encounters. This was an assemblage in large part of fighting men. But some sense of decency led the partisans to hurry away, out of sight and hearing of the womenfolk.

The bell-top cottonwood stood in a little space which had been a duelling ground for thirty years. The grass was firm and even for a distance of fifty yards in any direction, and the light at that hour favoured neither man.

For Banion, who was prompt, Jackson brought with him two men. One of them was a planter by name of Dillon, the other none less than stout Caleb Price, one of Wingate's chosen captains.

'I'll not see this made a thing of politics,' said he. 'I'm Northern, but I like the way that young man has acted. He hasn't had a fair deal from the officers of this train. He's going to have a fair deal now.'

'We allow he will,' said Dillon grimly.

He was fully armed, and so were all the seconds. For Woodhull showed the Kentuckian, Kelsey, young Jed Wingate – the latter by Woodhull's own urgent request – and the other train captain, Hall. So in its way the personal quarrel of these two hotheads did in a way involve the entire train.

'Strip yore man,' commanded the tall mountaineer. 'We're ready. It's go till one hollers enough; fa'r stand up, heel an' toe, no buttin' er gougin'. Fust man ter break them rules gits shot. Is that yore understandin', gentlemen.'

'How we get it, yes,' assented Kelsey.

'See you enforce it then, fer we're a-goin' to,' concluded Jackson.

He stepped back. From the opposite sides the two antagonists stepped forward. There was no ring, there was no timekeeper, no single umpire. There were no rounds, no duration set. It was man to man, for cause the most ancient and most bitter of all causes – sex.

CHAPTER 9

The Brute

Between the two stalwart men who fronted one another, stripped to trousers and shoes, there was not so much to choose. Woodhull perhaps had the better of it by a few pounds in weight, and forsooth looked less slouchy out of his clothes than in them. His was the long and sinewy type of muscle. He was in hard condition.

Banion, two years younger than his rival, himself was round and slender, thin of flank, a trace squarer and fuller of shoulder. His arms showed easily rippling bands of muscles, his body was hard in the natural vigour of youth and life in the open air. His eye was fixed all the time on his man. He did not speak or turn aside, but walked on in.

There were no preliminaries, there was no delay. In a flash the Saxon ordeal of combat was joined. The two fighters met in a rush.

At the centre of the fighting space they hung, body to body, in a whirling *mêlée*. Neither had much skill in real boxing, and such fashion of fight was unknown in that region, the offensive being the main thing and defence remaining incidental. The thud of fist on face, the discoloration that rose under the savage blows, the blood that oozed and scattered, proved that the fighting blood of both these mad creatures was up, so that they felt no pain, even as they knew no fear.

In their first fly, as witnesses would have termed it, there was no advantage to either, and both came out well marked. In the combat of the time and place there were no rules, no periods, no resting times. Once they were dispatched to it, the fight was the affair of the fighters, with no more than a very limited number of restrictions as to fouls.

They met and broke, bloody, gasping, once, twice, a dozen times. Banion was fighting slowly, carefully.

'I'll make it free, if you dare!' panted Woodhull at length.

They broke apart once more by mutual need of breath. He meant he would bar nothing; he would go back to the days of Boone and Kenton and Girty, when hair, eye, any part of the body was fair aim.

'You can't dare me!' rejoined Will Banion. 'It's as my seconds say.'

Young Jed Wingate, suddenly pale, stood by and raised no protest. Kelsey's face was stony calm. The small eye of Hall narrowed, but he too held to the etiquette of non-interference in this matter of man and man, though what had passed here was a deadly thing. Mutilation, death might now ensue, and not mere defeat. But they all waited for the other side.

'Air ye game to hit, Will?' demanded Jackson at length.

'I don't fear him, anyway he comes,' replied Will Banion. 'I don't like it, but all of this was forced on me.'

'The hell it was!' exclaimed Kelsey. 'I heard ye call my man a liar.'

'An' he called my man a coward!' cut in Jackson.

'He is a coward,' sneered Woodhull, panting, 'or he'd not flicker now. He's afraid I'll take his eye out, damn him!'

Will Banion turned to his friends.

'Are we gentlemen at all?' said he. 'Shall we go back a hundred years?'

'If your man's afraid, we claim the fight!' exclaimed Kelsey. 'Breast yore bird!'

'So be it then!' said Will Banion. 'Don't mind me, Jackson! I don't fear him and I think I can beat him. It's free! I bar nothing, nor can he! Get back!'

Woodhull rushed first in the next assault, confident of his skill in rough-and-tumble. He felt at his throat the horizontal arm of his enemy. He caught away the wrist in his own hand, but sustained a heavy blow at the side of his head. The defence of his adversary angered him to blind rage. He forgot everything but contact, rushed, closed and caught his antagonist in the brawny grip of his arms. The battle at once resolved itself into the wrestling and battering match of the frontier. And it was free! Each might kill or maim if so he could.

The wrestling grips of the frontiersmen were few and primitive, efficient when applied by masters; and no schoolboy but studied all the holds as matter of religion, in a time when physical prowess was the most admirable quality a man might have.

Each fighter tried the forward jerk and trip which sometimes would do with an opponent not much skilled; but this primer work got results for neither. Banion evaded and swung into a hip lock, so swift that Woodhull left the ground. But his instinct gave him hold with one hand at his enemy's collar. He spread wide his feet and cast his weight aside, so that he came standing, after all. He well knew that a man must keep his feet. Woe to him who fell when it all was free! His own riposte was a snakelike glide close into his antagonist's arms, a swift thrust of his leg between the other's – the grapevine, which sometimes served if done swiftly.

It was done swiftly, but it did not serve. The other spread his legs, leaned against him, and in a flash came back in the dreaded crotch lock of the frontier, which some men boasted no one could escape at their hands. Woodhull was flung fair, but he broke wide and rose and rushed back and joined again, grappling; so that they stood once more body to body, panting, red, savage as any animals that fight, and more cruel. The seconds all were on their feet, scarce breathing.

They pushed in sheer test, and each found the other's stark strength. Yet Banion's breath still came even, his eye betokened no anxiety of the issue. Both were bloody now, clothing and all. Then in a flash the scales turned against the challenger *à l'outrance*.

Banion caught his antagonist by the wrist, and swift as a flash stooped, turning his own back and drawing the arm of his enemy over his own shoulder, slightly turned, so that the elbow joint was in peril and so that the pain must be intense. It was one of the ju-jitsu holds, discovered independently perhaps at that instant; certainly a new hold for the wrestling school of the frontier.

Woodhull's seconds saw the look of pain come on his face, saw him wince, saw him writhe, saw him rise on his toes. Then, with a sudden squatting heave, Banion cast him full length in front of him, upon his back! Before he had time to move he was upon him, pinning him down. A growl came from six observers.

In an ordinary fall a man might have turned, might have escaped. But Woodhull had planned his own undoing when he had called it free. Eyeless men, usually old men, in this day brought up talk of the ancient and horrible warfare of a past generation, when destruction of the adversary was the one purpose and any means called fair when it was free.

But the seconds of both men raised no hand when they saw the balls of Will Banion's thumbs pressed against the upper orbit edge of his enemy's eyes.

'Do you say enough?' panted the victor.

A groan from the helpless man beneath.

'Am I the best man? Can I whip you?' demanded the voice above him, in the formula prescribed.

'Go on – do it! Pull out his eyes!' commanded Bill Jackson savagely. 'He called it free to you! But don't wait!'

But the victor sprang free, stood, dashed the blood from his own eyes, wavered on his feet.

The hands of his fallen foe were across his eyes. But even as his men ran in, stooped and drew them away, the conqueror exclaimed, 'I'll not! I tell you I won't maim you, free or no free! Get up!'

So Woodhull knew his eyes were spared, whatever might be the pain of the sore nerves along the socket bone.

He rose to his knees, to his feet, his face ghastly in his own sudden sense of defeat, the worse for his victor's magnanimity, if such it might be called. Humiliation was worse than pain. He staggered, sobbing.

'I won't take nothing for a gift from you!'

But now the men stood between them, like and like. Young Jed Wingate pushed back his man.

'It's done!' said he. 'You shan't fight no more with the man that let you up. You're whipped, and by your own word it'd have been worse!'

He himself handed Will Banion his coat.

'Go get a pail of water,' he said to Kelsey, and the latter departed.

Banion stepped apart, battered and pale beneath his own wounds.

'I didn't want to fight him this way,' said he. 'I left him his eyes so he can see me again. If so he wants, I'll meet him any way. I hope he won't rue back.'

'You fool!' said old Bill Jackson, drawing Banion to one side. 'Do ye know what ye're a-sayin'? Whiles he was a-layin' thar I seen the bottoms o' his boots. Right fancy they was, with smallish heels! That skunk'll kill ye in the dark, Will. Ye'd orto hev put out'n both his two eyes!'

A sudden sound made them all turn. Above crackling of down brush, came the scream of a woman's voice. At the side of the great tree stood a figure that had no right there. They turned mute.

It was Molly Wingate who faced them all now, turning from one bloody, naked figure to the other. She saw Sam Woodhull standing, his hands still at his face; caught some sense out of Jackson's words, overheard as she came into the clearing.

'You!' she blazed at Will Banion. 'You'd put out a man's eyes! You brute!'

CHAPTER 10

Ole Missoury

Molly Wingate looked from one to the other of the group of silent, shame-faced men. Puzzled, she turned again to the victor in the savage combat.

'You!'

Will Banion caught up his clothing, turned away.

'You are right!' said he. 'I have been a brute! Goodbye!'

An instant later Molly found herself alone with the exception of her brother.

'You, Jed, what was this?' she demanded.

Jed took a deep and heartfelt chew of plug.

'Well, it was a little argument between them two,' he said finally. 'Like enough a little jealousy, like, you know – over place in the train, or something. This here was for men. You'd no business here.'

'But it was a shame!'

'I reckon so.'

'Who started this?'

'Both of them. All we was here for was to see fair. Men got to fight sometimes.'

'But not like animals, not worse than savages!'

'Well, it was right savage, some of the time, sis.'

'They said – about eyes – oh!'

The girl shivered, her hands at her own eyes.

'Yes, they called it free. Anybody else, Sam Woodhull'd be sorry enough right now. T'other man throwed him clean and had him down, but he let him up. He didn't never hurt Sam's eyes, only pinched his head a little. He had a right, but didn't. It had to be settled and it was settled, fair and more'n fair, by him.'

'But, Jed' – the eternal female now – 'then, which one really whipped?'

'Will Banion did, ain't I told you? You insulted him, and he's gone. Having come in here where you wasn't no ways wanted, I reckon the best thing you can do is to go back to your own wagon and stay there. What with riding horses you hadn't ought, and seeing fights when you don't know a damned thing about nothing, I reckon you've made trouble about enough. Come on!'

936

'Price,' said Bill Jackson to the grave and silent man who walked with him towards the wagon train beyond the duelling ground, 'this settles hit. Us Missoury wagons won't go on under no sech man as Sam Woodhull. We didn't no ways eleck him – he was app'inted. Mostly, elected is better'n app'inted. An' I seen afore now, no man can hold his place on the trail unless'n he's fitten. We'll eleck Will Banion our cap'n, an' you fellers kin go to hell. What us fellers started out to do was to go to Oregon.'

'But that'll mean the train's split!'

'Shore hit will! Hit is split right now. But thar's enough o' the Liberty wagons to go through without no help. We kin whup all the rest o' this train, give we need ter, let alone a few Injuns now an' then.

'Tonight,' he concluded, 'we'll head up the river, an' leave you fellers the boat an' all o' Papin's Ferry to git acrost the way you want. Thar hain't no manner o' man, outfit, river er redskin that Ole Missoury kain't lick, take 'em as they come, them to name the holts an' the rules. We done showed you-all that. We're goin' to show you some more. So goodbye.' He held out his hand. 'Ye helped see far, an' ye're a far man, an' we'll miss ye. Ef ye git in need o' help come to us. Ole Missoury won't need no help.'

'Well, Woodhull's one of you Missourians,' remarked Price.

'Yes, but he ain't bred true. Major Banion is. Hit was me that made him fight knuckle an' skull an' not with weapons. He didn't want to, but I had a reason. I'm content an' soothe jest the way she lies. Ef Will never sees the gal agin she ain't wuth the seem'.

'Ye'll find Colonel William Banion at the head o' his own train. He's fitten, an' he's fout an' proved hit.'

CHAPTER 11

When All the World was Young

Molly Wingate kneeled by her cooking fire the following morning, her husband meantime awaiting the morning meal impatiently. All along the medley of crowded wagons rose confused sounds of activity at a hundred similar firesides.

'Where's Little Molly?' demanded Wingate. 'We got to be up and coming.'

'Her and Jed is off after the cattle. Well, you heard the news last night. You've got to get someone else to run the herd. If each family drives its own loose stock everything'll be all mixed up. The Liberty outfit pulled on by at dawn. Well, anyways they left us the sawmill and the boat.

'Sam Woodhull, he's anxious to get on ahead of the Missourians,' she added. 'He says he'll take the boat anyhow, and not pay them Kaws any such hold-up price like they ask.'

'All I got to say is, I wish we were across,' grumbled Wingate, stooping to the bacon spider.

'Huh! So do I – me and my bureau and my hens. Yes, after you've fussed around a while you men'll maybe come to the same conclusion your head cowguard had; you'll be making more boats and doing less swimming. I'm sorry he quit us.'

'It's the girl,' said her husband sententiously.

'Yes. But' – smiling grimly – 'one furse don't make a parting.'

'She's same as promised Sam Woodhull, Molly, and you know that.'

'Before he got whipped by Colonel Banion.'

'Colonel! Fine business for an officer! Woodhull told me he tripped and this other man was on top of him and nigh gouged out his two eyes. And he told me other things too. Banion's a traitor, to split the train. We can spare all such.'

'Can we?' rejoined his wife. 'I sort of thought – '

'Never mind what you thought. He's one of the unruly, servigerous sort; can't take orders, and a trouble maker always. We'll show that outfit. I've ordered three more scows built and the seams calked in the wagon boxes.'

Surely enough, the Banion plan of crossing, after all, was carried out, and although the river dropped a foot meantime, the attempt to ford *en masse* was abandoned. Little by little the wagon parks gathered on the north bank, each family assorting its own goods and joining in the general *sauve qui peut*.

Nothing was seen of the Missouri column, but rumour said they were ferrying slowly, with one boat and their doubled wagon boxes, over which they had nailed hides. Woodhull was keen to get on north ahead of this body. He had personal reasons for that. None too well pleased at the smiles with which his explanations of his bruised face were received, he made a sudden resolution to take a band of his own immediate neighbours and adherents and get on ahead of the Missourians. He based his decision, as he announced it, on the necessity of a scouting party to locate grass and water.

Most of the men who joined him were single men, of the more

restless sort. There were no family wagons with them. They declared their intention of travelling fast and light until they got among the buffalo. This party left in advance of the main caravan, which had not yet completed the crossing of the Kaw.

'Roll out! Ro–o–o–ll out!' came the mournful command at last, once more down the line.

It fell on the ears of some who were unwilling to obey. The caravan was disintegrating at the start. The gloom cast by the long delay at the ford had now resolved itself in certain instances into fear amounting half to panic. Some companies of neighbours said the entire train should wait for the military escort; others declared they would not go farther west, but would turn back and settle here, where the soil was so good. Still others said they all should lie here, with good grass and water, until further word came from the Platte Valley train and until they had more fully decided what to do. In spite of all the officers could do, the general advance was strung out over two or three miles. The rapid loss in order, these premature divisions of the train, augured ill enough.

The natural discomforts of the trail now also began to have their effect. A plague of green-headed flies and flying ants assailed them by day, and at night the mosquitoes made an affliction well-nigh insufferable. The women and children could not sleep, the horses groaned all night under the clouds of tormentors which gathered on them. Early as it was, the sun at times blazed with intolerable fervour, or again the heat broke in savage storms of thunder, hail and rain. All the elements, all the circumstances seemed in league to warn them back before it was too late, for indeed they were not yet more than on the threshold of the Plains.

The spring rains left the ground soft in places, so that in creek valleys stretches of corduroy sometimes had to be laid down. The high waters made even the lesser fords difficult and dangerous, and all knew that between them and the Platte ran several strong and capricious rivers, making in general to the southeast and necessarily trans-sected by the great road to Oregon.

They still were in the eastern part of what is now the state of Kansas, one of the most beautiful and exuberantly rich portions of the country, as all early travellers declared. The land lay in a succession of timber-lined valleys and open prairie ridges. Groves of walnut, oak, hickory, elm, ash at first were frequent, slowly changing, farther west, to larger proportions of poplar, willow and cottonwood. The white dogwood passed to make room for scattering thickets of wild plum. Wild tulips, yellow or of broken colours; the campanula, the wild honeysuckle, lupins – not yet quite in bloom – the sweetbrier and increasing quantities of the wild rose gave life to the always changing scene. Wild game of every sort was unspeakably abundant – deer and turkey in every bottom, thousands of grouse on the hills, vast flocks of snipe and plover, even numbers of the green parrakeets then so numerous along that latitude. The streams abounded in game fish. All nature was easy and generous.

Men and women grumbled at leaving so rich and beautiful a land lying waste. None had seen a country more supremely attractive. Emotions of tenderness, of sadness, also came to many. Nostalgia was not yet shaken off. This strained condition of nerves, combined with the trail hardships, produced the physical irritation which is inevitable in all amateur pioneer work. Confusions, discordances, arising over the most trifling circumstances, grew into petulance, incivility, wrangling and intrigue, as happened in so many other earlier caravans. In the Babel-like excitement of the morning catch-up, amid the bellowing and running of the cattle evading the yoke, more selfishness, less friendly accommodation now appeared, and men met without speaking, even this early on the road.

The idea of four parallel columns had long since been discarded. They broke formation, and at times the long caravan, covering the depressions and eminences of the prairie, wound along in mile-long detachments, each of which hourly grew more surly and more independent. Overdriven oxen now began to drop. By the time the prairies proper were reached more than a score of oxen had died. They were repeating trail history as recorded by the travellers of that day.

Personal and family problems also made divisions more natural. Many suffered from ague; fevers were very common. An old woman past seventy died one night and was buried by the wayside the next day. Ten days after the start twins were born to parents moving out to Oregon. There were numbers of young children, many of them in arms, who became ill. For one or other cause, wagons continually were dropping out. It was difficult for some wagons to keep up, the unseasoned oxen showing distress under loads too heavy for their draft. It was by no means a solid and compact army, after all, this west-bound wave of the first men with ploughs. All these things sat heavily on the soul of Jesse Wingate, who daily grew more morose and grim.

As the train advanced bands of antelope began to appear. The striped prairie gophers gave place to the villages of countless barking prairie dogs, curious to the eyes of the newcomers. At night the howling and snarling of grey wolves now made regular additions to the coyote chorus and the voices of the owls and whippoorwills. Little by little, day by day, civilisation was passing, the need for organisation daily became more urgent. Yet the original caravan had split practically into three divisions within a hundred and fifty miles from the jump-off, although the bulk of the train hung to Wingate's company and began to shake down, at least into a sort of tolerance.

Granted good weather, as other travellers had written, it was indeed impossible to evade the sense of exhilaration in the bold, free life. At evening encampment the scene was one worthy of any artist of all the world. The oblong of the wagon park, the white tents, the many fires, made a spectacle of marvellous charm and power. Perhaps within sight, at one time, under guard for the evening feed on the fresh young grass, there would be two thousand head of cattle. In the wagon village men, women and children would be engaged as though at home. There was little idleness in the train, and indeed there was much gravity and devoutness in the personnel. At one fireside the young men might be roaring 'Old Grimes is dead, that good old man', or 'Oh, then, Susannah'; but quite as likely close at hand some family group would be heard in sacred hymns. A strange envisagement it all made, in a strange environment, a new atmosphere, here on the threshold of the wilderness.

CHAPTER 12

The Dead Men's Tale

The wilderness, close at hand, soon was to make itself felt. Wingate's outriders moved out before noon of one day, intending to locate camp at the ford of the Big Vermilion. Four miles in advance they unexpectedly met the scout of the Missouri column, Bill Jackson, who had passed the Wingate train by a cut-off of his own on a solitary ride ahead for sake of information. He was at a gallop now, and what he said sent them all back at full speed to the head of the Wingate column.

Jackson riding ahead, came up with his hand raised for a halt.

'My God, cap'n, stop the train!' he called. 'Hit won't do for the womern and children to see what's on ahead yan!'

'What's up – where?' demanded Wingate.

'On three mile, on the water where they camped night afore last. Thar they air ten men, an' the rest's gone. Woodhull's wagons, but he ain't thar. Wagons burned, mules standing with arrers in them, rest all dead but a few. Hit's the Pawnees!'

The column leaders all galloped forward, seeing first what later most of the entire train saw – the abominable phenomenon of Indian warfare on the Plains.

Scattered over a quarter of a mile, where the wagons had stood not grouped and perhaps not guarded, lay heaps of wreckage beside heaps of ashes. One by one the corpses were picked out, here, there, over more than a mile of ground. They had fought, yes, but fought each his own losing individual battle after what had been a night surprise.

The swollen and blackened features of the dead men stared up, mutilated as savages alone mark the fallen. Two were staked out, hand and foot, and ashes lay near them, upon them. Arrows stood up between the ribs of the dead men, driven through and down into the ground. A dozen mules, as Jackson had said, drooped with low heads and hanging ears, arrow shafts standing out of their haunches, waiting for death to end their agony.

'Finish them, Jackson.'

Wingate handed the hunter his own revolver, signalling for Kelsey and Hall to do the same. The methodical cracking of the hand arms began to end the suffering of the animals.

They searched for scraps of clothing to cover the faces of the dead, the bodies of some dead. They motioned the women and children back when the head of the train came up. Jackson beckoned the leaders to the side of one wagon, partially burned.

'Look,' said he, pointing.

A long stick, once a whipstock, rose from the front of the wagon bed. It had been sharpened and thrust under the wrist skin of a human hand – a dried hand, not of a white man, but a red. A half-corroded bracelet of copper still clung to the wrist.

'If I read signs right, that's why!' commented Bill Jackson.

'But how do you explain it?' queried Hall. 'Why should they do that? And how could they, in so close a fight?'

'They couldn't,' said Jackson. 'That hand's a day an' a half older than these killings. Hit's Sam Woodhull's wagon. Well, the Pawnees like enough counted 'coup on the man that swung that hand up for a sign, even if hit wasn't one o' their own people.'

'Listen, men,' he concluded, 'hit was Woodhull's fault. We met some friendlies – Kaws – from the mission, an' they was mournin'. A half dozen o' them follered Woodhull out above the ferry when he pulled out. They told him he hadn't paid them for their boat, asked him for more presents. He got mad, so they say, an' shot down one o' them an' stuck up his hand – fer a warnin', so he said.

'The Kaws didn't do this killin'. This band of Pawnees was away down below their range. The Kaws said they was comin' fer a peace council, to git the Kaws an' Otoes to raise against us whites, comin' out so many, with ploughs and womenfolks – they savvy. Well, the Kaws has showed the Pawnees. The Pawnees has showed us.'

'Yes,' said the deep voice of Caleb Price, property owner and head of a family; 'they've showed us that Sam Woodhull was not fit to trust. There's one man that is.'

'Do you want him along with your wagons?' demanded Jackson. He turned to Wingate.

'Well,' said the train captain after a time, 'we are striking the Indian country now.'

'Shall I bring up our wagons an' jine ye all here at the ford this evenin'?'

'I can't keep you from coming on up the road if you want to. I'll not ask you.'

'All right! We'll not park with ye then. But we'll be on the same water. Hit's my own fault we split. We wouldn't take orders from Sam Woodhull, an' we never will.'

He nodded to the blackened ruins, to the grim dead hand pointing to the sky, left where it was by the superstitious blood avengers.

Wingate turned away and led the wagon train a half mile up the stream, pitching camp above the ford where the massacre had occurred. The duties of the clergy and the appointed sextons were completed. Silence and sadness fell on the encampment.

Jackson, the scout of the Missouri column, still lingered for some sort of word with Molly Wingate. Some odds and ends of brush lay about. Of the latter Molly began casting a handful on the fire and covering it against the wind with her shawl, which at times she quickly removed. As a result the confined smoke arose at more or less well defined intervals, in separate puffs or clouds.

'Ef ye want to know how to give the smoke signal right an' proper, Miss Molly,' said he at length, quietly, 'I'll larn ye how.'

The girl looked up at him.

'Well, I don't know much about it.'

'This way: it takes two to do hit best. You catch holt two corners o' the shawl now. Hoist it on a stick in the middle. Draw it down all over the fire. Let her simmer under some green stuff. Now! Lift her clean off, sideways, so's not ter break the smoke ball. See 'em go up? That's how.'

He looked at the girl keenly under his bushy grey brows.

'That's the Injun signal fer "Enemy in the country". S'pose you ever wanted to signal, say to white folks, "Friend in the country", you might remember – three short puffs an' one long one. That might bring up a friend. Sech a signal can be seed a long ways.'

Molly flushed to the eyes.

'What do you mean?'

'Nothin' at all, any more'n you do.'

Jackson rose and left her.

CHAPTER 13

Wild Fire

The afternoon wore on, much occupied with duties connected with the sad scenes of the tragedy. No word came of Woodhull, or of two others who could not be identified as among the victims at the death camp. No word, either, came from the Missourians, and so cowed or dulled were most of the men of the caravan that they did not venture far, even to undertake trailing out after the survivors of the massacre. In sheer indecision the great aggregation of wagons, piled up along the stream, lay apathetic, and no order came for the advance.

Jed and his cow guards were obliged to drive the cattle back into the ridges for better grazing, for the valley and adjacent country, which had not been burned over by the Indians the preceding fall, held a lower matting of heavy dry grass through which the green grass of springtime appeared only in sparser and more smothered growth. As many of the cattle and horses even now showed evil results from injudicious driving on the trail, it was at length decided to make a full day's stop so that they might feed up.

Molly Wingate, now assured that the Pawnees no longer were in the vicinity, ventured out for pasturage with her team of mules, which she had kept tethered close to her own wagon. She now rapidly was becoming a good frontierswoman and thoughtful of her locomotive power. Taking the direction of the cattle herd, she drove from camp a mile or two, resolving to hobble and watch her mules while they grazed close to the cattle guards.

She was alone. Around her, untouched by any civilisation, lay a wild, free world. The ceaseless wind of the prairie swept old and new grass into a continuous undulating surface, silver crested, a wave always passing, never past. The sky was unspeakably fresh and blue, with its light clouds, darker edged towards the far horizon of the unbounded, unbroken expanse of alternating levels and low hills. Across the broken ridges passed the teeming bird life of the land. The Eskimo plover in vast bands circled and sought their nesting places. Came also the sweep of cinnamon wings as the giant sickle-billed curlews wheeled in vast aerial phalanx, with their eager cries, 'Curlee! Curlee! Curlee!' – the wildest cry of the old prairies. Again, from some unknown, undiscoverable place, came the liquid, baffling, mysterious note of the nesting upland plover, sweet and clean as pure white honey.

Now and again a band of antelope swept ghostlike across a ridge. A great grey wolf stood contemptuously near on a hillock, gazing speculatively at the strange creature, the white woman, new come to his lands. It was the wilderness, rude, bold, yet sweet.

Who shall say what thoughts the flowered wilderness of spring carried to the soul of a young woman beautiful and ripe for love, her heart as sweet and melting as that of the hidden plover telling her mate of happiness? Surely a strange spell, born of youth and all this free world of things beginning, fell on the soul of Molly Wingate. She sat and dreamed, her hands idle, her arms empty, her beating pulses full, her heart full of a maid's imaginings.

How long she sat alone, miles apart, an unnoticed figure, she herself could not have said – surely the sun was past its zenith – when, moved by some vague feeling of her own, she noticed the uneasiness of her feeding charges.

The mules, hobbled and side-lined as Jed had shown her, turned face to the wind, down the valley, standing for a time studious and uncertain rather than alarmed. Then, their great ears pointed, they became uneasy; stirred, stamped, came back again to their position, gazing steadily in the one direction.

The ancient desert instinct of the wild ass, brought down through thwarted generations, never had been lost to them. They had foreknowledge of danger long before horses or human beings could suspect it.

Danger? What was it? Something, surely. Molly sprang to her feet. A band of antelope, running, had paused a hundred yards away, gazing back. Danger – yes; but what?

The girl ran to the crest of the nearest hillock and looked back. Even as she did so, it seemed that she caught touch of the great wave of apprehension spreading swiftly over the land.

Far off, low lying like a pale blue cloud, was a faint line of something that seemed to alter in look, to move, to rise and fall, to advance – down the wind. She never had seen it, but knew what it must be – the prairie fire! The lack of fall burning had left it fuel even now.

Vast numbers of prairie grouse came by, hurtling through the silence, alighting, strutting with high heads, fearlessly close. Grey creatures came hopping, halting or running fully extended – the prairie hares, fleeing far ahead. Band after band of antelope came on, running easily, but looking back. A heavy line of large birds, black to the eye, beat on laboriously, alighted, and ran onward with incredible speed – the wild turkeys, fleeing the terror. Came also broken bands of white-tailed deer, easy, elastic, bounding irregularly, looking back at the miles-wide cloud, which now and then spun up, black as ink towards the sky, but always flattened and came onward with the wind.

Danger? Yes! Worse than Indians, for yonder were the cattle; there lay the parked train, two hundred wagons, with the household goods that meant their life savings and their future hope in far-off Oregon. Women were there, and children – women with babes that could not walk. True, the water lay close, but it was narrow and deep and offered no salvation against the terror now coming on the wings of the wind.

That the prairie fire would find in this strip fuel to carry it even at this green season of the grass the wily Pawnees had known. This was cheaper than assault by arms. They would wither and scatter the white nation here! Worse than plumed warriors was yonder broken undulating line of the prairie fire.

Instinct told the white girl, gave her the same terror as that which inspired all these fleeing creatures. But what could she do? This was an elemental, gigantic wrath, and she but a frightened girl. She guessed rather than reasoned what it would mean when yonder line came closer, when it would sweep down, roaring, over the wagon train.

The mules began to bray, to plunge, too wise to undertake flight. She would at least save them. She would mount one and ride with the alarm for the camp.

The wise animals let her come close, did not plunge, knew that she meant help, allowed her trembling hands to loose one end of the hobble straps, but no more. As soon as each mule got its feet it whirled and was away. No chance to hold one of them now, and if she had mounted a hobbled animal it had meant nothing. But she saw them go towards the stream, towards the camp. She must run that way herself.

It was so far! There was a faint smell of smoke and a mysterious low humming in the air. Was it too late?

A swift, absurd, wholly useless memory came to her from the preceding day. Yes, it would be no more than a prayer, but she would send it out blindly into the air . . . Some instinct – yes, quite likely.

Molly ran to her abandoned wagonette, pushed in under the white tilt where her pallet bed lay rolled, her little personal plunder stored about. Fumbling, she found her sulphur matches. She would build her signal fire. It was all that she could do. It might at least alarm the camp.

Trembling, she looked about her, tore her hands breaking off little faggots of tall dry weed stems, a very few bits of wild thorn and fragments of a plum thicket in the nearest shallow coulee. She ran to her hillock, stooped and broke a dozen matches, knowing too little of fire-making in the wind. But at last she caught a wisp of dry grass, a few dry stems – others, the bits of wild plum branches. She shielded her tiny blaze with her frock, looking back over her shoulder, where the black curtain was rising taller. Now and then, even in the blaze of full day, a red, dull gleam rose and passed swiftly. The entire country was afire. Fuel? Yes; and a wind.

The humming in the air grew, the scent of fire came plainly. The plover rose around their nests and circled, crying piteously. The scattered hares became a great body of moving grey, like camouflage blots on the still undulating waves of green and silver, passing but not yet past – soon now to pass.

The girl, her hands arrested, her arms out, in her terror, stood trying to remember. Yes, it was three short puffs and a long pillar. She caught her shawl from her shoulders, stooped, spread it with both hands, drove in her stiffest bough for a partial support, cast in under the edge, timidly, green grass enough to make smoke, she hoped.

An instant and she sprang up, drawing the shawl swiftly aside, the next moment jealously cutting through the smoke with a side sweep of the covering.

It worked! The cut-off column rose, bent over in a little detached cloud. Again, with a quick flirt, eager eyed, and again the detached irregular ball! A third time – Molly rose, and now cast on dry grass and green grass till a tall and moving pillar of cloud by day arose.

At least she had made her prayer. She could do no more. With vague craving for any manner of refuge, she crawled to her wagon seat and covered her eyes. She knew that the wagon train was warned – they now would need but little warning, for the menace was written all across the world.

She sat she knew not how long, but until she became conscious of a roaring in the air. The line of fire had come astonishingly soon, she reasoned. But she forgot that. All the vanguard and the full army of wild creatures had passed by now. She alone, the white woman, most helpless of the great creatures, stood before the terror.

She sprang out of the wagon and looked about her. The smoke crest, black, red-shot, was coming close. The grass here would carry it. Perhaps yonder on the flint ridge where the cover was short – why had she not thought of that long ago? It was half a mile, and no sure haven then.

She ran, her shawl drawn about her head – ran with long, free stride, her limbs envigored by fear, her full-bosomed body heaving chokingly. The smoke was now in the air, and up the unshorn valley came the fire remorselessly, licking up the underlying layer of sun-cured grass which a winter's snow had matted down.

She could never reach the ridge now. Her overburdened lungs functioned but little. The world went black, with many points of red. Everywhere was the odour and feel of smoke. She fell and gasped, and knew little, cared little what might come. The elemental terror at last had caught its prey – soft, young, beautiful prey, this huddled form, a bit of brown and grey, edged with white of windblown skirt. It would be a sweet morsel for the flames.

Along the knife-edged flint ridge which Molly had tried to reach there came the pounding of hoofs, heavier than any of those that had passed. The cattle were stampeding directly down wind and before the fire. Dully, Molly heard the lowing, heard the far shouts of human voices. Then, it seemed to her, she heard a rush of other hoofs coming towards her. Yes, something was pounding down the slope towards her wagon, towards her. Buffalo, she thought, not knowing the buffalo were gone from that region.

But it was not the buffalo, nor yet the frightened herd, nor yet her mules. Out of the smoke curtain broke a rider, his horse flatout; a black horse with flying frontlet – she knew what horse. She knew what man rode him, too, black with smoke as he was now. He swept close to the wagon and was off. Something flickered there, with smoke above it, beyond the wagon by some yards. Then he was in saddle and racing again, his eyes and teeth white in the black mask of his face.

She heard no call and no command. But an arm reached down to hers, swept her up – and she was going onward, the horn of a saddle under her, her body held to that of the rider, swung sidewise. The horse was guided not down but across the wind.

Twice and three times, silent, he flung her off and was down, kindling his little back fires – the only defence against a wildfire. He breathed thickly, making sounds of rage.

'Will they never start?' he broke out at last. 'The fools – the fools!'

But by now it was too late. A sudden accession in the force of the wind increased the speed of the fire. The little line near Molly's wagon spared it, but caught strength. Could she have seen through the veils of smoke she would have seen a half-dozen fires this side the line of the great fire. But fire is fire.

Again he was in saddle and had her against his thigh, his body, flung any way so she came with the horse. And now the horse swerved, till he drove in the steel again and again, heading him not away from the fire but straight into it!

Molly felt a rush of hot air; surging, actual flame singed the ends of her hair. She felt his hand again and again sweep over her skirts, wiping out the fire as it caught. It was blackly hot, stifling – and then it was past!

Before her lay a wide black world. Her wagon stood, even its white top spared by miracle of the back fire. But beyond came one more line of smoke and flame. The black horse neighed now in the agony of his hot hoofs. His rider swung him to a lower level, where under the tough cover had lain moist ground, on which uncovered water now glistened. He flung her into the mire of it, pulled up his horse there and himself lay down, full length, his blackened face in the moist mud above which still smoked stubbles of the flame-shorn grass. He had not spoken to her, nor she to him. His eyes rested on the singed ends of her blown hair, her charred garments, in a frowning sympathy which found no speech. At length he brought the reins of his horse to her, flirting up the singed ends of the long mane, further proof of their narrow escape.

'I must try once more,' he said. 'The main fire might catch the wagon.'

He made off afoot. She saw him start a dozen nucleuses of fires; saw them advance till they halted at the edge of the burned ground, beyond the wagon, so that it stood safe in a vast black island. He came to her, drove his scorched boots deep as he could into the mud and sat looking up the valley towards the emigrant train. An additional curtain of smoke showed that the men there now were setting out back fires of their own. He heard her voice at last, 'It is the second time you have saved me – saved my life, I think. Why did you come?'

He turned to her as she sat in the edge of the wallow, her face streaked with smoke, her garments half burned off her limbs. She now saw his hands, which he was thrusting out on the mud to cool them, and sympathy was in her gaze also.

'I don't know why I came,' said he. 'Didn't you signal for me? Jackson told me you could.'

'No, I had no hope. I meant no one. It was only a prayer.'

'It carried ten miles. We were all back-firing. It caught in the sloughs – all the strips of old grass. I thought of your camp, of you. At least your signal told me where to ride.'

At length he waved his hand.

'They're safe over there,' said he. 'Think of the children!'

'Yes, and you gave me my one chance. Why?'

'I don't know. I suppose it was because I am a brute!' The bitterness of his voice was plain.

'Come, we must go to the wagons,' said Molly at length, and would have risen.

'No, not yet. The burned ground must cool before we can walk on it. I would not even take my horse out on it again.' He lifted a foot of the black Spaniard, whose muzzle quivered whimperingly. 'All right, old boy!' he said, and stroked the head thrust down to him. 'It might have been worse.'

His voice was so gentle that Molly Wingate felt a vague sort of jealousy. He might have taken her scorched hand in his, might at least have had some thought for her welfare. He did speak at last as to that.

'What's in your wagon?' he asked. 'We had better go there to wait. Have you anything along – oil, flour, anything to use on burns? You're burned. It hurts me to see a woman suffer.'

'Are not you burned too?'

'Yes.'

'It pains you?'

'Oh, yes, of course.'

He rose and led the way over the damper ground to the wagon, which stood smoke-stained but not charred, thanks to his own resourcefulness.

Molly climbed up to the seat, and rummaging about found a jar of butter, a handful of flour.

'Come up on the seat,' said she. 'This is better medicine than nothing.'

He climbed up and sat beside her. She frowned again as she now saw how badly scorched his hands were, his neck, his face. His eyebrows, caught by one wisp of flame, were rolled up at the ends, whitened. One cheek was a dull red.

Gently, without asking his consent, she began to coat his burned skin as best she might with her makeshift of alleviation. His hand trembled under hers.

'Now,' she said, 'hold still. I must fix your hand some more.'

She still bent over, gently, delicately touching his flesh with hers. And then all in one mad, unpremeditated instant it was done!

His hand caught hers, regardless of the pain to either. His arm went about her, his lips would have sought hers.

It was done! Now he might repent.

A mad way of wooing, inopportune, fatal as any method he possibly could have found, moreover a cruel, unseemly thing to do, here and with her situated thus. But it was done.

Till now he had never given her grounds for more than guessing. Yet now here was this!

He came to his senses as she thrust him away; saw her cheeks whiten, her eyes grow wide.

'Oh!' she said. 'Oh! Oh! Oh!'

'Oh!' whispered Will Banion to himself, hoarsely.

He held his two scorched hands each side her face as she drew back, sought to look into her eyes, so that she might believe either his hope, his despair or his contrition.

But she turned her eyes away. Only he could hear her outraged protest – 'Oh! Oh! Oh!'

CHAPTER 14

The Kiss

'It was the wind!' Will Banion exclaimed. 'It was the sky, the earth! It was the fire! I don't know what it was! I swear it was not I who did it! Don't forgive me, but don't blame me. Molly! Molly!

'It had to be sometime,' he went on, since she still drew away from him. 'What chance have I had to ask you before now? It's little I have to offer but my love.'

'What do you mean? It will never be at any time!' said Molly Wingate slowly, her hand touching his no more.

'What do you yourself mean?' He turned to her in agony of soul. 'You will not let me repent? You will not give me some sort of chance?'

'No,' she said coldly. 'You have had chance enough to be a gentleman – as much as you had when you were in Mexico with other women. But Major William Banion falsified the regimental accounts. I know that too. I didn't – I couldn't believe it – till now.'

He remained dumb under this. She went on mercilessly.

'Oh, yes, Captain Woodhull told us. Yes, he showed us the very vouchers. My father believed it of you, but I didn't. Now I do. Oh, fine! And you an officer of our army!'

She blazed out at him now, her temper rising.

'Chance? What more chance did you need? No wonder you couldn't love a girl – any other way than this. It would have to be sometime, you say. What do you mean? That I'd ever marry a thief?'

Still he could not speak. The fire marks showed livid against a paling cheek.

'Yes, I know you saved me – twice, this time at much risk,' resumed the girl. 'Did you want pay so soon? You'd – you'd – '

'Oh! Oh! Oh!'

It was his voice that now broke in. He could not speak at all beyond the exclamation under torture.

'I didn't believe that story about you,' she added after a long time. 'But you are not what you looked, not what I thought you were. So what you say must be sometime is never going to be at all.'

'Did he tell you that about me?' demanded Will Banion savagely. 'Woodhull – did he say that?'

'I have told you, yes. My father knew. No wonder he didn't trust you. How could he?'

She moved now as though to leave the wagon, but he raised a hand.

'Wait!' said he. 'Look yonder! You'd not have time now to reach camp.'

In the high country a great prairie fire usually or quite often was followed by a heavy rainstorm. What Banion now indicated was the approach of yet another of the epic phenomena of the prairies, as rapid, as colossal and as merciless as the fire itself.

On the western horizon a low dark bank of clouds lay for miles, piled, serrated, steadily rising opposite to the course of the wind that had driven the fire. Along it more and more visibly played almost incessant sheet lightning, broken with ripping zigzag flames. A hush had fallen close at hand, for now even the frightened breeze of evening had fled. Now and then, at first doubtful, then unmistakable and continuous, came the mutter and rumble and at length the steady roll of thunder.

They lay full in the course of one of the tremendous storms of the high country, and as the cloud bank rose and came on swiftly, spreading its flanking wings so that nothing might escape, the spectacle was terrifying almost as much as that of the fire, for, unprotected as they were, they could make no counter battle against the storm.

The air grew supercharged with electricity. It dripped, literally, from the barrel of Banion's pistol when he took it from its holster to carry it to the wagon. He fastened the reins of his horse to a wheel and hastened with other work. A pair of trail ropes lay in the wagon. He netted them over the wagon top and lashed the ends to the wheels to make the top securer, working rapidly, eyes on the advancing storm.

There came a puff, then a gust of wind. The sky blackened. The storm caught the wagon train first. There was no interval at all between the rip of the lightning and the crash of thunder as it rolled down on the clustered wagons. The electricity at times came not in a sheet or a ragged bolt, but in a ball of fire, low down, close to the ground, exploding with giant detonations.

Then came the rain, with a blanketing rush of level wind, sweeping away the last vestige of the wastrel fires of the emigrant encampment. An instant and every human being in the train, most of them ill defended by their clothing, was drenched by the icy flood. One moment and the battering of hail made climax of it all. The groaning animals plunged and fell at their picket ropes, or broke and fled into the open. The remaining cattle caught terror, and since there was no corral, most of the cows and oxen stampeded down the wind.

The canvas covers of the wagons made ill defence. Many of them were stripped off, others leaked like sieves. Mothers sat huddled in their calicoes, bending over their tow-shirted young, some of them babes in arms. The single jeans garments of the boys gave them no comfort. Under the wagons and carts, wrapped in blankets or patched quilts whose colours dripped, they crawled and sat as the air grew strangely chill. Only wreckage remained when they saw the storm muttering its way across the prairies, having done what it could in its elemental wrath to bar the road to the white man.

As for Banion and Molly, they sat it out in the light wagon, the girl wrapped in blankets, Banion much of the time out in the storm, swinging on the ropes to keep the wagon from overturning. He had no apparent fear. His calm assuaged her own new terrors. In spite of her bitter arraignment, she was glad that he was here, though he hardly spoke to her at all.

'Look!' he exclaimed at last, drawing back the flap of the wagon cover. 'Look at the rainbow!'

Over the cloud banks of the rain-wet sky there indeed now was flung the bow of promise. But this titanic land did all things gigantically. This was no mere prismatic arch bridging the clouds. The colours all were there, yes, and of an unspeakable brilliance and individual distinctness in the scale; but they lay like a vast painted mist, a mural of some celestial artist flung *en masse* against the curtain of the night. The entire clouded sky, miles on untold miles, was afire. All the opals of the universe were melted and cast into a tremendous picture painted by the Great Spirit of the Plains.

'Oh, wonderful!' exclaimed the girl. 'It might be the celestial city in the desert, promised by the Mormon prophet!'

'It may be so to them. May it be so to us. Blessed be the name of the Lord God of Hosts!' said Will Banion.

She looked at him suddenly, strangely. What sort of man was he, after all, so full of strange contradictions – a savage, a criminal, yet reverent and devout?

'Come,' he said, 'we can get back now, and you must go. They will think you are lost.'

He stepped to the saddle of his shivering horse and drew off the poncho, which he had spread above the animal instead of using it himself. He was wet to the bone. With apology he cast the waterproof over Molly's shoulders, since she now had discarded her blankets. He led the way, his horse following them.

They walked in silence in the deep twilight which began to creep across the blackened land. All through the storm he had scarcely spoken to her, and he spoke but rarely now. He was no more than guide. But as she approached safety Molly Wingate began to reflect how much she really owed this man. He had been a pillar of strength, elementally fit to combat all the elements, else she had perished.

'Wait!'

She had halted at the point of the last hill which lay between them and the wagons. They could hear the wailing of the children close at hand. He turned enquiringly. She handed back the poncho.

'I am all right now. You're wet, you're tired, you're burned to pieces. Won't you come on in?'

'Not tonight!'

But still she hesitated. In her mind there were going on certain processes she could not have predicted an hour earlier.

'I ought to thank you,' she said. 'I do thank you.'

His utter silence made it hard for her. He could see her hesitation, which made it hard for him, coveting sight of her always, loath to leave her.

Now a sudden wave of something, a directness and frankness born in some way in this new world apart from civilisation, like a windblown flame, irresponsible and irresistible, swept over Molly Wingate's soul as swiftly, as unpremeditatedly as it had over his. She was a young woman fit for love, disposed for love, at the age for love. Now, to her horror, the clasp of this man's arm, even when repelled in memory, returned, remained in memory! She was frightened that it still remained – frightened at her own great curiousness.

'About – that' – he knew what she meant – 'I don't want you to think anything but the truth of me. If you have deceived people, I don't want to deceive you.'

'What do you mean?' He was a man of not very many words.

'About – that!'

'You said it could never be.'

'No. If it could, I would not be stopping here now to say so much.'

He stepped closer, frowning.

'What is it you are saying then – that a man's a worse brute when he goes mad, as I did?'

'I expect not,' said Molly Wingate queerly. 'It is very far, out here. It's some other world, I believe. And I suppose men have kissed girls. I suppose no girl ever was married who was not ever kissed.'

'What are you saying?'

'I said I wanted you to know the truth about a woman – about me. That's just because it's not ever going to be between us. It can't be, because of that other matter in Mexico. If it had not been for that, I suppose after a time I wouldn't have minded what you did back there. I might have kissed you. It must be terrible to feel as you feel now, so ashamed. But after all – '

'It was criminal!' he broke out. 'But even criminals are loved by women. They follow them to jail, to the gallows. They don't mind what the man is – they love him, they forgive him. They stand by him to the very end!'

'Yes, I suppose many a girl loves a man she knows she never can marry. Usually she marries someone else. But kissing! That's terrible!'

'Yes. But you will not let me make it splendid and not terrible. You say it never can be – that means we've got to part. Well, how can I forget?'

'I don't suppose you can. I don't suppose that – that I can!'

'What are you going to say? Don't! Oh, please don't!'

But she still went on, strangely, not in the least understanding her own swift change of mood, her own intent with him, *vis-à-vis*, here in the wilderness.

'While we were walking down here just now,' said she, 'somehow it all began to seem not so wrong. It only seemed to stay wrong for you to have deceived me about yourself – what you really were – when you were in the army. I could maybe forgive you up to that far, for you did – for men are – well, men. But about that other – you knew all the time we couldn't – couldn't ever – I'd never marry a thief.'

The great and wistful regret of her voice was a thing not to be escaped. She stood, a very splendid figure, clean and marvellous of heart as she was begrimed and bedraggled of body now, her great vital force not abated by what she had gone through. She spread her hands just apart and looked at him in what she herself felt was to be the last meeting of their lives; in which she could afford to reveal all her soul for once to a man, and then go about a woman's business of living a life fed on the husks of love given her by some other man.

He knew that he had seen one more miracle. But, chastened now, he could, he must, keep down his own eager arms. He heard her speak once more, her voice like some melancholy bell of vespers of a golden evening.

'Oh, Will Banion, how could you take away a girl's heart and leave her miserable all her life?'

The cry literally broke from her. It seemed in her own ears the sudden voice of some other woman speaking – some unaccountable, strange woman whom she never had seen or known in all her life.

'Your – heart?' he whispered, now close to her in the dusk. 'You were not – you did not – you – '

But he choked. She nodded, not brazenly or crudely or coarsely, not even bravely, but in utter simplicity. For the time she was wholly free of woman's coquetry. It was as though the elements had left her also elemental. Her words now were of the earth, the air, the fire, the floods of life.

'Yes,' she said, 'I will tell you now, because of what you have done for me. If you gave me life, why shouldn't I give you love – if so I could?'

'Love? Give me love?'

'Yes! I believe I was going to love you, until now, although I had promised him – you know – Captain Woodhull. Oh, you see, I under-stand a little of what it was to you – what made you – ' She spoke disconnectedly. 'I believe – I believe I'd not have cared. I believe I could follow a man to the gallows. Now I will not, because you didn't tell me you were a thief. I can't trust you. But I'll kiss you once for goodbye. I'm sorry. I'm so sorry.'

Being a man, he never fathomed her mind at all. But being a man, slowly, gently, he took her in his arms, drew her tight. Long, long it was till their lips met – and long then. But he heard her whisper, 'Goodbye,' saw her frank tears, felt her slowly, a little by a little, draw away from him.

'Goodbye,' she said. 'Goodbye. I would not dare, any more, ever again. Oh, Will Banion, why did you take away my heart? I had but one!'

'It is mine!' he cried savagely. 'No other man in all the world shall ever have it! Molly!'

But she now was gone.

He did not know how long he stood alone, his head bowed on his saddle. The raucous howl of a great grey wolf near by spelled out the lonesome tragedy of his future life for him.

Quaint and sweet philosopher, and bold as she but now had been in one great and final imparting of her real self, Molly Wingate was only a wet, weary and bedraggled maid when at length she entered the desolate encampment which stood for home. She found her mother sitting on a box under a crude awning, and cast herself on her knees, her head on that ample bosom that she had known as haven in her childhood. She wept now like a little child.

'It's bad!' said stout Mrs Wingate, not knowing. 'But you're back and alive. It looks like we're wrecked and everything lost, and we come nigh about getting all burned up, but you're back alive to your ma! Now, now!'

That night Molly turned on a sodden pallet which she had made down beside her mother in the great wagon. But she slept ill. Over and over to her lips rose the same question, 'Oh, Will Banion, Will Banion, why did you take away my heart?'

CHAPTER 15

The Division

The great wagon train of 1848 lay banked along the Vermilion in utter and abject confusion. Organisation there now was none. But for Banion's work with the back fires the entire train would have been wiped out. The effects of the storm were not so capable of evasion. Sodden, wretched, miserable, chilled, their goods impaired, their cattle stampeded, all sense of gregarious self-reliance gone, two hundred wagons were no more than two hundred individual units of discontent and despair. So far as could be prophesied on facts apparent, the journey out to Oregon had ended in disaster almost before it was well begun.

Bearded men at smoking fires looked at one another in silence, or would not look at all. Elan, morale, esprit de corps were gone utterly.

Stout Caleb Price walked down the wagon lines, passing fourscore men shaking in their native agues, not yet conquered. Women, pale, gaunt, grim, looked at him from limp sunbonnets whose stays had been half dissolved. Children whimpered. Even the dogs, curled nose to tail under the wagons, growled surlily. But Caleb Price found at last the wagon of the bugler who had been at the wars and shook him out.

'Sound, man!' said Caleb Price. 'Play up 'Oh, Susannah'! Then sound the Assembly. We've got to have a meeting.'

They did have a meeting. Jesse Wingate scented mutiny and remained away.

'There's no use talking, men,' said Caleb Price, 'no use trying to fool ourselves. We're almost done, the way things are. I like Jess Wingate as well as any man I ever knew, but Jess Wingate's not the man. What shall we do?'

He turned to Hall, but Hall shook his head; to Kelsey, but Kelsey only laughed. 'I could get a dozen wagons through, maybe,' said the latter. 'Here's two hundred. Woodhull's the man, but Woodhull's gone – lost, I reckon, or maybe killed and lying out somewhere on these prairies. You take it, Cale.'

Price considered for a time.

'No,' said he at length. 'It's no time for one of us to take on what may be done better by someone else, because our women and children are at stake. The very best man's none too good for this job, and the more experience he has the better. The man who thinks fastest and clearest at the right time is the man we want, and the man we'd follow – the only man. Who'll he be?'

'Oh, I'll admit Banion had the best idea of crossing the Kaw,' said Kelsey. 'He got his own people over, too, somehow.'

'Yes, and they're together now ten miles below us. And Molly Wingate – she was caught out with her team by the fire – says it was Banion who started the back-fire. That saved his train and ours. Ideas that come too late are no good. We need some man with the right ideas at the right time.'

'You think it's Banion?' Hall spoke.

'I do think it's Banion. I don't see how it can be anyone else.'

'Woodhull'd never stand for it.'

'He isn't here.'

'Wingate won't.'

'He'll have to.'

The chief of mutineers, a grave and bearded man, waited for a time.

'This is a meeting of the train,' said he. 'In our government the majority rules. Is there any motion on this?'

Silence. Then rose Hall of Ohio, slowly, a solid man, with three wagons of his own.

'I've been against the Missouri outfit,' said he. 'They're a wild bunch, with no order or discipline to them. They're not all free-soilers, even if they're going out to Oregon. But if one man can handle them, he can handle us. An army man with a Western experience – who'll it be unless it is their man? So, Mr Chairman, I move for a committee of three, yourself to be one, to ride down and ask the Missourians to join on again, all under Major Banion.'

'I'll have to second that,' said a voice. Price saw a dozen nods. 'You've heard it, men,' said he. 'All in favour rise up.'

They stood, with not many exceptions – rough-clad, hard-headed, hard-handed men of the nation's vanguard. Price looked them over soberly.

'You see the vote, men,' said he. 'I wish Jess had come, but he didn't. Who'll be the man to ride down? Wingate?'

'He wouldn't go,' said Kelsey. 'He's got something against Banion; says he's not right on his war record – something – '

'He's right on his train record this far,' commented Price. 'We're not electing a Sabbath-school superintendent now, but a train captain who'll make these wagons cover twelve miles a day, average.

'Hall, you and Kelsey saddle up and ride down with me. We'll see what we can do. One thing sure, something has got to be done, or we might as well turn back. For one, I'm not used to that.'

They did saddle and ride – to find the Missouri column coming up with intention of pitching below, at the very scene of the massacre, which was on the usual Big Vermilion ford, steep-banked on either side, but with hard bottom.

Ahead of the train rode two men at a walk, the scout Jackson, and the man they sought. They spied him as the man on the black Spanish horse, found him a pale and tired young man, who apparently had slept as ill as they themselves. But in straight and manful fashion they told him their errand.

The pale face of Will Banion flushed, even with the livid scorch marks got in the prairie fire the day before. He considered.

'Gentlemen,' he said after a time, 'you don't know what you are asking of me. It would be painful for me to take that work on now.'

'It's painful for us to see our property lost and our families set afoot,' rejoined Caleb Price. 'It's not pleasant for me to do this. But it's no question, Major Banion, what you or I find painful or pleasant. The question is on the women and children. You know; that very well.'

'I do know it – yes. But you have other men. Where's Woodhull?'

'We don't know. We think the Pawnees got him among the others.'

'Jackson' – Banion turned to his companion – 'we've got to make a look-around for him. He's probably across the river somewhere.'

'Like enough,' rejoined the scout. 'But the first thing is for all us folks to git acrost the river too. Let him go to hell.'

'We want you, major,' said Hall quietly, and even Kelsey nodded.

'What shall I do, Jackson?' demanded Banion.

'Fly inter hit, Will,' replied that worthy. 'Leastways, take hit on long enough so's to git them acrost an' help git their cattle together. Ye couldn't git Wingate to work under ye no ways. But mebbe-so we can show 'em fer a day er so how Old Missoury gits acrost a country. Uh–huh?'

Again Banion considered, pondering many things of which none of these knew anything at all. At length he drew aside with the men of the main train.

'Park our wagons here, Bill,' he said. 'See that they are well parked, too. Get out your guards. I'll go up and see what we can do. We'll all cross here. Have your men get all the trail ropes out and lay in a lot of dry cottonwood logs. We'll have to raft some of the stuff over. See if there's any wild grapevines along the bottoms. They'll help hold the logs. So long.'

He turned, and with the instinct of authority rode just a half length ahead of the others on the return.

Jesse Wingate, a sullen and discredited Achilles, held to his tent, and Molly did as much, her stout-hearted and just-minded mother being the main source of Wingate news. Banion kept as far away from them as possible, but had Jed sent for.

'Jed,' said he, 'first thing, you get your boys together and go after the cattle. Most of them went downstream with the wind. The hobbled stuff didn't come back down the trail and must be below there too. The cows wouldn't swim the big river on a run. If there's rough country, with any shelter, they'd like enough begin to mill – it might be five miles, ten – I can't guess. You go find out.

'Now, you others, first thing, get your families all out in the sun. Spread out the bedclothes and get them dried. Build fires and cook your best right away – have the people eat. Get that bugle going and play something fast – 'Sweet Hour of Prayer' is for evening, not now. Give 'em Reveille, and then the cavalry charge. Play 'Susannah'.

'I'm going to ride the edge of the burning to look for loose stock. You others get a meal into these people – coffee, quinine, more coffee. Then hook up all the teams you can and move down to the ford. We'll be on the Platte and among the buffalo in a week or ten days. Nothing can stop us. All you need is just a little more coffee and a little more system, and then a good deal more of both.

'Now's a fine time for this train to shake into place,' he added. 'You, Price, take your men and go down the lines. Tell your kinfolk and families and friends and neighbours to make bands and hang together. Let 'em draw cuts for place if they like, but stick where they go. We can't tell how the grass will be on ahead, and we may have to break the train into sections on the Platte; but we'll break it ourselves, and not see it fall apart or fight apart. So?'

He wheeled and went away at a trot. All he had given them was the one thing they lacked.

The Wingate wagons came in groups and halted at the river bank, where the work of rafting and wagon boating went methodically forward. Scores of individual craft, tipsy and risky, two or three logs lashed together, angled across and landed far below. Horsemen swam across with lines and larger rafts were steadied fore and aft with ropes snubbed around tree trunks on either bank. Once started, the resourceful pioneer found a dozen ways to skin his cat, as one man phrased it, and presently the falling waters permitted swimming and fording the stock. It all seemed ridiculously simple and ridiculously cheerful.

Towards evening a great jangling of bells and shouting of young captains announced the coming of a great band of the stampeded livestock – cattle, mules and horses mixed. Afar came the voice of Jed Wingate singing, 'Oh, then Susannah', and urging Susannah to have no concern.

But Banion, aloof and morose, made his bed that night apart even from his own train. He had not seen Wingate – did not see him till the next day, noon, when he rode up and saluted the former leader, who sat on his own wagon seat and not in the saddle.

'My people are all across, Mr Wingate,' he said, 'and the last of your wagons will be over by dark and straightened out. I'm parked a mile ahead.'

'You are parked? I thought you were elected – by my late friends – to lead this whole train.'

He spoke bitterly and with a certain contempt that made Banion colour.

'No. We can travel apart, though close. Do you want to go ahead, or shall I?'

'As you like. The country's free.'

'It's not free for some things, Mr Wingate,' rejoined the younger man hotly. 'You can lead or not, as you like; but I'll not train up with a man who thinks of me as you do. After this think what you like, but don't speak any more.'

'What do you mean by that?'

'You know very well. You've believed another man's word about my personal character. It's gone far enough and too far.'

'The other man is not here. He can't face you.'

'No, not now. But if he's on earth he'll face me sometime.'

Unable to control himself further, Banion wheeled and galloped away to his own train.

'You ask if we're to join in with the Yankees,' he flared out to Jackson. 'No! We'll camp apart and train apart. I won't go on with them.'

'Well,' said the scout, 'I didn't never think we would, er believe ye could; not till they git in trouble agin – er till a certain light wagon an' mules throws in with us, huh?'

'You'll say no more of that, Jackson! But one thing: you and I have got to ride and see if we can get any trace of Woodhull.'

'Like looking for a needle in a haystack, an' a damn bad needle at that,' was the old man's comment.

CHAPTER 16

The Plains

'On to the Platte! The buffalo!' New cheer seemed to come to the hearts of the emigrants now, and they forgot bickering. The main train ground grimly ahead, getting back, if not all its egotism, at least more and more of its self-reliance. By courtesy, Wingate still rode ahead, though orders came now from a joint council of his leaders, since Banion would not take charge.

The great road to Oregon was even now not a trail but a road, deep cut into the soil, though no wheeled traffic had marked it until within the past five years. A score of paralled paths it might be at times, of tentative location along a hillside or a marshy level; but it was for the most part a deep-cut, unmistakable road from which it had been impossible to wander. At times it lay worn into the sod a half-foot, a foot in depth. Sometimes it followed the ancient buffalo trails to water – the first roads of the Far West, quickly seized on by hunters and engineers – or again it trans-sected these, hanging to the ridges after frontier-road fashion, heading out for the proved fords of the greater streams. Always the wheelmarks of those who had gone ahead in previous years, the continuing thread of the trail itself, worn in by trader and trapper and Mormon and Oregon or California man, gave hope and cheer to these who followed with the plough.

Stretching out, closing up, almost inch by inch, like some giant measuring worm in its slow progress, the train held on through a vast and stately landscape, which some travellers had called the Eden of America, such effect was given by the series of altering scenes. Small imagination, indeed, was needed to picture here a long-established civilisation, although there was not a habitation. They were beyond organised society and beyond the law.

Game became more abundant, wild turkeys still appeared in the timbered creek bottoms. Many elk were seen, more deer and very many antelope, packed in northward by the fires. A number of panthers and giant grey wolves beyond counting kept the hunters always excited. The wild abundance of an unexhausted nature offered at every hand. The sufficiency of life brought daily growth in the self-reliance which had left them for a time.

The wide timberlands, the broken low hills of the green prairie at length began to give place to a steadily rising inclined plane. The soil became less black and heavy, with more sandy ridges. The oak and hickory, stout trees of their forefathers, passed, and the cottonwoods appeared. After they had crossed the ford of the Big Blue – a hundred yards of racing water – they passed what is now the line between Kansas and Nebraska, and followed up the Little Blue, beyond whose ford the trail left these quieter river valleys and headed out over a high tableland in a keen straight flight over the great valley of the Platte, the highway to the Rockies.

Now the soil was sandier; the grass changed yet again. They had rolled under wheel by now more than one hundred different varieties of wild grasses. The vegetation began to show the growing altitude. The cactus was seen now and then. On the far horizon the wavering mysteries of the mirage appeared, marvellous in deceptiveness, mystical, alluring, the very spirits of the Far West appearing to move before their eyes in giant pantomime. They were passing from the Prairies to the Plains.

Shouts and cheers arose as the word passed back that the sand-hills known as the Coasts of the Platte were in sight. Some mothers told their children they were now almost in Oregon. The whips cracked more loudly, the tired teams, tongues lolling, quickened their pace as they struck the down-grade gap leading through the sand-ridges.

Two thousand Americans, some of them illiterate and ignorant, all of them strong, taking with them law, order, society, the church, the school, anew were staging the great drama of human life, act and scene and episode, as though upon some great moving platform drawn by invisible cables beyond the vast proscenium of the hills.

CHAPTER 17

The Great Encampment

As the long columns of the great wagon train broke through the screening sand-hills there was disclosed a vast and splendid panorama. The valley of the Platte lay miles wide, green in the full covering of spring. A crooked and broken thread of timber growth appeared, marking the moister soil and outlining the general course of the shallow stream, whose giant cottonwoods were dwarfed now by the distances. In between, and for miles up and down the flat expanse, there rose the blue smoke of countless camp fires, each showing the location of some white-topped ship of the Plains. Black specks, grouped here and there, proved the presence of the livestock under herd.

Over all shone a pleasant sun. Now and again the dark shadow of a moving cloud passed over the flat valley, softening its highlights for the time. At times, as the sun shone full and strong, the faint loom of the mirage added the last touch of mysticism, the figures of the wagons rising high, multiplied many-fold, with giant creatures passing between, so that the whole seemed, indeed, some wild phantasmagoria of the desert.

'Look!' exclaimed Wingate, pulling up his horse. 'Look, Caleb, the Northern train is in and waiting for us! A hundred wagons! They're camped over the whole bend.'

The sight of this vast reinforcement brought heart to every man, woman and child in all the advancing train. Now, indeed, Oregon was sure. There would be, all told, four hundred – five hundred – above six hundred wagons. Nothing could withstand them. They were the same as arrived!

As the great trains blended before the final emparkment men and women who had never met before shook hands, talked excitedly, embraced, even wept, such was their joy in meeting their own kind. Soon the vast valley at the foot of the Grand Island of the Platte – ninety miles in length it then was – became one vast bivouac whose parallel had not been seen in all the world.

Even so, the Missouri column held back, an hour or two later on the trail. Banion, silent and morose, still rode ahead, but all the flavour of his adventure out to Oregon had left him – indeed, the very savour of life itself. He looked at his arms, empty; touched his lips, where once her kiss had been, so infinitely and ineradicably sweet. Why should he go on to Oregon now?

As they came down through the gap in the Coasts, looking out over the Grand Island and the great encampment, Jackson pulled up his horse.

'Look! Someone comin' out!'

Banion sat his horse awaiting the arrival of the rider, who soon cut down the intervening distance until he could well be noted. A tall, spare man he was, middle-aged, of long lank hair and grey stubbled beard, and eyes overhung by bushy brows. He rode an Indian pad saddle, without stirrups, and was clad in the old costume of the hunter of the Far West – fringed shirt and leggings of buckskin. Moccasins made his foot-covering, though he wore a low, wide hat. As he came on at speed, guiding his wiry mount with a braided rope looped around the lower jaw, he easily might have been mistaken for a savage himself had he not come alone and from such company as that ahead. He jerked up his horse close at hand and sat looking at the newcomers, with no salutation beyond a short, 'How!'

Banion met him.

'We're the Westport train. Do you come from the Bluffs? Are you for Oregon?'

'Yes. I seen ye comin'. Thought I'd projeck some. Who's that back of ye?' He extended an imperative skinny finger toward Jackson. 'If it hain't Bill Jackson hit's his ghost!'

'The same to you, Jim. How!'

The two shook hands without dismounting.

Jackson turned grinning to Banion. 'Major,' said he, 'this is Jim Bridger, the oldest scout in the Rockies, an' a man that knows more West than any man this side the Missoury. I never thought to see him agin, sartain not this far east.'

'Ner me,' retorted the other, shaking hands with one man after another.

'Jim Bridger? That's a name we know,' said Banion. 'I've heard of you back in Kentucky.'

'Whar I come from, gentlemen – whar I come from more'n forty year ago, near's I can figger. Leastways I was borned in Virginny an' must of crossed Kentucky sometime. I kain't tell right how old I am, but I rek'lect perfect when they turned the water inter the Missoury River.' He looked at them solemnly.

'I come back East to the new place, Kansas City. It didn't cut no mustard, an' I drifted to the Bluffs. This train was pullin' West, an' I hired on for guide. I've got a few wagons o' my own – iron, flour an' bacon for my post beyant the Rockies – ef we don't all git our ha'r lifted afore then!

'We're in between the Sioux and the Pawnees now,' he went on. 'They're huntin' the bufflers not ten mile ahead. But when I tell these pilgrims, they laugh at me. The hull Sioux nation is on the spring hunt right now. I'll not have it said Jim Bridger led a wagon train into a massacree. If ye'll let me, I'm for leavin' 'em an' trainin' with you-all, especial since you got anyhow one good man along. I've knowed Bill Jackson many a year at the Rendyvous afore the fur trade petered. Damn the pilgrims! The hull world's broke loose this spring. There's five thousand Mormons on ahead, praisin' God every jump an' eatin' the grass below the roots. Womern an' children – so many of 'em, so many! I kain't talk about hit! Women don't belong out here! An' now here you come bringin' a thousand more!

'There's a woman an' a baby layin' dead in oar camp now,' he concluded. 'Died last night. The pilgrims is tryin' to make coffins fer 'em out'n cottonwood logs.'

'Lucky for all!' Jackson interrupted the garrulity of the other. 'We buried men in blankets on the Vermilion a few days back. The Pawnees got a small camp o' our own folks.'

'Yes, I know all about that.'

'What's that?' cut in Banion. 'How do you know?'

'Well, we've got the survivors – three o' them, countin' Woodhull, their captain.'

'How did they get here?'

'They came in with a small outfit o' Mormons that was north o' the Vermilion. They'd come out on the St Jo road. They told me – '

'Is Woodhull here – can you find him?'

'Shore! Ye want to see him?'

'Yes.'

'He told me all about hit – '

'We know all about it, perhaps better than you do – after he's told you all about it.'

Bridger looked at him, curious.

'Well, anyhow, hit's over,' said he. 'One of the men had a Pawnee arrer in his laig. Reckon hit hurt. I know, fer I carried a Blackfoot arrerhead under my shoulder blade fer sever'l years.

'But come on down and help me make these pilgrims set guards. Do-ee mind, now, the hull Sioux nation's just in ahead o' us, other side the river! Yet these people didn't want to ford to the south side the Platte; they wanted to stick north o' the river. Ef we had, we'd have our ha'r dryin' by now. I tell ye, the tribes is out to stop the wagon trains this spring. They say too many womern and children is comin', an' that shows we want to take their land away fer keeps.

'From now on to Oregon – look out! The Cayuses cleaned out the Whitman mission last spring in Oregon. Even the Shoshones is dancin'. The Crows is out, the Cheyennes is marchin', the Bannocks is east o' the Pass, an' ye kain't tell when ter expeck the Blackfoots an' Grow Vaws. Never was gladder to see a man than I am to see Bill Jackson.'

'Stretch out!'

Banion gave the order. The Missouri wagons came on, filed through the gap in order and with military exactness wheeled into a perfect park at one side the main caravan.

As the outer columns swung in, the inner spread out till the lapped wagons made a great oblong, Bridger watching them. Quickly the animals were outspanned, the picket ropes put down and the loose horses driven off to feed while the cattle were close herded. He nodded his approval.

'Who's yer train boss, Bill?' he demanded. 'That's good work.'

'Major Banion, of Doniphan's column in the war.'

'Will he fight?'

'Try him!'

News travels fast along a wagon train. Word passed now that there was a big Sioux village not far ahead, on the other side of the river, and that the caravan should be ready for a night attack. Men and women from the earlier train came into the Westport camp and the leaders formulated plans. More than four hundred families ate in sight of one another's fires that evening.

Again on the still air of the Plains that night rose the bugle summons, by now become familiar. In groups the wagon folk began to assemble at the council fire. They got instructions which left them serious. The camp fell into semi-silence. Each family returned to its own wagon. Out in the dark, flung around in a wide circle, a double watch stood guard. Wingate and his aids, Banion, Jackson, Bridger, the pick of the hardier men, went out for all the night. It was to Banion, Bridger and Jackson that most attention now was paid. Banion could not yet locate Woodhull in the train.

The scouts crept out ahead of the last picket line, for though an attack *en masse* probably would not come before dawn, if the Sioux really should cross the river, some horse stealing or an attempted stampede might be expected before midnight or soon after.

The night wore on. The fires of willow twigs and *bois des vaches* fell into pale coals, into ashes. The chill of the Plains came, so that the sleepers in the great wagon corral drew their blankets closer about them as they lay.

It was approaching midnight when the silence was ripped apart by the keen crack of a rifle – another and yet another.

Then, in a ripple of red detonation, the rifle fire ran along the upper front of the entire encampment.

'Turn out! Turn out, men!' called the high, clear voice of Banion, riding back. 'Barricade! Fill in the wheels!'

CHAPTER 18

Arrow and Plough

The night attack on the great emigrant encampment was a thing which had been preparing for years. The increasing number of the white men, the lessening numbers of the buffalo, meant inevitable combat with all the tribes sooner or later.

Now the spring hunt of the northern Plains tribes was on. Five hundred lodges of the Sioux stood in one village on the north side of the Platte. The scaffolds were red with meat, everywhere the women were dressing hides and the camp was full of happiness. For a month the great Sioux nation had prospered, according to its lights. Two hundred stolen horses were under the wild herdsmen, and any who liked the meat of the spotted buffalo might kill it close to camp from the scores taken out of the first caravans up the Platte that year – the Mormons and other early trailers whom the Sioux despised because their horses were so few.

But the Sioux, fat with *boudins* and *depouille* and marrowbones, had waited long for the great Western train which should have appeared on the north side of the Platte, the emigrant road from the Council Bluffs.

For some days now they had known the reason, as Jim Bridger had explained – the wagons had forded the river below the Big Island. The white men's medicine was strong.

The Sioux did not know of the great rendezvous at the forks of the Great Medicine Road. Their watchmen, stationed daily at the eminences along the river bluffs of the north shore, brought back scoffing word of the carelessness of the whites. When they got ready they, too, would ford the river and take them in. They had not heeded the warning sent down the trail that no more whites should come into this country of the tribes. It was to be war.

And now the smoke signals said yet more whites were coming in from the south! The head men rode out to meet their watchmen. News came back that the entire white nation now had come into the valley from the south and joined the first train.

Here then was the chance to kill off the entire white nation, their women and their children, so there would be none left to come from towards the rising sun! Yes, this would end the race of the whites without doubt or question, because they all were here. After killing these it would be easy to send word West to the Arapahoes and Gros Ventres and Cheyennes, the Crows, the Blackfeet, the Shoshones, the Utes, to follow west on the Medicine Road and wipe out all who had gone on West that year and the year before. Then the Plains and the mountains would all belong to the red men again.

The chiefs knew that the hour just before dawn is when an enemy's heart is like water, when his eyes are heavy, so they did not order the advance at once. But a band of the young men who always fought together, one of the inner secret societies or clans of the tribe, could not wait so long. First come, first served. Daylight would be time to look over the children and to keep those not desired for killing, and to select and distribute the young women of the white nation. But the night would be best for taking the elk-dogs and the spotted buffalo.

Accordingly a band from this clan swam and forded the wide river, crossed the island, and in the early evening came downstream back of a shielding fringe of cottonwoods. Their scouts saw with amazement the village of tepees that moved on wheels. They heard the bugle, saw the white nation gather at the medicine fire, heard them chant their great medicine song; then saw them disperse; saw the fires fall low.

They laughed. The white nation was strong, but they did not put out guards at night! For a week the Sioux had watched them, and they knew about that. It would be easy to run off all the herd and to kill a few whites even now, beginning the sport before the big battle of tomorrow, which was to wipe out the white nation altogether.

But when at length, as the handle of the Great Dipper reached the point agreed, the line of the Sioux clansmen crawled away from the fringe of trees and out into the cover of a little slough that made towards the village of tepees on wheels, a quarter of a mile in front of the village men arose out of the ground and shot into them. Five of their warriors fell. Tall men in the dark came out and counted coup on them, took off their war bonnets; took off even more below the bonnets. And there was a warrior who rode this way and that, on a great black horse, and who had a strange war cry not heard before, and who seemed to have no fear. So said the clan leader when he told the story of the repulse.

Taken aback, the attacking party found cover. But the Sioux would charge three times. So they scattered and crawled in again over a half circle. They found the wall of tepees solid; found that the white nation knew more of war than they had thought. They sped arrow after arrow, ball after ball, against the circle of the white tepees, but they did not break, and inside no one moved or cried out in terror; whereas outside, in the grass, men rose up and fired into them and did not run back, but came forward. Some had short rifles in their hands that did not need to be loaded, but kept on shooting. And none of the white nation ran away. And the elk-dogs with long ears, and the spotted buffalo, were no longer outside the village in the grass, but inside the village. What men could fight a nation whose warriors were so unfair as all this came to?

The tribesmen drew back to the cottonwoods a half-mile.

'My heart is weak,' said their clan leader. 'I believe they are going to shoot us all. They have killed twenty of us now, and we have not taken a scalp.'

'I was close,' said a young boy, whom they called Bull Gets Up or Sitting Bull. 'I was close, and I heard the spotted buffalo running about inside the village; I heard the children. Tomorrow we can run them away.'

'But tonight what man knows the gate into their village? They have got a new chief today. They are many as the grass leaves. Their medicine is strong. I believe they are going to kill us all if we stay here.' Thus the partisan.

So they did not stay there, but went away. And at dawn Banion and Bridger and Jackson and each of the column captains – others also – came into the corral carrying war bonnets, shields and bows; and some had things which had been once below war bonnets. The young men of this clan always fought on foot or on horse in full regalia of their secret order, day or night. The emigrants had plenty of this savage war gear now.

'We've beat them off,' said Bridger, 'an' maybe they won't ring us now. Get the cookin' done, Cap'n Banion, an' let's roll out. But for your wagon park they'd have cleaned us.'

The whites had by no means escaped scathless. A dozen arrows stood sunk into the sides of the wagons inside the park, hundreds had thudded into the outer sides, nearest the enemy. One shaft was driven into the hard wood of a plough beam. Eight oxen staggered, legs wide apart, shafts fast in their bodies; four lay dead; two horses also; as many mules.

This was not all. As the fighting men approached the wagons they saw a group of stern-faced women weeping around something which lay covered by a blanket on the ground. Molly Wingate stooped, drew it back to show them. Even Bridger winced.

An arrow, driven by a buffalo bow, had glanced on the spokes of a wheel, risen in its flight and sped entirely across the enclosure of the corral. It had slipped through the canvas cover of a wagon on the opposite side as so much paper and caught fair a woman who was lying there, a nursing baby in her arms, shielding it, as she thought, with her body. But the missile had cut through one of her arms, pierced the head of the child and sunk into the bosom of the mother deep enough to kill her also. The two lay now, the shaft transfixing both; and they were buried there; and they lie there still, somewhere near the Grand Island, in one of a thousand unknown and unmarked graves along the Great Medicine Road. Under the ashes of a fire they left this grave, and drove six hundred wagons over it, and the Indians never knew.

The leaders stood beside the dead woman, hats in hand. This was part of the price of empire – the life of a young woman, a bride of a year.

The wagons all broke camp and went on in a vast caravan, the Missourians now at the front. Noon, and the train did not halt. Banion urged the teamsters. Bridger and Jackson were watching the many signal smokes.

'I'm afeard o' the next bend,' said Jackson at length.

The fear was justified. Early in the afternoon they saw the outriders turn and come back to the train at full run. Behind them, riding out from the concealment of a clump of cottonwoods on the near side of the scattering river channels, there appeared rank after rank of the Sioux, more than two thousand warriors bedecked in all the savage finery of their war dress. They were after their revenge. They had left their village and, paralleling the white men's advance, had forded on ahead.

They came out now, five hundred, eight hundred, a thousand, two thousand strong, and the ground shook under the thunder of the hoofs. They were after their revenge, eager to inflict the final blow upon the white nation.

The spot was not ill chosen for their tactics. The alkali plain of the valley swung wide and flat, and the trail crossed it midway, far back from the water and not quite to the flanking sand-hills. While a few dashed at the cattle, waving their blankets, the main body, with workmanlike precision, strung out and swung wide, circling the train and riding into arrow range.

The quick orders of Banion and his scouts were obeyed as fully as time allowed. At a gallop, horse and ox transport alike were driven into a hurried park and some at least of the herd animals enclosed. The riflemen flanked the train on the danger side and fired continually at the long string of running horses, whose riders had flung themselves off-side so that only a heel showed above a pony's back, a face under his neck. Even at this range a half-dozen ponies stumbled, figures crawled off for cover. The emigrants were stark men with rifles. But the circle went on until, at the running range selected, the crude wagon park was entirely surrounded by a thin racing ring of steel and fire stretched out over two or three miles.

The Sioux had guns also, and though they rested most on the bow, their chance rifle fire was dangerous. As for the arrows, even from this disadvantageous station these peerless bowmen sent them up in a high arc so that they fell inside the enclosure and took their toll. Three men, two women lay wounded at the first ride, and the animals were plunging.

The war chief led his warriors in the circle once more, chanting his own song to the continuous chorus of savage ululations. The entire fighting force of the Sioux village was in the circle.

The ring ran closer. The Sioux were inside seventy-five yards, the dust streaming, the hideously painted faces of the riders showing through, red, saffron, yellow, as one after another warrior twanged a bow under his horse's neck as he ran.

But this was easy range for the steady rifles of men who kneeled and fired with careful aim. Even the six-shooters, then new to the Sioux, could work. Pony after pony fell, until the line showed gaps; whereas now the wagon corral showed no gap at all, while through the wheels, and over the tongue spaces, from every crevice of the grey towering wall came the fire of more and more men. The medicine of the white men was strong.

Three times the ring passed, and that was all. The third circuit was wide and ragged. The riders dared not come close enough to carry off their dead and wounded. Then the attack dwindled, the savages scattering and breaking back to the cover of the stream.

'Now, men, come on!' called out Banion. 'Ride them down! Give them a trimming they'll remember! Come on, boys!'

Within a half-hour fifty more Sioux were down, dead or very soon to die. Of the living not one remained in sight.

'They wanted hit, an' they got hit!' exclaimed Bridger, when at length he rode back, four war bonnets across his saddle and scalps at his cantle. He raised his voice in a fierce yell of triumph, not much other than savage himself, dismounted and disdainfully cast his trophies across a wagon tongue.

'I've et horse an' mule an' dog,' said he, 'an' wolf, wil'cat an' skunk, an' perrairy dog an' snake an' most ever'thing else that wears a hide, but I never could eat Sioux. But tomorrer we'll have ribs in camp. I've seed the buffler, an' we own this side the river now.'

Molly Wingate sat on a bedroll near by, knitting as calmly as though at home, but filled with wrath.

'Them nasty, dirty critters!' she exclaimed. 'I wish't the boys had killed them all. Even in daylight they don't stand up and fight fair like men. I lost a whole churnin' yesterday. Besides, they killed my best cow this mornin', that's what they done. And lookit this thing!'

She held up an Indian arrow, its strap-iron head bent over at right angles. 'They shot this into our plough beam. Looks like they got a spite at our plough.'

'Ma'am, they have got a spite at hit,' said the old scout, seating himself on the ground near by. 'They're scared o' hit. I've seed a bunch o' Sioux out at Laramie with a plough some Mormon left around when he died. They'd walk around and around that thing by the hour, talkin' low to theirselves. They couldn't figger hit out no ways a-tall.

'That season they sent a runner down to the Pawnees to make a peace talk, an' to find out what this yere thing was the whites had brung out. Pawnees sent to the Otoes, an' the Otoes told them. They said hit was the white man's big medicine, an' that hit buried all the buffler under the ground wherever hit come, so no buffler ever could git out again. Nacherl, when the runners come back an' told what that thing really was, all the Injuns, every tribe, said if the white man was goin' to bury the buffler the white man had got to stay back.

'Us trappers an' traders got along purty well with the Injuns – they could get things they wanted at the posts or the Rendyvous, an' that was all right. They had pelts to sell. But now these movers didn't buy nothin' an' didn't sell nothin'. They just went on through, a-carryin' this thing for buryin' the buffler. From now on the Injuns is goin' to fight the whites. Ye kain't blame 'em, ma'am; they only see their finish.

'Five years ago nigh a thousand whites drops down in Oregon. Next year come fifteen hundred, an' in '45 twicet that many, an' so it has went, doublin' an' doublin'. Six or seven thousand whites go up the Platte this season, an' a right smart sprinklin' o' them'll git through to Oregon. Them 'at does'll carry ploughs.

'Ma'am, if the brave that sunk a arrer in yore plough beam didn't kill yore plough hit warn't because he didn't want to. Hit's the truth – the plough does bury the buffler, an' fer keeps! Ye kain't kill a plough, ner neither kin yer scare hit away. Hit's the holdin'est thing ther is, ma'am – hit never does let go.'

'How long'll we wait here?' the older woman demanded.

'Anyhow fer two-three days, ma'am. Thar's a lot has got to sort out stuff an' throw hit away here. One man has drug a pair o' millstones all the way to here from Ohio. He allowed to get rich startin' a gris'mill out in Oregon. An' then ther's chairs an' tables, an' God knows what – '

'Well, anyhow,' broke in Mrs Wingate truculently, 'no difference what you men say, I ain't going to leave my bureau, nor my table, nor my chairs! I'm going to keep my two churns and my featherbed too. We've had butter all the way so far, and I mean to have it all the way – and eggs. I mean to sleep at nights, too, if the pesky muskeeters'll let me. They most have et me up. And I'd give a dollar for a drink of real water now. It's all right to settle this water overnight, but that don't take the sody out of it.

'Besides,' she went on, 'I got four quarts o' seed wheat in one of them bureau drawers, and six cuttings of my best rose-bush I'm taking out to plant in Oregon. And I got three pairs of Jed's socks in another bureau drawer. It's flat on its back, bottom of the load. I ain't going to dig it out for no man.'

'Well, hang on to them socks, ma'am. I've wintered many a time without none – only grass in my moccasins. There's outfits in this train that's low on flour an' side meat right now, let alone socks. We got to cure some meat. There's a million buffler just south in the breaks wantin' to move on north, but scared of us an' the Injuns. We'd orto make a good hunt inside o' ten mile tomorrer. We'll git enough meat to take us a week to jerk hit all, or else Jim Bridger's a liar – which no one never has said yit, ma'am.

'Flowers?' he added. 'You takin' flowers acrost? Flowers – do they go with the plough, too, as well as weeds? Well, well! Wimminfolks shore air a strange race o' people, hain't that the truth? Buryin' the buffler an' plantin' flowers on his grave!

'But speakin' o' buryin' things,' he suddenly resumed, 'an' speakin' o' ploughs, 'minds me o' what's delayin' us all right now. Hit's a fool thing, too – buryin' Injuns!'

'As which, Mr Bridger? What you mean?' enquired Molly Wingate, looking over her spectacles.

'This new man, Banion, that come in with the Missouri wagons – he taken hit on hisself to say, atter the fight was over, we orto stop an' bury all them Injuns! Well, I been on the Plains an' in the Rockies all my life, an' I never yit, before now, seed a Injun buried. Hit's onnatcherl. But this here man he, now, orders a ditch ploughed an' them Injuns hauled in an' planted. Hit's wastin' time. That's what's keepin' him an' yore folks an' sever'l others. Yore husband an' yore son is both out yan with him. Hit beats hell, ma'am, these new-fangled ways!'

'So that's where they are? I wanted them to fetch me something to make a fire.'

'I kain't do that, ma'am. Mostly my squaws – '

'Your what? Do you mean to tell me you got squaws, you old heathen?'

'Not many, ma'am – only two. Times is hard sence beaver went down. I kain't tell ye how hard this here depressin' has set on us folks out here.'

'Two squaws! My laws! Two – what's their names?' This last with feminine curiosity.

'Well now, ma'am, I call one on 'em Blast Yore Hide – she's a Ute. The other is younger an' pertier. She's a Shoshone. I call her Dang Yore Eyes. Both them women is powerful fond o' me, ma'am. They both are right proud o' their names, too, because they air white names, ye see. Now when time comes fer a fire, Blast Yore Hide an' Dang Yore Eyes, they fight hit out between 'em which gits the wood. I don't study none over that, ma'am.'

Molly Wingate rose so ruffled that, like an angered hen, she seemed twice her size.

'You old heathen!' she exclaimed. 'You old murderin' lazy heathen man! How dare you talk like that to me?'

'As what, ma'am? I hain't said nothin' out'n the way, have I? O' course, ef ye don't want to git the fire stuff, thar's yer darter – she's young an' strong. Yes, an' perty as a picter besides, though like enough triflin', like her maw. Where's she at now?'

'None of your business where.'

'I could find her.'

'Oh, you could! How?'

'I'd find that young feller Sam Woodhull that come in from below, renegadin' away from his train with that party o' Mormons – him that had his camp jumped by the Pawnees. I got a eye fer a womern, ma'am, but so's he – more'n fer Injuns, I'd say. I seed him with yore darter right constant, but I seemed to miss him in the ride. Whar was he at?'

'I don't know and it's none of your business, anyways.'

'No? Well, I was just wonderin', ma'am, because I heerd Cap'n Banion ast that same question o' yore husband, Cap'n Wingate, an' Cap'n Wingate done said jest what ye said yerself – that hit wasn't none o' his business. Which makes things look shore hopeful an' pleasant in this yere train o' pilgrims, this bright and pleasant summer day, huh?'

Grinning amicably, the incorrigible old mountaineer rose and went his way, and left the irate goodwife to gather her apron full of plains fuel for herself.

CHAPTER 19

Banion of Doniphan's

Molly Wingate was grumbing over her fire when at length her husband and son returned to their wagon. Jed was vastly proud over a bullet crease he had got in a shoulder. After his mother's alarm had taken the form of first aid he was all for showing his battle scars to a certain damsel in Caleb Price's wagon. Wingate remained dour and silent, as was now his wont, and cursed his luck that he had had no horse to carry him up in the late pursuit of the Sioux. He also was bitter over the delay in making a burial trench.

'Some ways, Jess,' commented his spouse, 'I'd a'most guess you ain't got much use for Will Banion.'

'Why should I have? Hasn't he done all he could to shoulder me out of my place as captain of this train? And wasn't I elected at Westport before we started?'

'Mostly, a man has to stay elected, Jess.'

'Well, I'm going to! I had it out with that young man right now. I told him I knew why he wanted in our train – it was Molly.'

'What did he say?'

'What could he say? He admitted it. And he had the gall to say I'd see it his way some day. Huh! That's a long day off, before I do. Well, at least he said he was going back to his own men, and they'd fall behind again. That suits me.'

'Did he say anything about finding Sam Woodhull?'

'Yes. He said that would take its time, too.'

'Didn't say he wouldn't?'

'No, I don't know as he did.'

'Didn't act scared of it?'

'He didn't say much about it.'

'Sam does.'

'I reckon – and why shouldn't he? He'll play evens some day, of course. But now, Molly,' he went on, with heat, 'what's the use talking? We both know that Molly's made up her mind. She loves Sam and don't love this other man any more than I do. He's only a drift-about back from the war, and wandering out to Oregon. He'll maybe not have a cent when he gets there. He's got one horse and his clothes, and one or two wagons, maybe not paid for. Sam's got five wagons of goods to start a store with, and three thousand in gold – so he says – as much as we have. The families are equal, and that's always a good thing. This man Banion can't offer Molly nothing, but Sam Woodhull can give her her place right from the start, out in Oregon. We got to think of all them things.

'And I've got to think of a lot of other things, too. It's our girl. It's all right to say a man can go out to Oregon and live down his past, but it's a lot better not to have no past to live down. You know what Major Banion done, and how he left the army – even if it wasn't why, it was how, and that's bad enough. Sam Woodhull has told us both all about Banion's record. If he'd steal in Mexico he'd steal in Oregon.'

'You didn't ever get so far along as to talk about that!'

'We certainly did – right now, him and me, not half an hour ago, while we was riding back.'

'I shouldn't have thought he'd of stood it,' said his wife, 'him sort of fiery-like.'

'Well, it did gravel him. He got white, but wouldn't talk. Asked if Sam Woodhull had the proof, and I told him he had. That was when he said he'd go back to his own wagons. I could see he was avoiding Sam. But I don't see how, away out here, and no law nor nothing, we're ever going to keep the two apart.'

'They wasn't.'

'No. They did have it out, like schoolboys behind a barn. Do you suppose that'll ever do for a man of spirit like Sam Woodhull? No, there's other ways. And as I said, it's a far ways from the law out here, and getting farther every day, and wilder and wilder every day. It's only putting it off, Molly, but on the whole I was glad when Banion said he'd give up looking for Sam Woodhull this morning and go on back to his own men.'

'Did he say he'd give it up?'

'Yes, he did. He said if I'd wait I'd see different. Said he could wait – said he was good at waiting.'

'But he didn't say he'd give it up?'

'I don't know as he did in so many words.'

'He won't,' said Molly Wingate.

CHAPTER 20

The Buffalo

The emigrants had now arrived at the eastern edge of the great region of free and abundant meat. They now might count on at least six or seven hundred miles of buffalo to subsist them on their way to Oregon. The cry of 'Buffalo! Buffalo!' went joyously down the lines of wagons, and every man who could muster a horse and a gun made ready for that chase which above all others meant most, whether in excitement or in profit.

Of these hundreds of hunters, few had any experience on the Plains. It was arranged by the head men that the hunt should be strung out over several miles, the Missourians farthest down the river, the others to the westward, so that all might expect a fairer chance in an enterprise of so much general importance.

Banion and Jackson, in accordance with the former's promise to Wingate, had retired to their own train shortly after the fight with the Sioux. The Wingate train leaders therefore looked to Bridger as their safest counsel in the matter of getting meat. That worthy headed a band of the best equipped men and played his own part in full character. A wild figure he made as he rode, hatless, naked to the waist, his legs in Indian leggings and his feet in moccasins. His mount, a compact cayuse from west of the Rockies, bore no saddle beyond a folded blanket cinched on with a rawhide band.

For weapons Bridger carried no firearms at all, but bore a short buffalo bow of the Pawnees – double-curved, sinew-backed, made of the resilient *bois d'arc*, beloved bow wood of all the Plains tribes. A thick sheaf of arrows, newly sharpened, swung in the beaver quiver at his back. Lean, swart, lank of hair, he had small look of the white man left about him as he rode now, guiding his horse with a jaw rope of twisted hair and playing his bow with a half-dozen arrows held along it with the fingers of his left hand.

'For buffler the bow's the best,' said he. 'I'll show ye before long.'

They had not too far to go. At that time the short-grass country of the Platte Valley was the great centre of the bison herds. The wallows lay in thousands, the white alkali showing in circles which almost touched edge to edge. The influx of emigrants had for the time driven the herds back from their ancient fords and watering places, to which their deep-cut trails led down, worn ineradicably into the soil. It was along one of the great buffalo trails that they now rode, breasting the line of hills that edged the Platte to the south.

When they topped the flanking ridge a marvellous example of wild abundance greeted them. Bands of elk, yet more numerous bands of antelope, countless curious grey wolves and more than one grizzly bear made away before them, but by orders were left unpursued. Of the feathered game they had now forgot all thought. The buffalo alone was of interest. The wild guide rode silent, save for a low Indian chant he hummed, his voice at times rising high, as though importunate.

'Ye got to pray to the Great Speret when-all ye hunt, men,' he explained. 'An' ye got to have someone that can call the buffler, as the Injuns calls them when they hunt on foot. I kin call 'em, too, good as any Injun. Why shouldn't I?

'Thar now!' he exclaimed within the next quarter of an hour. 'What did

Jim Bridger tell ye? Lookee yonder! Do-ee say Jim Bridger can't make buffler medicine? Do-ee see 'em over yan ridge – thousands?'

The others felt their nerves jump as they topped the ridge and saw fully the vast concourse of giant black-topped, beard-fronted creatures which covered the plateau in a body a mile and more across – a sight which never failed to thrill any who saw it.

It was a rolling carpet of brown, like the prairie's endless wave of green. Dust clouds of combat rose here and there. A low muttering rumble of hoarse dull bellowing was audible, even at that distance. The spectacle was to the novice not only thrilling – it was terrifying.

The general movement of the great pack was towards the valley; closest to them a smaller body of some hundreds that stood, stupidly staring, not yet getting the wind of their assailants.

Suddenly rose the high-pitched yell of the scout, sounding the charge. Snorting, swerving, the horses of the others followed his, terror smitten but driven in by men most of whom at least knew how to ride.

Smoothly as a bird in flight, Bridger's trained buffalo horse closed the gap between him and a plunging bunch of the buffalo. The white savage proved himself peer of any savage of the world. His teeth bared as he threw his body into the bow with a short, savage jab of the left arm as he loosed the sinew cord. One after another feather showed, clinging to a heaving flank; one after another muzzle dripped red with the white foam of running; then one after another great animal began to slow; to stand braced, legs apart; soon to begin slowly kneeling down. The living swept ahead, the dying lay in the wake.

The insatiate killer clung on, riding deep into the surging sea of rolling humps. At times, in savage sureness and cruelty, he did not ride abreast and drive the arrow into the lungs, but shot from the rear, quartering, into the thin hide back of the ribs, so that the shaft ranged forward into the intestines of the victim. If it did not bury, but hung free as the animal kicked at it convulsively, he rode up, and with his hand pushed the shaft deeper, feeling for the life, as the Indians called it, with short jabs of the embedded missile. Master of an old trade he was, and stimulated by the proofs of his skill, his followers emulated him with their own weapons. The report of firearms, muffled by the rolling thunder of hoofs, was almost continuous so long as the horses could keep touch with the herd.

Bridger paused only when his arrows were out, and grumbled to himself that he had no more, so could count only a dozen fallen buffalo for his product. That others, wounded, carried off arrows, he called bad luck and bad shooting. When he trotted back on his reeking horse, his quiver dancing empty, he saw other black spots than his own on the short grass. His followers had picked up the art not so ill. There was meat in sight now, certainly – as well as a half-dozen unhorsed riders and three or four wounded buffalo disposed to fight.

The old hunter showed his men how to butcher the buffalo, pulling them on their bellies, if they had not died thus, and splitting the hide down the back, to make a receptacle for the meat as it was dissected; showed them how to take out the tongue beneath the jaw, after slitting open the lower jaw. He besought them not to throw away the back fat, the hump, the boss ribs or the intestinal *boudins*; in short, gave them their essential buffalo-hunting lessons. Then he turned for camp, he himself having no relish for squaw's work, as he called it, and well assured the wagons would now have abundance.

Banion and Jackson, with their followers, held their hunt some miles below the scene of Bridger's chase, and had no greater difficulty in getting among the herds.

'How're ye ridin', Will?' asked Jackson before they mounted for the start from camp.

Banion slapped the black stallion on the neck.

'Not his first hunt!' said he.

'I don't mean yore hoss, but yore shootin' irons. Whar's yore guns?'

'I'll risk it with the dragoon revolvers,' replied Banion, indicating his holsters. 'Not the first time for them, either.'

'No? Well, maybe-so they'll do; but fer me, I want a hunk o' lead. Fer approachin' a buffler, still-huntin', the rifle's good, fer ye got time an' kin hold close. Plenty o' our men'll hunt thataway today, an' git meat; but fer me, give me a hunk o' lead. See here now, I got only a shotgun, cap an' ball, fourteen gauge, she is, an' many a hide she's stretched. I kerry my bullets in my mouth an' don't use no patchin' – ye hain't got time, when ye're runnin' in the herd. I let go a charge o' powder out'n my horn, clos't as I kin guess hit, spit in a bullet, and roll her home on top the powder with a jar o' the butt on top my saddle horn. That sots her down, an' she holds good enough to stay in till I ram the muzzle inter ha'r an' let go. She's the same as meat on the fire.'

'Well,' laughed Banion, 'you've another case of de gustibus, I suppose.'

'You're another, an' I call it back!' exclaimed the old man so truculently that his friend hastened to explain.

'Well, I speak Blackfoot, Crow, Bannack, Grow Vaw, Snake an' Ute,' grumbled the scout, 'but I never run acrost no Latins out here. I allowed maybe-so ye was allowin' I couldn't kill buffler with Ole Sal. That's what I keep her fer – just buffler. I'll show ye afore long.'

And even as Bridger had promised for his favourite weapon, he did prove beyond cavil the efficiency of Old Sal. Time after time the roar or the double roar of his fusee was heard, audible even over the thunder of the hoofs; and quite usually the hunk of lead, driven into heart or lights, low down, soon brought down the game, stumbling in its stride. The old half-breed style of loading, too, was rapid enough to give Jackson as many buffalo as Bridger's bow had claimed before his horse fell back and the dust cloud lessened in the distance.

The great speed and bottom of Banion's horse, as well as the beast's savage courage and hunting instinct, kept him in longer touch with the running game. Banion was in no haste. From the sound of firing he knew his men would have meat. Once in the surge of the running herd, the rolling backs, low heads and lolling tongues, shaggy frontlets and gleaming eyes all about him, he dropped the reins on Pronto's neck and began his own work carefully, riding close and holding low, always ready for the sudden swerve of the horse away from the shot to avoid the usual rush of the buffalo when struck. Since he took few chances, his shot rarely failed. In a mile or so, using pains, he had exhausted all but two shots, one in each weapon, and of course no man could load the old cap-and-ball revolver while in the middle of a buffalo run. Now, out of sheer pride in his own skill with small arms, he resolved upon attempting a feat of which he once had heard but never had seen.

Jackson, at a considerable distance to the rear, saw his leader riding back of two bulls which he had cut off and which were making frantic efforts to overtake the herd. After a time they drew close together, running parallel and at top speed. At the distance, what Jackson saw was a swift rush of the black horse between the two bulls. For an instant the three seemed to run neck and neck. Then the rider's arms seemed extended, each on its side. Two puffs of blue smoke stained the grey dust. The black horse sprang straight ahead, not swerving to either side. Two stumbling forms slowed, staggered and presently fell. Then the dust passed, and he saw the rider trot back, glancing here and there over the broad rolling plain at the work of himself and his men.

'I seed ye do hit, boy!' exclaimed the grizzled old hunter when they met. 'I seed ye plain, an' ef I hadn't, an' ye'd said ye'd did hit, I'd of said ye was a liar.'

'Oh, the double?' Banion coloured, not ill pleased at praise from Sir Hubert, praise indeed. 'Well, I'd heard it could be done.'

'Once is enough. Let 'em call ye a liar atter this! Ef any one o' them bulls had hit ye ye'd have had no hoss; an' any one was due to hit ye, or drive ye against the other, an' then he would. That's a trap I hain't ridin' inter noways, not me!'

He looked at his own battered piece a trifle ruefully.

'Well, Ole Sal,' said he, ' 'pears like you an' me ain't newfangled enough for these times, not none! When I git to Oregon, ef I ever do, I'm a goin' to stay thar. Times back, five year ago, no one dreamed o' wagons, let alone ploughs. Fust thing, they'll be makin' ploughs with wheels, an' rifles that's six-shooters too!'

He laughed loud and long at his own conceit.

'Well, anyways,' said he, 'we got meat. We've licked one red nation an' got enough meat to feed the white nation, all in a couple o' days. Not so bad – not so bad.'

And that night, in the two separate encampments, the white nation, in bivouac, on its battle ground, sat around the fires of *bois des vaches* till near morning, roasting boss ribs, breaking marrowbones, laughing, singing,

boasting, shaking high their weapons of war, men making love to their women – the Americans, most terrible and most successful of all savages in history.

But from one encampment two faces were missing until late – Banion and Jackson of the Missourians. Sam Woodhull, erstwhile column captain of the great train, of late more properly to be called unattached, also was absent. It was supposed by their friends that these men might be out late, superintending the butchering, or that at worst they were benighted far out and would find their way to camp the next morning.

Neither of these guesses was correct. Any guess, to be correct, must have included in one solution the missing men of both encampments, who had hunted miles apart.

CHAPTER 21

The Quicksands

As Banion and Jackson ended their part in the buffalo running and gave instructions to the wagon men who followed to care for the meat, they found themselves at a distance of several miles from their starting point. They were deep into a high rolling plateau where the going was more difficult than in the level sunken valley of the Platte. Concluding that it would be easier to ride the two sides of the triangle than the one over which they had come out, they headed for the valley at a sharp angle. As they rode, the keen eye of Jackson caught sight of a black object apparently struggling on the ground at the bottom of a little swale which made down in a long ribbon of green.

'Look-ee yan!' he exclaimed. 'Some feller's lost his buffler, I expect. Let's ride down an' put him out'n his misery afore the wolves does.'

They swung off and rode for a time towards the strange object.

Banion pulled up. 'That's no buffalo! That's a man and his horse! He's bogged down!'

'You're right, Will, an' bogged bad! I've knew that light-green slough grass to cover the wurst sort o' quicksand. She runs black sand under the mud, God knows how deep. Ye kain't run a buffler inter hit – he knows. Come on!'

They spurred down a half-mile of gentle slope, hard and firm under

985

foot, and halted at the edge of one of the strange man-traps which some-times were found in the undrained Plains – a slough of tall, coarse, waving grass which undoubtedly got its moisture from some lower stratum.

In places a small expanse of glistening black mud appeared, although for the most part the mask of innocent-looking grass covered all signs of danger. It was, in effect, the dreaded quicksand, the octopus of the Plains, which covered from view more than one victim and left no discoverable trace.

The rider had attempted to cross a narrow neck of the slough. His mount had begun to sink and flounder, had been urged forward until the danger was obvious. Then, too late, the rider had flung off and turned back, sinking until his feet and legs were gripped by the layer of deep soft sand below. It was one of the rarest but most terrible accidents of the savage wilderness.

Blackened by the mud which lay on the surface, his hat half buried, his arms beating convulsively as he threw himself forward again and again, the victim must in all likelihood soon have exhausted himself. The chill of night on the high Plains soon would have done the rest, and by good fortune he might have died before meeting his entombment. His horse ere this had accepted fate, and ceasing to struggle lay almost buried, his head and neck supported by a trembling bit of floating grass roots.

'Steady, friend!' called out Banion as he ran to the edge. 'Don't fight it! Spread out your arms and lie still! We'll get you out!'

'Quick! My lariat, Jackson, and yours!' he added.

The scout was already freeing the saddle ropes. The two horses stood, reins down, snorting at the terror before them, whose menace they now could sense.

'Take the horse!' called Banion. 'I'll get the man!'

He was coiling the thin, braided-hide *reata*, soft as a glove and strong as steel, which always hung at the Spanish saddle.

He cast, and cast again – yet again, the loop at forty feet gone to nothing. The very silence of the victim nerved him to haste, and he stepped in knee deep, finding only mud, the trickle of black sands being farther out. The rope sped once more, and fell within reach – was caught. A sob or groan came, the first sound. Even then from the imprisoned animal beyond him came that terrifying sound, the scream of a horse in mortal terror. Jackson's rope fell short.

'Get the rope under your arms!' called Banion to the blackened, sodden figure before him. Slowly, feebly, his order was obeyed. With much effort the victim got the loop below one arm, across a shoulder, and then paused.

'Your rope, quick, Bill!'

Jackson hurried and they joined the ends of the two ropes.

'Not my horse – he's wild. Dally on to your own saddle, Bill, and go slow or you'll tear his head off.'

The scout's pony, held by the head and backed slowly, squatted to its haunches, snorting, but heaving strongly. The head of the victim was drawn oddly towards his shoulder by the loop, but slowly, silently, his hands clutching at the rope, his body began to rise, to slip forward.

Banion, deep as he dared, at last caught him by the collar, turned up his face. He was safe. Jackson heard the rescuer's deep exclamation, but was busy.

'Cast free, Will, cast free quick, and I'll try for the horse!'

He did try, with the lengthened rope, cast after cast, paying little attention to the work of Banion, who dragged out his man and bent over him as he lay motionless on the safe edge of the treacherous sunken sands which still half buried him.

'No use!' exclaimed the older man. He ran to his saddle and got his deadly double barrel, then stepped as close as possible to the sinking animal as he could. There came a roar. The head of the horse dropped flat, began to sink. 'Pore critter!' muttered the old man, capping his reloaded gun. He now hastened to aid Banion.

The latter turned a set face towards him and pointed. The rescued man had opened his eyes. He reached now convulsively for a tuft of grass, paused, stared.

'Hit's Sam Woodhull!' ejaculated the scout. Then, suddenly, 'Git away, Will – move back!'

Banion looked over his shoulder as he stood, his own hands and arms, his clothing, black with mire. The old man's grey eye was like a strange gem, gleaming at the far end of the deadly double tube, which was levelled direct at the prostrate man's forehead.

'No!' Banion's call was quick and imperative. He flung up a hand, stepped between. 'No! You'd kill him – now?'

With a curse Jackson flung his gun from him, began to recoil the muddied ropes. At length, without a word, he came to Banion's side. He reached down, caught an arm and helped Banion drag the man out on the grass. He caught off a handful of herbage and thrust it out to Wood-hull, who remained silent before what seemed his certain fate.

'Wipe off yore face, you skunk!' said the scout. Then he seated himself, morosely, hands before knees.

'Will Banion,' said he, 'ye're a fool – a nacherl-borned, congenual, ingrain damned fool! Ye're flyin' in the face o' proverdence, which planted this critter right here fer us ter leave where no one'd ever be the wiser, an' where he couldn't never do no more devilment. Ye idjit, leave me kill him, ef ye're too chicken-hearted yoreself! Or leave us throw him back in again!'

Banion would not speak at first, though his eyes never left Woodhull's streaked, ghastly face.

'By God!' said he slowly, at length, 'if we hadn't joined Scott and climbed Chapultepec together, I'd kill you like a dog, right here! Shall I give you one more chance to square things for me? You know what I mean! Will you promise?'

'Promise?' broke in Jackson. 'Ye damned fool, would ye believe any promise he made, even now? I tell ye, boy, he'll murder ye the fust chanct he gits! He's tried hit one night afore. Leave me cut his throat, Will! Ye'll never be safe ontel I do. Leave me cut his throat er kill him with a rock. Hit's only right.'

Banion shook his head.

'No,' he said slowly, 'I couldn't, and you must not.'

'Do you promise?' he repeated to the helpless man. 'Get up – stand up! Do you promise – will you swear?'

'Swear? Hell!' Jackson also rose as Woodhull staggered to his feet. 'Ye knew this man or to kill ye, an' ye sneaked hit, didn't ye? Whar's yer gun?'

'There!' Woodhull nodded to the bog, over which no object now showed. 'I'm helpless! I'll promise! I'll swear!'

'Then we'll not sound the No-quarter charge that you and I have heard the Spanish trumpets blow. You will remember the shoulder of a man who fought with you? You'll do what you can now – at any cost?'

'What cost?' demanded Woodhull thickly.

Banion's own white teeth showed as he smiled.

'What difference?' said he. 'What odds?'

'That's hit!' Again Jackson cut in, inexorable. 'Hit's no difference to him what he sw'ars, yit he'd bargain even now. Hit's about the gal!'

'Hush!' said Banion sternly. 'Not another word!'

'Figure on what it means to you.' He turned to Woodhull. 'I know what it means to me. I've got to have my own last chance, Woodhull, and

I'm saving you for that only. Is your last chance now as good as mine? This isn't mercy – I'm trading now. You know what I mean.'

Woodhull had freed his face of the mud as well as he could. He walked away, stooped at a trickle of water to wash himself. Jackson quietly rose and kicked the shotgun back farther from the edge. Woodhull now was near to Banion's horse, which, after his fashion, always came and stood close to his master. The butts of the two dragoon revolvers showed in their holsters at the saddle. When he rose from the muddy margin, shaking his hands as to dry them, he walked towards the horse. With a sudden leap, without a word, he sprang beyond the horse with a swift clutch at both revolvers, all done with a catlike quickness not to have been predicted. He stood clear of the plunging horse, both weapons levelled, covering his two rescuers.

'Evener now!' His teeth bared. 'Promise *me*!'

Jackson's deep curse was his answer. Banion rose, his arms folded.

'You're a liar and a coward, Sam!' said he. 'Shoot, if you've got the nerve!'

Incredible, yet the man was a natural murderer. His eye narrowed. There came a swift motion, a double empty click!

'Try again, Sam!' said Banion, taunting him. 'Bad luck – you landed on an empty!'

He did try again. Swift as an adder, his hands flung first one and then the other weapon into action.

Click after click, no more; Jackson sat dumb, expecting death.

'They're all empty, Sam,' said Banion at last as the murderer cast down the revolvers and stood with spread hands. 'For the first time, I didn't reload. I didn't think I'd need them.'

'You can't blame me!' broke out Woodhull. 'You said it was no quarter! Isn't a prisoner justified in trying to escape?'

'You've not escaped,' said Banion, coldly now. 'Rope him, Jackson.'

The thin, soft hide cord fell around the man's neck, tightened.

'Now,' shrilled Jackson, 'I'll give ye a dog's death!'

He sprang to the side of the black Spaniard, who by training had settled back, tightening the rope.

CHAPTER 22

A Secret of Two

Catching the intention of the maddened man, now bent only on swift revenge, Banion sprang to the head of his horse, flinging out an arm to keep Jackson out of the saddle. The horse, frightened at the stubborn struggle between the two, sprang away. Woodhull was pulled flat by the rope about his neck, nor could he loosen it now with his hands, for the horse kept steadily away. Any instant and he might be off in a mad flight, dragging the man to his death.

'Ho! Pronto – *Vien aqui*!'

Banion's command again quieted the animal. His ears forward, he came up, whickering his own query as to what really was asked of him.

Banion caught the bridle rein once more and eased the rope. Jackson by now had his shotgun and was shouting, crazed with anger. Woodhull's life chance was not worth a bawbee.

It was his enemy who saved it once again, for inscrutable but unaltered reasons of his own.

'Drop that, Jackson!' called Banion. 'Do as I tell you! This man's mine!'

Cursing himself, his friend, their captive, the horse, his gun and all animate and inanimate nature in his blood rage, the old man, livid in wrath, stalked away at length. 'I'll kill him sometime, ef ye don't yerself!' he screamed, his beard trembling. 'Ye damned fool!'

'Get up, Woodhull!' commanded Banion. 'You've tried once more to kill me. Of course, I'll not take any oath or promise from you now. You don't understand such things. The blood of a gentleman isn't anywhere in your strain. But I'll give you one more chance – give myself that chance too. There's only one thing you understand. That's fear. Yet I've seen you on a firing line, and you started with Doniphan's men. We didn't know we had a coward with us. But you are a coward.

'Now I leave you to your fear! You know what I want – more than life it is to me; but your life is all I have to offer for it. I'm going to wait till then.

'Come on, now! You'll have to walk. Jackson won't let you have his horse. My own never carried a woman but once, and he's never carried a coward at all. Jackson shall not have the rope. I'll not let him kill you.'

'What do you mean?' demanded the prisoner, not without his effrontery.

The blood came back to Banion's face, his control breaking.

'I mean for you to walk, trot, gallop, damn you! If you don't you'll strangle here instead of somewhere else in time.'

He swung up, and Jackson sullenly followed.

'Give me that gun,' ordered Banion, and took the shotgun and slung it in the pommel loop of his own saddle.

The gentle amble of the black stallion kept the prisoner at a trot. At times Banion checked, never looking at the man following, his hands at the rope, panting.

'Ye'll try him in the camp council, Will?' began Jackson once more. 'Anyways that? He's a murderer. He tried to kill us both, an' he will yit. Boy, ye rid with Doniphan, an' don't know the *lex refugio*. Hasn't the prisoner tried to escape? Ain't that old as Mayheeco Veeayho? Take this skunk in on a good rope like that? Boy, ye're crazy!'

'Almost,' nodded Banion. 'Almost. Come on. It's late.'

It was late when they rode down into the valley of the Platte. Below them twinkled hundreds of little fires of the white nation, feasting. Above, myriad stars shone in a sky unbelievably clear. On every hand rose the roaring howls of the great grey wolves, also feasting now; the lesser chorus of yapping coyotes. The savage night of the Plains was on. Through it passed three savage figures, one a staggering, stumbling man with a rope around his neck.

They came into the guard circle, into the dog circle of the encampment; but when challenged answered, and were not stopped.

'Here, Jackson,' said Banion at length, 'take the rope. I'm going to our camp. I'll not go into this train. Take this pistol – it's loaded now. Let off the *reata*, walk close to this man. If he runs, kill him. Find Molly Wingate. Tell her Will Banion has sent her husband to her – once more. It's the last time.'

He was gone in the dark. Bill Jackson, having first meticulously exhausted the entire vituperative resources of the English, the Spanish and all the Indian languages he knew, finally poked the muzzle of the pistol into Woodhull's back.

'Git, damn ye!' he commanded. 'Centre, guide! Forrerd, march! Ye – '

He improvised now, all known terms of contempt having been heretofore employed.

Threading the way past many feast fires, he did find the Wingate wagons at length, did find Molly Wingate. But there his memory failed him. With a skinny hand at Sam Woodhull's collar, he flung him forward.

'Here, Miss Molly,' said he, 'this thing is somethin' Major Banion sont in ter ye by me. We find hit stuck in the mud. He said ye're welcome.'

But neither he nor Molly really knew why that other man had spared Sam Woodhull's life, or what it was he awaited in return for Sam Woodhull's life.

All that Jackson could do he did. As he turned in the dark he implanted a heartfelt kick which sent Sam Woodhull on his knees before Molly Wingate as she stood in wondering silence.

Then arose sudden clamourings of those who had seen part of this – seen an armed man assault another, unarmed and defenceless, at their very firesides. Men came running up. Jesse Wingate came out from the side of his wagon.

'What's all this?' he demanded. 'Woodhull, what's up? What's wrong here?'

CHAPTER 23

An Armistice

To the challenge of Wingate and his men Jackson made answer with a high-pitched fighting yell. Sweeping his pistol muzzle across and back again over the front of the closing line, he sprang into saddle and wheeled away.

'Hit means we've brung ye back a murderer. Git yer own rope – ye kain't have mine! If ye-all want trouble with Old Missoury over this, er anything else, come runnin' in the mornin'. Ye'll find us sp'ilin' fer a fight!'

He was off in the darkness.

Men clustered around the draggled man, one of their own men, recently one in authority. Their indignation rose, well grounded on the growing feeling between the two segments of the train. When Woodhull had told his own story, in his own way, some were for raiding the Missouri detachment forthwith. Soberer counsel prevailed. In the morning Price, Hall and Kelsey rode over to the Missouri encampment and asked for their leader. Banion met them while the work of breaking camp went on, the cattle herd being already driven in and held at the rear by lank, youthful riders, themselves sp'lin' fer a fight.

'Major Banion,' began Caleb Price, 'we've come over to get some sort of understanding between your men and ours. It looks like trouble. I don't want trouble.'

'Nor do I,' rejoined Banion. 'We started out for Oregon as friends. It seems to me that should remain our purpose. No little things should alter that.'

'Precisely. But little things have altered it. I don't propose to pass on any quarrel between you and one of our people – a man from your own town, your own regiment. But that has now reached a point where it might mean open war between two parts of our train. That would mean ruin. That's wrong.'

'Yes,' replied Banion, 'surely it is. You see, to avoid that, I was just ordering my people to pull out. I doubt if we could go on together now. I don't want war with any friends. I reckon we can take care of any enemies. Will this please you?'

Caleb Price held out his hand.

'Major, I don't know the truth of any of the things I've heard, and I think those are matters that may be settled later on. But I am obliged to say that many of our people trust you and your leadership more than they do our own. I don't like to see you leave.'

'Well, then we won't leave. We'll hold back and follow you. Isn't that fair?'

'It is more than fair, for you can go faster now than we can, like enough. But will you promise me one thing, sir?'

'What is it?'

'If we get in trouble and send back for you, will you come?'

'Yes, we'll come. But pull on out now, at once. My men want to travel. We've got our meat slung on lines along the wagons to cure as we move. We'll wait till noon for you.'

'It is fair.' Price turned to his associates. 'Ride back, Kelsey, and tell Wingate we all think we should break camp at once.

'You see,' he added to Banion, 'he wouldn't even ride over with us. I regret this break between you and him. Can't it be mended?'

A sudden spasm passed across Will Banion's browned face.

'It cannot,' said he, 'at least not here and now. But the women and children shall have no risk on that account. If we can ever help, we'll come.'

The two again shook hands, and the Wingate lieutenants rode away, so ratifying a formal division of the train.

'What do you make of all this, Hall?' asked sober-going Caleb Price at last. 'What's the real trouble? Is it about the girl?'

'Oh, yes; but maybe more. You heard what Woodhull said. Even if Banion denied it, it would be one man's word against the other's. Well, it's wide out here, and no law.'

'They'll fight?'

'Will two roosters that has been breasted?'

CHAPTER 24

The Road West

Came now once more the notes of the bugle in signal for the assembly. Word passed down the scattered Wingate lines, 'Catch up! Catch up!'

Riders went out to the day guards with orders to round up the cattle. Dark lines of the driven stock began to dribble in from the edge of the valley. One by one the corralled vehicles broke park, swung front or rear, until the columns again held on the beaten road up the valley in answer to the command, 'Roll out! Roll out!' The Missourians, long aligned and ready, fell in far behind and pitched camp early. There were two trains, not one.

Now, hour after hour and day by day, the toil of the trail through sand flats and dog towns, deadly in its monotony, held them all in apathy. The light-heartedness of the start in early spring was gone. By this time the spare spaces in the wagons were kept filled with meat, for always there were buffalo now. Lines along the sides of the wagons held loads of rudely made jerky – pieces of meat slightly salted and exposed to the clear dry air to finish curing.

But as the people fed full there began a curious sloughing off of the social compact, a change in personal attitude. A dozen wagons, short of supplies or guided by faint hearts, had their fill of the Far West and sullenly started back east. Three dozen broke train and pulled out independently for the West, ahead of Wingate, mule and horse transport again rebelling against being held back by the ox teams. More and more community cleavages began to define. The curse of flies by day, of mosquitoes by night added increasing miseries for the travellers. The hot midday sun wore sore on them. Restless high spirits, grief over personal losses, fear of the future, alike combined to lessen the solidarity of the great train; but still it inched along on its way to Oregon, putting behind mile after mile of the great valley of the Platte.

The grass now lay yellow in the blaze of the sun, the sandy dust was inches deep in the great road, cut by thousands of wheels. Flotsam and jetsam, wreckage, showed more and more. Skeletons of cattle, bodies not yet skeletons, aroused no more than a casual look. Furniture lay cast aside, even broken wagons, their wheels fallen apart, showing intimate disaster. The actual hardships of the great trek thrust themselves into evidence on every hand, at every hour. Often was passed a little cross, half buried in the sand, or the tail gate of a wagon served as head board for some ragged epitaph of some ragged man.

It was decided to cross the South Fork at the upper ford, so called. Here was pause again for the Wingate train. The shallow and fickle stream, fed by the June rise in the mountains, now offered a score of channels, all treacherous. A long line of oxen, now wading and now swimming, dragging a long rope to which a chain was rigged – the latter to pull the wagon forward when the animals got footing on ahead – made a constant sight for hours at a time. One wagon after another was snaked through rapidly as possible. Once bogged down in a fast channel, the fluent sand so rapidly filled in the spokes that the settling wagon was held as though in a giant vice. It was new country, new work for them all; but they were Americans of the frontier.

The men were in the water all day long, for four days, swimming, wading, digging. Perhaps the first plough furrow west of the Kaw was cast when some ploughs eased down the precipitous bank which fronted one of the fording places. Beyond that lay no mark of any plough for more than a thousand miles.

They now had passed the Plains, as first they crossed the Prairie. The thin tongue of land between the two forks, known as the Highlands of the Platte, made vestibule to the mountains. The scenery began to change, to become rugged, semi-mountainous. They noted and held in sight for a day the Courthouse Rock, the Chimney Rock, both long known to the fur traders, which opened up wide vistas of desert architecture new to their experience.

They were now amid great and varied abundance of game. A thousand buffalo, five, ten, might be in sight at one time, and the ambition of every man to kill his buffalo long since had been gratified. Black-tailed deer and antelope were common, and even the mysterious bighorn sheep of which some of them had read. Each tributary stream now had its delicious mountain trout. The fires at night had abundance of the best of food, cooked for the most part over the native fuel of the *bois des vaches*.

The grass showed yet shorter, proving the late presence of the toiling Mormon caravan on ahead. The weather of late June was hot, the glare of the road blinding. The wagons began to fall apart in the dry, absorbent air of the high country. And always skeletons lay along the trail. An ox abandoned by its owners as too footsore for further travel might better have been shot than abandoned. The grey wolves would surely pull it down before another day. Continuously such tragedies of the wilderness went on before their wearying eyes.

Breaking down from the highlands through the Ash Hollow gap, the train felt its way to the level of the North Fork of the great river which had led them for so long. Here some trapper once had built a cabin – the first work of the sort in six hundred miles – and by some strange concert this deserted cabin had years earlier been constituted a post office of the desert. Hundreds of letters, bundles of papers were addressed to people all over the world, east and west. No government recognised this office, no postage was employed in it. Only, in the hope that someone passing east or west would carry on the enclosures without price, folk here sent out their souls into the invisible.

'How far'll we be out at Laramie?' demanded Molly Wingate of the train scout, Bridger, whom Banion had sent on to Wingate in spite of his protest.

'Nigh on to six hundred an' sixty-seven mile they call hit, ma'am, from Independence to Laramie, an' we'll be two months a-makin' hit, which everges around ten mile a day.'

'But it's most to Oregon, hain't it?'

'Most to Oregon? Ma'am, it's nigh three hundred mile beyond Laramie to the South Pass, an' the South Pass hain't halfway to Oregon. Why, ma'am, we ain't well begun!'

CHAPTER 25

Old Laramie

An old grey man in buckskins sat on the ground in the shade of the adobe stockade at old Fort Laramie, his knees high in front of him, his eyes fixed on the ground. His hair fell over his shoulders in long curls which had once been brown. His pointed beard fell on his breast. He sat silent and motionless, save that constantly he twisted a curl around a forefinger, over and over again. It was his way. He was a long-hair, a man of another day. He had seen the world change in six short years, since the first wagon crossed yonder ridges, where now showed yet one more wagon train approaching.

He paid no attention to the debris and discard of this new day which lay all about him as he sat and dreamed of the days of trap and packet. Near at hand were pieces of furniture leaning against the walls, not bought or sold, but abandoned as useless here at Laramie. Wagon wheels, tyreless, their felloes falling apart, lay on the ground, and other ruins of great wagons, dried and disjointed now.

Dust lay on the ground. The grass near by was all cropped short. Far off, a village of the Cheyennes, come to trade, and sullen over the fact that little now could be had for robes or peltries, grazed their ponies aside from the white man's road. Six hundred lodges of the Sioux were on the tributary river a few miles distant. The old West was making a last gallant stand at Laramie.

Inside the gate a mob of white men, some silent and businesslike, many drunken and boisterous, pushed here and there for access to the trading shelves, long since almost bare of goods. Six thousand emigrants passed that year.

It was the Fourth of July in Old Laramie, and men in jeans and wool and buckskin were celebrating. Old Laramie had seen life – all of life, since the fur days of La Ramée in 1821. Having now superciliously sold out to these pilgrims, reserving only alcohol enough for its own consumption, Old Laramie was willing to let the world wag, and content to twiddle a curl around a finger.

But yet another detachment of the great army following the hegira of the Mormons was now approaching Laramie. In the warm sun of mid-morning, its worn wheels rattling, its cattle limping and with lolling tongues, this caravan forded and swung wide into a corral below the crowded tepees of the sullen tribesmen.

Ahead of it now dashed a horseman, swinging his rifle over his head and uttering Indian yells. He pulled up at the very door of the old adobe guard tower with its mounted swivel guns, swung off and pushed on into the honeycomb of the inner structure.

The famous border fortress was built around a square, the living quarters on one side, the trading rooms on another. Few Indians were admitted at one time, other than the Indian wives of the *engagés*, the officials of the fur company or of the attached white or half-breed hunters.

Above some of the inner buildings were sleeping lofts. The inner open space served as a general meeting ground. Indolent but on guard, Old Laramie held her watch, a rear guard of the passing West in its wild days before the plough.

All residents here knew Jim Bridger. He sought out the man in charge.

'How, Bordeaux?' he began. 'Whar's the bourgeois, Papin?'

'Down river – h'east h'after goods.' The trader, hands on his little counter, nodded to his shelves. 'Nada!' he said in his polyglot speech. 'Hi'll not got a damned thing lef'. How many loads you'll got for your h'own post, Jeem?'

'Eight wagons. Iron, flour and bacon.'

'Hi'll pay ye double here what you'll kin git retail there, Jeem, and take it h'all h'off your hand. This h'emigrant, she'll beat the fur.'

'I'll give ye half,' said Bridger. 'Thar's people here needs supplies that ain't halfway acrost. But what's the news, Bordeaux? Air the Crows down?'

'H'on the Sweetwater, h'awaitin' for the peelgrim. Hi'll heard of your beeg fight on the Platte. Plenty beeg fight on ahead, too, maybe-so. You'll bust h'up the trade, Jeem. My Sioux, she's scare to come h'on the post h'an' trade. He'll stay h'on the veelage, her.'

'Every dog to his own yard. Is that all the news?'

'Five thousand Mormons, he'll gone by h'already. H'womans pullin' the han'cart, *sacre Enfant*! News – you'll h'ought to know the news. You'll been h'on the settlement six mont'!'

'Hit seemed six year. The hull white nation's movin'. So. That all?'

'Well, go h'ask Keet. He's come h'up South Fork yesterdays. Maybe-so *quelq' cho' des nouvelles* h'out West. I dunno, me.'

'Kit – Kit Carson, you mean? What's Kit doing here?'

'*Oui*. I dunno, me.'

He nodded to a door. Bridger pushed past him. In an inner room a party of border men were playing cards at a table. Among these was a slight, sandy-haired man of middle age and mild, blue eye. It was indeed Carson, the redoubtable scout and guide, a better man even than Bridger in the work of the wilderness.

'How are you, Jim?' he said quietly, reaching up a hand as he sat. 'Haven't seen you for five years. What are you doing here?'

He rose now and put down his cards. The game broke up. Others gathered around Bridger and greeted him. It was some time before the two mountain men got apart from the others.

'What brung ye north, Kit?' demanded Bridger at length. 'You was in California in '47, with the General.'

'Yes, I was in California this spring. The treaty's been signed with Mexico. We get the country from the Rio Grande west, including California. I'm carrying dispatches to General Kearny at Leavenworth. There's talk about taking over Laramie for an army post. The tribes are up in arms. The trade's over, Jim.'

'What I know, an' have been sayin'! Let's have a drink, Kit, fer old times.'

Laughing, Carson turned his pockets inside out. As he did so something heavy fell from his pocket to the floor. In courtesy as much as curiosity Bridger stooped first to pick it up. As he rose he saw Carson's face change as he held out his hand.

'What's this stone, Kit – yer medicine?'

But Bridger's own face altered suddenly as he now guessed the truth. He looked about him suddenly, his mouth tight. Kit Carson rose and they passed from the room.

'Only one thing heavy as that, Mister Kit!' said Bridger fiercely. 'Where'd you git hit? My gran'pap had some o' that. Hit come from North Carliny years ago. I know what hit is – hit's gold! Kit Carson, damn ye, hit's the gold!'

'Shut your mouth, you fool!' said Carson. 'Yes, it's gold. But do you want me to be a liar to my general? That's part of my dispatches.'

'Hit' come from Californy?'

'Curse me, yes, California! I was ordered to get the news to the army first. You're loose-tongued, Jim. Can you keep this?'

'Like a grave, Kit.'

'Then here!'

Carson felt inside his shirt and pulled out a meagre and ill-printed sheet which told the most epochal news that this or any country has known – the midwinter discovery of gold at Sutter's Mills.

A flag was flying over Laramie stockade, and this flag the mountain men saw fit to salute with many libations, hearing now that it was to fly for ever over California as over Oregon. Crowding the stockade enclosure full was a motley throng – border men in buckskins, *engagés* swart as Indians, French breeds, full-blood Cheyennes and Sioux of the northern hills, all mingling with the curious emigrants who had come in from the wagon camps. Plump Indian girls, many of them very comely, some of them wives of the trappers who still hung about Laramie, ogled the newcomers, laughing, giggling together as young women of any colour do, their black hair sleek with oil, their cheeks red with vermilion, their wrists heavy with brass or copper or pinchbeck circlets, their small moccasined feet peeping beneath gaudy calico given them by their white lords. Older squaws, envious but perforce resigned, muttered as their own stern-faced stolid red masters ordered them to keep close. Of the full-bloods, whether Sioux or Cheyennes, only those drunk were other than sullenly silent and resentful as they watched the white man's orgy at Old Laramie on the Fourth of July of 1848.

Far flung along the pleasant valley lay a vast picture possible in no other land or day. The scattered covered wagons, the bands of cattle and horses, the white tents rising now in scores, the blue of many fires, all proved that now the white man had come to fly his flag over a new frontier.

Bridger stood, chanting an Indian song. A group of men came out, all excited with patriotic drink. A tall man in moccasins led, his fringed shirt open over a naked breast, his young squaw following him.

'Let me see one o' them damned things!' he was exclaiming. 'That's why I left home fifty year ago. Pap wanted to make me plough! I ain't seed one since, but I'll bet a pony I kin run her right now! Go git yer plough things, boys, an' fotch on any sort of cow critter suits ye, I'll bet I kin hook 'em up an' plough with 'em, too, right yere!'

The old grey man at the gate sat and twisted his long curls.

The sweet wind of the foothills blew aslant the smoke of a thousand fires. Over the vast landscape passed many moving figures. Young Indian men, mostly Sioux, some Cheyennes, a few Gros Ventres of the Prairie, all peaceable under the tacit truce of the trading post, rode out from their villages to their pony herds. From the post came the occasional note of an inharmonic drum, struck without rhythm by a hand gone lax. The singers no longer knew they sang. The border feast had lasted long. Keg after keg had been broached. The Indian drums were going. Came the sound of monotonous chants, broken with staccato yells as the border dance, two races still mingling, went on with aboriginal excesses on either side. On the slopes as dusk came twinkled countless tepee fires. Dogs barked mournfully a-distant. The heavy half-roar of the buffalo wolves, superciliously confident, echoed from the broken country.

Now and again a tall Indian, naked save where he clutched his robe to him unconsciously, came staggering to his tepee, his face distorted, yelling obscene words and not knowing what he said. Patient, his youngest squaw stood by his tepee, his spear held aloft to mark his door plate, waiting for her lord to come. Wolfish dogs lay along the tepee edges, noses in tails, eyeing the master cautiously. A grumbling old woman mended the fire at her own side of the room, nearest the door, spreading smooth robes where the man's medicine hung at the willow tripod, his slatted lazyback near by. In due time all would know whether at the game of 'hands', while the feast went on, the little elusive bone had won or lost for him. Perhaps he had lost his horses, his robes, his weapons – his squaws. The white man's medicine was strong, and there was much of it on his feasting day.

From the stockade a band of mounted Indians, brave in new finery, decked with eagle bonnets and gaudy in beaded shirts and leggings, rode out into the slopes, chanting maudlin songs. They were led by the most beautiful young woman of the tribe, carrying a wand topped by a gilded ball, and ornamented with bells, feathers, natural flowers. As the wild pageant passed the proud savages paid no attention to the white men.

The old grey man at the gate sat and twisted his long curls.

And none of them knew the news from California.

CHAPTER 26

The First Gold

The purple mantle of the mountain twilight was dropping on the hills when Bridger and Carson rode out together from the Laramie stockade to the Wingate encampment in the valley. The extraordinary capacity of Bridger in matters alcoholic left him still in fair possession of his faculties; but some new purpose, born of the exaltation of alcohol now, held his mind.

'Let me see that little dingus ye had, Kit,' said he – 'that piece o' gold.'

Carson handed it to him.

'Ye got any more o' hit, Kit?'

'Plenty! You can have it if you'll promise not to tell where it came from, Jim.'

'If I do, Jim Bridger's a liar, Kit!'

He slipped the nugget into his pocket. They rode to the head of the train, where Bridger found Wingate and his aids, and presented his friend. They all, of course, knew of Fremont's famous scout, then at the height of his reputation, and greeted him with enthusiasm. As they gathered around him Bridger slipped away. Searching among the wagons, he at last found Molly Wingate and beckoned her aside with portentous injunctions of secrecy.

In point of fact, a sudden maudlin inspiration had seized Jim Bridger, so that a promise to Kit Carson seemed infinitely less important than a promise to this girl, whom, indeed, with an old man's inept infatuation, he had worshipped afar after the fashion of white men long gone from society of their kind. Liquor now made him bold. Suddenly he reached out a hand and placed in Molly's palm the first nugget of California gold that ever had come thus far eastward. Physically heavy it was; of what tremendous import none then could have known.

'I'll give ye this!' he said. 'An' I know whar's plenty more.'

She dropped the nugget because of the sudden weight in her hand; picked it up.

'Gold!' she whispered, for there is no mistaking gold.

'Yes, gold!'

'Where did you get it?'

She was looking over her shoulder instinctively.

'Listen! Ye'll never tell? Ye mustn't! I swore to Kit Carson, that give hit to me, I'd never tell no one. But I'll set you ahead o' any livin' bein', so maybe some day ye'll remember old Jim Bridger.

'Yes, hit's gold! Kit Carson brung it from Sutter's Fort, on the Sacramenty, in Californy. They've got it thar in wagonloads. Kit's on his way east now to tell the army!'

'Everyone will know!'

'Yes, but not now! Ef ye breathe this to a soul, thar won't be two wagons left together in the train. Thar'll be bones o' womern from here to Californy!'

Wide-eyed, the girl stood, weighing the nugget in her hands.

'Keep hit, Miss Molly,' said Bridger simply. 'I don't want hit no more. I only got hit fer a bracelet fer ye, or something. Goodbye. I've got to leave the train with my own wagons afore long an' head fer my fort. Ye'll maybe see me – old Jim Bridger – when ye come through.

'Yes, Miss Molly, I ain't as old as I look, and I got a fort o' my own beyant the Green River. This year, what I'll take in for my cargo, what I'll make cash money fer work fer the immygrints, I'll salt down anyways ten thousand; next year maybe twicet that, or even more. I sartainly will do a good trade with them Mormons.'

'I suppose,' said the girl, patient with what she knew was alcoholic garrulity.

'An' out there's the purtiest spot west o' the Rockies, My valley is ever'thing a man er a womern can ask or want. And me, I'm a permanent man in these yere parts. It's me, Jim Bridger, that fust diskivered the Great Salt Lake. It's me, Jim Bridger, fust went through Colter's Hell up in the Yellowstone. Ain't a foot o' the Rockies I don't know. I eena'most built the Rocky Mountains, me.' He spread out his hands. 'And I've got to be eena'most all Injun myself.'

'I suppose.' The girl's light laugh cut him.

'But never so much as not to rever'nce the white woman, Miss Molly. Ye're all like angels to us wild men out yere. We – we never have forgot. And so I give ye this, the fust gold from Californy. There may be more. I don't know.'

'But you're going to leave us? What are you going to do?' A sudden kindness was in the girl's voice.

'I'm a-goin' out to Fort Bridger, that's what I'm a-goin' to do; an' when I git thar I'm a-goin' to lick hell out o' both my squaws, that's what I'm a-goin' to do! One's named Blast Yore Hide, an' t'other Dang Yore Eyes. Which, ef ye ask me, is two names right an' fitten, way I feel now.'

All at once Jim Bridger was all Indian again. He turned and stalked away. She heard his voice rising in his Indian chant as she turned back to her own wagon fire.

But now shouts were arising, cries coming up the line. A general movement was taking place towards the lower end of the camp, where a high quavering call rose again and again.

'There's news!' said Carson to Jesse Wingate quietly. 'That's old Bill Jackson's war cry, unless I am mistaken. Is he with you?'

'He was,' said Wingate bitterly. 'He and his friends broke away from the train and have been flocking by themselves since then.'

Three men rode up to the Wingate wagon, and two flung off. Jackson was there, yes, and Jed Wingate, his son. The third man still sat his horse. Wingate straightened.

'Mr Banion! So you see fit to come into my camp?' For the time he had no answer.

'How are you, Bill?' said Kit Carson quietly, as he now stepped forward from the shadows. The older man gave him a swift glance.

'Kit! You here – why?' he demanded. 'I've not seed ye, Kit, sence the last Rendyvous on the Green. Ye've been with the army on the coast?'

'Yes. Going East now.'

'Allus ridin' back and forerd acrost the hull country. I'd hate to keep ye in buckskin breeches, Kit. But ye're carryin' news?'

'Yes,' said Carson. 'Dispatches about new army posts – to General Kearny. Some other word for him, and some papers to the Adjutant General of the Army. Besides, some letters from Lieutenant Beale in Mexico, about war matters and the treaty, like enough. You know, we'll get all the southern country to the coast?'

'An' welcome ef we didn't! Not a beaver to the thousand miles, Kit. I'm goin' to Oregon – goin' to settle in the Nez Perce country, whar there's horses an' beaver.'

'But wait a bit afore you an' me gits too busy talkin'. Ye see, I'm with Major Banion, yan, an' the Missoury train. We're in camp ten mile below. We wouldn't mix with these people no more – only one way – but I reckon the major's got some business o' his own that brung him up. I rid with him. We met the boy an' ast him to bring us in. We wasn't sure how friendly our friends is feelin' towards him an' me.'

He grinned grimly. As he spoke they both heard a woman's shrilling, half greeting, half terror. Wingate turned in time to see his daughter fall to the ground in a sheer faint.

Will Banion slipped from his saddle and hurried forward.

CHAPTER 27

Two Who Loved

Jesse Wingate made a swift instinctive motion towards the revolver which swung at his hip. But Jed sprang between him and Banion.

'No! Hold on, pap – stop!' cried Jed. 'It's all right. I brought him in.'

'As a prisoner?'

'I am no man's prisoner, Captain Wingate,' said Banion's deep voice.

His eyes were fixed beyond the man to whom he spoke. He saw Molly, to whom her mother now ran, to take the white face in her own hands. Wingate looked from one to the other.

'Why do you come here? What do I owe you that you should bring more trouble, as you always have? And what do you owe me?'

'I owe you nothing!' said Banion. 'You owe me nothing at all. I have not travelled in your train, and I shall not travel in it. I tell you once more, you're wrong in your beliefs; but till I can prove that I'll not risk any argument about it.'

'Then why do you come to my camp now?'

'You should know.'

'I do know. It's Molly!'

'It's Molly, yes. Here's a letter from her. I found it in the cabin at Ash Hollow. Your friend Woodhull could have killed me – we passed him just now. Jed could have killed me – you can now; it's easy. But that wouldn't change me. Perhaps it wouldn't change her.'

'You come here to face me down?'

'No, sir. I know you for a brave man, at least. I don't believe I'm a coward – I never asked. But I came to see Molly, because here she's asked it. I don't know why. Do you want to shoot me like a coyote?'

'No. But I ask you, what do I owe you?'

'Nothing. But can we trade? If I promise to leave you with my train?'

'You want to steal my girl!'

'No! I want to earn her – someday.'

The old Roman before him was a man of quick and strong decisions. The very courage of the young man had its appeal.

'At least you'll eat,' said he. 'I'd not turn even a black Secesh away hungry – not even a man with your record in the army.'

'No, I'll not eat with you.'

'Wait then! I'll send the girl pretty soon, if you are here by her invitation. I'll see she never invites you again.'

Wingate walked toward his wagon. Banion kept out of the light circle and found his horse. He stood, leaning his head on his arms in the saddle, waiting, until after what seemed an age she slipped out of the darkness, almost into his arms, standing pale, her fingers lacing and unlacing – the girl who had kissed him once – to say goodbye.

'Will Banion!' she whispered. 'Yes, I sent for you. I felt you'd find the letter.'

'Yes, Molly.' It was long before he would look at her. 'You're the same,' said he. 'Only you've grown more beautiful every day. It's hard to leave you – awfully hard. I couldn't, if I saw you often.'

He reached out again and took her in his arms, softly, kissed her tenderly on each cheek, whispered things that lovers do say. But for his arms she would have dropped again, she was so weak. She fought him off feebly.

'No! No! It is not right! No! No! . . . 'You're not going to be with us any more?' she said at last.

He shook his head. They both looked at his horse, his rifle, swung in its sling strap at the saddle horn. She shook her head also.

'Is this the real goodbye, Will?' Her lips trembled.

'It must be. I have given my word to your father. But why did you send for me? Only to torture me? I must keep my word to hold my train apart. I've promised my men to stick with them.'

'Yes, you mustn't break your word. And it was fine just to see you a minute, Will; just to tell you – oh, to say I love you, Will! But I didn't think that was why I sent. I sent to warn you – against him. It seems always to come to the same thing.'

She was trying not to sob. The man was in but little better case. The stars did not want them to part. All the sombre wilderness world whispered for them to love and not to part at all. But after a time they knew that they again had parted, or now were able to do so.

'Listen, Will,' said the girl at last, putting back a lock of her fallen hair. 'I'll have to tell you. We'll meet in Oregon? I'll be married then. I've promised. Oh, God help me! I think I'm the wickedest woman in all the world, and the most unhappy. Oh, Will Banion, I – I love a thief! Even as you are, I love you! I guess that's why I sent for you, after all.

'Go find the scout – Jim Bridger!' she broke out suddenly. 'He's going on ahead. Go on to his fort with him – he'll have wagons and horses. He knows the way. Go with Bridger, Will! Don't go to Oregon! I'm afraid for you. Go to California – and forget me! Tell Bridger –

'Why, where is it?' she exclaimed.

She was feeling in the pocket of her apron, and it was empty.

'I've lost it!' she repeated. 'I lose everything!'

'What was it, Molly?'

She leaned her lips to his ear.

'It was gold!'

He stood, the magic name of that metal which shows the colour in the shade electrifying even his ignorance of the truth.

'Gold?'

She told him, breaking her own promise magnificently, as women will.

'Go, ride with Bridger,' she went on. 'Don't tell him you ever knew me. He'll not be apt to speak of me. But they found it, in California, the middle of last winter – gold! Gold! Carson's here in our camp – Kit Carson. He's the first man to bring it to the Valley of the Platte. He was sworn to keep it secret; so was Bridger, and so am I. Not to Oregon, Will – California! You can live down your past. If we die, God bless the man I do love. That's you, Will! And I'm going to marry – him. Ten days! On the trail! And he'll kill you, Will! Oh, keep away!'

She paused, breathless from her torrent of incoherent words, jealous of the passing moments. It was vague, it was desperate, it was crude. But they were in a world vague, desperate and crude.

'I've promised my men I'll not leave them,' he said at last. 'A promise is a promise.'

'Then God help us both! But one thing – when I'm married, that's the end between us. So goodbye.'

He leaned his head back on his saddle for a time, his tired horse turning back its head. He put out his hand blindly; but it was the muzzle of his horse that had touched his shoulder. The girl was gone.

The Indian drums at Laramie thudded through the dark. The great wolf in the breaks lifted his hoarse, raucous roar once more. The wilderness was afoot or bedding down, according to its like.

CHAPTER 28

When a Maid Marries

Carson, Bridger and Jackson, now reunited after years, must pour additional libations to Auld Lang Syne at Laramie, so they were soon off together. The movers sat around their thrifty cooking fires outside the wagon corral. Wingate and his wife were talking heatedly, she in her nervousness not knowing that she fumbled over and over in her fingers the heavy bit of rock which Molly had picked up and which was in her handkerchief when it was requisitioned by her mother to bathe her face just now. After a time she tossed the nugget aside into the grass. It was trodden by a hundred feet ere long.

But gold will not die. In three weeks a prowling Gros Ventre squaw found it and carried it to the trader, Bordeaux, asking, 'Shoog?'

'Non, non!' replied the Laramie trader. 'Pas de shoog!' But he looked curiously at the thing, so heavy.

'How, cola!' wheedled the squaw. 'Shoog!' She made the sign for sugar, her finger from her palm to her lips. Bordeaux tossed the thing into the tin can on the shelf and gave her what sugar would cover a spoon.

'Where?' he asked her, his fingers loosely shaken, meaning, 'Where did you get it?'

The Gros Ventre lied to him like a lady, and told him, on the South Fork, on the Creek of Bitter Cherries – near where Denver now is; and where placers once were. That was hundreds of miles away. The Gros Ventre woman had been there once in her wanderings and had seen some heavy metal.

Years later, after Fort Laramie was taken over by the government, Bordeaux as sutler sold much flour and bacon to men hurrying down the South Fork to the early Colorado diggings. Meantime, in his cups, he often told the mythical tale of the Gros Ventre woman – long after California, Idaho, Nevada, Montana were all afire. But one of his half-breed children very presently had commandeered the tin cup and its contents, so that to this day no man knows whether the child swallowed the nugget or threw it into the Laramie River or the Platte River or the sagebrush. Some depose that an emigrant bought it off the baby; but no one knows.

What all men do know is that gold does not die; nay, nor the news of it. And this news now, like a multiplying germ, was in the wagon train that had started out for Oregon.

As for Molly, she asked no questions at all about the lost nugget, but hurried to her own bed, supperless, pale and weeping. She told her father nothing of the nature of her meeting with Will Banion, then nor at any time for many weeks.

'Molly, come here, I want to talk to you.' Wingate beckoned to his daughter the second morning after Banion's visit.

The order for the advance was given. The men had brought in the cattle and the yoking up was well forward. The rattle of pots and pans was dying down. Dogs had taken their places on flank or at the wagon rear, women were climbing up to the seats, children clinging to pieces of dried meat. The train was waiting for the word.

The girl followed him calmly, high-headed.

'Molly, see here,' he began. 'We're all ready to move on. I don't know where Will Banion went, but I want you to know, as I told him, that he can't travel in our train.'

'He'll not ask to, father. He's promised to stick to his own men.'

'He's left you at last! That's good. Now I want you to drop him from your thoughts. Hear that, and heed it. I tell you once more, you're not treating Sam Woodhull right.'

She made him no answer.

'You're still young, Molly,' he went on. 'Once you're settled you'll find

Oregon all right. Time you were marrying. You'll be twenty and an old maid first thing you know. Sam will make you a good husband. Heed what I say.'

But she did not heed, though she made no reply to him. Her eye, 'scornful, threatening and young', looked yonder where she knew her lover was; nor was it in her soul ever to return from following after him. The name of her intended husband left her cold as ice.

'Roll out! Roll out! Ro–o–o–ll ou–t!'

The call went down the line once more. The pistolry of the wagon whips made answer, the drone of the drivers rose as the sore-necked oxen bowed their heads again, with less strength even for the lightened loads.

The old man who sat by the gate at Fort Laramie, twisting a curl around his finger, saw the plain clearing now, as the great train swung out and up the river trail. He perhaps knew that Jim Bridger, with his own freight wagons, going light and fast with mules, was on West, ahead of the main caravan. But he did not know the news Jim Bridger carried, the same news that Carson was carrying East. The three old mountain men, for a few hours meeting after years, now were passing far apart, never to meet again. Their chance encountering meant much to hundreds of men and women then on the road to Oregon; to untold thousands yet to come.

As for one Samuel Woodhull, late column captain, it was to be admitted that for some time he had been conscious of certain buffetings of fate. But as all thoroughbred animals are thin-skinned, so are all the short-bred pachydermatous, whereby they endure and mayhap arrive at the manger well as the next. True, even Woodhull's vanity and self-content had everything asked of them in view of his late series of mishaps; but by now he had somewhat chirked up under rest and good food, and was once more the dandy and hail fellow. He felt assured that very presently bygones would be bygones. Moreover – so he reasoned – if he, Sam Woodhull, won the spoils, what matter who had won any sort of victory? He knew, as all these others knew and as all the world knows, that a beautiful woman is above all things *spolia opima* of war. Well, in ten days he was to marry Molly Wingate, the most beautiful woman of the train and the belle of more than one community. Could he not afford to laugh best, in spite of all events, even if some of them had not been to his own liking?

But the girl's open indifference was least of all to his liking. It enraged his vain, choleric nature to its inner core. Already he planned dominance; but, willing to wait and to endure for ten days, meantime he employed innocence, reticence, dignity, attentiveness, so that he seemed a suitor misunderstood, misrepresented, unjustly used – to whose patient soul none the less presently must arrive justice and exoneration, after which all would be happier even than a marriage bell. After the wedding bells he, Samuel Woodhull, would show who was master.

Possessed once more of horse, arms and personal equipment, and having told his own story of persecution to good effect throughout the train, Woodhull had been allowed to resume a nominal command over a part of the Wingate wagons. The real control lay in the triumvirate who once had usurped power, and who might do so again.

Wingate himself really had not much more than nominal control of the general company, although he continued to give what Caleb Price called the easy orders. His wagons, now largely changed to ox transport, still travelled at the head of the train, Molly continuing to drive her own light wagon and Jed remaining on the cow column.

The advance hardly had left Fort Laramie hidden by the rolling ridges before Woodhull rode up to Molly's wagon and made excuse to pass his horse to a boy while he himself climbed up on the seat with his fiancée.

She made room for him in silence, her eyes straight ahead. The wagon cover made good screen behind, the herdsmen were far in the rear, and from the wagons ahead none could see them. Yet when her affianced husband dropped an arm about her waist the girl flung it off impatiently.

'Don't!' she exclaimed. 'I detest love-making in public. We see enough that can't be hid. It's getting worse, more open, the farther we get out.'

'The train knows we are to be married at the halfway stop, Molly. Then you'll change wagons and will not need to drive.'

'Wait till then.'

'I count the hours. Don't you, dearest?'

She turned a pallid face to him at last, resentful of his endearments.

'Yes, I do,' she said. But he did not know what she meant, or why she was so pale.

'I think we'll settle in Portland,' he went on. 'The travellers' stories say that place, at the head of navigation on the Willamette, has as good a chance as Oregon City, at the Falls. I'll practice law. The goods I am taking out will net us a good sum, I'm hoping. Oh, you'll see the day when you'll not regret that I held you to your promise! I'm not playing this Oregon game to lose it.'

'Do you play any game to lose it?'

'No! Better to have than to explain have not – that's one of my mottoes.'

'No matter how?'

'Why do you ask?'

'I was only wondering.'

'About what?'

'About men – and the differences.'

'My dear, as a schoolteacher you have learned to use a map, a black-board. Do you look on us men as ponderable, measurable, computable?'

'A girl ought to if she's going to marry.'

'Well, haven't you?'

'Have I?'

She still was staring straight ahead, cold, making no silent call for a lover's arms or arts. Her silence was so long that at length even his thick hide was pierced.

'Molly!' he broke out. 'Listen to me! Do you want the engagement broken? Do you want to be released?'

'What would they all think?'

'Not the question. Answer me!'

'No, I don't want it broken. I want it over with. Isn't that fair?'

'Is it?'

'Didn't you say you wanted me on any terms?'

'Surely!'

'Don't you now?'

'Yes, I do, and I'm going to have you, too!'

His eye, covetous, turned to the ripe young beauty of the maid beside him. He was willing to pay any price.

'Then it all seems settled.'

'All but one part. You've never really and actually told me you loved me.'

A wry smile.

'I'm planning to do that after I marry you. I suppose that's the tendency of a woman? Of course, it can't be true that only one man will do for a woman to marry, or one woman for a man? If anything went wrong on that basis – why, marrying would stop! That would be foolish, wouldn't it? I suppose women do adjust? Don't you think so?'

His face grew hard under this cool reasoning.

'Am I to understand that you are marrying me as a second choice, and so that you can forget some other man?'

'Couldn't you leave a girl a secret if she had one? Couldn't you be happier if you did? Couldn't you take your chance and see if there's anything under the notion about more than one man and more than one woman in the world? Love? Why, what is love? Something to marry on?

They say it passes. They tell me that marriage is more adjustable, means more interests than love; that the woman who marries with her eyes open is apt to be the happiest in the long run. Well, then, you said you wanted me on any terms. Does not that include open eyes?'

'You're making a hard bargain – the hardest a man can be obliged to take.'

'It was not of my seeking.'

'You said you loved me – at first.'

'No. Only a girl's in love with love – at first. I've not really lied to you. I'm trying to be honest before marriage. Don't fear I'll not be afterwards. There's much in that, don't you think? Maybe there's something, too, in a woman's ability to adjust and compromise? I don't know. We ought to be as happy as the average married couple, don't you think? None of them are happy for so very long, they say. They say love doesn't last long. I hope not. One thing, I believe marriage is easier to beat than love is.'

'How old are you, really, Molly?'

'I am just over nineteen, sir.'

'You are wise for that; you are old.'

'Yes – since we started for Oregon.'

He sat in sullen silence for a long time, all the venom of his nature gathering, all his savage jealousy.

'You mean since you met that renegade, traitor and thief, Will Banion! Tell me, isn't that it?'

'Yes, that's true. I'm older now. I know more.'

'And you'll marry me without love. You love him without marriage? Is that it?'

'I'll never marry a thief.'

'But you love one?'

'I thought I loved you.'

'But you do love him, that man!'

Now at last she turned to him, gazing straight through the mist of her tears.

'Sam, if you really loved me, would you ask that? Wouldn't you just try to be so gentle and good that there'd no longer be any place in my heart for any other sort of love, so I'd learn to think that our love was the only sort in the world? Wouldn't you take your chance and make good on it, believing that it must be in nature that a woman can love more than one man, or love men in more than one way? Isn't marriage broader and with more chance for both? If you love me and not just yourself alone, can't you take your chance as I am taking mine? And after all, doesn't a woman give the odds? If you do love, me – '

'If I do, then my business is to try to make you forget Will Banion.'

'There is no other way you could. He may die. I promise you I'll never see him after I'm married.

'And I'll promise you another thing' – her strained nerves now were speaking truth for her – 'if by any means I ever learn – if I ever believe – that Major Banion is not what I now think him, I'll go on my knees to him. I'll know marriage was wrong and love was right all the time.'

'Fine, my dear! Much happiness! But unfortunately for Major Banion's passing romance, the official records of a military court-martial and a dishonourable discharge from the army are facts which none of us can doubt or deny.'

'Yes, that's how it is. So that's why.'

'What do you really mean then, Molly – you say, that's why?'

'That's why I'm going to marry you, Sam. Nine days from today, at the Independence Rock, if we are alive. And from now till then, and always, I'm going to be honest, and I'm going to pray God to give you power to make me forget every other man in all the world except my – my – ' But she could not say the word 'husband'.

'Your husband!'

He said it for her, and perhaps then reached his zenith in approximately unselfish devotion, and in good resolves at least.

The sun shone blinding hot. The white dust rose in clouds. The plague of flies increased. The rattle and creak of wheel, the monotone of the drivers, the cough of dust-afflicted kine made the only sounds for a long time.

'You can't kiss me, Molly?'

He spoke not in dominance but in diffidence. The girl awed him.

'No, not till after, Sam; and I think I'd rather be left alone from now till then. After – Oh, be good to me, Sam! I'm trying to be honest as a woman can. If I were not that I'd not be worth marrying at all.'

Without suggestion or agreement on his part she drew tighter the reins on her mules. He sprang down over the wheel. The sun and the dust had their way again; the monotony of life, its drab discontent, its yearnings and its sense of failure once more resumed sway in part or all of the morose caravan. They all sought new fortunes, each of these. One day each must learn that, travel far as he likes, a man takes himself with him for better or for worse.

CHAPTER 29

The Broken Wedding

Banion allowed the main caravan two days' start before he moved beyond Fort Laramie. Every reason bade him to cut entirely apart from that portion of the company. He talked with every man he knew who had any knowledge of the country on ahead, read all he could find, studied such maps as then existed, and kept an open ear for advice of old-time men who in hard experience had learned how to get across a country.

Two things troubled him: the possibility of grass exhaustion near the trail and the menace of the Indians. Squaw men in from the north and west said that the Arapahoes were hunting on the Sweetwater, and sure to make trouble; that the Blackfeet were planning war; that the Bannacks were east of the Pass; that even the Crows were far down below their normal range and certain to harass the trains. These stories, not counting the hostility of the Sioux and Cheyennes of the Platte country, made it appear that there was a tacit suspense of intertribal hostility and a general and joint uprising against the migrating whites.

These facts Banion did not hesitate to make plain to all his men; but, descendants of pioneers, with blood of the wilderness in their veins, and each tempted by adventure as much as by gain, they laughed long and loud at the thought of danger from all the Indians of the Rockies. Had they not beaten the Sioux? Could they not in turn humble the pride of any other tribe? Had not their fathers worked with rifle lashed to the plough beam? Indians? Let them come!

Founding his own future on this resolute spirit of his men, Banion next looked to the order of his own personal affairs. He found prices so high at Fort Laramie, and the stock of all manner of goods so low, that he felt it needless to carry his own trading wagons all the way to Oregon, when a profit of 400 per cent lay ready not a third of the way across and less the further risk and cost. He accordingly cut down his own stocks to one wagon, and sold off wagons and oxen as well, until he found himself possessed of considerably more funds than when he had started out.

He really cared little for these matters. What need had he for a fortune or a future now? He was poorer than any jeans-clad ox driver with a sunbonnet on the seat beside him and tow-headed children on the flour and bacon sacks, with small belongings beyond the plough lashed at the tail gate, the axe leaning in the front corner of the box and the rifle swinging in its loops at the wagon bows. They were all beginning life again. He was done with it.

The entire caravan now had passed in turn the Prairies and the Plains. In the vestibule of the mountains they had arrived in the most splendid out-of-doors country the world has ever offered. The climate was superb, the scenery was a constant succession of changing beauties new to the eyes of all. Game was at hand in such lavish abundance as none of them had dreamed possible. The buffalo ranged always within touch, great bands of elk now appeared, antelope always were in sight. The streams abounded in noble game fish, and the lesser life of the open was threaded across continually by the presence of the great predatory animals – the grizzly, the grey wolf, even an occasional mountain lion. The guarding of the cattle herds now required continual exertion, and if any weak or crippled draft animal fell out its bones were clean within the hour. The feeling of the wilderness now was distinct enough for the most adventurous. They fed fat, and daily grew more like savages in look and practice.

Wingate's wagons kept well apace with the average schedule of a dozen miles a day, at times spurting to fifteen or twenty miles, and made the leap over the heights of land between the North Platte and the Sweetwater, which latter stream, often winding among defiles as well as pleasant meadows, was to lead them to the summit of the Rockies at the South Pass, beyond which they set foot on the soil of Oregon, reaching thence to the Pacific. Before them now lay the entry mark of the Sweetwater Valley, that strange oblong upthrust of rock, rising high above the surrounding plain, known for two thousand miles as Independence Rock.

At this point, more than eight hundred miles out from the Missouri, a custom of unknown age seemed to have decreed a pause. The great rock was an unmistakable landmark, and time out of mind had been a register of the wilderness. It carried hundreds of names, including every prominent one ever known in the days of the fur trade or the new day of the wagon trains. It became known as a resting place; indeed, many rested there for ever, and never saw the soil of Oregon. Many an emigrant woman, sick well-nigh to death, held out so that she might be buried among the many other graves that clustered there. So, she felt, she had the final company of her kind. And to those weak or faint of heart the news that this was not halfway across often smote with despair and death, and they, too, laid themselves down here by the road to Oregon.

But here also were many scenes of cheer. By this time the new life of the trail had been taken on, rude and simple. Frolics were promised when the wagons should reach the Rock. Neighbours made reunions there. Weddings, as well as burials, were postponed till the train got to Independence Rock.

Here then, a sad-faced girl, true to her promise and true to some strange philosophy of her own devising, was to become the wife of a suitor whose persistency had brought him little comfort beyond the wedding date. All the train knew that Molly Wingate was to be married there to Sam Woodhull, now restored to trust and authority. Some said it was a good match, others shook their heads, liking well to see a maid either blush or smile in such case as Molly's whereas she did neither.

At all events, Mrs Wingate was two days baking cakes at the train stops. Friends got together little presents for the bride. Jed, Molly's brother, himself a fiddler of parts, organised an orchestra of a dozen pieces. The Reverend Henry Doak, a Baptist divine of much nuptial diligence *en route*, made ready his best coat. They came into camp. In the open spaces of the valley hundreds of wagons were scattered, each to send representatives to Molly Wingate's wedding. Some insisted that the ceremony should be performed on the top of the Rock itself, so that no touch of romance should lack.

Then approached the very hour – ten of the night, after duties of the day were done. A canopy was spread for the ceremony. A central campfire set the place for the wedding feast. Within a half-hour the bride would emerge from the secrecy of her wagon to meet at the canopy under the Rock the impatient groom, already clad in his best, already giving largess to the riotous musicians, who now attuned instruments, now broke out into rude jests or pertinent song.

But Molly Wingate did not appear, nor her father, nor her mother. A hush fell on the rude assemblage. The minister of the gospel departed to the Wingate encampment to learn the cause of the delay. He found Jesse Wingate irate to open wrath, the girl's mother stony calm, the girl herself white but resolute.

'She insists on seeing the marriage licence, Mr Doak,' began Jesse Wingate. 'As though we could have one! As though she should care more for that than her parents!'

'Quite so,' rejoined the reverend man. 'That is something I have taken up with the happy groom. I have with all the couples I have joined in wedlock on the trail. Of course, being a lawyer, Mr Woodhull knows that even if they stood before the meeting and acknowledged themselves man and wife it would be a lawful marriage before God and man. Of course, also we all know that since we left the Missouri River we have been in unorganised territory, with no courts and no form of government, no society as we understand it at home. Very well. Shall loving hearts be kept asunder for those reasons? Shall the natural course of life be thwarted until we get to Oregon? Why, sir, that is absurd! We do not even know much of the government of Oregon itself, except that it is provisional.'

The face of Molly Wingate appeared at the drawn curtains of her transient home. She stepped from her wagon and came forward. Beautiful, but not radiant, she was; cold and calm, but not blushing and uncertain. Her wedding gown was all in white, true enough to tradition, though but of delaine, pressed new from its packing trunk by her mother's hands. Her bodice, long and deep in front and at back, was plain entirely, save for a treasure of lace from her mother's trunk and her mother's wedding long ago. Her hands had no gloves, but white short-fingered mitts, also cherished remnants of days of schoolgirl belledom, did service. Over white stockings, below the long and full-bodied skirt, showed the crossed bands of long elastic tapes tied in an ankle bow to hold in place her little slippers of black high-finished leather. Had they seen her, all had said that Molly Wingate was the sweetest and the most richly clad bride of any on all the long, long trail across the land that had no law. And all she lacked for her wedding costume was the bride's bouquet, which her mother now held out to her, gathered with care that day of the mountain flowers – blue harebells, forget-me-nots of varied blues and the blossom of the gentian, bold and blue in the sunlight, though at night enfolded and abashed, its petals turning in and waiting for the sun again to warm them.

Molly Wingate, stout and stern, full bosomed, wet eyed, held out her one little present to her girl, her ewe lamb, whom she was now surrendering. But no hand of the bride was extended for the bride's bouquet. The voice of the bride was not low and diffident, but high-pitched, insistent.

'Provisional? Provisional? What is it you are saying, sir? Are you asking me to be married in a provisional wedding? Am I to give all I have provisionally? Is my oath provisional, or his?'

'Now, now, my dear!' began the minister.

Her father broke out into a half-stifled oath.

'What do you mean?'

Her mother's face went pale under its red bronze.

'I mean this,' broke out the girl, still in the strained high tones that betokened her mental state: 'I'll marry no man in any halfway fashion! Why didn't you tell me? Why didn't I think? How could I have forgotten? Law, organisation, society, convention, form, custom – haven't I got even those things to back me? No? Then I've nothing! It was – it was those things – form, custom – that I was going to have to support me. I've got nothing else. Gone – they're gone, too! And you ask me to marry him – provisionally – provisionally! Oh, my God! what awful thing was this? I wasn't even to have that solid thing to rest on, back of me, after it all was over!'

They stood looking at her for a time, trying to catch and weigh her real intent, to estimate what it might mean as to her actions.

'Like images, you are!' she went on hysterically, her physical craving for one man, her physical loathing of another, driving her well-nigh mad. 'You wouldn't protect your own daughter!' – to her stupefied parents. 'Must I think for you at this hour of my life? How near – oh, how near! But not now – not this way! No! No!'

'What do you mean, Molly?' demanded her father sternly. 'Come now, we'll have no woman tantrums at this stage! This goes on! They're waiting! He's waiting!'

'Let him wait!' cried the girl in sudden resolution. All her soul was in the cry, all her outraged, self-punished heart. Her philosophy fell from her swiftly at the crucial moment when she was to face the kiss, the embrace of another man. The great inarticulate voice of her woman nature suddenly sounded, imperative, terrifying, in her own ears – 'Oh, Will Banion, Will Banion, why did you take away my heart?' And now she had been on the point of doing this thing! An act of God had intervened.

Jesse Wingate nodded to the minister. They drew apart. The holy man nodded assent, hurried away – the girl sensed on what errand.

'No use!' she said. 'I'll not!'

Stronger and stronger in her soul surged the yearning for the dominance of one man, not this man yonder – a yearning too strong now for her to resist.

'But, Molly, daughter,' her mother's voice said to her, 'girls has – girls does. And like he said, it's the promise, it's the agreement they both make, with witnesses.'

'Yes, of course,' her father chimed in. 'It's the consent in the contract when you stand before them all.'

'I'll not stand before them. I don't consent! There is no agreement!'

Suddenly the girl reached out and caught from her mother the pitiful little bride's bouquet.

'Look!' she laughed. 'Look at these!'

One by one, rapidly, she tore out and flung down the folded gentian flowers.

'Closed, closed! When the night came, they closed! They couldn't! They couldn't! I'll not – I can't!'

She had the hand's clasp of mountain blossoms stripped down to a few small flowers of varied blooms. They heard the coming of the groom, half running. A silence fell over all the great encampment. The girl's father made a half-step forward, even as her mother sank down, cowering, her hands at her face.

Then, without a word, with no plan or purpose, Molly Wingate turned, sprang away from them and fled out into a night that was black indeed.

Truly she had but one thought, and that in negation only. Yonder came to claim her a man suddenly odious to her senses. It could not be. His kiss, his arms – if these were of this present time and place, then no place in all the world, even the world of savage blackness that lay about, could be so bad as this. At the test, her philosophy had forsaken her, reason now almost as well, and sheer terrified flight remained her one reaction.

She was gone, a white ghost in her wedding gown, her little slippers stumbling over the stones, her breath coming sobbingly as she ran. They followed her. Back of them, at the great fire whose illumination deepened the shadows here, rose a murmur, a rising of curious people, a pressing forward to the Wingate station. But of these none knew the truth, and it was curiosity that now sought answer for the delay in the anticipated divertisement.

Molly Wingate ran for some moments, to some distance – she knew of neither. Then suddenly all her ghastly nightmare of terror found climax in a world of demons. Voices of the damned rose around her. There came a sudden shock, a blow. Before she could understand, before she could determine the shadowy form that rose before her in the dark, she fell forward like the stricken creature.

CHAPTER 30

The Dance in the Desert

There was no wedding that night at the Independence Rock. The Arapahoes saw to that. But there were burials the day following, six of them – two women, a child, three men. The night attack had caught the company wholly off guard, and the bright fire gave good illumination for shaft and ball.

'Put out the fires! Corral! Corral!'

Voices of command arose. The wedding guests rushed for the shelter of their own wagons. Men caught up their weapons and a steady fire at the unseen foe held the latter at bay after the first attack.

Indeed, a sort of panic seized the savages. A warrior ran back exclaiming that he had seen a spirit, all in white, not running away from the attack, but towards them as they lay in cover. He had shot an arrow at the spirit, which then had vanished. It would be better to fall back and take no more like chances.

For this reason the family of Molly Wingate, pursuing her closely as they could, found her at last, lying face down in the grass, her arms outspread, her white wedding gown red with blood. An arrow, its shaft cracked by her fall, was embedded in her shoulder, driven deep by the savage bowman who had fired in fear at an object he did not recognise. So they found her, still alive, still unmutilated, still no prisoner. They carried the girl back to her mother, who reached out her arms and laid her child down behind the barricaded wagon wheels.

'Bring me a candle, you!' she called to the nearest man. It chanced to be Sam Woodhull.

Soon a woman came with a light.

'Go away now!' the mother commanded the disappointed man.

He passed into the dark. The old woman opened the bodice over the girl's heart, stripped away the stained lace that had served in three weddings on two sides of the Appalachians, and so got to the wound.

'It's in to the bone,' she said. 'It won't come out. Get me my scissors out of my bag. It's hanging right 'side the seat, our wagon.'

'Ain't there no doctor?' she demanded, her own heart weakening now. But none could tell. A few women grouped around her.

'It won't come out of that little hole it went in,' said stout Molly Wingate, not quite sobbing. 'I got to cut it wider.'

Silence held them as she finished the shreds of the ashen shaft and pressed to one side the stub of it. So with what tools she knew best she cut into the fabric of her own weaving, out of her own blood and bone; cut mayhap in steady snippings at her own heart, pulling and wrenching until the flesh, now growing purple, was raised above the girl's white breast. Both arms, in their white sleeves, lay on the trodden grass motionless, and had not shock and strain left the victim unconscious the pain must now have done so.

The sinew wrappings held the strap-iron head, wetted as they now were with blood. The sighing surgeon caught the base of the arrowhead in thumb and finger. There was no stanching of the blood. She wrenched it free at last, and the blood gushed from a jagged hole which would have meant death in any other air or in any patient but the vital young.

Now they disrobed the bride that was no bride, even as the rifle fire died away in the darkness. Women brought frontier drafts of herbs held sovereign, and laid her upon the couch that was not to have been hers alone.

She opened her eyes, moaning, held out her arms to her mother, not to any husband; and her mother, bloody, unnerved, weeping, caught her to her bosom.

'My lamb! My little lamb! Oh, dear me! Oh, dear me!'

The wailing of others for their dead arose. The camp dogs kept up a continual barking, but there was no other sound. The guards now lay out in the dark. A figure came creeping towards the bridal tent.

'Is she alive? May I come in? Speak to me, Molly!'

'Go on away, Sam!' answered the voice of the older woman. 'You can't come in.'

'But is she alive? Tell me!' His voice was at the door which he could not pass.

'Yes, more's the pity!' he heard the same voice say.

But from the girl who should then have been his, to have and to hold, he heard no sound at all, nor could he know her frightened gaze into her mother's face, her tight clutch on her mother's hand.

This was no place for delay. They made graves for the dead, pallets for the wounded. At sunrise the train moved on, grim, grave, dignified and silent in its very suffering. There was no time for reprisal or revenge. The one idea as to safety was to move forward in hope of shaking off pursuit.

But all that morning and all that day the mounted Arapahoes harassed them. At many bends of the Sweetwater they paused and made sorties; but the savages fell back, later to close in, sometimes under cover so near that their tauntings could be heard.

Wingate, Woodhull, Price, Hall, Kelsey stationed themselves along the line of flankers, and as the country became flatter and more open they had better control of the pursuers, so that by nightfall the latter began to fall back.

The end of the second day of forced marching found them at the Three Crossings of the Sweetwater, deep in a cheerless alkaline desert, and on one of the most depressing reaches of the entire journey. That night such gloom fell on their council as had not yet been known.

'The Watkins boy died today,' said Hall, joining his colleagues at the guarded fire. 'His leg was black where it was broke. They're going to bury him just ahead, in the trail. It's not best to leave headboards here.'

Wingate had fallen into a sort of apathy. For a time Woodhull did not speak to him after he also came in.

'How is she, Mr Wingate?' he asked at last. 'She'll live?'

'I don't know,' replied the other. 'Fever. No one can tell. We found a doctor in one of the Iowa wagons. He don't know.'

Woodhull sat silent for a time, exclaimed at last, 'But she will – she must! This shames me! We'll be married yet.'

'Better wait to see if she lives or dies,' said Jesse Wingate succinctly.

'I know what I wish,' said Caleb Price at last as he stared moodily at the coals, 'and I know it mighty well – I wish the other wagons were up. Yes, and – '

He did not finish. A nod or so was all the answer he got. A general apprehension held them all.

'If Bridger hadn't gone on ahead, damn him!' exclaimed Kelsey at last.

'Or if Carson hadn't refused to come along, instead of going on east,' assented Hall. 'What made him so keen?'

Kelsey spoke morosely.

'Said he had papers to get through. Maybe Kit Carson'll sometime carry news of our being wiped out somewhere.'

'Or if we had Bill Jackson to trail for us,' ventured the first speaker again. 'If we could send back word – '

'We can't, so what's the use?' interrupted Price. 'We were all together, and had our chance – once.'

But buried as they were in their gloomy doubts, regrets, fears, they got through that night and the next in safety. They dared not hunt, though the buffalo and antelope were in swarms, and though they knew they now were near the western limit of the buffalo range. They urged on, mile after mile. The sick and the wounded must endure as they might.

Finally they topped the gentle incline which marked the heights of land between the Sweetwater and the tributaries of the Green, and knew they had reached the South Pass, called halfway to Oregon. There was no timber here. The pass itself was no winding canyon, but only a flat, broad valley. Bolder views they had seen, but none of greater interest.

Now they would set foot on Oregon, passing from one great series of waterways to another, and even vaster, leading down to the western sea – the unknown South Sea marked as the limits of their possessions by the gallants of King Charles when, generations earlier, and careless of all these intervening generations of toil and danger, they had paused at the summit of Rockfish Gap in the Appalachians and waved a gay hand each towards the unknown continent that lay they knew not how far to the westward.

But these, now arrived halfway of half that continent, made no merriment in their turn. Their wounded and their sick were with them. The blazing sun tried them sore. Before them also lay they knew not what.

And now, coming in from the northeast in a vast braided tracing of travois poles and trampling hoofs, lay a trail which fear told them was that of yet another war party waiting for the white-topped wagons. It led on across the Pass. It could not be more than two days old.

'It's the Crows!' exclaimed Sam Woodhull, studying the broad trail. 'They've got their women and children with them.'

'We have ours with us,' said Caleb Price simply.

Every man who heard him looked back at the lines of gaunt cattle, at the dust-stained canvas coverings that housed their families. They were far afield from home or safety.

'Call Wingate. Let's decide what to do,' exclaimed Price again. 'We'll have to vote.'

They voted to go on, fault of any better plan. Some said Bridger's post was not far ahead. A general impatience, fretful, querulous, manifested itself. Ignorant, many of these wanted to hurry on to Oregon, which for most meant the Williamette Valley, in touch with the sea, marked as the usual end of the great trek. Few knew that they now stood on the soil of the Oregon country. The maps and journals of Molly Wingate were no more forthcoming, for Molly Wingate no more taught the evening school, but lay delirious under the hothouse canvas cover that intensified the rays of the blazing sun. It was life or death, but by now a life-and-death issue had become no unusual experience.

It was August, midsummer, and only half the journey done. The heat was blinding, blistering. For days now, in the dry sage country, from the ford of the North Fork of the Platte, along the Sweetwater and down the Sandy, the white alkali dust had sifted in and over everything. Lips cracked open, hands and arms either were raw or black with tan. The wagons were ready to drop apart. A dull silence had fallen on the people; but fatuously following the great Indian trail they made camp at last at the ford of the Green River, the third day's march down the Pacific Slope. No three days of all the slow trail had been harder to endure than these.

'Play for them, Jed,' counselled Caleb Price, when that hardy youth, leaving his shrunken herd, came in for his lunch that day at the ford.

'Yes, but keep that fiddle in the shade, Jed, or the sun certainly will pop it open.'

Jed's mother, her apron full of broken bits of sagebrush, turned to see that her admonishment was heeded before she began her midday coffee fire. As for Jed himself, with a wide grin he crouched down at the side of the wagon and leaned against a wheel as he struck up a lively air, roaring joyously to his accompaniment:

> 'Git out o' the way, old Dan Tucker,
> You're too late to git yore supper!'

Unmindful of the sullen apathy of men and women, the wailing of children stifling under the wagon tops, the moans of the sick and wounded in their ghastly discomfort, Jed sang with his cracked lips as he swung from one jig to the next, the voice of the violin reaching all the wagons of the shortened train.

'Choose yore pardners!' rang his voice in the joyous jesting of youth. And – marvel and miracle – then and there, those lean brown folk did take up the jest, and laughingly gathered on the sun-seared sands. They formed sets and danced – danced a dance of the indomitable, at high noon, the heat blinding, the sand hot under feet not all of which were shod. Molly Wingate, herself fifty and full-bodied, cast down her firewood, caught up her skirt with either hand and made good an old-time jig to the tune of the violin and the roaring accompaniment of many voices and of patted hands. She paused at length, dropping her calico from between her fingers, and hastened to a certain wagon side as she wiped her face with her apron.

'Didn't you hear it, Molly?' she demanded, parting the curtain and looking in.

'Yes, I did. I wanted – I almost wanted to join. Mother, I almost wanted to hope again. Am I to live? Where are we now?'

'By a right pretty river, child, and eena'most to Oregon. Come, kiss your mother, Molly. Let's try.'

Whereupon, having issued her orders and set everyone to work at something after her practical fashion, the first lady of the train went frizzling her shaved buffalo meat with milk in the frying pan; grumbling that milk now was almost at the vanishing point, and that now they wouldn't see another buffalo; but always getting forward with her meal. This she at last amiably announced.

'Well, come an' git it, people, or I'll throw it to the dogs.'

Flat on the sand, on blankets or odds and ends of hide, the emigrants sat and ate, with the thermometer – had they had one – perhaps a hundred and ten in the sun. The men were silent for the most part, with now and then a word about the ford, which they thought it would be wise to make at once, before the river perchance might rise, and while it still would not swim the cattle.

'We can't wait for anyone, not even the Crows,' said Wingate, rising and ending the mealtime talk. 'Let's get across.'

Methodically they began the blocking up of the wagon bodies to the measurement established by a wet pole.

'Thank the Lord,' said Wingate, 'they'll just clear now if the bottom is hard all the way.'

One by one the teams were urged into the ticklish crossing. The line of wagons was almost all at the farther side when all at once the rear guard came back, spurring.

'Corral! Corral!' he called.

He plunged into the stream as the last driver urged his wagon up the bank. A rapid dust cloud was approaching down the valley.

'Indians!' called out a dozen voices. 'Corral, men! For God's sake, quick – corral!'

They had not much time or means to make defence, but with training now become second nature they circled and threw the dusty caravan into the wonted barricade, tongue to tail gate. The oxen could not all be driven within, the loose stock was scattered, the horses were not on picket lines at that time of day; but driving what stock they could, the boy herders came in at a run when they saw the wagons parking.

There was no time to spare. The dust cloud swept on rapidly. It could not spell peace, for no men would urge their horses at such pace under such a sun save for one purpose – to overtake this party at the ford.

'It's Bill Jackson!' exclaimed Caleb Price, rifle in hand, at the river's edge. 'Look out, men! Don't shoot! Wait! There's fifty Indians back of him, but that's Jackson ahead. Now what's wrong?'

The riddle was not solved even when the scout of the Missouri train, crowded ahead by the steady rush of the shouting and laughing savages, raised his voice as though in warning and shouted some word, unintelligible, which made them hold their fire.

The wild cavalcade dashed into the stream, crowding their prisoner – he was no less – before them, bent bows back of him, guns ready.

They were stalwart, naked men, wide of jaw, great of chest, not a woman or child among them, all painted and full armed.

'My God, men!' called Wingate, hastening under cover. 'Don't let them in! Don't let them in! It's the Crows!'

CHAPTER 31

How, Cola!

'How, cola!' exclaimed the leader of the band of Indians, crowding up to the gap in the corral where a part of the stock had just been driven in. He grinned maliciously and made the sign for 'Sioux' – the edge of the hand across the throat.

But men, rifles crosswise, barred him back, while others were hurrying, strengthening the barricade. A half-dozen rifles, thrust out through wheels or levelled across wagon togues, now covered the front rank of the Crows; but the savages, some forty or fifty in number, only sat their horses laughing. This was sport to them. They had no doubt at all that they would have their will of this party of the whites as soon as they got ready, and they planned further strategy. To drive a prisoner into camp before killing him was humorous from their point of view, and practical withal, like driving a buffalo close to the village before shooting it.

But the white men were not deceived by the trading-post salutation.

'He's a liar!' called out the voice of Jackson. 'They're not Sioux – they're Crows, an' out for war! Don't let 'em in, boys! For God's sake, keep 'em out!'

It was a brave man's deed. The wonder was his words were not his last, for though the Crows did not understand all his speech, they knew well enough what he meant. One brave near him struck him across the mouth with the heavy wooden stock of his Indian whip, so that his lips gushed blood. A half-dozen arrows turned towards him, trembling on the strings. But the voice of their partisan rose in command. He preferred a parley, hoping a chance might offer to get inside the wagon ring. The loose stock he counted safe booty any time they liked. He did not relish the look of the rifle muzzles at a range of twenty feet. The riders were now piled in almost against the wheels.

'Swap!' exclaimed the Crow leader ingratiatingly, and held out his hand. 'How, cola!'

'Don't believe him! Don't trust him, men!'

Again Jackson's voice rose. As the savages drew apart from him, to hold him in even better bow range – one young brave, hideously barred in vermilion and yellow, all the time with an arrow at the prisoner's back – the men in the wagon corral now saw that Jackson's hands were tied behind his back, so that he was helpless. But still he sat his own horse, and still he had a chance left to take.

'Look out!' he called high and clear. 'Get away from the hole! I'm comin' in!'

Before anyone fully caught his meaning he swung his horse with his legs, lifted him with his heels and made one straight, desperate plunge for the gap, jostling aside the nearest two or three of his oppressors.

It was a desperate man's one hope – no hope at all, indeed, for the odds were fifty to one against him. Swift as was his movement, and unprepared as his tormentors were for it, just as the horse rose to his leap over the wagon tongue, and as the rider flung himself low on his neck to escape what he knew would come, a bow twanged back of him. They all heard the zhut! of the arrow as it struck. Then, in a stumbling heap, horse and rider fell, rolled over, as a sleet of arrows followed through.

Jackson rolled to one side, rose to his knees. Molly Wingate chanced to be near. Her scissors, carefully guarded always, because priceless, hung at her neck. Swiftly she began to saw at the thong which held Jackson's wrists, bedded almost to the bone and twisted with a stick. She severed the cord somehow and the man staggered up. Then they saw the arrow standing out at both sides of his shoulder, driven through the muscles with the hasty snap of the painted bowman's shot.

'Cut it – break it!' he demanded of her; for all the men now were at the edge, and there was no one else to aid. And staunch Molly Wingate, her eyes staring again in horror, took the bloody stem and tried to break it off, in her second case of like surgery that week. But the shaft was flexible, tough and would not break.

'A knife – quick! Cut it off above the feather!'

He himself caught the front of the shaft and pushed it back, close to the head. By chance she saw Jed's knife at his belt as he kneeled at the barricade, and drew it. Clumsily but steadily she slashed into the shaft, weakened it, broke it, pushed the point forward. Jackson himself unhesitatingly pulled it through, a gush of blood following on either side the shoulder. There was no time to notice that. Crippled as he was, the man only looked for weapons. A pistol lay on the ground and he caught it up.

But for the packs and bales that had been thrown against the wheels, the inmates of the corral would all have fallen under the rain of arrows that now slatted and thudded in. But they kept low, and the Indians were so close against the wagons that they could not see under the bodies or through the wheels. The chocks had not yet been taken out from under the boxes, so that they stood high. Against such a barricade cavalry was helpless. There was no warrior who wanted to follow Jackson's example of getting inside.

For an instant there came no order to fire. The men were reaching into the wagons to unsling their rifles from the riding loops fastened to the bows. It all was a trample and a tumult and a whirl of dust under thudding hoofs outside and in, a phase which could last no more than an instant. Of a sudden, came the thin crack of a squirrel rifle from the far corner of the wagon park. The Crow partisan sat his horse just a moment, the expression on his face frozen there, his mouth slowly closing. Then he slid off his horse close to the gap, now piled high with goods and gear.

A boy's high quaver rose.

'You can't say nothing this time! You didn't shoot at all now!'

An emigrant boy was jeering at his father.

But by that time no one knew or cared who shot. The fight was on. Every rifle was emptied in the next instant, and at that range almost every shot was fatal or disabling. In sudden panic at the powder flare in their faces, the Crows broke and scattered, with no time to drag away their wounded.

The fight, or this phase of it, was over almost before it was begun. It all was one more repetition of border history. Almost never did the Indians make a successful attack on a trading post, rarely on an emigrant train in full corral. The cunning of the Crow partisan in driving in a prisoner as a fence had brought him close, yes – too close. But the line was not yet broken.

Firing with a steady aim, the emigrants added to the toll they took. The Crows bent low and flogged their horses. Only in the distant willow thickets did they pause. They even left their dead.

There were no wounded, or not for long. Jackson, the pistol in his hand, his face grey with rage and pain, stepped outside the corral. The Crow chief, shot through the chest, turned over, looked up dully.

'How, cola!' said his late prisoner, baring his teeth.

And what he did with this brave he did with all the others of the wounded able to move a hand. The debt to savage treachery was paid, savagely enough, when he turned back to the wagons, and such was the rage of all at this last assault that no voice was raised to stay his hand.

'There's nothing like tobacker,' asserted Jackson coolly when he had re-entered the corral and it came to the question of caring for his arrow wound. 'Jest tie on a good chaw o' tobacker on each side o' that hole an' 'twon't be long afore she's all right. I'm glad it went plumb through. I've knowed a arrerhead to pull off an' stay in when the sinew wroppin's got loose from soakin'.

'Look at them wrists,' he added, holding up his hands. 'They twisted that rawhide clean to the bone, damn their skins! Pertendin' to be friends! They put me in front sos't you'd let 'em ride up clost – that's the Crow way, to come right inter camp if they can, git in close an' play friends. But, believe me, this ain't but the beginnin'. They'll be back, an' plenty with 'em. Them Crows ain't west of the Pass fer only one thing, an' that's this wagon train.'

They gathered around him now, plying him with questions. Sam Woodhull was among those who came, and him Jackson watched narrowly every moment, his own weapon handy, as he now described the events that had brought him hither.

'Our train come inter the Sweetwater two days back o' you all,' he said. 'We seed you'd had a fight but had went on. We knowed some was hurt, fer we picked up some womern fixin's – tattin', hit were – with blood on hit. And we found buryin's, the dirt different colour.'

They told him now of the first fight, of their losses, of the wounded;

told him of the near escape of Molly Wingate, though out of courtesy to Woodhull, who stood near, they said nothing of the interrupted wedding. The old mountain man's face grew yet more stern.

'That gal!' he said. 'Her shot by a sneakin' Rapa-hoe? Ain't that a shame! But she's not bad – she's comin' through?'

Molly Wingate, who stood ready now with bandages, told him how alike the two arrow wounds had been.

'Take an' chaw tobacker, ma'am,' said he. 'Put a hunk on each side, do-ee mind, an' she'll be well.'

'Go on and tell us the rest,' someone demanded.

'Not much to tell that ye couldn't of knew, gentlemen,' resumed the scout. 'Ef ye'd sont back fer us we'd of jined ye, shore, but ye didn't send.'

'How could we send, man?' demanded Woodhull savagely. 'How could we know where you were, or whether you'd come – or whether you'd have been of any use if you had?'

'Well, we knew whar you-all was, 't any rate,' rejoined Jackson. 'We was two days back o' ye, then one day. Our captain wouldn't let us crowd in, fer he said he wasn't welcome an' we wasn't needed.

'That was ontel we struck the big Crow trail, with you all a follerin' o' hit blind, a-chasin' trouble as hard as ye could. Then he sont me on ahead to warn ye an' to ask ef we should jine on. We knowed the Crows was down atter the train.

'I laid down to sleep, I did, under a sagebrush, in the sun, like a fool. I was beat out an' needed sleep, an' I thought I was safe fer a leetle while. When I woke up it was a whoop that done hit. They was around me, laughin', twenty arrers p'inted, an' some shot inter the ground by my face. I taken my chance, an' shook hands. They grabbed me an' tied me. Then they made me guide them in, like ye seen. They maybe didn't know I come from the east an' not from the west.

'Their village is on some creek above here. I think they're on a visit to the Shoshones. Eight hundred men they are, or more. Hit's more'n what it was with the Sioux on the Platte, fer ye're not so many now. An' any time now the main band may come. Git ready, men. Fer me, I must git back to my own train. They may be back twenty mile, or thirty. Would any man want to ride with me? Would ye, Sam Woodhull?'

The eyes of his associates rested on Woodhull.

'I think one man would be safer than two,' said he. 'My own place is here if there's sure to be a fight.'

'Mebbe so,' assented Jackson. 'In fack, I don't know as more'n one'd git through if you an' me both started.' His cold grey eye was fixed on Woodhull carelessly. 'An' ef hit was the wrong man got through he'd never lead them Missouri men for'rerd to where this fight'll be.

'An' hit'll be right here. Look yan!' he added.

He nodded to the westward, where a great dust cloud arose.

'More is comin',' said he. 'Yan's Bannack like as not, er even the Shoshones, all I know, though they're usual quiet. The runners is out atween all the tribes. I must be on my way.'

He hurried to find his own horse and looked to its welfare, for it, too, had an arrow wound. As he passed a certain wagon he heard a voice call to him, saw a hand at the curtained front.

'Miss Molly! Hit's you! Ye're not dead no ways, then?'

'Come,' said the girl.

He drew near, fell back at sight of her thin face, her pallor; but again she commanded him.

'I know,' said she. 'He's – he's safe?'

'Yes, Miss Molly, a lot safer'n any of us here.'

'You're going back to him?'

'Yes. When he knows ye're hurt he'll come. Nothin'll stop him, once I tell him.'

'Wait!' she whispered. 'I heard you talk. Take him this.' She pushed into his hand a folded paper, unsealed, without address. 'To him!' she said, and fell back on the blankets of her rude pallet.

At that moment her mother was approaching, and at her side walked Woodhull, actuated by his own suspicions about Jackson. He saw the transaction of the passed note and guessed what he could not know. He tapped Jackson on the shoulder, drew him aside, his own face pale with anger.

'I'm one of the officers of this train,' said he. 'I want to know what's in that note. We have no truck with Banion, and you know that. Give it to me.'

Jackson calmly tucked the paper into the fire bag that hung at his belt.

'Come an' take it, Sam, damn ye!' said he. 'I don't know what's in hit, an' won't know. Who it's to ain't none o' yore damn business!'

'You're a cursed meddler!' broke out Woodhull. 'You're a spy in our camp, that's all you are!'

'So! Well, cussed meddler er not, I'm a cussed shore shot. An' I advise ye to give over on all this an' mind yore business. Ye'll have plenty to do by midnight, an' by that time all yore womern an' children, all yore old men an' all yore cowards'll be prayin' fer Banion an' his men to come. That there includes you somewhere's, Sam. Don't temp' me too much ner too long. I'll kill ye yit ef ye do! Git on away!'

They parted, each with eye over shoulder. Their talk had been aside and none had heard it in full. But when Woodhull again joined Mrs Wingate that lady conveyed to him Molly's refusal to see him or to set a time for seeing him. Bitterly angered, humiliated to the core, he turned back to the men who were completing the defences of the wagon park.

'I kain't start now afore dark,' said Jackson to the train command. 'They're a-goin' to jump the train. When they do come they'll surround ye an' try to keep ye back from the water till the stock goes crazy. Lay low an' don't let a Injun inside. Hit may be a hull day, er more, but when Banion's men come they'll come a-runnin' – allowin' I git through to tell 'em.

'Dig in a trench all the way aroun',' he added finally. 'Put the womern an' children in hit an' pile up all yer flour on top. Don't waste no powder – let 'em come up clost as they will. Hold on ontel we come.'

At dusk he slipped away, the splash of his horse's feet in the ford coming fainter and fainter, even as the hearts of some felt fainter as his wise and sturdy counsel left them. Naught to do now but to wait.

They did wait – the women and children, the old, the ill and the wounded huddled shivering and crying in the scooped-out sand, hardest and coldest of beds; the men in line against the barricade, a circle of guards outside the wagon park. But midnight passed, and the cold hours of dawn, and still no sign came of an attack. Men began to believe the dust cloud of yesterday no more than a false alarm, and the leaders were of two minds, whether to take Jackson's counsel and wait for the Missourians, or to hook up and push on as fast as possible to Bridger's fort, scarce more than two hard days' journey on ahead. But before this breakfast-hour discussion had gone far events took the decision out of their hands.

'Look!' cried a voice. 'Open the gate!'

The cattle guards and outposts who had just driven the herd to water were now spurring for shelter and hurrying on the loose stock ahead of them. And now, from the willow growth above them, from the trail that led to the ford and from the more open country to the westward there came, in three great detachments, not a band or a body, but an army of the savage tribesmen, converging steadily upon the wagon train.

They came slowly, not in a wild charge, not yelling, but chanting.

The upper and right-hand bodies were Crows. Their faces were painted black, for war and for revenge. The band on the left were wild men, on active half-broke horses, their weapons for the most part bows and arrows. They later found these to be Bannacks, belonging anywhere but here, and in any alliance rather than with the Crows from east of the Pass.

Nor did the latter belong here to the south and west, far off their own great hunting range. Obviously what Carson, Bridger and Jackson had said was true. All the tribes were in league to stop the great invasion of the white nation, who now were bringing their women and children and this thing with which they buried the buffalo. They meant extermination now. They were taking their time and would take their revenge for the dead who lay piled before the white man's barricade.

The emigrants rolled back a pair of wagons, and the cattle were crowded through, almost over the human occupants of the oblong. The gap was closed. All the remaining cargo packages were piled against the wheels, and the noncombatants sheltered in that way. Shovels deepened the trench here or there as men sought better to protect their families.

And now in a sudden *mêlée* of shouts and yells, of trampling hoofs and whirling colours, the first bands of the Crows came charging up in the attempt to carry away their dead of yesterday. Men stooped to grasp a stiffened wrist, a leg, a belt; the ponies squatted under ghastly dragging burdens.

But this brought them within pistol range. The reports of the white men's weapons began, carefully, methodically, with deadly accuracy. There was no panic. The motionless or the struggling blotches ahead of the wagon park grew and grew. A few only of the Crows got off with bodies of their friends or relatives. One warrior after another dropped. They were used to killing buffalo at ten yards. The white rifles killed their men now regularly at a hundred. They drew off, out of range.

Meantime the band from the westward was rounding up and driving off every animal that had not been corralled. The emigrants saw themselves in fair way to be set on foot.

Now the savage strategy became plain. The fight was to be a siege.

'Look!' Again a leader pointed.

Crouched now, advancing under cover of the shallow cut-bank, the headdresses of a score of the western tribesmen could be seen. They sank down. The ford was held, the water was cut off! The last covering fringe of willows also was held. On every side the black-painted savages sat their ponies, out of range. There could be no more water or grass for the horses and cattle, no wood for the camp.

There was no other concerted charge for a long time. Now and then some painted brave, chanting a death song, would ride slowly towards the wagon park, some dervish vow actuating him or some bravado impelling him. But usually he fell.

It all became a quiet, steady, matter-of-fact performance on both sides. This very freedom from action and excitement, so different from the gallant riding of the Sioux, was more terrifying than direct attack *en masse*, so that when it came to a matter of shaken morale the whites were in as bad a case as their foes, although thus far they had had no casualty at all.

There lacked the one leader, cool, calm, skilled, experienced, although courage did not lack. Yet even the best courage suffers when a man hears the wailing of his children back of him, the groans of his wife. As the hours passed, with no more than an occasional rifle shot or the zhut! of an arrow ending its high arc, the tension on the nerves of the beleaguered began to manifest itself.

At midday the children began to cry for water. They were appeased with milk from the few cows offering milk; but how long might that last, with the cattle themselves beginning to moan and low?

'How far are they back?'

It was Hall, leader of the Ohio wagons. But none could tell him where the Missouri train had paused. Wingate alone knew why Banion had not advanced. He doubted if he would come now.

'And this all was over the quarrel between two men,' said Caleb Price to his friend Wingate.

'The other man is a thief, Cale,' reiterated Wingate. 'He was court-martialed and broke, dishonourably discharged from the army. He was under Colonel Doniphan, and had control of subsistence in upper Mexico for some time. He had the regimental funds. Doniphan was irregular. He ran his regiment like a mess, and might order first this officer, then that, of the line or staff, to take on his free-for-all quartermaster trains. But he was honest. Banion was not. He had him broken. The charges were filed by Captain Woodhull. Well, is it any wonder there is no love lost? And is it any wonder I wouldn't train up with a thief, or allow him to visit in my family? By God! right now I wouldn't; and I didn't send for him to help us!'

'So!' said Caleb Price. 'So! And that was why the wedding –'

'Yes! A foolish fancy of a girl. I don't know what passed between her and Banion. I felt it safer for my daughter to be married, as soon as could be, to another man, an honest man. You know how that came out. And now, when she's as apt to die as live, and we're all as apt to, you others send for that renegade to save us! I have no confidence that he will come. I hope he will not. I'd like his rifles, but I don't want him.'

'Well,' said Caleb Price, 'it is odd how his rifles depend on him and not on the other man. Yet they both lived in the same town.'

'Yes, one man may be more plausible than another.'

'Yes? I don't know that I ever saw a man more plausible with his fists than Major Banion was. Yes, I'll call him plausible. I wish some of us – say, Sam Woodhull, now – could be half as plausible with these Crows. Difference in men, Jess!' he concluded. 'Woodhull was there – and now he's here. He's here – and now we're sending there for the other man.'

'You want that other man, thief and dishonest as he is?'

'By God! yes! I want his rifles and him too. Women, children and all, the whole of us, will die if that thief doesn't come inside of another twenty-four hours.'

Wingate flung out his arms, walked away, hands clasped behind his back. He met Woodhull.

'Sam, what shall we do?' he demanded. 'You're sort of in charge now. You've been a soldier, and we haven't had much of that.'

'There are fifteen hundred or two thousand of them,' said Woodhull slowly – 'a hundred and fifty of us that can fight. Ten to one, and they mean no quarter.'

'But what shall we do?'

'What can we but lie close and hold the wagons?'

'And wait?'

'Yes.'

'Which means only the Missouri men!'

'There's no one else. We don't know that they're alive. We don't know that they will come.

'But one thing I do know' – his dark face gathered in a scowl – 'if he doesn't come it will not be because he was not asked! That fellow carried a letter from Molly to him. I know that. Well, what do you-all think of me? What's my standing in all this? If I've not been shamed and humiliated, how can a man be? And what am I to expect?'

'If we get through, if Molly lives, you mean?'

'Yes. I don't quit what I want. I'll never give her up. You give me leave to try again? Things may change. She may consider the wrong she's done me, an honest man. It's his hanging around all the time, keeping in her mind. And now we've sent for him – and so has she!'

They walked apart, Wingate to his wagon.

'How is she?' he asked of his wife, nodding to Molly's wagon.

'Better some ways, but low,' replied his stout helpmate, herself haggard, dark circles of fatigue about her eyes. 'She won't eat, even with the fever down. If we was back home where we could get things! Jess, what made us start for Oregon?'

'What made us leave Kentucky for Indiana, and Indiana for Illinois? I don't know. God help us now!'

'It's bad, Jesse.'

'Yes, it's bad.' Suddenly he took his wife's face in his hands and kissed her quietly. 'Kiss Little Molly for me,' he said. 'I wish – I wish –'

'I wish them other wagons'd come,' said Molly Wingate. 'Then we'd see!'

CHAPTER 32

The Fight at the Ford

Jackson, wounded and weary as he was, drove his crippled horse so hard all the night through that by dawn he had covered almost fifty miles, and was in sight of the long line of wagons, crawling like a serpent down the slopes west of the South Pass, a cloud of bitter alkali dust hanging like a blanket over them. No part of the way had been more cheerless than this grey, bare expanse of more than a hundred miles, and none offered less invitation for a bivouac. But now both man and horse were well-nigh spent.

Knowing that he would be reached within an hour or so at best, Jackson used the last energies of his horse in riding back and forth at right angles across the trail, the Plains sign of 'Come to me!' He hoped it would be seen. He flung himself down across the road, in the dust, his bridle tied to his wrist. His horse, now nearly gone, lay down beside him, nor ever rose again. And here, in the time a gallop could bring them up, Banion and three of his men found them, one dead, the other little better.

'Bill! Bill!'

The voice of Banion was anxious as he lightly shook the shoulder of the prone man, half afraid that he, too, had died. Stupid in sleep, the scout sprang up, rifle in hand.

'Who's thar?'

'Hold, Bill! Friends! Easy now!'

The old man pulled together, rubbed his eyes.

'I must of went to sleep agin,' said he. 'My horse – pshaw now, pore critter, do-ee look now!'

In rapid words he now told his errand. They could see the train accelerating its speed. Jackson felt in the bag at his belt and handed Banion the folded paper. He opened the folds steadily, read the words again and again.

' "Come to us," ' is what it says. He spoke to Jackson.

'Ye're a damned liar, Will,' remarked Jackson.

'I'll read it all!' said Banion suddenly.

' "Will Banion, come to me, or it may be too late. There never was any wedding. I am the most wicked and most unhappy woman in the world. You owe me nothing! But come! M.W."

'That's what it says. Now you know. Tell me – you heard of no wedding back at Independence Rock? They said nothing? He and she –'

'Ef they was ever any weddin' hit was a damned pore sort, an' she says thar wasn't none. She'd orto know.'

'Can you ride, Jackson?'

'Span in six fast mules for a supply wagon, such as kin gallop. I'll sleep in that a hour or so. Git yore men started, Will. We may be too late. It's nigh fifty mile to the ford o' the Green.'

It came near to mutiny when Banion ordered a third of his men to stay back with the ox teams and the families. Fifty were mounted and ready in five minutes. They were followed by two fast wagons. In one of these rolled Bill Jackson, unconscious of the roughness of the way.

On the Sandy, twenty miles from the ford, they wakened him.

'Now tell me how it lies,' said Banion. 'How's the country?'

Jackson drew a sketch on the sand.

'They'll surround, an' they'll cut off the water.'

'Can we ford above and come in behind them?'

'We mout. Send half straight to the ford an' half come in behind, through the willers, huh? That'd put 'em atween three fires. Ef we driv' 'em on the wagons they'd get hell thar, an' ef they broke, the wagons could chase 'em inter us again. I allow we'd give 'em hell. Hit's the Crows

I'm most a-skeered of. The Bannacks – ef that's who they was – 'll run easy.'

At sunset of that day the emigrants, now half mad of thirst, and half ready to despair of succour or success, heard the Indian drums sound and the shrilling of the eagle-bone whistles. The Crows were chanting again. Whoops arose along the river bank.

'My God! they're coming!' called out a voice.

There was a stir of uneasiness along the line, an ominous thing. And then the savage hosts broke from their cover, more than a thousand men, ready to take some loss in their hope that the whites were now more helpless. In other circumstances it must have been a stirring spectacle for any who had seen it. To these, cowering in the sand, it brought terror.

But before the three ranks of the Crows had cleared the cover the last line began to yell, to whip, to break away. Scattering but continuous rifle fire followed them, war cries arose, not from savages, but white men. A line of riders emerged, coming straight through to the second rank of the Crow advance. Then the beleaguered knew that the Missourians were up.

'Banion, by God!' said a voice which few stopped to recognise as Woodhull's.

He held his fire, his rifle resting so long through the wagon wheel that Caleb Price in one swift motion caught it away from him.

'No harm, friend,' said he, 'but you'll not need this just now!'

His cold eye looked straight into that of the intending murderer.

The men in the wagon park rose to their work again. The hidden Bannacks began to break away from their lodgment under the river bank. The sound of hoofs and of shouts came down the trail. The other wing of the Missourians flung off and cleared the ford before they undertook to cross, their slow, irregular, deadly rifle fire doing its work among the hidden Bannacks until they broke and ran for their horses in the cotton-woods below. This brought them partly into view, and the rifles of the emigrants on that side bore on them till they broke in sheer terror and fled in a scattered *sauve qui peut*.

The Crows swerved under the enfilading fire of the men who now crossed the ford. Caught between three fires, and meeting for their first time the use of the revolver, then new to them, they lost heart and once more left their dead, breaking away into a mad flight west and north which did not end till they had forded the upper tributaries of the Green and Snake, and found their way back west of the Tetons to their own country far east and north of the Two-go-tee crossing of the Wind

River Mountains; whence for many a year they did not emerge again to battle with the white nation on the Medicine Road. At one time there were forty Crow squaws, young and old, with gashed breasts and self-amputated fingers, given in mourning over the unreturning brave.

What many men had not been able to do of their own resources, less than a fourth their number now had done. Side by side Banion, Jackson, a half-dozen others, rode up to the wagon gap, now opened. They were met by a surge of the rescued. Women, girls threw themselves upon them, kissing them, embracing them hysterically. Where had been gloom, now was rejoicing, laughter, tears.

The leaders of the emigrants came up to Banion and his men, Wingate in advance. Banion still sat his great black horse, coldly regarding them.

'I have kept my promise, Captain Wingate,' said he. 'I have not come until you sent for me. Let me ask once more, do I owe you anything now?'

'No, sir, you do not,' replied the older man.

'And do you owe me anything?'

Wingate did not answer.

'Name what you like, Major Banion,' said a voice at his shoulder – Caleb Price.

Banion turned to him slowly.

'Some things have no price, sir,' said he. 'For other things I shall ask a high price in time. Captain Wingate, your daughter asked me to come. If I may see her a moment, and carry back to my men the hope of her recovery, we shall all feel well repaid.'

Wingate made way with the others. Banion rode straight through the gap, with no more than one unseeing glance at Woodhull, near whom sat Jackson, a pistol resting on his thigh. He came to the place under a wagon where they had made a hospital cot for Molly Wingate. It was her own father and mother who lifted her out as Will Banion sprang down, hat in hand, pale in his own terror at seeing her so pale.

'No, don't go!' said the girl to her parents. 'Be here with us – and God."

She held out her arms and he bent above her, kissing her forehead gently and shyly as a boy.

'Please get well, Molly Wingate,' said he. 'You are Molly Wingate?'

'Yes. At the end – I couldn't! I ran away, all in my wedding clothes, Will. In the dark. Someone shot me. I've been sick, awfully sick, Will.'

'Please get well, Molly Wingate! I'm going away again. This time, I don't know where. Can't you forget me, Molly Wingate?'

'I'm going to try, Will. I did try. Go on ahead, Will,' she added. 'You know what I mean. Do what I told you. I – why, Will!'

'My poor lamb!' said the strong voice of her mother, who gathered her in her arms, looking over her shoulder at this man to whom her child had made no vows. But Banion, wet eyed, was gone once more.

Jackson saw his leader out of the wagon gap, headed for a camping spot far apart. He stumbled up to the cot where Molly lay, her silent parents still close by.

'Here, Miss Molly, gal,' said he, holding out some object in his hand. 'We both got a arrer through the shoulder, an' mine's a'most well a'ready. Ain't nothin' in the world like a good chaw o' tobacker to put on a arrer cut. Do-ee, now!'

CHAPTER 33

The Families are Coming!

The Missourians camped proudly and coldly apart, the breach between the two factions by no means healed, but rather deepened, even if honourably so, and now well understood of all.

Most men of both parties now knew of the feud between Banion and Woodhull, and the cause underlying it. Woman gossip did what it might. A half-dozen determined men quietly watched Woodhull. As many continually were near Banion, although for quite a different reason. All knew that time alone must work out the answer to this implacable quarrel, and that the friends of the two men could not possibly train up together.

After all, when in sheer courtesy the leaders of the Wingate train came over to the Missouri camp on the following day, there came nearer to being a good understanding than there ever had been since the first break. It was agreed that all the wagons should go on together as far as Fort Bridger, and that beyond that point the train should split into two or perhaps three bodies – a third if enough Woodhull adherents could be found to make him up a train. First place, second and third were to be cast by lot. They all talked soberly, fairly, with the dignity of men used to good standing among men. These matters concluded, and it having been agreed that all should lie by for another day, they resolved the meeting into one of better fellowship.

Old Bill Jackson, lying against his blanket roll, fell into reminiscence.

'Times past,' said he, 'the Green River Rendyvous was helt right in here. I've seed this place spotted with tepees – hull valley full o' Company men an' free trappers an' pack-train people – time o' Ashley an' Sublette an' my Uncle Jackson an' all them traders. That was right here on the Green. Ever'body drunk an' happy, like I ain't now. Mounting men togged out, new leggin's an' moccasins their womern had made, warriors painted up a inch o' their lives, an' women with brass wire an' calico all they wanted – maybe two-three thousand people in the Rendyvous.

'But I never seed the grass so short, an' I never seed so much fightin' afore in all my life as I have this trip. This is the third time we're jumped, an' this time we're lucky, shore as hell. Pull on through to Bridger an' fix yer wagons afore they tumble apart. Leave the grass fer them that follows, an' git on fur's you kin, every wagon. We ain't likely to have no more trouble now. Pile up them braves in one heap fer a warnin' to any other bunch o' reds that may come along to hide around the wagon ford. New times has come on the Green.'

'Can you travel, Jackson?' asked Hall of Ohio. 'You've had a hard time.'

'Who? Me? Why shouldn't I? Give me time to pick up some o' them bows an' arrers an' I'm ready to start. I noticed a right fine horn bow one o' them devils had – the Crows allus had good bows. That's the yaller-an'-red brave that was itchin' so long to slap a arrer through my ribs from behind. I'd like to keep his bow fer him, him not needin' it now.'

Before the brazen sun had fully risen on the second day these late peaceful farmers of Ohio, Iowa, Illinois, Indiana, Missouri, were plodding along once more beside their sore-footed oxen; passing out unaided into a land which many leading men in the government, North and South, and quite aside from political affiliations, did not value at five dollars for it all, though still a thousand miles of it lay ahead.

' "Oh, then, Susannah!" ' roared Jed Wingate, trudging along beside Molly's wagon in the sand. ' "Don't you cry fer me – I'm going through to Oregon, with my banjo on my knee!" '

Fair as a garden to the sun-seared eyes of the emigrants seemed the mountain post, Fort Bridger, when its rude stockade separated itself from the distortions of the desert mirage, whose citadels of silence, painted temples fronted with colossal columns, giant sphinxes, vast caryatids, lofty arches, fretwork façades, fantastically splendid castles and palaces now resolved themselves into groups of squat pole structures and a rude stock corral.

The site of the post itself could not better have been chosen. Here the flattened and dividing waters of the Black's Fork, icy cold and fresh from the Uintah Mountains to the southward, supported a substantial growth of trees, green now and wonderfully refreshing to desert-weary eyes.

'The families are coming!'

Bridger's clerk, Chardon, raised the new cry of the trading post.

'Broke an' hungry, I'll bet!' swore old Jim Bridger in his beard.

But he retired into his tepee and issued orders to his Shoshone squaw, who was young and pretty. Her name, as he once had said, was Dang Yore Eyes – and she was very proud of it. Philosophical withal, though smarting under recent blows of her white lord, she now none the less went out and erected once more in front of the tepee the token Bridger had kicked down – the tufted lance, the hair-fringed bull-neck shield, the sacred medicine bundle which had stood in front of Jeem's tepee in the Rendezvous on Horse Creek, what time he had won her in a game of hands. Whereupon the older squaw, not young, pretty or jealous, abused him in Ute and went out after wood. Her name was Blast Your Hide, and she also was very proud of her white name. Whereafter both Dang Yore Eyes and Blast Yore Hide, female, and hence knowing the moods of man, wisely hid out for a while. They knew when Jeem had the long talk with the sick white squaw, who was young, but probably needed bitter bark of the cottonwood to cure her fever.

Painted Utes and Shoshones stood about, no more silent than the few local mountaineers, bearded, beaded and fringed, who still after some mysterious fashion clung to the old life at the post. Against the new-comers, profitable as they were, still existed the ancient antipathy of the resident for the non-resident.

'My land sakes alive!' commented stoical Molly Wingate, after they had made some enquiries into the costs of staples here. 'This store ain't no place to trade. They want fifty dollars a sack for flour – what do you think of that? We got it for two dollars back home. And sugar a dollar a tin cup, and just plain salt two bits a pound, and them to guess at the pound. Do they think we're Indians, or what?'

'It's the tenth day of August, and a thousand miles ahead,' commented Caleb Price. 'And we're beyond the buffalo now.'

'And Sis is in trouble,' added Jed Wingate. 'The light wagon's got one hind spindle half in two, and I've spliced the hind ex for the last time.'

Jackson advanced an idea.

'At Fort Hall,' he said, 'I've seed 'em cut a wagon in two an' make a two-wheel cart out'n hit. They're easier to git through mountains that way.'

'Now listen to that, Jesse!' Mrs Wingate commented. 'It's getting down to less and less every day. But I'm going to take my bureau through, and my wheat, and my rose plants, if I have to put wheels on my bureau.'

The men determined to saw down three wagons of the train which now seemed doubtful of survival as quadrupeds, and a general rearrangement of cargoes was agreed. Now they must jettison burden of every dispensable sort. Some of the sore-necked oxen were to be thrown into the loose herd and their places taken for a time by cows no longer offering milk.

A new soberness began to sit on all. The wide reaches of desert with which they here were in touch appalled their hearts more than anything they yet had met. The grassy valley of the Platte, where the great fourfold tracks of the trail cut through a waving sea of green belly deep to the oxen, had seemed easy and inviting, and since then hardship had at least been spiced with novelty and change. But here was a new and forbidding land. This was the Far West itself; silent, inscrutable, unchanged, irreducible. The mightiness of its calm was a smiting thing. The awesomeness of its chill, indifferent nights, the unsparing ardours of its merciless noons, the measureless expanses of its levels, the cold barrenness of its hills – these things did not invite as to the bosom of a welcoming mother; they repelled, as with the chill gesture of a stranger turning away outcasts from the door.

'Here resolution almost faints!' wrote one.

A general requisition was made on the scant stores Bridger had hurried through. To their surprise, Bridger himself made no attempt at frontier profits.

'Chardon,' commanded the moody master of the post to his head clerk, 'take down your tradin' bar an' let my people in. Sell them their flour an' meal at what it has cost us here – all they want, down to what the post will need till my partner Vasquez brings in more next fall, if he ever does. Sell 'em their flour at four dollars a sack, an' not at fifty, boy. Git out that flag I saved from Sublette's outfit, Chardon. Put it on a pole for these folks, an' give it to them so's they kin carry it on acrost to Oregon. God's got some use for them folks out yan or hit wouldn't be happenin' this way. I'm goin' to help 'em acrost. Ef I don't, old Jim Bridger is a liar!'

That night Bridger sat in his lodge alone, moodily smoking. He heard a shaking at the pegs of the door flap.

'Get out!' he exclaimed, thinking that it was his older associate, or else some intruding dog.

His order was not obeyed. Will Banion pulled back the flap, stooped and entered.

'How!' exclaimed Bridger, and with fist smitten on the blankets made the sign to 'Sit!' Banion for a time also smoked in silence, knowing the moody ways of the old-time men.

'Ye came to see me about her, Miss Molly, didn't ye?' began Bridger after a long time, kicking the embers of the tepee fire together with the toe of his moccasin.

'How do you know that?'

'I kin read signs.'

'Yes, she sent me.'

'When?'

'That was at Laramie. She told me to come on with you then. I could not.'

'Pore child, they mout 'a' killed her! She told me she'd git well, though – told me so today. I had a talk with her.' His wrinkled face broke into additional creases. 'She told me more!'

'I've no wonder.'

'Ner me. Ef I was more young and less Injun I'd love that gal! I do, anyhow, fer sake o' what I might of been ef I hadn't had to play my game the way the cards said fer me.

'She told me she was shot on her weddin' night, in her weddin' clothes – right plum to the time an' minute o' marryin, then an' thar. She told me she thanked God the Injun shot her, an' she wished to God he'd killed her then an' thar. I'd like such fer a bride, huh? That's one hell of a weddin', huh? Why?'

Banion sat silent, staring at the embers.

'I know why, or part ways why. Kit an' me was drunk at Laramie. I kain't remember much. But I do ree-colleck Kit said something to me about you in the army, with Donerphan in Mayheeco. Right then I gits patriotic. "Hooray!" says I. Then we taken another drink. After that we fell to arguin' how much land we'd git out o' Mayheeco when the treaty was signed. He said hit war done signed now, or else hit warn't. I don't ree-colleck which, but hit was one or t'other. He had papers. Ef I see Kit agin any time now I'll ast him what his papers was. I don't ree-colleck exact.

'All that, ye see, boy,' he resumed, 'was atter I was over to the wagons at Laramie, when I seed Miss Molly to say goodbye to her. I reckon maybe I was outside o' sever'l horns even then.'

'And that was when you gave her the California nugget that Kit Carson had given you!' Banion spoke at last.

'Oh, ye spring no surprise, boy! She told me today she'd told you then; said she'd begged you to go on with me an' beat all the others to Californy; said she wanted you to git rich; said you an' her had parted, an' she wanted you to live things down. I was to tell ye that.

'Boy, she loves ye – not me ner that other man. The Injun womern kin love a dozen men. The white womern kain't. I'm still fool white enough fer to believe that. Of course she'd break her promise not to tell about the gold. I might 'a' knowed she'd tell the man she loved. Well, she didn't wait long. How long was hit afore she done so – about ten minutes? Boy, she loves ye. Hit ain't no one else.'

'I think so. I'm afraid so.'

'Why don't ye marry her then, damn ye, right here? Ef a gal loves a man he orto marry her, ef only to cure her o' bein' a damn fool to love any man. Why don't you marry her right now?'

'Because I love her!'

Bridger sat in disgusted silence for some time.

'Well,' said he at last, 'there's some kinds o' damned fools that kain't be cured noways. I expect you're one o' them. Me, I hain't so highfalutin'. Ef I love a womern, an' her me, somethin's goin' to happen. What's this here like? Nothin' happens. Son, it's when nothin' happens that somethin' else does happen. She marries another man – barrin' 'Rapahoes. A fool fer luck – that's you. But there mightn't always be a Injun hidin' to shoot her when she gits dressed up agin an' the minister is a-waitin' to pernounce 'em man an' wife. Then whar air ye?'

He went on more kindly after a time, as he reached out a hard, sinewy hand.

'Such as her is fer the young man that has a white man's full life to give her. She's purty as a doe fawn an' kind as a thoroughbred filly. In course ye loved her, boy. How could ye a-help hit? An' ye was willin' to go to Oregon – ye'd plough rather'n leave sight o' her? I don't blame ye, boy. Such as her is not supported by rifle an' trap. Hit's the home smoke, not the tepee fire, for her. I ask ye nothin' more, boy. I'll not ask ye what ye mean. Man an' boy, I've follered the tepee smokes – blue an' a-movin' an' a-beckonin' they was – an' I never set this hand to no plough in all my life. But in my heart two things never was wiped out – the sight o' the white womern's face an' the sight o' the flag with stars. I'll help ye all I can, an' good luck go with ye. Work hit out yore own way. She's worth more'n all the gold Californy's got buried!'

This time it was Will Banion's hand that was suddenly extended.

'Take her secret an' take her advice then,' said Bridger after a time. 'Ye must git in ahead to Californy. Fust come fust served, on any beaver water. Fer me 'tis easy. I kin hold my hat an' the immigrints'll throw money into hit. I've got my fortune here, boy. I can easy spare ye what ye need, ef ye do need a helpin' out'n my plate. Fer sake o' the finest gal that ever crossed the Plains, that's what we'll do! Ef I don't, Jim Bridger's a putrefied liar, so help me God!'

Banion made no reply at once, but could not fail of understanding.

'I'll not need much,' said he. 'My place is to go on ahead with my men. I don't think there'll be much danger now from Indians, from what I hear. At Fort Hall I intend to split off for California. Now I make you this proposition, not in payment for your secret, or for anything else: If I find gold I'll give you half of all I get, as soon as I get out or as soon as I can send it.'

'What do ye want o' me, son?'

'Six mules and packs. All the shovels and picks you have or can get for me at Fort Hall. There's another thing.'

'An' what is that?'

'I want you to find out what Kit Carson said and what Kit Carson had. If at any time you want to reach me – six months, a year – get word through by the wagon trains next year, in care of the District Court at Oregon City, on the Willamette.'

'Why, all right, all right, son! We're all maybe talkin' in the air, but I more'n half understand ye. One thing, ye ain't never really intendin' to give up Molly Wingate! Ye're a fool not to marry her now, but ye're reckonin' to marry her sometime – when the moon turns green, huh? When she's old an' shrivelled up, then ye'll marry her, huh?'

Banion only looked at him, silent.

'Well, I'd like to go on to Californy with ye, son, ef I didn't know I'd make more here, an' easier, out'n the crazy fools that'll be pilin' in here next year. So good luck to ye.

'Kit had more o' that stuff,' he suddenly added. 'He give me some more when I told him I'd lost that fust piece he give me. I'll give ye a piece fer sample, son. I've kep' hit close.'

He begun fumbling in the tobacco pouch which he found under the head of his blanket bed. He looked up blankly, slightly altering the name of his younger squaw.

'Well, damn her hide!' said he fervently. 'Ye kain't keep nothin' from 'em! An' they kain't keep nothin' when they git hit.'

CHAPTER 34

A Matter of Friendship

Once more the train, now permanently divided into two, faced the desert, all the men and many women now afoot, the kine low-headed, stepping gingerly in their new rawhide shoes. Grey, grim work, toiling over the dust and sand. But at the head wagon, taking over an empire foot by foot, flew the great flag. Half fanatics? That may be. Fanatics, so called, also had prayed and sung and taught their children, all the way across to the Great Salt Lake. They, too, carried books. And within one hour after their halt near the Salt Lake they began to plough, began to build, began to work, began to grow and make a country.

The men at the trading post saw the Missouri wagons pull out ahead. Two hours later the Wingate train followed, as the lot had determined. Woodhull remained with his friends in the Wingate group, regarded now with an increasing indifference, but biding his time.

Bridger held back his old friend Jackson even after the last train pulled out. It was mid afternoon when the start was made.

'Don't go just yet, Bill,' said he. 'Ride on an' overtake 'em. Nothin' but rattlers an' jack rabbits now fer a while. The Shoshones won't hurt 'em none. I'm powerful lonesome, somehow. Let's you an' me have one more drink.'

'That sounds reas'nble,' said Jackson. 'Shore that sounds reas'nble to me.'

They drank of a keg which the master of the post had hidden in his lodge, back of his blankets; drank again of high wines diluted but uncoloured – the 'likker' of the fur trade.

They drank from tin cups, until Bridger began to chant, a deepening sense of his old melancholy on him.

'Goodbye!' he said again and again, waving his hand in general vagueness to the mountains.

'We was friends, wasn't we, Bill?' he demanded again and again; and Jackson, drunk as he, nodded in like maudlin gravity. He himself began to chant. The two were savages again.

'Well, we got to part, Bill. This is Jim Bridger's last Rendyvous. I've rid around an' said goodbye to the mountings. Why don't we do it the way the big partisans allus done when the Rendyvous was over? 'Twas old Mike Fink an' his friend Carpenter begun hit, fifty year ago. Keelboat men on the river, they was. There's as good shots left today as then, an' as good friends. You an' me has seed hit; we seed hit at the very last meetin' o' the Rocky Mountain Company men, before the families come. An 'nary a man spilled the whiskey on his partner's head.'

'That's the truth,' assented Jackson. 'Though some I wouldn't trust now.'

'Would ye trust me, Bill, like I do you, fer sake o' the old times, when friends was friends?'

'Shore I would, no matter how come, Jim. My hand's stiddy as a rock, even though my shootin' shoulder's a leetle stiff from that Crow arrer.'

Each man held out his firing arm, steady as a bar.

'I kin still see the nail heads on the door, yan. Kin ye, Bill?'

'Plain! It's a waste o' likker, Jim, fer we'd both drill the cups.'

'Are ye a-skeered?'

'I told ye not.'

'Chardon!' roared Bridger to his clerk. 'You, Chardon, come here!'

The clerk obeyed, though he and others had been discreet about remaining visible as this bout of old-timers at their cups went on. Liquor and gunpowder usually went together.

'Chardon, git ye two fresh tin cups an' bring 'em here. Bring a piece o' charcoal to spot the cups. We're goin' to shoot 'em off each other's heads in the old way. You know what I mean?'

Chardon, trembling, brought the two tin cups, and Bridger with a burnt ember sought to mark plainly on each a black bull's-eye. Silence fell on the few observers, for all the emigrants had now gone and the open space before the rude trading building was vacant, although a few faces peered around corners. At the door of the tallest tepee two native women sat, a young and an old, their blankets drawn across their eyes, accepting fate, and not daring to make a protest.

'How!' exclaimed Bridger as he filled both cups and put them on the ground. 'Have ye wiped yer bar'l?'

'Shore I have. Let's wipe agin.'

Each drew his ramrod from the pipes and attached the cleaning worm with its twist of tow, kept handy in belt pouch in muzzle-loading days.

'Clean as a whistle!' said Jackson, holding out the end of the rod.

'So's mine, pardner. Old Jim Bridger never disgraced hisself with a rifle.'

'Ner me,' commented Jackson. 'Hold a hair full, Jim, an' cut nigh the top o' the tin. That'll be safer fer my skelp, an' hit'll let less whisky out'n the hole. We got to drink what's left. S'pose'n we have a snort now?'

'Atter we both shoot we kin drink,' rejoined his friend, with a remaining trace of judgement. 'Go take stand whar we marked the scratch. Chardon, damn ye, carry the cup down an' set hit on his head, an' ef ye spill a drop I'll drill ye, d'ye hear?'

The *engagé*'s face went pale.

'But Monsieur Jim – ' he began.

'Don't "Monsieur Jim" me or I'll drill a hole in ye anyways! Do-ee-do what I tell ye, boy! Then if ye crave fer to see some ol'-time shootin' come on out, the hull o' ye, an' take a lesson, damn ye!'

'Do-ee ye shoot first, Bill,' demanded Bridger. 'The light's soft, an' we'll swap atter the fust fire, to git hit squar for the hindsight, an' no shine on the side o' the front sight.'

'No, we'll toss fer fust,' said Jackson, and drew out a Spanish dollar. 'Tails fer me last!' he called as it fell. 'An' I win! You go fust, Jim.'

'Shore I will ef the toss-up says so,' rejoined his friend. 'Step off the fifty yard. What sort o' iron ye carryin', Bill?'

'Why do ye ask? Ye know ol' Mike Sheets in Virginia never bored a better. I've never changed.'

'Ner I from my old Hawken. Two good guns, an' two good men, Bill, o' the ol' times – the ol' times! We kain't say fairer'n this, can we, at our time o' life, fer favour o' the old times, Bill? We got to do somethin', so's to kind o' git rested up.'

'No man kin say fairer,' said his friend.

They shook hands solemnly and went onward with their devil-may-care test, devised in a historic keel-boat man's brain, as inflamed then by alcohol as their own were now.

Followed by the terrified clerk, Bill Jackson, tall, thin and grizzled, stoical as an Indian, and too drunk to care much for consequences, so only he proved his skill and his courage, walked steadily down to the chosen spot and stood, his arms folded, after leaning his own rifle against the door of the trading room. He faced Bridger without a tremor, his head bare, and cursed Chardon for a coward when his hand trembled as he balanced the cup on Jackson's head.

'Damn ye,' he exclaimed, 'there'll be plenty lost without any o' your spillin'!'

'Air ye all ready, Bill?' called Bridger from his station, his rifle cocked and the delicate triggers set, so perfect in their mechanism that the lightest touch against the trigger edge would loose the hammer.

'All ready!' answered Jackson.

The two, jealous still of the ancient art of the rifle, which nowhere in the world obtained nicer development than among men such as these, faced each other in what always was considered the supreme test of nerve and skill; for naturally a man's hand might tremble, sighting three inches above his friend's eye, when it would not move a hair sighting centre between the eyes of an enemy.

Bridger spat out his tobacco chew and steadily raised his rifle. The man opposite him stood steady as a pillar, and did not close his eyes. The silence that fell on those who saw became so intense that it seemed veritably to radiate, reaching out over the valley to the mountains as in a hush of leagues.

For an instant, which to the few observers seemed an hour, these two figures, from which motion seemed to have passed for ever, stood frozen. Then there came a spurt of whitish-blue smoke and the thin dry crack of the border rifle.

The hand and eye of Jim Bridger, in spite of advancing years, remained true to their long training. At the rifle crack the tin cup on the head of the statue-like figure opposite him was flung behind as though by the blow of an invisible hand. The spin of the bullet acting on the liquid contents, ripped apart the seams of the cup and flung the fluid wide. Then and not till then did Jackson move.

He picked up the empty cup, bored centre directly through the black spot, and turning walked with it in his hand toward Bridger, who was wiping out his rifle once more.

'I call hit mighty careless shootin',' said he, irritated. 'Now lookee what ye done to the likker! Ef ye'd held a leetle higher, above the level o' the likker, like I told ye, she wouldn't o' busted open thataway now. It's nacherl, thar warn't room in the cup fer both the likker an' the ball. That's wastin' likker, Jim, an' my mother told me when I was a boy, "Wilful waste makes woeful want!"'

'I call hit a plum-centre shot,' grumbled Bridger. 'Do-ee look now! Maybe ye think ye kin do better shoot'in yerself than old Jim Bridger!'

'Shore I kin, an' I'll show ye! I'll bet my rifle against yourn – ef I wanted so sorry a piece as yourn – kin shoot that clost to the mark an' not spill no likker a-tall! An' ye can fill her two-thirds full an' put yer thumb in fer the balance ef ye like.'

'I'll just bet ye a new mule agin yer pony ye kain't do nothin' o' the sort!' retorted Bridger.

'All right, I'll show ye. O' course, ye got to hold still.'

'Who said I wouldn't hold still?'

'Nobody. Now you watch me.'

He stooped at the little water ditch which had been led in among the buildings from the stream and kneaded up a little ball of mud. This he forced into the handle of the tin cup, entirely filling it, then washed off the body of the cup.

'I'll shoot the fillin' out'n the handle an' not out'n the cup!' said he. 'Mud's cheap, an' all the diff'runce in holdin' is ef I nicked the side o' yer haid it'd hurt ye 'bout the same as ef what I nicked the centre o' hit. Ain't that so? We'd orto practise inderstry an' 'conomy, Jim. Like my mother said, "Penny saved is er penny yearned." "Little drops o' water, little gains o' sand," says she, "a-makes the mighty o–o–ocean, an the plea–ea–sant land." '

'I never seed it tried,' said Bridger, with interest, 'but I don't see why hit hain't practical. Whang away, an ef ye spill the whiskey shootin' to one side, or cut har shootin' too low, your *caballo* is mine – an' he hain't much!'

With no more argument, he in turn took up his place, the two changing positions so that the light would favour the rifleman. Again the fear-smitten Chardon adjusted the filled cup, this time on his master's bared head.

'Do-ee turn her sideways now, boy,' cautioned Bridger. 'Set the han'le sideways squar', so she looks wide. Give him a fa'r shot now, fer I'm interested in this yere thing, either way she goes. Either I lose ha'r er a mule.'

But folding his arms he faced the rifle without batting an eye, as steady as had been the other in his turn.

Jackson extended his long left arm, slowly and steadily raising the silver bead up from the chest, the throat, the chin, the forehead of his friend, then lowered it, rubbing his sore shoulder.

'Tell him to turn that han'le squar' to me, Jim!' he called. 'The damn fool has got her all squegeed eroun' to one side.'

Bridger reached up a hand and straightened the cup himself.

'How's that?' he asked.

'All right! Now hold stiddy a minute.'

Again the Indian women covered their faces, sitting motionless. And at last came again the puff of smoke, the faint crack of the rifle, never loud in the high, rarefied air.

The straight figure of the scout never wavered. The cup still rested on his head. The rifleman calmly blew the smoke from his barrel, his eye on Bridger as the latter now raised a careful hand to his head. Chardon hastened to aid, with many ejaculations.

The cup still was full, but the mud was gone from inside the handle as though poked out with a finger! 'That's what I call shootin', Jim,' said Jackson, 'an' reas'nable shootin' too. Now spill half o' her where she'll do some good, an' give me the rest. I got to be goin' now. I don't want yer mule. I fust come away from Missouri to git shet o' mules.'

Chardon, cupbearer, stood regarding the two wild souls whom he never in his own more timid nature was to understand. The two mountain men shook hands. The alcohol had no more than steadied them in their rifle work, but the old exultation of their wild life came to them now once more. Bridger clapped hand to mouth and uttered his old war cry before he drained his share of the fiery fluid.

'To the ol' days, friend!' said he once more; 'the days that's gone, when men was men, an' a friend could trust a friend!'

'To the ol' days!' said Jackson in turn. 'An' I'll bet two better shots don't stand today on the soil o' Oregon! But I got to be goin', Jim. I'm goin' on to the Columby. I may not see ye soon. It's far.'

He swung into his saddle, the rifle in its loop at the horn. But Bridger came to him, a hand on his knee.

'I hate to see ye go, Bill.'

'Shore!' said Jackson. 'I hate to go. Take keer yerself, Jim.'

The two Indian women had uncovered their faces and gone inside the lodge. But old Jim Bridger sat down, back against a cottonwood, and watched the lopping figure of his friend jog slowly out into the desert. He himself was singing now, chanting monotonously an old Indian refrain that lingered in his soul from the days of the last Rendezvous.

At length he arose, and animated by a sudden thought sought out his tepee once more. Dang Yore Eyes greeted him with shy smiles of pride.

'Heap shoot, Jeem!' said she. 'No kill-um. Why?'

She was decked now in her finest, ready to use all her blandishments on her lord and master. Her cheeks were painted red, her wrists were heavy with copper. On a thong at her neck hung a piece of yellow stone which she had bored through with an awl, or rather with three or four awls, after much labour, that very day.

Bridger picked up the ornament between thumb and finger. He said no word, but his fingers spoke.

'Other pieces. Where?'

'White man. Gone – out there.' She answered in the same fashion. 'How, cola!' she spoke aloud. 'Him say, "How, cola", me.' She smiled with much pride over her conquest, and showed two silver dollars. 'Swap!'

In silence Bridger went into the tepee and pulled the door flaps.

CHAPTER 35

Gee – Whoa – Haw!

Midsummer in the desert. The road now, but for the shifting of the sands, would have been marked by the bodies of dead cattle, in death scarcely more bone and parchment than for days they had been while alive. The horned toad, the cactus, the rattlesnake long since had replaced the prairie dogs of the grassy floor of the eastern Plains. A scourge of great black crickets appeared, crackling loathsomely under the wheels. Sagebrush and sand took the place of trees and grass as they left the river valley and crossed a succession of ridges or plateaus. At last they reached vast black basaltic masses and lava fields, proof of former subterranean fires which seemingly had for ever dried out the life of the earth's surface. The very vastness of the views might have had charm but for the tempering feeling of awe, of doubt, of fear.

They had followed the trail over the immemorial tribal crossings over heights of land lying between the heads of streams. From the Green River, which finds the great canyons of the Colorado, they came into the vast horseshoe valley of the Bear, almost circumventing the Great Salt Lake, but unable to forsake it at last. West and south now rose bold mountains around whose northern extremity the river had felt its way, and back of these lay fold on fold of lofty ridges, now softened by the distances. Of all the splendid landscapes of the Oregon Trail, this one had few rivals. But they must leave this and cross to yet another though less inviting vast river valley of the series which led them across the continent.

Out of the many wagons which Jesse Wingate originally had captained, now not one hundred remained in his detachment when it took the sagebrush plateaus below the great Snake River. They still were back of the Missouri train, no doubt several days, but no message left on a cleft stick at camp cheered them or enlightened them. And now still another defection had cut down the train.

Woodhull, moody and irascible, feverish and excited by turns, ever since leaving Bridger had held secret conclaves with a few of his adherents, the nature of which he did not disclose. There was no great surprise and no extreme regret when, within safe reach of Fort Hall, he had announced his intention of going on ahead with a dozen wagons. He went without obtaining any private interview with Molly Wingate.

These matters none the less had their depressing effect. Few illusions remained to any of them now, and no romance. Yet they went on – ten miles, fifteen sometimes, though rarely twenty miles a day. Women fell asleep, babes in arms, jostling on the wagon seats; men almost slept as they walked, ox whip in hand; the cattle slept as they stumbled on, tongues dry and lolling. All the earth seemed strange, unreal. They advanced as though in a dream through some inferno of a crazed imagination.

About them now often rose the wavering images of the mirage, offering water, trees, wide landscapes; beckoning in such desert deceits as they often now had seen. One day as the brazen sun mocked them from its zenith they saw that they were not alone on the trail.

'Look, mother!' exclaimed Molly Wingate – she now rode with her mother on the seat of the family wagon, Jed driving her cart when not on the cow column. 'See! There's a caravan!'

Her cry was echoed or anticipated by scores of voices of others who had seen the same thing. They pointed west and south.

Surely there was a caravan – a phantom caravan! Far off, gigantic, looming and lowering again, it paralleled the advance of their own train, which in numbers it seemed to equal. Slowly, steadily, irresistibly, awesomely, it kept pace with them, sending no sign to them, mockingly indifferent to them – mockingly so, indeed; for when the leaders of the Wingate wagons paused the riders of the ghostly train paused also, biding their time with no action to indicate their intent. When the advance was resumed the uncanny *pari passu* again went on, the rival caravan going forward as fast, no faster than those who regarded it in a fascinated interest that began to become fear. Yonder caravan could bode no good. Without doubt it planned an ambush farther on, and this sinister indifference meant only its certainty of success.

Or were there, then, other races of men out here in this unknown world of heat and sand? Was this a treasure train of old Spanish *cargadores*? Did ghosts live and move as men? If not, what caravan was this, moving alone, far from the beaten trail? What purpose had it here?

'Look, mother!'

The girl's voice rose eagerly again, but this time with a laugh in it. And her assurance passed down the line, others laughing in relief at the solution.

'It's ourselves!' said Molly. 'It's the Fata Morgana – but how marvellous! Who could believe it?'

Indeed, the mirage had taken that rare and extraordinary form. The mirage of their own caravan, rising, was reflected, mirrored, by some freak of the desert sun and air, upon the fine sand blown in the air at a distance from the train. It was, indeed, themselves they saw, not knowing it, in a vast primordial mirror of the desert gods. Nor did the discovery of the truth lessen the feeling of discomfort, of apprehension. The laughter was at best uneasy until at last a turn in the trail, a shift in the wizardry of the heat waves, broke up the ghostly caravan and sent it, figure by figure, vehicle by vehicle, into the unknown whence it had come.

'This country!' exclaimed Molly Wingate's mother. 'It scares me! If Oregon's like this – '

'It isn't, mother. It is rich and green, with rains. There are great trees, many mountains, beautiful rivers where we are going, and there are fields of grain. There are – why, there are homes!'

The sudden pathos of her voice drew her mother's frowning gaze.

'There, there, child!' said she. 'Don't you mind. We'll always have a home for you, your paw and me.'

The girl shook her head.

'I sometimes think I'd better teach school and live alone.'

'And leave your parents?'

'How can I look my father in the face every day, knowing what he feels about me? Just now he accuses me of ruining Sam Woodhull's life – driving him away, out of the train. But what could I do? Marry him, after all? I can't – I can't! I'm glad he's gone, but I don't know why he went.'

'In my belief you haven't heard or seen the last of Sam Woodhull yet,' mused her mother. 'Sometimes a man gets sort of peeved – wants to marry a girl that jilts him more'n if she hadn't. And you certainly jilted him at the church door, if there'd been any church there. It was an awful thing, Molly. I don't know as I see how Sam stood it long as he did.'

'Haven't I paid for it, mother?'

'Why, yes, one way of speaking. But that ain't the way men are going to call theirselves paid. Until he's married, a man's powerful set on having a woman. If he don't, he thinks he ain't paid, it don't scarcely make no difference what the woman does. No, I don't reckon he'll forget. About Will Banion –'

'Don't let's mention him, mother. I'm trying to forget him.'

'Yes? Where do you reckon he is now – how far ahead?'

'I don't know. I can't guess.'

The colour on her cheek caught her mother's gaze.

'Gee-whoa-haw! Git along Buck and Star!' commanded the buxom dame to the swaying ox team that now followed the road with no real need of guidance. They took up the heat and burden of the desert.

CHAPTER 36

Two Love Letters

'The families are coming – again the families!' It was again the cry of the passing fur post, looking eastward at the caravan of the west-bound ploughs; much the same here at old Fort Hall, on the Snake River, as it was at Laramie on the North Platte, or Bridger on the waters tributary to the Green.

The company clerks who looked out over the sandy plain saw miles away a dust cloud which meant but one thing. In time they saw the Wingate train come on, slowly, steadily, and deploy for encampment a mile away. The dusty wagons, their double covers stained, mildewed, torn, were scattered where each found the grass good. Then they saw scores of the emigrants, women as well as men, hastening into the post.

It was now past midsummer, around the middle of the month of August, and the Wingate wagons had covered some twelve hundred and eighty miles since the start at mid-May of the last spring – more than three months of continuous travel; a trek before which the passage over the Appalachians, two generations earlier, wholly pales.

What did they need, here at Fort Hall, on the Snake, third and last settlement of the two thousand miles of toil and danger and exhaustion? They needed everything. But one question first was asked by these travel-sick home-loving people: What was the news?

News? How could there be news when almost a year would elapse before Fort Hall would know that on that very day – in that very month of August 1848 – Oregon was declared a territory of the Union?

News? How could there be news, when these men could not know for much more than a year that, as they outspanned here in the sage, Abraham Lincoln had just declined the governorship of the new territory of Oregon? Why? He did not know. Why had these men come here? They did not know.

But news – the news! The families must have the news. And here – always there was news! Just beyond branched off the trail to California. Here the supply trains from the Columbia brought news from the Oregon settlements. News? How slow it was, when it took a letter more than two years to go one way from edge to edge of the American continent!

They told what news they knew – the news of the Mormons of 1847 and 1848; the latest mutterings over fugitive negro slaves; the growing feeling that the South would one day follow the teachings of secession. They heard in payment the full news of the Whitman massacre in Oregon that winter; they gave back in turn their own news of the battles with the Sioux and the Crows; the news of the new army posts then moving west into the Plains to clear them for the whites. News? Why, yes, large news enough, and on either hand, so the trade was fair.

But these matters of the outside world were not the only ones of interest, whether to the post traders or the newly arrived emigrants. Had others preceded them? How many? When? Why, yes, a week earlier fifty wagons of one train, Missouri men, led by a man on a great black horse and an old man, a hunter. Banion? Yes, that was the name, and the scout was Jackson – Bill Jackson, an old-time free trapper. Well, these two had split off for California, with six good pack mules, loaded light. The rest of the wagons had gone on to the Snake. But why these two had bought the last shovels and the only pick in all the supplies at old Fort Hall no man could tell. Crazy, of course; for who could pause to work on the trail with pick or shovel, with winter coming on at the Sierra crossing?

But not crazier than the other band who had come in three days ago, also ahead of the main train. Woodhull? Yes, that was the name –

Woodhull. He had twelve or fifteen wagons with him, and had bought supplies for California, though they all had started for Oregon. Well, they soon would know more about the Mary's River and the Humboldt Desert. Plenty of bones, there, sure!

But even so, a third of the trains, these past five years, had split off at the Raft River and given up hope of Oregon. California was much better – easier to reach and better when you got there. The road to Oregon was horrible. The crossings of the Snake, especially the first crossing, to the north bank, was a gamble with death for the whole train. And beyond that, to the Blue Mountains, the trail was no trail at all. Few ever would get through, no one knew how many had perished. Three years ago Joe Meek had tried to find a better trail west of the Blues. All lost, so the story said. Why go to Oregon? Nothing there when you got there. California, now, had been settled and proved a hundred years and more. Every year men came this far east to wait at Fort Hall for the emigrant trains and to persuade them to go to California, not to Oregon.

But what seemed strange to the men at the trading post was the fact that Banion had not stopped or asked a question. He appeared to have made up his mind long earlier, and beyond asking for shovels he had wanted nothing. The same way with Woodhull. He had come in fast and gone out fast, headed for the Raft River trail to California, the very next morning. Why? Usually men stopped here at Fort Hall, rested, traded, got new stock, wanted to know about the trail ahead. Both Banion and Woodhull struck Fort Hall with their minds already made up. They did not talk. Was there any new word about the California trail, down at Bridger? Had a new route over the Humboldt Basin been found, or something of that sort? How could that be? If so, it must be rough and needing work in places, else why the need for so many shovels?

But maybe the emigrants themselves knew about these singular matters, or would when they had read their letters. Yes, of course, the Missouri movers had left a lot of letters, some for their folks back East next year maybe, but some for people in the train. Banion, Woodhull – had they left any word? Why, yes, both of them. The trader smiled. One each. To the same person, yes. Well, lucky girl! But that black horse now – the Nez Perces would give a hundred ponies for him. But he wouldn't trade. A sour young man. But Woodhull, now, the one with the wagons, talked more. And they each had left a letter for the same girl! And this was Miss Molly Wingate? Well, the trader did not blame them! These American girls! They were like roses to the old traders, cast away this lifetime out here in the desert.

News? Why, yes, no train ever came through that did not bring news and get news at old Fort Hall – and so on.

The enclosure of the old adobe fur-trading post was thronged by the men and women of the Wingate train. Molly Wingate at first was not among them. She sat, chin on her hand, on a wagon tongue in the encampment, looking out over the blue-grey desert to the red-and-gold glory of the sinking sun. Her mother came to her and placed in her lap the two letters, stood watching her.

'One from each,' said she sententiously, and turned away.

The girl's face paled as she opened the one she had felt sure would find her again, somewhere, somehow. It said:

DEAREST – I write to Molly Wingate, because and only because I know she still is Molly Wingate. It might be kinder to us both if I did not write at all but went my way and left it all to time and silence. I found I could not.

There will be no other woman, in all my life, for me. I cannot lay any vow on you. If I could, if I dared, I would say: 'Wait for a year, while I pray for a year – and God help us both.'

As you know, I now have taken your advice. Bridger and I are joined for the California adventure. If the gold is there, as Carson thinks, I may find more fortune than I have earned. More than I could earn you gave me – when I was young. That was two months ago. Now I am old.

Keep the news of the gold, if it can be kept, as long as you can. No doubt it will spread from other sources, but so far as I know – and thanks only to you – I am well ahead of any other adventurer from the East this season, and, as you know, winter soon will seal the trails against followers. Next year, 1849, will be the big rush, if it all does not flatten.

I can think of no one who can have shared our secret. Carson will be East by now, but he is a government man, and close of mouth with strangers. Bridger, I am sure – for the odd reason that he worships you – will tell no one else, especially since he shares profits with me, if I survive and succeed. One doubt only rests in my mind. At his post I talked with Bridger, and he told me he had a few other bits of gold that Carson had given him at Laramie. He looked for them but had lost them. He suspected his Indian women, but he knew nothing. Of course, it would be one chance in a thousand that anyone would know the women had these things, and even so no one could tell where the gold came from, because not even the women would know that; not even Bridger does, exactly; not even I myself.

In general I am headed for the valley of the Sacramento. I shall work north. Why? Because that will be towards Oregon!

I write as though I expected to see you again, as though I had a right to expect or hope for that. It is only the dead young man, Will Banion, who unjustly and wrongly craves and calls out for the greatest of all fortune for a man – who unfairly and wrongly writes you now, when he ought to remember your word, to go to a land far from you, to forget you and to live down his past. Ah, if I could! Ah, if I did not love you!

But being perhaps about to die, away from you, the truth only must be between you and me. And the truth is I never shall forget you. The truth is I love you more than anything else and everything else in all the world.

If I were in other ways what the man of your choice should be, would this truth have any weight with you? I do not know and I dare not ask. Reason does tell me how selfish it would be to ask you to hold in your heart a memory and not a man. That is for me to do – to have a memory, and not you. But my memory never can content me.

It seems as though time had been invented so that, through all its aeons, our feet might run in search, one for the other – to meet, where? Well, we did meet – for one instant in the uncounted ages, there on the prairie. Well, if ever you do see me again you shall say whether I have been, indeed, tried by fire, and whether it has left me clean – whether I am a man and not a memory.

That I perhaps have been a thief, stealing what never could be mine, is my great agony now. But I love you. Goodbye.

WILLIAM HAYS BANION
To Margaret Wingate, Fort Hall, in Oregon

For an hour Molly sat, and the sun sank. The light of the whole world died.

*　　　*　　　*

The other letter rested unopened until later; when she broke the seal and read by the light of a sagebrush fire, she frowned. Could it be that in the providence of God she once had been within one deliberate step of marrying Samuel Payson Woodhull?

My Darling Molly – This I hope finds you well after the hard journey from Bridger to Hall.

They call it Cruel to keep a Secret from a Woman. If so, I have been Cruel, though only in Poor pay for your Cruelty to me. I have had a Secret – and this is it: I have left for California from this Point and shall not go to Oregon. I have learned of Gold in the State of California, and have departed to that State in the hope of early Success in Achieving a Fortune. So far as I know, I am the First to have this news of Gold, unless a certain man whose name and thought I execrate has by his Usual dishonesty fallen on the same information. If so, we two may meet where none can Interfere.

I do not know how long I may be in California, but be Sure I go for but the one purpose of amassing a Fortune for the Woman I love. I never have given you Up and never shall. Your promise is mine and our Engagement never has been Broken, and the Mere fact that accident for the time Prevented our Nuptials by no means shall ever mean that we shall not find Happy Consummation of our most Cherished Desire at some later Time.

I confidently Hope to arrive in Oregon a rich man not later than one or two years from Now. Wait for me. I am mad without you and shall count the Minutes until then when I can take you in my Arms and Kiss you a thousand Times. Forgive me; I have not Heretofore told you of these Plans, but it was best not and it was for You. Indeed you are so much in my Thoughts, my Darling, that each and Everything I do is for You and You only.

No more at present then, but should Opportunity offer I shall get word to you addressed to Oregon City which your father said was his general Destination, it being my own present purpose Ultimately to engage in the Practice of law either at that Point or the settlement of Portland which I understand is not far Below. With my Means, we should soon be Handsomely Settled.

May God guard you on the Way Thither and believe me, Darling, with more Love than I shall be ever able to Tell and a Thousand Kisses,

Your Affianced and Impatient Lover,

Sam'l Payson Woodhull

The little sagebrush fire flared up brightly for an instant as Molly Wingate dropped one of her letters on the embers.

CHAPTER 37

Jim Bridger Forgets

'What's wrong with the people, Cale?' demanded Jesse Wingate of his stout-hearted associate, Caleb Price. The sun was two hours high, but not all the breakfast fires were going. Men were moody, truculent, taciturn, as they went about their duties.

Caleb Price bit into his yellow beard as he gazed down the irregular lines of the encampment.

'Do you want me to tell you the truth, Jesse?'

'Why, yes!'

'Well, then, it seems to me the truth is that this train has lost focus.'

'I don't know what you mean.'

'I don't know that I'm right – don't know I can make my guess plain. Of course, every day we lay up, the whole train goes to pieces. The thing to do is to go a little way each day – get into the habit. You can't wear out a road as long as this one by spurts – it's steady does it.

'But I don't think that's all. The main trouble is one that I don't like to hint to you, especially since none of us can help it.'

'Out with it, Cale!'

'The trouble is, the people don't think they've got a leader.'

Jesse Wingate coloured above his beard.

'That's pretty hard,' said he.

'I know it's hard, but I guess it's the truth. You and I and Hall and Kelsey – we're accepted as the chief council. But there are four of us, and all this country is new to all of us. The men now are like a bunch of cattle ready to stampede. They're nervous, ready to jump at anything. Wrong way, Jesse. They ought to be as steady as any of the trains that have gone across; 1843, when the Applegates crossed; 1846, when the Donners went – every year since. Our folks – well, if you ask me, I really think they're scared.'

'That's hard, Cale!'

'Yes, hard for me to say to you, with your wife sad and your girl just now able to sit up – yes, it's hard. Harder still since we both know it's your own personal matter – this quarrel of those two young men, which I don't need explain. That's at the bottom of the train's uneasiness.'

'Well, they've both gone now.'

'Yes, both. If half of the both were here now you'd see the people quiet. Oh, you can't explain leadership, Jesse! Some have it, most don't. He had. We know he had. I don't suppose many of those folks ever figured it out, or do now. But they'd fall in, not knowing why.

'As it is, I'll admit, there seems to be something in the air. They say birds know when an earthquake is coming. I feel uneasy myself, and don't know why. I started for Oregon. I don't know why. Do you suppose – '

The speculations of either man ceased as both caught sight of a little dust cloud far off across the sage, steadily advancing down the slope.

'Hum! And who's that, Jesse?' commented the Ohio leader. 'Get your big glass, Jesse.'

Wingate went to his wagon and returned with the great telescope he sometimes used, emblem of his authority.

'One man, two packs,' said he presently. 'All alone so far as I can see. He's Western enough – some post-trapper, I suppose. Rides like an Indian and dressed like one, but he's white, because he has a beard.'

'Let me see.' Price took the glass. 'He looks familiar! See if you don't think it's Jim Bridger. What's he coming for – two hundred miles away from his own post?'

It was Jim Bridger, as the next hour proved, and why he came he himself was willing to explain after he had eaten and smoked.

'I camped twelve mile back,' said he, 'an' pushed in this mornin'. I jest had a idee I'd saunter over in here, see how ye was gittin' along. Is your hull train made here?'

'No,' Wingate answered. 'The Missouri wagons are ahead.'

'Is Woodhull with ye?'

'No.'

'Whar's he at?'

'We don't know. Major Banion and Jackson, with a half dozen packs, no wagons, have given up the trip. They've split off for California – left their wagons.'

'An' so has Sam Woodhull, huh?'

'We suppose so. That's the word. He took about fifteen wagons with him. That's why we look cut down.'

'Rest of ye goin' on through, huh?'

'I am. I hope the others will.'

'Hit's three days on to whar the road leaves for Californy – on the Raft River. Mebbe more'll leave ye thar, huh?'

'We don't know. We hope not. I hear the fords are bad, especially the crossing of the Snake. This is a big river. My people are uneasy about it.'

'Yes, hit's bad enough, right often. Thar's falls in them canyons hundreds o' feet high, makin' a roarin' ye kin hear forty mile, mebbe. The big ford's erroun' two hunderd mile ahead. That'd make me four hunderd mile away from home, an' four hunderd to ride back agin', huh? Is that fur enough fer a ol' man, with snow comin' on soon?'

'You don't mean you'd guide us on that far? What charge?'

'I come fer that, mainly. Charge ye? I won't charge ye nothin'. What do ye s'pose Jim Bridger'd care ef ye all was drownded in the Snake? Ain't thar plenty more pilgrims whar ye-all come from? Won't they be out here next year, with money ter spend with my pardner Vasquez an' me?'

'Then how could we pay you?'

'Ye kain't. Whar's Miss Molly?'

'You want to see her?'

'Yes, else why'd I ask?'

'Come,' said Wingate, and led the way to Molly's little cart. The girl was startled when she saw the old scout, her wide eyes asking her question.

'Mornin', Miss Molly!' he began, his leathery face wrinkling in a smile. 'Ye didn't expect me, an' I didn't neither. I'm glad ye're about well o' that arrer wound. I kerried a arrerhead under my shoulder blade sever'l years once, ontel Preacher Whitman cut hit out. Hit felt right crawly all the time till then.

'Yes, I jest sauntered up couple hundred mile this mornin', Miss Molly, ter see how ye-all was gettin' along – one thing er another.'

Without much regard to others, he now led Molly a little apart and seated her on the sage beside him.

'Will Banion and Bill Jackson has went on to Californy, Miss Molly,' said he. 'You know why.' Mollie nodded.

'Ye'd orto! Ye told him.'

'Yes, I did.'

'I know. Him an' me had a talk. Owin' you an' me all he'll ever make, he allowed to pay nothin'! Which is, admittin' he loves you, he don't take no advice, ter finish that weddin' with another man substertuted. No, says he, "I kain't marry her, because I love her!" says he. Now, that's crazy. Somethin' deep under that, Miss Molly.'

'Let's not talk about it, please.'

'All right. Let's talk erbout Sam Woodhull, huh?'

'No!'

'Then mebbe I'd better be goin'. I know you don't want ter talk erbout me!' His wrinkling smile said he had more to tell.

'Miss Molly,' said he at last, 'I mout as well tell ye. Sam Woodhull is on the way atter Will Banion. He's like enough picked out a fine bunch o' horse thieves ter go erlong with him. He knows somethin' erbout the gold – I jest found out how.

'Ye see, some men ain't above shinin' up to a Injun womern even, such bein' mebbe lonesome. Sam Woodhull wasn't. He seed one o' my fam'ly wearin' a shiny thing on her neck. Hit were a piece o' gold Kit give me atter I give you mine. He trades the womern out o' her necklace – fer all o' two pesos, Mexican. But she not talkin' Missoury, an' him not talkin' Shoshone, they don't git fur on whar the gold come from.

'She done told him she got hit from me, but he don't say a word ter me erbout that; he's too wise. But she did tell him how Will Banion gits some mules an' packs o' me. From then, plain guessin', he allows ter watch Banion.

'My womern keeps sayin' – not meanin' no harm – thet thar's plenty more necklaces in Cal'for; because she's heard me an' Banion say that word, "Californy".

'Slim guessin' hit were, Miss Molly, but enough fer a man keen as Sam, that's not pertickler, neither. His plan was ter watch whar the packs went. He knowed ef Banion went ter Oregon he'd not use packs.

'Huh! Fine time he'll have, follerin' that boy an' them mules with wagons! I'm easier when I think o' that. Because, Miss Molly, ef them two does meet away from friends o' both, thar's goin' to be trouble, an' trouble only o' one kind.'

Again Molly Wingate nodded, pale and silent.

'Well, a man has ter take keer o' his own self,' went on Bridger. 'But that ain't all ner most what brung me here.'

'What was it then?' demanded Molly. 'A long ride!'

'Yeh. Eight hunderd mile out an' back, ef I see ye across the Snake, like I allow I'd better do. I'm doin' hit fer you, Miss Molly. I'm ol' an' ye're young; I'm a wild man an' ye're one o' God's wimern. But I had sisters once – white they was, like you. So the eight hunderd mile is light. But thet ain't why I come, neither, or all why, yit.'

'What is it then you want to tell me? Is it about – him?'

Bridger nodded. 'Yes. The only trouble is, I don't know what it is.'

'Now you're foolish!'

'Shore I am! Ef I had a few drinks o' good likker mebbe I'd be foolisher – er wiser. Leastways, I'd be more like I was when I plumb forgot what 'twas Kit Carson said to me when we was spreein' at Laramie. He had somethin' ter do, somethin' he was goin' ter do, somethin' I was ter do fer him, er mebee-so, next season, atter he got East an' got things done he was goin' ter do. Ye see, Kit's in the army.'

'Was it about – him?'

'That's what I kain't tell. I jest sauntered over here a few hunderd mile ter ask ye what ye s'pose it is that I've plumb fergot, me not havin' the same kind o' likker right now.

'When me an' Bill was havin' a few afore he left I was right on the p'int o' rememberin' what it was I was fergittin'. I don't make no doubt, ef Kit an' me er Bill an' me could only meet an' drink a long day er so hit'd all come plain to me. But all by myself, an' sober, an' not sociable with Dang Yore Eyes jest now, I sw'ar, I kain't think o' nothin'. What's a girl's mind fer ef hit hain't to think o' things?'

'It was about – him? It was about Kit Carson, something he had – was it about the gold news?'

'Mebbe. I don't know.'

'Did he – Mr Banion – say anything?'

'Mostly erbout you, an' not much. He only said ef I ever got any mail to send it ter the judge in the Willamette settlements.'

'He does expect to come back to Oregon!'

'How can I tell? My belief, he'd better jump in the Percific Ocean. He's a damn fool, Miss Molly. Ef a man loves a womern, that's somethin' that never orto wait. Yit he goes teeterin' erroun' like he had from now ter doomsday ter marry the girl which he loves too much fer ter marry her. That makes me sick. Yit he has resemblances ter a man, too, some ways – faint resemblances, yes. Fer instance, I'll bet a gun flint these here people that's been hearin' erbout the ford o' the Snake'd be a hull lot gladder ef they knew Will Banion was erlong. Huh?'

Molly Wingate was looking far away, pondering many things.

'Well, anyways, hit's even-Stephen fer them both two now,' went on Bridger, 'an' may God perteck the right an' the devil take the him'mostest. They'll like enough both marry Injun wimern an' settle down in Californy. Out o' sight, out o' mind. Love me little, love me long. Lord Lovell, he's mounted his milk-white steed. Farewell, sweet sir, partin' is such sweet sorrer; like ol' Cap'n Bonneville uster say. But o' all the messes any fool bunch o' pilgrims ever got inter, this is the worstest, an' hit couldn't be no worser.

'Now, Miss Molly, ye're a plumb diserpintment ter me. I jest drapped in ter see ef ye couldn't tell me what hit was Kit done told me. But ye kain't. Whar is yer boasted superiorness as a womern?

'But now, me, havin' did forty mile a day over that country yan, I need sustenance, an' I'm goin' to see ef ol' Cap' Grant, the post trader, has any bit o' Hundson Bay rum left. Ef he has hit's mine, an' ef not, Jim Bridger's a liar, an' that I say deliberate. I'm goin' to try to git inter normal condition enough fer to remember a few plain, simple truths, seein' as you-all kain't. Way hit is, this train's in a hell of a fix, an' hit couldn't be no worser.'

CHAPTER 38

When the Rockies Fell

The news of Jim Bridger's arrival, and the swift rumour that he would serve as pilot for the train over the dangerous portion of the route ahead, spread an instantaneous feeling of relief throughout the hesitant encampment at this, the last touch with civilisation east of the destination. He paused briefly at one or another wagon after he had made his own animals comfortable, laughing and jesting in his own independent way, *en route* to fulfil his promise to himself regarding the trader's rum.

In most ways the old scout's wide experience gave his dicta value. In one assertion, however, he was wide of the truth, or short of it. So far from things being as bad as they could be, the rapid events of that same morning proved that still more confusion was to ensue, and that speedily.

There came riding into the post from the westward a little party of old-time mountain men, driving their near-spent mounts and packs at a speed unusual even in that land of vast distances. They were headed by a man well known in that vicinity who, though he had removed to California since the fur days, made annual pilgrimage to meet the emigrant trains at Fort Hall in order to do proselytising for California, extolling the virtues of that land and picturing in direst fashion the horrors of the road thence to Oregon and the worthlessness of Oregon if ever attained. 'Old Greenwood' was the only name by which he was known. He was an old, old man, past eighty then, some said, with a deep blue eye, long white hair, a long and unkempt beard and a tongue of unparalleled profanity. He came in now, shouting and singing, as did the men of the mountains making the Rendezvous in the old days.

'How, Greenwood! What brings ye here so late?' demanded his erstwhile crony, Jim Bridger, advancing, tin cup in hand, to meet him. ' 'Light. Eat. Special, drink. How – to the old times!'

'Old times be damned!' exclaimed Old Greenwood. 'These is new times.'

He lifted from above the chafed hips of his trembling horse two sacks of something very heavy.

'How much is this worth to ye?' he demanded of Bridger and the trader. 'Have ye any shovels? Have ye any picks? Have ye flour, meal, sugar – anything?'

'Gold!' exclaimed Jim Bridger. 'Kit Carson did not lie! He never did!'

And they did not know how much this was worth. They had no scales for raw gold, nor any system of valuation for it. And they had no shovels and no pickaxes; and since the families had come they now had very little flour at Fort Hall.

But now they had the news! This was the greatest news that ever came to old Fort Hall – the greatest news America knew for many a year, and the world – the news of the great gold strikes in California.

Old Greenwood suddenly broke out, 'Have we left the mines an' come this fur fer nothin'? I tell ye, we must have supplies! A hundred dollars fer a pick! A hundred dollars fer a shovel! A hundred dollars fer a pair o' blankets! An ounce fer a box of sardines, damn ye! An ounce fer half a pound o' butter! A half ounce fer a aig! Anything ye like fer anything that's green! Three hundred fer a gallon o' likker! A ounce for a box o' pills! Eight hundred fer a barrel o' flour! Same fer pork, same fer sugar, same fer coffee! Damn yer picayune hides, we'll show ye what prices is! What's money to us? We can git the pure gold that money's made out of, an' git it all we want! Hooray fer Californy!'

He broke into song. His comrades roared in Homeric chorus with him, passing from one to another of the current ditties of the mines. They declared in unison, 'Old Grimes is dead, that good old man!' Then they swung off to yet another classic ballad:

> There was an old woman who had three sons –
> Joshua, James and John!
> Josh got shot, and Jim got drowned,
> And John got lost and never was found,
> And that was the end of the woman's three sons,
> Joshua, James and John.

Having finished the obsequies of the three sons, not once but many times, they went forward with yet another adaptation, following Old Greenwood, who stood with head thrown back and sang with tones of Bashan:

> Oh, then Susannah,
> Don't you cry fer me!
> I'm goin' to Californuah,
> With my wash pan on my knee.

The news of the gold was out. Bridger forgot his cups, forgot his friends, hurried to Molly Wingate's cart again.

'Hit's true, Miss Molly!' he cried – 'truer'n true hisself! Yan's men just in from Californy, an' they've got two horseloads o' gold, an' they say hit's nothin' – they come out fer supplies. They tried to stop Will Banion – they did trade some with Woodhull. They're nigh to Humboldt by now an' goin' hard. Miss Molly, gal, he's in ahead o' the hull country, an' got six months by hisself! Lord give him luck! Hit'll be winter, afore the men back East kin know. He's one year ahead – thanks ter yer lie ter me, an ter Kit, and Kit's ter his General.

'Gold! Ye kain't hide hit an' ye kain't find hit an' ye kain't dig hit up an' ye kain't keep hit down. Miss Molly, gal, I like ye, but how I do wish't ye was a man, so's you an' me could celebrate this here fitten!'

'Listen!' said the girl. 'Our bugle! That's Assembly!'

'Yes, they'll all be there. Come when ye kin. Hell's a-poppin' now!'

The emigrants, indeed, deserted their wagons, gathering in front of the stockade, group after group. There was a strange scene on the far-flung, unknown, fateful borderlands of the country Senator McDuffie but now had not valued at five dollars for the whole. All these now, halfway across, and with the ice and snow of winter cutting off pursuit for a year, had the great news which did not reach publication in the press of New York and Baltimore until September of 1848. It did not attain notice of the floor of Congress until December 5th of that year, although this was news that went to the very foundation of this republic; which, indeed, was to prove the means of the perpetuity of this republic.

The drunken hunters in their ragged wools, their stained skins, the emigrants in their motley garb – come this far they knew not why, since men will not admit of destiny in nations – also knew not that they were joying over the death of slavery and the life of the Union. They did not know that now, in a flash, all the old arguments and citations over slavery and secession were ancient and of no avail. The wagoners of the Sangamon, in Illinois, gathered here, roistering, did not know that they were dancing on the martyr's grave of Lincoln, or weaving him his crown, or buying shot and shell for him to win his grievous ordeal, brother against brother. Yet all those things were settled then, beyond that range of the Rockies which senators had said they would not spend a dollar to remove, 'were they no more than ten feet high'.

Even then the Rockies fell. Even then the great trains of the covered wagons, driven by men who never heard of destiny, achieved their places on the unwritten scroll of time.

The newcomers from beyond the Sierras, crazed with their easy fortune, and now inflamed yet further by the fumes of alcohol, even magnified the truth, as it then seemed. They spent their dust by the handful. They asked for skillets, cooking pans, that they could wash more gold. They wanted saws, nails, axes, hammers, picks. They said they would use the wagon boxes for Long Toms. They said if men would unite in companies to dam and divert the California rivers they would lay bare ledges of broken gold which would need only scooping up. The miners would pay anything for labour in iron and wood. They would buy any food and all there was of it at a dollar a pound. They wanted pack horses to cross the Humboldt Desert loaded. They would pay any price for men to handle horses for a fast and steady flight.

Because, they said, there was no longer any use in measuring life by the old standards of value. Wages at four bits a day, a dollar a day, two dollars, the old prices – why, no man would work for a half-hour for such return when any minute he might lift twenty dollars in the hollow of an iron spoon. Old Greenwood had panned his five hundred in a day. Men had taken two thousand – three – in a week; in a week, men, not in a year! There could be no wage scale at all. Labour was a thing gone by. Wealth, success, ease, luxury was at hand for the taking. What a man had dreamed for himself he now could have. He could overleap all the confining limits of his life, and even if weak, witless, ignorant or in despair, throw all that aside in one vast bound into attainment and enjoyment.

Rich? Why should any man remain poor? Work? Why should work be known, save the labour of picking up pure gold – done, finished, delivered at hand to waiting and weary humanity? Human cravings could no longer exist. Human disappointment was a thing no more to be known. In California, just yonder, was gold, gold, gold! Do you mind – can you think of it, men? Gold, gold, gold! The sun had arisen at last on the millennial day! Now might man be happy and grieve no more for ever!

Arguments such as these did not lack and were not needed with the emigrants. It took but a leap to the last conclusion. Go to California? Why should they not go? Had it not been foreordained that they should get the news here, before it was too late? Fifty miles more and they had lost it. A week earlier and they would not have known it for a year. Go to Oregon and plough? Why not go to California and dig in a day what a plough would earn in a year?

Call it stubbornness or steadfastness, at least Jesse Wingate's strength of resolution now became manifest. At first almost alone, he stayed the stampede by holding out for Oregon in the council with his captains.

They stood near the Wingate wagon, the same which had carried him into Indiana, thence into Illinois, now this far on the long way to Oregon. Old and grey was Mary Ann, as he called his wagon, by now, the paint ground from felloe, spoke and hub, the sides dust covered, the tilt disfigured and discoloured. He gazed at the time-worn, sturdy frame with something akin to affection. The spokes were wedged to hold them tight, the rims were bound with hide, worn away at the edges where the tyre gave no covering; the tyres had been reset again and again. He shook the nearest wheel to test it.

'Yes,' said he, 'we all show wear. But I see little use in changing a plan once made in a man's best sober judgement. For me, I don't think all the world has been changed overnight.'

'Oh, well, now,' demanded Kelsey, his nomad Kentucky blood dominant, 'what use holding to any plan just for sake of doing it? If something better comes, why not take it? That stands to reason. We all came out here to better ourselves. These men have done in six months what you and I might not do in ten years in Oregon.'

'They'd guide us through to California, too,' he went on. 'We've no guide to Oregon.'

Even Caleb Price nodded.

'They all say that the part from here on is the worst – drier and drier, and in places very rough. And the two fords of the Snake – well, I for one wish we were across them. That's a big river, and a bad one. And if we crossed the Blue Mountains all right, there's the Cascades, worse than the Blues, and no known trail for wagons.'

'I may have to leave my wagons,' said Jesse Wingate, 'but if I do I aim to leave them as close to the Willamette Valley as I can. I came out to farm. I don't know California. How about you, Hall? What do your neighbours say?'

'Much as Price says. They're worn out and scared. They've been talking about the Snake crossings ever since we left the Soda Springs. Half want to switch for California. A good many others would like to go back home – if they thought they'd ever get there!'

'But we've got to decide,' urged Wingate. 'Can we count on thirty wagons to go through? Others have got through in a season, and so can we if we stick. Price?'

His hesitant glance at his staunch trail friend's face decided the latter.

'I'll stick for Oregon!' said Caleb Price. 'I've got my wife and children along. I want my donation lands.'

'You, Hall?'

'I'll go with you,' said Hall, the third column leader, slowly. 'Like to try a whirl in California, but if there's so much gold there next year'll do. I want my lands.'

'Why, there's almost ten thousand people in Oregon by now, or will be next year,' argued Wingate. 'It may get to be a territory – maybe not a state, but anyways a territory, sometime. And it's free! Not like Texas and all this new Mexican land just coming in by the treaty. What do you say, finally, Kelsey?'

The latter chewed tobacco for some time.

'You put it to me hard to answer,' said he. 'Any one of us'd like to try California. It will open faster than Oregon if all this gold news is true. Maybe ten thousand people will come out next year, for all we know.'

'Yes, with picks and shovels,' said Jesse Wingate. 'Did ever you see pick or shovel build a country? Did ever you see steel traps make or hold one? Oregon's ours because we went out five years ago with wagons and ploughs – we all know that. No, friends, waterways never held a country. No path ever held on a river – that's for exploring, not for farming. To hold a country you need wheels, you need a plough. I'm for Oregon!'

'You put it strong,' admitted Kelsey. 'But the only thing that holds me back from California is the promise we four made to each other when we started. Our train's fallen apart little by little. I'm ole Kaintucky. We don't rue back, and we keep our word. We four said we'd go through. I'll stand by that, I'm a man of my word.'

Imperiously as though he were Pizarro's self, he drew a line in the dust of the trail.

'Who's for Oregon?' he shouted; again demanded, as silence fell, 'This side for Oregon!' And Kelsey of Kentucky, man of his word, turned the stampede definitely.

Wingate, his three friends; a little group, augmenting, crossed for Oregon. The women and the children stood aloof – sun-bonneted women, brown, some with new-born trail babes in arms, silent as they always stood. Across from the Oregon band stood almost as many men, for the most part unmarried, who had not given hostages to fortune, and were resolved for California. A cheer arose from these.

'Who wants my plough?' demanded a stalwart farmer from Indiana, more than fifteen hundred miles from his last home. 'I brung her this fur into this damned desert. I'll trade her fer a shovel and make one more try fer my folks back home.'

He loosed the wires which had bound the implement to the tail of his wagon all these weary miles. It fell to the ground and he left it there.

'Do some thinking, men, before you count your gold and drop your plough. Gold don't last, but the soil does. Ahead of you is the Humboldt Desert. There's no good wagon road over the mountains if you get that far. The road down Mary's River is a real gamble with death. Men can go through and make roads – yes; but where are the women and the children to stay? Think twice, men, and more than twice!' Wingate spoke solemnly.

'Roll out! Roll out!' mocked the man who had abandoned his plough. 'This way for Californy!'

The council ended in turmoil, where hitherto had been no more than a sedate daily system. Routine, become custom, gave way to restless movement, excited argument. Of all these hundreds now encamped on the sandy sagebrush plain in the high desert there was not an individual who was not affected in one way or another by the news from California, and in most cases it required some sort of a personal decision, made practically upon the moment. Men argued with their wives heatedly; women gathered in groups, talking, weeping. The stoic calm of the trail was swept away in a sort of hysteria which seemed to upset all their world and all its old values.

Whether for Oregon or California, a revolution in prices was worked overnight for every purchase of supplies. Flour, horses, tools, everything merchantable, doubled and more than doubled. Some fifty wagons in all now formed train for California, which, in addition to the long line of pack animals, left the Sangamon caravan, so called, at best little more than half what it had been the day before. The men without families made up most of the California train.

The agents for California, by force of habit, still went among the wagons and urged the old arguments against Oregon – the savage tribes on ahead, the forbidding desolation of the land, the vast and dangerous rivers, the certainty of starvation on the way, the risk of arriving after winter had set in on the Cascade Range – all matters of which they themselves spoke by hearsay. All the great West was then unknown. Moreover, Fort Hall was a natural division point, as quite often a third of the wagons of a train might be bound for California even before the discovery of gold. But Wingate and his associates felt that the Oregon immigration for that year, even handicapped as now, ultimately would run into thousands.

It was mid-morning of the next blazing day when he beckoned his men to him.

'Lets pull out,' he said. 'Why wait for the Californians to move? Bridger will go with us across the Snake. 'Twill only be the worse the longer we lie here, and our wagons are two weeks late now.'

The others agreed. But there was now little train organisation. The old cheery call, 'Catch up! Catch up!' was not heard. The group, the family, the individual now began to show again. True, after their leaders came, one after another, rattling, faded wagons, until the dusty trail that led out across the sage flats had a tenancy stretched out for over a half mile, with yet other vehicles falling in behind; but silent and grim were young and old now over this last defection.

'About that old man, Greenwood,' said Molly Wingate to her daughter as they sat on the same jolting seat, 'I don't know about him. I've saw elders in the church with whiskers as long and white as his'n, but you'd better watch your hog pen. For me, I believe he's a liar. It like enough is true he used to live back in the Rockies in Injun times, and he may be eighty-five years old, as he says, and California may have a wonderful climate, the way he says; but some things I can't believe.

'He says, now, he knows a man out in California, a Spanish man, who was two hundred and fifty years old, and he had quite a lot of money, gold and silver, he'd dug out of the mountains. Greenwood says he's known of gold and silver for years, himself. Well, this Spanish man had relatives that wanted his property, and he'd made a will and left it to them; but he wouldn't die, the climate was so good. So his folks allowed maybe if they sent him to Spain on a journey he'd die and then they'd get the property legal. So he went, and he did die; but he left orders for his body to be sent back to California to be buried. So when his body came they buried him in California, the way he asked – so Greenwood says.

'But did they get his property? Not at all! The old Spanish man, almost as soon as he was buried in California dirt, he came to life again! He's alive today out there, and this man Greenwood says he's a neighbour of his and he knows him well! Of course, if that's true you can believe almost anything about what a wonderful country California is. But for one, I ain't right sure. Maybe not everybody who goes to California is going to find a mountain of gold, or live to be three hundred years old!

'But to think, Molly! Here you knew all this away back to Laramie! Well, if the hoorah had started there 'stead of here there'd be dead people now back of us more'n there is now. That old man Bridger told you – why? And how could you keep the secret?'

'It was for Will,' said Molly simply. 'I had given him up. I told him to go to California and forget me, and to live things down. Don't chide me any more. I tried to marry the man you wanted me to marry. I'm tired. I'm going to Oregon – to forget. I'll teach school. I'll never marry – that's settled at last.'

'You got a letter from Sam Woodhull too.'

'Yes, I did.'

'Huh! Does he call that settled? Is he going to California to forget you and live things down?'

'He says not. I don't care what he says.'

'He'll be back.'

'Spare his journey! It will do him no good. The Indian did me a kindness, I tell you!'

'Well, anyways, they're both off on the same journey now, and who knows what or which? They both may be three hundred years old before they find a mountain of gold. But to think – I had your chunk of gold right in my own hands, but didn't know it! The same gold my mother's wedding ring was made of, that was mine. It's right thin now, child. You could of made a dozen out of that lump, like enough.'

'I'll never need one, mother,' said Molly Wingate.

The girl, weeping, threw her arms about her mother's neck. 'You ask why I kept the secret, even then. He kissed me, mother – and he was a thief!'

'Yes, I know. A man he just steals a girl's heart out through her lips. Yore paw done that way with me once. Git up, Dan! You, Daisy!'

'And from that time on,' she added laughing, 'I been trying to forget him and to live him down!'

CHAPTER 39

The Crossing

Three days out from Fort Hall the vanguard of the remnant of the train, less than a fourth of the original number, saw leaning against a gnarled sagebrush a box lid which had scrawled upon it in straggling letters one word – 'California'. Here now were to part the pick and the plough.

Jim Bridger, sitting his gaunt horse, rifle across saddle horn, halted for the head of the train to pull even with him.

'This here's Cassia Creek,' said he. 'Yan's the trail down Raft River ter the Humboldt and acrost the Sierrys ter Californy. A long, dry jump hit is, by all accounts. The Oregon road goes on down the Snake. Hit's longer, if not so dry.'

Small invitation offered in the physical aspect of either path. The journey had become interminable. The unspeakable monotony, whose only variant was peril, had smothered the spark of hope and interest. The allurement of mystery had wholly lost its charm.

The train halted for some hours. Once more discussion rose.

'Last chance for Californy, men,' said old Jim Bridger calmly. 'Do-ee see the tracks? Here's Greenwood come in. Yan's where Woodhull's wagons left the road. Below that, one side, is the tracks o' Banion's mules.

'I wonder,' he added, 'why thar hain't any letter left fer none o' us here at the fork o' the road.'

He did not know that, left in a tin at the foot of the board sign certain days earlier, there had rested a letter addressed to Miss Molly Wingate. It never was to reach her. Sam Woodhull knew the reason why. Having opened it and read it, he had possessed himself of exacter knowledge than ever before of the relations of Banion and Molly Wingate. Bitter as had been his hatred before, it now was venomous. He lived thenceforth no more in hope of gold than of revenge.

The decision for or against California was something for serious weighing now at the last hour, and it affected the fortune and the future of every man, woman and child in all the train. Never a furrow was ploughed in early Oregon but ran in bones and blood; and never a dollar was dug in gold in California – or ever gained in gold by any man – which did not cost two in something else but gold.

Twelve wagons pulled out of the trail silently, one after another, and took the winding trail that led to the left, to the west and south. Others watched them, tears in their eyes, for some were friends.

Alone on her cart seat, here at the fateful parting of the ways, Molly Wingate sat with a letter clasped in her hand, frank tears standing in her eyes. It was no new letter, but an old one. She pressed the pages to her heart, to her lips, held them out at arm's length before her in the direction of the far land which somewhere held its secrets.

'Oh, God keep you, Will!' she said in her heart, and almost audibly. 'Oh, God give you fortune, Will, and bring you back to me!'

But the Oregon wagons closed up once more and held their way, the stop not being beyond one camp, for Bridger urged haste.

The caravan course now lay along the great valley of the Snake. The giant deeds of the river in its canyons they could only guess. They heard of tremendous falls, of gorges through which no boat could pass, vague rumours of days of earlier exploration; but they kept to the high plateaus, dipping down to the crossings of many sharp streams, which in the first month of their journey they would have called impassable. It all took time. They were averaging now not twenty miles daily, but no more than half that, and the season was advancing. It was fall. Back home the wheat would be in stack, the edges of the corn would be seared with frost.

The vast abundance of game they had found all along now lacked. Some rabbits, a few sage grouse, nightly coyotes – that made all. The savages who now hung on their flanks lacked the stature and the brave trappings of the buffalo plainsmen. They lived on horse meat and salmon, so the rumour came. Now their environment took hold of the Pacific. They had left the East wholly behind.

On the salmon run they could count on food, not so good as the buffalo, but better than bacon grown soft and rusty. Changing, accepting, adjusting, prevailing, the wagons went on, day after day, fifty miles, a hundred, two hundred. But always a vague uneasiness pervaded. The crossing of the Snake lay on ahead. The moody river had cast upon them a feeling of awe. Around the sage fires at night the families talked of little else but the ford of the Snake, two days beyond the Salmon Falls.

It was morning when the wagons, well drawn together now, at last turned down the precipitous decline which took them from the high plateau to the water level. Here a halt was called. Bridger took full charge. The formidable enterprise confronting them was one of the real dangers of the road.

The strong green waters of the great river were divided at this ancient ford by two midstream islands, which accounted for the selection of the spot for the daring essay of a bridgeless and boatless crossing. There was something mockingly relentless in the strong rippling current, which cut off more than a guess at the actual depth. There was no ferry, no boat nor means of making one. It was not even possible to shore up the wagon beds so they might be dry. One thing sure was that if ever a wagon was swept below the crossing there could be no hope for it.

But others had crossed here, and even now a certain rough chart existed, handed down from these. Time now for a leader, and men now were thankful for the presence of a man who had seen this crossing made.

The old scout held back the company leaders and rode into the stream alone, step by step, scanning the bottom. He found it firm. He saw wheel marks on the first island. His horse, ears ahead, saw them also, and staggeringly felt out the way. Belly-deep and passable – yes.

Bridger turned and moved a wide arm. The foremost wagons came on to the edge.

The men now mounted the wagon seats, two to each wagon. Flankers drove up the loose cattle, ready for their turn later. Men rode on each side the lead yoke of oxen to hold them steady on their footing, Wingate, Price, Kelsey and Hall, bold men, well mounted, taking this work on themselves.

The plunge once made, they got to the first island, all of them, without trouble. But a dizzying flood lay on ahead to the second wheel-marked island in the river. To look at the rapid surface was to lose all sense of direction. But again the gaunt horse of the scout fell out, the riders waded in, their devoted saddle animals trembling beneath them. Bridger, student of fast fords, followed the bar upstream, angling with it, till a deep channel offered between him and the island. Unable to evade this, he drove into it, and his gallant mount breasted up and held its feet all the way across.

The thing could be done! Jim Bridger calmly turned and waved to the wagons to come on from the first island.

'Keep them jest whar we was!' he called back to Hall and Kelsey, who had not passed the last stiff water. 'Put the heavy cattle in fust! Hit maybe won't swim them. If the stuff gets wet we kain't help that. Tell the wimern hit's all right.'

He saw his friends turn back, their horses, deep in the flood, plunging through water broken by their knees; saw the first wagons lead off and crawl out upstream, slowly and safely, till within reach of his voice. Molly now was in the main wagon, and her brother Jed was driving.

Between the lines of wading horsemen the draft oxen advanced, following the wagons, strung out, but all holding their footing in the green water that broke white on the upper side of the wagons. A vast murmuring roar came up from the water thus retarded.

They made their way to the edge of the deep channel, where the cattle stood, breasts submerged.

Bridger rose in his stirrups and shouted, 'Git in thar! Come on through!'

They plunged, wallowed, staggered; but the lead yokes saw where the ford climbed the bank, made for it, caught footing, dragged the others through!

Wagon after wagon made it safe. It was desperate, but, being done, these matter-of-fact folk wasted no time in imaginings of what might have happened. They were safe, and the ford thus far was established so that the others need not fear.

But on ahead lay what they all knew was the real danger – the last channel, three hundred yards of racing, heavy water which apparently no sane man ever would have faced. But there were wheel marks on the farther shore. Here ran the road to Oregon.

The dauntless old scout rode in again, alone, bending to study the water and the footing. A gravel bar led off for a couple of rods, flanked by deep potholes. Ten rods out the bar turned. He followed it up, foot by foot, for twenty rods, quartering. Then he struck out for the shore.

The bottom was hard, yes; but the bar was very crooked, with swimming water on either hand, with potholes ten feet deep and more all alongside. And worst of all, there was a vast sweep of heavy water below the ford, which meant destruction and death for any wagon carried down. Well had the crossing of the Snake earned its sinister reputation. Courage and care alone could give any man safe-conduct here.

The women and children, crying, sat in the wagons, watching Bridger retrace the ford. Once his stumbling horse swam, but caught footing. He joined them, very serious.

'Hit's fordin' men,' said he, 'but she's mean, she shore is mean. Double up all the teams, yoke in every loose ox an' put six yoke on each wagon, er they'll get swep' down, shore's hell. Some o' them will hold the others ef we have enough. I'll go ahead, an' I want riders all along the teams, above and below, ter hold them ter the line. Hit can be did – hit's wicked water, but hit can be did. Don't wait – always keep things movin'.'

By this time the island was packed with the loose cattle, which had followed the wagons, much of the time swimming. They were lowing meaningly, in terror – a gruesome thing to hear.

The leader called to Price's oldest boy, driving Molly's cart, 'Tie on behind the big wagon with a long rope, an' don't drive in tell you see the fust two yoke ahead holdin'. Then they'll drag you through anyhow. Hang on to the cart whatever happens, but if you do get in, keep upstream of any animal that's swimmin'.

'All set, men? Come ahead!'

He led off again at last, after the teams were doubled and the loads had been piled high as possible to keep them dry. Ten wagons were left behind, it being needful to drive back, over the roaring channel, some of the doubled heavy teams for them.

They made it well, foot by foot, the cattle sometimes swimming gently, confidently, as the line curved down under the heavy current, but always enough holding to keep the team safe. The horsemen rode alongside, exhorting, assuring. It was a vast relief when at the last gravel stretch they saw the wet backs of the oxen rise high once more.

'I'll go back, Jesse,' said Kelsey, the man who had wanted to go to California. 'I know her now.'

'I'll go with you,' added young Jed Wingate, climbing down from his wagon seat and demanding his saddle horse, which he mounted bare-backed.

It was they two who drove and led the spare yokes back to repeat the crossing with the remaining wagons. Those on the bank watched them anxiously, for they drove straighter across to save time, and were carried below the trail on the island. But they came out laughing, and the oxen were rounded up once more and doubled in, so that the last of the train was ready.

'That's a fine mare of Kelsey's,' said Wingate to Caleb Price, who with him was watching the daring Kentuckian at his work on the downstream and more dangerous side of the linked teams. 'She'll go anywhere.'

Price nodded, anxiously regarding the labouring advance of the last wagons.

'Too light,' said he. 'I started with a ton and a half on the National Pike across Ohio and Indiana. I doubt if we average five hundred now. They ford light.'

'Look!' he cried suddenly, and pointed.

They all ran to the brink. The horsemen were trying to stay the drift of the line of cattle. They had worked low and missed footing. Many were swimming – the wagons were afloat!

The tired lead cattle had not been able to withstand the pressure of the heavy water a second time. They were off the ford!

But the riders from the shore, led by Jim Bridger, got to them, caught a rope around a horn, dragged them into line, dragged the whole gaunt team to the edge and saved the day for the lead wagon. The others caught and held their footing, laboured through.

But a shout arose. Persons ran down the bank, pointing. A hundred yards below the ford, in the full current of the Snake, the lean head of Kelsey's mare was flat, swimming hard and steadily, being swept downstream in a current which swung off shore below the ford.

'He's all right!' called Jed, wet to the neck, sitting his own wet mount, safe ashore at last. 'He's swimming too. They'll make it, sure! Come on!'

He started off at a gallop downstream along the shore, his eyes fixed on the two black objects, now steadily losing distance out beyond. But old Jim Bridger put his hands across his eyes and turned away his face. He knew!

It was now plain to all that yonder a gallant man and a gallant horse were making a fight for life. The grim river had them in its grip at last.

In a moment the tremendous power of the heavy water had swept Kelsey and his horse far below the ford. The current there was swifter, noisier, as though exultant in the success of the scheme the river all along had proposed.

As to the victims, the tragic struggle went on in silence. If the man called, no one could hear him above the rush and roar of the waters. None long had any hope as they saw the white rollers bury the two heads, of the horse and the man, while the set of the current steadily carried them away from the shore. It was only a miracle that the two bobbing black dots again and again came into view.

They could see the mare's muzzle flat, extended towards the shore; back of it, upstream, the head of the man. Whichever brain had decided, it was evident that the animal was staking life to reach the shore from which it had been swept away.

Far out in midstream some conformation of the bottom turned the current once more in a long slant shoreward. A murmur, a sob of hundreds of observers packed along the shore broke out as the two dots came closer, far below. More than a quarter of a mile downstream a sand point made out, offering a sort of beach where for some space a landing might be made. Could the gallant mare make this point? Men clenched their hands. Women began to sob, to moan gently.

When with a shout Jed Wingate turned his horse and set off at top speed down the shore some followed him. The horses and oxen, left alone, fell into confusion, the wagons tangled. One or two teams made off at a run into the desert. But these things were nothing.

Those behind hoped Jed would not try any rescue in that flood. Molly stood wringing her hands. The boy's mother began praying audibly. The voice of Jim Bridger rose in an Indian chant. It was for the dead!

They saw the gallant mare plunge up, back and shoulders and body rising as her feet found bottom a few yards out from shore. She stood free of the water, safe on the bar; stood still, looking back of her and down. But no man rose to his height beside her. There was only one figure on the bar.

They saw Jed fling off; saw him run and stoop, lifting something long and heavy from the water. Then the mare stumbled away. At length she lay down quietly. She never rose.

'She was standing right here,' said Jed as the others came. 'He had hold of the reins so tight I couldn't hardly open his hand. He must have been dead before the mare hit bottom. He was laying all under water, hanging to the reins, and that was all that kept him from washing on down.'

They made some rude and unskilled attempt at resuscitation, but had neither knowledge nor confidence. Perhaps somewhere out yonder the strain had been too great; perhaps the sheer terror had broken the heart of both man and horse. The mare suddenly began to tremble as she lay, her nostrils shivering as though in fright. And she died, after bringing in the dead man whose hand still gripped her rein.

They buried Kelsey of Kentucky – few knew him otherwise – on a hillock by the road at the first fording place of the Snake. They broke out the top board of another tail gate, and with a hot iron burned in one more record of the road: 'Rob't Kelsey, Ky. Drowned Sept. 7, 1848. A Brave Man.'

The sand long ago cut out the lettering, and long ago the ford passed to a ferry. But there lay, for a long time known, Kelsey of Kentucky, a brave man, who kept his promise and did not rue back, but who never saw either California or Oregon.

'Catch up the stock, men,' said Jesse Wingate dully, after a time. 'Let's leave this place.'

Loads were repacked, broken gear adjusted. Inside the hour the silent grey wagon train held on, leaving the waters to give shriving. The voice of the river rose and fell mournfully behind them in the changing airs.

'I knowed hit!' said old Jim Bridger, now falling back from the lead and breaking off his Indian dirge. 'I knowed all along the Snake'd take somebody – she does every time. This mornin' I seed two ravens that flew acrost the trail ahead. Yesterday I seed a rabbit settin' squar' in the trail. I thought hit was me the river wanted, but she's done took a younger an' a better man.'

'Man, man,' exclaimed stout-hearted Molly Wingate, 'what kind of a country have you brought us women to? One more thing like that and my nerve's gone. Tell me, is this the last bad river? And when will we get to Oregon?'

'Don't be a-skeered, ma'am,' rejoined Bridger. 'A accident kin happen anywheres. Hit's a month on ter Oregon, whar ye're headed. Some fords on ahead, yes; we got ter cross back ter the south side the Snake again.'

'But you'll go on with us, won't you?' demanded young Molly Wingate.

They had halted to breathe the cattle at the foot of a lava dust slope. Bridger looked at the young girl for a time in silence.

'I'm off my country, Miss Molly,' said he. 'Beyant the second ford, at Fort Boise, I ain't never been. I done aimed ter turn back here an' git back home afore the winter come. Ain't I did enough fer ye?'

But he hesitated. There was a kindly light on the worn old face, in the sunken blue eye.

'Ye want me ter go on, Miss Molly?'

'If you could it would be a comfort to me, a protection to us all.'

'Is hit so! Miss Molly, ye kin talk a ol'-time man out'n his last pelt! But sence ye do want me, I'll saunter along a leetle ways furtherer with ye. Many a good fight is spoiled by wonderin' how hit's goin' to come out. An' many a long trail's lost by wonderin' whar hit runs. I hain't never yit been plumb to Californy er Oregon. But ef ye say I must, Miss Molly, why I must; an' ef I must, why here goes! I reckon my wimern kin keep my fire goin' ontel I git back next year.'

CHAPTER 40

Oregon! Oregon!

The freakish resolves of the old-time trapper at least remained unchanged for many days, but at last one evening he came to Molly's wagon, his face grim and sad.

'Miss Molly,' he said, 'I'm come to say goodbye now. Hit's for keeps.'

'No? Then why? You are like an old friend to me. What don't I owe to you?'

'Ye don't owe nothin' ter me yit, Miss Molly. But I want ye ter think kindly o' old Jim Bridger when he's gone. I allow the kindest thing I kin do fer ye is ter bring Will Banion ter ye.'

'You are a good man, James Bridger,' said Molly Wingate. 'But then?'

'Ye see, Miss Molly, I had six quarts o' rum I got at Boise. Some folks says rum is wrong. Hit ain't. I'll tell ye why. Last night I drinked up my lastest bottle o' that Hundson's Bay rum. Hit war right good rum, an ez I lay lookin' up at the stars, all ter once hit come ter me that I was jest exactly, no more an' no less, jest ter the ha'r, ez drunk I was on the leetle spree with Kit at Laramie. Warn't that fine? An' warn't hit useful? Nach'el, bein' jest even up, I done thought o' everything I been fer-gettin'. Hit all come ter me ez plain ez a streak o' lightnin'. What it was Kit Carson told me I know now, but no one else shall know. No, not even you, Miss Molly. I kain't tell ye, so don't ask.

'Now I'm goin' on a long journey, an' a resky one; I kain't tell ye no more. I reckon I'll never see ye agin. So goodbye.'

With a swift grasp of his hand he caught the dusty edge of the white woman's skirt to his bearded lips.

'But, James – '

Suddenly she reached out a hand. He was gone.

*   *   *

One winter day, rattling over the icy fords of the road winding down the Sandy from the white Cascades, crossing the Clackamas, threading the intervening fringe of forest, there broke into the clearing at Oregon City the head of the wagon train of 1848. A fourth of the wagons abandoned and broken, a half of the horses and cattle gone since they had left the

1084

banks of the Columbia east of the mountains, the cattle leaning one against the other when they halted, the oxen stumbling and limping, the calluses of their necks torn, raw and bleeding from the swaying of the yokes on the rocky trail, their tongues out, their eyes glassy with the unspeakable toil they so long had undergone; the loose wheels wobbling, the thin boards rattling, the canvas sagged and stained, the bucket under each wagon empty, the plough at each tailgate thumping in its lashings of rope and hide – the train of the covered wagons now had, indeed, won through. Now may the picture of our own Ark of Empire never perish from our minds.

On the front seat of the lead wagon sat stout Molly Wingate and her husband. Little Molly's cart came next. Alongside the Caleb Price wagon, wherein now sat on the seat – hugging a sore-footed dog whose rawhide boots had worn through – a long-legged, barefoot girl who had walked twelve hundred miles since spring, trudged Jed Wingate, now grown from a tousled boy into a lean, self-reliant young man. His long whip was used in baseless threatenings now, for any driver must spare cattle such as these, gaunt and hollow-eyed. Tobacco protuberant in cheek, his feet half bare, his trousers ragged and fringed to the knee, his sleeves rolled up over brown and brawny arms, Jed Wingate now was enrolled on the list of men.

'Gee-whoa-haw! You Buck an' Star, git along there, damn ye!' So rose his voice, automatically but affectionately.

Certain French Canadians, old-time *engagés* of the fur posts now become *habitants*, landowners, on their way home from Sunday chapel, hastened to summon others.

'The families have come!' they called at the Falls, as they had at Portland town.

But now, though safely enlarged at last of the confinement and the penalties of the wagon train, the emigrants, many of them almost destitute, none of them of great means, needed to cast about them at once for their locations and to determine what their occupations were to be. They scattered, each seeking his place, like new trout in a stream.

CHAPTER 41

The Secret of the Sierras

Sam Woodhull carried in his pocket the letter which Will Banion had left for Molly Wingate at Cassia Creek in the Snake Valley, where the Oregon road forked for California. There was no post office there, yet Banion felt sure that his letter would find its way, and it had done so, save for the treachery of this one man. Naught had been sacred to him. He had read the letter without an instant's hesitation, feeling that anything was fair in his love for this woman, in his war with this man. Woodhull resolved that they should not both live.

He was by nature not so much a coward as a man without principle or scruple. He did not expect to be killed by Banion. He intended to use such means as would give Banion no chance. In this he thought himself fully justified, as a criminal always does.

But hurry as he might, his overdriven teams were no match for the tireless desert horse, the wiry mountain mount and the hardy mules of the tidy little pack train of Banion and his companion Jackson. These could go on steadily where wagons must wait. Their trail grew fainter as they gained.

At last, at the edge of a waterless march of whose duration they could not guess, Woodhull and his party were obliged to halt. Here by great good fortune they were overtaken by the swift pack train of Greenwood and his men, hurrying back with fresh animals on their return march to California. The two companies joined forces. Woodhull now had a guide. Accordingly when, after such dangers and hardships as then must be inevitable to men covering the gruesome trail between the Snake and the Sacramento, he found himself late that fall arrived west of the Sierras and in the gentler climate of the central valley, he looked about him with a feeling of exultation. Now, surely, fate would give his enemy into his hand.

Men were spilling south into the valley of the San Joaquin, coming north with proofs of the Stanislaus, the Tuolumne, the Merced. Greenwood insisted on working north into the country where he had found gold, along all the tributaries of the Sacramento. Even then, too, before the great year of '49 had dawned, prospectors were pushing to the head

1086

of the creeks making into the American Fork, the Feather River, all the larger and lesser streams heading on the west slopes of the Sierras; and Greenwood even heard of a band of men who had stolen away from the lower diggings and broken off to the north and east – some said, heading far up for the Trinity, though that was all unproved country so far as most knew.

And now the hatred in Woodhull's sullen heart grew hotter still, for he heard that not fifty miles ahead there had passed a quiet dark young man, riding a black Spanish horse; with him a bearded man who drove a little band of loaded mules! Their progress, so came the story, was up a valley whose head was impassable. The trail could not be obliterated back of them. They were in a trap of their own choosing. All that he needed was patience and caution.

Ships and wagon trains came in on the Willamette from the East. They met the coast news of gold. Men of Oregon also left in a mad stampede for California. News came that all the world now was in the mines of California. All over the East, as the later ships also brought in reiterated news, the mad craze of '49 even then was spreading.

But the men of '48 were in ahead. From them, scattering like driven game among the broken country, over hundreds of miles of forest, plain, bench land and valley lands, no word could come out to the waiting world. None might know the countless triumphs, the unnumbered tragedies – none ever did know.

There, beyond the law, one man might trail another with murder stronger than avarice in his heart, and none ever be the wiser. To hide secrets such as these the unfathomed mountains reached out their shadowy arms.

* * *

Now the winter wore on with such calendar as altitude, latitude, longitude gave it, and the spring of '49 came, East and West, in Washington and New York; at Independence on the Missouri; at Deseret by the Great Salt Lake; in California; in Oregon.

Above the land of the early Willamette settlements, forty or fifty miles up the Yamhill Valley, so a letter from Mrs Caleb Price to her relatives in Ohio said, the Wingates, leaders of the train, had a beautiful farm, near by the Cale Price Mill, as it was known. They had up a good house of five rooms, and their cattle were increasing now. They had forty acres in wheat, with what help the neighbours had given in housing and planting;

and wheat would run fifty bushels to the acre there. They had bought young trees for an orchard. The mother had planted roses; they now were fine. She believed they were as good as those she planted in Portland, when first she went through there – cuttings she had carried with her seed wheat in the bureau drawer, all the way across from the Saganon. Yes, Jesse Wingate and his wife had done well. Molly, their daughter, was still living with them and still unmarried, she believed.

There were many things which Mrs Caleb Price believed; also many things she did not mention.

She said nothing, for she knew nothing, of a little scene between these two as they sat on their little sawn-board porch before their door one evening, looking out over the beautiful and varied landscape that lay spread before them. Their wheat was in the green now. Their hogs revelled in their little clover field. 'We've done well, Jesse,' at length said portly Molly Wingate. 'Look at our place! A mile square, for nothing! We've done well, Jesse, I'll admit it.'

'For what?' answered Jesse Wingate. 'What's it for? What has it come to? What's it all about?'

He did not have any reply. When he turned he saw his wife wiping tears from her hard, lined face.

'It's Molly,' said she.

CHAPTER 42

Kit Carson Rides

Following the recession of the snow, men began to push westward up the Platte in the great spring gold rush of 1849. In the forefront of these, outpacing them in his tireless fashion, now passed westward the greatest traveller of his day, the hunter and scout, Kit Carson. The new post of Fort Kearny on the Platte; the old one, Fort Laramie in the foothills of the Rockies – he touched them soon as the grass was green; and as the sun warmed the grass slopes of the North Platte and the Sweetwater, so that his horses could paw out a living, he crowded on westward. He was a month ahead of the date for the wagon trains at Fort Bridger.

'How, Chardon!' said he as he drove in his two light packs, riding alone as was his usual way, evading Indian eyes as he of all men best knew how.

'How, Kit! You're early. Why?' The trader's chief clerk turned to send a boy for Vasquez, Bridger's partner. ' 'Light, Kit, and eat.'

'Where's Bridger?' demanded Carson. 'I've come out of my country to see him. I have government mail – for Oregon.'

'For Oregon? *Mon Dieu!* But Jeem' – he spread out his hands – 'Jeem he's dead, we'll think. We do not known. Now we know the gold news. Maybe-so we know why Jeem he's gone!'

'Gone? When?'

'Las' H'august-Settemb. H'all of an' at once he'll took the trail h'after the h'emigrant train las' year. He'll caught him h'on Fort Hall; we'll heard. But then he go h'on with those h'emigrant beyon' Hall, beyon' the fork for Californ'. He'll not come back. No one know what has become of Jeem. He'll been dead, maybe-so.'

'Yes? Maybe-so not! That old rat knows his way through the mountains, and he'll take his own time. You think he did not go on to California?'

'We'll know he'll didn't.'

Carson stood and thought for a time.

'Well, its bad for you, Chardon!'

'How you mean, M'sieu Kit?'

'Eat your last square meal. Saddle your best horse. Drive four packs and two saddle mounts along.'

'*Oui?* And where?'

'To Oregon!'

'To Oregon? *Sacre 'Fan!'* What you mean?'

'By authority of the government, I command you to carry this packet on to Oregon this season, as fast as safety may allow. Take a man with you – two; pick up any help you need. But go through.

'I cannot go further west myself, for I must get back to Laramie. I had counted on Jim, and Jim's post must see me through. Make your own plans to start tomorrow morning. I'll arrange all that with Vasquez.'

'But, M'sieu Kit, I cannot!'

'But you shall, you must, you will! If I had a better man I'd send him, but you are to do what Jim wants done.'

'*Mais, oui,* of course.'

'Yes. And you'll do what the President of the United States commands.'

'*Bon Dieu,* Kit!'

'That packet is over the seal of the United States of America, Chardon. It carries the signature of the president. It was given to the army to deliver. The army has given it to me. I give it to you, and you must go. It is for Jim. He would know. It must be placed in the hands of the Circuit Judge acting under the laws of Oregon, whoever he may be, and wherever. Find him in the Willamette country. Your pay will be more than you think, Chardon. Jim would know. Dead or alive, you do this for him.

'You can do thirty miles a day. I know you as a mountain man. Ride! Tomorrow I start east to Laramie – and you start west for Oregon!'

And in the morning following two riders left Bridger's for the trail. They parted, each waving a hand to the other.

CHAPTER 43

The Killer Killed

A rough low cabin of logs, hastily thrown together, housed through the winter months of the Sierra foothills the two men who now, in the warm days of early June, sat by the primitive fireplace cooking a midday meal. The older man, thin, bearded, who now spun a side of venison ribs on a cord in front of the open fire, was the mountain man, Bill Jackson, as anyone might tell who ever had seen him, for he had changed but little.

That his companion, younger, bearded, dressed also in buckskins, was Will Banion it would have taken closer scrutiny even of a friend to determine, so much had the passing of these few months altered him in appearance and in manner. Once light of mien, now he smiled never at all. For hours he would seem to go about his duties as an automaton. He spoke at last to his ancient and faithful friend, kindly as ever, and with his own alertness and decision.

'Let's make it our last meal on the Trinity, Bill. What do you say?'

'Why? What's eatin' ye, boy? Gittin' restless agin?'

'Yes, I want to move.'

'Most does.'

'We've got enough, Bill. The last month has been a crime. The spring snows uncovered a fortune for us, and you know it!'

'Oh, yes, eight hundred in one day ain't bad for two men that never had saw a gold pan a year ago. But she ain't petered yit. With what we've learned, an' what we know, we kin stay in here an' git so rich that hit shore makes me cry ter think o' trappin' beaver, even before 1836, when the beaver market busted. Why, rich? Will, hit's like you say, plumb wrong – we done hit so damned easy! I lay awake nights plannin' how ter spend my share o' this pile. We must have fifty-sixty thousand dollars o' dust buried under the floor, don't ye think?'

'Yes, more. But if you'll agree, I'll sell this claim to the company below us and let them have the rest. They offer fifty thousand flat, and it's enough – more than enough. I want two things – to get Jim Bridger his share safe and sound; and I want to go to Oregon.'

The old man paused in the act of splitting off a deer rib from his roast.

'Ye're one awful damn fool, ain't ye, Will? I did hope ter finish up here, a-brilin' my meat in a yaller-gold fireplace; but no matter how plain an' simple a man's tastes is, allus somethin' comes along ter bust 'em up.'

'Well, go on and finish your meal in this plain fireplace of ours, Bill. It has done us very well. I think I'll go down to the sluice a while.'

Banion rose and left the cabin, stooping at the low door. Moodily he walked along the side of the steep ravine to which the little structure clung. Below him lay the ripped-open slope where the little stream had been diverted. Below again lay the bared bed of the exploited water course, floored with boulders set in deep gravel, at times with seamy dams of flat rock lying under and across the gravel stretches; the bedrock, ages old, holding in its hidden fingers the rich secrets of immemorial time.

Here he and his partner had in a few months of strenuous labour taken from the narrow and unimportant rivulet more wealth than most could save in a lifetime of patient and thrifty toil. Yes, fortune had been kind. And it all had been so easy, so simple, so unagitating, so matter-of-fact! The hillside now looked like any other hillside, innocent as a woman's eyes, yet covering how much! Banion could not realise that now, young though he was, he was a rich man.

He climbed down the side of the ravine, the little stones rattling under his feet, until he stood on the bared floor of the bedrock which had proved so unbelievably prolific in coarse gold.

There was a sharp bend in the ravine, and here the unpaid toil of the little waterway had, ages long, carried and left especially deep strata of gold-shot gravel. As he stood, half musing, Will Banion heard, on the ravine side around the bend, the tinkle of a falling stone, lazily rolling from one impediment to another. It might be some deer or other animal, he thought. He hastened to get view of the cause, whatever it might be.

And then fate, chance, the goddess of fortune which some men say does not exist, but which all wilderness-goers know does exist, for one instant paused, with Will Banion's life and wealth and happiness lightly a-balance in cold, disdainful fingers.

He turned the corner. Almost level with his own, he looked into the eyes of a crawling man who – stooped, one hand steadying himself against the slant of the ravine, the other below, carrying a rifle – was peering frowningly ahead.

It was an evil face, bearded, aquiline, not unhandsome; but evil in its plain meaning now. The eyes were narrowed, the full lips drawn close, as though some tense emotion now approached its climax. The appearance was that of strain, of nerves stretched in some purpose long sustained.

And why not? When a man would do murder, when that has been his steady and premeditated purpose for a year, waiting only for opportunity to serve his purpose, that purpose itself changes his very lineaments, alters his whole cast of countenance. Other men avoid him, knowing unconsciously what is in his soul because of what is written on his face.

For months most men had avoided Woodhull. It was known that he was on a manhunt. His questions, his movements, his changes of locality showed that; and Woodhull was one of those who cannot avoid asseverance, needing it for their courage's sake. Now morose and brooding, now loudly profane, now laughing or now aloof, his errand in these unknown hills was plain. Well, he was not alone among men whose depths were loosed. Some time his hour might come.

It had come! He stared now full into the face of his enemy! He at last had found him. Here stood his enemy, unarmed, delivered into his hands.

For one instant the two stood, staring into one another's eyes. Banion's advance had been silent. Woodhull was taken as much unawares as he.

It had been Woodhull's purpose to get a stand above the sluices, hidden by the angle, where he could command the reach of the stream bed where Banion and Jackson last had been working. He had studied the place before, and meant to take no chances. His shot must be sure.

But now, in his climbing on the steep hillside, his rifle was in his left hand, downhill, and his footing, caught as he was with one foot half raised, was insecure. At no time these last four hours had his opportunity been so close – or so poor – as precisely now!

He saw Will Banion's eyes, suddenly startled, quickly estimating, looking into his own. He knew that behind his own eyes his whole foul soul lay bared – the soul of a murderer.

Woodhull made a swift spring down the hill, scrambling, half erect, and caught some sort of stance for the work which now was his to do. He snarled, for he saw Banion stoop, unarmed. It would do his victim no good to run. There was time even to exult, and that was much better in a long-deferred matter such as this.

'Now, damn you, I've got you!'

He gave Banion that much chance to see that he was now to die.

Half leaning, he raised the long rifle to its line and touched the trigger.

The report came; and Banion fell. But even as he wheeled and fell, stumbling down the hillside, his flung arm apparently had gained a weapon. It was not more than the piece of rotten quartz he had picked up and planned to examine later. He flung it straight at Woodhull's face – an act of chance, of instinct. By a hair it saved him.

Firing and missing at a distance of fifty feet, Woodhull remained not yet a murderer in deed. In a flash Banion gathered and sprang towards him as he stood in a half–second of consternation at seeing his victim fall and rise again. The rifle carried but the one shot. He flung it down, reached for his heavy knife, raising an arm against the second piece of rock which Banion flung as he closed. He felt his wrist caught in an iron grip, felt the blood gush where his temple was cut by the last missile. And then once more, on the narrow bared floor that but now was patterned in parquetry traced in yellow, and soon must turn to red, it came to man and man between them – and it was free!

They fell and stumbled so that neither could much damage the other at first. Banion knew he must keep the impounded hand back from the knife sheath or he was done. Thus close, he could make no escape. He fought fast and furiously, striving to throw, to bend, to beat back the body of a man almost as strong as himself, and now a maniac in rage and fear.

*　　*　　*

The sound of the rifle shot rang through the little defile. To Jackson, shaving off bits of sweet meat between thumb and knife blade, it meant the presence of a stranger, friend or foe, for he knew Banion had carried no weapon with him. His own long rifle he snatched from its pegs. At a long, easy lope he ran along the path which carried across the face of the ravine. His moccasined feet made no sound. He saw no one in the creek bed or at the long turn. But now, there came a loud, wordless cry which he knew was meant for him. It was Will Banion's voice.

The two struggling men grappled below him had no notion of how long they had fought. It seemed an age, and the denouement yet another age deferred. But to them came the sound of a voice, 'Git away, Will! Stand back!'

It was Jackson.

They both, still gripped, looked up the bank. The long barrel of a rifle, foreshortened to a black point, above it a cold eye, fronted and followed them as they swayed. The crooked arm of the rifleman was motionless, save as it just moved that deadly circle an inch this way, an inch back again.

Banion knew that this was murder, too, but he knew that naught on earth could stay it now. To guard as much as he could against a last desperate knife thrust even of a dying man, he broke free and sprang back as far as he could, falling prostrate on his back as he did so, tripped by an unseen stone. But Sam Woodhull was not upon him now, was not willing to lose his own life in order to kill. For just one instant he looked up at the death staring down on him, then turned to run.

There was no place where he could run. The voice of the man above him called out sharp and hard.

'Halt! Sam Woodhull, look at me!'

He did turn, in horror, in fascination at sight of the Bright Angel. The rifle barrel to his last gaze became a small, round circle, large as a bottle top, and around it shone a fringed aura of red and purple light. That might have been the eye.

Steadily as when he had held his friend's life in his hand, sighting five inches above his eyes, the old hunter drew now above the eyes of his enemy. When the dry report cut the confined air of the valley, the body of Sam Woodhull started forward. The small blue hole an inch above the eyes showed the murderer's manhunt done.

CHAPTER 44

Yet If Love Lack

Winding down out of the hills into the grassy valley of the Upper Sacramento, the little pack train of Banion and Jackson, six hardy mules beside the black horse and Jackson's mountain pony, picked its way along a gashed and trampled creek bed. The kayaks which swung heavy on the strongest two mules might hold salt or lead or gold. It all was one to any who might have seen, and the two silent men, the younger ahead, the older behind, obviously were men able to hold their counsel or to defend their property.

The smoke of a distant encampment caught the keen eye of Jackson as he rode, humming, carefree, the burden of a song.

' "Oh, then, Susannah!" ' admonished the old mountain man, and bade the said Susannah to be as free of care as he himself then and there was.

'More men comin' in,' said he presently. 'Wonder who them people is, an' ef hit's peace er war.'

'Three men. A horse band. Two Indians. Go in easy, Bill.'

Banion slowed down his own gait. His companion had tied the six mules together, nose and tail, with the halter of the lead mule wrapped on his own saddle horn. Each man now drew his rifle from the swing loop. But they advanced with the appearance of confidence, for it was evident that they had been discovered by the men of the encampment.

Apparently they were identified as well as discovered. A tall man in leggings and moccasins, a flat felt hat over his long grey hair, stood gazing at them, his rifle butt resting on the ground. Suddenly he emitted an unearthly yell, whether of defiance or of greeting, and springing to his own horse's picket pin gathered in the lariat, and mounting bareback came on, his rifle high above his head, and repeating again and again his war cry or salutation.

Jackson rose in his stirrups, dropped his lead line and forsook more than a hundred and fifty thousand dollars, some two mule-pack loads of gold. His own yell rose high in answer.

'I told ye all the world'd be here!' he shouted back over his shoulder. 'Do-ee see that old thief Jim Bridger? Him I left drunk an' happy last summer? Now what in hell brung him here?'

The two old mountain men flung off and stood hand in hand before Banion had rescued the precious lead line and brought on the little train.

Bridger threw his hat on the ground, flung down his rifle and cast his stoic calm aside. Both his hands caught Banion's and his face beamed, breaking into a thousand lines.

'Boy, hit's you, then! I knowed yer hoss – he has no like in these parts. I've traced ye by him this hundred miles below an' up agin, but I've had no word this two weeks. Mostly I've seed that when ye ain't lookin' fer a b'ar, thar he is. Well, here we air, fine an' fatten, an' me with two bottles left o' somethin' they call cognac down in Yerba Buena. Come on in an' we'll make medicine.'

They dismounted. The two Indians, short, deep-chested, bow-legged men, went to the packs. They gruntled as they unloaded the two larger mules.

The kayaks were lined up and the mantas spread over them, the animals led away for feed and water. Bridger produced a ham of venison, some beans, a bannock and some coffee – not to mention his two bottles of fiery fluid – before any word was passed regarding future plans or past events.

'Come here, Jim,' said Jackson after a time, tin cup in hand. The other followed him, likewise equipped.

'Heft this pannier, Jim.'

'Uh-huh? Well, what of hit? What's inter hit?'

'Not much, Jim. Jest three-four hunderd pounds o' gold settin' there in them four packs. Hit hain't much, but hit'll help some.'

Bridger stooped and uncovered the kayaks, unbuckled the cover straps.

'Hit's a true fack!' he exclaimed. 'Gold! Ef hit hain't, I'm a putrified liar, an' that's all I got to say!'

Now, little by little, they told, each to other, the story of the months since they had met, Bridger first explaining his own movements.

'I left the Malheur at Boise, an' brung along yan two boys. Ye needn't be a-skeered they'll touch the cargo. The gold means nothin' ter 'em, but horses does. We've got a good band ter drive north now. Some we bought an' most they stole, but no rancher cares fer horses here an' now.

'We come through the Klamaths, ye see, an' on south – the old horse trail up from the Spanish country, which only the Injuns knows. My boys say they kin take us ter the head o' the Willamette.'

'So ye did get the gold! Eh, sir?' said Bridger, his eyes narrowing. 'The tip the gal give ye was a good one?'

'Yes,' rejoined Banion. 'But we came near losing it and more. It was Woodhull, Jim. He followed us in.'

'Yes, I know. His wagons was not fur behind ye on the Humboldt. He left right atter ye did. He made trouble, huh? He'll make no more? Is that hit, huh?'

Bill Jackson slapped the stock of his rifle in silence. Bridger nodded. He had been close to tragedies all his life. They told him now of this one. He nodded again, close lipped.

'An' ye want courts an' the settlements, boys?' said he. 'Fer me, when I kill a rattler, that's enough. Ef ye're touchy an' want yer ree-cord clean, why, we kin go below an' fix hit. Only thing is, I don't want ter waste no more time'n I kin help, fer some o' them horses has a ree-cord that ain't maybe so plumb clean their own selves. Ye ain't goin' out east – ye're goin' north. Hit's easier, an' a month er two closter, with plenty o' feed an' water – the old Cayuse trail, huh?

'So Sam Woodhull got what he's been lookin' fer so long!' he added presently. 'Well, that simples up things some.'

'He'd o' got hit long ago, on the Platte, ef my partner hadn't been a damned fool,' confirmed Jackson. 'He was where we could a' buried him nach'erl, in the sands. I told Will then that Woodhull'd murder him the fust chancet he got. Well, he did – er ef he didn't hit wasn't no credit ter either one o' them two.'

'What differ does hit make, Bill?' remarked Bridger indifferently. 'Let bygones be bygones, huh? That's the pleasantest way, sence he's dead.

'Now here we air, with all the gold there ever was moulded, an' a hull two bottles o' cognac left, which takes holt e'enamost better'n Hundson's Bay rum. Ain't it a perty leetle ol' world to play with, all with nice pink stripes erroun' hit?'

He filled his tin and broke into a roaring song:

> 'There was a ol' widder which had three sons –
> Joshuway, James an' John.
> An' one got shot, an' one got drowned,
> An' th' last un got losted an' never was found.

'Ain't hit funny, son,' said he, turning to Banion with cup uplifted, 'how stiff likker allus makes me remember what I done fergot? Now Kit told me that at Laramie – '

' "Fer I'm goin' out to Oregon, with my wash pan on my knee!" ' chanted Bill Jackson, now solemnly oblivious of most of his surroundings and hence not consciously discourteous to his friends; ' "Susannah, don't ye cry!" '

They sat, the central figures of a scene wild enough, in a world still primitive and young. Only one of the three remained sober and silent, wondering, if one thing lacked, why the world was made.

CHAPTER 45

The Light of the Whole World

At the new farm of Jesse Wingate on the Yamhill, the wheat was in stack and ready for the flail, his deerskin sacks made ready to carry it to market after the threshing. His grim and weather-beaten wagon stood, now unused, at the barnyard fence of rails.

It was evening. Wingate and his wife again sat on their little stoop, gazing down the path that led to the valley road. A mounted man was opening the gate, someone they did not recognise.

'Maybe from below,' said Molly Wingate. 'Jed's maybe sent up another letter. Leave it to him, he's going to marry the most wonderful girl! Well, I'll call it true, she's a wonderful walker. All the Prices was.'

'Or maybe it's for Molly,' she added. 'Ef she's ever heard a word from either Sam Woodhull or – '

'Hush! I do not want to hear that name!' broke in her husband. 'Trouble enough he has made for us!'

His wife made no comment for a moment, still watching the stranger, who was now riding up the long approach, little noted by Wingate as he sat, moody and distrait.

'Jess,' said she, 'let's be fair and shame the devil. Maybe we don't know all the truth about Will Banion. You go in the house. I'll tend to this man, whoever he may be.'

But she did not. With one more look at the advancing figure, she herself rose and followed her husband. As she passed she cast a swift glance at her daughter, who had not joined them for the twilight hour. Hers was the look of the mother – maternal, solicitous, yet wise and resolved withal; woman understanding woman. And now was the hour for her ewe lamb to be alone.

Molly Wingate sat in her own little room, looking through her window at the far forest and the mountain peaks in their evening dress of many colours. She was no longer the tattered emigrant girl in fringed frock and mended moccasins. Ships from the world's great ports served the new market of the Columbia Valley. It was a trim and trig young woman in the habiliments of sophisticated lands who sat here now, her heavy hair, piled high, lighted warmly in the illumination of the window. Her skin, clear white, had lost its sunburn in the moister climate between the two ranges of mountains. Quiet, reticent, reserved – cold, some said; but all said Molly Wingate, teacher at the mission school, was beautiful, the most beautiful young woman in all the great Willamette settlements. Her hands were in her lap now, and her face as usual was grave. A sad young woman, her Oregon lovers all said of her. They did not know why she should be sad, so fit for love was she.

She heard now a knock at the front door, to which, from her position, she could not have seen anyone approach. She called out, 'Come!' but did not turn her head.

A horse stamped, neighed near her door. Her face changed expression. Her eyes grew wide in some strange association of memories suddenly revived.

She heard a footfall on the gallery floor, then on the floor of the hall. It stopped. Her heart almost stopped with it. Some undiscovered sense warned her, cried aloud to her. She faced the door, wide-eyed, as it was flung open.

'Molly!'

Will Banion's deep-toned voice told her all the rest. In terror, her hands to her face, she stood an instant, then sprang towards him, her voice almost a wail in its incredulous joy.

'Will! Will! Oh, Will! Oh! Oh!'

'Molly!'

They both paused.

'It can't be! Oh, you frightened me, Will! It can't be you!'

But he had her in his arms now. At first he could only push back her hair, stroke her cheek, until at last the rush of life and youth came back to them both, and their lips met in the sealing kiss of years. Then both were young again. She put up a hand to caress his brown cheek. Tenderly he pushed back her hair.

'Will! Oh, Will! It can't be!' she whispered again and again.

'But it is! It had to be! Now I'm paid! Now I've found my fortune!'

'And I've had my year to think it over, Will. As though the fortune mattered!'

'Not so much as that one other thing that kept you and me apart. Now I must tell you – '

'No, no, let be! Tell me nothing! Will, aren't you here?'

'But I must! You must hear me! I've waited two years for this!'

'Long, Will! You've let me get old!'

'You old?' He kissed her in contempt of time. 'But now wait, dear, for I must tell you.

'You see, coming up the valley I met the clerk of the court of Oregon City, and he knew I was headed up for the Yamhill. He asked me to serve as his messenger. "I've been sending up through all the valley settlements in search of one William Banion," he said to me. Then I told him who I was. He gave me this.'

'What is it?' She turned to her lover. He held in his hands a long package, enfolded in an otter skin. 'Is it a court summons for Will Banion? They can't have you, Will!'

He smiled, her head held between his two hands.

' "I have a very important document for Colonel William Banion," the clerk said to me. "It has been for some time in our charge, for delivery to him at once should he come into the Oregon settlements. It is from His Excellency, the President of the United States. Such messages do not wait. Seeing it to be of such importance, and knowing it to be military, Judge Lane opened it, since we could not trace the addressee. If you like – if you are, indeed, Colonel William Banion" – that was what he said.'

He broke off, choking.

'Ah, Molly, at last and indeed I am again Colonel William Banion!'

He took from the otter skin – which Chardon once had placed over the oilskin used by Carson to protect it – the long and formal envelope of heavy linen. His finger pointed – 'On the Service of the United States'.

'Why, Will!'

He caught the envelope swiftly to his lips, holding it there an instant before he could speak.

'My pardon! From the President! Not guilty – oh, not guilty! And I never was!'

'Oh, Will, Will! That makes you happy?'

'Doesn't it you?'

'Why, yes, yes! But I knew that always! And I know now that I'd have followed you to the gallows if that had had to be.'

'Though I were a thief?'

'Yes! But I'd not believe it! I didn't! I never did! I could not!'

'You'd take my word against all the world – just my word, if I told you it wasn't true? You'd want no proof at all? Will you always believe in me in that way? No proof?'

'I want none now. You do tell me that? No, no! I'm afraid you'd give me proofs! I want none! I want to love you for what you are, for what we both are, Will! I'm afraid!'

He put his hands on her shoulders, held her away arms' length, looked straight into her eyes.

'Dear girl,' said he, 'you need never be afraid any more.'

She put her head down contentedly against his shoulder, her face nestling sidewise, her eyes closed, her arms again quite around his neck.

'I don't care, Will,' said she. 'No, no, don't talk of things!'

He did not talk. In the sweetness of the silence he kissed her tenderly again and again.

And now the sun might sink. The light of the whole world by no means died with it.

THE VIRGINIAN

OWEN WISTER

Contents

To the Reader

Certain of the newspapers, when this book was first announced, made a mistake most natural upon seeing the subtitle as it then stood, *A Tale of Sundry Adventures*. 'This sounds like a historical novel,' said one of them, meaning (I take it) a colonial romance. As it now stands, the title will scarce lead to such interpretation; yet none the less is this book historical – quite as much so as any colonial romance. Indeed, when you look at the root of the matter, it is a colonial romance. For Wyoming between 1874 and 1890 was a colony as wild as was Virginia one hundred years earlier. As wild, with a scantier population, and the same primitive joys and dangers. There were, to be sure, not so many Chippendale settees.

We know quite well the common understanding of the term 'historical novel'. *Hugh Wynne* exactly fits it. But *Silas Lapham* is a novel as perfectly historical as is *Hugh Wynne*, for it pictures an era and personifies a type. It matters not that in the one we find George Washington and in the other none save imaginary figures; else *The Scarlet Letter* were not historical. Nor does it matter that Dr Mitchell did not live in the time of which he wrote, while Mr Howells saw many Silas Laphams with his own eyes; else *Uncle Tom's Cabin* were not historical. Any narrative which presents faithfully a day and a generation is of necessity historical; and this one presents Wyoming between 1874 and 1890.

Had you left New York or San Francisco at ten o'clock this morning, by noon the day after tomorrow you could step out at Cheyenne. There you would stand at the heart of the world that is the subject of my picture, yet you would look around you in vain for the reality. It is a vanished world. No journeys, save those which memory can take, will bring you to it now. The mountains are there, far and shining, and the sunlight, and the infinite earth, and the air that seems forever the true fountain of youth – but where is the buffalo, and the wild antelope, and where the horseman with his pasturing thousands? So like its old self does the sagebrush seem when revisited, that you wait for the horseman to appear.

But he will never come again. He rides in his historic yesterday. You will no more see him gallop out of the unchanging silence than you will see Columbus on the unchanging sea come sailing from Palos with his caravels.

And yet the horseman is still so near our day that in some chapters of this book, which were published separate at the close of the nineteenth century, the present tense was used. It is true no longer. In those chapters it has been changed, and verbs like 'is' and 'have' now read 'was' and 'had'. Time has flowed faster than my ink.

What is become of the horseman, the cowpuncher, the last romantic figure upon our soil? For he was romantic. Whatever he did, he did with his might. The bread that he earned was earned hard, the wages that he squandered were squandered hard – half a year's pay sometimes gone in a night – 'blown in', as he expressed it, or 'blowed in', to be perfectly accurate. Well, he will be here among us always, invisible, waiting his chance to live and play as he would like. His wild kind has been among us always, since the beginning: a young man with his temptations, a hero without wings.

The cowpuncher's ungoverned hours did not unman him. If he gave his word, he kept it; Wall Street would have found him behind the times. Nor did he talk lewdly to women; Newport would have thought him old-fashioned. He and his brief epoch make a complete picture, for in themselves they were as complete as the pioneers of the land or the explorers of the sea. A transition has followed the horseman of the plains; a shapeless state, a condition of men and manners as unlovely as is that moment in the year when winter is gone and spring not come, and the face of Nature is ugly. I shall not dwell upon it here. Those who have seen it know well what I mean. Such transition was inevitable. Let us give thanks that it is but a transition, and not a finality.

Sometimes readers enquire, Did I know the Virginian? As well, I hope, as a father should know his son. And sometimes it is asked, Was such and such a thing true? Now to this I have the best answer in the world. Once a cowpuncher listened patiently while I read him a manuscript. It concerned an event upon an Indian reservation. 'Was that the Crow reservation?' he enquired at the finish. I told him that it was no real reservation and no real event; and his face expressed displeasure. 'Why,' he demanded, 'do you waste your time writing what never happened, when you know so many things that did happen?'

And I could no more help telling him that this was the highest compliment ever paid me than I have been able to help telling you about it here!

Charleston, SC
31 March 1902

CHAPTER 1

Enter the Man

SOME NOTABLE SIGHT was drawing the passengers, both men and women, to the window; and therefore I rose and crossed the car to see what it was. I saw near the track an enclosure, and round it some laughing men, and inside it some whirling dust, and amid the dust some horses, plunging, huddling, and dodging. They were cow ponies in a corral, and one of them would not be caught, no matter who threw the rope. We had plenty of time to watch this sport, for our train had stopped that the engine might take water at the tank before it pulled us up beside the station platform of Medicine Bow. We were also six hours late, and starving for entertainment. The pony in the corral was wise, and rapid of limb. Have you seen a skilful boxer watch his antagonist with a quiet, incessant eye? Such an eye as this did the pony keep upon whatever man took the rope. The man might pretend to look at the weather which was fine; or he might affect earnest conversation with a bystander: it was bootless. The pony saw through it. No feint hoodwinked him. This animal was thoroughly a man of the world. His undistracted eye stayed fixed upon the dissembling foe, and the gravity of his horse-expression made the matter one of high comedy. Then the rope would sail out at him, but he was already elsewhere; and if horses laugh, gaiety must have abounded in that corral. Sometimes the pony took a turn alone; next he had slid in a flash among his brothers, and the whole of them like a school of playful fish whipped round the corral, kicking up the fine dust, and (I take it) roaring with laughter. Through the window-glass of our Pullman the thud of their mischievous hoofs reached us, and the strong, humorous curses of the cowboys. Then for the first time I noticed a man who sat on the high gate of the corral, looking on. For he now climbed down with the undulations of a tiger, smooth and easy, as if his muscles flowed beneath his skin. The others had all visibly whirled the rope, some of them even shoulder high. I did not see his arm lift or move. He appeared to hold the rope down low, by his leg. But like a sudden snake I saw the noose go out its length and fall true; and the thing was done. As the captured pony walked in with a sweet, church-door expression, our train moved slowly on to the station, and a passenger remarked, 'That man knows his business.'

But the passenger's dissertation upon roping I was obliged to lose, for Medicine Bow was my station. I bade my fellow-travellers goodbye, and descended, a stranger, into the great cattle land. And here in less than ten minutes I learned news which made me feel a stranger indeed.

My baggage was lost; it had not come on my train; it was adrift somewhere back in the two thousand miles that lay behind me. And by way of comfort, the baggage-man remarked that passengers often got astray from their trunks, but the trunks mostly found them after a while. Having offered me this encouragement, he turned whistling to his affairs and left me planted in the baggage-room at Medicine Bow. I stood deserted among crates and boxes, blankly holding my check, furious and forlorn. I stared out through the door at the sky and the plains; but I did not see the antelope shining among the sagebrush, nor the great sunset light of Wyoming. Annoyance blinded my eyes to all things save my grievance: I saw only a lost trunk. And I was muttering half-aloud, 'What a forsaken hole this is!' when suddenly from outside on the platform came a slow voice – 'Off to get married *again*? Oh, don't!'

The voice was Southern and gentle and drawling; and a second voice came in immediate answer, cracked and querulous – 'It ain't again. Who says it's again? Who told you, anyway?'

And the first voice responded caressingly – 'Why, your Sunday clothes told me, Uncle Hughey. They are speakin' mighty loud o' nuptials.'

'You don't worry me!' snapped Uncle Hughey, with shrill heat.

And the other gently continued, 'Ain't them gloves the same yu' wore to your last weddin'?'

'You don't worry me! You don't worry me!' now screamed Uncle Hughey.

Already I had forgotten my trunk; care had left me; I was aware of the sunset, and had no desire but for more of this conversation. For it resembled none that I had heard in my life so far. I stepped to the door and looked out upon the station platform.

Lounging there at ease against the wall was a slim young giant, more beautiful than pictures. His broad, soft hat was pushed back; a loose knotted, dull-scarlet handkerchief sagged from his throat; and one casual thumb was hooked in the cartridge-belt that slanted across his hips. He had plainly come many miles from somewhere across the vast horizon, as the dust upon him showed. His boots were white with it. His overalls were grey with it. The weather-beaten bloom of his face shone through it duskily, as the ripe peaches look upon their trees in a dry season. But no dinginess of travel or shabbiness of attire could tarnish the splendour that radiated from his youth and strength. The old man upon whose temper his remarks were doing such deadly work was combed and curried to a finish, a bridegroom swept and garnished; but alas for age! Had I been the bride, I should have taken the giant, dust and all.

He had by no means done with the old man.

'Why, yu've hung weddin' gyarments on every limb!' he now drawled, with admiration. 'Who is the lucky lady this trip?'

The old man seemed to vibrate. 'Tell you there ain't been no other! Call me a Mormon, would you?'

'Why, that – '

'Call me a Mormon? Then name some of my wives. Name two. Name one. Dare you!'

' – that Laramie wido' promised you – '

'Shucks!'

' – only her docter suddenly ordered Southern climate and – '

'Shucks! You're a false alarm.'

' – so nothing but her lungs came between you. And next you'd most got united with Cattle Kate, only – '

'Tell you you're a false alarm!'

' – only she got hung.'

'Where's the wives in all this? Show the wives! Come now!'

'That corn-fed biscuit-shooter at Rawlins yu' gave the canary – '

'Never married her. Never did marry – '

'But yu' come so near, uncle! She was the one left yu' that letter explaining how she'd got married to a young cyard-player the very day before her ceremony with you was due, and – '

'Oh, you're nothing; you're a kid; you don't amount to – '

' – and how she'd never, never forgot to feed the canary.'

'This country's getting full of kids,' stated the old man, witheringly. 'It's doomed.' This crushing assertion plainly satisfied him. And he blinked his eyes with renewed anticipation. His tall tormentor continued with a face of unchanging gravity, and a voice of gentle solicitude – 'How is the health of that unfortunate – '

'That's right! Pour your insults! Pour 'em on a sick, afflicted woman!' The eyes blinked with combative relish.

'Insults? Oh, no, Uncle Hughey!'

'That's all right! Insults goes!'

'Why, I was mighty relieved when she began to recover her mem'ry. Las' time I heard, they told me she'd got it pretty near all back. Remembered her father, and her mother, and her sisters and brothers, and her friends, and her happy childhood, and all her doin's except only your face. The boys was bettin' she'd get that far too, give her time. But I reckon afteh such a turrable sickness as she had, that would be expectin' most too much.'

At this Uncle Hughey jerked out a small parcel. 'Shows how much you know!' he cackled 'There! See that! That's my ring she sent me back, being too unstrung for marriage. So she don't remember me, don't she? Ha-ha! Always said you were a false alarm.'

The Southerner put more anxiety into his tone. 'And so you're a-takin' the ring right on to the next one!' he exclaimed. 'Oh, don't go to get married again, Uncle Hughey! What's the use o' being married?'

'What's the use?' echoed the bridegroom, with scorn. 'Hm! When you grow up you'll think different.'

'Course I expect to think different when my age is different. I'm havin' the thoughts proper to twenty-four, and you're havin' the thoughts proper to sixty.'

'Fifty!' shrieked Uncle Hughey, jumping in the air.

The Southerner took a tone of self-reproach. 'Now, how could I forget you was fifty,' he murmured, 'when you have been telling it to the boys so careful for the last ten years!'

Have you ever seen a cockatoo – the white kind with the topknot – enraged by insult? The bird erects every available feather upon its person. So did Uncle Hughey seem to swell, clothes, moustache, and woolly white beard; and without further speech he took himself on board the East-bound train, which now arrived from its siding in time to deliver him.

Yet this was not why he had not gone away before. At any time he could have escaped into the baggage-room or withdrawn to a dignified distance until his train should come up. But the old man had evidently got a sort of joy from this teasing. He had reached that inevitable age when we are tickled to be linked with affairs of gallantry, no matter how.

With him now the East-bound departed slowly into that distance whence I had come. I stared after it as it went its way to the far shores of civilisation. It grew small in the unending gulf of space, until all sign of its presence was gone save a faint skein of smoke against the evening sky. And now my lost trunk came back into my thoughts, and Medicine Bow seemed a lonely spot. A sort of ship had left me marooned in a foreign ocean; the Pullman was comfortably steaming home to port, while I – how was I to find Judge Henry's ranch? Where in this unfeatured wilderness was Sunk Creek? No creek or any water at all flowed here that I could perceive. My host had written he should meet me at the station and drive me to his ranch. This was all that I knew. He was not here. The baggage-man had not seen him lately. The ranch was almost certain to be too far to walk to, tonight. My trunk – I discovered myself still staring dolefully after the vanished East-bound; and at the same instant I became aware that the tall man was looking gravely at me – as gravely as he had looked at Uncle Hughey throughout their remarkable conversation.

To see his eye thus fixing me and his thumb still hooked in his cartridge-belt, certain tales of travellers from these parts forced themselves disquietingly into my recollection. Now that Uncle Hughey was gone, was I to take his place and be, for instance, invited to dance on the platform to the music of shots nicely aimed?

'I reckon I am looking for you, seh,' the tall man now observed.

CHAPTER 2

'When you call me that, smile!'

We cannot see ourselves as others see us, or I should know what appearance I cut at hearing this from the tall man. I said nothing, feeling uncertain.

'I reckon I am looking for you, seh,' he repeated politely.

'I am looking for Judge Henry,' I now replied. He walked towards me, and I saw that in inches he was not a giant. He was not more than six feet. It was Uncle Hughey that had made him seem to tower. But in his eye, in his face, in his step, in the whole man, there dominated a something potent to be felt, I should think, by man or woman.

'The Judge sent me afteh you, seh,' he now explained, in his civil Southern voice; and he handed me a letter from my host. Had I not witnessed his facetious performances with Uncle Hughey, I should have judged him wholly ungifted with such powers. There was nothing external about him but what seemed the signs of a nature as grave as you could meet. But I had witnessed; and therefore supposing that I knew him in spite of his appearance, that I was, so to speak, in his secret and could give him a sort of wink, I adopted at once a method of easiness. It was so pleasant to be easy with a large stranger, who instead of shooting at your heels had very civilly handed you a letter.

'You're from old Virginia, I take it?' I began.

He answered slowly, 'Then you have taken it correct, seh.'

A slight chill passed over my easiness, but I went cheerily on with a further enquiry. 'Find many oddities out here like Uncle Hughey?'

'Yes, seh, there is a right smart of oddities around. They come in on every train.'

At this point I dropped my method of easiness.

'I wish that trunks came on the train,' said I. And I told him my predicament.

It was not to be expected that he would be greatly moved at my loss; but he took it with no comment whatever. 'We'll wait in town for it,' said he, always perfectly civil.

Now, what I had seen of 'town' was, to my newly arrived eyes, altogether horrible. If I could possibly sleep at the Judge's ranch, I preferred to do so.

'Is it too far to drive there tonight?' I enquired.

He looked at me in a puzzled manner.

'For this valise,' I explained, 'contains all that I immediately need; in fact, I could do without my trunk for a day or two, if it is not convenient to send. So if we could arrive there not too late by starting at once – ' I paused.

'It's two hundred and sixty-three miles,' said the Virginian.

To my loud ejaculation he made no answer, but surveyed me a moment longer, and then said, 'Supper will be about ready now.' He took my valise and I followed his steps towards the eating-house in silence. I was dazed.

As we went, I read my host's letter – a brief, hospitable message. He was very sorry not to meet me himself. He had been getting ready to drive over, when the surveyor appeared and detained him. Therefore in his stead he was sending a trustworthy man to town, who would look after me and drive me over. They were looking forward to my visit with much pleasure. This was all.

Yes, I was dazed. How did they count distance in this country? You spoke in a neighbourly fashion about driving over to town, and it meant – I did not know yet how many days. And what would be meant by the term 'dropping in', I wondered. And how many miles would be considered

'WHEN YOU CALL ME THAT, SMILE!'

really far? I abstained from further questioning the 'trustworthy man'. My questions had not fared excessively well. He did not propose making me dance, to be sure: that would scarcely be trustworthy. But neither did he propose to have me familiar with him. Why was this? What had I done to elicit that veiled and skilful sarcasm about oddities coming in on every train? Having been sent to look after me, he would do so, would even carry my valise; but I could not be jocular with him. This handsome, ungrammatical son of the soil had set between us the bar of his cold and perfect civility. No polished person could have done it better. What was the matter? I looked at him, and suddenly it came to me. If he had tried familiarity with me the first two minutes of our acquaintance, I should have resented it; by what right, then, had I tried it with him? It smacked of patronising: on this occasion he had come off the better gentleman of the two. Here in flesh and blood was a truth which I had long believed in words, but never met before. The creature we call a *gentleman* lies deep in the hearts of thousands that are born without chance to master the outward graces of the type.

Between the station and the eating-house I did a deal of straight thinking. But my thoughts were destined presently to be drowned in amazement at the rare personage into whose society fate had thrown me.

Town, as they called it, pleased me the less, the longer I saw it. But until our language stretches itself and takes in a new word of closer fit, town will have to do for the name of such a place as was Medicine Bow. I have seen and slept in many like it since. Scattered wide, they littered the frontier from the Columbia to the Rio Grande, from the Missouri to the Sierras. They lay stark, dotted over a planet of treeless dust, like soiled packs of cards. Each was similar to the next, as one old five-spot of clubs resembles another. Houses, empty bottles, and garbage, they were forever of the same shapeless pattern. More forlorn they were than stale bones. They seemed to have been strewn there by the wind and to be waiting till the wind should come again and blow them away. Yet serene above their foulness swam a pure and quiet light, such as the East never sees; they might be bathing in the air of creation's first morning. Beneath sun and stars their days and nights were immaculate and wonderful.

Medicine Bow was my first, and I took its dimensions, twenty-nine buildings in all – one coal shute, one water tank, the station, one store, two eating-houses, one billiard hall, two tool-houses, one feed stable, and twelve others that for one reason and another I shall not name. Yet this wretched husk of squalor spent thought upon appearances; many houses in it wore a false front to seem as if they were two stories high. There they stood, rearing their pitiful masquerade amid a fringe of old tin cans, while at their very doors began a world of crystal light, a land without end, a space across which Noah and Adam might come straight from Genesis. Into that space went wandering a road, over a hill and down out of sight, and up again smaller in the distance, and down once more, and up once more, straining the eyes, and so away.

Then I heard a fellow greet my Virginian. He came rollicking out of a door, and made a pass with his hand at the Virginian's hat. The Southerner dodged it, and I saw once more the tiger undulation of body, and knew my escort was he of the rope and the corral.

'How are yu', Steve?' he said to the rollicking man. And in his tone I heard instantly old friendship speaking. With Steve he would take and give familiarity.

Steve looked at me, and looked away – and that was all. But it was enough. In no company had I ever felt so much an outsider. Yet I liked the company, and wished that it would like me.

'Just come to town?' enquired Steve of the Virginian.

'Been here since noon. Been waiting for the train.'

'Going out tonight?'

'I reckon I'll pull out tomorro'.'

'Beds are all took,' said Steve. This was for my benefit.

'Dear me!' said I.

'But I guess one of them drummers will let yu' double up with him.' Steve was enjoying himself, I think. He had his saddle and blankets, and beds were nothing to him.

'Drummers, are they?' asked the Virginian.

'Two Jews handling cigars, one American with consumption killer, and a Dutchman with jew'll'ry.'

The Virginian set down my valise, and seemed to meditate. 'I did want a bed tonight,' he murmured gently.

'Well,' Steve suggested, 'the American looks like he washed the oftenest.'

'That's of no consequence to me,' observed the Southerner.

'Guess it'll be when yu' see 'em.'

'Oh, I'm meaning something different. I wanted a bed to myself.'

'Then you'll have to build one.'

'Bet yu' I have the Dutchman's.'

'Take a man that won't scare. Bet yu' drinks yu' can't have the American's.'

'Go yu',' said the Virginian. 'I'll have his bed without any fuss. Drinks for the crowd.'

'I suppose you have me beat,' said Steve, grinning at him affectionately. 'You're such a son-of-a-bitch when you get down to work. Well, so long! I got to fix my horse's hoofs.'

I had expected that the man would be struck down. He had used to the Virginian a term of heaviest insult, I thought. I had marvelled to hear it come so unheralded from Steve's friendly lips. And now I marvelled still more. Evidently he had meant no harm by it, and evidently no offence had been taken. Used thus, this language was plainly complimentary. I had stepped into a world new to me indeed, and novelties were occurring with scarce any time to get breath between them. As to where I should sleep, I had forgotten that problem altogether in my curiosity. What was the Virginian going to do now? I began to know that the quiet of this man was volcanic.

'Will you wash first, sir?'

We were at the door of the eating-house, and he set my valise inside. In my tenderfoot innocence I was looking indoors for the washing arrangements.

'It's out hyeh, seh,' he informed me gravely, but with strong Southern accent. Internal mirth seemed often to heighten the local flavour of his speech. There were other times when it had scarce any special accent or fault in grammar.

A trough was to my right, slippery with soapy water; and hanging from a roller above one end of it was a rag of discouraging appearance. The Virginian caught it, and it performed one whirling revolution on its roller. Not a dry or clean inch could be found on it. He took off his hat, and put his head in the door.

'Your towel, ma'am,' said he, 'has been too popular.'

She came out, a pretty woman. Her eyes rested upon him for a moment, then upon me with disfavour; then they returned to his black hair.

'The allowance is one a day,' said she, very quietly. 'But when folks are particular – ' She completed her sentence by removing the old towel and giving a clean one to us.

'Thank you, ma'am,' said the cowpuncher.

She looked once more at his black hair, and without any word returned to her guests at supper.

A pail stood in the trough, almost empty; and this he filled for me from a well. There was some soap sliding at large in the trough, but I got my own. And then in a tin basin I removed as many of the stains of travel as I was able. It was not much of a toilet that I made in this first wash-trough of my experience, but it had to suffice, and I took my seat at supper.

Canned stuff it was – corned beef. And one of my table companions said the truth about it. 'When I slung my teeth over that,' he remarked, 'I thought I was chewing a hammock.' We had strange coffee, and condensed milk; and I have never seen more flies. I made no attempt to talk, for no one in this country seemed favourable to me. By reason of something – my clothes, my hat, my pronunciation, whatever it might be – I possessed the secret of estranging people at sight. Yet I was doing better than I knew; my strict silence and attention to the corned beef made me in the eyes of the cowboys at table compare well with the over-talkative commercial travellers.

The Virginian's entrance produced a slight silence. He had done wonders with the wash-trough, and he had somehow brushed his clothes. With all the roughness of his dress, he was now the neatest of us. He nodded to some of the other cowboys, and began his meal in quiet.

But silence is not the native element of the drummer. An average fish can go a longer time out of water than this breed can live without talking. One of them now looked across the table at the grave, flannel-shirted Virginian; he inspected, and came to the imprudent conclusion that he understood his man.

'Good-evening,' he said briskly.

'Good-evening,' said the Virginian.

'Just come to town?' pursued the drummer.

'Just come to town,' the Virginian suavely assented.

'Cattle business jumping along?' enquired the drummer.

'Oh, fair.' And the Virginian took some more corned beef.

'Gets a move on your appetite, anyway,' suggested the drummer.

The Virginian drank some coffee. Presently the pretty woman refilled his cup without his asking her.

'Guess I've met you before,' the drummer stated next.

The Virginian glanced at him for a brief moment.

'Haven't I, now? Ain't I seen you somewheres? Look at me. You been in Chicago, ain't you? You look at me well. Remember Ikey's, don't you?'

'I don't reckon I do.'

'See, now! I knowed you'd been in Chicago. Four or five years ago. Or maybe it's two years. Time's nothing to me. But I never forget a face. Yes, sir. Him and me's met at Ikey's, all right.' This important point

the drummer stated to all of us. We were called to witness how well he
had proved old acquaintanceship. 'Ain't the world small, though!' he
exclaimed complacently. 'Meet a man once and you're sure to run on to
him again. That's straight. That's no bar-room josh.' And the drummer's
eye included us all in his confidence. I wondered if he had attained that
high perfection when a man believes his own lies.

The Virginian did not seem interested. He placidly attended to his
food, while our landlady moved between dining-room and kitchen, and
the drummer expanded.

'Yes, sir! Ikey's over by the stockyards, patronised by all cattlemen that
know what's what. That's where. Maybe it's three years. Time never was
nothing to me. But faces! Why, I can't quit 'em. Adults or children, male
and female; onced I seen 'em I couldn't lose one off my memory, not if
you were to pay me bounty, five dollars a face. White men, that is. Can't
do nothing with Niggers or Chinese. But you're white, all right.' The
drummer suddenly returned to the Virginian with this high compliment.
The cowpuncher had taken out a pipe, and was slowly rubbing it. The
compliment seemed to escape his attention, and the drummer went on.

'I can tell a man when he's white, put him at Ikey's or out loose here in
the sagebrush.' And he rolled a cigar across to the Virginian's plate.

'Selling them?' enquired the Virginian.

'Solid goods, my friend. Havana wrappers, the biggest tobacco proposition for five cents got out yet. Take it, try it, light it, watch it burn.
Here.' And he held out a bunch of matches.

The Virginian tossed a five-cent piece over to him.

'Oh, no, my friend! Not from you! Not after Ikey's. I don't forget you.
See? I knowed your face right away. See? That's straight. I seen you at
Chicago all right.'

'Maybe you did,' said the Virginian. 'Sometimes I'm mighty careless
what I look at.'

'Well, py damn!' now exclaimed the Dutch drummer, hilariously. 'I
am ploom disappointed. I vas hoping to sell him somedings myself.'

'Not the same here,' stated the American. 'He's too healthy for me. I
gave him up on sight.'

Now it was the American drummer whose bed the Virginian had in
his eye. This was a sensible man, and had talked less than his brothers in
the trade. I had little doubt who would end by sleeping in his bed; but
how the thing would be done interested me more deeply than ever.

The Virginian looked amiably at his intended victim, and made one or two remarks regarding patent medicines. There must be a good deal of money in them, he supposed, with a live man to manage them. The victim was flattered. No other person at the table had been favoured with so much of the tall cowpuncher's notice. He responded, and they had a pleasant talk. I did not divine that the Virginian's genius was even then at work, and that all this was part of his satanic strategy. But Steve must have divined it. For while a few of us still sat finishing our supper, that facetious horseman returned from doctoring his horse's hoofs, put his head into the dining-room, took in the way in which the Virginian was engaging his victim in conversation, remarked aloud, 'I've lost!' and closed the door again.

'What's he lost?' enquired the American drummer.

'Oh, you mustn't mind him,' drawled the Virginian. 'He's one of those box-head jokers goes around openin' and shuttin' doors that-a-way. We call him harmless. Well,' he broke off, 'I reckon I'll go smoke. Not allowed in hyeh?' This last he addressed to the landlady, with especial gentleness. She shook her head, and her eyes followed him as he went out.

Left to myself I meditated for some time upon my lodging for the night, and smoked a cigar for consolation as I walked about. It was not a hotel that we had supped in. Hotel at Medicine Bow there appeared to be none. But connected with the eating-house was that place where, according to Steve, the beds were all taken, and there I went to see for myself. Steve had spoken the truth. It was a single apartment containing four or five beds, and nothing else whatever. And when I looked at these beds, my sorrow that I could sleep in none of them grew less. To be alone in one offered no temptation, and as for this courtesy of the country, this doubling up – !

'Well, they have got ahead of us.' This was the Virginian standing at my elbow.

I assented.

'They have staked out their claims,' he added.

In this public sleeping-room they had done what one does to secure a seat in a railroad train. Upon each bed, as notice of occupancy, lay some article of travel or of dress. As we stood there, the two Jews came in and opened and arranged their valises, and folded and refolded their linen dusters. Then a railroad employee entered and began to go to bed at this hour, before dusk had wholly darkened into night. For him, going to bed meant removing his boots and placing his overalls and waistcoat beneath his pillow. He had no coat. His work began at three in the morning; and even as we still talked he began to snore.

'The man that keeps the store is a friend of mine,' said the Virginian; 'and you can be pretty near comfortable on his counter. Got any blankets?'

I had no blankets.

'Looking for a bed?' enquired the American drummer, now arriving.

'Yes, he's looking for a bed,' answered the voice of Steve behind him.

'Seems a waste of time,' observed the Virginian. He looked thoughtfully from one bed to another. 'I didn't know I'd have to lay over here. Well, I have sat up before.'

'This one's mine,' said the drummer, sitting down on it. 'Half's plenty enough room for me.'

'You're cert'nly mighty kind,' said the cowpuncher. 'But I'd not think o' disconveniencing yu'.'

'That's nothing. The other half is yours. Turn in right now if you feel like it.'

'No. I don't reckon I'll turn in right now. Better keep your bed to yourself.'

'See here,' urged the drummer, 'if I take you I'm safe from drawing some party I might not care so much about. This here sleeping proposition is a lottery.'

'Well,' said the Virginian (and his hesitation was truly masterly), 'if you put it that way – '

'I do put it that way. Why, you're clean! You've had a shave right now. You turn in when you feel inclined, old man! I ain't retiring just yet.'

The drummer had struck a slightly false note in these last remarks. He should not have said 'old man'. Until this I had thought him merely an amiable person who wished to do a favour. But 'old man' came in wrong. It had a hateful taint of his profession; the being too soon with everybody, the celluloid good-fellowship that passes for ivory with nine in ten of the city crowd. But not so with the sons of the sagebrush. They live nearer nature, and they know better.

But the Virginian blandly accepted 'old man' from his victim: he had a game to play.

'Well, I cert'nly thank yu',' he said. 'After a while I'll take advantage of your kind offer.'

I was surprised. Possession being nine points of the law it seemed his very chance to entrench himself in the bed. But the cowpuncher had planned a campaign needing no entrenchments. Moreover, going to bed before nine o'clock upon the first evening in many weeks that a town's resources were open to you, would be a dull proceeding. Our entire company, drummer and all, now walked over to the store, and here my sleeping arrangements were made easily. This store was the cleanest place and the best in Medicine Bow, and would have been a good store anywhere, offering a multitude of things for sale, and kept by a very civil proprietor. He bade me make myself at home, and placed both of his counters at my disposal. Upon the grocery side there stood a cheese too large and strong to sleep near comfortably, and I therefore chose the dry-goods side. Here thick quilts were unrolled for me, to make it soft; and no condition was placed upon me, further than that I should remove my boots, because the quilts were new, and clean, and for sale. So now my rest was assured. Not an anxiety remained in my thoughts. These therefore turned themselves wholly to the other man's bed, and how he was going to lose it.

I think that Steve was more curious even than myself. Time was on the wing. His bet must be decided, and the drinks enjoyed. He stood against the grocery counter, contemplating the Virginian. But it was to me that he spoke. The Virginian, however, listened to every word.

'Your first visit to this country?'

I told him yes.

'How do you like it?'

I expected to like it very much.

'How does the climate strike you?'

I thought the climate was fine.

'Makes a man thirsty though.'

This was the sub-current which the Virginian plainly looked for. But he, like Steve, addressed himself to me.

'Yes,' he put in, 'thirsty while a man's soft yet. You'll harden.'

'I guess you'll find it a drier country than you were given to expect,' said Steve.

'If your habits have been frequent that way,' said the Virginian.

'There's parts of Wyoming,' pursued Steve, 'where you'll go hours and hours before you'll see a drop of wetness.'

'And if yu' keep a-thinkin' about it,' said the Virginian, 'it'll seem like days and days.'

Steve, at this stroke, gave up, and clapped him on the shoulder with a joyous chuckle. 'You old son-of-a-bitch!' he cried affectionately.

'Drinks are due now,' said the Virginian. 'My treat, Steve. But I reckon your suspense will have to linger a while yet.'

Thus they dropped into direct talk from that speech of the fourth dimension where they had been using me for their telephone.

'Any cyards going tonight?' enquired the Virginian.

'Stud and draw,' Steve told him. 'Strangers playing.'

'I think I'd like to get into a game for a while,' said the Southerner. 'Strangers, yu' say?'

And then, before quitting the store, he made his toilet for this little hand at poker. It was a simple preparation. He took his pistol from its holster, examined it, then shoved it between his overalls and his shirt in front, and pulled his waistcoat over it. He might have been combing his hair for all the attention anyone paid to this, except myself. Then the two friends went out, and I bethought me of that epithet which Steve again had used to the Virginian as he clapped him on the shoulder. Clearly this wild country spoke a language other than mine – the word here was a term of endearment. Such was my conclusion.

The drummers had finished their dealings with the proprietor, and they were gossiping together in a knot by the door as the Virginian passed out.

'See you later, old man!' This was the American drummer accosting his prospective bedfellow.

'Oh, yes,' returned the bedfellow, and was gone.

The American drummer winked triumphantly at his brethren. 'He's all right,' he observed, jerking a thumb after the Virginian. 'He's easy. You got to know him to work him. That's all.'

'Und vat is your point?' enquired the German drummer.

'Point is – he'll not take any goods off you or me; but he's going to talk up the killer to any consumptive he runs acrost. I ain't done with him yet. Say' (he now addressed the proprietor), 'what's her name?'

'Whose name?'

'Woman runs the eating-house.'

'Glen. Mrs Glen.'

'Ain't she new?'

'Been settled here about a month. Husband's a freight conductor.'

'Thought I'd not seen her before. She's a good looker.'

'Hm! Yes. The kind of good looks I'd sooner see in another man's wife than mine.'

'So that's the gait, is it?'

'Hm! well, it don't seem to be. She come here with that reputation. But there's been general disappointment.'

'Then she ain't lacked suitors any?'

'Lacked! Are you acquainted with cowboys?'

'And she disappointed 'em? Maybe she likes her husband?'

'Hm! well, how are you to tell about them silent kind?'

'Talking of conductors,' began the drummer. And we listened to his anecdote. It was successful with his audience; but when he launched fluently upon a second I strolled out. There was not enough wit in this narrator to relieve his indecency, and I felt shame at having been surprised into laughing with him.

I left that company growing confidential over their leering stories, and I sought the saloon. It was very quiet and orderly. Beer in quart bottles at a dollar I had never met before; but saving its price, I found no complaint to make of it. Through folding doors I passed from the bar proper with its bottles and elk head back to the hall with its various tables. I saw a man sliding cards from a case, and across the table from him another man laying counters down. Near by was a second dealer pulling cards from the bottom of a pack, and opposite him a solemn old rustic piling and changing coins upon the cards which lay already exposed.

But now I heard a voice that drew my eyes to the far corner of the room.

'Why didn't you stay in Arizona?'

Harmless looking words as I write them down here. Yet at the sound of them I noticed the eyes of the others directed to that corner. What answer was given to them I did not hear, nor did I see who spoke. Then came another remark.

'Well, Arizona's no place for amateurs.'

This time the two card dealers that I stood near began to give a part of their attention to the group that sat in the corner. There was in me a desire to leave this room. So far my hours at Medicine Bow had seemed to glide beneath a sunshine of merriment, of easy-going jocularity. This was suddenly gone, like the wind changing to north in the middle of a warm day. But I stayed, being ashamed to go.

Five or six players sat over in the corner at a round table where counters were piled. Their eyes were close upon their cards, and one seemed to be dealing a card at a time to each, with pauses and betting between. Steve was there and the Virginian; the others were new faces.

'No place for amateurs,' repeated the voice; and now I saw that it was the dealer's. There was in his countenance the same ugliness that his words conveyed.

'Who's that talkin'?' said one of the men near me, in a low voice.

'Trampas.'

'What's he?'

'Cowpuncher, bronco-buster, tinhorn, most anything.'

'Who's he talkin' at?'

'Think it's the black-headed guy he's talking at.'

'That ain't supposed to be safe, is it?'

'Guess we're all goin' to find out in a few minutes.'

'Been trouble between 'em?'

'They've not met before. Trampas don't enjoy losin' to a stranger.'

'Fello's from Arizona, yu' say?'

'No. Virginia. He's recently back from havin' a look at Arizona. Went down there last year for a change. Works for the Sunk Creek outfit.' And then the dealer lowered his voice still further and said something in the other man's ear, causing him to grin. After which both of them looked at me.

There had been silence over in the corner; but now the man Trampas spoke again.

'*And* ten,' said he, sliding out some chips from before him. Very strange it was to hear him, how he contrived to make those words a personal taunt. The Virginian was looking at his cards. He might have been deaf.

'*And* twenty,' said the next player, easily.

The next threw his cards down.

It was now the Virginian's turn to bet, or leave the game, and he did not speak at once.

Therefore Trampas spoke. 'Your bet, you son-of-a-bitch.'

The Virginian's pistol came out, and his hand lay on the table, holding it unaimed. And with a voice as gentle as ever, the voice that sounded almost like a caress, but drawling a very little more than usual, so that there was almost a space between each word, he issued his orders to the man Trampas – 'When you call me that, smile!' And he looked at Trampas across the table.

Yes, the voice was gentle. But in my ears it seemed as if somewhere the bell of death was ringing; and silence, like a stroke, fell on the large room. All men present, as if by some magnetic current, had become aware of this crisis. In my ignorance, and the total stoppage of my thoughts, I stood stock-still, and noticed various people crouching, or shifting their positions.

'Sit quiet,' said the dealer, scornfully to the man near me. 'Can't you see he don't want to push trouble? He has handed Trampas the choice to back down or draw his steel.'

Then, with equal suddenness and ease, the room came out of its strangeness. Voices and cards, the click of chips, the puff of tobacco, glasses lifted to drink – this level of smooth relaxation hinted no more plainly of what lay beneath than does the surface tell the depth of the sea.

For Trampas had made his choice. And that choice was not to 'draw his steel'. If it was knowledge that he sought, he had found it, and no mistake! We heard no further reference to what he had been pleased to style 'amateurs'. In no company would the black-headed man who had visited Arizona be rated a novice at the cool art of self-preservation.

One doubt remained: what kind of a man was Trampas? A public back-down is an unfinished thing – for some natures at least. I looked at his face, and thought it sullen, but tricky rather than courageous.

Something had been added to my knowledge also. Once again I had heard applied to the Virginian that epithet which Steve so freely used. The same words, identical to the letter. But this time they had produced a pistol. 'When you call me that, *smile*!' So I perceived a new example of the old truth, that the letter means nothing until the spirit gives it life.

CHAPTER 3

Steve Treats

It was for several minutes, I suppose, that I stood drawing these silent morals. No man occupied himself with me. Quiet voices, and games of chance, and glasses lifted to drink, continued to be the peaceful order of the night. And into my thoughts broke the voice of that card-dealer who had already spoken so sagely. He also took his turn at moralising.

'What did I tell you?' he remarked to the man for whom he continued to deal, and who continued to lose money to him.

'Tell me when?'

'Didn't I tell you he'd not shoot?' the dealer pursued with complacence. 'You got ready to dodge. You had no call to be concerned. He's not the kind a man need feel anxious about.'

The player looked over at the Virginian, doubtfully. 'Well,' he said, 'I don't know what you folks call a dangerous man.'

'Not him!' exclaimed the dealer with admiration. 'He's a brave man. That's different.'

The player seemed to follow this reasoning no better than I did.

'It's not a brave man that's dangerous,' continued the dealer. 'It's the cowards that scare me.' He paused that this might sink home.

'Fello' came in here las' Toosday,' he went on. 'He got into some misunderstanding about the drinks. Well, sir, before we could put him out of business, he'd hurt two perfectly innocent onlookers. They'd no more to do with it than you have,' the dealer explained to me.

'Were they badly hurt?' I asked.

'One of 'em was. He's died since.'

'What became of the man?'

'Why, we put him out of business, I told you. He died that night. But there was no occasion for any of it; and that's why I never like to be around where there's a coward. You can't tell. He'll always go to shooting before it's necessary, and there's no security who he'll hit. But a man like that black-headed guy is' (the dealer indicated the Virginian) 'need never worry you. And there's another point why there's no need to worry about him: *it'll be too late!*'

These good words ended the moralising of the dealer. He had given us a piece of his mind. He now gave the whole of it to dealing cards. I loitered here and there, neither welcome nor unwelcome at present, watching the cowboys at their play. Saving Trampas, there was scarce a face among them that had not in it something very likeable. Here were lusty horsemen ridden from the heat of the sun, and the wet of the storm, to divert themselves awhile. Youth untamed sat here for an idle moment, spending easily its hard-earned wages. City saloons rose into my vision, and I instantly preferred this Rocky Mountain place. More of death it undoubtedly saw, but less of vice, than did its New York equivalents. And death is a thing much cleaner than vice. Moreover, it was by no means vice that was written upon these wild and manly faces. Even where baseness was visible, baseness was not uppermost. Daring, laughter, endurance – these were what I saw upon the countenances of the cowboys. And this very first day of my knowledge of them marks a date with me. For something about them, and the idea of them, smote my American heart, and I have never forgotten it nor ever shall, as long as I live. In their flesh our natural passions ran tumultuous; but often in their spirit sat hidden a true nobility, and often beneath its unexpected shining their figures took on heroic stature.

The dealer had styled the Virginian 'a black-headed guy'. This did well enough as an unflattered portrait. Judge Henry's trustworthy man, with whom I was to drive two hundred and sixty-three miles, certainly had a very black head of hair. It was the first thing to notice now, if one glanced generally at the table where he sat at cards. But the eye came back to him – drawn by that inexpressible something which had led the dealer to speak so much at length about him.

Still, 'black-headed guy' justly fits him and his next performance. He had made his plan for this like a true and (I must say) inspired devil. And now the highly appreciative town of Medicine Bow was to be treated to a manifestation of genius.

He sat playing his stud-poker. After a decent period of losing and winning, which gave Trampas all proper time for a change of luck and a repairing of his fortunes, he looked at Steve and said amiably – 'How does bed strike you?'

I was beside their table, learning gradually that stud-poker has in it more of what I will call red pepper than has our Eastern game. The Virginian followed his own question – 'Bed strikes me,' he stated.

Steve feigned indifference. He was far more deeply absorbed in his bet and the American drummer than he was in this game; but he chose to take out a fat, florid gold watch, consult it elaborately, and remark, 'It's only eleven.'

'Yu' forget I'm from the country,' said the black-headed guy. 'The chickens have been roostin' a right smart while.'

His sunny Southern accent was again strong. In that brief passage with Trampas it had been almost wholly absent. But different moods of the spirit bring different qualities of utterance – where a man comes by these naturally. The Virginian cashed in his checks.

'Awhile ago,' said Steve, 'you had won three months' salary.'

'I'm still twenty dollars to the good,' said the Virginian. 'That's better than breaking a laig.'

Again, in some voiceless, masonic way, most people in that saloon had become aware that something was in process of happening. Several left their games and came to the front by the bar.

'If he ain't in bed yet – ' mused the Virginian.

'I'll find out,' said I. And I hurried across to the dim sleeping-room, happy to have a part in this.

They were all in bed; and in some beds two were sleeping. How they could do it – but in those days I was fastidious. The American had come in recently and was still awake.

'Thought you were to sleep at the store?' said he. So then I invented a little lie, and explained that I was in search of the Virginian.

'Better search the dives,' said he. 'These cowboys don't get to town often.'

At this point I stumbled sharply over something.

'It's my box of Consumption Killer,' explained the drummer. 'Well, I hope that man will stay out all night.'

'Bed narrow?' I enquired.

'For two it is. And the pillows are mean. Takes both before you feel anything's under your head.'

He yawned, and I wished him pleasant dreams.

At my news the Virginian left the bar at once, and crossed to the sleeping-room. Steve and I followed softly, and behind us several more strung out in an expectant line. 'What is this going to be?' they enquired curiously of each other. And upon learning the great novelty of the event, they clustered with silence intense outside the door where the Virginian had gone in.

We heard the voice of the drummer, cautioning his bedfellow. 'Don't trip over the Killer,' he was saying. 'The Prince of Wales barked his shin just now.' It seemed my English clothes had earned me this title.

The boots of the Virginian were next heard to drop.

'Can yu' make out what he's at?' whispered Steve.

He was plainly undressing. The rip of swift unbuttoning told us that the black-headed guy must now be removing his overalls.

'Why, thank yu', no,' he was replying to a question of the drummer. 'Outside or in's all one to me.'

'Then, if you'd just as soon take the wall –'

'Why, cert'nly.' There was a sound of bedclothes, and creaking. 'This hyeh pillo' needs a Southern climate,' was the Virginian's next observation.

Many listeners had now gathered at the door. The dealer and the player were both here. The storekeeper was present, and I recognised the agent of the Union Pacific Railroad among the crowd. We made a large company, and I felt that trembling sensation which is common when the cap of a camera is about to be removed upon a group.

'I should think,' said the drummer's voice, 'that you'd feel your knife and gun clean through that pillow.'

'I do,' responded the Virginian.

'I should think you'd put them on a chair and be comfortable.'

'I'd be uncomfortable, then.'

'Used to the feel of them, I suppose?'

'That's it. Used to the feel of them. I would miss them, and that would make me wakeful.'

'Well, good-night.'

'Good-night. If I get to talkin' and tossin', or what not, you'll understand you're to – '

'Yes, I'll wake you.'

'No, don't yu', for God's sake!'

'Not?'

'Don't yu' touch me.'

'What'll I do?'

'Roll away quick to your side. It don't last but a minute.' The Virginian spoke with a reassuring drawl.

Upon this there fell a brief silence, and I heard the drummer clear his throat once or twice.

'It's merely the nightmare, I suppose?' he said after a throat clearing.

'Lord, yes. That's all. And don't happen twice a year. Was you thinkin' it was fits?'

'Oh, no! I just wanted to know. I've been told before that it was not safe for a person to be waked suddenly that way out of a nightmare.'

'Yes, I have heard that too. But it never harms me any. I didn't want you to run risks.'

'Me?'

'Oh, it'll be all right now that yu' know how it is.' The Virginian's drawl was full of assurance.

There was a second pause, after which the drummer said – 'Tell me again how it is.'

The Virginian answered very drowsily: 'Oh, just don't let your arm or your laig touch me if I go to jumpin' around. I'm dreamin' of Indians when I do that. And if anything touches me then, I'm liable to grab my knife right in my sleep.'

'Oh, I understand,' said the drummer, clearing his throat. 'Yes.'

Steve was whispering delighted oaths to himself, and in his joy applying to the Virginian one unprintable name after another.

We listened again, but now no further words came. Listening very hard, I could half make out the progress of a heavy breathing, and a restless turning I could clearly detect. This was the wretched drummer. He was waiting. But he did not wait long. Again there was a light creak, and after it a light step. He was not even going to put his boots on in the fatal neighbourhood of the dreamer. By a happy thought Medicine Bow formed into two lines, making an avenue from the door. And then the commercial traveller forgot his Consumption Killer. He fell heavily over it.

Immediately from the bed the Virginian gave forth a dreadful howl.

And then everything happened at once; and how shall mere words narrate it? The door burst open, and out flew the commercial traveller in his stockings. One hand held a lump of coat and trousers with suspenders dangling, his boots were clutched in the other. The sight of us stopped his flight short. He gazed, the boots fell from his hand; and at his profane explosion, Medicine Bow set up a united, unearthly noise and began to play Virginia reel with him. The other occupants of the beds had already sprung out of them, clothed chiefly with their pistols, and ready for war.

'What is it?' they demanded. 'What is it?'

'Why, I reckon it's drinks on Steve,' said the Virginian from his bed. And he gave the first broad grin that I had seen from him.

'I'll set 'em up all night!' Steve shouted, as the reel went on regardless. The drummer was bawling to be allowed to put at least his boots on. 'This way, Pard,' was the answer; and another man whirled him round. 'This way, Beau!' they called to him; 'This way, Budd!' and he was passed like a shuttlecock down the line. Suddenly the leaders bounded into the sleeping-room. 'Feed the machine!' they said. 'Feed her!' And seizing the German drummer who sold jewellery, they flung him into the trough of the reel. I saw him go bouncing like an ear of corn to be shelled, and the dance engulfed him. I saw a Jew sent rattling after him; and next they threw in the railroad employee, and the other Jew; and while I stood mesmerised, my own feet left the earth. I shot from the room and sped like a bobbing cork into this mill race, whirling my turn in the wake of the others amid cries of, 'Here comes the Prince of Wales!' There was soon not much English left about my raiment.

They were now shouting for music. Medicine Bow swept in like a cloud of dust to where a fiddler sat playing in a hall; and gathering up fiddler and dancers, swept out again, a larger Medicine Bow, growing all the while. Steve offered us the freedom of the house, everywhere. He implored us to call for whatever pleased us, and as many times as we should please. He ordered the town to be searched for more citizens to come and help him pay his bet. But changing his mind, kegs and bottles were now carried along with us. We had found three fiddlers, and these played busily for us; and thus we set out to visit all cabins and houses where people might still by some miracle be asleep. The first man put out his head to decline. But such a possibility had been foreseen by the proprietor of the store. This seemingly respectable man now came dragging some sort of apparatus from his place, helped by the Virginian. The cowboys cheered, for they knew what this was. The man in his window likewise recognised it, and uttering a groan, came immediately out and joined us. What it was, I also learned in a few minutes. For we found a house where the people made no sign at either our fiddlers or our knocking. And then the infernal machine was set to work. Its parts seemed to be no more than an empty keg and a plank. Some citizen informed me that I should soon have a new idea of noise; and I nerved myself for something severe in the way of gunpowder. But the Virginian and the proprietor now sat on the ground holding the keg braced, and two others got down apparently to play see-saw over the top of it with the plank. But the keg and plank had been rubbed with rosin, and they drew the plank back and forth over the keg. Do you know the sound made in a narrow street by a dray loaded with strips of iron? That noise is a lullaby compared with the staggering, blinding bellow which rose from the keg. If you were to try it in your native town, you would not merely be arrested, you would be hanged, and everybody would be glad, and the clergyman would not bury you. My head, my teeth, the whole system of my bones leaped and chattered at the din, and out of the house like drops squirted from a lemon came a man and his wife. No time was given them. They were swept along with the rest; and having been routed from their own bed, they now became most furious in assailing the remaining homes of Medicine Bow. Everybody was to come out. Many were now riding horses at top speed out into the plains and back, while the procession of the plank and keg continued its work, and the fiddlers played incessantly.

Suddenly there was a quiet. I did not see who brought the message; but the word ran among us that there was a woman – the engineer's woman down by the water-tank – very sick. The doctor had been to see her from Laramie. Everybody liked the engineer. Plank and keg were heard no more. The horsemen found it out and restrained their gambols. Medicine Bow went gradually home. I saw doors shutting, and lights go out; I saw a late few reassemble at the card tables, and the drummers gathered themselves together for sleep; the proprietor of the store (you could not see a more respectable-looking person) hoped that I would be comfortable on the quilts; and I heard Steve urging the Virginian to take one more glass.

'We've not met for so long,' he said.

But the Virginian, the black-headed guy who had set all this nonsense going, said no to Steve. 'I have got to stay responsible,' was his excuse to his friend. And the friend looked at me. Therefore I surmised that the Judge's trustworthy man found me an embarrassment to his holiday. But if he did, he never showed it to me. He had been sent to meet a stranger and drive him to Sunk Creek in safety, and this charge he would allow no temptation to imperil. He nodded good-night to me. 'If there's anything I can do for yu', you'll tell me.'

I thanked him. 'What a pleasant evening!' I added.

'I'm glad yu' found it so.'

Again his manner put a bar to my approaches. Even though I had seen him wildly disporting himself, those were matters which he chose not to discuss with me.

Medicine Bow was quiet as I went my way to my quilts. So still, that through the air the deep whistles of the freight trains came from below the horizon across great miles of silence. I passed cowboys, whom half an hour before I had seen prancing and roaring, now rolled in their blankets beneath the open and shining night.

'What world am I in?' I said aloud. 'Does this same planet hold Fifth Avenue?'

And I went to sleep, pondering over my native land.

CHAPTER 4

Deep into Cattle Land

Morning had been for some while astir in Medicine Bow before I left my quilts. The new day and its doings began around me in the store, chiefly at the grocery counter. Dry goods were not in great request. The early rising cowboys were off again to their work; and those to whom their night's holiday had left any dollars were spending these for tobacco, or cartridges, or canned provisions for the journey to their distant camps. Sardines were called for, and potted chicken, and devilled ham: a sophisticated nourishment, at first sight, for these sons of the sagebrush. But portable ready-made food plays of necessity a great part in the opening of a new country. These picnic pots and cans were the first of her trophies that Civilisation dropped upon Wyoming's virgin soil. The cowboy is now gone to worlds invisible; the wind has blown away the white ashes of his camp-fires; but the empty sardine box lies rusting over the face of the Western earth.

So through my eyes half closed I watched the sale of these tins, and grew familiar with the ham's inevitable trade mark – that label with the devil and his horns and hoofs and tail very pronounced, all coloured a sultry prodigious scarlet. And when each horseman had made his purchase, he would trail his spurs over the floor, and presently the sound of his horse's hoofs would be the last of him. Through my dozing attention came various fragments of talk, and sometimes useful bits of knowledge. For instance, I learned the true value of tomatoes in this country. One fellow was buying two cans of them.

'Meadow Creek dry already?' commented the proprietor.

'Been dry ten days,' the young cowboy informed him. And it appeared that along the road he was going, water would not be reached much before sundown, because this Meadow Creek had ceased to run. His tomatoes were for drink. And thus they have refreshed me many times since.

'No beer?' suggested the proprietor.

The boy made a shuddering face. 'Don't say its name to me!' he exclaimed. 'I couldn't hold my breakfast down.' He rang his silver money upon the counter. 'I've swore off for three months,' he stated. 'I'm going to be as pure as the snow!' And away he went jingling out of the door, to ride seventy-five miles. Three more months of hard, unsheltered work, and he would ride into town again, with his adolescent blood crying aloud for its own.

'I'm obliged,' said a new voice, rousing me from a new doze. 'She's easier this morning, since the medicine.' This was the engineer, whose sick wife had brought a hush over Medicine Bow's rioting. 'I'll give her them flowers soon as she wakes,' he added.

'Flowers?' repeated the proprietor.

'You didn't leave that bunch at our door?'

'Wish I'd thought to do it.'

'She likes to see flowers,' said the engineer. And he walked out slowly, with his thanks unachieved. He returned at once with the Virginian; for in the band of the Virginian's hat were two or three blossoms.

'It don't need mentioning,' the Southerner was saying, embarrassed by any expression of thanks. 'If we had knowed last night –'

'You didn't disturb her any,' broke in the engineer. 'She's easier this morning. I'll tell her about them flowers.'

'Why, it don't need mentioning,' the Virginian again protested, almost crossly. 'The little things looked kind o' fresh, and I just picked them.' His eye now fell upon me, where I lay upon the counter. 'I reckon breakfast will be getting through,' he remarked.

I was soon at the wash-trough. It was only half-past six, but many had been before me – one glance at the roller-towel told me that. I was afraid to ask the landlady for a clean one, and so I found a fresh handkerchief, and accomplished a sparing toilet. In the midst of this the drummers joined me, one by one, and they used the degraded towel without hesitation. In a way they had the best of me; filth was nothing to them.

The latest risers in Medicine Bow, we sat at breakfast together; and they essayed some light familiarities with the landlady. But these experiments were failures. Her eyes did not see, nor did her ears hear them. She brought the coffee and the bacon with a sedateness that propriety itself could scarce have surpassed. Yet impropriety lurked noiselessly all over her. You could not have specified how; it was interblended with her sum total. Silence was her apparent habit and her weapon; but the American drummer found that she could speak to the point when need came for this. During the meal he had praised her golden hair. It was golden indeed, and worth a high compliment; but his kind displeased her. She had let it pass, however, with no more than a cool stare. But on taking his leave, when he came to pay for the meal, he pushed it too far.

'Pity this must be our last,' he said; and as it brought no answer, 'Ever travel?' he enquired. 'Where I go, there's room for a pair of us.'

'Then you'd better find another jackass,' she replied quietly.

I was glad that I had not asked for a clean towel.

From the commercial travellers I now separated myself, and wandered alone in pleasurable aimlessness. It was seven o'clock. Medicine Bow stood voiceless and unpeopled. The cowboys had melted away. The inhabitants were indoors, pursuing the business or the idleness of the forenoon. Visible motion there was none. No shell upon the dry sands could lie more lifeless than Medicine Bow. Looking in at the store, I saw the proprietor sitting with his pipe extinct. Looking in at the saloon, I saw the dealer dealing dumbly to himself. Up in the sky there was not a cloud nor a bird, and on the earth the lightest straw lay becalmed. Once I saw the Virginian at an open door, where the golden-haired landlady stood talking with him. Sometimes I strolled in the town, and sometimes out on the plain I lay down with my day dreams in the sagebrush. Pale herds of antelope were in the distance, and near by the demure prairie-dogs sat up and scrutinised me. Steve, Trampas, the riot of horsemen, my lost trunk, Uncle Hughey, with his abortive brides – all things merged in my thoughts in a huge, delicious indifference. It was like swimming slowly at random in an ocean that was smooth, and neither too cool nor too warm. And before I knew it, five lazy imperceptible hours had gone thus. There was the Union Pacific train, coming as if from shores forgotten.

Its approach was silent and long drawn out. I easily reached town and the platform before it had finished watering at the tank. It moved up, made a short halt, I saw my trunk come out of it, and then it moved away silently as it had come, smoking and dwindling into distance unknown.

Beside my trunk was one other, tied extravagantly with white ribbon. The fluttering bows caught my attention, and now I suddenly saw a perfectly new sight. The Virginian was further down the platform, doubled up with laughing. It was good to know that with sufficient cause he could laugh like this; a smile had thus far been his limit of external mirth. Rice now flew against my hat, and hissing gusts of rice spouted on the platform. All the men left in Medicine Bow appeared like magic, and more rice choked the atmosphere. Through the general clamour a cracked voice said, 'Don't hit her in the eye, boys!' and Uncle Hughey rushed proudly by me with an actual wife on his arm. She could easily have been his granddaughter. They got at once into a vehicle. The trunk was lifted in behind. And amid cheers, rice, shoes, and broad felicitations, the pair drove out of town, Uncle Hughey shrieking to the horses and the bride waving unabashed adieus.

The word had come over the wires from Laramie: 'Uncle Hughey has made it this time. Expect him on today's number two.' And Medicine Bow had expected him.

Many words arose on the departure of the newly married couple.

'Who's she?'

'What's he got for her?'

'Got a gold mine up Bear Creek.'

And after comment and prophecy, Medicine Bow returned to its dinner.

This meal was my last here for a long while. The Virginian's responsibility now returned; duty drove the Judge's trustworthy man to take care of me again. He had not once sought my society of his own accord; his distaste for what he supposed me to be (I don't exactly know what this was) remained unshaken. I have thought that matters of dress and speech should not carry with them so much mistrust in our democracy; thieves are presumed innocent until proved guilty, but a starched collar is condemned at once. Perfect civility and obligingness I certainly did receive from the Virginian, only not a word of fellowship. He harnessed the horses, got my trunk, and gave me some advice about taking provisions for our journey, something more palatable than what food we should find along the road. It was well thought of, and I bought quite a parcel of dainties, feeling that he would despise both them and me. And thus I took my seat beside him, wondering what we should manage to talk about for two hundred and sixty-three miles.

Farewell in those days was not said in Cattle Land. Acquaintances watched our departure with a nod or with nothing, and the nearest approach to 'Goodbye' was the proprietor's 'So long'. But I caught sight of one farewell given without words.

As we drove by the eating-house, the shade of a side window was raised, and the landlady looked her last upon the Virginian. Her lips were faintly parted, and no woman's eyes ever said more plainly, 'I am one of your possessions.' She had forgotten that it might be seen. Her glance caught mine, and she backed into the dimness of the room. What look she may have received from him, if he gave her any at this too public moment, I could not tell. His eyes seemed to be upon the horses, and he drove with the same mastering ease that had roped the wild pony yesterday. We passed the ramparts of Medicine Bow – thick heaps and fringes of tin cans, and shelving mounds of bottles cast out of the saloons. The sun struck these at a hundred glittering points. And in a moment we were in the clean plains, with the prairie-dogs and the pale herds of antelope. The great, still air bathed us, pure as water and strong as wine; the sunlight flooded the world; and shining upon the breast of the Virginian's flannel shirt lay a long gold thread of hair! The noisy American drummer had met defeat, but this silent free lance had been easily victorious.

It must have been five miles that we travelled in silence, losing and seeing the horizon among the ceaseless waves of the earth. Then I looked back, and there was Medicine Bow, seemingly a stone's throw behind us. It was a full half-hour before I looked back again, and there sure enough was always Medicine Bow. A size or two smaller, I will admit, but visible in every feature, like something seen through the wrong end of a field glass. The East-bound express was approaching the town, and I noticed the white steam from its whistle; but when the sound reached us, the train had almost stopped. And in reply to my comment upon this, the Virginian deigned to remark that it was more so in Arizona.

'A man come to Arizona,' he said, 'with one of them telescopes to study the heavenly bodies. He was a Yankee, seh, and a right smart one, too. And one night we was watchin' for some little old fallin' stars that he said was due, and I saw some lights movin' along acrost the mesa pretty lively, an' I sang out. But he told me it was just the train. And I told him I didn't know yu' could see the cyars that plain from his place. "Yu' can see them," he said to me, "but it is las' night's cyars you're lookin' at." ' At this point the Virginian spoke severely to one of the horses. 'Of course,' he then resumed to me, 'that Yankee man did not mean quite all he said. – You, Buck!' he again broke off suddenly to the horse. 'But Arizona, seh,' he continued, 'cert'nly has a mos' deceivin' atmospheah. Another man told me he had seen a lady close one eye at him when he was two minutes hard run from her.' This time the Virginian gave Buck the whip.

'What effect,' I enquired with a gravity equal to his own, 'does this extraordinary foreshortening have upon a quart of whiskey?'

'When it's outside yu', seh, no distance looks too far to go to it.'

He glanced at me with an eye that held more confidence than hitherto he had been able to feel in me. I had made one step in his approval. But I had many yet to go. This day he preferred his own thoughts to my conversation, and so he did all the days of this first journey; while I should have greatly preferred his conversation to my thoughts. He dismissed some attempts that I made upon the subject of Uncle Hughey; so that I had not the courage to touch upon Trampas, and that chill brief collision which might have struck the spark of death. Trampas! I had forgotten him till this silent drive I was beginning. I wondered if I should ever see him, or Steve, or any of those people again. And this wonder I expressed aloud.

'There's no tellin' in this country,' said the Virginian. 'Folks come easy, and they go easy. In settled places, like back in the States, even a poor man mostly has a home. Don't care if it's only a barrel on a lot, the fello' will keep frequentin' that lot, and if yu' want him yu' can find him. But out hyeh in the sagebrush, a man's home is apt to be his saddle blanket. First thing yu' know, he has moved it to Texas.'

'You have done some moving yourself,' I suggested.

But this word closed his mouth. 'I have had a look at the country,' he said, and we were silent again. Let me, however, tell you here that he had set out for a 'look at the country' at the age of fourteen; and that by his present age of twenty-four he had seen Arkansas, Texas, New Mexico, Arizona, California, Oregon, Idaho, Montana, and Wyoming. Everywhere he had taken care of himself, and survived; nor had his strong heart yet waked up to any hunger for a home. Let me also tell you that he was one of thousands drifting and living thus, but (as you shall learn) one in a thousand.

Medicine Bow did not forever remain in sight. When next I thought of it and looked behind, nothing was there but the road we had come; it lay like a ship's wake across the huge ground swell of the earth. We were swallowed in a vast solitude. A little while before sunset, a cabin came in view; and here we passed our first night. Two young men lived here, tending their cattle. They were fond of animals. By the stable a chained coyote rushed nervously in a circle, or sat on its haunches and snapped at gifts of food ungraciously. A tame young elk walked in and out of the cabin door, and during supper it tried to push me off my chair. A half-tame mountain sheep practised jumping from the ground to the roof. The cabin was papered with posters of a circus, and skins of bear and silver fox lay upon the floor. Until nine o'clock one man talked to the Virginian, and one played gaily upon a concertina; and then we all went to bed. The air was like December, but in my blankets and a buffalo robe I kept warm, and luxuriated in the Rocky Mountain silence. Going to wash before breakfast at sunrise, I found needles of ice in a pail. Yet it was hard to remember that this quiet, open, splendid wilderness (with not a peak in sight just here) was six thousand feet high. And when breakfast was over there was no December left; and by the time the Virginian and I were ten miles upon our way, it was June. But always every breath that I breathed was pure as water and strong as wine.

We never passed a human being this day. Some wild cattle rushed up to us and away from us; antelope stared at us from a hundred yards; coyotes ran skulking through the sagebrush to watch us from a hill; at our noon meal we killed a rattlesnake and shot some young sage chickens, which were good at supper, roasted at our camp-fire.

By half-past eight we were asleep beneath the stars, and by half-past four I was drinking coffee and shivering. The horse, Buck, was hard to catch this second morning. Whether some hills that we were now in had excited him, or whether the better water up here had caused an effervescence in his spirits, I cannot say. But I was as hot as July by the time we had him safe in harness, or, rather, unsafe in harness. For Buck, in the mysterious language of horses, now taught wickedness to his side partner, and about eleven o'clock they laid their evil heads together and decided to break our necks.

We were passing, I have said, through a range of demi-mountains. It was a little country where trees grew, water ran, and the plains were shut out for a while. The road had steep places in it, and places here and there where you could fall off and go bounding to the bottom among stones. But Buck, for some reason, did not think these opportunities good enough for him. He selected a more theatrical moment. We emerged from a narrow canyon suddenly upon five hundred cattle and some cowboys branding calves by a fire in a corral. It was a sight that Buck knew by heart. He instantly treated it like an appalling phenomenon. I saw him kick seven ways; I saw Muggins kick five ways; our furious motion snapped my spine like a whip. I grasped the seat. Something gave a forlorn jingle. It was the brake.

'Don't jump!' commanded the trustworthy man.

'No,' I said, as my hat flew off.

Help was too far away to do anything for us. We passed scathless through a part of the cattle; I saw their horns and backs go by. Some earth crumbled, and we plunged downward into water, rocking among stones, and upward again through some more crumbling earth. I heard a crash, and saw my trunk landing in the stream.

'She's safer there,' said the trustworthy man.

'True,' I said.

'We'll go back for her,' said he, with his eye on the horses and his foot on the crippled brake. A dry gully was coming, and no room to turn. The farther side of it was terraced with rock. We should simply fall backward, if we did not fall forward first. He steered the horses straight over, and just at the bottom swung them, with astonishing skill, to the right along the hard baked mud. They took us along the bed up to the head of the gully, and through a thicket of quaking asps. The light trees bent beneath our charge and bastinadoed the wagon as it went over them. But their branches enmeshed the horses' legs, and we came to a harmless standstill among a bower of leaves.

I looked at the trustworthy man, and smiled vaguely. He considered me for a moment.

'I reckon,' said he, 'you're feelin' about halfway between "Oh, Lord!" and "Thank God!"'

'That's quite it,' said I, as he got down on the ground.

'Nothing's broke,' said he, after a searching examination. And he indulged in a true Virginian expletive. 'Gentlemen, hush!' he murmured gently, looking at me with his grave eyes; 'one time I got pretty near scared. You, Buck,' he continued, 'some folks would beat you now till yu'd be uncertain whether yu' was a hawss or a railroad accident. I'd do it myself, only it wouldn't cure yu'.'

I now told him that I supposed he had saved both our lives. But he detested words of direct praise. He made some grumbling rejoinder, and led the horses out of the thicket. Buck, he explained to me, was a good horse, and so was Muggins. Both of them generally meant well, and that was the Judge's reason for sending them to meet me. But these broncos had their off days. Off days might not come very often; but when the humour seized a bronco, he had to have his spree. Buck would now behave himself as a horse should for probably two months. 'They are just like humans,' the Virginian concluded.

Several cowboys arrived on a gallop to find how many pieces of us were left. We returned down the hill; and when we reached my trunk, it was surprising to see the distance that our runaway had covered. My hat was also found, and we continued on our way.

Buck and Muggins were patterns of discretion through the rest of the mountains. I thought when we camped this night that it was strange Buck should be again allowed to graze at large, instead of being tied to a rope while we slept. But this was my ignorance. With the hard work that he was gallantly doing, the horse needed more pasture than a rope's length would permit him to find. Therefore he went free, and in the morning gave us but little trouble in catching him.

We crossed a river in the forenoon, and far to the north of us we saw the Bow Leg Mountains, pale in the bright sun. Sunk Creek flowed from their western side, and our two hundred and sixty-three miles began to grow a small thing in my eyes. Buck and Muggins, I think, knew perfectly that tomorrow would see them home. They recognised this region; and once they turned off at a fork in the road. The Virginian pulled them back rather sharply.

'Want to go back to Balaam's?' he enquired of them. 'I thought you had more sense.'

I asked, Who was Balaam?

'A maltreater of hawsses,' replied the cowpuncher. 'His ranch is on Butte Creek oveh yondeh.' And he pointed to where the diverging road melted into space. 'The Judge bought Buck and Muggins from him in the spring.'

'So he maltreats horses?' I repeated.

'That's the word all through this country. A man that will do what they claim Balaam does to a hawss when he's mad, ain't fit to be called human.' The Virginian told me some particulars.

'Oh!' I almost screamed at the horror of it, and again, 'Oh!'

'He'd have prob'ly done that to Buck as soon as he stopped runnin' away. If I caught a man doin' that – '

We were interrupted by a sedate-looking traveller riding upon an equally sober horse.

'Mawnin', Taylor,' said the Virginian, pulling up for gossip. 'Ain't you strayed off your range pretty far?'

'You're a nice one!' replied Mr Taylor, stopping his horse and smiling amiably.

'Tell me something I don't know,' retorted the Virginian.

'Hold up a man at cards and rob him,' pursued Mr Taylor. 'Oh, the news has got ahead of you!'

'Trampas has been hyeh explainin', has he?' said the Virginian with a grin.

'Was that your victim's name?' said Mr Taylor, facetiously. 'No, it wasn't him that brought the news. Say, what did you do, anyway?

'So that thing has got around,' murmured the Virginian. 'Well, it wasn't worth such wide repawtin'.' And he gave the simple facts to Taylor, while I sat wondering at the contagious powers of Rumour. Here, through this voiceless land, this desert, this vacuum, it had spread like a change of weather. 'Any news up your way?' the Virginian concluded.

Importance came into Mr Taylor's countenance. 'Bear Creek is going to build a schoolhouse,' said he.

'Goodness gracious!' drawled the Virginian. 'What's that for?'

Now Mr Taylor had been married for some years. 'To educate the offspring of Bear Creek,' he answered with pride.

'Offspring of Bear Creek,' the Virginian meditatively repeated. 'I don't remember noticin' much offspring. There was some white-tail deer, and a right smart o' jack rabbits.'

'The Swintons have moved up from Drybone,' said Mr Taylor, always seriously. 'They found it no place for young children. And there's Uncle Carmody with six, and Ben Dow. And Westfall has become a family man, and – '

'Jim Westfall!' exclaimed the Virginian. 'Him a fam'ly man! Well, if this hyeh Territory is goin' to get full o' fam'ly men and empty o' game, I believe I'll –'

'Get married yourself,' suggested Mr Taylor.

'Me! I ain't near reached the marriageable age. No, seh! But Uncle Hughey has got there at last, yu' know.'

'Uncle Hughey!' shouted Mr Taylor. He had not heard this. Rumour is very capricious. Therefore the Virginian told him, and the family man rocked in his saddle.

'Build your schoolhouse,' said the Virginian. 'Uncle Hughey has qualified himself to subscribe to all such propositions. Got your eye on a schoolmarm?'

CHAPTER 5

Enter the Woman

'We are taking steps,' said Mr Taylor. 'Bear Creek ain't going to be hasty about a schoolmarm.'

'Sure,' assented the Virginian. 'The children wouldn't want yu' to hurry.'

But Mr Taylor was, as I have indicated, a serious family man. The problem of educating his children could appear to him in no light except a sober one. 'Bear Creek,' he said, 'don't want the experience they had over at Calef. We must not hire an ignoramus.'

'Sure!' assented the Virginian again.

'Nor we don't want no gad-a-way flirt,' said Mr Taylor.

'She must keep her eyes on the blackboa'd,' said the Virginian, gently.

'Well, we can wait till we get a guaranteed article,' said Mr Taylor. 'And that's what we're going to do. It can't be this year, and it needn't to be. None of the kids is very old, and the schoolhouse has got to be built.' He now drew a letter from his pocket, and looked at me. 'Are you acquainted with Miss Mary Stark Wood of Bennington, Vermont?' he enquired.

I was not acquainted with her at this time.

'She's one we are thinking of. She's a correspondent with Mrs Balaam.' Taylor handed me the letter. 'She wrote that to Mrs Balaam, and Mrs Balaam said the best thing was for to let me see it and judge for myself. I'm taking it back to Mrs Balaam. Maybe you can give me your opinion how it sizes up with the letters they write back East?'

The communication was mainly of a business kind, but also personal, and freely written. I do not think that its writer expected it to be exhibited as a document. The writer wished very much that she could see the West. But she could not gratify this desire merely for pleasure, or she would long ago have accepted the kind invitation to visit Mrs Balaam's ranch. Teaching school was something she would like to do, if she were fitted for it. 'Since the mills failed' (the writer said), 'we have all gone to work and done a lot of things so that mother might keep on living in the old house. Yes, the salary would be a temptation. But, my dear, isn't Wyoming bad for the complexion? And could I sue them if mine got damaged? It is still admired. I could bring one male witness *at least* to prove that!' Then the writer became businesslike again. Even if she came to feel that she could leave home, she did not at all know that she could teach school. Nor did she think it right to accept a position in which one had had no experience. 'I do love children, boys especially,' she went on. 'My small nephew and I get on famously. But imagine if a whole benchful of boys began asking me questions that I couldn't answer! What should I do? For one could not spank them all, you know! And mother says that I ought not to teach anybody spelling, because I leave the *u* out of *honour*.'

Altogether it was a letter which I could assure Mr Taylor 'sized up' very well with the letters written in my part of the United States. And it was signed, 'Your very sincere spinster, Molly Stark Wood.'

'I never seen *honour* spelled with a *u*,' said Mr Taylor, over whose not highly civilised head certain portions of the letter had lightly passed.

I told him that some old-fashioned people still wrote the word so.

'Either way would satisfy Bear Creek,' said Mr Taylor, 'if she's otherwise up to requirements.'

The Virginian was now looking over the letter musingly, and with awakened attention.

' "Your very sincere spinster," ' he read aloud slowly.

'I guess that means she's forty,' said Mr Taylor.

'I reckon she is about twenty,' said the Virginian. And again he fell to musing over the paper that he held.

'Her handwriting ain't like any I've saw,' pursued Mr Taylor. 'But Bear Creek would not object to that, provided she knows 'rithmetic and George Washington, and them kind of things.'

'I expect she is not an awful sincere spinster,' surmised the Virginian, still looking at the letter, still holding it as if it were some token.

Has any botanist set down what the seed of love is? Has it anywhere been set down in how many ways this seed may be sown? In what various vessels of gossamer it can float across wide spaces? Or upon what different soils it can fall, and live unknown, and bide its time for blooming?

The Virginian handed back to Taylor the sheet of notepaper where a girl had talked as the women he had known did not talk. If his eyes had ever seen such maidens, there had been no meeting of eyes; and if such maidens had ever spoken to him, the speech was from an established distance. But here was a free language, altogether new to him. It proved, however, not alien to his understanding, as it was alien to Mr Taylor's.

We drove onward, a mile perhaps, and then two. He had lately been full of words, but now he barely answered me, so that a silence fell upon both of us. It must have been all of ten miles that we had driven when he spoke of his own accord.

'Your real spinster don't speak of her lot that easy,' he remarked. And presently he quoted a phrase about the complexion, ' "Could I sue them if mine got damaged?" ' and he smiled over this to himself, shaking his head. 'What would she be doing on Bear Creek?' he next said. And finally: 'I reckon that witness will detain her in Vermont. And her mother'll keep livin' at the old house.'

Thus did the cowpuncher deliver himself, not knowing at all that the seed had floated across wide spaces, and was biding its time in his heart.

On the morrow we reached Sunk Creek. Judge Henry's welcome and his wife's would have obliterated any hardships that I had endured, and I had endured none at all.

For a while I saw little of the Virginian. He lapsed into his native way of addressing me occasionally as 'seh' – a habit entirely repudiated by this land of equality. I was sorry. Our common peril during the runaway of Buck and Muggins had brought us to a familiarity that I hoped was destined to last. But I think that it would not have gone farther, save for a certain personage – I must call her a personage. And as I am indebted to her for gaining me a friend whose prejudice against me might never have been otherwise overcome, I shall tell you her little story, and how her misadventures and her fate came to bring the Virginian and me to an appreciation of one another. Without her, it is likely I should also not have heard so much of the story of the schoolmarm, and how that lady at last came to Bear Creek.

CHAPTER 6

Em'ly

My personage was a hen, and she lived at the Sunk Creek Ranch.

Judge Henry's ranch was notable for several luxuries. He had milk, for example. In those days his brother ranchmen had thousands of cattle very often, but not a drop of milk, save the condensed variety. Therefore they had no butter. The Judge had plenty. Next rarest to butter and milk in the cattle country were eggs. But my host had chickens. Whether this was because he had followed cock-fighting in his early days, or whether it was due to Mrs Henry, I cannot say. I only know that when I took a meal elsewhere, I was likely to find nothing but the eternal 'sowbelly', beans, and coffee; while at Sunk Creek the omelette and the custard were frequent. The passing traveller was glad to tie his horse to the fence here, and sit down to the Judge's table. For its fame was as wide as Wyoming. It was an oasis in the Territory's desolate bill-of-fare.

The long fences of Judge Henry's home ranch began upon Sunk Creek soon after that stream emerged from its canyon through the Bow Leg. It was a place always well cared for by the owner, even in the days of his bachelorhood. The placid regiments of cattle lay in the cool of the cottonwoods by the water, or slowly moved among the sagebrush, feeding upon the grass that in those forever departed years was plentiful and tall. The steers came fat off his unenclosed range and fattened still more in his large pasture; while his small pasture, a field some eight miles square, was for several seasons given to the Judge's horses, and over this ample space there played and prospered the good colts which he raised from Paladin, his imported stallion. After he married, I have been assured that his wife's influence became visible in and about the house at once. Shade trees were planted, flowers attempted, and to the chickens was added the much more troublesome turkey. I, the visitor, was pressed into service when I arrived, green from the East. I took hold of the farmyard and began building a better chicken-house, while the Judge was off creating meadow land in his grey and yellow wilderness. When any cowboy was unoccupied, he would lounge over to my neighbourhood, and silently regard my carpentering.

Those cowpunchers bore names of various denominations. There was Honey Wiggin; there was Nebrasky, and Dollar Bill, and Chalkeye. And

1146

they came from farms and cities, from Maine and from California. But the romance of American adventure had drawn them all alike to this great playground of young men, and in their courage, their generosity, and their amusement at me they bore a close resemblance to each other. Each one would silently observe my achievements with the hammer and the chisel. Then he would retire to the bunkhouse, and presently I would overhear laughter. But this was only in the morning. In the afternoon on many days of the summer which I spent at the Sunk Creek Ranch I would go shooting, or ride up towards the entrance of the canyon and watch the men working on the irrigation ditches. Pleasant systems of water running in channels were being led through the soil, and there was a sound of rippling here and there among the yellow grain; the green thick alfalfa grass waved almost, it seemed, of its own accord, for the wind never blew; and when at evening the sun lay against the plain, the rift of the canyon was filled with a violet light, and the Bow Leg Mountains became transfigured with hues of floating and unimaginable colour. The sun shone in a sky where never a cloud came, and noon was not too warm nor the dark too cool. And so for two months I went through these pleasant uneventful days, improving the chickens, an object of mirth, living in the open air, and basking in the perfection of content.

I was justly styled a tenderfoot. Mrs Henry had in the beginning endeavoured to shield me from this humiliation; but when she found that I was inveterate in laying my inexperience of Western matters bare to all the world, begging to be enlightened upon rattlesnakes, prairie-dogs, owls, blue and willow grouse, sage-hens, how to rope a horse or tighten the front cinch of my saddle, and that my spirit soared into enthusiasm at the mere sight of so ordinary an animal as a white-tailed deer, she let me rush about with my firearms, and made no further effort to stave off the ridicule that my blunders perpetually earned from the ranch hands, her own humorous husband, and any chance visitor who stopped for a meal or stayed the night.

I was not called by my name after the first feeble etiquette due to a stranger in his first few hours had died away. I was known simply as 'the tenderfoot'. I was introduced to the neighbourhood (a circle of eighty miles) as 'the tenderfoot'. It was thus that Balaam, the maltreater of horses, learned to address me when he came a two days' journey to pay a visit. And it was this name and my notorious helplessness that bid fair to end what relations I had with the Virginian. For when Judge Henry ascertained that nothing could prevent me from losing myself, that it was not uncommon for me to saunter out after breakfast with a gun and in thirty minutes cease to know north from south, he arranged for my protection. He detailed an escort for me; and the escort was once more the trustworthy man! The poor Virginian was taken from his work and his comrades and set to playing nurse for me. And for a while this humiliation ate into his untamed soul. It was his lugubrious lot to accompany me in my rambles, preside over my blunders, and save me from calamitously passing into the next world. He bore it in courteous silence, except when speaking was necessary. He would show me the lower ford, which I could never find for myself, generally mistaking a quicksand for it. He would tie my horse properly. He would recommend me not to shoot my rifle at a white-tailed deer in the particular moment that the outfit wagon was passing behind the animal on the further side of the brush. There was seldom a day that he was not obliged to hasten and save me from sudden death or from ridicule, which is worse. Yet never once did he lose his patience; and his gentle, slow voice, and apparently lazy manner remained the same, whether we were sitting at lunch together, or up in the mountains during a hunt, or whether he was bringing me back my horse, which had run away because I had again forgotten to throw the reins over his head and let them trail.

'He'll always stand if yu' do that,' the Virginian would say. 'See how my hawss stays right quiet yondeh.'

After such admonition he would say no more to me. But this tame nursery business was assuredly gall to him. For though utterly a man in countenance and in his self-possession and incapacity to be put at a loss, he was still boyishly proud of his wild calling, and wore his leathern chaps and jingled his spurs with obvious pleasure. His tiger limberness and his beauty were rich with unabated youth; and that force which lurked beneath his surface must often have curbed his intolerance of me. In spite of what I knew must be his opinion of me, the tenderfoot, my liking for him grew, and I found his silent company more and more agreeable. That he had spells of talking, I had already learned at Medicine Bow. But his present taciturnity might almost have effaced this impression, had I not happened to pass by the bunkhouse one evening after dark, when Honey Wiggin and the rest of the cowboys were gathered inside it.

That afternoon the Virginian and I had gone duck shooting. We had found several in a beaver dam, and I had killed two as they sat close together; but they floated against the breastwork of sticks out in the water some four feet deep, where the escaping current might carry them down the stream. The Judge's red setter had not accompanied us, because she was expecting a family.

'We don't want her along anyways,' the cowpuncher had explained to me. 'She runs around mighty irresponsible, and she'll stand a prairie-dog 'bout as often as she'll stand a bird. She's a triflin' animal.'

My anxiety to own the ducks caused me to pitch into the water with all my clothes on, and subsequently crawl out a slippery, triumphant, weltering heap. The Virginian's serious eyes had rested upon this spectacle of mud; but he expressed nothing, as usual.

'They ain't overly good eatin',' he observed, tying the birds to his saddle. 'They're divers.'

'Divers!' I exclaimed. 'Why didn't they dive?'

'I reckon they was young ones and hadn't experience.'

'Well,' I said, crestfallen, but attempting to be humorous, 'I did the diving myself.'

But the Virginian made no comment. He handed me my double-barrelled English gun, which I was about to leave deserted on the ground behind me, and we rode home in our usual silence, the mean little white-breasted, sharp-billed divers dangling from his saddle.

It was in the bunkhouse that he took his revenge. As I passed I heard his gentle voice silently achieving some narrative to an attentive audience, and just as I came by the open window where he sat on his bed in shirt and drawers, his back to me, I heard his concluding words, 'And the hat on his haid was the one mark showed yu' he weren't a snappin'-turtle.'

The anecdote met with instantaneous success and I hurried away into the dark.

The next morning I was occupied with the chickens. Two hens were fighting to sit on some eggs that a third was daily laying, and which I did not want hatched, and for the third time I had kicked Em'ly off seven potatoes she had rolled together and was determined to raise I know not what sort of family from. She was shrieking about the hen-house as the Virginian came in to observe (I suspect) what I might be doing now that could be useful for him to mention in the bunkhouse.

He stood awhile, and at length said, 'We lost our best rooster when Mrs Henry came to live hyeh.'

I paid no attention.

'He was a right elegant Dominicker,' he continued.

I felt a little ruffled about the snapping-turtle, and showed no interest in what he was saying, but continued my functions among the hens. This unusual silence of mine seemed to elicit unusual speech from him.

'Yu' see, that rooster he'd always lived round hyeh when the Judge was a bachelor, and he never seen no ladies or any persons wearing female gyarments. You ain't got rheumatism, seh?'

'Me? No.'

'I reckoned maybe them little old divers yu' got damp goin' afteh –' he paused.

'Oh, no, not in the least, thank you.'

'Yu' seemed sort o' grave this mawnin', and I'm cert'nly glad it ain't them divers.'

'Well, the rooster?' I enquired finally.

'Oh, him! He weren't raised where he could see petticoats. Mrs Henry she come hyeh from the railroad with the Judge afteh dark. Next mawnin' early she walked out to view her new home, and the rooster was a-feedin' by the door, and he seen her. Well, seh, he screeched that awful I run out of the bunkhouse; and he jus' went over the fence and took down Sunk Creek shoutin' fire, right along. He has never come back.'

'There's a hen over there now that has no judgement,' I said, indicating Em'ly. She had got herself outside the house, and was on the bars of a corral, her vociferations reduced to an occasional squawk. I told him about the potatoes.

'I never knowed her name before,' said he. 'That runaway rooster, he hated her. And she hated him same as she hates 'em all.'

'I named her myself,' said I, 'after I came to notice her particularly. There's an old maid at home who's charitable, and belongs to the Cruelty to Animals, and she never knows whether she had better cross in front of a street car or wait. I named the hen after her. Does she ever lay eggs?'

The Virginian had not 'troubled his haid' over the poultry.

'Well, I don't believe she knows how. I think she came near being a rooster.'

'She's sure manly-lookin',' said the Virginian. We had walked towards the corral, and he was now scrutinising Em'ly with interest.

She was an egregious fowl. She was huge and gaunt, with great yellow beak, and she stood straight and alert in the manner of responsible people. There was something wrong with her tail. It slanted far to one side, one feather in it twice as long as the rest. Feathers on her breast there were none. These had been worn entirely off by her habit of sitting upon potatoes and other rough abnormal objects. And this lent to her

EM'LY

appearance an air of being décolleté, singularly at variance with her otherwise prudish ensemble. Her eye was remarkably bright, but somehow it had an outraged expression. It was as if she went about the world perpetually scandalised over the doings that fell beneath her notice. Her legs were blue, long, and remarkably stout.

'She'd ought to wear knickerbockers,' murmured the Virginian. 'She'd look a heap better'n some o' them college students. And she'll set on potatoes, yu' say?'

'She thinks she can hatch out anything. I've found her with onions, and last Tuesday I caught her on two balls of soap.'

In the afternoon the tall cowpuncher and I rode out to get an antelope.

After an hour, during which he was completely taciturn, he said: 'I reckon maybe this hyeh lonesome country ain't been healthy for Em'ly to live in. It ain't for some humans. Them old trappers in the mountains gets skewed in the haid mighty often, an' talks out loud when nobody's nigher 'n a hundred miles.'

'Em'ly has not been solitary,' I replied. 'There are forty chickens here.'

'That's so,' said he. 'It don't explain her.'

He fell silent again, riding beside me, easy and indolent in the saddle. His long figure looked so loose and inert that the swift, light spring he made to the ground seemed an impossible feat. He had seen an antelope where I saw none.

'Take a shot yourself,' I urged him, as he motioned me to be quick. 'You never shoot when I'm with you.'

'I ain't hyeh for that,' he answered. 'Now you've let him get away on yu'!'

The antelope had in truth departed.

'Why,' he said to my protest, 'I can hit them things any day. What's your notion as to Em'ly?'

'I can't account for her,' I replied.

'Well,' he said musingly, and then took one of those particular turns that made me love him, 'Taylor ought to see her. She'd be just the schoolmarm for Bear Creek!'

'She's not much like the eating-house lady at Medicine Bow,' I said.

He gave a hilarious chuckle. 'No, Em'ly knows nothing o' them joys. So yu' have no notion about her? Well, I've got one. I reckon maybe she was hatched after a big thunderstorm.'

'A big thunderstorm!' I exclaimed.

'Yes. Don't yu' know about them, and what they'll do to aiggs? A big case o' lightnin' and thunder will addle aiggs and keep 'em from hatchin'. And I expect one came along, and all the other aiggs of Em'ly's set didn't hatch out, but got plumb addled, and she happened not to get addled that far, and so she just managed to make it through. But she cert'nly ain't got a strong haid.'

'I fear she has not,' said I.

'Mighty hon'ble intentions,' he observed. 'If she can't make out to lay anything, she wants to hatch somethin', and be a mother anyways.'

'I wonder what relation the law considers that a hen is to the chicken she hatched but did not lay?' I enquired.

The Virginian made no reply to this frivolous suggestion. He was gazing over the wide landscape gravely and with apparent inattention. He invariably saw game before I did, and was off his horse and crouched among the sage while I was still getting my left foot clear of the stirrup. I succeeded in killing an antelope, and we rode home with the head and hind quarters.

'No,' said he. 'It's sure the thunder, and not the lonesomeness. How do yu' like the lonesomeness yourself?'

I told him that I liked it.

'I could not live without it now,' he said. 'This has got into my system.' He swept his hand out at the vast space of world. 'I went back home to see my folks onced. Mother was dyin' slow, and she wanted me. I stayed a year. But them Virginia mountains could please me no more. Afteh she was gone, I told my brothers and sisters goodbye. We like each other well enough, but I reckon I'll not go back.'

We found Em'ly seated upon a collection of green California peaches, which the Judge had brought from the railroad.

'I don't mind her any more,' I said; 'I'm sorry for her.'

'I've been sorry for her right along,' said the Virginian. 'She does hate the roosters so.' And he said that he was making a collection of every class of object which he found her treating as eggs.

But Em'ly's egg-industry was terminated abruptly one morning, and her unquestioned energies diverted to a new channel. A turkey which had been sitting in the root-house appeared with twelve children, and a family of bantams occurred almost simultaneously. Em'ly was importantly scratching the soil inside Paladin's corral when the bantam tribe of newly born came by down the lane, and she caught sight of them through the bars. She crossed the corral at a run, and intercepted two of the chicks that were trailing somewhat behind their real mamma. These she undertook to appropriate, and assumed a high tone with the bantam, who was the smaller, and hence obliged to retreat with her still numerous family. I interfered, and put matters straight; but the adjustment was only temporary. In an hour I saw Em'ly immensely busy with two more bantams, leading them about and taking a care of them which I must admit seemed perfectly efficient.

And now came the first incident that made me suspect her to be demented.

She had proceeded with her changelings behind the kitchen, where one of the irrigation ditches ran under the fence from the hayfield to supply the house with water. Some distance along this ditch inside the field were the twelve turkeys in the short, recently cut stubble. Again Em'ly set off instantly like a deer. She left the dismayed bantams behind her. She crossed the ditch with one jump of her stout blue legs, flew over the grass, and was at once among the turkeys, where, with an instinct of maternity as undiscriminating as it was reckless, she attempted to huddle some of them away. But this other mamma was not a bantam, and in a few moments Em'ly was entirely routed in her attempt to acquire a new variety of family.

This spectacle was witnessed by the Virginian and myself, and it overcame him. He went speechless across to the bunkhouse, by himself, and sat on his bed, while I took the abandoned bantams back to their own circle.

I have often wondered what the other fowls thought of all this. Some impression it certainly did make upon them. The notion may seem out of reason to those who have never closely attended to other animals than man; but I am convinced that any community which shares some of our instincts will share some of the resulting feelings, and that birds and beasts have conventions, the breach of which startles them. If there be anything in evolution, this would seem inevitable. At all events, the chicken-house was upset during the following several days. Em'ly disturbed now the bantams and now the turkeys, and several of these latter had died, though I will not go so far as to say that this was the result of her misplaced attentions. Nevertheless, I was seriously thinking of locking her up till the broods should be a little older, when another event happened, and all was suddenly at peace.

The Judge's setter came in one morning, wagging her tail. She had had her puppies, and she now took us to where they were housed, in between the floor of a building and the hollow ground. Em'ly was seated on the whole litter.

'No,' I said to the Judge, 'I am not surprised. She is capable of anything.'

In her new choice of offspring, this hen had at length encountered an unworthy parent. The setter was bored by her own puppies. She found the hole under the house an obscure and monotonous residence compared with the dining-room, and our company more stimulating and sympathetic than that of her children. A much-petted contact with our superior race had developed her dog intelligence above its natural level, and turned her into an unnatural, neglectful mother, who was constantly forgetting her nursery for worldly pleasures.

At certain periods of the day she repaired to the puppies and fed them, but came away when this perfunctory ceremony was accomplished; and she was glad enough to have a governess bring them up. She made no quarrel with Em'ly, and the two understood each other perfectly. I have never seen among animals any arrangement so civilised and so perverted. It made Em'ly perfectly happy. To see her sitting all day jealously spreading her wings over some blind puppies was sufficiently curious; but when they became large enough to come out from under the house and toddle about in the proud hen's wake, I longed for some distinguished naturalist. I felt that our ignorance made us inappropriate spectators of such a phenomenon. Em'ly scratched and clucked, and the puppies ran to her, pawed her with their fat limp little legs, and retreated beneath her feathers in their games of hide-and-seek. Conceive, if you can, what confusion must have reigned in their infant minds as to who the setter was!

'I reckon they think she's the wet-nurse,' said the Virginian.

When the puppies grew to be boisterous, I perceived that Em'ly's mission was approaching its end. They were too heavy for her, and their increasing scope of playfulness was not in her line. Once or twice they knocked her over, upon which she arose and pecked them severely, and they retired to a safe distance, and sitting in a circle, yapped at her. I think they began to suspect that she was only a hen after all. So Em'ly resigned with an indifference which surprised me, until I remembered that if it had been chickens, she would have ceased to look after them by this time.

But here she was again 'out of a job', as the Virginian said.

'She's raised them puppies for that triflin' setter, and now she'll be huntin' around for something else useful to do that ain't in her business.'

Now there were other broods of chickens to arrive in the hen-house, and I did not desire any more bantam and turkey performances. So, to avoid confusion, I played a trick upon Em'ly. I went down to Sunk Creek and fetched some smooth, oval stones. She was quite satisfied with these, and passed a quiet day with them in a box. This was not fair, the Virginian asserted.

'You ain't going to jus' leave her fooled that-a-way?'

I did not see why not.

'Why, she raised them puppies all right. Ain't she showed she knows how to be a mother anyways? Em'ly ain't going to get her time took up for nothing while I'm round hyeh,' said the cowpuncher.

He laid a gentle hold of Em'ly and tossed her to the ground. She, of course, rushed out among the corrals in a great state of nerves.

'I don't see what good you do meddling,' I protested.

To this he deigned no reply, but removed the unresponsive stones from the straw.

'Why, if they ain't right warm!' he exclaimed plaintively. 'The poor, deluded son-of-a-gun!' And with this unusual description of a lady, he sent the stones sailing like a line of birds. 'I'm regular getting stuck on Em'ly,' continued the Virginian. 'Yu' needn't to laugh. Don't yu' see she's got sort o' human feelin's and desires? I always knowed hawsses was like people, and my collie, of course. It is kind of foolish, I expect, but that hen's goin' to have a real aigg di-rectly, right now, to set on.' With this he removed one from beneath another hen. 'We'll have Em'ly raise this hyeh,' said he, 'so she can put in her time profitable.'

It was not accomplished at once; for Em'ly, singularly enough, would not consent to stay in the box whence she had been routed. At length we found another retreat for her, and in these new surroundings, with a new piece of work for her to do, Em'ly sat on the one egg which the Virginian had so carefully provided for her.

Thus, as in all genuine tragedies, was the stroke of Fate wrought by chance and the best intentions.

Em'ly began sitting on Friday afternoon near sundown. Early next morning my sleep was gradually dispersed by a sound unearthly and continuous. Now it dwindled, receding to a distance; again it came near, took a turn, drifted to the other side of the house; then, evidently, whatever it was, passed my door close, and I jumped upright in my bed. The high, tense strain of vibration, nearly, but not quite, a musical note, was like the threatening scream of machinery, though weaker, and I bounded out of the house in my pyjamas.

There was Em'ly, dishevelled, walking wildly about, her one egg miraculously hatched within ten hours. The little lonely yellow ball of down went cheeping along behind, following its mother as best it could.

What, then, had happened to the established period of incubation? For an instant the thing was like a portent, and I was near joining Em'ly in her horrid surprise, when I saw how it all was. The Virginian had taken an egg from a hen which had already been sitting for three weeks.

I dressed in haste, hearing Em'ly's distracted outcry. It steadily sounded, without perceptible pause for breath, and marked her erratic journey back and forth through stables, lanes, and corrals. The shrill disturbance brought all of us out to see her, and in the hen-house I discovered the new brood making its appearance punctually.

But this natural explanation could not be made to the crazed hen. She continued to scour the premises, her slant tail and its one preposterous feather waving as she aimlessly went, her stout legs stepping high with an unnatural motion, her head lifted nearly off her neck, and in her brilliant yellow eye an expression of more than outrage at this overturning of a natural law. Behind her, entirely ignored and neglected, trailed the little progeny. She never looked at it. We went about our various affairs, and all through the clear, sunny day that unending metallic scream pervaded the premises. The Virginian put out food and water for her, but she tasted nothing. I am glad to say that the little chicken did. I do not think that the hen's eyes could see, except in the way that sleep-walkers' do.

The heat went out of the air, and in the canyon the violet light began to show. Many hours had gone, but Em'ly never ceased. Now she suddenly flew up in a tree and sat there with her noise still going; but it had risen lately several notes into a slim, acute level of terror, and was not like machinery any more, nor like any sound I ever heard before or since. Below the tree stood the bewildered little chicken, cheeping, and making tiny jumps to reach its mother.

'Yes,' said the Virginian, 'it's comical. Even her aigg acted different from anybody else's.' He paused, and looked across the wide, mellowing plain with the expression of easy-going gravity so common with him. Then he looked at Em'ly in the tree and the yellow chicken. 'It ain't so damned funny,' said he.

We went in to supper, and I came out to find the hen lying on the ground, dead. I took the chicken to the family in the hen-house.

No, it was not altogether funny any more. And I did not think less of the Virginian when I came upon him surreptitiously digging a little hole in the field for her.

'I have buried some citizens here and there,' said he, 'that I have respected less.'

And when the time came for me to leave Sunk Creek, my last word to the Virginian was, 'Don't forget Em'ly.'

'I ain't likely to,' responded the cowpuncher. 'She is just one o' them parables.'

Save when he fell into his native idioms (which, they told me, his wanderings had well-nigh obliterated until that year's visit to his home again revived them in his speech), he had now for a long while dropped the 'seh', and all other barriers between us. We were thorough friends, and had exchanged many confidences both of the flesh and of the spirit. He even went the length of saying that he would write me the Sunk Creek news if I would send him a line now and then. I have many letters from him now. Their spelling came to be faultless, and in the beginning was little worse than George Washington's.

The Judge himself drove me to the railroad by another way – across the Bow Leg Mountains, and south through Balaam's Ranch and Drybone to Rock Creek.

'I'll be very homesick,' I told him.

'Come and pull the latch-string whenever you please,' he bade me.

I wished that I might! No lotus land ever cast its spell upon man's heart more than Wyoming had enchanted mine.

CHAPTER 7

Through Two Snows

'Dear friend [thus in the spring the Virginian wrote me], Yours received. It must be a poor thing to be sick. That time I was shot at Cañada de Oro would have made me sick if it had been a little lower or if I was much of a drinking man. You will be well if you give over city life and take a hunt with me about August or say September for then the elk will be out of the velvet.

'Things do not pleaze me here just now and I am going to settel it by vamoosing. But I would be glad to see you. It would be pleasure not business for me to show you plenty elk and get you strong. I am not cry-babying to the Judge or making any kick about things. He will want me back after he has swallowed a littel tincture of time. It is the best dose I know.

'Now to answer your questions. Yes the Emmily hen might have ate loco weed if hens do. I never saw anything but stock and horses get poisoned with loco weed. No the school is not built yet. They are always big talkers on Bear Creek. No I have not seen Steve. He is around but I am sorry for him. Yes I have been to Medicine Bow. I had the welcome I wanted. Do you remember a man I played poker and he did not like it? He is working on the upper ranch near Ten Sleep. He does not amount to a thing except with weaklings. Uncle Hewie has twins. The boys got him vexed some about it, but I think they are his. Now that is all I know today and I would like to see you poco presently as they say at Los Cruces. There's no sense in you being sick.'

The rest of this letter discussed the best meeting point for us should I decide to join him for a hunt.

That hunt was made, and during the weeks of its duration something was said to explain a little more fully the Virginian's difficulty at the Sunk Creek Ranch, and his reason for leaving his excellent employer the Judge. Not much was said, to be sure; the Virginian seldom spent many words upon his own troubles. But it appeared that owing to some jealousy of him on the part of the foreman, or the assistant foreman, he found himself continually doing another man's work, but under circumstances so skilfully arranged that he got neither credit nor pay for it. He would not stoop to telling tales out of school. Therefore his ready and prophetic mind devised the simple expedient of going away altogether. He calculated that Judge Henry would gradually perceive there was a connection between his departure and the cessation of the satisfactory work. After a judicious interval it was his plan to appear again in the neighbourhood of Sunk Creek and await results.

Concerning Steve he would say no more than he had written. But it was plain that for some cause this friendship had ceased.

Money for his services during the hunt he positively declined to accept, asserting that he had not worked enough to earn his board. And the expedition ended in an untravelled corner of the Yellowstone Park, near Pitchstone Canyon, where he and young Lin McLean and others were witnesses of a sad and terrible drama that has been elsewhere chronicled.

His prophetic mind had foreseen correctly the shape of events at Sunk Creek. The only thing that it had not foreseen was the impression to be made upon the Judge's mind by his conduct.

Towards the close of that winter, Judge and Mrs Henry visited the East. Through them a number of things became revealed. The Virginian was back at Sunk Creek.

'And,' said Mrs Henry, 'he would never have left you if I had had my way, Judge H.!'

'No, Madam Judge,' retorted her husband; 'I am aware of that. For you have always appreciated a fine appearance in a man.'

'I certainly have,' confessed the lady, mirthfully. 'And the way he used to come bringing my horse, with the ridges of his black hair so carefully brushed and that blue spotted handkerchief tied so effectively round his throat, was something that I missed a great deal after he went away.'

'Thank you, my dear, for this warning. I have plans that will keep him absent quite constantly for the future.'

And then they spoke less flightily. 'I always knew,' said the lady, 'that you had found a treasure when that man came.'

The Judge laughed. 'When it dawned on me,' he said, 'how cleverly he caused me to learn the value of his services by depriving me of them, I doubted whether it was safe to take him back.'

'Safe!' cried Mrs Henry.

'Safe, my dear. Because I'm afraid he is pretty nearly as shrewd as I am. And that's rather dangerous in a subordinate.' The Judge laughed again. 'But his action regarding the man they call Steve has made me feel easy.'

And then it came out that the Virginian was supposed to have discovered in some way that Steve had fallen from the grace of that particular honesty which respects another man's cattle. It was not known for certain. But calves had begun to disappear in Cattle Land, and cows had been found killed. And calves with one brand upon them had been found with mothers that bore the brand of another owner. This industry was taking root in Cattle Land, and of those who practised it, some were beginning to be suspected. Steve was not quite fully suspected yet. But that the Virginian had parted company with him was definitely known. And neither man would talk about it.

There was the further news that the Bear Creek schoolhouse at length stood complete, floor walls, and roof; and that a lady from Bennington, Vermont, a friend of Mrs Balaam's, had quite suddenly decided that she would try her hand at instructing the new generation.

The Judge and Mrs Henry knew this because Mrs Balaam had told them of her disappointment that she would be absent from the ranch on Butte Creek when her friend arrived, and therefore unable to entertain her. The friend's decision had been quite suddenly made, and must form the subject of the next chapter.

CHAPTER 8

The Sincere Spinster

I do not know with which of the two estimates – Mr Taylor's or the Virginian's – you agreed. Did you think that Miss Mary Stark Wood of Bennington, Vermont, was forty years of age? That would have been an error. At the time she wrote the letter to Mrs Balaam, of which letter certain portions have been quoted in these pages, she was in her twenty-first year; or, to be more precise, she had been twenty some eight months previous.

Now, it is not usual for young ladies of twenty to contemplate a journey of nearly two thousand miles to a country where Indians and wild animals live unchained, unless they are to make such journey in the company with a protector, or are going to a protector's arms at the other end. Nor is schoolteaching on Bear Creek a usual ambition for such young ladies.

But Miss Mary Stark Wood was not a usual young lady for two reasons.

First, there was her descent. Had she so wished, she could have belonged to any number of those patriotic societies of which our American ears have grown accustomed to hear so much. She could have been enrolled in the Boston Tea Party, the Ethan Allen Ticonderogas, the Green Mountain Daughters, the Saratoga Sacred Circle, and the Confederated Colonial Chatelaines. She traced direct descent from the historic lady whose name she bore, that Molly Stark who was not a widow after the battle where her lord, her Captain John, battled so bravely as to send his name thrilling down through the blood of generations of schoolboys. This ancestress was her chief claim to be a member of those shining societies which I have enumerated. But she had been willing to join none of them, although invitations to do so were by no means lacking. I cannot tell you her reason. Still, I can tell you this. When these societies were much spoken of in her presence, her very sprightly countenance became more sprightly, and she added her words of praise or respect to the general chorus. But when she received an invitation to join one of these bodies, her countenance, as she read the missive, would assume an expression which was known to her friends as 'sticking her nose in the air'. I do not think that Molly's reason for refusing to join could have been a truly good one. I should add that her most precious possession – a treasure which accompanied her even if she went away for only one night's absence – was an heirloom, a little miniature portrait of the old Molly Stark, painted when that far-off dame must have been scarce more than twenty. And when each summer the young Molly went to Dunbarton, New Hampshire, to pay her established family visit to the last survivors of her connection who bore the name of Stark, no word that she heard in the Dunbarton houses pleased her so much as when a certain great-aunt would take her by the hand, and, after looking with fond intentness at her, pronounce – 'My dear, you're getting more like the General's wife every year you live.'

'I suppose you mean my nose,' Molly would then reply.

'Nonsense, child. You have the family length of nose, and I've never heard that it has disgraced us.'

'But I don't think I'm tall enough for it.'

'There now, run to your room, and dress for tea. The Starks have always been punctual.'

And after this annual conversation, Molly would run to her room, and there in its privacy, even at the risk of falling below the punctuality of the Starks, she would consult two objects for quite a minute before she began to dress. These objects, as you have already correctly guessed, were the miniature of the General's wife and the looking-glass.

So much for Miss Molly Stark Wood's descent.

The second reason why she was not a usual girl was her character. This character was the result of pride and family pluck battling with family hardship.

Just one year before she was to be presented to the world – not the great metropolitan world, but a world that would have made her welcome and done her homage at its little dances and little dinners in Troy and Rutland and Burlington – fortune had turned her back upon the Woods. Their possessions had never been great ones; but they had sufficed. From generation to generation the family had gone to school like gentlefolk, dressed like gentlefolk, used the speech and ways of gentlefolk, and as gentlefolk lived and died. And now the mills failed.

Instead of thinking about her first evening dress, Molly found pupils to whom she could give music lessons. She found handkerchiefs that she could embroider with initials. And she found fruit that she could make into preserves. That machine called the typewriter was then in existence, but the day of women typewriters had as yet scarcely begun to dawn, else

I think Molly would have preferred this occupation to the handkerchiefs and the preserves.

There were people in Bennington who 'wondered how Miss Wood could go about from house to house teaching the piano, and she a lady'. There always have been such people, I suppose, because the world must always have a rubbish heap. But we need not dwell upon them further than to mention one other remark of theirs regarding Molly. They all with one voice declared that Sam Bannett was good enough for anybody who did fancy embroidery at five cents a letter.

'I dare say he had a great-grandmother quite as good as hers,' remarked Mrs Flynt, the wife of the Baptist minister.

'That's entirely possible,' returned the Episcopal rector of Hoosic, 'only we don't happen to know who she was.' The rector was a friend of Molly's. After this little observation, Mrs Flynt said no more, but continued her purchases in the store where she and the rector had happened to find themselves together. Later she stated to a friend that she had always thought the Episcopal Church a snobbish one, and now she knew it.

So public opinion went on being indignant over Molly's conduct. She could stoop to work for money, and yet she pretended to hold herself above the most rising young man in Hoosic Falls, and all just because there was a difference in their grandmothers!

Was this the reason at the bottom of it? The very bottom? I cannot be certain, because I have never been a girl myself. Perhaps she thought that work is not a stooping, and that marriage may be. Perhaps – But all I really know is that Molly Wood continued cheerfully to embroider the handkerchiefs, make the preserves, teach the pupils – and firmly to reject Sam Bannett.

Thus it went on until she was twenty. Then certain members of her family began to tell her how rich Sam was going to be – was, indeed, already. It was at this time that she wrote Mrs Balaam her doubts and her desires as to migrating to Bear Creek. It was at this time also that her face grew a little paler, and her friends thought that she was overworked, and Mrs Flynt feared she was losing her looks. It was at this time, too, that she grew very intimate with that great-aunt over at Dunbarton, and from her received much comfort and strengthening.

'Never!' said the old lady, 'especially if you can't love him.'

'I do like him,' said Molly; 'and he is very kind.'

'Never!' said the old lady again. 'When I die, you'll have something – and that will not be long now.'

Molly flung her arms around her aunt, and stopped her words with a kiss.

And then one winter afternoon, two years later, came the last straw.

*　　*　　*

The front door of the old house had shut. Out of it had stepped the persistent suitor. Mrs Flynt watched him drive away in his smart sleigh.

'That girl is a fool!' she said furiously; and she came away from her bedroom window where she had posted herself for observation.

Inside the old house a door had also shut. This was the door of Molly's own room. And there she sat, in floods of tears. For she could not bear to hurt a man who loved her with all the power of love that was in him.

It was about twilight when her door opened, and an elderly lady came softly in. 'My dear,' she ventured, 'and you were not able – '

'Oh, mother!' cried the girl, 'have you come to say that too?'

The next day Miss Wood had become very hard. In three weeks she had accepted the position on Bear Creek. In two months she started, heart-heavy, but with a spirit craving the unknown.

CHAPTER 9

The Spinster Meets the Unknown

On a Monday noon a small company of horsemen strung out along the trail from Sunk Creek to gather cattle over their allotted sweep of range. Spring was backward, and they, as they rode galloping and gathering upon the cold week's work, cursed cheerily and occasionally sang. The Virginian was grave in bearing and of infrequent speech; but he kept a song going – a matter of some seventy-nine verses. Seventy-eight were quite unprintable, and rejoiced his brother cowpunchers monstrously. They, knowing him to be a singular man, forebore ever to press him, and awaited his own humour, lest he should weary of the lyric; and when after a day of silence apparently saturnine, he would lift his gentle voice and begin –

> 'If you go to monkey with my Looloo girl,
> Ill tell you what I'll do:
> I'll cyarve your heart with my razor, and
> I'll shoot you with my pistol, too – '

then they would stridently take up each last line, and keep it going three, four, ten times, and kick holes in the ground to the swing of it.

By the levels of Bear Creek that reach like inlets among the promontories of the lonely hills, they came upon the schoolhouse, roofed and ready for the first native Wyoming crop. It symbolised the dawn of a neighbourhood, and it brought a change into the wilderness air. The feel of it struck cold upon the free spirits of the cowpunchers, and they told each other that, what with women and children and wire fences, this country would not long be a country for men. They stopped for a meal at an old comrade's. They looked over his gate, and there he was pottering among garden furrows.

'Pickin' nosegays?' enquired the Virginian; and the old comrade asked if they could not recognise potatoes except in the dish. But he grinned sheepishly at them, too, because they knew that he had not always lived in a garden. Then he took them into his house, where they saw an object crawling on the floor with a handful of sulphur matches. He began to remove the matches, but stopped in alarm at the vociferous result; and his wife looked in from the kitchen to caution him about humouring little Christopher.

When she beheld the matches she was aghast, but when she saw her baby grow quiet in the arms of the Virginian, she smiled at that cowpuncher and returned to her kitchen.

Then the Virginian slowly spoke again – 'How many little strangers have yu' got, James?'

'Only two.'

'My! Ain't it most three years since yu' married? Yu' mustn't let time creep ahaid o' yu' James.'

The father once more grinned at his guests, who themselves turned sheepish and polite; for Mrs Westfall came in, brisk and hearty, and set the meat upon the table. After that, it was she who talked. The guests ate scrupulously, muttering, 'Yes, ma'am', and 'No, ma'am', in their plates, while their hostess told them of increasing families upon Bear Creek, and the expected schoolteacher, and little Alfred's early teething, and how it was time for all of them to become husbands like James. The bachelors of the saddle listened, always diffident, but eating heartily to the end; and soon after they rode away in a thoughtful clump. The wives of Bear Creek were few as yet, and the homes scattered; the schoolhouse was only a sprig on the vast face of a world of elk and bear and uncertain Indians; but that night, when the earth near the fire was littered with the cowpunchers' beds, the Virginian was heard drawling to himself: 'Alfred and Christopher. Oh, sugar!'

They found pleasure in the delicately chosen shade of this oath. He also recited to them a new verse about how he took his Looloo girl to the schoolhouse for to learn her A B C; and as it was quite original and unprintable, the camp laughed and swore joyfully, and rolled in its blankets to sleep under the stars.

*   *   *

Upon a Monday noon likewise (for things will happen so) some tearful people in petticoats waved handkerchiefs at a train that was just leaving Bennington, Vermont. A girl's face smiled back at them once, and withdrew quickly, for they must not see the smile die away.

She had with her a little money, a few clothes, and in her mind a rigid determination neither to be a burden to her mother nor to give in to that mother's desires. Absence alone would enable her to carry out this determination. Beyond these things, she possessed not much except spelling-books, a colonial miniature, and that craving for the unknown which has been mentioned. If the ancestors that we carry shut up inside us take turns in dictating to us our actions and our state of mind, undoubtedly Grandmother Stark was empress of Molly's spirit upon this Monday.

At Hoosic Junction, which came soon, she passed the up-train bound back to her home, and seeing the engineer and the conductor – faces that she knew well – her courage nearly failed her, and she shut her eyes against this glimpse of the familiar things that she was leaving. To keep herself steady she gripped tightly a little bunch of flowers in her hand.

But something caused her eyes to open; and there before her stood Sam Bannett, asking if he might accompany her so far as Rotterdam Junction.

'No!' she told him with a severity born from the struggle she was making with her grief. 'Not a mile with me. Not to Eagle Bridge. Goodbye.'

And Sam – what did he do? He obeyed her. I should like to be sorry for him. But obedience was not a lover's part here. He hesitated, the golden moment hung hovering, the conductor cried 'All aboard!' the train went, and there on the platform stood obedient Sam, with his golden moment gone like a butterfly.

After Rotterdam Junction, which was some forty minutes farther, Molly

Wood sat bravely up in the through car, dwelling upon the unknown. She thought that she had attained it in Ohio, on Tuesday morning, and wrote a letter about it to Bennington. On Wednesday afternoon she felt sure, and wrote a letter much more picturesque. But on the following day, after breakfast at North Platte, Nebraska, she wrote a very long letter indeed, and told them that she had seen a black pig on a white pile of buffalo bones, catching drops of water in the air as they fell from the railroad tank. She also wrote that trees were extraordinarily scarce. Each hour westward from the pig confirmed this opinion, and when she left the train at Rock Creek, late upon that fourth night – in those days the trains were slower – she knew that she had really attained the unknown, and sent an expensive telegram to say that she was quite well.

At six in the morning the stage drove away into the sagebrush, with her as its only passenger; and by sundown she had passed through some of the primitive perils of the world. The second team, virgin to harness, and displeased with this novelty, tried to take it off, and went down to the bottom of a gully on its eight hind legs, while Miss Wood sat mute and unflinching beside the driver. Therefore he, when it was over, and they on the proper road again, invited her earnestly to be his wife during many of the next fifteen miles, and told her of his snug cabin and his horses and his mine. Then she got down and rode inside, Independence and Grandmother Stark shining in her eye. At Point of Rocks, where they had supper and his drive ended, her face distracted his heart, and he told her once more about his cabin, and lamentably hoped she would remember him. She answered sweetly that she would try and gave him her hand. After all, he was a frank-looking boy, who had paid her the highest compliment that a boy (or a man for that matter) knows; and it is said that Molly Stark, in her day, was not a New Woman.

The new driver banished the first one from the maiden's mind. He was not a frank-looking boy, and he had been taking whiskey. All night long he took it, while his passenger, helpless and sleepless inside the lurching stage, sat as upright as she possibly could; nor did the voices that she heard at Drybone reassure her. Sunrise found the white stage lurching eternally on across the alkali, with a driver and a bottle on the box, and a pale girl staring out at the plain, and knotting in her handkerchief some utterly dead flowers. They came to a river where the man bungled over the ford. Two wheels sank down over an edge, and the canvas toppled like a descending kite. The ripple came sucking through the upper spokes, and as she felt the seat career, she put out her head and tremulously asked if anything was wrong. But the driver was addressing his team with much language, and also with the lash.

Then a tall rider appeared close against the buried axles, and took her out of the stage on his horse so suddenly that she screamed. She felt splashes, saw a swimming flood, and found herself lifted down upon the shore. The rider said something to her about cheering up, and its being all right, but her wits were stock-still, so she did not speak and thank him. After four days of train and thirty hours of stage, she was having a little too much of the unknown at once. Then the tall man gently withdrew, leaving her to become herself again. She limply regarded the river pouring round the slanted stage, and a number of horsemen with ropes, who righted the vehicle, and got it quickly to dry land, and disappeared at once with a herd of cattle, uttering lusty yells.

She saw the tall one delaying beside the driver, and speaking. He spoke so quietly that not a word reached her, until of a sudden the driver protested loudly. The man had thrown something, which turned out to be a bottle. This twisted loftily and dived into the stream. He said something more to the driver, then put his hand on the saddle horn, looked half-lingeringly at the passenger on the bank, dropped his grave eyes from hers, and swinging upon his horse, was gone just as the passenger opened her mouth and with inefficient voice murmured, 'Oh, thank you!' at his departing back.

The driver drove up now, a chastened creature. He helped Miss Wood in, and enquired after her welfare with a hanging head; then meek as his own drenched horses, he climbed back to his reins, and nursed the stage on towards the Bow Leg Mountains much as if it had been a perambulator.

As for Miss Wood, she sat recovering, and she wondered what the man on the horse must think of her. She knew that she was not ungrateful, and that if he had given her an opportunity she would have explained to him. If he supposed that she did not appreciate his act – Here into the midst of these meditations came an abrupt memory that she had screamed – she could not be sure when. She rehearsed the adventure from the beginning, and found one or two further uncertainties – how it had all been while she was on the horse, for instance. It was confusing to determine precisely what she had done with her arms. She knew where one of his arms had been. And the handkerchief with the flowers was gone. She made a few rapid dives in search of it. Had she, or had she not, seen him putting something in his pocket? And why had she behaved so unlike herself? In a few miles Miss Wood entertained sentiments of maidenly resentment towards her rescuer, and of maidenly hope to see him again.

* * *

To that river crossing he came again, alone, when the days were growing short. The ford was dry sand, and the stream a winding lane of shingle. He found a pool – pools always survive the year round in this stream – and having watered his pony, he lunched near the spot to which he had borne the frightened passenger that day. Where the flowing current had been, he sat, regarding the now extremely safe channel.

'She cert'nly wouldn't need to grip me so close this mawnin',' he said, as he pondered over his meal. 'I reckon it will mightily astonish her when I tell her how harmless the torrent is lookin'.' He held out to his pony a slice of bread matted with sardines, which the pony expertly accepted. 'You're a plumb pie-biter, you Monte,' he continued. Monte rubbed his nose on his master's shoulder. 'I wouldn't trust you with berries and cream. No, seh; not though yu' did rescue a drownin' lady.'

Presently he tightened the forward cinch, got in the saddle, and the pony fell into his wise mechanical jog; for he had come a long way, and was going a long way, and he knew this as well as the man did.

To use the language of Cattle Land, steers had 'jumped to seventy-five'. This was a great and prosperous leap in their value. To have flourished in that golden time you need not be dead now, nor even middle-aged; but it is Wyoming mythology already – quite as fabulous as the high-jumping cow. Indeed, people gathered together and behaved themselves much in the same pleasant and improbable way. Johnson County, and Natrona, and Converse, and others, to say nothing of the Cheyenne Club, had been jumping over the moon for some weeks, all on account of steers; and on the strength of this vigorous price of seventy-five, the Swinton Brothers were giving a barbecue at the Goose Egg outfit, their ranch on Bear Creek. Of course the whole neighbourhood was bidden, and would come forty miles to a man; some would come further – the Virginian was coming a hundred and eighteen. It had struck him – rather suddenly, as shall be made plain – that he should like to see how they were getting along up there on Bear Creek. 'They', was how he put it to his acquaintances. His acquaintances did not know that he had bought himself a pair of trousers and a scarf, unnecessarily excellent for such a general visit. They did not know that in the spring, two days after the adventure with the stage, he had learned accidentally who the lady in the stage was. This he had kept to himself; nor did the camp ever notice that he had ceased to sing that eightieth stanza he had made about the A B C – the stanza which was not printable. He effaced it imperceptibly, giving the boys the other seventy-nine at judicious intervals. They dreamed of no guile, but merely saw in him, whether frequenting camp or town, the same not over-angelic comrade whom they valued and could not wholly understand.

All spring he had ridden trail, worked at ditches during summer, and now he had just finished with the beef round-up. Yesterday, while he was spending a little comfortable money at the Drybone hog-ranch, a casual traveller from the north gossiped of Bear Creek, and the fences up there, and the farm crops, the Westfalls, and the young schoolmarm from Vermont, for whom the Taylors had built a cabin next door to theirs. The traveller had not seen her, but Mrs Taylor and all the ladies thought the world of her, and Lin McLean had told him she was 'away up in G'. She would have plenty of partners at this Swinton barbecue. Great boom for the country, wasn't it, steers jumping that way?

The Virginian heard, asking no questions; and left town in an hour, with the scarf and trousers tied in his slicker behind his saddle. After looking upon the ford again, even though it was dry and not at all the same place, he journeyed inattentively. When you have been hard at work for months with no time to think, of course you think a great deal during your first empty days. 'Step along, you Monte hawss!' he said, rousing after some while. He disciplined Monte, who flattened his ears affectedly and snorted. 'Why, you surely ain' thinkin' of you'-self as a hero? She wasn't really a-drowndin', you pie-biter.' He rested his serious glance upon the alkali. 'She's not likely to have forgot that mix-up, though. I guess I'll not remind her about grippin' me, and all that. She wasn't the kind a man ought to josh about such things. She had a right clear eye.' Thus, tall and loose in the saddle, did he jog along the sixty miles which still lay between him and the dance.

CHAPTER 10

Where Fancy was Bred

Two camps in the open, and the Virginian's Monte horse, untired, brought him to the Swintons' in good time for the barbecue. The horse received good food at length, while his rider was welcomed with good whiskey. *Good* whiskey – for had not steers jumped to seventy-five?

Inside the Goose Egg kitchen many small delicacies were preparing, and a steer was roasting whole outside. The bed of flame under it showed steadily brighter against the dusk that was beginning to veil the lowlands. The busy hosts went and came, while men stood and men lay near the fireglow. Chalkeye was there, and Nebrasky, and Trampas, and Honey Wiggin, with others, enjoying the occasion; but Honey Wiggin was enjoying himself: he had an audience; he was sitting up discoursing to it.

'Hello!' he said, perceiving the Virginian. 'So you've dropped in for your turn! Number – six, ain't he, boys?'

'Depends who's a-runnin' the countin',' said the Virginian, and stretched himself down among the audience.

'I've saw him number one when nobody else was around,' said Trampas.

'How far away was you standin' when you beheld that?' enquired the lounging Southerner.

'Well, boys,' said Wiggin, 'I expect it will be Miss Schoolmarm says who's number one tonight.'

'So she's arrived in this hyeh country?' observed the Virginian, very casually.

'Arrived!' said Trampas again. 'Where have you been grazing lately?'

'A right smart way from the mules.'

'Nebrasky and the boys was tellin' me they'd missed yu' off the range,' again interposed Wiggin. 'Say, Nebrasky, who have yu' offered your canary to the schoolmarm said you mustn't give her?'

Nebrasky grinned wretchedly.

'Well, she's a lady, and she's square, not takin' a man's gift when she don't take the man. But you'd ought to get back all them letters yu' wrote her. Yu' sure ought to ask her for them telltales.'

'Ah, pshaw, Honey!' protested the youth. It was well known that he could not write his name.

'Why, if here ain't Bokay Baldy!' cried the agile Wiggin, stooping to fresh prey. 'Found them slippers yet, Baldy? Tell yu' boys, that was turruble sad luck Baldy had. Did yu' hear about that? Baldy, yu' know, he can stay on a tame horse most as well as the schoolmarm. But just you give him a pair of young knittin'-needles and see him make 'em sweat! He worked an elegant pair of slippers with pink cabbages on 'em for Miss Wood.'

'I bought 'em at Medicine Bow,' blundered Baldy.

'So yu' did!' assented the skilful comedian. 'Baldy he bought 'em. And on the road to her cabin there at the Taylors' he got thinkin' they might be too big, and he got studyin' what to do. And he fixed up to tell her about his not bein' sure of the size, and how she was to let him know if they dropped off her, and he'd exchange' em, and when he got right near her door, why, he couldn't find his courage. And so he slips the parcel under the fence and starts serenadin' her. But she ain't inside her cabin at all. She's at supper next door with the Taylors, and Baldy singin' "Love has conqwered pride and angwer" to a lone house. Lin McLean was comin' up by Taylor's corral, where Taylor's Texas bull was. Well, it was turruble sad. Baldy's pants got tore, but he fell inside the fence, and Lin druv the bull back and somebody stole them Medicine Bow goloshes. Are you goin' to knit her some more, Bokay?'

'About half that ain't straight,' Baldy commented, with mildness.

'The half that was tore off yer pants? Well, never mind, Baldy; Lin will get left too, same as all of yu'.'

'Is there many?' enquired the Virginian. He was still stretched on his back, looking up at the sky.

'I don't know how many she's been used to where she was raised,' Wiggin answered. 'A kid stage-driver come from Point of Rocks one day and went back the next. Then the foreman of the 76 outfit, and the horse-wrangler from the Bar-Circle-L, and two deputy marshals, with punchers, stringin' right along – all got their tumble. Old Judge Burrage from Cheyenne come up in August for a hunt and stayed round here and never hunted at all. There was that horse thief – awful good-lookin'. Taylor wanted to warn her about him, but Mrs Taylor said she'd look after her if it was needed. Mr Horse-thief gave it up quicker than most; but the schoolmarm couldn't have knowed he had a Mrs Horse-thief camped on Poison Spider till afterwards. She wouldn't go ridin' with him. She'll go with some, takin' a kid along.'

'Bah!' said Trampas.

The Virginian stopped looking at the sky, and watched Trampas from where he lay.

'I think she encourages a man some,' said poor Nebrasky.

'Encourages? Because she lets yu' teach her how to shoot?' said Wiggin. ' Well – I don't guess I'm a judge. I've always kind o' kep' away from them good women. Don't seem to think of anything to chat about to 'em. The only folks I'd say she encourages is the school kids. She kisses them.'

'Riding and shooting and kissing the kids,' sneered Trampas. 'That's a heap too pussy-kitten for me.'

They laughed. The sagebrush audience is readily cynical.

'Look for the man, I say,' Trampas pursued. 'And ain't he there? She leaves Baldy sit on the fence while she and Lin McLean – '

They laughed loudly at the blackguard picture which he drew; and the laugh stopped short, for the Virginian stood over Trampas.

'You can rise up now, and tell them you lie,' he said.

The man was still for a moment in the dead silence. 'I thought you claimed you and her wasn't acquainted,' said he then.

'Stand on your laigs, you polecat, and say you're a liar!'

Trampas's hand moved behind him.

'Quit that,' said the Southerner, 'or I'll break your neck!'

The eye of a man is the prince of deadly weapons. Trampas looked in the Virginian's, and slowly rose. 'I didn't mean – ' he began, and paused, his face poisonously bloated.

'Well, I'll call that sufficient. Keep a-standin' still. I ain' going to trouble yu' long. In admittin' yourself to be a liar you have spoke God's truth for onced. Honey Wiggin, you and me and the boys have hit town too frequent for any of us to play Sunday on the balance of the gang.' He stopped and surveyed Public Opinion, seated around in carefully inexpressive attention. 'We ain't a Christian outfit a little bit, and maybe we have most forgotten what decency feels like. But I reckon we haven't *plumb* forgot what it means. You can sit down now, if you want.'

The liar stood and sneered experimentally, looking at Public Opinion. But this changeful deity was no longer with him, and he heard it variously assenting, 'That's so', and 'She's a lady', and otherwise excellently moralising. So he held his peace. When, however, the Virginian had departed to the roasting steer, and Public Opinion relaxed into that comfort which we all experience when the sermon ends, Trampas sat down amid the reviving cheerfulness, and ventured again to be facetious.

'Shut your rank mouth,' said Wiggin to him, amiably. 'I don't care whether he knows her or if he done it on principle. I'll accept the roundin' up he gave us – and say! you'll swallo' your dose, too! Us boys'll stand in with him in this.'

So Trampas swallowed. And what of the Virginian?

He had championed the feeble, and spoken honourably in meeting, and according to all the constitutions and by-laws of morality, he should have been walking in virtue's especial calm. But there it was! he had spoken; he had given them a peep through the keyhole at his inner man; and as he prowled away from the assemblage before whom he stood convicted of decency, it was vicious rather than virtuous that he felt. Other matters also disquieted him – so Lin McLean was hanging round that schoolmarm! Yet he joined Ben Swinton in a seemingly Christian spirit. He took some whiskey and praised the size of the barrel, speaking with his host like this – 'There cert'nly ain' goin' to be trouble about a second helpin'.'

'Hope not. We'd ought to have more trimmings, though. We're shy on ducks.'

'Yu' have the barrel. Has Lin McLean seen that?'

'No. We tried for ducks away down as far as the Laparel outfit. A real barbecue – '

'There's large thirsts on Bear Creek. Lin McLean will pass on ducks.'

'Lin's not thirsty this month.'

'Signed for one month, has he?'

'Signed! He's spooning our schoolmarm!'

'They claim she's a right sweet-faced girl.'

'Yes; yes; awful agreeable. And next thing you're fooled clean through.'

'Yu' don't say!'

'She keeps a-teaching the darned kids, and it seems like a good growed-up man can't interest her.'

'Yu' don't say!'

'There used to be all the ducks you wanted at the Laparel, but their fool cook's dead stuck on raising turkeys this year.'

'That must have been mighty close to a drowndin' the schoolmarm got at South Fork.'

'Why, I guess not. When? She's never spoken of any such thing – that I've heard.'

'Mos' likely the stage-driver got it wrong, then.'

'Yes. Must have drownded somebody else. Here they come! That's her ridin' the horse. There's the Westfalls. Where are you running to?'

'To fix up. Got any soap around hyeh?'

'Yes,' shouted Swinton, for the Virginian was now some distance away; 'towels and everything in the dugout.' And he went to welcome his first formal guests.

The Virginian reached his saddle under a shed. 'So she's never mentioned it,' said he, untying his slicker for the trousers and scarf. 'I didn't notice Lin anywheres around her.' He was over in the dugout now, whipping off his overalls; and soon he was excellently clean and ready, except for the tie in his scarf and the part in his hair. 'I'd have knowed her in Greenland,' he remarked. He held the candle up and down at the looking-glass, and the looking-glass up and down at his head. 'It's mighty strange why she ain't mentioned that.' He worried the scarf a fold or two further, and at length, a trifle more than satisfied with his appearance, he proceeded most serenely towards the sound of the tuning fiddles. He passed through the storeroom behind the kitchen, stepping lightly lest he should rouse the ten or twelve babies that lay on the table or beneath it. On Bear Creek babies and children always went with their parents to a dance, because nurses were unknown. So little Alfred and Christopher lay there among the wraps, parallel and crosswise with little Taylors, and little Carmodys, and Lees, and all the Bear Creek offspring that was not yet able to skip at large and hamper its indulgent elders in the ballroom.

'Why, Lin ain't hyeh yet!' said the Virginian, looking in upon the people. There was Miss Wood, standing up for the quadrille. 'I didn't remember her hair was that pretty,' said he. 'But ain't she a little, little girl!'

Now she was in truth five feet three; but then he could look away down on the top of her head.

'Salute your honey!' called the first fiddler. All partners bowed to each other, and as she turned, Miss Wood saw the man in the doorway. Again, as it had been at South Fork that day, his eyes dropped from hers, and she divining instantly why he had come after half a year, thought of the handkerchief and of that scream of hers in the river, and became filled with tyranny and anticipation; for indeed he was fine to look upon. So she danced away, carefully unaware of his existence.

'First lady, centre!' said her partner, reminding her of her turn. 'Have you forgotten how it goes since last time?'

Molly Wood did not forget again, but quadrilled with the most sprightly devotion.

'I see some new faces tonight,' said she, presently.

'Yu' always do forget our poor faces,' said her partner.

'Oh, no! There's a stranger now. Who is that black man?'

'Well – he's from Virginia, and he ain't allowin' he's black.'

'He's a tenderfoot, I suppose?'

'Ha, ha, ha! That's rich, too!' and so the simple partner explained a great deal about the Virginian to Molly Wood. At the end of the set she saw the man by the door take a step in her direction.

'Oh,' said she, quickly, to the partner, 'how warm it is! I must see how those babies are doing.' And she passed the Virginian in a breeze of unconcern.

His eyes gravely lingered where she had gone. 'She knowed me right away,' said he. He looked for a moment, then leaned against the door. ' "How warm it is!" said she. Well, it ain't so screechin' hot hyeh; and as for rushin' after Alfred and Christopher when their natural motheh is bumpin' around handy – she cert'nly can't be offended?' he broke off, and looked again where she had gone. And then Miss Wood passed him brightly again, and was dancing the schottische almost immediately. 'Oh, yes, she knows me,' the swarthy cowpuncher mused. 'She has to take trouble not to see me. And what she's a-fussin' at is mighty interestin'. Hello!'

'Hello!' returned Lin McLean, sourly. He had just looked into the kitchen.

'Not dancin'?' the Southerner enquired.

'Don't know how.'

'Had scyarlet fever and forgot your past life?'

Lin grinned.

'Better persuade the schoolmarm to learn yu'. She's goin' to give me instruction.'

'Huh!' went Mr McLean, and skulked out to the barrel.

'Why, they claimed you weren't drinkin' this month!' said his friend, following.

'Well, I am. Here's luck!' The two pledged in tin cups. 'But I'm not waltzin' with her,' blurted Mr McLean grievously. 'She called me an exception.'

'Waltzin',' repeated the Virginian quickly, and hearing the fiddles he hastened away.

Few in the Bear Creek Country could waltz, and with these few it was mostly an unsteered and ponderous exhibition; therefore was the Southerner bent upon profiting by his skill. He entered the room, and his lady saw him come where she sat alone for the moment, and her thoughts grew a little hurried.

'Will you try a turn, ma'am?'

'I beg your pardon?' It was a remote, well-schooled eye that she lifted now upon him.

'If you like a waltz, ma'am, will you waltz with me?'

'You're from Virginia, I understand?' said Molly Wood, regarding him politely, but not rising. One gains authority immensely by keeping one's seat. All good teachers know this.

'Yes, ma'am, from Virginia.'

'I've heard that Southerners have such good manners.'

'That's correct.' The cowpuncher flushed, but he spoke in his unvaryingly gentle voice.

'For in New England, you know,' pursued Miss Molly, noting his scarf and clean-shaven chin, and then again steadily meeting his eye, 'gentlemen ask to be presented to ladies before they ask them to waltz.'

He stood a moment before her, deeper and deeper scarlet; and the more she saw his handsome face, the keener rose her excitement. She waited for him to speak of the river; for then she was going to be surprised, and gradually to remember, and finally to be very nice to him. But he did not wait. 'I ask your pardon, lady,' said he, and bowing, walked off, leaving her at once afraid that he might not come back. But she had altogether mistaken her man. Back he came serenely with Mr Taylor, and was duly presented to her. Thus were the conventions vindicated.

It can never be known what the cowpuncher was going to say next; for Uncle Hughey stepped up with a glass of water which he had left Miss Wood to bring, and asking for a turn, most graciously received it. She danced away from a situation where she began to feel herself getting the worst of it. One moment the Virginian stared at his lady as she lightly circulated, and then he went out to the barrel.

Leave him for Uncle Hughey! Jealousy is a deep and delicate thing, and works its spite in many ways. The Virginian had been ready to look at Lin McLean with a hostile eye; but finding him now beside the barrel, he felt a brotherhood between himself and Lin, and his hostility had taken a new and whimsical direction.

'Here's how!' said he to McLean. And they pledged each other in the tin cups.

'Been gettin' them instructions?' said Mr McLean, grinning. 'I thought I saw yu' learning your steps through the window.'

'Here's your good health,' said the Southerner. Once more they pledged each other handsomely.

'Did she call you an exception, or anything?' said Lin.

'Well, it would cipher out right close in that neighbourhood.'

'Here's how, then!' cried the delighted Lin, over his cup.

'Jest because yu' happen to come from Vermont,' continued Mr McLean, 'is no cause for extra pride. Shoo! I was raised in Massachusetts myself, and big men have been raised there, too – Daniel Webster and Israel Putnam, and a lot of them politicians.'

'Virginia is a good little old state,' observed the Southerner.

'Both of 'em's a sight ahead of Vermont. She told me I was the first exception she'd struck.'

'What rule were you provin' at the time, Lin?'

'Well, yu' see, I started to kiss her.'

'Yu' didn't!'

'Shucks! I didn't mean nothin'.'

'I reckon yu' stopped mighty sudden?'

'Why, I'd been ridin' out with her – ridin' to school, ridin' from school, and a-comin' and a-goin', and she chattin' cheerful and askin' me a heap o' questions all about myself every day, and I not lyin' much neither. And so I figured she wouldn't mind. Lots of 'em like it. But she didn't, you bet!'

'No,' said the Virginian, deeply proud of his lady who had slighted him. He had pulled her out of the water once, and he had been her unrewarded knight even today, and he felt his grievance; but he spoke not of it to Lin; for he felt also, in memory, her arms clinging round him as he carried her ashore upon his horse. But he muttered, 'Plumb ridiculous!' as her injustice struck him afresh, while the outraged McLean told his tale.

'Trample is what she has done on me tonight, and without notice. We was startin' to come here; Taylor and Mrs were ahead in the buggy, and I was holdin' her horse, and helpin' her up in the saddle, like I done for days and days. Who was there to see us? And I figured she'd not mind, and she calls me an exception! Yu'd ought to've just heard her about Western men respectin' women. So that's the last word we've spoke. We come twenty-five miles then, she scootin' in front, and her horse kickin' the sand in my face. Mrs Taylor, she guessed something was up, but she didn't tell.'

'Miss Wood did not tell?'

'Not she! She'll never open her head. She can take care of herself, you bet!'

The fiddles sounded hilariously in the house, and the feet also. They had warmed up altogether, and their dancing figures crossed the windows back and forth. The two cowpunchers drew near to a window and looked in gloomily.

'There she goes,' said Lin.

'With Uncle Hughey again,' said the Virginian, sourly. 'Yu' might suppose he didn't have a wife and twins, to see the way he goes gambollin' around.'

'Westfall is takin' a turn with her now,' said McLean.

'James!' exclaimed the Virginian. 'He's another with a wife and fam'ly, and he gets the dancin', too.'

'There she goes with Taylor,' said Lin, presently.

'Another married man!' the Southerner commented. They prowled round to the storeroom, and passed through the kitchen to where the dancers were robustly tramping. Miss Wood was still the partner of Mr Taylor. 'Let's have some whiskey,' said the Virginian. They had it, and returned, and the Virginian's disgust and sense of injury grew deeper. 'Old Carmody has got her now,' he drawled. 'He polkas like a landslide. She learns his monkey-faced kid to spell dog and cow all the mawnin'. He'd ought to be tucked up cosy in his bed right now, old Carmody ought.'

They were standing in that place set apart for the sleeping children; and just at this moment one of two babies that were stowed beneath a chair uttered a drowsy note. A much louder cry, indeed a chorus of lament, would have been needed to reach the ears of the parents in the room beyond, such was the noisy volume of the dance. But in this quiet place the light sound caught Mr McLean's attention, and he turned to see if anything were wrong. But both babies were sleeping peacefully.

'Them's Uncle Hughey's twins,' he said.

'How do you happen to know that?' enquired the Virginian, suddenly interested.

'Saw his wife put 'em under the chair so she could find 'em right off when she come to go home.'

'Oh,' said the Virginian, thoughtfully. 'Oh, find 'em right off. Yes. Uncle Hughey's twins.' He walked to a spot from which he could view the dance. 'Well,' he continued, returning, 'the schoolmarm must have taken quite a notion to Uncle Hughey. He has got her for this quadrille.' The Virginian was now speaking without rancour; but his words came with a slightly augmented drawl, and this with him was often a bad omen. He now turned his eyes upon the collected babies wrapped in various coloured shawls and knitted work. 'Nine, ten, eleven, beautiful sleepin' strangers,' he counted, in a sweet voice. 'Any of 'em yourn, Lin?'

'Not that I know of,' grinned Mr McLean.

'Eleven, twelve. This hyeh is little Christopher in the blue-stripe quilt – or maybe that other yello'-head is him. The angels have commenced to drop in on us right smart along Bear Creek, Lin.'

'What trash are yu' talkin' anyway?'

'If they look so awful alike in the heavenly gyarden,' the gentle Southerner continued, 'I'd just hate to be the folks that has the cuttin' of 'em out o' the general herd. And that's a right quaint notion too,' he added softly. 'Them under the chair are Uncle Hughey's, didn't you tell me?' And stooping, he lifted the torpid babies and placed them beneath a table. 'No, that ain't thorough,' he murmured. With wonderful dexterity and solicitude for their welfare, he removed the loose wrap which was around them, and this soon led to an intricate process of exchange. For a moment Mr McLean had been staring at the Virginian, puzzled. Then, with a joyful yelp of enlightenment, he sprang to abet him.

And while both busied themselves with the shawls and quilts, the unconscious parents went dancing vigorously on, and the small, occasional cries of their progeny did not reach them.

CHAPTER 11

'You're going to love me before we get through'

The Swinton barbecue was over. The fiddles were silent, the steer was eaten, the barrel emptied, or largely so, and the tapers extinguished; round the house and sunken fire all movement of guests was quiet; the families were long departed homeward, and after their hospitable turbulence, the Swintons slept.

Mr and Mrs Westfall drove through the night, and as they neared their cabin there came from among the bundled wraps a still, small voice.

'Jim,' said his wife, 'I said Alfred would catch cold.'

'Bosh! Lizzie, don't you fret. He's a little more than a yearlin', and of course he'll snuffle.' And young James took a kiss from his love.

'Well, how you can speak of Alfred that way, calling him a yearling, as if he was a calf, and he just as much your child as mine, I don't see, James Westfall!'

'Why, what under the sun do you mean?'

'There he goes again! Do hurry up home, Jim. He's got a real strange cough.'

So they hurried home. Soon the nine miles were finished, and good James was unhitching by his stable lantern, while his wife in the house hastened to commit their offspring to bed. The traces had dropped, and each horse marched forward for further unbuckling, when James heard himself called. Indeed, there was that in his wife's voice which made him jerk out his pistol as he ran. But it was no bear or Indian – only two strange children on the bed. His wife was glaring at them.

He sighed with relief and laid down the pistol.

'Put that on again, James Westfall. You'll need it. Look here!'

'Well, they won't bite. Whose are they? Where have you stowed our'n?'

'Where have I – ' Utterance forsook this mother for a moment. 'And you ask me!' she continued. 'Ask Lin McLean. Ask him that sets bulls on folks and steals slippers, what he's done with our innocent lambs, mixing them up with other people's coughing, unhealthy brats. That's Charlie Taylor in Alfred's clothes, and I know Alfred didn't cough like that, and I said to you it was strange; and the other one that's been put in Christopher's new quilts is not even a bub – bub – boy!'

As this crime against society loomed clear to James Westfall's understanding, he sat down on the nearest piece of furniture, and heedless of his wife's tears and his exchanged children, broke into unregenerate laughter. Doubtless after his sharp alarm about the bear, he was unstrung. His lady, however, promptly restrung him; and by the time they had repacked the now clamorous changelings, and were rattling on their way to the Taylors', he began to share her outraged feelings properly, as a husband and a father should; but when he reached the Taylors' and learned from Miss Wood that at this house a child had been unwrapped whom nobody could at all identify, and that Mr and Mrs Taylor were already far on the road to the Swintons', James Westfall whipped up his horses and grew almost as thirsty for revenge as was his wife.

* * *

Where the steer had been roasted, the powdered ashes were now cold white, and Mr McLean, feeling through his dreams the change of dawn come over the air, sat up cautiously among the outdoor slumberers and waked his neighbour.

'Day will be soon,' he whispered, 'and we must light out of this. I never suspicioned yu' had that much of the devil in you before.'

'I reckon some of the fellows will act haidstrong,' the Virginian murmured luxuriously, among the warmth of his blankets.

'I tell yu' we must skip,' said Lin, for the second time; and he rubbed the Virginian's black head, which alone was visible.

'Skip, then, you,' came muffled from within, 'and keep you'self mighty sca'ce till they can appreciate our frolic.'

The Southerner withdrew deeper into his bed, and Mr McLean, informing him that he was a fool, arose and saddled his horse. From the saddlebag he brought a parcel, and lightly laying this beside Bokay Baldy, he mounted and was gone. When Baldy awoke later, he found the parcel to be a pair of flowery slippers.

In selecting the inert Virginian as the fool, Mr McLean was scarcely wise; it is the absent who are always guilty.

Before ever Lin could have been a mile in retreat, the rattle of the wheels roused all of them, and here came the Taylors. Before the Taylors' knocking had brought the Swintons to their door, other wheels sounded, and here were Mr and Mrs Carmody, and Uncle Hughey with his wife, and close after them Mr Dow, alone, who told how his wife had gone into one of her fits – she upon whom Dr Barker at Drybone had enjoined total abstinence from all excitement. Voices of women and children began to be uplifted; the Westfalls arrived in a lather, and the Thomases; and by sunrise, what with fathers and mothers and spectators and loud offspring, there was gathered such a meeting as has seldom been before among the generations of speaking men. Today you can hear legends of it from Texas to Montana; but I am giving you the full particulars.

Of course they pitched upon poor Lin. Here was the Virginian doing his best, holding horses and helping ladies descend, while the name of McLean began to be muttered with threats. Soon a party led by Mr Dow set forth in search of him, and the Southerner debated a moment if he had better not put them on a wrong track. But he concluded that they might safely go on searching.

Mrs Westfall found Christopher at once in the green shawl of Anna Maria Dow, but all was not achieved thus in the twinkling of an eye. Mr McLean had, it appeared, as James Westfall lugubriously pointed out, not merely 'swapped the duds; he had shuffled the whole doggone deck';

and they cursed this Satanic invention. The fathers were but of moderate assistance; it was the mothers who did the heavy work; and by ten o'clock some unsolved problems grew so delicate that a ladies' caucus was organised in a private room – no admittance for men – and what was done there I can only surmise.

During its progress the search party returned. It had not found Mr McLean. It had found a tree with a notice pegged upon it, reading, 'God bless our home!' This was captured.

But success attended the caucus; each mother emerged, satisfied that she had received her own, and each sire, now that his family was itself again, began to look at his neighbour sideways. After a man has been angry enough to kill another man, after the fire of righteous slaughter has raged in his heart as it had certainly raged for several hours in the hearts of these fathers, the flame will usually burn itself out. This will be so in a generous nature, unless the cause of the anger is still unchanged. But the children had been identified; none had taken hurt. All had been humanely given their nourishment. The thing was over. The day was beautiful. A tempting feast remained from the barbecue. These Bear Creek fathers could not keep their ire at red heat. Most of them, being as yet more their wives' lovers than their children's parents, began to see the mirthful side of the adventure; and they ceased to feel very severely towards Lin McLean.

Not so the women. They cried for vengeance; but they cried in vain, and were met with smiles.

Mrs Westfall argued long that punishment should be dealt the offender. 'Anyway,' she persisted, 'it was real defiant of him putting that up on the tree. I might forgive him but for that.'

'Yes,' spoke the Virginian in their midst, 'that wasn't sort o' right. Especially as I am the man you're huntin'.'

They sat dumb at his assurance.

'Come and kill me,' he continued, looking round upon the party. 'I'll not resist.'

But they could not resist the way in which he had looked round upon them. He had chosen the right moment for his confession, as a captain of horse awaits the proper time for a charge. Some rebukes he did receive; the worst came from the mothers. And all that he could say for himself was, 'I am getting off too easy.'

'But what was your point?' said Westfall.

'Blamed if I know any more. I expect it must have been the whiskey.'

'I would mind it less,' said Mrs Westfall, 'if you looked a bit sorry or ashamed.'

The Virginian shook his head at her penitently. 'I'm tryin' to,' he said.

And thus he sat disarming his accusers until they began to lunch upon the copious remnants of the barbecue. He did not join them at this meal. In telling you that Mrs Dow was the only lady absent upon this historic morning, I was guilty of an inadvertence. There was one other.

*   *   *

The Virginian rode away sedately through the autumn sunshine; and as he went he asked his Monte horse a question. 'Do yu' reckon she'll have forgotten you too, you pie-biter?' said he. Instead of the new trousers, the cowpuncher's leathern chaps were on his legs. But he had the new scarf knotted at his neck. Most men would gladly have equalled him in appearance. 'You Monte,' said he, 'will she be at home?'

It was Sunday, and no school day, and he found her in her cabin that stood next the Taylors' house. Her eyes were very bright.

'I'd thought I'd just call,' said he.

'Why, that's such a pity! Mr and Mrs Taylor are away.'

'Yes; they've been right busy. That's why I thought I'd call. Will yu' come for a ride, ma'am?'

'Dear me! I – '

'You can ride my hawss. He's gentle.'

'What! And you walk?'

'No, ma'am. Nor the two of us ride him *this* time, either.' At this she turned entirely pink and he, noticing, went on quietly: 'I'll catch up one of Taylor's hawsses. Taylor knows me.'

'No. I don't really think I could do that. But thank you. Thank you very much. I must go now and see how Mrs Taylor's fire is.'

'I'll look after that, ma'am. I'd like for yu' to go ridin' mighty well. Yu' have no babies this mawnin' to be anxious after.'

At this shaft, Grandmother Stark flashed awake deep within the spirit of her descendant, and she made a haughty declaration of war. 'I don't know what you mean, sir,' she said.

Now was his danger; for it was easy to fall into mere crude impertinence and ask her why, then, did she speak thus abruptly? There were various easy things of this kind for him to say. And any rudeness would have lost him the battle. But the Virginian was not the man to lose such a battle in such a way. His shaft had hit. She thought he referred to those babies about whom last night she had shown such superfluous solicitude. Her conscience was guilty. This was all that he had wished to make sure of before he began operations.

'Why, I mean,' said he, easily, sitting down near the door, 'that it's Sunday. School don't hinder yu' from enjoyin' a ride today. You'll teach the kids all the better for it tomorro', ma'am. Maybe it's your duty.' And he smiled at her.

'My duty! It's quite novel to have strangers – '

'Am I a stranger?' he cut in, firing his first broadside. 'I was introduced, ma'am,' he continued, noting how she had flushed again. 'And I would not be oversteppin' for the world. I'll go away if yu' want.' And hereupon he quietly rose, and stood, hat in hand.

Molly was flustered. She did not at all want him to go. No one of her admirers had ever been like this creature. The fringed leathern *chaparajos*, the cartridge-belt, the flannel shirt, the knotted scarf at the neck, these things were now an old story to her. Since her arrival she had seen young men and old in plenty dressed thus. But worn by this man now standing by her door, they seemed to radiate romance. She did not want him to go – and she wished to win her battle. And now in her agitation she became suddenly severe, as she had done at Hoosic Junction. He should have a punishment to remember!

'You call yourself a man, I suppose,' she said.

But he did not tremble in the least. Her fierceness filled him with delight, and the tender desire of ownership flooded through him.

'A grown-up, responsible man,' she repeated.

'Yes, ma'am. I think so.' He now sat down again.

'And you let them think that – that Mr McLean – You dare not look me in the face and say that Mr McLean did that last night!'

'I reckon I dassent.'

'There! I knew it! I said so from the first!'

'And me a stranger to you!' he murmured.

It was his second broadside. It left her badly crippled. She was silent.

'Who did yu' mention it to, ma'am?'

She hoped she had him. 'Why, are you afraid?' And she laughed lightly.

'I told 'em myself. And their astonishment seemed so genu-wine I'd just hate to think they had fooled me that thorough when they knowed it all along from you seeing me.'

'I did not see you. I knew it must – Of course I did not tell anyone.

When I said I said so from the first, I meant – you can understand perfectly what I meant.'

'Yes, ma'am.'

Poor Molly was near stamping her foot. 'And what sort of a trick,' she rushed on, 'was that to play? Do you call it a manly thing to frighten and distress women because you – for no reason at all? I should never have imagined it could be the act of a person who wears a big pistol and rides a big horse. I should be afraid to go riding with such an immature protector.'

'Yes; that was awful childish. Your words do cut a little; for maybe there's been times when I have acted pretty near like a man. But I cert'nly forgot to be introduced before I spoke to yu' last night. Because why? You've found me out dead in one thing. Won't you take a guess at this too?'

'I cannot sit guessing why people do not behave themselves – who seem to know better.'

'Well, ma'am, I've played square and owned up to yu'. And that's not what you're doin' by me. I ask your pardon if I say what I have a right to say in language not as good as I'd like to talk to yu' with. But at South Fork Crossin' who did any introducin'? Did yu' complain I was a stranger then?'

'I – no!' she flashed out; then, quite sweetly, 'The driver told me it wasn't *really* so dangerous there, you know.'

'That's not the point I'm makin'. You are a grown-up woman, a responsible woman. You've come ever so far, and all alone, to a rough country to instruct young children that play games – tag, and hide-and-seek, and fooleries they'll have to quit when they get old. Don't you think pretendin' yu' don't know a man – his name's nothin', but *him* – a man whom you were glad enough to let assist yu' when somebody was needed – don't you think that's mighty close to hide-and-seek them children plays? I ain't so sure but what there's a pair of us children in this hyeh room.'

Molly Wood was regarding him saucily. 'I don't think I like you,' said she.

'That's all square enough. You're goin' to love me before we get through. I wish yu'd come a-ridin, ma'am.'

'Dear, dear, dear! So I'm going to love you? How will you do it? I know men think that they only need to sit and look strong and make chests at a girl – '

'Goodness gracious! I ain't makin' any chests at yu'!' Laughter overcame him for a moment, and Miss Wood liked his laugh very much. 'Please come a-ridin',' he urged. 'It's the prettiest kind of a day.'

She looked at him frankly, and there was a pause. 'I will take back two things that I said to you,' she then answered him. 'I believe that I do like you. And I know that if I went riding with you, I should not have an immature protector.' And then, with a final gesture of acknowledgement, she held out her hand to him. 'And I have always wanted,' she said, 'to thank you for what you did at the river.'

He took her hand, and his heart bounded. 'You're a gentleman!' he exclaimed.

It was now her turn to be overcome with merriment. 'I've always wanted to be a man,' she said.

'I am mighty glad you ain't,' said he, looking at her.

But Molly had already received enough broadsides for one day. She could allow no more of them, and she took herself capably in hand. 'Where did you learn to make such pretty speeches?' she asked. 'Well, never mind that. One sees that you have had plenty of practice for one so young.'

'I am twenty-seven,' blurted the Virginian, and knew instantly that he had spoken like a fool.

'Who would have dreamed it!' said Molly, with well-measured mockery. She knew that she had scored at last, and that this day was hers. 'Don't be too sure you are glad I'm not a man,' she now told him. There was something like a challenge in her voice.

'I risk it,' he remarked.

'For I am almost twenty-three myself,' she concluded. And she gave him a look on her own account.

'And you'll not come a-ridin'?' he persisted.

'No,' she answered him; 'no.' And he knew that he could not make her.

'Then I will tell yu' goodbye,' said he. 'But I am comin' again. And next time I'll have along a gentle hawss for yu'.'

'Next time! Next time! Well, perhaps I will go with you. Do you live far?'

'I live on Judge Henry's ranch, over yondeh.' He pointed across the mountains. 'It's on Sunk Creek. A pretty rough trail; but I can come hyeh to see you in a day, I reckon. Well, I hope you'll cert'nly enjoy good health, ma'am.'

'Oh, there's one thing!' said Molly Wood, calling after him rather quickly. 'I – I'm not at all afraid of horses. You needn't bring such a gentle one. I – was very tired that day, and – and I don't scream as a rule.'

He turned and looked at her so that she could not meet his glance. 'Bless your heart!' said he. 'Will yu' give me one o' those flowers?'

'Oh, certainly! I'm always so glad when people like them.'

'They're pretty near the colour of your eyes.'

'Never mind my eyes.'

'Can't help it, ma'am. Not since South Fork.'

He put the flower in the leather band of his hat, and rode away on his Monte horse. Miss Wood lingered a moment, then made some steps towards her gate, from which he could still be seen; and then, with something like a toss of the head, she went in and shut her door.

Later in the day the Virginian met Mr McLean, who looked at his hat and innocently quoted, 'My Looloo picked a daisy.'

'Don't yu', Lin,' said the Southerner.

'Then I won't,' said Lin.

Thus, for this occasion, did the Virginian part from his lady – and nothing said one way or another about the handkerchief that had disappeared during the South Fork incident.

As we fall asleep at night, our thoughts will often ramble back and forth between the two worlds.

'What colour were his eyes?' wondered Molly on her pillow. 'His moustache is not bristly like so many of them. Sam never gave me such a look as . . . Hoosic Junction . . . No . . . You can't come with me . . . Get off your horse . . . The passengers are all staring . . . '

And while Molly was thus dreaming that the Virginian had ridden his horse into the railroad car, and sat down beside her, the fire in the great stone chimney of her cabin flickered quietly, its gleams now and again touching the miniature of Grandmother Stark upon the wall.

Camped on the Sunk Creek trail, the Virginian was telling himself in his blankets – 'I ain't too old for education. Maybe she will lend me books. And I'll watch her ways and learn . . . stand still, Monte . . . I can learn a lot more than the kids on that . . . There's Monte . . . you pie-biter, stop . . . He has ate up your book, ma'am, but I'll get yu' . . . '

And then the Virginian was fast asleep.

CHAPTER 12

Quality and Equality

To the circle at Bennington, a letter from Bear Creek was always a welcome summons to gather and hear of doings very strange to Vermont. And when the tale of the changed babies arrived duly by the post, it created a more than usual sensation, and was read to a large number of pleased and scandalised neighbours. 'I hate her to be where such things can happen,' said Mrs Wood. 'I wish I could have been there,' said her son-in-law, Andrew Bell. 'She does not mention who played the trick,' said Mrs Andrew Bell. 'We shouldn't be any wiser if she did,' said Mrs Wood. 'I'd like to meet the perpetrator,' said Andrew. 'Oh, no!' said Mrs Wood. 'They're all horrible.' And she wrote at once, begging her daughter to take good care of herself, and to see as much of Mrs Balaam as possible. 'And of any other ladies that are near you. For you seem to me to be in a community of roughs. I wish you would give it all up. Did you expect me to laugh about the babies?'

Mrs Flynt, when this story was repeated to her (she had not been invited in to hear the letter), remarked that she had always felt that Molly Wood must be a little vulgar, ever since she began to go about giving music lessons like any ordinary German.

But Mrs Wood was considerably relieved when the next letter arrived. It contained nothing horrible about barbecues or babies. It mentioned the great beauty of the weather, and how well and strong the fine air was making the writer feel. And it asked that books might be sent, many books of all sorts, novels, poetry, all the good old books and any good new ones that could be spared. Cheap editions, of course. 'Indeed she shall have them!' said Mrs Wood. 'How her mind must be starving in that dreadful place!' The letter was not a long one, and, besides the books, spoke of little else except the fine weather and the chances for outdoor exercise that this gave. 'You have no idea,' it said, 'how delightful it is to ride, especially on a spirited horse, which I can do now quite well.'

'How nice that is!' said Mrs Wood, putting down the letter. 'I hope the horse is not too spirited.' – 'Who does she go riding with?' asked Mrs Bell. 'She doesn't say, Sarah. Why?' – 'Nothing. She has a queer way of not mentioning things, now and then.' – 'Sarah!' exclaimed Mrs Wood, reproachfully. 'Oh, well, mother, you know just as well as I do that she can be very independent and unconventional.' – 'Yes; but not in that way. She wouldn't ride with poor Sam Bannett, and after all he is a suitable person.'

Nevertheless, in her next letter, Mrs Wood cautioned her daughter about trusting herself with anyone of whom Mrs Balaam did not thoroughly approve. The good lady could never grasp that Mrs Balaam lived a long day's journey from Bear Creek, and that Molly saw her about once every three months. 'We have sent your books,' the mother wrote; 'everybody has contributed from their store – Shakespeare, Tennyson, Browning, Longfellow; and a number of novels by Scott, Thackeray, George Eliot, Hawthorne, and lesser writers; some volumes of Emerson; and Jane Austen complete, because you admire her so particularly.'

This consignment of literature reached Bear Creek about a week before Christmas time.

By New Year's Day, the Virginian had begun his education.

'Well, I have managed to get through 'em,' he said, as he entered Molly's cabin in February. And he laid two volumes upon her table.

'And what do you think of them?' she enquired.

'I think that I've cert'nly earned a good long ride today.'

'Georgie Taylor has sprained his ankle.'

'No, I don't mean that kind of a ride. I've earned a ride with just us two alone. I've read every word of both of 'em, yu' know.'

'I'll think about it. Did you like them?'

'No. Not much. If I'd knowed that one was a detective story, I'd have got yu' to try something else on me. Can you guess the murderer, or is the author too smart for yu'? That's all they amount to. Well, he was too smart for me this time, but that didn't distress me any. That other book talks too much.'

Molly was scandalised, and she told him it was a great work.

'Oh, yes, yes. A fine book. But it will keep up its talkin'. Don't let you alone.'

'Didn't you feel sorry for poor Maggie Tulliver?'

'Hmp. Yes. Sorry for her, and for Tawmmy, too. But the man did right to drownd 'em both.'

'It wasn't a man. A woman wrote that.'

'A woman did! Well, then, o' course she talks too much.'

'I'll not go riding with you!' shrieked Molly.

But she did. And he returned to Sunk Creek, not with a detective story, but this time with a Russian novel.

It was almost April when he brought it back to her – and a heavy sleet storm lost them their ride. So he spent his time indoors with her, not speaking a syllable of love. When he came to take his departure, he asked her for some other book by this same Russian. But she had no more.

'I wish you had,' he said. 'I've never saw a book could tell the truth like that one does.'

'Why, what do you like about it?' she exclaimed. To her it had been distasteful.

'Everything,' he answered. 'That young come-outer, and his fam'ly that can't understand him – for he is broad gauge, yu' see, and they are narro' gauge.' The Virginian looked at Molly a moment almost shyly. 'Do you know,' he said, and a blush spread over his face, 'I pretty near cried when that young come-outer was dyin', and said about himself, "I was a giant". Life made him broad gauge, yu' see, and then took his chance away.

Molly liked the Virginian for his blush. It made him very handsome. But she thought that it came from his confession about 'pretty near crying', The deeper cause she failed to divine – that he, like the dying hero in the novel, felt himself to be a giant whom life had made 'broad gauge', and denied opportunity. Fecund nature begets and squanders thousands of these rich seeds in the wilderness of life.

He took away with him a volume of Shakespeare. 'I've saw good plays of his,' he remarked.

Kind Mrs Taylor in her cabin next door watched him ride off in the sleet, bound for the lonely mountain trail.

'If that girl don't get ready to take him pretty soon,' she observed to her husband, 'I'll give her a piece of my mind.'

Taylor was astonished. 'Is he thinking of *her*?' he enquired.

'Lord, Mr Taylor, and why shouldn't he?'

Mr Taylor scratched his head and returned to his newspaper.

* * *

It was warm – warm and beautiful upon Bear Creek. Snow shone upon the peaks of the Bow Leg range; lower on their slopes the pines were stirring with a gentle song; and flowers bloomed across the wide plains at their feet.

Molly and her Virginian sat at a certain spring where he had often ridden with her. On this day he was bidding her farewell before under-taking the most important trust which Judge Henry had as yet given him. For this journey she had provided him with Sir Walter Scott's *Kenilworth*. Shakespeare he had returned to her. He had bought Shake-speare for himself. 'As soon as I got used to readin' it,' he had told her, 'I knowed for certain that I liked readin' for enjoyment.'

But it was not of books that he had spoken much today. He had not spoken at all. He had bade her listen to the meadow-lark, when its song fell upon the silence like beaded drops of music. He had showed her where a covey of young willow-grouse were hiding as their horses passed. And then, without warning, as they sat by the spring, he had spoken potently of his love.

She did not interrupt him. She waited until he was wholly finished.

'I am not the sort of wife you want,' she said, with an attempt of airiness.

He answered roughly, 'I am the judge of that.' And his roughness was a pleasure to her, yet it made her afraid of herself. When he was absent from her, and she could sit in her cabin and look at Grandmother Stark, and read home letters, then in imagination she found it easy to play the part which she had arranged to play regarding him – the part of the guide, and superior, and indulgent companion. But when he was by her side, that part became a difficult one. Her woman's fortress was shaken by a force unknown to her before. Sam Bannett did not have it in him to look as this man could look, when the cold lustre of his eyes grew hot with internal fire. What colour they were baffled her still. 'Can it possibly change?' she wondered. It seemed to her that sometimes when she had been looking from a rock straight down into clear sea water, this same colour had lurked in its depths. 'Is it green, or is it grey?' she asked herself, but did not turn just now to see. She kept her face towards the landscape.

'All men are born equal,' he now remarked slowly.

'Yes,' she quickly answered, with a combative flash. 'Well?'

'Maybe that don't include women?' he suggested.

'I think it does.'

'Do yu' tell the kids so?'

'Of course I teach them what I believe!'

He pondered. 'I used to have to learn about the Declaration of Independence. I hated books and truck when I was a kid.'

'But you don't any more.'

'No. I cert'nly don't. But I used to get kep' in at recess for bein' so dumb. I was most always at the tail end of the class. My brother, he'd be head sometimes.'

'Little George Taylor is my prize scholar,' said Molly.

'Knows his tasks, does he?'

'Always. And Henry Dow comes next.'

'Who`s last?'

'Poor Bob Carmody. I spend more time on him than on all the rest put together.'

'My!' said the Virginian. 'Ain't that strange!'

She looked at him, puzzled by his tone. 'It's not strange when you know Bob,' she said.

'It's very strange,' drawled the Virginian. 'Knowin' Bob don't help it any.'

'I don't think that I understand you,' said Molly, stiffly.

'Well, it *is* mighty confusin'. George Taylor, he's your best scholar, and poor Bob, he's your worst, and there's a lot in the middle – and you tell me we're all born equal!'

Molly could only sit giggling in this trap he had so ingeniously laid for her. 'I'll tell you what,' pursued the cowpuncher, with slow and growing intensity, 'equality is a great big bluff. It's easy called.'

'I didn't mean – ' began Molly.

'Wait, and let me say what I mean.' He had made an imperious gesture with his hand. 'I know a man that mostly wins at cyards. I know a man that mostly loses. He says it is his luck. All right. Call it his luck. I know a man that works hard and he's gettin' rich, and I know another that works hard and is gettin' poor. He says it is his luck. All right. Call it his luck. I look around and I see folks movin' up or movin' down, winners or losers everywhere. All luck, of course. But since folks can be born that different in their luck, where's your equality? No, seh! call your failure luck, or call it laziness, wander around the words, prospect all yu' mind to, and yu'll come out the same old trail of inequality.' He paused a moment and looked at her. 'Some holds four aces,' he went on, 'and some holds nothin', and some poor fello' gets the aces and no show to play 'em; but a man has got to prove himself my equal before I'll believe him.'

Molly sat gazing at him, silent.

'I know what yu' meant,' he told her now, 'by sayin' you're not the wife I'd want. But I am the kind that moves up. I am goin' to be your best scholar.' He turned towards her, and that fortress within her began to shake.

'Don't,' she murmured. 'Don't, please.'

'Don't what?'

'Why – spoil this.'

'Spoil it?'

'These rides – I don't love you – I can't – but these rides are – '

'What are they?'

'My greatest pleasure. There! And, please, I want them to go on so.'

'Go on so! I don't reckon yu' know what you're sayin'. Yu' might as well ask fruit to stay green. If the way we are now can keep bein' enough for you, it can't for me. A pleasure to you, is it? Well, to me it is – I don't know what to call it. I come to yu' and I hate it, and I come again and I hate it, and I ache and grieve all over when I go. No! You will have to think of some other way than just invitin' me to keep green.'

'If I am to see you – ' began the girl.

'You're not to see me. Not like this. I can stay away easier than what I am doin'.'

'Will you do me a favour, a great one?' said she, now.

'Make it as impossible as you please!' he cried. He thought it was to be some action.

'Go on coming. But don't talk to me about – don't talk in that way – if you can help it.'

He laughed out, not permitting himself to swear.

'But,' she continued, 'if you can't help talking that way – sometimes – I promise I will listen. That is the only promise I make.'

'That is a bargain,' he said.

Then he helped her mount her horse, restraining himself like a Spartan, and they rode home to her cabin.

'You have made it pretty near impossible,' he said, as he took his leave. 'But you've been square today, and I'll show you I can be square when I come back. I'll not do more than ask you if your mind's the same. And now I'll not see you for quite a while. I am going a long way. But I'll be very busy. And bein' busy always keeps me from grievin' too much about you.'

Strange is woman! She would rather have heard some other last remark than this.

'Oh, very well!' she said. 'I'll not miss you either.'

He smiled at her. 'I doubt if yu' can help missin' me,' he remarked. And he was gone at once, galloping on his Monte horse.

Which of the two won a victory this day?

CHAPTER 13

The Game and the Nation – Act First

There can be no doubt of this – All America is divided into two classes – the quality and the equality. The latter will always recognise the former when mistaken for it. Both will be with us until our women bear nothing but kings.

It was through the Declaration of Independence that we Americans acknowledged the *eternal inequality* of man. For by it we abolished a cut-and-dried aristocracy. We had seen little men artificially held up in high places, and great men artificially held down in low places, and our own justice-loving hearts abhorred this violence to human nature. Therefore, we decreed that every man should thenceforth have equal liberty to find his own level. By this very decree we acknowledged and gave freedom to true aristocracy, saying, 'Let the best man win, whoever he is.' Let the best man win! That is America's word. That is true democracy. And true democracy and true aristocracy are one and the same thing. If anybody cannot see this, so much the worse for his eyesight.

The above reflections occurred to me before reaching Billings, Montana, some three weeks after I had unexpectedly met the Virginian at Omaha, Nebraska. I had not known of that trust given to him by Judge Henry, which was taking him East. I was looking to ride with him before long among the clean hills of Sunk Creek. I supposed he was there. But I came upon him one morning in Colonel Cyrus Jones's eating palace.

Did you know the palace? It stood in Omaha, near the trains, and it was ten years old (which is middle-aged in Omaha) when I first saw it. It was a shell of wood, painted with golden emblems – the steamboat, the eagle, the Yosemite – and a live bear ate gratuities at its entrance. Weather permitting, it opened upon the world as a stage upon the audience. You sat in Omaha's whole sight and dined, while Omaha's dust came and settled upon the refreshments. It is gone the way of the Indian and the buffalo, for the West is growing old. You should have seen the palace and sat there. In front of you passed rainbows of men – Chinese, Indian chiefs, Africans, General Miles, younger sons, Austrian nobility, wide females in pink. Our continent drained prismatically through Omaha once.

So I was passing that way also, walking for the sake of ventilation from

1194

a sleeping-car towards a bath, when the language of Colonel Cyrus Jones came out to me. The actual colonel I had never seen before. He stood at the rear of his palace in grey flowery moustaches and a Confederate uniform, telling the wishes of his guests to the cook through a hole. You always bought meal tickets at once, else you became unwelcome. Guests here had foibles at times, and a rapid exit was too easy. Therefore I bought a ticket. It was spring and summer since I had heard anything like the colonel. The Missouri had not yet flowed into New York dialect freely, and his vocabulary met me like the breeze of the plains. So I went in to be fanned by it, and there sat the Virginian at a table, alone.

His greeting was up to the code of indifference proper on the plains; but he presently remarked, 'I'm right glad to see somebody,' which was a good deal to say. 'Them that comes hyeh,' he observed next, 'don't eat. They feed.' And he considered the guests with a sombre attention. 'D' yu' reckon they find joyful di-gestion in this swallo'-an'-get-out trough?'

'What are you doing here, then?' said I.

'Oh, pshaw! When yu' can't have what you choose, yu' just choose what you have.' And he took the bill-of-fare. I began to know that he had something on his mind, so I did not trouble him further.

Meanwhile he sat studying the bill-of-fare.

'Ever heard o' them?' he enquired, shoving me the spotted document.

Most improbable dishes were there – salamis, canapés, suprêmes – all perfectly spelt and absolutely transparent. It was the old trick of copying some metropolitan menu to catch travellers of the third and last dimension of innocence; and whenever this is done the food is of the third and last dimension of awfulness, which the cowpuncher knew as well as anybody.

'So they keep that up here still,' I said.

'But what about them?' he repeated. His finger was at a special item, *Frogs' legs à la Delmonico*. 'Are they true anywheres?' he asked. And I told him, certainly. I also explained to him about Delmonico of New York and about Augustin of Philadelphia.

'There's not a little bit o' use in lyin' to me this mawnin',' he said, with his engaging smile. 'I ain't goin' to awdeh anything's laigs.'

'Well, I'll see how he gets out of it,' I said, remembering the old Texas legend. (The traveller read the bill-of-fare, you know, and called for a *vol-au-vent*. And the proprietor looked at the traveller, and running a pistol into his ear, observed, 'You'll take hash.') I was thinking of this and wondering what would happen to me. So I took the step.

'Wants frogs' legs, does he?' shouted Colonel Cyrus Jones. He fixed his eye upon me, and it narrowed to a slit. 'Too many brain workers breakfasting before yu' came in, professor,' said he. 'Missionary ate the last leg off me just now. Brown the wheat!' he commanded, through the hole to the cook, for someone had ordered hot cakes.

'I'll have fried aiggs,' said the Virginian. 'Cooked both sides.'

'White wings!' sang the colonel through the hole. 'Let 'em fly up and down.'

'Coffee an' no milk,' said the Virginian.

'Draw one in the dark!' the colonel roared.

'And beefsteak, rare.'

'One slaughter in the pan, and let the blood drip!'

'I should like a glass of water, please,' said I.

The colonel threw me a look of pity.

'One Missouri and ice for the professor!' he said.

'That fello's a right live man,' commented the Virginian. But he seemed thoughtful. Presently he enquired, 'Yu' say he was a foreigner, an' learned fancy cookin' to New Yawk?'

That was this cowpuncher's way. Scarcely ever would he let drop a thing new to him until he had got from you your whole information about it. So I told him the history of Lorenzo Delmonico and his pioneer work, as much as I knew, and the Southerner listened intently.

'Mighty inter-estin',' he said, ' – mighty. He could just take little old o'rn'ry frawgs, and dandy 'em up to suit the bloods. Mighty inter-estin'. I expaict, though, his cookin' would give an outraiged stomach to a plain-raised man.'

'If you want to follow it up,' said I, by way of a sudden experiment, 'Miss Molly Wood might have some book about French dishes.'

But the Virginian did not turn a hair. 'I reckon she wouldn't,' he answered. 'She was raised in Vermont. They don't bother overly about their eatin' up in Vermont. Hyeh's what Miss Wood recommended the las' time I was seein' her,' the cowpuncher added, bringing *Kenilworth* from his pocket. 'Right fine story. That Queen Elizabeth must have cert'nly been a competent woman.'

'She was,' said I. But talk came to an end here. A dusty crew, most evidently from the plains, now entered and drifted to a table; and each man of them gave the Virginian about a quarter of a slouchy nod. His greeting to them was very serene. Only, *Kenilworth* went back into his pocket, and he breakfasted in silence. Among those who had greeted him I now recognised a face.

'Why, that's the man you played cards with at Medicine Bow!' I said.

'Yes. Trampas. He's got a job at the ranch now.' The Virginian said no more, but went on with his breakfast.

His appearance was changed. Aged I would scarcely say, for this would seem as if he did not look young. But I think that the boy was altogether gone from his face – the boy whose freak with Steve had turned Medicine Bow upside down, whose other freak with the babies had outraged Bear Creek, the boy who had loved to jingle his spurs. But manhood had only trained, not broken, his youth. It was all there, only obedient to the rein and curb.

Presently we went together to the railway yard.

'The Judge is doing a right smart o' business this year,' he began, very casually indeed, so that I knew this was important. Besides bells and coal smoke, the smell and crowded sounds of cattle rose in the air around us. 'Hyeh's our first gather o' beeves on the ranch,' continued the Virginian. 'The whole lot's shipped through to Chicago in two sections over the Burlington. The Judge is fighting the Elkhorn road.' We passed slowly along the two trains – twenty cars, each car packed with huddled, round-eyed, gazing steers. He examined to see if any animals were down. 'They ain't ate or drank anything to speak of,' he said, while the terrified brutes stared at us through their slats. 'Not since they struck the railroad they've not drank. Yu' might suppose they know somehow what they're travellin' to Chicago for.' And casually, always casually, he told me the rest. Judge Henry could not spare his foreman away from the second gather of beeves. Therefore these two ten-car trains with their double crew of cowboys had been given to the Virginian's charge. After Chicago, he was to return by St Paul over the Northern Pacific; for the Judge had wished him to see certain of the road's directors and explain to them persuasively how good a thing it would be for them to allow especially cheap rates to the Sunk Creek outfit henceforth. This was all the Virginian told me; and it contained the whole matter, to be sure.

'So you're acting foreman,' said I.

'Why, somebody has to have the say, I reckon.'

'And of course you hated the promotion?'

'I don't know about promotion,' he replied. 'The boys have been used to seein' me one of themselves. Why don't you come along with us far as Plattsmouth?' Thus he shifted the subject from himself, and called to my notice the locomotives backing up to his cars, and reminded me that from Plattsmouth I had the choice of two trains returning. But he could not hide or belittle this confidence of his employer in him. It was the care of several thousand perishable dollars and the control of men. It was a compliment. There were more steers than men to be responsible for; but none of the steers had been suddenly picked from the herd and set above his fellows. Moreover, Chicago finished up the steers; but the new-made deputy foreman had then to lead his six highly unoccupied brethren away from towns, and back in peace to the ranch, or disappoint the Judge, who needed their services. These things sometimes go wrong in a land where they say you are all born equal; and that quarter of a nod in Colonel Cyrus Jones's eating palace held more equality than any whole nod you could see. But the Virginian did not see it, there being a time for all things.

We trundled down the flopping, heavy-eddied Missouri to Platts-mouth, and there they backed us on to a siding, the Christian Endeavour being expected to pass that way. And while the equality absorbed them-selves in a deep but harmless game of poker by the side of the railway line, the Virginian and I sat on the top of a car, contemplating the sandy shallows of the Platte.

'I should think you'd take a hand,' said I.

'Poker? With them kittens?' One flash of the inner man lightened in his eyes and died away, and he finished with his gentle drawl, 'When I play, I want it to be interestin'.' He took out Sir Walter's *Kenilworth* once more, and turned the volume over and over slowly, without opening it. You cannot tell if in spirit he wandered on Bear Creek with the girl whose book it was. The spirit will go one road, and the thought another, and the body its own way sometimes. 'Queen Elizabeth would have played a mighty pow'ful game,' was his next remark.

'Poker?' said I.

'Yes, seh. Do you expaict Europe has got any queen equal to her at present?'

I doubted it.

'Victoria'd get pretty nigh slain sliding chips out agaynst Elizabeth. Only mos' prob'ly Victoria she'd insist on a half-cent limit. You have read this hyeh *Kenilworth*? Well, deal Elizabeth ace high, an' she could scare Robert Dudley with a full house plumb out o' the bettin'.'

I said that I believed she unquestionably could.

'And,' said the Virginian, 'if Essex's play got next her too near, I reckon she'd have stacked the cyards. Say, d' yu' remember Shakespeare's fat man?'

'Falstaff? Oh, yes, indeed.'

'Ain't that grand? Why, he makes men talk the way they do in life. I reckon he couldn't get printed today. It's a right down shame Shakespeare couldn't know about poker. He'd have had Falstaff playing all day at that Tearsheet outfit. And the Prince would have beat him.'

'The Prince had the brains,' said I.

'Brains?'

'Well, didn't he?'

'I neveh thought to notice. Like as not he did.'

'And Falstaff didn't, I suppose?'

'Oh, yes, seh! Falstaff could have played whist.'

'I suppose you know what you're talking about; I don't,' said I, for he was drawling again.

The cowpuncher's eye rested a moment amiably upon me. 'You can play whist with your brains,' he mused, 'brains and cyards. Now cyards are only one o' the manifestations of poker in this hyeh world. One o' the shapes yu' fool with it in when the day's work is oveh. If a man is built like that Prince boy was built (and it's away down deep beyond brains), he'll play winnin' poker with whatever hand he's holdin' when the trouble begins. Maybe it will be a mean, triflin' army, or an empty six-shooter, or a lame hawss, or maybe just nothin' but his natural countenance. 'Most any old thing will do for a fello' like that Prince boy to play poker with.'

'Then I'd be grateful for your definition of poker,' said I.

Again the Virginian looked me over amiably. 'You put up a mighty pretty game o' whist yourself,' he remarked. 'Don't that give you the contented spirit?' And before I had any reply to this, the Christian Endeavour began to come over the bridge. Three instalments crossed the Missouri from Pacific Junction, bound for Pike's Peak, every car swathed in bright bunting, and at each window a Christian with a hand-kerchief, joyously shrieking. Then the cattle trains got the open signal, and I jumped off.

'Tell the Judge the steers was all right this far,' said the Virginian.

That was the last of the deputy foreman for a while.

CHAPTER 14

Between the Acts

My road to Sunk Creek lay in no straight line. By rail I diverged northwest to Fort Meade, and thence, after some stay with the kind military people, I made my way on a horse. Up here in the Black Hills it sluiced rain most intolerably. The horse and I enjoyed the country and ourselves but little; and when finally I changed from the saddle into a stagecoach, I caught a thankful expression upon the animal's face, and returned the same.

'Six legs inside this jerky tonight?' said somebody, as I climbed the wheel. 'Well, we'll give thanks for not havin' eight,' he added cheerfully. 'Clamp your mind on to that, Shorty.' And he slapped the shoulder of his neighbour. Naturally I took these two for old companions. But we were all total strangers. They told me of the new gold excitement at Rawhide, and supposed it would bring up the Northern Pacific; and when I explained the millions owed to this road's German bondholders, they were of opinion that a German would strike it richer at Rawhide. We spoke of all sorts of things, and in our silence I gloated on the autumn holiday promised me by Judge Henry. His last letter had said that an outfit would be starting for his ranch from Billings on the seventh, and he would have a horse for me. This was the fifth. So we six legs in the jerky travelled harmoniously on over the rain-gutted road, getting no deeper knowledge of each other than what our outsides might imply.

Not that we concealed anything. The man who had slapped Shorty introduced himself early. 'Scipio le Moyne, from Gallipolice, Ohio,' he said. 'The eldest of us always gets called Scipio. It's French. But us folks have been white for a hundred years.' He was limber and light-muscled, and fell skilfully about, evading bruises when the jerky reeled or rose on end. He had a strange, long, jocular nose, very wary-looking, and a bleached blue eye. Cattle was his business, as a rule, but of late he had been 'looking around some', and Rawhide seemed much on his brain. Shorty struck me as 'looking around' also. He was quite short, indeed, and the jerky hurt him almost every time. He was light-haired and mild. Think of a yellow dog that is lost, and fancies each newcomer in sight is going to turn out his master, and you will have Shorty.

It was the Northern Pacific that surprised us into intimacy. We were nearing Medora. We had made a last arrangement of our legs. I lay stretched in silence, placid in the knowledge it was soon to end. So I drowsed. I felt something sudden, and, waking, saw Scipio passing through the air. As Shorty next shot from the jerky, I beheld smoke and the locomotive. The Northern Pacific had changed its schedule. A valise is a poor companion for catching a train with. There was rutted sand and lumpy, knee-high grease wood in our short cut. A piece of stray wire sprang from some hole and hung caracoling about my ankle. Tin cans spun from my stride. But we made a conspicuous race. Two of us waved hats, and there was no moment that some one of us was not screeching. It meant twenty-four hours to us.

Perhaps we failed to catch the train's attention, though the theory seems monstrous. As it moved off in our faces, smooth and easy and insulting, Scipio dropped instantly to a walk, and we two others outstripped him and came desperately to the empty track. There went the train. Even still its puffs were the separated puffs of starting, that bitten-off, snorty kind, and sweat and our true natures broke freely forth.

I kicked my valise, and then sat on it, dumb.

Shorty yielded himself up aloud. All his humble secrets came out of him. He walked aimlessly round, lamenting. He had lost his job, and he mentioned the ranch. He had played cards, and he mentioned the man. He had sold his horse and saddle to catch a friend on this train, and he mentioned what the friend had been going to do for him. He told a string of griefs and names to the air, as if the air knew.

Meanwhile Scipio arrived with extreme leisure at the rails. He stuck his hands into his pockets and his head out at the very small train. His bleached blue eyes shut to slits as he watched the rear car in its smoke-blur ooze away westward among the mounded bluffs. 'Lucky it's out of range,' I thought. But now Scipio spoke to it.

'Why, you seem to think you've left me behind,' he began easily, in fawning tones. 'You're too much of a kid to have such thoughts. Age some.' His next remark grew less wheedling. 'I wouldn't be a bit proud to meet yu'. Why, if I was seen travellin' with yu', I'd have to explain it to my friends! Think you've got me left, do yu'? Just because yu' ride through this country on a rail, do yu' claim yu' can find your way around? I could take yu' out ten yards in the brush and lose yu' in ten seconds, you spangle-roofed hobo! Leave *me* behind? you recent blanket-mortgage yearlin'! You plush-lined, nickel-plated, whistlin' washroom, d' yu' figure I can't go east just as soon as west? Or I'll stay right here if it suits me, yu' dude-inhabited hot-box! Why, yu' coon-bossed face-towel – ' But from here he rose in flights of novelty that appalled and held me spellbound and which are not for me to say to you. Then he came down easily again, and finished with expressions of sympathy for it because it could never have known a mother.

'Do you expaict it could show a male parent offhand?' enquired a slow voice behind us. I jumped round, and there was the Virginian.

'Male parent!' scoffed the prompt Scipio. 'Ain't you heard about *them* yet?'

'Them? Was there two?'

'Two? The blamed thing was sired by a whole doggone Dutch syndicate.'

'Why, the piebald son of a gun!' responded the Virginian, sweetly. 'I got them steers through all right,' he added to me. 'Sorry to see yu' get so out o' breath afteh the train. Is your valise sufferin' any?'

'Who's he?' enquired Scipio, curiously, turning to me.

The Southerner sat with a newspaper on the rear platform of a caboose. The caboose stood hitched behind a mile or so of freight train, and the train was headed west. So here was the deputy foreman, his steers delivered in Chicago, his men (I could hear them) safe in the caboose, his paper in his lap, and his legs dangling at ease over the railing. He wore the look of a man for whom things are going smooth. And for me the way to Billings was smooth now, also.

'Who's he?' Scipio repeated.

But from inside the caboose loud laughter and noise broke on us. Someone was reciting 'And it's my night to howl.'

'We'll all howl when we get to Rawhide,' said some other one; and they howled now.

'These hyeh steam cyars,' said the Virginian to Scipio, 'make a man's language mighty nigh as speedy as his travel.' Of Shorty he took no notice whatever – no more than of the manifestations in the caboose.

'So yu' heard me speakin' to the express,' said Scipio. 'Well, I guess, sometimes I – See here,' he exclaimed, for the Virginian was gravely considering him, 'I may have talked some, but I walked a whole lot. You didn't catch *me* squandering no speed. Soon as – '

'I noticed,' said the Virginian, 'thinkin' came quicker to yu' than runnin'.'

I was glad I was not Shorty, to have my measure taken merely by my way of missing a train. And of course I was sorry that I had kicked my valise.

'Oh, I could tell yu'd been enjoyin' us!' said Scipio. 'Observin' somebody else's scrape always kind o' rests me too. Maybe you're a philosopher, but maybe there's a pair of us drawd in this deal.'

Approval now grew plain upon the face of the Virginian. 'By your laigs,' said he, 'you are used to the saddle.'

'I'd be called used to it, I expect.'

'By your hands,' said the Southerner, again 'you ain't roped many steers lately. Been cookin' or something?'

'Say,' retorted Scipio, 'tell my future some now. Draw a conclusion from my mouth.'

'I'm right distressed,' answered the gentle Southerner, 'we've not a drop in the outfit.'

'Oh, drink with me uptown!' cried Scipio. 'I'm pleased to death with yu'.'

The Virginian glanced where the saloons stood just behind the station, and shook his head.

'Why, it ain't a bit far to whiskey from here!' urged the other, plaintively. 'Step down, now. Scipio le Moyne's my name. Yes, you're lookin' for my brass earrings. But there ain't no earrings on me. I've been white for a hundred years. Step down. I've a forty-dollar thirst.'

'You're certainly white,' began the Virginian. 'But – '

Here the caboose resumed –

> 'I'm wild, and woolly, and full of fleas;
> I'm hard to curry above the knees;
> I'm a she-wolf from Bitter Creek, and
> It's my night to ho–o–wl – '

And as they howled and stamped, the wheels of the caboose began to turn gently and to murmur.

The Virginian rose suddenly. 'Will yu' save that thirst and take a forty-dollar job?'

'Missin' trains, profanity, or what?' said Scipio.

'I'll tell yu' soon as I'm sure.'

At this Scipio looked hard at the Virginian. 'Why, you're talkin' business!' said he, and leaped on the caboose, where I was already. 'I *was* thinkin' of Rawhide,' he added, 'but I ain't any more.'

'Well, good luck!' said Shorty, on the track behind us.

'Oh, say!' said Scipio, 'he wanted to go on that train, just like me.'

'Get on,' called the Virginian. 'But as to getting a job, he ain't just like you.' So Shorty came, like a lost dog when you whistle to him.

Our wheels clucked over the main-line switch. A train-hand threw it shut after us, jumped aboard, and returned forward over the roofs. Inside the caboose they had reached the third howling of the she-wolf.

'Friends of yourn?' said Scipio.

'My outfit,' drawled the Virginian.

'Do yu' always travel outside?' enquired Scipio.

'It's lonesome in there,' returned the deputy foreman. And here one of them came out, slamming the door.

'Hell!' he said, at sight of the distant town. Then, truculently, to the Virginian, 'I told you I was going to get a bottle here.'

'Have your bottle, then,' said the deputy foreman, and kicked him off into Dakota. (It was not North Dakota yet; they had not divided it.) The Virginian had aimed his pistol at about the same time with his boot. Therefore the man sat in Dakota quietly, watching us go away into Montana, and offering no objections. Just before he became too small to make out, we saw him rise and remove himself back towards the saloons.

CHAPTER 15

The Game and the Nation – Act Second

'That is the only step I have had to take this whole trip,' said the Virginian. He holstered his pistol with a jerk. 'I have been fearing he would force it on me.' And he looked at empty, receding Dakota with disgust. 'So nyeh back home!' he muttered.

'Known your friend long?' whispered Scipio to me.

'Fairly,' I answered.

Scipio's bleached eyes brightened with admiration as he considered the Southerner's back. 'Well,' he stated judicially, 'start awful early when yu' go to fool with him, or he'll make you feel onpunctual.'

'I expaict I've had them almost all of three thousand miles,' said the Virginian, tilting his head towards the noise in the caboose. 'And I've strove to deliver them back as I received them. The whole lot. And I would have. But he has spoiled my hopes.' The deputy foreman looked again at Dakota. 'It's a disappointment,' he added. 'You may know what I mean.'

I had known a little, but not to the very deep, of the man's pride and purpose in this trust. Scipio gave him sympathy. 'There must be quite a balance of 'em left with yu' yet,' said Scipio, cheeringly.

'I had the boys plumb contented,' pursued the deputy foreman, hurt into open talk of himself. 'Away along as far as Saynt Paul I had them reconciled to my authority. Then this news about gold had to strike us.'

'And they're a-dreamin' nuggets and Parisian bowleyvards,' suggested Scipio.

The Virginian smiled gratefully at him.

'Fortune is shinin' bright and blindin' to their delicate young eyes,' he said, regaining his usual self.

We all listened a moment to the rejoicings within.

'Energetic, ain't they?' said the Southerner. 'But none of 'em was whelped savage enough to sing himself bloodthirsty. And though they're strainin' mighty earnest not to be tame, they're goin' back to Sunk Creek with me accordin' to the Judge's awdehs. Never a calf of them will desert to Rawhide, for all their dangerousness; nor I ain't goin' to have any fuss over it. Only one is left now that don't sing. Maybe I will have to make some arrangements about him. The man I have parted with,' he said, with another glance at Dakota, 'was our cook, and I will ask yu' to replace him, Colonel.'

Scipio gaped wide. 'Colonel! Say!' He stared at the Virginian. 'Did I meet yu' at the palace?'

'Not exackly meet,' replied the Southerner. 'I was praisent one mawnin' las' month when this gentleman awdehed frawgs' laigs.'

'Sakes and saints, but that was a mean position!' burst out Scipio. 'I had to tell all comers anything all day. Stand up and jump language hot off my brain at 'em. And the pay don't near compensate for the drain on the system. I don't care how good a man is, you let him keep a-tappin' his presence of mind right along, without takin' a lay-off, and you'll have him sick. Yes, sir. You'll hit his nerves. So I told them they could hire some fresh man, for I was goin' back to punch cattle or fight Indians, or take a rest somehow, for I didn't propose to get jaded, and me only twenty-five years old. There ain't no regular Colonel Cyrus Jones any more, yu' know. He met a Cheyenne telegraph pole in seventy-four, and was buried. But his palace was doin' big business, and he had been a kind of attraction, and so they always keep a live bear outside, and some poor fello', fixed up like the Colonel used to be, inside. And it's a turrible mean position. Course I'll cook for yu'. Yu've a dandy memory for faces!'

'I wasn't right convinced till I kicked him off and you gave that shut to your eyes again,' said the Virginian.

Once more the door opened. A man with slim black eyebrows, slim black moustache, and a black shirt tied with a white handkerchief was looking steadily from one to the other of us.

'Good-day!' he remarked generally and without enthusiasm; and to the Virginian, 'Where's Schoffner?'

'I expaict he'll have got his bottle by now, Trampas.'

Trampas looked from one to the other of us again. 'Didn't he say he was coming back?'

'He reminded me he was going for a bottle, and afteh that he didn't wait to say a thing.'

Trampas looked at the platform and the railing and the steps. 'He told me he was coming back,' he insisted.

'I don't reckon he has come, not without he clumb up ahaid somewhere. An' I mus' say, when he got off he didn't look like a man does when he has the intention o' returnin'.'

At this Scipio coughed, and pared his nails attentively. We had already been avoiding each other's eye. Shorty did not count. Since he got aboard, his meek seat had been the bottom step.

The thoughts of Trampas seemed to be in difficulty. 'How long's this train been started?' he demanded.

'This hyeh train?' The Virginian consulted his watch. 'Why, it's been fanning it a right smart little while,' said he, laying no stress upon his indolent syllables.

'Huh!' went Trampas. He gave the rest of us a final unlovely scrutiny. 'It seems to have become a passenger train,' he said. And he returned abruptly inside the caboose.

'Is he the member who don't sing?' asked Scipio.

'That's the specimen,' replied the Southerner.

'He don't seem musical in the face,' said Scipio.

'Pshaw!' returned the Virginian. 'Why, you surely ain't the man to mind ugly mugs when they're hollow!'

The noise inside had dropped quickly to stillness. You could scarcely catch the sound of talk. Our caboose was clicking comfortably westward, rail after rail, mile upon mile, while night was beginning to rise from earth into the clouded sky.

'I wonder if they have sent a search party forward to hunt Schoffner?' said the Virginian. 'I think I'll maybe join their meeting.' He opened the door upon them. 'Kind o' dark hyeh, ain't it?' said he. And lighting the lantern, he shut us out.

'What do yu' think?' said Scipio to me. 'Will he take them to Sunk Creek?'

'He evidently thinks he will,' said I. 'He says he will, and he has the courage of his convictions.'

'That ain't near enough courage to have!' Scipio exclaimed. 'There's times in life when a man has got to have courage *without* convictions – *without* them – or he is no good. Now your friend is that deep constitooted that you don't know and I don't know what he's thinkin' about all this.'

'If there's to be any gun-play,' put in the excellent Shorty, 'I'll stand in with him.'

'Ah, go to bed with your gun-play!' retorted Scipio, entirely good-humoured. 'Is the Judge paying for a carload of dead punchers to gather his beef for him? And this ain't a proposition worth a man's gettin' hurt for himself, anyway.'

'That's so,' Shorty assented.

'No,' speculated Scipio, as the night drew deeper round us and the caboose click-clucked and click-clucked over the rail joints; 'he's waitin' for somebody else to open this pot. I'll bet he don't know but one thing now, and that's that nobody else shall know he don't know anything.'

Scipio had delivered himself. He lighted a cigarette, and no more wisdom came from him. The night was established. The rolling bad-lands sank away in it. A train-hand had arrived over the roof, and hanging the red lights out behind, left us again without remark or symptom of curiosity. The train-hands seemed interested in their own society and lived in their own caboose. A chill wind with wet in it came blowing from the invisible draws, and brought the feel of the distant mountains.

'That's Montana!' said Scipio, snuffing. 'I am glad to have it inside my lungs again.'

'Ain't yu' getting cool out there?' said the Virginian's voice. 'Plenty room inside.'

Perhaps he had expected us to follow him; or perhaps he had meant us to delay long enough not to seem like a reinforcement. 'These gentlemen missed the express at Medora,' he observed to his men, simply.

What they took us for upon our entrance I cannot say, or what they believed. The atmosphere of the caboose was charged with voiceless currents of thought. By way of a friendly beginning to the three hundred miles of caboose we were now to share so intimately, I recalled myself to them. I trusted no more of the Christian Endeavour had delayed them. 'I am so lucky to have caught you again,' I finished. 'I was afraid my last chance of reaching the Judge's had gone.'

Thus I said a number of things designed to be agreeable, but they met my small talk with the smallest talk you can have. 'Yes,' for instance, and 'Pretty well, I guess,' and grave strikings of matches and thoughtful looks at the floor. I suppose we had made twenty miles to the imperturbable clicking of the caboose when one at length asked his neighbour had he ever seen New York.

'No,' said the other. 'Flooded with dudes, ain't it?'

'Swimmin',' said the first.

'Leakin', too,' said a third.

'Well, my gracious!' said a fourth, and beat his knee in private delight. None of them ever looked at me. For some reason I felt exceedingly ill at ease.

'Good clothes in New York,' said the third.

'Rich food,' said the first.

'Fresh eggs, too,' said the third.

'Well, my gracious!' said the fourth, beating his knee.

'Why, yes,' observed the Virginian, unexpectedly; 'they tell me that aiggs there ain't liable to be so rotten as yu'll strike 'em in this country.'

None of them had a reply for this, and New York was abandoned. For some reason I felt much better.

It was a new line they adopted next, led off by Trampas.

'Going to the excitement?' he enquired, selecting Shorty.

'Excitement?' said Shorty, looking up.

'Going to Rawhide?' Trampas repeated. And all watched Shorty.

'Why, I'm all adrift missin' that express,' said Shorty.

'Maybe I can give you employment,' suggested the Virginian. 'I am taking an outfit across the basin.'

'You'll find most folks going to Rawhide, if you're looking for company,' pursued Trampas, fishing for a recruit.

'How about Rawhide, anyway?' said Scipio, skilfully deflecting this missionary work. 'Are they taking much mineral out? Have yu' seen any of the rock?'

'Rock?' broke in the enthusiast who had beaten his knee. 'There!' And he brought some from his pocket.

'You're always showing your rock,' said Trampas, sulkily; for Scipio now held the conversation, and Shorty returned safely to his dozing.

'H'm!' went Scipio at the rock. He turned it back and forth in his hand, looking it over; he chucked and caught it slightingly in the air, and handed it back. 'Porphyry, I see.' That was his only word about it. He said it cheerily. He left no room for discussion. You could not damn a thing worse. 'Ever been in Santa Rita?' pursued Scipio, while the enthusiast slowly pushed his rock back into his pocket. 'That's down in New Mexico. Ever been to Globe, Arizona?' And Scipio talked away about the mines he had known. There was no getting at Shorty any more that evening. Trampas was foiled of his fish, or of learning how the fish's heart lay. And by morning Shorty had been carefully instructed to change his mind about once an hour. This is apt to discourage all but very superior missionaries. And I too escaped for the rest of this night. At Glendive we had a dim supper, and I bought some blankets; and after that it was late, and sleep occupied the attention of us all.

We lay along the shelves of the caboose, a peaceful sight I should think, in that smoothly trundling cradle. I slept almost immediately, so tired that not even our stops or anything else waked me, save once, when the air I was breathing grew suddenly pure, and I roused. Sitting in the door was the lonely figure of the Virginian. He leaned in silent contemplation of the occasional moon, and beneath it the Yellowstone's swift ripples. On the caboose shelves the others slept sound and still, each stretched or coiled as he had first put himself. They were not untrustworthy to look at, it seemed to me – except Trampas. You would have said the rest of that young humanity was average rough male blood, merely needing to be told the proper things at the right time; and one big bunchy stocking of the enthusiast stuck out of his blanket, solemn and innocent, and I laughed at it. There was a light sound by the door, and I found the Virginian's eye on me. Finding who it was, he nodded and motioned with his hand to go to sleep. And this I did with him in my sight, still leaning in the open door, through which came the interrupted moon and the swimming reaches of the Yellowstone.

CHAPTER 16

The Game and the Nation – Last Act

It has happened to you, has it not, to wake in the morning and wonder for a while where on earth you are? Thus I came half to life in the caboose, hearing voices, but not the actual words at first.

But presently, 'Hathaway!' said someone more clearly. 'Portland 1291!'

This made no special stir in my intelligence, and I drowsed off again to the pleasant rhythm of the wheels. The little shock of stopping next brought me to, somewhat, with the voices still round me; and when we were again in motion, I heard: 'Rosebud! Portland 1279!' These figures jarred me awake, and I said, 'It was 1291 before,' and sat up in my blankets.

The greeting they vouchsafed and the sight of them clustering expressionless in the caboose brought last evening's uncomfortable memory back to me. Our next stop revealed how things were going today.

'Forsythe,' one of them read on the station. 'Portland 1266.'

They were counting the lessening distance westward. This was the undercurrent of war. It broke on me as I procured fresh water at Forsythe and made some toilet in their stolid presence. We were drawing nearer the Rawhide station – the point, I mean, where you left the railway for the new mines. Now Rawhide station lay this side of Billings. The broad path of desertion would open ready for their feet when the narrow path to duty and Sunk Creek was still some fifty miles more to wait. Here was Trampas's great strength; he need make no move meanwhile, but lie low for the immediate temptation to front and waylay them and win his battle over the deputy foreman. But the Virginian seemed to find nothing save enjoyment in this sunny September morning, and ate his breakfast at Forsythe serenely.

That meal done and that station gone, our caboose took up again its easy trundle by the banks of the Yellowstone. The mutineers sat for a while digesting in idleness.

'What's your scar?' enquired one at length, inspecting casually the neck of his neighbour.

'Foolishness,' the other answered.

'Yourn?'

'Mine.'

'Well, I don't know but I prefer to have myself to thank for a thing,' said the first.

'I was displaying myself,' continued the second. 'One day last summer it was. We come on a big snake by Torrey Creek corral. The boys got betting pretty lively that I dassent make my word good as to dealing with him, so I loped my cayuse full tilt by Mr Snake, and swung down and catched him up by the tail from the ground, and cracked him same as a whip, and snapped his head off. You've saw it done?' he said to the audience.

The audience nodded wearily.

'But the loose head flew agin me, and the fangs caught. I was pretty sick for a while.'

'It don't pay to be clumsy,' said the first man. 'If you'd snapped the snake away from yu' instead of towards yu', its head would have whirled off into the brush, same as they do with me.'

'How like a knife-cut your scar looks!' said I.

'Don't it?' said the snake-snapper. 'There's many that gets fooled by it.'

'An antelope knows a snake is his enemy,' said another to me. 'Ever seen a buck circling round and round a rattler?'

'I have always wanted to see that,' said I, heartily. For this I knew to be a respectable piece of truth.

'It's worth seeing,' the man went on. 'After the buck gets close in, he gives an almighty jump up in the air, and down comes his four hoofs in a bunch right on top of Mr Snake. Cuts him all to hash. Now you tell me how the buck knows that.'

Of course I could not tell him. And again we sat in silence for a while – friendlier silence, I thought.

'A skunk'll kill yu' worse than a snake bite,' said another, presently. 'No, I don't mean that way,' he added. For I had smiled. 'There is a brown skunk down in Arkansaw. Kind of prairie-dog brown. Littler than our variety, he is. And he is mad the whole year round, same as a dog gets. Only the dog has a spell and dies; but this here Arkansaw skunk is mad right along, and it don't seem to interfere with his business in other respects. Well, suppose you're camping out, and suppose it's a hot night, or you're in a hurry, and you've made camp late, or anyway you haven't got inside any tent, but you have just bedded down in the open. Skunk comes travelling along and walks on your blankets. You're warm. He likes that, same as a cat does. And he tramps with pleasure and comfort, same as a cat. And you move. You get bit, that's all. And you die of hydrophobia. Ask anybody.'

'Most extraordinary!' said I. 'But did you ever see a person die from this?'

'No, sir. Never happened to. My cousin at Bald Knob did.'

'Died?'

'No, sir. Saw a man.'

'But how do you know they're not sick skunks?'

'No, sir! They're well skunks. Well as anything. You'll not meet skunks in any state of the Union more robust than them in Arkansaw. And thick.'

'That's awful true,' sighed another. 'I have buried hundreds of dollars' worth of clothes in Arkansaw.'

'Why didn't yu' travel in a sponge bag?' enquired Scipio. And this brought a slight silence.

'Speakin' of bites,' spoke up a new man, 'how's that?' He held up his thumb.

'My!' breathed Scipio. 'Must have been a lion.'

The man wore a wounded look. 'I was huntin' owl eggs for a botanist from Boston,' he explained to me.

'Chiropodist, weren't he?' said Scipio. 'Or maybe a sonnabulator?'

'No, honest,' protested the man with the thumb; so that I was sorry for him, and begged him to go on.

'I'll listen to you,' I assured him. And I wondered why this politeness of mine should throw one or two of them into stifled mirth. Scipio, on the other hand, gave me a disgusted look and sat back sullenly for a moment, and then took himself out on the platform, where the Virginian was lounging.

'The young feller wore knee-pants and ever so thick spectacles with a half-moon cut in 'em,' resumed the narrator, 'and he carried a tin box strung to a strap I took for his lunch till it flew open on him and a horn toad hustled out. Then I was sure he was a botanist – or whatever yu' say they're called. Well, he would have owl eggs – them little prairie-owl that some claim can turn their head clean around and keep a-watchin' yu', only that's nonsense. We was ridin' through that prairie-dog town, used to be on the flat just after yu' crossed the south fork of Powder River on the Buffalo trail, and I said I'd dig an owl nest out for him if he was willin' to camp till I'd dug it. I wanted to know about them owls some myself – if they did live with the dogs and snakes, yu' know,' he broke off, appealing to me.

'Oh, yes,' I told him eagerly.

'So while the botanist went glarin' around the town with his glasses to see if he could spot a prairie-dog and an owl usin' the same hole, I was diggin' in a hole I'd seen an owl run down. And that's what I got.' He held up his thumb again.

'The snake!' I exclaimed.

'Yes, sir. Mr Rattler was keepin' house that day. Took me right there. I hauled him out of the hole hangin' to me. Eight rattles.'

'Eight!' said I. 'A big one.'

'Yes, sir. Thought I was dead. But the woman – '

'The woman?' said I.

'Yes, woman. Didn't I tell yu' the botanist had his wife along? Well, he did. And she acted better than the man, for he was losin' his head, and shoutin' he had no whiskey, and he didn't guess his knife was sharp enough to amputate my thumb, and none of us chewed, and the doctor was twenty miles away, and if he had only remembered to bring his ammonia – well, he was screeching out 'most everything he knew in the world, and without arranging it any, neither. But she just clawed his pocket and burrowed and kep' yelling, "Give him the stone, Augustus!" And she whipped out one of them Injun medicine-stones – first one I ever seen – and she clapped it on to my thumb, and it started in right away.'

'What did it do?' said I.

'Sucked. Like blotting-paper does. Soft and funny it was, and grey. They get 'em from elks' stomachs, yu' know. And when it had sucked the poison out of the wound, off it falls of my thumb by itself! And I thanked the woman for saving my life that capable and keeping her head that cool. I never knowed how excited she had been till afterward. She was awful shocked.'

'I suppose she started to talk when the danger was over,' said I, with deep silence around me.

'No; she didn't say nothing to me. But when her next child was born, it had eight rattles.'

Din now rose wild in the caboose. They rocked together. The enthusiast beat his knee tumultuously. And I joined them. Who could help it? It had been so well conducted from the imperceptible beginning. Fact and falsehood blended with such perfect art. And this last, an effect so new made with such world-old material! I cared nothing that I was the victim, and I joined them; but ceased, feeling suddenly somehow estranged or chilled. It was in their laughter. The loudness was too loud. And I caught the eyes of Trampas fixed upon the Virginian with exultant malevolence. Scipio's disgusted glance was upon me from the door.

Dazed by these signs, I went out on the platform to get away from the noise. There the Virginian said to me: 'Cheer up! You'll not be so easy for 'em that-a-way next season.'

He said no more; and with his legs dangled over the railing, appeared to resume his newspaper.

'What's the matter?' said I to Scipio.

'Oh, I don't mind if he don't,' Scipio answered. 'Couldn't yu' see? I tried to head 'em off from yu' all I knew, but yu' just ran in among 'em yourself. Couldn't yu' see? Kep' hinderin' and spoilin' me with askin' those urgent questions of yourn – why, I had to let yu' go your way! Why, that wasn't the ordinary play with the ordinary tenderfoot they treated you to! You ain't a common tenderfoot this trip. You're the foreman's friend. They've hit him through you. That's the way they count it. It's made them encouraged. Can't yu' see?'

Scipio stated it plainly. And as we ran by the next station, 'Howard!' they harshly yelled. 'Portland 1256!'

We had been passing gangs of workmen on the track. And at that last yell the Virginian rose. 'I reckon I'll join the meeting again,' he said. 'This filling and repairing looks like the washout might have been true.'

'Washout?' said Scipio.

'Big Horn bridge, they say – four days ago.'

'Then I wish it came this side Rawhide station.'

'Do yu'?' drawled the Virginian. And smiling at Scipio, he lounged in through the open door.

'He beats me,' said Scipio, shaking his head. 'His trail is turrible hard to anticipate.'

We listened.

'Work bein' done on the road, I see,' the Virginian was saying, very friendly and conversational.

'We see it too,' said the voice of Trampas.

'Seem to be easin' their grades some.'

'Roads do.'

'Cheaper to build 'em the way they want 'em at the start, a man would think,' suggested the Virginian, most friendly. 'There go some more I–talians.'

'They're Chinese,' said Trampas.

'That's so,' acknowledged the Virginian, with a laugh.

'What's he monkeyin' at now?' muttered Scipio.

'Without cheap foreigners they couldn't afford all this hyeh new gradin',' the Southerner continued.

'Grading! Can't you tell when a flood's been eating the banks?'

'Why, yes,' said the Virginian, sweet as honey. 'But 'ain't yu' heard of the improvements west of Big Timber, all the way to Missoula, this season? I'm talkin' about them.'

'Oh! Talking about them. Yes, I've heard.'

'Good money-savin' scheme, ain't it?' said the Virginian. 'Lettin' a freight run down one hill an' up the next as far as she'll go without steam, an' shavin' the hill down to that point.' Now this was an honest engineering fact. 'Better'n settin' dudes squintin' through telescopes an' cipherin' over one per cent re-ductions,' the Southerner commented.

'It's common sense,' assented Trampas. 'Have you heard the new scheme about the water-tanks?'

'I ain't right certain,' said the Southerner.

'I must watch this,' said Scipio, 'or I shall bust.' He went in, and so did I.

They were all sitting over this discussion of the Northern Pacific's recent policy as to betterments, as though they were the board of directors. Pins could have dropped. Only nobody would have cared to hear a pin.

'They used to put all their tanks at the bottom of their grades,' said Trampas.

'Why, yu' get the water easier at the bottom.'

'You can pump it to the top, though,' said Trampas, growing superior. 'And it's cheaper.'

'That gets me,' said the Virginian, interested.

'Trains after watering can start down hill now and get the benefit of the gravity. It'll cut down operating expenses a heap.'

'That's cert'nly common sense!' exclaimed the Virginian, absorbed. 'But ain't it kind o' tardy?'

'Live and learn. So they gained speed, too. High speed on half the coal this season, until the accident.'

'Accident!' said the Virginian, instantly.

'Yellowstone Limited. Man fired at engine-driver. Train was flying past that quick the bullet broke every window and killed a passenger on the back platform. You've been running too much with aristocrats,' finished Trampas, and turned on his heel.

'Haw, haw!' began the enthusiast, but his neighbour gripped him to silence. This was a triumph too serious for noise. Not a mutineer moved; and I felt cold.

'Trampas,' said the Virginian, 'I thought yu'd be afeared to try it on me.'

Trampas whirled round. His hand was at his belt. 'Afraid!' he sneered.

'Shorty!' said Scipio, sternly, and leaping upon that youth, took his half-drawn pistol from him.

'I'm obliged to yu',' said the Virginian to Scipio.

Trampas's hand left his belt. He threw a slight, easy look at his men, and keeping his back to the Virginian, walked out on the platform and sat on the chair where the Virginian had sat so much.

'Don't you comprehend,' said the Virginian to Shorty, amiably, 'that this hyeh question has been discussed peaceable by civilised citizens? Now you sit down and be good, and Mr le Moyne will return your gun when we're across that broken bridge, if they have got it fixed for heavy trains yet.'

'This train will be lighter when it gets to that bridge,' spoke Trampas, out on his chair.

'Why, that's true, too!' said the Virginian. 'Maybe none of us are crossin' that Big Horn bridge now, except me. Funny if yu' should end by persuadin' me to quit and go to Rawhide myself! But I reckon I'll not. I reckon I'll worry along to Sunk Creek, somehow.'

'Don't forget I'm cookin' for yu',' said Scipio, gruffly.

'I'm obliged to yu',' said the Southerner.

'You were speaking of a job for me,' said Shorty.

'I'm right obliged. But yu' see – I ain't exackly foreman the way this comes out, and my promises might not bind Judge Henry to pay salaries.'

A push came through the train from forward. We were slowing for the Rawhide station, and all began to be busy and to talk. 'Going up to the mines today?' 'Oh, let's grub first.' 'Guess it's too late, anyway.' And so forth; while they rolled and roped their bedding, and put on their coats with a good deal of elbow motion, and otherwise showed off. It was wasted. The Virginian did not know what was going on in the caboose. He was leaning and looking out ahead, and Scipio's puzzled eye never left him. And as we halted for the water-tank, the Southerner exclaimed, 'They 'ain't got away yet!' as if it were good news to him.

He meant the delayed trains. Four stalled expresses were in front of us, besides several freights. And two hours more at least before the bridge would be ready.

Travellers stood and sat about forlorn, near the cars, out in the sagebrush, anywhere. People in hats and spurs watched them, and Indian chiefs offered them painted bows and arrows and shiny horns.

'I reckon them passengers would prefer a laig o' mutton,' said the Virginian to a man loafing near the caboose.

'Bet your life!' said the man. 'First lot has been stuck here four days.'

'Plumb starved, ain't they?' enquired the Virginian.

'Bet your life! They've eat up their dining-cars and they've eat up this town.'

'Well,' said the Virginian, looking at the town, 'I expaict the dining-cyars contained more nourishment.'

'Say, you're about right there!' said the man. He walked beside the caboose as we puffed slowly forward from the water-tank to our siding. 'Fine business here if we'd only been ready,' he continued. 'And the Crow agent has let his Indians come over from the reservation. There has been a little beef brought in, and game, and fish. And big money in it, bet your life! Them Eastern passengers has just been robbed. I wisht I had somethin' to sell!'

'Anything starting for Rawhide this afternoon?' said Trampas, out of the caboose door.

'Not until morning,' said the man. 'You going to the mines?' he resumed to the Virginian.

'Why,' answered the Southerner, slowly and casually, and addressing himself strictly to the man, while Trampas, on his side, paid obvious inattention, 'this hyeh delay, yu' see, may unsettle our plans some. But it'll be one of two ways – we're all goin' to Rawhide, or we're all goin' to Billings. We're all one party, yu' see.'

Trampas laughed audibly inside the door as he rejoined his men. 'Let him keep up appearances,' I heard him tell them. 'It don't hurt us what he says to strangers.'

'But I'm goin' to eat hearty either way,' continued the Virginian. 'And I ain' goin' to be robbed. I've been kind o' promisin' myself a treat if we stopped hyeh.'

'Town's eat clean out,' said the man.

'So yu' tell me. But all you folks has forgot one source of revenue that yu' have right close by, mighty handy. If you have got a gunny sack, I'll show you how to make some money.'

'Bet your life!' said the man.

'Mr le Moyne,' said the Virginian, 'the outfit's cookin' stuff is aboard, and if you'll get the fire ready, we'll try how frawgs' laigs go fried.' He walked off at once, the man following like a dog. Inside the caboose rose a gust of laughter.

'Frogs!' muttered Scipio. And then turning a blank face to me, 'Frogs?'

'Colonel Cyrus Jones had them on his bill of fare,' I said. ' "*Frogs' Legs à la Delmonico*".'

'Shoo! I didn't get up that thing. They had it when I came. Never looked at it. Frogs?' He went down the steps very slowly, with a long frown. Reaching the ground, he shook his head. 'That man's trail is surely hard to anticipate,' he said. 'But I must hurry up that fire. For his appearance has given me encouragement,' Scipio concluded, and became brisk. Shorty helped him, and I brought wood. Trampas and the other people strolled off to the station, a compact band.

Our little fire was built beside the caboose, so the cooking things might be easily reached and put back. You would scarcely think such operations held any interest, even for the hungry, when there seemed to be nothing to cook. A few sticks blazing tamely in the dust, a frying-pan, half a tin bucket of lard, some water, and barren plates and knives and forks, and three silent men attending to them – that was all. But the travellers came to see. These waifs drew near us, and stood, a sad, lorn, shifting fringe of audience; four to begin with; and then two wandered away; and presently one of these came back, finding it worse elsewhere. 'Supper, boys?' said he. 'Breakfast,' said Scipio, crossly. And no more of them addressed us. I heard them joylessly mention Wall Street to each other, and Saratoga; I even heard the name Bryn Mawr, which is near Philadelphia. But these fragments of home dropped in the wilderness here in Montana beside a freight caboose were of no interest to me now.

'Looks like frogs down there, too,' said Scipio. 'See them marshy sloos full of weeds?' We took a little turn and had a sight of the Virginian quite active among the ponds. 'Hush! I'm getting some thoughts,' continued Scipio. 'He wasn't sorry enough. Don't interrupt me.'

'I'm not,' said I.

'No. But I'd 'most caught a-hold.' And Scipio muttered to himself again, 'He wasn't sorry enough.' Presently he swore loud and brilliantly. 'Tell yu'!' he cried. 'What did he say to Trampas after that play they exchanged over railroad improvements and Trampas put the josh on him? Didn't he say, "Trampas, I thought you'd be afraid to do it?" Well, sir, Trampas had better have been afraid. And that's what he meant. There's where he was bringin' it to. Trampas made an awful bad play then. You wait. Glory, but he's a knowin' man! Course he wasn't sorry. I guess he had the hardest kind of work to look as sorry as he did. You wait.'

'Wait? What for? Go on, man! What for?'

'I don't know! I don't know! Whatever hand he's been holdin' up, this is the showdown. He's played for a showdown here before the caboose gets off the bridge. Come back to the fire, or Shorty'll be leavin' it go out. Grow happy some, Shorty!' he cried on arriving, and his hand cracked on Shorty's shoulder. 'Supper's in sight, Shorty. Food for reflection.'

'None for the stomach?' asked the passenger who had spoken once before.

'We're figuring on that too,' said Scipio. His crossness had melted entirely away.

'Why, they're cowboys!' exclaimed another passenger; and he moved nearer.

From the station Trampas now came back, his herd following him less compactly. They had found famine, and no hope of supplies until the next train from the East. This was no fault of Trampas's; but they were following him less compactly. They carried one piece of cheese, the size of a fist, the weight of a brick, the hue of a corpse. And the passengers, seeing it, exclaimed, 'There's Old Faithful again!' and took off their hats.

'You gentlemen met that cheese before, then?' said Scipio, delighted.

'It's been offered me three times a day for four days,' said the passenger. 'Did he want a dollar or a dollar and a half?'

'Two dollars!' blurted out the enthusiast. And all of us save Trampas fell into fits of imbecile laughter.

'Here comes our grub, anyway,' said Scipio, looking off towards the marshes. And his hilarity sobered away in a moment.

'Well, the train will be in soon,' stated Trampas. 'I guess we'll get a decent supper without frogs.'

All interest settled now upon the Virginian. He was coming with his man and his gunny sack, and the gunny sack hung from his shoulder heavily, as a full sack should. He took no notice of the gathering, but sat down and partly emptied the sack. 'There,' said he, very businesslike, to his assistant, 'that's all we'll want. I think you'll find a ready market for the balance.'

'Well, my gracious!' said the enthusiast. 'What fool eats a frog?'

'Oh, I'm fool enough for a tadpole!' cried the passenger. And they began to take out their pocket-books.

'You can cook yours right hyeh, gentlemen,' said the Virginian, with his slow Southern courtesy. 'The dining-cyars don't look like they were fired up.'

'How much will you sell a couple for?' enquired the enthusiast.

The Virginian looked at him with friendly surprise. 'Why, help yourself! We're all together yet awhile. Help yourselves,' he repeated, to Trampas and his followers. These hung back a moment, then, with a slinking motion, set the cheese upon the earth and came forward nearer the fire to receive some supper.

'It won't scarcely be Delmonico style,' said the Virginian to the passengers, 'nor yet Saynt Augustine.' He meant the great Augustin, the traditional *chef* of Philadelphia, whose history I had sketched for him at Colonel Cyrus Jones's eating palace.

Scipio now officiated. His frying-pan was busy, and prosperous odours rose from it.

'Run for a bucket of fresh water, Shorty,' the Virginian continued, beginning his meal. 'Colonel, yu' cook pretty near good. If yu' had sold' em as advertised, yu'd have cert'nly made a name.'

Several were now eating with satisfaction, but not Scipio. It was all that he could do to cook straight. The whole man seemed to glisten. His eye was shut to a slit once more, while the innocent passengers thankfully swallowed.

'Now, you see, you have made some money,' began the Virginian to the native who had helped him get the frogs.

'Bet your life!' exclaimed the man. 'Divvy, won't you?' And he held out half his gains.

'Keep 'em,' returned the Southerner. 'I reckon we're square. But I expaict they'll not equal Delmonico's, seh?' he said to a passenger.

'Don't trust the judgement of a man as hungry as I am!' exclaimed the traveller, with a laugh. And he turned to his fellow-travellers. 'Did you ever enjoy supper at Delmonico's more than this?'

'Never!' they sighed.

'Why, look here,' said the traveller, 'what fools the people of this town are! Here we've been all these starving days, and you come and get ahead of them!'

'That's right easy explained,' said the Virginian. 'I've been where there was big money in frawgs, and they 'ain't been. They're all cattle hyeh.

Talk cattle, think cattle, and they're bankrupt in consequence. Fallen through. Ain't that so?' he enquired of the native.

'That's about the way,' said the man.

'It's mighty hard to do what your neighbours ain't doin',' pursued the Virginian. 'Montana is all cattle, an' these folks must be cattle, an' never notice the country right hyeh is too small for a range, an' swampy, anyway, an' just waitin' to be a frawg ranch.'

At this, all wore a face of careful reserve.

'I'm not claimin' to be smarter than you folks hyeh,' said the Virginian, deprecatingly, to his assistant. 'But travellin' learns a man many customs. You wouldn't do the business they done at Tulare, California, north side o' the lake. They cert'nly utilised them hopeless swamps splendid. Of course they put up big capital and went into it scientific, gettin' advice from the government Fish Commission, an' suchlike knowledge. Yu' see, they had big markets for their frawgs – San Francisco, Los Angeles, and clear to New York afteh the Southern Pacific was through. But up hyeh yu' could sell to passengers every day like yu' done this one day. They would get to know yu' along the line. Competing swamps are scarce. The dining-cyars would take your frawgs, and yu' would have the Yellowstone Park for four months in the year. Them hotels are anxious to please, an' they would buy off yu' what their Eastern patrons esteem as fine-eatin'. And you folks would be sellin' something instead o' nothin'.'

'That's a practical idea,' said a traveller. 'And little cost.'

'And little cost,' said the Virginian.

'Would Eastern people eat frogs?' enquired the man.

'Look at us!' said the traveller.

'Delmonico doesn't give yu' such a treat!' said the Virginian.

'Not exactly!' the traveller exclaimed.

'How much would be paid for frogs?' said Trampas to him. And I saw Scipio bend closer to his cooking.

'Oh, I don't know,' said the traveller. 'We've paid pretty well, you see.'

'You're late for Tulare, Trampas,' said the Virginian.

'I was not thinking of Tulare,' Trampas retorted. Scipio's nose was in the frying-pan.

'Mos' comical spot you ever struck!' said the Virginian, looking round upon the whole company. He allowed himself a broad smile of retrospect. 'To hear 'em talk frawgs at Tulare! Same as other folks talks hawsses or steers or whatever they're raising to sell. Yu'd fall into it yourselves if yu' started the business. Anything a man's bread and butter depends on, he's going to be earnest about. Don't care if it is a frawg.'

'That's so,' said the native. 'And it paid good?'

'The only money in the county was right there,' answered the Virginian. 'It was a dead county, and only frawgs was movin'. But that business was a-fannin' to beat four of a kind. It made yu' feel strange at first, as I said. For all the men had been cattle-men at one time or another. Till yu' got accustomed, it would give 'most anybody a shock to hear 'em speak about herdin' the bulls in a pasture by themselves.' The Virginian allowed himself another smile, but became serious again. 'That was their policy,' he explained. 'Except at certain times o' year they kept the bulls separate. The Fish Commission told 'em they'd better, and it cert'nly worked mighty well. It or something did – for, gentlemen, hush! but there was millions. You'd have said all the frawgs in the world had taken charge at Tulare. And the money rolled in! Gentlemen, hush! 'twas a gold mine for the owners. Forty per cent they netted some years. And they paid generous wages. For they could sell to all them French restaurants in San Francisco, yu' see. And there was the Cliff House. And the Palace Hotel made it a specialty. And the officers took frawgs at the Presidio, an' Angel Island, an' Alcatraz, an' Benicia. Los Angeles was beginnin' its boom. The corner-lot sharps wanted something by way of varnish. An' so they dazzled Eastern investors with advertisin' Tulare frawgs clear to N' Yol'ans an' New York. 'Twas only in Sacramento frawgs was dull. I expaict the California legislature was too or'n'ry for them fine-raised luxuries. They tell of one of them senators that he raked a million out of Los Angeles real estate, and started in for a bang-up meal with champagne. Wanted to scatter his new gold thick an' quick. But he got astray among all the fancy dishes, an' just yelled right out before the ladies, "Damn it! bring me forty dollars' worth of ham and aiggs." He was a funny senator, now.'

The Virginian paused, and finished eating a leg. And then with diabolic art he made a feint at wandering to new fields of anecdote. 'Talkin' of senators,' he resumed, 'Senator Wise – '

'How much did you say wages were at Tulare?' enquired one of the Trampas faction.

'How much? Why, I never knew what the foreman got. The regular hands got a hundred. Senator Wise – '

'A hundred a *month*?'

'Why, it was wet an' muddy work, yu' see. A man risked rheumatism some. He risked it a good deal. Well, I was going to tell about Senator Wise. When Senator Wise was speaking of his visit to Alaska – '

'Forty per cent, was it?' said Trampas.

'Oh, I must call my wife!' said the traveller behind me. 'This is what I came West for.' And he hurried away.

'Not forty per cent the bad years,' replied the Virginian. 'The frawgs had enemies, same as cattle. I remember when a pelican got in the spring pasture, and the herd broke through the fence – '

'Fence?' said a passenger.

'Ditch, seh, and wire net. Every pasture was a square swamp with a ditch around, and a wire net. Yu've heard the mournful, mixed-up sound a big bunch of cattle will make? Well, seh, as yu' druv from the railroad to the Tulare frawg ranch yu' could hear 'em a mile. Springtime they'd sing like girls in the organ loft, and by August they were about ready to hire out for bass. And all was fit to be soloists, if I'm a judge. But in a bad year it might only be twenty per cent. The pelican rushed 'em from the pasture right into the San Joaquin River, which was close by the property. The big balance of the herd stampeded, and though of course they came out on the banks again, the news had went around, and folks below at Hemlen eat most of 'em just to spite the company. Yu' see, a frawg in a river is more hopeless than any maverick loose on the range. And they never struck any plan to brand their stock and prove ownership.'

'Well, twenty per cent is good enough for me,' said Trampas, 'if Rawhide don't suit me.'

'A hundred a month!' said the enthusiast. And busy calculations began to arise among them.

'It went to fifty per cent,' pursued the Virginian, 'when New York and Philadelphia got to biddin' agaynst each other. Both cities had signs all over 'em claiming to furnish the Tulare frawg. And both had 'em all right. And same as cattle trains, yu'd see frawg trains tearing acrosst Arizona – big glass tanks with wire over 'em – through to New York, an' the frawgs starin' out.'

'Why, George,' whispered a woman's voice behind me, 'he's merely deceiving them! He's merely making that stuff up out of his head.'

'Yes, my dear, that's merely what he's doing.'

'Well, I don't see why you imagined I should care for this. I think I'll go back.'

'Better see it out, Daisy. This beats the geysers or anything we're likely to find in the Yellowstone.'

'Then I wish we had gone to Bar Harbour as usual,' said the lady, and she returned to her Pullman.

But her husband stayed. Indeed, the male crowd now was a goodly sight to see, how the men edged close, drawn by a common tie. Their different kinds of feet told the strength of the bond – yellow sleeping-car slippers planted miscellaneous and motionless near a pair of Mexican spurs. All eyes watched the Virginian and gave him their entire sympathy. Though they could not know his motive for it, what he was doing had fallen as light upon them – all except the excited calculators. These were loudly making their fortunes at both Rawhide and Tulare, drugged by their satanically aroused hopes of gold, heedless of the slippers and the spurs. Had a man given any sign to warn them, I think he would have been lynched. Even the Indian chiefs had come to see in their show war bonnets and blankets. They naturally understood nothing of it, yet magnetically knew that the Virginian was the great man. And they watched him with approval. He sat by the fire with the frying-pan, looking his daily self – engaging and saturnine. And now as Trampas declared tickets to California would be dear and Rawhide had better come first, the Southerner let loose his heaven-born imagination.

'There's a better reason for Rawhide than tickets, Trampas,' said he. 'I said it was too late for Tulare.'

'I heard you,' said Trampas. 'Opinions may differ. You and I don't think alike on several points.'

'Gawd, Trampas!' said the Virginian, 'd' yu reckon I'd be rotting hyeh on forty dollars if Tulare was like it used to be? Tulare is broke.'

'What broke it? Your leaving?'

'Revenge broke it, and disease,' said the Virginian, striking the frying-pan on his knee, for the frogs were all gone. At those lurid words their untamed child minds took fire, and they drew round him again to hear a tale of blood. The crowd seemed to lean nearer.

But for a short moment it threatened to be spoiled. A passenger came along, demanding in an important voice, 'Where are these frogs?' He was a prominent New York after-dinner speaker, they whispered me, and out for a holiday in his private car. Reaching us and walking to the Virginian, he said cheerily, 'How much do you want for your frogs, my friend?'

'You got a friend hyeh?' said the Virginian. 'That's good, for yu' need care taken of yu'.' And the prominent after-dinner speaker did not further discommode us.

'That's worth my trip,' whispered a New York passenger to me.

'Yes, it was a case of revenge,' resumed the Virginian, 'and disease. There was a man named Saynt Augustine got run out of Domingo, which is a Dago island. He come to Philadelphia, an' he was dead broke. But Saynt Augustine was a live man, an' he saw Philadelphia was full o' Quakers that dressed plain an' eat humdrum. So he started cookin' Domingo way for 'em, an' they caught right ahold. Terrapin, he gave 'em, an' croakeets, an' he'd use forty chickens to make a broth he called consommay. An' he got rich, and Philadelphia got well known, an' Delmonico in New York he got jealous. He was the cook that had the say-so in New York.'

'Was Delmonico one of them I–talians?' enquired a fascinated mutineer.

'I don't know. But he acted like one. Lorenzo was his front name. He aimed to cut – '

'Domingo's throat?' breathed the enthusiast.

'Aimed to cut away the trade from Saynt Augustine an' put Phila-delphia back where he thought she belonged. Frawgs was the fashionable rage then. These foreign cooks set the fashion in eatin', same as foreign dressmakers do women's clothes. Both cities was catchin' and swallowin' all the frawgs Tulare could throw at 'em. So he – '

'Lorenzo?' said the enthusiast.

'Yes, Lorenzo Delmonico. He bid a dollar a tank higher. An' Saynt Augustine raised him fifty cents. An' Lorenzo raised him a dollar. An' Saynt Augustine shoved her up three. Lorenzo he didn't expect Phila-delphia would go that high, and he got hot in the collar, an' flew round his kitchen in New York, an' claimed he'd twist Saynt Augustine's Domingo tail for him and crack his ossified system. Lorenzo raised his language to a high temperature, they say. An' then quite sudden off he starts for Tulare. He buys tickets over the Santa Fe, and he goes a-fannin' and a-foggin'. But, gentlemen, hush! The very same day Saynt Augustine he tears out of Philadelphia. He travelled by the way o' Washington, an' out he comes a-fannin' an' a-foggin' over the Southern Pacific. Of course Tulare didn't know nothin' of this. All it knowed was how the frawg market was on soarin' wings, and it was feelin' like a flight o' rawckets. If only there'd been some preparation – a telegram or something – the disaster would never have occurred. But Lorenzo and Saynt Augustine was that absorbed watchin' each other – for, yu' see, the Santa Fe and the Southern Pacific come together at Mojave, an' the two cooks travelled a matter of two hundred an' ten miles in the same cyar –

they never thought about a telegram. And when they arruv, breathless, an' started in to screechin' what they'd give for the monopoly, why, them unsuspectin' Tulare boys got amused at 'em. I never heard just all they done, but they had Lorenzo singin' and dancin', while Saynt Augustine played the fiddle for him. And one of Lorenzo's heels did get a trifle grazed. Well, them two cooks quit that ranch without disclosin' their identity, and soon as they got to a safe distance they swore eternal friendship, in their excitable foreign way. And they went home over the Union Pacific, sharing the same stateroom. Their revenge killed frawgs. The disease – '

'How killed frogs?' demanded Trampas.

'Just killed 'em. Delmonico and Saynt Augustine wiped frawgs off the slate of fashion. Not a banker in Fifth Avenue'll touch one now if another banker's around watchin' him. And if ever yu' see a man that hides his feet an' won't take off his socks in company, he has worked in them Tulare swamps an' got the disease. Catch him wadin', and yu'll find he's web-footed. Frawgs are dead, Trampas, and so are you.'

'Rise up, liars, and salute your king!' yelled Scipio. 'Oh, I'm in love with you!' And he threw his arms round the Virginian.

'Let me shake hands with you,' said the traveller, who had failed to interest his wife in these things. 'I wish I was going to have more of your company.'

'Thank yu', seh,' said the Virginian.

Other passengers greeted him, and the Indian chiefs came, saying, 'How!' because they followed their feelings without understanding.

'Don't show so humbled, boys,' said the deputy foreman to his most sheepish crew. 'These gentlemen from the East have been enjoying yu' some, I know. But think what a weary wait they have had hyeh. And you insisted on playing the game with me this way, yu' see. What outlet did yu' give me? Didn't I have it to do? And I'll tell yu' one thing for your consolation: when I got to the middle of the frawgs I 'most believed it myself.' And he laughed out the first laugh I had heard him give.

The enthusiast came up and shook hands. That led off, and the rest followed, with Trampas at the end. The tide was too strong for him. He was not a graceful loser; but he got through this, and the Virginian eased him down by treating him precisely like the others – apparently. Possibly the supreme – the most American – moment of all was when word came that the bridge was open, and the Pullman trains, with noise and triumph, began to move westward at last. Everyone waved farewell to everyone, craning from steps and windows, so that the cars twinkled with hilarity; and in twenty minutes the whole procession in front had moved, and our turn came.

'Last chance for Rawhide,' said the Virginian.

'Last chance for Sunk Creek,' said a reconstructed mutineer, and all sprang aboard. There was no question who had won his spurs now.

Our caboose trundled on to Billings along the shingly cottonwooded Yellowstone; and as the plains and bluffs and the distant snow began to grow well known, even to me, we turned to our baggage that was to come off, since camp would begin in the morning. Thus I saw the Virginian carefully rewrapping *Kenilworth*, that he might bring it to its owner unharmed; and I said, 'Don't you think you could have played poker with Queen Elizabeth?'

'No; I expaict she'd have beat me,' he replied. 'She was a lady.'

It was at Billings, on this day, that I made those reflections about equality. For the Virginian had been equal to the occasion: that is the only kind of equality which I recognise.

CHAPTER 17

Scipio Moralises

Into what mood was it that the Virginian now fell? Being less busy, did he begin to 'grieve' about the girl on Bear Creek? I only know that after talking so lengthily he fell into a nine days' silence. The talking part of him deeply and unbrokenly slept.

Official words of course came from him as we rode southward from the railroad, gathering the Judge's stray cattle. During the many weeks since the spring round-up, some of these animals had as usual got very far off their range, and getting them on again became the present business of our party.

Directions and commands – whatever communications to his subordinates were needful to the forwarding of this – he duly gave. But routine has never at any time of the world passed for conversation. His utterances, such as, 'We'll work Willo' Creek tomorro' mawnin',' or, 'I want the wagon to be at the fawks o' Stinkin' Water by Thursday,' though on some occasions numerous enough to sound like discourse, never once broke the man's true silence. Seeming to keep easy company with the camp, he yet kept altogether to himself. That talking part of him – the mood which brings out for you your friend's spirit and mind as a free gift or as an exchange – was down in some dark cave of his nature, hidden away. Perhaps it had been dreaming; perhaps completely reposing. The Virginian was one of those rare ones who are able to refresh themselves in sections. To have a thing on his mind did not keep his body from resting. During our recent journey – it felt years ago now! – while our caboose on the freight train had trundled endlessly westward, and the men were on the ragged edge, the very jumping-off place, of mutiny and possible murder, I had seen him sleep like a child. He snatched the moments not necessary for vigil. I had also seen him sit all night watching his responsibility, ready to spring on it and fasten his teeth in it. And now that he had confounded them with their own attempted weapon of ridicule, his powers seemed to be profoundly dormant. That final pitched battle of wits had made the men his captives and admirers – all save Trampas. And of him the Virginian did not seem to be aware.

But Scipio le Moyne would say to me now and then, 'If I was Trampas, I'd pull my freight.' And once he added, 'Pull it kind of casual, yu' know, like I wasn't noticing myself do it.'

'Yes,' our friend Shorty murmured pregnantly, with his eye upon the quiet Virginian, 'he's sure studying his revenge.'

'Studying your pussy-cat,' said Scipio. 'He knows what he'll do. The time 'ain't arrived.' This was the way they felt about it; and not unnaturally this was the way they made me, the inexperienced Easterner, feel about it. That Trampas also felt something about it was easy to know. Like the leaven which leavens the whole lump, one spot of sulkiness in camp will spread its dull flavour through any company that sits near it; and we had to sit near Trampas at meals for nine days.

His sullenness was not wonderful. To feel himself forsaken by his recent adherents, to see them gone over to his enemy, could not have made his reflections pleasant. Why he did not take himself off to other climes – 'pull his freight casual', as Scipio said – I can explain only thus: pay was due him – 'time', as it was called in cow-land; if he would have this money, he must stay under the Virginian's command until the Judge's ranch on Sunk Creek should be reached; meanwhile, each day's work added to the wages in store for him; and finally, once at Sunk Creek, it would be no more the Virginian who commanded him; it would be the real ranch foreman. At the ranch he would be the Virginian's equal again, both of them taking orders from their officially recognised superior, this foreman. Shorty's word about 'revenge' seemed to me like putting the thing backwards. Revenge, as I told Scipio, was what I should be thinking about if I were Trampas.

'He dassent,' was Scipio's immediate view. 'Not till he's got strong again. He got laughed plumb sick by the bystanders, and whatever spirit he had was broke in the presence of us all. He'll have to recuperate.' Scipio then spoke of the Virginian's attitude. 'Maybe revenge ain't just the right word for where this affair has got to now with him. When yu' beat another man at his own game like he done to Trampas, why, yu've had all the revenge yu' can want, unless you're a hog. And he's no hog. But he has got it in for Trampas. They've not reckoned to a finish. Would you let a man try such spitework on you and quit thinkin' about him just because yu'd headed him off?' To this I offered his own notion about hogs and being satisfied. 'Hogs!' went on Scipio, in a way that dashed my suggestion to pieces; 'hogs ain't in the case. He's got to deal with Trampas somehow – man to man. Trampas and him can't stay this way when they get back and go workin' same as they worked before. No, sir; I've seen his eye twice, and I know he's goin' to reckon to a finish.'

I still must, in Scipio's opinion, have been slow to understand, when on the afternoon following this talk I invited him to tell me what sort of 'finish' he wanted, after such a finishing as had been dealt Trampas already. Getting 'laughed plumb sick by the bystanders' (I borrowed his own not overstated expression) seemed to me a highly final finishing. While I was running my notions off to him, Scipio rose, and, with the frying-pan he had been washing, walked slowly at me.

'I do believe you'd oughtn't to be let travel alone the way you do.' He put his face close to mine. His long nose grew eloquent in its shrewdness, while the fire in his bleached blue eye burned with amiable satire. 'What has come and gone between them two has only settled the one point he was aimin' to make. He was appointed boss of this outfit in the absence of the regular foreman. Since then all he has been playin' for is to hand back his men to the ranch in as good shape as they'd been handed to him, and without losing any on the road through desertion or shooting or what not. He had to kick his cook off the train that day, and the loss made him sorrowful, I could see. But I'd happened to come along, and he jumped me into the vacancy, and I expect he is pretty near consoled. And as boss of the outfit he beat Trampas, who was settin' up for opposition boss. And the outfit is better than satisfied it come out that way, and they're stayin' with him; and he'll hand them all back in good condition, barrin' that lost cook. So for the present his point is made, yu' see. But look ahead a little. It may not be so very far ahead yu'll have to look. We get back to the ranch. He's not boss there any more. His responsibility is over. He is just one of us again, taking orders from a foreman they tell me has showed partiality to Trampas more'n a few times. Partiality! That's what Trampas is plainly trusting to. Trusting it will fix him all right and fix his enemy all wrong. He'd not otherwise dare to keep sour like he's doing. Partiality! D' yu' think it'll scare off the enemy?' Scipio looked across a little creek to where the Virginian was helping throw the gathered cattle on the bed-ground. 'What odds' – he pointed the frying-pan at the Southerner – 'd' yu' figure Trampas's being under any foreman's wing will make to a man like him? He's going to remember Mr Trampas and his spite-work if he's got to tear him out from under the wing, and maybe tear off the wing in the operation. And I am goin' to advise your folks,' ended the complete Scipio, 'not to leave you travel so much alone – not till you've learned more life.'

He had made me feel my inexperience, convinced me of innocence, undoubtedly; and during the final days of our journey I no longer invoked his aid to my reflections upon this especial topic: What would the Virginian do to Trampas? Would it be another intellectual crushing of him, like the frog story, or would there be something this time more material – say muscle, or possibly gunpowder – in it? And was Scipio, after all, infallible? I didn't pretend to understand the Virginian; after several years' knowledge of him he remained utterly beyond me. Scipio's experience was not yet three weeks long. So I let him alone as to all this, discussing with him most other things good and evil in the world, and being convinced of much further innocence; for Scipio's twenty odd years were indeed a library of life. I have never met a better heart, a shrewder wit, and looser morals, with yet a native sense of decency and duty somewhere hard and fast enshrined.

But all the while I was wondering about the Virginian: eating with him, sleeping with him (only not so sound as he did), and riding beside him often for many hours.

Experiments in conversation I did make – and failed. One day particularly while, after a sudden storm of hail had chilled the earth numb and white like winter in fifteen minutes, we sat drying and warming ourselves by a fire that we built, I touched upon that theme of equality on which I knew him to hold opinions as strong as mine. 'Oh,' he would reply, and 'Cert'nly'; and when I asked him what it was in a man that made him a leader of men, he shook his head and puffed his pipe. So then, noticing how the sun had brought the earth in half an hour back from winter to summer again, I spoke of our American climate.

It was a potent drug, I said, for millions to be swallowing every day.

'Yes,' said he, wiping the damp from his Winchester rifle.

Our American climate, I said, had worked remarkable changes, at least.

'Yes,' he said; and did not ask what they were.

So I had to tell him. 'It has made successful politicians of the Irish. That's one. And it has given our whole race the habit of poker'

Bang went his Winchester. The bullet struck close to my left. I sat up angrily.

'That's the first foolish thing I ever saw you do!' I said.

'Yes,' he drawled slowly, 'I'd ought to have done it sooner. He was pretty near lively again.' And then he picked up a rattlesnake six feet behind me. It had been numbed by the hail, part revived by the sun, and he had shot its head off.

CHAPTER 18

'Would you be a Parson?'

After this I gave up my experiments in conversation. So that by the final afternoon of our journey, with Sunk Creek actually in sight, and the great grasshoppers slatting their dry song over the sagebrush, and the time at hand when the Virginian and Trampas would be 'man to man', my thoughts rose to a considerable pitch of speculation.

And now that talking part of the Virginian, which had been nine days asleep, gave its first yawn and stretch of waking. Without preface, he suddenly asked me, 'Would you be a parson?'

I was mentally so far away that I couldn't get back in time to comprehend or answer before he had repeated – 'What would yu' take to be a parson?'

He drawled it out in his gentle way, precisely as if no nine days stood between it and our last real intercourse.

'Take?' I was still vaguely moving in my distance. 'How?'

His next question brought me home.

'I expect the Pope's is the biggest of them parson jobs?'

It was with an 'Oh!' that I now entirely took his idea. 'Well, yes; decidedly the biggest.'

'Beats the English one? Archbishop – ain't it? – of Canterbury? The Pope comes ahead of him?'

'His Holiness would say so if his Grace did not.'

The Virginian turned half in his saddle to see my face – I was, at the moment, riding not quite abreast of him – and I saw the gleam of his teeth beneath his moustache. It was seldom I could make him smile, even to this slight extent. But his eyes grew, with his next words, remote again in their speculation.

'His Holiness and his Grace. Now if I was to hear 'em namin' me that-a-way every mawnin' I'd sca'cely get down to business.'

'Oh, you'd get used to the pride of it.'

' 'Tisn't the pride. The laugh is what would ruin me. 'Twould take 'most all my attention keeping a straight face. The Archbishop –' here he took one of his wide mental turns – 'is apt to be a big man in them Shakespeare plays. Kings take talk from him they'd not stand from anybody else; and he talks fine, frequently. About the bees, for instance, when Henry is going to fight France. He tells him a beehive is similar to a kingdom. I learned that piece.' The Virginian could not have expected to blush at uttering these last words. He knew that his sudden colour must tell me in whose book it was he had learned the piece. Was not her copy of *Kenilworth* even now in his cherishing pocket? So he now, to cover his blush, very deliberately recited to me the Archbishop's discourse upon bees and their kingdom –

> 'Where some, like magistrates, correct at home . . .
> Others, like soldiers, armèd in their stings,
> Make boot upon the summer's velvet buds;
> Which pillage they with merry march bring home
> To the tent-royal of their emperor:
> Who, busied in his majesty, surveys
> The singing masons building roofs of gold.

'Ain't that a fine description of bees a-workin'? "The singing masons building roofs of gold!" Puts 'em right before yu', and is poetry without bein' foolish. His Holiness and his Grace. Well, they could not hire me for either o' those positions. How many religions are there?'

'All over the earth?'

'Yu' can begin with ourselves. Right hyeh at home I know there's Romanists, and Episcopals – '

'Two kinds!' I put in. 'At least two of Episcopals.'

'That's three. Then Methodists and Baptists, and – '

'Three Methodists!'

'Well, you do the countin'.'

I accordingly did it, feeling my revolving memory slip cogs all the way round. 'Anyhow, there are safely fifteen.'

'Fifteen.' He held this fact a moment. 'And they don't worship a whole heap o' different gods like the ancients did?

'Oh, no!'

'It's just` the same one?'

'The same one.'

The Virginian folded his hands over the horn of his saddle, and leaned forward upon them in contemplation of the wide, beautiful landscape.

'One God and fifteen religions,' was his reflection. 'That's a right smart of religions for just one God.'

This way of reducing it was, if obvious to him, so novel to me that my laugh evidently struck him as a louder and livelier comment than was required. He turned on me as if I had somehow perverted the spirit of his words.

'I ain't religious. I know that. But I ain't *un*religious. And I know that too.'

'So do I know it, my friend.'

'Do you think there ought to be fifteen varieties of good people?' His voice, while it now had an edge that could cut anything it came against, was still not raised. 'There ain't fifteen. There ain't two. There's one kind. And when I meet it, I respect it. It is not praying nor preaching that has ever caught me and made me ashamed of myself, but one or two people I have knowed that never said a superior word to me. They thought more o' me than I deserved, and that made me behave better than I naturally wanted to. Made me quit a girl onced in time for her not to lose her good name. And so that's one thing I have never done. And if ever I was to have a son or somebody I set store by, I would wish their lot to be to know one or two good folks mighty well – men or women – women preferred.'

He had looked away again to the hills behind Sunk Creek ranch, to which our walking horses had now almost brought us.

'As for parsons – ' the gesture of his arm was a disclaiming one, 'I reckon some parsons have a right to tell yu' to be good. The bishop of this hyeh Territory has a right. But I'll tell yu' this: a middlin' doctor is a pore thing, and a middlin' lawyer is a pore thing; but keep me from a middlin' man of God.'

Once again he had reduced it, but I did not laugh this time. I thought there should in truth be heavy damages for malpractice on human souls. But the hot glow of his words, and the vision of his deepest inner man it revealed, faded away abruptly.

'What do yu' make of the proposition yondeh?' As he pointed to the cause of this question he had become again his daily, engaging, saturnine self.

Then I saw over in a fenced meadow, to which we were now close, what he was pleased to call 'the proposition'. Proposition in the West does, in fact, mean whatever you at the moment please – an offer to sell you a mine, a cloudburst, a glass of whiskey, a steamboat. This time it meant a stranger clad in black, and of a clerical deportment which would in that atmosphere and to a watchful eye be visible for a mile or two.

'I reckoned yu' hadn't noticed him,' was the Virginian's reply to my ejaculation. 'Yes. He set me goin' on the subject a while back. I expect he is another missionary to us pore cowboys.'

I seemed from a hundred yards to feel the stranger's forceful personality. It was in his walk – I should better say stalk – as he promenaded along the creek. His hands were behind his back, and there was an air of waiting, of displeased waiting, in his movement.

'Yes, he'll be a missionary,' said the Virginian, conclusively; and he took to singing, or rather to whining, with his head tilted at an absurd angle upward at the sky –

    'Dar is a big Car'lina nigger,
    About de size of dis chile or p'raps a little bigger,
        By de name of Jim Crow.
    Dat what de white folks call him.
    If ever I sees him I 'tends for to maul him,
        Just to let de white folks see
        Such an animos as he
    Can't walk around the streets and scandalise me.'

The lane which was conducting us to the group of ranch buildings now turned a corner of the meadow, and the Virginian went on with his second verse –

'Great big fool, he hasn't any knowledge.
  Gosh! how could he, when he's never been to scollege?
    Neither has I.
    But I'se come mighty nigh;
  I peaked through de door as I went by.'

He was beginning a third stanza, but stopped short; a horse had neighed close behind us.

'Trampas,' said he, without turning his head, 'we are home.'

'It looks that way.' Some ten yards were between ourselves and Trampas, where he followed.

'And I'll trouble yu' for my rope yu' took this mawnin' instead o' your own.'

'I don't know as it's your rope I've got.' Trampas skilfully spoke this so that a precisely opposite meaning flowed from his words.

If it was discussion he tried for, he failed. The Virginian's hand moved, and for one thick, flashing moment my thoughts were evidently also the thoughts of Trampas. But the Virginian only held out to Trampas the rope which he had detached from his saddle.

'Take your hand off your gun, Trampas. If I had wanted to kill yu' you'd be lying nine days back on the road now. Here's your rope. Did yu' expect I'd not know it? It's the only one in camp the stiffness ain't all drug out of yet. Or maybe yu' expected me to notice and – not take notice?'

'I don't spend my time in expectations about you. If – '

The Virginian wheeled his horse across the road. 'Yu're talkin' too soon after reachin' safety, Trampas. I didn't tell yu' to hand me that rope this mawnin', because I was busy. I ain't foreman now; and I want that rope.'

Trampas produced a smile as skilful as his voice. 'Well, I guess your having mine proves this one is yours.' He rode up and received the coil which the Virginian held out, unloosing the disputed one on his saddle. If he had meant to devise a slippery, evasive insult, no small trick in cowland could be more offensive than this taking another man's rope. And it is the small tricks which lead to the big bullets. Trampas put a smooth coating of plausibility over the whole transaction. 'After the rope corral we had to make this morning – ' his tone was mock explanatory – 'the ropes was all strewed round camp, and in the hustle I – '

'Pardon me,' said a sonorous voice behind us, 'do you happen to have seen Judge Henry?' It was the reverend gentleman in his meadow, come to the fence. As we turned round to him he spoke on, with much rotund authority in his eye. 'From his answer to my letter, Judge Henry undoubtedly expects me here. I have arrived from Fetterman according to my plan which I announced to him, to find that he has been absent all day – absent the whole day.'

The Virginian sat sidewise to talk, one long, straight leg supporting him on one stirrup, the other bent at ease, the boot half lifted from its dangling stirrup. He made himself the perfection of courtesy. 'The Judge is frequently absent all night, seh.'

'Scarcely tonight, I think. I thought you might know something about him.'

'I have been absent myself, seh.'

'Ah! On a vacation, perhaps?' The divine had a ruddy face. His strong glance was straight and frank and fearless; but his smile too much reminded me of days bygone, when we used to return to school from the Christmas holidays, and the masters would shake our hands and welcome us with: 'Robert, John, Edward, glad to see you all looking so well! Rested, and ready for hard work, I'm sure!'

That smile does not really please even good, tame little boys; and the Virginian was nearing thirty.

'It has not been vacation this trip, seh,' said he, settling straight in his saddle. 'There's the Judge driving in now, in time for all questions yu' have to ask him.'

His horse took a step, but was stopped short. There lay the Virginian's rope on the ground. I had been aware of Trampas's quite proper departure during the talk; and as he was leaving, I seemed also to be aware of his placing the coil across the cantle of its owner's saddle. Had he intended it to fall and have to be picked up? It was another evasive little business, and quite successful, if designed to nag the owner of the rope. A few hundred yards ahead of us Trampas was now shouting loud cowboy shouts. Were they to announce his return to those at home, or did they mean derision? The Virginian leaned, keeping his seat, and, swinging down his arm, caught up the rope, and hung it on his saddle somewhat carefully. But the hue of rage spread over his face.

From his fence the divine now spoke, in approbation, but with another strong, cheerless smile. 'You pick up that rope as if you were well trained to it.'

'It's part of our business, seh, and we try to mind it like the rest.' But this, stated in a gentle drawl, did not pierce the missionary's armour; his superiority was very thick.

We now rode on, and I was impressed by the reverend gentleman's robust, dictatorial back as he proceeded by a short cut through the meadow to the ranch. You could take him for nothing but a vigorous, sincere, dominating man, full of the highest purpose. But whatever his creed, I already doubted if he were the right one to sow it and make it grow in these new, wild fields. He seemed more the sort of gardener to keep old walks and vines pruned in their antique rigidity. I admired him for coming all this way with his clean, short, grey whiskers and his black, well-brushed suit. And he made me think of a powerful locomotive stuck puffing on a grade.

Meanwhile, the Virginian rode beside me, so silent in his volcanic wrath that I did not perceive it. The missionary coming on top of Trampas had been more than he could stand. But I did not know, and I spoke with innocent cheeriness.

'Is the parson going to save us?' I asked; and I fairly jumped at his voice – 'Don't talk so much!' he burst out. I had got the whole accumulation!

'Who's been talking!' I in equal anger screeched back. 'I'm not trying to save you. I didn't take your rope.' And having poured this out, I whipped up my pony.

But he spurred his own alongside of me; and glancing at him, I saw that he was now convulsed with internal mirth. I therefore drew down to a walk, and he straightened into gravity.

'I'm right obliged to yu',' he laid his hand in its buckskin gauntlet upon my horse's mane as he spoke, 'for bringing me back out o' my nonsense. I'll be as serene as a bird now – whatever they do. A man,' he stated reflectively, 'any full-sized man, ought to own a big lot of temper. And like all his valuable possessions, he'd ought to keep it and not lose any.' This was his full apology. 'As for salvation, I have got this far: somebody,' he swept an arm at the sunset and the mountains, 'must have made all that, I know. But I know one more thing I would tell Him to His face: if I can't do nothing long enough and good enough to earn eternal happiness, I can't do nothing long enough and bad enough to be damned. I reckon He plays a square game with us if He plays at all, and I ain't bothering my haid about other worlds.'

As we reached the stables, he had become the serene bird he promised, and was sentimentally continuing:

'De sun is made of mud from de bottom of de river;
De moon is made o' fox-fire, as you might disciver;
De stars like de ladies' eyes,
All round de world dey flies,
To give a little light when de moon don't rise.'

If words were meant to conceal our thoughts, melody is perhaps a still thicker veil for them. Whatever temper he had lost, he had certainly found again; but this all the more fitted him to deal with Trampas, when the dealing should begin. I had half a mind to speak to the Judge, only it seemed beyond a mere visitor's business. Our missionary was at this moment himself speaking to Judge Henry at the door of the home ranch.

'I reckon he's explaining he has been a-waiting.' The Virginian was throwing his saddle off as I loosened the cinches of mine. 'And the Judge don't look like he was hopelessly distressed.'

I now surveyed the distant parley, and the Judge, from the wagonful of guests whom he had evidently been driving upon a day's excursion, waved me a welcome, which I waved back. 'He's got Miss Molly Wood there!' I exclaimed.

'Yes.' The Virginian was brief about this fact. 'I'll look afteh your saddle. You go and get acquainted with the company.'

This favour I accepted; it was the means he chose for saying he hoped, after our recent boiling over, that all was now more than right between us. So for the while I left him to his horses, and his corrals, and his Trampas, and his foreman, and his imminent problem.

CHAPTER 19

Dr MacBride Begs Pardon

Judge and Mrs Henry, Molly Wood, and two strangers, a lady and a gentleman, were the party which had been driving in the large three-seated wagon. They had seemed a merry party. But as I came within hearing of their talk, it was a fragment of the minister's sonority which reached me first – '. . . more opportunity for them to have the benefit of hearing frequent sermons,' was the sentence I heard him bring to completion.

'Yes, to be sure, sir.' Judge Henry gave me (it almost seemed) additional warmth of welcome for arriving to break up the present discourse. 'Let me introduce you to the Revd Dr Alexander MacBride. Doctor, another guest we have been hoping for about this time,' was my host's cordial explanation to him of me. There remained the gentleman with his wife from New York, and to these I made my final bows. But I had not broken up the discourse.

'We may be said to have met already.' Dr MacBride had fixed upon me his full, mastering eye; and it occurred to me that if they had policemen in heaven, he would be at least a centurion in the force. But he did not mean to be unpleasant; it was only that in a mind full of matters less worldly, pleasure was left out. 'I observed your friend was a skilful horseman,' he continued. 'I was saying to Judge Henry that I could wish such skilful horsemen might ride to a church upon the Sabbath. A church, that is, of right doctrine, where they would have opportunity to hear frequent sermons.'

'Yes,' said Judge Henry, 'yes. It would be a good thing.'

Mrs Henry, with some murmur about the kitchen, here went into the house.

'I was informed,' Dr MacBride held the rest of us, 'before undertaking my journey that I should find a desolate and mainly godless country. But nobody gave me to understand that from Medicine Bow I was to drive three hundred miles and pass no church of any faith.'

The Judge explained that there had been a few a long way to the right and left of him. 'Still,' he conceded, 'you are quite right. But don't forget that this is the newest part of a new world.'

'Judge,' said his wife, coming to the door, 'how can you keep them standing in the dust with your talking?'

This most efficiently did break up the discourse. As our little party, with the smiles and the polite holdings back of new acquaintanceship, moved into the house, the Judge detained me behind all of them long enough to whisper dolorously, 'He's going to stay a whole week.'

I had hopes that he would not stay a whole week when I presently learned of the crowded arrangements which our hosts, with many hospitable apologies, disclosed to us. They were delighted to have us, but they hadn't foreseen that we should all be simultaneous. The foreman's house had been prepared for two of us, and did we mind? The two of us were Dr MacBride and myself; and I expected him to mind. But I wronged him grossly. It would be much better, he assured Mrs Henry, than straw in a stable, which he had tried several times, and was quite ready for. So I saw that though he kept his vigorous body clean when he could, he cared nothing for it in the face of his mission. How the foreman and his wife relished being turned out during a week for a missionary and myself was not my concern, although while he and I made ready for supper over there, it struck me as hard on them. The room with its two cots and furniture was as nice as possible; and we closed the door upon the adjoining room, which, however, seemed also untenanted.

Mrs Henry gave us a meal so good that I have remembered it, and her husband the Judge strove his best that we should eat it in merriment. He poured out his anecdotes like wine, and we should have quickly warmed to them; but Dr MacBride sat among us, giving occasional heavy ha-has, which produced, as Miss Molly Wood whispered to me, a 'dreadfully cavernous effect'. Was it his sermon, we wondered, that he was thinking over? I told her of the copious sheaf of them I had seen him pull from his wallet over at the foreman's. 'Goodness!' said she. 'Then are we to hear one every evening?' This I doubted; he had probably been picking one out suitable for the occasion. 'Putting his best foot foremost,' was her comment; 'I suppose they have best feet, like the rest of us.' Then she grew delightfully sharp. 'Do you know, when I first heard him I thought his voice was hearty. But if you listen, you'll find it's merely militant. He never really meets you with it. He's off on his hill watching the battlefield the whole time.'

'He will find a hardened pagan here.'

'Judge Henry?'

'Oh, no! The wild man you're taming. He's brought you *Kenilworth* safe back.'

She was smooth. 'Oh, as for taming him! But don't you find him intelligent?'

Suddenly I somehow knew that she didn't want to tame him. But what did she want to do? The thought of her had made him blush this afternoon. No thought of him made her blush this evening.

A great laugh from the rest of the company made me aware that the Judge had consummated his tale of the 'Sole Survivor'.

'And so,' he finished, 'they all went off as mad as hops because it hadn't been a massacre.' Mr and Mrs Ogden – they were the New Yorkers – gave this story much applause, and Dr MacBride half a minute later laid his 'ha-ha', like a heavy stone, upon the gaiety.

'I'll never be able to stand seven sermons,' said Miss Wood to me.

'Talking of massacres' – I now hastened to address the already saddened table – 'I have recently escaped one myself.'

The Judge had come to an end of his powers. 'Oh, tell us!' he implored.

'Seriously, sir, I think we grazed pretty wet tragedy; but your extraordinary man brought us out into comedy safe and dry.'

This gave me their attention; and, from that afternoon in Dakota when I had first stepped aboard the caboose, I told them the whole tale of my experience: how I grew immediately aware that all was not right, by the Virginian's kicking the cook off the train; how, as we journeyed, the dark bubble of mutiny swelled hourly beneath my eyes; and how, when it was threatening I know not what explosion, the Virginian had pricked it with humour, so that it burst in nothing but harmless laughter.

Their eyes followed my narrative: the New Yorkers, because such events do not happen upon the shores of the Hudson; Mrs Henry, because she was my hostess; Miss Wood followed for whatever her reasons were – I couldn't see her eyes; rather, I *felt* her listening intently to the deeds and dangers of the man she didn't care to tame. But it was the eyes of the Judge and the missionary which I saw riveted upon me indeed until the end; and they forthwith made plain their quite dissimilar opinions.

Judge Henry struck the table lightly with his fist. 'I knew it!' And he leaned back in his chair with a face of contentment. He had trusted his man, and his man had proved worthy.

'Pardon me.' Dr MacBride had a manner of saying 'pardon me', which rendered forgiveness well-nigh impossible.

The Judge waited for him.

'Am I to understand that these – a – cowboys attempted to mutiny, and were discouraged in this attempt upon finding themselves less skilful at lying than the man they had plotted to depose?'

I began an answer. 'It was other qualities, sir, that happened to be revealed and asserted by what you call his lying that – '

'And what am I to call it, if it is not lying? A competition in deceit in which, I admit, he outdid them.'

'It's their way to – '

'Pardon me. Their way to lie? They bow down to the greatest in this?'

'Oh,' said Miss Wood in my ear, 'give him up.'

The Judge took a turn. 'We-ell, Doctor – ' He seemed to stick here.

Mr Ogden handsomely assisted him. 'You've said the word yourself, Doctor. It's the competition, don't you see? The trial of strength by no matter what test.'

'Yes,' said Miss Wood, unexpectedly. 'And it wasn't that George Washington couldn't tell a lie. He just wouldn't. I'm sure if he'd undertaken to he'd have told a much better one than Cornwallis.'

'Ha-ha, madam! You draw an ingenious subtlety from your books.'

'It's all plain to me,' Ogden pursued. 'The men were morose. This foreman was in the minority. He cajoled them into a bout of tall stories, and told the tallest himself. And when they found they had swallowed it whole – well, it would certainly take the starch out of me,' he concluded. 'I couldn't be a serious mutineer after that.'

Dr MacBride now sounded his strongest bass. 'Pardon me. I cannot accept such a view, sir. There is a levity abroad in our land which I must deplore. No matter how leniently you may try to put it, in the end we have the spectacle of a struggle between men where lying decides the survival of the fittest. Better, far better, if it was to come, that they had shot honest bullets. There are worse evils than war.'

The Doctor's eye glared righteously about him. None of us, I think, trembled; or, if we did, it was with emotions other than fear. Mrs Henry at once introduced the subject of trout-fishing, and thus happily removed us from the edge of whatever sort of precipice we seemed to have approached; for Dr MacBride had brought his rod. He dilated upon this sport with fervour, and we assured him that the streams upon the west slope of the Bow Leg Mountains would afford him plenty of it. Thus we ended our meal in carefully preserved amity.

CHAPTER 20

The Judge Ignores Particulars

'Do you often have these visitations?' Ogden enquired of Judge Henry. Our host was giving us whiskey in his office, and Dr MacBride, while we smoked apart from the ladies, had repaired to his quarters in the foreman's house previous to the service which he was shortly to hold.

The Judge laughed. 'They come now and then through the year. I like the bishop to come. And the men always like it. But I fear our friend will scarcely please them so well.'

'You don't mean they'll – '

'Oh, no. They'll keep quiet. The fact is, they have a good deal better manners than he has, if he only knew it. They'll be able to bear him. But as for any good he'll do – '

'I doubt if he knows a word of science,' said I, musing about the Doctor.

'Science! He doesn't know what Christianity is yet. I've entertained many guests, but none – The whole secret,' broke off Judge Henry, 'lies in the way you treat people. As soon as you treat men as your brothers, they are ready to acknowledge you – if you deserve it – as their superior. That's the whole bottom of Christianity, and that's what our missionary will never know.'

There was a somewhat heavy knock at the office door, and I think we all feared it was Dr MacBride. But when the Judge opened, the Virginian was standing there in the darkness.

'So!' The Judge opened the door wide. He was very hearty to the man he had trusted. 'You're back at last.'

'I came to repawt.'

While they shook hands, Ogden nudged me. 'That the fellow?' I nodded. 'Fellow who kicked the cook off the train?' I again nodded, and he looked at the Virginian, his eye and his stature.

Judge Henry, properly democratic, now introduced him to Ogden.

The New Yorker also meant to be properly democratic. 'You're the man I've been hearing such a lot about.'

But familiarity is not equality. 'Then I expect yu' have the advantage of me, seh,' said the Virginian, very politely. 'Shall I repawt tomorro'?' His grave eyes were on the Judge again. Of me he had taken no notice; he had come as an employee to see his employer.

'Yes, yes; I'll want to hear about the cattle tomorrow. But step inside a moment now. There's a matter – ' The Virginian stepped inside, and took off his hat. 'Sit down. You had trouble – I've heard something about it,' the Judge went on.

The Virginian sat down, grave and graceful. But he held the brim of his hat all the while. He looked at Ogden and me, and then back at his employer. There was reluctance in his eye. I wondered if his employer could be going to make him tell his own exploits in the presence of us outsiders; and there came into my memory the Bengal tiger at a trained-animal show I had once seen.

'You had some trouble,' repeated the Judge.

'Well, there was a time when they maybe wanted to have notions. They're good boys.' And he smiled a very little.

Contentment increased in the Judge's face. 'Trampas a good boy too?'

But this time the Bengal tiger did not smile. He sat with his eye fastened on his employer.

The Judge passed rather quickly on to his next point. 'You've brought them all back, though, I understand, safe and sound, without a scratch?'

The Virginian looked down at his hat, then up again at the Judge, mildly. 'I had to part with my cook.'

There was no use; Ogden and myself exploded. Even upon the embarrassed Virginian a large grin slowly forced itself. 'I guess yu' know about it,' he murmured. And he looked at me with a sort of reproach. He knew it was I who had told tales out of school.

'I only want to say,' said Ogden, conciliatingly, 'that I know I couldn't have handled those men.'

The Virginian relented. 'Yu' never tried, seh.'

The Judge had remained serious; but he showed himself plainly more and more contented. 'Quite right,' he said. 'You had to part with your cook. When I put a man in charge, I put him in charge. I don't make particulars my business. They're to be always his. Do you understand?'

'Thank yu'.' The Virginian understood that his employer was praising his management of the expedition. But I don't think he at all discerned – as I did presently – that his employer had just been putting him to a further test, had laid before him the temptation of complaining of a fellow-workman and blowing his own trumpet, and was delighted with his reticence. He made a movement to rise.

'I haven't finished,' said the Judge. 'I was coming to the matter. There's one particular – since I do happen to have been told. I fancy Trampas has learned something he didn't expect.'

This time the Virginian evidently did not understand, any more than I did. One hand played with his hat, mechanically turning it round.

The Judge explained. 'I mean about Roberts.'

A pulse of triumph shot over the Southerner's face, turning it savage for that fleeting instant. He understood now, and was unable to suppress this much answer. But he was silent.

'You see,' the Judge explained to me, 'I was obliged to let Roberts, my old foreman, go last week. His wife could not have stood another winter here, and a good position was offered to him near Los Angeles.'

I did see. I saw a number of things. I saw why the foreman's house had been empty to receive Dr MacBride and me. And I saw that the Judge had been very clever indeed. For I had abstained from telling any tales about the present feeling between Trampas and the Virginian; but he had divined it. Well enough for him to say that 'particulars' were something he let alone; he evidently kept a deep eye on the under-currents at his ranch. He knew that in Roberts, Trampas had lost a powerful friend. And this was what I most saw, this final fact, that Trampas had no longer any intervening shield. He and the Virginian stood indeed man to man.

'And so,' the Judge continued speaking to me, 'here I am at a very inconvenient time without a foreman. Unless,' I caught the twinkle in his eyes before he turned to the Virginian, 'unless you're willing to take the position yourself. Will you?'

I saw the Southerner's hand grip his hat as he was turning it round. He held it still now, and his other hand found it and gradually crumpled the soft crown in. It meant everything to him: recognition, higher station, better fortune, a separate house of his own, and – perhaps – one step nearer to the woman he wanted. I don't know what words he might have said to the Judge had they been alone, but the Judge had chosen to do it in our presence, the whole thing from beginning to end. The Virginian sat with the damp coming out on his forehead, and his eyes dropped from his employer's.

'Thank yu',' was what he managed at last to say.

'Well, now, I'm greatly relieved!' exclaimed the Judge, rising at once. He spoke with haste, and lightly. 'That's excellent. I was in something of a hole,' he said to Ogden and me; 'and this gives me one thing less to think of. Saves me a lot of particulars,' he jocosely added to the Virginian, who was now also standing up. 'Begin right off. Leave the bunk house. The gentlemen won't mind your sleeping in your own house.'

Thus he dismissed his new foreman gaily. But the new foreman, when he got outside, turned back for one gruff word – 'I'll try to please yu'.' That was all. He was gone in the darkness. But there was light enough for me, looking after him, to see him lay his hand on a shoulder-high gate and vault it as if he had been the wind. Sounds of cheering came to us a few moments later from the bunk house. Evidently he had 'begun right away', as the Judge had directed. He had told his fortune to his brother cowpunchers, and this was their answer.

'I wonder if Trampas is shouting too?' enquired Ogden.

'Hm!' said the Judge. 'That is one of the particulars I wash my hands of.'

I knew that he entirely meant it. I knew, once his decision taken of appointing the Virginian his lieutenant for good and all, that, like a wise commander-in-chief, he would trust his lieutenant to take care of his own business.

'Well,' Ogden pursued with interest, 'haven't you landed Trampas plump at his mercy?'

The phrase tickled the Judge. 'That is where I've landed him!' he declared. 'And here is Dr MacBride.'

CHAPTER 21

In a State of Sin

Thunder sat imminent upon the missionary's brow. Many were to be at his mercy soon. But for us he had sunshine still. 'I am truly sorry to be turning you upside down,' he said importantly. 'But it seems the best place for my service.' He spoke of the tables pushed back and the chairs gathered in the hall, where the storm would presently break upon the congregation. 'Eight-thirty?' he enquired.

This was the hour appointed, and it was only twenty minutes off. We threw the unsmoked fractions of our cigars away, and returned to offer our services to the ladies. This amused the ladies. They had done without us. All was ready in the hall.

'We got the cook to help us,' Mrs Ogden told me, 'so as not to disturb your cigars. In spite of the cowboys, I still recognise my own country.'

'In the cook?' I rather densely asked.

'Oh, no! I don't have a Chinaman. It's in the length of after-dinner cigars.'

'Had you been smoking,' I returned, 'you would have found them short this evening.'

'You make it worse,' said the lady; 'we have had nothing but Dr MacBride.'

'We'll share him with you now,' I exclaimed.

'Has he announced his text? I've got one for him,' said Molly Wood, joining us. She stood on tiptoe and spoke it comically in our ears. ' "I said in my haste, All men are liars." ' This made us merry as we stood among the chairs in the congested hall.

I left the ladies, and sought the bunk house. I had heard the cheers, but I was curious also to see the men, and how they were taking it. There was but little for the eye. There was much noise in the room. They were getting ready to come to church – brushing their hair, shaving, and making themselves clean, amid talk occasionally profane and continuously diverting.

'Well, I'm a Christian, anyway,' one declared.

'I'm a Mormon, I guess,' said another.

'I belong to the Knights of Pythias,' said a third.

'I'm a Mohammedist,' said a fourth; 'I hope I ain't goin' to hear nothin' to shock me.'

And they went on with their joking. But Trampas was out of the joking. He lay on his bed reading a newspaper, and took no pains to look pleasant. My eyes were considering him when the blithe Scipio came in.

'Don't look so bashful,' said he. 'There's only us girls here.'

He had been helping the Virginian move his belongings from the bunk house over to the foreman's cabin. He himself was to occupy the Virginian's old bed here. 'And I hope sleepin' in it will bring me some of his luck,' said Scipio. 'Yu'd ought to've seen us when he told us in his quiet way. Well,' Scipio sighed a little, 'it must feel good to have your friends glad about you.'

'Especially Trampas,' said I. 'The Judge knows about that,' I added.

'Knows, does he? What's he say?' Scipio drew me quickly out of the bunk house.

'Says it's no business of his.'

'Said nothing but that?' Scipio's curiosity seemed strangely intense. 'Made no suggestion? Not a thing?'

'Not a thing. Said he didn't want to know and didn't care.'

'How did he happen to hear about it?' snapped Scipio. 'You told him!' he immediately guessed. '*He* never would.' And Scipio jerked his thumb at the Virginian, who appeared for a moment in the lighted window of the new quarters he was arranging. 'He never would tell,' Scipio repeated. 'And so the Judge never made a suggestion to him,' he muttered, nodding in the darkness. 'So it's just his own notion. Just like him, too, come to think of it. Only I didn't expect – well, I guess he could surprise me any day he tried.'

'You're surprising me now,' I said. 'What's it all about?'

'Oh, him and Trampas.'

'What? Nothing surely happened yet?' I was as curious as Scipio had been.

'No, not yet. But there will.'

'Great Heavens, man! when?'

'Just as soon as Trampas makes the first move,' Scipio replied easily.

I became dignified. Scipio had evidently been told things by the Virginian.

'Yes, I up and asked him plumb out,' Scipio answered. 'I was liftin' his trunk in at the door, and I couldn't stand it no longer, and I asked him plumb out. "Yu've sure got Trampas where yu' want him." That's what I said. And he up and answered and told me. So I know.' At this point Scipio stopped; I was not to know.

'I had no idea,' I said, 'that your system held so much meanness.'

'Oh, it ain't meanness!' And he laughed ecstatically.

'What do you call it, then?'

'He'd call it discretion,' said Scipio. Then he became serious. 'It's too blamed grand to tell yu'. I'll leave yu' to see it happen. Keep around, that's all. Keep around. I pretty near wish I didn't know it myself.'

What with my feelings at Scipio's discretion, and my human curiosity, I was not in that mood which best profits from a sermon. Yet even though my expectations had been cruelly left quivering in mid air, I was not sure how much I really wanted to 'keep around'. You will therefore understand how Dr MacBride was able to make a prayer and to read Scripture without my being conscious of a word that he had uttered. It was when I saw him opening the manuscript of his sermon that I suddenly remembered I was sitting, so to speak, in church, and began once more to think of the preacher and his congregation. Our chairs were in the front line, of course; but, being next the wall, I could easily see the cowboys behind me. They were perfectly decorous. If Mrs Ogden had looked for pistols, daredevil attitudes, and so forth, she must have been greatly disappointed. Except for their weather-beaten cheeks and eyes, they were simply American young men with moustaches and without, and might have been sitting, say, in Danbury, Connecticut. Even Trampas merged quietly with the general placidity. The Virginian did not, to be sure, look like Danbury, and his frame and his features showed out of the mass; but his eyes were upon Dr MacBride with a creamlike propriety.

Our missionary did not choose Miss Wood's text. He made his selection from another of the Psalms; and when it came, I did not dare to look at anybody; I was much nearer unseemly conduct than the cowboys. Dr MacBride gave us his text sonorously, ' "They are altogether become filthy; There is none of them that doeth good, no, not one".' His eye showed us plainly that present company was not excepted from this. He repeated the text once more, then, launching upon his discourse, gave none of us a ray of hope.

I had heard it all often before; but preached to cowboys it took on a new glare of untimeliness, of grotesque obsoleteness – as if someone should say, 'Let me persuade you to admire woman,' and forthwith hold out her bleached bones to you. The cowboys were told that not only they could do no good, but that if they did contrive to, it would not help them. Nay, more: not only honest deeds availed them nothing, but even if they accepted this especial creed which was being explained to them as necessary for salvation, still it might not save them. Their sin was indeed the cause of their damnation, yet, keeping from sin, they might nevertheless be lost. It had all been settled for them not only before they were born, but before Adam was shaped. Having told them this, he invited them to glorify the Creator of the scheme. Even if damned, they must praise the person who had made them expressly for damnation. That is what I heard him prove by logic to these cowboys. Stone upon stone he built the black cellar of his theology, leaving out its beautiful park and the sunshine of its garden. He did not tell them the splendour of its past, the noble fortress for good that it had been, how its tonic had strengthened generations of their fathers. No; wrath he spoke of, and never once of love. It was the bishop's way, I knew well, to hold cowboys by homely talk of their special hardships and temptations. And when they fell he spoke to them of forgiveness and brought them encouragement. But Dr MacBride never thought once of the lives of these waifs. Like himself, like all mankind, they were invisible dots in creation; like him, they were to feel as nothing, to be swept up in the potent heat of his faith. So he thrust out to them none of the sweet but all the bitter of his creed, naked and stern as iron. Dogma was his all in all, and poor humanity was nothing but flesh for its canons.

Thus to kill what chance he had for being of use seemed to me more deplorable than it did evidently to them. Their attention merely wandered. Three hundred years ago they would have been frightened; but not in this electric day. I saw Scipio stifling a smile when it came to the doctrine of original sin. 'We know of its truth,' said Dr MacBride, 'from the severe troubles and distresses to which infants are liable, and from death passing upon them before they are capable of sinning.' Yet I knew he was a good man; and I also knew that if a missionary is to be tactless, he might almost as well be bad.

I said their attention wandered, but I forgot the Virginian. At first his attitude might have been mere propriety. One can look respectfully at a preacher and be internally breaking all the commandments. But even with the text I saw real attention light in the Virginian's eye. And keeping track of the concentration that grew on him with each minute made the sermon short for me. He missed nothing. Before the end his gaze at the preacher had become swerveless. Was he convert or critic? Convert was incredible. Thus was an hour passed before I had thought of time.

When it was over we took it variously. The preacher was genial and spoke of having now broken ground for the lessons that he hoped to instil. He discoursed for a while about trout fishing and about the rumoured uneasiness of the Indians northward where he was going. It was plain that his personal safety never gave him a thought. He soon bade us good-night. The Ogdens shrugged their shoulders and were amused. That was their way of taking it. Dr MacBride sat too heavily on the Judge's shoulders for him to shrug them. As a leading citizen in the Territory he kept open house for all comers. Policy and good nature made him bid welcome a wide variety of travellers. The cowboy out of employment found bed and a meal for himself and his horse, and missionaries had before now been well received at Sunk Creek Ranch.

'I suppose I'll have to take him fishing,' said the Judge, ruefully.

'Yes, my dear,' said his wife, 'you will. And I shall have to make his tea for six days.'

'Otherwise,' Ogden suggested, 'it might be reported that you were enemies of religion.'

'That's about it,' said the Judge. 'I can get on with most people. But elephants depress me.'

So we named the Doctor 'Jumbo', and I departed to my quarters.

At the bunk house, the comments were similar but more highly salted. The men were going to bed. In spite of their outward decorum at the service, they had not liked to be told that they were 'altogether become filthy', It was easy to call names; they could do that themselves. And they appealed to me, several speaking at once, like a concerted piece at the opera: 'Say, do you believe babies go to hell?' – 'Ah, of course he don't.' – 'There ain't no hereafter, anyway.' – 'Ain't there?' – 'Who told yu'?' – 'Same man as told the preacher we were all a sifted set of sons-of-guns.' – 'Well, I'm going to stay a Mormon.' – 'Well, I'm going to quit fleeing from temptation.' – 'That's so! Better get it in the neck after a good time than a poor one.' And so forth. Their wit was not extreme, yet I should like Dr MacBride to have heard it. One fellow put his natural soul pretty well into words, 'If I happened to learn what they had predestinated me to do, I'd do the other thing, just to show 'em!'

And Trampas? And the Virginian? They were out of it. The Virginian had gone straight to his new abode. Trampas lay in his bed, not asleep, and sullen as ever.

'He 'ain't got religion this trip,' said Scipio to me.

'Did his new foreman get it?' I asked.

'Huh! It would spoil him. You keep around, that's all. Keep around.'

Scipio was not to be probed; and I went, still baffled, to my repose.

No light burned in the cabin as I approached its door.

The Virginian's room was quiet and dark; and that Dr MacBride slumbered was plainly audible to me, even before I entered. Go fishing with him! I thought, as I undressed. And I selfishly decided that the Judge might have this privilege entirely to himself. Sleep came to me fairly soon, in spite of the Doctor. I was wakened from it by my bed's being jolted – not a pleasant thing that night. I must have started. And it was the quiet voice of the Virginian that told me he was sorry to have accidentally disturbed me. This disturbed me a good deal more. But his steps did not go to the bunk house, as my sensational mind had suggested. He was not wearing much, and in the dimness he seemed taller than common. I next made out that he was bending over Dr MacBride. The divine at last sprang upright.

'I am armed,' he said. 'Take care. Who are you?'

'You can lay down your gun, seh. I feel like my spirit was going to bear witness. I feel like I might get an enlightening.'

He was using some of the missionary's own language. The baffling I had been treated to by Scipio melted to nothing in this. Did living men petrify, I should have changed to mineral between the sheets. The Doctor got out of bed, lighted his lamp, and found a book; and the two retired into the Virginian's room, where I could hear the exhortations as I lay amazed. In time the Doctor returned, blew out his lamp, and settled himself. I had been very much awake, but was nearly gone to sleep again, when the door creaked and the Virginian stood by the Doctor's side.

'Are you awake, seh?'

'What? What's that? What is it?'

'Excuse me, seh. The enemy is winning on me. I'm feeling less inward opposition to sin.'

The lamp was lighted, and I listened to some further exhortations. They must have taken half an hour. When the Doctor was in bed again,

I thought that I heard him sigh. This upset my composure in the dark; but I lay face downward in the pillow, and the Doctor was soon again snoring. I envied him for a while his faculty of easy sleep. But I must have dropped off myself; for it was the lamp in my eyes that now waked me as he came back for the third time from the Virginian's room. Before blowing the light out he looked at his watch, and thereupon I enquired the hour of him.

'Three,' said he.

I could not sleep any more now, and I lay watching the darkness.

'I'm afeared to be alone!' said the Virginian's voice presently in the next room. 'I'm afeared.' There was a short pause, and then he shouted very loud, 'I'm losin' my desire afteh the sincere milk of the Word!'

'What? What's that? What?' The Doctor's cot gave a great crack as he started up listening, and I put my face deep in the pillow.

'I'm afeared! I'm afeared! Sin has quit being bitter in my belly.'

'Courage, my good man.' The Doctor was out of bed with his lamp again, and the door shut behind him. Between them they made it long this time. I saw the window become grey; then the corners of the furniture grow visible; and outside, the dry chorus of the blackbirds began to fill the dawn. To these the sounds of chickens and impatient hoofs in the stable were added, and some cow wandered by loudly calling for her calf. Next, someone whistling passed near and grew distant. But although the cold hue that I lay staring at through the window warmed and changed, the Doctor continued working hard over his patient in the next room. Only a word here and there was distinct; but it was plain from the Virginian's fewer remarks that the sin in his belly was alarming him less. Yes, they made this time long. But it proved, indeed, the last one. And though some sort of catastrophe was bound to fall upon us, it was myself who precipitated the thing that did happen.

Day was wholly come. I looked at my own watch, and it was six. I had been about seven hours in my bed, and the Doctor had been about seven hours out of his. The door opened, and he came in with his book and lamp. He seemed to be shivering a little, and I saw him cast a longing eye at his couch. But the Virginian followed him even as he blew out the now quite superfluous light. They made a noticeable couple in their under-clothes: the Virginian with his lean racehorse shanks running to a point at his ankle, and the Doctor with his stomach and his fat sedentary calves.

'You'll be going to breakfast and the ladies, seh, pretty soon,' said the Virginian, with a chastened voice. 'But I'll worry through the day somehow without yu'. And tonight you can turn your wolf loose on me again.'

Once more it was no use. My face was deep in the pillow, but I made sounds as of a hen who has laid an egg. It broke on the Doctor with a total instantaneous smash, quite like an egg.

He tried to speak calmly. 'This is a disgrace. An infamous disgrace. Never in my life have I – ' Words forsook him, and his face grew redder. 'Never in my life – ' He stopped again, because, at the sight of him being dignified in his red drawers, I was making the noise of a dozen hens. It was suddenly too much for the Virginian. He hastened into his room, and there sank on the floor with his head in his hands. The Doctor immediately slammed the door upon him, and this rendered me easily fit for a lunatic asylum. I cried into my pillow, and wondered if the Doctor would come and kill me. But he took no notice of me whatever. I could hear the Virginian's convulsions through the door, and also the Doctor furiously making his toilet within three feet of my head; and I lay quite still with my face the other way, for I was really afraid to look at him. When I heard him walk to the door in his boots, I ventured to peep; and there he was, going out with his bag in his hand. As I still continued to lie, weak and sore, and with a mind that had ceased all operation, the Virginian's door opened. He was clean and dressed and decent, but the devil still sported in his eye. I have never seen a creature more irresistibly handsome.

Then my mind worked again. 'You've gone and done it,' said I. 'He's packed his valise. He'll not sleep here.'

The Virginian looked quickly out of the door. 'Why, he's leavin' us!' he exclaimed. 'Drivin' away right now in his little old buggy!' He turned to me, and our eyes met solemnly over this large fact. I thought that I perceived the faintest tincture of dismay in the features of Judge Henry's new, responsible, trusty foreman. This was the first act of his administration. Once again he looked out at the departing missionary. 'Well,' he vindictively stated, 'I cert'nly ain't goin' to run afteh him.' And he looked at me again.

'Do you suppose the Judge knows?' I enquired.

He shook his head. 'The windo' shades is all down still oveh yondeh.' He paused. 'I don't care,' he stated, quite as if he had been ten years old. Then he grinned guiltily. 'I was mighty respectful to him all night.'

'Oh, yes, respectful! Especially when you invited him to turn his wolf loose.'

The Virginian gave a joyous gulp. He now came and sat down on the edge of my bed. 'I spoke awful good English to him most of the time,' said he. 'I can, yu' know, when I cinch my attention tight on to it. Yes, I cert'nly spoke a lot o' good English. I didn't understand some of it myself!'

He was now growing frankly pleased with his exploit. He had builded so much better than he knew. He got up and looked out across the crystal world of light. 'The Doctor is at one-mile crossing,' he said. 'He'll get breakfast at the N-lazy-Y.' Then he returned and sat again on my bed, and began to give me his real heart. 'I never set up for being better than others. Not even to myself. My thoughts ain't apt to travel around making comparisons. And I shouldn't wonder if my memory took as much notice of the meannesses I have done as of – as of the other actions. But to have to sit like a dumb lamb and let a stranger tell yu' for an hour that yu're a hawg and a swine, just after you have acted in a way which them that know the facts would call pretty near white – '

'Trampas!' I could not help exclaiming. For there are moments of insight when a guess amounts to knowledge.

'Has Scipio told – '

'No. Not a word. He wouldn't tell me.'

'Well, yu' see, I arrived home hyeh this evenin' with several thoughts workin' and stirrin' inside me. And not one o' them thoughts was what yu'd call Christian. I ain't the least little bit ashamed of 'em. I'm a human. But after the Judge – well, yu' heard him. And so when I went away from that talk and saw how positions was changed – '

A step outside stopped him short. Nothing more could be read in his face, for there was Trampas himself in the open door.

'Good-morning,' said Trampas, not looking at us. He spoke with the same cool sullenness of yesterday.

We returned his greeting.

'I believe I'm late in congratulating you on your promotion,' said he.

The Virginian consulted his watch. 'It's only half afteh six,' he returned.

Trampas's sullenness deepened. 'Any man is to be congratulated on getting a rise, I expect.'

This time the Virginian let him have it. 'Cert'nly. And I ain't forgetting how much I owe mine to you.'

Trampas would have liked to let himself go. 'I've not come here for any forgiveness,' he sneered.

'When did yu' feel yu' needed any?' The Virginian was impregnable.

Trampas seemed to feel how little he was gaining this way. He came out straight now. 'Oh, I haven't any Judge behind me, I know. I heard you'd be paying the boys this morning, and I've come for my time.'

'You're thinking of leaving us?' asked the new foreman. 'What's your dissatisfaction?'

'Oh, I'm not needing anybody back of me. I'll get along by myself.' It was thus he revealed his expectation of being dismissed by his enemy.

This would have knocked any meditated generosity out of my heart. But I was not the Virginian. He shifted his legs, leaned back a little, and laughed. 'Go back to your job, Trampas, if that's all your complaint. You're right about me being in luck. But maybe there's two of us in luck.'

It was this that Scipio had preferred me to see with my own eyes. The fight was between man and man no longer. The case could not be one of forgiveness; but the Virginian would not use his official position to crush his subordinate.

Trampas departed with something muttered that I did not hear, and the Virginian closed intimate conversation by saying, 'You'll be late for breakfast.' With that he also took himself away.

The ladies were inclined to be scandalised, but not the Judge. When my whole story was done, he brought his fist down on the table, and not lightly this time. 'I'd make him lieutenant-general if the ranch offered that position!' he declared.

Miss Molly Wood said nothing at the time. But in the afternoon, by her wish, she went fishing, with the Virginian deputed to escort her. I rode with them, for a while. I was not going to continue a third in that party; the Virginian was too becomingly dressed, and I saw *Kenilworth* peeping out of his pocket. I meant to be fishing by myself when that volume was returned.

But Miss Wood talked with skilful openness as we rode. 'I've heard all about you and Dr MacBride,' she said. 'How could you do it, when the Judge places such confidence in you?'

He looked pleased. 'I reckon,' he said, 'I couldn't be so good if I wasn't bad onced in a while.'

'Why, there's a skunk,' said I, noticing the pretty little animal trotting in front of us at the edge of the thickets.

'Oh, where is it? Don't let me see it!' screamed Molly. And at this deeply feminine remark, the Virginian looked at her with such a smile that, had I been a woman, it would have made me his to do what he pleased with on the spot.

Upon the lady, however, it seemed to make less impression. Or rather, I had better say, whatever were her feelings, she very naturally made no display of them, and contrived not to be aware of that expression which had passed over the Virginian's face.

It was later that these few words reached me while I was fishing alone – 'Have you anything different to tell me yet?' I heard him say.

'Yes; I have.' She spoke in accents light and well entrenched. 'I wish to say that I have never liked any man better than you. But I expect to!'

He must have drawn small comfort from such an answer as that. But he laughed out indomitably – 'Don't yu' go betting on any such expectation!' And then their words ceased to be distinct, and it was only their two voices that I heard wandering among the windings of the stream.

CHAPTER 22

'What is a Rustler?'

We all know what birds of a feather do. And it may be safely surmised that if a bird of any particular feather has been for a long while unable to see other birds of its kind, it will flock with them all the more assiduously when they happen to alight in its vicinity.

Now the Ogdens were birds of Molly's feather. They wore Eastern, and not Western, plumage, and their song was a different song from that which the Bear Creek birds sang. To be sure, the piping of little George Taylor was full of hopeful interest; and many other strains, both striking and melodious, were lifted in Cattle Land, and had given pleasure to Molly's ear. But although Indians, and bears, and mavericks, make worthy themes for song, these are not the only songs in the world. Therefore the Eastern warblings of the Ogdens sounded doubly sweet to Molly Wood. Such words as Newport, Bar Harbor, and Tiffany's thrilled her exceedingly. It made no difference that she herself had never been to Newport or Bar Harbor, and had visited Tiffany's more often to admire than to purchase. On the contrary, this rather added a dazzle to the music of the Ogdens. And Molly, whose Eastern song had been silent in this strange land, began to chirp it again during the visit that she made at the Sunk Creek Ranch.

Thus the Virginian's cause by no means prospered at this time. His forces were scattered, while Molly's were concentrated. The girl was not at that point where absence makes the heart grow fonder. While the Virginian was trundling his long, responsible miles in the caboose, delivering the cattle at Chicago, vanquishing Trampas along the Yellow-stone, she had regained herself.

Thus it was that she could tell him so easily during those first hours that they were alone after his return, 'I expect to like another man better than you.'

Absence had recruited her. And then the Ogdens had re-enforced her. They brought the East back powerfully to her memory, and her thoughts filled with it. They did not dream that they were assisting in any battle. No one ever had more unconscious allies than did Molly at that time. But she used them consciously, or almost consciously. She frequented them; she spoke of Eastern matters; she found that she had acquaintances whom the Ogdens also knew, and she often brought them into the conversation. For it may be said, I think, that she was fighting a battle – nay, a campaign. And perhaps this was a hopeful sign for the Virginian (had he but known it), that the girl resorted to allies. She surrounded herself, she steeped herself, with the East, to have, as it were, a sort of counteractant against the spell of the black-haired horseman.

And his forces were, as I have said, scattered. For his promotion gave him no more time for love-making. He was foreman now. He had said to Judge Henry, 'I'll try to please yu'.' And after the throb of emotion which these words had both concealed and conveyed, there came to him that sort of intention to win which amounts to a certainty. Yes, he would please Judge Henry!

He did not know how much he had already pleased him. He did not know that the Judge was humorously undecided which of his new fore-man's first acts had the more delighted him: his performance with the missionary, or his magnanimity to Trampas.

'Good feeling is a great thing in anyone,' the Judge would say; 'but I like to know that my foreman has so much sense.'

'I am personally very grateful to him,' said Mrs Henry.

And indeed so was the whole company. To be afflicted with Dr MacBride for one night instead of six was a great liberation.

But the Virginian never saw his sweetheart alone again; while she was at the Sunk Creek Ranch, his duties called him away so much that there was no chance for him. Worse still, that habit of birds of a feather brought about a separation more considerable. She arranged to go East with the Ogdens. It was so good an opportunity to travel with friends, instead of making the journey alone!

Molly's term of ministration at the schoolhouse had so pleased Bear Creek that she was warmly urged to take a holiday. School could afford to begin a little late. Accordingly, she departed.

The Virginian hid his sore heart from her during the moment of farewell that they had.

'No, I'll not want any more books,' he said, 'till yu' come back.' And then he made cheerfulness. 'It's just the other way round!' said he.

'What is the other way round?'

'Why, last time it was me that went travelling, and you that stayed behind.'

'So it was!' And here she gave him a last scratch. 'But you'll be busier than ever,' she said; 'no spare time to grieve about me!'

She could wound him, and she knew it. Nobody else could. That is why she did it.

But he gave her something to remember, too.

'Next time,' he said, 'neither of us will stay behind. We'll both go together.'

And with these words he gave her no laughing glance. It was a look that mingled with the words; so that now and again in the train, both came back to her, and she sat pensive, drawing near to Bennington and hearing his voice and seeing his eyes.

How is it that this girl could cry at having to tell Sam Bannett she could not think of him, and then treat another lover as she treated the Virginian? I cannot tell you, having never (as I said before) been a woman myself.

Bennington opened its arms to its venturesome daughter. Much was made of Molly Wood. Old faces and old places welcomed her. Fatted calves of varying dimensions made their appearance. And although the fatted calf is an animal that can assume more divergent shapes than any other known creature – being sometimes champagne and partridges, and again cake and currant wine – through each disguise you can always identify the same calf. The girl from Bear Creek met it at every turn.

The Bannetts at Hoosic Falls offered a large specimen to Molly – a dinner (perhaps I should say a banquet) of twenty-four. And Sam Bannett of course took her to drive more than once.

'I want to see the Hoosic Bridge,' she would say. And when they reached that well-remembered point, 'How lovely it is!' she exclaimed.

And as she gazed at the view up and down the valley, she would grow pensive. 'How natural the church looks,' she continued. And then, having crossed both bridges, 'Oh, there's the dear old lodge gate!' Or again, while they drove up the valley of the little Hoosic: 'I had forgotten it was so nice and lonely. But after all, no woods are so interesting as those where you might possibly see a bear or an elk.' And upon another occasion, after a cry of enthusiasm at the view from the top of Mount Anthony, 'It's lovely, lovely, lovely,' she said, with diminishing cadence, ending in pensiveness once more. 'Do you see that little bit just there? No, not where the trees are – that bare spot that looks brown and warm in the sun. With a little sagebrush, that spot would look something like a place I know on Bear Creek. Only of course you don't get the clear air here.'

'I don't forget you,' said Sam. 'Do you remember me? Or is it out of sight out of mind?'

And with this beginning he renewed his suit. She told him that she forgot no one; that she should return always, lest they might forget her.

'Return always!' he exclaimed. 'You talk as if your anchor was dragging.'

Was it? At all events, Sam failed in his suit.

Over in the house at Dunbarton, the old lady held Molly's hand and looked a long while at her. 'You have changed very much,' she said finally.

'I am a year older,' said the girl.

'Pshaw, my dear!' said the great-aunt. 'Who is he?'

'Nobody!' cried Molly, with indignation.

'Then you shouldn't answer so loud,' said the great-aunt.

The girl suddenly hid her face. 'I don't believe I can love anyone,' she said, 'except myself.'

And then that old lady, who in her day had made her courtesy to Lafayette, began to stroke her niece's buried head, because she more than half understood. And understanding thus much, she asked no prying questions, but thought of the days of her own youth, and only spoke a little quiet love and confidence to Molly.

'I am an old, old woman,' she said. 'But I haven't forgotten about it. They objected to him because he had no fortune. But he was brave and handsome, and I loved him, my dear. Only I ought to have loved him more. I gave him my promise to think about it. And he and his ship were lost.' The great-aunt's voice had become very soft and low, and she spoke with many pauses. 'So then I knew. If I had – if – perhaps I should have lost him; but it would have been after – ah, well! So long as you can help it, never marry! But when you cannot help it a moment longer, then listen to nothing but that; for, my dear, I know your choice would be worthy of the Starks. And now – let me see his picture.'

'Why, aunty!' said Molly.

'Well, I won't pretend to be supernatural,' said the aunt, 'but I thought you kept one back when you were showing us those Western views last night.'

Now this was the precise truth. Molly had brought a number of photographs from Wyoming to show to her friends at home. These, however, with one exception, were not portraits. They were views of scenery and of cattle round-ups, and other scenes characteristic of ranch life. Of young men she had in her possession several photographs, and all but one of these she had left behind her. Her aunt's penetration had in a way mesmerised the girl; she rose obediently and sought that picture of the Virginian. It was full length, displaying him in all his cowboy trappings – the leathern chaps, the belt and pistol, and in his hand a coil of rope.

Not one of her family had seen it, or suspected its existence. She now brought it downstairs and placed it in her aunt's hand.

'Mercy!' cried the old lady.

Molly was silent, but her eye grew warlike.

'Is that the way – ' began the aunt. 'Mercy!' she murmured; and she sat staring at the picture.

Molly remained silent.

Her aunt looked slowly up at her. 'Has a man like that presumed – '

'He's not a bit like that. Yes, he's exactly like that,' said Molly. And she would have snatched the photograph away, but her aunt retained it.

'Well,' she said, 'I suppose there are days when he does not kill people.'

'He never killed anybody!' And Molly laughed.

'Are you seriously – ' said the old lady.

'I almost might – at times. He is perfectly splendid.'

'My dear, you have fallen in love with his clothes.'

'It's not his clothes. And I'm not in love. He often wears others. He wears a white collar like anybody.'

'Then that would be a more suitable way to be photographed, I think. He couldn't go round like that here. I could not receive him myself.'

'He'd never think of such a thing. Why, you talk as if he were a savage.'

The old lady studied the picture closely for a minute. 'I think it is a good face,' she finally remarked. 'Is the fellow as handsome as that, my dear?'

More so, Molly thought. And who was he, and what were his prospects? were the aunt's next enquiries. She shook her head at the answers which she received; and she also shook her head over her niece's emphatic denial that her heart was lost to this man. But when their parting came, the old lady said – 'God bless you and keep you, my dear. I'll not try to manage you. They managed me – ' A sigh spoke the rest of this sentence. 'But I'm not worried about you – at least, not very much. You have never done anything that was not worthy of the Starks. And if you're going to take him, do it before I die so that I can bid him welcome for your sake. God bless you, my dear.'

And after the girl had gone back to Bennington, the great-aunt had this thought: 'She is like us all. She wants a man that is a man.' Nor did the old lady breathe her knowledge to any member of the family. For she was a loyal spirit, and her girl's confidence was sacred to her.

'Besides,' she reflected, 'if even *I* can do nothing with her, what a mess *they'd* make of it! We should hear of her elopement next.'

So Molly's immediate family never saw that photograph, and never heard a word from her upon this subject. But on the day that she left for Bear Creek, as they sat missing her and discussing her visit in the evening, Mrs Bell observed: 'Mother, how did you think she was?' – 'I never saw her better, Sarah. That horrible place seems to agree with her.' – 'Oh, yes, agree. It seemed to me – ' – 'Well?' – 'Oh, just somehow that she was thinking.' – 'Thinking?' – 'Well, I believe she has something on her mind.' – 'You mean a man,' said Andrew Bell. – 'A man, Andrew?' – 'Yes, Mrs Wood, that's what Sarah always means.'

It may be mentioned that Sarah's surmises did not greatly contribute to her mother's happiness. And rumour is so strange a thing that presently from the malicious outside air came a vague and dreadful word – one of those words that cannot be traced to its source. Somebody said to Andrew Bell that they heard Miss Molly Wood was engaged to marry a *rustler*.

'Heavens, Andrew!' said his wife; 'what is a rustler?'

It was not in any dictionary, and current translations of it were inconsistent. A man at Hoosic Falls said that he had passed through Cheyenne, and heard the term applied in a complimentary way to people who were alive and pushing. Another man had always supposed it meant some kind of horse. But the most alarming version of all was that a rustler was a cattle-thief.

Now the truth is that all these meanings were right. The word ran a sort of progress in the cattle country, gathering many meanings as it went. It gathered more, however, in Bennington. In a very few days, gossip had it that Molly was engaged to a gambler, a gold miner, an escaped stage robber, and a Mexican bandit; while Mrs Flynt feared she had married a Mormon.

Along Bear Creek, however, Molly and her 'rustler' took a ride soon after her return. They were neither married nor engaged, and she was telling him about Vermont.

'I never was there,' said he. 'Never happened to strike in that direction.'

'What decided your direction?'

'Oh, looking for chances. I reckon I must have been more ambitious than my brothers – or more restless. They stayed around on farms. But I got out. When I went back again six years afterward, I was twenty. They was talking about the same old things. Men of twenty-five and thirty – yet just sittin' and talkin' about the same old things. I told my mother about what I'd seen here and there, and she liked it, right to her death. But the others – well, when I found this whole world was hawgs and turkeys to them, with a little gunnin' afteh small game throwed in, I put on my hat one mawnin' and told 'em maybe when I was fifty I'd look in on 'em again to see if they'd got any new subjects. But they'll never. My brothers don't seem to want chances.'

'You have lost a good many yourself,' said Molly.

'That's correct.'

'And yet,' said she, 'sometimes I think you know a great deal more than I ever shall.'

'Why, of course I do,' said he, quite simply. 'I have earned my living since I was fourteen. And that's from old Mexico to British Columbia. I have never stolen or begged a cent. I'd not want yu' to know what I know.'

She was looking at him, half listening and half thinking of her great-aunt.

'I am not losing chances any more,' he continued. 'And you are the best I've got.'

She was not sorry to have Georgie Taylor come galloping along at this moment and join them. But the Virginian swore profanely under his breath. And on this ride nothing more happened.

CHAPTER 23

Various Points

Love had been snowbound for many weeks. Before this imprisonment its course had run neither smooth nor rough, so far as eye could see; it had run either not at all, or, as an undercurrent, deep out of sight. In their rides, in their talks, love had been dumb, as to spoken words at least; for the Virginian had set himself a heavy task of silence and of patience. Then, where winter barred his visits to Bear Creek, and there was for the while no ranch work or responsibility to fill his thoughts and blood with action, he set himself a task much lighter. Often, instead of Shakespeare and fiction, school books lay open on his cabin table; and penmanship and spelling helped the hours to pass. Many sheets of paper did he fill with various exercises, and Mrs Henry gave him her assistance in advice and corrections.

'I shall presently be in love with him myself,' she told the Judge. 'And it's time for you to become anxious.'

'I am perfectly safe,' he retorted. 'There's only one woman for him any more.'

'She is not good enough for him,' declared Mrs Henry. 'But he'll never see that.'

So the snow fell, the world froze, and the spelling-books and exercises went on. But this was not the only case of education which was progressing at the Sunk Creek Ranch while love was snowbound.

* * *

One morning Scipio le Moyne entered the Virginian's sitting-room – that apartment where Dr MacBride had wrestled with sin so courageously all night.

The Virginian sat at his desk. Open books lay around him; a half-finished piece of writing was beneath his fist; his fingers were coated with ink. Education enveloped him, it may be said. But there was none in his eye. That was upon the window, looking far across the cold plain.

The foreman did not move when Scipio came in, and this humorous spirit smiled to himself. 'It's Bear Creek he's havin' a vision of,' he concluded. But he knew instantly that this was not so. The Virginian was looking at something real, and Scipio went to the window to see for himself.

'Well,' he said, having seen, 'when is he going to leave us?'

The foreman continued looking at two horsemen riding together. Their shapes, small in the distance, showed black against the universal whiteness.

'When d' yu' figure he'll leave us?' repeated Scipio.

'He,' murmured the Virginian, always watching the distant horsemen; and again, 'he'.

Scipio sprawled down, familiarly, across a chair. He and the Virginian had come to know each other very well since that first meeting at Medora. They were birds many of whose feathers were the same, and the Virginian often talked to Scipio without reserve. Consequently, Scipio now understood those two syllables that the Virginian had pronounced precisely as though the sentences which lay between them had been fully expressed.

'Hm,' he remarked. 'Well, one will be a gain, and the other won't be no loss.'

'Poor Shorty!' said the Virginian. 'Poor fool!'

Scipio was less compassionate. 'No,' he persisted, 'I ain't sorry for him. Any man old enough to have hair on his face ought to see through Trampas.'

The Virginian looked out of the window again, and watched Shorty and Trampas as they rode in the distance. 'Shorty is kind to animals,' he said. 'He has gentled that hawss Pedro he bought with his first money. Gentled him wonderful. When a man is kind to dumb animals, I always say he had got some good in him.'

'Yes,' Scipio reluctantly admitted. 'Yes. But I always did hate a fool.'

'This hyeh is a mighty cruel country,' pursued the Virginian. 'To animals that is. Think of it! Think what we do to hundreds an' thousands of little calves! Throw 'em down, brand 'em, cut 'em, ear mark 'em, turn 'em loose, and on to the next. It has got to be, of course. But I say this. If a man can go jammin' hot irons on to little calves and slicin' pieces off 'em with his knife, and live along, keepin' a kindness for animals in his heart, he has got some good in him. And that's what Shorty has got. But he is lettin' Trampas get a hold of him, and both of them will leave us.'

And the Virginian looked out across the huge winter whiteness again. But the riders had now vanished behind some foothills.

Scipio sat silent. He had never put these thoughts about men and animals to himself, and when they were put to him, he saw that they were true.

'Queer,' he observed finally.

'What?'

'Everything.'

'Nothing's queer,' stated the Virginian, 'except marriage and lightning. Them two occurrences can still give me a sensation of surprise.'

'All the same it is queer,' Scipio insisted.

'Well, let her go at me.'

'Why, Trampas. He done you dirt. You pass that over. You could have fired him, but you let him stay and keep his job. That's goodness. And badness is resultin' from it, straight. Badness right from goodness.'

'You're off the trail a whole lot,' said the Virginian.

'Which side am I off, then?'

'North, south, east, and west. First point: I didn't expect to do Trampas any good by not killin' him, which I came pretty near doin' three times. Nor I didn't expect to do Trampas any good by lettin' him keep his job. But I am foreman of this ranch. And I can sit and tell all men to their face: "I was above that meanness". Point two: it ain't any *goodness*, it is *Trampas* that badness has resulted from. Put him anywhere and it will be the same. Put him under my eye, and I can follow his moves a little, anyway. You have noticed, maybe, that since you and I run on to that dead Polled Angus cow, that was still warm when we got to her, we have found no more cows dead of sudden death. We came mighty close to catchin' whoever it was that killed that cow and ran her calf off to his own bunch. He wasn't ten minutes ahead of us. We can prove nothin'; and he knows that just as well as we do. But our cows have all quit dyin' of sudden death. And Trampas he's gettin' ready for a change of residence. As soon as all the outfits begin hirin' new hands in the spring, Trampas will leave us and take a job with some of them. And maybe our cows'll commence gettin' killed again, and we'll have to take steps that will be more emphatic – maybe.'

Scipio meditated. 'I wonder what killin' a man feels like?' he said.

'Why, nothing to bother yu' – when he'd ought to have been killed. Next point: Trampas he'll take Shorty with him, which is certainly bad for Shorty. But it's me that has kept Shorty out of harm's way this long. If I had fired Trampas, he'd have worked Shorty into dissatisfaction that much sooner.'

Scipio meditated again. 'I knowed Trampas would pull his freight,' he said. 'But I didn't think of Shorty. What makes you think it?'

'He asked me for a raise.'

'He ain't worth the pay he's getting now.'

'Trampas has told him different.'

'When a man ain't got no ideas of his own,' said Scipio, 'he'd ought to be kind o' careful who he borrows 'em from.'

'That's mighty correct,' said the Virginian. 'Poor Shorty! He has told me about his life. It is sorrowful. And he will never get wise. It was too late for him to get wise when he was born. D' yu' know why he's after higher wages? He sends most all his money East.'

'I don't see what Trampas wants him for,' said Scipio.

'Oh, a handy tool someday.'

'Not very handy,' said Scipio.

'Well, Trampas is aimin' to train him. Yu' see, supposin' yu' were figuring to turn professional thief – yu'd be lookin' around for a nice young trustful accomplice to take all the punishment and let you take the rest.'

'No such thing!' cried Scipio, angrily. 'I'm no shirker.' And then, perceiving the Virginian's expression, he broke out laughing. 'Well,' he exclaimed, 'yu' fooled me that time.'

'Looks that way. But I do mean it about Trampas.'

Presently Scipio rose, and noticed the half-finished exercise upon the Virginian's desk. 'Trampas is a rolling stone,' he said.

'A rolling piece of mud,' corrected the Virginian.

'Mud! That's right. I'm a rolling stone. Sometimes I'd most like to quit being.'

'That's easy done,' said the Virginian.

'No doubt, when yu've found the moss yu' want to gather.' As Scipio glanced at the school books again, a sparkle lurked in his bleached blue eye. 'I can cipher some,' he said. 'But I expect I've got my own notions about spelling.'

'I retain a few private ideas that way myself,' remarked the Virginian, innocently; and Scipio's sparkle gathered light.

'As to my geography,' he pursued, 'that's away out loose in the brush. Is Bennington the capital of Vermont? And how d' yu' spell bridegroom?'

'Last point!' shouted the Virginian, letting a book fly after him: 'don't let badness and goodness worry yu', for yu'll never be a judge of them.'

But Scipio had dodged the book, and was gone. As he went his way, he said to himself, 'All the same, it must pay to fall regular in love.' At the bunk house that afternoon it was observed that he was unusually silent.

His exit from the foreman's cabin had let in a breath of winter so chill that the Virginian went to see his thermometer, a Christmas present from Mrs Henry. It registered twenty below zero. After reviving the fire to a white blaze, the foreman sat thinking over the story of Shorty: what its useless, feeble past had been; what would be its useless, feeble future. He shook his head over the sombre question, Was there any way out for Shorty? 'It may be,' he reflected, 'that them whose pleasure brings yu' into this world owes yu' a living. But that don't make the world responsible. The world did not beget you. I reckon man helps them that help themselves. As for the universe, it looks like it did too wholesale a business to turn out an article up to standard every clip. Yes, it is sorrowful. For Shorty is kind to his hawss.'

In the evening the Virginian brought Shorty into his room. He usually knew what he had to say; usually found it easy to arrange his thoughts; and after such arranging the words came of themselves. But as he looked at Shorty, this did not happen to him. There was not a line of badness in the face; yet also there was not a line of strength; no promise in eye, or nose, or chin; the whole thing melted to a stubby, featureless mediocrity. It was a countenance like thousands; and hopelessness filled the Virginian as he looked at this lost dog, and his dull, wistful eyes.

But some beginning must be made.

'I wonder what the thermometer has got to be,' he said. 'Yu' can see it, if yu'll hold the lamp to that right side of the window.'

Shorty held the lamp. 'I never used any,' he said, looking out at the instrument, nevertheless.

The Virginian had forgotten that Shorty could not read. So he looked out of the window himself, and found that it was twenty-two below zero. 'This is pretty good tobacco,' he remarked; and Shorty helped himself, and filled his pipe.

'I had to rub my left ear with snow today,' said he. 'I was just in time.'

'I thought it looked pretty freezy out where yu' was riding,' said the foreman.

The lost dog's eyes showed plain astonishment. 'We didn't see you out there,' said he.

'Well,' said the foreman, 'it'll soon not be freezing any more; and then we'll all be warm enough with work. Everybody will be working all over the range. And I wish I knew somebody that had a lot of stable work to be attended to. I cert'nly do for your sake.'

'Why?' said Shorty.

'Because it's the right kind of a job for you.'

'I can make more – ' began Shorty, and stopped.

'There is a time coming,' said the Virginian, 'when I'll want somebody that knows how to get the friendship of hawsses. I'll want him to handle some special hawsses the Judge has plans about. Judge Henry would pay fifty a month for that.'

'I can make more,' said Shorty, this time with stubbornness.

'Well, yes. Sometimes a man can – when he's not worth it, I mean. But it don't generally last.'

Shorty was silent.

'I used to make more myself,' said the Virginian.

'You're making a lot more now,' said Shorty.

'Oh, yes. But I mean when I was fooling around the earth, jumping from job to job, and helling all over town between whiles. I was not worth fifty a month then, nor twenty-five. But there was nights I made a heap more at cyards.'

Shorty's eyes grew large.

'And then, bang! it was gone with treatin' the men and the girls.'

'I don't always – ' said Shorty, and stopped again.

The Virginian knew that he was thinking about the money he sent East. 'After a while,' he continued, 'I noticed a right strange fact. The money I made easy that I *wasn't* worth, it went like it came. I strained myself none gettin' or spendin' it. But the money I made hard that I *was* worth, why I began to feel right careful about that. And now I have got savings stowed away. If once yu' could know how good that feels – '

'So I would know,' said Shorty, 'with your luck.'

'What's my luck?' said the Virginian, sternly.

'Well, if I had took up land along a creek that never goes dry and proved upon it like you have, and if I had saw that land raise its value on me with me lifting no finger – '

'Why did you lift no finger?' cut in the Virginian. 'Who stopped yu' taking up land? Did it not stretch in front of yu', behind yu', all around yu', the biggest, baldest opportunity in sight? That was the time I lifted my finger; but yu' didn't.'

Shorty stood stubborn.

'But never mind that,' said the Virginian. 'Take my land away tomorrow, and I'd still have my savings in bank. Because, you see, I had to work right hard gathering them in. I found out what I could do, and I settled down and did it. Now you can do that too. The only tough part is the finding out what you're good for. And for you, that is found. If you'll just decide to work at this thing you can do, and gentle those hawsses for the Judge, you'll be having savings in a bank yourself.'

'I can make more,' said the lost dog.

The Virginian was on the point of saying, 'Then get out!' But instead, he spoke kindness to the end. 'The weather is freezing yet,' he said, 'and it will be for a good long while. Take your time, and tell me if yu' change your mind.'

After that Shorty returned to the bunk house, and the Virginian knew that the boy had learned his lesson of discontent from Trampas with a thoroughness past all unteaching. This petty triumph of evil seemed scarce of the size to count as any victory over the Virginian. But all men grasp at straws. Since that first moment, when in the Medicine Bow saloon the Virginian had shut the mouth of Trampas by a word, the man had been trying to get even without risk; and at each successive clash of his weapon with the Virginian's, he had merely met another public humiliation. Therefore, now at the Sunk Creek Ranch in these cold white days, a certain lurking insolence in his gait showed plainly his opinion that by disaffecting Shorty he had made some sort of reprisal.

Yes, he had poisoned the lost dog. In the springtime, when the neighbouring ranches needed additional hands, it happened as the Virginian had foreseen – Trampas departed to a 'better job', as he took pains to say, and with him the docile Shorty rode away upon his horse Pedro.

* * *

Love now was not any longer snowbound. The mountain trails were open enough for the sure feet of love's steed – that horse called Monte. But duty blocked the path of love. Instead of turning his face to Bear Creek, the foreman had other journeys to make, full of heavy work, and watchfulness, and councils with the Judge. The cattle thieves were growing bold, and winter had scattered the cattle widely over the range. Therefore the Virginian, instead of going to see her, wrote a letter to his sweetheart. It was his first.

CHAPTER 24

A Letter with a Moral

The letter which the Virginian wrote to Molly Wood was, as has been stated, the first that he had ever addressed to her. I think, perhaps, he may have been a little shy as to his skill in the epistolary art, a little anxious lest any sustained production from his pen might contain blunders that would too staringly remind her of his scant learning. He could turn off a business communication about steers or stock cars, or any other of the subjects involved in his profession, with a brevity and a clearness that led the Judge to confide three-quarters of such correspondence to his foreman. 'Write to the 76 outfit,' the Judge would say, 'and tell them that my wagon cannot start for the round-up until,' etc.; or 'Write to Cheyenne and say that if they will hold a meeting next Monday week, I will,' etc. And then the Virginian would write such communications with ease.

But his first message to his lady was scarcely written with ease. It must be classed, I think, among those productions which are styled literary *efforts*. It was completed in pencil before it was copied in ink; and that first draft of it in pencil was well-nigh illegible with erasures and amendments. The state of mind of the writer during its composition may be gathered without further description on my part from a slight interruption which occurred in the middle.

The door opened, and Scipio put his head in. 'You coming to dinner?' he enquired.

'You go to hell,' replied the Virginian.

'My jinks!' said Scipio, quietly, and he shut the door without further observation.

To tell the truth, I doubt if this letter would ever have been undertaken, far less completed and despatched, had not the lover's heart been wrung with disappointment. All winter long he had looked to that day when he should knock at the girl's door, and hear her voice bid him come in. All winter long he had been choosing the ride he would take her. He had imagined a sunny afternoon, a hidden grove, a sheltering cleft of rock, a running spring, and some words of his that should conquer her at last and leave his lips upon hers. And with this controlled fire pent up within him, he had counted the days, scratching them off his calendar with a dig each night that once or twice snapped the pen. Then, when the trail stood open, this meeting was deferred, put off for indefinite days, or weeks; he could not tell how long. So, gripping his pencil and tracing heavy words, he gave himself what consolation he could by writing her.

The letter, duly stamped and addressed to Bear Creek, set forth upon its travels; and these were devious and long. When it reached its destination, it was some twenty days old. It had gone by private hand at the outset, taken the stagecoach at a way point, become late in that stagecoach, reached a point of transfer, and waited there for the postmaster to begin, continue, end, and recover from a game of poker, mingled with whiskey. Then it once more proceeded, was dropped at the right way point, and carried by private hand to Bear Creek. The experience of this letter, however, was not at all a remarkable one at that time in Wyoming.

Molly Wood looked at the envelope. She had never before seen the Virginian's handwriting. She knew it instantly. She closed her door, and sat down to read it with a beating heart.

Skunk Creek Ranch
5 May 188—

My dear Miss Wood – I am sorry about this. My plan was different. It was to get over for a ride with you about now or sooner. This year Spring is early. The snow is off the flats this side the range and where the sun gets a chance to hit the earth strong all day it is green and has flowers too, a good many. You can see them bob and mix together in the wind. The quaking-asps down low on the South side are in small leaf and will soon be twinkling like the flowers do now. I had planned to take a look at this with you and that was a better plan than what I have got to do. The water is high but I could have got over and as for the snow on top of the mountain a man told me nobody could cross it for a week yet, because he had just done it himself. Was not he a funny man? You ought to see how the birds have streamed across the sky while Spring was coming. But you have seen them on your side of the mountain. But I can't come now Miss Wood. There is a lot for me to do that has to be done and Judge Henry needs more than two eyes just now. I could not think much of myself if I left him for my own wishes.

But the days will be warmer when I come. We will not have to quit by five, and we can get off and sit too. We could not sit now unless for a very short while. If I know when I can come I will try to let you know, but I think it will be this way. I think you will just see me coming for I have things to do of an unsure nature and a good number of such. Do not believe reports about Indians. They are started by editors to keep the soldiers in the country. The friends of the editors get the hay and beef contracts. Indians do not come to settled parts like Bear Creek is. It is all editors and politicianists.

Nothing has happened worth telling you. I have read that play Othello. No man should write down such a thing. Do you know if it is true? I have seen one worse affair down in Arizona. He killed his little child as well as his wife but such things should not be put down in fine language for the public. I have read Romeo and Juliet. That is beautiful language but Romeo is no man. I like his friend Mercutio that gets killed. He is a man. If he had got Juliet there would have been no foolishness and trouble.

Well Miss Wood I would like to see you today. Do you know what I think Monte would do if I rode him out and let the rein slack? He would come straight to your gate for he is a horse of great judgment. ['That's the first word he has misspelled,' said Molly.] I suppose you are sitting with George Taylor and those children right now. Then George will get old enough to help his father but Uncle Hewie's twins will be ready for you about then and the supply will keep coming from all quarters all sizes for you to say big A little a to them. There is no news here. Only calves and cows and the hens are laying now which does always seem news to a hen every time she does it. Did I ever tell you about a hen Emily we had here? She was venturesome to an extent I have not seen in other hens only she had poor judgement and would make no family ties. She would keep trying to get interest in the ties of others taking charge of little chicks and bantams and turkeys and puppies one time, and she thought most anything was an egg. I will tell you about her sometime. She died without family ties one day while I was building a house for her to teach school in. ['The outrageous wretch!' cried Molly. And her cheeks turned deep pink as she sat alone with her lover's letter.]

I am coming the first day I am free. I will be a hundred miles from you most of the time when I am not more but I will ride a hundred miles for one hour and Monte is up to that. After never seeing you for so long I will make one hour do if I have to. Here is a flower I have just been out and picked. I have kissed it now. That is the best I can do yet.

Molly laid the letter in her lap and looked at the flower. Then suddenly she jumped up and pressed it to her lips, and after a long moment held it away from her.

'No,' she said. 'No, no, no.' She sat down.

It was some time before she finished the letter. Then once more she got up and put on her hat.

Mrs Taylor wondered where the girl could be walking so fast. But she was not walking anywhere, and in half an hour she returned, rosy with her swift exercise, but with a spirit as perturbed as when she had set out.

Next morning at six, when she looked out of her window, there was Monte tied to the Taylor's gate. Ah, could he have come the day before, could she have found him when she returned from that swift walk of hers!

CHAPTER 25

Progress of the Lost Dog

It was not even an hour's visit that the Virginian was able to pay his lady love. But neither had he come a hundred miles to see her. The necessities of his wandering work had chanced to bring him close enough for a glimpse of her, and this glimpse he took, almost on the wing. For he had to rejoin a company of men at once.

'Yu' got my letter?' he said.

'Yesterday.'

'Yesterday! I wrote it three weeks ago. Well, yu' got it. This cannot be the hour with you that I mentioned. That is coming, and maybe very soon.'

She could say nothing. Relief she felt, and yet with it something like a pang.

'Today does not count,' he told her, 'except that every time I see you counts with me. But this is not the hour that I mentioned.'

What little else was said between them upon this early morning shall be told duly. For this visit in its own good time did count momentously, though both of them took it lightly while its fleeting minutes passed. He returned to her two volumes that she had lent him long ago, and with Taylor he left a horse which he had brought for her to ride. As a goodbye, he put a bunch of flowers in her hand. Then he was gone, and she watched him going by the thick bushes along the stream. They were pink with wild roses; and the meadow-larks, invisible in the grass, like hiding choristers, sent up across the empty miles of air their unexpected song. Earth and sky had been propitious, could he have stayed; and perhaps one portion of her heart had been propitious too. So, as he rode away on Monte, she watched him, half chilled by reason, half melted by passion, self-thwarted, self-accusing, unresolved. Therefore the days that came for her now were all of them unhappy ones, while for him they were filled with work well done and with changeless longing.

* * *

One day it seemed as if a lull was coming, a pause in which he could at last attain that hour with her. He left the camp and turned his face towards Bear Creek. The way led him along Butte Creek. Across the stream lay Balaam's large ranch; and presently on the other bank he saw Balaam himself, and reined in Monte for a moment to watch what Balaam was doing.

'That's what I've heard,' he muttered to himself. For Balaam had led some horses to the water, and was lashing them heavily because they would not drink. He looked at this spectacle so intently that he did not see Shorty approaching along the trail.

'Morning,' said Shorty to him, with some constraint.

But the Virginian gave him a pleasant greeting.

'I was afraid I'd not catch you so quick,' said Shorty. 'This is for you.' He handed his recent foreman a letter of much battered appearance. It was from the Judge. It had not come straight, but very gradually, in the pockets of three successive cowpunchers. As the Virginian glanced over it and saw that the enclosure it contained was for Balaam, his heart fell. Here were new orders for him, and he could not go to see his sweetheart.

'Hello, Shorty!' said Balaam, from over the creek. To the Virginian he gave a slight nod. He did not know him, although he knew well enough who he was.

'Hyeh's a letter from Judge Henry for yu',' said the Virginian, and he crossed the creek.

Many weeks before, in the early spring, Balaam had borrowed two horses from the Judge, promising to return them at once. But the Judge, of course, wrote very civilly. He hoped that 'this dunning reminder' might be excused. As Balaam read the reminder, he wished that he had sent the horses before. The Judge was a greater man than he in the

Territory. Balaam could not but excuse the 'dunning reminder', but he was ready to be disagreeable to somebody at once.

'Well,' he said, musing aloud in his annoyance, 'Judge Henry wants them by the 30th. Well, this is the 24th, and time enough yet.'

'This is the 27th,' said the Virginian, briefly.

That made a difference! Not so easy to reach Sunk Creek in good order by the 30th! Balaam had drifted three sunrises behind the progress of the month. Days look alike, and often lose their very names in the quiet depths of Cattle Land. The horses were not even here at the ranch. Balaam was ready to be very disagreeable now. Suddenly he perceived the date of the Judge's letter. He held it out to the Virginian, and struck the paper.

'What's your idea in bringing this here two weeks late?' he said.

Now, when he had struck that paper, Shorty looked at the Virginian. But nothing happened beyond a certain change of light in the Southerner's eyes. And when the Southerner spoke, it was with his usual gentleness and civility. He explained that the letter had been put in his hands just now by Shorty.

'Oh,' said Balaam. He looked at Shorty. How had he come to be a messenger? 'You working for the Sunk Creek outfit again?' said he.

'No,' said Shorty.

Balaam turned to the Virginian again. 'How do you expect me to get those horses to Sunk Creek by the 30th?'

The Virginian levelled a lazy eye on Balaam. 'I ain' doin' any expecting,' said he. His native dialect was on top today. 'The Judge has friends goin' to arrive from New Yawk for a trip across the Basin,' he added. 'The hawsses are for them.'

Balaam grunted with displeasure, and thought of the sixty or seventy days since he had told the Judge he would return the horses at once. He looked across at Shorty seated in the shade, and through his uneasy thoughts his instinct irrelevantly noted what a good pony the youth rode. It was the same animal he had seen once or twice before! But something must be done. The Judge's horses were far out on the big range, and must be found and driven in, which would take certainly the rest of this day, possibly part of the next.

Balaam called to one of his men and gave some sharp orders, emphasising details, and enjoining haste, while the Virginian leaned slightly against his horse, with one arm over the saddle, hearing and understanding, but not smiling outwardly. The man departed to saddle up for his search on the big range, and Balaam resumed the unhitching of his team.

'So you're not working for the Sunk Creek outfit now?' he enquired of Shorty. He ignored the Virginian. 'Working for the Goose Egg?'

'No,' said Shorty.

'Sand Hill outfit, then?'

'No,' said Shorty.

Balaam grinned. He noticed how Shorty's yellow hair stuck through a hole in his hat, and how old and battered were Shorty's overalls. Shorty had been glad to take a little accidental pay for becoming the bearer of the letter which he had delivered to the Virginian. But even that sum was no longer in his possession. He had passed through Drybone on his way, and at Drybone there had been a game of poker. Shorty's money was now in the pocket of Trampas. But he had one valuable possession in the world left to him, and that was his horse Pedro.

'Good pony of yours,' said Balaam to him now, from across Butte Creek. Then he struck his own horse in the jaw because he held back from coming to the water as the other had done.

'Your trace ain't unhitched,' commented the Virginian, pointing,

Balaam loosed the strap he had forgotten, and cut the horse again for consistency's sake. The animal, bewildered, now came down to the water, with its head in the air, and snuffing as it took short, nervous steps.

The Virginian looked on at this, silent and sombre. He could scarcely interfere between another man and his own beast. Neither he nor Balaam was among those who say their prayers. Yet in this omission they were not equal. A half-great poet once had a wholly great day, and in that great day he was able to write a poem that has lived and become, with many, a household word. He called it *The Rime of the Ancient Mariner*. And it is rich with many lines that possess the memory; but these are the golden ones –

> He prayeth well, who loveth well
> Both man and bird and beast.
>
> He prayeth best, who loveth best
> All things both great and small;
> For the dear God who loveth us,
> He made and loveth all.

These lines are the pure gold. They are good to teach children; because after the children come to be men, they may believe at least some part of them still. The Virginian did not know them – but his heart had taught him many things. I doubt if Balaam knew them either. But on him they would have been as pearls to swine.

'So you've quit the round-up?' he resumed to Shorty.

Shorty nodded and looked sidewise at the Virginian.

For the Virginian knew that he had been turned off for going to sleep while night-herding.

Then Balaam threw another glance on Pedro the horse.

'Hello, Shorty!' he called out, for the boy was departing. 'Don't you like dinner any more? It's ready about now.'

Shorty forded the creek and slung his saddle off, and on invitation turned Pedro, his buckskin pony, into Balaam's pasture. This was green, the rest of the wide world being yellow, except only where Butte Creek, with its bordering cottonwoods, coiled away into the desert distance like a green snake without end. The Virginian also turned his horse into the pasture. He must stay at the ranch till the Judge's horses should be found.

'Mrs Balaam's East yet,' said her lord, leading the way to his dining-room.

He wanted Shorty to dine with him, and could not exclude the Virginian, much as he should have enjoyed this.

'See any Indians?' he enquired.

'Na-a!' said Shorty, in disdain of recent rumours.

'They're headin' the other way,' observed the Virginian; 'Bow Laig Range is where they was repawted.'

'What business have they got off the reservation, I'd like to know,' said the ranchman – 'Bow Leg, or anywhere?'

'Oh, it's just a hunt, and a kind of visitin' their friends on the South Reservation,' Shorty explained. 'Squaws along and all.'

'Well, if the folks at Washington don't keep squaws and all where they belong,' said Balaam, in a rage, 'the folks in Wyoming Territory 'ill do a little job that way themselves.'

'There's a petition out,' said Shorty. 'Paper's goin' East with a lot of names to it. But they ain't no harm, them Indians ain't.'

'No harm?' rasped out Balaam. 'Was it white men druv off the O. C. yearlings?'

Balaam's Eastern grammar was sometimes at the mercy of his Western feelings. The thought of the perennial stultification of Indian affairs at Washington, whether by politician or philanthropist, was always sure to arouse him. He walked impatiently about while he spoke, and halted impatiently at the window. Out in the world the unclouded day was shining, and Balaam's eye travelled across the plains to where a blue line, faint and pale, lay along the end of the vast yellow distance. That was the beginning of the Bow Leg Mountains. Somewhere over there were the red men, ranging in unfrequented depths of rock and pine – their forbidden ground.

Dinner was ready, and they sat down.

'And I suppose,' Balaam continued, still hot on the subject, 'you'd claim Indians object to killing a white man when they run on to him good and far from human help? These peaceable Indians are just the worst in the business.'

'That's so,' assented the easy-opinioned Shorty, exactly as if he had always maintained this view. 'Chap started for Sunk Creek three weeks ago. Trapper he was; old like, with a red shirt. One of his horses come into the round-up Toosday. Man ain't been heard from.' He ate in silence for a while, evidently brooding in his childlike mind. Then he said, querulously, 'I'd sooner trust one of them Indians than I would Trampas.'

Balaam slanted his fat bullet head far to one side, and laying his spoon down (he had opened some canned grapes) laughed steadily at his guest with a harsh relish of irony.

The guest ate a grape, and perceiving he was seen through, smiled back rather miserably.

'Say, Shorty,' said Balaam, his head still slanted over, 'what's the figures of your bank balance just now?'

'I ain't usin' banks,' murmured the youth.

Balaam put some more grapes on Shorty's plate, and drawing a cigar from his waistcoat, sent it rolling to his guest.

'Matches are behind you,' he added. He gave a cigar to the Virginian as an afterthought, but to his disgust, the Southerner put it in his pocket and lighted a pipe.

Balaam accompanied his guest, Shorty, when he went to the pasture to saddle up and depart. 'Got a rope?' he asked the guest, as they lifted down the bars.

'Don't need to rope him. I can walk right up to Pedro. You stay back.'

Hiding his bridle behind him, Shorty walked to the river bank, where the pony was switching his long tail in the shade; and speaking persuasively to him, he came nearer, till he laid his hand on Pedro's dusky mane, which was many shades darker than his hide. He turned expectantly, and his master came up to his expectations with a piece of bread.

'Eats that, does he?' said Balaam, over the bars.

'Likes the salt,' said Shorty. 'Now, n-n-ow, here! Yu' don't guess yu'll be bridled, don't you? Open your teeth! Yu'd like to play yu' was nobody's horse and live private? Or maybe yu'd prefer ownin' a saloon?'

Pedro evidently enjoyed this talk, and the dodging he made about the bit. Once fairly in his mouth, he accepted the inevitable, and followed Shorty to the bars. Then Shorty turned and extended his hand.

'Shake!' he said to his pony, who lifted his forefoot quietly and put it in his master's hand. Then the master tickled his nose, and he wrinkled it and flattened his ears, pretending to bite. His face wore an expression of knowing relish over this performance. 'Now the other hoof,' said Shorty; and the horse and master shook hands with their left. 'I learned him that,' said the cowboy, with pride and affection. 'Say, Pede,' he continued, in Pedro's ear, 'ain't yu' the best little horse in the country? What? Here, now! Keep out of that, you deadbeat! There ain't no more bread.' He pinched the pony's nose, one-quarter of which was wedged into his pocket.

'Quite a lady's little pet!' said Balaam, with the rasp in his voice 'Pity this isn't New York, now, where there's a big market for harmless horses. Gee-gees, the children call them.'

'He ain't no gee-gee,' said Shorty, offended. 'He'll beat any cow-pony workin' you've got. Yu' can turn him on a half-dollar. Don't need to touch the reins. Hang 'em on one finger and swing your body, and he'll turn.'

Balaam knew this, and he knew that the pony was only a four-year-old. 'Well,' he said, 'Drybone's had no circus this season. Maybe they'd buy tickets to see Pedro. He's good for that, anyway.'

Shorty became gloomy. The Virginian was grimly smoking. Here was something else going on not to his taste, but none of his business.

'Try a circus,' persisted Balaam. 'Alter your plans for spending cash in town, and make a little money instead.'

Shorty having no plans to alter and no cash to spend, grew still more gloomy.

'What'll you take for that pony?' said Balaam.

Shorty spoke up instantly. 'A hundred dollars couldn't buy that piece of stale mud off his back,' he asserted, looking off into the sky grandiosely.

But Balaam looked at Shorty. 'You keep the mud,' he said, 'and I'll give you thirty dollars for the horse.'

Shorty did a little professional laughing, and began to walk towards his saddle.

'Give you thirty dollars,' repeated Balaam, picking a stone up and slinging it into the river.

'How far do yu' call it to Drybone?' Shorty remarked, stooping to investigate the bucking strap on his saddle – a superfluous performance, for Pedro never bucked.

'You won't have to walk,' said Balaam. 'Stay all night, and I'll send you over comfortably in the morning, when the wagon goes for the mail.'

'Walk!' Shorty retorted. 'Drybone's twenty-five miles. Pedro'll put me there in three hours and not know he done it.' He lifted the saddle on the horse's back. 'Come, Pedro,' said he.

'Come, Pedro!' mocked Balaam.

There followed a little silence.

'No, sir,' mumbled Shorty, with his head under Pedro's belly, busily cinching. 'A hundred dollars is bottom figures.'

Balaam, in his turn, now duly performed some professional laughing, which was noted by Shorty under the horse's belly. He stood up and squared round on Balaam. 'Well, then,' he said, 'what'll yu' give for him?'

'Thirty dollars,' said Balaam, looking far off into the sky, as Shorty had looked.

'Oh, come, now,' expostulated Shorty.

It was he who now did the feeling for an offer, and this was what Balaam liked to see. 'Why, yes,' he said, 'thirty,' and looked surprised that he should have to mention the sum so often.

'I thought yu'd quit them first figures,' said the cowpuncher, 'for yu' can see I ain't goin' to look at 'em.'

Balaam climbed on the fence and sat there.

'I'm not crying for your Pedro,' he observed dispassionately. 'Only it struck me you were dead broke, and wanted to raise cash and keep yourself going till you hunted up a job and could buy him back.' He hooked his right thumb inside his waistcoat pocket. 'But I'm not cryin' for him,' he repeated. 'He'd stay right here, of course. I wouldn't part with him. Why does he stand that way? Hello!' Balaam suddenly straightened himself, like a man who has made a discovery.

'Hello, what?' said Shorty, on the defensive.

Balaam was staring at Pedro with a judicial frown. Then he stuck out a finger at the horse, keeping the thumb hooked in his pocket. So meagre a gesture was felt by the ruffled Shorty to be no just way to point at Pedro. 'What's the matter with that foreleg there?' said Balaam.

'Which? Nothin's the matter with it!' snapped Shorty.

Balaam climbed down from his fence and came over with elaborate deliberation. He passed his hand up and down the off foreleg. Then he spit slenderly. 'Mm!' he said thoughtfully; and added, with a shade of sadness, 'that's always to be expected when they're worked too young.'

Shorty slid his hand slowly over the disputed leg. 'What's to be expected?' he enquired – 'that they'll eat hearty? Well, he does.'

At this retort the Virginian permitted himself to laugh in audible sympathy.

'Sprung,' continued Balaam, with a sigh. 'Whirling round short when his bones were soft did that. Yes.'

'Sprung!' Shorty said, with a bark of indignation. 'Come on, Pede; you and me'll spring for town.'

He caught the horn of the saddle, and as he swung into place the horse rushed away with him. 'O-ee! yoi-yup, yup, yup!' sang Shorty, in the shrill cow dialect. He made Pedro play an exhibition game of speed, bringing him round close to Balaam in a wide circle, and then he vanished in dust down the left-bank trail.

Balaam looked after him and laughed harshly. He had seen trout dash about like that when the hook in their jaw first surprised them. He knew Shorty would show the pony off, and he knew Shorty's love for Pedro was not equal to his need of money. He called to one of his men, asked something about the dam at the mouth of the canyon, where the main irrigation ditch began, made a remark about the prolonged drought, and then walked to his dining-room door, where, as he expected, Shorty met him.

'Say,' said the youth, 'do you consider that's any way to talk about a good horse?'

'Any dude could see the leg's sprung,' said Balaam. But he looked at Pedro's shoulder, which was well laid back; and he admired his points, dark in contrast with the buckskin, and also the width between the eyes.

'Now you know,' whined Shorty, 'that it ain't sprung any more than your leg's cork. If you mean the right leg ain't plumb straight, I can tell you he was born so. That don't make no difference, for it ain't weak. Try him onced. Just as sound and strong as iron. Never stumbles. And he don't never go to jumpin' with yu'. He's kind and he's smart.' And the master petted his pony, who lifted a hoof for another handshake.

Of course Balaam had never thought the leg was sprung, and he now took on an unprejudiced air of wanting to believe Shorty's statements if he only could.

'Maybe there's two years' work left in that leg,' he now observed.

'Better give your hawss away, Shorty,' said the Virginian.

'Is this your deal, my friend?' enquired Balaam. And he slanted his bullet head at the Virginian.

'Give him away, Shorty,' drawled the Southerner. 'His laig is busted. Mr Balaam says so.'

Balaam's face grew evil with baffled fury. But the Virginian was gravely considering Pedro. He, too, was not pleased. But he could not interfere. Already he had overstepped the code in these matters. He would have dearly liked – for reasons good and bad, spite and mercy mingled – to have spoiled Balaam's market, to have offered a reasonable or even an unreasonable price for Pedro, and taken possession of the horse himself. But this might not be. In bets, in card games, in all horse transactions and other matters of similar business, a man must take care of himself, and wiser onlookers must suppress their wisdom and hold their peace.

That evening Shorty again had a cigar. He had parted with Pedro for forty dollars, a striped Mexican blanket, and a pair of spurs. Undressing over in the bunk house, he said to the Virginian, 'I'll sure buy Pedro back off him just as soon as ever I rustle some cash.' The Virginian grunted. He was thinking he should have to travel hard to get the horses to the Judge by the 30th; and below that thought lay his aching disappointment and his longing for Bear Creek.

In the early dawn Shorty sat up among his blankets on the floor of the bunk house and saw the various sleepers coiled or sprawled in their beds; their breathing had not yet grown restless at the nearing of day. He stepped to the door carefully, and saw the crowding blackbirds begin their walk and chatter in the mud of the littered and trodden corrals. From beyond among the cotton woods, came continually the smooth unemphatic sound of the doves answering each other invisibly; and against the empty ridge of the river-bluff lay the moon, no longer shining, for there was established a new light through the sky. Pedro stood in the pasture close to the bars. The cowboy slowly closed the door behind him, and sitting down on the step, drew his money out and idly handled it, taking no comfort just then from its possession. Then he put it back, and after dragging on his boots, crossed to the pasture, and held a last talk with his pony, brushing the cakes of mud from his hide where he had rolled, and passing a lingering hand over his mane. As the sounds of the morning came increasingly from tree and plain, Shorty glanced back to see that no one was yet out of the cabin, and then put his arms round the horse's neck, laying his head against him. For a moment the cowboy's insignificant face was exalted by the emotion he would never have let others see. He hugged tight this animal, who was dearer to his heart than anybody in the world.

'Goodbye, Pedro,' he said – 'goodbye.' Pedro looked for bread.

'No,' said his master, sorrowfully, 'not any more. Yu' know well I'd give it yu' if I had it. You and me didn't figure on this, did we, Pedro? Goodbye!'

He hugged his pony again, and got as far as the bars of the pasture, but returned once more. 'Goodbye, my little horse, my dear horse, my little, little Pedro,' he said, as his tears wet the pony's neck. Then he wiped them with his hand, and got himself back to the bunk house. After breakfast he and his belongings departed to Drybone, and Pedro from his field calmly watched this departure; for horses must recognise even less than men the black corners that their destinies turn. The pony stopped feeding to look at the mail-wagon pass by; but the master sitting in the wagon forebore to turn his head.

CHAPTER 26

Balaam and Pedro

Resigned to wait for the Judge's horses, Balaam went into his office this dry, bright morning and read nine accumulated newspapers; for he was behindhand. Then he rode out on the ditches, and met his man returning with the troublesome animals at last. He hastened home and sent for the Virginian. He had made a decision.

'See here,' he said; 'those horses are coming. What trail would you take over to the Judge's?'

'Shortest trail's right through the Bow Laig Mountains,' said the foreman, in his gentle voice.

'Guess you're right. It's dinner-time. We'll start right afterward. We'll make Little Muddy Crossing by sundown, and Sunk Creek tomorrow, and the next day'll see us through. Can a wagon get through Sunk Creek Canyon?'

The Virginian smiled. 'I reckon it can't, seh, and stay resembling a wagon.'

Balaam told them to saddle Pedro and one pack-horse, and drive the bunch of horses into a corral, roping the Judge's two, who proved extremely wild. He had decided to take this journey himself on remembering certain politics soon to be rife in Cheyenne. For Judge Henry was indeed a greater man than Balaam.

This personally conducted return of the horses would temper its tardiness, and, moreover, the sight of some New York visitors would be a good thing after seven months of no warmer touch with that metropolis than the Sunday *Herald*, always eight days old when it reached the Butte Creek Ranch.

They forded Butte Creek, and, crossing the well-travelled trail which follows down to Drybone, turned their faces towards the uninhabited country that began immediately, as the ocean begins off a sandy shore. And as a single mast on which no sail is shining stands at the horizon and seems to add a loneliness to the surrounding sea, so the long grey line of fence, almost a mile away, that ended Balaam's land on this side the creek, stretched along the waste ground and added desolation to the plain. No solitary watercourse with margin of cottonwoods or willow thickets flowed here to stripe the dingy, yellow world with interrupting green, nor were cattle to be seen dotting the distance, nor moving objects at all, nor any bird in the soundless air. The last gate was shut by the Virginian, who looked back at the pleasant trees of the ranch, and then followed on in single file across the alkali of No Man's Land.

No cloud was in the sky. The desert's grim noon shone sombrely on flat and hill. The sagebrush was dull like zinc. Thick heat rose near at hand from the caked alkali, and pale heat shrouded the distant peaks.

There were five horses. Balaam led on Pedro, his squat figure stiff in the saddle, but solid as a rock, and tilted a little forward, as his habit was.

One of the Judge's horses came next, a sorrel, dragging back continually on the rope by which he was led. After him ambled Balaam's wise pack-animal, carrying the light burden of two days' food and lodging. She was an old mare who could still go when she chose, but had been schooled by the years, and kept the trail, giving no trouble to the Virginian who came behind her. He also sat solid as a rock, yet subtly bending to the struggles of the wild horse he led, as a steel spring bends and balances and resumes its poise.

Thus they made but slow time, and when they topped the last dull rise of ground and looked down on the long slant of ragged, caked earth to the crossing of Little Muddy, with its single tree and few mean bushes, the final distance where eyesight ends had deepened to violet from the thin, steady blue they had stared at for so many hours, and all heat was gone from the universal dryness. The horses drank a long time from the sluggish yellow water, and its alkaline taste and warmth were equally welcome to the men. They built a little fire, and when supper was ended, smoked but a short while and in silence, before they got in the blankets that were spread in a smooth place beside the water.

They had picketed the two horses of the Judge in the best grass they could find, letting the rest go free to find pasture where they could. When the first light came, the Virginian attended to breakfast, while Balaam rode away on the sorrel to bring in the loose horses. They had gone far out of sight, and when he returned with them, after some two hours, he was on Pedro. Pedro was soaking with sweat, and red froth creamed from his mouth. The Virginian saw the horses must have been hard to drive in, especially after Balaam brought them the wild sorrel as a leader.

'If you'd kep' ridin' him, 'stead of changin' off on your hawss, they'd have behaved quieter,' said the foreman.

'That's good seasonable advice,' said Balaam, sarcastically. 'I could have told you that now.'

'I could have told you when you started,' said the Virginian, heating the coffee for Balaam.

Balaam was eloquent on the outrageous conduct of the horses. He had come up with them evidently striking back for Butte Creek, with the old mare in the lead.

'But I soon showed her the road she was to go,' he said, as he drove them now to the water.

The Virginian noticed the slight limp of the mare, and how her pastern was cut as if with a stone or the sharp heel of a boot.

'I guess she'll not be in a hurry to travel except when she's wanted to,' continued Balaam. He sat down, and sullenly poured himself some coffee. 'We'll be in luck if we make any Sunk Creek this night.'

He went on with his breakfast, thinking aloud for the benefit of his companion, who made no comments, preferring silence to the discomfort of talking with a man whose vindictive humour was so thoroughly uppermost. He did not even listen very attentively, but continued his preparations for departure, washing the dishes, rolling the blankets, and moving about in his usual way of easy and visible good nature.

'Six o'clock, already,' said Balaam, saddling the horses. 'And we'll not get started for ten minutes more.' Then he came to Pedro. 'So you haven't quit fooling yet, haven't you?' he exclaimed, for the pony shrank as he lifted the bridle. 'Take that for your sore mouth!' and he rammed the bit in, at which Pedro flung back and reared.

'Well, I never saw Pedro act that way yet,' said the Virginian.

'Ah, rubbish!' said Balaam. 'They're all the same. Not a bastard one but's laying for his chance to do for you. Some'll buck you off, and some'll roll with you, and some'll fight you with their fore feet. They may play good for a year, but the Western pony's man's enemy, and when he judges he's got his chance, he's going to do his best. And if you come out alive it won't be his fault.' Balaam paused for a while, packing. 'You've got to keep them afraid of you,' he said next; 'that's what you've got to do if you don't want trouble. That Pedro horse there has been fed, hand-fed, and fooled with like a damn pet, and what's that policy done? Why, he goes ugly when he thinks it's time, and decides he'll not drive any horses into camp this morning. He knows better now.'

'Mr Balaam,' said the Virginian, 'I'll buy that hawss off yu' right now.'

Balaam shook his head. 'You'll not do that right now or any other time,' said he. 'I happen to want him.'

The Virginian could do no more. He had heard cowpunchers say to refractory ponies, 'You keep still, or I'll Balaam you!' and he now understood the aptness of the expression.

Meanwhile Balaam began to lead Pedro to the creek for a last drink before starting across the torrid drought. The horse held back on the rein a little, and Balaam turned and cut the whip across his forehead. A delay of forcing and backing followed, while the Virginian, already in the saddle, waited. The minutes passed, and no immediate prospect, apparently, of getting nearer Sunk Creek.

'He ain' goin' to follow you while you're beatin' his haid,' the Southerner at length remarked.

'Do you think you can teach me anything about horses?' retorted Balaam.

'Well, it don't look like I could,' said the Virginian, lazily.

'Then don't try it, so long as it's not your horse, my friend.'

Again the Southerner levelled his eye on Balaam. 'All right,' he said, in the same gentle voice. 'And don't you call me your friend. You've made that mistake twiced.'

The road was shadeless, as it had been from the start, and they could not travel fast. During the first few hours all coolness was driven out of the glassy morning, and another day of illimitable sun invested the world with its blaze. The pale Bow Leg Range was coming nearer, but its hard hot slants and rifts suggested no sort of freshness, and even the pines that spread for wide miles along near the summit counted for nothing in the distance and the glare, but seemed mere patches of dull dry discoloration. No talk was exchanged between the two travellers, for the cowpuncher had nothing to say and Balaam was sulky, so they moved along in silent endurance of each other's company and the tedium of the journey.

But the slow succession of rise and fall in the plain changed and shortened. The earth's surface became lumpy, rising into mounds and knotted systems of steep small hills cut apart by staring gashes of sand, where water poured in the spring from the melting snow. After a time they ascended through the foothills till the plain below was for a while concealed, but came again into view in its entirety, distant and a thing of the past, while some magpies sailed down to meet them from the new country they were entering. They passed up through a small transparent forest of dead trees standing stark and white, and a little higher came on a line of narrow moisture that crossed the way and formed a stale pool among some willow thickets. They turned aside to water their horses, and found near the pool a circular spot of ashes and some poles lying, and beside these a cage-like edifice of willow wands built in the ground.

'Indian camp,' observed the Virginian.

There were the tracks of five or six horses on the farther side of the pool, and they did not come into the trail, but led off among the rocks on some system of their own.

'They're about a week old,' said Balaam. 'It's part of that outfit that's been hunting.'

'They've gone on to visit their friends,' added the cowpuncher.

'Yes, on the Southern Reservation. How far do you call Sunk Creek now?'

'Well,' said the Virginian, calculating, 'it's mighty nigh fo'ty miles from Muddy Crossin', an' I reckon we've come eighteen.'

'Just about. It's noon.' Balaam snapped his watch shut. 'We'll rest here till 12.30.'

When it was time to go, the Virginian looked musingly at the mountains. 'We'll need to travel right smart to get through the canyon tonight,' he said.

'Tell you what,' said Balaam; 'we'll rope the Judge's horses together and drive 'em in front of us. That'll make speed.'

'Mightn't they get away on us?' objected the Virginian. 'They're pow'ful wild.'

'They can't get away from me, I guess,' said Balaam, and the arrangement was adopted. 'We're the first this season over this piece of the trail,' he observed presently.

His companion had noticed the ground already, and assented. There were no tracks anywhere to be seen over which winter had not come and gone since they had been made. Presently the trail wound into a sultry gulch that hemmed in the heat and seemed to draw down the sun's rays more vertically. The sorrel horse chose this place to make a try for liberty. He suddenly whirled from the trail, dragging with him his less inventive fellow. Leaving the Virginian with the old mare, Balaam headed them off, for Pedro was quick, and they came jumping down the bank together, but swiftly crossed up on the other side, getting much higher before they could be reached. It was no place for this sort of game, as the sides of the ravine were ploughed with steep channels, broken with jutting knobs of rock, and impeded by short twisted pines that swung out from their roots horizontally over the pitch of the hill. The Virginian helped, but used his horse with more judgement, keeping as much on the level as possible, and endeavouring to anticipate the next turn of the runaways before they made it, while Balaam attempted to follow them close, wheeling short when they doubled, heavily beating up the face of the slope, veering again to come down to the point he had left, and whenever he felt Pedro begin to flag, driving his spurs into the horse and forcing him to keep up the pace. He had set out to overtake and capture on the side of the mountain these two animals who had been running wild for many weeks, and now carried no weight but themselves, and the futility of such work could not penetrate his obstinate and rising temper. He had made up his mind not to give in. The Virginian soon decided to move slowly along for the present, preventing the wild horses from passing down the gulch again, but otherwise saving his own animal from useless fatigue. He saw that Pedro was reeking wet, with mouth open, and constantly stumbling, though he galloped on. The cowpuncher kept the group in sight, driving the pack-horse in front of him, and watching the tactics of the sorrel, who had now undoubtedly become the leader of the expedition, and was at the top of the gulch, in vain trying to find an outlet through its rocky rim to the levels above. He soon judged this to be no thoroughfare, and changing his plan, trotted down to the bottom and up the other side, gaining more and more; for in this new descent Pedro had fallen twice. Then the sorrel showed the cleverness of a genuinely vicious horse. The Virginian saw him stop and fall to kicking his companion with all the energy that a short rope would permit. The rope slipped, and both, unencumbered, reached the top and disappeared. Leaving the pack-horse for Balaam, the Virginian started after them and came into a high tableland, beyond which the mountains began in earnest. The runaways were moving across towards these at an easy rate. He followed for a moment, then looking back, and seeing no sign of Balaam, waited, for the horses were sure not to go fast when they reached good pasture or water.

He got out of the saddle and sat on the ground, watching, till the mare came up slowly into sight, and Balaam behind her. When they were near, Balaam dismounted and struck Pedro fearfully, until the stick broke, and he raised the splintered half to continue.

Seeing the pony's condition, the Virginian spoke, and said, 'I'd let that hawss alone.'

Balaam turned to him, but wholly possessed by passion did not seem to hear, and the Southerner noticed how white and like that of a maniac his face was. The stick slid to the ground.

'He played he was tired,' said Balaam, looking at the Virginian with glazed eyes. The violence of his rage affected him physically, like some stroke of illness. 'He played out on me on purpose.' The man's voice was dry and light. 'He's perfectly fresh now,' he continued, and turned again to the coughing, swaying horse, whose eyes were closed. Not having the stick, he seized the animal's unresisting head and shook it. The Virginian watched him a moment, and rose to stop such a spectacle. Then, as if conscious he was doing no real hurt, Balaam ceased, and turning again in slow fashion looked across the level, where the runaways were still visible.

'I'll have to take your horse,' he said, 'mine's played out on me.'

'You ain' goin' to touch my hawss.'

Again the words seemed not entirely to reach Balaam's understanding, so dulled by rage were his senses. He made no answer, but mounted Pedro; and the failing pony walked mechanically forward, while the Virginian, puzzled, stood looking after him. Balaam seemed without purpose of going anywhere, and stopped in a moment. Suddenly he was at work at something. This sight was odd and new to look at. For a few seconds it had no meaning to the Virginian as he watched. Then his mind grasped the horror, too late. Even with his cry of execration and the tiger spring that he gave to stop Balaam, the monstrosity was wrought. Pedro sank motionless, his head rolling flat on the earth. Balaam was jammed beneath him. The man had struggled to his feet before the Virginian reached the spot, and the horse then lifted his head and turned it piteously round.

Then vengeance like a blast struck Balaam. The Virginian hurled him to the ground, lifted and hurled him again, lifted him and beat his face and struck his jaw. The man's strong ox-like fighting availed nothing. He fended his eyes as best he could against these sledge-hammer blows of justice. He felt blindly for his pistol. That arm was caught and wrenched backward, and crushed and doubled. He seemed to hear his own bones, and set up a hideous screaming of hate and pain. Then the pistol at last came out, and together with the hand that grasped it was instantly stamped into the dust. Once again the creature was lifted and slung so that he lay across Pedro's saddle a blurred, dingy, wet pulp.

Vengeance had come and gone. The man and the horse were motionless. Around them, silence seemed to gather like a witness.

'If you are dead,' said the Virginian, 'I am glad of it.' He stood looking down at Balaam and Pedro, prone in the middle of the open tableland. Then he saw Balaam looking at him. It was the quiet stare of sight without thought or feeling, the mere visual sense alone, almost frightful in its separation from any self. But as he watched those eyes, the self came back into them. 'I have not killed you,' said the Virginian. 'Well, I ain't goin' to go any more to yu' – if that's a satisfaction to know.'

Then he began to attend to Balaam with impersonal skill, like someone hired for the purpose. 'He ain't hurt bad,' he asserted aloud, as if the man were some nameless patient; and then to Balaam he remarked, 'I reckon it might have put a less tough man than you out of business for quite a while. I'm goin' to get some water now.' When he returned with the water, Balaam was sitting up, looking about him. He had not yet spoken, nor did he now speak. The sunlight flashed on the six-shooter where it lay, and the Virginian secured it. 'She ain't so pretty as she was,' he remarked, as he examined the weapon. 'But she'll go right handy yet.'

Strength was in a measure returning to Pedro. He was a young horse, and the exhaustion neither of anguish nor of over-riding was enough to affect him long or seriously. He got himself on his feet and walked waveringly over to the old mare, and stood by her for comfort. The cowpuncher came up to him, and Pedro, after starting back slightly, seemed to comprehend that he was in friendly hands. It was plain that he would soon be able to travel slowly if no weight was on him, and that he would be a very good horse again. Whether they abandoned the runaways or not, there was no staying here for night to overtake them without food or water. The day was still high, and what its next few hours had in store the Virginian could not say, and he left them to take care of themselves, determining meanwhile that he would take command of the minutes and maintain the position he had assumed both as to Balaam and Pedro. He took Pedro's saddle off, threw the mare's pack to the ground, put Balaam's saddle on her, and on that stowed or tied her original pack, which he could do, since it was so light. Then he went to Balaam, who was sitting up.

'I reckon you can travel,' said the Virginian. 'And your hawss can. If you're comin' with me, you'll ride your mare. I'm goin' to trail them hawsses. If you're not comin' with me, your hawss comes with me, and you'll take fifty dollars for him.'

Balaam was indifferent to this good bargain. He did not look at the other or speak, but rose and searched about him on the ground. The Virginian was also indifferent as to whether Balaam chose to answer or not. Seeing Balaam searching the ground, he finished what he had to say.

'I have your six-shooter, and you'll have it when I'm ready for you to. Now, I'm goin',' he concluded.

Balaam's intellect was clear enough now, and he saw that though the rest of this journey would be nearly intolerable, it must go on. He looked at the impassive cowpuncher getting ready to go and tying a rope on Pedro's neck to lead him, then he looked at the mountains where the runaways had vanished, and it did not seem credible to him that he had come into such straits. He was helped stiffly on the mare, and the three horses in single file took up their journey once more, and came slowly among the mountains. The perpetual desert was ended, and they crossed a small brook, where they missed the trail. The Virginian dismounted to find where the horses had turned off, and discovered that they had gone straight up the ridge by the watercourse.

'There's been a man camped in hyeh inside a month,' he said, kicking up a rag of red flannel.

'White man and two hawsses. Ours have went up his old tracks.'

It was not easy for Balaam to speak yet, and he kept his silence. But he remembered that Shorty had spoken of a trapper who had started for Sunk Creek.

For three hours they followed the runaways' course over softer ground, and steadily ascending, passed one or two springs, at length, where the mud was not yet settled in the hoof-prints. Then they came through a corner of pine forest and down a sudden bank among quaking-asps to a green park. Here the runaways beside a stream were grazing at ease, but saw them coming, and started on again, following down the stream. For the present all to be done was to keep them in sight. This creek received tributaries and widened, making a valley for itself. Above the bottom, lining the first terrace of the ridge, began the pines, and stretched back, unbroken over intervening summit and basin, to cease at last where the higher peaks presided.

'This hyeh's the middle fork of Sunk Creek,' said the Virginian. 'We'll get on to our right road again where they join.'

Soon a game trail marked itself along the stream. If this would only continue, the runaways would be nearly sure to follow it down into the canyon. Then there would be no way for them but to go on and come out into their own country, where they would make for the Judge's ranch of their own accord. The great point was to reach the canyon before dark. They passed into permanent shadow; for though the other side of the creek shone in full day, the sun had departed behind the ridges immediately above them. Coolness filled the air, and the silence, which in this deep valley of invading shadow seemed too silent, was relieved by the birds. Not birds of song, but a freakish band of grey talkative observers, who came calling and croaking along through the pines, and inspected the cavalcade, keeping it company for a while, and then flying up into the woods again. The travellers came round a corner on a little spread of marsh, and from somewhere in the middle of it rose a buzzard and sailed on its black pinions into the air above them, wheeling and wheeling, but did not grow distant. As it swept over the trail, something fell from its claw, a rag of red flannel; and each man in turn looked at it as his horse went by.

'I wonder if there's plenty elk and deer hyeh?' said the Virginian.

'I guess there is,' Balaam replied, speaking at last. The travellers had become strangely reconciled.

'There's game 'most all over these mountains,' the Virginian continued; 'country not been settled long enough to scare them out.' So they fell into casual conversation, and for the first time were glad of each other's company.

The sound of a new bird came from the pines above – the hoot of an owl – and was answered from some other part of the wood. This they did not particularly notice at first, but soon they heard the same note, unexpectedly distant, like an echo. The game trail, now quite a defined path beside the river, showed no sign of changing its course or fading out into blank ground, as these uncertain guides do so often. It led consistently in the desired direction, and the two men were relieved to see it continue. Not only were the runaways easier to keep track of, but better speed was made along this valley. The pervading imminence of night more and more dispelled the lingering afternoon, though there was yet no twilight in the open, and the high peaks opposite shone yellow in the invisible sun. But now the owls hooted again. Their music had something in it that caused both the Virginian and Balaam to look up at the pines and wish that this valley would end. Perhaps it was early for night-birds to begin; or perhaps it was that the sound never seemed to fall behind, but moved abreast of them among the trees above, as they rode on without pause down below; some influence made the faces of the travellers grave. The spell of evil which the sight of the wheeling buzzard had begun, deepened as evening grew, while ever and again along the creek the singular call and answer of the owls wandered among the darkness of the trees not far away.

The sun was gone from the peaks when at length the other side of the stream opened into a long wide meadow. The trail they followed, after crossing a flat willow thicket by the water, ran into dense pines, that here for the first time reached all the way down to the water's edge. The two men came out of the willows, and saw ahead the capricious runaways leave the bottom and go up the hill and enter the wood.

'We must hinder that,' said the Virginian; and he dropped Pedro's rope. 'There's your six-shooter. You keep the trail, and camp down there' – he pointed to where the trees came to the water – 'till I head them hawsses off. I may not get back right away.' He galloped up the open hill and went into the pine, choosing a place above where the vagrants had disappeared.

Balaam dismounted, and picking up his six-shooter, took the rope off Pedro's neck and drove him slowly down towards where the wood began. Its interior was already dim, and Balaam saw that here must be their stopping-place tonight, since there was no telling how wide this pine strip might extend along the trail before they could come out of it and reach another suitable camping-ground. Pedro had recovered his strength, and he now showed signs of restlessness. He shied where there was not even a stone in the trail, and finally turned sharply round. Balaam expected he was going to rush back on the way they had come; but the horse stood still, breathing excitedly. He was urged forward again, though he turned more than once. But when they were a few paces from the wood, and Balaam had got off preparatory to camping, the horse snorted and dashed into the water, and stood still there. The astonished Balaam followed to turn him; but Pedro seemed to lose control of himself, and plunged to the middle of the river, and was evidently intending to cross. Fearing that he would escape to the opposite meadow and add to their difficulties, Balaam, with the idea of turning him round, drew his six-shooter and fired in front of the horse, divining, even as the flash cut the dusk, the secret of all this – the Indians; but too late. His bruised hand had stiffened, marring his aim, and he saw Pedro fall over in the water, then rise and struggle up the bank on the farther shore, where he now hurried also, to find that he had broken the pony's leg.

He needed no interpreter for the voices of the seeming owls that had haunted the latter hour of their journey, and he knew that his beast's keener instinct had perceived the destruction that lurked in the interior of the wood. The history of the trapper whose horse had returned without him might have been – might still be – his own; and he thought of the rag that had fallen from the buzzard's talons when he had been disturbed at his meal in the marsh. 'Peaceable' Indians were still in these mountains, and some few of them had for the past hour been skirting his journey unseen, and now waited for him in the wood, which they expected him to enter. They had been too wary to use their rifles or show themselves, lest these travellers should be only part of a larger company following, who would hear the noise of a shot, and catch them in the act of murder. So, safe under the cover of the pines, they had planned to sling their silent noose, and drag the white man from his horse as he passed through the trees.

Balaam looked over the river at the ominous wood, and then he looked at Pedro, the horse that he had first maimed and now ruined, to whom he probably owed his life. He was lying on the ground, quietly looking over the green meadow, where dusk was gathering. Perhaps he was not suffering from his wound yet, as he rested on the ground; and into his animal intelligence there probably came no knowledge of this final stroke of his fate. At any rate, no sound of pain came from Pedro, whose friendly and gentle face remained turned towards the meadow. Once more Balaam fired his pistol, and this time the aim was true, and the horse rolled over, with a ball through his brain. It was the best reward that remained for him.

Then Balaam rejoined the old mare, and turned from the middle fork of Sunk Creek. He dashed across the wide field, and went over a ridge, and found his way along in the night till he came to the old trail – the road which they would never have left but for him and his obstinacy. He unsaddled the weary mare by Sunk Creek, where the canyon begins, letting her drag a rope and find pasture and water, while he, lighting no fire to betray him, crouched close under a tree till the light came. He thought of the Virginian in the wood. But what could either have done for the other had he stayed to look for him among the pines? If the cowpuncher came back to the corner, he would follow Balaam's tracks or not. They would meet, at any rate, where the creeks joined.

But they did not meet. And then to Balaam the prospect of going onward to the Sunk Creek Ranch became more than he could bear. To come without the horses, to meet Judge Henry, to meet the guests of the Judge's, looking as he did now after his punishment by the Virginian, to give the news about the Judge's favourite man – no, how could he tell such a story as this? Balaam went no farther than a certain cabin, where he slept, and wrote a letter to the Judge. This the owner of the cabin delivered. And so, having spread news which would at once cause a search for the Virginian, and having constructed such sentences to the Judge as would most smoothly explain how, being overtaken by illness, he had not wished to be a burden at Sunk Creek, Balaam turned homeward by himself. By the time he was once more at Butte Creek, his general appearance was a thing less to be noticed. And there was Shorty, waiting!

One way and another, the lost dog had been able to gather some ready money. He was cheerful because of this momentary purseful of prosperity.

'And so I come back, yu' see,' he said. 'For I figured on getting Pedro back as soon as I could when I sold him to yu'.'

'You're behind the times, Shorty,' said Balaam.

Shorty looked blank. 'You've sure not sold Pedro?' he exclaimed.

'Them Indians,' said Balaam, 'got after me on the Bow Leg trail. Got after me and that Virginia man. But they didn't get *me*.'

Balaam wagged his bullet head to imply that this escape was due to his own superior intelligence. The Virginian had been stupid, and so the Indians had got him. 'And they shot your horse,' Balaam finished. 'Stop and get some dinner with the boys.'

Having eaten, Shorty rode away in mournful spirits. For he had made so sure of once more riding and talking with Pedro, his friend whom he had taught to shake hands.

CHAPTER 27

Grandmother Stark

Except for its chair and bed, the cabin was stripped almost bare. Amid its emptiness of dismantled shelves and walls and floor, only the tiny ancestress still hung in her place, last token of the home that had been. This miniature, tacked against the despoiled boards, and its descendant, the angry girl with her hand on an open box-lid, made a sort of couple in the loneliness: she on the wall sweet and serene, she by the box sweet and stormy. The picture was her final treasure waiting to be packed for the journey. In whatever room she had called her own since childhood, there it had also lived and looked at her, not quite familiar, not quite smiling, but in its prim colonial hues delicate as some pressed flower. Its pale oval, of colour blue and rose and flaxen, in a battered, pretty gold frame, unconquerably pervaded any surroundings with a something like last year's lavender. Till yesterday a Crow Indian war-bonnet had hung next it, a sumptuous cascade of feathers; on the other side a bow with arrows had dangled; opposite had been the skin of a silver fox; over the door had spread the antlers of a black-tail deer; a bearskin stretched beneath it. Thus had the whole cosy log cabin been upholstered, lavish with trophies of the frontier; and yet it was in front of the miniature that the visitors used to stop.

Shining quietly now in the cabin's blackness this summer day, the heirloom was presiding until the end. And as Molly Wood's eyes fell upon her ancestress of Bennington, 1777, there flashed a spark of steel in them, alone here in the room that she was leaving forever. She was not going to teach school any more on Bear Creek, Wyoming; she was going home to Bennington, Vermont. When time came for school to open again, there should be a new schoolmarm.

This was the momentous result of that visit which the Virginian had paid her. He had told her that he was coming for his hour soon. From that hour she had decided to escape. She was running away from her own heart. She did not dare to trust herself face to face again with her potent, indomitable lover. She longed for him, and therefore she would never see him again. No great-aunt at Dunbarton, or anybody else that knew her and her family, should ever say that she had married below her station, had been an unworthy Stark! Accordingly, she had written to the Virginian, bidding him goodbye, and wishing him everything in the world. As she happened to be aware that she was taking everything in the world away from him, this letter was not the most easy of letters to write. But she had made the language very kind. Yes; it was a thoroughly kind communication. And all because of that momentary visit, when he had brought back to her two novels, *Emma* and *Pride and Prejudice*.

'How do you like them?' she had then enquired; and he had smiled slowly at her. 'You haven't read them!' she exclaimed.

'No.'

'Are you going to tell me there has been no time?'

'No.'

Then Molly had scolded her cowpuncher, and to this he had listened with pleasure undisguised, as indeed he listened to every word that she said.

'Why, it has come too late,' he had told her when the scolding was over. 'If I was one of your little scholars hyeh in Bear Creek schoolhouse, yu' could learn me to like such frillery I reckon. But I'm a mighty ignorant, growed-up man.'

'So much the worse for you!' said Molly.

'No. I am pretty glad I am a man. Else I could not have learned the thing you have taught me.'

But she shut her lips and looked away. On the desk was a letter written from Vermont. 'If you don't tell me at once when you decide,' had said the arch writer, 'never hope to speak to me again. Mary Wood, seriously, I am suspicious. Why do you never mention him nowadays? How exciting to have you bring a live cowboy to Bennington! We should all come to dinner. Though of course I understand now that many of them have excellent manners. But would he wear his pistol at table?' So the letter ran on. It recounted the latest home gossip and jokes. In answering it Molly Wood had taken no notice of its childish tone here and there.

'Hyeh's some of them cactus blossoms yu' wanted,' said the Virginian. His voice recalled the girl with almost a start. 'I've brought a good hawss I've gentled for yu', and Taylor'll keep him till I need him.'

'Thank you so much! but I wish –'

'I reckon yu' can't stop me lendin' Taylor a hawss. And you cert'nly 'll get sick schoolteachin' if yu' don't keep outdoors some. Goodbye – till that next time.'

'Yes; there's always a next time,' she answered, as lightly as she could.

'There always will be. Don't yu' know that?'

She did not reply.

'I have discouraged spells,' he pursued, 'but I down them. For I've told yu' you were going to love me. You are goin' to learn back the thing you have taught me. I'm not askin' anything now; I don't want you to speak a word to me. But I'm never goin' to quit till "next time" is no more, and it's "all the time" for you and me.'

With that he had ridden away, not even touching her hand. Long after he had gone she was still in her chair, her eyes lingering upon his flowers, those yellow cups of the prickly pear. At length she had risen impatiently, caught up the flowers, gone with them to the open window – and then, after all, set them with pains in water.

But today Bear Creek was over. She was going home now. By the week's end she would be started. By the time the mail brought him her goodbye letter she would be gone. She had acted.

To Bear Creek, the neighbourly, the friendly, the not comprehending, this move had come unlooked for, and had brought regret. Only one hard word had been spoken to Molly, and that by her next-door neighbour and kindest friend. In Mrs Taylor's house the girl had daily come and gone as a daughter, and that lady reached the subject thus – 'When I took Taylor,' said she, sitting by as Robert Browning and Jane Austen were going into their box, 'I married for love.'

'Do you wish it had been money?' said Molly, stooping to her industries.

'You know both of us better than that, child.'

'I know I've seen people at home who couldn't possibly have had any other reason. They seemed satisfied, too.'

'Maybe the poor ignorant things were!'

'And so I have never been sure how I might choose.'

'Yes, you are sure, deary. Don't you think I know you? And when it comes over Taylor once in a while, and he tells me I'm the best thing in his life, and I tell him he ain't merely the best thing but the only thing in mine – him and the children – why, we just agree we'd do it all over the same way if we had the chance.'

Molly continued to be industrious.

'And that's why,' said Mrs Taylor, 'I want every girl that's anything to me to know her luck when it comes. For I was that near telling Taylor I wouldn't!'

'If ever my luck comes,' said Molly, with her back to her friend, 'I shall say "I will" at once.'

'Then you'll say it at Bennington next week.'

Molly wheeled round.

'Why, you surely will. Do you expect he's going to stay here, and you in Bennington?' And the campaigner sat back in her chair.

'He? Goodness! Who is he?'

'Child, child, you're talking cross today because you're at outs with yourself. You've been at outs ever since you took this idea of leaving the school and us and everything this needless way. You have not treated him right. And why, I can't make out to save me. What have you found out all of a sudden? If he was not good enough for you, I – But, oh, it's a prime one you're losing, Molly. When a man like that stays faithful to a girl 'spite all the chances he gets, her luck is come.'

'Oh, my luck! People have different notions of luck.'

'Notions!'

'He has been very kind.'

'Kind!' And now without further simmering, Mrs Taylor's wrath boiled up and poured copiously over Molly Wood. 'Kind! There's a word you shouldn't use, my dear. No doubt you can spell it. But more than its spelling I guess you don't know. The children can learn what it means from some of the rest of us folks that don't spell so correct, maybe.'

'Mrs Taylor, Mrs Taylor – '

'I can't wait, deary. Since the roughness looks bigger to you than the diamond, you had better go back to Vermont. I expect you'll find better grammar there, deary.'

The good dame stalked out, and across to her own cabin, and left the angry girl among her boxes. It was in vain she fell to work upon them. Presently something had to be done over again, and when it was, the box held several chattels less than before the readjustment. She played a sort of desperate dominoes to fit these objects in the space, but here were a paperweight, a portfolio, with two wretched volumes that no chink would harbour; and letting them fall all at once, she straightened herself, still stormy with revolt, eyes and cheeks still hot from the sting of long-parried truth. There, on her wall still, was the miniature, the little silent ancestress; and upon this face the girl's glance rested. It was as if she appealed to Grandmother Stark for support and comfort across the hundred years which lay between them. So the flaxen girl on the wall and she among the boxes stood a moment face to face in seeming communion, and then the descendant turned again to her work. But after a desultory touch here and there she drew a long breath and walked to the open door. What use was in finishing today, when she had nearly a week? This first spurt of toil had swept the cabin bare of all indwelling charm, and its look was chill. Across the lane, his horse, the one he had 'gentled' for her, was grazing idly. She walked there and caught him, and led him to her gate. Mrs Taylor saw her go in, and soon come out in riding-dress; and she watched the girl throw the saddle on with quick ease – the ease he had taught her. Mrs Taylor also saw the sharp cut she gave the horse, and laughed grimly to herself in her window as horse and rider galloped into the beautiful sunny loneliness.

To the punished animal this switching was new, and at its third repetition he turned his head in surprise, but was no more heeded than were the bluffs and flowers where he was taking his own undirected choice of way. He carried her over ground she knew by heart – Corncliff Mesa, Crowheart Butte, Westfall's Crossing, Upper Canyon; open land and woodland, pines and sagebrush, all silent and grave and lustrous in the sunshine. Once and again a ranchman greeted her, and wondered if she had forgotten who he was; once she passed some cowpunchers with a small herd of steers, and they stared after her too. Bear Creek narrowed, its mountainsides drew near, its little falls began to rush white in midday shadow, and the horse suddenly pricked his ears. Unguided, he was taking this advantage to go home. Though he had made but little way – a mere beginning yet – on this trail over to Sunk Creek, here was already a Sunk Creek friend whinnying good-day to him, so he whinnied back and quickened his pace, and Molly started to life. What was Monte doing here? She saw the black horse she knew also, saddled, with reins dragging on the trail as the rider had dropped them to dismount. A cold spring bubbled out beyond the next rock, and she knew her lover's horse was waiting for him while he drank. She pulled at the reins, but loosed them, for to turn and escape now was ridiculous; and riding boldly round the rock, she came upon him by the spring. One of his arms hung up to its elbow in the pool, the other was crooked beside his head, but the face was sunk downward against the shelving rock, so that she saw only his black, tangled hair. As her horse snorted and tossed his head she looked swiftly at Monte, as if to question him. Seeing now the sweat matted on his coat, and noting the white rim of his eye, she sprang and ran to the motionless figure. A patch of blood at his shoulder behind stained the soft flannel shirt, spreading down beneath his belt, and the man's whole strong body lay slack and pitifully helpless.

She touched the hand beside his head, but it seemed neither warm nor cold to her; she felt for the pulse, as nearly as she could remember the doctors did, but could not tell whether she imagined or not that it was still; twice with painful care her fingers sought and waited for the heat, and her face seemed like one of listening. She leaned down and lifted his other arm and hand from the water, and as their ice-coldness reached her senses, clearly she saw the patch near the shoulder she had moved grow wet with new blood, and at that sight she grasped at the stones upon which she herself now sank. She held tight by two rocks, sitting straight beside him, staring, and murmuring aloud, 'I must not faint; I will not faint'; and the standing horses looked at her, pricking their ears.

In this cuplike spread of the ravine the sun shone warmly down, the tall red cliff was warm, the pines were a warm film and filter of green; outside the shade across Bear Creek rose the steep, soft, open yellow hill, warm and high to the blue, and Bear Creek tumbled upon its sun-sparkling stones. The two horses on the margin trail still looked at the spring and trees, where sat the neat flaxen girl so rigid by the slack prone body in its flannel shirt and leathern chaps. Suddenly her face livened. 'But the blood ran!' she exclaimed, as if to the horses, her companions in this. She moved to him, and put her hand in through his shirt against his heart.

Next moment she had sprung up and was at his saddle, searching, then swiftly went on to her own and got her small flask and was back beside him. Here was the cold water he had sought, and she put it against his forehead and drenched the wounded shoulder with it. Three times she tried to move him, so he might lie more easy, but his dead weight was too much, and desisting, she sat close and raised his head to let it rest against her. Thus she saw the blood that was running from in front of the shoulder also; but she said no more about fainting. She tore strips from her dress and soaked them, keeping them cold and wet upon both openings of his wound, and she drew her pocket-knife out and cut his shirt away from the place. As she continually rinsed and cleaned it, she watched his eyelashes, long and soft and thick, but they did not stir. Again she tried the flask, but failed from being still too gentle, and her searching eyes fell upon ashes near the pool. Still undispersed by the weather lay the small charred ends of a fire he and she had made once here together, to boil coffee and fry trout. She built another fire now, and when the flames were going well, filled her flask-cup from the spring and set it to heat. Meanwhile, she returned to nurse his head and wound. Her cold water had stopped the bleeding. Then she poured her brandy in the steaming cup, and, made rough by her desperate helplessness, forced some between his lips and teeth.

Instantly, almost, she felt the tremble of life creeping back, and as his deep eyes opened upon her she sat still and mute. But the gaze seemed luminous with an unnoting calm, and she wondered if perhaps he could not recognise her; she watched this internal clearness of his vision, scarcely daring to breathe, until presently he began to speak, with the same profound and clear impersonality sounding in his slowly uttered words.

'I thought they had found me. I expected they were going to kill me.' He stopped, and she gave him more of the hot drink, which he took, still lying and looking at her as if the present did not reach his senses. 'I knew hands were touching me. I reckon I was not dead. I knew about them soon as they began, only I could not interfere.' He waited again. 'It is mighty strange where I have been. No. Mighty natural.' Then he went back into his reverie, and lay with his eyes still full open upon her where she sat motionless.

She began to feel a greater awe in this living presence than when it had been his body with an ice-cold hand; and she quietly spoke his name, venturing scarcely more than a whisper.

At this, some nearer thing wakened in his look. 'But it was you all along,' he resumed. 'It is you now. You must not stay – ' Weakness overcame him, and his eyes closed. She sat ministering to him; and when he roused again, he began anxiously at once: 'You must not stay. They would get you, too.'

She glanced at him with a sort of fierceness, then reached for his pistol, in which was nothing but blackened empty cartridges. She threw these out and drew six from his belt, loaded the weapon, and snapped shut its hinge.

'Please take it,' he said, more anxious and more himself. 'I ain't worth tryin' to keep. Look at me!'

'Are you giving up?' she enquired, trying to put scorn in her tone. Then she seated herself.

'Where is the sense in both of us – '

'You had better save your strength,' she interrupted.

He tried to sit up.

'Lie down!' she ordered.

He sank obediently, and began to smile.

When she saw that, she smiled too, and unexpectedly took his hand. 'Listen, friend,' said she. 'Nobody shall get you, and nobody shall get me. Now take some more brandy.'

'It must be noon,' said the cowpuncher, when she had drawn her hand away from him. 'I remember it was dark when – when – when I can remember. I reckon they were scared to follow me in so close to settlers. Else they would have been here.'

'You must rest,' she observed.

She broke the soft ends of some evergreen, and putting them beneath his head, went to the horses, loosened the cinches, took off the bridles, led them to drink, and picketed them to feed. Further still, to leave nothing undone which she could herself manage, she took the horses' saddles off to refold the blankets when the time should come, and meanwhile brought them for him. But he put them away from him. He was sitting up against a rock, stronger evidently, and asking for cold water. His head was fire-hot, and the paleness beneath his swarthy skin had changed to a deepening flush.

'Only five miles!' she said to him, bathing his head.

'Yes. I must hold it steady,' he answered, waving his hand at the cliff.

She told him to try and keep it steady until they got home.

'Yes,' he repeated. 'Only five miles. But it's fightin' to turn around.' Half aware that he was becoming light-headed, he looked from the rock to her and from her to the rock with dilating eyes.

'We can hold it together,' she said. 'You must get on your horse.' She took his handkerchief from round his neck, knotting it with her own, and to make more bandage she ran to the roll of clothes behind his saddle and tore in halves a clean shirt. A handkerchief fell from it, which she seized also, and opening, saw her own initials by the hem. Then she remembered: she saw again their first meeting, the swollen river, the overset stage, the unknown horseman who carried her to the bank on his saddle and went away unthanked – her whole first adventure on that first day of her coming to this new country – and now she knew how her long-forgotten handkerchief had gone that day. She refolded it gently and put it back in his bundle, for there was enough bandage without it. She said not a word to him, and he placed a wrong meaning upon the look which she gave him as she returned to bind his shoulder.

'It don't hurt so much,' he assured her (though extreme pain was clearing his head for the moment, and he had been able to hold the cliff from turning). 'Yu' must not squander your pity.'

'Do not squander your strength,' said she.

'Oh, I could put up a pretty good fight now!' But he tottered in showing her how strong he was, and she told him that, after all, he was a child still.

'Yes,' he slowly said, looking after her as she went to bring his horse, 'the same child that wanted to touch the moon, I guess.' And during the slow climb down into the saddle from a rock to which she helped him he said, 'You have got to be the man all through this mess.'

She saw his teeth clenched and his drooping muscles compelled by will; and as he rode and she walked to lend him support, leading her horse by a backward-stretched left hand, she counted off the distance to him continually – the increasing gain, the lessening road, the landmarks nearing and dropping behind; here was the tree with the wasp-nest gone; now the burned cabin was passed; now the cottonwoods at the ford were in sight. He was silent, and held to the saddle horn, leaning more and more against his two hands clasped over it; and just after they had made the crossing he fell, without a sound, slipping to the grass, and his descent broken by her. But it started the blood a little, and she dared not leave him to seek help. She gave him the last of the flask and all the water he craved.

Revived, he managed to smile. 'Yu' see, I ain't worth keeping.'

'It's only a mile,' said she. So she found a log, a fallen trunk, and he crawled to that, and from there crawled to his saddle, and she marched on with him, talking, bidding him note the steps accomplished. For the next half-mile they went thus, the silent man clinched on the horse, and by his side the girl walking and cheering him forward, when suddenly he began to speak – 'I will say goodbye to you now, ma'am.'

She did not understand, at first, the significance of this.

'He is getting away,' pursued the Virginian. 'I must ask you to excuse me, ma'am.'

It was a long while since her lord had addressed her as 'ma'am'. As she looked at him in growing apprehension, he turned Monte and would have ridden away, but she caught the bridle.

'You must take me home,' said she, with ready inspiration. 'I am afraid of the Indians.'

'Why, you – why, they've all gone. There he goes. Ma'am – that hawss –'

'No,' said she, holding firmly his rein and quickening her step. 'A gentleman does not invite a lady to go out riding and leave her.'

His eyes lost their purpose. 'I'll cert'nly take you home. That sorrel
has gone in there by the wallow, and Judge Henry will understand.' With
his eyes watching imaginary objects, he rode and rambled, and it was now
the girl who was silent, except to keep his mind from its half-fixed idea of
the sorrel. As he grew more fluent she hastened still more, listening to
head off that notion of return, skilfully inventing questions to engage
him, so that when she brought him to her gate she held him in a manner
subjected, answering faithfully the shrewd unrealities which she devised,
whatever makeshifts she could summon to her mind; and next she had
got him inside her dwelling and set him down docile, but now completely
wandering; and then – no help was at hand, even here. She had made sure
of aid from next door, and there she hastened, to find the Taylor's cabin
locked and silent; and this meant that parents and children were gone to
drive; nor might she be luckier at her next nearest neighbours', should
she travel the intervening mile to fetch them. With a mind jostled once
more into uncertainty, she returned to her room, and saw a change in
him already. Illness had stridden upon him; his face was not as she had
left it, and the whole body, the splendid supple horseman, showed
sickness in every line and limb, its spurs and pistol and bold leather chaps
a mockery of trappings. She looked at him, and decision came back to
her, clear and steady. She supported him over to her bed and laid him on
it. His head sank flat, and his loose, nerveless arms stayed as she left them.
Then among her packing-boxes and beneath the little miniature, blue
and flaxen and gold upon its lonely wall, she undressed him. He was cold,
and she covered him to the face, and arranged the pillow, and got from its
box her scarlet and black Navajo blanket and spread it over him. There
was no more that she could do, and she sat down by him to wait. Among
the many and many things that came into her mind was a word he said to
her lightly a long while ago. 'Cowpunchers do not live long enough to
get old,' he had told her. And now she looked at the head upon the
pillow, grave and strong, but still the head of splendid, unworn youth.

At the distant jingle of the wagon in the lane she was out, and had met
her returning neighbours midway. They heard her with amazement, and
came in haste to the bedside; then Taylor departed to spread news of the
Indians and bring the doctor, twenty-five miles away. The two women
friends stood alone again, as they had stood in the morning when anger
had been between them.

'Kiss me, deary,' said Mrs Taylor. 'Now I will look after him – and
you'll need some looking after yourself.'

THE VIRGINIAN

But on returning from her cabin with what store she possessed of lint and stimulants, she encountered a rebel, independent as ever. Molly would hear no talk about saving her strength, would not be in any room but this one until the doctor should arrive; then perhaps it would be time to think about resting. So together the dame and the girl rinsed the man's wound and wrapped him in clean things, and did all the little that they knew – which was, in truth, the very thing needed. Then they sat watching him toss and mutter. It was no longer upon Indians or the sorrel horse that his talk seemed to run, or anything recent, apparently, always excepting his work. This flowingly merged with whatever scene he was inventing or living again, and he wandered unendingly in that incompatible world we dream in. Through the medley of events and names, often thickly spoken, but rising at times to grotesque coherence, the listeners now and then could piece out the reference from their own knowledge. 'Monte', for example, continually addressed, and Molly heard her own name, but invariably as 'Miss Wood'; nothing less respectful came out, and frequently he answered someone as 'ma'am'. At these fragments of revelation Mrs Taylor abstained from speech, but eyed Molly Wood with caustic reproach. As the night wore on, short lulls of silence intervened, and the watchers were deceived into hope that the fever was abating. And when the Virginian sat quietly up in bed, essayed to move his bandage, and looked steadily at Mrs Taylor, she rose quickly and went to him with a question as to how he was doing.

'Rise on your laigs, you polecat,' said he, 'and tell them you're a liar.'

The good dame gasped, then bade him lie down, and he obeyed her with that strange double understanding of the delirious; for even while submitting, he muttered 'liar', 'polecat', and then 'Trampas'.

At that name light flashed on Mrs Taylor, and she turned to Molly; and there was the girl struggling with a fit of mirth at his speech; but the laughter was fast becoming a painful seizure, Mrs Taylor walked Molly up and down, speaking immediately to arrest her attention.

'You might as well know it,' she said. 'He would blame me for speaking of it, but where's the harm all this while after? And you would never hear it from his mouth. Molly, child, they say Trampas would kill him if he dared, and that's on account of you.'

'I never saw Trampas,' said Molly, fixing her eyes upon the speaker.

'No, deary. But before a lot of men – Taylor has told me about it – Trampas spoke disrespectfully of you, and before them all he made Trampas say he was a liar. That is what he did when you were almost a stranger among us, and he had not started seeing so much of you. I expect Trampas is the only enemy he ever had in this country. But he would never let you know about that.'

'No,' whispered Molly; 'I did not know.'

'Steve!' the sick man now cried out, in poignant appeal. 'Steve!' To the women it was a name unknown – unknown as was also this deep inward tide of feeling which he could no longer conceal, being himself no longer. 'No, Steve,' he said next, and muttering followed. 'It ain't so!' he shouted; and then cunningly in a lowered voice, 'Steve, I have lied for you.'

In time Mrs Taylor spoke some advice.

'You had better go to bed, child. You look about ready for the doctor yourself.'

'Then I will wait for him,' said Molly.

So the two nurses continued to sit until darkness at the windows weakened into grey, and the lamp was no more needed. Their patient was rambling again. Yet, into whatever scenes he went, there in some guise did the throb of his pain evidently follow him, and he lay hitching his great shoulder as if to rid it of the cumbrance. They waited for the doctor, not daring much more than to turn pillows and give what other ease they could; and then, instead of the doctor, came a messenger, about noon, to say he was gone on a visit some thirty miles beyond, where Taylor had followed to bring him here as soon as might be. At this Molly consented to rest and to watch, turn about; and once she was over in her friend's house lying down, they tried to keep her there. But the revolutionist could not be put down, and when, as a last pretext, Mrs Taylor urged the proprieties and conventions, the pale girl from Vermont laughed sweetly in her face and returned to sit by the sick man. With the approach of the second night his fever seemed to rise and master him more completely than they had yet seen it, and presently it so raged that the women called in stronger arms to hold him down. There were times when he broke out in the language of the round-up, and Mrs Taylor renewed her protests. 'Why,' said Molly, 'don't you suppose I knew they could swear?' So the dame, in deepening astonishment and affection, gave up these shifts at decorum. Nor did the delirium run into the intimate, coarse matters that she dreaded. The cowpuncher had lived like his kind, but his natural daily thoughts were clean, and came from the untamed but unstained mind of a man. And towards morning, as Mrs Taylor sat taking her turn, suddenly he asked had he been sick long, and looked at her with a quieted eye. The wandering seemed to drop from him at a stroke, leaving him altogether himself. He lay very feeble, and enquired once or twice of his state and how he came here; nor was anything left in his memory of even coming to the spring where he had been found.

When the doctor arrived, he pronounced that it would be long – or very short. He praised their clean water treatment; the wound was fortunately well up on the shoulder, and gave so far no bad signs; there were not any bad signs; and the blood and strength of the patient had been as few men's were; each hour was now an hour nearer certainty, and meanwhile – meanwhile the doctor would remain as long as he could. He had many enquiries to satisfy. Dusty fellows would ride up, listen to him, and reply, as they rode away, 'Don't yu' let him die, Doc.' And Judge Henry sent over from Sunk Creek to answer for any attendance or medicine that might help his foreman. The country was moved with concern and interest; and in Molly's ears its words of good feeling seemed to unite and sum up a burden, 'Don't yu' let him die, Doc.' The Indians who had done this were now in military custody. They had come unpermitted from a southern reservation, hunting, next thieving, and as the slumbering spirit roused in one or two of the young and ambitious, they had ventured this in the secret mountains, and perhaps had killed a trapper found there. Editors immediately reared a tall war out of it; but from five Indians in a guardhouse waiting punishment not even an editor can supply war for more than two editions, and if the recent alarm was still a matter of talk anywhere, it was not here in the sick-room. Whichever way the case should turn, it was through Molly alone (the doctor told her) that the wounded man had got this chance – this good chance, he repeated. And he told her she had not done a woman's part, but a man's part, and now had no more to do; no more till the patient got well, and could thank her in his own way, said the doctor, smiling, and supposing things that were not so – misled perhaps by Mrs Taylor.

'I'm afraid I'll be gone by the time he is well,' said Molly, coldly; and the discreet physician said ah, and that she would find Bennington quite a change from Bear Creek.

But Mrs Taylor spoke otherwise, and at that the girl said: 'I shall stay as long as I am needed. I will nurse him. I want to nurse him. I will do everything for him that I can!' she exclaimed, with force.

'And that won't be anything, deary,' said Mrs Taylor, harshly. 'A year of nursing don't equal a day of sweetheart.'

The girl took a walk – she was of no more service in the room at present – but she turned without going far, and Mrs Taylor spied her come to lean over the pasture fence and watch the two horses – that one the Virginian had 'gentled' for her, and his own Monte. During this suspense came a new call for the doctor, neighbours profiting by his visit to Bear Creek; and in his going away to them, even under promise of quick return, Mrs Taylor suspected a favourable sign. He kept his word as punctually as had been possible, arriving after some six hours with a confident face, and spending now upon the patient a care not needed, save to reassure the bystanders. He spoke his opinion that all was even better than he could have hoped it would be, so soon. Here was now the beginning of the fifth day; the wound's look was wholesome, no further delirium had come, and the fever had abated a degree while he was absent. He believed the serious danger-line lay behind, and (short of the unforeseen) the man's deep untainted strength would reassert its control. He had much blood to make, and must be cared for during weeks – three, four, five – there was no saying how long yet. These next few days it must be utter quiet for him; he must not talk nor hear anything likely to disturb him; and then the time for cheerfulness and gradual company would come – sooner than later, the doctor hoped. So he departed, and sent next day some bottles, with further cautions regarding the wound and dirt, and to say he should be calling the day after tomorrow.

Upon that occasion he found two patients. Molly Wood lay in bed at Mrs Taylor's, filled with apology and indignation. With little to do, and deprived of the strong stimulant of anxiety and action, her strength had quite suddenly left her, so that she had spoken only in a sort of whisper. But upon waking from a long sleep, after Mrs Taylor had taken her firmly, almost severely, in hand, her natural voice had returned, and now the chief treatment the doctor gave her was a sort of scolding, which it pleased Mrs Taylor to hear. The doctor even dropped a phrase concerning the arrogance of strong nerves in slender bodies, and of undertaking several people's work when several people were at hand to do it for themselves, and this pleased Mrs Taylor remarkably. As for the wounded man, he was behaving himself properly. Perhaps in another week he could be moved to a more cheerful room. Just now, with cleanliness and pure air, any barn would do.

'We are real lucky to have such a sensible doctor in the country,' Mrs Taylor observed, after the physician had gone.

'No doubt,' said Molly. 'He said my room was a barn.'

'That's what you've made it, deary. But sick men don't notice much.'

Nevertheless, one may believe, without going widely astray, that illness, so far from veiling, more often quickens the perceptions – at any rate those of the naturally keen. On a later day – and the interval was brief – while Molly was on her second drive to take the air with Mrs Taylor, that lady informed her that the sick man had noticed. 'And I could not tell him things liable to disturb him,' said she, 'and so I – well, I expect I just didn't exactly tell him the facts. I said yes, you were packing up for a little visit to your folks. They had not seen you for quite a while, I said. And he looked at those boxes kind of silent like.'

'There's no need to move him,' said Molly. 'It is simpler to move them – the boxes. I could take out some of my things, you know, just while he has to be kept there. I mean – you see, if the doctor says the room should be cheerful – '

'Yes, deary.'

'I will ask the doctor next time,' said Molly, 'if he believes I am – competent – to spread a rug upon a floor.' Molly's references to the doctor were usually acid these days. And this he totally failed to observe, telling her when he came, why, to be sure! the very thing! And if she could play cards or read aloud, or afford any other light distractions, provided they did not lead the patient to talk and tire himself, that she would be most useful. Accordingly she took over the cribbage-board, and came with unexpected hesitation face to face again with the swarthy man she had saved and tended. He was not so swarthy now, but neat, with chin clean, and hair and moustache trimmed and smooth, and he sat propped among pillows watching for her.

'You are better,' she said, speaking first, and with uncertain voice.

'Yes. They have given me awdehs not to talk,' said the Southerner, smiling.

'Oh, yes. Please do not talk – not today.'

'No. Only this – ' he looked at her, and saw her seem to shrink, 'thank you for what you have done,' he said simply.

She took tenderly the hand he stretched to her; and upon these terms they set to work at cribbage. She won, and won again, and the third time laid down her cards and reproached him with playing in order to lose.

'No,' he said, and his eye wandered to the boxes. 'But my thoughts get away from me. I'll be strong enough to hold them on the cyards next time, I reckon.'

Many tones in his voice she had heard, but never the tone of sadness until today.

Then they played a little more, and she put away the board for this first time.

'You are going now?' he asked.

'When I have made this room look a little less forlorn. They haven't wanted to meddle with my things, I suppose.' And Molly stooped once again among the chattels destined for Vermont. Out they came; again the bearskin was spread on the floor, various possessions and ornaments went back into their ancient niches, the shelves grew comfortable with books, and, last, some flowers were stood on the table.

'More like old times,' said the Virginian, but sadly.

'It's too bad,' said Molly, 'you had to be brought into such a looking place.'

'And your folks waiting for you,' said he.

'Oh, I'll pay my visit later,' said Molly, putting the rug a trifle straighter.

'May I ask one thing?' pleaded the Virginian, and at the gentleness of his voice her face grew rosy, and she fixed her eyes on him with a sort of dread.

'Anything that I can answer,' said she.

'Oh, yes. Did I tell yu' to quit me, and did yu' load up my gun and stay? Was that a real business? I have been mixed up in my haid.'

'That was real,' said Molly. 'What else was there to do?'

'Just nothing – for such as you!' he exclaimed. 'My haid has been mighty crazy; and that little grandmother of yours yondeh, she – but I can't just quite catch a-hold of these things ' – he passed a hand over his forehead – 'so many – or else one right along – well, it's all foolishness!' he concluded, with something almost savage in his tone. And after she had gone from the cabin he lay very still, looking at the miniature on the wall.

He was in another sort of mood the next time, cribbage not interesting him in the least. 'Your folks will be wondering about you,' said he.

'I don't think they will mind which month I go to them,' said Molly. 'Especially when they know the reason.'

'Don't let me keep you, ma'am,' said he. Molly stared at him; but he pursued, with the same edge lurking in his slow words: 'Though I'll never forget. How could I forget any of all you have done – and been? If there had been none of this, why, I had enough to remember! But please don't stay, ma'am. We'll say I had a claim when yu' found me pretty well dead, but I'm gettin' well, yu' see – right smart, too!'

'I can't understand, indeed I can't,' said Molly, 'why you're talking so!'

He seemed to have certain moods when he would address her as 'ma'am', and this she did not like, but could not prevent.

'Oh, a sick man is funny. And yu' know I'm grateful to you.'

'Please say no more about that, or I shall go this afternoon. I don't want to go. I am not ready. I think I had better read something now.'

'Why, yes. That's cert'nly a good notion. Why, this is the best show you'll ever get to give me education. Won't yu' please try that *Emma* book now, ma'am? Listening to you will be different.' This was said with softness and humility.

Uncertain – as his gravity often left her – precisely what he meant by what he said, Molly proceeded with *Emma*; slackly at first, but soon with the enthusiasm that Miss Austen invariably gave her. She held the volume and read away at it, commenting briefly, and then, finishing a chapter of the sprightly classic, found her pupil slumbering peacefully. There was no uncertainty about that.

'You couldn't be doing a healthier thing for him, deary,' said Mrs Taylor. 'If it gets to make him wakeful, try something harder.' This was the lady's scarcely sympathetic view.

But it turned out to be not obscurity in which Miss Austen sinned.

When Molly next appeared at the Virginian's threshold, he said plaintively, 'I reckon I am a dunce.' And he sued for pardon. 'When I waked up,' he said, 'I was ashamed of myself for a plumb half-hour.' Nor could she doubt this day that he meant what he said. His mood was again serene and gentle, and without referring to his singular words that had distressed her, he made her feel his contrition, even in his silence. 'I am right glad you have come,' he said. And as he saw her going to the bookshelf, he continued, with diffidence: 'As regyards that *Emma* book, yu' see – yu' see, the doin's and sayin's of folks like them are above me. But I think' (he spoke most diffidently), 'if yu' could read me something that was *about* something, I – I'd be liable to keep awake.' And he smiled with a certain shyness.

'Something *about* something?' queried Molly, at a loss.

'Why, yes. Shakespeare. *Henry the Fourth*. The British king is fighting, and there is his son the prince. He cert'nly must have been a jimdandy boy if that is all true. Only he would go around town with a mighty triflin' gang. They sported and they held up citizens. And his father hated his travelling with trash like them. It was right natural – the boy and the old man! But the boy showed himself a man too. He killed a big fighter on the other side who was another jimdandy – and he was sorry for having it to do.' The Virginian warmed to his recital. 'I understand most all of that. There was a fat man kept everybody laughing. He was awful natural too; except yu' don't commonly meet 'em so fat. But the prince – that play is bedrock, ma'am! Have you got something like that?'

'Yes, I think so,' she replied. 'I believe I see what you would appreciate.'

She took her Browning, her idol, her imagined affinity. For the pale decadence of New England had somewhat watered her good old Revolutionary blood too, and she was inclined to think under glass and to live underdone – when there were no Indians to shoot! She would have joyed to venture 'Paracelsus' on him, and some lengthy rhymed discourses; and she fondly turned leaves and leaves of her pet doggerel analytics. 'Pippa Passes' and others she had to skip, from discreet motives – pages which he would have doubtless stayed awake at; but she chose a poem at length. This was better than *Emma*, he pronounced. And short. The horse was a good horse. He thought a man whose horse must not play out on him would watch the ground he was galloping over for holes, and not be likely to see what colour the rims of his animal's eye-sockets were. You could not see them if you sat as you ought to for such a hard ride. Of the next piece that she read him he thought still better. 'And it is short,' said he. 'But the last part drops.'

Molly instantly exacted particulars.

'The soldier should not have told the general he was killed,' stated the cowpuncher.

'What should he have told him, I'd like to know?' said Molly.

'Why, just nothing. If the soldier could ride out of the battle all shot up, and tell his general about their takin' the town – that was being gritty, yu' see. But that truck at the finish – will yu' please say it again?'

So Molly read –

> ' "You're wounded!" "Nay," the soldier's pride
>   Touched to the quick, he said,
> "I'm killed, sire!" And, his chief beside,
>   Smiling the boy fell dead.'

' "Nay, I'm killed, sire," ' drawled the Virginian, amiably; for (symptom of convalescence) his freakish irony was revived in him. 'Now a man who was man enough to act like he did, yu' see, would fall dead without mentioning it.'

None of Molly's sweet girlfriends had ever thus challenged Mr Browning. They had been wont to cluster over him with a joyous awe that deepened proportionally with their misunderstanding. Molly paused to consider this novelty of view about the soldier. 'He was a Frenchman, you know,' she said, under inspiration.

'A Frenchman,' murmured the grave cowpuncher. 'I never knowed a Frenchman, but I reckon they might perform that class of foolishness.'

'But why was it foolish?' she cried. 'His soldier's pride – don't you see?'

'No.'

Molly now burst into a luxury of discussion. She leaned towards her cowpuncher with bright eyes searching his; with elbow on knee and hand propping chin, her lap became a slant, and from it Browning the poet slid and toppled, and lay unrescued. For the slow cowpuncher unfolded his notions of masculine courage and modesty (though he did not deal in such high-sounding names), and Molly forgot everything to listen to him, as he forgot himself and his inveterate shyness and grew talkative to her. 'I would never have supposed that!' she would exclaim as she heard him; or, presently again, 'I never had such an idea!' And her mind opened with delight to these new things which came from the man's mind so simple and direct. To Browning they did come back, but the Virginian, though interested, conceived a dislike for him. 'He is a smarty,' said he, once or twice.

'Now here is something,' said Molly. 'I have never known what to think.'

'Oh, Heavens!' murmured the sick man, smiling. 'Is it short?'

'Very short. Now please attend.' And she read him twelve lines about a lover who rowed to a beach in the dusk, crossed a field, tapped at a pane, and was admitted.

'That is the best yet,' said the Virginian. 'There's only one thing yu' can think about that.'

'But wait,' said the girl, swiftly. 'Here is how they parted –

> Round the cape of a sudden came the sea,
>   And the sun looked over the mountain's rim:
>   And straight was a path of gold for him,
>   And the need of a world of men for me.'

'That is very, very true,' murmured the Virginian, dropping his eyes from the girl's intent ones.

'Had they quarrelled?' she enquired.

'Oh, no!'

'But –'

'I reckon he loved her very much.'

'Then you're sure they hadn't quarrelled?'

'Dead sure, ma'am. He would come back afteh he had played some more of the game.'

'The game?'

'Life, ma'am. Whatever he was a-doin' in the world of men. That's a bedrock piece, ma'am!'

'Well, I don't see why you think it's so much better than some of the others.'

'I could sca'cely explain,' answered the man. 'But that writer does know something.'

'I am glad they hadn't quarrelled,' said Molly, thoughtfully. And she began to like having her opinions refuted.

His bandages, becoming a little irksome, had to be shifted, and this turned their discourse from literature to Wyoming; and Molly enquired, had he ever been shot before? Only once, he told her. 'I have been lucky in having few fusses,' said he. 'I hate them. If a man has to be killed – '

'You never – ' broke in Molly. She had started back a little. 'Well,' she added hastily, 'don't tell me if – '

'I shouldn't wonder if I got one of those Indians,' he said quietly. 'But I wasn't waitin' to see! But I came mighty near doing for a white man that day. He had been hurtin' a hawss.'

'Hurting?' said Molly.

'Injurin'. I will not tell yu' about that. It would hurt yu' to hear such things. But hawsses – don't they depend on us? Ain't they somethin' like children? I did not lay up the man very bad. He was able to travel 'most right away. Why, you'd have wanted to kill him yourself!'

So the Virginian talked, nor knew what he was doing to the girl. Nor was she aware of what she was receiving from him as he unwittingly spoke himself out to her in these Browning meetings they held each day. But Mrs Taylor grew pleased. The kindly dame would sometimes cross the road to see if she were needed, and steal away again after a peep at the window. There, inside, among the restored home treasures, sat the two: the rosy alert girl, sweet as she talked or read to him; and he, the grave, half-weak giant among his wraps, watching her.

Of her delayed home visit he never again spoke, either to her or to Mrs Taylor; and Molly veered aside from any trend of talk she foresaw was leading towards that subject. But in those hours when no visitors came, and he was by himself in the quiet, he would lie often sombrely contemplating the girl's room, her little dainty knick-knacks, her home photographs, all the delicate manifestations of what she came from and what she was. Strength was flowing back into him each day, and Judge Henry's latest messenger had brought him clothes and mail from Sunk Creek and many enquiries of kindness, and returned taking the news of the cowpuncher's improvement, and how soon he would be permitted the fresh air. Hence Molly found him waiting in a flannel shirt of highly becoming shade, and with a silk handkerchief knotted round his throat; and he told her it was good to feel respectable again.

She had come to read to him for the allotted time; and she threw around his shoulders the scarlet and black Navajo blanket, striped with its splendid zigzags of barbarity. Thus he half sat, half leaned, languid but at ease. In his lap lay one of the letters brought over by the messenger; and though she was midway in a book that engaged his full attention – *David Copperfield* – his silence and absent look this morning stopped her, and she accused him of not attending.

'No,' he admitted; 'I am thinking of something else.'

She looked at him with that apprehension which he knew.

'It had to come,' said he. 'And today I see my thoughts straighter than I've been up to managing since – since my haid got clear. And now I must say these thoughts – if I can, if I can!' He stopped. His eyes were intent upon her; one hand was gripping the arm of his chair.

'You promised – ' trembled Molly.

'I promised you should love me,' he sternly interrupted. 'Promised that to myself. I have broken that word.'

She shut *David Copperfield* mechanically, and grew white.

'Your letter has come to me hyeh,' he continued, gentle again.

'My – ' She had forgotten it.

'The letter you wrote to tell me goodbye. You wrote it a little while ago – not a month yet, but it's away and away long gone for me.'

'I have never let you know – ' began Molly.

'The doctor,' he interrupted once more, but very gently now, 'he gave awdehs I must be kept quiet. I reckon yu' thought tellin' me might – '

'Forgive me!' cried the girl. 'Indeed I ought to have told you sooner! Indeed I had no excuse!'

'Why, should yu' tell me if yu' preferred not? You had written. And you speak' (he lifted the letter) 'of never being able to repay kindness; but you have turned the tables. I can never repay you by anything! by anything! So I had figured I would just jog back to Sunk Creek and let you get away, if you did not want to say that kind of goodbye. For I saw the boxes. Mrs Taylor is too nice a woman to know the trick of lyin', and she could not deceive me. I have knowed yu' were going away for good ever since I saw those boxes. But now hyeh comes your letter, and it seems no way but I must speak. I have thought a deal, lyin' in this room. And – today – I can say what I have thought. I could not make you happy.' He stopped, but she did not answer. His voice had grown softer than whispering, but yet was not a whisper. From its quiet syllables she turned away, blinded with sudden tears.

'Once, I thought love must surely be enough,' he continued. 'And I thought if I could make you love me, you could learn me to be less – less – more your kind. And I think I could give you a pretty good sort of love. But that don't help the little mean pesky things of day by day that make roughness or smoothness for folks tied together so awful close. Mrs Taylor hyeh – she don't know anything better than Taylor does. She don't want anything he can't give her. Her friends will do for him and his for her. And when I dreamed of you in my home – ' he closed his eyes and drew a long breath. At last he looked at her again. 'This is no country for a lady. Will yu' forget and forgive the bothering I have done?'

'Oh!' cried Molly. 'Oh!' And she put her hands to her eyes. She had risen and stood with her face covered.

'I surely had to tell you this all out, didn't I?' said the cowpuncher, faintly, in his chair.

'Oh!' said Molly again.

'I have put it clear how it is,' he pursued. 'I ought to have seen from the start I was not the sort to keep you happy.'

'But,' said Molly – 'but I – you ought – please try to keep me happy!' And sinking by his chair, she hid her face on his knees.

Speechless, he bent down and folded her round, putting his hands on the hair that had been always his delight. Presently he whispered – 'You have beat me; how can I fight this?'

She answered nothing. The Navajo's scarlet and black folds fell over both. Not with words, not even with meeting eyes, did the two plight their troth in this first new hour. So they remained long, the fair head nesting in the great arms, and the black head laid against it, while over the silent room presided the little Grandmother Stark in her frame, rosy, blue, and flaxen, not quite familiar, not quite smiling.

CHAPTER 28

No Dream to Wake From

For a long while after she had left him, he lay still, stretched in his chair. His eyes were fixed steadily upon the open window and the sunshine outside. There he watched the movement of the leaves upon the green cottonwoods. What had she said to him when she went? She had said, 'Now I know how unhappy I have been.' These sweet words he repeated to himself over and over, fearing in some way that he might lose them. They almost slipped from him at times; but with a jump of his mind he caught them again and held them – and then – 'I'm not all strong yet,' he murmured. 'I must have been very sick.' And, weak from his bullet wound and fever, he closed his eyes without knowing it. There were the cotton-woods again, waving, waving; and he felt the cool, pleasant air from the window. He saw the light draught stir the ashes in the great stone fireplace. 'I have been asleep,' he said. 'But she was cert'nly here herself. Oh, yes. Surely. She always has to go away every day because the doctor says – why, she was readin'!' he broke off, aloud. '*David Copperfield*.' There it was on the floor. 'Aha! nailed you anyway!' he said. 'But how scared I am of myself! – You're a fool. Of course it's so. No fever business could make yu' feel like this.'

His eye dwelt awhile on the fireplace, next on the deer horns, and next it travelled towards the shelf where her books were; but it stopped before reaching them.

'Better say off the names before I look,' said he. 'I've had a heap o' misleading visions. And – and supposin' – if this was just my sickness fooling me some more – I'd want to die. I would die! Now we'll see. If *Copperfield* is on the floor' (he looked stealthily to be sure that it was), 'then she was readin' to me when everything happened, and then there should be a hole in the book row, top, left. Top, left,' he repeated, and warily brought his glance to the place. 'Proved!' he cried. 'It's all so!'

He now noticed the miniature of Grandmother Stark. 'You are awful like her,' he whispered. 'You're cert'nly awful like her. May I kiss you too, ma'am?'

Then, tottering, he rose from his sick-chair. The Navajo blanket fell from his shoulders, and gradually, experimentally, he stood upright.

Helping himself with his hand slowly along the wall of the room, and round to the opposite wall with many a pause, he reached the picture, and very gently touched the forehead of the ancestral dame with his lips. 'I promise to make your little girl happy,' he whispered.

He almost fell in stooping to the portrait, but caught himself and stood carefully quiet, trembling, and speaking to himself. 'Where is your strength?' he demanded. 'I reckon it is joy that has unsteadied your laigs.'

The door opened. It was she, come back with his dinner.

'My Heavens!' she said; and setting the tray down, she rushed to him. She helped him back to his chair, and covered him again. He had suffered no hurt, but she clung to him; and presently he moved and let himself kiss her with fuller passion.

'I will be good,' he whispered.

You must,' she said. 'You looked so pale!'

'You are speakin' low like me,' he answered. 'But we have no dream we can wake from.'

Had she surrendered on this day to her cowpuncher, her wild man? Was she forever wholly his? Had the Virginian's fire so melted her heart that no rift in it remained? So she would have thought if any thought had come to her. But in his arms today, thought was lost in something more divine.

CHAPTER 29

Word to Bennington

They kept their secret for a while, or at least they had that special joy of believing that no one in all the world but themselves knew this that had happened to them. But I think that there was one person who knew how to keep a secret even better than these two lovers. Mrs Taylor made no remarks to anyone whatever. Nobody on Bear Creek, however, was so extraordinarily cheerful and serene. That peculiar severity which she had manifested in the days when Molly was packing her possessions, had now altogether changed. In these days she was endlessly kind and indulgent to her 'deary'. Although, as a housekeeper, Mrs Taylor believed in punctuality at meals, and visited her offspring with discipline when they were late without good and sufficient excuse, Molly was now exempt from the faintest hint of reprimand.

'And it's not because you're not her mother,' said George Taylor, bitterly. 'She used to get it, too. And we're the only ones that get it. There she comes, just as we're about ready to quit! Aren't you going to say *nothing* to her?'

'George,' said his mother, 'when you've saved a man's life it'll be time for you to talk.'

So Molly would come in to her meals with much irregularity; and her remarks about the imperfections of her clock met with no rejoinder. And yet one can scarcely be so severe as had been Mrs Taylor, and become wholly as mild as milk. There was one recurrent event that could invariably awaken hostile symptoms in the dame. Whenever she saw a letter arrive with the Bennington postmark upon it, she shook her fist at that letter.

'What's family pride?' she would say to herself. 'Taylor could be a Son of the Revolution if he'd a mind to. I wonder if she has told her folks yet.'

And when letters directed to Bennington would go out, Mrs Taylor would inspect every one as if its envelope ought to grow transparent beneath her eyes, and yield up to her its great secret if it had one. But in truth these letters had no great secret to yield up, until one day – yes; one day Mrs Taylor would have burst, were bursting a thing that people often did. Three letters were the cause of this emotion on Mrs Taylor's part; one addressed to Bennington, one to Dunbarton, and the third – here was the great excitement – to Bennington, but not in the little schoolmarm's delicate writing. A man's hand had traced those plain, steady vowels and consonants.

'It's come!' exclaimed Mrs Taylor, at this sight. 'He has written to her mother himself.'

That is what the Virginian had done, and here is how it had come about.

The sick man's convalescence was achieved. The weeks had brought back to him, not his whole strength yet – that could come only by many miles of open air on the back of Monte; but he was strong enough now to *get* strength. When a patient reaches this stage, he is out of the woods.

He had gone for a little walk with his nurse. They had taken (under the doctor's recommendation) several such little walks, beginning with a five-minute one, and at last today accomplishing three miles.

'No, it has not been too far,' said he. 'I am afraid I could walk twice as far.'

'Afraid?'

'Yes. Because it means I can go to work again. This thing we have had together is over.'

For reply, she leaned against him.

'Look at you!' he said. 'Only a little while ago you had to help me stand on my laigs. And now – ' For a while there was silence between them. 'I have never had a right down sickness before,' he presently went on. 'Not to remember, that is. If any person had told me I could *enjoy* such a thing – ' He said no more, for she reached up, and no more speech was possible.

'How long has it been?' he next asked her.

She told him.

'Well, if it could be forever – no. Not forever with no more than this. I reckon I'd be sick again! But if it could be forever with just you and me, and no one else to bother with. But any longer would not be doing right by your mother. She would have a right to think ill of me.'

'Oh!' said the girl. 'Let us keep it.'

'Not after I am gone. Your mother must be told.'

'It seems so – can't we – oh, why need anybody know?'

'Your mother ain't "anybody". She is your mother. I feel mighty responsible to her for what I have done.'

'But I did it!'

'Do you think so? Your mother will not think so. I am going to write to her today.'

'You! Write to my mother! Oh, then everything will be so different! They will all – ' Molly stopped before the rising visions of Bennington. Upon the fairytale that she had been living with her cowboy lover broke the voices of the world. She could hear them from afar. She could see the eyes of Bennington watching this man at her side. She could imagine the ears of Bennington listening for slips in his English. There loomed upon her the round of visits which they would have to make. The ringing of the doorbells, the waiting in drawing-rooms for the mistress to descend and utter her prepared congratulations, while her secret eye devoured the Virginian's appearance, and his manner of standing and sitting. He would be wearing gloves, instead of fringed gauntlets of buckskin. In a smooth black coat and waistcoat, how could they perceive the man he was? During those short formal interviews, what would they ever find out of the things that she knew about him? The things for which she was proud of him? He would speak shortly and simply; they would say, 'Oh, yes!' and 'How different you must find this from Wyoming!' – and then, after the door was shut behind his departing back they would say – He would be totally underrated, not in the least understood. Why should he be subjected to this? He should never be!

Now in all these half-formed, hurried, distressing thoughts which streamed through the girl's mind, she altogether forgot one truth. True it was that the voice of the world would speak as she imagined. True it was that in the eyes of her family and acquaintance this lover of her choice would be examined even more like a *specimen* than are other lovers upon these occasions: and all accepted lovers have to face this ordeal of being treated like specimens by the other family. But dear me! most of us manage to stand it, don't we? It isn't, perhaps, the most delicious experience that we can recall in connection with our engagement. But it didn't prove fatal. We got through it somehow. We dined with Aunt Jane, and wined with Uncle Joseph, and perhaps had two fingers given to us by old Cousin Horatio, whose enormous fortune was of the greatest importance to everybody. And perhaps fragments of the other family's estimate of us subsequently reached our own ears. But if a chosen lover cannot stand being treated as a specimen by the other family, he's a very weak vessel, and not worth any good girl's love. That's all I can say for him.

Now the Virginian was scarcely what even his enemy would term a weak vessel; and Molly's jealousy of the impression which he might make upon Bennington was vastly superfluous. She should have known that he would indeed care to make a good impression; but that such anxiety on his part would be wholly for her sake, that in the eyes of her friends she might stand justified in taking him for her wedded husband. So far as he was concerned apart from her, Aunt Jane and Uncle Joseph might say anything they pleased, or think anything they pleased. His character was open for investigation. Judge Henry would vouch for him.

This is what he would have said to his sweetheart had she but revealed to him her perturbations. But she did not reveal them; and they were not of the order that he with his nature was likely to divine. I do not know what good would have come from her speaking out to him, unless that perfect understanding between lovers which indeed is a good thing. But I do not believe that he could have reassured her; and I am certain that she could not have prevented his writing to her mother.

'Well, then,' she sighed at last, 'if you think so, I will tell her.'

That sigh of hers, be it well understood, was not only because of those far-off voices which the world would in consequence of her news be lifting presently. It came also from bidding farewell to the fairytale which she must leave now; that land in which she and he had been living close together alone, unhindered, unmindful of all things.

'Yes, you will tell her,' said her lover. 'And I must tell her too.'

'Both of us?' questioned the girl.

What would he say to her mother? How would her mother like such a letter as he would write to her? Suppose he should misspell a word? Would not sentences from him at this time – written sentences – be a further bar to his welcome acceptance at Bennington?

'Why don't you send messages by me?' she asked him.

He shook his head. 'She is not going to like it, anyway,' he answered. 'I must speak to her direct. It would be like shirking.'

Molly saw how true his instinct was here; and a little flame shot upward from the glow of her love and pride in him. Oh, if they could all only know that he was like this when you understood him! She did not dare say out to him what her fear was about this letter of his to her mother. She did not dare because – well, because she lacked a little faith. That is it, I am afraid. And for that sin she was her own punishment. For in this day, and in many days to come, the pure joy of her love was vexed and clouded, all through a little lack of faith; while for him, perfect in his faith, his joy was like crystal.

'Tell me what you're going to write,' she said.

He smiled at her. 'No.'

'Aren't you going to let me see it when it's done?'

'No.' Then a freakish look came into his eyes. 'I'll let yu' see anything I write to other women.' And he gave her one of his long kisses. 'Let's get through with it together,' he suggested, when they were once more in his sick-room, that room which she had given to him. 'You'll sit one side o' the table, and I'll sit the other, and we'll go ahaid; and pretty soon it will be done.'

'O dear!' she said. 'Yes, I suppose that is the best way.'

And so, accordingly, they took their places. The inkstand stood between them. Beside each of them she distributed paper enough, almost, for a presidential message. And pens and pencils were in plenty. Was this not the headquarters of the Bear Creek schoolmarm?

'Why, aren't you going to do it in pencil first?' she exclaimed, looking up from her vacant sheet. His pen was moving slowly, but steadily.

'No, I don't reckon I need to,' he answered, with his nose close to the paper. 'Oh, damnation, there's a blot!' He tore his spoiled beginning in small bits, and threw them into the fireplace. 'You've got it too full,' he commented; and taking the inkstand, he tipped a little from it out of the window. She sat lost among her false starts. Had she heard him swear, she would not have minded. She rather liked it when he swore. He possessed that quality in his profanity of not offending by it. It is quite wonderful how much worse the same word will sound in one man's lips than in another's. But she did not hear him. Her mind was among a litter of broken sentences. Each thought which she began ran out into the empty air, or came against some stone wall. So there she sat, her eyes now upon that inexorable blank sheet that lay before her, waiting, and now turned with vacant hopelessness upon the sundry objects in the room. And while she thus sat accomplishing nothing, opposite to her the black head bent down, and the steady pen moved from phrase to phrase.

She became aware of his gazing at her, flushed and solemn. That strange colour of the sea-water, which she could never name, was lustrous in his eyes. He was folding his letter.

'You have finished?' she said.

'Yes.' His voice was very quiet. 'I feel like an honester man.'

'Perhaps I can do something tonight at Mrs Taylor's,' she said, looking at her paper.

On it were a few words crossed out. This was all she had to show. At this set task in letter writing, the cowpuncher had greatly excelled the schoolmarm!

But that night, while he lay quite fast asleep in his bed, she was keeping vigil in her room at Mrs Taylor's.

Accordingly, the next day, those three letters departed for the mail, and Mrs Taylor consequently made her exclamation, 'It's come!'

On the day before the Virginian returned to take up his work at Judge Henry's ranch, he and Molly announced their news. What Molly said to Mrs Taylor and what Mrs Taylor said to her, is of no interest to us, though it was of much to them.

But Mr McLean happened to make a call quite early in the morning to enquire for his friend's health.

'Lin,' began the Virginian, 'there is no harm in your knowing an hour or so before the rest. I am – '

'Lord!' said Mr McLean, indulgently. 'Everybody has knowed that since the day she found yu' at the spring.'

'It was not so, then,' said the Virginian, crossly.

'Lord! Everybody has knowed it right along.'

'Hmp!' said the Virginian. 'I didn't know this country was that rank with gossips.'

Mr McLean laughed mirthfully at the lover. 'Well,' he said, 'Mrs McLean will be glad. She told me to give yu' her congratulations quite a while ago. I was to have 'em ready just as soon as ever yu' asked for 'em yourself.' Lin had been made a happy man some twelve months previous to this. And now, by way of an exchange of news, he added: 'We're expectin' a little McLean down on Box Elder. That's what you'll be expectin' some of these days, I hope.'

'Yes,' murmured the Virginian, 'I hope so too.'

'And I don't guess,' said Lin, 'that you and I will do much shufflin' of other folks' children any more.'

Whereupon he and the Virginian shook hands silently, and understood each other very well.

On the day that the Virginian parted with Molly, beside the weight of farewell which lay heavy on his heart, his thoughts were also grave with news. The cattle thieves had grown more audacious. Horses and cattle both were being missed, and each man began almost to doubt his neighbour.

'Steps will have to be taken soon by somebody, I reckon,' said the lover.

'By you?' she asked quickly.

'Most likely I'll get mixed up with it.'

'What will you have to do?'

'Can't say. I'll tell yu' when I come back.'

So did he part from her, leaving her more kisses than words to remember.

And what was doing at Bennington, meanwhile, and at Dunbarton? Those three letters which by their mere outside had so moved Mrs Taylor, produced by their contents much painful disturbance.

It will be remembered that Molly wrote to her mother, and to her great-aunt. That announcement to her mother was undertaken first. Its composition occupied three hours and a half, and it filled eleven pages, not counting a postscript upon the twelfth. The letter to the great-aunt took only ten minutes. I cannot pretend to explain why this one was so greatly superior to the other; but such is the remarkable fact. Its beginning, to be sure, did give the old lady a start; she had dismissed the cowboy from her probabilities.

'Tut, tut, tut!' she exclaimed out loud in her bedroom. 'She has thrown herself away on that fellow!'

But some sentences at the end made her pause and sit still for a long while. The severity upon her face changed to tenderness, gradually. 'Ah, me,' she sighed. 'If marriage were as simple as love!' Then she went slowly downstairs, and out into her garden, where she walked long between the box borders. 'But if she has found a great love,' said the old lady at length. And she returned to her bedroom, and opened an old desk, and read some old letters.

There came to her the next morning a communication from Bennington. This had been penned frantically by poor Mrs Wood. As soon as she had been able to gather her senses after the shock of her daughter's eleven pages and the postscript, the mother had poured out eight pages herself to the eldest member of the family. There had been, indeed, much excuse for the poor lady. To begin with, Molly had constructed her whole opening page with the express and merciful intention of preparing her mother. Consequently, it made no sense whatever. Its effect was the usual effect of remarks designed to break a thing gently. It merely made Mrs Wood's head swim, and filled her with a sickening dread. 'Oh, mercy, Sarah,' she had cried, 'come here. What does this mean?' And then, fortified by her elder daughter, she had turned over that first page and found what it meant on the top of the second. 'A savage with knives and pistols!' she wailed. 'Well, mother, I always told you so,' said her daughter Sarah. 'What is a foreman?' exclaimed the mother. 'And who is Judge Henry?' 'She has taken a sort of upper servant,' said Sarah. 'If it is allowed to go as far as a wedding, I doubt if I can bring myself to be present.' (This threat she proceeded to make to Molly, with results that shall be set forth in their proper place.) 'The man appears to have written to me himself,' said Mrs Wood. 'He knows no better,' said Sarah. 'Bosh!' said Sarah's husband later. 'It was a very manly thing to do.' Thus did consternation rage in the house at Bennington. Molly might have spared herself the many assurances that she gave concerning the universal esteem in which her cowpuncher was held, and the fair prospects which were his. So, in the first throes of her despair, Mrs Wood wrote those eight not maturely considered pages to the great-aunt.

'Tut, tut, tut!' said the great-aunt as she read them. Her face was much more severe today. 'You'd suppose,' she said, 'that the girl had been kidnapped! Why, she has kept him waiting three years!' And then she read more, but soon put the letter down with laughter. For Mrs Wood had repeated in writing that early outburst of hers about a savage with knives and pistols. 'Law!' said the great-aunt. 'Law, what a fool Lizzie is!'

So she sat down and wrote to Mrs Wood a wholesome reply about putting a little more trust in her own flesh and blood, and reminding her among other things that General Stark had himself been wont to carry knives and pistols owing to the necessities of his career, but that he had occasionally taken them off, as did probably this young man in Wyoming. 'You had better send me the letter he has written you,' she concluded. 'I shall know much better what to think after I have seen that.'

It is not probable that Mrs Wood got much comfort from this communication; and her daughter Sarah was actually enraged by it. 'She grows more perverse as she nears her dotage,' said Sarah. But the Virginian's letter was sent to Dunbarton, where the old lady sat herself down to read it with much attention.

Here is what the Virginian had said to the unknown mother of his sweetheart.

Mrs John Stark Wood
Bennington, Vermont

MADAM – If your daughter Miss Wood has ever told you about her saving a man's life here when some Indians had shot him that is the man who writes to you now. I don't think she can have told you right about that affair for she is the only one in this country who thinks it was a little thing. So I must tell you it, the main points. Such an action would have been thought highly of in a Western girl, but with Miss Wood's raising nobody had a right to expect it.

'Indeed!' snorted the great-aunt. 'Well, he would be right, if I had not had a good deal more to do with her "raising" than ever Lizzie had.' And she went on with the letter.

I was starting in to die when she found me. I did not know anything then, and she pulled me back from where I was half in the next world. She did not know but what Indians would get her too but I could not make her leave me. I am a heavy man one hundred and seventy-three stripped when in full health. She lifted me herself from the ground me helping scarce any for there was not much help in me that day. She washed my wound and brought me to with her own whiskey. Before she could get me home I was out of my head but she kept me on my horse somehow and talked wisely to me so I minded her and did not go clean crazy till she had got me safe to bed. The doctor says I would have died all the same if she had not nursed me the way she did. It made me love her more which I did not know I could. But there is no end, for this writing it down makes me love her more as I write it.

And now Mrs Wood I am sorry this will be bad news for you to hear. I know you would never choose such a man as I am for her for I have got no education and must write humble against my birth. I wish I could make the news easier but truth is the best.

I am of old stock in Virginia English and one Scotch Irish grandmother my father's father brought from Kentucky. We have always stayed at the same place farmers and hunters not bettering our lot and very plain. We have fought when we got the chance, under Old Hickory and in Mexico and my father and two brothers were killed in the Valley sixty-four. Always with us one son has been apt to run away and I was the one this time. I had too much older brothering to suit me. But now I am doing well being in full sight of prosperity and not too old and very strong my health having stood the sundries it has been put through. She shall teach school no more when she is mine. I wish I could make this news easier for you Mrs Wood. I do not like promises I have heard so many. I will tell any man of your family anything he likes to ask me, and Judge Henry would tell you about my reputation. I have seen plenty rough things but can say I have never killed for pleasure or profit and am not one of that kind, always preferring peace. I have had to live in places where they had courts and lawyers so called but an honest man was all the law you could find in five hundred miles. I have not told her about those things not because I am ashamed of them but there are so many things too dark for a girl like her to hear about.

I had better tell you the way I know I love Miss Wood. I am not a boy now, and women are no new thing to me. A man like me who has travelled meets many of them as he goes and passes on but I stopped when I came to Miss Wood. That is three years but I have not gone on. What right has such as he? you will say. So did I say it after she had saved my life. It was hard to get to that point and keep there with her around me all day. But I said to myself you have bothered her for three years with your love and if you let your love bother her you don't love her like you should and you must quit for her sake who has saved your life. I did not know what I was going to do with my life after that but I supposed I could go somewhere and work hard and so Mrs Wood I told her I would give her up. But she said no. It is going to be hard for her to get used to a man like me –

But at this point in the Virginian's letter, the old great-aunt could read no more. She rose, and went over to that desk where lay those faded letters of her own. She laid her head down upon the package, and as her tears flowed quietly upon it, 'O dear,' she whispered, 'O dear! And this is what I lost!'

To her girl upon Bear Creek she wrote the next day. And this word from Dunbarton was like balm among the harsh stings Molly was receiving. The voices of the world reached her in gathering numbers, and not one of them save that great-aunt's was sweet. Her days were full of hurts; and there was no one by to kiss the hurts away. Nor did she even hear from her lover any more now. She only knew he had gone into lonely regions upon his errand.

* * *

That errand took him far: Across the Basin, among the secret places of Owl Creek, past the Washakie Needles, over the Divide to Gros Ventre, and so through a final barrier of peaks into the borders of East Idaho. There, by reason of his bidding me, I met him, and came to share in a part of his errand.

It was with no guide that I travelled to him. He had named a little station on the railroad, and from thence he had charted my route by means of landmarks. Did I believe in omens, the black storm that I set out in upon my horse would seem like one today. But I had been living in cities and smoke; and Idaho, even with rain, was delightful to me.

CHAPTER 30

A Stable on the Flat

When the first landmark, the lone clump of cottonwoods, came at length in sight, dark and blurred in the gentle rain, standing out perhaps a mile beyond the distant buildings, my whole weary body hailed the approach of repose. Saving the noon hour, I had been in the saddle since six, and now six was come round again. The ranch, my resting-place for this night, was a ruin – cabin, stable, and corral. Yet after the twelve hours of pushing on and on through silence, still to have silence, still to eat and go to sleep in it, perfectly fitted the mood of both my flesh and spirit. At noon, when for a while I had thrown off my long oilskin coat, merely the sight of the newspaper half crowded into my pocket had been a displeasing reminder of the railway, and cities, and affairs. But for its possible help to build fires, it would have come no farther with me. The great levels around me lay cooled and freed of dust by the wet weather, and full of sweet airs. Far in front the foothills rose through the rain, indefinite and mystic. I wanted no speech with anyone, nor to be near human beings at all. I was steeped in a reverie as of the primal earth; even thoughts themselves had almost ceased motion. To lie down with wild animals, with elk and deer, would have made my waking dream complete; and since such dream could not be, the cattle around the deserted buildings, mere dots as yet across separating space, were my proper companions for this evening.

Tomorrow night I should probably be camping with the Virginian in the foothills. At his letter's bidding I had come eastward across Idaho, abandoning my hunting in the Saw Tooth Range to make this journey with him back through the Tetons. It was a trail known to him, and not to many other honest men. Horse Thief Pass was the name his letter gave it. Business (he was always brief) would call him over there at this time. Returning, he must attend to certain matters in the Wind River country. There I could leave by stage for the railroad, or go on with him the whole way back to Sunk Creek. He designated for our meeting the forks of a certain little stream in the foothills which today's ride had brought in sight. There would be no chance for him to receive an answer from me in the intervening time. If by a certain day – which was four days off still – I had not reached the forks, he would understand I had other plans. To me it was like living back in ages gone, this way of meeting my friend, this choice of a stream so far and lonely that its very course upon the maps was wrongly traced. And to leave behind all noise and mechanisms, and set out at ease, slowly, with one pack-horse, into the wilderness, made me feel that the ancient earth was indeed my mother and that I had found her again after being lost among houses, customs, and restraints. I should arrive three days early at the forks – three days of margin seeming to me a wise precaution against delays unforeseen. If the Virginian were not there, good; I could fish and be happy. If he were there but not ready to start, good; I could still fish and be happy. And remembering my Eastern helplessness in the year when we had met first, I enjoyed thinking how I had come to be trusted. In those days I had not been allowed to go from the ranch for so much as an afternoon's ride unless tied to him by a string so to speak; now I was crossing unmapped spaces with no guidance. The man who could do this was scarce any longer a 'tenderfoot'.

My vision, as I rode, took in serenely the dim foothills – tomorrow's goal – and nearer in the vast wet plain the clump of cottonwoods, and still nearer my lodging for tonight with the dotted cattle round it. And now my horse neighed. I felt his gait freshen for the journey's end, and leaning to pat his neck I noticed his ears no longer slack and inattentive, but pointing forward to where food and rest awaited both of us. Twice he neighed, impatiently and long; and as he quickened his gait still more, the pack-horse did the same, and I realised that there was about me still a spice of the tenderfoot: those dots were not cattle; they were horses.

My horse had put me in the wrong. He had known his kind from afar, and was hastening to them. The plainsman's eye was not yet mine; and I smiled a little as I rode. When was I going to know, as by instinct, the different look of horses and cattle across some two or three miles of plain?

These miles we finished soon. The buildings changed in their aspect as they grew to my approach, showing their desolation more clearly, and in some way bringing apprehension into my mood. And around them the horses, too, all standing with ears erect, watching me as I came – there was something about them; or was it the silence? For the silence which I had liked until now seemed suddenly to be made too great by the presence of the deserted buildings. And then the door of the stable opened, and men came out and stood, also watching me arrive. By the time I was dismounting more were there. It was senseless to feel as unpleasant as I did, and I strove to give to them a greeting that should sound easy. I told them that I hoped there was room for one more here tonight. Some of them had answered my greeting, but none of them answered this; and as I began to be sure that I recognised several of their strangely imperturbable faces, the Virginian came from the stable; and at that welcome sight my relief spoke out instantly.

'I am here, you see!'

'Yes, I do see.' I looked hard at him, for in his voice was the same strangeness that I felt in everything around me. But he was looking at his companions. 'This gentleman is all right,' he told them.

'That may be,' said one whom I now knew that I had seen before at Sunk Creek; 'but he was not due tonight.'

'Nor tomorrow,' said another.

'Nor yet the day after,' a third added.

The Virginian fell into his drawl. 'None of you was ever early for anything, I presume.'

One retorted, laughing, 'Oh, we're not suspicioning you of complicity.'

And another, 'Not even when we remember how thick you and Steve used to be.'

Whatever jokes they meant by this he did not receive as jokes. I saw something like a wince pass over his face, and a flush follow it. But he now spoke to me. 'We expected to be through before this,' he began. 'I'm right sorry you have come tonight. I know you'd have preferred to keep away.'

'We want him to explain himself,' put in one of the others. 'If he satisfies us, he's free to go away.'

'Free to go away!' I now exclaimed. But at the indulgence in their frontier smile I cooled down. 'Gentlemen,' I said, 'I don't know why my movements interest you so much. It's quite a compliment! May I get under shelter while I explain?'

No request could have been more natural, for the rain had now begun to fall in straight floods. Yet there was a pause before one of them said, 'He might as well.'

The Virginian chose to say nothing more; but he walked beside me into the stable. Two men sat there together, and a third guarded them. At that sight I knew suddenly what I had stumbled upon; and on the impulse I murmured to the Virginian – 'You're hanging them tomorrow.'

He kept his silence.

'You may have three guesses,' said a man behind me.

But I did not need them. And in the recoil of my insight the clump of cottonwoods came into my mind, black and grim. No other trees high enough grew within ten miles. This, then, was the business that the Virginian's letter had so curtly mentioned. My eyes went into all corners of the stable, but no other prisoners were here. I half expected to see Trampas, and I half feared to see Shorty; for poor stupid Shorty's honesty had not been proof against frontier temptations, and he had fallen away from the company of his old friends. Often of late I had heard talk at Sunk Creek of breaking up a certain gang of horse and cattle thieves that stole in one Territory and sold in the next, and knew where to hide in the mountains between. And now it had come to the point; forces had been gathered, a long expedition made, and here they were, successful under the Virginian's lead, but a little later than their calculations. And here was I, a little too early, and a witness in consequence. My presence seemed a simple thing to account for; but when I had thus accounted for it, one of them said with good nature – 'So you find us here, and we find you here. Which is the most surprised, I wonder?'

'There's no telling,' said I, keeping as amiable as I could; 'nor any telling which objects the most.'

'Oh, there's no objection here. You're welcome to stay. But not welcome to go, I expect. He ain't welcome to go, is he?'

By the answers that their faces gave him it was plain that I was not. 'Not till we are through,' said one.

'He needn't to see anything,' another added. 'Better sleep late tomorrow morning,' a third suggested to me.

I did not wish to stay here. I could have made some sort of camp apart from them before dark; but in the face of their needless caution I was helpless. I made no attempt to enquire what kind of spy they imagined I could be, what sort of rescue I could bring in this lonely country; my too early appearance seemed to be all that they looked at. And again my eyes sought the prisoners. Certainly there were only two. One was chewing tobacco, and talking now and then to his guard as if nothing were the matter. The other sat dull in silence, not moving his eyes; but his face worked, and I noticed how he continually moistened his dry lips. As I looked at these doomed prisoners, whose fate I was invited to sleep through tomorrow morning, the one who was chewing quietly nodded to me.

'You don't remember me?' he said.

It was Steve! Steve of Medicine Bow! The pleasant Steve of my first evening in the West. Some change of beard had delayed my instant recognition of his face. Here he sat sentenced to die. A shock, chill and painful, deprived me of speech.

He had no such weak feelings. 'Have yu' been to Medicine Bow lately?' he enquired. 'That's getting to be quite a while ago.'

I assented. I should have liked to say something natural and kind, but words stuck against my will, and I stood awkward and ill at ease, noticing idly that the silent one wore a grey flannel shirt like mine. Steve looked me over, and saw in my pocket the newspaper which I had brought from the railroad and on which I had pencilled a few expenses. He asked me, Would I mind letting him have it for a while? And I gave it to him eagerly, begging him to keep it as long as he wanted. I was overeager in my embarrassment. 'You need not return it at all,' I said; 'those notes are nothing. Do keep it.' He gave me a short glance and a smile. 'Thank you,' he said; 'I'll not need it beyond tomorrow morning.' And he began to search through it. 'Jake's election is considered sure,' he said to his companion, who made no response. 'Well, Fremont County owes it to Jake.' And I left him interested in the local news.

Dead men I have seen not a few times, even some lying pale and terrible after violent ends, and the edge of this wears off; but I hope I shall never again have to be in the company with men waiting to be killed. By this time tomorrow the grey flannel shirt would be buttoned round a corpse. Until what moment would Steve chew? Against such fancies as these I managed presently to barricade my mind, but I made a plea to be allowed to pass the night elsewhere, and I suggested the adjacent cabin. By their faces I saw that my words merely helped their distrust of me. The cabin leaked too much, they said; I would sleep drier here. One man gave it to me more directly: 'If you figured on camping in this stable, what has changed your mind?' How could I tell them that I shrunk from any contact with what they were doing, although I knew that only so could justice be dealt in this country? Their wholesome frontier nerves knew nothing of such refinements.

But the Virginian understood part of it. 'I am right sorry for your annoyance,' he said. And now I noticed he was under a constraint very different from the ease of the others.

After the twelve hours' ride my bones were hungry for rest. I spread my blankets on some straw in a stall by myself and rolled up in them; yet I lay growing broader awake, every inch of weariness stricken from my excited senses. For a while they sat over their councils, whispering cautiously, so that I was made curious to hear them by not being able; was it the names of Trampas and Shorty that were once or twice spoken? I could not be sure. I heard the whisperers cease and separate. I heard their boots as they cast them off upon the ground. And I heard the breathing of slumber begin and grow in the interior silence. To one after one sleep came, but not to me. Outside, the dull fall of the rain beat evenly, and in some angle dripped the spouting pulses of a leak. Sometimes a cold air blew in, bearing with it the keen wet odour of the sagebrush. On hundreds of other nights this perfume had been my last waking remembrance; it had seemed to help drowsiness; and now I lay staring, thinking of this. Twice through the hours the thieves shifted their positions with clumsy sounds, exchanging muffled words with their guard. So, often, had I heard other companions move and mutter in the darkness and lie down again. It was the very naturalness and usualness of every fact of the night – the stable straw, the rain outside, my familiar blankets, the cool visits of the wind – and with all this the thought of Steve chewing and the man in the grey flannel shirt, that made the hours unearthly and strung me tight with suspense. And at last I heard someone get up and begin to dress. In a little while I saw light suddenly through my closed eyelids, and then darkness shut again abruptly upon them. They had swung in a lantern and found me by mistake. I was the only one they did not wish to rouse. Moving and quiet talking set up around me, and they began to go out of the stable. At the gleams of new daylight which they let in my thoughts went to the clump of cottonwoods, and I lay still with hands and feet growing steadily cold. Now it was going to happen. I wondered how they would do it ; one instance had been described to me by a witness, but that was done from a bridge, and there had been but a single victim. This morning, would one have to wait and see the other go through with it first?

The smell of smoke reached me, and next the rattle of tin dishes. Breakfast was something I had forgotten, and one of them was cooking it now in the dry shelter of the stable. He was alone, because the talking and the steps were outside the stable, and I could hear the sounds of horses being driven into the corral and saddled. Then I perceived that the coffee was ready, and almost immediately the cook called them. One came in, shutting the door behind him as he re-entered, which the rest as they followed imitated; for at each opening of the door I saw the light of day leap into the stable and heard the louder sounds of the rain. Then the sound and the light would again be shut out, until someone at length spoke out bluntly, bidding the door be left open on account of the smoke. What were they hiding from? he asked. The runaways that had escaped? A laugh followed this sally, and the door was left open. Thus I learned that there had been more thieves than the two that were captured. It gave a little more ground for their suspicion about me and my anxiety to pass the night elsewhere. It cost nothing to detain me, and they were taking no chances, however remote.

The fresh air and the light now filled the stable, and I lay listening while their breakfast brought more talk from them. They were more at ease now than was I, who had nothing to do but carry out my rôle of slumber in the stall; they spoke in a friendly, ordinary way, as if this were like every other morning of the week to them. They addressed the prisoners with a sort of fraternal kindness, not bringing them pointedly into the conversation, nor yet pointedly leaving them out. I made out that they must all be sitting round the breakfast together, those who had to die and those who had to kill them. The Virginian I never heard speak. But I heard the voice of Steve; he discussed with his captors the sundry points of his capture.

'Do you remember a haystack?' he asked. 'Away up the south fork of Gros Ventre?'

'That was Thursday afternoon,' said one of the captors. 'There was a shower.'

'Yes. It rained. We had you fooled that time. I was laying on the ledge above to report your movements.'

Several of them laughed. 'We thought you were over on Spread Creek then.'

'I figured you thought so by the trail you took after the stack. Saturday we watched you turn your back on us up Spread Creek. We were snug among the trees the other side of Snake River. That was another time we had you fooled.'

They laughed again at their own expense. I have heard men pick to pieces a hand of whist with more antagonism.

Steve continued: 'Would we head for Idaho? Would we swing back over the Divide? You didn't know which! And when we generalled you on to that band of horses you thought was the band you were hunting – ah, we were a strong combination!' He broke off with the first touch of bitterness I had felt in his words.

'Nothing is any stronger than its weakest point.' It was the Virginian who said this, and it was the first word he had spoken.

'Naturally,' said Steve. His tone in addressing the Virginian was so different, so curt, that I supposed he took the weakest point to mean himself. But the others now showed me that I was wrong in this explanation.

'That's so,' one said. 'Its weakest point is where a rope or a gang of men is going to break when the strain comes. And you was linked with a poor partner, Steve.'

'You're right I was,' said the prisoner, back in his easy, casual voice.

'You ought to have got yourself separated from him, Steve.'

There was a pause. 'Yes,' said the prisoner, moodily. 'I'm sitting here because one of us blundered.' He cursed the blunderer. 'Lighting his fool fire queered the whole deal,' he added. As he again heavily cursed the blunderer, the others murmured to each other various 'I told you so's.'

'You'd never have built that fire, Steve,' said one. 'I said that when we spied the smoke,' said another. 'I said, "That's none of Steve's work, lighting fires and revealing to us their whereabouts."'

It struck me that they were plying Steve with compliments.

'Pretty hard to have the fool get away and you get caught,' a third suggested.

At this they seemed to wait. I felt something curious in all this last talk.

'Oh, did he get away?' said the prisoner, then.

Again they waited; and a new voice spoke huskily – 'I built that fire, boys.' It was the prisoner in the grey flannel shirt.

'Too late, Ed,' they told him kindly. 'You ain't a good liar.'

'What makes you laugh, Steve?' said someone.

'Oh, the things I notice.'

'Meaning Ed was pretty slow in backing up your play? The joke is really on you, Steve. You'd ought never to have cursed the fire-builder if you wanted us to believe he was present. But we'd not have done much to Shorty, even if we had caught him. All he wants is to be scared good and hard, and he'll go back into virtuousness, which is his nature when not travelling with Trampas.'

Steve's voice sounded hard now. 'You have caught Ed and me. That should satisfy you for one gather.'

'Well, we think different, Steve. Trampas escaping leaves this thing unfinished.'

'So Trampas escaped too, did he?' said the prisoner.

'Yes, Steve, Trampas escaped – this time; and Shorty with him – this time. We know it most as well as if we'd seen them go. And we're glad Shorty is loose, for he'll build another fire or do some other foolishness next time, and that's the time we'll get Trampas.'

Their talk drifted to other points, and I lay thinking of the skirmish that had played beneath the surface of their banter. Yes, the joke, as they put it, was on Steve. He had lost one point in the game to them. They were playing for names. He, being a chivalrous thief, was playing to hide names. They could only, among several likely confederates, guess Trampas and Shorty. So it had been a slip for him to curse the man who built the fire. At least, they so held it. For, they with subtlety reasoned, one curses the absent. And I agreed with them that Ed did not know how to lie well; he should have at once claimed the disgrace of having spoiled the expedition. If Shorty was the blunderer, then certainly Trampas was the other man; for the two were as inseparable as dog and master. Trampas had enticed Shorty away from good, and trained him in evil. It now struck me that after his single remark the Virginian had been silent throughout their shrewd discussion.

It was the other prisoner that I heard them next address. 'You don't eat any breakfast, Ed.'

'Brace up, Ed. Look at Steve, how hardy he eats!'

But Ed, it seemed, wanted no breakfast. And the tin dishes rattled as they were gathered and taken to be packed.

'Drink this coffee, anyway,' another urged; 'you'll feel warmer.'

These words almost made it seem like my own execution. My whole body turned cold in company with the prisoner's, and as if with a clank the situation tightened throughout my senses.

'I reckon if everyone's ready we'll start.' It was the Virginian's voice once more, and different from the rest. I heard them rise at his bidding, and I put the blanket over my head. I felt their tread as they walked out, passing my stall. The straw that was half under me and half out in the stable was stirred as by something heavy dragged or half lifted along over it. 'Look out, you're hurting Ed's arm,' one said to another, as the steps with tangled sounds passed slowly out. I heard another among those who followed say, 'Poor Ed couldn't swallow his coffee.' Outside they began getting on their horses; and next their hoofs grew distant, until all was silence round the stable except the dull, even falling of the rain.

CHAPTER 31

The Cottonwoods

I do not know how long I stayed there alone. It was the Virginian who came back, and as he stood at the foot of my blankets his eye, after meeting mine full for a moment, turned aside. I had never seen him look as he did now, not even in Pitchstone Canyon when we came upon the bodies of Hank and his wife. Until this moment we had found no chance of speaking together, except in the presence of others.

'Seems to be raining still,' I began after a little.

'Yes. It's a wet spell.'

He stared out of the door, smoothing his moustache.

It was again I that spoke. 'What time is it?'

He brooded over his watch. 'Twelve minutes to seven.'

I rose and stood drawing on my clothes.

'The fire's out,' said he; and he assembled some new sticks over the ashes. Presently he looked round with a cup.

'Never mind that for me,' I said.

'We've a long ride,' he suggested.

'I know. I've crackers in my pocket.'

My boots being pulled on, I walked to the door and watched the clouds. 'They seem as if they might lift,' I said. And I took out my watch.

'What time is it?' he asked.

'A quarter of – it's run down.'

While I wound it he seemed to be consulting his own.

'Well?' I enquired.

'Ten minutes past seven.'

As I was setting my watch he slowly said: 'Steve wound his all regular. I had to nightguard him till two.' His speech was like that of one in a trance: so, at least, it sounds in my memory today.

Again I looked at the weather and the rainy immensity of the plain. The foothills eastward where we were going were a soft yellow. Over the grey-green sagebrush moved shapeless places of light – not yet the uncovered sunlight, but spots where the storm was wearing thin; and wandering streams of warmth passed by slowly in the surrounding air. As I watched the clouds and the earth, my eyes chanced to fall on the distant clump of cottonwoods. Vapours from the enfeebled storm floated round them, and they were indeed far away; but I came inside and began rolling up my blankets.

'You will not change your mind?' said the Virginian by the fire. 'It is thirty-five miles.'

I shook my head, feeling a certain shame that he should see how unnerved I was.

He swallowed a hot cupful, and after it sat thinking; and presently he passed his hand across his brow, shutting his eyes. Again he poured out a cup, and emptying this, rose abruptly to his feet as if shaking himself free from something.

'Let's pack and quit here,' he said.

Our horses were in the corral and our belongings in the shelter of what had been once the cabin at this forlorn place. He collected them in silence while I saddled my own animal, and in silence we packed the two pack-horses, and threw the diamond hitch, and hauled tight the slack, damp ropes. Soon we had mounted, and as we turned into the trail I gave a look back at my last night's lodging.

The Virginian noticed me. 'Goodbye forever!' he interpreted.

'By God, I hope so!'

'Same here,' he confessed. And these were our first natural words this morning.

'This will go well,' said I, holding my flask out to him; and both of us took some, and felt easier for it and the natural words.

For an hour we had been shirking real talk, holding fast to the weather, or anything, and all the while that silent thing we were keeping off spoke plainly in the air around us and in every syllable that we uttered. But now we were going to get away from it; leave it behind in the stable, and set ourselves free from it by talking it out. Already relief had begun to stir in my spirits.

'You never did this before,' I said.

'No. I never had it to do.' He was riding beside me, looking down at his saddle horn.

'I do not think I should ever be able,' I pursued.

Defiance sounded in his answer. 'I would do it again this morning.'

'Oh, I don't mean that. It's all right here. There's no other way.'

'I would do it all over again the same this morning. Just the same.'

'Why, so should I – if I could do it at all.' I still thought he was justifying their justice to me.

He made no answer as he rode along, looking all the while at his saddle. But again he passed his hand over his forehead with that frown and shutting of the eyes.

'I should like to be sure I should behave myself if I were condemned,' I said next. For it now came to me – which should I resemble? Could I read the newspaper, and be interested in county elections, and discuss coming death as if I had lost a game of cards? Or would they have to drag me out? That poor wretch in the grey flannel shirt – 'It was bad in the stable,' I said aloud. For an after-shiver of it went through me.

A third time his hand brushed his forehead, and I ventured some sympathy.

'I'm afraid your head aches.'

'I don't want to keep seeing Steve,' he muttered.

'Steve!' I was astounded. 'Why he – why all I saw of him was splendid. Since it had to be. It was –'

'Oh, yes; Ed. You're thinking about him. I'd forgot him. So you didn't enjoy Ed?'

At this I looked at him blankly. 'It isn't possible that –'

Again he cut me short with a laugh almost savage. 'You needn't to worry about Steve. He stayed game.'

What then had been the matter that he should keep seeing Steve – that his vision should so obliterate from him what I still shivered at, and so shake him now? For he seemed to be growing more stirred as I grew less. I asked him no further questions, however, and we went on for several minutes, he brooding always in the same fashion, until he resumed with the hard indifference that had before surprised me – 'So Ed gave you feelings! Dumb ague and so forth.'

'No doubt we're not made the same way,' I retorted.

He took no notice of this. 'And you'd have been more comfortable if he'd acted same as Steve did. It cert'nly was bad seeing Ed take it that way, I reckon. And you didn't see him when the time came for business. Well, here's what it is: a man may be such a confirmed miscreant that killing's the only cure for him; but still he's your own species, and you don't want to have him fall around and grab your laigs and show you his fear naked. It makes you feel ashamed. So Ed gave you feelings, and Steve made everything right easy for you!' There was irony in his voice as he surveyed me, but it fell away at once into sadness. 'Both was miscreants. But if Steve had played the coward, too, it would have been a whole heap easier for me.' He paused before adding, 'And Steve was not a miscreant once.'

His voice had trembled, and I felt the deep emotion that seemed to gain upon him now that action was over and he had nothing to do but think. And his view was simple enough: you must die brave. Failure is a sort of treason to the brotherhood, and forfeits pity. It was Steve's perfect bearing that had caught his heart so that he forgot even his scorn of the other man.

But this was by no means all that was to come. He harked back to that notion of a prisoner helping to make it easy for his executioner. 'Easy plumb to the end,' he pursued, his mind reviewing the acts of the morning. 'Why, he tried to give me your newspaper. I didn't – '

'Oh, no,' I said hastily. 'I had finished with it.'

'Well, he took dying as naturally as he took living. Like a man should. Like I hope to.' Again he looked at the pictures in his mind. 'No play-acting nor last words. He just told goodbye to the boys as we led his horse under the limb – you needn't to look so dainty,' he broke off. 'You ain't going to get any more shocking particulars.'

'I know I'm white-livered,' I said with a species of laugh. 'I never crowd and stare when somebody is hurt in the street. I get away.'

He thought this over. 'You don't mean all of that. You'd not have spoke just that way about crowding and staring if you thought well of them that stare. Staring ain't courage; it's trashy curiosity. Now you did not have this thing – '

He had stretched out his hand to point, but it fell, and his utterance stopped, and he jerked his horse to a stand.

My nerves sprang like a wire at his suddenness, and I looked where he was looking. There were the cottonwoods, close in front of us. As we had travelled and talked we had forgotten them. Now they were looming within a hundred yards; and our trail lay straight through them.

'Let's go around them,' said the Virginian.

When we had come back from our circuit into the trail he continued: 'You did not have that thing to do. But a man goes through with his responsibilities – and I reckon you could.'

'I hope so,' I answered. 'How about Ed?'

'He was not a man, though we thought he was till this. Steve and I started punching cattle together at the Bordeaux outfit, north of Cheyenne. We did everything together in those days – work and play. Six years ago. Steve had many good points onced.'

We must have gone two miles before he spoke again. 'You prob'ly didn't notice Steve? I mean the way he acted to me?' It was a question, but he did not wait for my answer. 'Steve never said a word to me all through. He shunned it. And you saw how neighbourly he talked to the other boys.'

'Where have they all gone?' I asked.

He smiled at me. 'It cert'nly is lonesome now, for a fact.'

'I didn't know you felt it,' said I.

'Feel it! – they've went to the railroad. Three of them are witnesses in a case at Evanston, and the Judge wants our outfit at Medicine Bow. Steve shunned me. Did he think I was going back on him?'

'What if he did? You were not. And so nobody's going to Wind River but you?'

'No. Did you notice Steve would not give us any information about Shorty? That was right. I would have acted that way, too.' Thus, each time, he brought me back to the subject.

The sun was now shining warm during two or three minutes together, and gulfs of blue opened in the great white clouds. These moved and met among each other, and parted, like hands spread out, slowly weaving a spell of sleep over the day after the wakeful night storm. The huge contours of the earth lay basking and drying, and not one living creature, bird or beast, was in sight. Quiet was returning to my revived spirits, but there was none for the Virginian. And as he reasoned matters out aloud, his mood grew more overcast.

'You have a friend, and his ways are your ways. You travel together, you spree together confidentially, and you suit each other down to the ground. Then one day you find him putting his iron on another man's calf. You tell him fair and square those ways have never been your ways and ain't going to be your ways. Well, that does not change him any, for it seems he's disturbed over getting rich quick and being a big man in the Territory. And the years go on, until you are foreman of Judge Henry's ranch and he – is dangling back in the cottonwoods. What can he claim? Who made the choice? He cannot say, "Here is my old friend that I would have stood by". Can he say that?'

'But he didn't say it,' I protested.

'No. He shunned me.'

'Listen,' I said. 'Suppose while you were on guard he had whispered, "Get me off" – would you have done it?'

'No, sir!' said the Virginian, hotly.

'Then what do you want?' I asked. 'What did you want?'

He could not answer me – but I had not answered him, I saw; so I pushed it farther. 'Did you want endorsement from the man you were hanging? That's asking a little too much.'

But he had now another confusion. 'Steve stood by Shorty,' he said musingly. 'It was Shorty's mistake cost him his life, but all the same he didn't want us to catch – '

'You are mixing things,' I interrupted. 'I never heard you mix things before. And it was not Shorty's mistake.'

He showed momentary interest. 'Whose then?'

'The mistake of whoever took a fool into their enterprise.'

'That's correct. Well, Trampas took Shorty in, and Steve would not tell on him either.'

I still tried it, saying, 'They were all in the same boat.' But logic was useless; he had lost his bearings in a fog of sentiment. He knew, knew passionately, that he had done right; but the silence of his old friend to him through those last hours left a sting that no reasoning could assuage. 'He told goodbye to the rest of the boys; but not to me.' And nothing that I could point out in common sense turned him from the thread of his own argument. He worked round the circle again to self-justification. 'Was it him I was deserting? Was not the deserting done by him the day I spoke my mind about stealing calves? I have kept my ways the same. He is the one that took to new ones. The man I used to travel with is not the man back there. Same name, to be sure. And same body. But different in – and yet he had the memory! You can't never change your memory!'

He gave a sob. It was the first I had ever heard from him, and before I knew what I was doing I had reined my horse up to his and put my arm around his shoulders. I had no sooner touched him than he was utterly overcome. 'I knew Steve awful well,' he said.

Thus we had actually come to change places; for early in the morning he had been firm while I was unnerved, while now it was I who attempted to steady and comfort him.

I had the sense to keep silent, and presently he shook my hand, not looking at me as he did so. He was always very shy of demonstration. And he took to patting the neck of his pony. 'You Monte hawss,' said he, 'you think you are wise, but there's a lot of things you don't savvy.' Then he made a new beginning of talk between us.

'It is kind of pitiful about Shorty.'

'Very pitiful,' I said.

'Do you know about him?' the Virginian asked.

'I know there's no real harm in him, and some real good, and that he has not got the brains necessary to be a horse thief.'

'That's so. That's very true. Trampas has led him in deeper than his stature can stand. Now back East you can be middling and get along. But if you go to try a thing on in this Western country, you've got to do it *well*. You've got to deal cyards *well*; you've got to steal *well*; and if you claim to be quick with your gun, you must be quick, for you're a public temptation, and some man will not resist trying to prove he is the quicker. You must break all the Commandments *well* in this Western country, and Shorty should have stayed in Brooklyn, for he will be a novice his livelong days. You don't know about him? He has told me his circumstances. He don't remember his father, and it was like he could have claimed three or four. And I expect his mother was not much interested in him before or after he was born. He ran around, and when he was eighteen he got to be help to a grocery man. But a girl he ran with kept taking all his pay and teasing him for more, and so one day the grocery man caught Shorty robbing his till, and fired him. There wasn't no one to tell goodbye to, for the girl had to go to the country to see her aunt, she said. So Shorty hung around the store and kissed the grocery cat goodbye. He'd been used to feeding the cat, and she'd sit in his lap and purr, he told me. He sends money back to that girl now. This hyeh country is no country for Shorty, for he will be a conspicuous novice all his days.'

'Perhaps he'll prefer honesty after his narrow shave,' I said.

But the Virginian shook his head. 'Trampas has got hold of him.'

The day was now all blue above, and all warm and dry beneath. We had begun to wind in and rise among the first slopes of the foothills, and we had talked ourselves into silence. At the first running water we made a long nooning, and I slept on the bare ground. My body was lodged so fast and deep in slumber that when the Virginian shook me awake I could not come back to life at once; it was the clump of cottonwoods, small and far out in the plain below us, that recalled me.

'It'll not be watching us much longer,' said the Virginian. He made it a sort of joke; but I knew that both of us were glad when presently we rode into a steeper country, and among its folds and curvings lost all sight of the plain. He had not slept, I found. His explanation was that the packs needed better balancing, and after that he had gone up and down the stream on the chance of trout. But his haunted eyes gave me the real reason – they spoke of Steve, no matter what he spoke of; it was to be no short thing with him.

CHAPTER 32

Superstition Trial

We did not make thirty-five miles that day, nor yet twenty-five, for he had let me sleep. We made an early camp and tried some unsuccessful fishing, over which he was cheerful, promising trout tomorrow when we should be higher among the mountains. He never again touched or came near the subject that was on his mind, but while I sat writing my diary, he went off to his horse Monte, and I could hear that he occasionally talked to that friend.

Next day we swung southward from what is known to many as the Conant trail, and headed for that short cut through the Tetons which is known to but a few. Bitch Creek was the name of the stream we now followed, and here there was such good fishing that we idled; and the horses and I at least enjoyed ourselves. For they found fresh pastures and shade in the now plentiful woods; and the mountain odours and the mountain heights were enough for me when the fish refused to rise. This road of ours now became the road which the pursuit had taken before the capture. Going along, I noticed the footprints of many hoofs, rain-blurred but recent, and these were the tracks of the people I had met in the stable.

'You can notice Monte's,' said the Virginian. 'He is the only one that has his hind feet shod. There's several trails from this point down to where we have come from.'

We mounted now over a long slant of rock, smooth and of wide extent. Above us it went up easily into a little side canyon, but ahead, where our way was, it grew so steep that we got off and led our horses. This brought us to the next higher level of the mountain, a space of sagebrush more open, where the rain-washed tracks appeared again in the softer ground.

'Someone has been here since the rain,' I called to the Virginian, who was still on the rock, walking up behind the pack-horses.

'Since the rain!' he exclaimed. 'That's not two days yet.' He came and examined the footprints. 'A man and a hawss,' he said, frowning. 'Going the same way we are. How did he come to pass us, and us not see him?'

'One of the other trails,' I reminded him.

'Yes, but there's not many that knows them. They are pretty rough trails.'

'Worse than this one we're taking?'

'Not much; only how does he come to know any of them? And why don't he take the Conant trail that's open and easy and not much longer? One man and a hawss. I don't see who he is or what he wants here.'

'Probably a prospector,' I suggested.

'Only one outfit of prospectors has ever been here, and they claimed there was no mineral-bearing rock in these parts.'

We got back into our saddles with the mystery unsolved. To the Virginian it was a greater one, apparently, than to me; why should one have to account for every stray traveller in the mountains?

'That's queer, too,' said the Virginian. He was now riding in front of me, and he stopped, looking down at the trail. 'Don't you notice?'

It did not strike me.

'Why, he keeps walking beside his hawss; he don't get on him.'

Now we, of course, had mounted at the beginning of the better trail after the steep rock, and that was quite half a mile back. Still, I had a natural explanation. 'He's leading a pack-horse. He's a poor trapper, and walks.'

'Pack-horses ain't usually shod before and behind,' said the Virginian;

and sliding to the ground he touched the footprints. 'They are not four hours old,' said he. 'This bank's in shadow by one o'clock, and the sun has not cooked them dusty.'

We continued on our way; and although it seemed no very particular thing to me that a man should choose to walk and lead his horse for a while – I often did so to limber my muscles – nevertheless I began to catch the Virginian's uncertain feeling about this traveller whose steps had appeared on our path in mid-journey, as if he had alighted from the mid-air, and to remind myself that he had come over the great face of rock from another trail and thus joined us, and that indigent trappers are to be found owning but a single horse and leading him with their belongings through the deepest solitudes of the mountains – none of this quite brought back to me the comfort which had been mine since we left the cottonwoods out of sight down in the plain. Hence I called out sharply, 'What's the matter now?' when the Virginian suddenly stopped his horse again.

He looked down at the trail, and then he very slowly turned round in his saddle and stared back steadily at me. 'There's two of them,' he said.

'Two what?'

'I don't know.'

'You must know whether it's two horses or two men,' I said, almost angrily.

But to this he made no answer, sitting quite still on his horse and contemplating the ground. The silence was fastening on me like a spell, and I spurred my horse impatiently forward to see for myself. The footprints of two men were there in the trail.

'What do you say to that?' said the Virginian. 'Kind of ridiculous, ain't it?'

'Very quaint,' I answered, groping for the explanation. There was no rock here to walk over and step from into the softer trail. These second steps came more out of the air than the first. And my brain played me the evil trick of showing me a dead man in a grey flannel shirt.

'It's two, you see, travelling with one hawss, and they take turns riding him.'

'Why, of course!' I exclaimed; and we went along for a few paces.

'There you are,' said the Virginian, as the trail proved him right. 'Number one has got on. My God, what's that?'

At a crashing in the woods very close to us we both flung round and caught sight of a vanishing elk.

It left us confronted, smiling a little, and sounding each other with our eyes. 'Well, we didn't need him for meat,' said the Virginian.

'A spike-horn, wasn't it?' said I.

'Yes, just a spike-horn.'

For a while now as we rode we kept up a cheerful conversation about elk. We wondered if we should meet many more close to the trail like this; but it was not long before our words died away. We had come into a veritable gulf of mountain peaks, sharp at their bare summits like teeth, holding fields of snow lower down, and glittering still in full day up there, while down among our pines and parks the afternoon was growing sombre. All the while the fresh hoofprints of the horse and the fresh footprints of the man preceded us. In the trees, and in the opens, across the levels, and up the steeps, they were there. And so they were not four hours old! Were they so much? Might we not, round some turn, come upon the makers of them? I began to watch for this. And again my brain played me an evil trick, against which I found myself actually reasoning thus: if they took turns riding, then walking must tire them as it did me or any man. And besides, there was a horse. With such thoughts I combated the fancy that those footprints were being made immediately in front of us all the while, and that they were the only sign of any presence which our eyes could see. But my fancy overcame my thoughts. It was shame only which held me from asking this question of the Virginian: Had one horse served in both cases of Justice down at the cottonwoods? I wondered about this. One horse – or had the strangling nooses dragged two saddles empty at the same signal? Most likely; and therefore these people up here – Was I going back to the nursery? I brought myself up short. And I told myself to be steady; there lurked in this brain process which was going on beneath my reason a threat worse than the childish apprehensions it created. I reminded myself that I was a man grown, twenty-five years old, and that I must not merely seem like one, but feel like one. 'You're not afraid of the dark, I suppose?' This I uttered aloud, unwittingly.

'What's that?'

I started; but it was only the Virginian behind me. 'Oh, nothing. The air is getting colder up here.'

I had presently a great relief. We came to a place where again this trail mounted so abruptly that we once more got off to lead our horses. So likewise had our predecessors done; and as I watched the two different sets of bootprints, I observed something and hastened to speak of it.

'One man is much heavier than the other.'

'I was hoping I'd not have to tell you that,' said the Virginian.

'You're always ahead of me! Well, still my education is progressing.'

'Why, yes. You'll equal an Injun if you keep on.'

It was good to be facetious; and I smiled to myself as I trudged upward. We came off the steep place, leaving the canyon beneath us, and took to horseback. And as we proceeded over the final gentle slant up to the rim of the great basin that was set among the peaks, the Virginian was jocular once more.

'Pounds has got on,' said he, 'and Ounces is walking.'

I glanced over my shoulder at him, and he nodded as he fixed the weather-beaten crimson handkerchief round his neck. Then he threw a stone at a pack animal that was delaying on the trail. 'Damn your buckskin hide,' he drawled. 'You can view the scenery from the top.'

He was so natural, sitting loose in the saddle, and cursing in his gentle voice, that I laughed to think what visions I had been harbouring. The two dead men riding one horse through the mountains vanished, and I came back to everyday.

'Do you think we'll catch up with those people?' I asked.

'Not likely. They're travelling about the same gait we are.'

'Ounces ought to be the best walker.'

'Up hill, yes. But Pounds will go down a-foggin'.'

We gained the rim of the basin. It lay below us, a great cup of country – rocks, woods, opens, and streams. The tall peaks rose like spires around it, magnificent and bare in the last of the sun; and we surveyed this upper world, letting our animals get breath. Our bleak, crumbled rim ran like a rampart between the towering tops, a half circle of five miles or six, very wide in some parts, and in some shrinking to a scanty foothold, as here. Here our trail crossed over it between two eroded and fantastic shapes of stone, like mushrooms, or misshapen heads on pikes. Banks of snow spread up here against the black rocks, but half an hour would see us descended to the green and the woods. I looked down, both of us looked down, but our forerunners were not there.

'They'll be camping somewhere in this basin, though,' said the Virginian, staring at the dark pines. 'They have not come this trail by accident.'

A cold little wind blew down between our stone shapes, and upward again, eddying. And round a corner upward with it came fluttering a leaf of newspaper, and caught against an edge close to me.

'What's the latest?' enquired the Virginian from his horse. For I had dismounted, and had picked up the leaf.

'Seems to be inter–esting,' I next heard him say. 'Can't you tell a man what's making your eyes bug out so?'

'Yes,' my voice replied to him, and it sounded like some stranger speaking lightly near by; 'oh, yes! Decidedly interesting.' My voice mimicked his pronunciation. 'It's quite the latest, I imagine. You had better read it yourself.' And I handed it to him with a smile, watching his countenance, while my brain felt as if clouds were rushing through it.

I saw his eyes quietly run the headings over. 'Well?' he enquired, after scanning it on both sides. 'I don't seem to catch the excitement. Fremont County is going to hold elections. I see they claim Jake – '

'It's mine,' I cut him off. 'My own paper. Those are my pencil marks.'

I do not think that a microscope could have discerned a change in his face. 'Oh,' he commented, holding the paper, and fixing it with a critical eye. 'You mean this is the one you lent Steve, and he wanted to give me to give back to you. And so them are your own marks.' For a moment more he held it judicially, as I have seen men hold a contract upon whose terms they were finally passing. 'Well, you have got it back now, anyway.' And he handed it to me.

'Only a piece of it!' I exclaimed, always lightly. And as I took it from him his hand chanced to touch mine. It was cold as ice.

'They ain't through readin' the rest,' he explained easily. 'Don't you throw it away! After they've taken such trouble.'

'That's true,' I answered. 'I wonder if it's Pounds or Ounces I'm indebted to.'

Thus we made further merriment as we rode down into the great basin. Before us, the horse and boot tracks showed plain in the soft slough where melted snow ran half the day.

'If it's a paper chase,' said the Virginian, 'they'll drop no more along here.'

'Unless it gets dark,' said I.

'We'll camp before that. Maybe we'll see their fire.'

We did not see their fire. We descended in the chill silence, while the mushroom rocks grew far and the sombre woods approached. By a stream we got off where two banks sheltered us; for a bleak wind cut down over the crags now and then, making the pines send out a great note through the basin, like breakers in a heavy sea. But we made cosy in the tent. We pitched the tent this night, and I was glad to have it shut out the mountain peaks. They showed above the banks where we camped; and in the starlight their black shapes rose stark against the sky. They, with the pines and the wind, were a bedroom too unearthly this night. And as soon as our supper dishes were washed we went inside to our lantern and our game of cribbage.

'This is snug,' said the Virginian, as we played. 'That wind don't get down here.'

'Smoking is snug, too,' said I. And we marked our points for an hour, with no words save about the cards.

'I'll be pretty near glad when we get out of these mountains,' said the Virginian. 'They're most too big.'

The pines had altogether ceased; but their silence was as tremendous as their roar had been.

'I don't know, though,' he resumed. 'There's times when the plains can be awful big, too.'

Presently we finished a hand, and he said, 'Let me see that paper.'

He sat reading it apparently through, while I arranged my blankets to make a warm bed. Then, since the paper continued to absorb him, I got myself ready, and slid between my blankets for the night. 'You'll need another candle soon in that lantern,' said I.

He put the paper down. 'I would do it all over again,' he began. 'The whole thing just the same. He knowed the customs of the country, and he played the game. No call to blame me for the customs of the country. You leave other folks' cattle alone, or you take the consequences, and it was all known to Steve from the start. Would he have me take the Judge's wages and give him the wink? He must have changed a heap from the Steve I knew if he expected that I don't believe he expected that. He knew well enough the only thing that would have let him off would have been a regular jury. For the thieves have got hold of the juries in Johnson County. I would do it all over, just the same.'

The expiring flame leaped in the lantern, and fell blue. He broke off in his words as if to arrange the light, but did not, sitting silent instead, just visible, and seeming to watch the death struggle of the flame. I could find nothing to say to him, and I believed he was now winning his way back to serenity by himself. He kept his outward man so nearly natural that I forgot about that cold touch of his hand, and never guessed how far out from reason the tide of emotion was even now whirling him. 'I remember at Cheyenne onced,' he resumed. And he told me of a Thanksgiving visit to town that he had made with Steve. 'We was just colts then,' he said.

He dwelt on their coltish doings, their adventures sought and wrought in the perfect fellowship of youth. 'For Steve and me most always hunted in couples back in them gamesome years,' he explained. And he fell into the elemental talk of sex, such talk as would be an elk's or tiger's; and spoken so by him, simply and naturally, as we speak of the seasons, or of death, or of any actuality, it was without offence. But it would be offence should I repeat it. Then, abruptly ending these memories of himself and Steve, he went out of the tent, and I heard him dragging a log to the fire. When it had blazed up, there on the tent wall was his shadow and that of the log where he sat with his half-broken heart. And all the while I supposed he was master of himself, and self-justified against Steve's omission to bid him goodbye.

I must have fallen asleep before he returned, for I remember nothing except waking and finding him in his blankets beside me. The fire shadow was gone, and grey, cold light was dimly on the tent. He slept restlessly, and his forehead was ploughed by lines of pain. While I looked at him he began to mutter, and suddenly started up with violence. 'No!' he cried out; 'no! Just the same!' and thus wakened himself, staring. 'What's the matter?' he demanded. He was slow in getting back to where we were; and full consciousness found him sitting up with his eyes fixed on mine. They were more haunted than they had been at all, and his next speech came straight from his dream. 'Maybe you'd better quit me. This ain't your trouble.'

I laughed. 'Why, what is the trouble?'

His eyes still intently fixed on mine. 'Do you think if we changed our trail we could lose them from us?'

I was framing a jocose reply about Ounces being a good walker, when the sound of hoofs rushing in the distance stopped me, and he ran out of the tent with his rifle. When I followed with mine he was up the bank, and all his powers alert. But nothing came out of the dimness save our three stampeded horses. They crashed over fallen timber and across the open to where their picketed comrade grazed at the end of his rope. By him they came to a stand, and told him, I suppose, what they had seen; for all four now faced in the same direction, looking away into the mysterious dawn. We likewise stood peering, and my rifle barrel felt cold in my hand. The dawn was all we saw, the inscrutable dawn, coming and coming through the black pines and the grey open of the basin. There above lifted the peaks, no sun yet on them, and behind us our stream made a little tinkling.

'A bear, I suppose,' said I, at length.

His strange look fixed me again, and then his eyes went to the horses. 'They smell things we can't smell,' said he, very slowly. 'Will you prove to me they don't see things we can't see?'

A chill shot through me, and I could not help a frightened glance where we had been watching. But one of the horses began to graze and I had a wholesome thought. 'He's tired of whatever he sees, then,' said I, pointing.

A smile came for a moment in the Virginian's face. 'Must be a poor show,' he observed. All the horses were grazing now, and he added, 'It ain't hurt their appetites any.'

We made our own breakfast then. And what uncanny dread I may have been touched with up to this time henceforth left me in the face of a real alarm. The shock of Steve was working upon the Virginian. He was aware of it himself; he was fighting it with all his might; and he was being overcome. He was indeed like a gallant swimmer against whom both wind and tide have conspired. And in this now foreboding solitude there was only myself to throw him ropes. His strokes for safety were as bold as was the undertow that ceaselessly annulled them.

'I reckon I made a fuss in the tent?' said he, feeling his way with me.

I threw him a rope. 'Yes. Nightmare – indigestion – too much newspaper before retiring.'

He caught the rope. 'That's correct! I had a hell of a foolish dream for a growed-up man. You'd not think it of me.'

'Oh, yes, I should. I've had them after prolonged lobster and champagne.'

'Ah,' he murmured, 'prolonged! Prolonged is what does it.' He glanced behind him. 'Steve came back – '

'In your lobster dream,' I put in.

But he missed this rope. 'Yes,' he answered, with his eyes searching me. 'And he handed me the paper – '

'By the way, where is that?' I asked.

'I built the fire with it. But when I took it from him it was a six-shooter I had hold of, and pointing at my breast. And then Steve spoke. "Do you think you're fit to live?" Steve said; and I got hot at him, and I reckon I must have told him what I thought of him. You heard me, I expect?'

'Glad I didn't. Your language sometimes is – '

He laughed out. 'Oh, I account for all this that's happening just like you do. If we gave our explanations, they'd be pretty near twins.'

'The horses saw a bear, then?'

'Maybe a bear. Maybe –' but here the tide caught him again – 'What's your idea about dreams?'

My ropes were all out. 'Liver – nerves,' was the best I could do. But now he swam strongly by himself.

'You may think I'm discreditable,' he said, 'but I know I am. It ought to take more than – well, men have lost their friendships before. Feuds and wars have cloven a right smart of bonds in twain. And if my haid is going to get shook by a little old piece of newspaper – I'm ashamed I burned that. I'm ashamed to have been that weak.'

'Any man gets unstrung,' I told him. My ropes had become straws; and I strove to frame some policy for the next hours.

We now finished breakfast and set forth to catch the horses. As we drove them in I found that the Virginian was telling me a ghost story. 'At half-past three in the morning she saw her runaway daughter standing with a babe in her arms; but when she moved it was all gone. Later they found it was the very same hour the young mother died in Nogales. And she sent for the child and raised it herself. I knowed them both back home. Do you believe that?'

I said nothing.

'No more do I believe it,' he asserted. 'And see here! Nogales time is three hours different from Richmond. I didn't know about that point then.'

Once out of these mountains, I knew he could right himself; but even I, who had no Steve to dream about, felt this silence of the peaks was preying on me.

'Her daughter and her might have been thinkin' mighty hard about each other just then,' he pursued. 'But Steve is dead. Finished. You cert'nly don't believe there's anything more?'

'I wish I could,' I told him.

'No, I'm satisfied. Heaven didn't never interest me much. But if there was a world of dreams after you went –' He stopped himself and turned his searching eyes away from mine. 'There's a heap o' darkness wherever you try to step,' he said, 'and I thought I'd left off wasting thoughts on the subject. You see' – he dexterously roped a horse, and once more his splendid sanity was turned to gold by his imagination – 'I expect in many growed-up men you'd call sensible there's a little boy sleepin' – the little kid they onced was – that still keeps his fear of the dark. You mentioned the dark yourself yesterday. Well, this experience has woke up that kid in me, and blamed if I can coax the little cuss to go to sleep again! I keep a-telling him daylight will sure come, but he keeps a-crying and holding on to me.'

Somewhere far in the basin there was a faint sound, and we stood still. 'Hush!' he said.

But it was like our watching the dawn; nothing more followed.

'They have shot that bear,' I remarked.

He did not answer, and we put the saddles on without talk. We made no haste, but we were not over half an hour, I suppose, in getting off with the packs. It was not a new thing to hear a shot where wild game was in plenty; yet as we rode that shot sounded already in my mind different from others. Perhaps I should not believe this today but for what I look back to. To make camp last night we had turned off the trail, and now followed the stream down for a while, taking next a cut through the wood. In this way we came upon the tracks of our horses where they had been galloping back to the camp after their fright. They had kicked up the damp and matted pine needles very plainly all along.

'Nothing has been here but themselves, though,' said I.

'And they ain't showing signs of remembering any scare,' said the Virginian.

In a little while we emerged upon an open.

'Here's where they was grazing,' said the Virginian; and the signs were clear enough. 'Here's where they must have got their scare,' he pursued. 'You stay with them while I circle a little.' So I stayed; and certainly our animals were very calm at visiting this scene. When you bring a horse back to where he has recently encountered a wild animal his ears and his nostrils are apt to be wide awake.

The Virginian had stopped and was beckoning to me.

'Here's your bear,' said he, as I arrived. 'Two-legged, you see. And he had a hawss of his own.' There was a stake driven down where an animal had been picketed for the night.

'Looks like Ounces,' I said, considering the bootprints.

'It's Ounces. And Ounces wanted another hawss very bad, so him and Pounds could travel like gentlemen should.'

'But Pounds doesn't seem to have been with him.'

'Oh, Pounds, he was making coffee, somewheres in yonder, when this happened. Neither of them guessed there'd be other hawsses wandering here in the night, or they both would have come.' He turned back to our pack animals.

'Then you'll not hunt for this camp to make sure?'

'I prefer making sure first. We might be expected at that camp.'

He took out his rifle from beneath his leg and set it across his saddle at half-cock. I did the same; and thus cautiously we resumed our journey in a slightly different direction. 'This ain't all we're going to find out,' said the Virginian. 'Ounces had a good idea; but I reckon he made a bad mistake later.'

We had found out a good deal without any more, I thought. Ounces had gone to bring in their single horse, and coming upon three more in the pasture had undertaken to catch one and failed, merely driving them where he feared to follow.

'Shorty never could rope a horse alone,' I remarked.

The Virginian grinned. 'Shorty? Well, Shorty sounds as well as Ounces. But that ain't the mistake I'm thinking he made.'

I knew that he would not tell me, but that was just like him. For the last twenty minutes, having something to do, he had become himself again, had come to earth from that unsafe country of the brain where beckoned a spectral Steve. Nothing was left but in his eyes that question which pain had set there; and I wondered if his friend of old, who seemed so brave and amiable, would have dealt him that hurt at the solemn end had he known what a poisoned wound it would be.

We came out on a ridge from which we could look down. 'You always want to ride on high places when there's folks around whose intentions ain't been declared,' said the Virginian. And we went along our ridge for some distance. Then suddenly he turned down and guided us almost at once to the trail. 'That's it,' he said. 'See.'

The track of a horse was very fresh on the trail. But it was a galloping horse now, and no bootprints were keeping up with it any more. No boots could have kept up with it. The rider was making time today. Yesterday that horse had been ridden up into the mountains at leisure. Who was on him? There was never to be any certain answer to that. But who was not on him? We turned back in our journey, back into the heart of that basin with the tall peaks all rising like teeth in the cloudless sun, and the snow-fields shining white.

'He was afraid of us,' said the Virginian. 'He did not know how many of us had come up here. Three hawsses might mean a dozen more around.'

We followed the backward trail in among the pines, and came after a time upon their camp. And then I understood the mistake that Shorty had made. He had returned after his failure, and had told that other man of the presence of new horses. He should have kept this a secret; for haste had to be made at once, and two cannot get away quickly upon one horse. But it was poor Shorty's last blunder. He lay there by their extinct fire, with his wistful, lost-dog face upward, and his thick yellow hair unparted as it had always been. The murder had been done from behind. We closed the eyes.

'There was no natural harm in him,' said the Virginian. 'But you must do a thing well in this country.'

There was not a trace, not a clue, of the other man; and we found a place where we could soon cover Shorty with earth. As we lifted him we saw the newspaper that he had been reading. He had brought it from the clump of cottonwoods where he and the other man had made a later visit than ours to be sure of the fate of their friends – or possibly in hopes of another horse. Evidently, when the party were surprised, they had been able to escape with only one. All of the newspaper was there save the leaf I had picked up – all and more, for this had pencil writing on it that was not mine, nor did I at first take it in. I thought it might be a clue, and I read it aloud. 'Goodbye, Jeff,' it said. 'I could not have spoke to you without playing the baby.'

'Who's Jeff?' I asked. But it came over me when I looked at the Virginian. He was standing beside me quite motionless; and then he put out his hand and took the paper, and stood still, looking at the words. 'Steve used to call me Jeff,' he said, 'because I was Southern, I reckon. Nobody else ever did.'

He slowly folded the message from the dead, brought by the dead, and rolled it in the coat behind his saddle. For a half-minute he stood leaning his forehead down against the saddle. After this he came back and contemplated Shorty's face awhile. 'I wish I could thank him,' he said. 'I wish I could.'

We carried Shorty over and covered him with earth, and on that laid a few pine branches; then we took up our journey, and by the end of the forenoon we had gone some distance upon our trail through the Teton Mountains. But in front of us the hoofprints ever held their stride of haste, drawing farther from us through the hours, until by the next afternoon somewhere we noticed they were no longer to be seen; and after that they never came upon the trail again.

CHAPTER 33

The Spinster Loses Some Sleep

Somewhere at the eastern base of the Tetons did those hoofprints disappear into a mountain sanctuary where many crooked paths have led. He that took another man's possessions, or he that took another man's life, could always run here if the law or popular justice were too hot at his heels. Steep ranges and forests walled him in from the world on all four sides, almost without a break; and every entrance lay through intricate solitudes. Snake River came into the place through canyons and mournful pines and marshes, to the north, and went out at the south between formidable chasms. Every tributary to this stream rose among high peaks and ridges, and descended into the valley by well-nigh impenetrable courses: Pacific Creek from Two Ocean Pass, Buffalo Fork from no pass at all, Black Rock from the To-wo-ge-tee Pass – all these, and many more, were the waters of loneliness, among whose thousand hiding-places it was easy to be lost. Down in the bottom was a spread of level land, broad and beautiful, with the blue and silver Tetons rising from its chain of lakes to the west, and other heights presiding over its other sides. And up and down and in and out of this hollow square of mountains, where waters plentifully flowed, and game and natural pasture abounded, there skulked a nomadic and distrustful population. This in due time built cabins, took wives, begot children, and came to speak of itself as 'The honest settlers of Jackson's Hole'. It is a commodious title, and doubtless today more accurate than it was once.

Into this place the hoofprints disappeared. Not many cabins were yet built there; but the unknown rider of the horse knew well that he would find shelter and welcome among the felons of his stripe. Law and order might guess his name correctly, but there was no next step, for lack of evidence; and he would wait, whoever he was, until the rage of popular justice, which had been pursuing him and his brother thieves, should subside. Then, feeling his way gradually with prudence, he would let himself be seen again.

And now, as mysteriously as he had melted away, rumour passed over the country. No tongue seemed to be heard telling the first news; the news was there, one day, a matter of whispered knowledge. On Sunk

Creek and on Bear Creek, and elsewhere far and wide, before men talked men seemed secretly to know that Steve, and Ed, and Shorty, would never again be seen. Riders met each other in the road and drew rein to discuss the event, and its bearing upon the cattle interests. In town saloons men took each other aside, and muttered over it in corners.

Thus it reached the ears of Molly Wood, beginning in a veiled and harmless shape.

A neighbour joined her when she was out riding by herself.

'Good-morning,' said he. 'Don't you find it lonesome?' And when she answered lightly, he continued, meaning well: 'You'll be having company again soon now. He has finished his job. Wish he'd finished it *more!* Well, good-day.'

Molly thought these words over. She could not tell why they gave her a strange feeling. To her Vermont mind no suspicion of the truth would come naturally. But suspicion began to come when she returned from her ride. For, entering the cabin of the Taylors', she came upon several people who all dropped their talk short, and were not skilful at resuming it. She sat there awhile, uneasily aware that all of them knew something which she did not know, and was not intended to know. A thought pierced her: had anything happened to her lover? No; that was not it. The man she had met on horseback spoke of her having company soon again. How soon? she wondered. He had been unable to say when he should return, and now she suddenly felt that a great silence had enveloped him lately: not the mere silence of absence, of receiving no messages or letters, but another sort of silence which now, at this moment, was weighing strangely upon her.

And then the next day it came out at the schoolhouse. During that interval known as recess, she became aware through the open window that they were playing a new game outside. Lusty screeches of delight reached her ears.

'Jump!' a voice ordered. 'Jump!'

'I don't want to,' returned another voice, uneasily.

'You said you would,' said several. 'Didn't he say he would? Ah, he said he would. Jump now, quick!'

'But I don't want to,' quavered the voice in a tone so dismal that Molly went out to see.

They had got Bob Carmody on the top of the gate by a tree, with a rope round his neck, the other end of which four little boys were joyously holding. The rest looked on eagerly, three little girls clasping their hands, and springing up and down with excitement.

'Why, children!' exclaimed Molly.

'He's said his prayers and everything,' they all screamed out. 'He's a rustler, and we're lynchin' him. Jump, Bob!'

'I don't want – '

'Ah, coward, won't take his medicine!'

'Let him go, boys,' said Molly. 'You might really hurt him.' And so she broke up this game, but not without general protest from Wyoming's young voice.

'He said he would,' Henry Dow assured her.

And George Taylor further explained: 'He said he'd be Steve. But Steve didn't scare.' Then George proceeded to tell the schoolmarm, eagerly, all about Steve and Ed, while the schoolmarm looked at him with a rigid face.

'You promised your mother you'd not tell,' said Henry Dow, after all had been told. 'You've gone and done it,' and Henry wagged his head in a superior manner.

Thus did the New England girl learn what her cowboy lover had done. She spoke of it to nobody; she kept her misery to herself. He was not there to defend his act. Perhaps in a way that was better. But these were hours of darkness indeed to Molly Wood.

On that visit to Dunbarton, when at the first sight of her lover's photograph in frontier dress her aunt had exclaimed, 'I suppose there are days when he does not kill people,' she had cried in all good faith and mirth, 'He never killed anybody!' Later, when he was lying in her cabin weak from his bullet wound, but each day stronger beneath her nursing, at a certain word of his there had gone through her a shudder of doubt. Perhaps in his many wanderings he had done such a thing in self-defence, or in the cause of popular justice. But she had pushed the idea away from her hastily, back into the days before she had ever seen him. If this had ever happened, let her not know of it. Then, as a cruel reward for his candour and his laying himself bare to her mother, the letters from Bennington had used that very letter of his as a weapon against him. Her sister Sarah had quoted from it. 'He says with apparent pride,' wrote Sarah, 'that he has "never killed for pleasure or profit". Those are his exact words, and you may guess their dreadful effect upon mother. I congratulate you, my dear, on having chosen a protector so scrupulous.'

Thus her elder sister had seen fit to write; and letters from less near relatives made hints at the same subject. So she was compelled to accept this piece of knowledge thrust upon her. Yet still, still, those events had been before she knew him. They were remote, without detail or context. He had been little more than a boy. No doubt it was to save his own life. And so she bore the hurt of her discovery all the more easily because her sister's tone roused her to defend her cowboy.

But now!

In her cabin, alone, after midnight, she arose from her sleepless bed, and lighting the candle, stood before his photograph.

'It is a good face,' her great-aunt had said, after some study of it. And these words were in her mind now. There his likeness stood at full length, confronting her: the spurs on the boots, the fringed leathern *chaparajos*, the coiled rope in hand, the pistol at hip, the rough flannel shirt, and the scarf knotted at the throat – and then the grave eyes, looking at her. It thrilled her to meet them, even so. She could read life into them. She seemed to feel passion come from them, and then something like reproach. She stood for a long while looking at him, and then, beating her hands together suddenly, she blew out her light and went back into bed, but not to sleep.

'You're looking pale, deary,' said Mrs Taylor to her, a few days later.

'Am I?'

'And you don't eat anything.'

'Oh, yes, I do.' And Molly retired to her cabin.

'George,' said Mrs Taylor, 'you come here.'

It may seem severe – I think that it was severe. That evening when Mr Taylor came home to his family, George received a thrashing for disobedience.

'And I suppose,' said Mrs Taylor to her husband, 'that she came out just in time to stop 'em breaking Bob Carmody's neck for him.'

Upon the day following Mrs Taylor essayed the impossible. She took herself over to Molly Wood's cabin. The girl gave her a listless greeting, and the dame sat slowly down, and surveyed the comfortable room.

'A very nice home, deary,' said she, 'if it was a home. But you'll fix something like this in your real home, I have no doubt.'

Molly made no answer.

'What we're going to do without you I can't see,' said Mrs Taylor. 'But I'd not have it different for worlds. He'll be coming back soon, I expect.'

'Mrs Taylor,' said Molly, all at once, 'please don't say anything now. I can't stand it.' And she broke into wretched tears.

'Why, deary, he –'

'No; not a word. Please, please – I'll go out if you do.'

The older woman went to the younger one, and then put her arms round her. But when the tears were over, they had not done any good; it was not the storm that clears the sky – all storms do not clear the sky. And Mrs Taylor looked at the pale girl and saw that she could do nothing to help her towards peace of mind.

'Of course,' she said to her husband, after returning from her profitless errand, 'you might know she'd feel dreadful.'

'What about?' said Taylor.

'Why, you know just as well as I do. And I'll say for myself, I hope you'll never have to help hang folks.'

'Well,' said Taylor, mildly, 'if I had to, I'd have to, I guess.'

'Well, I don't want it to come. But that poor girl is eating her heart right out over it.'

'What does she say?'

'It's what she don't say. She'll not talk, and she'll not let me talk, and she sits and sits.'

'I'll go talk some to her,' said the man.

'Well, Taylor, I thought you had more sense. You'd not get a word in. She'll be sick soon if her worry ain't stopped someway, though.'

'What does she want this country to do?' enquired Taylor. 'Does she expect it to be like Vermont when it –'

'We can't help what she expects,' his wife interrupted. 'But I wish we could help *her*.'

They could not, however; and help came from another source. Judge Henry rode by the next day. To him good Mrs Taylor at once confided her anxiety. The Judge looked grave.

'Must I meddle?' he said.

'Yes, Judge, you must,' said Mrs Taylor.

'But why can't I send him over here when he gets back? Then they'll just settle it between themselves.'

Mrs Taylor shook her head. 'That would unsettle it worse than it is,' she assured him. 'They mustn't meet just now.'

The Judge sighed. 'Well,' he said, 'very well. I'll sacrifice my character, since you insist.'

Judge Henry sat thinking, waiting until school should be out. He did not at all relish what lay before him. He would like to have got out of it. He had been a federal judge; he had been an upright judge; he had met the responsibilities of his difficult office not only with learning, which is desirable, but also with courage and common sense besides, and these are essential. He had been a stanch servant of the law. And now he was invited to defend that which, at first sight, nay, even at second and third sight, must always seem a defiance of the law more injurious than crime itself. Every good man in this world has convictions about right and wrong. They are his soul's riches, his spiritual gold. When his conduct is at variance with these, he knows that it is a departure, a falling; and this is a simple and clear matter. If falling were all that ever happened to a good man, all his days would be a simple matter of striving and repentance. But it is not all. There come to him certain junctures, crises, when life, like a highwayman, springs upon him, demanding that he stand and deliver his convictions in the name of some righteous cause, bidding him do evil that good may come. I cannot say that I believe in doing evil that good may come. I do not. I think that any man who honestly justifies such course deceives himself. But this I can say: to call any act evil, instantly begs the question. Many an act that man does is right or wrong according to the time and place which form, so to speak, its context; strip it of its surrounding circumstances, and you tear away its meaning. Gentlemen reformers, beware of this common practice of yours! beware of calling an act evil on Tuesday because that same act was evil on Monday!

Do you fail to follow my meaning? Then here is an illustration. On Monday I walk over my neighbour's field; there is no wrong in such walking. By Tuesday he has put up a sign that trespassers will be prosecuted according to law. I walk again on Tuesday, and am a law-breaker. Do you begin to see my point? or are you inclined to object to the illustration because the walking on Tuesday was not *wrong*, but merely *illegal*? Then here is another illustration which you will find it a trifle more embarrassing to answer. Consider carefully, let me beg you, the case of a young man and a young woman who walk out of a door on Tuesday, pronounced man and wife by a third party inside the door. It matters not that on Monday they were, in their own hearts, sacredly vowed to each other. If they had omitted stepping inside that door, if they had dispensed with that third party, and gone away on Monday sacredly vowed to each other in their own hearts, you would have scarcely found their conduct moral. Consider these things carefully – the signpost and the third party – and the difference they make. And now, for a finish, we will return to the signpost.

Suppose that I went over my neighbour's field on Tuesday, after the signpost was put up, because I saw a murder about to be committed in the field, and therefore ran in and stopped it. Was I doing evil that good might come? Do you not think that to stay out and let the murder be done would have been the evil act in this case? To disobey the signpost was *right*; and I trust that you now perceive the same act may wear as many different hues of right or wrong as the rainbow, according to the atmosphere in which it is done. It is not safe to say of any man, 'He did evil that good might come.' Was the thing that he did, in the first place, evil? That is the question.

Forgive my asking you to use your mind. It is a thing which no novelist should expect of his reader, and we will go back at once to Judge Henry and his meditations about lynching.

He was well aware that if he was to touch at all upon this subject with the New England girl, he could not put her off with mere platitudes and humdrum formulas; not, at least, if he expected to do any good. She was far too intelligent, and he was really anxious to do good. For her sake he wanted the course of the girl's true love to run more smoothly, and still more did he desire this for the sake of his Virginian.

'I sent him myself on that business,' the Judge reflected uncomfortably. 'I am partly responsible for the lynching. It has brought him one great unhappiness already through the death of Steve. If it gets running in this girl's mind, she may – dear me!' the Judge broke off, 'what a nuisance!' And he sighed. For as all men know, he also knew that many things should be done in this world in silence, and that talking about them is a mistake.

But when school was out, and the girl gone to her cabin, his mind had set the subject in order thoroughly, and he knocked at her door, ready, as he had put it, to sacrifice his character in the cause of true love.

'Well,' he said, coming straight to the point, 'some dark things have happened.' And when she made no answer to this, he continued: 'But you must not misunderstand us. We're too fond of you for that.'

'Judge Henry,' said Molly Wood, also coming straight to the point, 'have you come to tell me that you think well of lynching?'

He met her. 'Of burning Southern Negroes in public, no. Of hanging Wyoming cattle thieves in private, yes. You perceive there's a difference, don't you?'

'Not in principle,' said the girl, dry and short.

'Oh – dear – me!' slowly exclaimed the Judge. 'I am sorry that you cannot see that, because I think that I can. And I think that you have just as much sense as I have.' The Judge made himself very grave and very good-humoured at the same time. The poor girl was strung to a high pitch, and spoke harshly in spite of herself.

'What is the difference in principle?' she demanded.

'Well,' said the Judge, easy and thoughtful, 'what do you mean by principle?'

'I didn't think you'd quibble,' flashed Molly. 'I'm not a lawyer myself.'

A man less wise than Judge Henry would have smiled at this, and then war would have exploded hopelessly between them, and harm been added to what was going wrong already. But the Judge knew that he must give to every word that the girl said now his perfect consideration.

'I don't mean to quibble,' he assured her. 'I know the trick of escaping from one question by asking another. But I don't want to escape from anything you hold me to answer. If you can show me that I am wrong, I want you to do so. But,' and here the Judge smiled, 'I want you to play fair, too.'

'And how am I not?'

'I want you to be just as willing to be put right by me as I am to be put right by you. And so when you use such a word as principle, you must help me to answer by saying what principle you mean. For in all sincerity I see no likeness in principle whatever between burning Southern Negroes in public and hanging Wyoming horse thieves in private. I consider the burning a proof that the South is semi-barbarous, and the hanging a proof that Wyoming is determined to become civilised. We do not torture our criminals when we lynch them. We do not invite spectators to enjoy their death agony. We put no such hideous disgrace upon the United States. We execute our criminals by the swiftest means, and in the quietest way. Do you think the principle is the same?'

Molly had listened to him with attention. 'The way is different,' she admitted.

'Only the way?'

'So it seems to me. Both defy law and order.'

'Ah, but do they both? Now we're getting near the principle.'

'Why, yes. Ordinary citizens take the law in their own hands.'

'The principle at last!' exclaimed the Judge.

'Now tell me some more things. Out of whose hands do they take the law?'

'The courts'.'

'What made the courts?'

'I don't understand.'

'How did there come to be any courts?'

'The Constitution.'

'How did there come to be any Constitution? Who made it?'

'The delegates, I suppose.'

'Who made the delegates?'

'I suppose they were elected, or appointed, or something.'

'And who elected them?'

'Of course the people elected them.'

'Call them the ordinary citizens,' said the Judge. 'I like your term. They are where the law comes from, you see. For they chose the delegates who made the Constitution that provided for the courts. There's your machinery. These are the hands into which ordinary citizens have put the law. So you see, at best, when they lynch they only take back what they once gave. Now we'll take your two cases that you say are the same in principle. I think that they are not. For in the South they take a Negro from jail where he was waiting to be duly hung. The South has never claimed that the law would let him go. But in Wyoming the law has been letting our cattle-thieves go for two years. We are in a very bad way, and we are trying to make that way a little better until civilisation can reach us. At present we lie beyond its pale. The courts, or rather the juries, into whose hands we have put the law, are not dealing the law. They are withered hands, or rather they are imitation hands made for show, with no life in them, no grip. They cannot hold a cattle-thief. And so when your ordinary citizen sees this, and sees that he has placed justice in a dead hand, he must take justice back into his own hands where it was once at the beginning of all things. Call this primitive, if you will. But so far from being a *defiance* of the law, it is an *assertion* of it – the fundamental assertion of self-governing men, upon whom our whole social fabric is based. There is your principle, Miss Wood, as I see it. Now can you help me to see anything different?'

She could not.

'But perhaps you are of the same opinion still?' the Judge enquired.

'It is all terrible to me,' she said.

'Yes; and so is capital punishment terrible. And so is war. And perhaps someday we shall do without them. But they are none of them so terrible as unchecked theft and murder would be.'

After the Judge had departed on his way to Sunk Creek, no one spoke to Molly upon this subject. But her face did not grow cheerful at once. It was plain from her fits of silence that her thoughts were not at rest. And sometimes at night she would stand in front of her lover's likeness, gazing upon it with both love and shrinking.

CHAPTER 34

To Fit her Finger

It was two rings that the Virginian wrote for when next I heard from him.

After my dark sight of what the Cattle Land could be, I soon had journeyed home by way of Washakie and Rawlins. Steve and Shorty did not leave my memory, nor will they ever, I suppose.

The Virginian had touched the whole thing the day I left him. He had noticed me looking a sort of farewell at the plains and mountains.

'You will come back to it,' he said. 'If there was a headstone for every man that once pleasured in his freedom here, yu' d see one most every time yu' turned your head. It's a heap sadder than a graveyard – but yu' love it all the same.'

Sadness had passed from him – from his uppermost mood, at least, when he wrote about the rings. Deep in him was sadness of course, as well as joy. For he had known Steve, and he had covered Shorty with earth. He had looked upon life with a man's eyes, very close; and no one, if he have a heart, can pass through this and not carry sadness in his spirit with him forever. But he seldom shows it openly; it bides within him, enriching his cheerfulness and rendering him of better service to his fellow-men.

It was a commission of cheerfulness that he now gave, being distant from where rings are to be bought. He could not go so far as the East to procure what he had planned. Rings were to be had in Cheyenne, and a still greater choice in Denver; and so far as either of these towns his affairs would have permitted him to travel. But he was set upon having rings from the East. They must come from the best place in the country; nothing short of that was good enough 'to fit her finger', as he said. The wedding ring was a simple matter. Let it be right, that was all: the purest gold that could be used, with her initials and his together graven round the inside, with the day of the month and the year.

The date was now set. It had come so far as this. July third was to be the day. Then for sixty days and nights he was to be a bridegroom, free from his duties at Sunk Creek, free to take his bride wheresoever she might choose to go. And she had chosen.

Those voices of the world had more than angered her; for after the anger a set purpose was left. Her sister should have the chance neither to come nor to stay away. Had her mother even answered the Virginian's letter, there could have been some relenting. But the poor lady had been inadequate in this, as in all other searching moments of her life: she had sent messages – kind ones, to be sure – but only messages. If this had hurt the Virginian, no one knew it in the world, least of all the girl in whose heart it had left a cold, frozen spot. Not a good spirit in which to be married, you will say. No; frozen spots are not good at any time. But Molly's own nature gave her due punishment. Through all these days of her warm happiness a chill current ran, like those which interrupt the swimmer's perfect joy. The girl was only half as happy as her lover; but she hid this deep from him – hid it until that final, fierce hour of reckoning that her nature had with her – nay, was bound to have with her, before the punishment was lifted, and the frozen spot melted at length from her heart.

So, meanwhile, she made her decree against Bennington. Not Vermont, but Wyoming, should be her wedding place. No world's voices should be whispering, no world's eyes should be looking on, when she made her vow to him and received his vow. Those vows should be spoken and that ring put on in this wild Cattle Land, where first she had seen him ride into the flooded river, and lift her ashore upon his horse. It was this open sky which should shine down on them, and this frontier soil upon which their feet should tread. The world should take its turn second.

After a month with him by stream and canyon, a month far deeper into the mountain wilds than ever yet he had been free to take her, a month with sometimes a tent and sometimes the stars above them, and only their horses besides themselves – after such a month as this, she would take him to her mother and to Bennington; and the old aunt over at Dunbarton would look at him, and be once more able to declare that the Starks had always preferred a man who was a man.

And so July third was to be engraved inside the wedding ring. Upon the other ring the Virginian had spent much delicious meditation, all in his secret mind. He had even got the right measure of her finger without her suspecting the reason. But this step was the final one in his plan.

During the time that his thoughts had begun to be busy over the other ring, by a chance he had learned from Mrs Henry a number of old fancies regarding precious stones. Mrs Henry often accompanied the Judge in venturesome mountain climbs, and sometimes the steepness of the rocks required her to use her hands for safety. One day when the Virginian went with them to help mark out certain boundary corners, she removed her rings lest they should get scratched; and he, being just behind her, took them during the climb.

'I see you're looking at my topaz,' she had said, as he returned them. 'If I could have chosen, it would have been a ruby. But I was born in November.'

He did not understand her in the least, but her words awakened exceeding interest in him; and they had descended some five miles of mountain before he spoke again. Then he became ingenious, for he had half worked out what Mrs Henry's meaning must be; but he must make quite sure. Therefore, according to his wild, shy nature, he became ingenious.

'Men wear rings,' he began. 'Some of the men on the ranch do. I don't see any harm in a man's wearin' a ring. But I never have.'

'Well,' said the lady, not yet suspecting that he was undertaking to circumvent her, 'probably those men have sweethearts.'

'No, ma'am. Not sweethearts worth wearin' rings for – in two cases, anyway. They won 'em at cyards. And they like to see 'em shine. I never saw a man wear a topaz.'

Mrs Henry did not have any further remark to make.

'I was born in January myself,' pursued the Virginian, very thoughtfully.

Then the lady gave him one look, and without further process of mind perceived exactly what he was driving at.

'That's very extravagant for rings,' said she. 'January is diamonds.'

'Diamonds,' murmured the Virginian, more and more thoughtfully. 'Well, it don't matter, for I'd not wear a ring. And November is – what did yu' say, ma'am?'

'Topaz.'

'Yes. Well, jewels are cert'nly pretty things. In the Spanish Missions yu'll see large ones now and again. And they're not glass, I think. And so they have got some jewel that kind of belongs to each month right around the twelve?'

'Yes,' said Mrs Henry, smiling. 'One for each month. But the opal is what you want.'

He looked at her, and began to blush.

'October is the opal,' she added, and she laughed outright, for Miss Wood's birthday was on the fifteenth of that month.

The Virginian smiled guiltily at her through his crimson.

'I've no doubt you can beat around the bush very well with men,' said Mrs Henry. 'But it's perfectly transparent with us – in matters of sentiment, at least.'

'Well, I am sorry,' he presently said. 'I don't want to give her an opal. I have no superstition, but I don't want to give her an opal. If her mother did, or anybody like that, why, all right. But not from me. D' yu' understand, ma'am?'

Mrs Henry did understand this subtle trait in the wild man, and she rejoiced to be able to give him immediate reassurance concerning opals.

'Don't worry about that,' she said. 'The opal is said to bring ill luck, but not when it is your own month stone. Then it is supposed to be not only deprived of evil influence, but to possess peculiarly fortunate power. Let it be an opal ring.'

Then he asked her boldly various questions, and she showed him her rings, and gave him advice about the setting. There was no special custom, she told him, ruling such rings as this he desired to bestow. The gem might be the lady's favourite or the lover's favourite; and to choose the lady's month stone was very well indeed.

Very well indeed, the Virginian thought. But not quite well enough for him. His mind now busied itself with this lore concerning jewels, and soon his sentiment had suggested something which he forthwith carried out.

When the ring was achieved, it was an opal, but set with four small embracing diamonds. Thus was her month stone joined with his, that their luck and their love might be inseparably clasped.

He found the size of her finger one day when winter had departed, and the early grass was green. He made a ring of twisted grass for her, while she held her hand for him to bind it. He made another for himself. Then, after each had worn their grass ring for a while, he begged her to exchange. He did not send his token away from him, but most carefully measured it. Thus the ring fitted her well, and the lustrous flame within the opal thrilled his heart each time he saw it. For now June was near its end; and that other plain gold ring, which, for safe keeping, he cherished suspended round his neck day and night, seemed to burn with an inward glow that was deeper than the opal's.

So in due course arrived the second of July. Molly's punishment had got as far as this: she longed for her mother to be near her at this time; but it was too late.

CHAPTER 35

With Malice Aforethought

Town lay twelve straight miles before the lover and his sweetheart, when they came to the brow of the last long hill. All beneath them was like a map: neither man nor beast distinguishable, but the veined and tinted image of a country, knobs and flats set out in order clearly, shining extensive and motionless in the sun. It opened on the sight of the lovers as they reached the sudden edge of the tableland, where since morning they had ridden with the head of neither horse ever in advance of the other.

At the view of their journey's end, the Virginian looked down at his girl beside him, his eyes filled with a bridegroom's light, and, hanging safe upon his breast, he could feel the gold ring that he would slowly press upon her finger tomorrow. He drew off the glove from her left hand, and stooping, kissed the jewel in that other ring which he had given her. The crimson fire in the opal seemed to mingle with that in his heart, and his arm lifted her during a moment from the saddle as he held her to him. But in her heart the love of him was troubled by that cold pang of loneliness which had crept upon her like a tide as the day drew near. None of her own people were waiting in that distant town to see her become his bride. Friendly faces she might pass on the way; but all of them new friends, made in this wild country: not a face of her childhood would smile upon her; and deep within her, a voice cried for the mother who was far away in Vermont. That she would see Mrs Taylor's kind face at her wedding was no comfort now.

There lay the town in the splendour of Wyoming space. Around it spread the watered fields westward for a little way, eastward to a great distance, making squares of green and yellow crops; and the town was but a poor rag in the midst of this quilted harvest. After the fields to the east, the tawny plain began; and with one faint furrow of river lining its undulations, it stretched beyond sight. But west of the town rose the Bow Leg Mountains, cool with their still unmelted snows and their dull blue gulfs of pine. From three canyons flowed three clear forks which began the river. Their confluence was above the town a good two miles; it looked but a few paces from up here, while each side the river straggled the margin cottonwoods, like thin borders along a garden walk. Over all this map hung silence like a harmony, tremendous yet serene.

'How beautiful! how I love it!' whispered the girl. 'But, oh, how big it is!' And she leaned against her lover for an instant. It was her spirit seeking shelter. Today, this vast beauty, this primal calm, had in it for her something almost of dread. The small, comfortable, green hills of home rose before her. She closed her eyes and saw Vermont: a village street, and the post office, and ivy covering an old front door, and her mother picking some yellow roses from a bush.

At a sound, her eyes quickly opened; and here was her lover turned in his saddle, watching another horseman approach. She saw the Virginian's hand in a certain position, and knew that his pistol was ready. But the other merely overtook and passed them, as they stood at the brow of the hill.

The man had given one nod to the Virginian, and the Virginian one to him; and now he was already below them on the descending road. To Molly Wood he was a stranger; but she had seen his eyes when he nodded to her lover, and she knew, even without the pistol, that this was not enmity at first sight.

It was not indeed. Five years of gathered hate had looked out of the man's eyes. And she asked her lover who this was.

'Oh,' said he, easily, 'just a man I see now and then.'

'Is his name Trampas?' said Molly Wood.

The Virginian looked at her in surprise. 'Why, where have you seen him?' he asked.

'Never till now. But I knew.'

'My gracious! Yu' never told me yu' had mind-reading powers.' And he smiled serenely at her.

'I knew it was Trampas as soon as I saw his eyes.'

'My gracious!' her lover repeated with indulgent irony. 'I must be mighty careful of my eyes when you're lookin' at 'em.'

'I believe he did that murder,' said the girl.

'Whose mind are yu' readin' now?' he drawled affectionately

But he could not joke her off the subject. She took his strong hand in hers, tremulously, so much of it as her little hand could hold. 'I know something about that – that – last autumn,' she said, shrinking from words more definite. 'And I know that you only did – '

'What I had to,' he finished, very sadly, but sternly, too.

'Yes,' she asserted, keeping hold of his hand. 'I suppose that – lynching – ' (she almost whispered the word) 'is the only way. But when they had to die just for stealing horses, it seems so wicked that this murderer – '

'Who can prove it?' asked the Virginian.

'But don't you know it?'

'I know a heap o' things inside my heart. But that's not proving. There was only the body, and the hoofprints – and what folks guessed.'

'He was never even arrested!' the girl said.

'No. He helped elect the sheriff in that county.'

Then Molly ventured a step inside the border of her lover's reticence. 'I saw – ' she hesitated, 'just now, I saw what you did.'

He returned to his caressing irony. 'You'll have me plumb scared if you keep on seein' things.'

'You had your pistol ready for him.'

'Why, I believe I did. It was mighty unnecessary.' And the Virginian took out the pistol again, and shook his head over it, like one who has been caught in a blunder.

She looked at him, and knew that she must step outside his reticence again. By love and her surrender to him their positions had been exchanged. He was not now, as through his long courting he had been, her half-obeying, half-refractory worshipper. She was no longer his half-indulgent, half-scornful superior. Her better birth and schooling that had once been weapons to keep him at his distance, or bring her off victorious in their encounters, had given way before the onset of the natural man himself. She knew her cowboy lover, with all that he lacked, to be more than ever she could be, with all that she had. He was her worshipper still, but her master, too. Therefore now, against the baffling smile he gave her, she felt powerless. And once again a pang of yearning for her mother to be near her today shot through the girl. She looked from her untamed man to the untamed desert of Wyoming, and the town where she was to take him as her wedded husband. But for his sake she would not let him guess her loneliness.

He sat on his horse Monte, considering the pistol. Then he showed her a rattlesnake coiled by the roots of some sagebrush. 'Can I hit it?' he enquired.

'You don't often miss them,' said she, striving to be cheerful.

'Well, I'm told getting married unstrings some men.' He aimed, and the snake was shattered. 'Maybe it's too early yet for the unstringing to begin!' And with some deliberation he sent three more bullets into the snake. 'I reckon that's enough,' said he.

'Was not the first one?'

'Oh, yes, for the snake.' And then, with one leg crooked cowboy fashion across in front of his saddle horn, he cleaned his pistol, and replaced the empty cartridges.

Once more she ventured near the line of his reticence. 'Has – has Trampas seen you much lately?'

'Why, no; not for a right smart while. But I reckon he has not missed me.'

The Virginian spoke this in his gentlest voice. But his rebuffed sweet-heart turned her face away, and from her eyes she brushed a tear.

He reined his horse Monte beside her, and upon her cheek she felt his kiss. 'You are not the only mind-reader,' said he, very tenderly. And at this she clung to him, and laid her head upon his breast. 'I had been thinking,' he went on, 'that the way our marriage is to be was the most beautiful way.'

'It is the most beautiful,' she murmured.

He slowly spoke out his thought, as if she had not said this. 'No folks to stare, no fuss, no jokes and ribbons and best bonnets, no public eye nor talkin' of tongues when most yu' want to hear nothing and say nothing.'

She answered by holding him closer.

'Just the bishop of Wyoming to join us, and not even him after we're once joined. I did think that would be ahead of all ways to get married I have seen.

He paused again, and she made no rejoinder.

'But we have left out your mother.'

She looked in his face with quick astonishment. It was as if his spirit had heard the cry of her spirit.

'That is nowhere near right,' he said. 'That is wrong.'

'She could never have come here,' said the girl.

'We should have gone there. I don't know how I can ask her to forgive me.'

'But it was not you!' cried Molly.

'Yes. Because I did not object. I did not tell you we must go to her. I missed the point, thinking so much about my own feelings. For you see – and I've never said this to you until now – your mother did hurt me. When you said you would have me after my years of waiting, and I wrote her that letter telling her all about myself, and how my family was not like yours, and – and – all the rest I told her, why you see it hurt me never to get a word back from her except just messages through you. For I had talked to her about my hopes and my failings. I had said more than ever I've said to you, because she was your mother. I wanted her to forgive me, if she could, and feel that maybe I could take good care of you after all. For it was bad enough to have her daughter quit her home to teach school out hyeh on Bear Creek. Bad enough without havin' me to come along and make it worse. I have missed the point in thinking of my own feelings.'

'But it's not your doing!' repeated Molly.

With his deep delicacy he had put the whole matter as a hardship to her mother alone. He had saved her any pain of confession or denial. 'Yes, it is my doing,' he now said. 'Shall we give it up?'

'Give what – ?' She did not understand.

'Why, the order we've got it fixed in. Plans are – well, they're no more than plans. I hate the notion of changing, but I hate hurting your mother more. Or, anyway, I *ought* to hate it more. So we can shift, if yu' say so. It's not too late.'

'Shift?' she faltered.

'I mean, we can go to your home now. We can start by the stage tonight. Your mother can see us married. We can come back and finish in the mountains instead of beginning in them. It'll be just merely shifting, yu' see.'

He could scarcely bring himself to say this at all; yet he said it almost as if he were urging it. It implied a renunciation that he could hardly bear to think of. To put off his wedding day, the bliss upon whose threshold he stood after his three years of faithful battle for it, and that wedding journey he had arranged: for there were the mountains in sight, the woods and canyons where he had planned to go with her after the bishop had joined them; the solitudes where only the wild animals would be, besides themselves. His horses, his tent, his rifle, his rod, all were waiting ready in the town for their start tomorrow. He had provided many dainty things to make her comfortable. Well, he could wait a little more, having waited three years. It would not be what his heart most desired: there would be the 'public eye and the talking of tongues' – but he could wait. The hour would come when he could be alone with his bride at last. And so he spoke as if he urged it.

'Never!' she cried. 'Never, never!'

She pushed it from her. She would not brook such sacrifice on his part. Were they not going to her mother in four weeks? If her family had warmly accepted him – but they had not; and in any case, it had gone too far, it was too late. She told her lover that she would not hear him, that if he said any more she would gallop into town separately from him. And for his sake she would hide deep from him this loneliness of hers, and the hurt that he had given her in refusing to share with her his trouble with Trampas, when others must know of it.

Accordingly, they descended the hill slowly together, lingering to spin out these last miles long. Many rides had taught their horses to go side by side, and so they went now: the girl sweet and thoughtful in her sedate grey habit; and the man in his leathern chaps and cartridge-belt and flannel shirt, looking gravely into the distance with the level gaze of the frontier.

Having read his sweetheart's mind very plainly, the lover now broke his dearest custom. It was his code never to speak ill of any man to any woman. Men's quarrels were not for women's ears. In his scheme, good women were to know only a fragment of men's lives. He had lived many outlaw years, and his wide knowledge of evil made innocence doubly precious to him. But today he must depart from his code, having read her mind well. He would speak evil of one man to one woman, because his reticence had hurt her – and was she not far from her mother, and very lonely, do what he could? She should know the story of his quarrel in language as light and casual as he could veil it with.

He made an oblique start. He did not say to her: 'I'll tell you about this. You saw me get ready for Trampas because I have been ready for him any time these five years.' He began far off from the point with that rooted caution of his – that caution which is shared by the primal savage and the perfected diplomat.

'There's cert'nly a right smart o' difference between men and women,' he observed.

'You're quite sure?' she retorted.

'Ain't it fortunate? – that there's both, I mean.'

'I don't know about fortunate. Machinery could probably do all the heavy work for us without your help.'

'And who'd invent the machinery?'

She laughed. 'We shouldn't need the huge, noisy things you do. Our world would be a gentle one.'

'Oh, my gracious!'

'What do you mean by that?'

'Oh, my gracious! Get along, Monte! A gentle world all full of ladies!'

'Do you call men gentle?' enquired Molly.

'Now it's a funny thing about that. Have yu' ever noticed a joke about fathers-in-law? There's just as many fathers- as mothers-in-law; but which side are your jokes?'

Molly was not vanquished. 'That's because the men write the comic papers,' said she.

'Hear that, Monte? The men write 'em. Well, if the ladies wrote a comic paper, I expect that might be gentle.'

She gave up this battle in mirth; and he resumed – 'But don't you really reckon it's uncommon to meet a father-in-law flouncin' around the house? As for gentle – Once I had to sleep in a room next a ladies' temperance meetin'. Oh, heavens! Well, I couldn't change my room, and the hotel man, he apologised to me next mawnin'. Said it didn't surprise him the husbands drank some.'

Here the Virginian broke down over his own fantastic inventions, and gave a joyous chuckle in company with his sweetheart. 'Yes, there's a big heap o' difference between men and women,' he said. 'Take that fello' and myself, now.'

'Trampas?' said Molly, quickly serious. She looked along the road ahead, and discerned the figure of Trampas still visible on its way to town.

The Virginian did not wish her to be serious – more than could be helped. 'Why, yes,' he replied, with a waving gesture at Trampas. 'Take him and me. He don't think much o' me. How could he? And I expect he'll never. But yu' saw just now how it was between us. We were not a bit like a temperance meetin'.'

She could not help laughing at the twist he gave to his voice. And she felt happiness warming her; for in the Virginian's tone about Trampas was something now that no longer excluded her. Thus he began his gradual recital, in a cadence always easy, and more and more musical with the native accent of the South. With the light turn he gave it, its pure ugliness melted into charm.

'No, he don't think anything of me. Once a man in the John Day Valley didn't think much, and by Cañada de Oro I met another. It will always be so here and there, but Trampas beats 'em all. For the others have always expressed themselves – got shut of their poor opinion in the open air.

'Yu' see, I had to explain myself to Trampas a right smart while ago, long before ever I laid my eyes on yu'. It was just nothing at all. A little matter of cyards in the days when I was apt to spend my money and my holidays pretty headlong. My gracious, what nonsensical times I have had! But I was apt to win at cyards, 'specially poker. And Trampas, he met me one night, and I expect he must have thought I looked kind o' young. So he hated losin' his money to such a young-lookin' man, and he took his way of sayin' as much. I had to explain myself to him plainly, so that he learned right away my age had got its growth.

'Well, I expect he hated that worse, having to receive my explanation with folks lookin' on at us publicly that-a-way, and him without further ideas occurrin' to him at the moment. That's what started his poor opinion of me, not havin' ideas at the moment. And so the boys resumed their cyards.

'I'd most forgot about it. But Trampas's mem'ry is one of his strong points. Next thing – oh, it's a good while later – he gets to losin' flesh because Judge Henry gave me charge of him and some other punchers taking cattle – '

'That's not next,' interrupted the girl.

'Not? Why – '

'Don't you remember?' she said, timid, yet eager. 'Don't you?'

'Blamed if I do!'

'The first time we met?'

'Yes; my mem'ry keeps that – like I keep this.' And he brought from his pocket her own handkerchief, the token he had picked up at a river's brink when he had carried her from an overturned stage.

'We did not exactly meet, then,' she said. 'It was at that dance. I hadn't seen you yet; but Trampas was saying something horrid about me, and you said – you said, "Rise on your legs, you pole cat, and tell them you're a liar". When I heard that, I think – I think it finished me.' And crimson suffused Molly's countenance.

'I'd forgot,' the Virginian murmured. Then sharply, 'How did you hear it?'

'Mrs Taylor – '

'Oh! Well, a man would never have told a woman that.'

Molly laughed triumphantly. 'Then who told Mrs Taylor?'

Being caught, he grinned at her. 'I reckon husbands are a special kind of man,' was all that he found to say. 'Well, since you do know about that, it was the next move in the game. Trampas thought I had no call to stop him sayin' what he pleased about a woman who was nothin' to me – then. But all women ought to be somethin' to a man. So I had to give Trampas another explanation in the presence of folks lookin' on, and it was just like the cyards. No ideas occurred to him again. And down goes his opinion of me some more!

'Well, I have not been able to raise it. There has been this and that and the other – yu' know most of the later doings yourself – and today is the first time I've happened to see the man since the doings last autumn. Yu' seem to know about them, too. He knows I can't prove he was with that gang of horse thieves. And I can't prove he killed poor Shorty. But he knows I missed him awful close, and spoiled his thieving for a while. So d' yu' wonder he don't think much of me? But if I had lived to be twenty-nine years old like I am, and with all my chances made no enemy, I'd feel myself a failure.'

His story was finished. He had made her his confidant in matters he had never spoken of before, and she was happy to be thus much nearer to him. It diminished a certain fear that was mingled with her love of him.

During the next several miles he was silent, and his silence was enough for her. Vermont sank away from her thoughts, and Wyoming held less of loneliness. They descended altogether into the map which had stretched below them, so that it was a map no longer, but earth with growing things, and prairie-dogs sitting upon it, and now and then a bird flying over it. And after a while she said to him, 'What are you thinking about?'

'I have been doing sums. Figured in hours it sounds right short. Figured in minutes it boils up into quite a mess. Twenty by sixty is twelve hundred. Put that into seconds, and yu' get seventy-two thousand seconds. Seventy-two thousand. Seventy-two thousand seconds yet before we get married.'

'Seconds! To think of its having come to seconds!'

'I am thinkin' about it. I'm choppin' sixty of 'em off every minute.'

With such chopping time wears away. More miles of the road lay behind them, and in the virgin wilderness the scars of new-scraped water ditches began to appear, and the first wire fences. Next, they were passing cabins and occasional fields, the outposts of habitation. The free road became wholly imprisoned, running between unbroken stretches of barbed wire. Far off to the eastward a flowing column of dust marked the approaching stage, bringing the bishop, probably, for whose visit here they had timed their wedding. The day still brimmed with heat and sunshine; but the great daily shadow was beginning to move from the feet of the Bow Leg Mountains outward towards the town. Presently they began to meet citizens. Some of these knew them and nodded, while some did not, and stared. Turning a corner into the town's chief street, where stood the hotel, the bank, the drug store, the general store, and the seven saloons, they were hailed heartily. Here were three friends – Honey Wiggin, Scipio le Moyne, and Lin McLean – all desirous of drinking the Virginian's health, if his lady – would she mind? The three stood grinning, with their hats off; but behind their gaiety the Virginian read some other purpose.

'We'll all be very good,' said Honey Wiggin.

'Pretty good,' said Lin.

'Good,' said Scipio.

'Which is the honest man?' enquired Molly, glad to see them.

'Not one!' said the Virginian. 'My old friends scare me when I think of their ways.'

'It's bein' engaged scares yu',' retorted Mr McLean. 'Marriage restores your courage, I find.'

'Well, I'll trust all of you,' said Molly. 'He's going to take me to the hotel, and then you can drink his health as much as you please.'

With a smile to them she turned to proceed, and he let his horse move with hers; but he looked at his friends. Then Scipio's bleached blue eyes narrowed to a slit, and he said what they had all come out on the street to say – 'Don't change your clothes.'

'Oh!' protested Molly, 'isn't he rather dusty and countrified?'

But the Virginian had taken Scipio's meaning. *'Don't change your clothes.'* Innocent Molly appreciated these words no more than the average reader who reads a masterpiece, complacently unaware that its style differs from that of the morning paper. Such was Scipio's intention, wishing to spare her from alarm.

So at the hotel she let her lover go with a kiss, and without a thought of Trampas. She in her room unlocked the possessions which were there waiting for her, and changed her dress.

Wedding garments, and other civilised apparel proper for a genuine frontiersman when he comes to town, were also in the hotel, ready for the Virginian to wear. It is only the somewhat green and unseasoned cowpuncher who struts before the public in spurs and deadly weapons. For many a year the Virginian had put away these childish things. He made a sober toilet for the streets. Nothing but his face and bearing remained out of the common when he was in a town. But Scipio had told him not to change his clothes; therefore he went out with his pistol at his hip. Soon he had joined his three friends.

'I'm obliged to yu',' he said. 'He passed me this mawnin'.'

'We don't know his intentions,' said Wiggin.

'Except that he's hangin' around,' said McLean.

'And fillin' up,' said Scipio, 'which reminds me – '

They strolled into the saloon of a friend, where, unfortunately, sat some foolish people. But one cannot always tell how much of a fool a man is, at sight.

It was a temperate health-drinking that they made. 'Here's how,' they muttered softly to the Virginian; and 'How,' he returned softly, looking away from them. But they had a brief meeting of eyes, standing and lounging near each other, shyly; and Scipio shook hands with the bridegroom. 'Someday,' he stated, tapping himself; for in his vagrant heart he began to envy the man who could bring himself to marry. And he nodded again, repeating, 'Here's how.'

They stood at the bar, full of sentiment, empty of words, memory and affection busy in their hearts. All of them had seen rough days together, and they felt guilty with emotion.

'It's hot weather,' said Wiggin.

'Hotter on Box Elder,' said McLean. 'My kid has started teething.'

Words ran dry again. They shifted their positions, looked in their glasses, read the labels on the bottles. They dropped a word now and then to the proprietor about his trade, and his ornaments.

'Good head,' commented McLean.

'Big old ram,' assented the proprietor. 'Shot him myself on Grey Bull last fall.'

'Sheep was thick in the Tetons last fall,' said the Virginian.

On the bar stood a machine into which the idle customer might drop his nickel. The coin then bounced among an arrangement of pegs, descending at length into one or another of various holes. You might win as much as ten times your stake, but this was not the most usual result; and with nickels the three friends and the bridegroom now mildly sported for a while, buying them with silver when their store ran out.

'Was it sheep you went after in the Tetons?' enquired the proprietor, knowing it was horse thieves.

'Yes,' said the Virginian. 'I'll have ten more nickels.'

'Did you get all the sheep you wanted?' the proprietor continued.

'Poor luck,' said the Virginian.

'Think there's a friend of yours in town this afternoon,' said the proprietor.

'Did he mention he was my friend?'

The proprietor laughed. The Virginian watched another nickel click down among the pegs.

Honey Wiggin now made the bridegroom a straight offer. 'We'll take this thing off your hands,' said he.

'Any or all of us,' said Lin.

But Scipio held his peace. His loyalty went every inch as far as theirs, but his understanding of his friend went deeper. 'Don't change your clothes,' was the first and the last help he would be likely to give in this matter. The rest must be as such matters must always be, between man and man. To the other two friends, however, this seemed a very special case, falling outside established precedent. Therefore they ventured offers of interference.

'A man don't get married every day,' apologised McLean. 'We'll just run him out of town for yu'.'

'Save yu' the trouble,' urged Wiggin. 'Say the word.'

The proprietor now added his voice. 'It'll sober him up to spend his night out in the brush. He'll quit his talk then.'

But the Virginian did not say the word, or any word. He stood playing with the nickels.

'Think of her,' muttered McLean.

'Who else would I be thinking of?' returned the Southerner. His face had become very sombre. 'She has been raised so different!' he murmured. He pondered a little, while the others waited, solicitous.

A new idea came to the proprietor. 'I am acting mayor of this town,' said he. 'I'll put him in the calaboose and keep him till you get married and away.'

'Say the word,' repeated Honey Wiggin.

Scipio's eye met the proprietor's, and he shook his head about a quarter of an inch. The proprietor shook his to the same amount. They understood each other. It had come to that point where there was no way out, save only the ancient, eternal way between man and man. It is only the great mediocrity that goes to law in these personal matters.

'So he has talked about me some?' said the Virginian.

'It's the whiskey,' Scipio explained.

'I expect,' said McLean, 'he'd run a mile if he was in a state to appreciate his insinuations.'

'Which we are careful not to mention to yu',' said Wiggin, 'unless yu' enquire for 'em.'

Some of the fools present had drawn closer to hear this interesting conversation. In gatherings of more than six there will generally be at least one fool; and this company must have numbered twenty men.

'This country knows well enough,' said one fool, who hungered to be important, 'that you don't brand no calves that ain't your own.'

The saturnine Virginian looked at him. 'Thank yu',' said he, gravely, 'for your endorsement of my character.' The fool felt flattered. The Virginian turned to his friends. His hand slowly pushed his hat back, and he rubbed his black head in thought.

'Glad to see yu've got your gun with you,' continued the happy fool. 'You know what Trampas claims about that affair of yours in the Tetons? He claims that if everything was known about the killing of Shorty – '

'Take one on the house,' suggested the proprietor to him, amiably. 'Your news will be fresher.' And he pushed him the bottle. The fool felt less important.

'This talk had went the rounds before it got to us,' said Scipio, 'or we'd have headed it off. He has got friends in town.'

Perplexity knotted the Virginian's brows. This community knew that a man had implied he was a thief and a murderer; it also knew that he knew it. But the case was one of peculiar circumstances, assuredly. Could he avoid meeting the man? Soon the stage would be starting south for the railroad. He had already today proposed to his sweetheart that they should take it. Could he for her sake leave unanswered a talking enemy upon the field? His own ears had not heard the enemy.

Into these reflections the fool stepped once more. 'Of course this country don't believe Trampas,' said he. 'This country – '

But he contributed no further thoughts. From somewhere in the rear of the building, where it opened upon the tin cans and the hinder purlieus of the town, came a movement, and Trampas was among them, courageous with whiskey.

All the fools now made themselves conspicuous. One lay on the floor, knocked there by the Virginian, whose arm he had attempted to hold. Others struggled with Trampas, and his bullet smashed the ceiling before they could drag the pistol from him. 'There now! there now!' they interposed; 'you don't want to talk like that,' for he was pouring out a tide of hate and vilification. Yet the Virginian stood quiet by the bar, and many an eye of astonishment was turned upon him. 'I'd not stand half that language,' some muttered to each other. Still the Virginian waited quietly, while the fools reasoned with Trampas. But no earthly foot can step between a man and his destiny. Trampas broke suddenly free.

'Your friends have saved your life,' he rang out, with obscene epithets. 'I'll give you till sundown to leave town.'

There was total silence instantly.

'Trampas,' spoke the Virginian, 'I don't want trouble with you.'

'He never has wanted it,' Trampas sneered to the bystanders. 'He has been dodging it five years. But I've got him coralled.'

Some of the Trampas faction smiled.

'Trampas,' said the Virginian again, 'are yu' sure yu' really mean that?'

The whiskey bottle flew through the air, hurled by Trampas, and crashed through the saloon window behind the Virginian.

'That was surplusage, Trampas,' said he, 'if yu' mean the other.'

'Get out by sundown, that's all,' said Trampas. And wheeling, he went out of the saloon by the rear, as he had entered.

'Gentlemen,' said the Virginian, 'I know you will all oblige me.'

'Sure!' exclaimed the proprietor, heartily. 'We'll see that everybody lets this thing alone.'

The Virginian gave a general nod to the company, and walked out into the street.

'It's a turrble shame,' sighed Scipio, 'that he couldn't have postponed it.'

The Virginian walked in the open air with thoughts disturbed. 'I am of two minds about one thing,' he said to himself uneasily.

Gossip ran in advance of him; but as he came by, the talk fell away until he had passed. Then they looked after him, and their words again rose audibly. Thus everywhere a little eddy of silence accompanied his steps.

'It don't trouble him much,' one said, having read nothing in the Virginian's face.

'It may trouble his girl some,' said another.

'She'll not know,' said a third, 'until it's over.'

'He'll not tell her?'

'I wouldn't. It's no woman's business.'

'Maybe that's so. Well, it would have suited me to have Trampas die sooner.'

'How would it suit you to have him live longer?' enquired a member of the opposite faction, suspected of being himself a cattle-thief.

'I could answer your question, if I had other folks' calves I wanted to brand.' This raised both a laugh and a silence.

Thus the town talked, filling in the time before sunset.

The Virginian, still walking aloof in the open air, paused at the edge of the town. 'I'd sooner have a sickness than be undecided this way,' he said, and he looked up and down. Then a grim smile came at his own expense. 'I reckon it would make me sick – but there's not time.'

Over there in the hotel sat his sweetheart, alone, away from her mother, her friends, her home, waiting his return, knowing nothing. He looked into the west. Between the sun and the bright ridges of the mountains was still a space of sky; but the shadow from the mountains' feet had drawn halfway towards the town. 'About forty minutes more,' he said aloud. 'She has been raised so different.' And he sighed as he turned back. As he went slowly, he did not know how great was his own unhappiness. 'She has been raised so different,' he said again.

Opposite the post office the bishop of Wyoming met him and greeted him. His lonely heart throbbed at the warm, firm grasp of this friend's hand. The bishop saw his eyes glow suddenly, as if tears were close. But none came, and no word more open than, 'I'm glad to see you.'

But gossip had reached the bishop, and he was sorely troubled also. 'What is all this?' said he, coming straight to it.

The Virginian looked at the clergyman frankly. 'Yu' know just as much about it as I do,' he said. 'And I'll tell yu' anything yu' ask.'

'Have you told Miss Wood?' enquired the bishop.

The eyes of the bridegroom fell, and the bishop's face grew at once more keen and more troubled. Then the bridegroom raised his eyes again, and the bishop almost loved him. He touched his arm, like a brother. 'This is hard luck,' he said.

The bridegroom could scarce keep his voice steady. 'I want to do right today more than any day I have ever lived,' said he.

'Then go and tell her at once.'

'It will just do nothing but scare her.'

'Go and tell her at once.'

'I expected you was going to tell me to run away from Trampas. I can't do that, yu' know.'

The bishop did know. Never before in all his wilderness work had he faced such a thing. He knew that Trampas was an evil in the country, and that the Virginian was a good. He knew that the cattle thieves – the rustlers – were gaining in numbers and audacity; that they led many weak young fellows to ruin; that they elected their men to office, and controlled juries; that they were a staring menace to Wyoming. His heart was with the Virginian. But there was his Gospel, that he preached, and believed, and tried to live. He stood looking at the ground and drawing a finger along his eyebrow. He wished that he might have heard nothing about all this. But he was not one to blink his responsibility as a Christian server of the church militant.

'Am I right,' he now slowly asked, 'in believing that you think I am a sincere man?'

'I don't believe anything about it. I know it.'

'I should run away from Trampas,' said the bishop.

'That ain't quite fair, seh. We all understand you have got to do the things you tell other folks to do. And you do them, seh. You never talk like anything but a man, and you never set yourself above others. You can saddle your own horses. And I saw yu' walk unarmed into that White River excitement when those two other parsons was a-foggin' and a-fannin' for their own safety. Damn scoundrels!'

The bishop instantly rebuked such language about brothers of his cloth, even though he disapproved both of them and their doctrines. 'Everyone may be an instrument of Providence,' he concluded.

'Well,' said the Virginian, 'if that is so, then Providence makes use of instruments I'd not touch with a ten-foot pole. Now if you was me, seh, and not a bishop, would you run away from Trampas?'

'That's not quite fair, either!' exclaimed the bishop, with a smile. 'Because you are asking me to take another man's convictions, and yet remain myself.'

'Yes, seh. I am. That's so. That don't get at it. I reckon you and I can't get at it.'

'If the Bible,' said the bishop, 'which I believe to be God's word, was anything to you – '

'It is something to me, seh. I have found fine truths in it.'

' "Thou shalt not kill," ' quoted the bishop. 'That is plain.'

The Virginian took his turn at smiling. 'Mighty plain to me, seh. Make it plain to Trampas, and there'll be no killin.' We can't get at it that way.'

Once more the bishop quoted earnestly. ' "Vengeance is mine, I will repay, saith the Lord".'

'How about instruments of Providence, seh? Why, we can't get at it that way. If you start usin' the Bible that way, it will mix you up mighty quick, seh.'

'My friend,' the bishop urged, and all his good, warm heart was in it, 'my dear fellow – go away for the one night. He'll change his mind.'

The Virginian shook his head. 'He cannot change his word, seh. Or at least I must stay around till he does. Why, I have given him the say-so. He's got the choice. Most men would not have took what I took from him in the saloon. Why don't you ask *him* to leave town?'

The good bishop was at a standstill. Of all kicking against the pricks none is so hard as this kick of a professing Christian against the whole instinct of human man.

'But you have helped me some,' said the Virginian. 'I will go and tell her. At least, if I think it will be good for her, I will tell her.'

The bishop thought that she saw one last chance to move him.

'You're twenty-nine,' he began.

'And a little over,' said the Virginian.

'And you were fourteen when you ran away from your family.'

'Well, I was weary, yu' know, of havin' elder brothers lay down my law night and mawnin'.'

'Yes, I know. So that your life has been your own for fifteen years. But it is not your own now. You have given it to a woman.'

'Yes; I have given it to her. But my life's not the whole of me. I'd give her twice my life – fifty – a thousand of 'em. But I can't give her – her nor anybody in heaven or earth – I can't give my – my – we'll never get at it, seh! There's no good in words. Goodbye.' The Virginian wrung the bishop's hand and left him.

'God bless him!' said the bishop. 'God bless him!'

*   *   *

The Virginian unlocked the room in the hotel where he kept stored his tent, his blankets, his pack-saddles, and his many accoutrements for the bridal journey in the mountains. Out of the window he saw the mountains blue in shadow, but some cottonwoods distant in the flat between were still bright green in the sun. From among his possessions he took quickly a pistol, wiping and loading it. Then from its holster he removed the pistol which he had tried and made sure of in the morning. This, according to his wont when going into a risk, he shoved between his trousers and his shirt in front. The untried weapon he placed in the holster, letting it hang visibly at his hip. He glanced out of the window again, and saw the mountains of the same deep blue. But the cottonwoods were no longer in the sunlight. The shadow had come past them, nearer the town; for fifteen of the forty minutes were gone. 'The bishop is wrong,' he said. 'There is no sense in telling her.' And he turned to the door, just as she came to it herself.

'Oh!' she cried out at once, and rushed to him.

He swore as he held her close. 'The fools!' he said. 'The fools!'

'It has been so frightful waiting for you,' said she, leaning her head against him.

'Who had to tell you this?' he demanded.

'I don't know. Somebody just came and said it.'

'This is mean luck,' he murmured, patting he 'This is mean luck.'

She went on: 'I wanted to run out and find you; but I didn't! I didn't! I stayed quiet in my room till they said you had come back.'

'It is mean luck. Mighty mean,' he repeated.

'How could you be so long?' she asked. 'Never mind, I've got you now. It is over.'

Anger and sorrow filled him. 'I might have known some fool would tell you,' he said.

'It's all over. Never mind.' Her arms tightened their hold of him. Then she let him go. 'What shall we do?' she said. 'What now?'

'Now?' he answered. 'Nothing now.'

She looked at him without understanding.

'I know it is a heap worse for you,' he pursued, speaking slowly. 'I knew it would be.'

'But it is over!' she exclaimed again.

He did not understand her now. He kissed her. 'Did you think it was over?' he said simply. 'There is some waiting still before us. I wish you did not have to wait alone. But it will not be long.' He was looking down, and did not see the happiness grow chilled upon her face, and then fade into bewildered fear. 'I did my best,' he went on. 'I think I did. I know I tried. I let him say to me before them all what no man has ever said, or ever will again. I kept thinking hard of you – with all my might, or I reckon I'd have killed him right there. And I gave him a show to change his mind. I gave it to him twice. I spoke as quiet as I am speaking to you now. But he stood to it. And I expect he knows he went too far in the hearing of others to go back on his threat. He will have to go on to the finish now.

'The finish?' she echoed, almost voiceless.

'Yes,' he answered very gently.

Her dilated eyes were fixed upon him. 'But – ' she could scarce form utterance, 'but you?'

'I have got myself ready,' he said. 'Did you think – why, what did you think?'

She recoiled a step. 'What are you going – ' She put her two hands to her head. 'Oh, God!' she almost shrieked, 'you are going – ' He made a step, and would have put his arm round her, but she backed against the wall, staring speechless at him.

'I am not going to let him shoot me,' he said quietly.

'You mean – you mean – but you can come away!' she cried. 'It's not too late yet. You can take yourself out of his reach. Everybody knows that you are brave. What is he to you? You can leave him in this place. I'll go with you anywhere. To any house, to the mountains, to anywhere away. We'll leave this horrible place together and – and – oh, won't you listen to me?' She stretched her hands to him. 'Won't you listen?'

He took her hands. 'I must stay here.'

Her hands clung to his. 'No, no, no. There's something else. There's something better than shedding blood in cold blood. Only think what it means! Only think of having to remember such a thing! Why, it's what they hang people for! It's murder!'

He dropped her hands. 'Don't call it that name,' he said sternly.

'When there was the choice!' she exclaimed, half to herself, like a person stunned and speaking to the air. 'To get ready for it when you have the choice!'

'He did the choosing,' answered the Virginian. 'Listen to me. Are you listening?' he asked, for her gaze was dull.

She nodded.

'I work hyeh. I belong hyeh. It's my life. If folks came to think I was a coward – '

'Who would think you were a coward?'

'Everybody. My friends would be sorry and ashamed, and my enemies would walk around saying they had always said so. I could not hold up my head again among enemies or friends.'

'When it was explained – '

'There'd be nothing to explain. There'd just be the fact.' He was nearly angry.

'There is a higher courage than fear of outside opinion,' said the New England girl.

Her Southern lover looked at her. 'Cert'nly there is. That's what I'm showing in going against yours.'

'But if you know that you are brave, and if I know that you are brave, oh, my dear, my dear! what difference does the world make? How much higher courage to go your own course – '

'I am goin' my own course,' he broke in. 'Can't yu' see how it must be about a man? It's not for their benefit, friends or enemies, that I have got this thing to do. If any man happened to say I was a thief and I heard about it, would I let him go on spreadin' such a thing of me? Don't I owe my own honesty something better than that? Would I sit down in a corner rubbin' my honesty and whisperin' to it, "There! there! I know you ain't a thief"? No, seh; not a little bit! What men say about my nature is not just merely an outside thing. For the fact that I let 'em keep on sayin' it is a proof I don't value my nature enough to shield it from their slander and give them their punishment. And that's being a poor sort of a jay.'

She had grown very white.

'Can't yu' see how it must be about a man?' he repeated.

'I cannot,' she answered, in a voice that scarcely seemed her own. 'If I ought to, I cannot. To shed blood in cold blood. When I heard about that last fall – about the killing of those cattle thieves – I kept saying to myself: "He had to do it. It was a public duty." And lying sleepless I got used to Wyoming being different from Vermont. But this – ' she gave a shudder – 'when I think of tomorrow, of you and me, and of – If you do this, there can be no tomorrow for you and me.'

At these words he also turned white.

'Do you mean – ' he asked, and could go no farther.

Nor could she answer him, but turned her head away.

'This would be the end – ?' he asked.

Her head faintly moved to signify yes.

He stood still, his hand shaking a little. 'Will you look at me and say that?' he murmured at length. She did not move. 'Can you do it?' he said.

His sweetness made her turn, but could not pierce her frozen resolve. She gazed at him across the great distance of her despair.

'Then it is really so?' he said.

Her lips tried to form words, but failed.

He looked out of the window, and saw nothing but shadow. The blue of the mountains was now become a deep purple. Suddenly his hand closed hard.

'Goodbye, then,' he said.

At that word she was at his feet, clutching him. 'For my sake,' she begged him. 'For my sake.'

A tremble passed through his frame. She felt his legs shake as she held them, and, looking up, she saw that his eyes were closed with misery.

Then he opened them, and in their steady look she read her answer. He unclasped her hands from holding him, and raised her to her feet.

'I have no right to kiss you any more,' he said. And then, before his desire could break him down from this, he was gone, and she was alone.

She did not fall, or totter, but stood motionless. And next – it seemed a moment and it seemed eternity – she heard in the distance a shot, and then two shots. Out of the window she saw people beginning to run. At that she turned and fled to her room, and flung herself face downward upon the floor.

* * *

Trampas had departed into solitude from the saloon, leaving behind him his ultimatum. His loud and public threat was town knowledge already, would very likely be county knowledge tonight. Riders would take it with them to entertain distant cabins up the river and down the river; and by dark the stage would go south with the news of it – and the news of its outcome. For everything would be over by dark. After five years, here was the end coming – coming before dark. Trampas had got up this morning with no such thought. It seemed very strange to look back upon the morning; it lay so distant, so irrevocable. And he thought of how he had eaten his breakfast. How would he eat his supper? For supper would come afterward. Some people were eating theirs now, with nothing like this before them. His heart ached and grew cold to think of them, easy and comfortable with plates and cups of coffee.

He looked at the mountains, and saw the sun above their ridges, and the shadow coming from their feet. And there close behind him was the morning he could never go back to. He could see it clearly; his thoughts reached out like arms to touch it once more, and be in it again. The night that was coming he could not see, and his eyes and his thoughts shrank from it. He had given his enemy until sundown. He could not trace the path which had led him to this. He remembered their first meeting – five years back, in Medicine Bow, and the words which at once began his hate. No, it was before any words; it was the encounter of their eyes. For out of the eyes of every stranger looks either a friend or an enemy, waiting to be known. But how had five years of hate come to play him such a trick, suddenly, today? Since last autumn he had meant sometime to get even with this man who seemed to stand at every turn of his crookedness, and rob him of his spoils. But how had he come to choose such a way of getting even as this, face to face? He knew many better ways; and now his own rash proclamation had trapped him. His words were like doors shutting him in to perform his threat to the letter, with witnesses at hand to see that he did so.

Trampas looked at the sun and the shadow again. He had till sundown. The heart inside him was turning it round in this opposite way: it was to *himself* that in his rage he had given this lessening margin of grace. But he dared not leave town in all the world's sight after all the world had heard him. Even his friends would fall from him after such an act. Could he – the thought actually came to him – could he strike before the time set? But the thought was useless. Even if his friends could harbour him after such a deed, his enemies would find him, and his life would be forfeit to a certainty. His own trap was closing upon him.

He came upon the main street, and saw some distance off the Virginian standing in talk with the bishop. He slunk between two houses, and cursed both of them. The sight had been good for him, bringing some warmth of rage back to his desperate heart. And he went into a place and drank some whiskey.

'In your shoes,' said the barkeeper, 'I'd be afraid to take so much.'

But the nerves of Trampas were almost beyond the reach of intoxication, and he swallowed some more, and went out again. Presently he fell in with some of his brothers in cattle stealing, and walked along with them for a little.

'Well, it will not be long now,' they said to him. And he had never heard words so desolate.

'No,' he made out to say; 'soon now.' Their cheerfulness seemed unearthly to him, and his heart almost broke beneath it.

'We'll have one to your success,' they suggested.

So with them he repaired to another place; and the sight of a man leaning against the bar made him start so that they noticed him. Then he saw that the man was a stranger whom he had never laid eyes on till now.

'It looked like Shorty,' he said, and could have bitten his tongue off.

'Shorty is quiet up in the Tetons,' said a friend. 'You don't want to be thinking about him. Here's how!'

Then they clapped him on the back and he left them. He thought of his enemy and his hate, beating his rage like a failing horse, and treading the courage of his drink. Across a space he saw Wiggin, walking with McLean and Scipio. They were watching the town to see that his friends made no foul play.

'We're giving you a clear field,' said Wiggin.

'This race will not be pulled,' said McLean.

'Be with you at the finish,' said Scipio.

And they passed on. They did not seem like real people to him.

Trampas looked at the walls and windows of the houses. Were they real? Was he here, walking in this street? Something had changed. He looked everywhere, and feeling it everywhere, wondered what this could be. Then he knew: it was the sun that had gone entirely behind the mountains, and he drew out his pistol.

*   *   *

The Virginian, for precaution, did not walk out of the front door of the hotel. He went through back ways, and paused once. Against his breast he felt the wedding ring where he had it suspended by a chain from his neck. His hand went up to it, and he drew it out and looked at it. He took it off the chain, and his arm went back to hurl it from him as far as he could. But he stopped and kissed it with one sob, and thrust it in his pocket. Then he walked out into the open, watching. He saw men here and there, and they let him pass as before, without speaking. He saw his three friends, and they said no word to him. But they turned and followed in his rear at a little distance, because it was known that Shorty had been found shot from behind. The Virginian gained a position soon where no one could come at him except from in front; and the sight of the mountains was almost more than he could endure, because it was there that he had been going tomorrow.

'It is quite a while after sunset,' he heard himself say.

A wind seemed to blow his sleeve off his arm, and he replied to it, and saw Trampas pitch forward. He saw Trampas raise his arm from the ground and fall again, and lie there this time, still. A little smoke was rising from the pistol on the ground, and he looked at his own, and saw the smoke flowing upward out of it.

'I expect that's all,' he said aloud.

But as he came nearer Trampas, he covered him with his weapon. He stopped a moment, seeing the hand on the ground move. Two fingers twitched, and then ceased; for it was all. The Virginian stood looking down at Trampas.

'Both of mine hit,' he said, once more aloud. 'His must have gone mighty close to my arm. I told her it would not be me.'

He had scarcely noticed that he was being surrounded and congratulated. His hand was being shaken, and he saw it was Scipio in tears.

Scipio's joy made his heart like lead within him. He was near telling his friend everything, but he did not.

'If anybody wants me about this,' he said, 'I will be at the hotel.'

'Who'll want you?' said Scipio. 'Three of us saw his gun out.' And he vented his admiration. 'You were that cool! That quick!'

'I'll see you boys again,' said the Virginian, heavily; and he walked away.

Scipio looked after him, astonished. 'Yu' might suppose he was in poor luck,' he said to McLean.

The Virginian walked to the hotel, and stood on the threshold of his sweetheart's room. She had heard his step, and was upon her feet. Her lips were parted, and her eyes fixed on him, nor did she move, or speak.

'Yu' have to know it,' said he. 'I have killed Trampas.'

'Oh, thank God!' she said; and he found her in his arms. Long they embraced without speaking, and what they whispered then with their kisses, matters not.

* * *

Thus did her New England conscience battle to the end, and, in the end, capitulate to love. And the next day, with the bishop's blessing, and Mrs Taylor's broadest smile, and the ring on her finger, the Virginian departed with his bride into the mountains.

CHAPTER 36

At Dunbarton

For their first bridal camp he chose an island. Long weeks beforehand he had thought of this place, and set his heart upon it. Once established in his mind, the thought became a picture that he saw waking and sleeping. He had stopped at the island many times alone, and in all seasons; but at this special moment of the year he liked it best. Often he had added several needless miles to his journey that he might finish the day at this point, might catch the trout for his supper beside a certain rock upon its edge, and fall asleep hearing the stream on either side of him.

Always for him the first signs that he had gained the true world of the mountains began at the island. The first pine trees stood upon it; the first white columbine grew in their shade; and it seemed to him that he always met here the first of the true mountain air – the coolness and the new fragrance. Below, there were only the cottonwoods, and the knolls and steep foothills with their sagebrush, and the great warm air of the plains; here at this altitude came the definite change. Out of the lower country and its air he would urge his horse upward, talking to him aloud, and promising fine pasture in a little while. Then, when at length he had ridden abreast of the island pines, he would ford to the sheltered circle of his camp-ground, throw off the saddle and blanket from the horse's hot, wet back, throw his own clothes off, and, shouting, spring upon the horse bare, and with a rope for bridle, cross with him to the promised pasture. Here there was a pause in the mountain steepness, a level space of open, green with thick grass. Riding his horse to this, he would leap off him, and with the flat of his hand give him a blow that cracked sharp in the stillness and sent the horse galloping and gambolling to his night's freedom. And while the animal rolled in the grass, often his master would roll also, and stretch, and take the grass in his two hands, and so draw his body along, limbering his muscles after a long ride. Then he would slide into the stream below his fishing place, where it was deep enough for swimming and cross back to his island, and dressing again, fit his rod together and begin his casting. After the darkness had set in, there would follow the lying drowsily with his head upon his saddle, the camp-fire sinking as he watched it, and sleep approaching to the murmur of the water on either side of him.

So many visits to this island had he made, and counted so many hours of reverie spent in its haunting sweetness, that the spot had come to seem his own. It belonged to no man, for it was deep in the unsurveyed and virgin wilderness; neither had he ever made his camp here with any man, nor shared with any the intimate delight which the place gave him. Therefore for many weeks he had planned to bring her here after their wedding, upon the day itself, and show her and share with her his pines and his fishing rock. He would bid her smell the first true breath of the mountains, would watch with her the sinking camp-fire, and with her listen to the water as it flowed round the island.

Until this wedding plan, it had by no means come home to him how deep a hold upon him the island had taken. He knew that he liked to go there, and go alone; but so little was it his way to scan himself, his mind, or his feelings (unless some action called for it), that he first learned his love of the place through his love of her. But he told her nothing of it. After the thought of taking her there came to him, he kept his island as something to let break upon her own eyes, lest by looking forward she should look for more than the reality.

Hence, as they rode along, when the houses of the town were shrunk to dots behind them, and they were nearing the gates of the foothills, she asked him questions. She hoped they would find a camp a long way from the town. She could ride as many miles as necessary. She was not tired. Should they not go on until they found a good place far enough within the solitude? Had he fixed upon any? And at the nod and the silence that he gave her for reply, she knew that he had thoughts and intentions which she must wait to learn.

They passed through the gates of the foothills, following the stream up among them. The outstretching fences and the widely trodden dust were no more. Now and then they rose again into view of the fields and houses down in the plain below. But as the sum of the miles and hours grew, they were glad to see the road less worn with travel, and the traces of men passing from sight. The ploughed and planted country, that quilt of many-coloured harvests which they had watched yesterday, lay in another world from this where they rode now. No hand but nature's had sown these crops of yellow flowers, these willow thickets and tall cottonwoods. Somewhere in a passage of red rocks the last sign of wagon wheels was lost, and after this the trail became a wild mountain trail. But it was still the warm air of the plains, bearing the sagebrush odour and not the pine, that they breathed; nor did any forest yet cloak the shapes of the tawny hills among which they were ascending. Twice the steepness loosened the pack ropes, and he jumped down to tighten them, lest the horses should get sore backs. And twice the stream that they followed went into deep canyons, so that for a while they parted from it. When they came back to its margin for the second time, he bade her notice how its water had become at last wholly clear. To her it had seemed clear enough all along, even in the plain above the town. But now she saw that it flowed lustrously with flashes; and she knew the soil had changed to mountain soil. Lower down, the water had carried the slightest cloud of alkali, and this had dulled the keen edge of its transparence. Full solitude was around them now, so that their words grew scarce, and when they spoke it was with low voices. They began to pass nooks and points favourable for camping, with wood and water at hand, and pasture for the horses. More than once as they reached such places, she thought he must surely stop; but still he rode on in advance of her (for the trail was narrow) until, when she was not thinking of it, he drew rein and pointed.

'What?' she asked timidly.

'The pines,' he answered.

She looked, and saw the island, and the water folding it with ripples and with smooth spaces. The sun was throwing upon the pine boughs a light of deepening red gold, and the shadow of the fishing rock lay over a little bay of quiet water and sandy shore. In this forerunning glow of the sunset, the pasture spread like emerald; for the dry touch of summer had not yet come near it. He pointed upward to the high mountains which they had approached, and showed her where the stream led into their first unfoldings.

'Tomorrow we shall be among them,' said he. 'Then,' she murmured to him, 'tonight is here?'

He nodded for answer, and she gazed at the island and understood why he had not stopped before; nothing they had passed had been so lovely as this place.

There was room in the trail for them to go side by side; and side by side they rode to the ford and crossed, driving the pack-horses in front of them, until they came to the sheltered circle, and he helped her down where the soft pine needles lay. They felt each other tremble, and for a moment she stood hiding her head upon his breast. Then she looked round at the trees, and the shores, and the flowing stream, and he heard her whispering how beautiful it was.

'I am glad,' he said, still holding her. 'This is how I have dreamed it would happen. Only it is better than my dreams.' And when she pressed him in silence, he finished, 'I have meant we should see our first sundown here, and our first sunrise.'

She wished to help him take the packs from their horses, to make the camp together with him, to have for her share the building of the fire, and the cooking. She bade him remember his promise to her that he would teach her how to loop and draw the pack-ropes, and the swing-ropes on the pack-saddles, and how to pitch a tent. Why might not the first lesson be now? But he told her that this should be fulfilled later. This night he was to do all himself And he sent her away until he should have camp ready for them. He bade her explore the island, or take her horse and ride over to the pasture, where she could see the surrounding hills and the circle of seclusion that they made.

'The whole world is far from here,' he said. And so she obeyed him, and went away to wander about in their hiding-place; nor was she to return, he told her, until he called her.

Then at once, as soon as she was gone, he fell to. The packs and saddles came off the horses, which he turned loose upon the pasture on the main land. The tent was unfolded first. He had long seen in his mind where it should go, and how its white shape would look beneath the green of the encircling pines. The ground was level in the spot he had chosen, without stones or roots, and matted with the fallen needles of the pines. If there should come any wind, or storm of rain, the branches were thick overhead, and around them on three sides tall rocks and undergrowth made a barrier. He cut the pegs for the tent, and the front pole, stretching and tightening the rope, one end of it pegged down and one round a pine tree. When the tightening rope had lifted the canvas to the proper height from the ground, he spread and pegged down the sides and back, leaving the opening so that they could look out upon the fire and a piece of the stream beyond. He cut tufts of young pine and strewed them thickly for a soft floor in the tent, and over them spread the buffalo hide and the blankets. At the head he placed the neat sack of her belongings. For his own he made a shelter with crossed poles and a sheet of canvas beyond the first pines. He built the fire where its smoke would float outward from the trees and the tent, and near it he stood the cooking things and his provisions, and made this first supper ready in the twilight. He had brought much with him; but for ten minutes he fished, catching trout enough. When at length she came riding over the stream at his call, there was nothing for her to do but sit and eat at the table he had laid. They sat together, watching the last of the twilight and the gentle oncoming of the dusk. The final afterglow of day left the sky, and through the purple which followed it came slowly the first stars, bright and wide apart. They watched the spaces between them fill with more stars, while near them the flames and embers of their fire grew brighter. Then he sent her to the tent while he cleaned the dishes and visited the horses to see that they did not stray from the pasture. Some while after the darkness was fully come, he rejoined her. All had been as he had seen it in his thoughts beforehand: the pines with the setting sun upon them, the sinking camp-fire, and now the sound of the water as it flowed murmuring by the shores of the island.

The tent opened to the east, and from it they watched together their first sunrise. In his thoughts he had seen this morning beforehand also: the waking, the gentle sound of the water murmuring ceaselessly, the growing day, the vision of the stream, the sense that the world was shut away far from them. So did it all happen, except that he whispered to her again – 'Better than my dreams.'

They saw the sunlight begin upon a hilltop; and presently came the sun itself, and lakes of warmth flowed into the air, slowly filling the green solitude. Along the island shores the ripples caught flashes from the sun.

'I am going into the stream,' he said to her; and rising, he left her in the tent. This was his side of the island, he had told her last night; the other was hers, where he had made a place for her to bathe. When he was gone, she found it, walking through the trees and rocks to the water's edge. And so, with the island between them, the two bathed in the cold stream. When he came back, he found her already busy at their camp. The blue smoke of the fire was floating out from the trees, loitering undispersed in the quiet air, and she was getting their breakfast. She had been able to forestall him because he had delayed long at his dressing, not willing to return to her unshaven. She looked at his eyes that were clear as the water he had leaped into, and at his soft silk neckerchief, knotted with care.

'Do not let us ever go away from here!' she cried, and ran to him as he came.

They sat long together at breakfast, breathing the morning breath of the earth that was fragrant with woodland moisture and with the pines. After the meal he could not prevent her helping him make everything clean. Then, by all customs of mountain journeys, it was time they should break camp and be moving before the heat of the day. But first, they delayed for no reason, save that in these hours they so loved to do nothing. And next, when with some energy he got upon his feet and declared he must go and drive the horses in, she asked, Why? Would it not be well for him to fish here, that they might be sure of trout at their nooning? And though he knew that where they should stop for noon, trout would be as sure as here, he took this chance for more delay.

She went with him to his fishing rock, and sat watching him. The rock was tall, higher than his head when he stood. It jutted out halfway across the stream, and the water flowed round it in quick foam, and fell into a pool. He caught several fish; but the sun was getting high, and after a time it was plain the fish had ceased to rise.

Yet still he stood casting in silence, while she sat by and watched him. Across the stream, the horses wandered or lay down in their pasture. At length he said with half a sigh that perhaps they ought to go.

'Ought?' she repeated softly.

'If we are to get anywhere today,' he answered.

'Need we get anywhere?' she asked.

Her question sent delight through him like a flood. 'Then you do not want to move camp today?' said he.

She shook her head.

At this he laid down his rod and came and sat by her. 'I am very glad we shall not go till tomorrow,' he murmured.

'Not tomorrow,' she said. 'Nor next day. Nor any day until we must.' And she stretched her hands out to the island and the stream exclaiming, 'Nothing can surpass this!'

He took her in his arms. 'You feel about it the way I do,' he almost whispered. 'I could not have hoped there'd be two of us to care so much.'

Presently, while they remained without speaking by the pool, came a little wild animal swimming round the rock from above. It had not seen them, nor suspected their presence. They held themselves still, watching its alert head cross through the waves quickly and come down through the pool, and so swim to the other side. There it came out on a small stretch of sand, turned its grey head and its pointed black nose this way and that, never seeing them, and then rolled upon its back in the warm dry sand. After a minute of rolling, it got on its feet again, shook its fur, and trotted away.

Then the bridegroom husband opened his shy heart deep down.

'I am like that fellow,' he said dreamily. 'I have often done the same.' And stretching slowly his arms and legs, he lay full length upon his back, letting his head rest upon her. 'If I could talk his animal language, I could talk to him,' he pursued. 'And he would say to me: "Come and roll on the sands. Where's the use of fretting? What's the gain in being a man? Come roll on the sands with me." That's what he would say.' The Virginian paused. 'But,' he continued, 'the trouble is, I am responsible. If that could only be forgot forever by you and me!' Again he paused and went on, always dreamily. 'Often when I have camped here, it has made me want to become the ground, become the water, become the trees, mix with the whole thing. Not know myself from it. Never unmix again. Why is that?' he demanded, looking at her. 'What is it? You don't know, nor I don't. I wonder would everybody feel that way here?'

'I think not everybody,' she answered.

'No; none except the ones who understand things they can't put words to. But you did!' He put up a hand and touched her softly. 'You understood about this place. And that's what makes it – makes you and me as we are now – better than my dreams. And my dreams were pretty good.'

He sighed with supreme quiet and happiness, and seemed to stretch his length closer to the earth. And so he lay, and talked to her as he had never talked to anyone, not even to himself. Thus she learned secrets of his heart new to her: his visits here, what they were to him, and why he had chosen it for their bridal camp. 'What I did not know at all,' he said, 'was the way a man can be pining for – for this – and never guess what is the matter with him.'

When he had finished talking, still he lay extended and serene; and she looked down at him and the wonderful change that had come over him, like a sunrise. Was this dreamy boy the man of two days ago? It seemed a distance immeasurable; yet it was two days only since that wedding eve when she had shrunk from him as he stood fierce and implacable. She could look back at that dark hour now, although she could not speak of it. She had seen destruction like sharp steel glittering in his eyes. Were these the same eyes? Was this youth with his black head of hair in her lap the creature with whom men did not trifle, whose hand knew how to deal death? Where had the man melted away to in this boy? For as she looked at him, he might have been no older than nineteen today. Not even at their first meeting – that night when his freakish spirit was uppermost – had he looked so young. This change their hours upon the island had wrought, filling his face with innocence.

By and by they made their nooning. In the afternoon she would have explored the nearer woods with him, or walked up the stream. But since this was to be their camp during several days, he made it more complete. He fashioned a rough bench and a table; around their tent he built a tall windbreak for better shelter in case of storm; and for the fire he gathered and cut much wood, and piled it up. So they were provided for, and so for six days and nights they stayed, finding no day or night long enough.

Once his hedge of boughs did them good service, for they had an afternoon of furious storm. The wind rocked the pines and ransacked the island, the sun went out, the black clouds rattled, and white bolts of lightning fell close by. The shower broke through the pine branches and poured upon the tent. But he had removed everything inside from where it could touch the canvas and so lead the water through, and the rain ran off into the ditch he had dug round the tent. While they sat within, looking out upon the bounding floods and the white lightning, she saw him glance at her apprehensively, and at once she answered his glance.

'I am not afraid,' she said. 'If a flame should consume us together now, what would it matter?'

And so they sat watching the storm till it was over, he with his face changed by her to a boy's, and she leavened with him.

When at last they were compelled to leave the island, or see no more of the mountains, it was not a final parting. They would come back for the last night before their journey ended. Furthermore, they promised each other like two children to come here every year upon their wedding day, and like two children they believed that this would be possible. But in after years they did come, more than once, to keep their wedding day upon the island, and upon each new visit were able to say to each other, 'Better than our dreams.'

For thirty days by the light of the sun and the camp-fire light they saw no faces except their own; and when they were silent it was all stillness, unless the wind passed among the pines, or some flowing water was near them. Sometimes at evening they came upon elk, or black-tailed deer, feeding out in the high parks of the mountains; and once from the edge of some concealing timber he showed her a bear, sitting with an old log lifted in its paws. She forbade him to kill the bear, or any creature that they did not require. He took her upward by trail and canyon, through the unfooted woods and along dwindling streams to their headwaters, lakes lying near the summit of the range, full of trout, with meadows of long grass and a thousand flowers, and above these the pinnacles of rock and snow.

They made their camps in many places, delaying several days here, and one night there, exploring the high solitudes together, and sinking deep in their romance. Sometimes when he was at work with their horses, or intent on casting his brown hackle for a fish, she would watch him with eyes that were fuller of love than of understanding. Perhaps she never came wholly to understand him; but in her complete love for him she found enough. He loved her with his whole man's power. She had listened to him tell her in words of transport, 'I could enjoy dying'; yet she loved him more than that. He had come to her from a smoking pistol, able to bid her farewell – and she could not let him go. At the last white-hot edge of ordeal, it was she who renounced, and he who had his way. Nevertheless she found much more than enough, in spite of the sigh that now and again breathed through her happiness when she would watch him with eyes fuller of love than of understanding.

They could not speak of that grim wedding eve for a long while after; but the mountains brought them together upon all else in the world and their own lives. At the end they loved each other doubly more than at the beginning, because of these added confidences which they exchanged and shared. It was a new bliss to her to know a man's talk and thoughts, to be given so much of him; and to him it was a bliss still greater to melt from that reserve his lonely life had bred in him. He never would have guessed so much had been stored away in him, unexpressed till now. They did not want to go to Vermont and leave these mountains, but the day came when they had to turn their backs upon their dream. So they came out into the plains once more, well established in their familiarity, with only the journey still lying between themselves and Bennington.

'If you could,' she said, laughing. 'If only you could ride home like this.'

'With Monte and my six-shooter?' he asked. 'To your mother?'

'I don't think mother could resist the way you look on a horse.'

But he said, 'It is this way she's fearing I will come.'

'I have made one discovery,' she said. 'You are fonder of good clothes than I am.'

He grinned. 'I cert'nly like 'em. But don't tell my friends. They would say it was marriage. When you see what I have got for Bennington's special benefit, you – why, you'll just trust your husband more than ever.'

She undoubtedly did. After he had put on one particular suit, she arose and kissed him where he stood in it.

'Bennington will be sorrowful,' he said. 'No wild-west show, after all. And no ready-made guy, either.' And he looked at himself in the glass with unhidden pleasure.

'How did you choose that?' she asked. 'How did you know that homespun was exactly the thing for you?'

'Why, I have been noticing. I used to despise an Eastern man because his clothes were not Western. I was very young then, or maybe not so very young, as very – as what you saw I was when you first came to Bear Creek. A Western man is a good thing. And he generally knows that. But he has a heap to learn. And he generally don't know that. So I took to watching the Judge's Eastern visitors. There was that Mr Ogden especially, from New Yawk – the gentleman that was there the time when I had to sit up all night with the missionary, yu' know. His clothes pleased me best of all. Fit him so well, and nothing flash. I got my ideas, and when I knew I was going to marry you, I sent my measure East – and I and the tailor are old enemies now.'

Bennington probably was disappointed. To see get out of the train merely a tall man with a usual straw hat, and Scotch homespun suit of a rather better cut than most in Bennington – this was dull. And his conversation – when he indulged in any – seemed fit to come inside the house.

Mrs Flynt took her revenge by sowing broadcast her thankfulness that poor Sam Bannett had been Molly's rejected suitor. He had done so much better for himself. Sam had married a rich Miss Van Scootzer, of the second families of Troy; and with their combined riches this happy couple still inhabit the most expensive residence in Hoosic Falls.

But most of Bennington soon began to say that Molly's cowboy could be invited anywhere and hold his own. The time came when they ceased to speak of him as a cowboy, and declared that she had shown remarkable sense. But this was not quite yet.

Did this bride and groom enjoy their visit to her family? Well – well, they did their best. Everybody did their best, even Sarah Bell. She said that she found nothing to object to in the Virginian; she told Molly so. Her husband Sam did better than that. He told Molly he considered that she was in luck. And poor Mrs Wood, sitting on the sofa, conversed scrupulously and timidly with her novel son-in-law, and said to Molly that she was astonished to find him so gentle. And he was undoubtedly fine-looking; yes, very handsome. She believed that she would grow to like the Southern accent. Oh, yes! Everybody did their best; and, dear reader, if ever it has been your earthly portion to live with a number of people who were all doing their best, you do not need me to tell you what a heavenly atmosphere this creates.

And then the bride and groom went to see the old great-aunt over at Dunbarton.

Their first arrival, the one at Bennington, had been thus: Sam Bell had met them at the train, and Mrs Wood, waiting in her parlour, had embraced her daughter and received her son-in-law. Among them they had managed to make the occasion as completely mournful as any family party can be, with the window blinds up. 'And with you present, my dear,' said Sam Bell to Sarah, 'the absence of a coffin was not felt.'

But at Dunbarton the affair went off differently. The heart of the ancient lady had taught her better things. From Bennington to Dunbarton is the good part of a day's journey, and they drove up to the gate in the afternoon. The great-aunt was in her garden, picking some August flowers, and she called as the carriage stopped, 'Bring my nephew here, my dear, before you go into the house.'

At this, Molly, stepping out of the carriage, squeezed her husband's hand. 'I knew that she would be lovely,' she whispered to him. And then she ran to her aunt's arms, and let him follow. He came slowly, hat in hand.

The old lady advanced to meet him, trembling a little, and holding out her hand to him. 'Welcome, nephew,' she said. 'What a tall fellow you are, to be sure. Stand off, sir, and let me look at you.'

The Virginian obeyed, blushing from his black hair to his collar.

Then his new relative turned to her niece, and gave her a flower. 'Put this in his coat, my dear,' she said. 'And I think I understand why you wanted to marry him.'

After this the maid came and showed them to their rooms. Left alone in her garden, the great-aunt sank on a bench and sat there for some time; for emotion had made her very weak.

Upstairs, Molly, sitting on the Virginian's knee, put the flower in his coat, and then laid her head upon his shoulder.

'I didn't know old ladies could be that way,' he said. 'D' yu' reckon there are many?'

'Oh, I don't know,' said the girl. 'I'm so happy!'

Now at tea, and during the evening, the great-aunt carried out her plans still further. At first she did the chief part of the talking herself. Nor did she ask questions about Wyoming too soon. She reached that in her own way, and found out the one thing that she desired to know. It was through General Stark that she led up to it.

'There he is,' she said, showing the family portrait. 'And a rough time he must have had of it now and then. New Hampshire was full of fine young men in those days. But nowadays most of them have gone away to seek their fortunes in the West. Do they find them, I wonder?'

'Yes, ma'am. All the good ones do.'

'But you cannot all be – what is the name? – Cattle Kings.'

'That's having its day, ma'am, right now. And we are getting ready for the change – some of us are.'

'And what may be the change, and when is it to come?'

'When the natural pasture is eaten off,' he explained. 'I have seen that coming a long while. And if the thieves are going to make us drive our stock away, we'll drive it. If they don't, we'll have big pastures fenced, and hay and shelter ready for winter. What we'll spend in improvements, we'll more than save in wages. I am well fixed for the new conditions. And then, when I took up my land, I chose a place where there is coal. It will not be long before the new railroad needs that.'

Thus the old lady learned more of her niece's husband in one evening than the Bennington family had ascertained during his whole sojourn with them. For by touching upon Wyoming and its future, she roused him to talk. He found her mind alive to Western questions: irrigation, the Indians, the forests; and so he expanded, revealing to her his wide observation and his shrewd intelligence. He forgot entirely to be shy. She sent Molly to bed, and kept him talking for an hour. Then she showed him old things that she was proud of, 'because,' she said, 'we, too, had something to do with making our country. And now go to Molly, or you'll both think me a tiresome old lady.'

'I think – ' he began, but was not quite equal to expressing what he thought, and suddenly his shyness flooded him again.

'In that case, nephew,' said she, 'I'm afraid you'll have to kiss me good-night.'

And so she dismissed him to his wife, and to happiness greater than either of them had known since they had left the mountains and come to the East. 'He'll do,' she said to herself, nodding.

Their visit to Dunbarton was all happiness and reparation for the doleful days at Bennington. The old lady gave much comfort and advice to her niece in private, and when they came to leave, she stood at the front door holding both their hands a moment.

'God bless you, my dears,' she told them. 'And when you come next time, I'll have the nursery ready.'

And so it happened that before she left this world, the great-aunt was able to hold in her arms the first of their many children.

Judge Henry at Sunk Creek had his wedding present ready. His growing affairs in Wyoming needed his presence in many places distant from his ranch, and he made the Virginian his partner. When the thieves prevailed at length, as they did, forcing cattle owners to leave the country or be ruined, the Virginian had forestalled this crash. The herds were driven away to Montana. Then, in 1892, came the cattle war, when, after putting their men in office, and coming to own some of the newspapers, the thieves brought ruin on themselves as well. For in a broken country there is nothing left to steal.

But the railroad came, and built a branch to that land of the Virginian's where the coal was. By that time he was an important man, with a strong grip on many various enterprises, and able to give his wife all and more than she asked or desired. Sometimes she missed the Bear Creek days, when she and he had ridden together, and sometimes she declared that his work would kill him. But it does not seem to have done so. Their eldest boy rides the horse Monte; and, strictly between ourselves, I think his father is going to live a long while.